The Hill : Hobbiton-across-the Water

Chronology 1419.	Frodo & Samwise	Gandalf. Gondor	Aragorn. Théoden	Enemies
		somewhat after midnight 7/8		
March 8 Th. ○ PM.	See Moon set about 5 a.m. Recapture Gollum. Leave Henneth Annûn in morning. Sleep in woods of Ithilien.	Pippin sees Moon, and beacons in Anórien. Errand-riders of Gondor pass, ~~Gandalf halts~~ 176 miles from Edoras. Gandalf halts 192 miles from Edoras. Faramir leaves Henneth Annûn in morning and goes to Cair Andros.	Aragorn leaves Dunharrow by the Paths of Dead. Reaches Erech at midnight. In the hills.	
9 F	Reach Osgiliath Road at dusk. Ominous sunset. Sleep in tree at midnight.	Gandalf rides through night and reaches Rammas Echor about 6.15 a.m. Conference with Denethor. Pippin sees the Captains ride in at end of day. Ominous sunset.	Aragorn leaves Erech at 8 a.m. and crosses Tarlang's Neck into Lamedon. reaches Calembel on Ciril. Théoden reaches Harrowdale at dusk, and finds muster nearly ready. Errand-riders of Gondor arrive at night.	Orc-host from Morannon with Easterlings assaults Cair Andros after Faramir has gone. They cross into Anórien and march west at great speed.
9/10 10 S.	Darkness begins to flow out of Mordor at night. F. & S. go on during early hours, and reach Hogback. No dawn. Lie hid till afternoon. Reach Cross-Roads at dusk, & see last gleam of sun. Pass Minas Morgul, and see host ride out. Begin climbing in Ephel Duath.	Dark Dawn. Pippin sees rescue of Faramir (riding in from Cair Andros) by Gandalf. Conference of Faramir and Denethor.	Théoden rides out onward to Minas Tirith. Leaves Dunharrow in morn; reaches Edoras. Leaves Edoras after midday and camps 30 miles east on way. Aragorn crosses the Ringlo. Darkness spreads over lens and dismays even the allies (Haradrim) of Mordor.	Great Signal of war in Mordor. ~~Another host leaves Morannon and makes for Cair Andros.~~ Main host under Lord of Nazgûl (King of Angmar) sets out at evening from Minas Morgul to attack crossing at Osgiliath. Force of Orcs repulsed at Lórien invade northern Rohan.
11 S	Climbing in Ephel Duath. They rest and sleep in a crevice of rocks. (Gollum slips off to see Shelob: nearly repents, but finally surrenders to evil).	Faramir sent to Osgiliath. Battle begins. News of the presence of the "Black Captain" (Lord of Nazgûl) reaches Minas Tirith.	Théoden rides on and camps 110 miles east. Aragorn reaches Linhir on Gilrain and forces crossing into Lebennin.	Morgul-host assaults ford at Osgiliath. ~~Another host takes Cair Andros, and holds the crossings against the Rohirrim~~ North of the City.
12 M.	Gollum returns and leads F. and S. into Shelob's lair (in afternoon)	Faramir retreats to Causeway forts. Gandalf goes to his aid.	Théoden rides on, and camps under Min-Rimmon. Aragorn drives enemy across Lebennin towards Pelargir	Morgul-host forces crossing of Anduin and assails the Rammas Echor at Causeway. Ents destroy Orc-host in plains of Rohan and so save Rohirrim from flank-attack or destruction of Edoras behind them. Easterlings pass the Pelennor and march west to waylay Rohirrim.

THE LORD OF THE RINGS
A Reader's Companion

Also by Wayne G. Hammond and Christina Scull:

J.R.R. Tolkien: Artist & Illustrator
Letters by J.R.R. Tolkien [*Index*]
The J.R.R. Tolkien Companion and Guide

As editors of works by J.R.R. Tolkien

Roverandom
Farmer Giles of Ham (50th anniversary edition)
The Lord of the Rings (50th anniversary edition)

The Lord of the Rings
A Reader's Companion

BY

Wayne G. Hammond

AND

Christina Scull

HOUGHTON MIFFLIN COMPANY
BOSTON · NEW YORK

First published in Great Britain by HarperCollins*Publishers*, 2005

For information about permission to reproduce selections from this book, write to Permissions, Houghton Mifflin Company, 215 Park Avenue South, New York, New York 10003

Visit our Web site: www.houghtonmifflinbooks.com

Details of all quotations reproduced on page vi

Cataloging-in-Publication Data is available.

ISBN-13 978-0-618-64267-0

Set in PostScript Minion by
Rowland Phototypesetting Ltd,
Bury St Edmunds, Suffolk, England

Printed and bound in China

In Memory of Our Parents

Luella Belle Thauvette
Wayne Gordon Hammond, Sr.

Eileen Hannah Abbott
Robert Stanley Scull

CONTENTS

THE TWO TOWERS

BOOK THREE

BOOK FOUR

THE RETURN OF THE KING

BOOK FIVE

PREFACE

The Lord of the Rings is a masterpiece of storytelling, and needs no assistance to entertain those sensitive to its qualities. Millions of readers have embraced its special blend of fantasy and adventure, its richness of language, its exploration of universal questions of life and death, friendship and love, duty and heroism, perseverance and sacrifice, the lust for war and the desire for peace, for more than fifty years unaided by *enchiridia* like the present book. One might say, as Tolkien did of the Appendices to his great work, that those who enjoy *The Lord of the Rings* as an 'heroic romance' only, without further explanation, will very properly neglect this volume. And yet, like all great works of literature, *The Lord of the Rings* repays close scrutiny with deeper understanding and appreciation, and to that end many of its readers may after all welcome assistance to some degree. It is a complicated work, with questions of content, vocabulary, antecedents, and variant texts. And it is unusual in that its setting, characters, and events continued to acquire new facets within the author's imagination as long as he lived.

As the reader will see, we have not produced an annotated edition of Tolkien's work in the manner of Douglas A. Anderson's *Annotated Hobbit* (1988; 2nd edn. 2003) or of our own editions of *Roverandom* (1998) and *Farmer Giles of Ham* (1999), in which text and notes are contained within the same covers, either parallel to each other or in discrete sections. Originally we had thought to follow one of these approaches for *The Lord of the Rings*, but practical difficulties soon became apparent. At some 1,200 pages *The Lord of the Rings* is a much longer work than *The Hobbit*, and of a much greater order of magnitude than that work, or than *Roverandom* and *Farmer Giles of Ham*, in its possibilities for commentary. At the same time, we were aware of the phenomenal growth in sales of *The Lord of the Rings* in recent years which brought the market in Tolkien's work to a high level of saturation, new editions of importance such as those published for the fiftieth anniversary of *The Lord of the Rings* notwithstanding. These issues led us to consider, and to reject for a variety of reasons – complexity of layout and typography, ease of handling, and cost – the models of annotation used earlier for Tolkien, and instead to devise a separate volume of notes and other material to accompany any edition of *The Lord of the Rings* the reader may have at hand.

In choosing what to gloss we have been guided by a sense, honed by decades of work in Tolkien studies and of reading the comments of scholars, enthusiasts, and ordinary readers, of those details of *The Lord of the Rings* that have been found of special interest, or that have given readers special difficulty. We have not glossed every detail, by any means. The late

Dr. Richard E. Blackwelder once counted in *The Lord of the Rings* 632 named individuals (of which 314 are in the Appendices), a number which soars to 1,648 when one adds titles, nicknames, and descriptive epithets (Sauron alone has 103) – to say nothing of place-names, battle names, etc. – far too many for the present book to cover exhaustively, if it is to stay within reasonable bounds. We are indebted, and recommend the reader also to refer, to invaluable encyclopedic works such as Robert Foster's *Complete Guide to Middle-earth.* Nor have we felt it advisable to try to predict every word which a reader might not understand among Tolkien's extensive and often very precise lexicon (to say nothing of that employed in our notes). We have glossed some of these words, in particular if they are obsolete, archaic, colloquial, rare, or otherwise (according to our judgement) unusual or liable to be misinterpreted; but readers' vocabularies vary widely, and what is an unfamiliar word to one may be commonplace to another. To the former group we recommend the use of a good (British) English language dictionary, such as the *Concise Oxford English Dictionary,* if not the larger *OED.* As Tolkien wrote in a draft letter to Walter Allen, April 1959, in regard to writing for children but also more generally true: 'an honest word is an honest word, and its acquaintance can only be made by meeting it in a right context. A good vocabulary is not acquired by reading books written according to some notion of the vocabulary of one's age-group. It comes from reading books above one' (*Letters of J.R.R. Tolkien*, pp. 298–9).

For the basis of our annotations we have naturally looked first to Tolkien's own writings and comments. *The Lord of the Rings* is a sequel to *The Hobbit,* and echoes elements of the earlier book; and it is a continuation of the 'Silmarillion' mythology which occupied Tolkien all of his life, with strong ties to that work (such as the parallel love-stories of Aragorn and Arwen in *The Lord of the Rings,* and Beren and Lúthien in a previous age) and references to its places, people, and events. It has been instructive sometimes to refer as well to the volumes of drafts and ancillary writings by Tolkien edited by his son and literary executor, Christopher, as *Unfinished Tales* (1980) and the twelve volumes of *The History of Middle-earth* (1983–96), in particular vols. VI–IX and XII which trace the evolution of *The Lord of the Rings* in detail; and also to miscellaneous linguistic writings by Tolkien published in the journal *Vinyar Tengwar.* These works reveal the often tortuous progress of Tolkien's thoughts as he crafted *The Lord of the Rings* and continued, after publication, to add to his creation and further interweave it with 'The Silmarillion'. It is not been our aim, however, to repeat here every variant idea or name considered by Tolkien in the course of writing or revision – these are legion, and best comprehended in the context of the drafts to which they belong – but rather to illuminate *The Lord of the Rings* as published, occasionally by pointing to texts ultimately altered or rejected, or to post-publication writings by Tolkien containing further development or invention.

Tolkien's letters have been a particularly important source of authoritative comment, both published, for the most part in the selected *Letters of J.R.R. Tolkien* (1981), and in various library and archival collections. Most important among the latter are the files of correspondence between Tolkien and his publisher George Allen & Unwin, now held by HarperCollins in London, and the main Allen & Unwin archive in the library of Reading University. *Letters* includes much about *The Lord of the Rings*, during its writing and after publication, as Tolkien sought to answer queries from friends and enthusiasts. The reader should be aware, however, that Tolkien's thoughts sometimes changed with the years and his memories varied, so that a comment at one moment may be contradicted by another written at a different time (see, for instance, his comments on the name *Elrond*, note for p. 15). Although he was concerned, by and large, when adding to his invention not to contradict what had been said in print, statements sent privately in correspondence were of a different order, to be held or discarded as the author wished.

The correspondence files at HarperCollins yielded, among much else, several pages which Tolkien wrote to the translator of the Dutch *Lord of the Rings* (1956–7), commenting on the meanings of various names. He later prepared a more extensive guide for translators, *Nomenclature of The Lord of the Rings*, which was first published as *Guide to the Names in The Lord of the Rings* in the first edition of *A Tolkien Compass*, edited by Jared Lobdell (1975), but omitted from the second (2003). It has seemed more appropriate to us and to the Tolkien Estate that the *Nomenclature* be reprinted in the present book, newly transcribed and with additions from the original manuscript and typescripts. These papers were kindly provided to us by Christopher Tolkien, along with photocopies of a glossary-index his father began to prepare for *The Lord of the Rings* probably in 1953 but never finished (it includes only place-names), quotations from his father's check copies of *The Lord of the Rings*, and a copy of the portion (omitted from *Letters*) of Tolkien's important letter to publisher Milton Waldman, written probably in late 1951, which describes *The Lord of the Rings* as part of his larger mythology. We have referred to the unfinished index and check copies freely in our notes, and include the extract from Tolkien's letter to Milton Waldman as an appendix.

For some notes, primarily questions of textual development and matters of chronology, we have consulted the invaluable collection of original manuscripts, typescripts, and proofs of *The Lord of the Rings* held in the Department of Special Collections and University Archives of the Marquette University Libraries, Milwaukee, Wisconsin. Notable among these materials is a series of time-schemes, especially those in Marquette MSS Series 4, Box 2, Folder 18, with which Tolkien kept track of the whereabouts and actions of his various characters, and the plot outlines and time-schemes in Marquette MSS 4/2 comprising *The Hunt for the Ring* (some of which is published in *Unfinished Tales*).

These and other sources, especially the enormous (if extremely variable) body of criticism and comment on *The Lord of the Rings* that has grown up since the first publication of that work, presented us with a wealth of material which we have winnowed and boiled down into this 'reader's companion'. The list of 'Works Consulted' near the end of this book includes only those that we cite or quote in our notes, or otherwise found particularly useful; it does not nearly approach a complete list of the books, articles, and even videos that we reviewed as sources. There is, of course, much more that could be said about *The Lord of the Rings*, of use and of interest, and no doubt much that readers will wish we had included, or had said differently (as they themselves have said, or would say); but as it is, we have written a volume at least twice as long as our publisher expected.

There is a strong desire, in writing this sort of book, to want to explain, and in trying to explain thoroughly there is a danger of venturing too far into speculation, until reach exceeds grasp. Therefore, although we have occasionally ventured to speculate, we have tried to do so very conservatively, and have thought it best for an understanding of Tolkien's work to prefer fact to interpretation, and the author's own views when they are available, together with a selection of well founded observations as they have appeared in the literature of Tolkien studies. We will be glad to receive corrections, and suggestions for further annotations along the same lines.

*

The structure of this book may be described as follows. Selected names, words, and other features of *The Lord of the Rings* are annotated at their first appearance in that work, except when a note seems more logically placed at a later point: in such cases we have included a cross-reference at the earlier location. Each note is keyed in the first instance, by page, to the emended text of 2004 (published, with continuous pagination, by HarperCollins, London, and by the Houghton Mifflin Company, Boston, Massachusetts), reprinted with further corrections in 2005, and to the previous standard second edition, first published in three individually paginated volumes by George Allen & Unwin, London, in 1966 (further revised in the second printing of 1967), and by the Houghton Mifflin Company in 1967, and reprinted many times. (In fact the pagination of the first edition is almost entirely identical to that of the second, except for preliminary matter and the Appendices.) Thus, for example, **1 (I: 10)** indicates p. 1 in the current edition, and p. 10 of vol. I in the old standard edition. To help readers who have other editions at hand locate the text in question, we have divided our annotations also according to section (Foreword, Prologue, Books I–VI, Appendices) and subsection (part or chapter), and have quoted the first few words of each paragraph which contains text that is the basis for comment. For this purpose, poems are considered self-contained 'paragraphs'.

Inevitably in a set of annotations for *The Lord of the Rings* one must refer forward and back, among Prologue, main text, and Appendices, as well as to outside sources, and in the process of glossing one term or phrase, will use terms which themselves have not been glossed because they have not yet been introduced in Tolkien's text. In such cases we have preferred generally not to cross-reference to other notes, or to nest note within note, but to rely on our index, so as to keep our apparatus as straightforward as possible. On this point also, in the unlikely event that we are now addressing someone consulting this book while reading *The Lord of the Rings* for the first time, be advised that we necessarily assume a familiarity with the story, and sometimes refer ahead to events later in the work (as, indeed, does Tolkien's Prologue, though most readers seem not to have noticed, so immersed do they become in the events of the story once it begins, or else leave the Prologue until they have come to the end of the book).

Our notes are preceded by a general history of *The Lord of the Rings* and comments on the process by which the 2004 text was edited; and are followed by a list of changes made in the editions of 2004 and 2005.

Titles of Tolkien's works are *italicized* with two exceptions: chapter titles; and 'The Silmarillion', which designates Tolkien's larger mythology, as distinct from *The Silmarillion*, the book first published in 1977. We have made no distinction between titles devised by J.R.R. Tolkien and those assigned by Christopher Tolkien to gatherings of like works by his father, e.g. *The Hunt for the Ring* in *Unfinished Tales.*

Readers should note the following abbreviations frequently used in this book:

Artist and Illustrator – Wayne G. Hammond and Christina Scull, *J.R.R. Tolkien: Artist and Illustrator* (1995)

Biography – Humphrey Carpenter, *J.R.R. Tolkien: A Biography* (1977)

Concise OED – *The Concise Oxford English Dictionary* (2002)

Descriptive Bibliography – Wayne G. Hammond, with the assistance of Douglas A. Anderson, *J.R.R. Tolkien: A Descriptive Bibliography* (1993)

Index – J.R.R. Tolkien, manuscript glossary-index to place-names in *The Lord of the Rings*; also cited as the 'unfinished index'

1966 Index – Expanded index first published in the George Allen & Unwin second edition of *The Lord of the Rings* (1966; in America by the Houghton Mifflin Co., 1967, but not by Ballantine Books)

Letters – *Letters of J.R.R. Tolkien*, selected and edited by Humphrey Carpenter, with the assistance of Christopher Tolkien (1981)

Marquette – J.R.R. Tolkien Papers, Marquette University Libraries

Nomenclature – J.R.R. Tolkien, *Nomenclature of The Lord of the Rings*

OED – *Oxford English Dictionary* (1987)

Scheme – J.R.R. Tolkien, latest and only complete manuscript time-scheme for *The Lord of the Rings* (Marquette MSS 4/2/18)

S.R. – Shire Reckoning

The Tale of Years – Appendix B of *The Lord of the Rings*

Waldman LR – Portion of letter by Tolkien to Milton Waldman, ?late 1951, concerning *The Lord of the Rings*, published at the end of the present book

Frequent reference is also made to 'the edition of 1994', i.e. the HarperCollins resetting of *The Lord of the Rings* issued that year, in which many errors were introduced (including its date of publication, at first given as '1991'; but its 'Note on the Text' by Douglas A. Anderson is correctly dated 1993).

Quotations have been transcribed generally as found, except that in quoting from the *Nomenclature*, with its many abbreviations of language names (e.g. *OE* for Old English), we have expanded these for ease of reading; but in the complete *Nomenclature* the abbreviations are (by and large) retained. Similarly we have given names from Tolkien's works, some of which he spelt or accented in different ways at different times, according to their sources. Dates internal to *The Lord of the Rings*, when not qualified as by 'Third Age' etc., are expressed in Shire Reckoning. Long vowels in Old English have been marked with a macron by convention, but in some quoted matter with an acute accent, according to the source.

Some of the material presented here as a 'Brief History of *The Lord of the Rings*' was prepared originally for our forthcoming *J.R.R. Tolkien Companion and Guide*, in which a more detailed chronology of the writing, production, and publication of *The Lord of the Rings* will be found, but which in the event has had to be temporarily set aside in order to give priority to *The Lord of the Rings: A Reader's Companion.*

For assistance and advice in the production of this book and of the anniversary edition of *The Lord of the Rings*, for providing the copies of papers and quotations by his father referred to above, and for his trust in our ability to write a book of annotations worthy to be a companion to his father's masterpiece, we are once again exceedingly grateful to Christopher Tolkien. Our thanks go also to Chris Smith, our patient editor at HarperCollins; to David Brawn, also at HarperCollins, with whom we had our earliest discussions about an annotated *Lord of the Rings*; to other members of the HarperCollins staff for assistance during our research visits; to Cathleen Blackburn of Manches Solicitors LLP, representing the Tolkien Estate; to Matt Blessing, Head of Special Collections and University Archives, Marquette University Libraries, and his staff, and to the previous director, Charles Elston; to Michael Bott and his staff in the Department of Archives and Manuscripts, Reading University Library; to Colin Harris, Judith Priestman, and their staff in the Department of Western Manuscripts, Bodleian Library, University of Oxford; to the staff of the British Library; to Neil Somerville and other staff of the BBC Written Archives Centre, Caversham Park, Reading; and to the staffs of the Williams College Library and the Chapin Library of Rare Books at Williams College.

Arden Smith kindly and meticulously read this book in draft and advised us on linguistic matters. We are also indebted to Carl Hostetter, especially for his editorial work on Tolkien's essay *The Rivers and Beacon-hills of Gondor* in *Vinyar Tengwar*, from which we have frequently quoted. For information on textual differences in *The Lord of the Rings* we are particularly grateful to Douglas Anderson, Dainis Bisenieks, David Bratman, Steve Frisby, Yuval Kfir, Nancy Martsch, Charles Noad, Kenzo Sasakawa, and Makoto Takahashi. Finally, for miscellaneous points of information and encouragement, we would like to thank Helen Armstrong, David Cofield, Graeme Cree, Gustav Dahlander (Rúmil), Christopher Gilson, Jeremy Marshall, John Rateliff and Janice Coulter, Alan Reynolds, René van Rossenberg, Anders Stenström (Beregond), Mary Stolzenbach, Patrick Wynne, and many other Tolkien scholars and enthusiasts who have examined the minutiae of *The Lord of the Rings*, an inexhaustible subject.

Wayne G. Hammond
Christina Scull
Williamstown, Massachusetts
May 2005

A BRIEF HISTORY OF THE LORD OF THE RINGS

J.R.R. Tolkien began to write *The Lord of the Rings* in December 1937, not, as he erroneously recalled in the Foreword to its second edition (1965; see note to p. xxii, below) and as numerous critics have repeated, 'soon after *The Hobbit* was written and before its publication' (i.e. between late 1936 and September 1937). Indeed he might never have written his masterpiece if *The Hobbit* had not been an immediate success, and publisher Stanley Unwin, of the London firm George Allen & Unwin, had not encouraged him to produce a sequel. Within only a few weeks of the publication of *The Hobbit* on 21 September 1937 Unwin warned Tolkien that 'a large public' would be 'clamouring next year to hear more from you about Hobbits!' (quoted in *Letters*, p. 23). Tolkien was flattered but 'a little perturbed. I cannot think of anything more to say about *hobbits*. . . . But I have only too much to say, and much already written, about the world into which the hobbit intruded' (letter to Stanley Unwin, 15 October 1937, *Letters*, p. 24). For more than twenty years he had been concerned with the development of a private mythology broadly called 'The Silmarillion'. Scattered elements of this appeared first in poems he wrote before and during the First World War; then, in 1916–17, with the writing of the prose *Book of Lost Tales*, his great creation began to take fuller form. At the same time, in parallel with his stories, he devised languages for the Elves, Men, Dwarves, and other peoples of his invented world. *The Hobbit* seems originally not to have been set within the same world, but Tolkien borrowed from his mythology to enrich what was, to begin with, no more than a long story told to his children.

Now, with *The Hobbit* in print, Tolkien wished to return to his 'secret vice', the creation of languages and stories set in the world of Arda and the lands of Middle-earth. But Unwin aroused in him 'a faint hope. . . . I have spent nearly all the vacation-times of seventeen years examining, and doing things of that sort, driven by immediate financial necessity (mainly medical and educational)' – that is, earning money to supplement his teaching salaries from the universities of Leeds and Oxford, in order to pay doctor's bills and support his children's schooling. 'Writing stories in prose or verse has been stolen, often guiltily, from time already mortgaged, and has been broken and ineffective. I may perhaps now do what I much desire to do, and not fail of financial duty' (letter to Stanley Unwin, 15 October 1937, *Letters*, p. 24). On 19 October 1937 Unwin wrote again with encouragement ('You are one of those rare people with genius', quoted in *Letters*, p. 25), to which Tolkien replied: 'I will start something soon, &

submit it to your boy [Rayner Unwin, who had enjoyed *The Hobbit*] at the earliest opportunity' (23 October, *Letters*, p. 25). But he did not do so at once. On 15 November he met Stanley Unwin in London, handed over for consideration by Allen & Unwin parts of 'The Silmarillion' and other stories, including the brief *Farmer Giles of Ham*, and then continued to work on his mythology.

On 15 December Stanley Unwin expressed his opinion that 'The Silmarillion' contained 'plenty of wonderful material' which might be mined to produce 'further books like *The Hobbit* rather than a book in itself' (quoted in *The Lays of Beleriand*, p. 366). What Allen & Unwin needed, he felt, was another *Hobbit*, or failing that, a volume of stories like *Farmer Giles of Ham*. On 16 December Tolkien replied that it was now clear to him that 'a sequel or successor to *The Hobbit*' was called for, to which he promised to give thought and attention. But it was difficult with 'the construction of elaborate and consistent mythology (and two languages)' occupying his mind, and the Silmarils in his heart. Hobbits, he said, 'can be comic, but their comedy is suburban unless it is set against things more elemental' (*Letters*, p. 26). He did not need to add, for Unwin knew it already, that his academic and administrative duties as a professor in the Oxford English School consumed many hours of his time, and he had responsibilities also to his wife and four children. Nonetheless, inspiration seems to have struck at once – happily, at a free moment during the Christmas vacation – for on 19 December he informed C.A. Furth at Allen & Unwin that he had 'written the first chapter of a new story about Hobbits – "A long expected party"' (*Letters*, p. 27).

In this as first conceived Bilbo Baggins, the hero of *The Hobbit*, gives a magnificent party to celebrate his seventieth (not yet 'eleventy-first') birthday, then disappears from Hobbiton. The treasure he had gained in *The Hobbit* is now depleted, and he has a renewed desire to travel again outside his own land. But Tolkien did not yet know what adventures might be in store for Bilbo, or whether his new story would be about Bilbo or one of Bilbo's descendants. After five pages he abandoned this version of the opening chapter, though many aspects, even some of its phrasing, survived with little change into the published book. He then wrote a second version, closely based on the first, with much new material, including the presence of the wizard Gandalf; but after heavy emendation left this draft unfinished. A third version soon followed, in which the party is given not by Bilbo, who has left his homeland, but by his son Bingo (so called, perhaps, because Tolkien's children owned a 'family' of stuffed koala bears, the 'Bingos'), and then a fourth, in which the party is given by Bilbo's adopted cousin Bingo Bolger-Baggins. On 1 February 1938 Tolkien wrote to C.A. Furth: 'Would you ask Mr Unwin whether his son [Rayner], a very reliable critic, would care to read the first chapter of the sequel to *The Hobbit*? . . . I have no confidence in it, but if he thought it a promising beginning, could add to it the tale that is brewing' (*Letters*, p. 28).

A few jottings from this time reveal the ideas that Tolkien was now considering. In one he noted: 'Make return of ring a motive', that is, the magic ring that Bilbo found in *The Hobbit* and which in the third and fourth versions of the new chapter is Bilbo's parting gift to Bingo (*The Return of the Shadow*, p. 41). In another memo Tolkien began to consider the nature of the ring:

> *The Ring*: whence its origin. Necromancer [an evil figure mentioned but not seen in *The Hobbit*]? Not very dangerous, when used for good purpose. But it exacts its penalty. You must either lose it, or *yourself*. Bilbo could not bring himself to lose it. He starts on a holiday handing over ring to Bingo. But he vanishes. Bingo worried. Resists desire to go and find him – though he does travel round a lot looking for news. Won't lose ring as he feels it will ultimately bring him to his father.
>
> At last he meets Gandalf. Gandalf's advice. You must stage a *disappearance*, and the ring may then be cheated into letting you follow a similar path. But you have got to *really disappear* and give up the past. Hence the 'party'.
>
> Bingo confides in his friends. Odo, Frodo, and Vigo (?) [> Marmaduke] insist on coming too. . . . [*The Return of the Shadow*, p. 42]

From these and similar thoughts Tolkien began to write a tale in which the hobbits Bingo, Frodo, and Odo set out for Rivendell. On the road they are overtaken by a rider wrapped in a great cloak and hood, who after a moment of tension is comically revealed to be Gandalf. But Tolkien immediately abandoned this idea, already beginning to conceive a story much darker than *The Hobbit*, and instead decided that Bingo and company were being pursued by Black Riders. He began the chapter anew, and much as in the finished *Lord of the Rings* (if with many differences of detail) brought the hobbits to a meeting with elves in the Woody End, to Farmer Maggot's house, and to a house in Buckland with their friend Marmaduke (precursor of Merry) Brandybuck. On 4 March 1938 Tolkien wrote to Stanley Unwin: 'The sequel to *The Hobbit* has now progressed as far as the end of the third chapter. But stories tend to get out of hand, and this has taken an unpremeditated turn' (*Letters*, p. 34). 'Beyond any doubt', Christopher Tolkien has said, that turn was 'the appearance of the Black Riders' (*Return of the Shadow*, p. 44). But it would be some time yet before their nature and purpose became clear.

After a pause, from the end of August to mid-September 1938 Tolkien continued *The Lord of the Rings* as far as the middle of Bingo's conversation with the dwarf Glóin during the feast at Rivendell (the equivalent of published Book II, Chapter 1). During this period the story continued to change and evolve, and new ideas arose in the process. When Tolkien reached the point at which the hobbits are captured by a Barrow-wight, he made a rough plot outline for the story as far as the hobbits' arrival at Rivendell, and already foresaw a journey to the Fiery Mountain (Mount

Doom). But he had doubts about some of the story he had written to date, and considered possible changes. The character Trotter, a hobbit 'ranger' who joins Bingo and company in Bree, was a particular mystery; and as Tolkien considered the powers and history of Bingo's ring, the idea that it is the Ruling Ring began to emerge.

From probably late September to the end of 1938 Tolkien altered the cast of hobbits, introducing Sam Gamgee, and added a new second chapter, 'Ancient History' (later 'The Shadow of the Past', published Book I, Chapter 2), in which Gandalf tells Bingo about the Ring and Gollum, and advises Bingo to leave the Shire. Also added was an account of the Black Riders' attack on Crickhollow. Tolkien now made a new fair copy manuscript of the work as far as the conversation between Frodo (the name now replacing 'Bingo') and Glóin out of existing drafts, incorporating many small changes and moving generally closer to the published text. Here in places, as in later workings, he tried out several versions of new or revised material before he was satisfied. He also wrote a new text to provide background information about Hobbits – the precursor of the Prologue – and drew a first selection of Hobbit family trees.

On 31 August he had written to C.A. Furth that *The Lord of the Rings* was 'getting quite out of hand' and progressing 'towards quite unforeseen goals' (*Letters*, p. 40). On 13 October he wrote to Stanley Unwin that the work was 'becoming more terrifying than *The Hobbit.* It may prove quite unsuitable [for its original intended audience of children]. It is more "adult". . . . The darkness of the present days [as war with Germany was an evident possibility] has had some effect on it. Though it is not an "allegory"' (*Letters*, p. 41). *The Lord of the Rings* now ran to over 300 manuscript pages, and according to the author's overly optimistic estimate, required at least another 200 to complete. He was eager to finish it. 'I am at the "peak" of my educational financial stress,' he wrote to C.A. Furth on 2 February 1939, 'with a second son [Michael] clamouring for a university and the youngest [Christopher] wanting to go to school (after a year under heart-specialists), and I am obliged to do exams and lectures and what not.' *The Lord of the Rings* was 'in itself a good deal better than *The Hobbit*,' he felt, 'but it may not prove a very fit sequel. It is more grown-up – but the audience for which *The Hobbit* was written [his children] has done that also.' Although his eldest son (John) was enthusiastic about the new work, 'it would be a relief to me to know that my publishers were satisfied. . . . The writing of *The Lord of the Rings* is laborious, because I have been doing it as well as I know how, and considering every word' (*Letters*, p. 42). On 10 February he wrote again to Furth, vowing to make a special effort to complete *The Lord of the Rings* before 15 June; but other duties occupied his time, and later that summer he had an accident while gardening which resulted in concussion and required stitches.

Tolkien's injury left him unwell for a long time, 'and that combined with the anxieties and troubles that all share [with the outbreak of war], and with the lack of any holiday, and with the virtual headship of a department in this bewildered university have made me unpardonably neglectful', he wrote to Stanley Unwin on 19 December 1939 (*Letters*, p. 44). Nonetheless, during the second half of the year Tolkien produced rough 'plot-outlines, questionings, and portions of the text' which show the author temporarily 'at a halt, even at a loss, to the point of a lack of confidence in radical components of the narrative structure that had been built up with such pains' (Christopher Tolkien, *The Return of the Shadow*, p. 370). He considered, *inter alia*, a version of the story once more with Bilbo as the hero, that the hobbit Trotter was actually Bilbo's well-travelled cousin Peregrin Boffin, that a dragon should invade the Shire, and that Frodo should meet the 'Giant Treebeard'; and he accurately foresaw final elements of the story yet to be written: a snowstorm in the pass over the mountains, the Mines of Moria, the loss of Gandalf, a siege, that Frodo would find himself unable to destroy the Ring, that Gollum would seize it and fall, the devastation of the Shire.

Tolkien now, after several false starts, completed a version of 'The Council of Elrond' (published Book II, Chapter 2), still far from its final form, in which the Fellowship consisted of Gandalf, Boromir, and five hobbits, one of whom was Peregrin Boffin (alias Trotter). He then wrote first drafts of 'The Ring Goes South' (Book II, Chapter 3) and 'The Mines of Moria' (later 'A Journey in the Dark', Book II, Chapter 4), and substantially revised his account of the journey to Rivendell told in Book I in order to clarify Gandalf's part in events. To this end he made many outlines, notes, and time-schemes co-ordinating events and the movements of Gandalf, the Black Riders, and Frodo and his companions. In the process, he decided that Trotter was not a Hobbit but a Man, whose true name was Aragorn.

In his Foreword to the second edition of *The Lord of the Rings* (1965) Tolkien said that in writing the story he suffered delays because of his academic duties, which were

> increased by the outbreak of war in 1939, by the end of which year the tale had not yet reached the end of Book I. In spite of the darkness of the next five years I found that the story could not now be wholly abandoned, and I plodded on, mostly by night, till I stood by Balin's tomb in Moria. There I halted for a long while. It was almost a year later when I went on and so came to Lothlórien and the Great River late in 1941.

But in his letter to Stanley Unwin of 19 December 1939 (*Letters*, p. 44) Tolkien wrote that he had 'never quite ceased work' on *The Lord of the Rings*, which had 'reached Chapter XVI' – a clear indication that he was at work on 'The Mines of Moria' (published as 'A Journey in the Dark'), and in Book II, during 1939. From this Christopher Tolkien has convincingly argued that his father's hiatus in writing must have begun in that year rather than 1940 as the Foreword implies. He comments in *The Return of the Shadow* (p. 461): 'I feel sure . . . that – more than a quarter of a century later – [my father] erred in his recollection of the year' – a memory, perhaps, of his revision of the Moria episode rather than of its initial writing.

Tolkien returned to *The Lord of the Rings* evidently in late August 1940, continued to work on it probably until the beginning of Michaelmas Term at Oxford in October of that year, picked up the story again during the Christmas vacation, and returned to it again at times during 1941. It is not possible to date his writing or revision during this period more precisely except for a narrative outline, headed 'New Plot. Aug. 26–27, 1940': in this Tolkien decided that Gandalf's unexplained absence in Book I was caused by the wizard Sarumond/Saramund/Saruman, who betrayed Gandalf to the Black Riders. He also wrote an account of Gandalf and the hobbit Hamilcar (later Fredegar 'Fatty') Bolger telling Frodo in Rivendell of their adventures, and of Gandalf's rescue of Hamilcar from Black Riders, added other passages to agree with this account, but in the end rejected the episode.

Various decisions that Tolkien now made entailed considerable emendation and rewriting, especially of the second part of 'At the Sign of the Prancing Pony' (later 'Strider', Book I, Chapter 10). He also revised 'Many Meetings' (Book II, Chapter 1), with an addition in which Bilbo tells Frodo of Aragorn's background, and the third of ultimately fifteen versions of the poem Bilbo recites at Rivendell (evolved in stages from Tolkien's *Errantry*, an independent poem published in 1933). At least three new versions of 'The Council of Elrond' date from this time as well, as Tolkien worked out additional material to be discussed, mainly arising from the position of Aragorn as the heir of Elendil. At this stage the chapter included material that was later removed to the Appendices, or that became the basis of the separate work *Of the Rings of Power and the Third Age* (published in 1977 in *The Silmarillion*).

Having settled most of his doubts and made necessary changes in Book I and the beginning of Book II, Tolkien revised the account already written of the journey of the Company of the Ring from Rivendell as far as Balin's tomb. He wrote a fresh manuscript of 'The Ring Goes South' (Book III, Chapter 3), advancing confidently and making changes in the process, and rewrote the first part of the Moria episode. At last he moved the story beyond the discovery of Balin's tomb until the surviving members of the Fellowship emerged from Moria. It was probably not until towards the end of 1941 that he wrote of the Company in Lothlórien and their farewell from that golden land (published Book II, Chapters 6–8, 'Lothlórien', 'The Mirror of Galadriel', and 'Farewell to Lórien'): here too, the story evolved as it progressed, requiring many emendations to earlier parts of the episode. 'By this time,' Christopher Tolkien has said, 'it had become my father's method to begin making a fair copy before a new stretch of the narrative had proceeded very far' (*The Treason of Isengard*, p. 267), built up in stages as different parts of the draft text were completed. During the writing of the chapters set in Lothlórien Tolkien temporarily rejected *Aragorn* as Trotter's true name in favour first of *Elfstone* (and replaced the name *Aragorn* with *Elfstone* haphazardly in earlier text as far back as the chapter at Bree and the fifth version of the Council of Elrond), then rejected *Elfstone* for *Ingold*, before returning to *Elfstone*. He also drafted a substantial outline of subsequent chapters in which he imagined Boromir's encounter with Frodo, his attempt to seize the Ring, Frodo's flight, and Frodo and Sam's journey in Mordor.

Tolkien then continued *The Lord of the Rings* with a new chapter, 'The Scattering of the Company' (later divided into 'The Great River' and 'The Breaking of the Fellowship', published Book II, Chapters 9–10). Uncertain as to whether time moved at a different pace, or no time passed at all, while the Company was in Lothlórien, he wrote several versions of the conversation on the subject (ultimately in 'The Great River') and devised variant time-schemes. At the end of 1941 and the beginning of 1942 he finished Book II and began to write Book III, completing Chapters 1–4 ('The Departure of Boromir', 'The Riders of Rohan', 'The Uruk-hai', and 'Treebeard') around the end of January. The next two chapters ('The White Rider' and 'The King of the Golden Hall') were written probably by Midsummer, along with two outlines of the course of the story foreseen from Fangorn, though Tolkien still had not conceived many significant parts of the story yet to be told. He devoted spare time in summer and autumn 1942 to the remainder of Book III ('Helm's Deep', 'The Road to Isengard', 'Flotsam and Jetsam', 'The Voice of Saruman', and 'The Palantír'), which he seems to have worked on as a whole rather than bringing each part to a developed state before beginning work on the next.

As he developed the story of Helm's Deep in successive drafts, its fortifications became more elaborate and the account of its defence more complex. He completed 'The Road to Isengard' (Book III, Chapter 8) only after writing seven versions of Théoden and Gandalf's conversation about riding to Saruman's fortress, and four of Merry's lecture on pipe-weed, besides much other preliminary drafting. Apparently satisfied at last, he made a fair copy, but removed most of the material on pipe-weed into the preliminary section that became the Prologue; then he rejected much of what he had written and began to draft again, with a different chronology and changes in the route to Isengard. In 'The Voice of Saruman' (Book III, Chapter 10) he completed the interview with Saruman only after several drafts. And when he came to 'The Palantír' (Book III, Chapter 11) the appearance of that object was unexpected, and he did not know immediately how to use it in the story. As he later wrote: 'I knew nothing of the *Palantíri*, though from the moment the Orthanc-stone was cast from the window, I recognized it, and knew the meaning of the "rhyme of lore" that had been running through my mind: *seven stars and seven stones and one white tree*' (letter to W.H. Auden, 7 June 1955, *Letters*, p. 217).

On 7 December 1942 Tolkien wrote to Stanley Unwin, wondering if, because of the war, it was 'of any use, other than private and family amusement, to endeavour to complete the sequel to *The Hobbit.* I have worked on it at intervals since 1938, all such intervals in fact as trebled official work, quadrupled domestic work, and "Civil Defence" have left. It is now approaching completion' (*Letters*, p. 58). He hoped to have free time to work on *The Lord of the Rings* during the Christmas vacation, and thought that he might finish it early in 1943. It had now reached 'Chapter 31' (i.e. 'The Palantír'), and Tolkien believed that it needed at least six more chapters to be finished, which were already sketched. But he did no further work on the book until spring 1944.

On 3 April he wrote to his son Christopher that he had begun 'to nibble at [the] Hobbit again' (i.e. *The Lord of the Rings*) and had 'started to do some (painful) work on the chapter which picks up the adventures of Frodo and Sam again; and to get myself attuned have been copying and polishing the last written chapter (Orthanc-Stone ['The Palantír'])' (*Letters*, p. 69). Apart from occasional revisions to earlier parts of the tale, during the rest of April and May 1944 Tolkien brought Frodo, Sam, and Gollum through the Dead Marshes, into Ithilien and a meeting with men of Gondor, to Shelob's Lair and the pass of Kirith (later Cirith) Ungol. Christopher's keen interest in the story, while in South Africa for training in the Royal Air Force, encouraged his father to work on his book, as did the enthusiasm of friends such as C.S. Lewis. During this period Tolkien had chapters typed and sent them to Christopher by post; and his frequent letters to Christopher allow us to date the progress of *The Lord of the Rings* for a while with some precision.

On 6 May 1944 Tolkien informed Christopher that a new character had come on the scene: '(I am sure I did not invent him, I did not even want him, though I like him, but there he came walking into the woods of Ithilien): Faramir, the brother of Boromir' (*Letters*, p. 79). By 21 May he struck a difficult patch: 'All that I had sketched or written before proved of little use, as times, motives etc., have all changed. However at last with v[ery] great labour, and some neglect of other duties, I have now written or nearly written all the matter up to the capture of Frodo in the high pass on the very brink of Mordor' (letter to Christopher Tolkien, *Letters*, p. 81). 'The matter' comprised the final three chapters of Book IV ('The Stairs of Cirith Ungol', 'Shelob's Lair', and 'The Choices of Master Samwise'), in which Tolkien decided to alter the sequence of events as the hobbits and Gollum climbed to the pass, from a stair, then a tunnel, then a stair to stair, stair, and tunnel. On 15 May he wrote to Christopher that he was 'now coming to the nub, when the threads must be gathered and the times synchronized and the narrative interwoven; while the whole thing has grown so large in significance that the sketches of concluding chapters (written ages ago) are quite inadequate, being on a more "juvenile" level' (*Letters*, pp. 80–1). On 31 May he reported that he had just spent all the time he could spare in a 'desperate attempt to bring "The Ring" to a suitable pause, the capture of Frodo by the Orcs in the passes of Mordor, before I am obliged to break off by examining', and achieved this only 'by sitting up all hours' (letter to Christopher Tolkien, 31 May 1944, *Letters*, p. 83). On 12 August 1944 he wrote that he was now 'absolutely dry of any inspiration for the Ring [*The Lord of the Rings*] and am back where I was in the Spring, with all the inertia to overcome again. What a relief it would be to get it done' (*Letters*, p. 91).

He returned to the story in October 1944, with abortive beginnings of 'Minas Tirith' and 'The Muster of Rohan' (published Book V, Chapters 1 and 3). He now mistakenly thought that Book V would be the final part of *The Lord of the Rings*, and again was uncertain of events to come. On 16 October he wrote to Christopher that he had 'been struggling with the dislocated chronology of the Ring,' that is the timeline of *The Lord of the Rings* as a whole, 'which has proved most vexatious, and has not only interfered with other more urgent and duller duties, but has stopped me getting on. I think I have solved it all at last by small map alterations, and by inserting [in Books III and IV] an extra day's Entmoot, and extra days into Trotter's chase and Frodo's journey' (*Letters*, p. 97). In fact, some of his changes to the chronology required substantial emendation to the text. And it was probably at this point that he made a new, elaborate working time-scheme which shows the actions of all the major characters synoptically from 19 January, the fifth day of the voyage of the Fellowship down the Anduin, until 8 February.

Tolkien remained optimistic about Book V into the next spring. On ?18 March 1945 he told Stanley Unwin that given 'three weeks with nothing else to do – and a little rest and sleep first' he probably would be able to finish *The Lord of the Rings*, but 'I don't see any hope of getting them'. He remembered that he had promised to let Unwin see part of what was written, but

> it is so closely knit, and under a process of growth in all its parts, that I find I have to have all the chapters by me – I am always, you see, hoping to get at it. And anyway only one copy (home-typed or written by various filial hands and my own), that is legible by others, exists, and I've feared to let go of it; and I've shirked the expense of professional typing in these hard days, at any rate until the end, and the whole is corrected. [*Letters*, pp. 113–14]

But he made little or no further progress until the middle of the following year. On 21 July 1946 he wrote to Stanley Unwin:

> I have been ill, worry and overwork mainly, but am a good deal recovered; and am at last able to take some steps to see that at least the overwork, so far as it is academic, is alleviated. For the first time in 25 years, except the year I went on crutches (just before *The Hobbit* came

> out, I think), I am free of examining, and though I am still battling with a mountain of neglects . . . and with a lot of bothers in this time of chaos and 'reconstruction', I hope after this week actually to – write.

But after a long gap since he had last worked on *The Lord of the Rings* 'I shall now have to study my own work in order to get back into it. But I really do hope to have it done before the autumn term, and at any rate before the end of the year' (*Letters*, pp. 117–18).

Around the end of September 1946 he returned to Book V, now with more developed ideas than two years previously. He completed it probably by the end of October 1947, with the usual succession of drafts and fair copies, and uncertainties as to how to proceed. As first written, the whole of Aragorn's journey from Helm's Deep to Minas Tirith was told in retrospect on the day following the Battle of the Pelennor Fields. At a later date, Tolkien decided to tell the first part of this tale, as far as the Stone of Erech, as narrative in a new chapter preceding 'The Muster of Rohan' (Book V, Chapter 3).

Also during the period 1946–7 Tolkien made further revisions to Books I and II, and wrote as a 'specimen' a revised account of Bilbo's encounter with Gollum in Chapter 5 of *The Hobbit*, which he sent to Allen & Unwin on 21 September 1947. In the first edition of *The Hobbit* Gollum offers the Ring to Bilbo as a 'present'; but this was now unlikely, given the dark possessive nature of the Ring as conceived in *The Lord of the Rings*, as well as the more sinister personality of Gollum in the sequel. Tolkien changed the episode so that Gollum offers to show Bilbo the way out of the goblin-caves if the hobbit should be successful at the riddle-game.

Tolkien completed *The Lord of the Rings* at last, at least in draft, in the period 14 August to 14 September 1948 in the quiet of his son Michael's home at Payables Farm, Woodcote, while Michael and his family were away on holiday. Some parts of Book VI were achieved, for once, with little difficulty. As Christopher Tolkien has said about 'Mount Doom' (Book VI, Chapter 3), for instance, it

> is remarkable in that the primary drafting constitutes a completed text, with scarcely anything in the way of preparatory sketching of individual passages, and while the text is rough and full of corrections made at the time of composition it is legible almost throughout; moreover many passages underwent only the most minor changes later. It is possible that some more primitive material has disappeared, but it seems to me . . . that the long thought which my father had given to the ascent of Mount Doom and the destruction of the Ring enabled him, when at last he came to write it, to achieve it more quickly and surely than almost any earlier chapter in *The Lord of the Rings*. [*Sauron Defeated*, p. 37]

But other parts were not so easy to write. Tolkien seems to have felt his way in 'The Scouring of the Shire', with much revision and significant changes. Although he realized that Saruman was behind the troubles in the Shire, it was only after several false starts that he made the character actually present among the hobbits. Christopher Tolkien has said that 'it is very striking that here, virtually at the end of *The Lord of the Rings* and in an element in the whole that my father had long meditated, the story when he first wrote it down should have been so different from its final form (or that he so signally failed to see "what really happened"!)' (*Sauron Defeated*, p. 93). Also at this stage Tolkien conceived Book VI as ending not with the present final chapter, 'The Grey Havens', but with an Epilogue featuring Sam and his children reading from the Red Book, ultimately omitted (but published in *Sauron Defeated*).

Over the next year Tolkien made fair copies and typescripts of *The Lord of the Rings*, finishing the complete work in October 1949. In doing so he incorporated late changes and additions already in draft, and made new changes as well. Not until this late date was the name of Elrond's daughter changed from *Finduilas* to *Arwen Evenstar*, and Frodo's role in the Scouring of the Shire made passive rather than active. Tolkien also now further developed background and ancillary material for the Prologue and Appendices, concerning the history, peoples, languages, alphabets, and calendars of Middle-earth.

*

Although he had written *The Lord of the Rings* nominally for publication by George Allen & Unwin, at length Tolkien began to resent their rejection of 'The Silmarillion' in 1937 and came increasingly to feel that *The Lord of the Rings* and 'The Silmarillion' should be published together – indeed, that the former needed the latter to make its full impact. Thus when in autumn 1949 he was introduced to Milton Waldman, a senior editor at the London publisher Collins, and Waldman expressed an interest in publishing both books if 'The Silmarillion' could be finished, Tolkien responded eagerly. The question now arose, however, whether Tolkien had any moral or legal commitment to Allen & Unwin. In a draft letter to Waldman of 5 February 1950 Tolkien wrote that he believed himself to have

> no *legal* obligation to Allen & Unwin, since the clause in *The Hobbit* contract with regard to offering the next book seems to have been satisfied either (a) by their rejection of *The Silmarillion* or (b) by their eventual acceptance and publication of *Farmer Giles*. I should . . . be glad to leave them, as I have found them in various ways unsatisfactory. But I have friendly personal relations with Stanley (whom all the same I do not much like) and with his second son Rayner (whom I do like very much). [*Letters*, p. 135]

And since *The Lord of the Rings* had always been considered a sequel to *The Hobbit*, he thought that he might have a moral obligation to the publisher of the earlier work.

On 24 February 1950 he wrote to Stanley Unwin about *The Lord of the Rings*, deliberately putting it in a poor light:

> And now I look at it, the magnitude of the disaster is apparent to me. My work has escaped from my control, and I have produced a monster: an immensely long, complex, rather bitter, and very terrifying romance, quite unfit for children (if fit for anybody); and it is not really a sequel to *The Hobbit*, but to *The Silmarillion*. My estimate is that it contains, even without certain necessary adjuncts, about 600,000 words. . . . I can see only too clearly how impracticable this is. But I am tired. It is off my chest, and I do not feel that I can do anything more about it, beyond a little revision of inaccuracies. Worse still: I feel that it is tied to the *Silmarillion*. . . .
>
> Ridiculous and tiresome as you may think me, I want to publish them both – *The Silmarillion* and *The Lord of the Rings* – in conjunction or in connexion . . . that is what I should like. Or I will let it all be. I cannot contemplate any drastic re-writing or compression. . . . But I shall not have any just grievance (nor shall I be dreadfully surprised) if you decline so obviously unprofitable a proposition. . . . [*Letters*, pp. 136–7]

Unwin replied on 6 March that it would be difficult to publish both 'The Silmarillion' and *The Lord of the Rings*, especially with the costs of book production three times what they were before the war. Would there be any possibility, he asked, of breaking the work into, say, 'three or four to some extent self-contained volumes' (quoted in *Letters*, p. 137)? 'A work of great length can, of course, be divided artificially', Tolkien replied on 10 March.

> But the whole Saga of the Three Jewels and the Rings of Power has only one natural division into two parts . . . : *The Silmarillion* and other legends; and *The Lord of the Rings*. The latter is as indivisible and unified as I could make it.
>
> It is, of course, divided into sections for narrative purposes (six of them), and two or three of these, which are of more or less equal length, could be bound separately, but they are not in any sense self-contained. [*Letters*, p. 138]

He wondered, moreover, if many beyond his friends would read, or purchase, so long a work. He understood the financial barriers to publication, and said that he would not feel aggrieved should Allen & Unwin decline.

Stanley Unwin did not reply at once, but on 3 April informed Tolkien that he was still studying the problem of how *The Lord of the Rings* might be published. To print 2,500 copies in two large volumes, each of 1392 pages, 'would involve an outlay of well over £5,000, and each volume would actually cost for paper, printing, and binding, without allowing anything for overheads, author or publisher, about 22/-' (Tolkien-George Allen & Unwin archive, HarperCollins). Rayner Unwin by now also supplied an opinion, requested by his father, which the elder Unwin sent to Tolkien though it had never been intended for Tolkien's eyes:

> *The Lord of the Rings* is a very great book in its own curious way and deserves to be produced somehow. *I* never felt the lack of a *Silmarillion* when reading it. But although he claims not to contemplate any drastic rewriting, etc., surely this is a case for an editor who would incorporate any *really* relevant material from *The Silmarillion* into *The Lord of the Rings* without increasing the enormous bulk of the latter and, if feasible, even cutting it. Tolkien wouldn't do it, but someone whom he would trust and who had sympathy (one of his sons?) might possibly do it. If this is not workable I would say publish *The Lord of the Rings* as a prestige book, and after having a second look at it, drop *The Silmarillion.* [quoted in *Biography*, p. 210]

This infuriated Tolkien, who on 14 April demanded that Unwin give an immediate answer to his proposal for publication of both works. Unwin replied on 17 April that he was sorry that Tolkien felt it necessary to present an ultimatum,

> particularly one in connection with a manuscript which I have never seen in its final and complete form. We have not even had an opportunity of checking whether it does in fact run to one million, two hundred thousand words.... As you demand an *immediate* 'yes' or 'no' the answer is 'no'; but it might well have been yes given adequate time and the sight of the complete typescript. [Tolkien-George Allen & Unwin archive, HarperCollins; partly quoted in *Letters*, p. 141]

Tolkien now was able to tell Milton Waldman that *The Lord of the Rings* was free of any entanglements. But once Collins' staff considered the work in earnest, Waldman informed Tolkien that it would have to be cut for publication. Dismayed, Tolkien said that he would try to comply, but appears never to have begun to do so; indeed, he continued to expand Appendix A. Waldman then left England for Italy where he lived for much of the year, and also fell ill, leaving *The Lord of the Rings* and the still unfinished 'Silmarillion' in the hands of colleagues who did not share Waldman's enthusiasm for what Tolkien had written. Probably in late 1951 and apparently at Waldman's suggestion, Tolkien wrote a long letter, about 10,000 words, explaining the two works and demonstrating his view that they are interdependent and indivisible. (Much of this statement is published in *Letters*, pp. 143–61. An account of *The Lord of the Rings*, omitted from the transcription in *Letters*, is included as an appendix to the present book.)

Stanley Unwin meanwhile had written to Tolkien, taking note of his problems with Collins and letting him know that the door had not closed for him at Allen & Unwin. Then on 22 June 1952 Tolkien wrote humbly to Rayner Unwin, in reply to a query:

> As for *The Lord of the Rings* and *The Silmarillion*, they are where they were. The one finished (and the end revised), the other still unfinished (or unrevised), and both gathering dust. I have been both off and on too unwell, and too burdened to do much about them, and too downhearted. Watching paper-shortages and costs mounting against me. But I have rather modified my views. Better something than nothing! Although to me all are one, and the 'L[ord] of the Rings' would be better far (and eased) as part of the whole, I would gladly consider the publication of any part of this stuff. Years are becoming precious. And retirement (not far off) will, as far as I can see, bring not leisure but a poverty that will necessitate scraping a living by 'examining' and such like tasks.
>
> When I have a moment to turn round I will collect the *Silmarillion* fragments in process of completion – or rather the original outline which is more or less complete, and you can read it. My difficulty is, of course, that owing to the expense of typing and the lack of time to do my own (I typed nearly all of *The Lord of the Rings*!) I have no spare copies to let out. But what about *The Lord of the Rings*? Can anything be done about that, to unlock gates I slammed myself? [*Letters*, p. 163, corrected from the Tolkien-George Allen & Unwin archive, HarperCollins]

Rayner quickly replied, asking to see a copy of the complete *Lord of the Rings* to 'give us a chance to refresh our memories and get a definite idea of the best treatment for it'. The capital outlay would be great, he advised, but less serious if Allen & Unwin did not publish *The Lord of the Rings* and 'The Silmarillion' all at once. 'We do *want* to publish for you – it's only ways and means that have held us up. So please let us have the Ring now, and when you are able the Silmarillion too (I've never read it at all you see) and by the time you are freer we shall be ready to discuss it' (1 July 1952, Tolkien-George Allen & Unwin archive, HarperCollins, partly quoted in *Letters*, pp. 163–4).

Tolkien now retreated again to his son Michael's home at Woodcote to read through and correct *The Lord of the Rings*. Since he had written the work over such a long span of years, he found that some of its elements needed to be changed, and even in later parts Tolkien needed to ensure that all of the adjustments consequent upon changes in the story's chronology had been made. Other alterations now occurred to him as well; and if he had not done so already, he also had to consider which version of Bilbo's encounter with Gollum was to be considered 'true', his revision for *The Hobbit* having been included in the 1951 second edition.

In early November 1952, having obtained cost estimates for printing *The Lord of the Rings*, Rayner Unwin sent a telegram to his father, who was on a business trip in the Far East. Rayner admitted that publication of *The Lord of the Rings* would be a big risk for their firm, and believed that Allen & Unwin might lose up to a thousand pounds in the process; but in his opinion Tolkien had written a work of genius. He asked his father if he might offer Tolkien a contract. Stanley Unwin famously cabled in reply: '*If* you believe it is a work of genius, *then* you may lose a thousand pounds' (quoted in Rayner Unwin, *George Allen & Unwin: A Remembrancer* (1999), p. 99). Allen & Unwin minimized their risk, however, by offering Tolkien a profit-sharing agreement, by which no royalties would be paid to him until all of the publisher's costs had been recovered, but thereafter he would receive half-profits. Tolkien quickly agreed.

By 17 November 1952 Allen & Unwin decided that the most economical way to publish *The Lord of the Rings* was in three volumes, at a price not exceeding 25*s* each. This unfortunately has led many of its readers to speak of it as three separate but interconnected works, a 'trilogy', though it is no such thing. Tolkien himself considered its important division to be its six books, to each of which he had given a title, not the three volumes into which these were artificially broken. He wrote to Rayner Unwin on 24 March 1953:

> I have given some thought to the matter of sub-titles for the volumes, which you thought were desirable. But I do not find it easy, as the 'books', though they must be grouped in pairs, are not really paired; and the middle pair (III/IV) are not really related.
>
> Would it not do if the 'book-titles' were used: e.g. *The Lord of the Rings*: Vol. I *The Ring Sets out* and *The Ring Goes South*; Vol. II *The Treason of Isengard*, and *The Ring goes East*; Vol. III *The War of the Ring*, and *The End of the Third Age*?
>
> If not, I can at the moment think of nothing better than: I *The Shadow Grows* II *The Ring in the Shadow* III *The War of the Ring* or *The Return of the King*. [*Letters*, p. 167]

(Alternate book titles are preserved in a galley proof of the combined tables of contents of the three volumes, Marquette MSS 4/2/16: Book I *The First Journey*; Book II *The Journey of the Nine Companions*; Book III *The Treason of Isengard*; Book IV *The Journey of the Ring-bearers*; Book V *The War of the Ring*; Book VI *The End of the Third Age*. All of these were ultimately abandoned.)

On 11 April 1953 Tolkien reported to Rayner Unwin that he had 'at last completed the revision for press – I hope to the last comma – of Part I: *The Return of the Shadow*: of *The Lord of the Rings*, Books I and II' (*Letters*, p. 167). He was also prepared to send his Foreword, but still had not decided what would appear in the Appendices, or what he would be able to provide in the time remaining before publication. By now he had proposed that the book contain a facsimile of the burnt pages of the Book of Mazarbul (which figures in Book II, Chapter 5), but expensive halftones were ruled out. Allen & Unwin also suggested economies for the Moria Gate illustration in Book II, Chapter 2, and for the three maps that Tolkien thought necessary. Although Tolkien had originally hoped that *The Lord of the Rings* could contain illustrations, the cost was prohibitive, given the great length of the book and the difficulties of Britain's postwar economy. In the event, only a few essential blocks could be included, and all in line. In the process of writing *The Lord of the Rings*, however, Tolkien drew a number of quick sketches to aid his thoughts, such as a diagram of Helm's Deep, different conceptions of Saruman's fortress Orthanc and of Minas Tirith, and a plan of Farmer Cotton's house. He also made several more finished drawings in coloured pencil, of Old Man Willow, Moria Gate, Lothlórien, Dunharrow, and Barad-dûr – not all of which are actual scenes from *The Lord of the Rings*, or accord in every detail with the final text. (See further, *Artist and Illustrator*, Chapter 5.)

Galley proofs began to arrive for Tolkien's attention in July 1953. On 4 August he wrote to his son Christopher:

> There seem such an endless lot of them; and they have put me very much out of conceit with parts of the Great Work, which seems, I must confess, in print very long-winded in parts. But the printing is very good, as it ought to be from an almost faultless copy; except that the impertinent compositors have taken it upon themselves to correct, as they suppose, my spelling and grammar: altering throughout *dwarves* to *dwarfs*; *elvish* to *elfish*; *further* to *farther*; and worst of all, *elven-* to *elfin*. [*Letters*, p. 169]

He complained, and his original readings were restored.

On 28 July Rayner Unwin pressed Tolkien that each of the three volumes needed a title, and made his own suggestions; among these, he felt that *The Lord of the Rings* could be applied to Volume I, and did not propose an overall title for the complete work. Tolkien countered that he preferred *The Lord of the Rings* for the whole, with *The Return of the Shadow*, *The Shadow Lengthens*, and *The Return of the King* for the volumes. After further discussion, on 17 August he proposed

> as titles of the *volumes*, under the overall title of *The Lord of the Rings*: Vol. I The Fellowship of the Ring. Vol. II The Two Towers. Vol. III The War of the Ring (or, if you still prefer that: The Return of the King).
>
> The Fellowship of the Ring will do, I think; and fits well with the fact that the last chapter of the Volume is The Breaking of the Fellowship. The Two Towers gets as near as possible to finding a title to cover the widely divergent Books 3 and 4; and can be left ambiguous – it might refer to Isengard and Barad-dûr, or to Minas Tirith and B[arad-dûr]; or to Isengard and Cirith Ungol. On reflection I prefer for Vol. III The War of the Ring, since it gets in the Ring again; and also is more non-committal, and gives less hint about the turn of the story: the chapter titles have been chosen also to give away as little as possible in advance. But I am not set in my choice. [*Letters*, pp. 170–1]

Unwin agreed, but preferred *The Return of the King* for Volume III.

During the rest of 1953, through 1954, and for the first half of 1955 Tolkien worked with Allen & Unwin on production of *The Lord of the Rings*. Proofs arrived at intervals for correction. Frequent correspondence was needed to deal with these, to arrange the completion of miscellaneous art (for the most part redrawn by a printer's copyist after Tolkien's originals), to transmit and correct the three maps (drawn by Christopher Tolkien; see below, 'The Maps of *The Lord of the Rings*'), and to settle the dust-jacket designs (see below, 'Preliminaries'). Probably during 1953 Tolkien began to prepare a glossary-index to *The Lord of the Rings*, as promised in the original Foreword to *The Fellowship of the Ring*, and continued to work on it at least into 1954, but completed only a list of place-names. And in the second half of 1954 and early 1955 he wrote additional material for the Appendices, but had to omit most of this for lack of space: it included the works now known as *The Quest of Erebor* and *The Hunt for the Ring*, parts of which (in different versions) were eventually published in *Unfinished Tales* (1980).

Early in the process he was asked by Allen & Unwin to write, for publicity purposes, a description of *The Lord of the Rings* in not more than 100 words, with biographical details of the author. He felt that he could not write the briefest sketch concerning his work in fewer than 300 or 400 words. His friend George Sayer, English Master at Malvern, agreed to help, and sent Allen & Unwin a blurb of 95 words. The publisher itself drafted a blurb for Tolkien's approval, drawing mainly upon his effort, with a reduced comment by Sayer about poetry in *The Lord of the Rings*. A shortened version of the final text appeared in the publisher's catalogue *Autumn & Winter Books 1953* (omitting the second paragraph), but the complete text was in *Autumn Books 1954*:

> Mr. Tolkien's long and enthralling tale is cast in the same imaginary period of history as was *The Hobbit*, and some of the chief characters, notably Gandalf and the sinister Gollum, appear again. It is a story of mounting excitement which sweeps the reader into a world of heroic endeavour and high romance.
>
> *The Lord of the Rings* begins in the homely village from which the Hobbit set forth, but it passes soon into the presence of the Great. It depicts the supreme crisis of its time when the dark power of Sauron threatened to overwhelm the world, and the heroism with which that evil was met. Yet it differs from most heroic romances (and there are very few in English) in that the large events are seen through the eyes of simple folk, the smallest and humblest of human-kind, as they themselves grow to great heights of achievement and nobility.
>
> Behind the exciting adventure-story and the variety and freshness of Mr. Tolkien's imaginary world the reader will find a study of the noble and heroic in relation to the commonplace. Throughout, this great

> prose epic is illuminated with songs and verses which show Mr. Tolkien to be an outstanding poet.
>
> The book will be published in three volumes. It is not a children's book, neither is it necessary to have read *The Hobbit* first. But readers of *The Hobbit* of all ages will be amongst the most insistent in demanding *The Lord of the Rings*. [Tolkien-George Allen & Unwin archive, HarperCollins]

Volume I, *The Fellowship of the Ring*, was published by George Allen & Unwin in London on 29 July 1954 in 3,000 copies (plus 1,500 for its American edition, published on 21 October 1954 by the Houghton Mifflin Company, Boston). Volume II, *The Two Towers*, was published by Allen & Unwin on 11 November 1954 in 3,250 copies (plus 1,000 copies for Houghton Mifflin, published on 21 April 1955). Volume III, *The Return of the King*, was published by Allen & Unwin on 20 October 1955 in 7,000 copies (plus 5,000 copies for Houghton Mifflin, published on 5 January 1956). The lesser print runs for Volumes I and II reflect the publishers' initial level of expectations of sales, while the much higher quantity for Volume III indicates the demand for the conclusion of the work, delayed nearly a year while Tolkien completed a revision of Books V and VI and then the Appendices, the latter selected and reduced from an abundance of material.

*

The initial critical response to *The Lord of the Rings* was mixed, but on the whole mostly positive, a state of affairs which has continued to the present day. Some of its first reviewers were puzzled: it was not the sort of book they were accustomed to read, nor the sort they might have expected from Tolkien, whose two previous works of fiction (*The Hobbit* and *Farmer Giles of Ham*) had been marketed for children, nor could it be read complete until 1955 (in America, 1956). Some were put off by comments by its advance readers, who compared it grandly to Spenser, Malory, and Ariosto. But not a few were impressed by what they read.

The anonymous reviewer of *The Fellowship of the Ring* for the *Times Literary Supplement*, describing Hobbits, wrote that 'it is as though these Light Programme types had intruded into the domain of the Nibelungs'. He felt, however, that Tolkien had just managed to pull off the difficult 'change of key' within the first volume; and yet 'the plot lacks balance. All right-thinking hobbits, dwarfs, elves and men can combine against Sauron, Lord of Evil; but their only code is the warrior's code of courage, and the author never explains what it is they consider the Good.' Perhaps, he thought, 'this is the point of a subtle allegory', of the West against the Communist East. In any case, '*The Fellowship of the Ring* is a book to be read for sound prose and rare imagination' ('Heroic Endeavour', *Times Literary Supplement*, 27 August 1954, p. 541). In contrast, Peter Green in the *Daily Telegraph* ('Outward Bound by Air to an Inappropriate Ending',

27 August 1954, p. 8) remarked that Tolkien had 'written, with the interminable prosiness of a bazaar story-teller, an adventure yarn about magic rings and Black Riders which should prove immensely popular with those 10-year-olds who don't prefer space-fiction. . . . It's a bewildering amalgam of Malory, Grimm, the Welsh *Mabinogion*, T.H. White and "Puck of Pook's Hill". The style veers from pre-Raphaelite to Boy's Own Paper.' But even so, he concluded, 'this shapeless work has an undeniable fascination'. In the *New Statesman and Nation* Naomi Mitchison praised Tolkien's book for its details of geography and language, but regretted that certain aspects of its world were not worked out, and that there were 'uncertainties on the scientific side. But on the fully human side, from the standpoint of history and semantics, everything is there' ('One Ring to Bind Them', 18 September 1954, p. 331).

Much firmer and unequivocal support for *The Fellowship of the Ring* came from Tolkien's friend C.S. Lewis (who had read the work or heard it read to him in draft) in a review for *Time and Tide* ('The Gods Return to Earth', 14 August 1954):

> This book is like lightning from a clear sky: as sharply different, as unpredictable in our age as *Songs of Innocence* [by William Blake] were in theirs. To say that in it heroic romance, gorgeous, eloquent, and unashamed, has suddenly returned at a period almost pathological in its anti-romanticism, is inadequate. To us, who live in that odd period, the return – and the sheer relief of it – is doubtless the important thing. But in the history of Romance itself – a history which stretches back to the *Odyssey* and beyond – it makes not a return but an advance or revolution: the conquest of new territory. [p. 1082]

With the publication of *The Two Towers* the *Times Literary Supplement* proclaimed the work to be 'a prose epic in praise of courage', and noted that 'within his imagined world the author continually unveils fresh countries of the mind, convincingly imagined and delightful to dwell in.' But 'large sectors of this mythic world are completely omitted; women play no part; no one does anything to get money; oddly enough, no one uses the sea, though that may come in the final volume. And though the allegory is now plainer there is still no explanation of wherein lies the wickedness of Sauron' ('The Epic of Westernesse', 17 December 1954, p. 817). Maurice Richardson in the *New Statesman and Nation* thought that *The Two Towers* would 'do quite nicely as an allegorical adventure story for very leisured boys, but as anything else . . . it has been widely overpraised'. The work had begun as 'a charming children's book' but 'proliferated into an endless worm', its fantasy 'thin and pale'. He liked its scenes of battle and the 'atmosphere of doom and danger and perilous night-riding', though, and thought that the allegory (as he perceived it to be) raised 'interesting speculations' as to whether the Ring related to the atomic nucleus, and Orcs perhaps with materialist scientists ('New Novels', 18 December 1954, pp. 835–6).

The *Times Literary Supplement* praised the completion of *The Lord of the Rings* upon the appearance of *The Return of the King*: 'At last the great edifice shines forth in all its splendour, with colonnades stretching beyond the ken of mortal eye, dome rising behind dome to hint at further spacious halls as yet unvisited.' The reviewer felt that *The Lord of the Rings* was 'not a work that many adults will read right through more than once; though even a single reading will not be quickly forgotten' ('The Saga of Middle Earth', 25 November 1955, p. 704). But he thought that Tolkien could have distinguished Good and Evil better. In response to a reader's letter, the reviewer wrote, with an astonishing lack of perception, that 'throughout the book the good try to kill the bad, and the bad try to kill the good. We never see them doing anything else. Both sides are brave. Morally there seems nothing to choose between them' (*TLS*, 9 December 1955, p. 743). C.S. Lewis answered such criticism in his combined review of *The Two Towers* and *The Return of the King* for *Time and Tide* ('The Dethronement of Power', 22 October 1955): 'Since the climax of Volume I was mainly concerned with the struggle between good and evil in the mind of Boromir', it was not easy to see how anyone could complain that the characters in *The Lord of the Rings* 'are all either black or white'; and even those who do complain

> will hardly brazen it out through the two last volumes. Motives, even in the right side, are mixed. Those who are now traitors usually began with comparatively innocent intentions. Heroic Rohan and imperial Gondor are partly diseased. Even the wretched Sméagol, till quite late in the story, has good impulses; and (by a tragic paradox) what finally pushes him over the brink is an unpremeditated speech by the most selfless character of all [Sam]. [p. 1373]

By now *The Lord of the Rings* had been widely reviewed, and the critical climate was such that W.H. Auden would later write: 'I rarely remember a book about which I have had such violent arguments. Nobody seems to have a moderate opinion; either, like myself, people find it a masterpiece of its genre or they cannot abide it' ('At the End of the Quest, Victory', *New York Times Book Review*, 22 January 1956, p. 5). He himself had given it high praise. On the other hand there was (most famously) Edmund Wilson, who wrote of *The Lord of the Rings* in *The Nation* ('Oo, Those Awful Orcs!' 14 April 1956, pp. 312–13) that there was little in the book 'over the head of a seven-year-old child', that it dealt with 'a simple confrontation – of the Forces of Evil with the Forces of Good, the remote and alien villain with the plucky little home-grown hero', that Tolkien's 'poverty of imagination' was so pathetic that to have critics such as C.S. Lewis, Naomi Mitchison, and Richard Hughes pay tribute to *The Lord of the Rings* (on the original dust-jackets) could be explained only by the 'lifelong appetite' that 'certain people – especially, perhaps, in Britain – have . . . for juvenile trash'. In 1962 Edmund Fuller observed that the critical acclaim with which *The Lord of the Rings* was received was so great as to carry in it 'an inevitable counterreaction – a natural hazard of any work unique in its time that kindles a joy by its very freshness' ('The Lord of the Hobbits: J.R.R. Tolkien', reprinted in *Tolkien and the Critics: Essays on J.R.R. Tolkien's The Lord of the Rings* (1968), ed. by Neil D. Isaacs and Rose A. Zimbardo, p. 36). Or, as Tolkien himself put it,

> *The Lord of the Rings*
> is one of those things:
> if you like it you do:
> if you don't, then you boo!

(quoted in *Biography*, p. 223). He took note of criticism as it came to his attention. On 9 September 1954, following the first reviews of *The Fellowship of the Ring*, he wrote to Rayner Unwin:

> As for the reviews they were a great deal better than I feared, and I think might have been better still, if we had not quoted the Ariosto remark, or indeed got involved at all with the extraordinary animosity that C.S. L[ewis] seems to excite in certain quarters. He warned me long ago that his support might do me as much harm as good. I did not take it seriously, though in any case I should not have wished other than to be associated with him – since only by his support and friendship did I ever struggle to the end of the labour. All the same many commentators seem to have preferred lampooning his remarks or his review to reading the book.
>
> The (unavoidable) disadvantage of issuing in three parts has been shown in the 'shapelessness' that several readers have found, since that is true if one volume is supposed to stand alone. 'Trilogy', which is not really accurate, is partly to blame. There is too much 'hobbitry' in Vol. I taken by itself; and several critics have obviously not got far beyond Chapter I.
>
> I must say that I was unfortunate in coming into the hands of the D[aily] Telegraph, during the absence of [John] Betjeman. My work is not in his line, but he at any rate is neither ignorant nor a gutter-boy. Peter Green seems to be both. I do not know him or of him, but he is so rude as to make one suspect malice. . . .
>
> I am most puzzled by the remarks on the style. I do not expect, and did not expect, many to be amused by hobbits, or interested in the general story and its modes, but the discrepancy in the judgements on the style (which one would have thought referable to standards independent of personal liking) are very odd – from laudatory quotation to 'Boys Own Paper' (which has no one style)! [*Letters*, p. 184]

Critical attitudes towards *The Lord of the Rings* continue to vary. No one explanation will account for this phenomenon, or for the basis of the work's popularity. When, at the 1983 Tolkien conference at Marquette

University, the late Lester Simons asked two or three dozen Tolkien scholars and enthusiasts to explain the popularity of *The Lord of the Rings*, he received almost as many answers. It is a gripping adventure story; it is a glimpse into another world, with its own history, geography, languages, a fictional world but one which seems real while the reader is 'inside' it; it is a work utterly different from fiction praised by critics for dealing with 'real life', that is, with the dysfunctional lives and petty relationships of uninteresting and unpleasant people whom most readers would prefer not to meet; it is a story in which ethics and morality are more clear-cut than in contemporary life, a story in which even the 'weak' have a part to play in great events; and so forth, not forgetting its sympathetic characters and carefully crafted prose. At the close of the twentieth century *The Lord of the Rings* came first in several opinion polls as readers' choice for best or favourite book – much to the dismay of certain critics, some of whom cried foul. As Tolkien wrote already on 3 March 1955 to one of his readers, Dora Marshall: 'It remains an unfailing delight to me to find my own belief justified: that the "fairy-story" is really an adult genre, and one for which a starving audience exists' (*Letters*, p. 209). That audience has increased substantially from time to time, as a result of publicity surrounding adaptations of *The Lord of the Rings* for radio and film; but the book has always sold well on its own, on its merits as literature and, at least since the mid-1960s, an icon of popular culture.

*

Far from losing a thousand pounds, as Rayner Unwin had feared, *The Lord of the Rings* proved a commercial success. Allen & Unwin quickly ordered new printings of Volumes I and II to satisfy orders, and more copies continued to be needed, both domestically and overseas. Since its first publication *The Lord of the Rings* has never been out of print. In 1954–5, as a matter of course, Allen & Unwin instructed its printer to keep the (metal) type of the three volumes standing, ready for additional impressions. But the printer failed to do so for *The Fellowship of the Ring*, and on receiving an order for more copies quickly reset that volume so that it would appear to be identical to the original setting. This was done, however, without notifying either Allen & Unwin or Tolkien, thus without fresh proofreading by publisher or author, and in the process numerous errors were introduced, mainly the substitution of a word with a similar word, a change in the order of words, or a change in punctuation. The fact of the resetting was not discovered until 1992.

Small corrections were made to *The Lord of the Rings* in its early printings, before the standing type was cast into more durable printing plates for subsequent impressions. Then in 1965 Tolkien learned that his American copyright in *The Lord of the Rings*, and in *The Hobbit*, could be open to legal challenge. He was asked to revise both works so that new U.S. copyrights could be obtained. But before he could act, Ace Books of

New York, a well-known publisher of science fiction, issued their own paperback edition of *The Lord of the Rings* at the cheap price of seventy-five cents. Ace Books held that *The Lord of the Rings* was in the public domain in the United States, due to improper attention to details of copyright (a claim later taken up by others, and at last disproved in court). From July to September 1965 Tolkien sent material for a revised *Lord of the Rings* to the Houghton Mifflin Company; this was incorporated in an authorized paperback edition by Ballantine Books of New York and first published in October 1965. These revisions were then made to the George Allen & Unwin second edition of 1966, which in turn was the basis for the Houghton Mifflin second edition of 1967. (N.B. in the present book, references to the 'second edition (1965)' of *The Lord of the Rings* are dated from the first appearance of the revised text, though the primary, hardcover editions did not appear until one or two years later.) Further emendations were made to later Ballantine printings, and notably to the second printing of the Allen & Unwin second edition in 1967 – Tolkien had continued to work on the text beyond his deadline for changes in 1965. In the process, however, errors and omissions were variously made, and the texts of these different editions diverged.

As Tolkien, and later Christopher Tolkien acting as his father's literary executor, discovered errors in *The Lord of the Rings*, they were sent to Allen & Unwin for action. But with every resetting of the text, new errors have been introduced. In 1987 Douglas A. Anderson, working with Christopher Tolkien, encouraged Houghton Mifflin to bring its standard edition of *The Lord of the Rings* (unchanged since 1966) into line with the standard British edition (to which emendations had been made from time to time), and to make additional corrections to the text as needed. For several years this was the most accurate edition available. Then in 1994 HarperCollins, successor to Allen & Unwin (and its successor, Unwin Hyman) as Tolkien's primary publisher, reset *The Lord of the Rings* again, now in electronic form for ease of correction; but in doing so, once again many errors were made, which in turn were carried into later printings and into other editions (by HarperCollins, Houghton Mifflin, and Ballantine Books) based on the 1994 setting. Some of these errors were corrected in the HarperCollins edition of 2002, others not until the HarperCollins edition of 2004 (also published by Houghton Mifflin) and its further corrected reprint of 2005.

*

For the fiftieth anniversary of *The Lord of the Rings* in 2004 we proposed, and it was agreed by Tolkien's publishers and the Tolkien Estate, that a fresh effort should be made to produce a text as close as possible to what its author intended, as far as that could be very conservatively determined. Already for many years we had studied *The Lord of the Rings* textually and bibliographically, and had published thoughts on the subject (Hammond,

J.R.R. Tolkien: A Descriptive Bibliography (1993), A5; Scull, 'A Preliminary Study of Variations in Editions of *The Lord of the Rings*', *Beyond Bree*, April and August 1985); and we had become aware of lingering errors and inconsistencies which we thought should be addressed. To that end we now compiled an exhaustive and up to date catalogue of known errors, corrections, and emendations throughout the publishing history of *The Lord of the Rings*. In doing so we made use of similar lists prepared by J.R.R. and Christopher Tolkien to guide earlier emendation and resetting; notes by Christopher Tolkien in the *Lord of the Rings* volumes of *The History of Middle-earth*; the results of an invaluable comparison of copies of *The Lord of the Rings* by Steven M. Frisby, together with his research in the J.R.R. Tolkien Papers in the Marquette University Libraries; our own examination of the Marquette papers, of the Tolkien-Allen & Unwin correspondence archive held by HarperCollins, and of the Allen & Unwin archive at the University of Reading; 'A Corrigenda to *The Lord of the Rings*' by David Bratman, in *Tolkien Collector* 6 (March 1994); independent lists and comments by Douglas Anderson, Charles Noad, and Arden Smith; private correspondence with fellow Tolkien enthusiasts; and references in Tolkien-related journals, bulletins, and Internet forums.

This analysis allowed us to see where most (if not all) errors and corrections had been made previously. It showed that five dozen compositor's errors made in the unauthorized resetting of *The Fellowship of the Ring* in 1954 still survived in the latest edition (2002). And it revealed patterns of emendation by Tolkien, particularly in the second edition. At the same time, we made a careful reading of our copy-text, the 2002 HarperCollins edition, and with the aid of searchable computer files provided by HarperCollins we charted variant spellings and punctuation in *The Lord of the Rings*, to determine if Tolkien had preferred usages in addition to those he had expressed in correspondence, on proof sheets, or in his personal check copies of the book, and which had not been consistently followed.

As we remarked in our editors' note in the 2004 edition, Tolkien's point of view in regard to errors seemed clear, both from the textual evidence we had gathered and from a letter he wrote on 30 October 1967 to Joy Hill at George Allen & Unwin, concerning a reader's query he had received about points in the Appendices to *The Lord of the Rings*:

> Personally I have ceased to bother about these minor 'discrepancies', since if the genealogies and calendars etc. lack verisimilitude it is in their general excessive accuracy: as compared with real annals or genealogies! Anyway the slips were few, have now mostly been removed, and the discovery of what remain seems an amusing pastime! *But errors in the text are another matter.* [italics ours; Tolkien-George Allen & Unwin archive, HarperCollins]

In fact, Tolkien had not 'ceased to bother', and 'slips' were dealt with as opportunities arose. His emendations to the second edition of *The Lord of the Rings* show that he was concerned with both accuracy and consistency – of spelling, capitalization, and punctuation, as well as details of story. Even so, he left unchanged much that might have been a candidate for change, and we wondered: was this because he did not notice some of the (mostly minor) typographic errors, or because he saw the errors but felt them to be not worth correction (or even that they were improvements), or because of the difficulties and expense of correction to (metal) type or plates, or because he simply did not have the time to carry it through? Since, today, electronic typesetting allows corrections to be made more easily, quickly, and cheaply, and since the type of *The Lord of the Rings* was to be reformatted for the anniversary edition in any case, how far would Tolkien now want to impose consistency on (say) the capitalization of *Orcs* versus *orcs*, or the hyphenation of *birthday-present* versus *birthday present*? And how far should an editor go, in the author's absence, in imposing such changes?

After long thought we decided upon a general working policy in which, wherever the latest text of *The Lord of the Rings* differed from readings which could be shown with comfortable certainty to have been intended or preferred by Tolkien, it should be changed accordingly. Typographical errors, or unintended omissions of text, should be repaired or restored; and spelling and capitalization should be regularized wherever a clear preference by Tolkien could be discerned. More substantive textual questions would be considered case by case. At all times we would be conservative in our judgement and hold to high standards of evidence; and every point would be considered by Christopher Tolkien as our supervisor.

With this in mind, we prepared for Christopher Tolkien's approval a list of 229 points of discussion, concerning errors and inconsistencies in *The Lord of the Rings*, and issues such as the varying capitalization of *Sun* and *Moon*, the differentiation of Gollum's *precious* and *Precious* (depending upon capitalization), and whether *Númenórean(s)* should have one or two accented letters. Most of these points described the current text, sometimes in multiple instances, and included a recommendation whether or not to make a change, with a possible revision and evidence to justify our stance. We looked always for at least a preponderance of evidence to support a suggested change. In cases such as 'a great paved highway had wound upwards from the lowlands of the Dwarf-kingdom' (Book II, Chapter 6), where the Dwarf-kingdom clearly did not have lowlands, and the first printing had 'from the lowlands *to* the Dwarf-kingdom' (italics ours), a correction was called for without question. In some instances we had extensive documentary evidence of an error, as in the case of *glistered/ glistened* ('glistered and sparkled on the grass') in Book I, Chapter 8. Steve Frisby had shown that this phrase began in manuscript as 'glittering in the sun', but was immediately revised to 'glistered and sparkled in the grass'. When a typescript was made of this chapter 'glistered' was keyed as 'glistened', but corrected by Tolkien in manuscript back to 'glistered'. The printer's typescript once again contained the error 'glistened', which Tolkien again corrected; and the correct form 'glistered' then was set in type and appeared in the first printing – only to revert to 'glistened' in the unauthorized resetting of the volume. In this, as well as in the other fifty-nine errors that still survived from the 1954 reset *Fellowship of the Ring*, although each was not necessarily incorrect in meaning or style, the substituted reading was invariably less appropriate or felicitous than the original.

We did not recommend a change in every case. Sometimes we considered instances of usage in which we could find no clear pattern in *The Lord of the Rings*, or where otherwise we could not be sure of Tolkien's intent. *Hobbit(s)/hobbit(s)*, *Orc(s)/orc(s)*, and the like, and *Sun/sun*, *Moon/moon*, *inter alia*, thus remain as they were. Christopher Tolkien commented to us that some apparent inconsistencies of form in his father's work indeed may have been deliberate: for instance, although Tolkien carefully distinguished *house* 'dwelling' from *House* 'noble family or dynasty', in two instances he used *house* in the latter sense but in lower case, perhaps because a capital letter would have detracted from the importance of the adjective with which the word was paired ('royal house', 'golden house'). In other cases variations in usage probably were no more than the result of natural but unnoticed changes of mind over the long period in which *The Lord of the Rings* was written.

Nonetheless it seemed to us appropriate to regularize, carefully and very selectively – in so far as we detected variation – words or phrases such as *any one* and *birthday present* to *anyone* and *birthday-present*, according to predominant usage in the book and other compelling evidence. Christopher Tolkien told us that his father would not have 'bothered his head' about such things, where there was no clear difference in meaning; but that he always intended to be consistent in his writing, even if he did not always succeed. 'However much my father desired to achieve consistency at every level of his work,' Christopher wrote,

> from capital letters to the dates of dynasties, he was bound to fail. He didn't go in for steady, meticulous, plodding reading (re-reading) of his texts; rather, his eye lit upon things that struck him, & he made a hasty note in the margin. His life was a perpetual battle against time (& tiredness), and for a world-class niggler (as he cheerfully recognized himself to be) this was a perpetual frustration. But he 'niggled' on a grand and noble conception, & indeed its coherence in fine detail is a part of its power. [private correspondence]

More substantive errors, many of them noted in *The History of Middle-earth*, were more difficult to analyze and to form a recommendation for or against correction. We were sometimes reluctant to suggest any change for these, and indeed recommended against change to any text whose correction could be accomplished only by significant rewriting. Thus (to name only two examples) the description of the doors of Moria as seen by moonlight, at a time when the moon was into its last quarter and rising late, and Gimli's statement at Helm's Deep that he had 'hewn naught but wood since I left Moria' (Book III, Chapter 7), though he had killed many orcs at Parth Galen, have been retained in the text unchanged – but they are described and discussed in our notes, as is any major alteration to the text at any time in its history. But simpler corrections to palpable errors, such as the number of ponies the hobbits took with them from Crickhollow (*six* had been evidently a 'shadow' of an earlier version, now emended to *five*), and the distance from the ferry to the Brandywine Bridge in Book I, Chapter 5 (now *ten* miles rather than *twenty*), were another matter. As Christopher Tolkien commented: 'I cannot see anything but advantage in getting rid of inconsistencies of this nature which puzzle observant readers and diminish the very credibility that my father was so anxious to maintain. Of course if he had noticed this inconsistency himself or had it pointed out to him he would have altered it without a second thought' (private correspondence). Thus most of the errors in *The Lord of the Rings* mentioned in *The History of Middle-earth* were corrected in the anniversary edition; but a few of these points, at the last, fell below our desired level of certainty for action, perhaps most notably the text of Bilbo's song of Eärendil at Rivendell, a different version of which Christopher Tolkien has surmised that his father meant to include rather than the one that was published.

Rayner Unwin once suggested, not entirely with tongue in cheek, that it will take three centuries of correction and emendation of *The Lord of the Rings* to achieve typographical perfection. Indeed, new errors have entered in with each resetting of type, sometimes even when only a single correction has been made. Even the edition of 2004, despite great care by its editors and publisher, still contains flaws, some of them survivals from previous settings not previously noticed, others newly introduced through what might be called misunderstandings by software. Additional corrections were identified by the present authors in the course of writing this *Reader's Companion*, or have been called to our attention by sharp-eyed readers of the anniversary edition; and these, in turn, have been made to the reprint of 2005.

CHRONOLOGIES, CALENDARS, AND MOONS

In *The Hobbit* Tolkien provides only a few specific dates, preferring general suggestions of the passing of time ('Long days after they had climbed out of the valley . . . they were still going up and up', Chapter 4). The situation in *The Lord of the Rings* is very different: even the first version of the first chapter provides a date for Bilbo's birthday, 22 September. And once Frodo leaves Bag End, both the narrative and *The Tale of Years* (Appendix B) give a detailed account of his and other characters' movements, more or less on a daily basis with the exception of periods in Rivendell and Lothlórien. In order to keep track of these, early in writing *The Lord of the Rings* Tolkien began to make lists and tables to record the chronology of events. As the story developed and changed, he emended these time-schemes or began new ones. From about the point that the Company of the Ring leave Lothlórien until the destruction of the Ring, many of Tolkien's time-schemes are synoptic, recording events day by day horizontally across a series of columns, with each column devoted to the movements of one or more members of the scattered Company or to a general group such as 'Enemies'.

Occasionally a new idea came to Tolkien, or one thread of the story required more time than he had first thought, requiring other threads to be adjusted so that they would come together at the right time; for instance, in remarking to himself on moving the Battle of the Pelennor Fields from 14 to 15 March, he wrote:

> But more time is needed for Aragorn. Fellowship could be broken sooner giving 2 days (5) [i.e. presumably 5 days instead of 3] to F[rodo and] S[am] in Emyn Muil and moving Hornburg ride back 2 days. But this would all throw out of gear in rest [of] story. Best would be to make Pelennor later. [Marquette MSS 4/2/17]

At other times more substantial shifts were needed: these generally had little effect on the details of the narrative since they did not alter the sequence of events, but they required the emendation of blocks of dates. The first such change was Tolkien's decision that the Company of the Ring should leave Rivendell on 25 December instead of 24 November 3018 (Third Age).

Although Tolkien could adjust the movements of his characters so that a journey took more or less time, the phases of the moon were beyond his control. He took great care, however, to ensure that the moons described in *The Lord of the Rings* acted according to the standard lunar cycle, and that the widely separated actors in his story saw the same moon on the same date. During 1944, for instance, while working on Book IV, he wrote to his son Christopher: 'at this point [24 April] I need to know how much later the moon gets up each night when nearing the full, and how to stew a rabbit'; and 'I found my moons in the crucial days between Frodo's flight and the present situation (arrival at Minas Morghul) were doing impossible things, rising in one part of the country and setting simultaneously in another' (14 May; *Letters*, pp. 74, 80).

In winter 1941–2, while writing of the journey of the Company of the Ring down the Anduin, he decided to base the moons in his book on the primary world lunar calendar. He wrote on one time-scheme (Marquette MSS 3/1/34 ADDS):

> Moons are after 1941–2 + 6 [> 5] days thus F[ull] M[oon] Jan 2 is Jan 7

In the first scheme in which this formula was applied, based on the calendar for (AD) 1942, the departure from Rivendell has been moved to 25 December, the Company arrive in Hollin on 6 January, and there is a full moon on 7 January. At this point in the development of the story, no time passes in Middle-earth while the Company are in Lórien. The same time-scheme also records a new moon on 21 January, the night before the Company are attacked by Orcs at Sarn Gebir. In 1942 the moon was full on 2 January, and new on 16 January. Since the Company still reach Hollin in January in the published *Lord of the Rings*, one would expect a full moon on 7/8 January (2 + 5), but instead it appears on 8/9 January.

The difference in dates is due to further developments in the story, centred on the full moon seen by Frodo early in the morning of 8 March at Henneth Annûn (Book IV, Chapter 6). When this episode was first written it took place on the night of 6/7 February, with a full moon on 6 February entered in time-schemes. *Whitaker's Almanack* for 1942 indicates that the moon became full on 1 February, and that 1/2 February was the night of the full moon. In Book V this same moon is seen by Pippin as he rides with Gandalf to Minas Tirith, and it also governs the date set for the muster of Rohan. But during the writing of Book V Tolkien made two important decisions: he concluded (after having twice changed his mind) that time in the outside world did continue to pass while the Company was in Lothlórien; and he decided to apply to the story a new calendar of his own invention, the 'Shire Reckoning'. In this every month has thirty days, there are two Yule days between 30 December and 1 January, and in a normal year three days (Lithe, Mid-year's Day, and Lithe) between 30 June and 1 July. To effect this, Tolkien now had to adjust his time-schemes to take account of such matters as February having thirty days rather than twenty-eight.

A scheme headed 'New Time Table; allowing 30 days sojourn in Lothlórien', Marquette MSS 4/2/17, originally showed the Company leaving Lothlórien on 14 February, Sam seeing the new moon on 20 February, and Frodo being at Henneth Annûn now on 7/8 March. In 1942 there was a new moon on 15 February and a full moon on 3 March – it became full just after midnight, therefore 2/3 March was the night of the full moon – thus the scheme applies the formula of date plus five days for a full moon on 7/8 March. But at the bottom of the first sheet of this scheme Tolkien struck through '[January] 31' and wrote beside it 'Feb 1' – clearly the introduction of Shire Reckoning into the chronology. He then adjusted the other dates in the scheme upward, so that the Company left Lothlórien on 15 rather than 14 February. He evidently soon realized, however, that although this adjustment accounted for one of the extra two days in February in the Shire Reckoning, the second extra day would place Frodo's night at Henneth Annûn on 6/7 March, not at the full moon. Therefore he altered the time-scheme yet again, so that the Company leaves Lothlórien on 16 February and Frodo is at Henneth Annûn correctly on 7/8 March. The new moon which had been on 20 February was now on 22 February. To the side of the entry for 16 February Tolkien scribbled a rough note:

> if dates at ?crucial points later Mar 1 – – > [*sic*] are to be correct then if S.R. to be used Lórien stay must be 2 days long [?longer]. Coy. [Company] must come out on Feb. 16 our ?reckoning = S.R. W[ed] Feb 16 and all other dates pushed back ?to ?agree after Feb. 30 all would then be ?correct ?again. [Marquette MSS 4/2/17]

This is the clue to his lunar calendar as finally conceived: the moons in *The Lord of the Rings* are based on those of 1941–2, but with their dates adjusted on either side of the full moon of 7/8 March to take account of Shire Reckoning. When this is checked against Tolkien's latest and only complete time-scheme (for the period 22 September 3018, S.R. 1418 – 6 October 3021, S.R. 1421), every phase of the moon entered there agrees. We have used this (Marquette MSS 4/2/18) frequently in the present book, where it is referred to as *Scheme*.

In the table given below, the first column **A** gives the dates and phases of the moon for the relevant parts of 1941–2 (Gregorian calendar); the second column **B** shows the same dates + 5; and the third column **C** shows dates in the Shire Reckoning adjusted from 7/8 March with the phases of the moon as they are entered on this final time-scheme. Entries are included at relevant points to clarify the adjustments to Shire Reckoning. Entries of date or phases of the moon in square brackets do not appear in the time-scheme, but are calculated from other entries.

Another piece of evidence supporting the accuracy of this table is the state of the moon when Gandalf escapes from Orthanc. *The Tale of Years* states that he left in the early hours of 18 September 3018 (Third Age). In one version of *The Hunt for the Ring* (Marquette MSS 4/2/33) it is said that 'Gandalf escapes night of 17/18. Full Moon 6 days waned'. *Whitaker's Almanack* for 1941 has the moon at full late on 5 September, therefore 5/6 September is the night of the full moon; in the chart this becomes S.R.

11/12 September, 6 days before 17/18. One aspect of the 1942 lunar calendar which Tolkien did not introduce into *The Lord of the Rings* was a complete lunar eclipse on 2 March beginning 22.31 GMT. On one time-scheme, however (Marquette MSS 3/1/36 ADDS, with dates altered from February to March), Tolkien notes between 7 and 8 March 'Total eclipse at 10.30'.

Tolkien often entered in his schemes specific times, sometimes to the odd minute, for the rising and setting of the sun and the moon, or when a journey began or ended. These aided him in judging what length of journey or sequence of events plausibly could be fitted into a given period of time. The times do not appear in the final text, where they were replaced by more general references such as 'at dawn', 'early morning', 'noon', 'dusk', etc. as witnessed by the characters. These more general terms did not need to be changed when events were moved forward, and differences of latitude or longitude need not be taken into account.

A		B	C	
5 Sep	FM	10 Sep	11 Sep	FM
11 Sep		16 Sep	17 Sep	
13 Sep	LQ	18 Sep	19 Sep	
16 Sep		21 Sep	22 Sep	
21 Sep	NM	26 Sep	27 Sep	NM
24 Sep		29 Sep	30 Sep	
25 Sep		30 Sep	1 Oct	
26 Sep		1 Oct	2 Oct	
27 Sep	FQ	2 Oct	3 Oct	FQ
30 Sep		5 Oct	6 Oct	
5 Oct	FM	10 Oct	11 Oct	FM
13 Oct	LQ	18 Oct	19 Oct	LQ
20 Oct	NM	25 Oct	26 Oct	NM
24 Oct		29 Oct	30 Oct	
25 Oct		30 Oct	1 Nov	
26 Oct		31 Oct	2 Nov	
27 Oct	FQ	1 Nov	3 Nov	[FQ]
3 Nov		8 Nov	10 Nov	
4 Nov	FM	9 Nov	11 Nov	[FM]
12 Nov	LQ	17 Nov	19 Nov	[LQ]
19 Nov	NM	24 Nov	26 Nov	[NM]
23 Nov		28 Nov	30 Nov	
24 Nov		29 Nov	1 Dec	
25 Nov	FQ	30 Nov	2 Dec	[FQ]
26 Nov		1 Dec	3 Dec	
3 Dec	FM	8 Dec	10 Dec	[FM]
11 Dec	LQ	16 Dec	18 Dec	[LQ]
18 Dec	NM	23 Dec	25 Dec	NM
23 Dec		28 Dec	30 Dec	

A		B	C	
24 Dec		29 Dec	1 Yule	
25 Dec	FQ	30 Dec	2 Yule	[FQ]
26 Dec		31 Dec	1 Jan	
27 Dec		1 Jan	2 Jan	
31 Dec		5 Jan	6 Jan	
1 Jan		6 Jan	7 Jan	
2 Jan	FM	7 Jan	8 Jan	FM
10 Jan	LQ	15 Jan	16 Jan	LQ
16 Jan	NM	21 Jan	22 Jan	NM
24 Jan	FQ	29 Jan	30 Jan	FQ
25 Jan		30 Jan	1 Feb	
26 Jan		31 Jan	2 Feb	
27 Jan		1 Feb	3 Feb	
31 Jan		5 Feb	7 Feb	
1 Feb	FM	6 Feb	8 Feb	FM
8 Feb	LQ	13 Feb	15 Feb	LQ
15 Feb	NM	20 Feb	22 Feb	NM
23 Feb	FQ	28 Feb	30 Feb	FQ
24 Feb		1 Mar	1 Mar	
28 Feb		5 Mar	5 Mar	
1 Mar		6 Mar	6 Mar	
3 Mar	FM	8 Mar	8 Mar	FM
9 Mar	LQ	14 Mar	14 Mar	LQ
16 Mar	NM	21 Mar	21 Mar	NM
20 Mar		25 Mar	25 Mar	
25 Mar	FQ	30 Mar	30 Mar	[FQ]
26 Mar		31 Mar	1 Apr	
27 Mar		1 Apr	2 Apr	
31 Mar		5 Apr	6 Apr	
1 Apr	FM	6 Apr	7 Apr	FM
2 Apr		7 Apr	8 Apr	
8 Apr		13 Apr	14 Apr	[LQ]
15 Apr	NM	20 Apr	21 Apr	[NM]
23 Apr	FQ	28 Apr	29 Apr	[FQ]
24 Apr		29 Apr	30 Apr	
25 Apr		30 Apr	1 May	
30 Apr	FM	5 May	6 May	[FM]
7 May	LQ	12 May	13 May	[LQ]
15 May	NM	20 May	21 May	
23 May	FQ	28 May	29 May	[FQ]
24 May		29 May	30 May	
25 May		30 May	1 Jun	
26 May		31 May	2 Jun	
27 May		1 Jun	3 Jun	

A		B	C	
30 May	FM	4 Jun	6 Jun	[FM]
31 May		5 Jun	7 Jun	
5 Jun	LQ	10 Jun	12 Jun	[LQ]
13 Jun	NM	18 Jun	20 Jun	[NM]
21 Jun	FQ	26 Jun	28 Jun	[FQ]
23 Jun		28 Jun	30 Jun	
24 Jun		29 Jun	Lithe	
25 Jun		30 Jun	Overlithe	
26 Jun		1 Jul	Lithe	
27 Jun		2 Jul	1 Jul	
28 Jun	FM	3 Jul	2 Jul	[FM]
30 Jun		5 Jul	4 Jul	
5 Jul	LQ	10 Jul	9 Jul	
13 Jul	NM	18 Jul	17 Jul	NM
26 Jul		31 Jul	30 Jul	
12 Aug	NM	17 Aug	17 Aug	NM
25 Aug		30 Aug	30 Aug	
26 Aug	FM	31 Aug	1 Sep	[FM]
31 Aug		5 Sep	6 Sep	
24 Sep		29 Sep	30 Sep	
25 Sep	FM	30 Sep	1 Oct	[FM]
24 Oct	FM	29 Oct	30 Oct	FM

NM = new moon; FQ = first quarter; FM = full moon; LQ = last quarter

PRELIMINARIES

Dust-jacket (1954–5) – Tolkien was consulted closely about the design of the dust-jacket for the first George Allen & Unwin edition. In January 1954 he was asked to suggest a design for the jacket of *The Fellowship of the Ring*, to be published six months later. He replied on 23 February that he had neither the time nor the inspiration to do so, but soon produced a series of sketches for jackets for both *The Fellowship of the Ring* and *The Two Towers* (see *Artist and Illustrator*, figs. 176–80).

For the first he envisioned a large gold ring in the centre, representing Sauron's Ring, surrounded by the fiery letters of its inscription. Above this would be a ring with a red jewel, representing Narya, the ruby Ring of Fire worn by Gandalf, in symbolic opposition to Sauron; and towards the bottom of the jacket would be the other two Elven-rings, Nenya and Vilya, the Rings of Water and Air, set with adamant and sapphire.

The Two Towers jacket also had the One Ring in the centre, but it was now flanked by two towers. One design for *The Two Towers* featured the Ring surrounded by the three Elven-rings and the seven Dwarf-rings, but containing the nine rings given to mortal Men. The most dramatic of the *Two Towers* designs, a moody painting in black, red, white, and grey on grey-brown paper (*Artist and Illustrator*, fig. 180), features the tower of Minas Morgul at left, headquarters of the Nazgûl, with their nine rings, and at right, the tower of Orthanc. Above the One Ring is a flying Nazgûl, and elsewhere are pertinent symbols such as the White Hand of Saruman.

In March 1954 Tolkien also made a dust-jacket design for *The Return of the King* which was even more elaborate and impressive. Drawn and painted on black paper, it features the empty winged throne of Gondor awaiting the return of the King. The circular form of the throne echoes and replaces that of the One Ring, destroyed in the course of the volume. Above this is the White Tree of Gondor and the Seven Stars of Elendil, and below it, a green jewel which represents the coming of the King Elessar, the 'Elfstone'. Finally, above and behind the throne is the shadow of Sauron stretching out his long arm across red and black mountains. (See *Artist and Illustrator*, figs. 181–2.)

Although superb designs, these were too costly to produce at that time, even if technically feasible, and it was felt by Allen & Unwin that a single design should be used for all three volumes of the original edition, with minor variation in paper or ink colour. In the event, this was a simplification of Tolkien's most developed design for *The Fellowship of the Ring* (*Artist and Illustrator*, fig. 177), which also included the Eye of Sauron within the One Ring. Two of the Elven-rings were omitted, retaining only

Narya, and Tolkien's calligraphy was replaced with titling set in type. The jacket for the second Allen & Unwin edition (1966) featured the same 'Ring and Eye' motif, reproduced at a smaller size.

In 1969 Allen & Unwin adapted Tolkien's design for the *Return of the King* jacket for the binding of the first de luxe one-volume edition of *The Lord of the Rings*. In 1998 HarperCollins adapted Tolkien's original designs on jackets for a new three-volume edition, with new lettering. The bindings of the HarperCollins and Houghton Mifflin fiftieth anniversary editions of 2004 featured, at last, Tolkien's design for the One Ring and the Three Rings together.

For details of other jackets and bindings, see *Descriptive Bibliography* A5.

In order to promote *The Lord of the Rings* George Allen & Unwin sent proof copies of the first volume to selected reviewers. Among these were Richard Hughes, who had enthusiastically reviewed *The Hobbit* in 1937; the author Naomi Mitchison; and Tolkien's friend C.S. Lewis. Extracts from their comments subsequently appeared on the front flap of the original dust-jacket:

> *The Lord of the Rings* is not a book to be described in a few sentences. It is an heroic romance – 'something which has scarcely been attempted on this scale since Spenser's *Faerie Queene*, so one can't praise the book by comparisons – there is nothing to compare it with. What can I say then?' continues RICHARD HUGHES, 'for *width* of imagination it almost beggars parallel, and it is nearly as remarkable for its vividness and for the narrative skill which carries the reader on, enthralled, for page after page.'
>
> By an extraordinary feat of the imagination Mr. Tolkien has created, and maintains in every detail, a new mythology in an invented world. As for the story itself, 'it's really super science fiction', declared NAOMI MITCHISON after reading the first part, *The Fellowship of the Ring*, 'but it is timeless and will go on and on. It's odd you know. One takes it completely seriously: as seriously as Malory'.
>
> C.S. LEWIS is equally enthusiastic. 'If Ariosto rivalled it in invention (in fact he does not) he would still lack its heroic seriousness. No imaginary world has been projected which is at once multifarious and so true to its own inner laws; none so seemingly objective, so disinfected from the taint of an author's merely individual psychology; none so relevant to the actual human situation yet so free from allegory. And what fine shading there is in the variations of style to meet the almost endless diversity of scenes and characters – comic, homely, epic, monstrous, or diabolic.'
>
> Spenser, Malory, Ariosto or Science Fiction? A flavour of all of them and a taste of its own. Only those who have read *The Lord of the Rings* will realise how impossible it is to convey all the qualities of a great book.

On seeing this blurb Tolkien wrote to publisher Rayner Unwin:

> I am pleased to find that the preliminary opinions are so good, though I feel that comparisons with Spenser, Malory, and Ariosto (not to mention super Science Fiction) are too much for my vanity! I showed your draft notice to Geoffrey Mure (Warden [at Merton College, Oxford, where Tolkien was a Fellow]), who was being tiresome this morning and threatening to eject me from my room in favour of a mere tutor. He was visibly shaken, and evidently did not know before what the college had been harbouring. . . . Anyway my stock went up sufficiently to obtain me an even better room, even at the cost of ejecting one so magnificent as the Steward. So if you have any more appreciations which I have not seen, please let me have a look at them. I promise not to become like Mr Toad [in *The Wind in the Willows*, vain and conceited]. [13 May 1954, *Letters*, pp. 181–2, corrected from the Tolkien-George Allen & Unwin archive, HarperCollins]

Title-page – The title-page inscription, also printed identically on the facing page, runs continuously in two alphabets by Tolkien, who also provided the calligraphy. The first line reads, in his runic *Cirth*, 'THE LORD OF THE RINGS TRANSLATED FROM THE RED BOOK', and the remainder reads, in the script *Tengwar*, 'of Westmarch by John Ronald Reuel Tolkien herein is set forth the history of the War of the Ring and the return of the King as seen by the Hobbits'. Tolkien drew the inscription for the first edition of *The Lord of the Rings*, but made minor errors in the lettering: these were corrected in the first printing of *The Return of the King* and the second printing of *The Fellowship of the Ring* and *The Two Towers*. Tolkien earlier drew inscriptions in runes for the dust-jacket of *The Hobbit* (1937).

The variety of Cirth used on the title-page differs slightly from the Dwarvish *Angerthas Moria* as described in Appendix E, but is essentially consistent with the 'usage of Erebor' employed by Tolkien in his 'facsimiles' of the Book of Mazarbul (see Book II, Chapter 5; *Artist and Illustrator*, fig. 156; *Pictures by J.R.R. Tolkien*, 2nd edn., no. 24). On the Tengwar employed on the title-page, Tolkien writes in Appendix E:

> There was of course no 'mode' [of Tengwar] for the representation of English. One adequate phonetically could be devised from the Fëanorian system [the letters said to be invented by the Noldorin Elf Fëanor]. The brief example on the title-page does not attempt to exhibit this. It is rather an example of what a man of Gondor might have produced, hesitating between the values of the letters familiar in his 'mode' and the traditional spelling of English. [p. 1122, III: 400]

The Ring-verse – Printed since the first edition in the preliminaries, and repeated by Gandalf to Frodo in Book I, Chapter 2 (see further, notes for

p. 50). Tolkien said in an interview that it had come to him while he was taking a bath, but he made several versions before reaching its final form. In the first complete text, for instance, published in *The Return of the Shadow*, p. 269, there were nine Elven-rings (rather than three) and only three for Men (rather than nine); and in a later version there were twelve rings for Men (rather than nine) and nine for the Dwarf-lords (rather than seven).

THE MAPS OF THE LORD OF THE RINGS

During the writing of *The Lord of the Rings* Tolkien made several working maps, some of which were published in *The History of Middle-earth*, vols. VI–VIII. From an early stage it was also his intention to include one or more finely drawn maps in the finished book, but he found them difficult to make. On 11 April 1953 he wrote to Rayner Unwin:

> Maps are worrying me. One at least (which would then have to be rather large) is absolutely essential. I think three are needed: 1. Of the Shire; 2. Of Gondor; and 3. A general small-scale map of the whole field of action. They exist, of course; though not in any form fit for reproduction – for of course in such a story one cannot make a map for the narrative, but must first make a map and make the narrative agree. 3 is needed throughout. 1 is needed in the first volume and the last. 2 is essential in vols II and III. [*Letters*, p. 168]

On 9 October 1953 he wrote to W.N. Beard at George Allen & Unwin that he was 'stumped' by the *Lord of the Rings* maps, 'indeed in a panic. They are essential; and urgent; but I just cannot get them done. I have spent an enormous amount of time on them without profitable result. Lack of skill combined with being harried. Also the shape and proportions of "The Shire" as described in the tale cannot (by me) be made to fit into shape of a page; nor at that size be contrived to be informative.' He felt that 'even at a little cost there should be picturesque maps, providing more than a mere index to what is said in the text. I could do maps suitable to the text. It is the attempt [for the sake of economy] to cut them down and omitting all their colour (verbal and otherwise) to reduce them to black and white bareness, on a scale so small that hardly any names can appear, that has stumped me' (*Letters*, p. 171).

Ultimately, in its first edition and many of its later hardcover editions, *The Lord of the Rings* featured three maps printed in black and red, with the two larger maps on fold-out sheets. All of these were drawn by Christopher Tolkien, a general map of Middle-earth in late 1953, a map of the Shire in March 1954, and a large-scale map in April 1955. On 18 April 1955 Tolkien wrote to Rayner Unwin: 'The map is hell! I have not been as careful as I should in keeping track of distances. I think a large scale map simply reveals all the chinks in the armour – besides being obliged to differ somewhat from the printed small scale version [in *The Fellowship of the Ring* and *The Two Towers*], which was semi-pictorial. May have to abandon it for this trip!' (*Letters*, p. 210). But he did not abandon it, as he recalled in April 1956 in a draft letter to H. Cotton Minchin:

> I had to call in the help of my son – the C.T. or C.J.R.T. of the modest initials on the maps – an accredited student of hobbit-lore. And neither of us had an entirely free hand. I remember that when it became apparent that the 'general map' would not suffice for the final Book [VI], or sufficiently reveal the courses of Frodo, the Rohirrim, and Aragorn, I had to devote many days, the last three virtually without food or bed, to drawing re-scaling and adjusting a large map, at which he [Christopher] then worked for 24 hours (6 a.m. to 6 a.m. without bed) in re-drawing just in time. [*Letters*, p. 247]

The scale of this third map, Tolkien informed Rayner Unwin, 'is 5 times enlarged exactly from that of the general map' (18 April 1955, *Letters*, p. 210).

A PART OF THE SHIRE

In *The Return of the Shadow* Christopher Tolkien lists four extant maps of the Shire made by his father, and two by himself. The earliest of these, by J.R.R. Tolkien, was published as the frontispiece to *The Return of the Shadow*, in colour in the British and American hardcover editions and in black and white in the British paperback (but omitted in the American paperback). The final version, drawn by Christopher, was first published in *The Fellowship of the Ring* in 1954 (but not, as Tolkien wished, also in *The Return of the King* in 1955, to accommodate the action of the final chapters of Book VI). That map, *A Part of the Shire*, was based on a large-scale map Christopher had drawn in 1943, in which he developed the villages and other features north of the Water. In that part of the 1954 map are ***Nobottle***, ***Little Delving***, ***Needlehole***, ***Rushock Bog***, ***Bindbole Wood***, ***Oatbarton***, ***Dwaling***, ***Brockenborings***, and ***Scary*** (with an adjoining quarry); the map of 1943 had, in addition, *Chivery*, *Goatacre*, *Ham Burrows*, *Ravenbeams*, *Ham's Barton*, *Grubb's Spinney*, *Windwhistle Wood*, *Ham Hall Woods*, *Long Cleeve*, and *Sandy Cleeve*, among others. Christopher Tolkien has told the present authors that he is

> virtually certain that my father allowed me some latitude of invention in that region of the Shire; and altogether certain that I proposed the name *Nobottle* and some (at least) of the others (*Needlehole*, *Rushock Bog*, *Scary*). I must have got them from browsing in my father's large collection of books on English place-names (including field-names, wood-names, stream-names, and their endlessly varying forms). It may be that we discussed each one that I proposed, but of that I have now no recollection. He would scarcely have tolerated any that he thought poorly of, and he certainly wouldn't have allowed anything of that sort to reappear on the 1954 map. (He certainly used the 1943 map himself – there are pencillings of his on it – 'Budgeford' and 'Bridgefields', with a road running north from Whitfurrows to Scary.) [private correspondence]

According to the Took family tree in Appendix C, Bandobras Took (the Bullroarer) had 'many descendants, including the North-tooks of Long Cleeve', and Peregrin Took eventually married 'Diamond of Long Cleeve' (*cleeve* from Old English *clif* 'cliff, hill').

Several of the names on the Shire map do not also appear in the text, or do not appear there in the same form.

Christopher Tolkien is certain that ***Bindbole Wood*** is a real place-name somewhere in England, but he has not been able to locate it again, nor we have been able to do so ourselves. *Bindbole* is presumably related to *bind* (or *bine*) 'bind' (compare *bindweed, woodbine*) and *bole* 'tree-trunk'. *Bindbole Wood*, however, sometimes has been misread as *Bindbale Wood*: as printed on the 1954 map the *o* of *Bindbole* resembles a compressed italic *a*. Christopher has confirmed to us that the intended reading is *Bindbole*, but the word is rendered *Bindbale* on the Shire map in the Ballantine Books edition of *The Lord of the Rings* (1965), in the cartography of Barbara Strachey and Karen Wynn Fonstad (see below), in Robert Foster's *Complete Guide to Middle-earth* (1978), and even, curiously, in a manuscript note by Tolkien himself which he prepared as part of comments on names suggested for the Dutch translation of *The Lord of the Rings* and submitted to him in 1956 (Tolkien-George Allen & Unwin archive, HarperCollins; letter from Tolkien to Rayner Unwin, 3 July 1956, cf. *Letters*, p. 251). The Dutch translator Max Schuchart had rendered *Bindbale Wood* (as he thought it was) as *Het Boze Woud* 'The Devil's Wood'. Tolkien replied: 'This at any rate does not and could not mean *het boze woud*! As it stands it means rather *pakke-baal* or *binde-balen*.' To which he added, unfortunately without elaboration (if he had any elaboration to give for *Bindbale* rather than *Bindbole*): 'The reason for the name is not, of course, given in the map – but there is one.' The Dutch translation as published renders the name as 'Pakkebaal Bos' after *pakken* 'to grab, pack' and *baal* 'bag, bale', with *bos* 'wood' – thus 'Bindbale Wood' once again. In writing his reply Tolkien evidently referred to the 1954 map, where 'Bindbole' might be mistaken for 'Bindbale'; according to Christopher Tolkien, 'Bindbole', so spelled, is unmistakable in his map of 1943.

Brockenborings is spelled thus on the Shire map, but is *Brockenbores* in the text (see note for p. 1021).

Budge Ford is spelled thus on the map, but 'Budgeford' in the text (see note for p. 108).

Deephallow is mentioned in a draft of 'A Short Cut to Mushrooms' (Book I, Chapter 4), in connection with the way south from the Brandywine Bridge ('the causeway that runs from the Bridge through Stock and past the Ferry down along the River to Deephallow', *The Return of the Shadow*, p. 286), but not in the final text. In his notes to the Dutch translator Tolkien says that *Deephallow* 'is not clear in etymology (not meant to be – not all names are!)', but probably contains the Old English element *-hall* (or *-healh*) 'recess, a piece of land half-enclosed (by slopes, woods, or a river-bend)', as also in *Woodhall*. Deephallow is 'in the angle between Shirebourn, and *Brandywine*'.

Dwaling suggests a form of 'dwelling' from the root *dwal-* (*dwel-*). In his notes to the Dutch translator, however, Tolkien wrote that 'according to English toponymy' *Dwaling* 'should be the settlement of (the descendants of) a person called *Dwale*, probably a nick-name and therefore also probably uncomplimentary: older English *dwale* "dull"?' The latter word is cognate with Gothic *dwals* 'foolish', which appears in Tolkien's 'Gothicization' of his surname, *Dwalakōneis* (see *Letters*, p. 357). But it is impossible to say whether he had considered the meaning of *Dwaling*, added to the map by Christopher, before this point. The German translator (1969) assumed that *Dwaling* was derived from the plant-name *dwale* 'deadly nightshade, belladonna', thus 'Nachtschatten'.

Girdley Island is so named probably because it is 'girdled' or enclosed by the branching river Brandywine. *Girdley* contains the element *-ey*, *y* 'small island' (from Old Norse *ey*).

Green-Hill Country is spelled thus on the map (with a hyphen), but 'Green Hill Country' in the text (see note for p. 71).

The village ***Little Delving*** is the smaller 'companion' of Michel Delving on the White Downs (see notes for pp. 5, 6), like other Hobbit place-names containing an element (*delve*) related to digging.

Needlehole is also the name of a village in Gloucestershire. Its elements *needle* + *hole* are simple, but 'hole' again suggests the Hobbit tendency to dig.

Newbury 'new burg or castle' is a name also found in Berkshire.

In *The Treason of Isengard* Christopher Tolkien notes that his father allowed him to add 'Nobottle', after the name of a village in Northamptonshire, to his 1943 Shire map. ***Nobottle*** is related to *Newbold* and *Nobold* 'new building', from Old English *bold* (*boðl*, *botl*) 'building' – though in 1943 Christopher 'was under the impression that the name meant that the village was so poor and remote that it did not even possess an inn' (p. 424). In *Nomenclature* Tolkien cautions that the element *-bottle* (as also in *Hardbottle*, see note for p. 1021) 'is not connected with *bottle* "glass container"'.

Oatbarton combines *oat*, for the grain, with the common English place-name element *-barton*, from Old English *beretūn* or **bærtūn*, generally 'corn farm' (from *bere* 'barley, corn' + *tūn* 'enclosure'), later usually 'outlying grange, demesne farm'. The artist of the Shire map in the 1965 Ballantine Books edition of *The Lord of the Rings* misread 'Oatbarton' as 'Catbarion'.

In the name ***Overbourn Marshes*** the element *-bourn* is straightforward 'stream', from Old English *burna*, and is common in English river- and place-names. As some readers have remarked, the marshes are indeed 'over (across) the bourn (stream)', i.e. the river Shirebourn (see below), but Old English *ōfer* 'border, margin, edge, brink, river-bank' is well attested.

Pincup, Tolkien wrote to the Dutch translator, 'would, of course, not be analyzable by a modern Englishman, but is of a well-known pattern, containing bird/animal name and *hop* "recess, retreat". In this case the bird-name is *pinnuc, pink* (a finch or sparrow)'.

Rushy is spelled thus on the map, but is 'Rushey' in the text (see note for p. 98).

Rushock (of ***Rushock*** Bog) is also the name of villages in Worcestershire and Herefordshire. It is related to Old English **riscuc* or **rixuc* 'a rushy place, a rush-bed'. In his notes for the Dutch translator Tolkien wrote that '*rushock* is a derivative of *rush* (water plant) or from *rush* + *hassock* (Old. E. *hassuc*) coarse grass'.

Shirebourn contains, like *Overbourn* (see above), *bourn* 'stream', but it 'has nothing to do with "The Shire". . . . It represents a genuine river-name, ancient *Scíre-burna* "bright-spring", or "bright-stream"' from Old English *scīr* 'bright, clear, pure' (Tolkien, notes to the Dutch translator). *The Cambridge Dictionary of English Place-Names* (2004) notes that Old English *burna* was used normally 'for a stream not large enough to be called a river, used especially for streams with clear water, flowing over gravelly beds from springs, with seasonally variable flow and distinctive plant association' (p. xliii) – though for Hobbits it evidently *was* large enough to be called a river, and is so labelled on the Shire map. The river Sherbourne which runs by Coventry in Warwickshire was recorded in the fourteenth century as 'Schirebourn' and 'Shirebourn' among other spellings. Tolkien expanded the geography of this part of the Shire in his Preface to *The Adventures of Tom Bombadil and Other Verses from the Red Book* (1962), in regard to his poem *Bombadil Goes Boating*:

> *Grindwall* was a small hythe on the north bank of the Withywindle; it was outside the Hay, and so was well watched and protected by a *grind* or fence extended into the water. *Breredon* (Briar Hill) was a little village on rising ground behind the hythe, in the narrow tongue between the end of the High Hay and the Brandywine. At the *Mithe* [from Old English *m?ðe* 'mouth of a stream'], the outflow of the Shirebourn, was a landing stage, from which a lane ran to Deephallow and so on to the Causeway road that went through Rushey and Stock. [p. 9, n. 1]

Standelf combines Old English *stān* 'stone, stones' and *delf* 'digging, mine, quarry, ditch', thus *stān-gedelf* 'quarry'; compare 'Stonydelph' in Warwickshire. In a draft of 'A Conspiracy Unmasked' (Book I, Chapter 5) the main road in Buckland is described as running 'from the Bridge to Standelf and Haysend'. Christopher Tolkien writes in *The Return of the Shadow*: 'Standelf is never mentioned in the text of [*The Lord of the Rings*], though marked on my father's map of the Shire and on both of mine [1943 and 1954]; on all three the road stops there and does not continue to Haysend, which is not shown as a village or any sort of habitation' (pp. 298–9).

Stockbrook is spelled thus on the map, but 'Stock-brook' in the text (see note for p. 89).

Thistle Brook is presumably a brook around which thistles grow.

The ***Three Farthing Stone*** is spelled thus on the map, without a hyphen, but 'Three-Farthing Stone' in the text (see note for p. 1003).

Tookbank combines the family name *Took* (the settlement is in the Tookland, see note for p. 71) and *-bank* 'slope, hillside'.

Waymoot is spelled thus on the map, but is 'Waymeet' in the text (see note for p. 1009).

The second element of ***Willowbottom*** is derived from Old English *botm* (or *boðm*) 'valley bottom'; compare *Longbottom* (note for p. 8). In his notes to the Dutch translator Tolkien commented that *bottom* 'is widespread in local toponymy in England (often in dialectal form *botham*) ref[erring] to "steep-sided valley" or especially a "deeplying flat"'.

The Yale was added to the Shire map in the Allen & Unwin second edition of *The Fellowship of the Ring* (1966). Christopher Tolkien comments in *The Return of the Shadow* that his father wrote 'The Yale' on the Shire map in a copy of the first edition,

> placing it south of Whitfurrows in the Eastfarthing, in such a way as to show that he intended a region, like 'The Marish', not a particular place of settlement (the road to Stock runs through it); and at the same time, on the same copy, he expanded the text in FR [*The Fellowship of the Ring*] p. 86, introducing the name: 'the lowlands of the Yale' [which revised text appeared in the second edition]. The Shire Map in the Second Edition has *The Yale* added here, but in relation to a small black square, as if it were the name of a farm or small hamlet; this must have been a misunderstanding. [p. 387]

(See note for p. 76.)

For *Brandywine* (Baranduin), *Bree*, *Bridgefields*, *Buckland*, *Bucklebury*, *Bywater*, *Crickhollow*, the *East Road*, the *Farthings*, *Frogmorton*, *Haysend*, the *Hedge*, the *Hill*, *Hobbiton*, *Longbottom*, the *Marish*, *Michel Delving on the White Downs*, the *Old Forest*, *Overhill*, *Sarn Ford*, *Stock*, *Tuckborough*, the *Water*, *Whitfurrows*, the *Withywindle*, the *Woody End*, and the *Yale*, see notes for the text.

Barbara Strachey points out in her *Journeys of Frodo: An Atlas of J.R.R. Tolkien's The Lord of the Rings* (1981) that Tolkien's illustration for *The Hobbit*, *The Hill: Hobbiton-across-the Water* (*Artist and Illustrator*, fig. 98), 'shows clearly that the road from Hobbiton to Overhill runs *west* of the Hill, not east, as drawn in the map *A Part of the Shire*' (n. 2). She altered her map accompanying this note accordingly. Karen Wynn Fonstad, *An Atlas of Middle-earth* (rev. edn. (1991), pp. 70–1), follows the 1954 map in depicting the road to Overhill.

In Book I, Chapter 4 of *The Lord of the Rings*, after meeting the elves in the Green Hill Country the hobbits decide to cut across country to the

Bucklebury Ferry. Frodo says: 'The Ferry is east from Woodhall; but the hard road curves away to the left – you can see a bend of it away north over there. It goes round the north end of the Marish so as to strike the causeway from the Bridge above Stock.' On the Shire map, however, the road meets the causeway in the village of Stock itself, not above it, and in this instance Tolkien made no change to the text to accommodate the map.

In the first edition of *The Fellowship of the Ring* the Shire map shows Buck Hill and Brandy Hall as a black mark of moderate size located to the east of the road running north from Standelf, with the road between Brandy Hall and the river Brandywine. But in Book I, Chapter 5 it is established that Brandy Hall was on the river-side, with the road behind it, and thus the hobbits 'passed Buck Hill and Brandy Hall on their left' on their way to Crickhollow. In *The Return of the Shadow* Christopher Tolkien comments that on his 1943 map of the Shire the text 'was already wrongly represented, since the main road is shown as passing between the River and Brandy Hall (and the lane to Crickhollow leaves the road south of the hall, so that the hobbits would in fact, according to this map, still pass it on their left). This must have been a simple misinterpretation of the text which my father did not notice . . . ; and it reappeared on my map published in the first edition' (p. 305). In the Allen & Unwin second edition (1966) the Shire map was corrected to show a large black square, representing Brandy Hall, between the road and the river.

On 28 July 1965 Tolkien wrote to Austin Olney at his American publisher, the Houghton Mifflin Company:

> I ran into some difficulties with the maps [for the second edition of *The Lord of the Rings*]. I have finally decided, where this is possible and does not damage the story, to take the *maps* as 'correct' and adjust the narrative. . . . The *small map* 'Part of the Shire' is most at fault and much needs correction (and some additions), and has caused a number of questions to be asked. The chief fault is that the Ferry at Bucklebury and to Brandy Hall and Crickhollow have shifted about 3 miles too far north (about 4 mm.). This cannot be altered at this time, but it is unfortunate that Brandy Hall clearly on the river-bank is placed so that the main road runs in front of it instead of behind. There is also no trace of the wood described at top of p. 99 [Book I, Chapter 4: 'Beyond that they came again to a belt of trees . . .']. I have had simply to disregard these map-errors. [Tolkien-George Allen & Unwin archive, HarperCollins, mostly printed in *Letters*, p. 358]

GENERAL MAP OF MIDDLE-EARTH

Like the Shire map, Christopher Tolkien's small-scale general map of Middle-earth for the first edition of *The Lord of the Rings* contains several features not mentioned in the text. (Those located in the South are shown also on the large-scale map of Rohan, Gondor, and Mordor: see below.)

The ***Mountains of Mirkwood*** had already appeared on the *Wilderland* map in *The Hobbit.* A note by Tolkien to his late (post-*Lord of the Rings*) work *The Disaster of the Gladden Fields* reports their Sindarin names:

> The Emyn Duir (Dark Mountains) were a group of high hills in the north-east of the Forest, so called because dense fir-woods grew upon their slopes; but they were not yet [at the beginning of the Third Age] of evil name. In later days when the shadow of Sauron spread through Greenwood the Great, and changed its name from Eryn Galen to Taur-nu-Fuin (translated Mirkwood), the Emyn Duir became a haunt of many of his most evil creatures, and were called Emyn-nu-Fuin, the Mountains of Mirkwood. [*Unfinished Tales*, pp. 280–1, n. 14]

The same note mentions, but does not name, the ***Old Forest Road***, also a feature of the *Wilderland* map in *The Hobbit.* In *The Disaster of the Gladden Fields* it is called 'the ancient Dwarf-Road (*Men-i-Naugrim*)' (*Unfinished Tales*, p. 280, n. 14). Christopher Tolkien comments that this

> is the Old Forest Road described in *The Hobbit*, Chapter 7. In the earlier draft of this section of the present narrative there is a note referring to 'the ancient Forest Road that led down from the Pass of Imladris and crossed Anduin by a bridge (that had been enlarged and strengthened for the passage of the armies of the Alliance), and so over the eastern valley into the Greenwood. . . . In *The Hobbit* the Forest Road traversed the great river by the Old Ford, and there is no mention of there having once been a bridge at the crossing. [p. 281]

Serni, one of the rivers of Lebennin in Gondor, is mentioned in another late work (*c.* 1967–9), *The Rivers and Beacon-hills of Gondor.* There it is said that *Serni* derives from

> an adjectival formation from S[indarin] *sarn* 'small stone, pebble' . . . or a collective, the equivalent of Quenya *sarnië* 'shingle, pebble-bank'. Though Serni was the shortest river its name was continued to the sea after its confluence with Gilrain. It was the only one of the five to fall into the delta of the Anduin. Its mouth was blocked with shingles, and at any rate in later times ships approaching Anduin and making for Pelargir went by the eastern side of Tol Falas and took the sea-way passage made by the Númenóreans in the midst of the Delta of the Anduin. [*Vinyar Tengwar* 42 (July 2001), p. 11, and *Unfinished Tales*, pp. 463–4]

The name of another river of the South, ***Sirith***, is said in *The Rivers and Beacon-hills of Gondor* to mean 'simply "a flowing": cf. *tirith* "watching, guarding" from the stem *tir-* "to watch"' (*Vinyar Tengwar* 42 (July 2001), p. 11).

Tolfalas, an island in the Bay of Belfalas just beyond the Mouths of

Anduin. Its name derives from Sindarin *tol* 'isle' + *falas* 'surf, wave-beaten shore'.

The ***Trollshaws***, referred to in the text as 'the Trolls' wood'. *Shaw* is an archaic word for 'thicket, small wood, copse, or grove'.

In *Unfinished Tales* Christopher Tolkien comments that the body of water marked on his 1954 map as 'The Icebay of Forochel' 'was in fact only a small part of the Bay (referred to in *The Lord of the Rings*, Appendix A I iii as "immense") which extended much further to the north-east: its northern and western shores being formed by the great Cape of Forochel, of which the tip, unnamed, appears on my original map' (p. 13, n.).

In notes for the Dutch translator of *The Lord of the Rings* Tolkien commented that 'the mapmaker *should* have written *Harondor (South Gondor)*', i.e. not 'South Gondor (Harondor)'. The latter appears on the 1954 map, but *Harondor* was omitted from the new map of 1980 (see below).

'Hithaeglir', the Sindarin name of the Misty Mountains, appears on the 1954 map as 'Hithaeglin'.

The valley in which Isengard is located appears on the 1954 map as 'Nan Gurunír', a spelling used through much of the writing of *The Lord of the Rings*. In the published text it is spelt *Nan Curunír*. The latter spelling is used on the Pauline Baynes map (see below); while on the *Unfinished Tales* map an arrow simply points to 'Isengard'.

In *The Return of the Shadow*, p. 441, Christopher Tolkien says that on his 1954 map 'the mountainous heights shown extending from the main range westwards north of Hollin are badly exaggerated from what my father intended: "about the feet of the main range there was tumbled an ever wider land of bleak hills, and deep valleys filled with turbulent water"'.

Here, in relation to the general map and purely as analogies of location, one might take note of Tolkien's remarks in a letter to Charlotte and Denis Plimmer of 8 February 1967:

> The action of the story [*The Lord of the Rings*] takes place in the North-west of 'Middle-earth', equivalent in latitude to the coastlands of Europe and the north shores of the Mediterranean. But this is not a purely 'Nordic' area in any sense. If Hobbiton and Rivendell are taken (as intended) to be at about the latitude of Oxford, then Minas Tirith, 600 miles south, is at about the latitude of Florence. The Mouths of the Anduin and the ancient city of Pelargir are at about the latitude of ancient Troy. [*Letters*, p. 376]

THE MAP OF ROHAN, GONDOR, AND MORDOR

On the 1955 large-scale map, as Tolkien wrote in his draft letter to H. Cotton Minchin, April 1956, 'inconsistencies of spelling are due to me. It was only in the last stages that (in spite of my son's protests: he still holds that no one will ever pronounce *Cirith* right, it appears as *Kirith* in his map, as formerly also in the text) I decided to be "consistent" and spell Elvish names and words throughout without *k*' (*Letters*, p. 247) – thus *Kelos, Kiril, Kirith Ungol* for *Celos, Ciril, Cirith Ungol.*

Dor-in-Ernil is not mentioned in the text of *The Lord of the Rings* but appears in the south-west corner of the large-scale map. In *The Rivers and Beacon-hills of Gondor* it is glossed as 'the Land of the Prince' (*Unfinished Tales*, p. 243). Christopher Tolkien has noted that on the large map 'it is placed on the other side of the mountains from Dol Amroth, but its occurrence in the present context [in an account of Amroth and Nimrodel] suggests that *Ernil* was the Prince of Dol Amroth (which might be supposed in any case)' (*Unfinished Tales*, p. 255, n. 14).

The ***Mering Stream*** is shown on the map north of the Firien Wood. According to *Cirion and Eorl and the Friendship of Gondor and Rohan* it rose in a cleft in a northward spur of the Ered Nimrais, and flowed through the Firien Wood and then over the plain to join the Entwash. In earlier days 'the line of the Mering Stream was fortified (between the impassable marshes of its confluence with the Entwash and the bridge where the Road passed westward out of the Firien Wood' (*Unfinished Tales*, p. 301). Both *Mering Stream* and its Sindarin name *Glanhír* mean 'boundary stream', from Old English *mēre* 'boundary'.

THE PAULINE BAYNES MAP

In 1969 Pauline Baynes, Tolkien's favoured illustrator for his books (*Farmer Giles of Ham, The Adventures of Tom Bombadil and Other Verses from the Red Book, Smith of Wootton Major,* etc.), was commissioned to produce a poster-map of Middle-earth for sale by George Allen & Unwin. She consulted with Tolkien, who sent her a marked photocopy of the general map, as well as additional names to include and advice on a few points of topography and nomenclature (e.g. that *Ciril* etc. should be spelled with *C* rather than *K*). Her *Map of Middle-earth* was published by Allen & Unwin in 1970. The following additions were supplied by Tolkien:

The ***Adorn***, a tributary of the River Isen which flows into it from the west of the Ered Nimrais (mentioned in Appendix A).

Andrast, Sindarin 'long cape', the 'dark cape of Ras Morthil' at the end of the northern arm of the Bay of Belfalas mentioned in *Aldarion and Erendis* (*Unfinished Tales*, p. 175).

The *Drúwaith Iaur* (Old Púkel-land), between the River Isen and the Ered Nimrais. *Drúwaith* is Sindarin *drú* 'wild' + *waith* 'folk, land'. In his late essay *The Drúedain* Tolkien says that the region at the eastern end of the Ered Nimrais, in Anórien, was called '"the Old Púkel-wilderness" (Drúwaith Iaur)' after the Púkel-men or 'Wild Men' believed to survive there at the end of the Third Age, after the coming of the Númenóreans drove the Púkel-men from the coastlands (*Unfinished Tales*, p. 384). In an editor's note Christopher Tolkien comments on the location of the name

Drúwaith Iaur (*Old Púkel-land*) on Pauline Baynes' map, 'placed well to the north of the mountains of the promontory of Andrast', not in Anórien. 'My father stated however that the name was inserted by him and was correctly placed' (*Unfinished Tales*, p. 387, n. 13).

Edhellond, an '"Elf-haven" [Sindarin *edhel* 'elf' + *lond* 'haven'] in Belfalas near the confluence of the rivers Morthond and Ringló, north of Dol Amroth' (*Unfinished Tales*, pp. 431–2). In his Preface to *The Adventures of Tom Bombadil and Other Verses from the Red Book* Tolkien writes, in relation to the poem *The Last Ship*: 'In the Langstrand and Dol Amroth there were many traditions of the ancient Elvish dwellings, and of the haven at the mouth of the Morthond from which "westward ships" had sailed as far back as the fall of Eregion in the Second Age' (p. 8).

Éothéod (Old English 'horse-people' or 'horse-land') in the far North near the sources of the Anduin; see note for p. 1063.

Eryn Vorn (Sindarin 'dark wood', i.e. 'Blackwood'), a cape at the mouth of the Baranduin. The surviving native forest-dwellers of Minhiriath fled here towards the end of the Second Age when their forests were destroyed by the Númenóreans, and themselves treated as enemies when they objected. See extract from *The Rivers and Beacon-hills of Gondor* in *Unfinished Tales*, pp. 262–3. In the first printing of the Pauline Baynes map the name was misspelled 'Erin Voru'.

Framsburg, near Éothéod, presumably a stronghold named for Fram, son of Frumgar, who slew the dragon Scatha; see note for p. 978.

Lond Daer, according to *The Rivers and Beacon-hills of Gondor* 'one of the earliest ports of the Númenóreans, begun by the renowned mariner-king Tar-Aldarion, and later enlarged and fortified. It was called Lond Daer Enedh, the Great Middle Haven (as being between Lindon in the North and Pelargir on the Anduin).' After the Downfall of Númenor 'in the early days of the kingdoms the most expeditious route' between Arnor and Gondor was generally by sea to Lond Daer 'at the head of the estuary of the Gwathló and so to the river-port of Tharbad, and thence by the Road. The ancient sea-port and its great quays were ruinous, but with long labour a port capable of receiving seagoing vessels had been made at Tharbad, and a fort raised there on great earthworks on both sides of the river, to guard the once famed Bridge of Tharbad' (*Unfinished Tales*, p. 264, n.). Christopher Tolkien comments that Lond Daer 'is of course the Vinyalondë or New Haven' mentioned in his father's unfinished story of Númenor, *Aldarion and Erendis* (published in *Unfinished Tales*); and that the (Sindarin) name *Lond Daer* 'must refer to a time long after the Númenórean intervention in the war against Sauron in Eriador; for according to *The Tale of Years* Pelargir was not built until the year 2350 of the Second Age, and became the chief haven of the Faithful Númenóreans' (*Unfinished Tales*, p. 265).

The ***Undeeps***, two great westward bends in the Anduin between the Brown Lands and the Wold of Rohan. They are described in a late note on languages in Middle-earth as 'the great loops of the Anduin (where it came down swiftly past Lórien and entered low flat lands before its descent again into the chasm of the Emyn Muil)'. It 'had many shallows and wide shoals over which a determined and well-equipped enemy could force a crossing by rafts or pontoons, especially in the two westward bends, known as the North and South Undeeps' (*Unfinished Tales*, p. 260).

In addition, ***R. Swanfleet*** is erroneously written on the map to mark the lower course of the river whose upper course is labelled ***R. Glanduin***, which rises in the Misty Mountains and flows south-west into the Gwathló (Greyflood). *Swanfleet* (Sindarin *Nîn-in-Eilph*) in fact is the name of the fens at the confluence of the Glanduin (Sindarin 'border-river') and Gwathló near Tharbad. The reference (since the second edition) to 'the Swanfleet river' in Book VI, Chapter 6 is to the river that *flows into* the Swanfleet, rather than that the Swanfleet is itself a river; see note for pp. 984–5. The label was corrected on a later printing of the Baynes map, among a handful of other errors, chiefly misreadings of the source maps provided to the artist, or continuation of errors on the 1954 map.

Three of the river-names, or supposed river-names, on the Pauline Baynes map – *Adorn*, *Glanduin*, and *Swanfleet* – were subsequently added to the general Middle-earth map published in various Allen & Unwin editions of *The Lord of the Rings*. At length problems with the map were brought to Christopher Tolkien's attention, and it was discovered not only that *Swanfleet* had been mistaken as the name of a river rather than of wetlands, but also that *Swanfleet* and *Glanduin* had been applied to the upper course of the Isen, far to the south of the correct location.

THE *UNFINISHED TALES* MAP

When preparing the volume *Unfinished Tales* (1980) Christopher Tolkien intended at first to include the general 1954 map from *The Lord of the Rings*, with corrections (such as to the *Swanfleet* and *Glanduin*) and the addition of further names, some of which had already appeared on the Pauline Baynes map. But, as he says in the Introduction to *Unfinished Tales*:

> it seemed to me on reflection that it would be better to copy my original map and take the opportunity to remedy some of its minor defects (to remedy the major ones being beyond my powers). I have therefore redrawn it fairly exactly, on a scale half as large again. . . . The area shown is smaller, but the only features lost are the Havens of Umbar and the Cape of Forochel. . . .
>
> All the more important place-names that occur in this book but not in *The Lord of the Rings* are included, such as *Lond Daer, Drúwaith Iaur, Edhellond, the Undeeps, Greylin*; and a few others that might have been, or should have been, shown on the original map, such as the rivers *Harnen* and *Carnen*, *Annúminas*, *Eastfold*, *Westfold*, the *Mountains of Angmar*. The mistaken inclusion of *Rhudaur* alone has been corrected

> by the addition of *Cardolan* and *Arthedain*, and I have shown the little island of *Himling* off the far north-western coast, which appears on one of my father's sketch-maps and on my own first draft. . . .
>
> I have thought it desirable to mark in the entire length of the Great Road linking Arnor and Gondor, although its course between Edoras and the Fords of Isen is conjectural (as also is the precise placing of Lond Daer and Edhellond). [pp. 13–14]

East Bight, added in this map, is the indentation in the eastern border of Mirkwood. (A *bight* is a curve or recess in a coastline or other geographical feature.) In *Cirion and Eorl and the Friendship of Gondor and Rohan* it is said that the Éothéod, ancestors of the Rohirrim,

> were a remnant of the Northmen, who had formerly been a numerous and powerful confederation of peoples living in the wide plains between Mirkwood and the River Running, great breeders of horses and riders renowned for their skill and endurance, though their settled homes were in the eaves of the Forest, and especially in the East Bight, which had largely been made by their felling of trees. [*Unfinished Tales*, p. 288]

The rivers ***Greylin*** and ***Langwell***, marked on the 1954 map but not named, were added to the *Unfinished Tales* map presumably from the information given in *Cirion and Eorl and the Friendship of Gondor and Rohan* concerning the lands into which the Northmen of Éothéod moved in Second Age 1977, as recorded in *The Tale of Years*; see note for p. 1063.

Regarding ***Himling***, a small island off the coast of Lindon, Christopher Tolkien writes: '*Himling* was the earlier form of *Himring* (the great hill on which Maedhros son of Fëanor had his fortress in *The Silmarillion*), and though the fact is nowhere referred to it is clear that Himring's top rose above the waters that covered drowned Beleriand' (*Unfinished Tales*, pp. 13–14).

On the original *Unfinished Tales* map the branching of the River Sirith and its western tributary, the Celos, were marked in reverse order. This was later corrected in some printings of the map, but not all.

*

The maps described here are the most common among the various editions of *The Lord of the Rings*, the American mass-market paperback editions notably excepted. Some differences, however, may be found between printings. Even in the 2004 fiftieth anniversary edition, the large-scale map in the Houghton Mifflin copies was emended to reflect Tolkien's later thinking on the spelling of *Celos*, *Ciril*, *Cirith Ungol*, while the otherwise identical map in the HarperCollins copies retained the original spellings in *K*. The HarperCollins large-scale map was corrected in 2005.

FOREWORD TO THE SECOND EDITION

In his Foreword to the first edition of *The Lord of the Rings* (1954–5) Tolkien adopted the same pose that he had used in his prefatory note to the second edition of *The Hobbit* (1951) and that survives in the Appendices of its sequel, that he was not the author of the work but merely its translator and editor. He also explicitly stated, anticipating comparison of the new work with his earlier book, that *The Lord of the Rings* was not written for children; he thanked his friends the Inklings, and his children, for their support during the long process of composition ('if "composition" is a just word' – returning to his 'editorial' pose); and he provided helpful information, before the text began, about the correct pronunciation of names. The original Foreword read in full (I: 7–8):

> This tale, which has grown to be almost a history of the great War of the Ring, is drawn for the most part from the memoirs of the renowned Hobbits, Bilbo and Frodo, as they are preserved in the Red Book of Westmarch. This chief monument of Hobbit-lore is so called because it was compiled, repeatedly copied, and enlarged and handed down in the family of the Fairbairns of Westmarch, descended from that Master Samwise of whom this tale has much to say.
>
> I have supplemented the account of the Red Book, in places, with information derived from the surviving records of Gondor notably the Book of the Kings; but in general, though I have omitted much, I have in this tale adhered more closely to the actual words and narrative of my original than in the previous selection from the Red Book, *The Hobbit*. That was drawn from the early chapters, composed originally by Bilbo himself. If 'composed' is a just word. Bilbo was not assiduous, nor an orderly narrator, and his account is involved and discursive, and sometimes confused: faults that still appear in the Red Book, since the copiers were pious and careful, and altered very little.
>
> The tale has been put into its present form in response to the many requests that I have received for further information about the history of the Third Age, and about Hobbits in particular. But since my children and others of their age, who first heard of the finding of the Ring, have grown older with the years, this book speaks more plainly of those darker things which lurked only on the borders of the earlier tale, but which have troubled Middle-earth in all its history. It is, in fact, not a book written for children at all; though many children will, of course, be interested in it, or parts of it, as they still are in the histories and legends of other times (especially in those not specially written for them).

I dedicate this book to all admirers of Bilbo, but especially to my sons and my daughter, and to my friends the Inklings. To the Inklings, because they have already listened to it with a patience, and indeed with an interest, that almost leads me to suspect that they have hobbit-blood in their venerable ancestry. To my sons and my daughter for the same reason, and also because they have all helped me in the labours of composition. If 'composition' is a just word, and these pages do not deserve all that I have said about Bilbo's work.

For if the labour has been long (more than fourteen years), it has been neither orderly nor continuous. But I have not had Bilbo's leisure. Indeed much of that time has contained for me no leisure at all, and more than once for a whole year the dust has gathered on my unfinished pages. I only say this to explain to those who have waited for this book why they have had to wait so long. I have no reason to complain. I am surprised and delighted to find from numerous letters that so many people, both in England and across the Water, share my interest in this almost forgotten history; but it is not yet universally recognized as an important branch of study. It has indeed no obvious practical use, and those who go in for it can hardly expect to be assisted.

Much information, necessary and unnecessary, will be found in the Prologue. To complete it some maps are given, including one of the Shire that has been approved as reasonably correct by those Hobbits that still concern themselves with ancient history. At the end of the third volume will be found also some abridged family-trees, which show how the Hobbits mentioned were related to one another, and what their ages were at the time when the story opens. There is an index of names and strange words with some explanations. And for those who like such lore in an appendix some brief account is given of the languages, alphabets, and calendars that were used in the West-lands in the Third Age of Middle-earth. Those who do not need such information, or who do not wish for it, may neglect these pages; and the strange names that they meet they may, of course, pronounce as they like. Care has been given to their transcription from the original alphabets, and some notes are offered on the intentions of the spelling adopted.* But not all are interested in such matters, and many who are not may still find the account of these great and valiant deeds worth the reading. It was in that hope that I began the work of translating and selecting the stories of the Red Book, part of which are now presented to Men of a later Age, one almost as darkling and ominous as was the Third Age that ended with the great years 1418 and 1419 of the Shire long ago.

*Some may welcome a preliminary note on the pronunciation actually intended by the spellings used in this history.

The letters *c* and *g* are always 'hard' (as *k*, and *g* in *get*), even before *e*, *i*, and *y*; *ch* is used as in Welsh or German, not as in English *church*.

> The diphthongs *ai* (*ae*), and *au* (*aw*), represent sounds like those heard in *brine* and *brown*, and *not* those in *brain* and *brawn*.
>
> Long vowels are all marked with an accent, or with a circumflex, and are usually also stressed. Thus *Legolas* has a short *o*, and is meant to be stressed on the initial syllable.
>
> These remarks do not apply to the names of the Hobbits or their Shire, which have all been anglicized, for reasons later explained.

For draft texts including some of these phrases, or words to the same effect, see *The Peoples of Middle-earth*, Chapters 1 and 2.

Tolkien wrote an entirely new Foreword for the second edition of *The Lord of the Rings*, first published by Ballantine Books in 1965. This was, in part, a response to the need for new text in order to establish new copyright in the work in the United States, where rival publisher Ace Books had argued that *The Lord of the Rings* had fallen into the public domain. But also Tolkien had come to dislike the approach he had taken in the Foreword of 1954. He wrote of this in one of his check copies of *The Lord of the Rings*: 'Confusing (as it does) real personal matters with the "machinery" of the Tale is a serious mistake' (quoted in *The Peoples of Middle-earth*, p. 26). He did not add, and in the event it may be that none of his readers noticed, that the original Foreword indicated that Frodo and Sam, at least, survived the War of the Ring – Sam to the extent that he had descendants; but the Prologue also included, and still includes, minor 'spoilers' in other respects.

xxii (I: 5): This tale grew

xxii (I: 5). This tale grew in the telling, until it became a history of the Great War of the Ring and included many glimpses of the yet more ancient history that preceded it. – As described more fully in the 'Brief History' above, *The Lord of the Rings* began as another children's story about Bilbo Baggins or one of his descendants, but soon became a much greater conception, far longer than Tolkien anticipated or was able accurately to project, darker and more complex than his earlier work about Bilbo, and as much a continuation of the 'Silmarillion' mythology on which Tolkien had worked for decades as it was a sequel to *The Hobbit*. On 20 September 1963 Tolkien wrote to Colonel Worskett (as at other times to other readers): 'Part of the attraction of The L.R. [*The Lord of the Rings*] is, I think, due to the glimpses of a large history in the background: an attraction like that of viewing far off an unvisited island, or seeing the towers of a distant city gleaming in a sunlit mist' (*Letters*, p. 333). The published *Silmarillion* (1977), *Unfinished Tales* (1980), and *History of Middle-earth* (1983–96) document the 'large history' referred to only in passing in *The Lord of the Rings*.

xxii (I: 5). It was begun soon after *The Hobbit* was written and before its publication in 1937; but I did not go on with this sequel, for I wished

first to complete and set in order the mythology and legends of the Elder Days, which had then been taking shape for some years. – In fact, Tolkien began *The Lord of the Rings* three months after *The Hobbit* was published on 21 September 1937. His correspondence with George Allen & Unwin leaves no doubt that once *The Hobbit* was published he wished to return to work on his 'mythology and legends of the Elder Days', i.e. 'The Silmarillion', concerned with the earlier ages of the world prior to that in which *The Lord of the Rings* is set, which had 'been taking shape' since at least 1916. On 16 December 1937 he wrote to Stanley Unwin, who had suggested a sequel to *The Hobbit*: 'I am sure you will sympathize when I say that the construction of elaborate and consistent mythology (and two languages) rather occupies the mind, and the Silmarils are in my heart' (*Letters*, p. 26). But by 19 December he was able to inform C.A. Furth at Allen & Unwin: 'I have written the first chapter of a new story about Hobbits – "A long expected party"' (*Letters*, p. 27). Tolkien now made little progress with 'The Silmarillion' until he had finished *The Lord of the Rings*.

xxii (I: 5). I had little hope that other people would be interested in this work ['The Silmarillion'] – On 15 November 1937 Tolkien handed over to Stanley Unwin the *Quenta Silmarillion*, the *Lay of Leithian*, and other 'Silmarillion' manuscripts, among works to be considered for publication. The critic Edward Crankshaw was impressed with a prose version accompanying the poetic *Lay of Leithian* (the story of Beren and Lúthien), despite 'eye-splitting' names which he took to be Celtic; but neither this, nor any of the other 'Silmarillion' writings, was of the sort that Allen & Unwin wanted from Tolkien to follow *The Hobbit*. The *Quenta Silmarillion*, in fact, was felt to be too peculiar and difficult even to be given to a publisher's reader. On 15 December Stanley Unwin wrote to Tolkien that he thought that 'The Silmarillion' contained 'plenty of wonderful material' which might be mined to produce 'further books like *The Hobbit* rather than a book in itself' (quoted in *The Lays of Beleriand*, p. 366).

xxii (I: 5). it ['The Silmarillion'] was primarily linguistic in inspiration and was begun in order to provide the necessary background of 'history' for Elvish tongues – So Tolkien said also at other times: his stories, he told W.H. Auden on 7 June 1955, 'are and were so to speak an attempt to give a background or a world in which my expressions of linguistic taste could have a function. The stories were comparatively late in coming' (*Letters*, p. 214). But while Tolkien's interest in the invention of languages dated from his youth, so too did an interest in the creation of imaginative poetry and prose. See further, note for pp. 80–1.

xxii (I: 5): When those whose advice

xxii (I: 5). When those whose advice and opinion I sought corrected *little hope* to *no hope*, I went back to the sequel, encouraged by requests

from readers for more information concerning hobbits and their adventures. – More precisely, when Allen & Unwin rejected 'The Silmarillion' Tolkien did not *go back to* the sequel but began to write it. It is true, however, that by December 1937 he was convinced that readers were interested in knowing more about the world of *The Hobbit.* On 15 October 1937 he wrote to Stanley Unwin: 'My daughter would like something [more] on the Took family. One reader wants fuller details about Gandalf and the Necromancer [as Sauron is called in *The Hobbit*]' (*Letters*, p. 24). And on 16 December of that year he informed Unwin that he had 'received several queries, on behalf of children and adults, concerning the *runes* [on the *Hobbit* dust-jacket and Thror's map] and whether they are real and can be read' (*Letters*, p. 27).

xxii (I: 5). But the story was drawn irresistibly towards the older world – On 24 February 1950 Tolkien wrote to Stanley Unwin that 'The Silmarillion' had 'bubbled up, infiltrated, and probably spoiled everything (that even remotely approached "Faery") which I have tried to write since. It was kept out of *Farmer Giles* [*of Ham*] with an effort', but there are points of convergence in his story *Roverandom* (published 1998) and his 'Father Christmas' letters (selection first published 1976). 'Its shadow was deep on the later parts of *The Hobbit.* It has captured *The Lord of the Rings*, so that that has become simply its continuation and completion . . .' (*Letters*, pp. 136–7).

xxii (I: 5). The process had begun in the writing of *The Hobbit*, in which there were already some references to the older matter: Elrond, Gondolin, the High-elves, and the orcs, as well as glimpses that had arisen unbidden of things higher or deeper or darker than its surface: Durin, Moria, Gandalf, the Necromancer, the Ring. – The extent of the influence of 'The Silmarillion' on *The Hobbit* is a matter of debate, and is discussed at length in the entry for *The Hobbit* in our *J.R.R. Tolkien Companion and Guide.* Here it will suffice to express our opinion that Tolkien occasionally 'borrowed' from his mythology in writing *The Hobbit*, but did not necessarily set that work in the world of 'The Silmarillion'. The jolly children's-book elves of Rivendell in *The Hobbit*, for instance, are not very like the noble and tragic race of Elves in Tolkien's legends of the Elder Days (or of *The Lord of the Rings*), though they share the same name; nor did the magic ring in *The Hobbit* do more than convey invisibility to its wearer – in that book it is merely a ring, not yet the terrible One Ring of Sauron. Only later, when *The Lord of the Rings* was consciously made an extension of 'The Silmarillion', did *The Hobbit* too become a part of the larger work, by virtue of its sequel.

xxii–xxiii (I: 5–6): Those who had asked

xxii (I: 5). the composition of *The Lord of the Rings* went on at intervals during the years 1936 to 1949, a period in which I had many duties that

I did not neglect, and many other interests as a learner and teacher that often absorbed me – The first date is incorrect, for the reason stated above. Tolkien brought the main text of *The Lord of the Rings* 'to a successful conclusion' in summer 1948 (letter to Hugh Brogan, 31 October 1948, *Letters*, p. 131), but did not complete a fair copy, further revised typescript until October 1949. 'Many duties' is an understatement: Tolkien was a busy professor in the Oxford English School, and served on many committees. In the absence of many of his colleagues during the war years he shouldered an even greater burden of responsibilities, including the organization of special courses for Navy and Air Force cadets. In 1945, on changing from the Rawlinson and Bosworth Professorship of Anglo-Saxon to the Merton chair of English Language and Literature, he had to develop new series of lectures.

xxii (I: 5). 1939, by the end of which year the tale had not yet reached the end of Book One – Once again Tolkien's memory (or records) failed. On 2 February 1939 he informed C.A. Furth at George Allen & Unwin (*Letters*, p. 41): 'By the end of last term [December 1938] the new story – *The Lord of the Rings* – had reached Chapter 12', i.e. Chapter 12 as originally conceived, Book II, Chapter 1 as published.

xxii–xxiii (I: 5). I plodded on, mostly by night, till I stood by Balin's tomb in Moria. There I halted for a long while. It was almost a year later when I went on and so came to Lothlórien and the Great River late in 1941. In the next year I wrote the first drafts of the matter that now stands as Book Three, and the beginnings of chapters I and III of Book Five – Tolkien's reference to 'a year later' in 1941 implies that he 'stood by Balin's tomb' in 1940. But there is clear evidence that he reached that point in the story by December 1939: see the 'Brief History', above, and Christopher Tolkien's argument in this regard in *The Return of the Shadow*, p. 461. Tolkien did indeed work on Book III in 1942 ('the next year' after 1941), but Christopher Tolkien has shown that his father did not begin to write Book V until autumn 1944 (see *The War of the Ring*, pp. 231–4).

xxiii (I: 6): It was during 1944

xxiii (I: 6). These chapters . . . were written and sent out as a serial to my son, Christopher – Christopher Tolkien was called up into the Royal Air Force in July 1943, and in January 1944 was sent to South Africa for pilot training. He returned to England in March 1945. During his absence his father wrote and had typed chapters in Book IV of *The Lord of the Rings* which he sent to Christopher in addition to frequent letters.

xxiii (I: 6). Nonetheless it took another five years before the tale was brought to its present end; in that time I changed my house, my chair, and my college – Tolkien, his wife, and their daughter moved from 20

Northmoor Road to 3 Manor Road, Oxford, in March 1947. In 1945 Tolkien was elected Merton Professor of English Language and Literature, following the death of Professor H.C. Wyld; in October of that year he was made a Fellow of Merton College, Oxford. Previously, as Rawlinson and Bosworth Professor of Anglo-Saxon, he had been a Fellow of Pembroke College.

xxiii (I: 6): ***The Lord of the Rings*** **has been read**

xxiii (I: 6). ***The Lord of the Rings*** **has been read by many people since it finally appeared in print** – In the second edition (1965) this continued: 'appeared in print ten years ago'. For the Allen & Unwin de luxe edition of 1969 the number was changed to 'fifteen'. On 27 December 1976 Christopher Tolkien wrote to Rayner Unwin: 'I don't think one can go on dating it year by year, can one? – or we shall end up making my father say "*The Lord of the Rings* has been read by many people since it finally appeared in print a century ago"!' (Tolkien-George Allen & Unwin archive, HarperCollins). The solution was to omit the number of years altogether.

xxiii (I: 6). The prime motive was the desire of a tale-teller to try his hand at a really long story that would hold the attention of readers, amuse them, delight them, and at times maybe excite them or deeply move them. – Here Tolkien is stating not so much his motive in writing *The Lord of the Rings* as his hopes for the effect of his work on its readers, and he is looking back at his accomplishment rather than at his thoughts at its inception – when he had no clear idea how to proceed. The immediate motive for the book, of course, was the desire of his publisher for another story about hobbits. Tolkien acknowledged this, but as the years passed following the publication of *The Lord of the Rings* he sometimes waxed philosophical about why he had written it, and his thoughts varied. On 7 June 1955, for instance, he said to W.H. Auden that he wrote *The Lord of the Rings* 'as a personal satisfaction, driven to it by the scarcity of literature of the sort that I wanted to read (and what there was was often heavily alloyed)' (*Letters*, p. 211). On 10 April 1958 he wrote to C. Ouboter: 'I was primarily writing an exciting story in an atmosphere and background such as I find personally attractive' (*Letters*, p. 267). And in autumn 1971 he wrote to Carole Batten-Phelps: 'Of course the book was written to please myself (at different levels), and as an experiment in the arts of long narrative, and of inducing "Secondary Belief"' (*Letters*, p. 412).

xxiii (I: 6). Some who have read the book, or at any rate reviewed it, have found it boring, absurd, or contemptible – Although reviews of *The Lord of the Rings* on its first publication were mixed, they were mostly positive, some even enthusiastic; but a few were so remarkably negative as to suggest, as Tolkien obviously felt, that their writers had not read his book very carefully. Robert H. Flood ('Hobbit Hoax?' *Books on Trial*, February 1955, pp. 169–70) felt that 'pretentious snobbery is the best description for this scholarly off-shoot of a once-done fairy tale [*The*

Fellowship of the Ring]. . . . It's the type of "quaint" thing that could well be a hoax to snare the hacks who would call it any more than a deadly, overlong bore.' Maurice Richardson ('New Novels', *New Statesman and Nation*, 18 December 1954, pp. 835–6) judged Tolkien to have 'a great deal of imagination [but] . . . of low potential. The various creatures, hobbits, elves, dwarfs [*sic*], orcs, ents [in *The Two Towers*] . . . [have no] real individuality; not one is a character. And though their dialogue is carefully varied, from colloquial-historical for men and wizards to prep school slang for hobbits and orcs, they all speak with the same flat, castrated voice.' Most notoriously, the American critic Edmund Wilson wrote of *The Lord of the Rings* ('Oo, Those Awful Orcs!' *Nation*, 14 April 1956, pp. 312–13) that there is little in the book 'over the head of a seven-year-old child. It is essentially . . . a children's book which has somehow got out of hand. . . .' It deals with 'a simple confrontation – of the Forces of Evil with the Forces of Good, the remote and alien villain with the plucky little home-grown hero.' Tolkien's 'poverty of imagination' was so pathetic, Wilson felt, that to have critics such as C.S. Lewis, Naomi Mitchison, and Richard Hughes pay tribute to *The Lord of the Rings* (in brief quotations printed on the original Allen & Unwin dust-jackets) could be explained only by the 'lifelong appetite' that 'certain people – especially, perhaps, in Britain – have . . . for juvenile trash.' Philip Toynbee, writing a few years later in the *Observer* (6 August 1961), took a similar and particularly ill-considered line: Tolkien's 'Hobbit fantasies', he said, are 'dull, ill-written, whimsical and childish', his 'more ardent supporters' were then 'beginning to sell out their shares' in him, and – most erroneously – *The Lord of the Rings* had already 'passed into a merciful oblivion'.

xxiii–xxiv (I: 6–7): As for any inner meaning

xxiv (I: 6). The crucial chapter, 'The Shadow of the Past' . . . was written long before the foreshadow of 1939 had yet become a threat of inevitable disaster. . . . Its sources are things long before in mind, or in some cases already written, and little or nothing in it was modified by the war that began in 1939 or its sequels. – 'The Shadow of the Past', originally 'Ancient History', was added to *The Lord of the Rings* in its revision of ?late September–early October 1938, one year before the official declaration of war between Germany and Great Britain; and even before then, Tolkien had developed many details concerning the nature of the Ring and the direction in which his tale was headed. At the end of September 1938 the British Prime Minister, Neville Chamberlain, returned from the Munich Conference and famously proclaimed 'peace in our time'; but many in Britain, who had viewed with mounting horror the rise to power of Adolf Hitler, already thought that war with Germany was, indeed, inevitable. On 13 October 1938 Tolkien wrote to Stanley Unwin that 'the darkness of the present days has had some effect' on his *Hobbit* sequel. 'Though it is not an "allegory"' (*Letters*, p. 41).

xxiv (I: 7): The real war

xxiv (I: 7). If it [the Second World War] had inspired or directed the development of the legend, then certainly the Ring would have been seized and used against Sauron. . . . Saruman, failing to get possession of the Ring, would in the confusion and treacheries of the time have found in Mordor the missing links in his own researches into Ring-lore, and before long he would have made a Great Ring of his own. . . . – The reference is surely to the development of the atomic bomb by the Allies, and to the subsequent proliferation of nuclear weapons to the Soviet Union. Of course the Ring was conceived by Tolkien long before such things came to public attention in 1945.

xxiv (I: 7): Other arrangements

xxiv (I: 7). I cordially dislike allegory in all its manifestations, and always have done so since I grew old and wary enough to detect its presence. I much prefer history, true or feigned, with its varied applicability to the thought and experience of readers. I think that many confuse 'applicability' with 'allegory'; but the one resides in the freedom of the reader, and the other in the purported domination of the author. – Some reviewers classified *The Lord of the Rings* as an allegory – as if a work of fantasy were necessarily allegorical – but as many, or more, acknowledged clearly that it was not an allegory but heroic romance, though allegorical meanings might be inferred. By the time he wrote his revised Foreword in 1965, and even before *The Lord of the Rings* was first published, Tolkien had argued in correspondence against an allegorical interpretation. When in 1947 Rayner Unwin, while reading the work still in manuscript, commented on its 'struggle between darkness and light' which sometimes seemed to leave 'the story proper to become pure allegory' (quoted in *Letters*, pp. 119–20), Tolkien advised Rayner's father, publisher Stanley Unwin, that he should

> not let Rayner suspect 'Allegory'. There is a 'moral', I suppose, in any tale worth telling. But that is not the same thing. Even the struggle between darkness and light (as he calls it, not me) is for me just a particular phase of history, one example of its pattern, perhaps, but not The Pattern; and the actors are individuals – they each, of course, contain universals, or they would not live at all, but they never represent them as such.
>
> Of course, Allegory and Story converge, meeting somewhere in Truth. So that the only perfectly consistent allegory is a real life; and the only fully intelligible story is an allegory. And one finds, even in imperfect human 'literature', that the better and more consistent an allegory is the more easily it can be read 'just as a story'; and the better and more closely woven a story is the more easily can those so minded find allegory in it. But the two start from opposite ends. You can make

> the Ring into an allegory of our own time, if you like: an allegory of the inevitable fate that waits for all attempts to defeat evil power by power. But that is only because all power magical or mechanical does always so work. You cannot write a story about an apparently simple magic ring without that bursting in, if you really take the ring seriously, and make things happen that would happen, if such things existed. [31 July 1947, *Letters*, p. 121]

In ?late 1951 Tolkien wrote to Milton Waldman about *The Lord of the Rings* and the larger mythology of which it is a part: 'I dislike Allegory – the conscious and intentional allegory [introduced deliberately by an author] – yet any attempt to explain the purport of myth or fairytale must use allegorical language' (*Letters*, p. 145). In an autobiographical statement written in 1955 Tolkien stated, similar to language in his revised Foreword, that *The Lord of the Rings* 'is not "about" anything but itself. Certainly it has *no* allegorical intentions, general, particular, or topical, moral, religious, or political' (*Letters*, p. 220). In a letter to Herbert Schiro on 17 November 1957 he wrote: 'There is *no* "symbolism" or conscious allegory in my story. Allegory of the sort "five wizards = five senses" is wholly foreign to my way of thinking. . . . To ask if the Orcs "are" Communists is to me as sensible as asking if Communists are Orcs. That there is no allegory does not, of course, say there is no applicability. There always is' (*Letters*, p. 262).

Critics have often pointed out that despite Tolkien's statement that he 'cordially dislike[d] allegory in all its manifestations', his stories *Leaf by Niggle* (first published 1945) and *Smith of Wootton Major* (1967) are indeed allegories, or at least (to give the author the benefit of the doubt) seem to include allegorical elements. It is not clear in either case that Tolkien set out consciously to write an allegory, and for each he denied that he had done so. Robert Murray has observed that Tolkien had an ambivalent attitude to allegory, but could not refuse it 'some place, provided it were kept in it. It could serve in an argument; there he was quite prepared to make up allegories and call them such, as he did twice in two pages of his great lecture on *Beowulf* [*Beowulf: The Monsters and the Critics*, 1936]' ('Sermon at Thanksgiving Service, Keble College Chapel, 23rd August 1992', *Proceedings of the J.R.R. Tolkien Centenary Conference 1992* (1995), p. 18).

See further, entry for 'Allegory' in Christina Scull and Wayne G. Hammond, *The J.R.R. Tolkien Companion and Guide* (forthcoming).

xxiv–xxv (I: 7–8): An author cannot

xxiv (I: 7). to be caught in youth by 1914 – The First World War broke out in August 1914, when Tolkien was twenty-two and still an undergraduate at Oxford. By October of that year many of his friends, and his brother Hilary, had already enlisted in the Army. Desiring to complete his studies, Tolkien joined the Officers Training Corps at Oxford, and as soon as he had his degree in June 1915 he applied for a commission.

xxiv (I: 7). By 1918 all but one of my close friends were dead. – Robert Quilter Gilson and Geoffrey Bache Smith died, respectively, in July 1916 (killed in action on the opening day of the Battle of the Somme) and December 1916 (from wounds inflicted by a bursting shell). They had been his closest friends from his days at King Edward's School, Birmingham, along with Christopher Wiseman, who survived the war. Tolkien had also been associated with Ralph S. Payton, who died in July 1916, and Thomas Kenneth Barnsley, killed in July 1917. Another special friend among Tolkien's classmates, Vincent Trought, had died earlier, in January 1912, after a severe illness.

xxiv (I: 7). it has been supposed by some that 'The Scouring of the Shire' reflects the situation in England at the time when I was finishing my tale. . . . It is an essential part of the plot, foreseen from the outset, though in the event modified by the character of Saruman as developed in the story – Not quite from the outset, but early in the development of the story. A partly illegible note by Tolkien among papers dated August 1939 possibly reads, as interpreted by Christopher Tolkien: 'What of Shire? Sackville-Baggins [and] his friends hurt [the] lands. There was war between the four quarters', i.e. of the Shire (*The Return of the Shadow*, p. 380). As the character of Saruman developed, so too did the idea that he had instigated the troubles in the Shire through hired ruffians. He was not physically present in 'The Scouring of the Shire' (Book VI, Chapter 8) until the chapter was half written in summer 1948, and Tolkien 'realized' that the chief ruffian 'Sharkey' and Saruman were one and the same.

xxv (I: 8). The country in which I lived in childhood was being stealthily destroyed before I was ten. . . . Recently I saw in a paper a picture of the last decrepitude of the once thriving corn-mill beside its pool that long ago seemed to me so important. I never liked the looks of the Young miller – For a few years from 1896 Tolkien lived with his widowed mother and his brother in the hamlet of Sarehole, south of Birmingham (now part of the suburb of Hall Green). In September 1900 the family moved closer to the city, in part so that Tolkien would have less far to travel to school. In memory Sarehole became an idyllic place, and an inspiration for the Shire. In an interview for the *Oxford Mail* (3 August 1966, p. 4) Tolkien said to John Ezard:

> I could draw you a map of every inch of [Sarehole]. . . . I loved it with an intensity of love that was a kind of nostalgia reversed. There was an old mill that really did grind corn [grain] with two millers . . . a great big pond with swans on it, a sandpit, a wonderful dell with flowers, a few old-fashioned village houses and further away a stream with another mill. . . . It was a kind of lost paradise and it was wonderful.

But after a visit to Sarehole in September 1933 Tolkien wrote in his diary:

> I pass over the pangs to me of passing through Hall Green – become a huge tram-ridden meaningless suburb where I actually lost my way – and eventually down what is left of beloved lanes of childhood, and past the very gate of our cottage, now in the midst of a sea of new red-brick. The old mill still stands and Mrs Hunt's still sticks out into the road as it turns uphill; but the crossing beyond the now fenced-in pool, where the bluebell lane ran down into the mill lane, is now a dangerous crossing alive with motors and red lights. The White Ogre's house . . . is become a petrol station, and most of Short Avenue and the elms between it and the crossing have gone. How I envy those whose precious early scenery has not been exposed to such violent and peculiarly hideous change. [quoted in *Biography*, pp. 124–5]

Tolkien had nicknamed the younger of the two men who operated the mill 'the White Ogre' because of his white dusty face. Hilary Tolkien recalled that in order to reach the place where he and his brother picked blackberries they had to pass through the 'White Ogre's' land, 'and he didn't like us very much because the path was very narrow through the field and we traipsed off after corncockles and other pretty things' (quoted in *Biography*, p. 21).

The mill at Sarehole that Tolkien knew, on Cole Bank Road, was built in the 1760s. Today it is the sole survivor of some fifty water-mills that once operated in Birmingham. A branch of the city Museums and Art Gallery, it is open to the public. In 1968 Tolkien subscribed to an appeal for its restoration.

xxv (I: 8): *The Lord of the Rings* is now issued

xxv (I: 8). *The Lord of the Rings* is now issued in a new edition, and the opportunity has been taken of revising it. A number of errors and inconsistencies that still remained in the text have been corrected, and an attempt has been made to provide information on a few points which attentive readers have raised. . . . In the meantime [in lieu of an 'accessory volume' with additional material] this edition offers this Foreword, an addition to the Prologue, some notes, and an index of the names of persons and places. – When the first sentences of this paragraph were written they referred specifically to the revisions undertaken for the edition published by Ballantine Books, and were specially mentioned in order to point out that extra material had been added, a prerequisite for establishing new United States copyright in *The Lord of the Rings*. Some later editions have retained the paragraph (the words continue to be apt), while others have replaced it with new text describing alterations (e.g. that the first Allen & Unwin paperback edition of 1968 omitted all of the Appendices except for *A Part of the Tale of Aragorn and Arwen*), or have omitted it altogether. The Ballantine Books edition uniquely included in 1965, and still includes, the paragraph '*The Lord of the Rings* is now issued

... rather to the accessory volume', as well as a further paragraph as follows:

> I hope that those who have read *The Lord of the Rings* with pleasure will not think me ungrateful: to please readers was my main object, and to be assured of this has been a great reward. Nonetheless, for all its defects of omission and inclusion, it was the product of long labour, and like a simple-minded hobbit I feel that it is, while I am still alive, my property in justice unaffected by copyright laws. It seems to me a grave discourtesy, to say no more, to issue my book without even a polite note informing me of the project: dealings one might expect of Saruman in his decay rather than from the defenders of the West. However that may be, this paperback edition and no other has been published with my consent and co-operation. Those who approve of courtesy (at least) to living authors will purchase it and no other. And if the many kind readers who have encouraged me with their letters will add to their courtesy by referring friends or enquirers to Ballantine Books, I shall be very grateful. To them, and to all who have been pleased by this book, especially those Across the Water for whom it is specially intended, I dedicate this edition.

In fact this statement is now irrelevant even to the Ballantine Books mass market paperback edition, since court decisions and new legislation have reaffirmed Tolkien's original American copyrights, and a second authorized paperback edition (in larger trade format) is published in the United States (the land 'Across the Water') by Houghton Mifflin.

xxv (I: 8). A complete index, making full use of the material prepared by Mrs. N. Smith, belongs rather to the accessory volume. – Tolkien states on this page that he desired to make an 'accessory volume' to satisfy readers' demands for further information about the world of *The Lord of the Rings*: 'many enquiries could only be answered by additional appendices, or indeed by the production of an accessory volume containing much of the material that I did not include in the original edition, in particular more detailed linguistic information'. But he had hoped to produce a book of this sort much earlier. In a letter to H. Cotton Minchin of April 1956 he wrote:

> I am ... primarily a philologist and to some extent a calligrapher. ... And my son [Christopher] after me. To us far and away the most absorbing interest is the Elvish tongues, and the nomenclature based on them; and the alphabets [see Appendix E]. My plans for the 'specialist volume' were largely linguistic. An index of names was to be produced, which by etymological interpretation would also provide quite a large Elvish vocabulary. ... I worked at it for months, and indexed the first two vols. (it was the chief cause of the delay of Vol iii) until it became clear that size and cost were ruinous. ...

> But the problems (delightful if I had time) which the extra volume will set, will seem clear if I tell you that while many like you demand *maps*, others wish for *geological* indications rather than places; many want Elvish grammars, phonologies, and specimens; some want metrics and prosodies. . . . Musicians want tunes, and musical notation; archaeologists want ceramics and metallurgy. Botanists want a more accurate description of the *mallorn*, of *elanor*, *niphredil*, *alfirin*, *mallos*, and *symbelmynë*; and historians want more details about the social and political structure of Gondor; general enquirers want information about the Wainriders, the Harad, Dwarvish origins, the Dead Men, the Beornings, and the missing two wizards (out of five). It will be a big volume, even if I attend only to the things revealed to my limited understanding! [*Letters*, pp. 247–8]

Unfortunately even the 'index of names and strange words with some explanations' promised in the Foreword to the first edition of *The Lord of the Rings* (I: 8) was not completed in time to appear in 1955 in *The Return of the King*. Tolkien seems to have begun work on it in summer 1954 but abandoned it by 1955. His statement to Minchin that he had 'indexed the first two volumes', i.e. *The Fellowship of the Ring* and *The Two Towers*, is curious, given that the manuscript of the unfinished index includes references, divided by book (not volume), to all parts of the Prologue and the text proper through Book VI (i.e. to the end of the story) – built up evidently in snatches of time, to judge by the great number of variations in Tolkien's handwriting; its citations do not correspond to the pagination of the first edition as published but rather, evidently, to working proofs; and the index covers only the names of places, natural features, and buildings. Christopher Tolkien drew upon this work in compiling his own indexes, with brief explanatory statements, to *The Silmarillion* and *Unfinished Tales*.

On 7 December 1957 Tolkien wrote to Rayner Unwin objecting to the draft Swedish translation of *The Lord of the Rings* by Åke Ohlmarks (published 1959–61), in which many of the names of people and places had been changed. By this date Tolkien had sent Ohlmarks a detailed criticism of a list of changes, which he had to complete at short notice; and it occurred to him that he could more easily deal with such questions of translation if he had an index of names in *The Lord of the Rings*. 'If I had an index of names', he wrote to Rayner Unwin,

> it would be a comparatively easy matter to indicate at once all names suitable for translation (as being themselves according to the fiction 'translated' into English), and to add a few notes on points where (I know now) translators are likely to trip. . . .
>
> This 'handlist' would be of *great use* to me in future corrections and in composing an index (which I think should replace some of the present appendices); also in dealing with *The Silmarillion* (into which

> some of the L.R. has to be written backwards to make the two coherent). Do you think you could do anything about this? [*Letters*, pp. 263–4]

Unwin replied on 12 December that if this were a job that 'could be done rather as an index is done without very much judgement, but a good deal of donkey work', Allen & Unwin can have a list made for him by one of their regular indexers. On 13 December Tolkien wrote to Unwin that he needed 'an alphabetical list of all proper names of persons, places, or things . . . in the *text* (including Foreword and Prologue, but *not* the Appendices)' (Tolkien-George Allen & Unwin archive, HarperCollins). By the end of January 1958 an indexer was found and work was begun; the index was completed in May 1958, at the last in a rush as the compiler was due to give birth. For some years Tolkien intended that a fuller index, on the lines he had originally drafted, should replace parts of the Appendices in a later edition of *The Lord of the Rings*. This was never accomplished, but Tolkien did produce an offshoot in 1967, his *Nomenclature of The Lord of the Rings* as an aid to translators (see appendix to the present volume). A revision of the index produced in 1958 was included in *The Lord of the Rings* beginning with the Ballantine Books edition of 1965, together with an index to songs and verses in the work, compiled by Tolkien's secretary Baillie Klass (later Mrs Christopher Tolkien). Tolkien emended the index for the Allen & Unwin second edition of 1966, adding a few notes and 'translations', and selected citations to the Appendices. It was replaced by a new, enlarged index by the present authors (but preserving Tolkien's added notes) beginning in 2005.

The compiler of the 1958 index was Nancy Smith, by curious chance the wife of a former university roommate of Christopher Tolkien.

PROLOGUE

For drafts and history of the Prologue, see *The Return of the Shadow*, pp. 310–14, and *The Peoples of Middle-earth*, Chapter 1.

1

Concerning Hobbits

1 (I: 10): This book is largely concerned

1 (I: 10). Hobbits – Tolkien first used the word *hobbit* when he wrote, *c.* 1929–30: 'In a hole in the ground there lived a hobbit.' He did not immediately know its meaning, in what would become the famous first sentence of *The Hobbit*, nor could he explain its inspiration. He conceived the race of Hobbits, especially the hero of *The Hobbit*, Bilbo Baggins, to fit the name. Critics have suggested, *inter alia*, that Tolkien may have unconsciously derived *hobbit* from *hob* 'hobgoblin, sprite, elf' or *hob* (*hobb, hobbe*) 'rustic, clown', words well known in English literature and folklore, or from the goblins known as 'Hobyahs' in a tale collected by Joseph Jacobs in *More English Fairy Tales* (1894). The word *hobbit* in fact had already appeared in *The Denham Tracts* (1892–5), a folklore collection by Michael Aislabie Denham, as a kind of spirit. Tolkien himself suspected an influence of the title of the novel *Babbit* by Sinclair Lewis (1922), but denied any connection with *rabbit*. In regard to the latter, Douglas A. Anderson argues in *The Annotated Hobbit*, 2nd edn. (2003), that a connection did exist, on the evidence of Tolkien's several comparisons in *The Hobbit* of Bilbo Baggins to a rabbit, and his (cancelled) footnote to a discussion of *hobbit* ('my own invention') in a draft of *Lord of the Rings* Appendix F written no later than summer 1950: 'I must admit that its faint suggestion of *rabbit* appealed to me. Not that hobbits at all resembled rabbits, unless it be in burrowing' (see *The Peoples of Middle-earth*, p. 49).

On 8 January 1971 Tolkien wrote to Roger Lancelyn Green that his claim to have invented *hobbit*, then being investigated by the *Oxford English Dictionary*, rested on

> unsupported assertion that I remember the occasion of its invention (by me); and that I had not *then* any knowledge of *Hobberdy, Hobbaty, Hobberdy Dick* etc. (for 'house-sprites') [dialectal forms that had been called to his attention; the latter was also, in 1955, the title of a book by folklorist Katharine Briggs]; and that my 'hobbits' were in any case of wholly dissimilar sort, a diminutive branch of the human race. Also that

> the only E[nglish] word that influenced the invention was 'hole'; that granted the description of *hobbits*, the trolls' use of *rabbit* was merely an obvious insult, of no more etymological significance than Thorin's insult [in *The Hobbit*] to Bilbo 'descendant of rats!' [*Letters*, p. 406]

The *OED* subsequently defined *hobbit* as 'a member of an imaginary race of half-sized people in stories by Tolkien . . . said by him to mean "hole-dweller"'. A good overview of this question is provided by Donald O'Brien in 'On the Origin of the Name "Hobbit"', *Mythlore* 16, no. 2, whole no. 60 (Winter 1989).

In Appendix F it is said that '*Hobbit* was the name usually applied by the Shire-folk to all their kind.' Its origin 'was by most forgotten. It seems, however, to have been at first a name given to the Harfoots by the Fallohides and Stoors [see note for p. 3], and to be a worn-down form of . . . *holbytla* "hole-builder"' (p. 1130, III: 408). Also in Appendix F is an 'internal' explanation of the word:

> *Hobbit* is an invention. In the Westron the word used, when this people was referred to at all, was *banakil* 'halfling'. But at this date the folk of the Shire and of Bree used the word *kuduk*, which was not found elsewhere. Meriadoc, however, actually records that the King of Rohan used the word *kûd-dûkan* 'hole-dweller'. Since, as has been noted, the Hobbits had once spoken a language closely related to that of the Rohirrim, it seems likely that *kuduk* was a worn-down form of *kûd-dûkan*. The latter I have translated . . . by *holbytla*; and *hobbit* provides a word that might well be a worn-down form of *holbytla*, if that name had occurred in our own ancient language [i.e. Old English *hol* 'hole' + *bytla* 'builder']. [pp. 1137–8, III: 416]

In *The Hunt for the Ring*, written after *The Lord of the Rings* and published in *Unfinished Tales*, it is said that the name *Hobbit* 'was local [to the Shire] and not a universal Westron word' (p. 342).

On the capitalization of *Hobbit(s)*, *hobbit(s)*, see note for p. 5 (*Orcs*).

1 (I: 10). Red Book of Westmarch – The name of Tolkien's fictitious source for *The Hobbit* and *The Lord of the Rings* echoes that of the 'Black Book of Carmarthen', a twelfth-century manuscript collection of ancient Welsh poetry with references to King Arthur, and the 'Red Book of Hergest', a fourteenth-century Welsh manuscript which contains, among other works, the *Mabinogion*. Here Tolkien continues the pose he first adopted in the first edition Foreword, as translator and editor of a work from antiquity, parts of which indeed were themselves based on still older works. The device of the 'found manuscript' was common in English fiction at least from the eighteenth century, in works such as *Pamela* and *Clarissa* by Samuel Richardson, and the *Pickwick Papers* of Charles Dickens. Tolkien also applied it in his *Notion Club Papers* (published in *Sauron Defeated*).

The name *Red Book of Westmarch* is supposedly derived from the colour of the red leather binding of Bilbo's diary, and of three other volumes, 'probably in a single red case' as described later in the Prologue (p. 14, I: 23), and from the place in the Shire where it was long preserved (see further, note for p. 14). It first appeared, however, in the author's note added by Tolkien to the second edition of *The Hobbit* (1951).

1 (I: 10): Hobbits are an unobtrusive but very ancient people

1 (I: 10). Hobbits ... love peace and quiet and good tilled earth: a well-ordered and well-farmed countryside was their favourite haunt. They do not and did not understand or like machines more complicated than a forge-bellows, a water-mill, or a hand-loom, though they were skilled with tools. – In a letter to Deborah Webster, 25 October 1958, Tolkien wrote:

> I am in fact a *Hobbit* (in all but size). I like gardens, trees, and unmechanized farmlands; I smoke a pipe, and like good plain food (unrefrigerated), but detest French cooking. I like, and even dare to wear in these dull days, ornamental waistcoats. I am fond of mushrooms (out of a field); have a very simple sense of humour (which even my appreciative critics find tiresome); I go to bed late and get up late (when possible). I do not travel much. [*Letters*, pp. 288–9]

Some of these similarities are mentioned later in the Prologue, and in Book I, Chapter 1.

1 (I: 10). the art of disappearing swiftly and silently – In *The Hobbit* it is said about Hobbits: 'There is little or no magic about them, except the ordinary everyday sort which helps them to disappear quietly and quickly when large stupid folk like you and me come blundering along' (Chapter 1).

1–2 (I: 10–11): For they are a little people

1–2 (I: 10–11). For they are a little people, smaller than Dwarves: less stout and stocky, that is, even when they are not actually much shorter. Their height is variable, ranging between two and four feet of our measure. They seldom now reach three feet; but they have dwindled, they say, and in ancient days they were taller. – In *The Hobbit* (2nd edn. and later) it is said only that Hobbits 'are (or were) a little people, about half our height, and smaller than the bearded dwarves' (Chapter 1). In a letter written to his American publisher, Houghton Mifflin, probably in March or April 1938, Tolkien gave the 'actual size' of Bilbo Baggins in *The Hobbit* as 'about three feet or three feet six inches' (*Letters*, p. 35). But in one of the Tolkien manuscripts in the Bodleian Library, Oxford are these three variant statements, written *c.* 1969, with some repetition as Tolkien develops the text (the second is partly printed in *Unfinished Tales*, pp. 286–7):

Halflings was derived from the Númenórean name for them (in Sindarin *Periannath*). It was given first to the Harfoots, who became known to the rulers of Arnor in the eleventh century of the Third Age . . . ; later it was also applied to the Fallohides and Stoors. The name thus evidently referred to their height as compared with Númenórean men, and was approximately accurate when first given. The Númenóreans were a people of great stature. . . . Their full-grown men were often seven feet tall.

The descriptions and assumptions of the text are not in fact haphazard, and are based on a standard: the average height of a male adult hobbit at the time of the story. For Harfoots this was taken as 3 ft. 6; Fallohides were slimmer and a little taller; and Stoors broader, stouter, and somewhat shorter. The remarks in the *Prologue* [concerning the height of Hobbits] . . . are unnecessarily vague and complicated, owing to the inclusion of references to supposed modern survivals of the race in later times; but as far as the LR [*Lord of the Rings*] is concerned they boil down to this: the hobbits of the Shire were in height between 3 and 4 feet in height, never less and seldom more. They did not of course call themselves *Halflings*.

The description of the height of hobbits is perhaps unnecessarily vague and complicated in the Prologue. . . . But it boils down to this: Dwarves were about 4 ft. high at least. Hobbits were lighter in build, but not much shorter; their tallest men were 4 ft., but seldom taller. Though nowadays their survivors are seldom 3 ft. high, in the days of the story they were taller which means that they usually exceeded 3 ft. and qualified for the name of halfling. But the name 'halfling' must have originated circa T[hird] A[ge] 1150, getting on for 2,000 years (1868) before the War of the Ring, during which the dwindling of the Númenóreans had shown itself in stature as well as in life-span. So that it referred to a height of full-grown males of an average of, say, 3 ft. 5. The dwindling of the Dúnedain was not a normal tendency, shared by peoples whose proper home was Middle-earth; but due to the loss of their ancient land far in the West, nearest of all mortal lands to 'The Undying Realm'. The much later dwindling of hobbits must be due to a change in their state and way of life; they became a fugitive and secret people, driven as Men, the Big Folk, became more and more numerous, usurping the more fertile and habitable lands, to refuge in forest or wilderness: a wandering and poor folk, forgetful of their arts and living a precarious life absorbed in the search for food and fearful of being seen; for cruel men would shoot them for sport as if they were animals. In fact they relapsed into the state of 'pygmies'. The other stunted race, the Drúedain, never rose much above that state.

In *The Marvellous Land of Snergs* (1927) by E.A. Wyke-Smith, a work acknowledged by Tolkien as 'an unconscious source-book for the Hobbits' (letter to W.H. Auden, 7 June 1955, *Letters*, p. 215), the title characters 'are a race of people only slightly taller than the average table but broad in the shoulders and of great strength. Probably they are some offshoot of the pixies who once inhabited the hills and forests of England, and who finally disappeared about the reign of Henry VIII' (p. 7). Critics of *The Hobbit* and *The Lord of the Rings* have often compared Hobbits to antecedents in fairy- and folk-tales, noting especially that hobs, brownies, leprechauns, and the like are also 'little people', who likewise often dress in green and live underground.

In his letter of ?late 1951 to Milton Waldman Tolkien said that he made Hobbits

> *small* (little more than half human stature, but dwindling as the years pass) partly to exhibit the pettiness of man, plain unimaginative parochial man – though not with either the smallness or the savageness of Swift, and mostly to show up, in creatures of very small physical power, the amazing and unexpected heroism of ordinary men 'at a pinch'. [*Letters*, p. 158]

Tolkien saw his Hobbits as different from Men only in size, and in being longer lived except in relation to Men of Númenórean descent (though at the end of the Third Age even their span of years was no longer as great as it once had been). The Dwarves are different again in size, mortal like Men and Hobbits, but unless slain usually lived at least 250 years. In Tolkien's mythology Elves, Men, Hobbits, and Dwarves are all basically human, but their division and differences enabled Tolkien to isolate and explore certain aspects of humankind. Inter-species relationships in his fiction to some extent replace interaction between different nationalities and races in reality.

1 (I: 10). Dwarves – Here, as earlier in *The Hobbit*, Tolkien uses *dwarves* as the plural of *dwarf*. He acknowledged in correspondence that in English grammar the 'correct' plural is *dwarfs*; 'but philology suggests that *dwarrows* would be the historical form [if developed from Old English *dweorgas*]. The real answer is that I knew no better' (letter to the *Observer*, ?February 1938, *Letters*, p. 31). Tolkien added a note about *dwarves* to *The Hobbit* with the Unwin Books edition of 1966, and inserted the following in Appendix F:

> It may be observed that in this book as in *The Hobbit* the form *dwarves* is used, although the dictionaries tell us that the plural of *dwarf* is *dwarfs*. It should be *dwarrows* (or *dwerrows*), if singular and plural had each gone its own way down the years, as have *man* and *men*, or *goose* and *geese*. But we no longer speak of a dwarf as often as we do of a man, or even of a goose, and memories have not been fresh enough

> among Men to keep hold of a special plural for a race now abandoned to folk-tales, where at least a shadow of truth is preserved, or at last to nonsense-stories in which they have become mere figures of fun. [pp. 1136–7, III: 415]

Tolkien does, however, use *dwarrow* in *Dwarrowdelf* 'Dwarf-delving', to represent in English the name of Moria in the Common Speech (*Phurunargian*).

When he received the first galley proofs of *The Fellowship of the Ring* Tolkien was annoyed to find that the compositors, following common practice, had 'corrected' *dwarves* to *dwarfs* (as well as *elvish* to *elfish*, *further* to *farther*, and *elven* to *elfin*). The original forms were quickly restored. It may be a measure of the influence of Tolkien's writings that the *Concise Oxford English Dictionary* gives both *dwarfs* and *dwarves* as the acceptable plural.

On Dwarves, see further, notes for pp. 228, 315.

2 (I: 11). Bandobras Took (Bullroarer), son of Isumbras the Third – In the Prologue as published in editions prior to 2004, Tolkien made Bandobras the 'son of Isengrim the Second', the Tenth Thain; but in doing so, he forgot that in the final Took family tree (Appendix C) he had moved Bandobras down one generation, so that he became the son of Isumbras III and the *grandson* of Isengrim II. See *The Return of the Shadow*, pp. 311, 316–17, and compare *The Peoples of Middle-earth*, pp. 109–11.

In *The Hobbit*, Chapter 1, Bandobras is described (relative to his 'gentler descendant', Bilbo Baggins) as the 'Old Took's great-grand-uncle Bullroarer, who was so huge (for a hobbit) that he could ride a horse. He charged the ranks of the goblins of Mount Gram in the Battle of the Green Fields, and knocked their king Golfimbul's head clean off with a wooden club. It sailed a hundred yards through the air and went down a rabbit-hole, and in this way the battle was won and the game of Golf invented at the same moment.' In *The Lord of the Rings* Appendix C, however, Bandobras is the Old Took's great-uncle, not great-grand-uncle.

In *Nomenclature* Tolkien comments that when he wrote the nickname 'Bullroarer' in *The Hobbit*, Chapter 1, he believed that '*bullroarer* was a word used by anthropologists, etc. for instrument(s) used by uncivilized peoples that made a roaring sound; but I cannot find it in any dictionaries (not even in O.E.D. Suppl[ement])'. But it does appear in the *Oxford English Dictionary*, under *Bull*, as 'a flat slip of wood a few inches long, narrowing to one or both ends, and fastened by one end to a thong for whirling it round, when it gives an intermittent whirring or roaring noise, heard a long way off'. See further, Steve Wood, 'Tolkien & the O.E.D.', *Amon Hen* 28 (August 1977), and Arden R. Smith, 'Possible Sources of Tolkien's Bullroarer', *Mythprint* 37, no. 12, whole no. 225 (December 2000).

Isumbras is the name also of the hero of a popular Middle English romance, *Sir Isumbras*. On the surname *Took*, see note for p. 4.

2 (I: 11). two famous characters – Merry Brandybuck and Pippin Took. At the field of Cormallen (Book VI, Chapter 4) Sam remarks on their height, gained by drinking ent-draughts: 'you're three inches taller than you ought to be' (p. 955, III: 234).

2 (I: 11): As for the Hobbits

2 (I: 11). Shire – The country of the Hobbits is thus named for the first time; in *The Hobbit* it is an unnamed part of the 'Western Lands' indicated on the map of *Wilderland* as lying off its western edge. *Shire* is a common English literary synonym for 'county', and an element in the name of certain regions of England, e.g. *Berkshire, Oxfordshire.* In notes for the Dutch translator of *The Lord of the Rings* Tolkien comments that it 'is an essentially English word of ancient historical association (& [I] have used [it] for that reason)'. In *Nomenclature* he notes that '*Shire*, Old English *scīr*, seems very early to have replaced the ancient Germanic word for a "district" found in its oldest form in Gothic *gawi*, surviving now in German *Gau*, Dutch *gouw*.' Compare, later in the Prologue: 'The Hobbits named [the land to which they moved] the Shire, as the region of the authority of their Thain, and a district of well-ordered business' (p. 5, I: 14).

In Appendix F it is said that the 'untranslated' name of the Shire was *Sûza*; this 'and all other places of the Hobbits [named in *The Lord of the Rings*] have thus been Englished' (p. 1134, III: 412–13).

On the Shire, see further, note for p. 5.

2 (I: 11). They dressed in bright colours, being notably fond of yellow and green; but they seldom wore shoes, since their feet had tough leathery soles and were clad in a thick curling hair, much like the hair of their heads, which was commonly brown. . . . Their faces were as a rule good-natured rather than beautiful, broad, bright-eyed, red-cheeked, with mouths apt to laughter, and to eating and drinking. And laugh they did, and eat, and drink, often and heartily, being fond of simple jests at all times, and of six meals a day (when they could get them). – A similar description is found in *The Hobbit*, Chapter 1:

> Hobbits have no beards. . . . They are inclined to be fat in the stomach; they dress in bright colours (chiefly green and yellow); wear no shoes, because their feet grow natural leathery soles and thick warm brown hair like the stuff on their heads (which is curly); have long clever brown fingers, good-natured faces, and laugh deep fruity laughs (especially after dinner, which they have twice a day when they can get it).

Tolkien drew several pictures for *The Hobbit* in which the hobbit Bilbo Baggins appears: *One Morning Early in the Quiet of the World, The Three Trolls Are Turned to Stone, Bilbo Woke Up with the Early Sun in His Eyes, Bilbo Comes to the Huts of the Raft-elves* and related sketches, *Conversation with Smaug,* and *The Hall at Bag-End, Residence of B. Baggins Esquire*

(*Artist and Illustrator*, figs. 89, 100, 113, 122–4, 133, 139). In only the last of these is the figure of Bilbo complete and distinct. In March or April 1938 Tolkien wrote to his American publisher, the Houghton Mifflin Company, in reply to a request for drawings of hobbits:

> I am afraid . . . I must leave it in the hands of someone who can draw. My own pictures are an unsafe guide – e.g. the picture of Mr. Baggins in Chapter VI and XII [*Bilbo Woke* and *Conversation with Smaug*]. The very ill-drawn one in Chapter XIX [*The Hall at Bag-End*] is a better guide than these in general impressions.
>
> I picture a fairly human figure, not a kind of 'fairy' rabbit as some of my British reviewers seem to fancy: fattish in the stomach, shortish in the leg. A round jovial face; ears only slightly pointed and 'elvish'; hair short and curling (brown). The feet from the ankles down, covered with brown hairy fur. Clothing: green velvet breeches; red or yellow waistcoat; brown or green jacket; gold (or brass) buttons; a dark green hood and cloak (belonging to a dwarf) . . . leathery soles, and well-brushed furry feet are a feature of essential hobbitness. . . . [*Letters*, p. 35]

Although Tolkien indicated that Hobbit ears should be drawn 'only slightly pointed', his own drawings, in particular an unpublished sketch (referred to in *Artist and Illustrator*, p. 99), suggest a 'pointedness' more than slight but less than that often seen in fan-drawn pictures of hobbits or elves.

Norman Talbot in 'Where Do Elves Go To?: Tolkien and a Fantasy Tradition', *Proceedings of the J.R.R. Tolkien Centenary Conference 1992* (1995), suggests that Hobbits may owe something of their appearance to Puck in Kipling's *Puck of Pook's Hill* (1906). In the first chapter of that book Puck is described as 'a small, brown, broad-shouldered, pointy-eared person with a snub nose, slanting blue eyes, and a grin that ran right across his freckled face' and with 'bare, hairy feet'.

2 (I: 11). comely things – *Comely* 'pleasant to look at'.

2 (I: 11). They were hospitable and delighted in parties, and in presents, which they gave away freely and eagerly accepted. – See note for p. 27.

2 (I: 11): It is plain indeed

2 (I: 11). Hobbits are relatives of ours – Tolkien wrote to Milton Waldman in ?late 1951: 'The Hobbits are, of course, really meant to be a branch of the specifically *human* race (not Elves or Dwarves) – hence the two kinds can dwell together (as at Bree), and are called just the Big Folk and Little Folk' (*Letters*, p. 158 n.).

2 (I: 11). Elves – Tolkien used *Elves* to denote the central race of beings in his mythology from its earliest expression in *The Book of Lost Tales*. In a letter to Naomi Mitchison on 25 April 1954 he commented that '"Elves" is a translation, not perhaps now very suitable, but originally good enough, of *Quendi* [Quenya 'the speakers', the name for all of elven-kind]. They are represented as a race similar in appearance (and more so the further back) to Men, and in former days of the same stature' (*Letters*, p. 176; cf. Appendix F). Later that year, on 18 September, he wrote to Hugh Brogan that he now deeply regretted having used *Elves* 'though this is a word in ancestry and original meaning suitable enough. But the disastrous debasement of this word, in which Shakespeare played an unforgiveable part, has really overloaded it with regrettable tones, which are too much to overcome' (*Letters*, p. 185). In *Nomenclature* (entry for *Elven-smiths*) he directs that a word be chosen to translate *Elf* which does not 'retain some of the associations of a kind that I should particularly desire not to be present (if possible): e.g. those of Drayton or of *A Midsummer Night's Dream*. . . . That is, the pretty fanciful reduction of *elf* to a butterfly-like creature inhabiting flowers.' A German translation in particular, he suggested, might use *Alp* or *Alb* as

> the true cognate of English *elf*; and if it has senses nearer to English *oaf*, referring to puckish and malicious sprites, or to idiots regarded as 'changelings', that is true also of English *elf*. I find these debased rustic associations less damaging than the 'pretty' literary fancies. The Elves of the 'mythology' of *The Lord of the Rings* are not actually equatable with the folklore traditions about 'fairies'. . . .

2 (I: 11). Elder Days – At the beginning of *The Tale of Years* (Appendix B) Tolkien notes that the term *Elder Days* 'was properly given only to the days before the casting out of Morgoth', i.e. the First Age of the world, before the Great Battle in which Morgoth was overthrown, and after which many elves returned from Middle-earth into the Far West (p. 1082, III: 363; see further in *The Silmarillion*). In *Nomenclature* he writes that it

> is naturally taken by English readers to mean 'older' (sc. former) but with an archaic flavour, since this original form of the comparative is now only applied to persons, or used as a noun in *Elders* (seniors). In inventing the expression I intended this, as well as association with the poetic *eld* 'old age, antiquity'. I have since (recently) come across the expression in early English: *be eldern dawes* 'in the days of our forefathers, long ago'.

2 (I: 11). Middle-earth – In *Nomenclature* Tolkien comments that *Middle-earth* is

> not a special land, or world, or 'planet' as too often supposed, though it is made plain in the prologue [to *The Lord of the Rings*] . . . text, and Appendices that the story takes place on this earth and under skies in general the same as now visible. The sense is 'the inhabited lands of

> (Elves and) Men', envisaged as lying between the Western Sea and that of the Far East (only known in the West by rumour). *Middle-earth* (see dictionaries) is a modern alteration of medieval *middel-erde* from Old English *middan-geard*. . . .

Middle-earth, recorded in the *Oxford English Dictionary* back to *c.* 1275 (as *middelerþe*, *middilerþe*, etc.), is defined as 'the earth, as placed between heaven and hell, or as supposed to occupy the centre of the universe'.

In the entry for *Isengard* in *Nomenclature* Tolkien indicates that

> the *gard* element ['enclosure'] appears in Old Norse *garðr* . . . and English *garth* (beside genuine English *yard*); this though usually of more lowly associations (as English *farmyard*) appears e.g. in Old Norse *Ás-garðr*, now widely known as *Asgard* in mythology. The word was early lost in German, except in Old High German *mittin-* or *mittil-gart* (the inhabited lands of Men) = Old Norse *miðgarðr*, and Old English *middan-geard*. . . .

2 (I: 11). Bilbo, and of Frodo – In regard to the name *Bilbo* several critics have noted that a *bilbo* is 'a sword noted for the temper and elasticity of its blade' and 'often used as the proper name of a sword personified; esp. that of a bully or swashbuckler' (*OED*). But there is no evidence that this was the source of *Bilbo* in *The Hobbit*.

On 7 September 1955 Tolkien wrote to Richard Jeffery that *Frodo* 'is a real name from the Germanic tradition. Its Old English form was *Fróda*. Its obvious connexion with the word *fród* meaning etymologically "wise by experience", but it had mythological connexions with legends of the Golden Age in the North' (*Letters*, p. 224). 'Frōda' is mentioned in the Old English poem *Beowulf*, as the father of Ingeld.

2–3 (I: 11–12): Those days, the Third Age

2 (I: 11). Third Age – The Third Age of the world in Tolkien's mythology is considered to have begun with the overthrow of Sauron by the Last Alliance of Elves and Men in Second Age 3441, and to have come to an end in the War of the Ring: see the beginning of *The Tale of Years*. In his letter to Milton Waldman in ?late 1951 Tolkien called the Third Age 'a Twilight Age, a Medium Aevum, the first of the broken and changed world [after the destruction of Númenor]; the last of the lingering dominion of visible fully incarnate Elves, and the last also in which Evil assumes a single dominant incarnate shape [Sauron]' (*Letters*, p. 154).

2 (I: 11). Old World, east of the Sea – In his unfinished index Tolkien defines *Old World* as 'Middle-earth before the change of land at [the] fall of Númenor', and he wrote expansively on the word *Sea*:

> Usually refers to the Western Ocean beyond which no mortal lands were yet known to exist (though the roundness of Middle-earth was

well-known). There was a tradition that anciently one could sail west until one came at last to Valinor, 'the Blessed Realm', but that had been veiled and beset with impenetrable shadows – for which reason 'the Shadowy Seas' was often said of the remote western sea; so that the Elves that had forsaken Valinor could not return. Cf. Galadriel's song in Book II. But after the overthrow of Morgoth and the downfall of Thangorodrim (cf. Elrond's words in [Book] II ch. 2), the return west had been re-opened for Elves. But Valinor was forbidden to Mortals. The Númenóreans (or Dúnedain), as a reward for their help in the overthrow of Morgoth, had been given the great Isle of Númenor to dwell in, furthest west of all mortal lands; but when they became proud, because of their great might and splendour, and tried to land in Valinor, the Blessed Realm was removed from the Circles of the World, and Númenor cast down into the Sea, and the fashion of the earth changed. A few only of the faithful Númenóreans escaped from the drowning of the land and returned to the West-shore of Middle-earth, and thereafter only elven-ships could sail into the 'true West' following the 'straight road', and so rising above the Circles of the World come again to Eldamar (Elvenhome) on the shores of Valinor. So *Sea* = Great Sea and frequently *Western Seas* or *Great Sea*(*s*); also called *the Sundering Seas.*

On the fall of Númenor, see Appendix A, Part I (i), and the *Akallabêth* in *The Silmarillion.*

3 (I: 12). the upper vales of Anduin, between the eaves of Greenwood the Great and the Misty Mountains – A *vale* is an area of land between two stretches of high ground or hills, usually traversed by a river or stream; the *Oxford English Dictionary* notes that in later usage *vale* is 'chiefly poetical' except in place-names, e.g. the 'Vale of Evesham'. The upper vales of the great river Anduin are north of Lothlórien in the geography of *The Lord of the Rings*, while the lower vales are south of Rauros. The name *Anduin* is derived from Sindarin *and* 'long' + *duin* 'large river'; in manuscripts Tolkien translates it as 'great river' and 'long river'.

Eaves is used here, and elsewhere in *The Lord of the Rings*, in the obsolete sense 'edge of a wood'.

Greenwood the Great is the great forest east of the Anduin and south of the Grey Mountains, later (and throughout *The Lord of the Rings* proper) known as Mirkwood (see below). *Greenwood* is an old word for a wood or forest when in leaf, which Tolkien uses for deliberate poetic or archaic effect. It is said in *The Tale of Years* that after the War of the Ring, in which there is a great battle under the trees in the North, Mirkwood is renamed *Eryn Lasgalen*, the Wood of Greenleaves.

The *Misty Mountains* are 'the great range (called in E[lvish] *Hithaeglir* "line of misty peaks"), running more or less from N[orth] to S[outh] from Mt. Gundabad about 200 miles n[orth] of Rivendell, to *Methedras* about 400 miles s[outh] of Rivendell' (*Index*). Tom Shippey has suggested that

Tolkien borrowed the name from the Eddic poem *Skirnismál*, which includes the phrase 'The mirk is outside, I call it our business to fare over the misty mountains, over the tribes of orcs' (*The Road to Middle-earth*, 2nd edn. (1992), p. 65). Tolkien depicted the Misty Mountains most notably in his colour illustration for *The Hobbit*, *Bilbo Woke Up with the Early Sun in His Eyes* (*Artist and Illustrator*, fig. 113): there the mountains were clearly influenced by the Swiss Alps, which Tolkien visited in 1911.

3 (I: 12). **Eriador** – The lands in Middle-earth west of the Misty Mountains and east of the Blue Mountains (Ered Luin). In Appendix A it is said that 'Eriador was of old the name of all the lands between the Misty Mountains and the Blue; in the South it was bounded by the Greyflood and the Glanduin that flows into it above Tharbad' (p. 1039, III: 319). A note among Tolkien's papers from *c.* 1949–53 (quoted in *Vinyar Tengwar* 42 (July 2001), p. 4) states that *Eriador* contains the element *eryā* 'isolated, lonely' in the Elvish language Noldorin (later called Sindarin); elsewhere Sindarin *dor* 'land' is well established. Thus the note translates *Eriador* as 'wilderness'. In his *Etymologies* Tolkien includes the stem ERE- 'be alone, deprived', and the example *erya* 'single, sole' (*The Lost Road and Other Writings*, p. 356).

Fredrik Ström has suggested, in a letter to *Vinyar Tengwar* 42, that the *Lone-lands* of *The Hobbit*, Chapter 2, introduced by Tolkien in the edition of 1966, are the linguistic equivalent of *Eriador*.

3 (I: 12). **Mirkwood** – The forest east of the Misty Mountains earlier known as Greenwood the Great, but at the time of the events of *The Hobbit* and *The Lord of the Rings* under the shadow of evil things, especially in the southern regions around the tower of Dol Guldur. In Appendix F it is said that to the Elves the forest was *Taur e-Ndaedelos* 'forest of the great fear'; *Mirkwood* is its equivalent in the Common Speech, but has a different meaning. *The Disaster of the Gladden Fields*, written by Tolkien after the publication of *The Lord of the Rings*, tells of 'days when the shadow of Sauron spread through Greenwood the Great, and changed its name from Eryn Galen to Taur-nu-Fuin (translated Mirkwood)'. Christopher Tolkien notes in *Unfinished Tales* that 'the name given here, Taur-nu-Fuin "forest under night", was the later name of Dorthonion, the forested highland on the northern borders of Beleriand in the Elder Days. The application of the same name, Taur-nu-Fuin, to both Mirkwood and Dorthonion is notable, in the light of the close relation of my father's pictures of them' (p. 281). Tolkien painted a watercolour picture, *Beleg Finds Flinding in Taur-na-Fúin*, in July 1928 (*Artist and Illustrator*, fig. 54), and in 1937 redrew it in ink as *Mirkwood* for the first edition of *The Hobbit* (*Artist and Illustrator*, fig. 88).

On 29 July 1966 Tolkien wrote to his grandson Michael George Tolkien:

> *Mirkwood* is not an invention of mine, but a very ancient name, weighted with legendary associations. It was probably the Primitive Germanic name for the great mountainous forest regions that anciently

formed a barrier to the south of the lands of Germanic expansion. In some traditions it became used especially of the boundary between Goths and Huns. I speak now from memory: its ancientness seems indicated by its appearance in very early German (11th c. ?) as *mirkiwidu* although the **merkw-* stem 'dark' is not otherwise found in German at all (only in O[ld] E[nglish], O[ld] S[axon], and O[ld] N[orse]), and the stem **widu- > witu* was in German (I think) limited to the sense 'timber', not very common, and did not survive into mod[ern] G[erman]. In O[ld] E[nglish] *mirce* only survives in poetry, and in the sense 'dark', or rather 'gloomy', only in *Beowulf* [line] 1405 *ofer myrcan mor*: elsewhere only with the sense 'murky' > wicked, hellish. It was never, I think, a mere 'colour' word: 'black', and was from the beginning weighted with the sense of 'gloom'. . . .

In O[ld] N[orse], *myrkviðr* is often found, mainly in Eddaic verse as a proper name. The best known examples are *Völundarkviða* 'Lay of Wayland' line 2 where swanmaidens are said to fly from the south through Mirkwood (*meyjar flugu sunnan Myrkvið ígegnum*). The legend and the lay are not of ultimately Norse origin, but derived from the area whence the English came. No doubt **Mircwudu* would have appeared in it. The other is in *Atlakviða* ['Lay of Atli'] the long and corrupt lay dealing with the way in which Atli (Ætla, Attila) got the brothers of Guðrún to come and visit him and then murdered them. Among the many gifts and territories that he promised to give them in stanza 5 is mentioned *hrís þat et mæra es menn Myrkvið kalla* 'that renowned forest that men call Mirkwood'.

It seemed to me too good a fortune that Mirkwood remained intelligible (with exactly the right tone) in modern English to pass over: whether *mirk* is a Norse loan or a freshment of the obsolescent O[ld] E[nglish] word. [British Library MS Add. 71657, partly printed in *Letters*, pp. 369–70]

The name 'Mirkwood' earlier figured also in *A Tale of the House of the Wolfings* (1888) by William Morris.

3 (I: 12): Before the crossing of the mountains

3 (I: 12). three somewhat different breeds: Harfoots, Stoors, and Fallohides – *Harfoot* is 'meant to be intelligible (in its context) and recognized as altered form of an old name = "hairfoot": sc. "one with hairy feet". (Technically supposed to represent archaic *hǣr-fōt > hērfot > hĕrfoot* with the usual change of *er > ar* in English. Modern English *hair*, though related, is not a direct descendant of Old English *hǣr/hēr* = German *Haar*)' (*Nomenclature*).

Stoor is the name of a 'kind of hobbit, of heavier build. This is early English *stor, stoor* "large, strong", now obsolete' (*Nomenclature*). Thus 'the Stoors were broader, heavier in build', etc. (p. 3, I: 12).

Fallohide is meant by Tolkien 'to represent a name with a meaning in Common Speech, though one devised in the past and so containing archaic elements. It is made of English *fallow* + *hide* and means 'paleskin'. It is archaic since *fallow* "pale, yellowish" is not now in use, except in *fallow deer*; and *hide* is no longer applied to human skin (except as a transference back from its modern use of animal hides, used for leather)' (*Nomenclature*). Thus 'the Fallohides were fairer of skin and also of hair' (3, I: 12).

The entry into Eriador by three 'breeds' of Hobbits no doubt deliberately echoes the entry into Britain in ancient days by the three Germanic 'invaders' described by the Venerable Bede, the Angles, Saxons, and Jutes. See also note for *Marcho* and *Blanco*, p. 4.

3 (I: 12): The Harfoots had much to do

3 (I: 12). They [the Harfoots] moved westward early, and roamed over Eriador – *The Tale of Years* records for Third Age 1050: 'The Periannath [Hobbits] are first mentioned in records, with the coming of the Harfoots to Eriador' (p. 1085, III: 366).

3 (I: 12). Weathertop – The tallest of the Weather Hills, east of Bree and north of the great East Road, called in Sindarin *Amon Sûl* 'hill of the wind'. The element *weather* in *Weathertop* and *Weather Hills* has a nautical sense 'windward', and is related to 'wind' also in the expression *wind and weather.*

3 (I: 12). Wilderland – 'Hobbit name for the lands beyond the Misty Mountains, [in] E[lvish, i.e. Sindarin] *Rhóvannion* [*sic*], but often used to include the wild lands on the west side of the range, that is Eastern *Eriador*' (*Index*). In *Nomenclature* Tolkien comments that *Wilderland* is 'an invention (not actually found in English), based on *wilderness* (originally meaning 'country of wild creatures, not inhabited by Men'), but with a side-reference to the verb *wilder* "wander astray", and *bewilder.* Supposed to be the Common Speech name of *Rhovanion* (in the map, not in the text), the lands east of the Misty Mountains (including Mirkwood) as far as the River Running.' *The Hobbit* includes a map of Wilderland, so titled.

3 (I: 12): The Stoors lingered

3 (I: 12). They [the Stoors] came west after the Harfoots and followed the course of the Loudwater southwards; and there many of them long dwelt between Tharbad and the borders of Dunland – *The Tale of Years* records for Third Age *c.* 1150: 'The Stoors come over the Redhorn Pass and move to the Angle [between the Hoarwell and the Loudwater], or to Dunland' (p. 1085, III: 366).

Loudwater represents the Common Speech word for Sindarin *Bruinen.* It is also an old name for the River Wye, still preserved in a place in Chipping Wycombe, Buckinghamshire, and 'derived from the noise incessantly made by the rapidity of the stream' (G. Lipscomb, quoted in Eilert Ekwall, *English River Names* (1928), p. 263).

Tharbad is a ruined town at the crossing over the river Gwathló (Greyflood); its name is Sindarin for 'road-crossing', as Tolkien states in his unfinished index.

Dunland is 'a country about the west skirts of the Misty M[oun]t[ai]ns at their far S[outhern] end, inhabited by the Dunlendings, remnant of an old race of Men (akin to the Breelanders?), hostile to the Rohirrim' (*Index*). In Appendix F Tolkien writes of the Dunlendings: '*Dunland* and *Dunlending* are the names that the Rohirrim gave to them, because they were swarthy and dark-haired; there is thus no connexion between the word *dunn* in these names and the Grey-elven [Sindarin] word *Dûn* "west"' (p. 1130, III: 408). Compare English *dun* 'dull greyish-brown'.

3–4 (I: 12–13): The Fallohides, the least numerous

3 (I: 12). They [the Fallohides] crossed the mountains north of Rivendell and came down the River Hoarwell. In Eriador they soon mingled with the other kinds that had preceded them – *The Tale of Years* records for Third Age *c.* 1150: 'The Fallohides enter Eriador' (p. 1085, III: 366).

Rivendell is 'the fair valley' in which Elrond Halfelven 'lives in the Last Homely House' (so introduced in *The Hobbit*, Chapter 3). The name ('cloven-dell') represents the Common Speech word for Sindarin *Imladris* 'deep dale of the cleft' (*Nomenclature*).

The *Hoarwell* flows south from the Ettenmoors to join the Loudwater (Bruinen); its English name contains the elements *hoar* 'greyish-white' + Old English *well* 'well, spring, stream'. In the context of *The Lord of the Rings* it represents the Common Speech word for Sindarin *Mitheithel* 'hoary spring' (*Index*). See further, note for p. 200.

4 (I: 13). the Tooks and the Masters of Buckland – In *Nomenclature* Tolkien defines *Took* as a 'Hobbit-name of unknown origin representing actual Hobbit *Tūk*'. Tom Shippey notes in *The Road to Middle-earth* that *Took* is 'a faintly comic name in modern English (people prefer to respell it "Tooke"), but it is only the ordinary Northern pronunciation [as for the word *too*] of the very common "Tuck"' (2nd edn, p. 93).

In Book I, Chapter 5 the head of the Brandybuck family is called 'Master of the Hall' (i.e. Brandy Hall). *Master* is used in this sense much as it is in the Scottish peerage. Elsewhere in *The Lord of the Rings* it is used as an honorific. On this, and for *Buckland*, see notes for p. 22.

4 (I: 13): In the westlands of Eriador

4 (I: 13). Mountains of Lune – Mountains to the north and south-west of the Shire, forming the ancient boundary of Beleriand (Lindon) and Eriador. The name is an adaptation of Sindarin *Ered Luin* 'blue mountains'.

Lune as used here should not be confused with the name of the river, gulf, or firth (see below).

4 (I: 13). Dúnedain, the kings of Men that came over the Sea out of Westernesse – *Dúnedain* 'Men of the West', from Sindarin *dûn* 'west' + *edain* 'men' (singular *Dúnadan*).

Westernesse is the name in the Common Speech for *Númenor* 'west-land' (see note for p. 15). Tolkien states in *Nomenclature* that it 'is meant to be *western* + *ess* an ending used in partly francized names of "romantic" lands, as *Lyonesse*, or *Logres* (England in Arthurian Romance). The name actually occurs in the early romance *King Horn*, of some kingdom reached by ship.' In a letter to Dick Plotz, 12 September 1965, Tolkien wrote that he had 'often used *Westernesse* as a translation. This is derived from rare Middle English *Westernesse* (known to me only in MS. C of *King Horn*) where the meaning is vague, but may be taken to mean "Western lands" as distinct from the East inhabited by the Paynim and Saracens' (*Letters*, p. 361).

4 (I: 13). North Kingdom – Arnor (see below).

4 (I: 13). Bree and in the Chetwood – *Bree* is a 'small land, 40 miles east of the Shire. The name properly means "hill" in a language older than Westron, and the country was also called "(the) Bree-land". The hill itself was often called "Bree-hill" . . . – or (in Bree) the Hill' (*Index*). The name is derived from Welsh *bre* 'hill', earlier Old British **brigā*. Christopher Tolkien has said that it is based on *Brill* in Buckinghamshire, a place his father 'knew well, for it sits on a hill in the Little Kingdom of *Farmer Giles of Ham*. The name *Brill* is derived from the old British word *bre* "hill", to which the English added their own word *hyll*' (*The Return of the Shadow*, p. 131). Tom Shippey suggests in *The Road to Middle-earth* that Tolkien 'borrowed' *Bree* 'for its faint Celtic "style", to make subliminally the point that the hobbits were immigrants too, that their land had had a history before them' (2nd edn., p. 99).

Chetwood is 'the woodlands east and south of Bree' (*Index*). The element *chet* (also in *Archet*, see note for p. 149) comes from a British name of a wood, *Cēt*, from Old Celtic **kaito-* 'wood'; to this was added Old English *wudu* 'wood'. Thus *Chetwood* is etymologically 'wood-wood', as *Bree-hill* is 'hill-hill'.

4 (I: 13): It was in these early days

4 (I: 13). Common Speech, the Westron as it was named – On 25 April 1954 Tolkien wrote to Naomi Mitchison: 'The Westron or C[ommon] S[peech] is supposed to be derived from the Mannish *Adunaic* language of the Númenóreans, spreading from the Númenórean Kingdoms in the days of the Kings, and especially from *Gondor*, where it remains spoken in nobler and rather more antique style (a style also usually adopted by the

Elves when they use this language)' (*Letters*, p. 175). Tolkien briefly discusses the Common Speech in Appendix F.

4 (I: 13). **Arnor to Gondor** – *Arnor* is the name of the Númenórean northern realm, derived from Sindarin *ar(a)-* 'high, noble, royal' + *dôr* 'land', hence 'royal land', 'land of the king'. On 17 December 1972 Tolkien wrote to Richard Jeffery that he 'retained' (from his fictional source manuscripts) *Arnor* 'because he desired to avoid *Ardor*', referring to a sound shift in the supposed later development of Sindarin. 'But it can now only (though reasonably) be explained after invention as due to a blending of Q[uenya] *arnanóre / arnanor* with S[indarin] *arn(a)dor* > *ardor*. The name was in any case given to mean "royal land" as being the realm of *Elendil* and so taking precedence of the southern realm' (*Letters*, p. 428). In Appendix A it is said that 'at its greatest Arnor included all Eriador, except the regions beyond the Lune, and the lands east of Greyflood and Loudwater, in which lay Rivendell and Hollin' (p. 1039, III: 319).

Gondor 'stone-land' is the name of the southern Númenórean kingdom in Middle-earth, established by Isildur and Anárion. In his unfinished index Tolkien describes Gondor as

> anciently including Calen-ardon (later called *Rohan*) from Isengard to Entwash; Anórien between Entwash and the White Mts. [Mountains] and all the land betw[een] west of Anduin from Rauros to River Erui; and Ithilien, the lands east of Anduin between the river and Ephel Dúath (the Mts. of Shadow), as far South as R[iver] Poros; also the 'faithful fiefs' of Lebennin, Belfalas and Anfalas (Langstrand), west of Anduin and Sirith, between the White Mts. and the Sea; and the 'lost fief' of S[outh] Gondor between R. Poros and Harnen. At the time of this history it included only Anórien and the 'faithful fiefs'.

Tolkien wrote to Graham Tayar in his letter of 4–5 June 1971:

> In the matter of *Gondar/Gondor* you touch on a difficult matter, but one of great interest: the nature of the process of 'linguistic invention' (including nomenclature) in general, and in *The Lord of the Rings* in particular. . . . As far as *Gondor* goes the facts (of which I am aware) are these: 1) I do not recollect ever having heard the name *Gondar* (in Ethiopia) before your letter; 2) *Gondor* is (a) a name fitted to the style and phonetics of *Sindarin*, and (b) has the sense 'Stone-land' sc. 'Stone (-using people's) land'. [*Author's note:* This meaning was understood by other peoples ignorant of Sindarin: cf. *Stoningland* . . . and in particular the conversation of *Théoden* and *Ghân*. . . . In fact it is probable within the historical fiction that the Númenóreans of the Southern kingdom adopted this name from the primitive inhabitants of *Gondor* and gave it a suitable version in Sindarin.] Outside the inner historical fiction, the name was a very early element in the invention of the whole story. Also in the linguistic construction of the tale, which is accurate

> and detailed, *Gondor* and *Gondar* would be two distinct words/names, and the latter would have no precise sense. Nonetheless one's mind is, of course, stored with a 'leaf-mould' of memories (submerged) of names, and these rise up to the surface at times, and may provide with modification the bases of 'invented' names. Owing to the prominence of Ethiopia in the Italian war *Gondar* may have been one such element. But no more than say *Gondwana-land* (that rare venture of geology into poetry). In this case I can actually recollect the reason why the element **gon(o)*, **gond(o)* was selected for the stem of words meaning stone, when I began inventing the 'Elvish' languages. When about 8 years old I read in a small book (professedly for the young) [*Celtic Britain* by John Rhys] that nothing of the language of primitive peoples (before the Celts or Germanic invaders) is now known, except perhaps *ond* = 'stone' (+ one other now forgotten). I have no idea how such a form could even be guessed, but the *ond* seemed to me fitting for the meaning. (The prefixing of g- was much later, after the invention of the history of the relation between *Sindarin* & *Quenya* in which primitive initial *g*- was lost in Q[uenya]: the Q[uenya] form of the word remained *ondo*.) [*Letters*, pp. 409–10]

See further, Carl F. Hostetter and Patrick Wynne, 'Stone Towers', *Mythlore* 19, no. 4, whole no. 74 (Autumn 1993).

4 (I: 13). all the coasts of the Sea from Belfalas to Lune – *Belfalas* is the name of a region on the south coast of Gondor, according to *Index* derived from Sindarin *bel* 'steep, sheer' + *falas* 'surf, wave-beaten shore'. In *The Rivers and Beacon-hills of Gondor* from more than a decade later (*c.* 1967–9), however, Tolkien considers, first, that 'the element *Bel-* in *Belfalas* has no suitable meaning in Sindarin', but that possibly it meant in the language of earlier inhabitants of the area the same as Sindarin *falas* 'shore', 'especially one exposed to great waves and breakers (cf. Q[uenya] *falma* "a wave-crest, wave")', and thus is

> an example of the type of place-name, not uncommon when a region is occupied by a new people, in which two elements of much the same topographical meaning are joined: the first being in the older and the second in the incoming language. Probably because the first was taken by the Incomers as a particular name. However, in Gondor the shoreland from the mouth of Anduin to Dol Amroth was called *Belfalas*, but actually usually referred to as *ifalas* 'the surf-beach' (or sometimes as *Then-falas* 'short-beach'), in contrast to *An-falas* 'long-beach', between the mouths of Morthond and Levnui [Lefnui]. But the great bay between Umbar and Angast [Andrast] (the Long Cape, beyond Levnui) was called the Bay of Belfalas (*Côf Belfalas*) or simply of Bel (*Côf gwaeren Bêl* 'the windy Bay of Bêl'). So that it is more probable that Bêl was the name or part of the name of the region afterward usually called

Dor-en-Ernil 'land of the Prince': it was perhaps the most important part of Gondor before the Númenórean settlement.

He then struck through this argument, posited *Bel-* as 'certainly an element derived from a pre-Númenórean name; but its source is known, and was in fact Sindarin', and began to write an experimental extension of his history of the Elves; but he broke off in mid-sentence, before saying more about the question of *Belfalas* (*Vinyar Tengwar* 42 (July 2001), pp. 15–16).

Lune here refers to the Gulf of Lune (Lhûn) in the north-west of Middle-earth, at the outlet of the River Lune. In Appendix A it is said that 'beyond the Lune was Elvish country, green and quiet, where no Men went; but Dwarves dwelt, and still dwell, in the east side of the Blue Mountains, especially in those parts south of the Gulf of Lune, where they have mines that are still in use' (p. 1039, III: 319). Ekwall, *English River-names*, records two rivers in Britain named *Lune*: one rises near Ravenstonedale in Westmorland and runs through Lonsdale to the Irish Sea south-west of Lancaster, the other is an affluent of the Tees in the North Riding of Yorkshire.

4 (I: 13): About this time legend among the Hobbits

4 (I: 13). Marcho and Blanco – The names of the Fallohide brothers, who with 'a great following of Hobbits' colonized the Shire, are a deliberate parallel to those of Hengest and Horsa, two Germanic chieftains who came to Britain with their warriors in the early fifth century, first of the Anglo-Saxons who eventually conquered the native Britons. *Hengest* is Old English for 'gelding, horse, steed', and *horsa* stems from Old English *hors* 'horse', while *Marcho* is derived from Old English *mearh* 'horse, steed' (compare Welsh *march* 'horse, stallion', *marchog* 'rider') and *blanca* is Old English for 'white or grey horse'.

4 (I: 13). Fornost – A Númenórean city on the North Downs in Eriador, the later seat of the Kings of Arnor. The name is 'translated' later in the Prologue as *Norbury* ('north' + 'city, fortress'). In full its name is *Fornost Erain* 'Norbury of the Kings' (or 'Kings' Norbury') from Sindarin *forn* 'north' + *ost* 'fortress', *erain* plural of *aran* 'king'. See also note for p. 9.

4 (I: 13). the brown river Baranduin – In *Nomenclature* Tolkien states that *Baranduin* means 'the long gold-brown river', from Sindarin *baran* 'brown, yellow-brown' + (given in the preliminary version of *Nomenclature*) *duin* 'large [or long] river'. 'The common Elvish was *duinē*: stem *dui-* "flow (in volume)". The Quenya form would have been *luine* (Quenya initial $d > l$), but the word was not used. . . . Usually by hobbits altered to *Brandywine*.' Compare, in the next paragraph of the Prologue, 'the Brandywine (as the Hobbits turned the name)'.

At the end of Appendix F Tolkien writes of *Brandywine* that the hobbit-names for this river were alterations of the Elvish *Baranduin* (accented on *and*), derived from *baran* 'golden brown' and *duin* '(large) river'. Of *Baranduin* Brandywine seemed a natural corruption in modern times. Actually the older hobbit-name was *Branda-nîn* 'border-water', which would have been more closely rendered by Marchbourn; but by a jest that had become habitual, referring again to its colour, at this time the river was usually called *Bralda-hîm* 'heady ale'. [p. 1138, III: 416]

4 (I: 13). Bridge of Stonebows, that had been built in the days of the power of the North Kingdom – *Bridge of Stonebows* is the older name of a Númenórean bridge with three arches over the Baranduin, usually called by Hobbits the Brandywine Bridge, 'from the east-end of which Hobbit land-measurement and distances were reckoned' (*Index*). *Stonebows* is derived from Old English *stānboȝa* 'stone-bow', i.e. 'arch'.

4 (I: 13). Far Downs – An area on the 'old west-borders of the Shire, before [the] occupation of Westmarch' (*Index*). Frodo, Sam, and company come to the Far Downs on their way to the Grey Havens in Book VI, Chapter 9. A *down*, generally speaking, is an area of open rolling land.

4 (I: 13). All that was demanded of them was that they should keep the Great Bridge in repair, and all other bridges and roads, speed the king's messengers, and acknowledge his lordship. – These are traditional responsibilities of a people to their lord, which also serve the general good.

4, n. 1 (I: 13, n. 1): As the records of Gondor relate

4, n. 1(I: 13, n. 1). the Northern line, which came to an end with Arvedui – *Arvedui* is Sindarin for 'last-king'.

4–5 (I: 13–14): Thus began the *Shire-reckoning*

4 (I: 13). *Shire-reckoning* – The count of years used by the Hobbits of the Shire. The term is printed in *The Lord of the Rings* as both *Shire-reckoning* (marginally predominant) and *Shire Reckoning*. The latter form (with two capitals and no hyphen, preferred in the present book), found in the Appendices, may have been influenced by *Kings' Reckoning*, *Stewards' Reckoning*, and *New Reckoning* used in Appendix D.

5 (I: 14). To the last battle at Fornost with the Witch-lord of Angmar – *Angmar* was an 'ancient kingdom in the far North of Middle-earth, ruled by the Witch-king (afterwards the Chief of the Nazgûl)' (*Index*). Its name is derived from Sindarin *ang* 'iron' + Quenya *mar* 'home'. In the manuscript of *Nomenclature* Tolkien notes that 'the name and origin of the Witch-king is not recorded, but he was probably (like the Lieutenant of Barad-dûr [the Mouth of Sauron]) of Númenórean descent. *Angmar* seems to be corrupt Sindarin or Quenya < *anga* "iron" + *mbar-* "habitation": pure Sindarin would be *angbar*, Quenya *angamar*.'

The *Witch-lord* (or *Witch-king*) *of Angmar* was the greatest of the nine Men to whom Sauron gave rings of power, and thus perverted them: 'those who used the Nine Rings became mighty in their day, kings, sorcerers, and warriors of old' (*Of the Rings of Power and the Third Age* in *The Silmarillion*, p. 289). He became chief of the Ringwraiths. The use of *witch* in his title seems odd to contemporary eyes, to whom the word is popularly associated only with females, but its oldest use recorded in the *Oxford English Dictionary* is 'a man who practises witchcraft or magic; a magician, sorcerer, wizard', and for most of its history it belonged to no gender.

In Third Age 1974 the Witch-king and his forces took Fornost; but in 1975 he was defeated in a great battle (the *last battle*) against the Host of the West and vanished from the North, escaping to Mordor.

5 (I: 14). Thain – *Thain* was obviously inspired by English *thane*, 'one who in Anglo-Saxon times held lands of the king or other superior by military service' (*OED*), most familiar today by its use in Shakespeare's *Macbeth*. The *Oxford English Dictionary* notes, however, that 'the regular modern representation of Old English *þegn*, if the word had lived on in spoken use, would have been *thain* (cf. *fain*, *main*, *rain*), as it actually appears in some writers, chiefly northern, from 1300 to near 1600'. The first Thain of the Shire was Bucca of the Marish, from whom were descended the Oldbucks; later the title was associated with the Tooks. Originally in the Prologue Tolkien gave the head of the Took family the title 'The Shirking': but it 'was no longer in use in Bilbo's time: it had been killed by the endless and inevitable jokes that had been made about it, in defiance of its obvious etymology ['shire-king', compare *Shire-reeve* > *Shirriff*]' (*The Peoples of Middle-earth*, pp. 5–6). Tolkien later changed *Shirking* to *Thane*, and then to *Thain*.

5 (I: 14). There for a thousand years they were little troubled by wars, and they prospered and multiplied after the Dark Plague (S.R. 37) until the disaster of the Long Winter and the famine that followed it. Many thousands then perished, but the Days of Dearth (1158–60) were at the time of this tale long past and the Hobbits had again become accustomed to plenty. – As first published this passage read more briefly: 'And thenceforward for a thousand years they lived in almost unbroken peace.' It was expanded in the second edition (1965). The *Dark Plague*, or Great Plague, spread out of Rhovanion into Gondor and Eriador in Third Age 1636; according to the late (post-*Lord of the Rings*) work *Cirion and Eorl and the Friendship of Gondor and Rohan* it appeared in Rhovanion in the winter of 1635, began the waning of the Northmen, and spread to Gondor where the mortality was great. 'When the Plague passed it is said that more than half of the folk of Rhovanion had perished, and of their horses also' (*Unfinished Tales*, p. 289). In a note related to *The Battles of the Fords of Isen* (another later work, also in *Unfinished Tales*) Tolkien dates the Great Plague to 1636–7.

The *Long Winter* is dated in *The Tale of Years* to Third Age 2758–9: 'Great suffering and loss of life in Eriador and Rohan. Gandalf comes to the aid of the Shire-folk' (p. 1088, III: 369). *Days of Dearth* refers to the period of suffering that followed the Long Winter.

5 (I: 14). cornlands, vineyards – *Corn* in British English usage means 'grain', not 'maize' (Indian corn) which was little known in England prior to the Second World War. Grape vines were being grown, and wine made, at a substantial number of monasteries in England already by the time of the Norman Conquest. England, especially southern England, and Wales are at the northern fringe of the climate suitable for viniculture.

5 (I: 14): Forty leagues it stretched

5 (I: 14). Forty leagues it stretched from the Far Downs to the Brandywine Bridge, and fifty from the northern moors to the marshes in the south. – As first published this passage read: 'Fifty leagues it stretched from the Westmarch under the Tower Hills to the Brandywine Bridge, and nearly fifty from the northern moors to the marshes in the south.' Its revision in the second edition (1965) has at least two possible explanations (or both): because the Westmarch was not added to the Shire until after the events of the story (though its addition must predate the Prologue); or because on the scale of the 1954 general map of Middle-earth, 50 leagues (150 miles) from the Brandywine Bridge extends beyond Westmarch, even beyond the Tower Hills, and it was easier to alter the text than to redraw the map. Tolkien had wished to retain 'and nearly fifty' for the north–south dimension, but it was wrongly typeset in the Ballantine Books edition (1965) and the error was continued in the Allen & Unwin second edition (1966). Tolkien noted the error and accepted it; but Ballantine Books also set 'Far Downs' as 'Fox Downs', and 'northern moors' as 'western moors', errors which were corrected in the Allen & Unwin edition.

One *league* is generally considered equal to about three miles. The unit of measure has never been usual in Britain, except for poetical or rhetorical purposes. Tolkien uses the term also in a note published in *Unfinished Tales* describing Númenórean linear measures, where it is defined as 'very nearly three of our miles' (p. 285); and also among unpublished manuscript workings of 'Hobbit long measures' (Marquette MSS 4/2/19):

1 nail (length of toe-nail) = ½ in. [*altered from* ¼]
3 nails [*altered from* 6] = 1 toe (sc. big toe), 1½ in.
6 toes = 1 foot, 9 in.
3 feet = 1 step, or *ell*, 2 ft. 3 in.
6 feet = 1 two-step, or long-gait (or fathom), 4 ft. 6 in.

land and road measures
(based on easy step, toe to toe without effort in walking)

1 pace or 'easy-step' = 2 ft.
2 paces = 1 gait or rod, 4 ft.
12 paces (or 6 gaits) = 1 stripe, 24 ft. (8 yds.)
144 paces (72 gaits, 12 stripes) = 1 run, 96 yds.
  2 runs = 1 sullong, 192 yds.
1,728 paces (864 gaits, 6 sullongs) = 1 (short) mile, or pace-mile, 1,152 yards
1,728 gaits (2 pace-miles) = 1 long mile, or gait mile or gaitway, 2,304 yds.

ell & *fathom* were always used of *rope* or cloth

On another page in this folder are related jottings:

12 paces / or 6 gaits (24 ft. or 8 yds.) = 1 [*deleted:* rackenty or] abain
120 paces / or 60 gaits (240 ft. or 80 yds.) = 1 run
  3 runs (240 yds.) = 1 sullong
1,200 paces / or 600 gaits (2,400 ft., 800 yds.) = 1 yong or half mile
2,400 paces / or 1,200 gaits (4,800 ft., 1,600 yds.) = 1 mile
  3 miles or 1 league (Bree tigh)
in Bree 12 same as 6 yong or 1,728 paces
[?] Bree mile [?] paces or 6,912 ft or 2,304 yds.
the Hobbit yong-mile or longmile = 2,304 yds.
pace-mile or (short) = 1,182 yds.

Sullong is an alternate spelling of *suling*, an historical measure of land in Kent, equivalent to the *hide* or *carucate* elsewhere in Britain. *Yong* is an obsolete word for 'going; gait; travelling, journey; course' (*OED*).

5 (I: 14). The Hobbits named it the Shire . . . and there in that pleasant corner of the world they plied their well-ordered business – The description of the Shire that follows in the Prologue and continues in Book I, Chapter 1 is a great deal more developed than the glimpse one finds in *The Hobbit*, before Bilbo is rushed out of Bag-End and into his adventure. On 3 July 1956 Tolkien wrote to Rayner Unwin that 'if we drop the "fiction" of long ago, "The Shire" is based on rural England and not any other country in the world. . . . The toponymy [place-names] of *The Shire* . . . is a "parody" of that of rural England, in much the same sense as are its inhabitants: they go together and are meant to. After all the book is English and by an Englishman' (*Letters*, p. 250). Elsewhere he commented that the Shire is more or less a rural Warwickshire village of about the time of Queen Victoria's Diamond Jubilee (1897).

5 (I: 14). the Guardians, and of the labours of those that made possible the long peace of the Shire – *Guardians* here clearly does not refer to the Valar (angelic powers in Tolkien's mythology, 'Guardians of the World'), but rather to the Rangers, the Dúnedain of the North. In Book I, Chapter 8, Tom Bombadil speaks of the Dúnedain, as the 'Men of Westernesse', 'walking in loneliness, guarding from evil things folk that are heedless' (p. 146, I: 157).

5 (I: 14–15): At no time had Hobbits of any kind

5 (I: 14). Battle of Greenfields – In his unfinished index Tolkien describes the *Greenfields* as 'a district between the Norbourn and Brandywine [rivers] in the Northfarthing, famous as the scene of [the] only battle (before this history began) in the Shire (S.R. 1147) in which the last Orcs to invade this part of the world were defeated by Bandobras Took'.

5 (I: 14). Orcs – In the edition of 1966 Tolkien added a note to *The Hobbit*: '*Orc* is not an English word. It occurs in one or two places but is usually translated *goblin* (or *hobgoblin* for the larger kinds). *Orc* is the hobbits' form of the name given at that time to these creatures, and it is not connected at all with our *orc*, *ork*, applied to sea-animals of dolphin kind.' The original edition of *The Hobbit* contained only one mention of the word (except as it appears in the sword-name *Orcrist* 'goblin-cleaver'), in the sentence: 'Before you could get round Mirkwood in the North you would be right among the slopes of the Grey Mountains, and they are simply stiff with goblins, hobgoblins, and orcs of the worst description' (Chapter 7). Another instance entered in the edition of 1951. In *The Lord of the Rings* Tolkien preferred *orc*, though for variety he used *goblin* numerous times also, as a synonym. In *Nomenclature* he comments that *orc*

> is supposed to be the Common Speech name of these creatures at that time [of the story]. . . . It was translated 'goblin' in *The Hobbit* . . . and other words of similar sense in other European languages (as far as I know), are not really suitable. The *orc* in *The Lord of the Rings* and *The Silmarillion*, though of course partly made out of traditional features, is not really comparable in supposed origin, functions, and relation to the Elves. In any case *orc* seemed to me, and seems, in sound a good name for these creatures.
>
> It should be spelt *ork* (so the Dutch translation) in a Germanic language of translation, but I had used the spelling *orc* in so many places that I have hesitated to change it in the English text, though the adjective is necessarily spelt *orkish*. The Grey-elven [Sindarin] form is *orch*, plural *yrch*.
>
> (I originally took the word from Old English *orc* (*Beowulf* 112, *orc-neas* and the gloss *orc* = *þyrs* 'ogre', *heldeofol* 'hell-devil'). This is supposed not to be connected with Modern English *orc*, *ork*, a name applied to various sea-beasts of the dolphin-order.)

In Appendix F of *The Lord of the Rings* it is said that 'Orc is the form of the name that other races had for this foul people as it was in the language of Rohan. In Sindarin it was *orch*' (p. 1131, III: 409).

In regard to the use of *orc* by both Tolkien and the poet William Blake, Tolkien wrote on 29 December 1968 to Sigrid Fowler that according to a note in one of his old diaries, dated 21 February 1919, he had then

> just been reading part of Blake's prophetic books, which I had never seen before, and discovered to my astonishment several similarities of nomenclature (though not necessarily in function) e.g. *Tiriel*, *Vala*, *Orc*. Whatever explanation of these similarities – few: most of Blake's invented names are as alien to me as his 'mythology' – may be, they are not 'prophetic' on Blake's part, nor due to any imitation on my part: his mind (as far as I have attempted to understand it) and art or conception of Art, have no attraction for me at all. Invented names are likely to show chance similarities between writers familiar with Greek, Latin, and especially Hebrew nomenclature. In my work *Orc* is not an 'invention' but a borrowing from Old English *orc* 'demon'. This is supposed to be derived from Latin *Orcus*, which Blake no doubt knew. And is also supposed to be unconnected with *orc* the name of a maritime animal. But I recently investigated *orc*, and find the matter complex. [Tolkien-George Allen & Unwin archive, HarperCollins]

In *The Return of the Shadow* Christopher Tolkien notes that the word *Orc* had appeared already years earlier in *The Book of Lost Tales* (1916–17), and 'had been pervasive in all my father's subsequent writings. In the *Lost Tales* the two terms [*Orc* and *Goblin*] were used as equivalents, though sometimes apparently distinguished. . . . A clue may be found in a passage in both the earlier and the later *Quenta* [in *The Shaping of Middle-earth* and *The Lost Road and Other Writings*] . . . : "Goblins they may be called, *but in ancient days they were strong and fell*"' (p. 437). At one stage in the writing of *The Lord of the Rings* Tolkien suggested that *orcs* was to distinguish a subset of goblins, those particularly large and evil.

One of the issues considered in the emendation of *The Lord of the Rings* in 2004 was that of consistency of capitalization of *orc(s)* and *Orc(s)*, as well as *hobbit(s)* and *Hobbit(s)*, etc. Christopher Tolkien had advised George Allen & Unwin in 1975:

> Simple consistency (i.e. either *orcs* or *Orcs* throughout) is highly undesirable, and should on no account be attempted, since the variation has significance, and was conscious and deliberate on the part of the author. Compare for example Vol. III p. 176 [in the previous standard edition] 'these are Men not Orcs' with III p. 177 'Presently two orcs came into view.' The capital should be reserved to cases where Orcs (etc.) are referred to as a race, a kind, or in some generalised sense. There will of course be marginal cases – no doubt also definite inconsistencies within the general scheme. Thus the foreword (written later) should have Orcs . . . and *H*obbits. . . . The same applies to Dwarves, Elves, Wizards. But on the whole I would strongly suggest leaving the text as it is in this

respect – and certainly if in any doubt. [Tolkien-George Allen & Unwin archive, HarperCollins]

Although this seems a simple rule to observe, there are many ambiguous cases in the text, where the author's intent could not be known with certainty. In the end, in 2004, it seemed safest to follow Christopher Tolkien's advice of 1975, to leave things as they stood in this regard.

The word *orc* having entered current usage, in fantasy fiction and gaming beyond its appearance in *The Lord of the Rings*, it has been added to the *Oxford English Dictionary.*

Artists inspired by *The Lord of the Rings* have tended to picture Orcs as monsters, hideous and grotesque, part animal (often with pig-like faces) and part Man. In June 1958 Tolkien wrote to Forrest J. Ackerman, regarding a proposed film treatment of *The Lord of the Rings*, that he intended Orcs to be 'corruptions of the "human" form seen in Elves and Men. They are (or were) squat, broad, flat-nosed, sallow-skinned, with wide mouths and slant eyes: in fact degraded and repulsive versions of the (to Europeans) least lovely Mongol-types' (*Letters*, p. 274).

On the nature of Orcs, see further, note for p. 444.

5 (I: 14). the weathers had grown milder, and the wolves that had once come ravening out of the North in bitter white winters – The plural *weathers* is now rare except in the phrase 'in all weathers'. The reference to 'wolves . . . ravening out of the North' looks ahead to mentions of the Fell Winter of Third Age 2911 (S.R. 1311), when white wolves entered the Shire over the frozen Brandywine.

5 (I: 14). Michel Delving – The chief township of the Shire, on the White Downs east of Hobbiton. *Michel* is derived from Old English *micel* 'great'. It survives in Modern English as *mickle* (and also *muckle*), and in place-names as *Michel*, *Mickle-* and *Much-* among other forms. *Delving* reflects the Hobbits' inclination towards digging.

5 (I: 14). mathom – In Appendix F Tolkien writes, concerning his 'editorial method' in *The Lord of the Rings*, that '*mathom* is meant to recall ancient English *máthm*, and so to represent the relationship of the actual Hobbit *kast* to R[ohirric] *kastu*' (p. 1136, III: 414–15). Bosworth and Toller's *Anglo-Saxon Dictionary* (1898) notes *māðum* 'a precious or valuable thing (often refers to gifts)'. Thus Tolkien uses *mathom* ironically for things which are *not* treasured, only for which there was 'no immediate use' or which the Hobbits 'were unwilling to throw away'. Although *museum* appears twice in *The Lord of the Rings*, the (English) Hobbits' *mathom-house*, based on an English word, is more 'appropriate' than *museum* which is of classical origin, ultimately from Greek *mouseion* 'seat of the Muses'.

6 (I: 15): Nonetheless, ease and peace

6 (I: 15). ease and peace had left this people curiously tough. They were, if it came to it, difficult to daunt or to kill; and they were, perhaps, so unwearyingly fond of good things not least because they could, when put to it, do without them, and could survive rough handling by grief, foe, or weather in a way that astonished those who did not know them well and looked no further than their bellies and their well-fed faces. – Tolkien said to Denys Gueroult, in an interview conducted for the British Broadcasting Corporation in 1964, that 'Hobbits are just rustic English people, small in size because it reflects (in general) the small reach of their imagination – not the small reach of their courage or latent power'. That they were 'difficult to daunt or to kill', could 'survive rough handling', and so forth reflects the popular view (at least by the people themselves) of the ability of the inhabitants of the British Isles to 'muddle through' any difficulty or disaster, a romantic view, but one wholly justified by their suffering and perseverance, shared by Tolkien, through two world wars.

6 (I: 15). If any Hobbit stooped for a stone, it was well to get quickly under cover, as all trespassing beasts knew very well. – Compare *The Hobbit*, Chapter 8: 'As a boy [Bilbo] used to practise throwing stones at things, until rabbits and squirrels, and even birds, got out of his way as quick as lightning if they saw him stoop. . . .'

6 (I: 15): All Hobbits had originally lived in holes

6 (I: 15). smials – In Appendix F Tolkien writes that '*smial* (or *smile*) is a likely form for a descendant of *smygel*, and represents well the relationship of Hobbit *trân* to R[ohirric] *trahan*' (p. 1136, III: 415). *Smygel* is Old English for 'burrow, place to creep into' (compare *Sméagol*, note for p. 53).

Aside from the historical fact of underground homes in our world (from ancient times to the present), hobbit-holes recall to Tolkien's intended audience the subterranean dwellings of English children's literature, such as the 'neatest sandiest hole' in *The Tale of Peter Rabbit* by Beatrix Potter, and the homes of Mole and Badger in *The Wind in the Willows* by Kenneth Grahame. See further, Wayne G. Hammond, 'All the Comforts: The Image of Home in *The Hobbit* and *The Lord of the Rings*', *Mythlore* 14, no. 1, whole no. 51 (Autumn 1987).

6 (I: 15). flats – Areas of level ground, distinct from hill country.

6 (I: 15). Tuckborough – The 'chief village of the Tooks at [the] west-end of the Green Hill Country' (*Index*). The element *Tuck* is a variant of the clan name *Took*, *borough* a modernization (as also *burg*, *burgh*) of Old English *burh* 'fortified place'.

6 (I: 15). White Downs – So called, presumably, because of a concentration of white chalky soil, as in many English place-names containing Old English *hwīt* 'white' (e.g. *Whitehorse Hill* in Berkshire).

6 (I: 15): The habit of building farmhouses

6 (I: 15). Marish – 'A district (of reclaimed marshland) on [the] east-side of [the] Eastfarthing' (*Index*). *Marish* is 'an old form of English *marsh*' (*Nomenclature*).

6–7 (I: 16): It is probable that the craft

7 (I: 16). Grey Havens – Havens, i.e. harbours, 'on either side of the narrows at the end of the Gulf of Lune, under the governance of *Círdan* "*Shipwright*", from which the Elven-ships set sail into the West' (*Index*). *Grey Havens* is a 'translation' of Sindarin *Mithlond* (*mith-* 'grey' + *lond* 'harbour').

7 (I: 16). Three Elf-towers of immemorial age were still to be seen on the Tower Hills beyond the western marches. They shone far off in the moonlight. The tallest was furthest away, standing alone upon a green mound. – As first published this passage read: 'Three Elf-towers of immemorial age were still to be seen beyond the western marches. They shone far off in the moonlight. The tallest was furthest away, standing alone upon a green hill.' It was revised in the second printing (1967) of the Allen & Unwin second edition.

Tower Hills is a 'translation' of Sindarin *Emyn Beraid* (*emyn* plural of *amon* 'hill' + *beraid* plural of *barad* 'tower'). In his unfinished index Tolkien describes the 'three green hills beyond the west-borders of the Shire, where three towers reputed to be built by the Elves stood', also called the White Towers. 'They were in fact built by Elendil and in one of the towers was set one of the Seven Palantíri or Stones of Seeing.' But in *Of the Rings of Power and the Third Age* it is said 'that the towers of Emyn Beraid were not built indeed by the Exiles of Númenor, but were raised by Gil-galad for Elendil, his friend' (*The Silmarillion*, p. 292).

March is used here in the sense 'tract of land on the border of a country', from Old English *mearc* 'boundary' (from which also is derived *mark*, hence *the Mark*, i.e. Rohan). Historically *marches* has been used to refer to the parts of England on the borders of Scotland and Wales.

7 (I: 16). The Hobbits of the Westfarthing said that one could see the Sea from the top of that tower; but no Hobbit had ever been known to climb it. Indeed, few Hobbits had ever seen or sailed upon the Sea, and fewer still had ever returned to report it. – A tower offering such a view figures in an 'allegory' within Tolkien's landmark lecture *Beowulf: The Monsters and the Critics*, delivered at the British Academy on 25 November 1936. In this a man has built a tower out of old stone. His friends, without themselves climbing its steps, perceive that its stones are ancient, and push the tower over to study the stuff from which it was made. The builder's descendants, left with a muddle of stones, wonder why he should have built a tower with them instead of restoring his old house. 'But from the top of that tower the man had been able to look out upon the sea' (*The Monsters and the Critics and Other Essays*, p. 8).

In Chapter 1 of *The Hobbit*, as revised in 1966, Bilbo says: 'Not the Gandalf who was responsible for so many quiet lads and lasses going off into the Blue for mad adventures? Anything from climbing trees to visiting elves – or sailing in ships, sailing to other shores!' Hobbits, by and large, are shown to prefer the quiet of their homes and the familiarity of their land, tightly circumscribed. In Book I, Chapter 2 of *The Lord of the Rings* 'Sam waved his arm vaguely: neither he nor any of them [in the *Green Dragon*] knew how far it was to the Sea, past the old towers beyond the western borders of the Shire' (p. 45, I: 54). The Sea, as the Prologue notes later in the present paragraph, 'became a word of fear among them, and a token of death'.

7 (I: 16). **Most Hobbits regarded even rivers and small boats with deep misgivings, and not many of them could swim.** – With the notable exception of Bucklanders such as Merry Brandybuck. 'Not all of us look on boats as wild horses', he tells Celeborn in Book II, Chapter 8. 'My people live by the banks of the Brandywine' (p. 368, I: 384).

7 (I: 16): The craft of building may have come

7 (I: 16). **thatched with dry grass or straw, or roofed with turves** – The thatched roof was a common feature of English houses until the sixteenth century, and though less common today remains a hallmark of the country village in popular thought, as it was in fact in Tolkien's youth. *Turves* is the plural of *turf*, a section of grass etc. with earth and matted roots.

7–8 (I: 16–17): The houses and the holes of Shire-hobbits

7 (I: 16). **Baggins** – See note for p. 21.

7 (I: 16). **Brandybucks of Brandy Hall** – In *Nomenclature* Tolkien writes that *Brandybuck* is 'a rare English name', which in *The Lord of the Rings* is 'meant to contain elements of the *Brandywine River* and the family name *Oldbuck*. The latter contains the word *buck* (animal); either Old English *bucc* "male deer" (fallow or roe), or *bucca* "he-goat"'. *Brandybuck* is not listed, however, in P.H. Reaney's *Dictionary of English Surnames* (rev. 3rd edn. 1997), though cf. *Buck*, *Bucke*; *Buckland*; etc.

Brandy Hall is the 'chief dwelling of the Masters of Buckland' (*Index*), begun *c.* S.R. 740, and where the orphaned Frodo Baggins spent his childhood. It occupies the whole of a low hill, with 'three large front-doors, many side-doors, and about a hundred windows' (Book I, Chapter 5, p. 98, I: 108). It may be seen faintly in a drawing by Tolkien (*Artist and Illustrator*, fig. 146).

7 (I: 16–17). The genealogical trees at the end of the Red Book of Westmarch – Some are included in *The Lord of the Rings* as Appendix C.

7 (I: 17). Hobbits delighted in such things, if they were accurate: they liked to have books filled with things they already knew – As first published this passage read: 'Hobbits delight in such things, if they are accurate: they like to have books filled with things that they already know'. The verbs were emended to the past tense in the second edition (1965).

2

Concerning Pipe-weed

8 (I: 17): There is another astonishing thing

8 (I: 17). an astonishing habit: they imbibed or inhaled, through pipes of clay or wood, the smoke of the burning leaves of a herb, which they called *pipe-weed* or *leaf*, a variety probably of *Nicotiana*. – Tolkien began this section of the Prologue as a lecture by Merry to Théoden, the King of Rohan, in Book III, Chapter 8, but moved it when it grew too long.

Pipe-weed here substitutes for *tobacco*, though Tolkien's mention of *Nicotiana* indicates that they are one and the same; or rather, that *pipe-weed* refers to the same group of plants, *tobacco* being the name for any plant of the genus *Nicotiana*. *Pipe-weed* is a more 'hobbitish' word, incorporating *weed* in the sense 'tobacco' which dates at least to the early seventeenth century, whereas *tobacco*, from Spanish *tabaco* (from American Indian origin), would have seemed linguistically out of place in Middle-earth. Tobacco itself is a New World plant, imported to England; compare tomatoes, likewise an American import, mentioned in the first edition of *The Hobbit* (1937), altered to *pickles* in the revision of 1966. (But see also *potatoes*, note for p. 22.) There were tobacco plantations in England in the seventeenth century, notably in Worcestershire and Gloucestershire, despite government prohibitions against the growth of the plant domestically, in favour of importation by the Virginia Company. Pipe-weed is similarly not native to Middle-earth, but (as Tolkien has Merry 'suspect') was 'originally brought over Sea by the Men of Westernesse' (p. 8, I: 17). See further, Anders Stenström (Beregond), 'Något om pipor, blad och rökning' ('Some Notes on Pipes, Leaf, and Smoking', in Swedish with a summary in English), *Arda* 4 (1988, for 1984).

Tolkien himself had the same 'astonishing habit' of smoking a pipe.

8 (I: 17). *Herblore of the Shire* – *Herblore* has the same sense as *herbal*, 'a book which describes the uses and virtues of plants'. *De Herba Panacea* by Giles Everard, published in Antwerp in 1587, is said to be the first book completely about tobacco.

8 (I: 17): 'This,' he says, 'is the one art

8 (I: 17). Tobold Hornblower – *Tobold* is an alternate spelling of *Theobald*, an English forename (*þeud-* 'people, race' + *bald* 'bold, brave'); a medieval variant, familiar from Shakespeare, was *Tybalt*.

In *Nomenclature* Tolkien writes that *Hornblower* in the Shire was 'evidently' an occupational surname. Reaney, *A Dictionary of English Surnames*, notes that 'in the Middle Ages workmen were called to work by the ringing of bells or by a horn' (p. 238).

8 (I: 17). Isengrim the Second – *Isengrim* 'is an old Germanic name, perhaps best known as the name adopted for the Wolf as a character in the romance of *Reynard the Fox*' (*Nomenclature*).

8 (I: 17). Longbottom – In his notes for the Dutch translator Tolkien commented that *bottom* (from Old English *boþm* 'valley') 'is widespread in local toponymy in England (often in dialectal form *botham*) ref[erring] to "steep-sided valley" or especially a "deeplying flat"'. In *Nomenclature* he writes that the second element of *Longbottom* 'retains its original sense (as locally and frequently in place-names and derived surnames such as *Ramsbottom*) of "valley" (especially the head or inner end of a valley)'.

8 (I: 17): 'How Old Toby came by the plant

8 (I: 17). Rangers – The Dúnedain of the North, protectors of Eriador. *Ranger* here has the sense 'wanderer'.

8 (I: 17). Wizards – '*Wizard* is a translation of Quenya istar (Sindarin *ithron*): one of the members of an "order" (as they called it), claiming to possess, and exhibiting, eminent knowledge of the history and nature of the World' (*The Istari*, in *Unfinished Tales*, p. 388). See further, notes for pp. 48, 502.

8 (I: 17). *The Prancing Pony* – No actual *Prancing Pony* is recorded in Britain, but there is a *Prancing Horse* in Thatcham, Berkshire, among hundreds of pub-names with *horse*, and a few with *pony* such as the *Welsh Pony* in George Street, Oxford.

8 (I: 17). Butterbur – See note for p. 148.

8–9 (I: 18): 'All the same, observations

9 (I: 18). Greenway – The name given by the Bree-folk to the little-used, grass-grown North–South Road 'originally running from Isengard to Fornost' (*Index*). It is described by Christopher Tolkien in *Unfinished Tales* as 'the great Númenórean road linking the Two Kingdoms, crossing the Isen at the Fords of Isen and the Greyflood at Tharbad and then on northwards to Fornost' (p. 314, n. 32).

9 (I: 18). the coming of Elendil – *Elendil* 'elf-friend' or 'star-lover' was a Man of Númenor, who with his sons Isildur and Anárion escaped the destruction of that land and came to Middle-earth in Second Age 3319. He was the first High King of Arnor and Gondor, slain with Gil-galad in the overthrow of Sauron at the end of the Second Age.

9 (I: 18). Not even the Wizards first thought of that before we did. Though one Wizard that I knew took up the art long ago – As first published, 'Wizards' was capitalized in the first of these sentences, but 'wizard' in the second sentence was in lower case (I: 19). With the second printing (1967) of the Allen & Unwin second edition Tolkien instituted a general rule, as he noted in one of his check copies: 'Caps (Wizard) to be used for reference to (any one of) the Five Wizards (Istari); or the Witch King; but not generally or (as often) when used contemptuously. But "wizard" is used as it were personally . . . with ref[erence] to Gandalf in narrative or dialogue.' The *one Wizard* referred to here is Gandalf.

3

Of the Ordering of the Shire

9 (I: 18): The Shire was divided

9 (I: 18). divided into four quarters, the Farthings – In *Nomenclature* Tolkien comments that *farthing* as used in *The Lord of the Rings*

> is the same word as English *farthing* (Old English *feorðing*, Middle English *ferthing*), quarter of a penny; but used in its original sense, 'a fourth part, a quarter'. This is modelled on *thriding* 'third part', still used of the divisions of Yorkshire, with loss of *th* after the *th*, *t* in *Northriding*, *Eastriding*, *Westriding*. The application to divisions of other measures than money has long been obsolete in English, and *farthing* has been used since early Middle English for a negligible amount, so that to English ears the application to the divisions of the Shire (an area of about 18,000 square miles) is comical.

The manuscript of *Nomenclature* also notes: 'There has long been some agitation in Yorkshire for the creation of a Fourth Division and it was seriously suggested in the *Yorkshire Post* soon after the first appearance of my book, that the *Farthings* of the Shire would provide a good model for a new nomenclature. But no doubt the comic associations would be against the word.'

9 (I: 18). Outside the Farthings were the East and West Marches: the Buckland (p. 98); and the Westmarch added to the Shire in S.R. 1452. – This sentence was added at the end of the paragraph in the second edition (1965). In editions prior to 2004 the page reference was sometimes in error or omitted, and the year in which the Westmarch was added to the Shire was wrongly given as '1462'. The latter error stemmed, probably, from the fact that in the first edition the Westmarch is noted only as part of the entry for 1462 in *The Tale of Years*, as 'a region newly inhabited'; but in the second edition Tolkien also added an entry for 1452 in *The Tale of Years* (p. 1097, III: 378): 'The Westmarch, from the Far Downs to the Tower Hills (*Emyn Beraid*), is added to the Shire by the gift of the King. Many hobbits remove to it.'

9 (I: 18). folklands – *Folkland* is a term of Old English law, denoting 'land of a folk or people', as opposed to a *bookland*, held by charter or deed.

9 (I: 18). Tookland – 'A district owned by (and mainly inhabited by) the Took family, south of the [East] Road, and over most of the western parts of the Green Hill Country' (*Index*).

9 (I: 18). Boffins – The *Oxford English Dictionary* dates the contemporary word *boffin* (etymology unknown) in the sense '"elderly" naval officer' only to 1941, and in the sense 'person engaged in "back-room" scientific or technical research' only to 1945, whereas the Hobbit surname *Boffin* appeared already in the first portion of *The Lord of the Rings* written in 1937. The name at the head of the family tree *Boffin of the Yale* (added to Appendix C in the edition of 2004), *Buffo Boffin*, suggests a derivation from *buffoon*. Joseph Wright's *English Dialect Dictionary* (1898–1905) records the Nottinghamshire word *bofin* 'dolt, dullard'. In Appendix F Tolkien gives the 'original' form of the name, before he 'anglicized' it, as *Bophîn*.

9 (I: 18): The Shire at this time

9 (I: 18). Growing food and eating it occupied most of their time. – In one version of *The Quest of Erebor* it is said that 'as far as he [Thorin Oakenshield] was concerned they [the Hobbits] were just food-growers who happened to work the fields on either side of the Dwarves' ancestral road to the mountains' (*The Annotated Hobbit*, 2nd edn., p. 371).

9 (I: 18): There remained, of course

9 (I: 18). Fornost, or Norbury as they called it . . . Kings' Norbury – See note for p. 4. Ekwall, *The Concise Oxford Dictionary of English Place-names*, records several places in England called *Norbury*. *Kings' Norbury* echoes the name *King's* (*Kings'*, *Kings*) *Norton* near Birmingham, where Tolkien lived briefly as a boy.

9 (I: 18). Hobbits still said of wild folk and wicked things (such as trolls) that they had not heard of the king. For they attributed to the king of old all their essential laws; and usually they kept the laws of free will, because they were The Rules (as they said), both ancient and just. – In ancient tradition the king or ruler is the source of all law and justice.

For *trolls*, see note for p. 44.

9–10 (I: 18–19): It is true that the Took family

9 (I: 18). Oldbucks – See note for p. 7 (*Brandybucks*).

9 (I: 19). The Thain was the master of the Shire-moot, and captain of the Shire-muster and the Hobbitry-in-arms – A *moot* is a public meeting (compare *entmoot* in Book III, Chapter 4). *Shire-moot* was an Anglo-Saxon institution, a county court or assembly of lords of estates, bishops, and representatives of villages, who met to make decisions and render judgements – in Britain, an ancestor of Parliament.

A *muster* is a calling together of an armed force (compare the *muster of Rohan* in Book V).

10 (I: 19): The only real official in the Shire

10 (I: 19). The only real official in the Shire at this date was the Mayor . . . who was elected every seven years at the Free Fair on the White Downs at the Lithe, that is at Midsummer. – The *Mayor* of the Shire was usually a ceremonial position, as the Prologue states, but it was not unusual in English history for a mayor (as chief official of a borough or municipality) also to act as local magistrate. In a draft letter to A.C. Nunn, probably written late 1958–early 1959, in commenting on Hobbit property law and customs of descent Tolkien referred to a ruling by Mayor Samwise on the disposition of property of an inhabitant of the Shire deemed to have passed 'over Sea in the presence of a reliable witness' (*Letters*, p. 294).

In Appendix D it is explained that in the Shire Calendar the 'months were all equal and had 30 days each; but they had 3 Summerdays, called in the Shire the Lithe or the Lithedays, between June and July. The last day of the year and the first of the next year were called the Yuledays. . . . The Lithedays and the Yuledays were the chief holidays and times of feasting' (p. 1109, III: 387). See further, notes for pp. 1106, 1109.

Criticizing errors in the Swedish translation of *The Lord of the Rings*, Tolkien notes that the event at which the Mayor of the Shire was elected

> was not a night festival or 'wake', but a day-celebration marked by a 'Free Fair' . . . so-called because anyone who wished could set up a booth without charge. The [Swedish] translator has assimilated the passage to the Scandinavian summer-solstice festival, christianized in name by association with St. John the Baptist's day (June 24), which occurred at more or less the right date. . . . [*Nomenclature*]

10 (I: 19). the offices of Postmaster and First Shirriff were attached to the mayoralty, so that he managed both the Messenger Service and the Watch – The Shire postal (or messenger) service, mentioned also in Book I, Chapter 1 (where it is overwhelmed by the invitations to Bilbo's party) and in Book VI, Chapter 8 (the 'Quick Post service'), is one of numerous features of Hobbit society which deliberately reflect the England of Tolkien's youth; see further, note for p. 26. It presupposes, *inter alia*, a literate (if not generally learned) culture, and the ability to manufacture or otherwise obtain the materials for writing, pens, ink, paper (or a substitute).

Shirriff is 'actually a now obsolete form of English *sheriff* "shire-officer", used by me to make the connexion with *Shire* plainer. In the story it and *Shire* are supposed to be special hobbit-words, not generally current in the Common Speech of the time, and so derived from their former language related to that of the *Rohirrim*' (*Nomenclature*). English *sheriff* is derived from *shire-reeve*, i.e. the *reeve* or local official of the *shire* (county).

Watch historically refers to keeping watch (for trespass or wrongdoing) by night (opposed to *ward*, guard by day), but the temporal distinction for *watch* is now rarely recognized.

10 (I: 19): The Shirriffs was the name

10 (I: 19). only a feather in their caps – A mild joke, referring in the first instance to the shirriff's 'badge' of office, but also to the phrase 'feather in his cap', derived from the old custom that the sportsman who kills the first woodcock in a hunt puts one of its feathers in his cap, and more anciently from the custom in Asia, North America, and elsewhere of adding a feather to one's headgear for each enemy slain.

10 (I: 19). haywards – The term *hayward* originally referred to one who protected the fences around lands enclosed for growing hay (Old English *hegeweard*), later more generally applied to one who prevents cattle from breaking through into enclosed fields with growing crops.

10 (I: 19–20): At the time when this story begins

10 (I: 19). Bounders – The body referred to in the preceding paragraph, 'varying at need . . . employed to "beat the bounds", and to see that Outsiders of any kind, great or small, did not make themselves a nuisance'. To 'beat the bounds' in the usual sense means 'to trace out the boundaries of a parish, striking certain points with rods, etc. by way of a sensible sign patent to witnesses' (*OED*, *beat* as verb, sense 41), which work was done by a *bounder* 'one who sets or marks out bounds or limits' (*OED*). Here, however, *bounders* is intended to mean 'persons watching the boundaries' of the Shire, and is a joke to anyone familiar with *bounder* as pejorative slang. In *Nomenclature* Tolkien says of *bounders* that the

> word exists in English and is not marked as obsolete in dictionaries, though I have seldom heard it used. Probably because the late nineteenth-century slang *bounder* – 'an offensively pushing and ill-bred man' – was for a time in very general use and soon became a term of contempt equivalent to 'cad'. It is a long time since I heard it, and I think it is now forgotten by younger people. . . .

In the text the sense 'cad' 'is meant to be recalled by English readers, but the primary functional sense to be clearly understood. (This slender jest, is not, of course, worth imitating [in translation], even if possible)' (*Nomenclature*).

10 (I: 20). How much or how little he revealed to no one, not even to Frodo his favourite 'nephew'. – As first published the final word of this sentence was not in quotation marks. It was emended in the second printing (1967) of the Allen & Unwin second edition. 'Nephew' is applied to Frodo only as a term of convenience: strictly speaking, he is Bilbo's 'first *and* second cousin, once removed', as Gaffer Gamgee says in Book I, Chapter 1 (see further, note for p. 23).

4

Of the Finding of the Ring

11 (I: 20): As is told in *The Hobbit*

11 (I: 20). Gandalf the Grey – Introduced in *The Hobbit*, the name *Gandalf* comes, like most of the names of Thorin's company of dwarves, from the *Dvergatal* or 'Roster of Dwarfs' contained in the *Völuspá*, one of the poems in the *Elder* (or *Poetic*) *Edda*. Tolkien applied it first to the chief dwarf (later renamed 'Thorin'), while the wizard in *The Hobbit* was originally called 'Bladorthin'. *Gandalf* contains the Old Norse elements *gandr* 'anything enchanted or an object used by sorcerers' + *alfr* 'elf'. In a note written after the publication of *The Lord of the Rings* but before its second edition (1965), Tolkien comments that

> *Gandalf* is a substitution in the English narrative on the same lines as the treatment of Hobbit and Dwarf names. It is an actual Norse name (found applied to a Dwarf in *Völuspá*) used by me since it appears to contain *gandr*, a staff, especially one used in 'magic', and might be supposed to mean 'Elvish wight with a (magic) staff'. Gandalf was not an Elf, but would be by Men associated with them, since his alliance and friendship with Elves was well-known. Since the name is attributed to 'the North' in general, *Gandalf* must be supposed to represent a Westron name, but one made up of elements not derived from Elvish tongues. [*The Istari* in *Unfinished Tales*, p. 399]

Gandalf belongs to an order of Wizards, each of whom bears the name of a colour or shade. See further, notes for pp. 48, 256.

11 (I: 20). Thorin Oakenshield . . . and his twelve companions in exile – The name *Thorin* is likewise from the *Dvergatal*, which also includes *Eikinskjaldi* 'oakenshield'. Thorin and his companions are 'in exile' from the former Dwarf-kingdom of Erebor, having been driven out by the dragon Smaug. Their story, and that of their 'quest of great treasure', is told in *The Hobbit*, in Appendix A, Part III ('Durin's Folk') of *The Lord of the Rings*, and in *The Quest of Erebor* in *Unfinished Tales* and *The Annotated Hobbit* (2nd edn.). One of the twelve companions, Glóin, appears in *The Lord of the Rings*, Book II, Chapter 1, and others are referred to there and elsewhere in Book II.

11 (I: 20). the dwarf-hoards of the Kings under the Mountain, beneath Erebor in Dale – In Appendix A it is said that, after dwarves in Moria aroused from sleep a Balrog of Morgoth, most of those who escaped fled to the North, where at Erebor Thráin I became the first King under the Mountain. *Erebor*, the Lonely Mountain, is an isolated peak to the east of the northernmost parts of Mirkwood; its Sindarin name contains the element *er* 'one, alone' (as in *Eriador*). There the dwarves prospered and became rich; but

> the rumour of the wealth of Erebor spread abroad and reached the ears of the dragons, and at last Smaug the Golden, greatest of the dragons of his day, arose and without warning came against King Thrór and descended on the Mountain in flames. It was not long before all that realm was destroyed, and the town of Dale nearby was ruined and deserted; but Smaug entered into the Great Hall and lay there upon a bed of gold. [p. 1072, III: 353]

Dale was later rebuilt under Bard the Bowman, slayer of Smaug, to whom men gathered 'from the Lake and from South and West, and all the valley had become tilled again and rich . . .' (*The Hobbit*, Chapter 19).

11 (I: 20). the Dragon that guarded the hoard – Smaug.

11 (I: 20). the Battle of Five Armies – The great battle fought at Dale in *The Hobbit*, Chapter 17: 'Upon one side were the Goblins and the wild Wolves, and upon the other were Elves and Men and Dwarves' (and at the last, the Eagles of the Misty Mountains).

11 (I: 20). but for an 'accident' by the way. . . . It seemed then like mere luck. – Tolkien suggests that fate, or providence, is at work. At the end of *The Hobbit*, Chapter 19, Gandalf says to Bilbo: 'You don't really suppose, do you, that all your adventures and escapes were managed by mere luck, just for your sole benefit?'

11 (I: 20): Trying to find his way out

11 (I: 20). Gollum – The name *Gollum* is said in *The Hobbit*, Chapter 5, to represent 'a horrible swallowing noise in his throat'. In *The Annotated Hobbit* Douglas A. Anderson suggests that it may have been influenced by Old Norse *gull, goll* 'gold', one inflected form of which is *gollum* 'gold, treasure, something precious' (2nd edn., p. 120). Anderson also notes that Gollum had an antecedent in Tolkien's writings, in the poem *Glip*, written probably around 1928 (published in *The Annotated Hobbit*, 2nd edn., p. 119).

11 (I: 20). a ring of gold that made its wearer invisible – In *The Hobbit* there is no hint that the ring found by Bilbo in Gollum's cave is anything more than a common fairy-tale device, such as figures in stories by Andrew Lang, in Chrétien's *Yvain*, and perhaps earliest of all, in the story of Gyges in Plato's *Republic*.

11 (I: 20). It was the one thing he loved, his 'Precious' – In editions prior to 2004 the word *Precious* here is spelt *precious*, without a capital letter. Here, as in several other instances, it was emended to 'Precious' in consequence of a note written by Tolkien in one of his check copies of *The Lord of the Rings*, stating that lower case *precious* should be used when Gollum is addressing himself in soliloquy, and capitalized *Precious* when it is a reference to the Ring. Tolkien did not follow this rule carefully in the Prologue or in Books I and II, but did so later in the work. When we raised the question of *precious* versus *Precious* (among other points) with Christopher Tolkien, he replied:

> I think there is a major difficulty in the search for consistency in all such matters. While my father very evidently cared greatly for consistency at every level, he equally evidently failed to achieve it, both when actually writing & subsequently. The reason is of course that the matters in question (hyphens, capitals etc.) are often not distinctive of meaning at all, while sometimes one may subjectively feel a difference (of tone, of emphasis . . .); and even when they are distinctions of meaning (as precious – Precious) the 'consistency rule' was often one which my father imposed subsequently on his text. . . . Of course Gollum's 'precious' is of its nature very ambiguous. [private correspondence]

11 (I: 20–1): Maybe he would have attacked

11 (I: 20). an Elvish knife, which served him as a sword – The blade 'Sting', acquired by Bilbo in the trolls' hoard described in *The Hobbit*, Chapter 2.

On the issue of *Elvish* so spelt and capitalized, see note for p. 192.

12 (I: 21–2). But pity stayed him – The fact that Bilbo showed mercy to Gollum, and later that Frodo and Sam also did so, will be of profound importance to the outcome of the story. See further, Gandalf's comments to Frodo in Book I, Chapter 2.

12–13 (I: 22): Now it is a curious fact

13 (I: 22). this is not the story as Bilbo first told it – In Chapter 5 of the first edition of *The Hobbit* Gollum promises that if he loses the riddle game he will give Bilbo a present: the magic ring that Bilbo has, in fact, already found where Gollum lost it. As Tolkien worked on *The Lord of the Rings*, however, he developed a very different view of the Ring: now it was to possess its bearer too strongly for it to be given up easily. On 31 July

1947 he wrote to Stanley Unwin, in response to comments on Book I by Rayner Unwin: 'Rayner has, of course, spotted a weakness (inevitable): the linking [between *The Hobbit* and *The Lord of the Rings*]. . . . The weakness is Gollum, and his action in offering the ring as a present' (*Letters*, p. 121). Then on 21 September 1947 Tolkien sent to Allen & Unwin 'a specimen of re-writing of Chapter V' of *The Hobbit*, 'which would simplify, though not necessarily improve, my present task' (letter to Stanley Unwin, *Letters*, p. 124). This revision altered Gollum's promise, now (if he loses the contest) to show Bilbo the way out of the goblin caves, and it made Gollum more wretched and treacherous.

Tolkien seems to have forgotten about the revision, until three years later when (after a gap not atypical of the postwar days of paper rationing) he received proof of a new edition of *The Hobbit*, including his specimen. He wrote to Stanley Unwin on 10 September 1950:

> Well, there it is: the alteration is now made, and cannot, I suppose, be unmade. . . .
>
> I have now on my hands two printed versions of a crucial incident. Either the first must be regarded as washed out, a mere miswriting that ought never to have seen the light; or the story as a whole must take into account the existence of two versions and use it. The former was my original simpleminded intention, though it is a bit awkward (since the Hobbit is fairly widely known in its older form) if the literary presence can be done convincingly (I think), but not briefly explained in a note. [p. 142]

On 14 September he wrote again to Unwin: 'I have decided to accept the existence of both versions of Chapter Five, so far as the sequel goes' (*Letters*, p. 142). His final solution was brilliant: that the Ring at once began to assert control over Bilbo, so that he lied about how he obtained it in order to strengthen his claim to ownership, and that it was this false account that 'Bilbo set down in his memoirs, and he seems never to have altered it himself, not even after the Council of Elrond. Evidently it still appeared in the original Red Book, as it did in several of the copies and abstracts' (p. 13, I: 22).

13 (I: 22). the Council of Elrond – See Book II, Chapter 2.

13 (I: 22). Samwise – The name *Samwise* (Sam Gamgee) is a modernization of Old English *samwīs* 'halfwise, simple'. In Appendix F it is said that Sam's 'true' Hobbit name was *Banazîr*, or *Ban* for short.

13 (I: 22): Gandalf, however, disbelieved

13 (I: 22). Gandalf, however, disbelieved Bilbo's first story – There is no hint in *The Hobbit*, even as revised, of Gandalf's curiosity about the Ring.

13 (I: 22). birthday-present – In editions prior to 2004 this was spelt *birthday present*, without a hyphen. The 2002 edition (copy-text for the 2004 edition) contains both *birthday present* and *birthday-present*, with the former the most common (also *birthday-parties*, *Birthday Party*, etc.); but the revised edition of *The Hobbit* contains *birthday-present*, and since Tolkien's general preference is clearly for hyphened forms, the emended text contains a certain amount of regularization in this regard. In the process of writing *The Lord of the Rings* Tolkien's practice varied widely, e.g. *birthday present*, *birthday-present*, *birth-day present*, *birth-day-present*.

13 (I: 22–3): His sword, Sting

13 (I: 22). Sting – So named by Bilbo after he used it to kill a great spider in Mirkwood; see *The Hobbit*, Chapter 8.

13 (I: 22–3). coat of marvellous mail – In Chapter 13 of *The Hobbit* (edition of 1966) Thorin Oakenshield puts on Bilbo 'a small coat of mail, wrought for some young elf-prince long ago. It was of silver-steel, which the elves call *mithril*. . . .' (In the first edition (1937) the coat 'was of silvered steel and ornamented with pearls'.) *Mail* is 'armour composed of interlaced rings or chain-work or of overlapping plates fastened upon a groundwork' (*OED*).

13 (I: 23). But he kept in a drawer at Bag End the old cloak and hood that he had worn on his travels – Not, however, the one in which he started his journey with the dwarves, 'a dark-green cloak borrowed from Dwalin' (*The Hobbit*, Chapter 2). In Chapter 6, after he has escaped from the goblins, it is said that Bilbo 'had lost hood, cloak, food, pony, his buttons, and his friends'.

For *Bag End*, see note for p. 21.

14–16 (I: 23–25): NOTE ON THE SHIRE RECORDS

The final section of the current Prologue entered only with the second edition of *The Lord of the Rings* (1965).

14 (I: 23): At the end of the Third Age

14 (I: 23). the Reunited Kingdom – Arnor and Gondor, reunited under the rule of Elessar (Aragorn) after the War of the Ring.

14 (I: 23): The largest of these collections

14 (I: 23). Undertowers, the home of the Fairbairns, Wardens of the Westmarch – *Undertowers* is an appropriate name for a Hobbit home built, presumably, beneath the Tower Hills.

In *Nomenclature* Tolkien explains that *Fairbairns* 'is an English surname, a northern variant of the name *Fairchild*. It is used by me to suggest that the Elvish beauty of Elanor daughter of Sam [Gamgee] was long inherited by her descendants. Elanor was also remarkable for her golden hair: and in modern English *fair*, when used of complexion or hair, means primarily blond. . . .'

The *Westmarch* is a 'region (beyond [the] original borders of the Shire) between [the] *Far Downs* and [the] *Tower Hills*. First occupied at the beginning of the Fourth Age. [Referred to] esp[ecially] in "the Red Book of Westmarch" . . .' (*Index*).

14 (I: 23–4): The original Red Book

14 (I: 23). The original Red Book has not been preserved, but many copies were made – This is often the case with early writings, when they are preserved at all.

14 (I: 23). Minas Tirith – Sindarin 'tower of guard', the name of the chief city in Gondor, formerly *Minas Anor* 'tower of the sun'. *The Silmarillion* tells of an earlier *Minas Tirith*, built by Finrod Felagund on Tol Sirion in the First Age.

14 (I: 23). Elessar – Quenya 'elfstone', the name of Aragorn as ruler of the Reunited Kingdom. See further, note for p. 375.

14 (I: 23). Periannath – Sindarin 'halflings'.

14–15 (I: 24): The Thain's book

15 (I: 24). *The Tale of Aragorn and Arwen* – See Appendix A. *Aragorn*, see note for p. 58.

15 (I: 24). Faramir – See note for p. 657.

15 (I: 24). the passing of the King – The King Elessar died on 1 March, S.R. 1541 (Fourth Age 120).

15 (I: 24). Bilbo's 'Translations from the Elvish'. These three volumes were found to be a work of great skill and learning in which, between 1403 and 1418, he had used all the sources available to him in Rivendell, both living and written. But since they were little used by Frodo, being almost entirely concerned with the Elder Days, no more is said of them here. – It is implied that these are to be the source of *The Silmarillion*, indeed that they are themselves 'The Silmarillion'; see Christopher Tolkien's comment on this subject, *The Book of Lost Tales, Part One*, p. 6.

15 (I: 24): Since Meriadoc and Peregrin

15 (I: 24). Meriadoc and Peregrin – In Appendix F Tolkien writes:

> The names of the Bucklanders were different from those of the rest of the Shire. The folk of the Marish and their offshoot across the Brandywine were in many ways peculiar, as has been told. It was from the former language of the southern Stoors, no doubt, that they inherited many of their very odd names. These I have usually left unaltered, for

> if queer now, they were queer in their own day. They had a style that we should perhaps feel vaguely to be 'Celtic'. [p. 1135, III: 413]

Meriadoc, the full given name of Merry Brandybuck, is shared by a sixth-century Welsh saint revered in Cornwall and Brittany, and by the hero of a thirteenth-century French Arthurian romance, *Mériadeuc* or *Le Chevalier aux deux épées*. Merry's 'true' shortened name is said in Appendix F to be *Kali*, Westron for 'jolly, gay', 'actually an abbreviation of the now unmeaning Buckland name Kalimac' (p. 1135, III: 414).

Tolkien also writes in Appendix F:

> In some old families, especially those of Fallohide origin such as the Tooks and the Bolgers, it was . . . the custom to give high-sounding first-names. Since most of these seem to have been drawn from legends of the past, of Men as well as of Hobbits, and many while now meaningless to Hobbits closely resembled the names of Men in the Vale of Anduin, or in Dale, or in the Mark, I have turned them into those old names, largely of Frankish and Gothic origin, that are still used by us or are met in our histories. [p. 1135, III: 413]

Hence *Peregrin* Took, usually called Pippin (also a name of Pépin III (714–768), King of the Franks, father of Charlemagne). On 7 September 1955 Tolkien wrote to Richard Jeffery: 'Peregrin is, of course, a real modern name, though it means "traveller in strange countries"' (*Letters*, p. 224), from Latin *peregrinari* 'to travel abroad'.

15 (I: 24). Rohan – See note for p. 262.

15 (I: 24). Bucklebury – In *Nomenclature* Tolkien writes that *Bucklebury* includes the *buck* element as in *Brandybuck* (see note for p. 7) + 'English *-bury* (= Old English *burg* "a place occupying a defensive position, walled or enclosed, a town". . . . The *-le* in *Buckle-* is either an alteration of *Buckenbury*, with old genitive plural *-en(a)*, or a reduction of *Buckland*.' In his notes for the Dutch translator Tolkien describes the name *Bucklebury* as 'a phonetic reduction of *Buckhall-bury* – in which *hall* does represent *hall* "large house/mansion"'.

15–16 (I: 24–5): At Great Smials the books

15 (I: 24). Númenor – Quenya 'west-land', in fuller form *Númenóre*, 'a great isle furthest west of all lands before the Lonely Isle, Eressëa, and the Shores of Valinor' (*Index*). See notes for pp. 2 (*Old World*) and 4 (*Westernesse*). On 12 September 1965 Tolkien wrote to Dick Plotz that *Númenor* has no connection to 'numinous', and 'no reference to "divinity" or sense of its presence. It is a construction from the Eldarin base NDU "below, down; descend"; Q[uenya] *núme* "going down, occident"; *númen* "the direction or region of the sunset" + *nóre* "land" as an inhabited area. I have often used *Westernesse* as a translation' (*Letters*, p. 361).

15 (I: 24). Sauron – The 'Dark Lord' of the Ring-verse, ruler of Mordor, once the lieutenant of the first Dark Lord, Melkor (Morgoth), whose story is told in *The Silmarillion*. In that work it is said that among all of Melkor's servants

> that have names the greatest was that spirit whom the Eldar [the High Elves] called Sauron, or [in Sindarin] Gorthaur the Cruel. In his beginning he was of the Maiar [beings in rank below the Valar] of Aulë [the Smith], and he remained mighty in the lore of that people. In all the deeds of Melkor the Morgoth upon Arda [the Earth], in his vast works and in the deceits of his cunning, Sauron had a part, and was only less evil than his master in that for long he served another and not himself. But in after years he rose like a shadow of Morgoth and a ghost of his malice, and walked behind him on the same ruinous path down into the Void. [pp. 31–2]

See further, Book I, Chapter 2, and Appendix A. In *The Hobbit* Sauron is called 'the Necromancer'.

In a draft letter to a Mr Rang, August 1967, Tolkien wrote that 'there is no linguistic connexion, and therefore no connexion in significance, between *Sauron* a contemporary form of an older **θaurond-* derivative from an adjectival **θaurā* (from a base THAW) "detestable", and the Greek *σαύρα* "a lizard"' (*Letters*, p. 380).

15 (I: 25). Elrond – Elrond Halfelven, master of Rivendell, was introduced in *The Hobbit*, Chapter 3 as

> an elf-friend – one of those people whose fathers came into the strange stories before the beginning of History, the wars of the evil goblins and the elves and the first men in the North. In those days of our tale there were still some people who had both elves and heroes of the North for ancestors, and Elrond the master of the house was their chief.
>
> He was as noble and as fair in face as an elf-lord, as strong as a warrior, as wise as a wizard, as venerable as a king of dwarves, and as kind as summer.

On 14 October 1958 Tolkien wrote to Rhona Beare concerning the 'etymology' of the name *Elrond*:

> *Elrond, Elros.* **rondō* was a prim[itive] Elvish word for 'cavern'. Cf. *Nargothrond* (fortified cavern by the R[iver] Narog), *Aglarond*, etc. **rossē* meant 'dew, spray (of fall or fountain)'. *Elrond* and *Elros*, children of *Eärendil* (sea-lover) and *Elwing* (Elf-foam), were so called, because they were carried off by the sons of Fëanor, in the last act of the feud between the high-elven houses of the Noldorin princes concerning the Silmarils; the Silmaril rescued from Morgoth by Beren and Lúthien, and given to King Thingol (Elwë) Lúthien's father, had descended to Elwing dtr. [daughter] of Dior, son of Lúthien. The infants were not slain, but left

> like 'babes in the wood', in a cave with a fall of water over the entrance. There they were found: Elrond within the cave, and Elros dabbling in the water. [*Letters*, p. 282]

But in late writings Tolkien said that *Elrond* meant 'Star-dome', from *el-* 'star' + *rond* 'hall or chamber with vaulted or arched roof' (*Quendi and Eldar* in *The War of the Jewels*, p. 414); that '*Elrond* was a word for the firmament, the starry dome as it appeared like a roof to Arda; and it was given by Elwing in memory of the great Hall of the Throne of Elwë in the midst of his stronghold of Menegroth that was called the *Menelrond*' (*The Problem of Ros*, in *The Peoples of Middle-earth*, p. 371); and that 'the names *Elros* and *Elrond* . . . were formed to recall the name of their mother *Elwing*' (*The Shibboleth of Fëanor* in *The Peoples of Middle-earth*, p. 349).

15 (I: 25). Celeborn went to dwell there [Rivendell] after the departure of Galadriel; but there is no record of the day when at last he sought the Grey Havens, and with him went the last living memory of the Elder Days in Middle-earth. – The elves Celeborn and Galadriel were the lord and lady of Lothlórien, the woodland realm where the Company of the Ring rests for a time (Book II). Their histories arose with the writing of *The Lord of the Rings* and were later refashioned as Tolkien brought the characters into 'The Silmarillion'. See further, note for p. 357.

Celeborn, a kinsman of King Thingol of Doriath, for a time dwelt in Lindon, south of the Lune; 'his wife was Galadriel, greatest of Elven women. She was sister of Finrod Felagund, Friend-of-Men, once king of Nargothrond, who gave his life to save Beren son of Barahir' (Appendix B, p. 1082, III: 363). Their daughter Celebrían married Elrond of Rivendell. Christopher Tolkien writes in *Unfinished Tales* that

> the name Celeborn when first devised was intended to mean 'Silver Tree'. . . . In my father's latest philological writings, however, the meaning 'Silver Tree' was abandoned: the second element of *Celeborn* (as the name of a person) was derived from the ancient adjectival form *ornā* 'uprising, tall', rather than from the related noun *ornē* 'tree'. (*Ornē* was originally applied to straighter and more slender trees such as birches, whereas stouter, more spreading trees such as oaks and beeches were called in the ancient language *galadā* 'great growth'; but this distinction was not always observed in Quenya and disappeared in Sindarin where all trees came to be called *galadh*, and *orn* fell out of common use, surviving only in verse and songs and in many names both of persons and of trees. [pp. 266–7]

Thus in late writings Tolkien conceived the meaning of *Celeborn* to be 'silver-tall' (*Unfinished Tales*, p. 286).

In a letter to Mrs Meriel Thurston, 30 November 1972, Tolkien wrote that *Galadriel* means 'glittering garland' (*Letters*, p. 423); and in a letter to Mrs Catharine Findlay, 6 March 1973, he said that *Galadriel*,

> like all other names of Elvish persons in *The Lord of the Rings*, is an invention of my own. It is in Sindarin form (see Appendices E and F) and means 'Maiden crowned with gleaming hair'. It is a secondary name given to her in her youth in the far past because she had long hair that glistened like gold but was also shot with silver. She was then of Amazon disposition and bound up her hair as a crown when taking part in athletic feats. [*Letters*, p. 428]

In the appendix of Quenya and Sindarin name-elements in *The Silmarillion*, in the entry for *kal-* (*gal-*), it is said that *Galadriel* has

> no connexion with Sindarin *galadh* 'tree', although in the case of Galadriel such a connexion was often made, and the name altered to *Galadhriel*. In the High-elven speech her name was *Al(a)táriel*, derived from *alata* 'radiance' (Sindarin *galad*) and *riel* 'garlanded maiden' (from a root *rig-* 'twine, wreathe'): the whole meaning 'maiden crowned with a radiant garland', referring to her hair. [p. 360]

In an addition to 'The Silmarillion' written after the completion of *The Lord of the Rings* but before its publication, Tolkien noted that in High-elvish Galadriel's 'name was *Altariellë* "Lady with garland of sunlight", *galata-rīgelle* = S[indarin] *Galadriel*. It was thus mere accident that her name resembled *galað* (Silvan *galad* "tree")' (*Morgoth's Ring*, p. 182). In a late essay on the customs of name-giving among the Eldar in Valinor, Tolkien wrote that *Alatáriel* was an *epessë* 'after-name' or nickname given to Galadriel by Celeborn, 'which she chose to use in Middle-earth, rendered into Sindarin as *Galadriel*, rather than her "father-name" *Artanis* ["noble woman"], or her "mother-name" *Nerwen* ["man-maiden"]' (Christopher Tolkien, *Unfinished Tales*, p. 266).

It is not clear what Tolkien meant by *the last living memory of the Elder Days in Middle-earth*. Some have queried if this should not be said instead of Treebeard the Ent, or of Tom Bombadil. In response to one such query, Christopher Tolkien remarked that his father was given to this kind of 'rhetorical superlative' (Tolkien-George Allen & Unwin archive, HarperCollins).

THE FELLOWSHIP OF THE RING

BOOK I

Chapter 1

A LONG-EXPECTED PARTY

For drafts and history of this chapter, see *The Return of the Shadow*, pp. 11–44, 233–41, 314–15, 370–4, 376–9, 384–6; *The Treason of Isengard*, pp. 18–21.

21 (I: 29). [chapter title] – The title of the first chapter of *The Lord of the Rings*, 'A Long-expected Party', is a deliberate echo of the title of the first chapter of *The Hobbit* (1937), 'An Unexpected Party'.

21 (I: 29): When Mr. Bilbo Baggins

21 (I: 29). Baggins of Bag End – In *Nomenclature* Tolkien notes that *Baggins* is 'intended to recall "bag" – compare Bilbo's conversation with Smaug in *The Hobbit* – and meant to be associated (by hobbits) with *Bag End* (sc. the end of a "bag" or "pudding bag" = cul-de-sac), the local name for Bilbo's house. (It was the local name for my aunt's [Jane Neave] farm in Worcestershire [Dormiston Manor], which was at the end of a lane leading to it and no further.)' In *The Hobbit*, Chapter 12, Bilbo says to the dragon Smaug: 'I came from the end of a bag, but no bag went over me.' Bag End (spelt *Bag-End* in *The Hobbit*) is at the end of a lane leading up The Hill, a high point in the village of Hobbiton, as shown in Tolkien's illustration for *The Hobbit, The Hill: Hobbiton-across-the Water* (*Artist and Illustrator*, fig. 98; see also figs. 89–97).

Tom Shippey comments in *The Road to Middle-earth* that

> *cul-de-sacs* are at once funny and infuriating. They belong to no language, since the French call such a thing an *impasse* and the English a 'dead-end'. The word has its origins in snobbery, the faint residual feeling that English words, ever since the Norman Conquest, have been 'low' and that French ones, or even *Frenchified* ones, would be better. *Cul-de-sac* is accordingly a peculiarly ridiculous piece of English class-feeling – and Bag End a defiantly English reaction to it. As for Mr Baggins, one thing he is more partial to than another is his tea, which he has at four o'clock. But over much of the country 'tea', indeed anything eaten between meals but especially afternoon tea 'in a substantial form' as the *OED* says, is called 'baggins'. The *OED* prefers the 'politer' form 'bagging', but Tolkien himself knew that people who used words like that were almost certain to drop the terminal -g (another post-Conquest confusion anyway). He would have found the term glossed under *bæggin* . . . in W.E. Haigh's [*New*] *Glossary of the Dialect of the Huddersfield District* (London: Oxford University Press), for which he had written an appreciative prologue in 1928. [2nd edn, p. 66]

Haigh defines the word as 'a meal, now usually "tea", but formerly any meal; a bagging. Probably so called because workers generally carried their meals to work in a bag of some kind' (p. 6). But 'baggin' also appears (under *Bagging*) in the great *English Dialect Dictionary* of Tolkien's friend and mentor Joseph Wright, in the example 'He did eit a looaf an' a peawnd o' ham an' three eggs at his baggin'. Douglas A. Anderson comments in *The Annotated Hobbit* that *Baggins* 'is therefore an appropriate name to be found among hobbits, who we are told have dinner twice a day, and for Bilbo, who later in Chapter 1, sits down to his second breakfast. In the Prologue to *The Lord of the Rings*, Tolkien notes that hobbits were fond of "six meals a day (when they could get them)"' (2nd edn., p. 30).

21 (I: 29). his eleventy-first birthday – The term *eleventy-first* (111) is in the humorous, sometimes childish vein of language (with other words such as *tweens*) found in parts of *The Hobbit*, and which Tolkien uses in *The Lord of the Rings* to characterize the Hobbits and their culture in contrast with other races of Middle-earth. The Tolkien scholar Arden R. Smith informs us that

> the word *eleventy* has a philological basis, seen in Old English *hundendleofantig* and Old Norse *ellifu tigir* '110'. The Old English word is attested in such forms as *hundendlyftig*, *hundændlæftig*, and *hundælleftig* (see *OED* s.v. †*hund*). Although the prefix *hund-* was often omitted in words of this type, there do not appear to be any attestations of **endleofantig* without the prefix. [private correspondence]

21 (I: 29): Bilbo was very rich

21 (I: 29). Bilbo . . . had been the wonder of the Shire for sixty years, ever since his remarkable disappearance and unexpected return. – For a bare summary of the story of Bilbo Baggins in *The Hobbit*, see part 4 of the Prologue, 'Of the Finding of the Ring' (pp. 11–14, I: 20–3). Bilbo 'disappeared' from the Shire in S.R. 1341, most remarkably for a quiet-loving hobbit, on the spur of the moment, and (though no eyewitnesses are reported) most publicly in the company of twelve dwarves and the wizard Gandalf from the Green Dragon Inn at Bywater. He returned to Hobbiton in S.R. 1342 to find himself presumed dead and his home and personal property being sold at auction. 'The return of Mr Bilbo Baggins created quite a disturbance, under the Hill and over the Hill, and across the Water; it was a great deal more than a nine days' wonder. The legal bother, indeed, lasted for years' (*The Hobbit*, Chapter 19).

21 (I: 29). the Hill – 'A small isolated hill on the south side of which lay Hobbiton' (*Index*). The name first appeared in *The Hobbit*, Chapter 1, with an illustration: see *Artist and Illustrator*, figs. 92–8. Tom Shippey comments in *The Road to Middle-earth* that at the time of *The Hobbit* it was Tolkien's common practice 'simply to make names out of capital letters. Thus Bilbo lives in a tunnel which goes "not quite straight into the side of the hill – The Hill, as all the people for many miles round called it"' (2nd edn, p. 87).

21 (I: 29). At ninety he [Bilbo] was much the same as at fifty. At ninety-nine they began to call him *well-preserved* – In ?late 1951 Tolkien wrote to Milton Waldman that 'the normal [life] span of hobbits is represented as being roughly in the proportion of 100 [years] to our 80' (*Waldman LR*). Indeed it is not unusual to find entries in the family trees of Appendix C for hobbits who lived to be 100 or more.

21 (I: 29): But so far trouble had not come

21 (I: 29). He remained on visiting terms with his relatives (except, of course, the Sackville-Bagginses) – '*Sackville* is an English name (of more aristocratic association than *Baggins*). It is of course joined in the story with *Baggins* because of the similar meaning in English (= Common Speech) *sack* and *bag*, and because of the slightly comic effect of this conjunction' (*Nomenclature*). In *The Road to Middle-earth* Tom Shippey remarks that Bilbo's cousins 'have severed their connection with Bag End while calling it *cul-de-sac(k)* and tagging on the French suffix *-ville*' (2nd edn., p. 66). In his draft letter to A.C. Nunn, probably late 1958–early 1959, Tolkien wrote that in some 'great families the headship might pass through a *daughter of the deceased* [head] to his *eldest* grandson. . . . In such cases the heir (if he accepted the courtesy title) took the name of his mother's family – though he often retained that of his father's family also (placed second). This was the case with *Otho Sackville-Baggins*. For the nominal headship of the *Sackvilles* had come to him through his mother *Camellia*' (*Letters*, p. 295).

In *The Hobbit*, when Bilbo returns from his adventure, the Sackville-Bagginses 'never admitted that the returned Baggins was genuine, and they were not on friendly terms with Bilbo ever after. They really had wanted to live in his hobbit-hole so very much' (Chapter 19).

21 (I: 29): The eldest of these

21 (I: 29). When Bilbo was ninety-nine he adopted Frodo as his heir . . . and the hopes of the Sackville-Bagginses were finally dashed. – At the end of *The Hobbit*, Chapter 19, 'Bilbo's cousins the Sackville-Bagginses were . . . busy measuring his rooms [at Bag End] to see if their own furniture would fit. In short Bilbo was "Presumed Dead", and not everybody that said so was sorry to find the presumption wrong.' Otho Sackville-Baggins was heir not only to the headship of the Sackville family, but also to that of the Baggins family on his cousin Bilbo's 'death' in S.R. 1342 (Bilbo had succeeded to the title on his mother's death in 1334), but Bilbo returned, and once Bilbo had adopted Frodo as his heir, Otho was denied 'his rather absurd ambition to achieve the rare distinction of being "head" of two families . . . a situation which will explain his exasperation with the adventures and disappearances of Bilbo, quite apart from any loss of property involved in the adoption of Frodo.' After the 'legal fiasco' of 1342 regarding Bilbo's 'death', 'no one dared to presume his death again' (draft letter to A.C. Nunn, probably late 1958–early 1959, *Letters*, pp. 294, 295).

21 (I: 29). *tweens*, as the hobbits called the irresponsible twenties between childhood and coming of age at thirty-three – *Tweens* is a play on 'teens', i.e. the teenage years, but also on 'between' and 'twenties'. In Tolkien's day, one legally 'came of age' at twenty-one.

21–2 (I: 29–30): Twelve more years passed

22 (I: 30). the Old Took – Gerontius Took (1190–1320). The Old Took was first mentioned in *The Hobbit*, Chapter 1, as the father of Bilbo Baggins' mother Belladonna Took and the friend of Gandalf. Frodo, Merry, and Pippin are also among his many descendants. In the fifth draft version of Book I, Chapter 1 (in which the Old Took lived only to 125) Tolkien wrote that 'the title Old was bestowed on him . . . not so much for his age as for his oddity, and because of the enormous number of the young, younger, and youngest Tooks' (*The Return of the Shadow*, p. 245). When preparing *The Tale of Years* Tolkien wanted to call the Old Took 'Isembard', but *The Two Towers* was already in print, in which Pippin refers to 'Old Gerontius' (Book III, Chapter 4). *Gerontius* is probably derived from the Greek for 'old man'; the poem *The Dream of Gerontius* by John Henry Newman was widely celebrated in the late 19th century. In an unpublished letter to Anneke C. Kloos-Adriaansen and P. Kloos, 18 April and 6 May 1963, Tolkien wrote that the Old Took

> has part of his origins in the fact that both my grandfathers were longeval. My father's father was in his eleventh year when Waterloo was fought; my mother's father, a much younger man, was born before Queen Victoria came to the throne, and survived till his ninety-ninth year [*Biography* gives his dates as 1833–1930], missing his 'hundred' (with which he was as much concerned as Bilbo was to surpass the Old Took) only because he mowed a large lawn that spring and then sat in the wind without a jacket. [courtesy of Christopher Tolkien]

22 (I: 30): Tongues began to wag

22 (I: 30). Bywater – 'Village name: as being beside the wide pool occurring in the course of the Water, the main river of the Shire, a tributary of the Brandywine' (*Nomenclature*). Bywater was first mentioned in *The Hobbit*, Chapter 2: Bilbo Baggins met Thorin and company there at the Green Dragon Inn.

22 (I: 30): No one had a more attentive audience

22 (I: 30). Ham Gamgee, commonly known as the Gaffer – *Ham* is intended to be short for *Hamfast*, from Old English *hāmfæst* 'stay at home'. In Appendix F it is said that the 'true' name of Hamfast is *Ranugad*, or *Ran* for short.

In the finished *Nomenclature* Tolkien notes that *Gamgee* is 'a surname found in England though uncommon. I do not know its origin; it does not appear to be English. It is also a word for "cotton-wool" (now obsolescent but known to me in childhood), derived from the name of S. [Sampson] *Gamgee*, died 1886, a distinguished surgeon, who invented "Gamgee tissue")'. But in a draft of this entry it is said that *Gamgee* is

> a difficult name, but important as that of one of the chief characters [Sam]. It has no recognizable meaning in this form, and therefore, according to the theory of translation from C[ommon] S[peech] into Anglicized names the actual CS name had no meaning still apparent in its own time. . . . Gamgee has the second *g* soft. . . .
>
> According to the general theory [described at the beginning of *Nomenclature*] a hobbit name that had no recognizable meaning should be retained, and its sound represented according to the habits of English, or any other Language of Translation. It might therefore be a reasonable procedure in this case to replace *Gamgee* by its real contemporary form, stated [at the end of Appendix F] to have been *Galbasi* or contracted *Galpsi*.
>
> *Gamgee* is however a borderline case. Though the origin or meaning of *Galbasi*, *Galpsi* was not at that time generally known, in the family it was said to be derived from the village name *Galabas*, which had a meaning, being composed of elements = English *play* + one of the words common in place-names, in full or reduced form, such as *-ham*, *-ton*, *-wich*, or *-stow*. . . . *Gamgee* is an English surname, though not a common one. To my surprise I once received a letter about my book from a living person bearing the name Sam Gamgee. He had not, and I have not any information about its origin, but some relationship to the surnames *Gammidge*, *Gam(m)age* is possible. . . .
>
> As a matter of personal history, distinct from the internal fictions of the tale, the use of *Gamgee* has a history that might interest some people. I knew the name as a child, and thought it amusingly odd and it stuck in my mind. But its oddity was largely due to the fact that *gamgee* was to me the ordinary name for (surgical) 'cottonwool'. I supposed that Dr. Gamgee got his name from it. Many years later for the amusement of my children a character, partly fictitious but based on an actual old rustic met on holiday, fond of talking to anybody over his garden fence, was invented and called Gaffer Gamgee. He did not get into *The Hobbit*, then beginning to be composed (1932 [a questionable date – *authors*]), but a few years later got into the early chapters of the sequel.

> It was, of course, due to my association of *gamgee* with *cottonwool* that determined the choice of *Cotton* for a family associated with Sam Gamgee (*Cotton Lane* was a name of importance in my early childhood), though I was of course by then aware that this name of places or persons had no connexion with 'cotton' [see note for p. 934]. But this [is] a purely private jest, of no importance to the tale, and actually not fitted to it, though it belongs to childhood memories which are a large ingredient in the make-up of the Shire.
>
> P.S. The surname *Gamage* is, according to English Place-Name Society, *Gloucestershire* [1964–5], III p. 168–9 derived from the French place-name *Gamaches.* Some of the forms of the derived surname *de Gamesches, de Gamagis, de Gemegis*, there cited from medieval records, resemble *Gamgee.* On reflection I therefore think it would be better if *Gamgee* in the tale were treated as a name of unknown origin (being derived from some place outside the Shire or some language not connected with the Common Speech) as *Took* etc. . . .

On 25 April 1954 Tolkien wrote to Naomi Mitchison that the name *Gamgee*

> would not have taken that form, if I had not heard of 'Gamgee tissue'; there was I believe a Dr. Gamgee (no doubt of the kin) in Birmingham when I was a child. The name was any way always familiar to me. Gaffer Gamgee arose first: he was a legendary character to my children (based on a real-life gaffer, not of that name). But, as you will find explained, in this tale the name is a 'translation' of the real Hobbit name, derived from a village (devoted to rope-making) anglicized as Gamwich (pron. Gammidge), near Tighfield. . . . [*Letters*, pp. 179–80; *Gamwich* is not on the Shire map, but named in the family tree of Samwise, Appendix C]

A *gaffer* is an elderly male rustic.

22 (I: 30). ***The Ivy Bush*** – An actual inn or pub name. The sign-emblem of a vintner was once traditionally an ivy bush.

22 (I: 30). Holman – 'An English surname; but here supposed to = "hole-man" (pronounced the same)' (*Nomenclature*).

22 (I: 30). They lived on the Hill itself, in Number 3 Bagshot Row just below Bag End. – *Bagshot Row* is 'the row of small "holes" in the lane below Bag End. (Said to have been so named because the earth removed in excavating 'Bag End' was shot over the edge of the sudden fall in the hillside on the ground which later became the gardens and earthwalls of the humbler dwelling' (*Nomenclature*). Tolkien's explanation of *bagshot* is invented folk-etymology. The first element of the name, *bag-* repeats that in *Bag End.* Its second element *-shot* may be related to the old dialect word *shot* 'division of land', but it is tempting to suggest a more likely derivation from **scēot* 'steep slope', an unrecorded Old English word assumed by Eilert Ekwall in his *Concise Oxford Dictionary of English Place-Names* (4th edn., 1960, entry for *Shottle*), thus a play on 'hill'. Compare *Shotover* ('hill with a steep slope') east of Oxford, where the ground rises sharply.

22 (I: 30): 'A very nice well-spoken gentlehobbit

22 (I: 30). gentlehobbit – A careful choice of word: Tolkien could not have used 'gentleman' in this context, as Bilbo is a hobbit. In the first edition of *The Hobbit* (1937), Chapter 1, Gandalf refers to Bilbo as an 'excitable little man'; this was emended in the second edition (1951) to 'excitable little fellow' after the noted children's author Arthur Ransome (*Swallows and Amazons*, etc.) suggested to Tolkien that the first form was 'a leak or a tear in the veil, undoing just a little of what you had done' to make Bilbo 'so Hobbitty' (letter of 17 December 1937, *Signalling from Mars: The Letters of Arthur Ransome* (1997), p. 251).

22 (I: 30). calling him 'Master Hamfast', and consulting him constantly upon the growing of vegetables – in the matter of 'roots', especially potatoes, the Gaffer was recognized as the leading authority – Tolkien uses the word *Master* here, as often in *The Lord of the Rings*, as an expression of respect, in the archaic sense of a title denoting high rank, learning, etc. – Bilbo respects Gaffer Gamgee as a master gardener – distinct from *Mister* (as 'Mr Bilbo Baggins', 'Mr Frodo') which is a title of respect in a broader sense, and occasionally *Master* as a title applied to males not yet 'come of age' (as in 'Master Everard Took' later in Book I, Chapter 1). Sam Gamgee himself becomes 'Master Samwise' at last in Book VI, Chapter 4, so called by Gandalf after the successful events on Mount Doom.

Potatoes, like tobacco, are an import to Europe from the Americas, with a name derived from the Spanish. But while Tolkien preferred *pipe-weed* for tobacco in *The Lord of the Rings*, he retained *potatoes*, altering it only when Sam uses the dialect form *taters*.

22 (I: 30): 'But what about this Frodo

22 (I: 30). Old Noakes – '*Noake(s), Noke(s)* is an English surname, derived probably from the not uncommon minor place-name *No(a)ke*, from early English *atten oke* "at the oak"' (*Nomenclature*). The surname *Nokes* also appears in Tolkien's *Smith of Wootton Major* (1967).

22 (I: 30). Baggins is his name, but he's more than half a Brandybuck – Frodo is technically only half a Brandybuck, through his mother Primula Brandybuck. Perhaps Noakes is referring to Frodo having spent his early life in Buckland.

22 (I: 30). Buckland – The place-name *Buckland*, denoting 'a strip of land occupied by Shire-hobbits, east of [the] Brandywine' (*Index*), like the surnames *Brandybuck* and *Oldbuck* is meant to contain the word *buck* from Old English *bucc* 'male deer' (fallow or roe) or *bucca* 'he-goat', 'though *Buckland*, an English place-name, is frequently in fact derived from "book-land", land originally held by a written charter' (*Nomenclature*, entry for *Brandybuck*). Tom Shippey observes in *The Road to Middle-earth* (2nd edn., p. 93) that Shire place-names

> sound funny but they ring true. . . . Buckland itself is an Oxfordshire placename, common all over England since it has the rather dull etymology of *bócland*, land 'booked' to the Church by charter, and so different from *folcland* or 'folkland' which was unalienable. That derivation was impossible in Middle-earth [where there is no established religion or church], so Tolkien constructed the more satisfactory one that the Buckland was where the Buck family lived, was indeed a 'folkland' centred on Bucklebury like the 'Tookland' centred on Tuckborough.

22 (I: 30). where folks are so queer – Suspicion of the 'other', to use a term from anthropology, is as common among hobbits as among humanity. Compare Farmer Maggot in Book I, Chapter 4, 'we do get queer folk wandering in these parts at times' (p. 92, I: 102), and 'You should never have gone mixing yourself up with Hobbiton folk, Mr. Frodo. Folk are queer up there' (p. 94, I: 104); and Book I, Chapter 9: 'The Shire-hobbits referred to those of Bree, and to any others that lived beyond the borders, as Outsiders, and took very little interest in them, considering them dull and uncouth' (p. 150, I: 162). Even Frodo is not immune: in Book II, Chapter 1 he tells Gandalf: 'I didn't know that any of the Big People were like that. I thought, well, that they were just big, and rather stupid: kind and stupid like Butterbur; or stupid and wicked like Bill Ferny. But then we don't know much about Men in the Shire, except perhaps the Bree-landers' (pp. 220–1, I: 233). On this theme, see further, Christina Scull, 'Open Minds, Closed Minds in *The Lord of the Rings*', *Proceedings of the J.R.R. Tolkien Centenary Conference 1992* (1995).

22 (I: 30): 'You're right, Dad!'

22 (I: 30). drownded – The *Oxford English Dictionary* gives this as an alternative to *drowned* with the comment 'now vulgar'. It is part of the flavour of the Gaffer's rustic speech, and not unique among those at *The Ivy Bush* (compare, for instance, *agin* 'against, near' in the preceding paragraph). In Appendix F Tolkien writes that 'the Hobbits of the Shire and of Bree had at this time . . . adopted the Common Speech. They used it in their own manner freely and carelessly . . .' (p. 1130, III: 408). At the time of the earliest radio adaptation of *The Lord of the Rings* (BBC, 1955–6) Tolkien pointed out to producer Terence Tiller (in correspondence preserved in the BBC Written Archives Centre) that most Hobbits spoke a rustic dialect, except for the Hobbit 'gentry': thus the speech of Ham Gamgee, and of his son Samwise, is 'rustic', but not that of Bilbo, Frodo, Merry, or Pippin. Bilbo and Frodo are set apart from other hobbits by their knowledge and interests, while Merry and Pippin are of high birth, heirs respectively of the Master of Buckland and of the Thain, and therefore brought up to be more 'cultured'.

In 'Studies in Tolkien's Language: III Sure as Shiretalk – On Linguistic Variation in Hobbit Speech', *Arda* 5 (1988, for 1985), Nils-Lennart Johannesson concludes that Tolkien's use of dialectal Warwickshire or Oxfordshire forms for Hobbit dialogue 'was selective rather than wholesale. His guiding principle seems to have been to avoid too markedly localized forms and only to rely on forms with a fairly wide distribution in English dialects, forms which could be slipped in unobtrusively in the speech of Shire hobbits' (p. 41).

23 (I: 31): 'Well, so they say'

23 (I: 31). Primula Brandybuck – In Appendix F it is said that 'to their maid-children [female children] Hobbits commonly gave the names of flowers or jewels' (p. 1135, III: 413). *Primula* is the name of a genus of flowers including primroses and cowslips. Compare, for instance, *Lobelia Sackville-Baggins, Salvia Brandybuck, Rose Cotton.*

23 (I: 31). She was our Mr. Bilbo's first cousin on the mother's side (her mother being the youngest of the Old Took's daughters) – Primula Brandybuck's mother was Mirabella Took, eleventh out of twelve children in her immediate family. The other two of 'the three remarkable daughters of the Old Took' (as they are called in *The Hobbit*, Chapter 1) were Belladonna, who married Bungo Baggins, and Donnamira, who married Hugo Boffin. Their names share the elements *bella*, *donna*, and *mira*. Bilbo is the son of Belladonna, Frodo the grandson of Mirabella, Merry Brandybuck the great-grandson of Mirabella, and Fredegar Bolger the great-grandson of Donnamira. Pippin Took is the great-grandson of Hildigrim, one of the nine brothers of Belladonna, Donnamira, and Mirabella.

23 (I: 31). Gorbadoc – In the Brandybuck family tree (Appendix C) Gorbadoc Brandybuck is called 'Broadbelt', presumably in connection with the Gaffer's description that he was 'partial to his vittles' and kept 'a mighty generous table'. *Gorbadoc* is a variant spelling of the name of a legendary British king, recalled by Geoffrey of Monmouth in his *Historia Regum Britanniae* (twelfth century), and of the title character of one of the earliest of English tragedies, *Gorboduc, or Ferrex and Porrex* (sixteenth century).

23 (I: 31). vittles – An obsolete or dialect variant of *victuals* 'prepared food', the spelling reflecting the Gaffer's rustic pronunciation of the word. Compare 'jools' later on p. 23.

23 (I: 31): 'And *I* heard she pushed him in

23 (I: 31). Sandyman, the Hobbiton miller – The Hobbiton water-mill is shown in Tolkien's pictures of Hobbiton for *The Hobbit* (see especially

Artist and Illustrator, fig. 98). The Gaffer does 'not much like the miller': in the medieval village the miller was the most prosperous and the least popular inhabitant, as the villagers had to bring their grain to him for milling, and he did the measuring. Naturally he was suspected of cheating, and in literature of the Middle Ages, such as Chaucer's *Canterbury Tales*, he is typically characterized as dishonest. In *The Lord of the Rings* the miller seems a genuinely unsavoury character, and his son (Ted Sandyman), who takes up with the ruffians, is even worse.

23 (I: 31): 'You shouldn't listen to all you hear

23 (I: 31). Brandy Hall. A regular warren – The word *warren*, 'network of rabbit burrows', suggests the similarity between *rabbit* and *hobbit*, but is not inapt for an elaborate Hobbit hole housing never fewer than 'a couple of hundred relations'.

23 (I: 31): 'But I reckon

23 (I: 31). it was a nasty knock – This is the reading prior to the edition of 1994, when 'knock' was mistakenly reset as 'shock'. The correct word was restored in the edition of 2004. *Knock* in this sense means 'misfortune, blow, setback'.

23–4 (I: 31–2): 'Then you've heard more

23 (I: 31–2). I saw Mr. Bilbo when he came back. . . . I'd not long come prentice to old Holman . . . but he had me up at Bag End helping him to keep folks from trampling and trapessing all over the garden while the sale was on. – *Prentice* is short for *apprentice*.

The double-*s* spelling 'trapessing' suggests that this is how the Gaffer pronounces *trapesing*, i.e. *traipsing*.

The *sale* was the auction of Bilbo's effects after he went to the Lonely Mountain and in his absence from Hobbiton was presumed dead, as told in *The Hobbit*, Chapter 19.

24 (I: 32). some mighty big bags and a couple of chests. I don't doubt they were mostly full of treasure – In *The Hobbit* Bilbo returns from the Lonely Mountain with 'only two small chests, one filled with silver, the other with gold, such as one strong pony could carry', to which he adds bags of gold from a trolls' hoard (Chapters 18, 19). But 'his gold and silver was largely spent in presents, both useful and extravagant – which to a certain extent accounts for the affection of his nephews and his nieces' (Chapter 19).

24 (I: 32). Mr. Bilbo has learned him his letters – meaning no harm, mark you, and I hope no harm will come of it. – *Learned* is used in the ancient sense 'taught', now considered archaic or slang. Cf. the fourteenth-century poem *Sir Gawain and the Green Knight*, 'if thou learnest him his lesson', or Mr Badger in *The Wind in the Willows* (1908) by Kenneth

Grahame, after he has had his grammar 'corrected' by the Water Rat: 'But we don't *want* to teach 'em. We want to *learn* 'em – learn 'em, learn 'em.' Thus *learned him his letters* 'taught him to read'. *Meaning no harm* suggests that the Gaffer thinks that such education is above Sam's station in life.

24 (I: 32): 'Ah, but he has likely enough been adding

24 (I: 32). outlandish folk that visit him: dwarves coming at night, and that old wandering conjuror, Gandalf – They are literally *outlandish*, i.e. foreign (as well as strange in Hobbit eyes): the dwarves are apparently from Dale (where Bilbo goes after he leaves Hobbiton), while Gandalf is from Valinor beyond the Western Seas.

A *conjuror* is a performer of 'magic' tricks. In his lecture *On Fairy-Stories* (delivered in 1939, first published in 1947) Tolkien wrote with disdain of 'high class conjuring', as opposed to true magic (*Tree and Leaf*, p. 47).

24 (I: 32): 'And you can say what *you* like

24 (I: 32). pint of beer – In Britain beer is customarily served in pints (or half-pints), imperial measure, 20 fluid ounces (or 0.568 litre).

24 (I: 32): That very month was September

24 (I: 32). fireworks, what is more, such as had not been seen in the Shire for nigh on a century, not indeed since the Old Took died – In *The Hobbit*, Chapter 1, Bilbo praises Gandalf as 'the man that used to make such particularly excellent fireworks! . . . Old Took used to have them on Midsummer's Eve. Splendid! They used to go up like great lilies and snapdragons and laburnums of fire and hang in the twilight all evening!'

24–5 (I: 32–3): Days passed and The Day grew nearer

24 (I: 33). dwarves with long beards and deep hoods – The appearance of bearded, hooded dwarves was established in *The Hobbit*.

24–5 (I: 33). An old man was driving it all alone. He wore a tall pointed blue hat, a long grey cloak, and a silver scarf. He had a long white beard and bushy eyebrows that stuck out beyond the brim of his hat. – Gandalf the Wizard is introduced in *The Hobbit*, Chapter 1, as 'an old man with a staff. He had a tall pointed blue hat, a long grey cloak, a silver scarf over which his long white beard hung down below his waist, and immense black boots.' He looks at Bilbo 'from under long bushy eyebrows that stuck out further than the brim of his shady hat'. Tolkien drew at least four pictures of Gandalf (see *Artist and Illustrator*, figs. 89, 91, 100, 104), in none of which did he attempt to represent the wizard's eyebrows with the same exaggeration as in the text.

In his biography of Tolkien Humphrey Carpenter links the wizard to a postcard depicting an old man in a red cloak and a long white beard, which Tolkien called the 'origin of Galdalf'. Carpenter believed that Tolkien purchased this reproduction of a work by the German painter Josef Madlener during a walking tour of Switzerland in 1911; but Manfred Zimmermann, 'The Origin of Gandalf and Josef Madlener', *Mythlore* 9, no. 4, whole no. 34 (Winter 1983), shows that the painting, *Der Berggeist* ('The Mountain Spirit', reproduced in *The Annotated Hobbit*, 2nd edn.), belongs rather to the mid-1920s.

Marjorie Burns in 'Gandalf and Odin', *Tolkien's* Legendarium*: Essays on* The History of Middle-earth (2000), suggests that Gandalf shares certain attributes with the Norse god Odin: 'the most distinctive features of Gandalf – his hat, beard, staff and penchant for wandering' are 'the key characteristics that Odin displays when he leaves Asgard, and travels in disguise through the plane of human existence, the middle-earth of Norse mythology. During these earthly journeys, Odin does not appear as a stern and forbidding deity or a bloodthirsty god of battle – but rather as a grey-bearded old man who carries a staff and wears a hood or cloak (usually blue) and a wide-brimmed floppy hat' (p. 220).

25 (I: 33). large red G . . . and the elf-rune – The first reproduced character is in the Elvish script *Tengwar*, and the second in the runic *Cirth* (see Appendix E). A *rune* is a letter formed with simple strokes so as to suit carving.

25 (I: 33): When the old man, helped by Bilbo

25 (I: 33). Bilbo gave a few pennies away – *Pennies* are also mentioned as currency in Bree ('silver pennies' as the price of ponies), but we are never told where or by whom they were minted.

25 (I: 33): Inside Bag End, Bilbo and Gandalf

25 (I: 33). Inside Bag End, Bilbo and Gandalf were sitting at the open window of a small room looking out west on to the garden. – Bilbo's hobbit-hole is already familiar to readers of *The Hobbit*:

> It had a perfectly round door like a porthole, painted green, with a shiny yellow brass knob in the exact middle. The door opened on to a tube-shaped hall like a tunnel: a very comfortable tunnel without smoke, with panelled walls, and floors tiled and carpeted, provided with polished chairs, and lots and lots of pegs for hats and coats. . . . The tunnel wound on and on, going fairly but not quite straight into the side of the hill . . . and many little round doors opened out of it, first on one side and then on another. No going upstairs for the hobbit: bedrooms, bathrooms, cellars, pantries (lots of these), wardrobes (he had whole rooms devoted to clothes), kitchens, dining-rooms, all were on the same floor, and indeed on the same passage. The best rooms were the only ones to have windows, deep-set round windows looking over his garden, and meadows beyond, sloping down to the river.

It was 'the most luxurious hobbit-hole . . . to be found either under The Hill or over The Hill or across The Water' (Chapter 1). Tolkien drew several illustrations of Bag End, or illustrations in which Bag End is an element, for *The Hobbit*: see *Artist and Illustrator*, figs. 89–98 and 139.

As in *The Hobbit*, the story of *The Lord of the Rings* takes the reader 'there and back again' with Bag End at its beginning and end. It, and (in the sequel) by extension the Shire, is a 'familiar' setting from which the reader is eased into a world containing elements of fantasy.

25 (I: 33). snap-dragons and sunflowers, and nasturtians – Snap-dragons (*Antirrhinum majus*, with flowers shaped like a dragon's mouth), sunflowers (*Helianthus*, with large golden flowers), and nasturtians are brightly-coloured plants often found in English gardens. *Nasturtians* is here deliberately used by Tolkien rather than the more familiar *nasturtiums*: this form, he wrote to Katharine Farrer on 7 August 1954, 'represents a final triumph' over the printer of *The Lord of the Rings* who appeared

> to have a highly educated pedant as a chief proof-reader, and they started correcting my English without reference to me: *elfin* for *elven*; *farther* for *further*; *try to say* for *try and say* and so on. I was put to the trouble of proving to him his own ignorance, as well as rebuking his impertinence. So, though I do not much care, I dug my toes in about *nasturtians*. I have always said this. It seems to be a natural anglicization that started soon after 'Indian Cress' was naturalized (from Peru, I think) in the 18th century; but it remains a minority usage. I prefer it because *nasturtium* is, as it were, bogusly botanical, and falsely learned.
>
> I consulted the [Merton] college gardener to this effect: 'What do you call these things, gardener?'
>
> 'I calls them *tropaeolum*, sir.'
>
> 'But, when you're just talking to dons?'
>
> 'I says *nasturtians*, sir.'
>
> 'Not *nasturtium*?'
>
> 'No sir, that's watercress.'
>
> And that seems to be the fact of botanical nomenclature. . . . [*Letters*, p. 183]

The *Oxford English Dictionary*, however, records *nasturtian* as a 'corrupt form' of *nasturtium* as applied to *tropaeolum*. *Nasturtium* is recorded first as the common name of a genus of cruciferous plants, of which watercress is the best-known representative, and second as the trailing plant with 'showy orange-coloured flowers', also known as 'Indian Cress'. In the second sense it 'now usually' denotes 'the larger species *Tropaeolum majus*, introduced from Peru in 1686, but at first applied to *T. minus* (also from Peru), known in this country (England) from 1596, and at first called *Nasturtium Indicum*'.

26 (I: 34): The next day more carts rolled up the Hill

26 (I: 34). they began to tick off the days on the calendar; and they watched eagerly for the postman, hoping for invitations – These and many other details confirm that the Shire is, as Tolkien said (see note for p. 5), based on rural England at the end of the nineteenth century: calendars on which one could tick off dates, a postal service (with local offices), written invitations to parties, fireworks, silk waistcoats, party crackers, tissue-paper, moth-balls, umbrellas, inkwells, bookcases, etc. The tone had been set in *The Hobbit*, with Bilbo's engagement tablet, door-bell, tea-kettle, clock on the mantelpiece, pocket handkerchiefs, and so forth.

26 (I: 34): One morning the hobbits woke

26 (I: 34). the large field, south of Bilbo's front door. . . . The three hobbit-families of Bagshot Row, adjoining the field – These features may be seen in Tolkien's illustrations of Hobbiton for *The Hobbit* (*Artist and Illustrator*, figs. 97–8).

26 (I: 34): The tents began to go up

26 (I: 34). draught – In this sense (= *draft*), a conscription of persons for a special purpose.

26–7 (I: 35): Bilbo Baggins called it a *party*

26 (I: 35). a few from outside the borders – This continues the theme of Bilbo's connection with *outlandish* folk. In an early version of this chapter the Brockhouses (see note for p. 28) were said to live 'not in the Shire at all, but in Combe-under-Bree', and to be 'remotely connected with the Tooks, but were also friends Bilbo had made in the course of his travels' (*The Return of the Shadow*, p. 236).

27 (I: 35). Hobbits give presents to other people on their own birthdays. – In the Prologue it is said that Hobbits 'were hospitable and delighted in parties, and in presents, which they gave away freely and eagerly accepted' (p. 2, I: 11). In his draft letter to A.C. Nunn, probably late 1958–early 1959, Tolkien expanded on this idea, *inter alia*:

> A person celebrating his/her birthday was called a *ribadyan* (which may be rendered according to the system [of 'translation'] described [in Appendix F] and adopted a *byrding*). . . . With regard to *presents*: on his birthday the 'byrding' both *gave* and *received* presents; but the processes were different in origin, function, and etiquette. The *reception* was omitted by the narrator (since it does not concern the [Bilbo's] Party). . . . [pp. 290–1]

27 (I: 35): On this occasion the presents

27 (I: 35). There were toys the like of which they [the hobbit-children] had never seen before, all beautiful and some obviously magical. Many of them had . . . come all the way from the Mountain and from Dale, and were of real dwarf-make. – The *Mountain* is Erebor, the Lonely Mountain, and *Dale* is at its foot. In *The Hobbit*, Chapter 1, Thorin Oakenshield talks of the days when he lived in Erebor, near 'the merry town of Dale', when Dwarves had 'leisure to make beautiful things just for the fun of it, not to speak of the most marvellous and magical toys, the like of which is not to be found in the world now-a-days. So my grandfather's halls became full of armour and jewels and carvings and cups, and the toy-market of Dale was the wonder of the North.'

27 (I: 35): When every guest had been welcomed

27 (I: 35). lunch, tea, and dinner (or supper) – *Lunch* is the midday meal; *tea* a light afternoon meal of tea, bread, cakes, etc.; and *dinner* or *supper* the main meal of the day, taken in the evening (*supper* sometimes connotes a light evening meal). Hobbits apparently made fine distinctions between these: in *The Hobbit*, Chapter 1, it is said that they have dinner 'twice a day when they can get it', and in the Prologue (see note for p. 2) that Hobbits had 'six meals a day (when they could get them)'.

27 (I: 35). elevenses – British colloquialism for light refreshment taken at about 11.00 a.m.

27 (I: 35): The fireworks were by Gandalf

27 (I: 35). The fireworks were by Gandalf – On 29 February 1968 Tolkien wrote to Donald Swann: 'Fireworks have no special relation to me. They appear in the books (and would have done even if I disliked them) because they are part of the representation of *Gandalf*, bearer of the Ring of Fire, the Kindler: the most childlike aspect shown to the Hobbits being fireworks' (*Letters*, p. 390). But this is an argument after the fact. Gandalf was already associated with fireworks in *The Hobbit*, and fireworks reappeared in *The Lord of the Rings* with the second version of 'A Long-expected Party', long before Tolkien conceived the three Elven-rings.

27 (I: 35). squibs, crackers, backarappers, sparklers, torches, dwarf-candles, elf-fountains, goblin-barkers and thunder-claps – A *squib* is a small firework which burns with a hissing sound. A *cracker* explodes with a sharp noise. A *backarraper* is a firecracker with several folds, which results in a rapid series of explosions. A *sparkler* is a sparkling (not explosive) firework held in the hand. *Torch* in fireworks parlance is a slow-burning wax candle used to illuminate the area in which fireworks are prepared. *Dwarf-candles* etc. are presumably specialty items made by dwarves, or by Gandalf. In general, a *candle* is a hand-held firework (such as *Roman candle*), and a *fountain* is a ground-mounted firework which forms sprays of coloured sparks.

27–8 (I: 35–6): There were rockets

27 (I: 35). a phalanx of flying swans – *Phalanx* in Greek antiquity denoted soldiers drawn up in a line of battle in close order; by extension, any common mass.

27 (I: 36). the Water – 'The Shire-water, full name of stream running down from the north (through Hobbiton and Bywater) and then along the line of the Road to the Brandywine which it joined just above the Bridge' (*Index*).

27 (I: 36). And there was also one last surprise, in honour of Bilbo. . . . It shaped itself like a mountain seen in the distance, and began to glow at the summit. It spouted green and scarlet flames. Out flew a red-golden dragon . . . passed like an express train – An allusion to Bilbo's adventures in *The Hobbit*, at the Lonely Mountain and menaced by the dragon Smaug. The reference to 'an express train' is often mentioned by critics as a glaring anachronism in Middle-earth.

28 (I: 36): 'That is the signal for supper!'

28 (I: 36). provender – Food, with the humorous connotation 'animal fodder'.

28 (I: 36): There were many Bagginses

28 (I: 36). Bagginses and Boffins, and also many Tooks and Brandybucks; there were various Grubbs (relations of Bilbo Baggins' grandmother), and various Chubbs (connexions of his Took grandfather); and a selection of Burrowses, Bolgers, Bracegirdles, Brockhouses, Goodbodies, Hornblowers and Proudfoots. – Except for *Baggins*, *Boffin*, and *Brandybuck*, all of these surnames are listed in *A Dictionary of English Surnames* by P.H. Reaney (rev. 3rd edn., 1997). For *Baggins*, *Boffin*, *Took*, *Brandybuck*, and *Hornblower*, see notes for pp. 21, 9, 4, 22, and 8 respectively.

In *Nomenclature* Tolkien comments that *Grubb* 'is meant to recall the English verb *grub* "dig, root in the ground"'. The auctioneers in *The Hobbit*, Chapter 19, are 'Messrs Grubb, Grubb, and Burrowes', and Bilbo's grandmother was Laura Grubb.

Chubb was 'chosen because its immediate association in English is with the adjective *chubby* "round and fat in bodily shape" (said to be derived from the *chub*, a name of a river-fish)' (*Nomenclature*). Bilbo's Took grandfather, Gerontius, married Adamanta Chubb.

In *Nomenclature* (in the entry for *Budgeford*) Tolkien comments that '*Bolger* and *Bulger* occur as surnames in England. Whatever their real origin, they are used in the story to suggest that they were in origin nicknames referring to fatness, tubbiness' (compare *bulge*). The Bolger family tree was added to Appendix C in the 2004 edition.

Bracegirdle also is 'used in the text, of course, with reference to the hobbit tendency to be fat and so to strain their belts' (*Nomenclature*).

Brockhouse is derived from the old country word *brock* 'badger' (from Old English *brocc*) + *house*. Tolkien explains in *Nomenclature* that *brock* 'occurs in numerous place-names, from which surnames are derived, such as *Brockbanks* [and compare *Brockenbores*, note for p. 1021]. *Brockhouse* is of course feigned to be a hobbit-name, because the "brock" builds complicated and well-ordered underground-dwellings or "setts"'.

The surname *Goodbody* is derived from Old English *gōd* 'good' and *bodig* 'frame, trunk of an animal'. Tolkien may have meant to suggest, again, a sense of corpulence.

According to Reaney, the English surname *Proudfoot* means 'one who walks with a haughty step'. Tolkien suggests that the Hobbit surname stems instead from a physical characteristic. The name of the 'elderly hobbit' who speaks up at Bilbo's party (see note for p. 29) is 'Proudfoot, and well merited; his feet were large, exceptionally furry, and both were on the table' (p. 29, I: 37).

In Appendix F Tolkien notes that 'in the case of persons . . . Hobbit-names in the Shire and in Bree were for those days peculiar, notably in the habit that had grown up, some centuries before this time, of having inherited names for families. Most of these surnames had obvious meanings (in the current language being derived from jesting nicknames, or from place-names, or – especially in Bree – from the names of plants and trees)' (pp. 1134–5, III: 413). Other peoples in Middle-earth, in contrast, used the patronymic system, e.g. 'Aragorn, son of Arathorn'.

29 (I: 37): ***My dear People***

29 (I: 37). his embroidered silk waistcoat – Tolkien does not say where in Middle-earth silk was produced, and how the Hobbits were able to obtain it, or whether Bilbo's garment was imported or made in the Shire. Tolkien himself, after the success of *The Lord of the Rings*, was able to indulge a personal taste in fancy waistcoats (i.e. close-fitting, waist-length, sleeveless garments, in the United States called *vests*).

29 (I: 37): ***My dear Bagginses***

29 (I: 37). ProudFEET! – Thus Bilbo's 'Proudfoots' is 'corrected', but Bilbo repeats 'Proudfoots'. Tolkien is making a linguistic joke about the plural of *foot*, which does not simply take an *-s* and become *foots*, but changes form to become *feet* (like *goose/geese*). The Old English word for *foot* is *fōt*, plural *fēt*, derived from Germanic **fōtiz*, which underwent '*i*-mutation' whereby the vowel sound changed to long *e*.

29 (I: 37–8): *I hope you are all enjoying yourselves*

29 (I: 37). crackers – In this context, paper cylinders which when pulled apart make a noise like a firework and release toys, sweets, or other small party gifts. They are an essential part of a typical British Christmas celebration. Those at Bilbo's party are 'musical': they contain 'trumpets and horns, pipes and flutes, and other musical instruments', a parallel to the dwarves' fiddles, flutes, drum, clarinets, viols, and harp in the 'unexpected party' of *The Hobbit*, Chapter 1.

29 (I: 38). Master Everard Took and Miss Melilot Brandybuck got on a table and with bells in their hands began to dance the Springle-ring: a pretty dance, but rather vigorous. – In *Nomenclature* Tolkien notes that *Springle-ring* is 'an invention', the name of which a translator should render by something in the language of translation which implies 'a vigorous ring-dance in which dancers often leaped up'. In Tolkien's poem *Bombadil Goes Boating* (in *The Adventures of Tom Bombadil and Other Verses from the Red Book*) Farmer Maggot's 'daughters did the Springle-ring, goodwife did the laughing'. In the second draft version of Book I, Chapter 1 the dance is called 'the flip-flap' (a step-dance of the nineteenth century).

29 (I: 38): But Bilbo had not finished

29 (I: 38). Seizing a horn from a youngster nearby – The reading is 'nearby' in the first and second printings; curiously, the word became 'near by' in the third printing (1955), though the words in that line were otherwise unchanged. It was restored to *nearby* in the edition of 2004. Both *near by* and *nearby* are correct – the first is the primary form in the *Oxford English Dictionary*, though only *nearby* now appears in the *Concise OED* – but a review of *The Lord of the Rings* shows that *nearby* was Tolkien's clear preference (if perhaps not always that of the printer). For the 2004 edition we regularized four long-standing instances of *near by* to *nearby*, two in the narrative and two in the Appendices.

30 (I: 38): *Together we score one hundred and forty-four*

30 (I: 38). *Together we score one hundred and forty-four. . . . One Gross* – *Gross* is indeed a word meaning (as a noun) 'twelve dozen' or 144, but also (as an adjective) 'fat, coarse, unrefined'. Tolkien is playing on the two meanings of word, having indeed already remarked that 'all the one hundred and forty-four guests . . . had a *very* pleasant feast, in fact an *engrossing* entertainment' (p. 28, I: 36–7, emphasis ours).

30 (I: 38): *It is also, if I may be allowed*

30 (I: 38). *the anniversary of my arrival by barrel at Esgaroth on the Long Lake. . . . The banquet was very splendid . . . though I had a bad cold at the time . . . and could only say 'thag you very buch'.* – In *The Hobbit* Bilbo's companions are captured by Wood-elves in Mirkwood, while he himself uses his magic ring to become invisible. He frees the dwarves from captivity by hiding them in barrels being taken by river to Lake-town, also known as *Esgaroth* (Sindarin 'reedlake', according to *The Etymologies* in *The Lost Road and Other Writings*, p. 356). Thorin Oakenshield proclaims his return as King under the Mountain, and he and the others are feted by the people. Bilbo, however, has 'a shocking cold. For three days he sneezed and coughed, and he could not go out, and even after that his speeches at banquets were limited to "Thag you very buch"' (Chapter 10).

30 (I: 39): He stepped down and vanished

30 (I: 39). One hundred and forty-four flabbergasted hobbits – Earlier in the chapter it is said that 'the invitations were limited to twelve dozen . . . and the guests were selected from all the families to which Bilbo and Frodo were related, with the addition of a few special unrelated friends (such as Gandalf)' (p. 28, I: 36). This suggests that Gandalf was counted among the 144; but since he knew Bilbo's plans, he could not be *flabbergasted* (to be astonished, struck dumb by amazement) – nor is he a hobbit. In the second draft version of this chapter Tolkien wrote that 'invitations had been limited to twelve dozen, or one gross (in addition to Gandalf and the host)' (*The Return of the Shadow*, p. 22). On his retained set of galley proofs for *The Fellowship of the Ring* he toyed with the idea of changing 144 flabbergasted hobbits to only 140, plus three dwarves and Gandalf (Marquette Series 3/2/16).

31–2 (I: 40): He walked briskly back

31 (I: 40). old cloak and hood . . . it might have been dark green . . . rather too large for him – See note for p. 13.

31 (I: 40). a bundle wrapped in old cloths, and a leather-bound manuscript – The bundle is presumably Bilbo's mithril coat, the manuscript the memoirs he is said to have been writing at the end of *The Hobbit*.

32 (I: 40): 'I do – when I know anything

32 (I: 40). something to talk about for nine days, or ninety-nine more likely – An allusion to the phrase *nine days' wonder*, something that causes a great sensation for a short while, and is then forgotten; but also a reference to the final chapter of *The Hobbit*, where 'the return of Mr Bilbo Baggins . . . was a great deal more than a nine days' wonder'.

32 (I: 41): 'Well, I've made up my mind

32 (I: 41). I want to see mountains again – Bilbo's adventures in *The Hobbit* took him over (and beneath) the Misty Mountains, east to the Lonely Mountain. On 31 July 1947 Tolkien wrote to Stanley Unwin, who was about to travel to Switzerland, 'how I long to see the snows and the great heights again!' (*Letters*, p. 123). His own holiday in Switzerland in 1911 inspired the mountains of *The Hobbit*, and evidently other features of the landscape of Middle-earth; see also notes for pp. 226, 283, 795.

32 (I: 41): 'I am old, Gandalf

32 (I: 41). I feel all thin, sort of *stretched* . . . like butter that has been scraped over too much bread – A warning sign that Bilbo's ring has extended his life, but at the cost of his health. In ?late 1951 Tolkien wrote to Milton Waldman: 'The view is taken [in *The Lord of the Rings*] (as clearly reappears later in the case of the Hobbits that have the Ring for a while) that each "Kind" has a natural span integral to its biological and spiritual nature. This cannot really be *increased* qualitatively or quantitatively; so that prolongation in time is like stretching a wire ever tauter, or "spreading butter ever thinner" – it becomes an intolerable torment' (*Letters*, p. 155).

33 (I: 41): 'Well yes – and no

33 (I: 41). Now it comes to it, I don't like parting with it at all – Tolkien subtly reveals through this conversation the hold that the Ring has on Bilbo. Years later, Gandalf will tell Frodo that on the night when Bilbo left Bag End 'he said and did things then that filled me with a fear that no words of Saruman could allay. I knew at last that something dark and deadly was at work' (Book I, Chapter 2, p. 48, I: 57).

34 (I: 42): Gandalf's eyes flashed

34 (I: 42). Gandalf the Grey – For Gandalf *the Grey*, see note for p. 258.

34 (I: 43): Bilbo drew his hand over his eyes

34 (I: 43). like an eye looking at me – A foreshadow of the Eye of Sauron, searching for the Ring. Compare the experience of Frodo on Amon Hen, in Book II, Chapter 10.

35 (I: 44): *The Road goes ever on and on*

35 (I: 44). *The Road goes ever on and on* – A recording by Tolkien of this poem is included on Disc 1 of *The J.R.R. Tolkien Audio Collection*. The composer Donald Swann set this and other poems by Tolkien to music, together published as *The Road Goes Ever On: A Song Cycle* (first edition 1967).

Bilbo's walking-song echoes the poem he recites in the final chapter of *The Hobbit*:

Roads go ever ever on,
Over rock and under tree,
By caves where never sun has shone,
By streams that never find the sea:

Over snow by winter sown,
And through the merry flowers of June,
Over grass and over stone,
And under mountains in the moon.

Roads go ever ever on
Under cloud and under star,
Yet feet that wandering have gone
Turn at last to home afar.
Eyes that fire and sword have seen
And horror in the halls of stone
Look at last on meadows green
And trees and hills they long have known.

Frodo will sing a variation of 'The Road goes ever on and on' in Book I, Chapter 3, and Bilbo yet another in Book VI, Chapter 6. In 1956 Tolkien commented in notes on W.H. Auden's review of *The Return of the King* that 'most men make some journeys. Whether long or short, with an errand or simply to go "there and back again", is not of primary importance. As I tried to express it in Bilbo's Walking Song, even an afternoon-to-evening walk may have important effects. When Sam had got no further than the Woody End [Book I, Chapter 3] he had already had an "eye-opener"' (*Letters*, p. 239).

Douglas A. Anderson has suggested in *The Annotated Hobbit* (pp. 360–1) that the inspiration for *The Road Goes Ever On* may be the poem 'Romance' by E.F.A. Geach, first published in the collection *Oxford Poetry 1918*, reprinted in 1922 immediately following Tolkien's poem *Goblin Feet* in the anthology *Fifty New Poems for Children*:

Round the Next Corner and in the next street
Adventure lies in wait for you.
Oh, who can tell what you may meet
Round the next corner and in the next street!
Could life be anything but sweet
When all is hazardous and new
Round the next corner and in the next street?
Adventure lies in wait for you.

36 (I: 44): He paused, silent

36 (I: 44). in the field and tents – Editions prior to 2004 have plural 'fields' ('in the fields and tents'), an error which entered in the typescript prepared for the printer and overlooked by Tolkien in proof. The manuscript and earlier typescript of the chapter have 'field'.

37 (I: 45): Inside in the hall

37 (I: 45). Inside in the hall there was piled a large assortment of packages and parcels and small articles of furniture. – A list of presents given by Bilbo with humorous messages existed in the first chapter from its earliest draft; as this progressed, Tolkien changed the details several times. On 25 September 1954 he wrote to Naomi Mitchison:

> I am more conscious of my sketchiness in the archaeology and *realien* [realities, technical facts] than in the economics: clothes, agricultural implements, metal-working, pottery, architecture and the like. Not to mention music and its apparatus. I am not incapable of or unaware of economic thought; and I think as far as the 'mortals' go, Men, Hobbits, and Dwarfs [*sic*], that the situations are so devised that economic likelihood is there and could be worked out: Gondor has sufficient 'townlands' and fiefs with a good water and road approach to provide for its population; and clearly has many industries though these are hardly alluded to. The Shire is placed in a water and mountain situation and a distance from the sea and a latitude that would give it a natural fertility, quite apart from the stated fact that it was a well-tended region when they took it over (no doubt with a good deal of older arts and crafts). The Shire-hobbits have no very great need of metals, but the Dwarfs are agents; and in the east of the Mountains of Lune are some of their mines. . . . Some of the modernities found among them (I think especially of *umbrellas*) are probably, I think certainly, a mistake, of the same order as their silly names, and tolerable with them only as a deliberate 'anglicization' to point the contrast between them and other peoples in the most familiar terms. I do not think people of that sort and stage of life and development can be both peaceable and very brave and tough 'at a pinch'. Experience in two wars has confirmed me in that view. [*Letters* pp. 196–7]

Critics have commented on the contrast between Hobbit culture and that of Gondor. The latter, as the older society, it is presumed, should be the more advanced, but the reverse seems to be true – at least, if one measures 'advancement' by material goods and familiar Western customs. The point has also been made that so many details of Hobbit society are anachronistic in a pre-industrial world; but China had clocks, silk, paper, printing, and gunpowder long before they were known in Europe. See further, Christina Scull, '*The Hobbit* and Tolkien's Other Pre-War Writings', *Mallorn* 30 (September 1993).

38 (I: 46): Every one of the various parting gifts

38 (I: 46). Old Winyards – 'A wine – but, of course, in fact a place-name, meaning "the Old Vineyards" [in the Southfarthing]. *Winyard* is actually preserved as a place-name in England, descending from Old English before the assimilation to French and Latin *vin-*' (*Nomenclature*).

39 (I: 47–8): 'Foiled again!'

39 (I: 47). Fiddlesticks! – Nonsense!

39 (I: 48): Then they went round the hole

39 (I: 48). legendary gold ... is, as everyone knows, anyone's for the finding – In editions prior to 2004 *everyone* and *anyone* were printed throughout the text either as single words or as *every one* and *any one*, with alternate forms even on the same page. In the current edition these have been regularized as *everyone* and *anyone*, according to the most predominant usage in the 2002 copy-text and with reference to the *Lord of the Rings* papers at Marquette.

40 (I: 48): 'Then I forgive you

40 (I: 48). pony-trap – A two-wheeled carriage pulled by a pony.

Chapter 2

THE SHADOW OF THE PAST

For drafts and history of this chapter, see *The Return of the Shadow*, pp. 75–87, 250–72, 318–23; *The Treason of Isengard*, pp. 21–9, 38–9.

42 (I: 51): But in the meantime

42 (I: 51). run off into the Blue. . . . The blame was mostly laid on Gandalf. – *Into the Blue* 'into the unknown, into the "wide (or wild) blue yonder"'. In *The Hobbit*, Chapter 1, Bilbo says: 'Not the Gandalf who was responsible for so many quiet lads and lasses going off into the Blue for mad adventures?'

42 (I: 51): 'If only that dratted wizard

42 (I: 51). a party in honour of Bilbo's hundred-and-twelfth birthday, which he called a Hundred-weight Feast – In Britain a *hundredweight* is 112 pounds.

42–3 (I: 51–2): He lived alone, as Bilbo had done

42 (I: 51). he had a good many friends, especially among the younger hobbits (mostly descendants of the Old Took). . . . Folco Boffin and Fredegar Bolger were two of these; but his closest friends were Peregrin Took (usually called Pippin), and Merry Brandybuck (his real name was Meriadoc – Frodo was born in S.R. 1368, Folco in 1378, Fredegar 'Fatty' in 1380 (as was Sam Gamgee), Merry in 1382, and Pippin in 1390. Of the four leading hobbits of *The Lord of the Rings*, Frodo is by far the eldest, twelve years older than Sam, fourteen older than Merry, and twenty-two older than Pippin. Folco helps Frodo pack for his move to Crickhollow in Book I, Chapter 3, then has no more part in the story. It has been noted that Folco, Fredegar, Pippin, and Merry are all great-great-grandsons of the Old Took (Frodo is a great-grandson).

43 (I: 52): There were rumours of strange things

43 (I: 52). Elves, who seldom walked in the Shire, could now be seen passing westward through the woods in the evening, passing and not returning; but they were leaving Middle-earth and were no longer concerned with its troubles. There were, however, dwarves on the road in unusual numbers. The ancient East–West Road ran through the Shire to its end at the Grey Havens, and dwarves had always used it on their way to their mines in the Blue Mountains. They were the hobbits' chief source of news. . . . – As first published this passage read: 'Elves, who seldom walked in the Shire, could now be seen passing westward through the woods in the evening, passing but not returning; but they shook their heads and went away singing sadly to themselves. There were, however, dwarves in unusual numbers. [*paragraph:*] The great West Road, of course, ran through the Shire over the Brandywine Bridge, and dwarves had always used it from time to time. They were the hobbits' chief source of news. . . .' Tolkien intended the revision to include 'through the Shire *over the Brandywine Bridge* to its end at the Grey Havens', but the words here italicized were omitted in the second edition (1965) by Ballantine Books, and Tolkien chose to accept the error.

On the elves passing westward, Tolkien wrote to Naomi Mitchison on 25 September 1954:

> But the promise was made to the Eldar (the High Elves – not to other varieties, they had long before made their irrevocable choice, preferring Middle-earth to paradise) for their sufferings in the struggle with the prime Dark Lord [Melkor] had still to be fulfilled: that they should always be able to leave Middle-earth, if they wished, and pass over Sea to the True West by the Straight Road, and so come to Eressëa – but so pass out of time and history, never to return. [*Letters*, p. 198]

In his unfinished index Tolkien defines the 'East Road' as 'the great ancient road from the Grey Havens to Rivendell, called by Hobbits the East Road (or great East Road from Brandywine Bridge eastwards)'.

The *Blue Mountains* are the Ered Luin; see note for p. 4.

43 (I: 52). But now Frodo often met strange dwarves of far countries, seeking refuge in the West. – As first published this sentence read: 'But now Frodo often met strange dwarves of different kinds, coming out of southern lands.' It was revised in the second edition (1965).

43 (I: 52). Mordor – *Mordor* 'black-land' (*Index*) is the land under the direct rule of Sauron, east of the mountains of the Ephel Dúath in the East of Middle-earth. The name is derived from Sindarin *morn* (adjective) 'dark, black' + *dôr* 'land'. In a letter to Alina Dadlez, foreign rights coordinator at George Allen & Unwin, 23 February 1961, Tolkien commented that

> the placing of Mordor in the east was due to simple narrative and geographical necessity, within my 'mythology'. The original stronghold of Evil was (as traditionally) in the North [the lands of Melkor/Morgoth in 'The Silmarillion']; but as that had been destroyed, and was indeed under the sea, there had to be a new stronghold, far removed from the Valar, the Elves, and the sea-power of Númenor. [*Letters*, p. 307]

44 (I: 53): That name the hobbits only knew in legends

44 (I: 53). the evil power in Mirkwood had been driven out by the White Council – See Gandalf's account in Book II, Chapter 2. In *The Hobbit*,

Chapter 19, it is revealed that 'Gandalf had been to a great council of the white wizards, masters of lore and good magic; and that they had at last driven the Necromancer from his dark hold in the south of Mirkwood'. In the first and second editions of *The Hobbit* (1937, 1951) Gandalf says of this that 'the North is freed from that horror for many long years, I hope'; but as revised in 1966, with the events of *The Lord of the Rings* in mind, he says instead that 'the North *will be* freed from that horror for many long years, *I hope*' (emphasis ours).

In *Of the Rings of Power and the Third Age* it is said that when, after a time of watchful peace, the shadow of evil fell upon Mirkwood, 'in that time was first made the Council of the Wise that is called the White Council, and therein were Elrond and Galadriel and Círdan, and other lords of the Eldar, and with them were Mithrandir [Gandalf] and Curunír [Saruman]' (*The Silmarillion*, p. 300). On the *White Council*, see further, *The Hunt for the Ring* in *Unfinished Tales*, especially pp. 349–52.

44 (I: 53). the Dark Tower had been rebuilt – Barad-dûr, the fortress of Sauron, built in Mordor as a stronghold against the power of the Númenóreans *c.* 1000–1600 (Second Age), besieged in Second Age 3434–41. In that conflict the tower itself was broken, but its foundations, built with the power of the Ring, were not destroyed. Sauron returned openly to power and began to rebuild Barad-dûr in Third Age 2951.

44 (I: 53). Trolls – In Appendix F it is said that

> *Troll* has been used to translate the Sindarin *Torog*. In their beginning far back in the twilight of the Elder Days, these were creatures of dull and lumpish nature. . . . But Sauron had made use of them, teaching them what little they could learn and increasing their wits with wickedness. . . .
>
> But at the end of the Third Age a troll-race not before seen appeared in southern Mirkwood and in the mountain borders of Mordor. . . . Olog-hai were they called in the Black Speech. That Sauron bred them none doubted, though from what stock was not known. . . . Trolls they were, but filled with the evil will of their master: a fell race, strong, agile, fierce and cunning, but harder than stone. [p. 1132, I: 410]

In Book III, Chapter 4, Treebeard states his belief that Trolls are counterfeits made by Morgoth, the Dark Lord of an earlier age, in mockery of Ents. See further, note for p. 205.

44 (I: 53): Little of all this

44 (I: 53). *The Green Dragon* – Dozens of pubs with this name are recorded in Britain. There was one in Oxford, in different buildings in St Aldates, from 1587 until its final demolition in 1926.

44 (I: 53). the spring of Frodo's fiftieth year – It is S.R. 1418.

44 (I: 53): Sam Gamgee was sitting

44 (I: 53). Sam Gamgee – On 24 December 1944 Tolkien wrote to his son Christopher:

> Cert[ainly] Sam is the most closely drawn character, the successor to Bilbo of the first book, the genuine hobbit. Frodo is not so interesting, because he has to be highminded, and has (as it were) a vocation. The book will prob[ably] end up with Sam. Frodo will naturally become too ennobled and rarefied by the achievement of the great Quest, and will pass West with all the great figures; but S[am] will settle down to the Shire and gardens and inns. [*Letters*, p. 105]

44 (I: 53): 'No thank 'ee'

44 (I: 53). No thank 'ee – 'No thank you'; *'ee* is a colloquial contraction for *ye*.

44 (I: 53): 'All right,' said Sam

44 (I: 53). Tree-men, these giants . . . one bigger than a tree was seen up away beyond the North Moors – As first written in draft, Sam spoke of 'giants . . . nigh as big as a tower or leastways a tree', changed at the time of writing to 'Tree-men'. Christopher Tolkien comments in *The Return of the Shadow*: 'Was this passage . . . the first premonition of the Ents? But long before my father had referred to "Tree-men" in connection with the voyages of Eärendel' (p. 254). In Appendix D it is said that it was 'a jesting idiom in the Shire to speak of "on Friday the first" when referring to a day that did not exist [since no month began on a Friday in the Shire Calendar], or to a day on which very unlikely events such as the flying of pigs or (in the Shire) the walking of trees might occur' (p. 1109, III: 387).

44 (I: 53). North Moors – 'The lower-slopes of the Hills of Evendim, and north-boundary of the Shire' (*Index*).

44 (I: 53): 'My cousin Hal for one

44 (I: 53). My cousin Hal for one. He works for Mr. Boffin at Overhill and goes up to the Northfarthing for the hunting. – *Cousin Hal* is Halfast Gamgee, son of Hamfast Gamgee's younger brother, Halfred of Overhill.

In a draft revision of this chapter the 'Tree-men' were seen by Jo Button, who worked for 'Mr Fosco Boffin of Northope', at that point in the development of the story Bilbo's first cousin once removed, the son of Jago Boffin and grandson of Hugo Boffin. Jago and Hugo survived into the final Boffin family tree (published at last in Appendix C in the edition of 2004), but in Fosco's place is 'Vigo'. Tolkien later changed *Northope* to *The Yale*, then to *Overhill* (moving 'The Yale' elsewhere; see note for p. 76). In his notes for the Dutch translator Tolkien said of *Overhill*: 'plainly the village received its name since it was *over* or beyond The Hill from Hobbiton'.

Hal's hunting in the Northfarthing is presumably for food: in the Prologue it is said that Hobbits killed nothing for sport.

44 (I: 53): 'But this one was as big as an elm tree

44 (I: 53). seven yards to a stride – If the 'giant' is an Ent, then this is an exaggeration: a true Ent-stride measures four feet (see note for p. 470).

45 (I: 54): 'And I've heard tell that Elves

45 (I: 54). the White Towers – The elf-towers on the Tower Hills; see note for p. 7.

45 (I: 54). elven-ships – One of the issues considered in preparing the anniversary edition of 2004 was that of compound words beginning *elven-* or *Elven-* (of which *elven-ships* is merely the first to appear in the text). In 1975 Christopher Tolkien advised Allen & Unwin, regarding a list of suggested emendations to a reprint of the 1974 Unwin Books edition of *The Lord of the Rings*, that in words such as *dwarf-candles*, *elf-fountains*, and *goblin-barkers* the first element is used attributively and is properly in lower case. Of similar kind are forms in *elven-* : *elven-blade*, *elven-blood*, *elven-boat*, *elven-bows*, *elven-brooch*, *elven-cake*, *elven-cloak(s)*, *elven-eyes*, *elven-fair*, *elven-fingers*, *elven-flowers*, *elven-glass*, *elven-grey*, *elven-hoods*, *elven-light*, *elven-maids* (excepting the poetic 'An Elven-maid there was of old', Book II, Chapter 6), *elven-mail*, *elven-princeling*, *elven-rope*, *elven-runes*, *elven-script*, *elven-sheath*, *elven-ship(s)*, *elven-skill*, *elven-song*, *elven-strands*, *elven-sword*, *elven-tongue*, *elven-tower*, *elven-voices*, *elven-white*, *elven-wise* (but compare 'the Elven-wise, lords of the Eldar', Book II, Chapter 1), and *elven-work*. In Tolkien's usage these are clearly in the majority compared with capitalized *Elven-folk*, *Elven-home* (as a place name), *Elven-kin*, *Elven-kind*, *Elven-king(s)*, *Elven-lady* ('the Elven-lady', lady of the Elves, i.e. Galadriel), *Elven-latin*, *Elven-lord(s)*, *Elven-lore*, *Elven-rings*, *Elven-river* (i.e. the Esgalduin), *Elven-smiths*, *Elven-speech* (but compare *elven-tongue*), *Elven-stars* (poetically), *Elven-tears* (poetically), *Elven-way* ('the Elven-way from Hollin'), and *(the) Elven-wise*. Of this second group, most appear to be specific names or titles, or to refer to specific groups, e.g. *Elven-rings* denotes the whole body of rings made by the Elves of Eregion, and *Elven-smiths* refers to those particular Elves; and on this basis we emended one instance of *elven-folk* in Appendix F ('the Elven-folk of Mirkwood and Lórien') to *Elven-folk*. *Elven-lore*, used only twice in *The Lord of the Rings*, seems of a more general nature, akin to *elven-runes*, *elven-script*, etc., unless it means a specific body of knowledge, the lore of the Elves; and *Elven-speech* is surely similar, if not equivalent, to *elven-tongue*, but in the context of its single use in *The Lord of the Rings* (Appendix F, 'the native speech of the Númenoreans remained for the most part their ancestral Mannish tongue, the Adûnaic, and to this in the latter days of their pride their kings and lords returned, abandoning the Elven-speech') it could be taken to mean the body of Elvish languages and was left unchanged. Capitalized *Elven-tongue* and lower case *elven-tongue* both appeared in *The Lord of the Rings* until the second printing (1967) of the Allen & Unwin second edition, when Tolkien made a deliberate effort to regularize these as *elven-tongue*, in the process overlooking five instances emended in 2004.

A related difficulty occurs with compounds beginning *elf-* or *Elf-*. Here too there is much variation: *elf-banes, elf-blade, elf-cake, elf-children, elf-cloak, elf-eyes, elf-faces, elf-fashion, elf-fountains, elf-hair, elf-horse, elf-letters, elf-runes, elf-speech, elf-stone, elf-sword, elf-tongue, elf-woman, elf-wrights,* and *elf-wrought*, but *Elf-friend(s), Elf-kin, Elf-kindred, Elf-kingdoms, Elf-kings, Elf-lady, Elf-lord(s), Elf-magic, Elf-minstrels, Elf-sires, Elf-towers, Elf-wardens,* and *Elf-warrior.* It has seemed correct to regularize stray instances of *Elf-runes* to *elf-runes*, *elf-friend(s)* to *Elf-friend(s)* ('friend of the Elves', i.e. the race as a whole), *elf-lord* to *Elf-lord*, and *elf-country* to *Elf-country*, both forms of each having appeared in previous editions.

45 (I: 54): 'Well, I don't know

45 (I: 54). Fair Folk – 'The beautiful people. (Based on Welsh *Tylwyth teg* "the Beautiful Kindred" = Fairies). Title of the Elves' (*Nomenclature*).

45 (I: 54): 'Oh, they're both cracked'

45 (I: 54). moonshine – In this sense, foolish talk, without substance.

46 (I: 55): Next morning after a late breakfast

46 (I: 55). the new green of spring – It seems clear from a thorough analysis of *The Lord of the Rings* that Tolkien preferred to use lower case letters for the names of seasons except in personifications, proverbs, and (usually) poetry. Here for *spring* (emended from *Spring*), and in a few other instances, capitalization of the names of seasons was regularized in the edition of 2004.

46 (I: 55): Gandalf was thinking of a spring

46 (I: 55). a spring, nearly eighty years before, when Bilbo had run out of Bag End without a handkerchief – At this moment in *The Lord of the Rings* it is 13 April 1418. Bilbo had left Hobbiton with Thorin and company in April 1341 (Third Age 2941), the day after the 'unexpected party', but the precise date is not clear: see *The Annotated Hobbit*, 2nd edn., pp. 56–7. In Chapter 1 of *The Hobbit* it is said that 'to the end of his days Bilbo could never remember how he found himself outside, without a hat, a walking-stick or any money, or anything that he usually took when he went out. . . . Very puffed he was, when he got to Bywater . . . and found he had come without a pocket-handkerchief!'

46 (I: 55). he smoked and blew smoke-rings with the same vigour and delight – At the 'unexpected party' in *The Hobbit*, Chapter 1, '[Thorin] was blowing the most enormous smoke-rings, and wherever he told one to go, it went . . . but wherever it went it was not quick enough to escape Gandalf. Pop! he sent a smaller smoke-ring from his short clay-pipe straight through each one of Thorin's. Then Gandalf's smoke-ring would go green and come back to hover over the wizard's head.'

47 (I: 56): 'In Eregion long ago

47 (I: 56). In Eregion long ago many Elven-rings were made, magic rings as you call them, and they were, of course, of various kinds: some more potent and some less. The lesser rings were only essays in the craft before it was full-grown, and to the Elven-smiths they were but trifles – yet still to my mind dangerous for mortals. But the Great Rings, the Rings of Power, they were perilous. – In his unfinished index Tolkien describes *Eregion* as a 'region of a dwelling of Elves in the Second Age, near the West-gate of Moria, famous for crafts (especially those of Celebrimbor "Silverhand") and the making of Rings of Power'. It was also called (by Men) *Hollin*; see note for p. 282. Sindarin *Eregion* 'holly-region' (*Nomenclature*, under *Hollin*) contains the element *ereg* 'thorn, holly'.

In *The Hobbit* Bilbo's ring is no more than a useful device for getting out of tough spots by means of invisibility. When it became a link between *The Hobbit* and its sequel, however, Tolkien needed to explore its nature and develop its history. As he wrote to Christopher Bretherton on 16 July 1964, 'to be the burden of a large story' the Ring 'had to be of supreme importance. I then linked it with the (originally) quite casual reference [in *The Hobbit*] to the Necromancer', who by other names already existed in the 'Silmarillion' mythology (*Letters*, p. 346). In an early draft of *The Lord of the Rings* 'the Ring-lord' made many rings

> and sent them out through the world to snare people. He sent them to all sorts of folk – the Elves had many, and there are now many elfwraiths in the world, but the Ring-lord cannot rule them; the goblins got many, and the invisible goblins are very evil and wholly under the Lord; dwarves I [Gandalf] don't believe had any; some say the rings don't work on them: they are too solid. Men had few, but they were most quickly overcome. . . . [*The Return of the Shadow*, p. 75]

Later Tolkien wrote:

> In ancient days the Necromancer, the Dark Lord Sauron, made many magic rings of various properties that gave various powers to their possessors. He dealt them out lavishly and sowed them abroad to ensnare all peoples, but specially Elves and Men. For those that used the rings, according to their strength and will and hearts, fell quicker or slower under the power of the rings, and the dominion of their

> maker. Three, Seven, Nine and One he made of special potency: for their possessors became not only invisible to all in this world, if they wished, but could see both the world under the sun and the other side in which invisible things move. And they had (what is called) good luck, and (what seemed) endless life. Though, as I [Gandalf] say, what power the Rings conferred on each possessor depended on what use they made of them – on what they were themselves, and what they desired. [*The Return of the Shadow*, p. 258]

Only after much further thought did the final history of the Rings emerge, expressed in the present chapter and in Book II, Chapter 2 ('The Council of Elrond'): that they were made by the Elven-smiths of Eregion, with Sauron's guidance, except for the One made by Sauron himself in the fires of Orodruin, and the Three which were made by the Elf Celebrimbor, greatest of the Elven-smiths. Even from the earliest conceptions of the Rings it is said that many were made, of which some were 'of special potency', and thus the 'Great Rings' were distinguished from 'the lesser rings'. See further, notes for pp. 50, 242.

47 (I: 56): 'A mortal, Frodo

47 (I: 56). the Dark Power that rules the Rings – Prior to the edition of 2004 'Dark Power' appeared, here and in two other instances on this page, as 'dark power', in reference to Sauron. All other instances of *Dark Power* in *The Lord of the Rings*, however (sometimes used to mean Morgoth), are consistently capitalized.

47 (I: 57): 'Known?' said Gandalf

47 (I: 57). the Wise – The Istari (Wizards) and the greatest of the Eldar in Middle-earth. Compare *White Council*, note for p. 44.

47–8 (I: 57): 'When did I first begin to guess?'

48 (I: 57). Saruman the White – *Saruman*, derived from Old English *searu* 'device, design, contrivance, art', is the name among Men of the Wizard called by the Eldar *Curunír* 'man of skill'.

48 (I: 57): 'Maybe not,' answered Gandalf

48 (I: 57). Hobbits are, or were, no concern of his. Yet he is great among the Wise. He is the chief of my order and the head of the Council. His knowledge is deep, but his pride has grown with it, and he takes ill any meddling. – In *The Tale of Years* it is said that 'when maybe a thousand years had passed' in the Third Age,

> and the first shadow had fallen on Greenwood the Great [Mirkwood], the *Istari* or Wizards appeared in Middle-earth. It was afterwards said that they came out of the Far West and were messengers sent to contest the power of Sauron, and to unite all those who had the will to resist

> him; but they were forbidden to match his power with power, or to seek to dominate Elves or Men by force and fear. [p. 1084, III: 365]

And further, in *Of the Rings of Power and the Third Age*:

> In the likeness of Men they appeared, old but vigorous, and they changed little with the years, and aged but slowly, though great cares lay on them; great wisdom they had, and many powers of mind and hand. Long they journeyed far and wide among Elves and Men, and held converse also with beasts and with birds; and the peoples of Middle-earth gave to them many names, for their true names they did not reveal. Chief among them were those whom the Elves called Mithrandir and Curunír, but Men in the North named Gandalf and Saruman. Of these Curunír was the eldest and came first, and after him came Mithrandir and Radagast, and others of the Istari who went into the east of Middle-earth, and do not come into these tales. [*The Silmarillion*, pp. 299–300]

An essay on this subject, with related writings, was published as *The Istari* in *Unfinished Tales*, pp. 388–402. There it is said that

> *Wizard* is a translation of Quenya istar (Sindarin *ithron*): one of the members of an 'order' (as they called it), claiming to possess, and exhibiting, eminent knowledge of the history and nature of the World. The translation (though suitable in its relation to 'wise' and other ancient words of knowing, similar to that of *istar* in Quenya) is not perhaps happy, since the *Heren Istarion* or 'Order of Wizards' was quite distinct from the 'wizards' and 'magicians' of later legend. . . . [*Unfinished Tales*, p. 388]

In the *Valaquenta* it is made clear that the Istari were Maiar, beings 'of the same order as the Valar but of less degree' (*The Silmarillion*, p. 30). In correspondence regarding the Wizards, Tolkien called them the equivalent of Angels. (In *The Silmarillion* the term *Ainur* 'the holy ones' is used to refer to both Valar and Maiar, but neither *Ainur* nor *Maiar* are used in *The Lord of the Rings*.)

Saruman first took an interest in Hobbits, and in the Shire, because they were an interest of Gandalf, of whom Saruman was jealous. See note for p. 75, and accounts in *The Hunt for the Ring* in *Unfinished Tales*, pp. 347–52.

48 (I: 57): 'And I waited

48 (I: 57). a fear that no words of Saruman could allay – The words referred to, to the effect that the One Ring would never be found in Middle-earth, are reported by Gandalf in Book II, Chapter 2.

48–9 (I: 58): 'He felt better at once,' said Gandalf

48 (I: 58). Among the Wise I am the only one that goes in for hobbit-lore – But in *The Hunt for the Ring* it is said that Saruman also studied the Hobbits, and that Gandalf knew that he did.

50 (I: 59). [Ring inscription] – Tolkien struggled to draw a 'facsimile' of the Ring inscription for reproduction that would be good enough to represent, to his eye, 'Elvish work', while suffering from fibrositis (rheumatic inflammation) which affected his writing. He was disappointed with proofs of his first attempts, which he felt too large and sprawling; and at the eleventh hour he noticed that he had written as the sixteenth letter in the second line (including vowels) *hwesta* (with extended stem), value *kh*, rather than *unque* (with extended stem), value *gh* (see Appendix E): the word in the Ring inscription (in the Black Speech) at this point is *agh*, not *akh* (see Book II, Chapter 2). Allen & Unwin replaced the block with the version subsequently printed in all editions except the fiftieth anniversary edition of 2004: there the earlier, rejected lettering was reproduced by mistake, rephotographed from the original art in the Bodleian Library, Oxford. In the first edition, as in most editions of *The Lord of the Rings*, the Ring inscription was printed in black as an economy measure, rather than red.

In some early Ballantine Books printings the inscription was printed upside-down.

50 (I: 59): 'I cannot read the fiery letters'

50 (I: 59). I cannot read the fiery letters – They are inscribed on the Ring in a heavily flourished Tengwar.

A recording by Tolkien of the passage from these words to the end of the Ring-verse is included on Disc 1 of *The J.R.R. Tolkien Audio Collection*.

50 (I: 59): It is only two lines

50 (I: 59). two lines of a verse long known in Elven-lore – The two lines, at least, must have been composed by Sauron, who engraved them on the Ring. They are 'the words that the Smiths of Eregion heard, and knew that they had been betrayed' (Book II, Chapter 2, p. 255, I: 267). It is not clear when the rest of the Ring-verse was written, or by whom.

The second line of the two lines quoted by Gandalf was mistakenly omitted in early printings of the HarperCollins edition of 1994, and in other British and American editions based on that resetting.

50 (I: 59–60): *Three Rings for the Elven-kings under the sky*

50 (I: 59–60). *Three Rings for the Elven-kings . . .* – In the earliest complete version of the Ring-verse there are nine Rings 'for the Elven-kings under moon and star' and three 'for Mortal Men that wander far' (*The Return of the Shadow*, p. 269, n. 14). Another had twelve Rings for Men, nine for the Dwarves, and three for the Elves. The numbers and powers of the Rings varied as the story developed. The term *Elven-kings* seems to be merely poetic; later in this chapter Gandalf refers, more appropriately, to 'the Elf-lords', i.e. the leaders of the Elves in Middle-earth.

51 (I: 60): 'Ah!' said Gandalf

51 (I: 60). the Black Years – The latter part of the Second Age marked by the forging of the Rings of Power, the dominion of Sauron over much of Middle-earth, his war against the Elves and Men, the fall of Númenor, and the defeat of Sauron by the Last Alliance. Called by the Elves the 'Days of Flight',

> in that time many of the Elves of Middle-earth fled to Lindon and thence over the seas never to return; and many were destroyed by Sauron and his servants. But in Lindon Gil-galad still maintained his power, and Sauron dared not as yet to pass the Mountains of Ered Luin nor to assail the Havens; and Gil-galad was aided by the Númenóreans. Elsewhere Sauron reigned, and those who would be free took refuge in the fastnesses of wood and mountain, and ever fear pursued them. [*Of the Rings of Power and the Third Age* in *The Silmarillion*, p. 289]

51 (I: 60): 'But last night I told you

51 (I: 60). hold in Mirkwood – Dol Guldur; see note for p. 250.

51 (I: 60–1): 'The Three, fairest of all

51 (I: 60). Nine he gave to Mortal Men – In *Of the Rings of Power and the Third Age* it is said that 'those who used the Nine Rings became mighty in their day' (*The Silmarillion*, p. 289); but according to the *Akallabêth* three of the Men whom Sauron ensnared were already 'great lords of Númenórean race' (*The Silmarillion*, p. 267). One of the nine, Khamûl, commander of Dol Guldur, was from the East; see further, *The Hunt for the Ring* in *Unfinished Tales*.

In 'Ðe Us Ðas Beagas Geaf (He Who Gave Us These Rings): Sauron and the Perversion of Anglo-Saxon Ethos', *Mythlore* 16, no. 1, whole no. 59 (Autumn 1989), Leslie Stratyner argues that Sauron's practice of giving rings is a perverted reflection that of the Anglo-Saxon lord, who gave his thanes rings and ornaments in exchange for their love and loyalty, but Sauron's rings, 'the ones that he controls, are tokens of evil, gifts designed not to reward but to enslave' (p. 6).

51 (I: 60). Ringwraiths – *Ringwraith* is a 'translation' of Black Speech *Nazgûl*, from *nazg* 'ring' + *gûl* 'wraith' (compare *ghoul*). In 'Orcs, Wraiths, Wights: Tolkien's Images of Evil', *Tolkien and his Literary Resonances: Views of Middle-earth* (2000), Tom Shippey contends that the wraith in *The Lord of the Rings* is strikingly original: there is nothing like it in any early epic, not even *Beowulf*. . . . The entry on 'wraith' in the *OED* shows a rather characteristic self-contradiction. Meaning 1 offers this definition: 'An apparition or spectre of a dead person: a phantom or ghost,' giving Gavin Douglas's 1513 translation of the *Aeneid* as its first citation. As sense b, however, and once again citing Douglas's *Aeneid* in support, the *OED* offers, "An immaterial or spectral appearance of a living being." Are wraiths, then, alive or dead? The *OED* editors accept both solutions . . . [but have] nothing at all to say about the word's etymology, commenting only of "obscure origin" – just the kind of puzzle that repeatedly caught Tolkien's attention. [p. 189]

51–2 (I: 61): 'So it is now

51 (I: 61). he [Sauron] let a great part of his own former power pass into it [the Ring] – On 14 October 1958 Tolkien wrote to Rhona Beare that 'the Ring of Sauron is only one of the various mythical treatments of the placing of one's life, or power, in some external object, which is thus exposed to capture or destruction with disastrous results to oneself' (*Letters*, p. 279). On this wider subject, see Sir James George Frazer, *The Golden Bough: A Study in Magic and Religion* (1922), Chapter 66, 'The External Soul in Folk-tales'. On this aspect of the One Ring, see further, note for pp. 1036–7.

52 (I: 61): 'And this is the dreadful chance, Frodo

52 (I: 61). He believed that the One had perished – Some readers have argued that if, as is said in Book II, Chapter 2, the Ring contained much of Sauron's former power and was the force that protected the foundations of Barad-dûr, Sauron could *not* have believed that the Ring had perished, for he still had his power, and the foundations of the Dark Tower survived. This, however, is to argue from known results following the destruction of the Ring in Book VI. The Ring was unique in history, and it may be that even its maker could not say what would happen to him were it to be destroyed, any more than the Wise could say with certainty whether the Three Rings would fail if the One were no more.

52 (I: 61): 'It was taken from him,' said Gandalf

52 (I: 61). estranged – Divided in feeling or affection.

52 (I: 61). The strength of the Elves to resist him was greater long ago. . . . The Men of Westernesse came to their aid. – The war of the Elves against Sauron began in Second Age 1693 and lasted until 1700, when a great navy from Númenor sailed to their aid. From 1701 Sauron concentrated his attention eastwards; but so great was the power of the Númenóreans that at last, in 3262, he surrendered and went to Númenor as a hostage. There he corrupted the hearts of most of the people, and encouraged them to make war on the Undying Lands in the West, as punishment for which Númenor was destroyed. Only the Faithful among the Númenóreans survived, cast up on the shores of Middle-earth, and Sauron, who returned to Mordor. Once again he took up the Ring, and warred against the Eldar and the Men of Westernesse (Númenor). Elendil, chief of the Númenóreans in exile, and the Elven-king Gil-galad formed the Last Alliance of Elves and Men and laid siege to the Dark Tower, as is told in this chapter and in Book II, Chapter 2.

52 (I: 61): 'But for the moment

52 (I: 61). It was Gil-galad, Elven-king and Elendil of Westernesse – *Gil-galad* is Sindarin for 'star of bright light'. In Tolkien's writings the character first appears in *The Fall of Númenor*, *c.* 1936–7, published in *The Lost Road and Other Writings*.

52 (I: 61): 'But the Ring was lost

52 (I: 61). Isildur was marching north along the east banks of the River, and near the Gladden Fields he was waylaid – This story is told at greater length in *The Disaster of the Gladden Fields* in *Unfinished Tales*, pp. 271–85. *Isildur* was the elder son of Elendil, who with his father and his brother Anárion escaped from the drowning of Númenor and founded in Middle-earth the Númenórean realms in exile. The *Gladden Fields* are 'great stretches of reeds and flags in and about the Anduin (about 100 miles south of Rivendell' (*Index*). In *Nomenclature* Tolkien comments that '*gladden* is here the name for the "flag" or iris (Old English *glædene*), now usually spelt *gladdon*, and has no connexion with English *glad*; *gladden*, verb.'

52–3 (I: 62): 'Long after, but still very long ago

52 (I: 62). Long after, but still very long ago – The story of Sméagol-Gollum builds on elements told in passing in *The Hobbit*, Chapter 5: that he had lived with his grandmother in a hole in a bank by a river, that he knew the concept of a birthday-present. But the comment that Gollum had 'lost all his friends and was driven away, alone, and crept down into the dark under the mountains' was added in the second edition (1951), as part of revisions to *The Hobbit* to bring it more into line with the developing *Lord of the Rings*.

53 (I: 62). Sméagol – The name is derived from Old English *smygel* 'a burrow, place to creep into'.

53 (I: 62): 'He had a friend called Déagol

53 (I: 62). Déagol – The name is derived from Old English *dēagol* (*dīgol*) 'secret, hidden'. Early in the writing of *The Lord of the Rings* it was (as *Dígol*) the true name of Gollum; he himself found the ring in the mud of the river-bank.

53 (I: 62): '"Give us that, Déagol, my love'

53 (I: 62). my love – A form of address to a friend or companion; compare 'my dear' occasionally used by Sam when referring to his master, Frodo. No romantic sentiment is intended. See also note for p. 730.

54 (I: 63): 'So he journeyed by night

54 (I: 63). The Ring went into the shadows with him, and even the maker, when his power had begun to grow again, could learn nothing of it. – According to *The Tale of Years*, Sméagol murdered Déagol around Third Age 2463, and took the Ring under the Misty Mountains around 2470. But already by 1050 a shadow had fallen on the Greenwood, and *c.* 1100 it was discovered that an evil power had entered Dol Guldur.

55 (I: 64–5): 'A Ring of Power looks after itself

55 (I: 64). its keeper never abandons it. At most he plays with the idea of handing it on to some one else's care – and that only at an early stage, when it first begins to grip. But as far as I know Bilbo alone in history has ever gone beyond playing, and really done it. – This is true of the One Ring, but not of all Rings of Power, of which Gandalf seems to be speaking generally. Celebrimbor gave away the Three Rings, Círdan gave his Ring to Gandalf, Gil-galad (when dying) gave his to Elrond, and Thrór gave his Ring to Thráin.

57 (I: 66): 'Light, light of Sun and Moon

57 (I: 66). Sun and Moon – The capitalization of *sun* and *moon* varies throughout *The Lord of the Rings*. When a proofreader queried this point in galleys of *The Two Towers*, Tolkien replied: 'The characters when actually "speaking" are represented as always personifying Sun (she) and Moon (he) (when not = sunlight moonlight). Occasionally this has filtered into the narrative where it was not intended, or where speech is rendered indirectly . . .' (Marquette Series 3/5/38). This, however, does not completely address instances of *Sun* and *Moon* used for poetic purposes, and otherwise there are too many debatable instances of *Sun/sun* and *Moon/moon* to judge Tolkien's intentions on the basis of a general rule.

58 (I: 67): 'The Wood-elves tracked him first

58 (I: 67). Wood-elves – The Elves of Mirkwood, first met in *The Hobbit*.

58 (I: 67): 'But at the western edge

58 (I: 67). ken – Knowledge. The Wood-elves are unfamiliar with lands south of Mirkwood.

58 (I: 67–8): 'Well, that was years ago

58 (I: 67). Aragorn – In a letter to Richard Jeffery, 17 December 1972, Tolkien replied to Jeffery's query whether *Aragorn* meant 'tree-king' (*orn* is Sindarin 'tree'):

> This cannot contain a 'tree' word. 'Tree-King' would have no special fitness for him. . . . The system by which all the names from *Malvegil* onwards [see Appendix A ii] are trisyllabic, and have only one 'significant' element (*ara* being used where the final element was of one syllable; but *ar* in other cases) is peculiar to this line of names. The *ara* is prob[ably] derived from cases where *aran* 'king' lost its *n* phonetically (as *Arathorn*), *ara-* then being used in other cases. [*Letters*, p. 426]

In a manuscript note among the Marquette Tolkien papers, quoted in *The Peoples of Middle-earth* (p. xii), Tolkien interpreted *Aragorn* to mean 'Kingly Valour'.

Here, at the first mention of his name in the text proper, Aragorn is described in superlatives: 'the greatest traveller and huntsman of this age of the world'. But the reader does not meet him for another seven chapters, and then, like the hobbits, must take his skills on trust until they are demonstrated.

58 (I: 68). turned to other paths – This was the reading in the first printing of the first edition (1954). In the unauthorized resetting of *The Fellowship of the Ring* for its second printing (1954) 'paths' was mistakenly altered to 'parts'. The error was corrected in the edition of 2004.

60 (I: 69): 'Of course, my dear Frodo

60 (I: 69). even when I was far away there has never been a day when the Shire has not been guarded by watchful eyes – That is, by the Rangers, the Dúnedain. In *The Tale of Years* it is said that *c.* 3000 (Third Age) 'the Shire is being closely guarded by the Rangers', and in 3001, when Gandalf suspects that Bilbo's ring is the One Ring, 'the guard on the Shire is doubled' (p. 1090, III: 371).

60 (I: 69). nine years ago, when I last saw you – In autumn of S.R. 1408; it is now spring of 1418.

60 (I: 70): Frodo drew the Ring out of his pocket

60 (I: 70). but he found that he had put it back in his pocket – John D. Rateliff notes in '*She* and Tolkien', *Mythlore* 8, no. 2, whole no. 28 (Summer 1981) a similarity between this incident in *The Lord of the Rings* and a passage in *She and Allan* by H. Rider Haggard, whose *She* Tolkien knew and admired:

There is also an echo of the One Ring . . . when Allan Quatermain is given a magic amulet which he is warned to keep safe. He wears it on a chain around his neck and keeps it hidden under his shirt [as Frodo does after leaving Rivendell], only bringing out on rare occasions or at great need. Soon after he receives it, a magician tells him he will not be able to throw it away even if he wanted to and challenges him to try:

> I did try, but something seemed to prevent me from accomplishing my purpose of giving the carving back to Zikali as I wished to do. First my pipe got in the way of my hand, then the elephant hairs caught in the collar of my coat; then a pang of rheumatism to which I was accustomed from an old injury, developed of a sudden in my left arm, and lastly I grew tired of bothering about the thing. [p. 7, Haggard quotation from Chapter 1]

61 (I: 70): 'Your small fire, of course

61 (I: 70). there is not now any dragon left on earth in which the old fire is hot enough – Tolkien wrote to Naomi Mitchison on 25 April 1954:

> *Dragons*. They had not stopped; since they were active in far later times, close to our own. Have I said anything to suggest a final ending of dragons? If so it should be altered. The only passage I can think of is . . . 'there is not now any dragon left on earth in which the old fire is hot enough'. But that implies, I think, that there are still dragons, if not of full primeval stature. [*Letters*, p. 177]

61 (I: 70). Ancalagon the Black – Greatest of the winged dragons of Morgoth, destroyed by Eärendil in the Great Battle at the end of the First Age. Its name contains Sindarin *anca* 'jaws' + a second element from Sindarin *alag* 'rushing'.

61 (I: 70): 'There is only one way

61 (I: 70). to find the Cracks of Doom in the depts of Orodruin, the Fire-mountain – Tolkien comments in *Nomenclature* that 'in modern use' *crack of doom* is

> derived from *Macbeth* IV, i, 117, in which *the cracke of Doome* means 'the announcement of the Last Day', by a crack/peal of thunder: so commonly supposed, but it may mean 'the sound of the last trump', since *crack* could be applied to the sudden sound of horns or trumpets (so *Sir Gawain* [*and the Green Knight*, lines] 116, 1166). In this story *crack* is here used in the sense 'fissure', and refers to the volcanic fissure in the crater of *Orodruin* in *Mordor*.

Sindarin *Orodruin* is 'translated' in the text; in *Nomenclature* Tolkien calls it 'mountain of red flame'. It is the volcano near Barad-dûr in Mordor. See further, note for p. 245.

61 (I: 70–1): 'No!' cried Gandalf, springing to his feet

61 (I: 71). Do not tempt me! For I do not wish to become like the Dark Lord himself. Yet the way of the Ring to my heart is pity, pity for weakness and the desire of strength to do good. – In a draft letter to Eileen Elgar, September 1963, Tolkien wrote: 'Gandalf as Ring-lord would have been far worse than Sauron. He would have remained "righteous", but self-righteous. He would have continued to rule and order things for "good", and the benefit of his subjects according to his wisdom (which was and would have remained great)' (*Letters*, pp. 332–3).

62–3 (I: 72): 'My dear Frodo!' exclaimed Gandalf

62 (I: 72). at a pinch – If hard pressed, if absolutely necessary. In *The Hobbit*, Chapter 1, Gandalf tells the dwarves that Bilbo 'as fierce as a dragon in a pinch' (at which the narrator comments: 'If you have ever seen a dragon in a pinch, you will realise that this was only a poetical exaggeration applied to any hobbit'). On 31 July 1947 Tolkien wrote to Stanley Unwin, in regard to Book I of *The Lord of the Rings*: 'I have failed if it does not seem possible that mere mundane hobbits could cope with such things [fear and horror]. I think that there is no horror conceivable that such creatures cannot surmount, by grace (here appearing in mythological forms) combined with a refusal of their nature and reason at the last pinch to compromise or submit' (*Letters*, pp. 120–1).

63 (I: 72). the Wild – Uninhabited lands, 'also called *the Wilderness*' (*Index*).

63 (I: 72): 'Well, well, bless my beard!'

63 (I: 72). bless my beard – Tolkien commented that Middle-earth in the Third Age is not a Christian world, but neither is it devoid of religion; rather, 'it is a monotheistic world of "natural theology"' (statement to the Houghton Mifflin Company, 30 June 1955, *Letters*, p. 220). 'Bless my beard' avoids the theological implications of 'bless my soul'. But Sam's 'Lor bless you, Mr. Gandalf, sir!' and 'Lor bless me, sir' later in this chapter are not far removed from a Christian invocation of the Lord.

63 (I: 72): 'Eavesdropping, sir?

63 (I: 72). Eavesdropping . . . There ain't no eaves at Bag End – An *eavesdropper* secretly listens to other people's conversations, originally someone who took up a position in the *eavesdrop* (or *eaves drip*), which received water dripping from the *eaves* (in this context, the edge of a projecting roof; compare different sense in note for p. 3). Sam is technically correct: there are no eaves at Bag End, which is built into the Hill; but he has been listening at the window.

64 (I: 73): 'It can't be helped, Sam'

64 (I: 73). I hope Gandalf will turn you into a spotted toad and fill the garden full of grass-snakes. – Grass-snakes eat toads.

Chapter 3

THREE IS COMPANY

For drafts and history of this chapter, see *The Return of the Shadow*, pp. 40–72, 273–85, 323–5, 330; *The Treason of Isengard*, pp. 29–32.

65 (I: 74). [chapter title] – 'Three Is Company' plays on the proverb *Two is company, three is a crowd*. The original draft of the chapter was called 'Three's Company and Four's More'.

65 (I: 74): He looked at Frodo

65 (I: 74). I shall really turn him into a toad – Nowhere in *The Hobbit* or *The Lord of the Rings* does Gandalf exercise the power to transform one kind of being into another, and one suspects that here he does not literally mean what he says. It makes no difference to Sam, however, who believes that Gandalf could, if he chose, change him into something 'unnatural', a belief which Frodo encourages ('if you even breathe a word of what you've heard here, then I hope Gandalf will turn you into a spotted toad and fill the garden full of grass-snakes', p. 64, I: 73).

65–6 (I: 74–5): 'I have been so taken up

66 (I: 75). Bilbo went to find a treasure, there and back again – *There and Back Again* is the subtitle of *The Hobbit*. Of course, Frodo too goes 'there' to Mount Doom, 'and back again' to Bag End.

66 (I: 75): 'Towards danger, but not too rashly

66 (I: 75). the Road . . . will grow worse as the year fails – *Fail* is used here in an obsolete sense, 'come to an end'.

66 (I: 75): 'Rivendell!' said Frodo

66 (I: 75). Halfelven – The forms *Halfelven* and *Half-elven* both appear in *The Lord of the Rings*, the former in the text proper, the latter in Appendix A (e.g. 'the long-sundered branches of the Half-elven were reunited') as also in *The History of Galadriel and Celeborn* in *Unfinished Tales*. Christopher Tolkien does not believe that his father ever intended a distinction between the forms, and no clear preference by Tolkien can be discerned. In the index to *The Silmarillion* the term *Half-elven* (thus) is glossed: 'translation of Sindarin *Peredhel*, plural *Peredhil*' (p. 334).

67 (I: 76): As a matter of fact

67 (I: 76). Crickhollow in the country beyond Bucklebury – In *Nomenclature* Tolkien states that *Crickhollow* 'is meant to be taken as composed of an obsolete element + known word *hollow*', in the sense 'a small depression in the ground'. In his notes for the Dutch translator Tolkien calls *crick-* 'another of the "Celtic" elements in Buckland and East-farthing names', thus probably from British *crūc* 'a hill' or Old Welsh **creic* 'rock, cliff'. In Book I, Chapter 5, when Frodo and his companions approach Crickhollow they follow a lane 'for a couple of miles as it climbed up and down into the country' (p. 100, I: 110).

67 (I: 76): 'Well no; but I have heard

67 (I: 76). I have heard something – How and from whom Gandalf heard something, while he 'kept himself very quiet and did not go about by day' (p. 66, I: 75), is not revealed; but clearly he has had a message or messages of some sort. Compare Book II, Chapter 2, in which Gandalf says merely that at this time 'a cloud of anxiety was on my mind' and 'I had a foreboding of some danger, still hidden from me but drawing near' (p. 256, I: 269). In notes dated 'Autumn 1939' Tolkien planned that 'it was a messenger of Trotter's [then a hobbit "ranger" who kept watch on the Shire] . . . that took Gandalf away – fearing Black Riders' (*The Treason of Isengard*, p. 9).

67 (I: 76–7): On September 20th two covered carts

67 (I: 77). Thursday, his birthday morning dawned – It is 22 September 1418.

67 (I: 77): The next morning they were busy packing

67 (I: 77). The next morning – 23 September.

68–9 (I: 77–8): After lunch, the Sackville-Bagginses

68 (I: 77). Lotho – During the writing of *The Lord of the Rings* the name of Otho and Lobelia Sackville-Baggins' son was *Cosimo*. Only after he completed the narrative did Tolkien replace it with *Lotho*, possibly formed from elements in the names of both his parents.

68 (I: 78). she was now a hundred years old – Lobelia was born in S.R. 1318. At 23 or 24 she was already married to Otho when Bilbo returned to the Shire in 1342 in *The Hobbit*. Lotho was not born for another twenty-two years. The Hobbit family-trees in Appendix C show that another young wife and mother, Rosa Baggins, who married Hildigrim Took, had a son when she was 24, but otherwise they suggest that female Hobbits generally married in their thirties. Christopher Tolkien points out that in early drafts of this chapter Lobelia was even younger: 'Lobelia was in both versions 92 years old at this time, and had had to wait seventy-seven years (as in FR [*The Fellowship of the Ring*]) for Bag-end, which makes her a grasping fifteen year old when Bilbo came back at the end of *The Hobbit* to find her measuring his rooms' (*The Return of the Shadow*, p. 283, n. 5).

69 (I: 78): He took his own tea

69 (I: 78). to do for Mr. Frodo – *To do for* 'to look after, keep house for'.

69 (I: 78): The sun went down

69 (I: 78). Hill Road – 'The road up the Hill to Bag End and Overhill beyond' (*Index*).

69 (I: 78): The sky was clear

69 (I: 78). I am going to start – Some have criticized Tolkien for taking so long to launch Frodo on his quest. Not until the third chapter does he start, and then proceeds at a leisurely pace, arriving at Crickhollow in Chapter 5. But as Wayne G. Hammond observes in 'All the Comforts: The Image of Home in *The Hobbit* and *The Lord of the Rings*', *Mythlore* 14, no. 1, whole no. 51 (Autumn 1987):

> If Tolkien had hurried Frodo and his companions into adventure . . . we would not appreciate so well the arcadia that Frodo is willing to give up for the sake of his people. . . . Proceeding at the author's deliberately casual pace, we grow to love the Shire as we never loved Bag End in *The Hobbit* (though we found it a desirable residence), having visited there so briefly before Bilbo was hurried away. [p. 31]

70 (I: 79): Pippin was sitting

70 (I: 79). Sam! Time! – Since Sam has been having a final drink before leaving, it may not be coincidental that Frodo's call is similar to that heard in an English pub at closing time.

70 (I: 79): 'All aboard, Sam?'

70 (I: 79). All aboard – A traditional call for passengers to board a vessel, signalling an imminent departure.

70 (I: 79): Frodo shut and locked

70 (I: 79). cut along – Run, move quickly.

70–1 (I: 80): For a short way they followed the lane

71 (I: 80). along hedgerows and the borders of coppices – A *hedgerow* is a row of bushes or shrubs, and sometimes trees, forming a living fence, boundary, or enclosure. Hedgerows are a quintessential part of the English landscape: some are centuries old.

A *coppice* is a small wood or thicket, grown for the purpose of periodic cutting.

71 (I: 80): After some time they crossed the Water

71 (I: 80). The stream was there no more than a winding black ribbon, bordered with leaning alder-trees. A mile or two further south they

hastily crossed the great road from the Brandywine Bridge; they were now in the Tookland and bending south-eastwards they made for the Green Hill Country. As they began to climb its first slopes they looked back and saw the lamps in Hobbiton far off twinkling in the gentle valley of the Water. – As first published this passage read: 'The stream was there no more than a winding black ribbon, bordered with leaning alder-trees. They were now in Tookland, and going southwards; but a mile or two further on they crossed the main road from Michel Delving to Bywater and Brandywine Bridge. Then they struck south-east and began to climb into the Green Hill Country south of Hobbiton. They could see the village twinkling down in the gentle valley of the Water.' It was revised in the second edition (1965).

Alders, in the birch family, commonly grow on riverbanks and in damp places.

Tolkien evidently concluded that the northern limit of the *Tookland* (or folkland of the Tooks; see note for p. 9) was not immediately across the Water from Hobbiton, but further south across the great East Road. That road, moreover, as drawn in the map *A Part of the Shire*, does not pass through Bywater, which is reached by a side road running north near the Three-Farthing Stone.

Green Hill Country was spelt with a hyphen ('Green-Hill Country') by Christopher Tolkien on the Shire map, but his father preferred the unhyphened form in the text. The name refers to a hilly region of the Shire from Tookbank in the west to the Woody End in the east.

71 (I: 80): When they had walked for about three hours

71 (I: 80). Soon they struck a narrow road, that went rolling up and down, fading grey into the darkness ahead: the road to Woodhall, and Stock, and the Bucklebury Ferry. – As first published this sentence read: 'Soon they struck a narrow road, that went rolling up and down, fading grey into the darkness ahead: the road to Woodhall and the Bucklebury Ferry.' The words 'and Stock' were added in the second edition (1965). In the map *A Part of the Shire* the village of Stock is too prominent not to be mentioned when referring to this particular road.

In a note for the Dutch translator of *The Lord of the Rings* Tolkien commented that the *-hall* of *Woodhall* 'in English toponymy is very commonly (as is here intended) a "recess, a piece of land half enclosed (by slopes, woods, or a river-bend)". The word (ancient *halh*, *hale*) is peculiar to English. . . .'

The name *Stock* probably derives from Old English *stoc* 'place'. It is common in English place-names as *stoke* or *stock*, but usually combined with some other element.

71 (I: 80). Woody End – 'A wooded district at east-end of the Green Hill Country' (*Index*). In the edition of 2004 'Woody-End' was here emended to 'Woody End', in accord with all other instances of the name.

72 (I: 81): 'Hobbits!' he thought

72 (I: 81). 'Hobbits!' he thought. 'Well, what next? I have heard of strange things in his land, but I have seldom heard of a hobbit sleeping out of doors under a tree. Three of them! There's something mighty queer behind this.' He was quite right, but he never found out any more about it. – To be told what the fox thought is a curious departure from the narrative, which otherwise records the experiences of those taking part. It is much more in the manner of *The Hobbit*, with an outside narrator inserting comments, a device Tolkien grew to dislike.

72 (I: 81): The morning came, pale and clammy

72 (I: 81). The morning came – It is 24 September 1418.

73–4 (I: 83): 'I don't know,' said Frodo

73 (I: 83). It came to me then, as if I was making it up; but I may have heard it long ago. – The reader will recognize the song as almost identical to the one Bilbo sang as he set out on his journey in Book I, Chapter 1. The only change is the replacement in the fifth line of 'eager feet' with 'weary feet'. In *The Road to Middle-earth* Tom Shippey comments that both Bilbo and Frodo 'are leaving Bag End, but the former cheerfully, without the Ring, without responsibility, for Rivendell, the latter with a growing sense of unwished involvement, carrying the Ring and heading in the end for Mordor' (2nd edn., p. 168).

73–4 (I: 83). He used often to say there was only one Road; that it was like a great river: its springs were at every doorstep, and every path was its tributary. "It's a dangerous business, Frodo, going out of your door," he used to say. "You step into the Road, and if you don't keep your feet, there is no knowing where you might be swept off to. – The *Road* is a recurring image in Tolkien's writings, often in contrast with the security and comfort of home. It was also a common literary motif when he was young, when there were fewer cars and people walked a great deal. The 'open road' held the promise of freedom and adventure, but also of risk and uncertainty. In *The Wind in the Willows* by Kenneth Grahame, Mr Toad praises 'the open road, the dusty highway, the heath, the common, the hedgerows, the rolling downs! Camps, villages, towns, cities! Here to-day, up and off to somewhere else to-morrow! Travel, change, interest, excitement!' (Chapter 2). The uncertainty of where the Road might lead can also be seen as a metaphor for life: no one knows what the future will bring, and at this point in the story Frodo can think no further than Rivendell. Roads and paths (and waterways) also figure in Tolkien's pictorial art: note especially, in this regard, *The Hall at Bag-End* (*Artist and Illustrator*, fig. 139) for *The Hobbit* with its open door and the road beyond.

74 (I: 83). the Lonely Mountain – Erebor; see note for p. 11.

74 (I: 84): Round the corner came a black horse

74 (I: 84). Round the corner came a black horse, no hobbit-pony but a full-sized horse; and on it sat a large man, who seemed to crouch in the saddle, wrapped in a great black cloak and hood, so that only his boots in the high stirrups showed below; his face was shadowed and invisible. – As this chapter was first written, the rider was Gandalf, disguised by a great cloak, who greeted the hobbits comically – Tolkien had not progressed far with the story, and still conceived it as a work for children. But he abandoned this idea, and decided that the hobbits were being pursued – 'an unpremeditated turn', as he wrote to Stanley Unwin on 4 March 1938 (*Letters*, p. 34). Instead of a pleasant farewell walk through the Shire, Frodo is being hunted, and the atmosphere is one of fear and urgency. The hobbits do not yet know that the man in black is one of the Ringwraiths mentioned by Gandalf in Book I, Chapter 2, and Tolkien is careful to tell the reader only what the hobbits know.

75 (I: 84): When it reached the tree

75 (I: 84). The riding figure sat quite still with its head bowed, as if listening. From inside the hood came a noise as of someone sniffing to catch an elusive scent; the head turned from side to side of the road. – In the second part of 1954 Tolkien wrote several, differing accounts of the Black Riders' search for the One Ring, summarized by Christopher Tolkien in *The Hunt for the Ring*, published in *Unfinished Tales*. At the end of one unpublished version it is said that the account was 'drawn up by Gandalf, Elrond, and told to Frodo in Rivendell' (Marquette MSS 4/2/36). It begins by noting that after the Black Riders overcame the Rangers guarding Sarn Ford, four of them, including the leader, the Witch-king, turned eastward (see note for p. 143), and five, including Khamûl, formerly the commander of Dol Guldur, entered the Shire and divided:

> [One] keeps to the east, passing northwards towards the Marish and Bridge. [One] takes road leading northwest to Michel Delving, and [another] goes with him, but there ?fares on and traverses the North Farthing. [The other two] go through the central Shire, until they reach the East Road, probably near the Three-Farthing Stone. ([These] were probably Khamûl and his companion, from Dol Guldur; and [Khamûl] [is] the most ready of all (save [the Witch-king]) to perceive the presence of the Ring, but also the one whose power was most confused and diminished by sunlight). Drawn by the Ring [Khamûl] goes to Hobbiton which he reaches *at evening on Fri. Sep. 23rd.* [His companion] keeps an eye on the East Road and Stock Road, lurking probably between the two, just south of Whitfurrows. [Khamûl] just misses Frodo, and misled by the Gaffers [*sic*] starts out east again.
>
> [On 24 September he] picks up the Stock Road, and overtakes Frodo at approaches to Woody End – probably by accident; he becomes

uneasily aware of the Ring, but is hesitant and uncertain because of the bright sun. He turns into the woods and waits for night.

75 (I: 84): 'There are some men about'

75 (I: 84). Down in the Southfarthing they have had trouble with Big People – These may have been refugees from lands in the South, such as the hobbits will encounter at Bree in Book I, Chapter 9, but possibly the first hint of Saruman's interest in the Shire:

> Saruman had long taken an interest in the Shire – because Gandalf did, and he was suspicious of him; and because (again in secret imitation of Gandalf) he had taken to the 'Halflings' leaf', and needed supplies. . . . Latterly other motives were added . . . he had begun to feel certain that in some way the Shire was connected with the Ring in Gandalf's mind. Why this strong guard upon it? He therefore began to collect detailed information about the Shire, its chief persons and families, its roads and other matters. For this he used Hobbits within the Shire, in the pay of the Bracegirdles and the Sackville-Bagginses, but his agents were Men, of Dunlendish origin. . . . The Rangers were suspicious, but did not actually refuse entry to the servants of Saruman. [*The Hunt for the Ring* in *Unfinished Tales*, p. 347]

76 (I: 86): The shadows of the trees

76 (I: 86). the grass was thick and tussocky . . . and the trees began to draw together into thickets. – *Tussocky* 'growing in dense clumps or tufts'.

A *thicket* is 'a dense growth of shrubs, underwood, and small trees' (*OED*).

76 (I: 86): The sun had gone down

76 (I: 86). The sun had gone down red behind the hills at their backs, and evening was coming on before they came back to the road at the end of the long level over which it had run straight for some miles. At that point it bent left and went down into the lowlands of the Yale making for Stock; but a lane branched right, winding through a wood of ancient oak-trees on its way to Woodhall. 'That is the way for us,' said Frodo. [*paragraph:*] Not far from the road-meeting they came on. . . . – As first published this passage read: 'The sun had gone down red behind the hills at their backs, and evening was coming on before they came to the end of the long level over which the road ran straight. At that point it bent somewhat southward, and began to wind again, as it entered a wood of ancient oak-trees. [*paragraph:*] Not far from the edge of the road they came on. . . .' It was revised in the second edition (1965). Later in the chapter, three references to 'road' were changed to 'lane' and three to 'path', and one omitted; and a reference to 'roadside' was changed to 'wayside'.

76 (I: 86). the Yale – The name may be derived from obsolete Welsh **iâl* 'hill-country'. Tolkien associated the Boffin family with the Yale: see their family tree in Appendix C. See also note on *Yale* in 'The Maps of *The Lord of the Rings*', above.

77 (I: 86): Twilight was about them

77 (I: 86). a tune that was as old as the hills – The traditional saying *as old as the hills* means 'very old indeed'.

77–8 (I: 86–7): *Upon the hearth the fire is red*

77–8 (I: 86–7). *Upon the hearth the fire is red . . .* – A recording by Tolkien of this poem is included on Disc 1 of *The J.R.R. Tolkien Audio Collection.*

77 (I: 86). *standing stone* – *Standing stone* is often used to refer to what an archaeologist would call a *menhir*, a single, tall, upright stone, erected in prehistoric times in Western Europe. The term is also used several times in Book I, Chapter 8.

77 (I: 87). *Apple, thorn, and nut and sloe* – Representative plants of the English countryside, e.g. crab-apple, hawthorn, hazel. *Sloe* is *Prunus spinosa* or blackthorn, a thorny shrub bearing white flowers and small blue-black fruit.

77 (I: 87). *dell* – A small, usually wooded hollow or valley (as also in *Rivendell*).

78 (I: 87). *wander back to home and bed* – When Bilbo taught this song to Frodo 'as they walked in the lanes of the Water-valley and talked about Adventure' (p. 77, I: 86) their 'home and bed' was not far away. Now the song seems to prophesy the future of the hobbits: before they can 'wander back to home and bed' they will indeed have to tread many paths 'through shadows to the edge of night'.

78 (I: 87): The hoofs drew nearer

78 (I: 87). tree-bole – A *bole* is a 'trunk below branches', as Tolkien noted on a galley proof for *The Fellowship of the Ring* in which the printer's reader queried its usage.

78 (I: 88): The sound of hoofs

78 (I: 88). It looked like the black shade of a horse led by a smaller black shadow – According to Marquette MSS 4/2/36 (*The Hunt for the Ring*): 'After dark, becoming acutely aware of the Ring, [Khamûl] goes in pursuit; but is daunted by the sudden appearance of the Elves and the song of Elbereth. While Frodo is surrounded by the Elves he cannot perceive the Ring clearly.'

79 (I: 88): 'Yes, it is Elves'

79 (I: 88). They don't live in the Shire, but they wander into it in spring and autumn, out of their own lands away beyond the Tower Hills – In matter appended to *The Road Goes Ever On: A Song Cycle* Tolkien speculates that these particular elves 'since they appear to have been going eastward, were Elves living in or near Rivendell returning from the *palantír* of the Tower Hills. On such visits they were sometimes rewarded by a vision, clear but remote, of Elbereth, as a majestic figure, shining white, standing upon the mountain *Oiolosse* [Quenya "ever-snow-white"] (S[indarin] *Uilos*)' (p. 66).

79 (I: 88–9): *Snow-white! Snow-white! O Lady clear!*

79 (I: 88–9). *Snow-white! Snow-white! O Lady clear! . . .* – A recording by Tolkien of this poem is included on Disc 1 of *The J.R.R. Tolkien Audio Collection.*

79 (I: 88). *Snow-white!* – *Snow-white* is a 'translation' of Sindarin *Fanuilos*, the title of Elbereth (see below, and note for p. 238), also known as Varda, lady of the Valar, the angelic powers, guardians of the world.

79 (I: 88). *beyond the Western Seas* – See note for p. 2. With her spouse, Manwë, lord of the Valar, Varda dwells in Valinor, in the land of Aman separated from Middle-earth by the Western Seas.

> Their halls are above the everlasting snow, upon Oiolossë, the uttermost tower of Taniquetil, tallest of all the mountains upon Earth. When Manwë there ascends his throne and looks forth, if Varda is beside him, he sees further than all other eyes, through mist, and through darkness, and over the leagues of the sea. And if Manwë is with her, Varda hears more clearly than all other ears the sound of voices that cry from east to west, from the hills and the valleys, and from the dark places that Melkor has made upon Earth. Of all the Great Ones who dwell in this world the Elves hold Varda most in reverence and love. Elbereth they name her, and they call upon her name out of the shadows of Middle-earth, and uplift it in song at the rising of the stars. [*Silmarillion*, p. 26]

79 (I: 88). *the world of woven trees!* – Middle-earth, the 'far land beyond the Sea' in the next stanza. Compare *galadhremmin ennorath* 'tree-tangled middle-lands' in the elves' hymn to Elbereth at the end of Book II, Chapter 1.

79 (I: 88). *Gilthoniel! O Elbereth!* – *Gilthoniel* is Sindarin 'star-kindler', containing the element *gil* 'bright spark'. Varda was honoured by the Elves above all as the creator of the stars, the lights under which the Elves first woke, in days before the Sun and Moon were created. Here, poetically, the 'windy fields' are the sky, 'silver blossom' the stars.

In *The Road Goes Ever On: A Song Cycle* Tolkien explains that '*Elbereth* was the usual name in S[indarin] of the *Vala*, called in Q[uenya] *Varda*, "the Exalted." It is more or less the equivalent of Q[uenya] *Elentári*, "Star-queen" but *bereth* actually meant "spouse," and was used of one who is "queen" as spouse of a king' (p. 66).

The elves who sing these words are Noldor, who once lived in Valinor but disobeyed the wishes of the Valar and followed their leader Fëanor to Middle-earth in a vain attempt to recover the great jewels, the Silmarils, stolen by Morgoth (see note for p. 193); now they 'dwell / In this far land beneath the trees' and remember 'thy starlight on the Western Seas'. Stratford Caldecott points out in *Secret Fire: The Spiritual Vision of J.R.R. Tolkien* (2003) that the Elves' hymn to Elbereth bears a similarity to a popular Catholic hymn to the Virgin Mary, venerated as Queen of Heaven and 'Star of the Sea' (*Stella Maris*):

> *Hail, Queen of Heaven, the ocean star,*
> *Guide of the wand'rer here below:*
> *Thrown on life's surge, we claim thy care –*
> *Save us from peril and from woe.*
> *Mother of Christ, star of the sea,*
> *Pray for the wanderer, pray for me.* [p. 57]

79 (I: 89): The song ended

79 (I: 89). These are High Elves! . . . Few of that fairest folk are ever seen in the Shire. Not many now remain in Middle-earth – On 14 April 1954 Tolkien wrote to Naomi Mitchison that his Elves

> are represented as having become early divided in to two, or three varieties. 1. The *Eldar* who heard the summons of the Valar or Powers to pass from Middle-earth over the Sea to the West; and 2. the Lesser Elves who did not answer it. Most of the *Eldar* after a great march reached the Western Shores and passed over Sea; these were the High Elves, who became immensely enhanced in powers and knowledge. But part of them in the event remained in the coast-lands of the North-west: these were the *Sindar* or Grey-elves. The lesser Elves hardly appear [in *The Lord of the Rings*], except as part of the people of The Elf-realm; of Northern Mirkwood, and of Lórien, ruled by *Eldar*; their languages do not appear.
>
> The High Elves met in this book are Exiles, returned back over Sea to Middle-earth, after events which are the main matter of the *Silmarillion*, part of one of the main kindreds of the *Eldar*: the Noldor (Masters of Lore). Or rather a last remnant of these. For the *Silmarillion* proper and the First Age ended with the destruction of the primeval Dark Power (of whom Sauron was a mere lieutenant), and the rehabilitation of the Exiles, who returned again over Sea. Those who lingered were those who were enamoured of Middle-earth and yet desired the unchanging beauty of the Land of the Valar. [*Letters*, pp. 176–7]

(Elsewhere Tolkien equates *Eldar* with the High Elves (see note for p. 43), or defines the term more narrowly as 'the West-elves' in contrast to 'the East-elves', p. 1127, III: 405. The classification of Elves in Tolkien's mythology according to their response to the summons of the Valar is a difficult issue; see further, *The Lost Road and Other Writings*, pp. 182–3.)

As commented earlier (see note for p. 2), Tolkien wished to distinguish his Elves, the central race in his mythology, from the general conception of elves or fairies in our own world. In his writings both Elves and Men are called the Children of Ilúvatar, because the One (God) alone introduced their theme into the Music of Creation (as told in the *Ainulindalë*, published in *The Silmarillion*). The Elves, who among the Children woke first in Middle-earth, are often referred to as the 'Firstborn', and Men, who woke much later, as the 'Followers'. Although the Elves are represented as similar in appearance to Men, they have different abilities and different fates, as Tolkien wrote in a draft letter to Michael Straight:

> Of course, in fact exterior to my story, Elves and Men are just different aspects of the Humane, and represent the problem of Death as seen by a finite but willing and self-conscious person. In this mythological world Elves and Men are in their incarnate forms kindred, but in the relation of their 'spirits' to the world in time represent different 'experiments', each of which has its own natural trend, and weakness. The Elves represent, as it were, the artistic, aesthetic, and purely scientific aspects of the Humane nature raised to a higher level than is actually seen in Men. That is: they have a devoted love of the physical world, and a desire to observe and understand it for its own sake and as 'other' – sc. as a reality derived from God in the same degree as themselves – not as a material for use or as a power-platform. They also possess a 'subcreational' or artistic faculty of great excellence. They are therefore 'immortal'. *Not* 'eternally', but to endure with and within the created world while its story lasts. When 'killed', by the injury or destruction of their incarnate form, they do not escape from time, but remain *in* the world, either discarnate, or being re-born. This becomes a great burden as the ages lengthen, especially in a world in which there is malice and destruction. . . . [*Letters*, p. 236, dated there to January or February 1956, but more likely end of 1955]

Elsewhere he explained more fully the different fates of Elves and Men:

> The doom of the Elves is to be immortal, to love the beauty of the world, to bring it to full flower with their gifts of delicacy and perfection, to last while it lasts, never leaving it even when 'slain', but returning – and yet, when the Followers come, to teach them, and make way for them, to 'fade' as the Followers grow and absorb the life from which both proceed. The Doom (or the Gift) of Men is mortality, freedom from the circles of the world . . . a mystery of God of which no more

is known than that 'what God has purposed for Men is hidden': a grief and an envy to the immortal Elves. [letter to Milton Waldman, ?late 1951, *Letters*, p. 147]

The elves now met by Frodo and company offer a serious contrast to those met by Bilbo at Rivendell in *The Hobbit*, who except for Elrond are hardly above the mischievous fairies of English tradition. One feels that the Elves of *The Lord of the Rings* would never sing 'tra-la-la-lally / here down in the valley' or say 'Just look! Bilbo the hobbit on a pony, my dear! Isn't it delicious!' (*The Hobbit*, Chapter 3). In Appendix F (referring specifically to the Noldor) it is said that the Elves

> were a race high and beautiful, the older Children of the world, and among them the Eldar were as kings, who now are gone: the People of the Great Journey, the People of the Stars. They were tall, fair of skin and grey-eyed, though their locks were dark, save in the golden house of Finarfin; and their voices had more melodies than any mortal voice that now is heard. They were valiant, but the history of those that returned to Middle-earth in exile was grievous; and though it was in far-off days crossed by the fate of the Fathers, their fate is not that of Men. Their dominion passed long ago, and they dwell now beyond the circles of the world, and do not return. [p. 1137, III: 415–16]

As first published, the passage 'Few of that fairest folk are ever seen in the Shire' read: 'I did not know that any of the fairest folk were ever seen in the Shire.' This was altered by Tolkien in the second edition (1965). In the later reading Frodo is made to appear more learned on the subject of Elves: compare, in Book I, Chapter 2, that Frodo often 'wandered by himself, and to the amazement of sensible folk he was sometimes seen far from home walking in the hills and woods under the starlight. Merry and Pippin suspected that he visited the Elves at times, as Bilbo had done' (pp. 42–3, I: 51–2).

80 (I: 89–90): 'I am Gildor'

80 (I: 89). Gildor Inglorion of the House of Finrod – *Gildor* probably means 'star-lord'. Its first element is definite, its second uncertain. *Inglorion* contains the element *-glor* 'gold'.

When *The Lord of the Rings* was published *Finrod* was the name of the third son of Finwë, leader of the Noldorin Elves, and Finrod had a son called Inglor Felagund. Some time later in his work on the 'Silmarillion' Tolkien changed the name of the son of Finwë to Finarfin, and *his* son became Finrod Felagund. To agree with this, in the second edition of *The Lord of the Rings* (1965) he changed the description of Galadriel at the beginning of Appendix B from 'sister of Felagund of the House of Finrod' to 'sister of Finrod Felagund', and in Appendix F 'Lady Galadriel of the royal house of Finrod, father of Felagund' became 'Lady Galadriel of the royal house of Finarfin'. Yet Tolkien left 'House of Finrod' unchanged in Book I, Chapter 3, probably an oversight, though a reference to 'Finrod Inglor' in papers associated with the telling of the story of Beren and Lúthien under Weathertop (Book I, Chapter 11) might indicate that Tolkien was already pondering the change of names.

It is strange that there is no mention of Gildor in the 'Silmarillion' papers, written either before or after the publication of *The Lord of the Rings*; yet Tolkien wrote Galadriel, Gil-galad, and even (briefly) the Ents into the earlier history. The only *Gildor* to be found there is a Man, one of the companions of Barahir, father of Beren, introduced after the completion of *The Lord of the Rings* but before its publication. *Inglorion* would seem to connect Gildor especially with Inglor Felagund, yet apart from briefly considering Inglor as a possible father for Gil-galad, Tolkien had him remain unmarried because his beloved had stayed in Valinor. Tolkien may have thought of Gildor as the son of one of Finrod Felagund's brothers, or may simply have used names which seemed suitable for the purpose; or he may have intended the phrase 'of the House of' to mean one closely associated with the family of Finrod, a member of the household.

80 (I: 89). We are Exiles – Noldor who came to Middle-earth with Fëanor, and have not yet returned into the West. See note for p. 79.

80–1 (I: 90): 'O Fair Folk!

81 (I: 90). '*Elen síla lúmenn' omentielvo*, a star shines on the hour of our meeting,' he added in the High-elven speech. – As first published, the last word of this Elvish phrase read *omentielmo*. It was changed to *omentielvo* in the second edition (1965). In ?1974 Christopher Tolkien wrote to Rayner Unwin to explain the alteration:

> The original edition had *omentielmo*. . . . My father changed the reading to *omentielvo*, and this was incorporated in the Revised edition. The reading in the Ballantine Books edition . . . *omentilmo*, is an error for *omentielmo*.
>
> The point is one of Elvish (Quenya) grammar. Quenya made a distinction in its dual inflexion which turns on the number of persons involved, and failure to understand this was, as my father remarked, 'a mistake generally made by mortals'. . . . A manuscript note in one of my father's copies of *The Lord of the Rings* says that the Thain's Book (see The Prologue) has *omentielvo*, but that Frodo's (lost) manuscript probably had *omentielmo*; and that *omentielvo* is the correct form in the context. [Tolkien-George Allen & Unwin archive, HarperCollins]

In fact the Ballantine Books *Fellowship of the Ring* as first published in 1965 had correct *omentielvo*, but in the sixth printing (1966) this word was changed to *omentilmo*. As Dick Plotz, the founder of the Tolkien Society of America, explained:

> The original version was *Elen síla lúmenn' omentielmo*, which means literally 'A star shines on the hour of our (my, his, her, NOT your) meeting.' Tolkien, on reflection, changed this to *omentielvo*, 'of our (my, your, possibly his, her) meeting.' This was, of course, a proper change. . . . *I*, however, saw it as an obvious error, and prevailed upon Ballantine to CORRECT it! The 'correction' introduced another error, since *omentilmo*, as far as I know, means nothing at all. Now they won't change it back, because it's too expensive. [*Mythprint* 10, no. 1 (July 1974), p. 3]

The word was finally corrected by Ballantine Books in their reset edition of autumn 2001.

Tolkien wrote to his son Christopher on 21 February 1958 that he had told an enquirer, who had asked what *The Lord of the Rings* 'was all about', that 'it was an effort to create a situation in which a common greeting would be *elen síla lúmenn' omentielmo*, and that the phrase long antedated the book' (*Letters*, pp. 264–5). This was, however, clearly not his primary intention when starting to write *The Lord of the Rings*; indeed, although Gildor appears in the first version of this chapter (written by 4 March 1938), the Elvish greeting does not appear until the third version, written in autumn 1938, and then in a different form. But Tolkien's passion for language was inextricably linked with another interest. As he wrote to Milton Waldman in ?late 1951:

> Many children make up, or begin to make up, imaginary languages. I have been at it since I could write. But I have never stopped, and of course, as a professional philologist (especially interested in linguistic aesthetics), I have changed in taste, improved in theory, and probably in craft. Behind my stories is now a nexus of languages (mostly only structurally sketched). But to those creatures which in English I call misleadingly Elves are assigned two related languages more nearly completed, whose history is written, and whose forms (representing two different sides of my own linguistic taste) are deduced scientifically from a common origin. Out of these languages are made nearly all the *names* that appear in my legends. This gives a certain character (a cohesion, a consistency of linguistic style, and an illusion of historicity) to the nomenclature, or so I believe, that is markedly lacking in other comparable things. . . .
>
> But an equally basic passion of mine *ab initio* was for myth (not allegory!) and for fairy-story, and above all for heroic legend on the brink of fairy-tale and history. . . . I was an undergraduate before thought and experience revealed to me that these were not divergent interests – opposite poles of science and romance – but integrally related. [*Letters*, pp. 143–4]

He explained this relationship further in a draft letter to a Mr Thompson, 14 January 1956: 'It was just as the 1914 War burst on me that I made the discovery that "legends" depend on the language to which they belong; but a living language depends equally on the "legends" which it conveys by tradition' (*Letters*, p. 231).

The 'two related languages' to which Tolkien refers in his letter to Milton Waldman are *Quenya*, which reflects his interest in Finnish, and *Sindarin*, influenced by Welsh. The greeting 'Elen síla lúmenn' omentielvo' is in Quenya.

An important element in the stories of the Elves told in 'The Silmarillion' is that their history explains why the languages they spoke diverged over time. In Appendix F Tolkien explains that Quenya was the language of the Elves in Valinor, where it had been spoken by the Noldor. But the Noldor who followed Fëanor to Middle-earth adopted for their daily use Sindarin, the language they found spoken there by the Grey-elves: 'in the long twilight their tongue had changed with the changefulness of mortal lands and had become far estranged from the speech of the Eldar from beyond the Sea'. Among the Noldor Quenya had become 'as it were, an "Elven-latin", still used for ceremony, and high matters of lore and song' (p. 1128, III: 406).

81 (I: 90): 'Be careful, friends!'

81 (I: 90). Elf-friend – *Elf-friend* was a name or title full of meaning for Tolkien. In *Nomenclature* he explains that 'it was suggested by *Ælfwine*, the English form of an old Germanic name (represented for instance in the Lombardic *Alboin*), though its analysable meaning was probably not recognized or thought significant by the many recorded bearers of the name *Ælfwine* in Old English'. In his 'Silmarillion' writings an Anglo-Saxon named Ælfwine was to witness or record much of the history of the Elves, and several of the component parts of the mythology are attributed to him as writer or transmitter. Verlyn Flieger has said of the term *Elf-friend* in *The Lord of the Rings* that readers of that work first meet it

> early in the story, in an exchange that at first reading seems of little significance. Responding to Frodo's Elvish greeting . . . the Elf Gildor replies. 'Hail, Elf-friend!' At this point in the story it seems to be simply polite elf-hobbit talk. Even when in a later, more serious moment Gildor says to Frodo, 'I name you Elf-friend,' this still seems largely a formal rather than a substantive locution. . . . With every repetition, however, the meaning deepens, and when in the house of Tom Bombadil, Goldberry says to Frodo, 'I see you are an Elf-friend; the light in your eyes and the ring in your voice tells it' . . . , we begin to realize that more than politeness is involved; Elf-friend is some kind of special identity. This is confirmed when, still later, the Elf Legolas introduces Aragorn to Haldir of Lórien as 'an Elf-friend of the folk of Westernesse'. . . .
>
> However, it is only at the Council of Elrond that we discover that the phrase has a history beyond the immediate present. Formally

accepting his offer to carry the Ring to Mount Doom, Elrond Halfelven tells Frodo, 'Though all the mighty Elf-friends of old, Hador and Húrin, and Túrin, and Beren himself were assembled together, your seat should be among them'. . . . What seemed at first a polite form of address, later a complimentary epithet, can here be seen as the sign of election to a special company. ['In the Footsteps of Ælfwine', *Tolkien's* Legendarium: *Essays on* The History of Middle-earth (2000), pp. 183–4]

In our analysis of the various editions of *The Lord of the Rings* the capitalized spelling *Elf-friend* was found to be Tolkien's clear preference ('friend of the Elves', of the entire race), rather than *elf-friend*, which had also appeared. Two instances of the latter form were emended to the former in the edition of 2004.

81 (I: 90): They now marched on again

81 (I: 90). a tall Elf – Although in his earliest poems and 'Silmarillion' writings Tolkien did not entirely reject the idea of fairies or elves being, or becoming, diminutive, he soon altered his opinion, and came to believe that the current conception of such creatures was a debasement of how they had once been regarded. In *On Fairy-Stories* he criticized the definition of *fairies* in the *Oxford English Dictionary*: 'As for *diminutive size*: I do not deny that the notion is a leading one in modern use. . . . Of old there were indeed some inhabitants of Faërie that were small (though hardly diminutive), but the smallness was not characteristic of the people as a whole' (*Tree and Leaf*, p. 11). In one of his late manuscripts he commented on the stature of his Elves:

> The *Quendi* [Elves] were in origin a tall people. The *Eldar* . . . were those . . . who accepted the invitation of the Valar to remove from Middle-earth and set forth on the Great March to the Western Shores of Middle-earth. They were in general the stronger and taller members of the Elvish folk at that time. In Eldarin tradition it was said that even their women were seldom less than six feet in height; their full-grown elfmen no less than six and a half feet, while some of the great kings and leaders were taller. [Tolkien Papers, Bodleian Library, Oxford]

81 (I: 90): The woods on either side

81 (I: 90). brakes of hazel – A *brake* is a clump of bushes or briers, a thicket. (Compare *thicket*, note for p. 76.)

81 (I: 90). green ride – A *ride* is a path through woods. In some printings of the Ballantine Books edition this was misprinted *ridge*.

81 (I: 91): The Elves sat on the grass

81 (I: 91). hillock – A small hill or mound.

81 (I: 91): Away high in the East

81 (I: 91). Remmirath, the Netted Stars – *Remmirath* contains Sindarin *rem* 'mesh' + *mîr* 'jewel' with *-ath* collective plural suffix. Commentators agree that this must be another name for the Pleiades, a cluster of seven stars in the constellation Taurus, named after the daughters of Atlas and Pleione in Greek mythology. Naomi Getty in 'Stargazing in Middle-earth', *Beyond Bree*, April 1984, quotes a description by Timothy Ferris (*Galaxies* (1980)): 'The light of the stars in the Pleiades cluster . . . reflecting off the dust of the cloud in which the cluster is embedded, forms a veil that glitters like diamonds.'

81 (I: 91). red Borgil . . . glowing like a jewel of fire – The name *Borgil* 'red star' is derived from Sindarin *bor(n)* 'hot, red' + *gil* 'star'. Naomi Getty, 'Stargazing in Middle-earth' identifies it as the red star Aldebaran, which like the Pleiades is in the constellation Taurus. But Jorge Quiñonez and Ned Raggett, in 'Nólë i Meneldilo: Lore of the Astronomer', *Vinyar Tengwar* 12 (July 1990), and others have argued that it is the red giant star Betelgeuse in the constellation Orion.

81 (I: 91). the Swordsman of the Sky, Menelvagor, with his shining belt – In Appendix E Tolkien identifies *Menelvagor* (from Sindarin *menel* 'firmament, heavens' + *magor* 'swordsman') as the constellation Orion. Orion is typically pictured as a hunter with a belt and sword. In the 'Silmarillion' it was one of the signs set in the heavens by Varda: when the Swordsman first strode up the sky, the Elves, first of the Children of Ilúvatar, woke in Middle-earth.

82 (I: 91): At the south end of the greensward

82 (I: 91). greensward – Grass-covered ground.

82 (I: 91): Pippin afterwards recalled

82 (I: 91). draught – In this sense, a drink drawn from a cask or other container.

82 (I: 92): After a while Pippin fell fast asleep

82 (I: 92). bower – 'A place closed in or overarched with branches of trees or shrubs, or other plants; a shady recess, leafy covert, arbour' (*OED*).

83 (I: 93): 'But it is not your own Shire

83 (I: 93). Others dwelt here before hobbits were; and others will dwell here again when hobbits are no more – It is said in the Prologue that 'though it [the Shire] had long been deserted when they [the Hobbits] entered it, it had before been well tilled, and there the king had once had many farms, cornlands, vineyards, and woods' (p. 5, I: 14). Gildor, an immortal Elf, takes a long view. Tolkien lived close to a countryside in which the passage of successive peoples was marked with stone monuments, burial mounds, Roman roads, village churches, railways, and the like. He was aware that a land can have a long history, and that in the past each wave of invaders or immigrants usually displaced its predecessor.

83 (I: 83). The wide world is all about you: you can fence yourselves in, but you cannot for ever fence it out – A foreshadow of the occupation of the Shire in Book VI. The Hobbits' lack of contact with, or concern about, the world outside their borders left them ill-prepared to deal with an invader.

84 (I: 93): Gildor was silent for a moment

84 (I: 94). ***Do not meddle in the affairs of Wizards, for they are subtle and quick to anger*** – *The Lord of the Rings* includes many such proverbs or sayings, some of them known outside of the story, or adaptations of old proverbs, but also many that were newly invented.

84 (I: 93): 'And it is also said'

84 (I: 93). ***Go not to the Elves for counsel, for they will say both no and yes*** – Bill Welden wryly comments in 'Negation in Quenya', *Vinyar Tengwar* 42 (July 2001), that this saying is in a sense literally true. 'The earliest versions of the Elvish languages had two distinct roots for negation', but Tolkien was dissatisfied with them. Probably at about the time *The Lord of the Rings* was published, he altered the meaning of one of them, which by 1959 had come to be 'an interjection of pleasure/assent'; then in a very late essay the same root reverted to being negative (pp. 32–4).

84 (I: 93–4): 'Is it indeed?'

84 (I: 94). In this meeting there may be more than chance – Throughout *The Lord of the Rings* there are suggestions that Providence is at work, or may be at work – Tolkien makes no overt statement. But Frodo and his companions meet the elves in the Woody End by chance (as it seems), when they have been menaced by a Black Rider. Later, in Book I, Chapter 7, they are rescued from Old Man Willow by Tom Bombadil: 'Just chance brought me then,' he says, 'if chance you call it' (p. 126, I: 137); and in Book II, Chapter 2, the Council of Elrond convenes though Elrond did not call its participants to Rivendell. 'You have come and are here met, in this very nick of time, by chance as it may seem. Yet it is not so. Believe rather that it is so ordered that we, who sit here, and none others, must now find counsel for the peril of the world' (p. 242, I: 255).

84 (I: 94): 'Is it not enough to know

84 (I: 94). Is it not enough to know that they are servants of the Enemy? – It is clear from what Gildor says, and from his earlier warning that 'peril is now both before you and behind you, and upon either side', that he knows exactly who the Black Riders are, but both Frodo and the reader must wait to learn more.

84 (I: 94). fell things – *Fell* in this context means 'dreadful, terrible'.

Chapter 4

A SHORT CUT TO MUSHROOMS

For drafts and history of this chapter, see *The Return of the Shadow*, chiefly pp. 88ff., 286–97, 325; *The Treason of Isengard*, p. 32.

86 (I: 95): In the morning Frodo woke

86 (I: 95). In the morning Frodo woke refreshed. – It is 26 September 1418.

87 (I: 96): 'They seem a bit above my likes and dislikes

87 (I: 96). so old and young, and so gay and sad – The immortal Elves are in fact centuries old but youthful in appearance, merry in manner but burdened with their own labours and sorrows.

87 (I: 96): 'Yes, sir. I don't know how to say it

87 (I: 96). I know we are going to take a very long road, into darkness; but I know I can't turn back. . . . I have something to do before the end, and it lies ahead, not in the Shire. I must see it through, sir, if you understand me. – Here is our first glimpse of Sam's strength of character: he is not merely a servant, or comic relief. We will see it again several times, especially near the end of Book IV, when Frodo is apparently dead and Sam must choose whether to stay with his fallen master or to continue the quest to Mount Doom: '"What am I to do then?" he cried again, and now he seemed plainly to know the hard answer: *see it through*' (p. 732, II: 341).

Some critics have described the relationship between Frodo and Sam as akin to that of a British army officer and his batman (servant), distinguished also by their middle- and working-class backgrounds respectively. Indeed Tolkien once remarked that Sam is 'a reflexion of the English soldier, of the privates and batmen I knew in the 1914 war, and recognised as so far superior to myself' (quoted in *Biography*, p. 81). But in dealing with an etymological point in his draft letter to Mr Rang, August 1967, Tolkien described Sam's relationship to Frodo as having the status of one who serves a legitimate master, but the spirit of a friend (if not an equal); see *Letters*, p. 386.

Late in 1964 Tolkien commented in a letter to Joan O. Falconer that Sam and Frodo have quite different characters, background, and education. Sam is sententious and cocksure, a 'rustic of limited outlook and knowledge'. He is a loyal servant, and has a personal love for Frodo, but also 'a touch of the contempt of his kind (moderated to tolerant pity) for motives above their reach'. His attitude towards Frodo is 'slightly paternal, not to say patronizing', but his protectiveness is 'largely forced on him by circumstance' after Frodo is injured on Weathertop (Book I, Chapter 11) and takes on the heavy burden of the Ring (Book II, Chapter 2) (*Mythprint* 8, no. 3 (September 1973), p. 3).

88 (I: 97): 'We can cut straighter than the road

88 (I: 97). The Ferry is east from Woodhall; but the hard road curves away to the left. . . . It goes round the north end of the Marish so as to strike the causeway from the Bridge above Stock. – As first published the first part of this passage read: '"The Ferry is south-east from Woodhall; but the road curves away to the left'. It was revised in the second printing (1967) of the Allen & Unwin second edition. In the map *A Part of the Shire* the road meets the causeway in the village of Stock itself, not above it, but in this instance Tolkien made no change to the text to accommodate the map.

A *causeway* is a raised road, usually over wet ground or water.

88 (I: 97): 'All right!' said Pippin

88 (I: 97). the *Golden Perch* – This name is not recorded for any inn or pub in Britain, though there are many with *Golden*, such as the *Golden Cross* once in Cornmarket Street, Oxford, and a few named *Perch*, including three in Oxfordshire. In *Nomenclature* Tolkien describes this as 'an inn name; probably one favoured by anglers. In any case *Perch* is the fish-name (and not a land-measure or bird-perch).'

88–9 (I: 97–8): It was already nearly as hot

88 (I: 98). Their course had been chosen to leave Woodhall to their left, and to cut slanting through the woods that clustered upon the eastern side of the hills – As first published the final word of this passage read 'hill'. It was emended to 'hills' in the edition of 1994.

89 (I: 98): 'Why, this is the Stock-brook!'

89 (I: 98). Stock-brook – 'A stream running from the Woody End by Stock to join the Brandywine River' (*Index*).

90 (I: 99–100): Frodo propped his back against the tree-trunk

90 (I: 99). *Ho! Ho! Ho! to the bottle I go . . .* – 'Rain may fall and wind may blow, / And many miles be still to go, / But under a tall tree I will lie, / And let the clouds go sailing by' recalls Amiens' song in Shakespeare's *As You Like It*: 'Under the Greenwood tree / Who loves to lie with me, / . . . . / Here shall he see / No enemy / But winter and rough weather' (Act II, Scene 5).

90 (I: 99). A long-drawn wail . . . . like the cry of some evil and lonely creature – 'The Nazgûl were they, the Ringwraiths, the Enemy's most terrible servants; darkness went with them, and they cried with the voices of death' (*Of the Rings of Power and the Third Age* in *The Silmarillion*, p. 289).

91 (I: 100): 'I know these fields and this gate!'

91 (I: 100). This is Bamfurlong, old Farmer Maggot's land. – As first published this passage read simply: 'We are on old Farmer Maggot's land.' It was revised, with the name of the property added, in the second printing (1967) of the Allen & Unwin second edition. The name *Bamfurlong* originally appeared in Book VI, Chapter 8, referring to an entirely different place. It is 'an English place-name, probably from *bean* "bean" + *furlong* (in sense: 'a division of a common field'), the name being given to a strip of land usually reserved for beans. The name is now, and so is supposed to have been at that time in the Shire, without clear meaning' (*Nomenclature*).

Maggot was intended by Tolkien 'to be a "meaningless" name, hobbit-like in sound. Actually it is an accident that *maggot* is an English word = "grub, larva"' (*Nomenclature*). Farmer Maggot appeared again, with his wife and daughters, in the poem *Bombadil Goes Boating*, in *The Adventures of Tom Bombadil and Other Verses from the Red Book* (1962).

91 (I: 100): 'One trouble after another!'

91 (I: 100). the slot leading to a dragon's den – *Slot* in this sense means 'track, marks of an animal's passage'.

91–2 (I: 101): 'I know,' said Frodo

92 (I: 101). When I was a youngster – Later in this chapter Frodo says that he has been in terror of Maggot and his dogs for over thirty years: this suggests that he was caught stealing mushrooms by Maggot in S.R. 1387 or earlier, when he was still in his 'tweens' and living at Brandy Hall.

92 (I: 101). varmint – Dialectal variant of *vermin* 'a troublesome person or animal'.

92 (I: 101): They went along the lane

92 (I: 101). Puddifoots – *Puddifoot*, a 'surname in the muddy Marish', is 'meant to suggest *puddle* + *foot*' (*Nomenclature*).

92 (I: 101): Suddenly as they drew nearer

92 (I: 101). Grip! Fang! Wolf! – The name is 'meant of course to be the English *fang* "canine or prominent tooth" . . . associated with *Grip*, the sense of the now lost verb *fang*' (*Nomenclature*).

95–6 (I: 105): Frodo now accepted the invitation

96 (I: 105). the fire was mended – Fuel was added to the fire.

96 (I: 105). bacon – Thus the Shire-Hobbits must have kept pigs.

96 (I: 105): 'I will!' said he

96 (I: 105). crossing a deep dike, and climbing a short slope up on to the high-banked causeway – The dike has probably been excavated to build the raised causeway beside the river. The *Oxford English Dictionary* notes that past use of *dike* 'varies between "ditch, dug out place" and "mound formed by throwing up the earth" and may include both'.

97 (I: 106): 'I want Mr. Baggins

97 (I: 106). a dark lantern was uncovered – A lantern with a moveable panel or shutter to hide or reveal the light.

97 (I: 106–7): 'No, I caught 'em trespassing'

97 (I: 107). worriting – Colloquial 'worrying, fretting, anxious'.

Chapter 5

A CONSPIRACY UNMASKED

For drafts and history of this chapter, see *The Return of the Shadow*, chiefly pp. 99–106, 298–302, 304–5, 326–7, 330; *The Treason of Isengard*, chiefly pp. 32–6, 39.

98 (I: 108): They turned down the Ferry Lane

98 (I: 108). Ferry Lane, which was straight and well-kept and edged with large white-washed stones. . . . The white bollards near the water's edge glimmered in the light of two lamps on high posts – These features are seen in a rough drawing made by Tolkien, as well as the further landing, the steep and winding path, and the lights of Brandy Hall described in the following paragraph. See *Artist and Illustrator*, fig. 146.

A *bollard* is a short post on a quay or ship for securing a rope.

98 (I: 108): Merry led the pony over a gangway

98 (I: 108). Buck Hill – The hill on the east bank of the Brandywine 'in which the great "smial" of Brandy Hall was built' (*Index*).

98 (I: 108): Long ago Gorhendad Oldbuck

98 (I: 108). Gorhendad Oldbuck – *Gorhendad* is Welsh 'great-grandfather'.

98 (I: 108–9): The people in the Marish

98 (I: 109). Rushey – '"Rush-isle" (sc. in origin a "hard" among the fens of the Marish). The [Old English] element *-ey, y* in the sense "small island" . . . is very frequent in English place-names' (*Nomenclature*). *Rushey* is misspelt *Rushy* on the map *A Part of the Shire*. There is a Rushy Weir in Oxfordshire, recorded in the sixteenth century as *Russhey*.

99 (I: 109): Their land was originally unprotected

99 (I: 109). the High Hay. It had been planted many generations ago, and was now thick and tall, for it was constantly tended. It ran all the way from Brandywine Bridge . . . to Haysend (where the Withywindle flowed out of the Forest into the Brandywine): well over twenty miles from end to end. – In his unfinished index Tolkien defines the *High Hay* as 'a great hedge fencing off the Old Forest from Buckland'. The High Hay appears on the map *A Part of the Shire* as 'The Hedge'. In notes for the Dutch translator of *The Lord of the Rings* Tolkien comments that '*Hay* is of course an archaic word for *hedge* still very frequent in place-names'. Dictionaries indicate that it might also be used to mean 'a fence; a boundary', and in medieval times it was often used to refer to a part of a forest within such a hedge or fence, reserved for hunting.

In *Nomenclature* Tolkien defines *Haysend* as 'the end of the *hay* or boundary hedge (not *hay* "dried grass")'.

In *Nomenclature* Tolkien also explains that the *Withywindle* is 'a winding river bordered by willows (withies). *Withy-* is not uncommon in English place-names, but *-windle* does not actually occur (*withywindle* was modelled on *withywind*, a name of the convolvulus or bindweed)'.

99 (I: 109): On the far stage, under the distant lamps

99 (I: 109). a dark black bundle – Marquette MSS 4/2/36 (*The Hunt for the Ring*) gives the following account of the Black Riders' pursuit of Frodo on 25 September 1418:

> As soon as the Elves depart [Khamûl] renews his hunt, and reaching the ridge above Woodhall is aware that the Ring has been there. Failing to find the Bearer and feeling that he is drawing away, he summons [his companion] by cries. [He] is aware of the general direction that the Ring has taken, but not knowing of Frodo's rest in the wood, and believing him to have made straight eastwards, he and [his companion] ride over the fields. They visit Maggot while Frodo is still under the trees. [Khamûl] then makes a mistake (probably because he imagines the Ringbearer as some mighty man, strong and swift): he does not look near the farm, but sends [his companion] *down* Causeway towards Overbourn, while he goes *north* along it towards the Bridge. They tryst to return and meet one another at night; but do so just too late. Frodo crosses by ferry just before [Khamûl] arrives. [His companion] joins him soon after. [Khamûl] is now well aware that the Ring has crossed the river; but the river is a barrier to his sense of its movement.

99 (I: 109): 'They can go ten miles north

99 (I: 109). ten miles north to Brandywine Bridge – In editions prior to 2004 this distance read 'twenty miles'. In *The Return of the Shadow* Christopher Tolkien notes that his father wrote 'twenty miles' (emended from 'fifteen') at a time when the length of the High Hay, and consequently the length of Buckland from north to south, was 'something over forty miles from end to end'. 'In [*The Fellowship of the Ring*] the High Hay is "well over *twenty* miles from end to end", yet Merry still says: "They can go *twenty* miles north to Brandywine Bridge." . . . It is in fact an error which my father never observed: when the length of Buckland from north to south was reduced, Merry's estimate of the distance of the Bridge from the Ferry should have been changed commensurately' (p. 298). For the correction in 2004, Christopher Tolkien suggested to the editors that 'ten miles' would be a good approximate figure.

101 (I: 111): 'Trust me to arrange things

101 (I: 111). *three* tubs, and a copper full of boiling water – The use of the more informal *tub* rather than *bath* or *bath-tub* suggests a portable container, probably wooden with a flat bottom.

A *copper* is a large vessel, usually made of copper, used to heat water for domestic purposes, especially for laundry. The bathing arrangements described are typical of the nineteenth century and earlier.

101 (I: 111): Merry and Fatty went into the kitchen

101 (I: 111). The voice of Pippin was suddenly lifted up . . . – A recording by Tolkien of the final part of this paragraph and the following song is included on Disc 1 of *The J.R.R. Tolkien Audio Collection.*

101 (I: 111): *Sing hey! for the bath at close of day*

101 (I: 111). loon – Informally, a silly or foolish person.

102 (I: 112): 'Lawks!' said Merry

102 (I: 112). Lawks! – An expression of surprise, possibly a deformation of 'Lord!'

102 (I: 113): 'Cousin Frodo has been very close

102 (I: 113). Cousin Frodo has been very close – The various marriages between Tooks, Brandybucks, and Bagginses created multiple relationships between Frodo and Pippin, and Frodo and Merry. Pippin is both Frodo's second and third cousin, once removed in each case, and Merry is his first, second, and third cousin, once removed in each case.

Close in this context means 'closed, shut, not forthcoming'.

103 (I: 113): Frodo opened his mouth

103 (I: 113). We have constantly heard you muttering: "Shall I ever look down into that valley again, I wonder" – One such instance is given in Chapter 3, not long after the hobbits set out.

105 (I: 115): 'Step forward, Sam!'

105 (I: 115). before he was finally caught. After which . . . he seemed to regard himself as on parole, and dried up.' – Before he *dried up* (ceased to be a source of information) Sam must, however, have made one final report with details of Gandalf's conversation with Frodo, otherwise Merry would not know about the Ring.

105 (I: 116): 'And after all, sir'

105 (I: 116). Gildor said you should take them as was willing – Gildor's actual words were: 'do not go alone. Take such friends as are trusty and willing' (Book I, Chapter 3, p. 84, I: 94). Gandalf's words in Book I, Chapter 2 had been similar: 'I don't think you need go alone. Not if you know of anyone you can trust, and who would be willing to go by your side' (p. 63, I: 72).

106 (I: 116): It was made on the model

106 (I: 116). It was made on the model of the dwarf-song that started Bilbo on his adventure long ago, and went to the same tune: – That song, 'Far over the misty mountains cold', etc., was published in *The Hobbit*, Chapter 1; it refers to Dwarf history, the coming of the dragon, and the quest the dwarves are about to begin ('We must away ere break of day, / To claim our long-forgotten gold'). The song here is less grim, more hopeful (in the Hobbit manner): the hobbits do not know where their journey will take them.

106 (I: 116): *Farewell we call to hearth and hall!*

106 (I: 116). *Farewell we call to hearth and hall!* . . . – A recording by Tolkien of this poem is included on Disc 1 of *The J.R.R. Tolkien Audio Collection.*

106–7 (I: 117): 'The answer to the second question

107 (I: 117). I have prepared practically everything – In the preceding chapters the reader has come to know Frodo, Sam, and Pippin. Now Tolkien establishes Merry as a responsible, thoughtful character able to plan and prepare, distinguishing him from the more impulsive, less mature Pippin.

107 (I: 117). five ponies – As first published these words read 'six ponies', a trace of an earlier version of the story, in which five hobbits were to journey together, requiring a pony each and one for baggage. This changed when it became Fredegar Bolger's task to stay behind, but the extra pony remained. See *The Return of the Shadow*, pp. 326–7. Although some readers have tried to explain the reading 'six ponies' by suggesting that one was for Fredegar to ride with his friends as far as the hedge, Merry is here answering Frodo's question about preparations, with details of transport and provisions specifically for the four hobbits who are to make the journey – excluding Fredegar.

107 (I: 117). stores and tackle – Provisions and equipment for their travels.

107 (I: 117): 'That all depends on what you think

107 (I: 117). if they were not stopped at the North-gate, where the Hedge runs down to the river-bank, just this side of the Bridge. The gate-guards would not let them through by night – In his unfinished index Tolkien notes that the *North-gate* is the same as the 'Buckland Gate' and the 'Hay Gate' referred to by Merry in Book VI, Chapters 7 and 8. The present passage makes it clear that anyone wishing to enter Buckland from the north had to pass through a gate and might be questioned by guards.

107 (I: 117). the Master of the Hall – In fact, Merry's father.

108 (I: 118): Fond as he was of Frodo

108 (I: 118). Budgeford in Bridgefields – In his unfinished index Tolkien describes *Budgeford* as a 'village by a ford over the Shire-water in Bridgefields (chief dwelling of the Bolgers)'. In *Nomenclature* he states that '*budge-* was an obscured element, having at the time no clear meaning. Since it [Budgeford] was the main residence of the *Bolger* family . . . it [*budge-*] may be regarded as a corruption of the element *bolge, bulge*.'

Bridgefields is described in *Index* simply as a 'district of the Shire, along the Brandywine, north of the main road (largely inhabited by the Bolgers)'.

108 (I: 118). but he had never been over the Brandywine Bridge – Fatty is now in Buckland, east of the Brandywine, but he has certainly been on the west side of the river, since he was present at Bilbo's party (indicated in Appendix C) as well as Frodo's birthday dinner at Bag End only a few days earlier, and earlier 'often in and out of Bag End' (Book I, Chapter 2, p. 42, I: 51). It seems unlikely that Tolkien meant to suggest that Fatty always crossed the river by the ferry, and not the bridge; presumably these words are meant to convey that he had never travelled further East on the Road than the Brandywine Bridge, beyond which is the wide world.

108 (I: 118–19): When at last he had got to bed

108 (I: 118–19). a vague dream, in which he seemed to be looking out of a high window over a dark sea of tangled trees. Down below among the roots there was sound of creatures crawling and snuffling. He felt sure they would smell him out sooner or later – Frodo's dream seems to anticipate his first night in Lothlórien, when he hears orcs pass by the tree in which he is sleeping, and Gollum sniffing and scrabbling at its foot; yet it goes back to the earliest version of the chapter, long before any idea of Lothlórien arose in Tolkien's mind.

108 (I: 119): Then he heard a noise in the distance

108 (I: 119). the Sound of the Sea far-off. . . . He was on a dark heath. . . . Looking up he saw before him a tall white tower, standing alone on a high ridge. A great desire came over him to climb the tower and see the Sea. He started to struggle up the ridge towards the tower: but suddenly a light came in the sky, and there was a noise of thunder. – The final paragraphs of this chapter are all that remain of a much longer dream which Tolkien introduced into the narrative in autumn 1939 to explain Gandalf's absence. Gandalf has been pursued by Black Riders, and has taken refuge in a tower. Black Riders are watching the tower, but withdraw when summoned by another Rider; then a grey-mantled figure on a white horse makes his escape. Tolkien was uncertain when Frodo should experience this dream: he tried to place it at Bree where, as the dream ended,

Frodo saw a light and heard thunder, then woke as Trotter (the hobbit 'ranger') drew the curtains and pushed back the shutters with a clang; then he moved it to the night at Crickhollow, adding it to a dream already written for that night. But when Tolkien replaced this idea for Gandalf's absence with his imprisonment at Orthanc by Saruman, he removed most of dream from the end of this chapter, leaving only the beginning in which Frodo sees a tall white tower, and added a desire to climb it for a view of the Sea (compare note for p. 7, on the Elf-towers at the edge of the Shire). Christopher Tolkien comments in *The Treason of Isengard*: 'And so the tall white tower of Frodo's dream at Crickhollow in the final tale remains from what was the precursor of Orthanc; and the thunder that he heard goes back to the interruption of his dream by Trotter's thrusting back the shutters at *The Prancing Pony*' (p. 36).

Chapter 6

THE OLD FOREST

For drafts and history of this chapter, see *The Return of the Shadow*, chiefly pp. 110–16, 302, 327–8; *The Treason of Isengard*, p. 36.

109 (I: 120): Frodo woke suddenly

109 (I: 120). Frodo woke – It is 26 September 1418.

109 (I: 120): 'What is it!' cried Merry

109 (I: 120). sluggard – A lazy, slow-moving person.

109 (I: 120): Soon after six o'clock

109 (I: 120). spinney – A small wood, a thicket. (Compare *thicket*, note for p. 76.)

109 (I: 120): In their shed they found the ponies

109 (I: 120). the Hedge – The High Hay; see note for p. 99.

110 (I: 121): 'I don't know what stories you mean

110 (I: 121). goblins – See note for p. 5 (*Orcs*).

110 (I: 121). In fact long ago they attacked the Hedge: they came and planted themselves right by it, and leaned over it. But the hobbits came and cut down hundreds of trees, and made a great bonfire in the Forest. . . . After that the trees gave up the attack, but they became very unfriendly. – In fact, the trees were naturally propagating. In a letter to the *Daily Telegraph*, 30 June 1972, Tolkien wrote: 'In all my works I take the part of trees as against all their enemies. Lothlórien is beautiful because there the trees were loved; elsewhere forests are represented as awakening to consciousness of themselves. The Old Forest was hostile to two legged creatures because of the memory of many injuries' (*Letters*, p. 419).

111–12 (I: 122–3): The light grew clearer

112 (I: 123). hemlocks and wood-parsley, fire-weed seeding into fluffy ashes, and rampant nettles and thistles – By *hemlocks* Tolkien may be referring to *Conium maculatum*, which Roger Philips in *Wild Flowers of Britain* (1977) describes as common in England and Wales, growing to a height of two metres, mainly in damp places but also on disturbed ground. But Tolkien often used *hemlocks* in a wider sense. Christopher Tolkien has said: 'My father used to refer to all the big white umbellifers as "hemlocks", although he was well aware that a lot of them were really cow parsley or chervil' (private correspondence). The *Oxford English Dictionary* notes that *hemlock* is 'also in rural use applied to the large *Umbelliferae* generally'.

Wood-parsley may be the same as the *cow parsley* (*Anthriscus sylvestris*) mentioned by Christopher Tolkien.

Fire-weed may be *Epilobium angustifolium*, a wildflower commonly found in woodland areas that have been cleared or burned off.

Nettles and *thistles* are prickly plants of various genera.

Plant names in *The Lord of the Rings* are discussed by J.A. Schulp in 'The Flora of Middle-earth', *Inklings-Jahrbuch für Literatur und Ästhetik* 3 (1985).

113–14 (I: 124–5): On the south-eastern side

114 (I: 125). the Barrow-downs – In *Nomenclature* Tolkien describes the *Barrow-downs* as 'low treeless hills on which there were many "barrows", sc. tumuli and other prehistoric grave-mounds. This *barrow* is not related to modern *barrow* "an implement with a wheel"; it is a recent adoption by archaeologists of dialectal *barrow* (< *berrow* < Old English *beorg, berg* "hill, mound").' See further, note for p. 130.

In Europe the custom of burying the dead in mounds began in the Neolithic period and continued through the Viking period. In the former, many barrows were family graves, but in later times burial mounds were raised mainly over the bodies of kings or chieftains, often interred with rich grave-goods. Tom Shippey points out that Tolkien would have seen many real barrows: 'Barely fifteen miles from Tolkien's study the Berkshire Downs rise from the Oxfordshire plain, thickly studded with Stone Age mounds, among them the famous Wayland's Smithy, from which a track leads to Nine Barrows Down' (*J.R.R. Tolkien: Author of the Century* (2000), p. 61).

115 (I: 126): After stumbling along for some way

115 (I: 126). a dark river of brown water, bordered with ancient willows, arched over with willows, blocked with fallen willows, and flecked with thousands of faded willow-leaves. The air was thick with them, fluttering yellow from the branches – These features are depicted in Tolkien's drawing *Old Man Willow* (*Artist and Illustrator*, fig. 147). The large willow in its foreground may have been suggested by tree-drawings by Arthur Rackham. Tom Shippey has pointed out that only a short walk from his home in Northmoor Road, Oxford Tolkien 'would have seen virtually the same sight: the slow, muddy, lazy river fringed with willows. The real river, the one that flows into the Thames at Oxford, is the Cherwell' (*J.R.R. Tolkien: Author of the Century*, p. 63). Eilert Ekwall, *English River-names*, suggests 'winding river' as a possible meaning of *Cherwell*; cf. 'Withywindle', note for p. 99.

115–16 (I: 127): There being nothing else for it

116 (I: 127). rills – A *rill* is a small stream.

117 (I: 128): Half in a dream

117 (I: 128). dragonets – Small dragons.

117 (I: 128): 'Do you know, Sam'

117 (I: 128). the beastly tree *threw* me in! – Verlyn Flieger points out in 'Taking the Part of Trees: Eco-Conflict in Middle-earth', *J.R.R. Tolkien and His Literary Resonances: Views of Middle-earth* (2000), that since Tolkien's love of trees is well known

> it may come as something of a shock to be reminded that the first real villain to be met in *LR* is a tree. I except the Black Riders, since at this point in the narrative we have not met, but only seen and heard them. We do not know who or what they are or what they want. But we know more than enough about Old Man Willow. Huge, hostile, malicious, his trapping of Merry and Pippin in his willowy toils, his attempt to drown Frodo, give the hobbits their first major setback, and come uncomfortably close to ending their journey before it has properly started. [p. 148]

Old Man Willow existed before Tolkien began *The Lord of the Rings*. He was one of the several adversaries encountered, and overcome, by Tom Bombadil in the poem *The Adventures of Tom Bombadil* published in the *Oxford Magazine* in 1934. Early in the writing of *The Lord of the Rings*, when Tolkien was trying to think of suitable adventures for the hobbits, he decided to incorporate elements from the poem into the story, among them that the hobbits would have 'Adventure with Willowman and Barrow-wights' (*The Return of the Shadow*, p. 43). In the poem, Old Man Willow catches Tom in a crack; therefore one or more hobbits were destined to suffer the same fate. Also, Tom is pulled into the river by Goldberry; thus in *The Lord of the Rings* Old Man Willow throws Frodo into the river. But the light-hearted tone of the poem had to be adapted to the more serious story. Old Man Willow became a much greater menace, and the source even of the hobbits' earlier difficulties in the Old Forest: 'his song and thought ran through the woods on both sides of the river. His grey thirsty spirit drew power out of the earth and spread like fine root-threads in the ground, and invisible twig fingers in the air, till it had under its dominion nearly all the trees of the Forest from the Hedge to the Downs' (Book I, Chapter 7, p. 130, I: 141).

118 (I: 129): 'We might try to hurt or frighten this tree

118 (I: 129). tinder-boxes – Equipment for lighting fires, with tinder (a dry substance that readily catches fire from a spark), flint (hard stone which when struck gives off a spark), and steel. This is in keeping with pre-industrial Hobbit society, though Bilbo in *The Hobbit* has matches. See further, Anders Stenström (Beregond), 'Striking Matches', *Arda* 5 (1988, for 1985).

119 (I: 130): ***Hey! Come merry dol! derry dol! My darling!***

119 (I: 130). ***Hey! Come merry dol! derry dol! My darling! . . .*** – A recording by Tolkien of this poem is included on Disc 1 of *The J.R.R. Tolkien Audio Collection.*

119 (I: 130). ***Old Tom Bombadil*** – Michael and Priscilla, Tolkien's second son and daughter, told members of the Tolkien Society in 1974 that *Tom Bombadil* was the name of a colourful Dutch doll owned by the Tolkien children, dressed exactly as Tom is described in *The Lord of the Rings.* (Another report, quoting Tolkien's eldest son, John, agrees; according to Humphrey Carpenter, *Biography,* the doll belonged to Michael.) As such, it may have been one of the Tolkien sons or daughter who chose its name rather than Tolkien himself; at any rate, the name was devised years before Tolkien began *The Lord of the Rings,* and the character had already appeared in a story and a poem.

The story apparently was told first in oral form. A written version was abandoned soon after it gave a description of a 'Tom Bombadil' similar to that in *The Lord of the Rings*: 'Tom Bombadil was the name of one of the oldest inhabitants of the kingdom; but he was a hale and hearty fellow. Four feet high in his boots he was, and three feet broad. He wore a tall hat with a blue feather, his jacket was blue, and his boots were yellow' (quoted in *Biography,* p. 162). Tolkien also wrote a poem about Tom Bombadil, published in the *Oxford Magazine* for 15 February 1934:

Old Tom Bombadil was a merry fellow;
bright blue his jacket was, and his boots were yellow.
He lived down under Hill; and a peacock's feather
nodded in his old hat, tossing in the weather.

Old Tom Bombadil walked about the meadows
gathering the buttercups, a-chasing of the shadows,
tickling the bumblebees a-buzzing in the flowers,
sitting by the waterside for hours upon hours.

There his beard dangled long down into the water:
up came Goldberry, the Riverwoman's daughter;
pulled Tom's hanging hair. In he went a-wallowing
under the waterlilies, bubbling and a-swallowing.

'Hey! Tom Bombadil, whither are you going?'
said fair Goldberry. 'Bubbles you are blowing,
frightening the finny fish and the brown water-rat,
startling the dabchicks, drowning your feather-hat!'

Back to her mother's house in the deepest hollow
swam young Goldberry; but Tom, he would not follow.
On knotted willow-roots he sat in sunny weather
drying his yellow boots and his draggled feather.

Up woke Willow-man, began upon his singing,
sang Tom fast asleep under branches swinging;
in a crack caught him tight: quiet it closed together,
trapped Tom Bombadil, coat and hat and feather.

'Ha! Tom Bombadil, what be you a-thinking,
peeping inside my tree, watching me a-drinking
deep in my wooden house, tickling me with feather,
dripping wet down my face like a rainy weather?'

'You let me out again, Old Man Willow!
I am stiff lying here; they're no sort of pillow,
your hard crooked roots. Drink your river water!
Go back to sleep again, like the River-daughter!'

Willow-man let him loose, when he heard him speaking;
locked fast his wooden house, muttering and creaking,
whispering inside the tree. Tom, he sat a-listening.
On the boughs piping birds were chirruping and whistling.
Tom saw butterflies quivering and winking;
Tom called the conies out, till the sun was sinking.

Then Tom went away. Rain began to shiver,
round rings spattering in the running river.
Clouds passed, hurrying drops were falling helter-skelter;
old Tom Bombadil crept into a shelter.

Out came Badger-brock with his snowy forehead
and his dark blinking eyes. In the hill he quarried
with his wife and many sons. By the coat they caught him,
pulled him inside the hole, down their tunnels brought him.

Inside their secret house, there they sat a-mumbling:
'Ho! Tom Bombadil, where have you come tumbling,
bursting in the front-door? Badgerfolk have caught you:
you'll never find it out, the way that we have brought you!'

'Now, old Badger-brock, do you hear me talking?
You show me out at once! I must be a-walking.

Show me to your backdoor under briar-roses;
then clean grimy paws, wipe your earthy noses!
Go back to sleep again on your straw pillow
like fair Goldberry and Old Man Willow!'

Then all the Badgerfolk said 'We beg your pardon!'
showed Tom out again to their thorny garden,
went back and hid themselves a-shivering and a-shaking,
blocked up all their doors, earth together raking.

Old Tom Bombadil hurried home to supper,
unlocked his house again, opened up the shutter,
let in the setting sun in the kitchen shining,
watched stars peering out and the moon climbing.

Dark came under Hill. Tom, he lit a candle,
up-stairs creaking went, turned the door handle.
'Hoo! Tom Bombadil, I am waiting for you
just here behind the door! I came up before you.
You've forgotten Barrow-wight dwelling in the old mound
up there a-top the hill with the ring of stones round.
He's got loose to-night: under the earth he'll take you!
Poor Tom Bombadil, pale and cold he'll make you!'

'Go out! Shut the door, and don't slam it after!
Take away gleaming eyes, take your hollow laughter!
Go back to grassy mound, on your stony pillow
lay down your bony head, like Old Man Willow,
like young Goldberry, and Badgerfolk in burrow!
Go back to buried gold and forgotten sorrow!'

Out fled Barrow-wight, through the window flying,
through yard, over wall, up the hill a-crying,
past white drowsing sheep, over leaning stone-rings,
back under lonely mound, rattling his bone-rings.

Old Tom Bombadil lay upon his pillow
sweeter than Goldberry, quieter than the Willow,
snugger than Badgerfolk, or the barrow-dwellers;
slept like a hummingtop, snored like a bellows.

He woke up in morning-light, whistled like a starling,
sang 'come, derry-dol, merry-dol, my darling!';
clapped on his battered hat, boots and coat and feather,
opened the window wide to the sunny weather.

Old Tom Bombadil was a clever fellow;
bright blue his jacket was, and his boots were yellow.
None ever caught old Tom, walking in the meadows
winter and summer-time, in the lights and shadows,
down dale, over hill, jumping over water –
but one day Tom he went and caught the River-daughter,
in green gown, flowing hair, sitting in the rushes,
an old song singing fair to birds upon the bushes.

He caught her, held her fast! Water-rats went scuttering,
reeds hissed, herons cried; and her heart was fluttering.
Said Tom Bombadil: 'Here's my pretty maiden!
You shall come home with me! The table is all laden:
yellow cream, honeycomb, white bread and butter;
roses at window-pane peeping through the shutter.
You shall come under Hill – never mind your mother
in her deep weedy pool: there you'll find no lover!'

Old Tom Bombadil had a merry wedding
crowned all in buttercups, his old feather shedding;
his bride with forgetmenots and flaglilies for garland,
robed all in silver-green. He sang like a starling,
hummed like a honeybee, lilted to the fiddle,
clasping his river-maid round her slender middle.

Lamps gleamed within his house, and white was the bedding;
in the bright honey-moon Badgerfolk came treading,
danced down under Hill, and Old Man Willow
tapped, tapped at window-pane, as they slept on the pillow;
on the bank in the reeds Riverwoman sighing
heard old Barrow-wight in his mound crying.

Old Tom Bombadil heeded not the voices,
taps, knocks, dancing feet, all the nightly noises;
slept till the sun arose, then sang like a starling:
'Hey! come, derry-rol, merry-dol, my darling!'
sitting on the doorstep chopping sticks of willow,
while fair Goldberry combed her tresses yellow.

On 16 December 1937, pressed for a new story about Hobbits but temporarily unable to think of one, Tolkien wrote to Stanley Unwin: 'Perhaps a new (if similar) line? Do you think Tom Bombadil, the spirit of the (vanishing) Oxford and Berkshire countryside, could be made into the hero of a story? Or is he, as I suspect, fully enshrined in the enclosed verses [from the *Oxford Magazine*]? Still I could enlarge the portrait'

(*Letters*, p. 26). He then almost immediately began a new story about Hobbits, but one in which he incorporated and enlarged in power or significance not only Tom Bombadil, but almost all of the other characters who appear in the poem, and recycled most of Tom's adventures. In his draft letter to Peter Hastings, September 1954, Tolkien commented that he put Tom Bombadil into *The Lord of the Rings* 'because I had already "invented" him independently . . . and wanted an "adventure" on the way' (*Letters*, p. 192). See further, Christina Scull, 'Tom Bombadil and *The Lord of the Rings*', and Patricia Reynolds, 'The Real Tom Bombadil', both in *Leaves from the Tree: J.R.R. Tolkien's Shorter Fiction* (1991).

In his Preface to *The Adventures of Tom Bombadil and Other Verses from the Red Book*, for which he revised the original poem, Tolkien states that the name 'Tom Bombadil' was probably given to him by the hobbits of Buckland 'to add to his many older ones', and is 'Bucklandish' in form. At the Council of Elrond (Book II, Chapter 2) we learn some of his other names. Elrond says: 'I had forgotten Bombadil, if indeed this is still the same that walked the woods and hills long ago, and even then was older than the old. That was not then his name. Iarwain Ben-adar we called him, oldest and fatherless. But many another name he has since been given by other folk: Forn by the Dwarves, Orald by Northern Men, and other names beside' (p. 265, I: 278). In an unpublished draft letter of late 1968 Tolkien wrote that '*Iarwain* = old-young, presumably because as far as anybody remembered he had always looked much the same: old but very vigorous' (private collection). In *Nomenclature* (under *Orald*) Tolkien states that *Forn* and *Orald* 'are meant to be names in foreign tongues (not Common Speech). . . . *Forn* is actually the Scandinavian word for "(belonging to) ancient (days)". . . . *Orald* is an Old English word for "very ancient", evidently meant [in *The Lord of the Rings*] to represent the language of the Rohirrim and their kin.'

119 (I: 130). ***water-lilies*** – White water-lilies, *Nymphaea alba*, are native to Britain. They float in lakes and ponds.

119 (I: 130). ***Goldberry*** – In both the *Bombadil* poem and *The Lord of the Rings* Goldberry is referred to as 'River-woman's daughter', with no further explanation. In the poem, where Goldberry pulls Tom into the river by his beard, she resembles the traditional beautiful, golden-haired water-sprite or nixie, sometimes accused of pulling humans into a river or lake to drown. Further, in the poem, Tom and Goldberry have a 'merry wedding', but in *The Lord of the Rings* their exact relationship is not made clear. Tolkien was startled when the 1955 BBC radio adaptation of *The Fellowship of the Ring* described Goldberry as Tom's *daughter*.

119 (I: 130–1): Frodo and Sam stood as if enchanted

119 (I: 130). an old battered hat with a tall crown and a long blue feather – In the *Bombadil* poem of 1934 Tom wears a peacock's feather in his hat;

in the 1962 revision this became 'a swan-wing feather'. Tolkien wrote to Rayner Unwin on 12 April 1962:

> You may note that I have written a new *Bombadil* poem [*Bombadil Goes Boating*], which I hope is adequate to go with the older one, though for its understanding it requires some knowledge of the *L.R.* At any rate it performs the service of further 'integrating' Tom with the world of the *L.R.* into which he was inserted. In the original poem he was said to wear a peacock's feather, which (I think you will agree) was entirely unsuitable for the situation in the *L.R.* In it his feather is merely reported as 'blue'. Its origin is now revealed. [*Letters*, p. 315]

In *Bombadil Goes Boating*, written for the 1962 *Adventures of Tom Bombadil* volume but based on older workings, Tom encounters a kingfisher as he travels down the Withywindle:

> *The King's fisher shut his beak, winked his eye, as singing*
> *Tom passed under bough. Flash! then he went winging;*
> *dropped down jewel-blue a feather, and Tom caught it*
> *gleaming in a sun-ray: a pretty gift he thought it.*
> *He stuck it in his tall hat, the old feather casting:*
> *'Blue now for Tom', he said, 'a merry hue and lasting!'*

In his Preface to *The Adventures of Tom Bombadil and Other Verses from the Red Book* Tolkien suggests that the two 'Bombadil' poems were written by hobbits in Buckland, and 'show that the Bucklanders knew Bombadil, though, no doubt, they had as little understanding of his powers as the Shire-folk had of Gandalf's: both were regarded as benevolent persons, mysterious maybe and unpredictable but nonetheless comic. [*The Adventures of Tom Bombadil*] is made up of various hobbit-versions of legends concerning Bombadil' (p. 9).

120 (I: 131): 'Whoa! Whoa! steady there!'

120 (I: 131). Now my little fellows, where be you a-going-to, puffing like a bellows? What's the matter here then? Do you know who I am? – All of Tom's speech, even that printed as prose, has a rhythm suggesting verse. Tom Shippey comments that Tom Bombadil

> does not yet seem to have discovered, or sunk into, prose. Much of what he says is printed by Tolkien as verse, but almost all of what he says can be *read* as verse, falling into strongly-marked two-stress phrases, with or without rhyme and alliteration, usually with feminine or unstressed endings. . . . The point is though that while we appreciate it as rhythmical (unlike prose), we also do not mark it as premeditated or artificial (unlike verse). [*The Road to Middle-earth*, 2nd edn., p. 97]

Shippey develops this theme further in *J.R.R. Tolkien: Author of the Century*, suggesting that the style of Tom's verse and speech reflect his closeness to nature:

> He is a kind of exhalation of the earth, a nature-spirit . . . a highly English one: cheerful, noisy, unpretentious to the point of shabbiness, extremely direct, apparently rather simple, not as simple as he looks. The fact that everything he says is in a sort of verse, whether printed as verse or not, and that the hobbits too find themselves 'singing merrily, as if it was easier and more natural than talking', make him seem, not an artist, but someone from an age before art and nature were distinguished, when magic needed no wizard's staff but came from words alone. Tolkien may have got the idea from the singing wizards of the Finnish epic the *Kalevala*, which he so much admired. . . . [p. 64]

120 (I: 131): 'What?' shouted Tom Bombadil

120 (I: 131). Old grey Willow-man! I'll freeze his marrow cold, if he don't behave himself. I'll sing his roots off. I'll sing a wind up and blow leaf and branch away. – But he never does. In his draft letter to Peter Hastings, September 1954, Tolkien notes that although he is master of 'his natural little realm', Tom Bombadil 'hardly even judges, and as far as can be seen makes no effort to reform or remove even the Willow' (*Letters*, p. 192).

121 (I: 132): *Hop along, my little friends, up the Withywindle!*

121 (I: 132). *Hop along, my little friends, up the Withywindle!* . . . – A recording by Tolkien of this poem is included on Disc 1 of *The J.R.R. Tolkien Audio Collection.*

121 (I: 132): It became difficult to follow the path

121 (I: 132). they caught sight of queer gnarled and knobbly faces that gloomed dark against the twilight, and leered down at them from the high bank and the edges of the wood – The image recalls pictures of trees by British artist Arthur Rackham, whose illustrations Tolkien admired.

121–2 (I: 133): The grass under their feet

121 (I: 133). knoll – A small hill or mound.

Chapter 7

IN THE HOUSE OF TOM BOMBADIL

For drafts and history of this chapter, see *The Return of the Shadow*, chiefly pp. 115–24, 303–4, 328–9; *The Treason of Isengard*, chiefly pp. 36–7.

123 (I: 134): In a chair, at the far side of the room

123 (I: 134). Her long yellow hair rippled down her shoulders; her gown was green, green as young reeds, shot with silver like beads of dew; and her belt was of gold, shaped like a chain of flag-lilies set with the pale-blue eyes of forget-me-nots. – The gown and belt of Goldberry, the 'River-woman's daughter', are described with appropriate water or river imagery. According to the *Bombadil* poem, at her wedding she wore a garland of forget-me-nots and flag-lilies, and a robe of silver-green.

Flag-lily or *yellow-flag* is another name for the same iris that gave its name to the Gladden Fields (see note for p. 52). It is a perennial, native to Britain, growing in marshes and in wet ground by rivers.

123 (I: 134). About her feet in wide vessels of green and brown earthenware, white water-lilies were floating, so that she seemed to be enthroned in the midst of a pool – Goldberry may have left the river to become Tom's wife, but she still surrounds herself with her element. Later, 'her gown rustled softly like the wind in the flowering borders of a river', and her shoes are said to be 'like fishes' mail'.

123 (I: 134): 'Enter, good guests!'

123 (I: 134). a fair young elf-queen – In 'Higher Argument: Tolkien and the Tradition of Vision, Epic and Prophecy', *Proceedings of the J.R.R. Tolkien Centenary Conference 1992* (1995), Deirdre Greene comments that

> Frodo's first sight of Goldberry in the house of Tom Bombadil tells the reader a great deal about the woman and, by association, her mate. . . . The dwelling has low roofs, indicating simple humility; it is filled with light, suggesting spiritual good; the furnishings and the candles are of natural materials, connoting rural closeness to nature. Goldberry's chair, far opposite the door, suggests a throne in a reception hall. Her yellow hair suggests innocence and goodness; it is yellow rather than gold, emphasizing her unassuming nature. Her gown associates her with lush, young vegetation. Her belt is the gold of purity and sovereignty, but it celebrates in its floral design the eternal, cyclical triumph of nature; she is encircled by water and flowers, symbols of purity and fertility. As a

> whole, the image asserts Goldberry as a queen or a local deity, whose power derives from nature. . . . [pp. 47–8]

Goldberry in *The Lord of the Rings* has stature, and powers, not even hinted at in the 1934 poem. In June 1958 Tolkien wrote to Forrest J. Ackerman that in *The Lord of the Rings* 'we are . . . in real river-lands in autumn. Goldberry represents the actual seasonal changes in such lands' (*Letters*, p. 272).

124 (I: 135): Frodo looked at her

124 (I: 135). He is, as you have seen him. . . . He is the Master of wood, water, and hill. – Soon after the publication of *The Fellowship of the Ring* Peter Hastings, the manager of a Catholic bookshop in Oxford, wrote to Tolkien querying Goldberry's description of Tom Bombadil as 'He is'. He said that this seemed to imply that Tom was God. In a draft reply of September 1954 Tolkien wrote:

> As for Tom Bombadil, I really do think you are being too serious, besides missing the point. . . . Lots of other characters [in *The Lord of the Rings*] are called Master; and if 'in time' Tom was primeval he was Eldest in Time. But Goldberry and Tom are referring to the mystery of *names* [see note for p. 131]. . . . You may be able to conceive of your unique relation to the Creator without a name – can you: for in such a relation pronouns become proper nouns? But as soon as you are in a world of other finites with a similar, if each unique and different relation to the Prime Being, who are you? Frodo has asked not 'what is Tom Bombadil' but 'Who is he'. We and he no doubt often laxly confuse the questions. Goldberry gives what I think is the correct answer. We need not go into the sublimities of 'I am that I am' [God's words to Moses in Exodus 3:14] – which is quite different from *he is*. She adds as a concession a statement of part of the 'what'. He is *master* in a peculiar way: he has no fear, and no desire of possessions or domination at all. He merely knows and understands about such things as concern him in his natural little realm. [*Letters*, pp. 191–2]

In notes Tolkien made before drafting this chapter, the emphasis of Goldberry's reply is somewhat different: 'He is not the possessor but the master, because he belongs to himself' (*The Return of the Shadow*, p. 117). This is perhaps a way of saying that Tom is master of himself, and fulfils the precept 'Know thyself' attributed to many ancient authorities.

Many readers of *The Lord of the Rings* would like fuller answers to the questions of who or what is Tom Bombadil, but Tolkien never provided them. He wrote to Naomi Mitchison on 25 April 1954:

> There is of course a clash between 'literary' technique, and the fascination of elaborating in detail an imaginary mythical Age. . . . As a story, I think it is good that there should be a lot of things unexplained

(especially if an explanation actually exists); and I have perhaps from this point of view erred in trying to explain too much, and give too much past history. . . . And even in a mythical Age there must be some enigmas, as there always are. Tom Bombadil is one (intentionally). . . .

Tom Bombadil is not an important person – to the narrative. I suppose he has some importance as a 'comment'. I mean, I do not really write like that: he is just an invention . . . and he represents something that I feel important, though I would not be prepared to analyze the feeling precisely. I would not, however, have left him in, if he did not have some kind of function. I might put it this way. The story is cast in terms of a good side, and a bad side, beauty against ruthless ugliness, tyranny against kingship, moderated freedom with consent against compulsion that has lost any object save mere power, and so on; but both sides in some degree, conservative or destructive, want a measure of control. But if you have, as it were taken 'a vow of poverty', renounced control, and take your delight in things for themselves without reference to yourself, watching, observing, and to some extent knowing, then the question of the rights and wrongs of power and control might become utterly meaningless to you, and the means of power quite valueless. It is a natural pacifist view, which always arises in the mind when there is a war. But the view of Rivendell seems to be that it is an excellent thing to have represented, but that there are in fact things with which it cannot cope; and upon which its existence nonetheless depends. Ultimately only the victory of the West will allow Bombadil to continue, or even to survive. Nothing would be left for him in the world of Sauron. [*Letters*, pp. 174, 178–9]

Tolkien used similar words about Tom Bombadil in his draft letter to Peter Hastings, September 1954:

I don't think Tom needs philosophizing about, and is not improved by it. . . . I kept him in, and as he was, because he represents certain things otherwise left out. I do not mean him to be an allegory – or I should not have given him so particular, individual, and ridiculous a name – but 'allegory' is the only mode of exhibiting certain functions: he is then an 'allegory', or an exemplar, a particular embodying of pure (real) natural science: the spirit that desires knowledge of other things, their history and nature, *because they are 'other'* and wholly independent of the enquiring mind, a spirit coeval with the rational mind, and entirely unconcerned with 'doing' anything with the knowledge: Zoology and Botany not Cattle-breeding or Agriculture. [*Letters*, p. 192]

In *Amon Hen* 173 (January 2002) Christopher Fettes quoted from a letter sent to him by Tolkien in 1961:

I think there are two answers: (i) External (ii) Internal; according to (i) Bombadil just came into my mind independently and got swept into

> the growing stream of *The Lord of the Rings*. The original poem about him, in the curious rhythm which characterizes him, appeared in the *Oxford Magazine* at some time not long before the war. According to (ii), I have left him where he is and not attempted to clarify his position, first of all because I like him and he has at any rate a satisfying geographical home in the lands of *The Lord of the Rings*; but more seriously because in any world or universe devised imaginatively (or imposed simply upon the actual world) there is always some element that does not fit and opens as it were a window into some other system. You will notice that though the Ring is a serious matter and has great power for all the inhabitants of the world of *The Lord of the Rings* even the best and the most holy, it does not touch Tom Bombadil at all. So Bombadil is 'fatherless', he has no historical origin in the world described in *The Lord of the Rings*. [pp. 31–2]

In an unpublished draft letter in 1968 Tolkien wrote: '*I* do *not* know his [Tom Bombadil's] origin though I might make guesses. He is best left as he is, a mystery. There are many mysteries in any closed/organized system of history/mythology' (private collection; see further, note for p. 131).

124 (I: 135): 'No, indeed!' she answered

124 (I: 135). No one ever caught old Tom walking in the forest, wading in the water, leaping on the hill-tops, under light and shadow. . . . He has no fear. Tom Bombadil is master. – Tom's ability to escape from every danger is the main theme of the 1934 poem. He is threatened or caught in turn by Goldberry, Old Man Willow, the Badgerfolk, and the Barrow-wight, but at his command each releases him. Goldberry's words echo those of the poem: 'None ever caught old Tom, walking in the meadows / winter and summer-time, in the lights and shadows, / down dale, over hill, jumping over water'.

124 (I: 135): 'Here's my pretty lady

124 (I: 135). I see yellow cream and honeycomb, and white bread, and butter; milk, cheese, and green herbs and ripe berries – In the 1934 poem 'the table is all laden: / yellow cream, honeycomb, white bread and butter'. Here more foods have been added – but no meats.

125 (I: 136): He opened the door

125 (I: 136). The floor was flagged, and strewn with fresh green rushes – That is, the floor was constructed of flagstones, flat rectangular stone slabs used for paving.

In medieval times and later in the country *rushes* (slender marsh plants of the family *Juncaceae*) or reeds were strewn on floors for warmth and were regularly replaced.

127 (I: 138): In the dead of night

127 (I: 138). Then he saw the young moon rising – In 'Tolkien's Calendar & Ithildin', *Mythlore* 9, no. 4, whole no. 34 (Winter 1982), Rhona Beare comments that 'this was a fantastic dream-moon; it was waxing and yet he [Frodo] saw it rise by night . . . the waxing moon always rises by day and sets before sunrise' (p. 23). The *young moon* in Frodo's dream may derive from Tolkien's first account, later changed, of Gandalf's escape from Orthanc on a night when 'the moon was still young' (*The Treason of Isengard*, p. 134).

127 (I: 138). A mighty eagle swept down and bore him away. – Frodo is dreaming of Gandalf's escape from Orthanc in the early hours of 18 September. Gandalf will give a detailed account of the escape in Book II, Chapter 2.

127 (I: 138). the sound of hoofs, galloping, galloping from the East. 'Black Riders!' – This part of the dream is probably linked in time with that of Gandalf's escape, and with the Riders' journey to the Shire, which they reached on the day Frodo left Bag End.

127 (I: 138): At his side Pippin lay dreaming

127 (I: 138). twig-fingers scraping wall and window . . . he had a dreadful feeling that he was still . . . inside the willow – In the *Bombadil* poem Old Man Willow 'tapped, tapped at window-pane' on Tom and Goldberry's wedding night.

128 (I: 139): As far as he could remember

128 (I: 139). Sam slept through the night in deep content, if logs are contented. – An oblique reference to the phrase *to sleep like a log*, i.e. to sleep soundly.

128 (I: 139): They woke up, all four at once

128 (I: 139). They woke – It is the morning of 27 September 1418.

128 (I: 139–40): 'Good morning, merry friends!'

128 (I: 139). nosing wind and weather – *To nose* 'to find out, discover by means of scent', but also, in this context, to enjoy a breath of fresh morning air.

128 (I: 139). naught wakes hobbit-folk – In editions prior to 2004 these words read 'nought wakes hobbit-folk'. On a proof of *The Return of the King* (Sotheby's catalogue, 21–2 July 1992, lot 183): Tolkien wrote in reply to a printer's query about *naught* versus *nought* that he did not mind which was used, since the English language had hesitated between *a* and *o* in this word for twelve centuries, and he did so himself. It is evident, however, that he decided in favour of *naught* as there were no instances of *nought* in the first printing of *The Return of the King*. Some instances of *nought* did appear in early printings of *The Fellowship of the Ring* and *The Two Towers*, but most of these were changed during Tolkien's lifetime on his instructions: one instance in *The Fellowship of the Ring* was changed in the second printing (1954), and is noted in correspondence with Allen & Unwin in September 1954, months before the printer's query mentioned above; a second example in *Fellowship* was changed in the second printing (1967) of the Allen & Unwin second edition; and six instances in *The Two Towers* all changed in the fourth printing (1956) of its first edition. Tolkien evidently authorized the change when it came to his notice, but missed four instances which it has seemed correct to emend in the new text.

129 (I: 140): As they looked out of the window

129 (I: 140). it seemed plain to them that it was a rain-song – The implication is clear that Goldberry can call up rain with her singing.

129 (I: 140): The upper wind settled in the West

129 (I: 140). waving his arms as if he was warding off the rain . . . he seemed quite dry, except for his boots – 'As if' is what the hobbits think as they watch Tom, but it seems clear that he *does* keep the rain from touching him.

130 (I: 141): Suddenly Tom's talk left the woods

130 (I: 141). the Great Barrows, and the green mounds, and the stone-rings upon the hills and in the hollows of the hills – This description recalls the prehistoric burial mounds and stone circles in England and elsewhere in Europe. According to Appendix A: 'It is said that the mounds of Tyrn Gorthad, as the Barrow-downs were called of old, are very ancient, and that many were built in the days of the old world of the First Age by the forefathers of the Edain, before they crossed the Blue Mountains into Beleriand, of which Lindon is all that now remains' (p. 1041, III: 321), i.e. early in human history: in Tolkien's mythology Men awoke only at the beginning of the First Age when the Sun first rose in the heavens. The Edain were the Men who joined the Elves in their fight against Morgoth, the first Dark Lord; most of them left Middle-earth at the end of the First Age.

130 (I: 141). Green walls and white walls rose. There were fortresses on the heights. Kings of little kingdoms fought together, and the young Sun shone like fire on the red metal of their new and greedy swords. There was victory and defeat; and towers fell, fortresses were burned, and flames went up into the sky. – This probably still relates to the 'forefathers of the Edain' mentioned above, supported by reference to the 'young Sun'. *Red metal* suggests the use of copper or bronze in an early period similar to the Bronze Age of our history.

130 (I: 141). Gold was piled on the biers of dead kings and queens; and mounds covered them, and the stone doors were shut; and the grass grew over all. Sheep walked for a while – It is not clear whether these dead kings and queens were the rulers of the 'little kingdoms' referred to above or from a later period, when Men who escaped the drowning of Númenor established new kingdoms in Middle-earth. The Barrow-downs became part of the kingdom of Cardolan. In Appendix A it is said that the hills where their forefathers had lived 'were . . . revered by the Dúnedain [Men of the West, Númenóreans] after their return; and there many of their lords and kings were buried' (p. 1041, III: 321).

Almost the whole of this paragraph, with its sense of fleeting time and the impermanence of human works, recalls Tolkien's poem *Iumonna Gold Galdre Bewunden* (1923; revised in 1937 and as *The Hoard* in 1962), in particular lines from the last verse:

> *There is an old hoard in a dark rock*
> *Forgotten behind doors none can unlock.*
> *The keys are lost and the path gone,*
> *The mound unheeded that the grass grows on:*
> *The sheep crop it and the larks rise*
> *From its green mantle. . . .* [*Oxford Magazine*, 4 March 1937]

130 (I: 141). A shadow came from dark places far away . . . Barrow-wights walked in the hollow places – The 'dark places' were the kingdom of Angmar in the far North, established *c.* Third Age 1300 by the Witch-king, the chief of the Ringwraiths, and the kingdom of Rhudaur which fell under his control.

In *Nomenclature* Tolkien writes that *barrow-wights* are 'creatures dwelling in a *barrow* "grave-mound". . . . It is an invented name. . . .' But the *Oxford English Dictionary* attributes the first use of this word combination to Andrew Lang, in *Essays in Little* (1891): 'In the graves where treasures were hoarded the Barrowwights dwelt, ghosts that were sentinels over the gold'. *Wight* is said in the *OED* to be 'originally and chiefly with a (good or bad) epithet, applied to supernatural, preternatural, or unearthly beings. *Obsolete* or *rare archaic*.'

In the *Dictionary of Northern Mythology* (1993) Rudolf Simek notes that 'the belief that life after death could take on the form of the living dead (see *draugr*) who inhabited the burial mound was frequently and vividly depicted in [Northern] literature, although belief in them was not restricted merely to those buried in burial mounds' (p. 49). He describes the *draugr* as

> the living dead who in folk-belief led a very real life after dying and being buried in a burial mound and who consequently represented a threat to the living. In the Middle Ages the idea of there being living dead in burial mounds became a popular literary topos, and the sagas

are full of descriptions of these wraiths who might involve grave robbers in fights and who became a threat to both men and animals especially at midwinter. [p. 65]

131 (I: 142): When they caught

131 (I: 142). when the world was wider, and the seas flowed straight to the western Shore – Before the shape of the world was changed, and Aman was physically present in the West beyond the Sea; see note for p. 2.

131 (I: 142). when only the Elf-sires were awake – Presumably, before the waking of Men at the rising of the Sun at the beginning of the First Age, when the Elves lived in a world lit only by stars. This seems to be the meaning in the first version of this text: 'Tom went singing back before the Sun and before the Moon, out into the old starlight' (*The Return of the Shadow*, p. 121).

131 (I: 142): 'Eh, what?'

131 (I: 142). Eldest, that's what I am – Most of the names by which Tom has been called refer to him as old or ancient; see note for p. 119. In the first complete text for this chapter he says: 'I am an Aborigine, that's what I am, the Aborigine of this land', changed to 'I am Ab-Origine' (*The Return of the Shadow*, pp. 121, 329). *Ab-origine* is Latin 'from the beginning'; in English *aborigine* is used to describe a people who has inhabited or existed in a land from earliest times.

131 (I: 142). Tom was here before the river and the trees; Tom remembers the first raindrop and the first acorn. – This may mean that Tom was present when the Ainur (the Valar and the Maiar) entered into the world and began their long task of shaping it according to the vision they had seen in the Music of Creation. In which case, Tom may be one of the Maiar, i.e. one of the lesser Ainur, who chose to remain in Middle-earth rather than to resettle in Aman in the West. Yet the passage could also be read to mean that Tom was *here*, specifically in this part of the world, before current features appeared in the local landscape. But Gandalf suggests at the Council of Elrond (Book II, Chapter 2) that Tom once ranged wider: 'And now he is withdrawn into a little land, within bounds that he has set' (p. 265, I: 279).

131 (I: 142). He made paths before the Big People, and saw the little people arrive – Tom knew the land before Men arrived in the First Age, and before the first Hobbits entered Eriador *c.* Third Age 1050, or perhaps came to Bree *c.* 1300 or settled the Shire in 1601.

131 (I: 142). When the Elves passed westward, Tom was already here, before the seas were bent. – According the *Annals of Aman*, written by Tolkien in 1951, the Elves passed West more than 3,000 years before the raising of the Sun.

131 (I: 142). He knew the dark under the stars when it was fearless – before the Dark Lord came from Outside. – The same words appear in the first text. Christopher Tolkien comments that Tom Bombadil is referring to 'the Ages of the Stars, before Morgoth came back to Middle-earth after the destruction of the Trees [the Two Trees of Valinor, in "The Silmarillion"]', but he is not sure what is meant by 'from Outside':

> It must be said that it seems unlikely that Bombadil would refer to Valinor across the Great Sea as 'Outside', especially since this was long ages 'before the seas were bent', when Númenor was drowned; it would seem much more natural to interpret the word as meaning 'the Outer Dark', 'the Void' beyond the Walls of the World. But in the mythology as it was when my father began *The Lord of the Rings* Melkor [Morgoth] entered 'the World' with the other Valar, and never left it until his final defeat. It was only with his [Tolkien's] return to *The Silmarillion* after *The Lord of the Rings* was completed that there entered the account found in the published work . . . in which Melkor was defeated . . . and driven into the Outer Dark, from which he returned in secret. . . . It seems then that either Bombadil must in fact refer to Morgoth's return from Valinor to Middle-earth, in company with Ungoliant and bearing the Silmarils, or else that my father had already at this date developed a new conception of the earliest history of Melkor. [*The Return of the Shadow*, p. 122]

Christopher later discovered that the conception that Melkor had withdrawn from the Earth arose earlier, *c.* 1946 (see *Morgoth's Ring*, especially pp. 4, 40), but this is still some eight years after Tolkien wrote the first text of 'In the House of Tom Bombadil'.

Like Frodo, we have learned more about Tom Bombadil as the story has progressed, but still cannot fit him neatly into any category. He remains, as Tolkien wished, an enigma. Nonetheless many readers have their pet theories about Tom. The furthest one can go is to state what he is not: he is not Man, Dwarf, or Hobbit, since he is not (like those races) mortal. He does not look like, nor does Elrond consider him to be, an Elf. Although it is not specifically stated that he never left Middle-earth, this is implied, in which case he is not one of the Valar. And in his letter to Peter Hastings, September 1954, Tolkien rejected the implication that Bombadil was Eru (God): such an identification would have been impossible for Tolkien, a devout Catholic. See further, the list of available information about Tom Bombadil and various comments on his nature compiled by Charles E. Noad, 'The Natures of Tom Bombadil: A Summary', in *Leaves from the Tree: J.R.R. Tolkien's Shorter Fiction* (1991). Gene Hargrove also provides a useful study of evidence and theories in the first part of 'Who is Tom Bombadil', *Mythlore* 13, no. 1, whole no. 47 (Autumn 1986), though his conclusion that Tom is the Vala Aulë seems unlikely.

132 (I: 143): He appeared already to know much about them

132 (I: 143). he owed his recent knowledge largely to Farmer Maggot – In early texts Tolkien considered whether to make Farmer Maggot distant kin to Tom, and not a hobbit. In the 1962 poem *Bombadil Goes Boating* Tom sets out to visit the Shire, rowing himself down the Withywindle. He lands at Mithe Steps, begins to walk up the Causeway, and is met by Maggot. They exchange insults, and

Laughing they drove away, in Rushey never halting,
though the inn open stood and they could smell the malting.
They turned down Maggot's Lane, rattling and bumping,
Tom in the farmer's cart dancing round and jumping.
Stars shone on Bamfurlong, and Maggot's house was lighted;
fire in the kitchen burned to welcome the benighted.

Maggot's sons bowed at the door, his daughters did their curtsy,
his wife brought tankards out for those that might be thirsty.
Songs they had and merry tales, the supping and the dancing;
Goodman Maggot there for all his belt was prancing,
Tom did a hornpipe when he was not quaffing,
daughters did the Springle-ring, goodwife did the laughing.

When the others went to bed in hay, fern, or feather,
close in the inglenook they laid their heads together,
old Tom and Muddy-feet [Maggot], swapping all the tidings
from Barrow-downs to Tower Hills: of walkings and of ridings;
of wheat-ears and barley-corn, of sowing and of reaping;
queer tales from Bree, and talk at smithy, mill, and cheaping;
rumours in whispering trees, south-wind in the larches,
tall Watchers by the Ford, Shadows on the marches.

132 (I: 143). There's earth under his old feet – A version of *to have one's feet on the ground*, 'to base oneself on realities, to be practical'.

132 (I: 144): 'Show me the precious Ring!'

132 (I: 144). handed it at once to Tom – Curiously, perhaps an indication of Tom's mastery, Frodo hands the Ring to him without any sense of reluctance (and 'to his own astonishment'), though he had hesitated when Gandalf asked for the Ring in Book I, Chapter 2.

133 (I: 144): Frodo looked at it closely

133 (I: 144). an absurd story about badgers – Perhaps the story of his capture by Badgerfolk in the 1934 poem.

133–4 (I: 145): 'Keep to the green grass

134 (I: 145). he advised them to pass barrows by on the west-side – As the hobbits are going north, passing the barrows on the west would be going *deasil* 'sunwise or clockwise', considered to be auspicious by the Celts; whereas to pass on the east would be going *withershins* or *widdershins* 'against the sun, anti-clockwise', which was considered unlucky and likely to cause disaster.

Chapter 8

FOG ON THE BARROW-DOWNS

For drafts and history of this chapter, see *The Return of the Shadow*, chiefly pp. 125–31, 329; *The Treason of Isengard*, p. 37.

135 (I: 146): That night they heard no noises

135 (I: 146). Frodo heard a sweet singing running in his mind: a song that seemed to come like a pale light behind a grey rain-curtain, and growing stronger to turn the veil all to glass and silver, until at last it was rolled back, and a far green country opened before him under a swift sunrise. – Frodo's dream foreshadows what he hears and sees as he nears the Undying Lands at the end of *The Lord of the Rings*, in Book VI, Chapter 9.

135 (I: 146): The vision melted into waking

135 (I: 146). The vision melted into waking – It is the morning of 28 September 1418.

138 (I: 149): Soon they were leading their ponies

138 (I: 149). When they reached the bottom it was so chill – This was the reading in the first printing of the first edition (1954). In the unauthorized resetting of *The Fellowship of the Ring* for its second printing (1954) the final word was mistakenly altered to 'cold'. The error was corrected in the edition of 2004.

141 (I: 152): *Cold be hand and heart and bone*

141 (I: 152). *Cold be hand and heart and bone . . .* – The wight's incantation, looking to the triumph of the 'dark lord', recalls the oath of the Orcs of Morgoth in *The Lay of Leithian* (written in the mid-1920s to 1931, published in *The Lays of Beleriand*, p. 230):

Death to light, to law, to love!
Cursed be moon and stars above!
May darkness everlasting old
that waits outside in surges cold
drown Manwë, Varda, and the sun!
May all in hatred be begun,
and all in evil ended be,
in the moaning of the endless Sea!

141 (I: 152). *till the Sun fails and the Moon is dead . . .* till the dark lord lifts his hand over dead sea and withered land. – The song seems to envisage some sort of resurrection when the world is cold, dead, and lightless, over which the Dark Lord will preside. This vision of utter desolation contrasts with suggestions in 'The Silmarillion' that one day the Marring of Arda (i.e. the evils inflicted on the Earth by Morgoth) will be healed, and with Galadriel's words to Treebeard that they may meet again when 'the lands that lie under the wave are lifted up again. Then in the willow-meads of Tasarinan we may meet in the Spring' (Book VI, Chapter 6, p. 981, I: 259).

141 (I: 152): He heard behind his head

141 (I: 152). a long arm was groping, walking on its fingers – Sinister hands and arms appear in Tolkien's art, in this regard most particularly in the picture *Maddo*, 'a gloved hand without an arm that opened curtains a crack after dark and crawled down the curtain' (quoted in *Artist and Illustrator*, p. 83, for fig. 78).

141 (I: 152). they were in a kind of passage which behind them turned a corner. – Many of the Neolithic barrows in England contain chambers opening off a central passage. The best known is probably the West Kennet barrow near Avebury, which was used as a communal grave, possibly for a thousand years, the last burial being *c.* 2200 BC. Communal burial was replaced during the Bronze Age by individual burials, presumably of persons of significance, and the tombs and mounds over them became smaller.

141 (I: 152–3): But the courage that had been awakened

141 (I: 152). But the courage that had been awakened in him was now too strong – In Book I, Chapter 3 Frodo was tempted to put on the Ring to escape from the Black Rider, but was saved when the Rider suddenly rode off. Here he is also tempted to use the Ring, and thinks of himself free but alive, though his friends were dead. Courage, however, and friendship, overcome temptation: his first triumph over the Ring, an indication of his strength of character. In Book II, Chapter 1 Gandalf says to Frodo: 'You have some strength in you, my dear hobbit! As you showed in the Barrow. That was touch and go: perhaps the most dangerous moment of all' (p. 219, I: 231).

142 (I: 153): *Old Tom Bombadil is a merry fellow*

142 (I: 153). *His songs are stronger songs* – Stronger, that is, than the wight's incantation. The power of Tom's music strongly begs comparison with that of the wizard Väinämöinen in the Finnish *Kalevala*, a significant influence on Tolkien's writings. David Elton Gay, in 'J.R.R. Tolkien and the *Kalevala*: Some Thoughts on the Finnish Origins of Tom Bombadil and Treebeard', *Tolkien and the Invention of Myth: A Reader* (2002), comments that for both Väinämöinen and Tom Bombadil power comes from their command of song and lore rather than from ownership and domination. Väinämöinen spends his time in endless singing, not singing songs of power, however, but rather songs of knowledge. Indeed, it would appear that he, like Tom Bombadil, sings for the simple pleasure of singing. . . . As Tom's conversations with the Hobbits make apparent, his mastery of his land, like Väinämöinen's, is through knowledge and experience rather than ownership.

. . . To have power over something in the mythology of the *Kalevala* one must know its origins and be able to sing the appropriate songs and incantations concerning these origins. Great power in the world of the *Kalevala* requires great age and great knowledge, and Väinämöinen has both. A large part of his power comes from the fact that as the oldest of all living things he saw the creation of things, heard their names, and knows the songs of their origins, and it was his works which helped give shape to the land. The same is clearly true of Tom Bombadil. [pp. 298–9]

142 (I: 153): There was a loud rumbling

142 (I: 153). the sun rising – It is the morning of 29 September.

142 (I: 153–4): ***Get out, you old Wight!***

142 (I: 154). ***darker than the darkness, / Where gates stand forever shut, till the world is mended.*** – Perhaps an allusion to the state of affairs at the end of the *Quenta Silmarillion*:

> But Morgoth himself the Valar thrust through the Door of Night beyond the Walls of the World, into the Timeless Void; and a guard is set for ever on those walls, and Eärendil keeps watch upon the ramparts of the sky. Yet the lies that Melkor, the mighty and accursed, Morgoth Bauglir, the Power of Terror and of Hate, sowed in the hearts of Elves and Men are a seed that does not die and cannot be destroyed; and ever and anon it sprouts anew, and will bear dark fruit even unto the latest days. [*The Silmarillion*, pp. 254–5]

143 (I: 154): 'What in the name of wonder?'

143 (I: 154). The men of Carn Dûm came on us at night and we were worsted. Ah! the spear in my heart! – *Carn Dûm* was the chief fortress of Angmar, the realm of the Witch-king, the leader of the Ringwraiths, in Third Age *c.* 1300–1973. In Appendix A it is said that, according to some, 'the mound in which the Ring-bearer was imprisoned had been the grave of the last prince of Cardolan, who fell in the war of 1409', and at about the time of the Great Plague of 1636 'an end came of the Dúnedain of Cardolan, and evil spirits out of Angmar and Rhudaur entered into the deserted mounds and dwelt there' (p. 1041, III: 321). *The Tale of Years* indicates for Third Age 1409: 'The Witch-king of Angmar invades Arnor . . . Fornost and Tyrn Gorthad [the Barrow-downs] are defended'. Merry's remarks indicate that in his dreams or trance he has been experiencing the last hours of the prince of Cardolan. But the barrow-wight is not the ghost of this prince, but one of the evil spirits who came to the mounds some two hundred years after the prince's death, as an agent of the Witch-king of Angmar.

In Marquette MSS 4/2/36 (*The Hunt for the Ring*) it is said that after the Black Riders had overcome the Rangers guarding Sarn Ford, four of the Riders

> pursue Rangers along Greenway, and having slain them or driven them off Eastwards, make a camp at Andrath (where the road passes between the Barrowdowns and the South Downs) [cf. note for p. 177]. [The Witch-king] now visits the Barrowdowns and stops there some days (probably until late on 27). This proves a main error, though in fact it was nearly successful, since the Barrowwights are roused, and all things of evil spirit hostile to Elves and Men are on the watch with malice in the Old Forest and on the Barrowdowns. [The other three Black Riders] are left to guard the eastern borders, to watch the Greenway, and guard against Elves or Dúnedain coming from eastwards.

Another text concerning *The Hunt for the Ring*, Marquette MSS 4/2/33, notes that 'the Witch-King . . . had known something of the country long ago, in his wars with the Dúnedain, and especially of the Tyrn Gorthad of Cardolan, now the Barrow-downs, whose evil wights had been sent there by himself' (see also *Unfinished Tales*, p. 348).

To be *worsted* is to be defeated, overcome.

144 (I: 155): *Hey! now! Come hoy now!*

144 (I: 155). *Sharp-ears, Wise-nose, Swish-tail and Bumpkin, / White-socks . . . and old Fatty Lumpkin!* – Four of the names that Tom gives the ponies were clearly chosen to suit their physical features or special abilities. In *Nomenclature* Tolkien states that the *-kin* of *Fatty Lumpkin* 'is of course a diminutive suffix'. When Fatty Lumpkin appears he is described as 'large, stronger, fatter (and older) than their own ponies'. The most common definition of *lump* is 'a compact mass of no definite shape', but colloquially or in dialect is used to describe a big, fat, or stupid person or animal. The *Concise Oxford English Dictionary* notes that *bumpkin* possibly derives from Middle Dutch *bommekijn* 'little barrel', 'denoting a dumpy person'.

145 (I: 156): The hobbits were delighted

145 (I: 156). my making – *Making* is an archaic word for the composition of poetry.

145 (I: 156–7): It was still fairly early by the sun

145 (I: 156). that glistered and sparkled – This was the reading in the first printing of the first edition (1954). In the unauthorized resetting of *The*

Fellowship of the Ring for its second printing (1954), 'glistered' was mistakenly altered to 'glistened'. The error was corrected in the edition of 2004.

145 (I: 156). for so the spell of the mound should be broken and scattered – A recurring theme in Tolkien's works is that of avarice, and of the evils that may come of it. In *The Hobbit* Smaug's hoard brings out feelings of greed in the dwarves, the Elves, and the Lakemen, but not Bilbo, who gives away the Arkenstone in an attempt to defuse hostilities; and in the poem *Iumonna Gold Galdre Bewunden* (and its revision *The Hoard*) a treasure passes from Elves, to Dwarves, to a dragon, to a young warrior, all of whom come to a violent end. Tom Shippey in *The Road to Middle-earth*, pp. 79–80 (2nd edn.), discusses the origin of the poem, based on a line in *Beowulf* ('the gold of ancient men, wound round with magic') which refers to the curse of avarice on another dragon's hoard. In *The Lord of the Rings* Tom Bombadil negates any such spell on the wight's treasures by giving them away.

145 (I: 156–7). with blue stones, many-shaded like flax-flowers – There are several wild species of flax in addition to *Linum usitatissimum* which is cultivated to produce linseed and fibre. The blueness of the flower varies.

145–6 (I: 157): For each of the hobbits

145 (I: 157). a dagger, long, leaf-shaped, and keen, . . . damasked with serpent-forms in red and gold – The acquiring of daggers 'long enough as swords' by the hobbits echoes Bilbo acquiring the elven-blade 'Sting' from the trolls' hoard in *The Hobbit*, Chapter 2.

In regard to *damasked*, the usual word when applied to metal is *damascened* 'ornamented with designs incised in the surface and inlaid with gold or silver'. The word is derived from the name of Damascus, a city famous for such work.

146 (I: 157): 'Old knives are long enough

146 (I: 157). these blades were forged many long years ago by Men of Westernesse: they were foes of the Dark Lord, but they were overcome by the evil king of Carn Dûm in the Land of Angmar – Though the Men of Westernesse who made these blades were defeated long before by the Witch-king of *Angmar* (see note for p. 5), yet one of these knives will be used to bring about his final destruction: Merry's blade, which in the battle of the Pelennor Fields in Book V, Chapter 6 pierces the Witch-king's sinew behind his knee. The blade having withered away, Tolkien writes:

> So passed the sword of the Barrow-downs, work of Westernesse. But glad would he have been to know its fate who wrought it slowly long ago in the North-kingdom when the Dúnedain were young, and chief among their foes was the dread realm of Angmar and its sorcerer king.

> No other blade, though mightier hands had wielded it, would have dealt that foe a wound so bitter, cleaving the undead flesh, breaking the spell that knit his unseen sinews to his will. [p. 844, III: 119–20]

146 (I: 157): 'Few now remember them

146 (I: 157). yet still some go wandering, sons of forgotten kings walking in loneliness, guarding from evil things folk that are heedless – The remnants of the Dúnedain of the North who, led by the descendants of the former kings, have become Rangers, constantly on guard to protect against evil those who live in their former realm. Only a few days earlier, the Rangers attempted to prevent the Black Riders from crossing Sarn Ford and entering the Shire; they failed, but delayed the Riders long enough that Frodo had just left Bag End when the first one arrived in Hobbiton. At the Council of Elrond (Book II, Chapter 2) Aragorn will tell Boromir:

> Peace and freedom do you say? The North would have known them little but for us. Fear would have destroyed them. But when dark things come from the houseless hills, or creep from sunless woods, they fly from us. What roads would any dare tread, what safety would there be in quiet lands, or in the houses of simple men at night, if the Dúnedain were asleep, or were all gone into the grave?
>
> And yet less thanks have we than you. . . . Yet we would not have it otherwise. If simple folk are free from care and fear, simple they will be, and we must be secret to keep them so. This has been the task of my kindred, while the years have lengthened and the grass has grown. [p. 248, I: 261–2]

146 (I: 157): The hobbits did not understand his words

146 (I: 157). they had a vision as it were of a great expanse of years behind them, like a vast shadowy plain over which there strode shapes of Men, tall and grim with bright swords, and last came one with a star on his brow – The Man 'with a star on his brow' is Aragorn, the last descendant of kings of Arnor, and ultimately of the kings of Númenor. The star is the Elendilmir, which he will later wear on the Pelennor Fields and at his coronation in Minas Tirith. The vision may owe something to that conjured by the witches for Macbeth in Shakespeare's play, showing the long line of Banquo's descendants who would succeed to Macbeth's crown.

146 (I: 158–9): They went forward steadily

146 (I: 158). The dark line they had seen was not a line of trees but a line of bushes growing on the edge of a deep dike with a steep wall on the further side. – There are several similar dikes in England set up as defences or to mark boundaries. Among these is the Wansdyke, which runs from Andover in Hampshire to Portishead on the shores of the Severn estuary, built probably as a defensive frontier in the sixth century when the Britons and Anglo-Saxons were fighting over the territory. Other examples are Fleam's Dyke and Devil's Ditch near Newmarket, Cambridgeshire, parts of a rampart system built in the sixth to eighth centuries during the wars between the Anglians and the Mercians. But the most famous is Offa's Dyke, said to have been built by King Offa in the eighth century to mark and protect Mercia's border with Wales. 'A formidable barrier, it consists of an earthen bank thirty feet (10 m) wide with a ditch six feet (2 m) deep and twelve feet wide (4 m) on the Welsh side. . . . The earthwork was carefully engineered to create the most effective barrier and to keep the best view into Wales, suggesting that its primary function was military and that the Mercians had a free choice of where to site it' (Margaret Worthington, 'Offa's Dyke', in *The Blackwell Encyclopaedia of Anglo-Saxon England* (1999), p. 341).

146–7 (I: 158). it had once been the boundary of a kingdom – Probably the northern boundary of Cardolan, south of Arthedain.

147 (I: 158): They climbed down and out of the dike

147 (I: 158). furlongs – A *furlong* is an eighth of a mile, 220 yards.

147 (I: 158–9): 'No, I hope not tonight'

147 (I: 159). Black Land – 'Common Speech translation of *Mordor*' (*Nomenclature*).

147–8 (I: 159): 'Tom will give you good advice

148 (I: 159). Barliman Butterbur – Tolkien comments in *Nomenclature*, regarding *Butterbur*, that it was, as far as he knew,

> not found as a name in England. Though *Butter* is so used, as well as combinations (in origin place-names) such as *Butterfield*. These have in the tale been modified, to fit the generally botanical names of Bree, to the plant-name *butterbur* (*Petasites vulgaris*). . . . (The butterbur is a fleshy plant with heavy flower-head on thick stalk, and very large leaves.)
>
> Butterbur's first name *Barliman* is simply an altered spelling of *barley* and *man* (suitable to an innkeeper and ale-brewer).

Until quite late in the writing of *The Lord of the Rings* Butterbur's first name was *Barnabas*. In an early version of Appendix F Tolkien wrote that he

> gave him this name for various reasons. First of all a personal one. On an old grey stone in a quiet churchyard in southern England I once saw in large letters the name *Barnabas Butter*. That was long ago and before I had seen the Red Book, but the name came back to me when the character of the stout innkeeper of Bree was presented to me in Frodo's record. The more so because his name, in agreement with the generally botanical type of name favoured in Bree, was actually *Butterburr* or in

the C[ommon] S[peech] *Zilbarāpha* [> *Zilbirāpha*]. [*The Peoples of Middle-earth*, p. 52]

148 (I: 160): Before them rose Bree-hill

148 (I: 160). a dark mass against misty stars – Tolkien correctly makes no mention of the moon. The moon is only just past new, and the hobbits are facing east: a thin crescent would have been visible briefly in the west just after sunset.

Chapter 9

AT THE SIGN OF THE PRANCING PONY

For drafts and history of this chapter, see *The Return of the Shadow*, pp. 132–47, 172, 331–6, 349–50; *The Treason of Isengard*, pp. 40–2, 62, 73–6.

149 (I: 161): Bree was the chief village

149 (I: 161). Bree – A sketch-plan of the village is reproduced in *The Return of the Shadow*, p. 335.

149 (I: 161). Staddle – In *Nomenclature* Tolkien notes that the name of this village derives from *staddle* which 'is now dialectal, but occurs in place-names = "foundation", of buildings, sheds, ricks, etc.: from Old English *staðol*'. Compare *Staddlethorpe* in Yorkshire.

149 (I: 161). Combe in a deep valley – In *Nomenclature* Tolkien comments that a *coomb* is 'a deep (but usually not very large) valley. [The word is] very frequent as an element in place-names spelt *-comb*, *-cumb*, *-combe*, etc.' The *Oxford English Dictionary* suggests that the similarity of Old English *cumb* 'vessel, cup' to British *cumbo-* (Modern Welsh *cwm*) 'valley' assisted the survival of the element in many place names and the adoption of *cumb* as an Old English word meaning 'a deep hollow or valley'. *Combe* or *Coomb* survives as a place name on its own (there is a Combe in Oxfordshire) or as one element of a place-name, e.g. *Compton*, *Ilfracombe*, *Winchcombe*.

149 (I: 161). Archet – In *Nomenclature* Tolkien writes that *Archet* is 'actually an English place-name of Celtic origin. Used in the nomenclature of Bree to represent a stratum of names older than those in Common Speech or the Hobbit language.' The manuscript of *Nomenclature* notes that *Archet* descended 'from British **ar(e)cait-* > Old English *ar-cæt* (Welsh *argoed* [obsolete 'trees, edge of forest'])'.

149 (I: 161): The Men of Bree were brown-haired

149 (I: 161). the original inhabitants – See first note for p. 130.

149 (I: 161). when the Kings returned again over the Great Sea . . . when the memory of the old Kings had faded into the grass – They were there when the Númenóreans returned to Middle-earth and established the kingdom of Arnor; and they were still there when the rulers of Arnor and its later sub-divisions (Arthedain, Rhudaur, and Cardolan) had been forgotten.

150 (I: 162): Down on the Road

150 (I: 162). ***Strange as news from Bree*** **was still a saying in the Eastfarthing . . . when news from North, South, and East could be heard in the inn** – That is, as opposed to news from the West, i.e. from the Shire itself, which was not 'strange'.

150 (I: 162). the Northern Lands – Arnor, the North Kingdom, the northern realm established by the Númenóreans, with its later centre at Fornost or Norbury some hundred miles north of Bree. The area had become depopulated and desolate as a result of the attacks of the Witch-king of Angmar.

152 (I: 164): The man stared after the hobbits

152 (I: 164). a dark figure climbed quickly in over the gate – When reading *The Lord of the Rings* for the first time, this seems a sinister figure; in fact it is Aragorn. Tolkien does not explain why Aragorn chose to enter Bree in this fashion.

152: (I: 164): The hobbits rode on

152 (I: 164). he was finding his first sight of Men and their tall houses quite enough – It is said in the Prologue that when Hobbits did build houses, they were 'usually long, low, and comfortable' (p. 7, I: 16).

152 (I: 164): Even from the outside

152 (I: 164). second-floor windows – In Britain (and in English (or British) English) the floor at street (or front door) level is the ground floor, and floors are numbered from the next floor up. The *second floor* is thus two floors above ground level, in the United States called the *third floor.*

153 (I: 165): 'Hi! Nob!' he shouted

153 (I: 165). Nob – *Nob* was perhaps chosen to rhyme with *Bob.* It does not seem to be a recognized diminutive or nickname.

153 (I: 165): 'There now!' said Mr. Butterbur

153 (I: 165). I'm run off my feet – That is, 'to be very busy; to be kept constantly on the move'. It will be noted that Butterbur likes to use commonplace sayings.

153 (I: 165). It never rains but it pours, we say in Bree. – And elsewhere, a common proverb meaning: 'One occurrence is frequently the harbinger of many more; strokes of good or ill fortune are often accompanied by additional benefits or misfortunes'.

153 (I: 165): 'Well now

153 (I: 165). One thing drives out another, so to speak – Another platitude from Mr Butterbur, similar to the proverb *One nail drives out another,* i.e.

'unable to keep two thoughts in his head at once'. Katharyn W. Crabbe comments in *J.R.R. Tolkien*:

> Barliman's string of platitudes . . . is perfect as a representation of the conversation of a man who is too busy to concentrate on what is before him. This sort of nearly meaningless utterance is only probable in a kind of semiconscious conversation that prepares us for a shock of recognition instead of a simple shock when Barliman reveals that he has forgotten to send Gandalf's warning letter to Frodo. [rev. and expanded edn. (1988), p. 100]

153 (I: 166): He led them a short way

153 (I: 166). parlour – *Parlour* is the usual word for a private room at an inn for conversation and dining, but not for sleeping.

154 (I: 166): The landlord hovered round for a little

154 (I: 166). and then prepared to leave them – As first published this passage read '*proposed* to leave them' (italics ours), an error which arose in typescript. It was emended in the edition of 1994.

154 (I: 166). We don't get Outsiders – travellers from the Shire – The Bree-folk use the same term to describe the Shire Hobbits as the Shire Hobbits use for Breelanders. See notes for pp. 22 and 992.

154 (I: 166): So refreshed and encouraged

154 (I: 166). Mind your Ps and Qs – To be careful in one's words and behaviour.

154–5 (I: 167): The company was in the big common-room

154 (I: 167). the big common-room of the inn – 'A room common to all; especially the public room at an inn' (*OED*). The *Oxford English Dictionary* prefers two words for this usage, restricting the hyphened form for a common-room in a school or college.

155 (I: 167): As soon as the Shire-hobbits entered

155 (I: 167). Rushlight, Goatleaf, Heathertoes, Appledore, Thistlewool and Ferny. . . . The Mugworts . . . Banks, Brockhouse, Longholes, Sandheaver and Tunnelly – A *rushlight* is 'a candle made by dipping the pith of a rush in tallow' (*Concise OED*).

Goatleaf, Tolkien explains in *Nomenclature*, is a 'Bree-name of botanical type, an old name of honeysuckle/woodbine. Cf. French *chèvrefeuille* (medieval Latin *caprifolium*, probably from the vernaculars).'

Heathertoes has 'no parallel in English, though *Heather-* appears in some surnames. . . . (Presumably a joke of the Big Folk, meaning that the Little Folk, wandering unshod, collected heather, twigs, and leaves between their toes)' (*Nomenclature*).

Appledore, Tolkien says in *Nomenclature*, is an 'old word for "apple-tree" (survives in English place-names)', from Old English *apuldor*.

In *Nomenclature* Tolkien instructs that *Thistlewool* should be translated by sense. It is presumably another word for *thistle-down* 'the light fluffy down of thistle seeds, enabling them to be blown about by the wind' (*Concise OED*). Although the *Oxford English Dictionary* has no entry for *thistlewool* it notes as a second sense for *wool* 'a downy substance or fibre found on certain trees or plants'.

'*Fern* and *Ferny*, *Fernie* are English surnames, but whatever their origin the name is here used to fit the predominantly botanical names current in Bree' (*Nomenclature*).

Mugwort is the name of a plant, '(*Artemisia*, French *armoise*, akin to Wormwood, French *armoise amère*). . . . There is no special reason for the choice of *Mugwort*, except its hobbit-like sound' (*Nomenclature*).

Tolkien comments in *Nomenclature* that *Banks* is 'clearly a topographical name containing *bank* in the sense "steep slope or hill-side"'.

For *Brockhouse*, see note for p. 28.

The names *Longholes*, *Sandheaver*, and *Tunnelly* continue the Hobbit tendency towards surnames related to digging.

155 (I: 168): The Men and Dwarves

155 (I: 168). There was trouble away in the South, and it seemed that the Men who had come up the Greenway were on the move looking for lands where they could find some peace – They were surely fleeing from the threat of war, rather than from war itself. At this point in the story the only overt action has been Sauron's attack on Osgiliath in June, and his forces (other than the Ringwraiths) have not yet crossed the Anduin.

155 (I: 168). a squint-eyed ill-favoured fellow – In American usage *squint* means 'to narrow, slit one's eyes'. Though *squint* can have this meaning in England, generally in English English it denotes a disorder of the eye. In response to an enquiry from Nancy Martsch, who knew only the American usage and wondered if by describing the Southerner as 'squint-eyed' Tolkien meant that he had narrow eyes, like an orc, or that he held his eyes half-closed, Christopher Tolkien replied:

> Just as you had never heard until recently of the use of the word *squint* to mean anything but 'to narrow the eyes', so I had never until your letter heard of *that* meaning. I believe that *squint* in 'English English' always carries the idea of *obliqueness*: a *squint* is a strabismus (muscular disorder that causes the eye to look obliquely) and *to squint* means to suffer from that condition – but also more generally, to *look* obliquely, 'to look out of the corner of the eye': it can thus very readily come to connote character, and naturally leads to the meaning very fully developed in French, where a main meaning of *louche* ('squinting') is 'ambiguous, dubious, suspicious, shady, fishy'.

> Just what my father meant to convey by the '*squint-eyed* Southerner' at Bree I'm not sure. I don't think that he can possibly have meant that the man had 'slit-eyes' (goblin-like). He may have meant that he actually had a squint (optical disorder), but that seems unnecessarily particular. So the likeliest meaning, I think, is that the man didn't look straight, but obliquely, watchfully, sideways, suggesting craftiness and *crooked*ness. [quoted in Nancy Martsch, 'The "Squint-eyed Southerner"', *Beyond Bree*, May 1990, p. 9]

In Book I, Chapter 11 the Southerner is described as having 'slanting eyes' and looking 'more than half like a goblin', suggesting that Tolkien envisioned orcs as having slanting eyes, but probably not slit-eyes (p. 180, I: 193). A great deal is revealed about the Southerner in *The Hunt for the Ring*:

> Some while ago one of Saruman's most trusted servants (yet a ruffianly fellow, an outlaw driven from Dunland, where many said that he had Orc-blood) had returned from the Shire, where he had been negotiating for the purchase of 'leaf' and other supplies. . . . This man was now on his way back to continue the business. . . . He had orders also to get into the Shire if possible and learn if there had been any departures of persons well-known recently. He was well-supplied with maps, lists of names, and notes concerning the Shire.
>
> This Dunlending was overtaken by several of the Black Riders as they approached the Tharbad crossing. In an extremity of terror he was haled to the Witch-king and questioned. He saved his life by betraying Saruman. . . . The Witch-king . . . obtained much information, including some about the only name that interested him: *Baggins*. It was for this reason that Hobbiton was singled out as one of the points for immediate visit and enquiry. . . .
>
> Seeing that his Master suspected some move between the Shire and Rivendell, he also saw that Bree . . . would be an important point, at least for information. He put therefore the Shadow of Fear on the Dunlending, and sent him on to Bree as an agent. [*Unfinished Tales*, pp. 347–8]

155 (I: 168). If room isn't found . . . They've a right to live – This seems more than an echo of the German claim to *Lebensraum* 'living space', one of the causes of the Second World War; it was a word Tolkien often would have heard used. In *The Gathering Storm* (1948) Winston Churchill summarized a discussion he had in 1937 with Herr von Ribbentrop, the German Ambassador to Britain:

> Germany would stand guard for the British Empire in all its greatness and extent. They might ask for the return of the German colonies, but this was evidently not cardinal. What was required was that Britain should give Germany a free hand in the East of Europe. She must

have her *Lebensraum*, or living space, for her increasing population. Therefore Poland and the Danzig Corridor must be absorbed. White Russia and the Ukraine were indispensable to the future life of the German Reich of more than seventy million souls. Nothing less would suffice. [pp. 222–3]

156 (I: 168): The hobbits did not pay much attention

156 (I: 168). the Town Hole – In his unfinished index Tolkien describes this as 'a tunnelled hall at Michel Delving in the White Downs'. *Town Hole* is obviously a punning play on *Town Hall*.

156 (I: 168). Will Whitfoot – In *Nomenclature* Tolkien instructs that *Whitfoot* should be translated 'by "white" and "foot"'.

156 (I: 168): Suddenly Frodo noticed

156 (I: 168). a strange-looking weather-beaten man – As first written and for some time considerable time in the history of *The Lord of the Rings*, Frodo saw 'a queer-looking, brown-faced *hobbit*' (*The Return of the Shadow*, p. 137, emphasis ours). Tolkien introduced the character without knowing who he was; he wrote to W.H. Auden on 7 June 1955 that 'Strider sitting in the corner at the inn was a shock, and I had no more idea who he was than had Frodo' (*Letters*, p. 216). This may be one reason why this scene works so well. Frodo, Tolkien, and the reader see Strider from the same point of view. In *The Return of the Shadow* and *The Treason of Isengard* one can trace Tolkien's doubts and hesitations about the identity of Strider (or 'Trotter' as he remained until after the completion of *The Lord of the Rings*; see further, Christina Scull, 'What Did He Know and When Did He Know It?: Planning, Inspiration, and *The Lord of the Rings*', in the proceedings of the October 2004 Marquette University Tolkien conference, forthcoming).

In *The Return of the Shadow* Christopher Tolkien remarks:

> It would obviously not be true to say merely that there was a rôle to be played in the story, and that at first this rôle was played by a Hobbit but afterwards by a Man. . . . I would be inclined to think that the original figure (the mysterious person who encounters the hobbits in the inn at Bree) was capable of development in different directions without losing important elements of his 'identity' as a recognisable character – even though the choice of one direction or another would lead to quite different historical and racial 'identities' in Middle-earth. So Trotter was not simply switched from Hobbit to Man. . . . Rather, he had been potentially Aragorn for a long time; and when my father decided that Trotter *was* Aragorn and *was not* Peregrin Boffin [a Hobbit] his stature and his history were totally changed, but a great deal of the 'indivisible' Trotter remained in Aragorn and determined his nature. [pp. 430–1]

157–8 (I: 170): Frodo suddenly felt very foolish

157 (I: 170). quite unaccountably the desire came over him to slip it on and vanish out of the silly situation. It seemed to him, somehow, as if the suggestion came to him from outside, from someone or something in the room. – Tolkien gave no further indication as to the source of this urge. It is implied (or one may infer) that the Ring sensed that Black Riders had entered Bree and was trying to reveal its presence.

158 (I: 170): For a moment Frodo stood gaping

158 (I: 170). a ridiculous song – Originally at this point in the story Tolkien inserted the 'Troll Song', i.e. *The Root of the Boot* (see note for p. 206), but almost at once decided to substitute a revision of his poem *The Cat and the Fiddle: A Nursery-Rhyme Undone and Its Scandalous Secret Unlocked*, which had been published in the journal *Yorkshire Poetry* for October–November 1923. The text as found in its original manuscript is printed in *The Return of the Shadow*, pp. 145–7. It is obviously indebted to the nursery rhyme 'Hey Diddle Diddle':

Hey diddle diddle
The cat and the fiddle,
The cow jumped over the moon;
The little dog laughed
To see such sport,
And the dish ran away with the spoon.

But George Burke Johnston, in his essay 'The Poetry of J.R.R. Tolkien', *The Tolkien Papers* (1967), suggests that Tolkien was inspired also by a similar poem by George MacDonald in *At the Back of the North Wind* (1870, Chapter 24), 'The True History of the Cat and the Fiddle', in which the nursery rhymes 'Hey Diddle Diddle' and 'The Man in the Moon Came Down Too Soon' are combined. The poem as published in *The Lord of the Rings* was reprinted in 1962 in *The Adventures of Tom Bombadil and Other Verses from the Red Book*, as *The Man in the Moon Stayed Up Too Late*.

See further, Thomas Honegger, 'The Man in the Moon: Structural Depth in Tolkien', in *Root and Branch: Approaches towards Understanding Tolkien* (1999).

158–60 (I: 170–2): *There is an inn, a merry old inn*

158–60 (I: 170–2). *There is an inn, a merry old inn . . .* – A recording by Tolkien of this poem is included on Disc 1 of *The J.R.R. Tolkien Audio Collection*.

158 (I: 170). *the Man in the Moon* – The Man in the Moon in this poem must be assumed to represent stories and legends among Men and Hobbits who had little idea of the 'real' state of affairs in Arda. In Tolkien's mythology, after the Two Trees of Valinor were wounded and poisoned by

Melkor and Ungoliant, before dying Telperion bore one last silver flower and Laurelin a last golden fruit. The Moon was created from that silver flower, and it was guided by Tilion, a Maia, one of the lesser Ainur. The phases of the Moon were ascribed to his uncertain pace, and evidently gave rise to stories such as the one told in this poem.

158 (I: 170). *ostler* – A man (or hobbit) who looks after the horses of people staying at an inn.

158 (I: 171). *For Sunday there's a special pair / And these they polish up with care / on Saturday afternoons.* – In Appendix D Tolkien says, regarding the names of the days of the week:

> I have translated these names also into our own names, naturally beginning with Sunday and Monday, which occur in the Shire week with the same names as ours, and re-naming the others in order. It must be noted, however, that the associations of the names were quite different in the Shire. The last day of the week, Friday (Highday), was the chief day, and one of holiday (after noon) and evening feasts. Saturday thus corresponds more nearly to our Monday, and Thursday to our Saturday. [*Author's footnote:* I have therefore in Bilbo's song . . . used Saturday and Sunday instead of Thursday and Friday.] [p. 1111, III: 389]

159 (I: 171). *The white horses of the Moon* – In mythological art the goddess Selene (Luna, the Moon) is sometimes depicted riding in a chariot drawn by white horses.

160, n. (I: 172, n.): Elves (and Hobbits)

160, n. (I: 172, n.). Elves (and Hobbits) always refer to the Sun as She. – Tolkien represents the Sun and Moon as female and male, the reverse of the genders depicted in Greek and Roman mythology. In 'The Silmarillion' the Sun formed from the fruit of Laurelin was guided by the maiden Arien, also a Maia.

160 (I: 172): The local hobbits stared in amazement

160 (I: 172). Presently he [Bill Ferny] slipped out of the door, followed by the squint-eyed southerner: the two had been whispering together a good deal during the evening. – In editions prior to 2004 this sentence was followed by: 'Harry the gatekeeper also went out just behind them.' In draft Book I, Chapter 9 contained three references to Harry Goatleaf at the inn, all of which Tolkien firmly deleted. On a page of notes concerning elements in the chapter, Tolkien wrote: 'Cut out Harry – he is unnecessary', i.e. that the references to him at the inn were not needed. But the final reference, 'Harry the gatekeeper also went out just behind them', somehow entered the typescript, and so the published text. In discussion of this point with us, Christopher Tolkien argued that it is not credible that if his father wanted to restore the motive of Harry at the inn he would have reinstated only the third reference, and not the two earlier references (in which Harry calls for relief at the gate, and Frodo sees him among the crowd) in order to explain his presence. As such, the surviving sentence presented an anomaly best removed, according to the author's clear intent. (See *The Treason of Isengard*, p. 42.)

161 (I: 173): 'Well?' said Strider

161 (I: 173). You have put your foot in it! Or should I say your finger – Tolkien is playing with the phrase *to put one's foot in it* 'to do something stupid or tactless'.

162 (I: 174): 'Certainly!' said Frodo

162 (I: 174). Were these people all in league against him? – *In league* 'conspiring together'.

Chapter 10

STRIDER

For drafts and history of this chapter, see *The Return of the Shadow*, pp. 148–63, 171–6, 336–54, 367–8; *The Treason of Isengard*, pp. 43–53, 62–4, 77–8.

164 (I: 175): Frodo, Pippin, and Sam

164 (I: 175). faggots – A *faggot* is a bundle of sticks or twigs used for fuel.

163–4 (I: 176–7): 'Too much; too many dark things'

163 (I: 176). old Bombadil – The familiar reference suggests that Strider knows Tom Bombadil well.

165 (I: 177): 'News of you, of course

165 (I: 177). I know all the lands between the Shire and the Misty Mountains, for I have wandered over them for many years. I am older than I look. – In Appendix A it is said that in Third Age 2951 'Aragorn took leave lovingly of Elrond . . . and he went out into the wild. For nearly thirty years he laboured in the cause against Sauron; and he became a friend of Gandalf the Wise, from whom he gained much wisdom. With him he made many perilous journeys, but as the years wore on he went more often alone' (p. 1060, III: 340). He was born on 1 March 2931 (S.R. 1331), thus when he met the hobbits in Bree he was eighty-seven years old.

165 (I: 177). Do you wish them to find you? They are terrible! – We are not told how Strider knows about the Ringwraiths, or why, on this page, 'his face was drawn as if with pain, and his hands clenched the arms of his chair'. The passage in fact is a shadow of drafts of this chapter in which Strider was still the Hobbit 'Trotter', who 'had been captured and imprisoned by the Dark Lord' and had his feet hurt by torture.

167 (I: 179): 'Where was I?

167 (I: 179). Three months back – On Mid-year's Day. It is now 29 September 1418.

167 (I: 179): 'It's addressed plain enough'

167 (I: 179). a lettered man – In this sense, one who can read.

167 (I: 179): Poor Mr. Butterbur looked troubled

167 (I: 179). I'm mortal afraid – *Mortal* is used here in the colloquial sense 'extremely great'.

167–8 (I: 180): 'These black men'

168 (I: 180). It was on Monday – It is the evening of Thursday, 29 September. The Black Riders reached Bree on the day the hobbits were in the Old Forest, and would certainly have found them if they had been on the road.

169 (I: 181): 'I'll do that'

169 (I: 181). his slow pate – *Pate* 'head', by extension the intellect. Nob's brain works slowly; he isn't 'quick on the uptake'.

169 (I: 182): *THE PRANCING PONY*

169 (I: 182). Midyear's Day – In the Shire Calendar there are three days between June and July, the middle one of these is *Midyear's Day* (also spelt *Mid-year's Day*). See Appendix D.

170 (I: 182): *PS. Do NOT use It again*

170 (I: 182). *PS.* – Latin *post scriptum*, from which English *postscript*, literally 'after written', something added at the end of a letter following the signature. For each additional note another *P* is added.

170 (I: 182). *Do not travel by night!* – In Book I, Chapter 11 Aragorn remarks that 'our shapes cast shadows in their minds, which only the noon sun destroys; and in the dark they [the Black Riders] perceive many signs and forms that are hidden from us: then they are most to be feared' (p. 189, I: 202).

170 (I: 182): *All that is gold does not glitter*

170 (I: 182). *All that is gold does not glitter* – Compare the traditional saying *all that glitters is not gold* (in Shakespeare's *Merchant of Venice*, 'All that glisters is not gold'). In his 'Canon's Yeoman's Tale' in the *Canterbury Tales* Chaucer says: 'But al thyng which that shyneth as the gold / Nis nat gold, as that I have heard told.'

170 (I: 182). *From the ashes a fire shall be woken* – For this Tom Shippey has suggested an inspiration by Spenser's *Faerie Queene*: 'There shall a sparke of fire, which hath long-while / Bene in his ashes raked up and hid / Be freshly kindled . . .' (quoted in *The Road to Middle-earth*, 2nd edn., p. 317, n. 9).

170 (I: 182): *PPPS. I hope Butterbur*

170 (I: 182). lumber-room – A room for the storage of unused or useless household articles.

170 (I: 183): 'Would it? Would any of you

170 (I: 182). The Enemy has set traps for me before now. – The Enemy (the forces of Sauron or his allies) are evidently aware of Aragorn as a leader of their foes, but are ignorant of his lineage.

171 (I: 183): 'That you are a stout fellow'

171 (I: 183). If I was after the Ring, I could have it – NOW! – Paul H. Kocher observes that 'like every other leader of the West' Aragorn is given 'one fateful chance' to yield to the temptation of the Ring. 'But he conquers it and is never bothered by it again. . . . And by his pledge of help he subordinates his own ambitions to their [the hobbits'] safety as bearers of the Ring' (*Master of Middle-earth: The Fiction of J.R.R. Tolkien* (1972), pp. 135–6).

171 (I: 183): 'But I *am* the real Strider

171 (I: 183). Arathorn – In his letter to Richard Jeffery, 17 December 1972, Tolkien wrote that *Arathorn* 'contains an abbreviated form of *þorono* (thorono) "eagle", seen in *Thoron- dor, Thorongil*: Q[uenya] *þorno / sorno*' (*Letters*, p. 427).

171 (I: 184): 'I did not know'

171 (I: 184). He drew out his sword, and they saw that the blade was indeed broken a foot below the hilt. – What was Aragorn to do if he needed to defend himself? The broken sword is with him as an heirloom of his house (see Book II, Chapter 2); presumably he carried some more effective weapon, though none is mentioned. His situation recalls the most famous broken sword of legend, Gram in the *Volsungasaga*, which Tolkien mentions in *On Fairy-Stories*. Odin gave the sword to Sigmund, but years later shattered it with a blow from his spear and turned the tide of battle. Hjordis, Sigmund's widow, saved the shards and gave them to her son Sigurd when he grew up. The sword was reforged for him by Regin, and with it he slew the dragon Fafnir. Tolkien first read Sigurd's story while still a child, in Andrew Lang's retelling in *The Red Fairy Book* (1890).

172 (I: 184): 'Well,' said Strider

172 (I: 184). Strider shall be your guide. And now I think it is time you went to bed and took what rest you can. We shall have a rough road tomorrow. – In editions prior to 2004 this passage read only: 'Strider shall be your guide. We shall have a rough road tomorrow.' Christopher Tolkien notes in *The Treason of Isengard*, p. 78, that the intervening sentence was present in the complex and difficult draft manuscript of the chapter, and indeed the words 'We shall have a rough road tomorrow' clearly depend on 'And now I think . . . what rest you can'. But 'And now I think . . .' was omitted from a later typescript, and so from the published *Lord of the*

Rings. In correspondence with the present authors Christopher commented that the words in question were omitted also from a fair copy manuscript preceding the typescript. There is no suggestion, he says, that his father was doubtful about the words in the original manuscript; their absence from the fair copy was probably a mere example of 'jumping', no more than the author inadvertently skipping over a sentence in the process of revising the 'chaotic' draft text, 'a mass of emendations, rejected pages, and inserted riders' (*The Treason of Isengard*, p. 78).

172 (I: 184): 'It is a hill, just to the north

172 (I: 184). about half way from here to Rivendell – But it does not appear to be 'half way' on the general map. In *Journeys of Frodo* (1981) Barbara Strachey remarks on this as a discrepancy, and speculates that Tolkien meant that Weathertop was half way to the Last Bridge. The Hobbits and Aragorn took seven days to reach Weathertop from Bree, involving a detour to the North, and seven days from Weathertop to the Bridge (with Frodo in a wounded condition and unable to hurry), while there was a *further* seven days from the Bridge to Rivendell. Aragorn is well aware of the distance: he says on Weathertop that it would take them fourteen days to reach the Ford, though it normally took him, by himself, twelve. In *The Return of the Shadow* Christopher Tolkien points to one of the drafts of this chapter, where Weathertop is said to be 'a hill, just north of the Road, somewhere about halfway to Rivendell from here' (p. 353), and comments on Strachey's suggestion that

> it is now seen that Aragorn's words 'about halfway from here (Bree) to Rivendell' in [*The Fellowship of the Ring*] go back to Trotter's here; and at this stage the River Hoarwell and the Last Bridge on the East Road did not yet exist. . . . I think that Trotter (Aragorn) was merely giving Folco (Sam) a rough but sufficient idea of the distances before them. – The relative distances go back to the original version . . . : about 120 miles from Bree to Weathertop, close on 200 from Weathertop to the Ford. [p. 368, n. 2]

See further, note for pp. 187–8.

172 (I: 184): Strider looked grave

172 (I: 184). We last met on the first of May: at Sarn Ford down the Brandywine. – In Book I, Chapter 2, however, it is said that Gandalf arrived at Bag End after a long absence on an evening in early April; and 'two or three weeks' later, in Book I, Chapter 3, he advised Frodo that he ought to leave soon; and in the end 'stayed in the Shire for over two months' before leaving (pp. 65, 67, III: 74, 76), i.e. in June 1418 (S.R.). Christopher Tolkien comments in *The Treason of Isengard* that 'there is no reference to his [Gandalf] having left Hobbiton during this time' (p. 80, n. 20).

Tolkien writes in the manuscript of *Nomenclature* that *Sarn Ford*

> is a half-translation (of *Sarn-athrad* 'stony-ford'), a process frequent in place-names. The [Sindarin] word *sarn* meant 'stony'; as a noun a 'stony place', an outcrop of rock in softer ground, or in a river-bed. The ancient ford over the Baranduin was so-called because, after passing through the flats of the Eastfarthing, it passed then over a wide area of shingles before turning south-west and falling swiftly down into lower lands on its way to the sea. (It was named by the Númenóreans after a ford in the River Gelion (in the lost land of Beleriand) famous in legend.)

173 (I: 186): 'I found him, sir'

173 (I: 186). South-gate – In his unfinished index Tolkien notes that the *South-gate* is the 'eastward gate of Bree (so-called because at that point the Road was running southwards)'.

174 (I: 186): 'No, I think not'

174 (I: 186). their power is in terror – In June 1958 Tolkien wrote to Forrest J. Ackerman that the Black Riders' peril

> is almost entirely due to the unreasoning *fear* which they inspire (like ghosts). They have no great physical power against the fearless; but what they have, and the fear they inspire, is enormously increased by *darkness*. The Witch-king, their leader, is more powerful in all ways than the others; but [in the first part of the story] he must not yet be raised to the stature of Vol. III. There, put in command by Sauron, he is given an added demonic force. [*Letters*, p. 272]

174 (I: 186): Their bags and gear

174 (I: 186). The Sickle – Glossed here as 'the Plough or Great Bear', i.e. Ursa Major, called in Britain the Plough or the Wain, and in America the Big Dipper.

Chapter 11

A KNIFE IN THE DARK

For drafts and history of this chapter, see *The Return of the Shadow*, pp. 162–71, 174–89, 354–9, 368; *The Treason of Isengard*, pp. 53–8, 64–5.

176 (I: 188): As they prepared for sleep

176 (I: 178). a black shadow moved under the trees – It is the night of 29 September 1418. Merry had told Frodo on the evening of 25 September that the Black Riders could have reached Crickhollow that evening if they were not stopped at the North-gate. In Marquette MSS 4/2/36 (*The Hunt for the Ring*) Tolkien explains their delay as follows. Khamûl, alarmed at the escape of the Ring over the river on the night of 25 September, summoned the other four Riders who had entered the Shire:

> (The Nazgûl found one another easily, since they were quickly aware of a companion presence, and could hear the cries over great distances. They could see one another also from far away, even by day when to them a Nazgûl was the one clearly visible thing in a mist.)
>
> As soon as he has assembled his force (in the early morning of 26th, probably) [Khamûl] leaves one to lurk near the Bridge and watch it; he sends [two] along the East Road, with orders to report to [the Witch-king] the eastward movement of the Ring; he himself with [his companion] passes secretly into Buckland by the north gate of that land. But desiring to attract as little notice as possible he (mistakenly and against Sauron's orders) sacrifices speed to stealth.
>
> [The two sent east] pass along the East Road, and visit Bree and 'The Prancing Pony'. They then go in search of [the Witch-king] but cannot at once find him [until 27th September. He] is elated to learn that the Ring was really in the Shire, but is alarmed and angry at its escape; and also by the fact that the Bearer must now certainly know that he is being hunted. (If he is a person of power and knowledge he may find out indeed how to use it, and compel a Nazgûl to leave him unmolested at the least. But [he is told that Khamûl] has discovered that the Bearer is a v[ery] small spiritless creature with no pride or will power, and is filled with terror at the approach of a Ringwraith.)
>
> [The Witch-king] is uncertain what to do. The Bearer seems to be making eastwards, he is therefore surely bound for Rivendell (not the Havens). He would have naturally used the East Road; but will he do so, now that he knows he is pursued? Probably he will attempt to escape from the Shire at some unexpected point, through the Old Forest and the Downs, and there make cross-country to strike the Road beyond

Weathertop, maybe. In that direction [he] now sends out [three Riders] separately, with orders to reassemble just east of Weathertop, and then return towards Bree along or near the Road. [He] himself, [with two other Riders] redoubles his vigilance on the east-borders along the Greenway . . . his counsels disturbed by threat of attack. Some of the Dúnedain have met Elvish messengers, and [he] is uneasily aware that many enemies are watching him and though none has yet come with power to challenge him.

Meanwhile [Khamûl and his companion] are searching Buckland, but can do little except at night; and they are at a loss, since the Buckland did not appear in Saruman's charts of the Shire at all. By good fortune they do not discover the Hay-gate or become aware that the Ring has departed. [In his unfinished index Tolkien says that *Hay-gate* is another name for the north gate. Perhaps here he is referring to the gate *through* the High Hay into the Old Forest.] On 28 September they find Crickhollow at night, but do not attack though [Khamûl] is aware that the Ring has been, or is still, there. [Khamûl] ?lurks near, and [his companion] is sent to bring [the rider left by the Bridge] and the horses. Road between Bridge and Bree is thus left unwatched. [Early on 29 September Khamûl and the other two Riders] come back to Crickhollow and watch it as night passes.

176 (I: 188): There was a faint stir

176 (I: 188). a cock crowed far away. The cold hour before dawn was passing. – *The cold hour before dawn* is perhaps a reference to the proverb *The darkest hour is just before dawn*. This may be the reason that the Riders waited so long before attacking. Yet traditionally the cock crows to signal dawn (compare the end of Book V, Chapter 4), at which time ghosts and apparitions must vanish, e.g. the ghost of Hamlet's father in *Hamlet*, Act I, Scene 2. Here the cock anticipates the dawn, and though the Riders are no apparitions, an attack before cock crow would seem more appropriate.

176 (I: 188). In the dark without moon or stars – The young moon would have set well before midnight, but the absence of stars suggests that the night became overcast.

177 (I: 189): The Brandybucks were blowing

177 (I: 189). not since the white wolves came in the Fell Winter, when the Brandywine was frozen over – An event analogous to the freezing of the Rhine at the end of 406 AD which enabled the Vandals (with some Alans, Suevi, and Burgundians) to invade the Western Roman Empire.

177 (I: 189): Far away answering horns

177 (I: 189). Far away answering horns were heard. – Prior to the edition of 2004 'Far away' read 'Far-away'. In *The Treason of Isengard* Christopher

Tolkien comments that 'in all the variant forms [drafts] of the "Crickhollow episode" the reading is "Far away" (adverbial). The reading of [*The Fellowship of the Ring*] (p. 189), "Far-away answering horns" (adjectival), which appears already in the first impression of the first edition, is I think an early error' (p. 64, n. 21).

177 (I: 189): Frodo soon went to sleep

177 (I: 189). the noise of wind and galloping hoofs . . . and far off he heard a horn blowing wildly – Frodo seems to be dreaming of events at Crickhollow.

177 (I: 189). He opened his eyes – It is now 30 September.

177 (I: 189): As soon as Strider had roused them all

177 (I: 189). the windows had been forced – In Marquette MSS 4/2/36 (*The Hunt for the Ring*) it is said that the three Black Riders who had been sent to Weathertop and told to ride back along the Road

> reached Bree at dusk [on 29 September], and soon learn from the Isengard spy of the events in the Inn, and guess the presence of the Ring. One is sent to the [Witch-king]. . . . [He] is waylaid by Dúnedain and driven away does not reach [the Witch-king] until the next day. . . . [The other two] foiled in their attempt to capture Merry make plans for attack on the Inn at night. . . . The Inn attacked by the two Riders in early hours before dawn. Crickhollow attacked at about the same time. . . . Both attacks fail. [The two Riders in Bree] go off in haste to find [the Witch-king] to report that Bearer has gone (without waiting for further news). [The three from Crickhollow] ride down the Buckland Gate and make also for Andrath [Sindarin 'long climb', the 'defile between the Barrow-downs and the South Downs through which the North–South Road (Greenway) passed', *Unfinished Tales*, p. 418]. The Nazgûl are thus all assembled at Andrath. [The Witch-king] is exceedingly wroth, and feels certain that Bearer has gone east from Bree. He is not yet aware of the presence of Gandalf, and does not learn anything of Aragorn beyond the report of the spy that 'a Ranger was in the Inn on the night of Sep[tember] 29'.
>
> [The Witch-king] now plans his pursuit. He sends four Riders across country from Andrath to Weathertop. He himself with the other four scour all round the borders from Sarn Ford to Bree at speed, but can find out nothing, or feel any trace of the Ring . . . [on 30 September] knowing now that Ring has escaped East [they] leave Greenway and take East Road; soon after midnight they ride through Bree like a storm, casting down the gates.

178 (I: 190): 'I doubt it,' said the landlord

178 (I: 190). horse or ponies for draught – Used for drawing a cart, plough, etc.

181 (I: 193): 'Morning, Longshanks!'

181 (I: 193). Longshanks – *Shanks* 'legs', thus *Longshanks* 'long-legs'. Aragorn, of Númenórean descent, is considerably taller than the Men of Bree; but Ferny means his greeting to be an insult. *Longshanks* was a nickname of Edward I, King of England (ruled 1272–1307).

181 (I: 193): 'Morning, my little friends!'

181 (I: 193). Stick-at-naught – Unscrupulous or ruthless, allowing nothing to hinder one in accomplishing one's desire.

181–2 (I: 194): His plan, as far as they

182 (I: 194). Midgewater Marshes – In his unfinished index Tolkien describes these as 'a fen between Chetwood and Weathertop'. In *Nomenclature* he says that 'the name was suggested by *Mývatn* in Iceland of the same meaning'. *Midge* is a colloquial name for any gnatlike insect.

182 (I: 194): Whether because of Strider's skill

182 (I: 194). The next day – It is 1 October 1418.

182 (I: 194). On the third day – On 2 October.

183 (I: 195): The next day, the fourth

183 (I: 195). The next day – It is now 3 October.

183 (I: 195). Neekerbreekers – In *Nomenclature* Tolkien describes *Neekerbreekers* as an 'invented insect-name', and states that their sound is 'supposed to be like that of a cricket'.

183 (I: 195): As Frodo lay, tired

183 (I: 195). there came a light in the eastern sky – This is the night of 3/4 October 1418. In *The Tale of Years* it is said that on 30 September Gandalf reached Bree, that he left on 1 October, and that on 3 October he was attacked at night on Weathertop. According to another account, on 2 October the four Black Riders who were sent ahead

> assemble near Weathertop. [One] remains [while three] go on eastwards on or near Road. . . . Oct. 3: Gandalf reaches Weathertop but does not overtake [Witch-king and other four Riders]; for they become aware of his approach as he overtakes them on Shadowfax, and withdraw into hiding beside the road. They close in behind. [The Witch-king] is both pleased and puzzled. For a while he had been in great fear, thinking that by some means Gandalf had got possession of the Ring and was

now the Bearer; but as Gandalf passes he is aware that Gandalf has not got the Ring. What is he pursuing? He himself must be after the escaping Bearer; and it must therefore somehow have gone on far ahead. But Gandalf is a great power and enemy. He must be dealt with, and yet that needs great force.

[The five] follow Gandalf hotly to Weathertop. Since Gandalf halts there, [the Witch-King] suspects that that is a trysting place.

Gandalf is attacked by [the five plus the rider who had stayed near Weathertop] on Weathertop on night 3–4. Frodo and Aragorn see the light of the battle in the sky from their camp.

Oct. 4: Gandalf repulses the Nazgûl and escapes northwards at Sunrise, and follows the Hoarwell up towards the mountains. [Four Riders] are sent in pursuit (mainly because [the Witch-king] thinks it possible he may know of the whereabouts or course of the Bearer). But [the Witch-king and Khamûl] remain watching Weathertop. Thus they become aware of the approach of Frodo on Oct. 5. [The other three] return from East. [Marquette MSS 4/2/36, *The Hunt for the Ring*]

183 (I: 195): They had not gone far

183 (I: 195). the fifth day – It is 4 October 1418.

183 (I: 195): 'That is Weathertop'

183 (I: 195). The Old Road – In his unfinished index Tolkien says that this 'refers to the great East Road'.

183 (I: 195–6): 'Yes, but the hope is faint

183 (I: 196). Not all the birds are to be trusted – In *The Hobbit* the eagles and Roäc the raven can converse with the dwarves and Bilbo, and are friendly and helpful. The thrush understands speech and informs Bard the Bowman of Smaug's weak spot. In *The Lord of the Rings* the eagles are again friendly, and it seems probable that the Elves use birds to carry messages (as Gildor sends news to Tom Bombadil, Aragorn, and Elrond). But later in *The Lord of the Rings* Aragorn and Gandalf will be (rightly) suspicious of the crows in Hollin.

184 (I: 196): At day's end they came

184 (I: 196). That night they set a watch – By implication they had not done so before, though Aragorn seems to have stayed awake most of the night of 3/4 October.

184 (I: 196). The moon was waxing – This is the night of 4/5 October. The moon reached its first quarter on 3 October.

184 (I: 196): Next morning they set out

184 (I: 196). Next morning – It is 5 October.

184 (I: 196). short commons – Insufficient rations, scant fare.

184–5 (I: 197): The hills drew nearer

184–5 (I: 197). the remains of green-grown walls and dikes, and in the clefts there stood the ruins of old works of stone – See entry for p. 146. Tolkien may also have been influenced by the Roman wall in the north of England, built by order of the Emperor Hadrian after his visit in AD 122, extending for seventy miles from Wallsend on the east coast to Bowness on the west.

185 (I: 197): In the morning they found

185 (I: 197). In the morning – It is 6 October.

185 (I: 197): 'No. There is no barrow

185 (I: 197). in their latter days they defended the hills for a while against the evil that came out of Angmar. This path was made – See further, Appendix A. The Witch-king established himself in Angmar (*c.* Third Age 1300), and in his realm in the North, on both sides of the Mountains, 'and there were gathered many evil men and Orcs, and other fell creatures'. It was not known until later that he was 'the chief of the Ringwraiths, who came north with the purpose of destroying the Dúnedain in Arnor'. By this time Arnor had become divided into three separate kingdoms, one of which, Rhudaur, was allied with Angmar. The line of Isildur survived only in Arthedain. King Argeleb I of Arthedain, who ruled from Third Age 1349, fortified the Weather Hills against Angmar and Rhudaur, but was slain in battle against them in 1356.

> Arveleg son of Argeleb, with the help of Cardolan [the third realm] and Lindon [the Elves living near the Gulf of Lune], drove back his enemies from the Hills; and for many years Arthedain and Cardolan held in force a frontier along the Weather Hills. . . . A great host came out of Angmar in 1409, and crossing the river entered Cardolan and surrounded Weathertop. The Dúnedain were defeated and Arveleg was slain. The Tower of Amon Sûl was burned and razed; but the *palantír* was saved and carried back in retreat to Fornost. [p. 1040, III: 320]

185 (I: 197). Amon Sûl – Sindarin 'hill of the wind'.

185 (I: 197). It is told that Elendil stood there watching for the coming of Gil-galad out of the West, in the days of the Last Alliance – Weathertop was in Arnor, Elendil's realm. According to *The Heirs of Elendil*, a working text for Appendix A, Elendil built the Tower of Amon Sûl on top of Weathertop 'in which was kept the chief *palantír* of the North' (*The Peoples of Middle-earth*, p. 193). Although it is not specifically stated in the published *Lord of the Rings* that Elendil built Amon Sûl, the fact that it is referred to several times as the place where the *palantír* was kept (see

Book III, Chapter 11), indicates that this probably remained Tolkien's view. Gil-galad's realm of Lindon was in the West. Both *The Tale of Years* and *Of the Rings of Power and the Third Age* (in *The Silmarillion*) indicate that the armies of the *Last Alliance* of Elves and Men against Sauron assembled in Rivendell, then crossed the Misty Mountains and marched south to Mordor. Had they planned to use the great North-South Road they would have met further west.

185 (I: 197–8): *Gil-galad was an Elven-king*

185 (I: 197–8). *Gil-galad was an Elven-king . . .* – A recording by Tolkien of this poem is included on Disc 1 of *The J.R.R. Tolkien Audio Collection*.

185 (I: 197). *the last whose realm was fair and free / between the Mountains and the Sea* – Gil-galad was the last of the Noldor in Middle-earth to be regarded as a king. Many of the Elves had been killed in the overthrow of Sauron at the end of the Second Age, and those that survived lived mainly in refuges or enclaves such as Rivendell or Lothlórien.

185 (I: 198). helm – Archaic 'helmet'.

185 (I: 198). *the countless stars of heaven's field / were mirrored in his silver shield* – Probably a poetic way of stating that stars were emblazoned on his shield, not actually reflected. Among the various devices that Tolkien drew in the early 1960s are two for Gil-galad, preliminary ideas rather than finished works, showing patterns of stars on a blue ground (see *Artist and Illustrator*, fig. 190).

186 (I: 199): 'He did not make it up'

186 (I: 189). the lay that is called *The Fall of Gil-galad* – A *lay* is 'a short lyric or narrative poem meant to be sung' (*OED*).

186 (I: 189). Bilbo must have translated it. I never knew that. – Strider reveals that he knows Bilbo, but the hobbits do not notice.

186 (I: 198–9): On the top they found

186 (I: 198). a cairn of broken stones had been piled – A *cairn* is 'a mound of rough stones built as a memorial or landmark' (*Concise OED*). Here, possibly built by Gandalf, to draw Aragorn's attention.

186–7 (I: 199): Standing upon the rim of the ruined circle

186–7 (I: 199). the glint of distant water . . . the Mountains – The *glint of distant water* is presumably a glimpse of the River Hoarwell.

The *Mountains* are the Misty Mountains.

187 (I: 199): 'I should say,' answered Strider

187 (I: 199). the light we saw three nights ago – In Book II, Chapter 2 it is revealed that Strider is correct in his interpretation of the scratches.

187–8 (I: 200): I don't know if the Road

187 (I: 200). the *Forsaken Inn*, a day's journey east of Bree – The *Forsaken Inn* is located 'where the East Road approached the old borders of the Bree-land' (*Index*). Aragorn probably means one day's journey on foot, not on horseback, perhaps about fifteen or twenty miles east of Bree. The name of the inn may be meant to indicate that it is now derelict.

187–8 (I: 200). Some say it is so far, and some say otherwise. It is a strange road.... But I know how long it would take me on my own feet ... twelve days from here to the Ford of Bruinen, where the Road crosses the Loudwater ... we have at least a fortnight's journey before us – In an early text, before the conception of Aragorn, Trotter the hobbit is more specific, following directly from the statement about the *Forsaken Inn*:

> the stages, in days taken by waggon, pony, or horse, or on foot, are pretty well known, of course. I should reckon it is about 120 long-miles from Bree to Weathertop – by the Road, which loops south and north. We have come a shorter but not quicker way: between 80 and 90 miles in the last six days. It is nearer 40 than 30 miles from Brandywine Bridge to Bree. I don't know, but I should make the count of miles from your Bridge to the Ford under the Misty Mountains a deal over 300 miles. So it must be close on 200 from Weathertop to the Ford. I have heard it said that from Bridge to Ford can be done in a fortnight going hard with fair weather; but I have never met any that had made the journey in that time. Most take nigh on a month, and poor hobbit-folk on foot take more. [*The Return of the Shadow*, p. 170]

But Tolkien found this 'too cut and dried', and through further revisions boiled it down to the final text.

In his unfinished index Tolkien locates the *Ford of Bruinen* 'at end of the East Road, over the River Bruinen about 20 miles SW [south-west] of Rivendell'. *Bruinen* is the Sindarin equivalent of *Loudwater.*

191 (I: 203): 'Then tell us some other tale

191 (I: 203). a tale about the Elves before the fading time – In *The Tale of Years* Tolkien says of the Third Age that 'these were the fading years of the Eldar. For long they were at peace, wielding the Three Rings while Sauron slept and the One Ring was lost; but they attempted nothing new, living in memory of the past' (p. 1084, III: 365). In his letter to Milton Waldman, ?late 1951, Tolkien suggests that the fading began in the Second Age:

> There was nothing wrong essentially in their lingering against counsel, still sadly with [*omission in typescript*] the mortal lands of their old heroic deeds. But they wanted to have their cake without eating it. They wanted peace and bliss and perfect memory of 'The West', and yet to

> remain on the ordinary earth where their prestige as the highest people, above wild Elves, dwarves, and Men, was greater than at the bottom of the hierarchy of Valinor. They thus became obsessed with 'fading', the mode in which the changes of time (the law of the world under the sun) was perceived by them. They became sad and their art (shall we say) antiquarian, and their efforts really a kind of embalming. [*Letters*, p. 151]

191 (I: 203): 'I will tell you the tale

191–3 (I: 203–5). I will tell you the tale of Tinúviel . . . – A recording by Tolkien of this paragraph and the following poem is included on Disc 1 of *The J.R.R. Tolkien Audio Collection.*

The poem that follows has several precursors in Tolkien's writings, of which the most direct is *Light as Leaf on Lindentree*, verses first published in the Leeds magazine *The Gryphon* for June 1925, but based on workings which date back to 1919–20. (See further, *The Lays of Beleriand*, pp. 120–4.) The tale of Beren and Lúthien, the love between a mortal Man and an immortal Elf, is a central element in his mythology and was close to his heart: for part of the inspiration for Lúthien was the woman he married (Edith Bratt). The names of Beren and Lúthien are carved, with their own, on their tombstone in Wolvercote Cemetery, Oxford. On 11 July 1972 Tolkien wrote to his son Christopher:

> I never called Edith *Lúthien* – but she was the source of the story that in time became the chief part of the *Silmarillion*. It was first conceived in a small woodland glade filled with hemlocks at Roos in Yorkshire (where I was for a brief time in command of an outpost of the Humber Garrison in 1917, and she was able to live with me for a while). In those days her hair was raven, her skin clear, her eyes brighter than you have seen them, and she could sing – and *dance*. But the story has gone crooked, & I am left [after her death], and *I* cannot plead before the inexorable Mandos. [*Letters*, p. 420]

191–3 (I: 204–5): *The leaves were long, the grass was green*

191 (I: 204). hemlock umbels – For *hemlock*, see note for p. 112. An *umbel* is 'a flower cluster in which stalks of nearly equal length spring from a common centre and form a flat or curved surface, characteristic of the parsley family' (*Concise OED*).

191 (I: 204). *Tinúviel was dancing there* – Her true name was *Lúthien* 'enchantress'. *Tinúviel* 'daughter of twilight', a poetic word for the nightingale, was the name Beren gave her when he saw her dancing and singing under the stars.

191 (I: 204). *music of a pipe unseen* – The musician is the Elf Daeron. In *The Book of Lost Tales* he is Tinúviel's brother; elsewhere he is a minstrel at Thingol's court and in love with Lúthien.

191 (I: 204). *raiment* – An archaic word for clothing.

191 (I: 204). *Beren came from mountains cold* – *Beren* (Sindarin 'bold, valiant') was the last survivor of a small band of outlaws who had resisted Morgoth in the forested northern highland called Dorthonion. He endured a terrible journey south through the Ered Gorgoroth and found his way into the realm of Doriath, ruled by Lúthien's father.

191 (I: 204). *the Elven-river* – The *Esgalduin* (Sindarin 'river under veil').

191 (I: 204). *mantle* – A sleeveless cloak.

192 (I: 204). *Through woven woods in Elvenhome* – *Elvenhome* usually means that part of the land of Aman in the West where the Elves dwell, but that is not possible in this context. Here the name must allude to the Elven realm of Doriath, in Beleriand during the Elder Days.

192 (I: 204). *Of feet as light as linden-leaves* – *Linden* is another name for the lime-tree.

192 (I: 204). *Of music welling underground* – Thingol and his court dwelt in Menegroth, 'The Thousand Caves', 'the fairest dwelling of any king that has ever been east of the Sea' (*The Silmarillion*, p. 93).

192 (I: 204). *Whispering fell the beechen leaves* – A reference to the beech-forest of Neldoreth, in the northern part of Doriath.

192 (I: 205). *He saw the elven-flowers spring* – This may refer to the white flowers of *niphredil* 'snowdrop' that also greeted Lúthien's birth.

192 (I: 205). *Elvish name* – In editions prior to 2004 this read 'elvish name'. Both *Elvish* and *elvish*, used adjectivally, appeared in *The Lord of the Rings*; but in a check copy of the second edition Tolkien wrote: 'Elvish as a separate adjective should always have capital (as English French etc.)'. Thus one finds *Elvish character, Elvish knife, Elvish smiths* as well as *Elvish language, Elvish speech*, etc., but *elvish minstrels, elvish robes*, etc. as well, capitals and lower case about evenly divided in occurrences. When editing the edition of 2004 we considered that some uses of *elvish*, as in *elvish air*, are of a more general nature, and do not necessarily mean 'of the Elves', but most of the instances cited seem more closely related: the 'elvish minstrels' *are* Elves, the 'elvish song' *is* in Elvish, 'Tinúviel' *is* an Elvish name (Sindarin), and so forth. Tolkien seems to have been of two minds about this rule, and did not follow his stated practice (stated after the fact) consistently except, in all but one instance, in *The Return of the King*.

193 (I: 205). *Immortal maiden elven-wise* – Lúthien's father was an Elf, but her mother was Melian, a Maia, akin to the Valar. Through her mother Lúthien inherited more than Elven immortality.

193 (I: 205). *Through halls of iron and darkling door, / And woods of*

nightshade morrowless. – The *halls of iron* are Morgoth's stronghold, Angband.

Darkling is a poetic adjective for 'in the dark'.

The *woods of nightshade* are Taur-nu-Fuin (Sindarin 'forest under night'), the name given to Dorthonion when it came under the sway of Morgoth.

193 (I: 205). ***The Sundering Seas between them lay*** – When Beren was killed his spirit passed to the halls of Mandos beyond the Western Seas in Aman, and as Lúthien had bade him tarried there,

> unwilling to leave the world, until Lúthien came to say her last farewell upon the dim shores of the Outer Sea, whence Men that die set out never to return. But the spirit of Lúthien fell down into darkness, and . . . came into the halls of Mandos . . . and she knelt before Mandos and sang to him.
>
> The song of Lúthien before Mandos was the song most fair that ever in words was woven, and the song most sorrowful that ever the world shall hear. . . . For Lúthien wove two themes of words, of the sorrow of the Eldar and the grief of Men, of the Two Kindreds that were made by Ilúvatar to dwell in Arda, the Kingdom of Earth amid the innumerable stars. And as she knelt before him her tears fell upon his feet like rain upon the stones; and Mandos was moved to pity, who never before was so moved, nor has been since.
>
> Therefore he summoned Beren, and even as Lúthien had spoken in the hour of his death they met again beyond the Western Sea. But Mandos had no power to withhold the spirits of Men that were dead within the confines of the world, after their time of waiting; nor could he change the fates of the Children of Ilúvatar. He went therefore to Manwë, Lord of the Valar . . . and Manwë sought counsel in his inmost thought, where the will of Ilúvatar was revealed. [*The Silmarillion*, pp. 186–7]

The choices offered to Lúthien were to dwell in Valinor with the Valar, where 'Beren could not come', or to become mortal and return to Middle-earth, to dwell there for a short time with Beren, but 'be subject to a second death, even as he; and ere long she would leave the world for ever. . . . This doom she chose' (p. 187).

193–4 (I: 205–6): Strider sighed and paused

193 (I: 205). ***ann-thennath*** – In 'Three Elvish Verse Modes', in *Tolkien's* Legendarium*: Essays on* The History of Middle-earth (2000), Patrick Wynne and Carl F. Hostetter comment that Aragorn's song is one of several English poems in *The Lord of the Rings* 'portrayed as translations from Elvish originals into Westron, the Common Speech' for which 'there is no evidence that Tolkien ever actually wrote any of the original Elvish poems said to underlie these "translated" versions, but such references provide an additional layer of depth to the sub-created world, implying that Middle-earth was home to a vast body of authentic Elvish verse of which we are shown only tantalizing glimpses' (p. 114). Since *ann-thennath* is Sindarin, Wynne and Hostetter assume that the 'original' poem was in Sindarin. They note that *ann-* means 'long', and cite evidence suggesting that *thenn* means 'short', and they state that *-ath* is 'a Sindarin suffix "used as a group plural, embracing all things of the same name, or those associated in some special arrangement or organization"', concluding:

> Thus *ann-thennath* appears to literally mean *'long-shorts,' or more freely *'longs and shorts (in some special arrangement or organization)' – not inappropriate as the name of a mode of verse, since the terms *long* and *short* are commonly used in prosody to describe syllables of contrasting length in quantitative verse (such as Latin), stressed versus unstressed syllables in accentual verse (such as English), and poetic lines consisting of varying numbers of syllables or metrical feet. [p. 115]

193 (I: 205). Barahir – Sindarin 'bold, eager lord'.

193 (I: 205). Thingol – Sindarin 'grey-cloak, grey-mantle'.

193 (I: 205–6). fairest maiden . . . the mists of the Northern lands – When Beren first sees Lúthien in *The Silmarillion* 'he fell into an enchantment; for Lúthien was the most beautiful of all the Children of Ilúvatar. Blue was her raiment as the unclouded sky, but her eyes were grey as the starlit evening; her mantle was sewn with golden flowers, but her hair was dark as the shadows of twilight' (p. 165).

In his unfinished index to *The Lord of the Rings* Tolkien defines *Northern lands* as 'the N.W. [north-west] of the world of the Elder Days, esp[ecially] Beleriand and adjacent regions, also called *Norland*'.

193 (I: 206). the Great Enemy, of whom Sauron of Mordor was but a servant – The 'Great Enemy' is the Vala whose name in Quenya was Melkor, 'he who arises in might'. 'Great might was given to him by Ilúvatar', but he turned his power and knowledge 'to evil purposes, and squandered his strength in violence and tyranny' and sought to make Middle-earth his realm (*The Silmarillion*, p. 31). He subtly poisoned the minds of many of the Noldor against the Valar, with the aid of Ungoliant (see note for p. 723) he destroyed the Two Trees which gave light to Valinor, and he stole the Silmarils, the creation of the Elf Fëanor, slaying Fëanor's father, Finwë, when he tried to oppose him. Fëanor then gave Melkor a new name, *Morgoth* 'the Black Enemy'.

193 (I: 206). the Silmarils – Fëanor was 'of all the Noldor . . . the most subtle in mind, and the most skilled in hand . . . he it was who first of the Noldor discovered how gems greater and brighter than those of the earth might be made with skill' (*The Silmarillion*, p. 64). The greatest of his creations were the three Silmarils, jewels like the crystal of diamonds within which was 'inner fire . . . made of the blended light of the Two Trees' (p. 67). The Silmarils were hallowed by Varda, and only in them was preserved the unsullied light of the Two Trees, poisoned by Melkor and Ungoliant. Quenya *silima* 'silver, shining white' was the name that Fëanor gave to their substance.

193 (I: 206). the Elves of the West – The Noldor only, of the three peoples of the Elves, returned to Middle-earth from Aman against the advice and warnings of the Valar.

193 (I: 206). the Mountains of Terror – A 'translation' of Sindarin *Ered Gorgoroth.*

193 (I: 206). Neldoreth – See notes for pp. 192, 469.

193 (I: 206). Tinúviel rescued Beren from the dungeons of Sauron – Beren was captured and imprisoned in Sauron's stronghold, Tol-in-Gaurhoth (Sindarin 'isle of werewolves'). With the aid of Huan, the great wolfhound of Valinor, Lúthien overcame Sauron, forced him to yield the mastery of his tower, and rescued Beren. Sauron fled in the form of a vampire.

193 (I: 206). and cast down even the Great Enemy from his throne, and took from his iron crown one of the three Silmarils – Beren and Lúthien, disguised as a werewolf and a bat, entered Morgoth's fortress, Angband, after Lúthien cast a spell of sleep on the wolf Carcharoth 'the Red Maw' who guarded its gate. When they came before Morgoth, and he stripped the disguise from Lúthien, she sang a song which sent him and all his court to sleep. Morgoth fell from his throne, and his crown which held the stolen Silmarils rolled from his head.

193 (I: 206). the bride-price of Lúthien – This was the reading in the first printing of the first edition (1954). In the unauthorized resetting of *The Fellowship of the Ring* for its second printing (1954) 'bride-price' was misprinted as 'bride-piece', an error which survived in subsequent printings and editions for some twenty years. In a 1975 accounting of textual changes in *The Lord of the Rings* Christopher Tolkien remarked of 'bride-piece': 'This is one of the most ancient and ineradicable errors and seems likely to become part of the English language in America to judge from the number of times it is quoted' (courtesy of Christopher Tolkien).

When Beren asked Thingol for Lúthien's hand, Thingol had declared: 'Bring to me in your hand a Silmaril from Morgoth's crown; and then if she will, Lúthien may set her hand in yours' (*The Silmarillion*, p. 167). In this way he hoped to keep a promise he had made to his daughter not to slay or imprison Beren, but also to bring about his death.

Authorities differ concerning the practice of demanding or paying a *bride-price.* The *Oxford English Dictionary* defines it as 'money paid for a bride' and cites a nineteenth-century text: 'By early Teutonic custom . . . the *bride-price or price paid by the intending husband to the family of the bride'. Yet according to Tacitus in *Germania*:

> marriage in Germany is austere. . . . The dowry is brought by husband to wife, not by wife to husband. Parents and kinsmen attend and approve the gifts, gifts not chosen to please a woman's whim or gaily deck a young bride, but oxen, horse with reins, shield, spear and sword. For such gifts a man gets his wife, and she in turn brings some presents of arms to her husband. . . . She is receiving something that she must hand over unspoilt and treasured to her children, for her sons' wives to receive in their turn and pass on to the grandchildren. [*Tacitus on Britain and Germany*, translated by H. Mattingly (1948), pp. 115–16]

Dorothy Whitelock in *The Beginnings of English Society* (1952) says that 'the wording of the earliest Kentish laws suggest a crude view of marriage, as the purchase of a wife', and comments:

> Yet the position of women in Anglo-Saxon society was a high one (already Tacitus had been struck by their influential position in the Germanic races), and very soon the bride-price came to be regarded as the property of the bride herself. It is probably what is referred to later on as what the suitor paid 'in order that she might accept his suit.' Before the end of the period the law states categorically: 'No woman or maiden shall ever be forced to marry one whom she dislikes, nor be sold for money.' [p. 151]

193 (I: 206). Beren was slain by the Wolf that came from the gates of Angband – When Beren and Lúthien left Angband they found that Carcharoth had woken. Lúthien was tired, and when Beren tried to daunt the wolf with the Silmaril, Carcharoth bit off his hand and devoured both it and the jewel. But the Silmaril burnt the wolf's flesh, and he fled howling and ravaging through the land. Beren and Lúthien were rescued by eagles from Morgoth's pursuit and came eventually to Doriath, where Thingol accepted Beren, for indeed there was now a Silmaril in his hand, though the hand was inside the wolf. But Carcharoth broke into Doriath, and Beren was slain defending Thingol from the assault.

Angband means 'iron prison', from Sindarin *ang* 'iron' + *band* 'prison, duress'.

194 (I: 206). There live still those of whom Lúthien was the foremother, and it is said that her line shall never fail. Elrond of Rivendell is of that Kin. – Elrond is Lúthien's great-grandson. Aragorn might have added that he too is descended from Lúthien, through Elrond's brother Elros, the first King of Númenor. The story of Beren and Lúthien has an even greater significance for Aragorn, to be revealed only later: he has fallen in love with Elrond's daughter, Arwen, who has returned his love and is willing to renounce her Elvish immortality, to become mortal like Lúthien before her. Elrond has told Aragorn, his foster-son, that: 'Maybe it has been appointed so, that by my loss the kingship of Men may be restored. Therefore, though I love you, I say to you: Arwen Undómiel shall not diminish her life's grace for less cause. She shall not be the bride of any Man less than the King of both Gondor and Arnor' (*The Tale of Aragorn and Arwen* in Appendix A, p. 1016, III: 342). Aragorn is the rightful heir to both thrones, but has small hope of being accepted in Gondor, or of recovering Arnor in the North. As he tells the story, does he wonder if he will succeed in fulfilling Elrond's conditions, and does he hope that the belief that the line of Lúthien 'shall never fail' is an omen for the future?

Of course, the first-time reader picks up none of these undertones. Paul H. Kocher comments:

> None of the hobbits has the faintest glimmer of an idea why Aragorn chooses this particular legend to recite, and neither have we at first reading, thanks to Tolkien's failure to mention Arwen at all up to that point. But in the light of later revelations it can dawn on us that the longing for Arwen is a torment, a joy, a despair, a comfort to Aragorn in a time of little hope. Small wonder that he is 'strange and grim at times,' but he seldom speaks of the life of private emotions stirring within. [*Master of Middle-earth*, p. 137]

194 (I: 206). Dior Thingol's heir; and of him Elwing the White – *Dior* (Sindarin 'successor') was also called *Eluchil* 'Heir of Thingol [also called *Elu*]'. Dior named his daughter *Elwing* 'which is "Star-spray", for she was born on a night of stars, whose light glittered in the spray of the waterfall of Lanthir Lamath ["waterfall of echoing voices"] beside her father's house' (*The Silmarillion*, p. 235). (Compare Tolkien's letter to Rhona Beare, 14 October 1958, in which *Elwing* is 'translated' as 'Elf-foam' (*Letters*, p. 282); and see note for p. 15, *Elrond*.)

194 (I: 206). Eärendil ... he that sailed his ship out of the mists of the world into the seas of heaven with the Silmaril upon his brow – Eärendil was the son of Tuor, a Man, and Idril, an Elf, the only child of Turgon, the King of Gondolin. By the time Eärendil wedded Elwing, Morgoth had conquered almost all of Beleriand. Eärendil set sail into the West to seek help from the Valar, but not until Elwing came to him with the Silmaril recovered by Beren and Lúthien was he able the pierce the barriers that the Valar had set to prevent anyone from Middle-earth reaching Valinor. There, speaking as a representative of Men and Elves: 'Pardon he asked for the Noldor and pity for their great sorrows, and mercy upon Men and Elves and succour in their need. And his prayer was granted' (*The Silmarillion*, p. 249). But neither he nor Elwing was allowed to return to Middle-earth. The Valar took his ship *Vingilot* 'foam-flower' and hallowed it and raised it into the heavens, where Eärendil sails with the Silmaril on his brow, seen most often at morning or at evening.

Eärendil is Quenya for 'lover of the sea'. In his draft letter to Mr Rang, August 1967, Tolkien wrote that it is 'the most important name' in his mythology inspired by the real world.

> This name is in fact (as is obvious) derived from A-S [Anglo-Saxon = Old English] *éarendel*. When first studying A-S professionally (1913–) – I had done so as a boyish hobby when supposed to be learning Greek and Latin – I was struck by the great beauty of this word (or name), entirely coherent with the normal style of A-S, but euphonic to a peculiar degree in that pleasing but not 'delectable' language. Also its form strongly suggests that it is in origin a proper name and not a common noun. This is borne out by the obviously related form in other Germanic languages; from which among the confusions and debasements of late traditions it at least seems certain that it belonged to an astronomical-myth, and was the name of a star or star-group. To my mind the A-S uses seem plainly to indicate that it was a star presaging the dawn (at any rate in English tradition): that is what we now call *Venus*: the morning-star as it may be seen shining brilliantly in the dawn, before the actual rising of the Sun. That is at any rate how I took it. Before 1914 I wrote a 'poem' upon Earendel who launched his ship like a bright spark from the havens of the Sun. I adopted him into my mythology – in which he became a prime figure as a mariner, and eventually as a herald star, and a sign of hope to men. [*Letters*, p. 385]

194 (I: 206). of Eärendil came the Kings of Númenor – Elros and Elrond, the sons of Eärendil, were allowed to choose to which kindred their fates should be joined, Elves or Men. Elrond chose to be of Elf-kind, but Elros of Man-kind. After the overthrow of Morgoth the Valar rewarded Men who had fought against him with a new dwelling place, an island in the West yet still distant from Valinor, called *Andor* 'the land of the Gift', and *Númenor* 'west-land'. Elros became the first King of Númenor.

195 (I: 208): Immediately, though everything else

195 (I: 208). Their eyes fell on him – When Frodo yields to the compulsion to put on the Ring, he is visible to the Ringwraiths. Gandalf tells him in Book II, Chapter 1: 'You were in gravest peril while you wore the Ring, for then you were half in the wraith-world yourself, and they might have seized you. You could see them, and they could see you' (p. 222, I: 234).

195–6 (I: 208): At that moment Frodo threw himself forward

195 (I: 208). *O Elbereth! Gilthoniel!* – Elbereth, or Varda, 'was often thought of, or depicted, as standing on a great height looking towards Middle-earth, with eyes that penetrated the shadows, and listening to the cries for aid of Elves (and Men) in peril or grief. Frodo . . . and Sam both invoke her in moments of extreme peril. . . . (These and other references to religion in *The Lord of the Rings* are frequently overlooked)' (*The Road Goes Ever On: A Song Cycle*, p. 65).

196 (I: 208). With a last effort Frodo, dropping his sword, slipped the Ring from his finger – As first published this passage read: 'With a last effort Frodo slipped the Ring from his finger', with no reference to his sword. It was revised to the current form in the Allen & Unwin second edition (1966). The Ballantine Books edition (1965) misprinted the passage as: 'With a last effort, dropping his sword, Frodo slipped the Ring from his finger'. In one of his check copies Tolkien noted the Ballantine divergence without comment.

In Marquette MSS 4/2/36 (*The Hunt for the Ring*) Tolkien wrote:

> Oct. 6. Frodo reaches Weathertop observed by the Nazgûl. Aragorn sees [three Riders] coming back from a patrol of the Road west of Weathertop.
>
> The camp is attacked at night by [five Riders]; but they are driven off by Aragorn; and withdraw after wounding Frodo. [The Witch-king] now knows who is the Bearer, and is greatly puzzled that it should be a small creature, and not Aragorn, who seems to be a great power though apparently 'only a Ranger'. But the Bearer has been marked with the Knife and (he thinks) cannot last more than a day or two.
>
> It is a strange thing that the camp was not watched while darkness lasted of the night Oct. 6–7, and the crossing of the Road into the southward lands seems not to have been observed, so that [the Witch-king] again lost track of the Ring. For this there were probably several reasons, the least to be expected being the most important, namely that [the Witch-king], the great captain, was actually dismayed. He had been shaken by the fire of Gandalf, and began to perceive that the mission on which Sauron had sent him was one of great peril to himself both by the way, and on his return to his Master (if unsuccessful); and he had been doing ill, so far achieving nothing save rousing the power of the Wise and directing them to the Ring. But above all the timid and terrified Bearer had resisted him, had dared to strike at him with an enchanted sword made by his own enemies long ago for his destruction. Narrowly it had missed him. How he had come by it – save in the Barrows of Cardolan. Then he was in some way mightier than the B[arrow]-wight; and he called on *Elbereth*, a name of terror to the Nazgûl. He was then in league with the High Elves of the Havens.
>
> Escaping a wound that would have been as deadly to him as the Mordor-knife to Frodo (as was proved at the end), he withdrew and hid for a while, out of doubt and *fear* both of Aragorn and especially of *Frodo*. But fear of Sauron, and the forces of Sauron's will was the stronger.
>
> Oct. 7. He arose and cried out to his companions, and drew [the

other four] back to him. He then patrols the Road to the Bridge of Mitheithel, knowing that it was practically impossible to cross the Greyflood between Tharbad and the Bridge (while [the four Riders who pursued Gandalf] are away north along the upper river). The Nazgûl search in vain for the Bearer while Aragorn leads Frodo in the pathless lands south of the Road.

Chapter 12

FLIGHT TO THE FORD

For drafts and history of this chapter, see *The Return of the Shadow*, pp. 190–205, 359–62, 368; *The Treason of Isengard*, pp. 58–62, 65–6.

198 (I: 210): Frodo dozed, though the pain

198 (I: 210). Dawn was growing in the sky – It is the morning of 7 October 1418.

198 (I: 210): 'Look!' he cried

198 (I: 210). all blades perish that pierce that dreadful King – This anticipates the withering of Merry's blade after he stabbed the Witch-king in Book V, Chapter 6.

198 (I: 210): 'And more deadly to Frodo

198 (I: 210). the blade seemed to melt – On 18 April and 6 May 1963 Tolkien wrote to Anneke C. Kloos-Adriaansen and P. Kloos:

> The melting of the sword-blade has a dramatic quality, which is attractive to a storyteller and makes it linger in the memory; but the dramatic effect is the only real connexion between the different uses of the motif. . . . I had read *Beowulf* before I wrote the *Lord of the Rings*, so there is probably an historical connexion between the melting of the Witchking's knife and the withering of Meriadoc's sword from the burial-mound [Book V, Chapter 6] . . . and the Anglo-Saxon poem. But that remains a fact of my personal biography (of which I was certainly not consciously aware when writing), and in no way enhances or explains the incidents in their places. [courtesy of Christopher Tolkien]

In *Beowulf* the blade of the ancient sword with which he kills Grendel's mother and cuts off Grendel's head 'began to waste away in gory fragments like icicles, by reason of the foeman's blood . . . .the sword was already melted, the damasked blade burnt up, – so hot had been the blood, the fiend so poisonous, who had died in that place' (*Beowulf and the Finnesburg Fragment*, translated by John R. Clark Hall (1940), p. 101).

198 (I: 210): He sat down on the ground

198 (I: 210). he sang over it a slow song in a strange tongue. . . . From the pouch at his belt he drew out the long leaves of a plant. – The healing of Frodo by Aragorn with herb (*athelas*) and song recalls the healing of Beren by Lúthien in *The Lay of Leithian*, a long poem in 'The Silmarillion':

Then Huan came and bore a leaf,
Of all the herbs of healing chief,
that evergreen in woodland glade
there grew with broad and hoary blade.

. . . .

Therewith the smart he swift allayed,
while Lúthien murmuring in the shade
the staunching song that Elvish wives
long years had sung in those sad lives
of war and weapons, wove o'er him.
[*The Lays of Beleriand*, p. 266]

198 (I: 210–11): 'These leaves,' he said

198 (I: 210). *Athelas* – A Sindarin word. Its second element is apparently *las(s)* 'leaf'. The first element is problematic; according to Arden R. Smith, an unpublished etymology connects it with Quenya *asëa*, as in *asëa aranion* 'kingsfoil' (but if so, *athelas* = 'leaf-leaf'); see note for p. 864.

200 (I: 212): Before the first day's march

200 (I: 212). Four days passed – The period 7–10 October.

200 (I: 212): At the end of the fifth day

200 (I: 212). At the end of the fifth day . . . and on the sixth day – The period 11–12 October.

200 (I: 212): 'I am afraid we must go back

200 (I: 212). River Hoarwell, that the Elves call Mitheithel. It flows down out of the Ettenmoors, the troll-fells north of Rivendell, and joins the Loudwater away in the South. Some call it the Greyflood after that. – In *Nomenclature* Tolkien glosses *Mitheithel* as 'pale grey' + 'spring, source'.

In the word *Ettenmoors* the element *etten* is derived from Old English *eōten* 'giant, troll', and *moor* is used here in the sense 'high barren land' – hence *troll-fells*, fells (i.e. hills or moorland) in which trolls lived.

Greyflood is a 'translation' of Sindarin *Gwathló*. Of this river Tolkien writes at great length in *The Rivers and Beacon-hills of Gondor* (this portion published chiefly in *Unfinished Tales*, pp. 261–3), e.g.:

> The river Gwathló is translated 'Greyflood'. But *gwath* is a Sindarin word for 'shadow', in the sense of dim light, owing to cloud or mist, or in deep valley. This does not seem to fit the geography. The wide lands divided by the Gwathló into the regions called by the Númenóreans Minhiriath ('Between the Rivers', Baranduin and Gwathló) and Enedwaith ('Middle-folk') were mainly plains, open and mountainless. At the point of the confluence of Glanduin and Mitheithel the land was

> almost flat, and the waters became sluggish and tended to spread into fenland. But some hundred miles below Tharbad the slope increased. The Gwathló, however, never became swift, and ships of smaller draught could without difficulty sail or be rowed as far as Tharbad. [*Unfinished Tales*, pp. 261–2]

Tolkien decided that the river had received its name from Númenóreans who explored it in small boats soon after they first returned to Middle-earth in the Second Age. 'As soon as the seaward region of salt airs and great winds was passed the forest drew down to the river-banks, and wide though the waters were the huge trees cast great shadows on the river, under which the boats of the adventurers crept silently up into the unknown land. So the first name they gave to it was "River of Shadow", *Gwath-hîr, Gwathir*' (*Unfinished Tales*, p. 263). But the Númenóreans denuded much of the area of trees, and by the Third Age the area was mainly grassland.

200 (I: 212): 'What is that other river

200 (I: 212). What is that other river we can see far away there? – In *The Return of the Shadow* Christopher Tolkien points out that Barbara Strachey, on her map of this region in *Journeys of Frodo*, brings the Loudwater further west

> because from the high ground above the Last Bridge the travellers could see not only the Hoarwell but also the Loudwater, whereas going by the published map [of 1954] the rivers 'would have been some 100 miles apart and the hill [on which they stood] would have had to have been a high mountain for it [the Loudwater] to have been visible.' By bringing this river so far to the west on her map the distance from the hill above the Last Bridge to the nearest point of the Loudwater is reduced to about 27 miles. On my father's [working] maps the shortest distance from the Last Bridge to the Loudwater varies between (approximately) 45 (on the earliest), 60, and 62 miles; on the published map it is about 75 miles. Thus the objection that the Loudwater was too far away to be seen is real; but it cannot be resolved in this way. [p. 202, note]

200 (I: 212–13): 'That is Loudwater, the Bruinen of Rivendell

200 (I: 212). The Road runs along the edge of the hills for many miles from the Bridge to the Ford of Bruinen. – As first published this passage read: 'The Road runs along it for many leagues to the Ford.' It was revised in the second edition (1965). In *The Return of the Shadow* Christopher Tolkien comments that this region appears on three of his father's sketch-maps, drawn during the writing of *The Lord of the Rings*: 'on two of these the Road is shown approaching the Loudwater at a fairly acute angle, but by no means running alongside it. On the third (the earliest) the Road runs close to the river for a long distance before the Ford; and this is less because the course of the Road is different than because on this map the river flows at first (after the Ford) in a more westerly direction towards the Hoarwell' (p. 202). The latter is also the case on the general map of Middle-earth Christopher drew for his father in 1943 (see 'The Maps of *The Lord of the Rings*', above); on the published (1954) map, however, the Road erroneously approaches the river at a wide angle. Christopher believes that the change described in the present annotation, 'with "runs along the edge of the hills" instead of "runs along it [the Loudwater]", was . . . made to save the appearance of the map' (p. 202). See also notes for pp. 202, 208.

200 (I: 213): Next day, early in the morning

200 (I: 213). Next day, early in the morning – It is 13 October.

201 (I: 213): They hurried along with all the speed

201 (I: 213). they saw the Last Bridge ahead, at the bottom of a short steep slope – In *The Lord of the Rings* the East Road crosses the River Hoarwell by the *Last Bridge.*

At this point in *The Lord of the Rings* there arises an inconsistency with *The Hobbit.* In the first and second editions of *The Hobbit* (1937, 1951), in Chapter 2, the dwarves and Bilbo travel beside a river with willows on its bank, and decide to camp for the night. The narrator comments: 'I don't know what river it was: a rushing red one, swollen with the rains of the last few days, that came down from the hills and mountains in front of them.' They see a fire (the trolls' campfire) on a hill some way off but clearly not far, for they reach it that night; in doing so they do not cross a bridge. But in *The Lord of the Rings* the travellers come to the Road early on the seventh day out from Weathertop, go along it for a mile or two to the Last Bridge, cross the river (the Hoarwell), and after another mile turn into the hills. Then, after six days' travel, they discover the old trolls turned to stone. As Karen Wynn Fonstad puts it, in *The Hobbit*

> the Trolls' fire was so close to the river that it could be seen 'some way off,' and it probably took the Dwarves no more than an hour to reach; whereas Strider led the Hobbits north of the road [turning off a mile beyond the Bridge], where they lost their way and spent six days reaching the clearing where they found the Stone-trolls. Lost or not, it seems almost impossible that that the time-pressed Ranger would have spent six days reaching a point the Dwarves found in an hour. [*The Atlas of Middle-earth*, rev. edn., p. 97]

In *The Return of the Shadow* Christopher Tolkien comments that his father 'was greatly concerned to harmonise Bilbo's journey [in *The Hobbit*] with the geography of *The Lord of the Rings*, especially in respect of the distance and time taken: in terms of *The Lord of the Rings* Gandalf, Bilbo, and the Dwarves took far too long, seeing that they were mounted' (p. 204). In 1960 Tolkien rewrote Chapter 2 of *The Hobbit*, introducing the Last

Bridge: in this Bilbo and company passed the river in the morning, and the camp from which the trolls' fire was seen was made at the end of the day, many miles further east. The revision was never finished, and was not used for the new (third) edition of 1966, but a small emendation was made nonetheless to Chapter 2: now the dwarves and Bilbo travel beside the same river with the willows when 'fortunately the road went over an ancient stone bridge, for the river swollen with the rains, came rushing down from the hills and mountains in the north'. After crossing over, they camp by the river, rescue a pony that has bolted into the water, and come upon the trolls that night.

201 (I: 213): He held out his hand

201 (I: 213). beryl, an elf-stone – A *beryl* is a transparent precious stone, pale green passing into light blue, yellow, and white.

201 (I: 213): The hobbits were glad

201 (I: 213). Here and there upon heights and ridges they caught glimpses of ancient walls of stone, and the ruins of towers. . . . Frodo . . . recalled Bilbo's account of his journey and the threatening towers on the hills north of the Road – In Chapter 2 of *The Hobbit*, as Bilbo and his companions travel through deserted lands, 'not far ahead were dreary hills, rising higher and higher, dark with trees. On some of them were old castles with an evil look, as if they had been built by wicked people.'

201 (I: 213). the Trolls' wood – Shown on the general map of Middle-earth as the 'Trollshaws' (see note in 'The Maps of *The Lord of the Rings*', above).

201 (I: 214): 'No!' said Strider

201 (I: 214). Men once dwelt here, ages ago; but none remain now. They became an evil people as legends tell, for they fell under the shadow of Angmar. But all were destroyed in the war that brought the North Kingdom to its end. – The travellers are now in Rhudaur; see note for p. 185.

201–2 (I: 214): 'The heirs of Elendil

201 (I: 214). heirs of Elendil do not forget . . . and many more things than I can tell are remembered in Rivendell – Thus the reader learns, if he notices so casual a remark, that Aragorn is himself of the illustrious line of Elendil, a living descendant of figures of legend. Having been fostered in Rivendell, no doubt he heard many tales there of his ancestors before Elrond revealed his lineage to him when he reached the age of twenty.

202 (I: 214): 'I have,' said Strider

202 (I: 214). I dwelt there once, and still I return when I may. There my heart is, but it is not my fate to sit in peace – A hint, but no more, that someone for whom Aragorn cares greatly dwells in Rivendell. On rereading this is clearly a reference to Arwen. When Elrond revealed to Aragorn his lineage and the shards of Elendil's sword, he said: 'With these you may yet do great deeds; for I foretell that the span of your life shall be greater than the measure of Men, unless evil befalls you or you fail at the test. But the test will be hard and long' (Appendix A, p. 1057, III: 338). *The Tale of Aragorn and Arwen* in Appendix A tells of Aragorn's labours against Sauron, his perilous journeys with Gandalf or alone, and his service under a different name in Rohan and Gondor, all before the events of *The Lord of the Rings*; and at the Council of Elrond he reveals the ceaseless watch of the Dúnedain in the north to protect simple people from fear and foes.

202 (I: 214): The hills now began to shut them in

202 (I: 214). The Road behind held on its way to the River Bruinen – As first published this passage read: 'The Road bent back again southward towards the River'. It was revised in the second edition (1965). In *The Return of the Shadow* Christopher Tolkien comments that from maps made by his father of the region in which the company is now moving 'there is no question that the Road after passing south of Weathertop made first a great swing or loop to the North-east. . . . The Road then made a great bend southwards, round the feet of the Trollshaws.' These 'great northward and southward swings' are correct on the 1943 map drawn by Christopher for his father, but on the published (1954) map 'the Road has only a feeble northward curve between Weathertop and the Hoarwell Bridge, and then runs in a straight line to the Ford. This was obviously simply carelessness due to haste on my part. My father doubtless observed it at the time but felt that on so small a scale the error was not very grievous: in any case the map was made, and it had been a matter of urgency.' But he thinks that this error was the reason for the change in the second edition described in the present note, to make 'the discrepancy with the map less obvious' (p. 200). See also notes for pp. 200 and 208.

202 (I: 214): The hobbits grew very weary

202 (I: 214). dales – Small valleys.

202 (I: 214). They had been two days in the country when the weather turned wet – The two fine days are 14 and 15 October 1418.

202 (I: 214). The next day – It is 16 October.

202 (I: 215): In the morning he woke

202 (I: 215). In the morning – It is 17 October.

203 (I: 215): When he returned he was not reassuring

203 (I: 215). the Ettendales – In his unfinished index Tolkien describes the *Ettendales* as 'the Dales of the Ettenmoors, running up into the foothills of the Misty Mountains'. In *Nomenclature* he comments that *Ettendales* was 'meant to be a Common Speech (not Elvish) name, though it contains an obsolete element *eten* "troll, ogre"' (from Old English *eōten*, compare note for p. 200).

204 (I: 216): Night was cold up on the high ridge

204 (I: 216). imagining that endless dark wings were sweeping by above him, and that on the wings rode pursuers that sought him – Frodo's dream presages the Ringwraiths on the winged creatures they will ride later in the story.

204 (I: 216): The morning dawned bright and fair

204 (I: 216). The morning dawned – It is 18 October.

204 (I: 217): When they came up with him

204 (I: 217). a path . . . In places it was now faint and overgrown, or choked with fallen stones and trees; but at one time it seemed to have been much used. It was a path made by strong arms and heavy feet. – The path made by the trolls who had been turned to stone over seventy-seven years earlier, as told in Chapter 2 of *The Hobbit*.

204–5 (I: 217): They followed the track

205 (I: 217). They followed the track . . . a door hanging crookedly ajar upon one hinge – In *The Hobbit*, Chapter 2, after the trolls have been turned to stone at sunrise, Gandalf, the dwarves, and Bilbo look for their cave and come upon 'a big door of stone leading to a cave'. They open it with a key Bilbo has found; the broken hinge is an unexplained later development.

205 (I: 217): Outside the door they all halted

205 (I: 217). on the floor lay many old bones . . . some great empty jars and broken pots – In *The Hobbit* Bilbo and company found, among other things, 'bones on the floor and . . . pots full of gold coins'.

205 (I: 218): The sun was now high

205 (I: 218). There stood the trolls: three large trolls. One was stooping, and the other two stood staring at him. – In *The Hobbit*, Chapter 2, three trolls capture the dwarves and argue how to cook them. Gandalf, imitating the trolls' voices, foments a dispute so that the trolls do not notice that sunrise is near. At that moment 'the light came over the hill. . . . William never spoke for he stood turned to stone as he stooped; and Bert and Tom were stuck like rocks as they looked at him . . . for trolls . . . must be underground before dawn, or they go back to the stuff of the mountains they are made of, and never move again.' In 1926 Helen Buckhurst, a friend and colleague of Tolkien, read a paper, 'Icelandic Folklore', to the Viking Society for Northern Research, in which she remarked that

> the Icelandic Trolls, as depicted both in the Sagas and in more recent tales, are huge, misshapen creatures, bearing some resemblance to human form, but always hideously ugly. They make their homes among the mountains, living generally in caves among the rocks or in the lava. They are almost always malignant in disposition, and frequently descend at night upon outlying farms in order to carry off sheep and horses, children, or even grown men and women, to devour in their mountain homes . . . some kinds of trolls have no power except during the hours of darkness; during the day they must remain hidden in their caves, for the rays of the sun turn them to stone. [published in *Saga-Book* 10 (1928–9), pp. 222–3, 229, quoted by Douglas A. Anderson in *The Annotated Hobbit*, 2nd edn., p. 80]

206 (I: 219): 'I don't know about that,' said Sam

206–8 (I: 219–20). Standing up, with his hands behind his back . . . – A recording by Tolkien from this sentence to the end of the following poem (but with 'John' and 'Jim' instead of 'Tom' and 'Tim') is included on Disc 1 of *The J.R.R. Tolkien Audio Collection.*

206–8 (I: 219–20): *Troll sat alone on his seat of stone*

206–8 (I: 219–20). *Troll sat alone on his seat of stone* . . . – Originally to be Frodo's song at the *Prancing Pony* in Book I, Chapter 9, the 'Troll Song' was moved here, following the discovery of the stone trolls from *The Hobbit.* It was based on a similar poem, called *Pēro & Pōdex* ('Boot and Bottom'), written by Tolkien in 1926 while he was at the University of Leeds. In 1936 that early version was privately printed, as *The Root of the Boot*, in the booklet *Songs for the Philologists* along with other poems devised at Leeds by Tolkien and his colleague E.V. Gordon. It is indeed sung 'to an old tune', 'The Fox Went Out on a Winter's Night'. *The Root of the Boot* was reprinted in 2003 in *The Annotated Hobbit* (2nd edn.), and with corrections by Tolkien in *The Return of the Shadow*, p. 143. After its appearance as revised in *The Lord of the Rings* the poem was reprinted as *The Stone Troll* in *The Adventures of Tom Bombadil and Other Verses from the Red Book* (1962).

206 (I: 219). *Done by! Gum by!* – In each verse the fifth line is mainly composed of nonsense phrases to rhyme with the last phrase of the fourth line.

206 (I: 219). ***my nuncle*** – That is, 'my uncle'. Tolkien is making a comment on the practice in Middle English whereby the *n* of a preceding indefinite article *an* or the possessive pronoun *myn* ('mine') was frequently transferred to a following word beginning with a vowel.

207 (I: 219). ***without axin' leave should go making free*** – *Axin'* is a dialectal form of 'asking'.

Making free is acting without permission.

207 (I: 219). ***For a couple o' pins . . . I'll eat thee too*** – *Pin* is often used to mean 'something cheap or worthless'; thus here 'it wouldn't take much to make me eat you too'.

207 (I: 220). ***gave him the boot to larn him . . . A bump o' the boot on the seat*** – *Larn* is a dialectal form of *learn*; see note for p. 24.

A bump o' the boot on the seat 'kick on his behind'.

208 (I: 220). ***the bone he boned from its owner*** – *Boned* is slang for 'stole, steal, made off with'.

208 (I: 220): In the afternoon

208 (I: 220). the Road had left the Hoarwell far behind in its narrow valley, and now clung close to the feet of the hills, rolling and winding eastward among woods – As first published this passage read: 'the Road had turned away from the river down in its narrow valley, and now clung close to the feet of the hills, rolling and winding northward among woods'. It was revised in the second edition (1965), but misprinted by Ballantine Books as 'the Road had left the Haarwell far behind the river down in its narrow valley, and now clung close to the feet of the hills, rolling and winding lastward among woods'. The passage was correct in the first printing of the Allen & Unwin second edition (1966) except for the repeated error 'Haarwell', and fully correct in the second printing (1967). Tolkien noted in one of his check copies, referring to the form 'Haarwell': 'So B(al[lantine]). Has 2nd [Allen & Unwin] ed. been taken from B(al)? But it does not include the B(al) error of keeping *the river* after *behind* nor B(al) *lastward* for *eastward*. If the error is independent it suggests the evil influence of *Harwell* (of same sense!).' In 1946 the Royal Air Force base at Harwell in Oxfordshire became the Atomic Energy Research Establishment.

In *The Return of the Shadow* Christopher Tolkien notes that here the first edition text seems to contradict Strider's earlier remark as published in 1954 (see note for p. 200): the Road runs along the river Loudwater 'for many leagues to the Ford', but when the travellers come down to the Road out of the Trollshaws it had turned away from the river. But this, Christopher thinks, 'is probably less a contradiction than a question of how closely "runs along the Loudwater" is interpreted'. One of the maps made by his father in aid of writing *The Lord of the Rings* shows the Road approaching the river, running alongside it for a stretch, and then bending somewhat away and "clinging to the feet of the hills" before returning to the Ford.

> The changed reading of the Second Edition [described in the present note] . . . – made so as not to alter the amount of text – makes the words 'narrow valley' refer to the Hoarwell, and there is no longer any statement at this point about the course of the Road in relation to the Loudwater. This was clearly another accommodation to the published map (and is not an entirely happy solution, as was also 'northward' to 'eastward'. [pp. 202–3]

208 (I: 220). Strider pointed out a stone in the grass. On it roughly cut and now much weathered could still be seen dwarf-runes and secret marks. – In *The Hobbit* the company took the pots of gold from the trolls' cave 'and buried them very secretly not far from the track . . . putting many spells over them, just in case they ever had a chance to come back and recover them' (Chapter 2). On their return journey Bilbo and Gandalf dug up the gold and shared it.

209 (I: 221): They were beginning

209 (I: 221). deep heather and bilberry brushwood – *Heather* is a native shrub, very common on moors and heathland in Britain, growing to about fifteen inches high, usually with purple or pinkish-purple flowers, but sometimes white.

Bilberry brushwood is a dwarf shrub also very common on moors and heathland, growing to a height of about twenty inches and producing small, edible, blue berries.

209 (I: 221): The light faded

209 (I: 221). its headstall flickered and flashed – As first published this passage read 'its bit and bridle flickered and flashed'. It was revised in the second edition (1965). In 1958 Rhona Beare wrote to Tolkien asking why Glorfindel's horse had a bridle and bit, when elsewhere in *The Lord of the Rings* Elves are said to ride without bit, bridle, and saddle. (In Book III, Chapter 2 Legolas says that he needs no saddle or rein; in Book III, Chapter 11 Gandalf describes riding without saddle or bridle as 'elf-fashion'.) Tolkien replied on 14 October 1958:

> I could, I suppose, answer: 'trick-cyclist can ride a bicycle with handle-bars!' But actually *bridle* was casually and carelessly used for what I suppose should have been called a *headstall* [the part of the halter or bridle that fits over the top of the horse's head]. Or rather, since *bit* was added . . . long ago ([Book I, Chapter 12] was written very early) I had not considered the natural ways of elves with animals. Glorfindel's horse would have an ornamental *headstall*, carrying a plume, and with the

> straps studded with jewels and small bells; but Glor[findel] would certainly not use a *bit.* I will change *bridle and bit* to *headstall.* [*Letters,* p. 279]

Tolkien removed the bit from Glorfindel's horse, and in this instance, the bridle. But later in the chapter Glorfindel says that he 'will shorten the stirrups up to the saddle-skirts' so that Frodo may ride; and while riding Frodo's hand is said to leave the bridle.

In a letter to *Amon Hen* 111 (August 1991, p. 17) Helen Armstrong writes:

> It's worth remembering that the Professor [Tolkien] wrote a lot straight out of his mind's eye, and only rationalised it later. Gut feeling should not be denied. Originally, Asfaloth appeared in a saddle and bridle. Someone pointed out that an elf-horse would not wear a bitted bridle, and the Professor changed it to 'headstall'. . . . He did not drop the harness altogether. Why not? I propose: 1) he liked the decorative effect of the flashing gems and bells, 2) his sense rebelled against a short-legged Frodo on a big horse in desperate flight without the help of a saddle (or: 'Glorfindel's wisdom warned him that a fugitive might need to ride his horse, and it would be easier for both if there was something to hang onto'), 3) Tolkien's encounters with cavalry people during the war taught him that a saddle creates a firm interface between horse and rider so that, under physical stress, they don't come apart so easily.

209 (I: 221–2): Strider sprang from hiding

209 (I: 222). ***Ai na vedui Dúnadan! Mae govannen!*** – Sindarin 'Hail at last, Dúnadan! Well met!' Glorfindel uses nearly the same greeting for Frodo, but in English (representing the Common Speech): 'Hail and well met at last'.

209 (I: 222): Soon Strider beckoned

209 (I: 222). This is Glorfindel, who dwells in the house of Elrond – Tolkien first gave the name *Glorfindel* to one of the Elf-lords of Gondolin in *The Fall of Gondolin*, written probably between the end of 1916 and the first half of 1917, the first written of the stories in *The Book of Lost Tales*, the earliest version of 'The Silmarillion'. The question of whether the Glorfindel of Rivendell in *The Lord of the Rings* was the same as the Elf of that name in *The Silmarillion* has been a subject of debate among readers; and Tolkien himself considered this question. In summer 1938, in a draft note for 'The Council of Elrond' (Book II, Chapter 2), an early signal of his thoughts, he had already written: 'Glorfindel tells of his ancestry in Gondolin' (*The Return of the Shadow*, p. 214). More than thirty years later, in late 1972–3, he produced two brief essays on the subject, published as *Glorfindel* in *The Peoples of Middle-earth.*

The name *Glorfindel*, he wrote,

> is in fact derived from the earliest work on the mythology: *The Fall of Gondolin*. . . . It was intended to mean 'Golden-tressed'. . . .
>
> Its use in *The Lord of the Rings* is one of the cases of somewhat random use of the names found in the older legends, now referred to as *The Silmarillion*, which escaped reconsideration in the final published form of *The Lord of the Rings*. [*The Peoples of Middle-earth*, p. 379]

He rejected the apparently simple solution that this was a mere duplication of names, that the two characters in question were different persons. 'This repetition of so striking a name, though possible, would not be credible. No other major character in the Elvish legends as reported in *The Silmarillion* and *The Lord of the Rings* has a name borne by another Elvish person of importance' (p. 380). Nor did he choose simply to alter the name *Glorfindel* in 'The Silmarillion', which was still unpublished. Instead, he decided that when Glorfindel of Gondolin was slain in combat with a Balrog in the First Age,

> his spirit would according to the laws established by the One be obliged at once to return to the land of the Valar. There he would go to Mandos and be judged, and would remain in the 'Halls of Waiting' until Manwë granted him release. Elves were destined to be 'immortal', that is not to die within the unknown limits decreed by the One, which at the most could be until the end of life on Earth as a habitable realm. Their death – by any injury to their bodies so severe that it could not be healed – and the disembodiment of their spirits was an 'unnatural' and grievous matter. It was therefore the duty of the Valar . . . to restore them to incarnate life, if they desired it. [*The Peoples of Middle-earth*, p. 380]

After minimizing Glorfindel's part in the revolt of the Noldor in returning to Middle-earth against the wishes of the Valar, and stressing the importance of his sacrifice on behalf of refugees from Gondolin (among whom was Eärendil), Tolkien continued:

> After his purging of any guilt that he had incurred in the rebellion, he was released from Mandos, and Manwë restored him. He then became again a living incarnate person, but was permitted to dwell in the Blessed Realm; for he had regained the primitive innocence and grace of the Eldar. For long years he remained in Valinor, in reunion with the Eldar who had not rebelled and in the companionship of the Maiar. To these he had now become almost an equal, for though he was an incarnate . . . his spiritual power had been greatly enhanced by his self-sacrifice. At some time . . . he became a follower, and a friend of Gandalf (Olórin). [*The Peoples of Middle-earth*, p. 381]

Tolkien concluded that Glorfindel must have returned to Middle-earth probably *c.* Second Age 1600, when the power of Sauron had become great, in response to 'urgent messages and prayers asking for help . . . received in Númenor and Valinor' (p. 382).

209–10 (I: 222): No. He had not when I departed

209–10 (I: 222). when I departed . . . nine days ago. . . . Elrond received news – In *Scheme* it is said that the news (presumably sent by Gildor on 25 September or soon after) reached Elrond on 8 October, and that Glorfindel set out from Rivendell on 9 October. It is now 18 October 1418.

210 (I: 222): It was my lot to take the Road

210 (I: 222). It was my lot to take the Road, and I came to the Bridge of Mitheithel . . . nigh on seven days ago. Three of the Servants of Sauron were on the Bridge, but they withdrew and I pursued them westward. I came also upon two others but they turned away southward. – *The Tale of Years* indicates that Glorfindel drove the Riders from the Bridge on 11 October, two days before Strider and the hobbits crossed it. It is said in Marquette MSS 4/2/36 (*The Hunt for the Ring*):

> Oct. 11: Glorfindel reaches Bridge of Mitheithel and there finds [three Riders, including Khamûl]. He drives them back well down the road, until they leave it and disperse. (Thus Aragorn and Frodo cross safely on Oct. 13). Glorfindel meets [the Witch-king and another Rider] coming east along road, but [the Witch-king] cannot challenge him (esp[ecially] by day) with so small help; he flees into the pathless lands.
>
> Oct. 14: [These five Riders] resassemble and start in pursuit again. [The Witch-king and Khamûl] perceive that Ring crossed Bridge but lose trail, and waste time hunting about.
>
> Oct. 19: They become aware of the Ring not far ahead.

211 (I: 223–4): To that Frodo had no answer

211 (I: 223). Not until the grey of dawn – It is 19 October.

212 (I: 224): They had rested rather less

212 (I: 224). In this way they covered almost twenty miles by nightfall – The company began the march when the sun had climbed far into the morning. Taking into account that it is now mid-October, they probably took about six hours, including the two brief halts, to cover nearly twenty miles.

212 (I: 224). the Road bent right and ran down towards the bottom of the valley, now making straight for the Bruinen. – As first published this passage read: 'the Road turned right and ran steeply down towards the bottom of the valley, making once more for the river'. It was revised in the second edition (1965).

212 (I: 224): The hobbits were still weary

212 (I: 224). early next morning – It is 20 October.

212 (I: 225): The white horse leaped forward

212 (I: 225). rear-guard – In military terms, troops detached to guard the rear of a larger body of soldiers. The hyphen is probably in error, previously overlooked; elsewhere in *The Lord of the Rings* the word is spelt *rearguard.*

213 (I: 225): 'Ride on! Ride on!'

213 (I: 225). ***noro lim, noro lim, Asfaloth!*** – According to Arden R. Smith, an unpublished text among Tolkien's private linguistic papers (Box-file Quenya B) explicitly states that Sindarin *noro lim* means 'run swift'.

213 (I: 226): Frodo looked back

213 (I: 226). He could see them clearly now – Gandalf explains in Book II, Chapter 1 that because of his wound Frodo was already on the threshold of becoming a wraith, and thus, even though he did not put on the Ring, he could see the Riders and they could see him.

214 (I: 226): But the pursuers were close behind

214 (I: 226). quailed – Withered, weakened due to fear.

214 (I: 226–7): 'By Elbereth and Lúthien the Fair'

214 (I: 226–7). 'By Elbereth and Lúthien the Fair,' said Frodo with a last effort, lifting up his sword – Despite his weakened state, Frodo resists to the last, showing strength of mind and character.

214 (I: 227): At that moment there came a roaring

214 (I: 227). Dimly Frodo saw the river below him rise, and down along its course there came a plumed cavalry of waves. White flames seemed to Frodo to flicker on their crests, and he half fancied that he saw amid the water white riders upon white horses with frothing manes. – When Frodo wakes in Rivendell at the beginning of the next book, Gandalf tells him that Elrond controls the river, and made it rise in anger in order to bar the Ford. The flood was released as soon as the Captain of the Ring-wraiths rode into the water. But Gandalf was responsible for the waves taking the form of white horses – a common (even clichéd) representation of waves in art.

215 (I: 227): The black horses were filled with madness

215 (I: 227). The black horses – Marquette MSS 4/2/36 (*The Hunt for the Ring*) gives the following account of the Black Riders at the Ford: on 20 October the four Riders who had pursued Gandalf return from the North, reaching the Fords of Bruinen, not long before Frodo comes there, pursued by the other five. After the Witch-king breaks Frodo's sword, he, Khamûl, and possibly some others dare to ford the water – 'for he is desperate, knows that the Ring is about to escape to Rivendell. But the water overwhelms him – and Aragorn and Glorfindel drive the others into River with fire'.

BOOK II

Chapter 1

MANY MEETINGS

For drafts and history of this chapter, see *The Return of the Shadow*, pp. 206–19, 362–8; *The Treason of Isengard*, pp. 68–70, 81–109.

219 (I: 231): Frodo woke and found himself lying in bed

219 (I: 231). Frodo woke – It is the morning of 24 October 1418.

219 (I: 231): 'In the house of Elrond

219 (I: 231). the house of Elrond – In editions prior to 2004 these words read 'the House of Elrond', with 'House' capitalized. It, and six similar phrases, were emended to 'house' in 2004, following Tolkien's lead in the second printing (1967) of the Allen & Unwin second edition, where he took care to distinguish *house* 'domicile' from *House* 'dynasty' (e.g. 'And here in the House of Elrond more shall be made clear to you' (1st edn., I: 259) > 'And here in the house of Elrond [= Rivendell] more shall be made clear to you') but overlooked a few instances.

In two cases in the 2004 edition, however, both in Appendix F, the existing reading was left unchanged: 'Noblest of all was the Lady Galadriel of the royal house of Finarfin' (p. 1128, III: 406) and 'They were tall, fair of skin and grey-eyed, though their locks were dark, save in the golden house of Finarfin' (p. 1137, III: 416). Each of these logically should have 'House' rather than 'house', but in correspondence with us on this point, Christopher Tolkien observed that to his '"inner ear" the capital letter imparts a slight additional emphasis and higher pitch, which reduces the significance of "royal"'. It may be that in these constructions 'house' becomes attached to the preceding adjective rather than to 'of Finarfin'.

220 (I: 232): 'I was delayed,' said Gandalf

220 (I: 232). 'I was delayed,' said Gandalf, 'and that nearly proved our ruin. And yet I am not sure: it may have been better so.' – Because Gandalf was delayed, the hobbits set out later than planned and were menaced by Black Riders. But because of this, Frodo has endured trials which help him to grow in character and ultimately to undertake his journey to Mount Doom, while Merry has obtained the knife from the barrow with which he will help to defeat the Witch-king. Todd Jensen explores this point in 'Frodo's Delay', *Beyond Bree*, May 1991; in response to which David Cremona comments that

> it is part of the *schema* of *The Lord of the Rings* that what seems to be setbacks, blunders and delays, turn out to have been useful shortcuts;

though I think Tolkien would have argued that, had they done otherwise, with a good intention, that too might have led to the quest's end, but by a different path. Ilúvatar, as ever, does not compel or predestine, but his plans are far-seeing and the roads to his ends, many. [letter to *Beyond Bree*, June 1991, p. 10]

220 (I: 232): 'Yes, I, Gandalf the Grey'

220 (I: 232). Morgul-lord – The chief of the Ringwraiths. In Third Age 2000 the Ringwraiths issued from Mordor and laid siege to Minas Ithil, the city built by Isildur on a western shoulder of the Mountains of Shadow, the eastern border of Mordor. The city fell to them in 2002 and became a place of fear, renamed Minas Morgul 'tower of black sorcery'.

220–1 (I: 232–3): 'I am glad,' said Frodo

221 (I: 233). Bree-landers – When preparing the edition of 2004 we compared the variants *Breeland/Bree-land* and *Breelanders/Bree-landers*, and found that Tolkien had a clear preference for the hyphened forms. Here 'Breelanders' was emended to 'Bree-landers'. In Book VI, Chapter 8, one instance of 'Breeland' was emended to 'Bree-land'.

221 (I: 233): 'You don't know much

221 (I: 233). The race of the Kings from over the Sea is nearly at an end. – Aragorn is the last descendant of Kings of Númenor; but this also means, perhaps, that there are few Men of Númenórean blood left in Middle-earth.

221 (I: 233): 'Only a Ranger!'

221 (I: 233). the last remnant in the North of the great people, the Men of the West – Tolkien wrote to Milton Waldman in ?late 1951: 'But in the north Arnor dwindles, is broken into petty kingdoms, and finally vanishes. The remnant of the Númenóreans becomes a hidden wandering Folk, and though their true line of Kings of Isildur's heirs never fails this is known only in the House of Elrond' (*Letters*, p. 157). See note for p. 5.

221 (I: 233–4): Well, four nights and three days

221 (I: 233). Elrond is a master of healing – Aragorn was able to ease Frodo's pain, and will achieve much more in the Houses of Healing after the Battle of the Pelennor Fields. But even there he will say: 'Would that Elrond were here, for he is the eldest of all our race, and has the greater power' (Book V, Chapter 8, p. 863, III: 139). See further, note for p. 871.

222 (I: 234): Frodo shuddered

222 (I: 234). which you bore for seventeen days – From the evening of 6 October to the evening of 23 October 1418.

222 (I: 234): 'Because these horses are born

222 (I: 234). chattels – Moveable possessions; in this sense, slaves.

222 (I: 234). wargs – *Wargs* first appeared in Tolkien's writings in Chapter 6 of *The Hobbit.* Gandalf, Bilbo, and the dwarves, having escaped from goblins, are attacked at night by wolves, but temporarily escape by climbing into trees: for 'even the wild Wargs (for so the evil wolves over the Edge of the Wild were named) cannot climb trees'. On 7 November 1966 Tolkien wrote to Gene Wolfe that *warg* 'is an old word for wolf, which also had the sense of an outlaw or hunted criminal. This is its usual sense in surviving texts. I adopted the word, which had a good sound for the meaning, as a name for this particular brand of demonic wolf in the story' ('The Tolkien Toll-free Fifties Freeway to Mordor & Points beyond Hurray!' *Vector*, 67/68 (Spring 1974), p. 9). In his draft letter to 'Mr Rang', August 1967, he said that 'the word *Warg* . . . is not supposed to be A-S [Anglo-Saxon] specifically, and is given prim[itive] Germanic form as representing the noun common to the Northmen of these creatures' (*Letters*, p. 381). Old Norse *vargr* means both 'wolf and outlaw'; the Old English noun *wearg(-h)* used of human beings means 'a criminal, an outcast', but of other creatures 'a monster, malignant being, evil spirit'; whence *wearg* as an adjective: 'evil, vile, malignant, accursed'. Jacob Grimm in *Teutonic Mythology* cites the Slavic name for the Devil, variations of *vrag*, also meaning 'malefactor', and comments that it 'is the same as Old High German *warg* (lupus). . . . The Devil has monstrous jaws and throat in common with the wolf and hell' (translated by James Steven Stallybrass, 1883 (2004), vol. 3, p. 998).

222 (I: 234). werewolves – A *werewolf* is a person who is transformed or is capable of transforming himself at times into a wolf.

222–3 (I: 234–5): Yes, at present, until all else is conquered

222 (I: 234–5). The Elves may fear the Dark Lord, and they may fly before him, but never again will they listen to him or serve him. – That is, they may flee Sauron by leaving Middle-earth and sailing to Valinor. *Never again will they listen to him* is probably a reference to the Elven-smiths of Eregion, who were ensnared by the knowledge that Sauron offered them; see note for p. 242. Tolkien does not tell of any instances of elves serving Sauron, or Morgoth, at least not by choice; in 'The Silmarillion' some elves are enslaved by Morgoth. But unexplained references like this in *The Lord of the Rings* suggest that the story rests upon a vast foundation of history.

222–3 (I: 235). the Elven-wise, lords of the Eldar from beyond the furthest seas – The *Elven-wise* are the Noldor who returned to Middle-earth from Aman in the West at the beginning of the First Age. The name *Noldor* 'meant "the Wise" (but wise in the sense of possessing knowledge, not in the sense of possessing sagacity, sound judgement)' (*The Silmarillion*, p. 344).

'According to Elvish legend the name *Eldar* "People of the Stars" was given to all Elves by the Vala Oromë' when he found them after they first awoke. 'It came, however, to be used to refer only to the Elves of the Three Kindreds (Vanyar, Noldor, and Teleri) who set out on the great westward march . . . (whether or not they remained in Middle-earth)' (*The Silmarillion*, p. 326). See also note for p. 79.

222–3 (I: 235). those who have dwelt in the Blessed Realm live at once in both worlds, and against both the Seen and the Unseen they have great power – In *Nomenclature* Tolkien defines *Blessed Realm* as the 'Common Speech name for the Far Western Land in which the Valar (guardian powers) and the High Elves dwelt, called in Quenya *Aman* ["blessed, free from evil"], the region where the Valar dwelt being *Valimar, Valinor*; that of the Elves *Eldamar*. The Blessed Realm was at this time no longer part of the physical world, and could not except in rare cases, be reached by mortals.'

223 (I: 235): Yes, you saw him for a moment

223 (I: 235). Firstborn – In *Nomenclature* Tolkien writes that the Elves are called the *Firstborn* because they 'appeared in the world before all other "speaking peoples", not only Men, but also Dwarves, of independent origin'.

225 (I: 237): Frodo was now safe

225 (I: 237). the Last Homely House east of the Sea. That house was, as Bilbo had long ago reported, 'a perfect house, whether you like food or sleep or story-telling or singing, or just sitting and thinking best, or a pleasant mixture of them all'. – The reference is to *The Hobbit*, Chapter 3: 'His [Elrond's] house was perfect whether you liked food, or sleep, or work, or story-telling, or singing, or just sitting and thinking best, or a pleasant mixture of them all. Evil things did not come into that valley.' There the house is called 'the Last Homely House west of the Mountains'.

225 (I: 237–8): 'I can take you to them

225 (I: 237–8). It's a big house, this, and very peculiar, always a bit more to discover, and no knowing what you may find round a corner. – In Tolkien's illustration *Rivendell* published in *The Hobbit* (*Artist and Illustrator*, fig. 108, and in other depictions, figs. 104–7) Elrond's house seems very small compared to its description in *The Lord of the Rings*. Sam's remark recalls the Cottage of Lost Play in *The Book of Lost Tales*, which looks small from the outside but is spacious inside.

226 (I: 238): Sam led him along

226 (I: 238). a high garden above the steep bank of the river. He found his friends sitting in a porch on the side of the house looking east. Shadows had fallen in the valley below, but there was still light on the face of the mountains far above. . . . The sound of running and falling water was loud – In the painting of Rivendell for *The Hobbit* Elrond's house is shown in a deep valley, built on a high bank above a river with a waterfall, with mountains in the background. Four of the extant drawings of the house include a portico or colonnade.

Marie Barnfield argues convincingly in 'The Roots of Rivendell', *Þe Lyfe ant þe Auncestrye* 3 (Spring 1996), that Tolkien's conception of the valley of Rivendell as depicted in his painting was inspired by his visit to Lauterbrunnen in Switzerland during a walking tour in 1911. Tolkien wrote to his son Michael in 1967/8 that he and his companions on the tour 'went on foot . . . practically all the way from Interlaken, mainly by mountain paths, to Lauterbrunnen and so to Mürren and eventually to the head of the Lauterbrunnenthal in a wilderness of morains' (*Letters*, pp. 391–2). Barnfield notes that the Lauterbrunnen Valley is set, like Rivendell, in a deep ravine. She compares Tolkien's painting with a photograph of Lauterbrunnen taken by her husband in 1990:

> the structure of the cliffs forming the valley walls is identical. . . . The course of the river is the same in each; the bridge in each picture is similarly placed. . . . The two valleys have the self-same area of vegetation, and both are backed by a range of snow-capped mountains. . . . Almost more importantly, the site of Elrond's house is occupied . . . by a collection of buildings of which one, with a roof similar to that of the tower of Elrond's house, rises, turret-style behind the rest. [p. 9]

226 (I: 238). as if summer still lingered in Elrond's gardens – It is 24 October, well into autumn, but as we learn near the end of the book, Elrond wears one of the Elven-rings, and seems to be able to control the extremes of climate. In Lothlórien, where Galadriel also wears a Ring, in winter 'no heart could mourn for summer or for spring' (Book II, Chapter 6, p. 350, I: 365).

226 (I: 238): The hall of Elrond's house

226 (I: 238). Elrond . . . sat in a great chair at the end of the long table upon the dais – The arrangement of a table raised on a dais for those of higher rank goes back to medieval times, but survives in college halls in Oxford. A photograph of the Hall in Exeter College, Oxford, where Tolkien took meals while an undergraduate, is reproduced in *The Tolkien Family Album* by John and Priscilla Tolkien (1992), p. 35. Later, as a Fellow of Pembroke and then of Merton, Tolkien would have sat at the table on the dais when he dined in college.

226 (I: 238–9): Frodo looked at them

226 (I: 239). Elrond, of whom so many tales spoke – Elrond entered Tolkien's mythology in 1926, in the *Sketch of the Mythology*: there his father was Eärendel, the son of a Man, Tuor, and an Elven princess, Idril, and his mother was Elwing, descendant of Beren and Lúthien. He is described as 'part mortal and part elfin and part of the race of Valar', and 'when later the Elves return to the West, bound by his mortal half he elects to stay on earth' (*The Shaping of Middle-earth*, p. 38, emendation p. 39). In subsequent 'Silmarillion' texts Elrond's parentage remained unchanged, but it was some time before his own history reached its final form in which, the younger son of Eärendil and Elwing, he chose to be numbered among the Elves and stayed in Middle-earth, while his elder brother, Elros, chose to be of Mankind and became the first King of Númenor.

Later Tolkien introduced Elrond into *The Hobbit*, or rather he introduced a character with that name. In his letter to Christopher Bretherton, 16 July 1964, he wrote concerning Elrond:

> The passage in Ch. iii relating him to the Half-elven of the mythology was a fortunate accident, due to the difficulty of constantly inventing good names for new characters. I gave him the name Elrond casually, but as this came from my mythology . . . I made him half-elven. Only in *The Lord* was he identified with the son of Eärendel, and so the great-grandson of Lúthien and Beren, a great power and a Ringholder. [*Letters*, pp. 346–7]

In Chapter 3 of *The Hobbit* Tolkien wrote:

> The master of the house was an elf-friend – one of those people whose fathers came into the strange stories before the beginning of History, the wars of the evil goblins and the elves and the first men in the North. In those days of our tale there were still some people who had both elves and heroes of the North for ancestors, and Elrond the master of the house was their chief.
>
> He was as noble and as fair in face as an elf-lord, as strong as a warrior, as wise as a wizard, as venerable as a king of dwarves, and as kind as summer. He comes into many tales.

In fact, when Tolkien wrote *The Hobbit* Elrond played only a minor role in 'The Silmarillion', and there were no particular tales of his exploits. It was only at about the time that *The Hobbit* was accepted for publication that Tolkien began to write about the Second Age, in which Elrond played an important part in the resistance to Sauron; but most of the mentions of him in 'The Silmarillion' are embedded in general histories. By the Third Age, as Tolkien wrote to Milton Waldman in ?late 1951, Elrond had come to symbolize

> the ancient wisdom, and his House [i.e. Rivendell] represents Lore – the preservation in reverent memory of all tradition concerning the

good, wise, and beautiful. It is not a scene of *action* but of *reflection*. Thus it is a place visited on the way to all deeds, or 'adventures'. It may prove to be on the direct road (as in *The Hobbit*); but it may be necessary to go from there in a totally unexpected course. So necessarily in *The Lord of the Rings*, having escaped to Elrond from the imminent pursuit of present evil, the hero departs in a wholly new direction: to go and face it at its source. [*Letters*, p. 153]

227 (I: 239): In the middle of the table

227 (I: 239). Young she was and yet not so. The braids of her dark hair were touched by no frost; her white arms and clear face were flawless and smooth, and the light of stars was in her bright eyes, grey as a cloudless night; yet queenly she looked – As first published this passage read: 'Young she was, and yet not so; for though the braids of her dark hair were touched by no frost and her white arms and clear face were hale and smooth, and the light of stars was in her bright eyes, grey as a cloudless night, yet queenly she looked'. It was revised in the second edition (1965).

Arwen was born in Third Age 241; at this point in the story she is 2,777 years old, though that is young for one of Elven blood. Her father, Elrond, is over 6,500 years old, and Glorfindel is far older.

227 (I: 239). a cap of silver lace netted with small gems, glittering white – In *The Rivers and Beacon-hills of Gondor* Tolkien calls this cap a *tressure* and says that the women of the Eldar were accustomed to wear them. Christopher Tolkien comments that '*tressure*, a net for confining the hair, is a word of medieval English which my father had used in his translation of *Sir Gawain and the Green Knight* (stanza 69): "the clear jewels / that were twined in her tressure by twenties in clusters", where the original has the form *tressour*' (*Vinyar Tengwar* 42 (July 2001), pp. 11–12).

227 (I: 239): So it was that Frodo saw her

227 (I: 239). whom few mortals had yet seen – This seems to be an 'editorial' comment by someone looking back from the time when Arwen lived among mortals as Queen of Gondor and wife of the King Elessar (Aragorn).

227 (I: 239). likeness of Lúthien – Arwen is Lúthien's great-great-granddaughter.

227 (I: 239). Arwen . . . Undómiel, for she was the Evenstar of her people – In a letter to a Mr Joukes on 28 August 1967 Tolkien wrote that *Arwen* 'means in Elvish "noble maiden", but . . . it is also a word in Welsh meaning "greatly blessed"' (reproduced in René van Rossenberg, *Hobbits in Holland: Leven en Werk van J.R.R. Tolkien* (1992), p. 68). *Arwen* is Sindarin, but *Undómiel* 'evening star' is Quẹnya. 'Evenstar of her people' means, perhaps, that Arwen was the last Elf of high rank born in Middle-earth, where the time of the Elves is now coming to its end.

227 (I: 239). the land of her mother's kin – Arwen's mother was Celebrían, daughter of Celeborn and Galadriel, rulers of Lothlórien on the eastern side of the Misty Mountains. According to *The Tale of Years*, Arwen returned from Lothlórien to Rivendell in Third Age 3009.

227 (I: 239). her brothers, Elladan and Elrohir, were out upon errantry – Elladan and Elrohir were twins born in Third Age 130. Tolkien wrote in a letter to Rhona Beare on 14 October 1958 that

> these names, given to his sons by Elrond, refer to the fact that they were 'half-elven'. . . . Both signify *elf* + *man*. *Elrohir* might be translated 'Elf-knight'; *rohir* being a later form . . . of *rochir* 'horse-lord' from *roch* 'horse' + *hir* 'master'. . . . *Elladan* might be translated 'Elf-Númenórean'. *Adan* (pl[ural] *Edain*) was the Sindarin form of the name given to the 'fathers of men', the members of the Three Houses of Elf-friends, whose survivors afterwards became the Númenóreans, or *Dún-edain*. [*Letters*, p. 282]

227 (I: 239). their mother's torment in the dens of the orcs – In Appendix A it is said that

> in [Third Age] 2509 Celebrían . . . was journeying to Lórien when she was waylaid in the Redhorn Pass, and her escort being scattered by the sudden assault of the Orcs, she was seized and carried off. She was pursued and rescued by Elladan and Elrohir, but not before she had suffered torment and had received a poisoned wound. She was brought back to Imladris [Rivendell], and though healed in body by Elrond, lost all delight in Middle-earth, and the next year went to the Havens and passed over Sea. [p. 1043, III: 323]

228 (I: 240): Next to Frodo on his right

228 (I: 240). a dwarf . . . richly dressed. His beard, very long and forked, was white, nearly as white as the snow-white cloth of his garments. He wore a silver belt, and round his neck hung a chain of silver and diamonds. – In *The Hobbit* Glóin wore a white hood. Beards are a sign of importance among Dwarves, and Glóin belongs to the descendants of Durin, the Longbeards (see note for p. 1071). The Dwarves' love of (even lust for) precious metals and stones was well established in *The Hobbit* (compare Balin in Chapter 19: 'his jewelled belt was of great magnificence'), as already in myth and folklore.

228 (I: 240): 'Welcome and well met!'

228 (I: 240). Glóin at your service – The name *Glóin*, like *Gandalf*, is from the *Dvergatal*; see note for p. 11. In *The Hobbit* his name is spelt without an accent.

'At your service' was established as a form of greeting in *The Hobbit*, Chapter 1.

In a letter to Naomi Mitchison on 8 December 1955 Tolkien commented on the recent BBC radio adaptation of *The Fellowship of the Ring*: 'I thought that [Glóin in the broadcast] was not too bad, if a bit exaggerated. I do think of the "Dwarves" like Jews: at once native and alien in their habitations, speaking the languages of the country, but with an accent due to their own private tongue' (*Letters*, p. 229).

228 (I: 240): 'Frodo Baggins at your service

228 (I: 240). 'Frodo Baggins at your service and your family's,' said Frodo correctly – This is the correct response, established in the first chapter of *The Hobbit*.

228 (I: 241): Throughout the rest of the meal

228 (I: 241). Grimbeorn the Old, son of Beorn – In *The Hobbit* Beorn is a 'skin-changer' who assists Gandalf, Bilbo, and the dwarves, and helps to win the Battle of Five Armies in the shape of a great bear. *Beorn* is an Old English word meaning 'prince, nobleman, warrior' or poetic 'man'.

228–9 (I: 241): 'Indeed,' said Glóin

228 (I: 241). Beornings – Men of the upper Vales of Anduin, the people of Beorn.

228 (I: 241). the High Pass and the Ford of Carrock – In his unfinished index Tolkien describes the *High Pass* as 'a pass over the Misty Mts. immediately east of Rivendell'. In *The Disaster of the Gladden Fields* the Elvish name of the pass is given as *Cirith Forn en Andrath*, 'the high-climbing pass of the North' (*Unfinished Tales*, p. 271; Sindarin *cirith* 'cleft, pass', *forn* 'north', *andrath* 'long climb'), and elsewhere in that work it is called the *Pass of Imladris*.

In Chapter 7 of *The Hobbit* as Bilbo and the dwarves are being carried by eagles they see 'cropping out of the ground, right in the path of the stream which looped itself about it . . . a great rock, almost a hill of stone', called by Beorn the *Carrock* (compare Old English *carr*, Welsh *carreg* 'rock, stone'). When they land they find 'a flat space on the top of the hill of stone and a well-worn path with many steps leading down to the river, across which a ford of huge flat stones led to the grassland beyond the stream'. The 'river' is actually the northern part of the Anduin.

229 (I: 241). the Bardings. The grandson of Bard the Bowman rules them – The Men of Dale, people of Bard the Bowman who, as told in *The Hobbit*, killed the dragon Smaug.

229 (I: 241): And with that Glóin embarked

229 (I: 241). Dáin was still King under the Mountain – Dáin II was a second cousin of Thorin Oakenshield. He succeeded as ruler of the restored Dwarf-kingdom at Erebor after Thorin's death in the Battle of Five Armies.

229 (I: 241). Of the ten companions who had survived the Battle of Five Armies seven were still with him: Dwalin, Glóin, Dori, Nori, Bifur, Bofur, and Bombur. Bombur was now so fat – Two of Thorin's companions were also killed in the Battle, Fíli and Kíli, the sons of his sister, who had fallen defending him. All but two of the dwarf-names mentioned in this and the following paragraph come from the *Dvergatal* (see note for p. 11); but *Óin* is included by Snorri Sturluson in the dwarf list in his *Prose Edda*. *Balin* is the odd dwarf out; possibly his name was chosen simply to rhyme with *Dwalin*.

In *The Hobbit* the dwarf *Bombur* (cf. Old Norse *bumba* 'drum') was already 'immensely fat and heavy' (Chapter 1).

229 (I: 241–2): Glóin began then to talk of the works

229 (I: 242). the fountains, and the pools! – This was the reading in the first printing of the first edition (1954). In the unauthorized resetting of *The Fellowship of the Ring* for its second printing (1954) 'fountains' was mistakenly altered to 'mountains'. The error was corrected in the edition of 2004.

229 (I: 242): 'I will come and see them

229 (I: 242). the Desolation of Smaug – In his unfinished index Tolkien defines this as the 'desert about Mt. Erebor in the days of the dragon, Smaug'.

For *Smaug*, see note for p. 11. On 20 February 1938 a letter by Tolkien was published in the newspaper *The Observer*, in reply to queries about *The Hobbit*. In this he noted that 'the dragon bears as name – a pseudonym – the past tense of the primitive Germanic verb *Smugan*, to squeeze through a hole: a low philological jest' (*Letters*, p. 31).

230 (I: 242): Frodo found himself walking with Gandalf

230 (I: 242). the Hall of Fire – This recalls, in function and in having a fire always burning, the Room of Logs with the Tale-fire in the Cottage of Lost Play, in *The Book of Lost Tales*.

231 (I: 243–4): 'I got here without much adventure

231 (I: 243). Time doesn't seem to pass here: it just is – Compare the similar experience by the Company of the Ring in Lothlórien. Elrond at Rivendell and Galadriel in Lothlórien wear two of the Three Rings, made to retard change and thus, apparently, time. See further, note for p. 370.

231 (I: 244): 'I hear all kinds of news

231 (I: 244). I have thought several times of going back to Hobbiton for it; but I am getting old, and they would not let me: Gandalf and Elrond, I mean. They seemed to think that the Enemy was looking high and low for me, and would make mincemeat of me, if he caught me tottering

about in the Wild. – Bilbo's statements raise unanswerable questions. When did Gandalf tell him about the Ring? Gandalf was not sure himself until he made the final test in Bag End in April. Did he confide his worries to Bilbo before he was certain that it was the Ring? Or did he tell him when passing through Rivendell on his way to Bag End the previous spring, after questioning Gollum?

To make mincemeat is 'to cut into very small pieces, destroy, annihilate'.

233 (I: 245): '*The* Dúnadan,' said Bilbo

233 (I: 245). Númenórean – In editions prior to 2004 this, and the great majority of some fifty-four other instances of the word (especially in the Appendices), read 'Númenorean', with one rather than two acute accents. But in his father's posthumously published writings, such as *The Silmarillion* and *Unfinished Tales*, editor Christopher Tolkien has preferred 'Númenórean', 'as my father often so wrote it in manuscript, though by no means always' (comment on an unpublished list of textual questions in *The Lord of the Rings*, 1975). At Marquette University we searched the manuscripts and typescripts of *The Lord of the Rings* and confirmed that Tolkien's practice varied, not unusually when writing at speed, or when making a typescript in which accents were inserted in pen (if not overlooked): sometimes one accent, sometimes two, sometimes none at all. The typesetters then had to make sense of this variation, if possible, and (perhaps with an eye to economy) a technical decision seems to have been made whereby 'Númenorean' was regularized with a single accent – though not in every instance. Tolkien, meanwhile, in writings after *The Lord of the Rings*, seems to have had a preference for 'Númenórean', which we chose to follow in preparing the 2004 edition. At the least, this form imposes on the reader the correct pronunciation, with stress on the first and third syllables of the word.

233 (I: 245). the Lady Arwen was there – This is the first clear indication that Arwen is of importance to Aragorn. She was added late to the story, but this did not involve much additional text or rewriting, since the tale is told mainly from the viewpoint of Frodo and the other hobbits, and we learn no more about the relationship than they do. They and we (on a first reading) are equally surprised when Arwen arrives at Minas Tirith to marry Aragorn.

233 (I: 245–6): At first the beauty of the melodies

233 (I: 245). Almost it seemed that the words took shape, and visions of far lands and bright things that he had never yet imagined opened out before him; and the firelit hall became like a golden mist of foam that sighed upon the margins of the world. – Elvish song has an effect on Frodo similar to that of 'Faërian Drama' described by Tolkien in *On Fairy-Stories*:

> 'Faërian Drama' – those plays which according to abundant records elves have often presented to men – can produce Fantasy with a realism and immediacy beyond the compass of any human mechanism. As a result their usual effect (upon a man) is to go beyond Secondary Belief. If you are present at a Faërian drama you yourself are, or think you are, bodily inside its Secondary World. The experience may be very similar to Dreaming. [*Tree and Leaf*, pp. 48–9]

233–6 (I: 246–9): *Eärendil was a mariner*

233 (I: 246). *Eärendil was a mariner . . .* – The long and complex history of this poem is discussed at length by Christopher Tolkien in *The Treason of Isengard*, Chapter 5. Here it will suffice to say that probably in the early 1930s Tolkien wrote a set of verses called *Errantry*. The earliest extant version begins: 'There was a merry passenger, / a messenger, an errander'. This developed through five further texts until the work was published in the *Oxford Magazine* for 9 November 1933 (reprinted in *The Treason of Isengard*). When, years later, Tolkien wanted a poem for Bilbo to recite at Rivendell in *The Lord of the Rings*, he developed *Errantry* further through fifteen more texts, until it was concerned with Eärendil, a pivotal figure in his mythology. The earlier of these versions begin 'There was a merry messenger' (or a variant); the six later texts, probably after a long interval of time, begin 'Eärendel [*or* Eärendil] was a mariner'. The third version in this second category was published in *The Lord of the Rings* in 1954; but three more, further revised versions followed. Christopher Tolkien believes that these final texts were mislaid by his father, and not to be found when the typescript of *The Lord of the Rings* had to be sent to the publisher, so that a less developed version came into print, 'as it should not have done. It looks also as if these lost texts did not turn up again until many years had passed, by which time my father no longer remembered the history' (*The Treason of Isengard*, p. 103). Following is the ultimate form of the poem, the *Eärendillinwë*:

> *Eärendil was a mariner*
> *that tarried in Arvernien:*
> *he built a boat of timber felled*
> *in Nimbrethil to journey in.*
> *Her sails he wove of silver fair,*
> *with silver were her banners sewn;*
> *her prow he fashioned like the swans*
> *that white upon the Falas roam.*
>
> *His coat that came from ancient kings*
> *of chainéd rings was forged of old;*
> *his shining shield all wounds defied,*
> *with runes entwined of dwarven gold.*

His bow was made of dragon-horn,
his arrows shorn of ebony,
of triple steel his habergeon,
his scabbard of chalcedony;
his sword was like a flame in sheath,
with gems was wreathed his helmet tall,
an eagle-plume upon his crest,
upon his breast an emerald.

Beneath the Moon and under star
he wandered far from northern strands,
bewildered on enchanted ways
beyond the days of mortal lands.
From gnashing of the Narrow Ice
where shadow lies on frozen hills,
from nether heats and burning waste
he turned in haste, and roving still
on starless waters far astray
at last he came to Night of Naught,
and passed, and never sight he saw
of shining shore nor light he sought.
The winds of fear came driving him,
and blindly in the foam he fled
from west to east, and errandless,
unheralded he homeward sped.

In might the Fëanorians
that swore the unforgotten oath
brought war into Arvernien
with burning and with broken troth;
and Elwing from her fastness dim
then cast her in the waters wide,
but like a mew was swiftly borne,
uplifted o'er the roaring tide.
Through hopeless night she came to him,
and flame was in the darkness lit,
more bright than light of diamond
the fire upon her carcanet.
The Silmaril she bound on him,
and crowned him with the living light,
and dauntless then with burning brow
he turned his prow at middle-night.
Beyond the world, beyond the Sea,
then strong and free a storm arose,
a wind of power in Tarmenel;

by paths that seldom mortal goes
from Middle-earth on mighty breath
as flying wraith across the grey
and long-forsaken seas distressed
from East to West he passed away.

Through Evernight he back was borne
on black and roaring waves that ran
o'er leagues unlit and foundered shores
that drowned before the Days began,
until he heard on strands of pearl
where ends the world the music long,
where ever-foaming billows roll
the yellow gold and jewels wan.
He saw the Mountain silent rise
where twilight lies upon the knees
of Valinor, and Eldamar
beheld afar beyond the seas.
A wanderer escaped from night
to haven white he came at last,
to Elvenhome the green and fair
where keen the air, where pale as glass
beneath the Hill of Ilmarin
a-glimmer in a valley sheer
the lamplit towers of Tirion
are mirrored on the Shadowmere.

He tarried there from errantry,
and melodies they taught to him,
and sages old him marvels told,
and harps of gold they brought to him.
They clothed him then in elven-white,
and seven lights before him sent,
as through the Calacirian
to hidden land forlorn he went.
He came unto the timeless halls
where shining fall the countless years,
and endless reigns the Elder King
for ever king on mountain sheer;
and words unheard were spoken then
of folk of Men and Elven-kin,
beyond the world were visions showed
forbid to those that dwell therein.

A ship then new they built for him
of mithril and of elvenglass
with crystal keel; no shaven oar
nor sail she bore, on silver mast
the Silmaril as lantern light
and banner bright with living flame
of fire unstained by Elbereth
herself was set, who thither came
and wings immortal made for him,
and laid on him undying doom,
to sail the shoreless skies and come
behind the Sun and light of Moon.

From Evereven's lofty hills
where softly silver fountains fall
his wings him bore, a wandering light,
beyond the mighty Mountain Wall.
From World's End then he turned away,
and yearned again to find afar
his home through shadows journeying,
and burning as an island star
on high above the mists he came,
a distant flame before the Sun,
a wonder ere the waking dawn
where grey the Norland waters run.

And over Middle-earth he passed
and heard at last the weeping sore
of women and of elven-maids
in Elder Days, in years of yore.
But on him mighty doom was laid,
till Moon should fade, an orbéd star
to pass, and tarry never more
on Hither Shores where mortals are;
till end of Days on errand high,
a herald bright that never rests,
to bear his burning lamp afar,
the Flammifer of Westernesse.

This, says Christopher Tolkien, is the form 'in which [the poem] should have been published' (*The Treason of Isengard*, p. 103). But when we came to consider the text of *The Lord of the Rings* for the edition of 2004, we hesitated to replace large portions of the established version of *Eärendil was a mariner*, even with lines very likely to have been preferred by its author. Our policy was to approach all emendations conservatively, and this seemed too great a change to contemplate, let alone to suggest, on a much different scale than the correction of clear errors or the alteration of small details for the sake of accuracy or consistency. Also, we felt that we should not ignore the fact that (even granting Christopher Tolkien's argument that his father had come to forget its textual history) Tolkien had not taken the opportunity to alter Bilbo's song at Rivendell for the second edition in 1965. It is a difficult issue, in which one could argue cogently either way, for replacement or for letting the 1954 text stand (though with minor typographical corrections). In the event it seemed prudent to do the latter, but to discuss the matter here and to include the final version in its entirety.

A revision of *Errantry* was published in 1962 in *The Adventures of Tom Bombadil and Other Verses from the Red Book*. In his Preface to that book Tolkien, again in his guise as 'editor' of a Hobbit manuscript, says that *Errantry*

> was evidently made by Bilbo. This is indicated by its obvious relationship to the long poem recited by Bilbo, as his own composition, in the house of Elrond. In origin a 'nonsense rhyme', it is in the Rivendell version found transformed and applied, somewhat incongruously, to the High-elvish and Númenórean legends of Eärendil. Probably because Bilbo invented its metrical devices and was proud of them. They do not appear in other pieces in the Red Book. The older form, here given, must belong to the early days after Bilbo's return from his journey [in *The Hobbit*]. Though the influence of Elvish traditions is seen, they are not seriously treated, and the names used (*Derrilyn, Thellamie, Belmarie, Aerie*) are mere inventions in the Elvish style, and are not in fact Elvish at all. [p. 8]

233 (I: 246). *Arvernien* – 'A southern region of the lost land of Beleriand' (*Index*). It appears on the *Map of Beleriand* in *The Silmarillion* to the west of the mouths of the river Sirion.

233 (I: 246). *Nimbrethil* – 'White-birches' (*Index*), a wooded region in Arvernien. In *The Silmarillion* it is said that 'with the aid of Círdan, Eärendil built Vingilot, the Foam-flower, fairest of the ships of song; golden were its oars and white its timbers, hewn in the birchwoods of Nimbrethil, and its sails were as the argent moon' (p. 246). (On Sindarin *brethil* 'birch', see note for p. 475.)

234 (I: 246). *her prow he fashioned like a swan* – This was the reading in the first printing of the first edition (1954). In the unauthorized resetting of *The Fellowship of the Ring* for its second printing (1954) 'he' was mistakenly altered to 'was'. The error was corrected in the edition of 2004.

The ships of the Teleri in Aman were 'made in the likeness of swans, with beaks of gold and eyes of gold and jet' (*The Silmarillion*, p. 61). In Book II, Chapter 8 of *The Lord of the Rings* Celeborn and Galadriel arrive in a ship wrought in the likeness of a swan.

234 (I: 246). ***panoply*** – A complete suit of armour. The *Oxford English Dictionary* notes that in medieval times 'its brightness and splendour are chiefly connoted'.

234 (I: 246). ***chainéd rings*** – Chain- or ring-mail; see note for p. 13.

234 (I: 246). ***his shining shield was scored with runes / to ward all wounds and harm from him*** – The magical power of runic inscriptions, on weapons, amulets, etc., is well established in Northern literature and tradition. Compare 'runes of power upon the door' in Gimli's poem of Durin, Book II, Chapter 4.

234 (I: 246). ***dragon-horn*** – The hard bony outgrowth of a dragon.

234 (I: 246). ***shorn of ebony*** – That is, cut from *ebony*, a hard black wood.

234 (I: 246). ***habergeon*** – 'A sleeveless coat or jacket of mail (or scale) armour' (*OED*).

234 (I: 246). ***his scabbard of chalcedony*** – *Chalcedony* is a precious or semi-precious stone such as onyx or agate.

This is the only line to survive intact from the original version of the poem: see last note for p. 236.

234 (I: 246). ***his sword of steel was valiant*** – For *valiant* in this context the *Oxford English Dictionary* gives two possible definitions, both obsolete: 'Of things: strong, firm' or 'Of material things: fine, splendid'.

234 (I: 246). ***adamant*** – A rock or mineral of legend or folklore, variously described, like the diamond or other hard gems, or like the magnetic lodestone. 'In modern use it is only a poetical or rhetorical name for the embodiment of surpassing hardness; that which is impregnable to any application of force' (*OED*).

234 (I: 246). ***plume upon his crest*** – In this sense, an ornament of feathers at the top of a helmet.

234 (I: 246). ***upon his breast an emerald*** – This must be the 'green stone' which, as Bilbo tells Frodo after the song is over, was Aragorn's only contribution. It presumably refers to the Elessar: see further, note for p. 375.

234 (I: 246). ***northern strands*** – The western shores (poetic *strands*) of the North of Middle-earth.

234 (I: 246). ***bewildered on enchanted ways*** – This is probably a reference to the Enchanted Isles which prevented mariners from reaching Valinor:

> And in that time also, which songs call . . . the Hiding of Valinor, the Enchanted Isles were set, and all the seas about them were filled with shadows and bewilderment. And these isles were strung in a net in the Shadowy Seas from the north to the south. . . . Hardly might any vessel

> pass between them, for in the dangerous sounds the waves sighed for ever upon dark rocks shrouded in mist. And in the twilight a great weariness came upon mariners and a loathing of the sea; but all that ever set foot upon the islands were there entrapped and slept until the Change of the World. Thus . . . of the many messengers that in after days sailed into the West none came ever to Valinor – save one only: the mightiest mariner of song [Eärendil]. [*The Silmarillion*, p. 102]

234 (I: 246). *from gnashing of the Narrow Ice* – In his unfinished index Tolkien describes the *Narrow Ice* as 'an ice-bound strait in the remote North between Middle-earth and the "Uttermost West" (Helcaraxë)'. In *The Silmarillion* it is said that in the extreme North 'only a narrow sea divided Aman upon which Valinor was built, from the Hither Lands [Middle-earth]; but this narrow sea was filled with grinding ice, because of the violence of the frosts of Melkor' (p. 57).

234 (I: 246). *Night of Naught* – In his unfinished index Tolkien writes that *Night of Naught* is the same as *Evernight* 'a dark region south of *Valinor*'.

234 (I: 247). *flying Elwing* – Eärendil's wife, Elwing, remained in Middle-earth, in havens near the mouths of Sirion, while her husband sailed into the West. The sons of Fëanor attacked the Havens in an attempt to seize the Silmaril recovered by Elwing's grandparents (see notes for pp. 193–4); but Elwing with the Silmaril on her breast cast herself into the sea. Then the Vala Ulmo

> bore Elwing up out of the waves, and he gave her the likeness of a great white bird, and upon her breast there shone as a star the Silmaril, as she flew over the water to seek Eärendil her beloved. . . . Eärendil at the helm of his ship saw her come towards him, as a white cloud exceeding swift beneath the moon, as a star over the sea moving in a strange course, a pale flame on wings of storm. [*The Silmarillion*, p. 247]

234 (I: 247). *carcanet* – An archaic word for 'an ornamental collar or necklace, usually of gold or set with jewels' (*OED*).

234 (I: 247). *Otherworld beyond the Sea* – Aman, Valinor.

235 (I: 247). *Tarmenel* – In his unfinished index Tolkien defines *Tarmenel* as 'high heaven, region of wind', and in *Nomenclature* (under *Over-heaven*) notes 'Elvish *menel* "firmament", *tar-menel* "high heaven", suggested by Old Norse *upphiminn*'. It is implied that Manwë, the chief of the Valar, lord of the winds, sent the 'wind of power' that blew Eärendil's ship into the West.

235 (I: 247). *foundered Shores / that drowned before the Days began* – A reference, perhaps, to Melkor casting down and destroying the two Lamps which had lit Middle-earth *before the Days began*, i.e. before the raising of the Sun at the beginning of the First Age, and the resulting floods and change in the shape of the lands, when shores *foundered*, i.e. were submerged.

235 (I: 247). *on strands of pearl / . . . where ever-foaming billows roll / the gold and jewels wan* – A reference to the shores of Aman, where the Teleri dwelt: 'Many jewels the Noldor gave them, opals and diamonds and pale crystals, which they strewed upon the shores and scattered in the pools; marvellous were the beaches of Elendë in those days. And many pearls they won for themselves from the sea' (*The Silmarillion*, p. 61).

235 (I: 247). *the Mountain* – Taniquetil (Quenya 'high white peak'), near the east coast of Aman. It is the highest mountain in Arda, and is also called *Oiolossë* 'ever-snow-white' or Mount Everwhite. In July 1928 Tolkien painted a watercolour picture of Taniquetil, *Halls of Manwë on the Mountains of the World above Faerie* (*Artist and Illustrator*, fig. 52).

235 (I: 247). *Valinor, and Eldamar* – *Valinor* '"land of the Valar" or "ruling powers"'; *Eldamar* 'land of the Eldar or "High-Elves" on the shores of Valinor' (*Index*).

235 (I: 247). *Elvenhome* – Eldamar.

235 (I: 247). *Ilmarin* – In his unfinished index Tolkien defines *Ilmarin* as '"mansion of the high airs", dwelling of Manwë, Lord of the *Valar* (the Elder King) upon *Oiolossë*; used in verse for *Valinor* [Book II, Chapter 8]. *The hill of Ilmarin* name (in verse) of Oiolossë.'

235 (I: 247). *lamplit towers of Tirion / are mirrored on the Shadowmere* – *Tirion* (Quenya 'watch-tower') was the city built by the Vanyar and Noldor in Eldamar, later inhabited only by the Noldor.

Shadowmere is a 'translation' of *Luvailin*, 'a mere in Eldamar under shadow of Oiolossë (Mt. Everwhite)' (*Index*).

235 (I: 248). *the Calacirian* – 'Region of Eldamar, near the Calacirya (ravine of light)' (*Index*). Tirion was built in the Calacirya, the pass in the mountains of the Pelóri which guarded the eastern shore of Aman.

235 (I: 248). *the Elder King* – Manwë, the chief of the Valar,

> is the dearest to Ilúvatar and understands most clearly his purposes. He was appointed to be, in the fullness of time, the first of all Kings: lord of the realm of Arda and ruler of all that dwell therein. In Arda his delight is in the winds and the clouds, and in all the regions of the air, from the heights to the depths, from the utmost borders of the Veil of Arda to the breezes that blow in the grass. Súlimo he is surnamed, Lord of the Breath of Arda. All swift birds, strong of wing. he loves, and they come and go at his bidding. [*The Silmarillion*, p. 26]

235 (I: 248). *words unheard were spoken then / of folk of Men and Elven-kin* – Because of his mixed descent, Eärendil spoke as ambassador of both Men and Elves seeking the aid of the Valar against Morgoth.

236 (I: 248). *mithril* – The Sindarin word (?'grey-glitter') for true-silver. Gandalf describes the metal in Book II, Chapter 4: 'It could be beaten like copper, and polished like glass; and the Dwarves could make of it a metal, light and yet harder than tempered steel. Its beauty was like to that of common silver, but the beauty of *mithril* did not tarnish or grow dim' (p. 317, I: 331).

236 (I: 248). *undying doom, / to sail the shoreless skies and come / behind the Sun and light of Moon* – *Doom* 'judgement'. See note for p. 194.

236 (I: 248). *Evereven's lofty hills* – 'Evereven, Ever-eve, names for Eldamar' (*Index*).

236 (I: 248). *the mighty Mountain Wall* – The Pelóri, 'the fencing or defensive heights' on the eastern shore of Aman.

236 (I: 248). *World's End* – 'The remote side of Valinor' (*Index*).

236 (I: 248). *a distant flame before the Sun, / a wonder ere the waking dawn* – Eärendil as Venus the morning star; see note for p. 194.

236 (I: 248). *the Norland waters* – The North-west of the world of the Elder Days, especially Beleriand and adjacent regions.

236 (I: 249). *Hither shores* – 'Middle-earth (especially the western coastlands)' (*Index*).

236 (I: 249). *Flammifer of Westernesse* – *Flammifer* means 'bearing a flame'. When men set sail for Númenor (Westernesse) they were guided by the light of Eärendil in the heavens.

237 (I: 249): 'You needn't,' said Bilbo

237 (I: 250). cheek to make verses about Eärendil in the house of Elrond – For Elrond is, after all, the *son* of Eärendil.

237 (I: 250): They got up and withdrew

237–8 (I: 250). They got up and withdrew . . . – A recording by Tolkien from this sentence to the end of the following poem is included on Disc 1 of *The J.R.R. Tolkien Audio Collection*. An alternate recording of the poem alone is included on Disc 2.

238 (I: 250): *A Elbereth Gilthoniel*

238 (I: 250). *A Elbereth Gilthoniel . . .* – Compare the hymn to Elbereth given in English in Book I, Chapter 3: see notes for page 79. On 8 June 1961 Tolkien sent a translation of *A Elbereth Gilthoniel . . .* to Rhona Beare:

> O Elbereth Kindler-of-the-Stars, radiant, fall slanting, glittering like jewels from the firmament, the glory of the star-host! To the far distance gazing afar from the tree-woven middle-land, Snow White, to you I will

> sing on this side of the sea, here on this side of the great sea. [*J.R.R. Tolkien's Letters to Rhona Beare* (1985), p. 18]

A different translation by Tolkien is included in *The Road Goes Ever On: A Song Cycle* (1967; here with a lacuna supplied from his accompanying analysis):

> O! Elbereth who lit the stars, from glittering crystal slanting falls with light like jewels from heaven on high the glory of the starry host. To lands remote I have looked afar [from tree-tangled middle-lands], and now to thee, Fanuilos, bright spirit clothed in ever-white, I here will sing beyond the Sea, beyond the wide and Sundering Sea. [p. 64]

The *Road Goes Ever On* volume also includes a rendering of the hymn by Tolkien in Tengwar.

238 (I: 250). ***palan-díriel*** – The reference to having looked afar (*palan-díriel*), Tolkien says in *The Road Goes Ever On: A Song Cycle*, is

> to the *palantír* upon the Tower Hills (the 'Stone of Elendil'). . . . This alone of the *palantíri* was so made as to look out only west over the Sea. After the fall of Elendil the High-Elves took back this Stone into their own care, and it was not destroyed, nor used again by Men.
>
> The High-Elves (such as did not dwell in or near the Havens) journeyed to the Tower Hills at intervals to look afar at *Eressëa* (the Elvish isle) and the Shores of Valinor, close to which it lay. The hymn . . . is one appropriate to Elves who have just returned from such a pilgrimage. [p. 65]

Compare the note in Appendix A:

> The only Stone left in the North [after the loss of those of Annúminas and Amon Sûl] was the one in the Tower on Emyn Beraid that looks towards the Gulf of Lune. . . . But we [the Hobbits] are told that it was unlike the others and not in accord with them; it looked only to the Sea. Elendil set it there so that he could look back with 'straight sight' and see Eressëa in the vanished West; but the bent seas below covered Númenor for ever. [p. 1042, III: 322]

238 (I: 250). ***Fanuilos*** – In *The Road Goes Ever On: A Song Cycle* Tolkien comments that *Fanuilos* is

> the title of Elbereth . . . which is rendered 'Snow-white' . . . though this is very inadequate. *Fana-* is an Elvish element, with primary meaning 'veil.' The S[indarin] form *fân, fan-* was usually applied to clouds, floating as veils over the blue sky or the sun or moon, or resting on hills.
>
> In Quenya, however, the simple word *fana* acquired a special sense. Owing to the close association of the High-Elves with the *Valar*, it was

> applied to the 'veils' or 'raiment' in which the *Valar* presented themselves to physical eyes. These were the bodies in which they were self-incarnated. They usually took the shape of the bodies of Elves (and Men). . . . In these *fanar* they later presented themselves to the Elves, and appeared as persons of majestic (but not gigantic) stature, vested in robes expressing their individual natures and functions. The High-Elves said that these forms were always in some degree radiant, as if suffused with a light from within. In Quenya, *fana* thus came to signify the radiant and majestic figure of one of the great *Valar*. In Sindarin, especially as used by the High-Elves, the originally identical word *fân* (*fan-*), 'cloud,' was also given the same sense. *Fan-uilos* thus in full signified 'bright (angelic) figure ever white (as snow)'. [p. 66]

238 (I: 250): Frodo halted for a moment

238 (I: 250). Near him sat the Lady Arwen. To his surprise Frodo saw that Aragorn stood beside her; his dark cloak was thrown back, and he seemed to be clad in elven-mail, and a star shone on his breast. – For the first time Frodo, and the reader, sees Aragorn as a regal figure. The star on his breast is perhaps similar to the brooches worn by Rangers in Book V, Chapter 2: 'of silver shaped like a rayed star'.

In an interview with Daphne Castell, Tolkien commented that even in a 'time of a great war and high adventure' love is in the background. In *The Lord of the Rings*

> there's surely enough given in flashes for an attentive reader to see, even without the Appendix (of Aragorn and Arwen [Appendix A]), the whole tale as one aspect of the love-story of this pair, and the achievement of a high, noble, and romantic love. . . . You get the scene in Rivendell, with Aragorn suddenly revealed in princely dignity to Frodo standing by Arwen. There's Aragorn's vision, after he had plighted his troth to Arwen and left her; and what were his thoughts after receiving the furled standard, or when he unfurled it after achieving the paths of the dead. ['The Realms of Tolkien', *New Worlds* 50 (November 1966), pp. 150–1]

238 (I: 250–1): He led Frodo back to his own little room

238 (I: 250). south across the ravine of the Bruinen – At several points in *The Lord of the Rings* it is made clear that the river Bruinen or Loudwater runs near to the house of Elrond. But in Christopher Tolkien's 1954 and 1980 maps of Middle-earth, and in the *Wilderland* map in *The Hobbit*, Rivendell is drawn north of the Ford between a larger river and a tributary. Neither of these is named on the *Hobbit* map, but in one of his check copies of *The Hobbit* Tolkien later added, *inter alia*, the names *Bruinen or Loudwater* against the river north of the house and (probably) *Merrill* against the tributary to the south of Rivendell. On one of his sketch-maps

Tolkien first drew the lines of the rivers (Mitheithel and Bruinen) and the Road to the Ford

> in ink, and subsequently coloured [them] over in blue and red chalk. When my father did this he changed the course of the 'tributary stream' south of Elrond's house by bending it up northwards and joining it to the Bruinen some way to the east; thus the house at Rivendell is at the western end of land enclosed by two streams coming down from the Mountains, parting, and then joining again. It might therefore be supposed that both were called 'Bruinen' (discounting the name 'Merrill' written on the Wilderland map in *The Hobbit*). But I do not think that detailed conclusions can be drawn from this sketch-map. [Christopher Tolkien, *The Return of the Shadow*, p. 205]

All of Tolkien's drawings of Rivendell show it on the north side of a river, with tall hills or cliffs north of the house.

Chapter 2

THE COUNCIL OF ELROND

For drafts and history of this chapter, see *The Return of the Shadow*, pp. 395–407, 409, 412–14; *The Treason of Isengard*, pp. 110–60.

239 (I: 252): Next day Frodo woke early

239 (I: 252). Next day Frodo woke – It is the morning of 25 October 1418.

239 (I: 252). woven nets of gossamer – Cobwebs twinkling with dew.

239 (I: 252): Suddenly as they were talking

239 (I: 252). the Council of Elrond – In *J.R.R. Tolkien: Author of the Century* Tom Shippey comments that the present chapter

> is a largely unappreciated *tour de force*, whose success may be gauged by the fact that few pause to recognize its complexity. It breaks, furthermore, most of the rules which might be given to an apprentice writer. For one thing, though it is fifteen thousand words long, in it nothing happens: it consists entirely of people talking. For another, it has an unusual number of speakers present (twelve), the majority of them (seven) unknown to the reader and appearing for the first time. Just to make things more difficult, the longest speech, by Gandalf, which takes up half the total, contains direct quotation from seven more speakers, or writers, all of them apart from Butterbur and Gaffer Gamgee new to the story, and some of them (Saruman, Denethor) to be extremely important to it later on. Other speakers, like Glóin, give quotations from yet more speakers, Dáin and Sauron's messenger. Like so many committee meetings, this chapter could very easily have disintegrated, lost its way, or simply become too boring to follow. The fact that it does not is brought about by two things, Tolkien's extremely firm grasp of the history . . . of Middle-earth; and his unusual ability to suggest cultural variation by differences in mode of speech. [pp. 68–9; see also more generally, pp. 68–82]

239 (I: 252): Gandalf led them to the porch

239 (I: 252). the porch where Frodo had found his friends the evening before – As described in the previous chapter, this is in 'a high garden above the steep bank of the river . . . on the side of the house looking east' (p. 226, I: 238). In draft the Council was held 'in a high glade among the trees on the valley-side far above the house' (*The Return of the Shadow*, p. 395), but Tolkien decided that it should be instead 'behind closed doors'. Nonetheless, the porch of the final text is open to the air and the sounds of nature.

240 (I: 253): He then pointed out and named

240 (I: 253). Gimli – In his draft letter to Mr Rang, August 1967, Tolkien wrote that Old English 'will have nothing to say about *Gimli*. Actually the poetic word *gim* in archaic O[ld] N[orse] verse is probably not related to *gimm* (an early loan < Latin *gemma*) "gem", though possibly it was later associated with it: its meaning seems to have been "fire"' (*Letters*, p. 382).

Manfred Zimmermann, in 'Miscellaneous Remarks: On Gimli and on Rhythmic Prose', *Mythlore* 11, no. 3, whole no. 41 (Winter–Spring 1985), argues that Old Norse *gim* 'fire' would be the best source for *Gimli*, as a philological joke: 'Who was Gimli's father? Of course, Gloin of Thorin & Co., whose name might be translated as "the Glowing One" (Old Norse *glóinn*). Now if we treat *Gimli* as the diminutive form of *gim* "fire", we would get a highly appropriate name for the son of the "Glowing One": "Little Fire" or "Spark"' (p. 32).

240 (I: 253). Erestor – In drafts of this chapter *Erestor* is called a 'Half-elf', a kinsman of Elrond, and briefly considered as one of the Company of the Ring.

240 (I: 253). Galdor, an Elf from the Grey Havens – In Tolkien's mythology the name *Galdor* was given earliest to the Lord of the People of the Tree, among the Elves of Gondolin; it is said in the name-list to *The Fall of Gondolin* (in *The Book of Lost Tales*) to be akin to the Gnomish word for 'tree'. In drafts of *The Lord of the Rings* the name was given first to the character later called *Legolas* (see below); and later in *The Silmarillion* to a Man of the First Age, the father of Húrin and Huor.

240 (I: 253). Círdan the Shipwright – A Telerin Elf, from that kindred known for their ships and seafaring, one of the great among the Eldar, keeper of the Grey Havens during the Second and Third Ages. *Círdan* is Sindarin for 'shipwright', from *cair* 'ship' + *-dan* 'maker'. For many years only he knew that the Istari (Wizards) had come over the Sea out of the West, for he saw their landings on the shores of Middle-earth. See further, note for p. 1030.

240 (I: 253). Legolas, a messenger from his father, Thranduil, King of the Elves of Northern Mirkwood – In his draft letter to Mr Rang, August 1967, Tolkien wrote that

> *Legolas* is translated *Greenleaf* . . . (II, 106, 154) a suitable name for a Woodland Elf, though one of royal and originally Sindarin line. . . . I think an investigator . . . might have perceived the relation of the element *-las* to *lassi* 'leaves' in Galadriel's lament [Book II, Chapter 8], *lasse-lanta* 'leaf-fall' = autumn . . . ; and *Eryn Lasgalen* [Appendix B]. . . . 'Technically' Legolas is a compound (according to rules) of S[indarin] *laeg* 'viridis' fresh and green, and *go-lass* 'collection of leaves, foliage'. [*Letters*, p. 382; see also p. 282]

Just as the name *Galdor* first appeared in *The Fall of Gondolin*, so too did *Legolas Greenleaf* – as well as *Glorfindel* – but only the last of these was retained by the same character in both stories.

Tolkien's regard for Legolas in *The Lord of the Rings* is reflected in a late comment, in response to a 'ladylike' illustration of the character: 'He was tall as a young tree, lithe, immensely strong, able swiftly to draw a great war-bow and shoot down a Nazgûl, endowed with the tremendous vitality of Elvish bodies, so hard and resistant to hurt that he went only in light shoes over rock or through snow, the most tireless of all the Fellowship' (quoted in *The Book of Lost Tales, Part Two*, p. 327).

Thranduil, the King of the Silvan Elves in the north of Mirkwood, already appeared in *The Hobbit*, named only the 'Elvenking'.

240 (I: 253): He was cloaked and booted

240 (I: 253). baldric – A belt for a sword or other piece of equipment, worn over the shoulder and reaching to the opposite hip.

240 (I: 253). He gazed at Frodo and Bilbo with sudden wonder. – He has never seen a hobbit, but (as revealed later in the chapter) has heard a voice in a dream speak of 'the Halfling'.

240 (I: 253): 'Here,' said Elrond

240 (I: 253). Boromir . . . arrived in the grey morning – *Boromir* of *The Lord of the Rings* shares a name with a Man of the First Age, the great-grandson of Bëor the Old and grandfather of Barahir, the father of Beren, as told in *The Silmarillion*. In the *Etymologies* Tolkien states that '*Boromir* is an old N[oldorin] name of ancient origin also borne by Gnomes: O[ld] N[oldorin] *Boronmíro, Boromíro*' (*The Lost Road and Other Writings*, p. 353). In Appendix F *Boromir* is said to be of 'mixed form' (p. 1128, III: 406, n.), that is, containing both Quenya and Sindarin elements (Sindarin *boro(n)* 'steadfast' + Quenya *míre* 'jewel').

Here Boromir *arrived in the grey morning*, but according to *The Tale of Years* he reached Rivendell on 24 October, the night before the Council.

240 (I: 253): 'It is now many years ago'

240 (I: 253). Moria: the mighty works of our fathers that are called in our own tongue Khazad-dûm – *Moria*, and the Mines of Moria, are mentioned several times in *The Hobbit*. In his draft letter to Mr Rang, August 1967, Tolkien says that *Moria* was there

> a casual 'echo' of *Soria Moria Castle* in one of the Scandinavian tales translated by Dasent [from the collection *Norske Folke Eventyr* by Peter Christen Asbjørnsen and Jørgen Moe (1852)]. (The tale had no interest for me: I had already forgotten it and have never since looked at it. It was thus merely the source of the sound-sequence *moria*, which might have been found or composed elsewhere.) I liked the sound-sequence;

> it alliterated with 'mines', and it connected itself with the MOR element in my linguistic construction. [*Letters*, p. 384]

The name *Moria* (stressed on the first syllable) is Sindarin, from *mor-* 'dark, black' (as in *Mordor, Morgoth*) + *iâ* 'void, abyss'.

In Appendix F it is said of Moria that 'the Dwarves themselves, and this name at least was never kept secret, called it *Khazad-dûm*, the Mansion of the Khazâd; for such is their own name for their own race' (p. 1137, III: 415). According to the index in *The Silmarillion*, the element *dûm* is probably a plural or collective, meaning 'excavations, halls, mansions' (p. 337). In his unfinished index Tolkien glosses *Khazad-dûm* as 'deeps of the *Khuzd* or Dwarves'. See further, note for p. 306.

240–1 (I: 253–4): Glóin sighed

240 (I: 253). too deep we delved there, and woke the nameless fear – In Appendix A it is said that in Moria

> the Dwarves delved deep ... seeking beneath Barazinbar [Caradhras] for *mithril*. ... Thus they roused from sleep a thing of terror that, flying from Thangorodrim, had lain hidden at the foundations of the earth since the coming of the Host of the West [and the Great Battle at the end of the First Age in which Thangorodrim was destroyed]: a Balrog of Morgoth. Durin was slain by it, and the year after Náin I, his son; and then the glory of Moria passed, and its people were destroyed or fled far away. [pp. 1071–2, III: 353]

See further, note for p. 330.

240 (I: 253). the children of Durin – The descendants of the eldest of the Seven Fathers of the Dwarves. According to Appendix A, Durin

> slept alone, until in the deeps of time and the awakening of his people he came to Azanulbizar, and in the caves above Kheled-zâram in the east of the Misty Mountains he made his dwelling, where afterwards were the Mines of Moria renowned in song.
>
> There he lived so long that he was known far and wide as Durin the Deathless. Yet in the end he died before the Elder Days had passed and his tomb was in Khazad-dûm; but his line never failed, and five times an heir was born in his House so like to his Forefather that he received the name Durin. [p. 1071, III: 352]

240 (I: 254). no dwarf has dared to pass the doors of Khazad-dûm for many lives of kings, save Thrór only, and he perished – In Appendix A it is told how Thrór, King under the Mountain at Erebor, with his family fled from the dragon Smaug 'into long and homeless wandering'. Years later, 'old, poor, and desperate', Thrór went to Moria in search of gold. 'He was a little crazed perhaps with age and misfortune and long brooding on the splendour of Moria in his forefathers' days; or the Ring [one of the

Seven Rings of the Dwarves, which Thrór had long held until giving it to his son Thráin], it may be, was turning to evil now that its master [Sauron] was awake, driving him to folly and destruction' (p. 1073, III: 354). He entered Moria proudly, and was slain by Azog, a great Orc. In *The Hobbit*, Chapter 1, Gandalf says to Thorin (son of Thráin): 'Your grandfather Thror was killed, you remember, in the mines of Moria by Azog the Goblin.'

241 (I: 254): 'At this we were greatly troubled

241 (I: 254). an earnest – A token.

241 (I: 254): 'At that his breath came like the hiss of snakes

241 (I: 254). I must consider this message and what it means under its fair cloak. – In *The Road to Middle-earth* Tom Shippey comments on the conversation between Dáin and the messenger from Mordor as an example of various dialogues in *The Lord of the Rings* whose

> unifying feature is delight in the contrast between passionate interior and polite or rational expression: the weakness of the latter is an index of the strength of the former. Thus the messenger's 'things will not seem so well' works as violent threat; 'not too long' means 'extremely rapidly'. In reply Dáin's 'fair cloak' implies 'foul body' and the obscure metaphor of spending the 'time of my thought' indicates refusal to negotiate under threat. Both participants seek to project a cool, ironic self-control. [2nd edn., p. 110]

242 (I: 255): They all listened while Elrond

242 (I: 255). the Elven-smiths of Eregion and their friendship with Moria – In *Of the Rings of Power and the Third Age* it is said that 'Eregion was nigh to the great mansions of the Dwarves that were named Khazad-dûm. . . . From Ost-in-Edhil, the city of the Elves, the highroad ran to the west gate of Khazad-dûm, for a friendship arose between Dwarves and Elves, such as has never elsewhere been, to the enrichment of both those peoples' (*The Silmarillion*, p. 286). In his draft letter to Peter Hastings, September 1954, Tolkien wrote that

> the particular branch of the High-Elves concerned [in *The Lord of the Rings*], the Noldor or Loremasters, were always on the side of 'science and technology', as we should call it: they wanted to have the knowledge that Sauron genuinely had, and those of Eregion refused the warnings of Gilgalad and Elrond. The particular 'desire' of the Eregion Elves – an 'allegory' if you like of the love of machinery, and technical devices – is also symbolised by their special friendship with the Dwarves of Moria. [*Letters*, p. 190]

See further, note for p. 303.

242 (I: 255). he was not yet evil to behold – In *Of the Rings of Power and the Third Age* it is told how Sauron the Maia 'became the greatest and most trusted of the servants of the Enemy [Morgoth], and the most perilous, for he could assume many forms, and for long if he willed he could still appear noble and beautiful, so as to deceive all but the most wary.' But his 'fair semblance' was lost for ever in the drowning of Númenor, and when his spirit returned to Mordor he 'wrought for himself a new shape; and it was terrible' (*The Silmarillion*, pp. 285, 292). In his draft letter to Eileen Elgar, September 1963, Tolkien wrote that

> in a tale which allows the incarnation of great spirits in a physical and destructible form their power must be far greater when actually physically present. Sauron should be thought of as very terrible. The form that he took was that of a man of more than human stature, but not gigantic. In his earlier incarnation he was able to veil his power (as Gandalf did) and could appear as a commanding figure of great strength of body and supremely royal demeanour and countenance. [*Letters*, p. 332]

242 (I: 255). the Mountain of Fire – Orodruin, Mount Doom.

242 (I: 255). Celebrimbor . . . hid the Three which he had made – *Celebrimbor* ('hand of silver', from Sindarin *celebrin* 'of silver' + *paur* 'fist, hand'), a Noldorin Elf, was the son of Curufin and a grandson of Fëanor. In the Second Age he was the greatest of the smiths of Eregion.

242 (I: 255): Then through all the years

242 (I: 255). since that history is elsewhere recounted, even as Elrond himself set it down in his books of lore, it is not here recalled – The history of the One Ring, and of the other Rings, grew in the process of writing the present chapter, until eventually Tolkien removed much of it into the essay *Of the Rings of Power and the Third Age*, originally intended to be included in the Appendices of *The Lord of the Rings* but not published until 1977 in *The Silmarillion*. In that work it is said that in Eregion

> the counsels of Sauron were most gladly received, for in that land the Noldor desired ever to increase the skill and subtlety of their works. Moreover they were not at peace in their hearts, since they had refused to return into the West, and they desired both to stay in Middle-earth, which indeed they loved, and yet to enjoy the bliss of those that had departed. Therefore they hearkened to Sauron, and they learned of him many things, for his knowledge was great. In those days the smiths of Ost-in-Edhil surpassed all that they had contrived before; and they took thought, and they made Rings of Power. But Sauron guided their labours, and he was aware of all that they did; for his desire was to set a bond upon the Elves and to bring them under his vigilance. [*The Silmarillion*, p. 287]

Tolkien also included an account of Eregion in his late work *Concerning Galadriel and Celeborn*. There Galadriel and Celeborn are said to have been the rulers of Eregion, and Celebrimbor one of their craftsmen. While this is not contradicted in *The Lord of the Rings*, it seems unlikely to have been Tolkien's conception of events while he was writing that work, but rather stems from a growing interest in his later years in the enhancement of Galadriel's role in the history of Middle-earth. Christopher Tolkien summarizes the later account as follows:

> In Eregion Sauron posed as an emissary of the Valar, sent by them to Middle-earth . . . or ordered by them to remain there to give aid to the Elves. He perceived at once that Galadriel would be his chief adversary and obstacle, and he endeavoured therefore to placate her, bearing her scorn with outward patience and courtesy. . . . Sauron used all his arts upon Celebrimbor and his fellow-smiths, who had formed a society or brotherhood, very powerful in Eregion, the Gwaith-i-Mírdain; but he worked in secret, unknown to Galadriel and Celeborn. Before long Sauron had the Gwaith-i-Mírdain under his influence, for at first they had great profit from his instruction in secret matters of their craft. So great became his hold on the Mírdain that at length he persuaded them to revolt against Galadriel and Celeborn and to seize power in Eregion; and that was at some time between 1350 and 1400 of the Second Age. Galadriel thereupon left Eregion. . . . [*Unfinished Tales*, pp. 236–7]

The work continues with Celebrimbor's discovery of the existence of the One Ring, his repentance, the hiding and dispersal of the Three Rings of the Elves, and Sauron's attack on Eregion, where he believed the Three Rings to be.

> At last the attackers broke into Eregion with ruin and devastation, and captured the chief object of Sauron's assault, the House of the Mírdain, where were their smithies and their treasures. Celebrimbor, desperate, himself withstood Sauron on the steps of the great door of the Mírdain; but he was grappled and taken captive, and the House was ransacked. There Sauron took the Nine Rings and other lesser works of the Mírdain; but the Seven and the Three he could not find. Then Celebrimbor was put to torment, and Sauron learned from him where the Seven were bestowed. This Celebrimbor revealed, because neither the Seven nor the Nine did he value as he valued the Three; the Seven and the Nine were made with Sauron's aid, whereas the Three were made by Celebrimbor alone, with a different power and purpose. [*Unfinished Tales*, p. 238]

The idea that the Three were made by the Elves, and finally by Celebrimbor alone, not by Sauron himself, and that Sauron had made the One Ring to be master of the other Rings, took long to develop in the writing of *The Lord of the Rings*. (Curiously, even in ?late 1951, in his letter to Milton

Waldman (*Letters*, p. 152), Tolkien wrote that 'the Elves of Eregion', rather than Celebrimbor specifically, 'made Three supremely beautiful and powerful rings, almost solely of their own imagination, and directed to the preservation of beauty: they did not confer invisibility'.)

242–3 (I: 255–6): Of Númenor he spoke

242 (I: 256). Elendil the Tall – In a note associated with *The Disaster of the Gladden Fields* it is said that the Númenórean unit of measurement for distance was the *ranga* or stride, 'slightly longer than our yard, approximately thirty-eight inches, owing to their [the Númenóreans'] greater stature'; and that

> two *rangar* was often called 'man-high', which at thirty-eight inches gives an average height of six feet four inches; but this was at a later date, when the stature of the Dúnedain appears to have decreased, and also was not intended to be an accurate statement of the observed average of male stature among them, but was an approximate length expressed in the well-known unit *ranga*. . . . It is however said of the great people of the past that they were more than man-high. Elendil was said to be 'more than man-high by nearly half a *ranga*'; but he was accounted the tallest of all the Númenóreans who escaped the Downfall. [*Unfinished Tales*, pp. 285–6]

Thus Elendil, by this account, was apparently almost eight feet tall. But in another late, unpublished note Tolkien wrote that

> the Númenoreans before the Downfall were a people of great stature and strength, the Kings of Men; their full grown men were commonly seven feet tall, especially in the royal and noble houses. In the North where men of other kinds were fewer and their race remained purer this stature remained more frequent, though in both Arnor and Gondor apart from mixture of race the Númenóreans showed a dwindling of height and of longevity in Middle-earth that became more marked as the Third Age passed. Aragorn, direct descendant of Elendil and his son Isildur, both of whom had been seven feet tall, must nonetheless have been a very tall man . . . , probably at least 6 ft. 6; and Boromir, of high Númenorean lineage, not much shorter (say 6 ft. 4). [Tolkien Papers, Bodleian Library, Oxford]

243 (I: 256). the hosts of Gil-galad and Elendil – *Host* is an archaic word for 'army', a body or group of things in great numbers.

243 (I: 256): Thereupon Elrond paused

243 (I: 256). Beleriand – The 'lost land of [the] Elder Days (of which Lindon was all that remained in the Third Age)' (*Index*). In the index to *The Silmarillion* Christopher Tolkien notes that *Beleriand*

> was said to have signified 'the country of Balar', and to have been given first to the lands about the mouths of Sirion that faced the Isle of Balar. Later the name spread to include all the ancient coast of the Northwest of Middle-earth south of the Firth of Drengist, and all the inner lands south of Hithlum and eastwards to the feet of the Blue Mountains, divided by the river Sirion into East and West Beleriand. Beleriand was broken in the turmoils at the end of the First Age, invaded by the sea, so that only Ossiriand (Lindon) remained. [*The Silmarillion*, p. 319]

In Tolkien's mythology Beleriand was originally called *Broseliand*: compare *Broceliande* in legends of King Arthur.

243 (I: 256). when Thangorodrim was broken – *Thangorodrim* was 'the great mountain-crown ([Sindarin] "mountain-chain of tyranny") above the vast underground fortress of Morgoth, the Dark Lord of the Elder Days' (*Index*). It was broken in the Great Battle at the end of the First Age. The name is sometimes used also to refer to Angband, the fortress beneath the mountain.

243 (I: 256). and the Elves deemed that evil was ended for ever, and it was not so – Tom Shippey has commented that 'the idea that evil could be ended "for ever" may recall the belief that World War I was fought as "the war to end all wars"; but Tolkien lived both through the time of that belief, or that assurance, and its total failure with the second outbreak of war in 1939' (*J.R.R. Tolkien: Author of the Century*, p. 165).

243 (I: 256): 'So it was indeed'

243 (I: 256). my memory reaches back even to the Elder Days – Late workings by Tolkien on the chronology of the First Age show the last war of the Elder Days occurring between F.A. 550 and 597 (changed to 545 and 587), and Elrond born in F.A. 528 (changed to 532).

243 (I: 256). Eärendil was my sire, who was born in Gondolin before its fall; and my mother was Elwing, daughter of Dior, son of Lúthien of Doriath – *Gondolin* was 'the hidden City of King Turgon in Beleriand in the Elder Days, destroyed by Morgoth' (*Index*); Eärendil, then only a boy, escaped from its ruin. See further, note for p. 316.

Doriath (Sindarin 'land of the fence', referring to the Girdle of Melian or protective enchantment around that land) was the 'the Guarded Realm, the secret country of King Thingol in the midst of Beleriand in the Elder Days' (*Index*).

243 (I: 256). three ages in the West of the world – See the preface to *The Tale of Years*, Appendix B.

243 (I: 256): 'I was the herald of Gil-galad

243 (I: 256). the Battle of Dagorlad before the Black Gate of Mordor – *Dagorlad* (Sindarin 'battle-plain') lay 'east of Emyn Muil and near [the]

Dead Marshes, scene of [the] first great Battle of the Last Alliance' (*Index*).

The *Black Gate* was 'the main northern entrance to Mordor, guarding the defile of Cirith Gorgor. Also called in Elvish *The Morannon*' (*Index*).

243 (I: 256). Aeglos and Narsil – In editions prior to 2005 'Aeglos' read 'Aiglos'. Tolkien comments in *The Rivers and Beacon-hills of Gondor* that 'originally the difference between correct Sindarin *ae* and *ai* was neglected, *ai* more usual in English being used for both in the general narrative. . . . So *Hithaiglir* on the map for *Hithaeglir* and *Aiglos* [for *Aeglos*]' (*Vinyar Tengwar* 42 (July 2001), p. 11). The *1966 Index* glosses *Aeglos* (*Aiglos*) as (Sindarin) 'icicle'. In *The Silmarillion* the name is glossed 'snow-point'.

In the *1966 Index Narsil* is glossed as 'red and white flame'. In his letter to Richard Jeffery, 17 December 1972, Tolkien wrote that '*Narsil* is a name composed of 2 basic stems without variation or adjuncts: √*NAR* "fire", & √*THIL* "white light". It thus symbolised the chief heavenly lights, as enemies of darkness, Sun (*Anar*) and Moon (in Q[uenya]) *Isil*' (*Letters*, p. 425).

243 (I: 256). hilt-shard – The fragment of the sword including its handle.

243 (I: 256): '"This I will have as weregild

243 (I: 256). weregild for my father, and my brother – *Weregild* (literally 'man-gold') under ancient Teutonic and English law was payment in compensation or fine for murder and other crimes.

Only later in this chapter is it said directly that Isildur's brother Anárion was also killed in the battle.

In *The Road to Middle-earth* Tom Shippey comments that

> Elrond's speech . . . as is only suitable for one so old, is full of old-fashioned inversions of syntax and words like 'weregild', 'esquire', 'shards'. Its burden is to state the Northern 'theory of courage', as Tolkien called it in his British Academy lecture, [*Beowulf: The Monsters and the Critics*] whose central thesis is that even ultimate defeat does not turn right into wrong. Elrond has seen 'many defeats and many fruitless victories', and in a way he has even given up hope, at least for his adopted people the elves . . . ; but this does not make him change his mind or look for easy options. [2nd edn., p. 109]

243 (I: 256). Isildur's Bane – That is, the cause of Isildur's death.

243–4 (I: 257): 'Only to the North did these tidings come

243–4 (I: 257). From the ruin of the Gladden Fields, where Isildur perished, three men only came ever back over the mountains after long wandering. One of these was Ohtar, the esquire of Isildur, who bore the shards of the sword of Elendil – *The Lord of the Rings* mentions only Ohtar; in *The Disaster of the Gladden Fields*, where the story of Isildur's fall is told at greater length, it is said that Isildur commanded Ohtar and a companion to flee with the sheath and shards of Narsil; and it is revealed that the third survivor was Estelmo, esquire of Elendur (the son of Isildur, killed with his father by attacking Orcs), 'one of the last to fall, but was stunned by a club, and not slain' (*Unfinished Tales*, p. 276).

In an author's note to the same work, Tolkien says that '*Ohtar* is the only name used in the legends; but it is probably only the title of address that Isildur used at this tragic moment, hiding his feelings under formality. *Ohtar* "warrior, soldier" was the title of all who, though fully trained and experienced, had not yet been admitted to the rank of *roquen*, "knight"' (*Unfinished Tales*, p. 282, n. 17) – hence *esquire* (or *squire*), the rank below *knight* in the hierarchy of knighthood in European history.

244 (I: 257). Valandil, the heir of Isildur – *Valandil* 'Vala-friend', like *Eärendil* and *Elendil*, contains the Quenya element or verbal base (N)DIL 'to love, be devoted to'. Valandil was the fourth son of Isildur, born in Rivendell.

244 (I: 257): 'Fruitless did I call the victory

244 (I: 257). the race of Númenor has decayed, and the span of their years has lessened – In Book V, Chapter 8 it is said that the span of the lives of the people of Gondor 'had now waned to little more than that of other men, and those among them who passed the tale of five score [one hundred] years with vigour were grown few, save in some houses of purer blood' (p. 860, III: 136). In Book VI, Chapter 5 Aragorn says that he is 'of the race of the West unmingled' (p. 971, III: 249).

244 (I: 257): 'In the North after the war

244 (I: 257). Annúminas beside Lake Evendim – *Annúminas* is Sindarin for 'tower of the west', from *annûn* 'west' + *minas* 'tower'.

Evendim is the Common Speech rendering of Sindarin *Nenuial* (*nen* 'water' + *uial* 'twilight'), where the river Baranduin rose.

244 (I: 257). North Downs – The 'low hills n[orth] of the Shire' (*Index*).

244 (I: 257): 'In the South the realm of Gondor long endured

244 (I: 257). Osgiliath, Citadel of the Stars – In his unfinished index Tolkien notes: '*Osgiliath* (*ost* "fort, citadel"; *giliath* hosts of stars (*gil*)), chief city of ancient Gondor on either side of Anduin; now ruined'.

244 (I: 257). Minas Ithil they built, Tower of the Rising Moon, eastward upon a shoulder of the Mountains of Shadow; and westward at the feet of the White Mountains Minas Anor they made, Tower of the Setting Sun – *Minas* is Sindarin 'tower' ('esp[ecially] one that is tall and isolated'), *ithil* '(full) moon', *anor* 'sun' (*Index*).

The *Mountains of Shadow* (Sindarin *Ephel Dúath*) are the western 'fence' of Mordor.

The *White Mountains* (Sindarin *Ered Nimrais*) are a great range of peaks in Gondor, south of the Misty Mountains, running from east to west.

244 (I: 257). Eressëa – Tol Eressëa, the 'Lonely Isle', home of many Elves in the Bay of Eldamar near the coasts of Aman.

244 (I: 257). Uttermost West – Aman.

244–5 (I: 257–8): 'But in the wearing of the swift years

244 (I: 257–8). the line of Meneldil – *Meneldil* is Sindarin 'astronomer', including (as for *Menelvagor*) the element *menel* 'firmament, heavens'.

244 (I: 258). Gorgoroth – A high plateau in Mordor, between the Mountains of Shadow and the Mountains of Ash. The name contains Sindarin *gorgor* 'terror, haunting fear'.

245 (I: 258). it is called Minas Morgul, the Tower of Sorcery – *Morgul* is derived from Sindarin *mor-* 'black' + *gûl* 'sorcery', thus 'black arts'.

245 (I: 258): 'So it has been for many lives of men

245 (I: 258). the Lords of Minas Tirith – The Stewards; see further, note for p. 670.

245 (I: 258). Argonath – The 'Pillars of the Kings' on the river Anduin at the entrance to Gondor; see note for p. 392.

245 (I: 258): 'Believe not that in the land of Gondor

245 (I: 258). bulwark – A defence.

245 (I: 258): 'Yet that hour, maybe, is not now far away

245 (I: 258). Mount Doom – The Common Speech name of the volcano Orodruin, but also 'a translation of its other name *Amon Amarth* "hill of doom", given to Sauron's forge-mountain because it was linked in little-understood prophecies with the "doom" that was foretold would befall' when the Ring was found again (*Nomenclature*).

245 (I: 258). Ithilien, our fair domain east of the River, though we kept a foothold there and strength of arms – In his unfinished index Tolkien writes of *Ithilien* (Sindarin 'land of the moon') as 'territory (in earliest time belonging to Isildur and governed from Minas Ithil)'. Its last inhabitants fled in Third Age 2954 (S.R. 1354) when Mount Doom burst into flame; but Gondor retained a secret refuge, Henneth Annûn, built in Third Age 2901 (see Book IV, Chapters 5–6).

245 (I: 258). this very year, in the days of June, sudden war came upon us – 20 June, according to *The Tale of Years.*

245 (I: 258). the Easterlings and the cruel Haradrim – The *Easterlings* are, simply, 'Men from the East', from the regions beyond the Sea of Rhûn.

The *Haradrim* are Men of Harad ('the South', i.e. the lands south of Mordor). In his letter to Naomi Mitchison, 25 April 1954, Tolkien wrote that 'in Grey-elven [Sindarin] the general plurals were very frequently made by adding to a name (or place-name) some word meaning "tribe, host, horde, people". So *Haradrim* the Southrons: Q[uenya] *rimbe*, S[indarin] *rim*, host' (*Letters*, p. 178).

245–6 (I: 259): 'I was in the company that held the bridge

245 (I: 259). my brother – Faramir, but not named until Book IV, Chapter 5.

246 (I: 259): 'In this evil hour

246 (I: 259). a hundred and ten days I have journeyed – According to *The Tale of Years* Boromir left Gondor on 4 July 1418. It is now 25 October.

246 (I: 259). a dream came to my brother . . . and afterwards a like dream came oft to him again, and once to me – Tom Shippey sees this as an example of free will:

> In Middle-earth, one may say, Providence or the Valar sent the dream that took Boromir to Rivendell. But they sent it first and most often to Faramir, who would no doubt have been a better choice. It was human decision, or human perversity, which led to Boromir claiming the journey, with what chain of ill-effects and casualties no one can tell. 'Luck', then, is a continuous interplay of providence and free will. . . . [*The Road to Middle-earth*, 2nd edn., pp. 136–7]

246 (I: 259): 'In that dream I thought

246 (I: 259). *Imladris* – The Sindarin name for Rivendell. It contains the element *imlad* 'narrow valley with steep sides but a flat habitable bottom' (*Index*). See also note for p. 3.

246 (I: 259). *Halfling* – 'Common Speech name for *Hobbit.* It is not actually an English word, but might be (i.e. it is suitably formed with an appropriate suffix). The sense is "a half-sized man/person"' (*Nomenclature*). See also note for pp. 1–2.

246 (I: 259). Denethor – In Appendix F it is said that *Denethor* is of Sindarin form, probably one of the 'names of Elves or Men remembered in the songs and histories of the First Age' (p. 1128, III: 406, n.). In *The Silmarillion* the name *Denethor* is given to a leader of the Green-elves that dwelt in Ossiriand; he was slain in the First Battle of Beleriand. According to notes by Tolkien in his *Lhammas* or 'Account of Tongues', *Denethor* (or *Denithor*) is said to be derived from *ndani-thārō* 'saviour of the Dani [the Green-elves]' (*The Lost Road and Other Writings*, p. 188).

246 (I: 259). Loth – Reluctant, unwilling.

247 (I: 260): 'I was not sent to beg any boon

247 (I: 260). boon – An archaic word for 'gift, favour'.

247 (I: 260). the Sword of Elendil would be a help beyond our hope – Boromir chooses his words carefully: he wishes that the *Sword* of Elendil may come to Gondor, but the question was whether he wished the *House* of Elendil to return.

248 (I: 261): Aragorn smiled at him

248 (I: 261). Little do I resemble the figures of Elendil and Isildur as they stand carven in their majesty in the halls of Denethor. – Compare the 'avenue of kings' Pippin sees in the great hall at Minas Tirith in Book V, Chapter 1. It is said, however, in *The Disaster of the Gladden Fields* 'that in later days those (such as Elrond) whose memories recalled him [Elendur, eldest son of Isildur, "one of the greatest, the fairest of the seed of Elendil, most like to his grandsire"] were struck by the great likeness to him, in body and mind, of King Elessar' (*Unfinished Tales*, pp. 283–4, n. 26; and p. 274). And after Aragorn's coronation 'all that beheld him gazed in silence, for it seemed to them that he was revealed to them now for the first time. Tall as the sea-kings of old, he stood above all that were near; ancient of days he seemed and yet in the flower of manhood; and wisdom sat upon his brow, and strength and healing were in his hands, and a light was about him' (Book VI, Chapter 5, p. 968, III: 246).

248 (I: 261). I have had a hard life and a long; and the leagues that lie between here and Gondor are a small part in the count of my journeys. I have crossed many mountains and many rivers, and trodden many plains, even into the far countries of Rhûn and Harad where the stars are strange. – In *The Tale of Aragorn and Arwen* (Appendix A) it is said of Aragorn:

> His ways were hard and long, and he became somewhat grim to look upon, unless he chanced to smile; and yet he seemed to Men worthy of honour, as a king that is in exile, when he did not hide his true shape. For he went in many guises, and won renown under many names. He rode in the host of the Rohirrim, and fought for the Lord of Gondor by land and by sea; and then in the hour of victory he passed out of the knowledge of Men of the West, and went alone far into the East and deep into the South, exploring the hearts of Men, both evil and good, and uncovering the plots and devices of the servants of Sauron. [p. 1060, III: 340–1]

Rhûn and *Harad* are Sindarin 'East' and 'South' respectively.

249 (I: 262): 'But not yet, I beg, Master!'

249 (I: 262). 'But not yet, I beg, Master!' cried Bilbo. – This was the reading in the first printing of the first edition (1954). In the unauthorized resetting of *The Fellowship of the Ring* for its second printing (1954) 'cried' was mistakenly altered to 'said'. The error was corrected in the edition of 2004.

249 (I: 262): 'Very well,' said Bilbo

249 (I: 262). true story – See note for p. 13.

250 (I: 263): 'Some, Galdor,' said Gandalf

250 (I: 263). The Nine the Nazgûl keep. – The *Nazgûl* are the Ringwraiths. In his draft letter to Mr Rang, August 1967, Tolkien mentions 'two cases where I was *not*, at the time of making use of them, aware of "borrowing", but where it is probable, but by no means certain, that the names were nonetheless "echoes"'. One of these was

> *nazg*: the word for 'ring' in the Black Speech. This was devised to be a vocable as distinct in style and phonetic content from words of the same meaning in Elvish or in other real languages that are most familiar: English, Latin, Greek, etc. Though actual congruences (of form + sense) occur in unrelated real languages, and it is impossible in constructing imaginary languages from a limited number of component sounds to avoid such resemblances (if one tries to – I do not), it remains remarkable that *nasc* is the word for 'ring' in Gaelic (Irish: in Scottish usually written *nasg*). It also fits well in meaning, since it also means, and prob[ably] originally meant, a *bond*, and can be used for an 'obligation'. Nonetheless I only became aware of, or again aware, of its existence recently in looking for something in a Gaelic dictionary. I have no great liking at all for Gaelic from Old Irish downwards, as a language, but it is of course of great historical and philological interest, and I have at various times studied it. (With alas! very little success.) It is thus probable that *nazg* is actually derived from it, and this short hard and clear vocable, sticking out from what seems to me (an unloving alien) a mushy language, became lodged in this connexion in my linguistic memory. [*Letters*, pp. 384–5]

Gandalf's statement that the Nazgûl 'keep' the Nine Rings suggests that they physically hold them. But in Book I, Chapter 2 he tells Frodo that 'the Nine [Sauron] has gathered to himself' (p. 51, I: 61), and in *The Hunt for the Ring* it is said that the Nazgûl 'were entirely enslaved to their Nine Rings, which [Sauron] now himself held', so that the Ringwraiths 'were quite incapable of acting against his will' (*Unfinished Tales*, p. 343). In his draft letter to Eileen Elgar, September 1963, Tolkien wrote that Sauron through the Nine Rings '(which he held) had primary control of their [the Nazgûl's] wills' (*Letters*, p. 331).

250 (I: 263). The Three we know of – Indeed, two of the Three Rings are present at the Council, held by Elrond and Gandalf.

250 (I: 263): 'There is indeed a wide waste of time

250 (I: 263). between the River and the Mountain – That is, between the loss of the Ring by Isildur in the Anduin, and the finding of the Ring by Bilbo in Gollum's cave beneath the Misty Mountains.

250 (I: 263). And well is it that not until this year, this very summer, as it seems, did he learn the full truth. – Between Third Age 3009 and 3017 Gollum was captured by Sauron (*The Tale of Years*; varying accounts are given in *The Hunt for the Ring* in *Unfinished Tales*). Under torture Gollum revealed information about the Ring from which Sauron realized that it was the One, and learned that it had been stolen by 'Baggins' from the 'Shire'. Although Gollum had some idea of the location of the Shire, he led Sauron to believe that it was near the Gladden River. In 3017 Sauron released Gollum, hoping that he might lead the Dark Lord's spies to the Ring. Gollum evaded them, but was captured by Aragorn and taken as a prisoner to Thranduil; see further, note for p. 1090.

250 (I: 263–4): 'Some here will remember

250 (I: 263). many years ago I myself dared to pass the doors of the Necromancer in Dol Guldur – In fact, according to *The Tale of Years* Gandalf did so twice, in Third Age 2063 (after the Wise began to fear that the growing power in Dol Guldur was Sauron taking shape again) and again in 2850 ('Gandalf again enters Dol Guldur, and discovers that its master is indeed Sauron, who is gathering all the Rings and seeking for news of the One, and of Isildur's Heir. He finds Thráin and receives the key of Erebor', p. 1088, III: 369). In *The Hobbit*, Chapter 1, the Necromancer is mentioned by Gandalf as 'an enemy far beyond the powers of all the dwarves put together'. Later he is called a 'black sorcerer' in a 'dark tower', and serves (for the purposes of the story) as a reason for Gandalf to leave Bilbo and his companions to their own devices. In Chapter 19 it is said that Gandalf 'had been to a great council of the white wizards, masters of lore and good magic; and . . . they had at last driven the Necromancer from his dark hold in the south of Mirkwood'.

Strictly speaking, a *necromancer* is one who communicates with the dead, sometimes for the purpose of telling the future; and in a late philosophical work (*Of Death and the Severance of Fëa and Hröa*, published in *Morgoth's Ring*) concerning the spirit and bodily forms of Elves Tolkien suggests that Sauron and his followers attempted to enslave spirits of the dead or to use the dead to enslave living hosts or displace their rightful inhabitants. But Tolkien seems to have intended the word to be read in its more general sense, 'wizard, magician', if with an evil connotation.

Dol Guldur means 'hill of sorcery', from Sindarin *dol* 'head' (often applied to hills and mountains), *gûl* 'sorcery' + *dûr* 'dark'. See further, note for p. 352.

250 (I: 263). Saruman dissuaded us from open deeds against him – *The Tale of Years* indicates for Third Age 2851: 'The White Council meets. Gandalf urges an attack on Dol Guldur. Saruman overrules him.' To this is appended the note: 'It afterwards became clear that Saruman had then begun to desire to possess the One Ring himself, and he hoped that it might reveal itself, seeking its master, if Sauron were let be for a time' (p. 1088, III: 369).

250 (I: 263). the Council – The White Council.

250 (I: 263). that was in the very year of the finding of this Ring – That is, the finding of the Ring by Bilbo, in Third Age 2941.

250 (I: 263): 'But we were too late

250 (I: 263). Sauron . . . had long prepared against our stroke, governing Mordor from afar through Minas Morgul, where his Nine servants dwelt – According to *The Tale of Years* the Nazgûl gathered in Mordor in Third Age 1980 and besieged Minas Ithil in 2000. In 2002 was the 'fall of Minas Ithil, afterwards known as Minas Morgul'.

250 (I: 264). soon after came to the Dark Tower and openly declared himself – In Third Age 2951.

250 (I: 264). Then for the last time the Council met – In Third Age 2953.

251 (I: 264): 'That was seventeen years ago

251 (I: 264). That was seventeen years ago. – At the time of Bilbo's 'long-expected party', Third Age 3001 (S.R. 1401).

251 (I: 264–5): Then Gandalf told how they had explored

251 (I: 265). the fences of Mordor – 'The Mountains of Shadow' (*Index*).

252 (I: 265): 'So said Denethor

252 (I: 265). records that few even of the lore-masters now can read – In editions prior to 2004 this passage read: 'records that few now can read, even of the lore-masters'. It was belatedly emended according to an instruction Tolkien wrote on the galley proof of *The Fellowship of the Ring*, but which was overlooked by the typesetters.

252 (I: 265). For Isildur did not march away straight from the war – See further, *The Tradition of Isildur*, part of *Cirion and Eorl and the Friendship of Gondor and Rohan* in *Unfinished Tales*.

252–3 (I: 266): ***It was hot when I first took it***

252 (I: 266). ***glede*** – An archaic word meaning 'live coal', commonly spelt *gleed*.

253 (I: 266). ***it seemeth to shrink*** – Tolkien's use of archaic verb constructions (*seemeth*, *loseth*, *fadeth*, *saith*, *misseth*) suggests, to the reader of

Modern English (and relative to the Common Speech of the Third Age of Middle-earth), a document from a much earlier time.

253 (I: 266). *It is precious to me* – The use of the word 'precious' is significant and ominous, deliberately recalling Gollum's name for the Ring and Bilbo's use of the word in speaking of it in Book I, Chapter 1.

253 (I: 266–7): 'There is little need to tell of them'

253 (I: 266). the deadly flowers of Morgul Vale – In Book IV, Chapter 8, when Frodo, Sam, and Gollum are in the *Morgul Vale*, the ravine in which Minas Morgul stands, they see 'shadowy meads filled with pale white flowers. Luminous these were too, beautiful yet horrible of shape, like the demented forms in an uneasy dream; and they gave forth a faint sickening charnel-smell; an odour of rottenness filled the air' (p. 704, II: 313).

253 (I: 266). the skirts of the Dead Marshes – *Skirts* in this sense means 'edges'.

The *Dead Marshes* are 'wide stagnant marshes [south-east] of [the] Emyn Muil and [east] of Nindalf' (*Index*). In one text of *The Hunt for the Ring* it is said that after his release from Mordor 'Gollum soon disappeared into the Dead Marshes, where Sauron's emissaries could not or would not follow him' (*Unfinished Tales*, p. 342). According to *The Tale of Years*, Aragorn captured Gollum in the Dead Marshes in Third Age 3017.

254 (I: 267): 'And if that is not proof enough

254 (I: 267). *Ash nazg durbatulûk . . .* – In Appendix F Tolkien writes of the Black Speech that it was devised by Sauron for his servants, though it failed in that purpose. The harshness of the language reflects the brutality of those who used it, and is expressed by Tolkien through hard consonants and unattractive (to English ears) vowel sounds.

255 (I: 268): 'He is in prison, but no worse'

255 (I: 268). I do not doubt that he was allowed to leave Mordor on some evil errand – This is confirmed by Shagrat's comment in Book IV, Chapter 10 that Gollum has 'been here [Cirith Ungol] before. Came *out* of Lugbúrz [Barad-dûr] the first time, years ago, and we had word from High Up to let him pass' (p. 738, II: 348). In *The Hunt for the Ring* it is said that

> Gollum was captured in Mordor . . . and taken to Barad-dûr, and there questioned and tormented. When he had learned what he could from him, Sauron released him and sent him forth again. He did not trust Gollum. . . . But Sauron perceived the depth of Gollum's malice towards those that had 'robbed' him, and guessing that he would go in search of them to avenge himself, Sauron hoped that his spies would thus be led to the Ring. [*Unfinished Tales*, p. 337]

255 (I: 268): 'You were less tender to me'

255 (I: 268). his imprisonment in the deep places of the Elven-king's halls – During his journey through Mirkwood, as told in *The Hobbit*, Chapter 9.

255 (I: 268): 'Now come!' said Gandalf

255 (I: 268). all the grievances that stand between Elves and Dwarves – In *The Silmarillion* it is said that 'ever cool was the friendship between the Naugrim [Dwarves] and the Eldar, though much profit they had one of the other'. At first the Sindar, the Grey-elves, welcomed them for their skills with metal and stone; 'but the Naugrim gave their friendship more readily to the Noldor in after days than to any others of Elves and Men, because of their love and reverence for Aulë [the Vala who created the Dwarves]; and the gems of the Noldor they praised above all other wealth' (*The Silmarillion*, p. 92). But in later days the Dwarves lusted after the Silmaril in the Nauglamír, the Necklace of the Dwarves that had come into the possession of the Sindarin King Thingol of Doriath, whom they slew; and in the resulting war of vengeance many Elves and Dwarves were slain, 'and it has not been forgotten' (p. 234).

255–6 (I: 269): 'It was that very night of summer

256 (I: 269). the year of the Dragon's fall – Third Age 2941 (S.R. 1341).

256 (I: 269): 'At the end of June

256 (I: 269). At the end of June I was in the Shire, but a cloud of anxiety was on my mind, and I rode to the southern borders of the little land; for I had a foreboding of some danger, still hidden from me but drawing near. There messages reached me – This is not quite the same as the story in Book I, Chapter 3, where Gandalf told Frodo: 'I have heard something that has made me anxious and needs looking into'. See note for p. 67.

256 (I: 269). There messages reached me telling me of war and defeat in Gondor, and when I heard of the Black Shadow a chill smote my heart. – The *defeat* was Sauron's attack on Osgiliath on 20 June.

256 (I: 269). Radagast the Brown, who at one time dwelt at Rhosgobel – Christopher Tolkien reports that 'in a very late note on the names of the Istari Radagast is said to be a name deriving from the Men of the Vales of Anduin, "not now clearly interpretable"' (*Unfinished Tales*, p. 401, n. 4). One of many who has suggested a source for *Radagast*, Douglas A. Anderson notes in *The Annotated Hobbit* that 'Edward Gibbon's *The History of the Decline and Fall of the Roman Empire* . . . tells of a Gothic leader named Radagaisus who invaded Italy in the early years of the fifth century. Other sources, including the eleventh-century German historian Adam of Bremen, tell of a possible Slavic deity called *Redigast*' (2nd edn., p. 167).

Jacob Grimm in *Teutonic Mythology* refers several times to a Slavic deity, variously as *Radigast*, *Radegast*, and derives his name from '*rad* glad, *radost* joy'. Radagast's affinity for birds is reflected in his name as it was in Valinor, *Aiwendil*, perhaps from Quenya *aiwe* 'a small bird' + *-ndil* 'devoted to'.

Gandalf refers to Radagast in *The Hobbit*, Chapter 7 as 'my good cousin . . . who lives near the southern borders of Mirkwood', and Beorn comments that Radagast is 'not a bad fellow as wizards go'. In *The Hunt for the Ring* Radagast is called a 'kinsman' to Gandalf (see note for p. 257). *Kinsman* and *cousin* may mean only that Gandalf and Radagast are of the same race, of the Maiar.

In the same note on the Istari cited above, *Rhosgobel* is said to have been 'in the forest borders between the Carrock and the Old Forest Road' (*Unfinished Tales*, p. 401, n. 4). Its name derives from Sindarin *rhosc* 'brown' + *gobel* 'walled house or village "town"'. In his unfinished index Tolkien defines *Rhosgobel* as 'russet village or "town" (enclosure)'.

256 (I: 269). He is one of my order – See note for p. 48.

256 (I: 270): '"Gandalf!" he cried

256 (I: 270). uncouth – Odd, strange.

256–7 (I: 270): '"I have an urgent errand," he said

257 (I: 270). The Nine are abroad again. They have crossed the River secretly and are moving westward. – Gandalf's account will make it clear that his meeting with Radagast took place on the same day that he wrote to Frodo from Bree, i.e. Mid-year's Day, only twelve days after Sauron's attack on Osgiliath. (In the first edition of *The Lord of the Rings*, *The Tale of Years* placed their meeting three days earlier, on 29 June.) This raises some problems of chronology, of which Tolkien himself became aware when writing his accounts of *The Hunt for the Ring*. Marquette MSS 4/2/35, a mainly unpublished text trailing into illegibility, shows Tolkien working on a solution to the problem:

> On June 29th Radagast could not know this [that the Nine were abroad, etc.], if B[lack] R[ider]s did not cross the Anduin till June 20. Saruman had to discover it; tell Radagast; and Radagast had to look for Shire. It must have taken 14 days *at least*.
>
> Therefore all the story of BRs going North etc. and then coming to Isengard on [the] day of Gandalf's release must be remodelled [e.g. the story told in *Unfinished Tales*, pp. 338–9, and similar versions].
>
> Something of this sort. Sauron did *not* know where 'Shire' was. Gollum had been unclear on that point (perhaps deliberately: but in any case S[auron]'s natural assumption was that all the events and the 'thief' belonged like Gollum to Anduin Vale). Nonetheless S[auron]'s chief fears were directed towards Havens and Rivendell: he naturally suspects the Westlands.

The Nazgûl are ordered to steal over Anduin one by one and make enquiries. This is ordered soon after S[auron] learns that Gollum (who disappeared into the D[ead] Marshes) has been captured and is with Thranduil, and that *Gandalf has visited that realm.* **Say sometime early in April.*

At first the Nazgûl investigate Anduin's Vale . . . but can find no trace of Ring or 'Baggins' . . . some begin to investigate Rohan. . . . Sauron is already in communication with Saruman [*illegible*] Palantír; but has not yet mastered him. Yet he reads enough of his mind to suspect (a) that he covets the Ring for himself and (b) that he knows something about it. The Nazgûl are ordered to visit Saruman. Saruman is v[ery] frightened at S[auron]'s suspicion of himself and his knowledge of the Ring. Though he dislikes Gandalf intensely and is v[ery] jealous of him, he believes G[andalf] knows something vital about the Ring because the Nazgûl [?ask] of the *Shire* which has always been a great concern of Gandalf, and because his agents have discovered that it is extraord[inarily] closely guarded; also that Gandalf is now actually there since 12 April. He [Saruman] therefore thinks of getting his [Gandalf's] help. . . .

The Nazgûl, then, came to Isengard towards early? June. Saruman was helped at this point [by] g[ood] fortune. Radagast becomes aware that Nazgûl are abroad in Anduin Vale spreading panic and searching for 'Shire'. He becomes v[ery] alarmed and can think of nothing but to go and consult Saruman head of order of Wizards. He does so . . . not long after visit of the Nazgûl to Isengard. Saruman knows that Radagast is a kinsman of Gandalf's and wholly trusted by him: he uses him as messenger, and sends him off to the Shire. Radagast leaves Isengard about June 15th. . . .

Soon after Sauron wishing to distract attention from the Nazgûl attacks Osgiliath. The Witch-King . . . captures bridge and passes into Gondor. . . .

What happens between June 20 and escape of Gandalf which cannot be earlier than night of Sept. 16/17? [17/18 September in *The Tale of Years*] Some 86 days!

Radagast's words 'they are moving westward' would apply in the situation up to visit of Nazgûl to Isengard. The westward move must then be delayed. And the race of the B[lack] R[ider]s for Shire in September must be due to some new definite information obtained just before Gandalf's escape.

Several of the Nazgûl must remain in A[nduin] Vale. One or more actually direct the attack on Thranduil when Gollum escapes. Sauron thinks it vital to have him captured again and/or killed. 2/3 Nazgûl still prowl about Rohan and [?] in Dunland, and up towards Eregion. They are rather timid and ineffectual without [the] W[itch]-king. Also they will not cross Greyflood into 'enemy Elvish country' without his leadership or express command. The ?major force of N[azgûl] 5/6 are engaged in hunt in Anduin Vale and forest etc. for Gollum. . . .

When no news of Gollum can be found Nazgûl asks for new orders. Sauron has now more information. Belated Sept. 1 he has learned of the 'oracular words' and of Boromir's mission (July 4). How? The words became widely? known in Gondor and Rohan, and Boromir's [?departure] was also known. This is enough to make S[auron] suspect that the Wise know about the Ring, and that some tryst is arranged in Rivendell. His suspicions of Saruman are redoubled. He has caught S[aruman] again in palantír.

257 (I: 270–1): '"Stay a moment!" I said

257 (I: 270). Orthanc – See note for p. 258.

258 (I: 271): 'However, I wrote a message to Frodo

258 (I: 271). Gap of Rohan – 'The opening (about twenty miles wide) between the last end of the Misty Mountains and the north-thrust spur of the White Mountains' (*Index*).

258 (I: 271). Ered Nimrais – Sindarin, 'translated' in the text 'White Mountains'.

258 (I: 271). But Isengard is a circle of sheer rocks that enclose a valley as with a wall, and in the midst of that valley is a tower of stone called Orthanc. It was not made by Saruman, but by the Men of Númenor long ago – *Isengard*, Tolkien writes in *Nomenclature*, is intended to represent a 'translation' into the Common Speech of Sindarin *Angrenost*, but 'made at so early a date that at the period of the tale' it 'had become archaic in form' and its original meaning was obscured. '*Isen* is an old variant form in English of *iron*; *gard* a Germanic word meaning "an enclosure", especially one round a dwelling, or group of buildings. . . . *Isengard* "the iron-court" was so called because of the great hardness of the stone in that place and especially in the central tower.' For *gard*, see further, note for p. 2.

In his unfinished index Tolkien notes '*Orthanc* "forked-height", Númenórean tower in the Circle of Isengard'. There also, and in the published text, it is said that *Orthanc* has a twofold meaning: in Sindarin it signifies 'Mount Fang', but in the language of Rohan 'the Cunning Mind'. Old English *orþanc* as an noun means 'original, inborn thought' or 'a skilful contrivance or work, artifice, device, design', and as an adjective 'cunning, skilful'.

It took Tolkien some time to decide on the exact form and shape of the tower of Orthanc. In the process, he made a series of drawings, some also showing the circle of Isengard: see *Artist and Illustrator*, pp. 169–71, figs. 162–4; *The Treason of Isengard*, frontispiece; *The War of the Ring*, pp. 31–5, with illustrations on pp. 33–4; and *Sauron Defeated*, p. 137, with illustrations on pp. 138–9. Isengard and Orthanc are described in detail in Book III, Chapters 8–10.

258 (I: 271): 'But I rode to the foot of Orthanc

258 (I: 271). He wore a ring on his finger. – Later in this chapter, in his talk with Gandalf, Saruman calls himself 'Saruman Ring-maker' (p. 259, I: 272). Nothing more is said of this ring, but it seems clear that Saruman's study of the Elven-rings has led him to try to make rings of power himself. See also note for p. xxiv.

258 (I: 271): '"Yes, I have come"

258 (I: 271). Saruman the White – In *The Lord of the Rings* only three Wizards are identified by name and colour, but in Appendix B it is said that five came to Middle-earth. In Tolkien's account of the Istari written in 1954 it is said that 'the first to come [Saruman] . . . was clad in white. . . . Others there were also: two clad in sea-blue [the Ithryn Luin, 'Blue Wizards'], and one in earthen brown [Radagast]; and last came one [Gandalf] who seemed least, less tall than the others, and in looks more aged, grey-haired and grey-clad' (*The Istari* in *Unfinished Tales*, p. 389). Tolkien seems to have forgotten this, however, when he replied to a query about the colours of the Wizards not named in *The Lord of the Rings*:

> I have not named the colours, because I do not know them. I doubt if they had distinctive colours. Distinction was only required in the case of the three who remained in the relatively small area of the North-west. . . . I really do not know anything clearly about the other two – since they do not concern the history of the N.W. [North-west]. I think they went as emissaries to distant regions, East and South, far out of Númenórean range: missionaries to 'enemy-occupied' lands, as it were. What success they had I do not know; but I fear they failed, as Saruman did, though doubtless in different ways; and I suspect they were founders or beginners of secret cults and 'magic' traditions that outlasted the fall of Sauron. [letter to Rhona Beare, 14 October 1958, *Letters*, p. 280]

In a hasty sketch by Tolkien of a council of the Valar at which it was decided to send the Istari to Middle-earth, the names in Valinor of the Blue Wizards are given as 'Alatar and Pallando' (*Unfinished Tales*, p. 394).

258–9 (I: 272): '"Radagast the Brown!" laughed Saruman

258 (I: 272). Radagast the Fool! Yet he had just the wit to play the part that I set him. – Late in life Tolkien looked again at the postcard of the Madlener pointing *Der Berggeist*, which he said had influenced his conception of Gandalf (but see note for pp. 24–5), and it inspired him to consider and compare Gandalf, Radagast, and Saruman:

> On a rock beneath a pine-tree is seated a small but broad old man with a wide brimmed round hat and a long cloak talking to a white fawn that is nuzzling his upturned hands. He has a humorous but at the

> same time compassionate expression – his mouth is visible and smiling, because he has a white beard but no hair on his upper lip. The scene is a wooded glade (pine, fir, and birch) beside a rivulet with a glimpse of mountain peaks in the distance. This [*sic*] an owl and four other smaller birds looking from branches of the trees. Gandalf or Radagast? Gandalf. He was the friend and confidant of all living creatures of good will [compare, Book II, Chapter 7, p. 359, I: 375: 'With Dwarf and Hobbit, Elves and Men, / with mortal and immortal folk, / with bird on bough and beast in den, / in their own secret tongues he spoke']. He differed from Radagast and Saruman in that he never turned aside from his appointed mission ('I was the Enemy of Sauron' [Book VI, Chapter 5, p. 971, III: 249]) and was unsparing of himself. Radagast was fond of beasts and birds, and found them easier to deal with; he did not become proud and domineering, but neglectful and easygoing, and he had very little to do with Elves or Men although obviously resistance to Sauron had to be sought chiefly in their cooperation. But since he remained of good will (though he had not much courage), his work in fact helped Gandalf at crucial moments. Saruman is sufficiently revealed in the story. No doubt he started with good will, and with higher authority and superior powers. But he was impatient with the sloth, stupidity, and obstinate free wills of the peoples he was sent to advise and encourage. It would seem that from the beginning he adopted a visible form of commanding stature and noble countenance. Unlike Gandalf, who in contrast would appear stumpy, and in certain respects comic or grotesque in looks and in manner. His pride grew and he became pitiless, valuing things inanimate or living and all persons high or lowly simply as tools for his designs, to be deceived or misdirected, when simple force was not available.

In a variant version of the last part of this text, Tolkien wrote that 'it is clear that Gandalf (with greater insight and compassion) had in fact more knowledge of birds and beasts than Radagast, and was regarded by them with more respect and affection'; and he added to his description of Saruman that 'he lost all sense of humour (always strong in Gandalf)' (Tolkien Papers, Bodleian Library, Oxford).

Der Berggeist is reproduced in *The Annotated Hobbit*, 2nd edn., colour plate between pp. 178 and 179.

259 (I: 272–3): '"And listen, Gandalf, my old friend and helper!"

259 (I: 272). the Wise, such as you and I, may with patience come at last to direct its courses, to control it – Tom Shippey comments on this:

> The idea of anyone, however wise, persuading Sauron, would sound simply silly if it were said in so many words. No sillier, though, than the repeated conviction of many British intellectuals before and after this time that they could somehow get along with Stalin, or with Hitler.

> Saruman, indeed, talks exactly like too many politicians. It is impossible to work out exactly what he means because of the abstract nature of his speech; in the end it is doubtful if he understands it himself. His message is in any case one of compromise and calculation. [*J.R.R. Tolkien: Author of the Century*, p. 75]

He describes Saruman as 'the most contemporary figure in Middle-earth, both politically and linguistically. He is on the road to "doublethink" (which Orwell was to invent, or describe [in *Nineteen-Eighty-Four*], at almost exactly the same time' (p. 76).

259 (I: 272). We can bide our time, we can keep our thoughts in our hearts, deploring maybe evils done by the way, but approving the high and ultimate purpose: Knowledge, Rule, Order; all the things that we have so far striven in vain to accomplish, hindered rather than helped by our weak or idle friends. There need not be, there would not be, any real change in our designs, only in our means. – In *The Road to Middle-earth* Tom Shippey comments:

> What Saruman says encapsulates many of the things the modern world has learned to dread most: the ditching of allies, the subordination of means to end, the 'conscious acceptance of guilt in the necessary murder'. But the way he puts it is significant too. No other character in Middle-earth has Saruman's trick of balancing phrases against each other so that incompatibles are resolved, and none comes out with words as empty as "deploring", "ultimate", worst of all "real".' [2nd edn., p. 108]

259–60 (I: 273): 'He came and laid his long hand

260 (I: 273). I have many eyes in my service, and I believe that you know where this precious thing now lies. Is it not so? Or why do the Nine ask for the Shire, and what is your business there? – At the same time that he was working out background details of Sauron's hunt for the Ring (in the second half of 1954 and in early 1955) Tolkien also gave his attention to the history of relations between Saruman and Gandalf in the years preceding Gandalf's identification of the One Ring. 'Saruman soon became jealous of Gandalf, and this rivalry turned at last to hatred, the deeper for being concealed, and the more bitter in that Saruman knew in his heart that the Grey Wanderer had the greater strength, and the greater influence upon the dwellers in Middle-earth, even though he hid his power and desired neither fear nor reverence' (*Unfinished Tales*, p. 349). Saruman secretly watched Gandalf, and seeing that

> Gandalf thought the Shire worth visiting, Saruman himself visited it, but disguised and in utmost secrecy, until he had explored and noted all its ways and lands, and thought then he had learned all there was to know of it. And even when it seemed to him no longer wise or profitable

> to go thither, he still had spies and servants that went in or kept an eye upon its borders. For he was still suspicious. He was himself so far fallen that he believed all others of the Council had each their deep and far-reaching policies for their own enhancement, to which all that they did must in some way refer. So when long after he learned something of the finding of Gollum's Ring by the Halfling, he could believe only that Gandalf had known of this all the time; and this was his greatest grievance, since all that concerned the Rings he deemed his especial province. That Gandalf's mistrust of him was merited and just in no way lessened his anger. [*The Hunt for the Ring* in *Unfinished Tales*, p. 349]

261 (I: 275): 'So it was that when summer waned

261 (I: 275). when summer waned, there came a night of moon – *The Tale of Years* says for 18 September 1418: 'Gandalf escapes from Orthanc in the early hours'. An account of Gandalf's escape among the *Hunt for the Ring* papers (Marquette MSS 4/2/33; see further, note for p. 262) agrees that this was on the night of 17/18 September, with the moon six days past the full (11/12 September).

261 (I: 275). Gwaihir the Windlord, swiftest of the Great Eagles – *Gwaihir* is derived from Sindarin *gwai* 'wind' + *hîr* 'lord'. In *The Silmarillion* 'spirits in the shape of hawks and eagles flew ever to and from' Manwë's halls upon Taniquetil in Valinor, and 'brought word to him of well nigh all that passed in Arda' (p. 40). Among other deeds in the First Age they kept watch on Thangorodrim, rescued Beren and Lúthien, attacked orcs who waylaid refugees from Gondolin, and led by Eärendil destroyed the winged dragons released by Morgoth in the Great Battle. In *The Hobbit* eagles rescue Gandalf, Bilbo, and the dwarves from wargs and orcs, and take part in the Battle of Five Armies. (See also note for p. 948.)

261–2 (I: 275): '"Then I will bear you to Edoras

261 (I: 275). Edoras – '*Edoras* "the courts", name in the Mark-speech of the royal town of Rohan on the N[orth] edge of the White Mts' (*Index*). The word is derived from Old English *edor, eodor* 'enclosure, dwelling, house', plural *edoras.*

261 (I: 275). Rohan – 'Form in Gondor of the Elvish name *Rochan* "Horse-country" (*roch* "a horse"), a wide region, formerly northern part of Gondor (and then called *Calenardon* [*sic*])' (*Index*). In his draft letter to Mr Rang, August 1967, Tolkien said that the name *Rohan*, 'stated to be Elvish', was not associated

> with anything Germanic; still less with the only remotely similar O[ld] N[orse] *rann* 'house', which is incidentally not at all appropriate to a still partly mobile and nomadic people of horse-breeders! ... *Rohan*

> . . . is derived from Elvish **rokkō* 'swift horse for riding' (Q[uenya] *rokko*, S[indarin] *roch*) + a suffix frequent in names of lands. . . .
>
> *Rohan* is a famous name, from Brittany, borne by an ancient proud and powerful family. I was aware of this, and liked its shape; but I had also (long before) invented the Elvish horse-word and saw how Rohan could be accommodated to the linguistic situation as a late Sindarin name of the Mark. . . . Nothing in the history of Brittany will throw any light on the Eorlingas. Incidentally the ending *-and* (*an*), *-end* (*en*) in land-names no doubt owes something to such (romantic and other) names as *Broceliand(e)*, but is perfectly in keeping with an already devised structure of primitive (common) Elvish . . . , or it would not have been used. [*Letters*, pp. 382, 383]

Rohan was the name in Gondor for the country which its own people called the Mark; and they called themselves *Rohirrim*. Tolkien comments on these names in a lengthy note to *Cirion and Eorl and the Friendship of Gondor and Rohan*:

> Their proper form was *Rochand* and *Rochir-rim*, and they were spelt as *Rochand*, or *Rochan*, and *Rochirrim* in the records of Gondor. They contain Sindarin *roch* 'horse', translating the *éo-* in *Éothéod* and in many personal names of the Rohirrim. In *Rochand* the Sindarin ending *-nd* (*-and*, *-end*, *-ond*) was added; it was commonly used in the names of regions or countries, but the *-d* was usually dropped in speech, especially in long names. . . . *Rochirrim* was modelled on *éo-herë*, the term used by the Éothéod for the full muster of their cavalry in time of war; it was made from *roch* + Sindarin *hîr* 'lord, master (entirely unconnected with [the Anglo-Saxon word] *herë*). In the names of peoples Sindarin *rim* 'great number, host' . . . was commonly used to form collective plurals. . . . The language of the Rohirrim contained the sound here represented by *ch* (a back spirant as *ch* in Welsh), and, though it was infrequent in the middle of words between vowels, it presented them with no difficulty. But the Common Speech did not possess it, and in pronouncing Sindarin (in which it was very frequent) the people of Gondor, unless learned, represented it by *h* in the middle of words and by *k* at the end of them (where it was most forcibly pronounced in correct Sindarin). Thus arose the names *Rohan* and *Rohirrim* as used in *The Lord of the Rings*. [*Unfinished Tales*, pp. 318–19, n. 49]

262 (I: 275). in the Riddermark of Rohan – In his unfinished index Tolkien equates *the Riddermark* with 'the Mark', 'name among the Rohirrim for their own country of Rohan; also the *Mark of Rohan*'. The *1966 Index* includes the entry 'Riddermark (Riddena-mearc), *land of the knights*, name in Rohan, of Rohan'. Eorl, to whom Gondor granted the lands later known as Rohan, 'took the title of King of the Mark of the Riders. . . . The term

Mark signified a borderland, especially one serving as a defence of the inner lands of a realm' (*Cirion and Eorl and the Friendship of Gondor and Rohan* in *Unfinished Tales*, p. 306). Tom Shippey comments in *The Road to Middle-earth* that

> there is no English county called 'the Mark', but the Anglo-Saxon kingdom which included both Tolkien's home-town Birmingham and his *alma mater* Oxford was 'Mercia' – a Latinism. . . . However the West Saxons called their neighbours the *Mierce*, clearly a derivation (by "i-mutation") from *Mearc*; the 'Mercians" own pronunciation of that would certainly have been the 'Mark', and that was no doubt once the everyday term for central England. [2nd edn., p. 111]

262 (I: 275). the Rohirrim, the Horse-lords – On 25 April 1954 Tolkien wrote to Naomi Mitchison: '*Rohir-rim* is the Elvish (Gondorian) name for the people that called themselves Riders of the Mark or Eorlingas. . . . The *Rohirrim* is derived from *roch* (Q[uenya] *rokko*) horse, and the Elvish stem *kher-* "possess"; whence Sindarin *Rochir* "horse-lord", and *Rochir-rim* [with Sindarin *rim* "host"] "the host of the Horse-lords"' (*Letters*, p. 178). See also the note for *Rohan*, above.

262 (I: 275): 'He set me down in the land of Rohan

262 (I: 275). The rest must be brief – Marquette MSS 4/2/33, probably the latest manuscript among the *Hunt for the Ring* papers (marked 'official & final'), gives the following account of Gandalf's escape to Rohan, with slight differences from *The Tale of Years*:

> Gandalf escapes night of 17/18. Full Moon 6 days waned, but bright because the weather after long cloud has become clear. Gandalf cannot descend on an Eagle before the Gates of Edoras, and in any case has to avoid the pursuit of Saruman. He is set down therefore by Gwaihir in the foothills of the White Mts. at dawn on Sept[ember] 18 (west of Edoras), and does not come to Edoras until Sept 19 – in a beggarly guise on foot. He cannot get an audience with Théoden [the king], and is treated as a beggar at the doors. It is not until Sept 20 that his persistence (and growing anger which alarms the doorwards) gains him entrance to Théoden warning him against Saruman. Wormtongue [secretly in Saruman's service, and with great influence over the king] is absent for some reason and Théodred [the king's son] is more favourable to Gandalf; so Théoden is troubled but will not make up his mind. He says he will speak of it again next day. But next day 21 [September] Wormtongue reappears. It was really for him that Théoden waited (since he has become enthralled by his counsel). Wormtongue now opposes Gandalf as Théoden bids him begone next morning: it then being late in the day. (W'tongue (as G. guesses or knows) sends off a messenger to Isengard that night. But the messenger even with utmost

haste does not reach Saruman until late on 24 [September]. It is about 250 miles from Edoras to Isengard.)

Gandalf says that this is ill-treatment which Théoden will rue. He does not understand the urgency of the times. He mentions the dreadful rumours of the passage of the Black Riders which have terrified all Rohan. Now said Gandalf if no one else dare oppose these evil things, I dare. But not on foot. One might look for aid in such business from a great king, lord of horses.

Then Théoden rashly exclaims: why take any horse you wish – and begone! This is much to dislike of W'tongue but Théoden is reluctant to take back his word, and Théodred opposes W'tongue, saying that a king cannot do so even to a beggar, but that for his part he thinks more honour and heed should be paid to Gandalf Greyhame.

So on 22 [September] Gandalf leaves Edoras and goes to the horse-sheds. (They are some way from Edoras. Gandalf does not get there until evening?) There he sees Shadowfax, and decides to have him alone. S'fax is wild wary and unwilling, and walks away whenever Gandalf approaches. It is not till late on 22 that S'fax will allow Gandalf to come up and speak to him; and not until Sept 23rd that he is tamed and will allow Gandalf to ride off. Gandalf sets off 6 pm 23rd of September.

The main chronological difference between this account and *The Tale of Years* is that in the latter Théoden dismisses Gandalf on 20 September, Gandalf takes longer to tame Shadowfax, but still sets off on the 23rd.

262 (I: 275–6): 'Not this at least

262 (I: 275). Not this at least . . . that they will buy their lives with their horses – Boromir judges the Rohirrim correctly. When, in Book III, Chapter 2 Aragorn asks Éomer about the rumour, Éomer says that Rohan does not pay tribute to Sauron 'though it comes to my ears that that lie has been told. Some years ago the Lord of the Black Land wished to purchase horses of us at great price, but we refused him, for he puts beasts to evil use. Then he sent plundering Orcs, and they carry off what they can, choosing always the black horses: few of these are now left' (p. 436, II: 39).

262 (I: 276): 'True indeed!' said Gandalf

262 (I: 276). Shadowfax – In *Nomenclature* Tolkien writes that *Shadowfax* 'is an anglicized form of Rohan (= Old English) *Sceadu-fæx* "having shadow-grey mane (and coat)". (It does not actually occur in Old English.) . . . *Fax* "hair" is now obsolete in English, except in the name *Fairfax* (no longer understood).'

262 (I: 276). Never before had any man mounted him – As first published this passage read: 'Never before had any man bestrode him'. It was revised in the second edition (1965). In an interview with Denys Gueroult of the

BBC early in 1965 Tolkien regretted that he, a Professor of English Language and Literature, had made errors in grammar in *The Lord of the Rings*, such as the use of *bestrode* as the past participle of *bestride*.

262–3 (I: 276): 'But fear grew in me as I rode

262–3 (I: 276). Ever as I came north I heard tidings of the Riders, and though I gained on them day by day, they were ever before me. . . . I came to Hobbiton and Frodo had gone – Marquette MSS 4/2/33 (*The Hunt for the Ring*, partly published in *Unfinished Tales*) describes the Black Riders' arrival at Isengard while Gandalf is still a prisoner:

> Saruman is terrified and desperate. The full horror of service to Mordor is perceived by him. He suddenly resolves to yield to Gandalf, and beg for his pardon & help. Temporizing at the gate, he admits he has Gandalf within, and says he will go and try to discover what he knows. If that is unavailing he will deliver Gandalf to them.
>
> Saruman then hastens to Orthanc. He goes to the summit – and finds Gandalf gone! Away south against the setting moon he sees a great Eagle apparently making for Edoras. Now his case is worse. If Gandalf has escaped there is still a real chance that Sauron will *not* get the Ring, and will be defeated. In his heart Saruman recognizes the great power and the strange 'good fortune' (we might say divine blessing and succour) that go with Gandalf. But now he is left alone to deal with the Dreadful Nine. His mood changes and his pride reasserts itself in anger at Gandalf's escape from impenetrable Isengard, and in furious jealousy.
>
> He goes to the Gate and says (lying) that he made Gandalf confess. He does not admit that this is his own knowledge, not being aware of how much Sauron knew of his mind and heart! 'I will report this myself to the Lord of Barad-dûr' he said loftily, 'to whom I speak from afar on great matters that concern us. But all that you need to know on the mission that he has given you is where "the Shire" lies. That, he says, is north-west from here, some 600 miles, on the borders of the sea-ward Elvish country'.

The Riders leave and move in haste to the Fords of Isen. (This agrees with *The Tale of Years*, which says that the Black Riders crossed the Isen on the same day that Gandalf escaped. See further, notes for p. 155.)

According to Marquette MSS 4/2/33, Gandalf himself

> starts from some point about 20 miles east of Edoras – S'fax [Shadowfax] has led him a good way, before being tamed. This would be about 620 miles to Sarn Ford, and S[arn] F[ord] was about 100 miles direct to Hobbiton. His great ride from 6 p.m. Sept 23 to 6 p.m Sept 28 when at latest he must have reached the Shire at Sarn Ford. . . . In that time G[andalf] covered 620 miles. . . .
>
> Start 6 p.m. 23 [September]. Rode through night (needing secrecy

until far from Isengard) Gandalf at [? this point] would be [?] Sept 24 would be just approaching the Fords of Isen. (Cross Isen Sept 24 morning 7 a.m.) He would probably push on and ride further west near Dol Baran. (Gandalf probably rode with frequent short halts; and actually rested for 8 hours. His average for the 16 hours going was not therefore very quick @ 120 m[iles] p[er] day, but one has to allow for 3 halts so that riding time was probably only 12 hours, and for difficulties of route – places where only a walking pace was possible, river crossings, detours for fen &c. So average even for S'fax was 10 m.p.h. [miles per hour])

He would reach Dol Baran another 30 miles on, about 9 a.m. Sept 24. He would start again about 5 p.m. At 9 a.m. Sept 25 he would be 145 miles on into Enedwaith (or 170 from Tharbad). He would go on again after 5 p.m. At 9 a.m. Sept 26 he would be 265 miles on in Enedwaith.

Start again 5 p.m. Cross Greyflood (Tharbad) 1 a.m. 27 [September]. At 9 a.m. Sept. 27th he would have passed Tharbad by 60 miles and be 90 miles from Sarn Ford. Go on at 5 p.m. He would reach Sarn Ford at about 2 a.m. 28 [September]. Aware of [?] of B. Rs [Black Riders] (he would meet Rangers no doubt who gave him the information cited Text I 276 [i.e. "I heard tidings . . ."]) would cross into Shire and [?maybe] rest while at [?Sarn Ford]. He came to Hobbiton some time during Sept 29.

263 (I: 277): '"Ass! Fool! Thrice worthy and beloved Barliman!"

263 (I: 277). Midsummer – In earlier editions of *The Lord of the Rings* this word was spelt variously *midsummer* and *Midsummer* (as well as *mid-summer*, which seems to have been an enduring typographical error). In the 2004 edition it was regularized as capitalized *Midsummer*, according to Tolkien's clear preference.

264 (I: 278): 'I reached here at last

264 (I: 278). It took me nearly fifteen days from Weathertop. . . . But so it was that I came to Rivendell only two days before the Ring. – In editions prior to 2004 this passage read: 'It took me nearly fourteen days from Weathertop. . . . But so it was that I came to Rivendell only three days before the Ring.' The narrative, *The Tale of Years*, and various unpublished time-schemes by Tolkien agree that Gandalf left Weathertop at dawn on 4 October, after being attacked by Ringwraiths during the night of 3/4 October, and that Frodo arrived at Rivendell on 20 October. But Gandalf's statement that he came to Rivendell only *three* days before the Ring does not agree with *The Tale of Years*, where he is said to have arrived on the *18th*, only *two* days before Frodo. One or the other must be wrong. Since various time-schemes also place Gandalf's arrival on 18 October, it seemed certain that the narrative was at fault, and an emendation of 'three' to 'two' was indicated. And although it would just be possible for 'nearly fourteen days' to stand if Gandalf arrived in the early hours of 18 October, well before dawn, since that expression of time was obviously dependent on 'three days', it too was emended in the 2004 edition.

264 (I: 278). and Shadowfax departed. I sent him back to his master – See note for p. 435.

265 (I: 278): 'This is grievous news

265 (I: 278). But such falls and betrayals ... have happened before – There are no precise parallels to Saruman's betrayal in Tolkien's writings. Celebrimbor was deceived by Sauron, but rejected him as soon as he realized his purposes. In the First Age some of the Swarthy Men from the East proved faithless to the Noldor and changed sides during the Battle of Unnumbered Tears.

265 (I: 278). I have known few hobbits, save Bilbo here; and it seems to me that he is perhaps not so alone and singular as I had thought him. – On 15 December 1965 Tolkien wrote to Rayner Unwin:

> Hobbits were a breed of which the chief physical mark was their stature; and the chief characteristic of their temper was the almost total eradication of any dormant 'spark', only about one per mil had any trace of it. Bilbo was especially selected by the authority and insight of Gandalf as *abnormal*: he had a good share of hobbit virtues: shrewd sense, generosity, patience, and fortitude, also a strong 'spark' yet unkindled. The story [*The Hobbit*] and its sequel are not about 'types' or the cure of bourgeois smugness by wider experience, but about the achievements of specially graced and gifted individuals. I would say, if saying such things did not spoil what it tries to make explicit, 'by ordained individuals, inspired and guided by an Emissary to ends beyond their individual education and enlargement'. This is clear in *The Lord of the Rings*; but it is present, if veiled, in *The Hobbit* from the beginning, and is alluded to in Gandalf's last words ['You don't really suppose, do you, that all your adventures and escapes were managed by mere luck, just for your sole benefit?']. [*Letters*, p. 365]

265 (I: 278): 'The Barrow-wights

265 (I: 278). of the Old Forest many tales have been told: all that now remains is but an outlier of its northern march – Most of the old forests west of the Misty Mountains were devastated by the Númenóreans, who felled trees for timber for their ships, or were burned by raiders of Sauron: see *Unfinished Tales*, pp. 261–3. For centuries in our own history the forests of Europe and North America were heavily cut for shipbuilding and to fuel ironworks.

An *outlier* is an outlying portion of something detached from its main body.

265 (I: 278). time was when a squirrel could go from tree to tree from what is now the Shire to Dunland west of Isengard – In their edition of *Sir Gawain and the Green Knight* (1925) Tolkien and E.V. Gordon cite an old saying: 'From Blacon Point to Helbree / A squirrel may leap from tree to tree' (p. 94).

265 (I: 278). Iarwain Ben-Adar . . . Forn . . . Orald – See note for p. 119.

267 (I: 280): 'None here can do so'

267 (I: 280). There lies our hope, if hope it be. – *Hope* is one of the three Christian virtues and an important theme in *The Lord of the Rings*, mentioned often. Aragorn's childhood name was *Estel*, Sindarin 'hope'. Many of the characters in the book struggle on with little hope of success or victory, but do not abandon hope: that route leads to despair, and in Denethor's case to suicide. Tolkien commented in a letter written to his son Christopher on 7–8 November 1944: 'in the last chapter of The Ring that I have yet written I hope you'll note, when you receive it . . . that Frodo's face goes livid and convinces Sam that he's dead, just when Sam gives up *hope*' (*Letters*, p. 101).

267 (I: 280). We must send the Ring to the Fire. – To the Cracks of Doom in the volcano Orodruin, as Gandalf explains to Frodo in Book I, Chapter 2.

267 (I: 280–1): 'I do not understand

267 (I: 280–1). Why should we not think that the Great Ring has come into our hands to serve us in the very hour of need? Wielding it the Free Lords of the Free may surely defeat the Enemy. – Even though Boromir accedes to Elrond's authority in this matter, he does not accept his reasoning ('Boromir looked at them doubtfully', this page). This paragraph is an early hint of his desire to possess the Ring, even though for a noble purpose.

267 (I: 281): 'Alas, no,' said Elrond

267 (I: 281). Its strength . . . is too great for anyone to wield at will, save only those who have already a great power of their own. But for them it holds a deadlier peril. The very desire of it corrupts the heart. – Anne C. Petty comments in *Tolkien in the Land of Heroes* (2003) that

> someone of extraordinary power might be able to bend the Ring to his or her own will, usurping the original owner's power. However, when worn by someone with the intent to wield power, whether for good or evil, the Ruling Ring will exert the nature of its maker, Sauron. This is precisely why the powerful characters of light such as Gandalf and Galadriel refuse it.
>
> By this we realize that as a talisman of power, the Ring is both actual and symbolic. It represents what happens when concentrated power

> (especially in a technological sense) takes our imagination in frightening directions. The inference to weapons and industries of war in our technological age is applicable, although not allegorical. [p. 155]

In *The Road to Middle-earth* Tom Shippey argues that the maxim 'Power corrupts, and absolute power corrupts absolutely' – a 'distinctly modern' opinion, first given expression by Lord Acton in 1887 – 'is the core of *The Lord of the Rings*', and is reflected in all that is said about the evil effects of the Ring on its bearers, regardless of their strength or good purpose (2nd edn., p. 124).

267 (I: 281). For nothing is evil in the beginning. Even Sauron was not so. – In September 1954 Tolkien wrote in his draft letter to Peter Hastings that

> Sauron was of course not 'evil' in origin. He was a 'spirit' corrupted by the Prime Dark Lord (the Prime sub-creative Rebel) Morgoth. He was given an opportunity of repentance, when Morgoth was overcome, but could not face the humiliation of recantation, and suing for pardon; and so his temporary turn to good and 'benevolence' ended in a greater relapse, until he became the main representative of Evil of later ages. But at the beginning of the Second Age he was still beautiful to look at, or could still assume a beautiful visible shape – and was not indeed wholly evil, not unless all 'reformers' who want to hurry up with 'reconstruction' and 'reorganization' are wholly evil, even before pride and the lust to exert their will eat them up. [*Letters*, p. 190]

And in notes he made in ?1956 on W.H. Auden's review of *The Return of the King* Tolkien states:

> In my story I do not deal in Absolute Evil. I do not think there is such a thing, since that is Zero. I do not think at any rate any 'rational being' is wholly evil. Satan fell. . . . In my story Sauron represents as near an approach to the wholly evil will as is possible. He had gone the way of all tyrants: beginning well, at least on the level that while desiring to order all things according to his own wisdom he still at first considered the (economic) well-being of other inhabitants of the Earth. But he went further than human tyrants in pride and the lust for domination, being in origin an immortal (angelic) spirit. In *The Lord of the Rings* the conflict is not basically about 'freedom', though that is naturally involved. It is about God, and His sole right to divine honour. The Eldar and the Númenóreans believed in The One, the true God, and held worship of any other person an abomination. Sauron desired to be a God-King, and was held to be this by his servants. . . . [*Letters*, p. 243]

Brian Rosebury comments in *Tolkien: A Cultural Phenomenon* (2003) that

> any analysis of the aesthetic power of *The Lord of the Rings* needs to take into account the fact that its values are organised around a moral conflict: Sauron's despotism is not only to be 'undesired', it is to be undesired in the specific sense of being perceived as categorically morally bad. Nothing could be more false, however, than the notion that *The Lord of the Rings* represents a deterministic, or Manichean, universe of struggle between the innately and unalterably good and the innately and unalterably evil. On the contrary . . . the imagined world is underpinned by an optimistic, and occasionally explicit theology of quite a different kind. Nothing is evil in the beginning'. . . . Though God is not referred to in *The Lord of the Rings* (except fleetingly in an Appendix [A, p. 1037, III: 317]) . . . , and though its world is pre-Christian, there is no doubt that we are in an Augustinian universe, in which all Creation is good, and evil is conceived in terms of freely-chosen negation, of a wilful abdication from the original state of created perfection. [p. 35]

267–8 (I: 281): Boromir looked at them doubtfully

268 (I: 281). Mayhap the Sword-that-was-Broken may still stem the tide – if the hand that wields it has inherited not an heirloom only, but the sinews of the Kings of Men. – In *Master of Middle-earth*, after analyzing the part played by Aragorn at the Council, and in particular his handling of Boromir, Paul H. Kocher concludes:

> By a combination of tact and boldness Aragorn has now won from Boromir everything he wants: recognition that the sword is Elendil's and that Aragorn is its rightful owner by unbroken succession, together with an invitation to accompany him back to Gondor without delay. Of course, Boromir is not yet yielding any specific admissions on the question of the succession. It is hard to visualize a man so dedicated to power eventually surrendering his position of advantage, as Faramir does afterward. What will happen when the two men reach Minas Tirith will happen. But Aragorn has already made a great stride towards his goal. [pp. 142–3]

And Tom Shippey comments that

> Aragorn and Boromir strike sparks off each other through their ways of speech as well as their claims, Aragorn's language deceptively modern, even easy-going on occasion, but with greater range than Boromir's slightly wooden magniloquence. There is even significance in Aragorn letting his rival have the last word in their debate, with a clause which is perfectly in line with modern speech – 'we will put it to the test one day' – but also relates easily to the vaunts of ancient heroes, like Ælfwine's *nú mæg cunnian hwá céne sý* in *The Battle of Maldon*, 'now who is bold can be put to the test'. [*The Road to Middle-earth*, 2nd edn., p. 110]

268 (I: 281–2): 'Balin will find no ring

268 (I: 281–2). Thrór gave it to Thráin his son, but not Thráin to Thorin. It was taken with torment from Thráin in the dungeons of Dol Guldur. – In Appendix A it is said that 'the Dwarves of Durin's folk' believed this ring

> to be the first of the Seven that was forged, and they say that it was given to the King of Khazad-dûm, Durin III, by the Elven-smiths themselves and not by Sauron, thought doubtless his evil power was on it, since he had aided in the forging of all the Seven. But the possessors of the Ring did not display it or speak of it, and they seldom surrendered it until near death, so that others did not know for certain where it was bestowed. . . .
>
> None the less it may well be as the Dwarves now believe, that Sauron by his arts had discovered who had this Ring, the last to remain free, and that the singular misfortunes of the heirs of Durin were largely due to his malice. [p. 1076, III: 357–8]

268 (I: 282): The Elves returned no answer

268 (I: 282). They were not made as weapons of war or conquest: that is not their power. Those who made them did not desire strength or domination or hoarded wealth, but understanding, making, and healing to preserve all things unstained. – Tolkien did not entirely approve of the purpose of preservation for which the Elven-rings were made. In his draft letter to Michael Straight, ?end of 1955, he explained that the Elves found their immortality a burden as time passed.

> Mere *change* as such is not represented [in *The Lord of the Rings*] as 'evil': it is the unfolding of the story and to refuse this is of course against the design of God. But the Elvish weakness is in these terms naturally to regret the past, and to become unwilling to face change: as if a man were to hate a very long book still going on, and wished to settle down in a favourite chapter. Hence they [the Elven-smiths] fell in a measure to Sauron's deceits: they desired some 'power' over things as they are (which is quite distinct from art), to make their particular will to preservation effective: to arrest change, and keep things always fresh and fair. The 'Three Rings' were 'unsullied', because this object was in a limited way good, it included the healing of the real damages of malice, as well as the mere arrest of change; and the Elves did not desire to dominate other wills, nor to usurp all the world to their particular pleasure. [*Letters*, p. 236]

269 (I: 283): 'Despair, or folly?'

269 (I: 283). Well, let folly be our cloak, a veil before the eyes of the Enemy! For he is very wise, and weighs all things to a nicety – *To a* *nicety* means 'precisely, exactly, as closely or completely as possible'; but the *Oxford English Dictionary* also gives an obsolete meaning, 'folly, stupidity', citing an instance in Chaucer.

269 (I: 283): 'At least for a while'

269 (I: 283). This quest may be attempted by the weak with as much hope as the strong. Yet such is oft the course of deeds that move the wheels of the world: small hands do them because they must, while the eyes of the great are elsewhere. – Tolkien said many times that this was one of the main themes of *The Lord of the Rings*, most notably in his letter to Milton Waldman in ?late 1951:

> But as the earliest Tales [in his larger mythology] are seen through Elvish eyes, as it were, this last great Tale [*The Lord of the Rings*], coming down from myth and legend to the earth, is seen mainly through the eyes of Hobbits; it thus becomes in fact anthropocentric. But through Hobbits, not Men so-called, because the last tale is to exemplify most clearly a recurrent theme: the place in 'world-politics' of the unforeseen and unforeseeable acts of will, and deeds of virtue of the apparently small, ungreat, forgotten in the places of the Wise and Great (good as well as evil). A moral of the whole (after the primary symbolism of the Ring, as the will to mere power, seeking to make itself objective by physical force and mechanism, and so also inevitably by lies) is the obvious one that without the high and noble the simple and vulgar is utterly mean; and without the simple and ordinary the noble and heroic is meaningless. [*Letters*, p. 160]

In his draft letter to Mr Thompson on 14 January 1956 Tolkien wrote that, like many readers, he loved the Hobbits, 'since I love the vulgar and simple as dearly as the noble, and nothing moves my heart (beyond all the passions and heartbreaks of the world) so much as "ennoblement" (from the Ugly Duckling to Frodo)' (*Letters*, p. 232).

269 (I: 283): 'Very well, very well'

269 (I: 283). ***and he lived happily ever afterwards to the end of his days.*** **It is a good ending, and none the worse for having been used before.** – 'And they lived happily ever after' is, of course, a traditional ending for fairy-stories, on which Tolkien comments in *On Fairy-Stories*, originally a lecture written and presented while he was working on the early chapters of *The Lord of the Rings*. There he says that such an ending is 'an artificial device. It does not deceive anybody. End-phrases of this kind are to be compared to the margins and frames of pictures, and are no more to be thought of as the real end of any particular fragment of the seamless Web of Story than the frame is of the visionary scene, or the casement of the Outer World' (*Tree and Leaf*, p. 72).

The Hobbit in fact has two endings. The first is a version of the ending

Bilbo wanted, of the fairy-tale type: 'and though few believed any of his tales, he remained very happy to the end of his days, and those were extraordinarily long'. Then follows a brief coda describing a visit by Gandalf and Balin to Bilbo some years later.

270 (I: 283–4): 'Exactly! And who are they to be?

270 (I: 284). Can't we think of some names now? – This was the reading in the first printing of the first edition (1954). In the unauthorized resetting of *The Fellowship of the Ring* for its second printing (1954) 'Can't we' was mistakenly altered to 'Can't you'. The error was corrected in the edition of 2004.

270–1 (I: 284): 'But it is a heavy burden'

270 (I: 284). I do not lay it on you. But if you take it freely, I will say that your choice is right – The import of Elrond's statements throughout this chapter is that events have occurred – such as the gathering of peoples for the Council itself – not by mere chance, but by Providence (though that word does not appear in *The Lord of the Rings*). He now says that Frodo has been chosen, that he is fated to bear the Ring; but Frodo nonetheless has free will, and may choose whether or not to accept his fate. In his draft letter to Eileen Elgar, September 1963, Tolkien calls Frodo 'an instrument of Providence' (p. 326), and makes it clear that his quest succeeded in the end, despite his failure himself to put the Ring into the Fire, because he undertook it with free will, with humility and out of love for the world he knew.

On the issue of choice and freedom in *The Lord of the Rings*, see especially Matthew T. Dickerson, *Following Gandalf: Epic Battles and Moral Victories in* The Lord of the Rings (2003), pp. 83–94.

270–1 (I: 284). all the mighty Elf-friends of old, Hador, and Húrin, and Túrin, and Beren himself – When Tolkien wrote the name *Hador* the Man he was referring to was the leader of the Third (and greatest) House of the Edain, who brought his people into Beleriand and entered the service of Fingolfin, High King of the Noldor. In the 'Silmarillion' mythology, Hador died defending the rearguard of Fingolfin after the Battle of Sudden Flame. But in writing dated possibly to 1958, Tolkien extended the length of the First Age and the generations of the Houses of the Edain. Thus Hador remained the hero who died after the Battle of Sudden Flame, but became the great-great-grandson of the Man who led the Third House into Beleriand. This latter story appears in *The Silmarillion*: 'Now Hador Lórindol, son of Hathol, son of Magor, son of Malach Aradan, entered the household of Fingolfin in his youth, and was loved by the King. Fingolfin therefore gave him the lordship of Dor-lómin, and into that land he gathered most of the people of his kin, and became the mightiest of the chieftains of the Edain' (p. 147). On a family tree Tolkien annotated the name *Hador Lorindol* as 'the warrior Goldenhead' (*The War of the Jewels*, p. 234).

Húrin, also called *Thalion* 'the steadfast, the strong', was the grandson of Hador. He succeeded to the lordship of Dor-lómin and was a vassal of Fingon, son of Fingolfin. In the Battle of Unnumbered Tears, which was almost a total victory for Morgoth and in which Fingon was slain, Húrin and his men 'held the rear', while Turgon of the hidden realm of Gondolin and the remnants of the host of Fingon retreated:

> Húrin fought until he alone was left. He threw away his shield and wielded an axe, and he slew well nigh a hundred Orcs; but he was taken alive by Morgoth's command, and dragged to Angband. But Húrin would not reveal whither Turgon was gone, and Morgoth cursed him, and he was chained upon Thangorodrim; and Morgoth gave him sight to see the evil that befell his kindred in the world. [*The Later Annals of Beleriand* in *The Lost Road and Other Writings*, p. 137]

Túrin, also called (among other names) *Turambar* 'master of doom', was the son of Húrin, and either through the curse of Morgoth or because of failings in his own character, was ill-fated in much that he did. He was one of the greatest warriors of the First Age, yet he slew his best friend, was instrumental in bringing about the fall of Nargothrond, and unknowingly married his own sister. But he also achieved the deed of a true hero in slaying the great dragon Glaurung. His story was one of the first written of those in *The Book of Lost Tales*, and Tolkien twice began to retell it at great length (but never finished), in alliterative verse in *The Lay of the Children of Húrin* in the early 1920s (published in *The Lays of Beleriand*), and in prose in the *Narn i Chîn Húrin* in the 1950s (published in *Unfinished Tales*).

For *Beren*, see notes for pp. 191–3.

271 (I: 284): Sam sat down

271 (I: 284). a nice pickle – A colloquial use of *pickle* 'a difficult situation, sorry plight'. *Nice* is used ironically.

Chapter 3

THE RING GOES SOUTH

For drafts and history of this chapter, see *The Return of the Shadow*, pp. 406–9, 415–41; *The Treason of Isengard*, pp. 161–75.

272–3 (I: 285–6): 'Yes,' said the wizard.

272 (I: 286). You will probably make quite a long stay here. – Some readers have thought it a mistake that the Company did not leave Rivendell sooner, before winter weather made it difficult to cross the Misty Mountains. In the original draft of the chapter their departure was on 24 November. See further, note for p. 279.

273 (I: 286): *When winter first begins to bite*

273 (I: 286). *When winter first begins to bite . . .* – Bilbo's poem echoes one in Act V, Scene 2 of Shakespeare's *Love's Labour's Lost*, a set play for Tolkien's final examinations at Oxford in 1915:

When icicles hang by the wall,
And Dick the shepherd blows his nail,
And Tom bears logs into the hall,
And milk comes frozen home in pail,
When blood is nipp'd, and ways be foul,
then nightly sings the staring owl. . . .

274 (I: 287): So the days slipped away

274 (I: 287). The Hunter's Moon waxed round in the night sky. . . . But low in the south one star shone red. Every night as the Moon waned again, it shone brighter – The *Oxford English Dictionary* defines the Harvest Moon as 'the moon which is full within a fortnight of the autumnal equinox (22 or 23 Sept.) and which rises for several nights nearly at the same hour, at points successively further north on the eastern horizon', and the *Hunter's Moon* as the full moon following the Harvest Moon. But it is clear in *The Lord of the Rings* that the Hunter's Moon is still waxing after the Council of Elrond, which took place on 25 October. In *Scheme* Tolkien shows a new moon on 26 October, the day after the Council, and must have regarded the full moon of 11 November as the Hunter's Moon. In early drafts he specifically noted a moon in November as being the Hunter's Moon.

Several readers have suggested that the *one star* that *shone red* is the planet Mars.

274 (I: 287): The hobbits had been nearly two months

274 (I: 287). sources of the Gladden River – In editions prior to 2004 'sources' was printed as 'source', singular, but the drafts and corrected typescript of this chapter have it in the plural.

The *Gladden River* flows from the Misty Mountains to join the Anduin in the Gladden Fields. Its sources are roughly halfway between the High Pass and the Redhorn Gate near Moria. Christopher Tolkien states that this phrase 'was obviously based on the Map of Wilderland in *The Hobbit*, where the Gladden, there of course unnamed, rises in several streams falling from the Misty Mountains' (*The Treason of Isengard*, p. 172, n. 9).

274 (I: 287). Radagast was not there; and they had returned over the high pass that was called the Redhorn Gate. – In editions prior to 2004 'Redhorn Gate' read 'Dimrill Stair'. In the process of writing this chapter Tolkien emended the name of the pass from 'Dimrill Stair' or 'Dimrill Pass' to 'Redhorn Gate', but overlooked this instance. In his unfinished index he glosses *Redhorn Gate* as the 'name of a pass under the sides of *Redhorn* [Caradhras] into Dimrill Dale'. In the Appendices it is called the Redhorn Pass. See further, *The Treason of Isengard*, p. 164.

274 (I: 287). The sons of Elrond, Elladan and Elrohir . . . had made a great journey, passing down the Silverlode into a strange country – In his unfinished index Tolkien notes that *Silverlode* is a 'translation' of *Celebrant* (Sindarin 'silver course'), 'a river running from Mirrormere through Lórien to join Anduin at the end of the Naith'. See also note for p. 283.

The *strange country* is obviously Lothlórien.

274–5 (I: 287–8): In no region had the messengers

275 (I: 288). Eight out of the Nine are accounted for at least – In this matter Marquette MSS 4/2/36 (*The Hunt for the Ring*) says:

> Only the bodies of 8 horses were discovered; but also the raiment of the Captain. It is probable that the Captain took the one horse that remained (he may have had strength to withdraw it from the flood) and unclad, naked, invisible, rode as swift as he could back to Mordor. At swiftest he could not accomplish that (for his horse at least would need some food and rest, though he needed none) ere November had passed. The wrath and fear of Sauron then may be guessed; yet if there was any in the world in whom he trusted it was the Lord of Angmar; and if his wrath were lessened by perceiving that his great servant had defeated by ill chance (and the craft of the Wise) rather than by faults of his own, his fear would be the more – seeing what power was yet in his Enemies, and how sharply fortune favoured them at each turn when all seemed lost. Help no doubt was sent out to the other Ringwraiths as they made their way back, and they were bidden to remain secret again. It was no doubt at the end of 1418 that Sauron (S. likely aided by

Angmar) bethought him of the winged mounts; and yet withheld them, until things became almost desperate and he was forced to launch his war in haste.

275 (I: 288): Elrond summoned the hobbits

275 (I: 288). Elrond summoned the hobbits – It is 18 December 1418.

276 (I: 289): 'Neither does Frodo'

276 (I: 289). I think, Elrond, in this matter it would be well to trust rather to their friendship than to great wisdom. – Gandalf is wise to say so. After the Battle of the Pelennor Fields he will remark to Pippin that had Elrond not yielded to him 'neither of you would have set out; and then far more grievous would the evils of this day have been' (Book V, Chapter 8, p. 859, III: 135–6).

276–7 (I: 290): The Sword of Elendil

276–7 (I: 290). The Sword of Elendil was forged anew . . . and on its blade was traced a device of seven stars set between the crescent moon and the rayed sun – The seven stars are the device of Elendil. According to a note in the *1966 Index* entry for 'Stars', the seven stars 'originally represented the single stars on the banners of each of seven ships (of 9) that bore a *palantír*'. In his letter to Richard Jeffery of 17 December 1972 Tolkien wrote that the sword's original name, *Narsil*, 'symbolised the chief heavenly lights, as enemies of darkness' (*Letters*, p. 425).

277 (I: 290). Andúril, Flame of the West – In his letter to Richard Jeffrey, 17 December 1972, Tolkien wrote that *Andúril* 'meant Flame of the West (as a region) not of the Sunset' (*Letters*, p. 425). The name is derived from Quenya *andúnë* 'sunset, west' + *ril* 'glitter, brilliance'.

277 (I: 290): Aragorn and Gandalf

277 (I: 290). Aragorn and Gandalf . . . pondered the storied and figured maps and books of lore – *Storied and figured*, i.e. pictorial, like the maps Tolkien drew for *The Hobbit*.

Later in this chapter Pippin says that he too looked at maps while at Rivendell, but does not remember them; while in Book III, Chapter 3 Merry is able to judge his location based on his own study of Elrond's maps, and in Book VI, Chapter 2 Frodo says that he was shown a map of Mordor as it was before Sauron returned.

279 (I: 292): It was a cold grey day

279 (I: 292). It was a cold grey day near the end of December. – According to *The Tale of Years*, it is 25 December 1418. As this chapter was first written, the Company departed on 24 November, but Tolkien decided to move the event later in the year: 'Too much takes place in *winter*', he noted. 'They should remain longer at Rivendell. This would have additional advantage of allowing Elrond's scouts and messengers far longer *time*. He should discover Black Riders have gone back. Frodo should not start until say Dec. 24th.' Christopher Tolkien comments that 'it seems likely that 24 December was chosen as being "numerically" one month later than the existing date . . . and it was changed to 25 December to make the new dates agree "numerically" with the existing time-structure (since November has 30 days but December 31) [before Tolkien introduced the concept of thirty-day months in the Shire Reckoning]' (*The Treason of Isengard*, pp. 422–3).

Henry Resnik reported that during an interview with Tolkien in early March 1966 he had commented to Tolkien on the date of the departure from Rivendell, and on certain aspects of Frodo which seemed to parallel Jesus Christ. To the question 'How do you feel about the idea that people might identify Frodo with Christ?' Tolkien replied:

> Well, you know, there've been saviours before; it is a very common thing. There've been heroes and patriots who have given up for their countries. You don't have to be Christian to believe that somebody has to die to save something. As a matter of fact, December 25th occurred strictly by accident, and I left it in to show that this was not a Christian myth anyhow. It was a purely unimportant date, and I thought, Well there it is, just an accident. ['An Interview with Tolkien', *Niekas* 18 (Spring 1967), p. 43]

In *Nomenclature*, however, Tolkien wrote that

> the midwinter festival was not an Elvish custom, and so would not have been celebrated at Rivendell. The Fellowship, however, left on Dec. 25, which [date] had then no significance, since the Yule, or its equivalent, was then the last day of the year and the first of the next year ['Yule' = the two Yule days between 30 December and 1 January in the Hobbit calendar, which were holidays and times of feasting]. Though Dec. 25 (setting out) and March 25 (accomplishment of quest) were intentionally chosen by me.

279 (I: 292): The Company took little gear

279 (I: 292). his war horn – In the previous chapter this is described as 'a great horn tipped with silver' (p. 240, I: 253); in Book IV, Chapter 5 Faramir describes it as 'a great horn of the wild ox of the East, bound with silver, and written with many characters. That horn the eldest son of our house [the House of Stewards] has borne for many generations; and it is said that if it be blown at need anywhere within the bounds of Gondor, as the realm was of old, its voice will not pass unheeded' (p. 666, II: 276). In Book V, Chapter 1 Denethor says that the horn has been born by the eldest son of his house 'since Vorondil [*d.* Third Age 2029] . . . hunted the wild kine of Araw in the far fields of Rhûn'. In a manuscript in the Bodleian Library, Oxford, Tolkien identifies the Wild Kine from which the horn came as an *aurochs*, which the *Concise Oxford English Dictionary* defines as 'a large extinct wild ox that was the ancestor of domestic cattle'.

279 (I: 292): 'Slow should you be

279 (I: 292). until you stand once more on the borders of your land and dire need is on you – Elrond's advice foreshadows Boromir's dire need under Amon Hen in Book III, Chapter 1.

279–80 (I: 293): Gimli the dwarf alone

279 (I: 293). Gandalf bore his staff – The mention of Gandalf's staff here among swords, knife, bow, and axe suggests that it may be considered a weapon, but it is never used as such. Wizards or magicians traditionally have staffs which sometimes seem essential to the performing of magic (Prospero in Shakespeare's *Tempest*, for instance, breaks his staff when he renounces magic). Gandalf often uses his when performing a supernormal act, such as lighting fire on Caradhras or breaking the bridge in Moria. But Rony Rojkin in 'The Istari' (*Beyond Bree*, April 1999) asks:

> How much 'magic' is actually in the staff? We know that the Istari came from the West with the staff and that they always kept them close at hand. In Théoden's Hall the staff is considered as a weapon: 'The staff in the hand of a wizard may be more than a prop for age', says Háma. There are many examples of Gandalf using the staff, but there are times he does 'magic' without it (or at least it isn't mentioned).
>
> When Gandalf and Saruman faced each other [in Book III, Chapter 10] . . . what makes the casting out of the Order official is the breaking of his [Saruman's] staff. Saruman's reaction may imply a physical anguish, but the whole episode is very much like the breaking of the sword of an army officer. . . . So maybe the staff is also a symbol of status. . . .
>
> Is the staff just a plain wood [object] the Istari use at their will, or is it a 'magical' item in its own right? If it is magical, is it in tune with the wizard, or could any man who would pick it up be able to use it? If the Istari do need the staff, does it have to be The Staff or perhaps they can use anything they happen to find? How exactly do they work magic? [p. 8]

280 (I: 293). the elven-sword Glamdring, the mate of Orcist that now lay upon the breast of Thorin under the Lonely Mountain – *Glamdring* (Sindarin 'foe-hammer') and *Orcrist* (Sindarin 'goblin-cleaver') were found in the same trolls' hoard as Bilbo's sword Sting in *The Hobbit*, Chapter 2. They were taken by Gandalf and Thorin. Orcrist was buried with Thorin after his death in the Battle of Five Armies.

280 (I: 293): Their farewells had been said

280 (I: 293). Aragorn sat with his head bowed to his knees; only Elrond knew fully what this hour meant to him. – He goes forth hoping to regain a crown and the hand of Arwen.

281 (I: 294): 'Faithless is he that says farewell

281 (I: 294). Faithless is he that says farewell when the road darkens – This introduces an exchange of proverbs and platitudes between Gimli and Elrond: 'Let him not vow to walk in the dark, who has not seen the nightfall', 'Sworn word may strengthen quaking heart', 'Or break it'. Katharyn W. Crabbe comments that Tolkien uses proverbs

> to build the sense of the familiar, but also to create a sense of the individuality of cultures. . . . The proverbs . . . have the effect, even for readers who do not recognize the references, of lending a solidity to the projection of Middle-earth. A culture that has its own folk-wisdom, whether it is the same as ours or only parallel to it, is a culture that seems to make sense, to have coherence, to operate by rules of some kind – in short, to seem real.

Further, Tolkien 'often amuses himself and the reader by creating situations in which obvious statements of traditional wisdom are set in opposition. . . . Gimli's exchange with Elrond suggests the limitations of the partial truths of proverbs as guides to action' (*J.R.R. Tolkien*, rev. edn., pp. 98–9).

282 (I: 295): They had been a fortnight

282 (I: 295). They had been a fortnight on the way when the weather changed. . . . There came a cold clear dawn – *The Tale of Years* indicates that the Company reached here on 8 January 1419, and thus had travelled fifteen nights (according to the Shire Reckoning).

282 (I: 296): Gandalf stood at Frodo's side

282 (I: 296). Hollin . . . Eregion – *Hollin* is the name in Common Speech, short for *Hollin-land*, 'of the country called in Elvish [Sindarin] *Eregion* = "Holly-region". *Hollin* is an old form, still used locally, of *holly*; the region abounded in holly-trees' (*Nomenclature*). See also note for p. 47.

283 (I: 296): I need no map

283 (I: 296). Baraz, Zirak, Shathûr – Shortened forms of the names in the Dwarf language of the three mountains above Khazad-dûm, given in full in the following paragraph: 'Barazinbar, the Redhorn, cruel Caradhras; and beyond him are Silvertine and Cloudyhead: Celebdil the White, and Fanuidhol the Grey, that we call Zirakzigil and Bundushathûr'.

In his unfinished index Tolkien gives *Barazinbar* as the 'Dwarves' name of Caradhras' and '*Caradhras* "redhorn"' as the 'Elvish [Sindarin] name of a mountain above Moria in the Hithaeglir or Misty Mountains, often called "the cruel"'. In notes on Dwarvish made by Tolkien after the publication of *The Lord of the Rings* it is said that 'Khuzdul [Dwarvish] *baraz* (BRZ) probably = "red or ruddy", and *inbar* (MBR) a horn, Sindarin *Caradhras* < *caran-rass* being a translation of the Dwarvish name' (*The Treason of Isengard*, p. 174).

In his unfinished index Tolkien gives *Zirak-zigil* (*sic*) as the 'Dwarf-name of Celebdil', and '*Celebdil* "Silvertine"' as the 'Elvish [Sindarin] name of one of the Mountains of Moria'. In his notes on Dwarvish he says that

> *Zirak-zigil* should mean 'Silver-spike' (cf. 'Silvertine', and *Celebdil* < Sindarin *celeb* 'silver' + *till* 'tine, spike, point'). But silver is evidently KBL in *Kibil-nâla* – KBL seems to have some connexion with Quenya *telep-* 'silver'. But all these peoples seem to have possessed various words for the precious metals, some referring to the material and its properties, some to their colour and other associations. So that *zirak* (ZRK) is probably another name for 'silver', or for its grey colour. *Zigil* is evidently a word for 'spike' (smaller and more slender than a 'horn'). Caradhras seems to have been a great mountain tapering upwards (like the Matterhorn), while Celebdil was simply crowned by a smaller pinnacle.

Christopher Tolkien reports that 'still later pencilled notes reversed this explanation, suggesting that *zigil* (ZGL) meant "silver" and *zirak* meant "spike"' (*The Treason of Isengard*, pp. 174–5).

In a letter to his son Michael in 1967/68, recalling his visit to Switzerland in 1911, Tolkien wrote: 'I left the view of *Jungfrau* with deep regret: eternal snow, etched as it seemed against eternal sunshine, and the *Silberhorn* sharp against dark blue: the *Silvertine* (*Celebdil*) of my dreams' (*Letters*, p. 392).

In *The Lord of the Rings* as first published the name *Zirakzigil* was spelt with a hyphen, as 'Zirak-zigil', except in one instance in *The Two Towers*. In the second printing (1967) of the Allen & Unwin second edition the form was changed generally to 'Zirakzigil', except for two instances of 'Zirak-zigil' overlooked in *The Return of the King*. In 2004 Christopher Tolkien determined that his father decisively preferred the unhyphened form 'Zirakzigil', on the basis of manuscript evidence in check copies of *The Fellowship of the Ring* and *The Two Towers*. In three copies of the former, Tolkien struck out the hyphen in 'Zirak-zigil' and noted in the margin 'See II 105', i.e. a page in *The Two Towers* with the form 'Zirakzigil'; and in a copy of the latter, in the margin by 'Zirakzigil', he wrote 'stet'. Christopher commented to us:

> I think this is a *locus classicus* for students of the textual criticism of my father's works. While it can't be said just *when* he made the annotation on his copy of the 1st printing of the 1st ed. of FR [*The Fellowship of the Ring*], p. 296 there is at least evidence of the clearest conceivable

> kind that he *did not want* 'Zirakzigil' to be hyphened! *But*, in the sets of LR [*The Lord of the Rings*] that he used as check-copies & on which he made many corrections he said nothing about the two occurrences of 'Zirak-zigil' in RK [*The Return of the King*]. Does this suggest that at some other and later time he changed his mind & decided to accept the hyphened form? Of course not. It is mere common sense to say that he didn't change them because (for whatever cause) he didn't observe them. The strong deletion of the hyphen on three successive copies, with reason for it given (& the note 'stet' in one copy at the place where the printed text had no hyphen), must count far more heavily than the mere retention of the hyphen without comment much further on in the book. [private correspondence]

The hyphen was removed from the two instances of *Zirak-zigil* in *The Return of the King* in 2004.

In his unfinished index Tolkien gives *Shathûr* as the 'Dwarf-name of Fanuidhol "Cloudyhead"' and *Cloudyhead* as a 'translation' of Sindarin 'Fanuidhol, one of the Mountains of Moria (Elvish [Sindarin] *fain* "cloud", *fanui* "cloudy"; *dol* "head" (often applied to hills and mountains))'. In his notes on Dwarvish he said that 'since *Shathûr* was the basic Dwarvish name the element probably refers to "cloud", and was probably a plural "clouds"; *Bund(u)* in the fuller name *Bundu-shathûr* "must therefore mean "head" or something similar. Possibly *bund* (BND) – *u* – *Shathûr* "head in/of clouds"' (*The Treason of Isengard*, p. 174).

283 (I: 296): Only once before

283 (I: 296). Dwarrowdelf – In a letter to Stanley Unwin on 15 October 1937 Tolkien mentioned his use of *dwarves* instead of *dwarfs* (see note for p. 1) and commented: 'The real "historical" plural of *dwarf* . . . is *dwarrows*, anyway: rather a nice word, but a bit too archaic. Still I rather wish I had used the word *dwarrow*' (*Letters*, pp. 23–4). In Appendix F he notes: 'I have used that form [*dwarrows*] only in the name *Dwarrowdelf*, to represent the name of Moria in the Common Speech: *Phurunargian*. For that meant "Dwarf-delving" and yet was already a word of antique form' (p. 1137, III: 415).

283 (I: 296): 'There the Misty Mountains divide

283 (I: 296). There the Misty Mountains divide, and between their arms lies the deep-shadowed valley which we cannot forget: Azanulbizar, the Dimrill Dale, which the Elves call Nanduhirion. – Tolkien made a small sketch of the Dimrill Dale with the three mountains of Moria behind: see *Artist and Illustrator*, fig. 158.

As told in 'Durin's Folk' in Appendix A, in Third Age 2799 the Dwarves attacked the Orcs then occupying Moria after the latter had killed Thrór and mutilated his body. A bitter battle was fought in Nanduhirion before the East-gate of Moria, and though the Dwarves won the battle 'their dead were beyond count of grief. Barely half of their number, it is said, could still stand or had hope of healing' (p. 1075, III: 356).

Concerning *Azanulbizar*, in the manuscript of *Nomenclature* Tolkien comments that it is the

> Dwarf name of *Nan Duhirion*, Common Speech *Dimrill Dale.* Sindarin *nan(d)* valley / *dû* dim, dark – *sîr* stream > *Duhir-ion* 'region of the dim streams'. It not is here genitive, but in apposition to *nan(d)* 'valley', though in English 'of' is often inserted in such cases (as the City of Rome): the valley (that is called) *Duhirion.*
>
> The analysis of the dwarf *Azanulbizar* is uncertain. *Azan* was probably a plural of *uzu* 'dimness, shadow' (cf. *Khazad – Khuzd*); *-ul* was a genitive ending of patronymics such as *Balin Fundinul* B[alin] (son of) F[undin]; *bizār* was probably a plural of a stem *b-z-r* a small stream (running down from a spring). 'The rills of the shadows'. The combination was used as a name of the valley, without expression of valley. (Dwarvish *d-b-n*) is merely an alteration of full name *duban azanulbizar.*

In the finished *Nomenclature* it is said that 'the Common Speech form is an accurate translation: the valley of the dim (overshadowed) rills that ran down the mountain-side'.

283 (I: 296): 'It is for the Dimrill Dale

283 (I: 296). There lies the Mirrormere – In his manuscripts and typescripts Tolkien hesitated between *Mirrormere* and hyphened *Mirror-mere*, but emended all instances with a hyphen to *Mirrormere* in typescript or proof. Among the extracts from the Book of Mazarbul in Book II, Chapter 5 the name appears as *Mirror mere*, a deliberate variation. The Dwarvish name for *Mirrormere*, given by Gimli in the following paragraph, is *Kheled-zâram*, which in notes on Dwarvish written after the publication of *The Lord of the Rings* Tolkien 'translated' as 'probably "glass-pool"'. He noted that '*kheled* was certainly a Dwarf word for "glass"' (*The Return of the Shadow*, p. 466, n. 39).

283 (I: 296): 'Dark is the water of Kheled-zâram

283 (I: 296). Kibil-nâla – The Silverlode. In his unfinished index Tolkien 'translates' the Dwarvish name as 'silver-channel'. In late notes on Dwarf names he wrote that 'the meaning of *nâla* is not known. If it corresponds to *rant* [in *Celebrant*] and *lode* [in *Silverlode*], it should mean "path, course, rivercourse, or bed".' He added later: 'It is probable that the Dwarves actually found silver in the river' (*The Treason of Isengard*, p. 175).

283 (I: 297): 'To the end of the journey

283 (I: 297). To the end of the journey. . . . We cannot look too far ahead. – In Book II, Chapter 8 Aragorn will tell Celeborn that he does not think that Gandalf had any clear plans beyond reaching Lothlórien.

284 (I: 297): 'I hope that is it'

284 (I: 297). I have a sense of watchfulness – In his letter to Milton Waldman, ?late 1951, Tolkien wrote: 'There is a sense throughout of a hidden watch on their movements, a constant hostility even of beasts and inanimate things. The Company is driven to attempt the passage of the ominous Mines of Moria, and there Gandalf falls into an abyss in the act of saving them from a trap' (*Waldman LR*).

Readers have long debated who was responsible for the *crebain* searching Hollin (see below, note for p. 285) and for the wargs that attack the Company later in this chapter, and whether the storm that prevents the crossing of the Misty Mountains by the Redhorn Gate at the end of the chapter is merely (if spectacularly) a phenomenon of nature, or a reflection of the malice of Caradhras (the mountain itself), or caused by some outside agency. Tolkien's words to Milton Waldman, written with deliberate brevity, could mean only that events drove the Company into Moria; but his use of 'driven' and 'trap' suggests that someone wanted the Company to go by that route – Sauron (whom Boromir believes can govern storms), or Saruman. The published text indicates that Saruman had influence in Dunland and Fangorn; that Sauron was keeping watch on the east bank of Anduin; that on 26 February the Company was attacked by an uneasy alliance of Orcs from Isengard, Moria, and Mordor; and that the orcs Uglúk and Grishnákh, and therefore their masters Saruman and Sauron, apparently had some knowledge associating hobbits with the Ring. To this may be added information from unpublished time-schemes and notes by Tolkien, plotting the plans and actions of Sauron, Saruman, and their agents, from 15 January 1419 when Gandalf falls in Moria and the rest of the Company make their escape. In *Scheme* it is said: '15 January Moria-orcs pursue Coy. [Company] over Silverlode. . . . Messengers leave Moria to *Isengard*, bringing news of events to Saruman, and also mentioning the appearance of Gollum. (Moria is 260 miles direct to Isengard; but orc-messengers cover this in less than 4 days.) Messages also go to Barad-dûr, some by evil birds.' In an earlier time-scheme, Marquette MSS 3/1/34, at a stage in the writing when no time passed while the Company was in Lothlórien, on the fourth day of their voyage down the Anduin 'messengers from Moria reach Isengard, where Saruman has already heard rumour by birds and spies of the hobbits'. Compare 'the crows of Saruman', p. 548, III: 154.

The *crebain*, however, and the unexplained shadow that Frodo sees or feels pass over the stars, and the snowstorm (but not the wargs) in this chapter existed in its earliest version, before Saruman had entered the story. Tolkien himself may not have known who was responsible for these events; in any case, here as elsewhere in *The Lord of the Rings* the work is improved by the reader experiencing the same uncertainty and suspense as the characters.

285 (I: 298): 'Regiments of black crows

285 (I: 298). *crebain* – A special kind of crow, singular **craban*. In *An Introduction to Elvish* (1978, p. 75) Jim Allan suggests that Sindarin **craban* is related to Old English *crāwan* 'to crow' (usually of a cock), Old High German *hraban*, Old Norse *hrafn*, Old English *hræfn* 'raven'. (Compare Old English *crāwe* 'a crow'.)

285 (I: 298). Fangorn – Sindarin 'Treebeard'. In his unfinished index Tolkien described *Fangorn* as the forest 'on the mountain-sides at extreme [south-east] of the Misty M[ountain]s, that still stretched some miles into the [north-east] plains of Rohan, about the upper waters of the Entwash and Limlight'.

286 (I: 299): Guided by Aragorn

286 (I: 299). The Moon now at the full – 8/9 January is the night of the full moon.

286 (I: 299). It was the cold chill hour before the first stir of dawn – It is 9 January 1419.

286 (I: 299). he saw or felt a shadow pass over the high stars – The *shadow* is never explained. For experienced readers of *The Lord of the Rings* it is instantly reminiscent of a winged Nazgûl; but at this point in the story the Nazgûl, newly mounted on fell creatures of the air, had not yet crossed west over the Anduin. In Book II, Chapter 9 a similar dark shape momentarily cuts off the moon's light and causes Frodo (as here) to feel a chill: there it is almost certainly a Nazgûl, but here Gandalf suggests that it is only a wisp of cloud. Christopher Tolkien comments in *The Treason of Isengard* (p. 365): 'it seems likely to me that the shadow that passed across the stars near Hollin was in fact the first precocious appearance of a Winged Nazgûl'.

286 (I: 299–300): Nothing further happened

286 (I: 300). For two more nights – The nights of 9/10 and 10/11 January.

286 (I: 300). On the third morning – It is 11 January 1419.

287 (I: 300): 'I think no good of our course

287 (I: 300). marshals of the Horse-lords – For *marshal*, see note for p. 432. The *Horse-lords* are the Rohirrim: see note for p. 262.

288 (I: 301): The Company set out again

288 (I: 301). The Company set out – It is the night of 11/12 January.

288 (I: 302): 'His arm has grown long

288 (I: 302). if he can draw snow down from the North to trouble us here three hundred leagues away – *Three hundred leagues* is 900 miles.

The text is not clear whether this relates to the distance between Caradhras and Barad-dûr, or between Caradhras and the North from which the snow may have been drawn.

289 (I: 302): The Company halted suddenly

289 (I: 302). the sounds were those of shrill cries, and wild howls of laughter. Stones began to fall from the mountain-side – The passage recalls the crossing of the Misty Mountains in *The Hobbit*, Chapter 4: 'the wind came shrill among the rocks. Boulders, too, at times, came galloping down the mountain-sides . . . the echoes were uncanny, and the silence seemed to dislike being broken'.

290 (I: 303–4): 'Give them this'

290 (I: 304). *miruvor*, the cordial of Imladris – Within the mythology, presumably named after a cordial (flavoured drink) of the Valar which Tolkien describes in *The Road Goes Ever On: A Song Cycle*, *miruvóre*. 'According to the Eldar, [it is] a word derived from the language of the Valar; the name that they gave to the drink poured out at their festivals. Its making and the meaning of its name were not known for certain, but the Eldar believed it to be made from the honey of the undying flowers in the gardens of Yavanna, though it was clear and translucent' (p. 61). 'Its actual origin as an "invention"', however, as Tolkien writes in a manuscript quoted in *Parma Eldalamberon* 12 (1998), p. xi, 'goes back to at least 1915, its real source being Gothic **midu* (=Gmc. [Germanic] *među*) ["mead"] + *wōþeis* ["sweet"], then supposed to have been developed so: *miđuwōþi* > *miđuwōði* > *miřuwōři* > *miruvóre*'.

290 (I: 304): But though they had brought wood

290 (I: 304). kindlings – Small sticks or twigs used for lighting fires.

290 (I: 304). *naur an edraith ammen!* – Sindarin 'Fire be for saving of us!' (see *The Treason of Isengard*, p. 175, n. 24).

291 (I: 304–5): Frodo gazed wearily

291 (I: 305). Very slowly a dim light began to grow – It is the morning of 12 January 1419.

292 (I: 305): Aragorn was the tallest

292 (I: 305). Aragorn was the tallest of the Company, but Boromir, little less in height, was broader – In a note written *c.* 1969 Tolkien said that 'Aragorn, direct descendant of Elendil and his son Isildur, both of whom had been seven feet tall, must nonetheless have been a very tall man (with a great stride), probably at least 6 ft. 6; and Boromir, of high Númenórean lineage, not much shorter (say 6 ft. 4)' (Tolkien Papers, Bodleian Library, Oxford).

292 (I: 306): The others waited huddled together

292 (I: 306). lowered – Looked dark and threatening.

293 (I: 306): He lifted up the hobbit

293 (I: 306–7). Pippin marvelled at his strength. . . . Even now, burdened as he was, he was widening the track – This is Boromir's finest hour; without his advice about taking wood for a fire, and his strength, the Company might not have survived the night or escaped the mountain. Pippin's admiration will grow even greater when Boromir defends him and Merry from orcs, and will influence him to offer his service to Boromir's father, Denethor.

Chapter 4

A JOURNEY IN THE DARK

For drafts and history of this chapter, see *The Return of the Shadow*, pp. 428–30, 437, 442–67; *The Treason of Isengard*, pp. 176–89.

295 (I: 308): It was evening

295 (I: 308). It was evening – It is still 12 January 1419.

296 (I: 309): 'It is a name of ill omen

296 (I: 309). Or we might pass by and cross the Isen into Langstrand and Lebennin – The river *Isen* flows from the Misty Mountains through Isengard and across the Gap of Rohan.

Langstrand is a 'translation' of *Anfalas*, coastland 'fief' of Gondor, west of Belfalas. In the Common Speech it means 'long strand' (a *strand* is the margin of a body of water).

In his unfinished index Tolkien notes that *Lebennin* means '"five rivers", land between the White Mts. and Ethir Anduin, from Anórien to Belfalas: one of the "faithful fiefs". (The rivers that gave it its name were *Erui*, *Sirith*, *Serni*, *Gilrain*, *Celos*.)'

296 (I: 309): 'As for the longer road

296 (I: 309). As for the longer road. . . . We might spend a year in such a journey – Gandalf is exaggerating the distance: even if the Company were to travel west almost to the sea before turning south (to avoid Isengard), the journey would be at most three times the route Frodo took, reaching Orodruin by 25 March, including a month's stay in Lothlórien.

296 (I: 309–10): 'You speak of what you do not know

296 (I: 309). Barad-dûr – *Barad-dûr* is Sindarin for 'dark tower', derived from '*barad* "tower" in the sense of a lofty fortress (as in the Tower of London) + *dûr* "dark" (connoting dread and evil)' (manuscript of *Nomenclature*).

297 (I: 310): 'Good, Gimli!'

297 (I: 310). I sought there long for Thráin son of Thrór after he was lost. – In Appendix A it is said that Thráin and his people, driven from Erebor by Smaug and kept from Moria by fear of Durin's Bane, settled east of the Ered Luin, and there prospered after a fashion by working iron. But the lust for gold was ever in Thráin's mind, and at last he and a few others attempted to return to Erebor and the treasure they had abandoned to the dragon. Now, 'as soon as he was abroad with few companions'

Thráin 'was hunted by the emissaries of Sauron. Wolves pursued him, Orcs waylaid him, evil birds shadowed his path, and the more he strove to go north the more misfortunes opposed him.' One dark night, while sheltering under the eaves of Mirkwood, Thráin disappeared from camp. His companions 'searched for him many days, until at last giving up hope they departed and came at length back to [his son] Thorin. Only long after was it learned that Thráin had been taken alive and brought to the pits of Dol Guldur' (p. 1077, III: 358).

In *The Hobbit*, Chapter 1 and elsewhere, Gandalf tells of finding Thráin in Dol Guldur, but only by chance, while on other business (seeking to learn if the Necromancer was Sauron). In one version of *The Quest of Erebor* (compare 'Durin's Folk' in Appendix A of *The Lord of the Rings*) Gandalf recalls a chance meeting with Thorin Oakenshield, who was brooding on the loss of the Dwarves' treasure to Smaug, and thinking of revenge. Then, says Gandalf,

> 'I remembered a dangerous journey of mine, ninety-one years before, when I had entered Dol Guldur in disguise, and had found there an unhappy Dwarf dying in the pits. I had no idea who he was. He had a map . . . and a key that seemed to go with it, though he was too far gone to explain it. And he said that he had possessed a great Ring.
>
> 'Nearly all his ravings were of that. *The last of the Seven* he said over and over again. But all these things he might have come by in many ways. He might have been a messenger caught as he fled, or even a thief trapped by a greater thief. But he gave the map and key to me. "For my son," he said; and then he died, and soon after I escaped myself. . . .
>
> 'Now I remembered . . . and it seemed clear that I had heard the last words of Thráin the Second, though he did not name himself or his son.' [*Unfinished Tales*, p. 324]

This explains well enough how Gandalf came to have the map of Erebor and the key to the mountain's secret door, as described in *The Hobbit*; and it clarifies Gandalf's statement at the Council of Elrond that Thráin's ring was taken from him in torment. But if, as Gandalf says in the present chapter of *The Lord of the Rings*, that he searched for Thráin when he was lost, it seems strange that he should come upon a Dwarf in Dol Guldur who has a map of the secret way into Erebor, and its key, and who evidently once possessed one of seven rings, and yet not consider at once that it might be Thráin (rather than a messenger or thief) – and this, according to *The Tale of Years*, only nine years after Thráin's disappearance, when (presumably) the loss of Thráin would still be fresh in Gandalf's mind.

297 (I: 310): 'I too once passed the Dimrill Gate'

297 (I: 310). 'I too once passed the Dimrill Gate,' said Aragorn . . . the memory is very evil – In the first version of this chapter Trotter the

Hobbit says much the same. For him the memory of Moria was 'evil' because he was caught there by forces of the Dark Lord.

The *Dimrill Gate* is 'the eastern or Great Gate of Moria' (*Index*).

297 (I: 310): 'I will,' said Aragorn

297 (I: 310). And I say to you: if you pass the doors of Moria, beware! – This is the first of many times that Aragorn shows remarkable foresight.

298 (I: 311): 'Then let us start

298 (I: 311). The wolf that one hears is worse than the orc that one fears. – This seems precisely the sort of proverb one would expect in Middle-earth, as does Aragorn's rejoinder: 'But where the warg howls, there also the orc prowls.'

298 (I: 311): 'My heart's right down

298 (I: 311). But we aren't etten yet – That is: 'We haven't been eaten yet.'

298 (I: 311): 'Listen, Hound of Sauron!'

298 (I: 311). Hound of Sauron – *Hound* is used here in the generic sense 'canine'. As told in *The Silmarillion*, Sauron was of old 'lord of werewolves' (p. 156).

298–9 (I: 312): The night was old

298 (I: 312). The night was old. – It is now early on 13 January 1419.

299 (I: 312): *Naur an edraith ammen! Naur dan i ngaurhoth!*

299 (I: 312). *Naur an edraith ammen! Naur dan i ngaurhoth!* – 'Fire save us! Fire drive back the werewolves!' For an analysis of these words in Sindarin, see Carl F. Hostetter, 'Settled Spells', *Amon Hen* 122 (July 1993).

299 (I: 312): There was a roar and a crackle

299 (I: 312). There was a roar and a crackle, and the trees above him burst into a leaf and bloom of blinding flame. The fire leapt from tree-top to tree-top. The swords of the defenders shone and flickered. – Gandalf now shows himself much more powerful than in the similar attack by wolves in *The Hobbit*, Chapter 6. In the latter he, the dwarves, and Bilbo climb into fir-trees, then: 'He gathered the huge pine-cones from the branches of his tree. Then he set one alight with bright blue fire, and threw it whizzing down among the circle of wolves. . . . Then another came and another, one in blue flames, one in red, and another in green. They burst on the ground in the middle of the circle and went off in coloured sparks and smoke.'

300 (I: 313): Gimli now walked ahead

300 (I: 313). Sirannon – In his unfinished index Tolkien defines *Sirannon* as '"stream of the Gate", tr[anslated] as Gate-stream . . . , that formerly flowed from springs near the West-door of Moria down the Stair Falls and beside the road from Eregion to Moria'.

301 (I: 314): At length they came

301 (I: 314). Rounding the corner they saw before them a low cliff some five fathoms high, with a broken and jagged top. Over it a trickling water dripped, through a wide cleft that seemed to have been carved out by a fall that had once been strong and full. – Tolkien made a carefully finished drawing showing this cliff, and the steps, lake, and west wall described in the following paragraphs. It does not quite agree with the description, and 'probably depicts the approach to the west gate of Moria as Tolkien conceived it before he wrote any of the relevant text. He later cut off the bottom quarter of the drawing . . . apparently in an attempt to salvage most of the picture by removing the more active part of the Stair Falls [which appear as more than a trickle]' (Wayne G. Hammond and Christina Scull, *Artist and Illustrator*, p. 159, figs. 148–9).

A *fathom* is 'a unit of length equal to six feet, chiefly used in reference to the depth of water', originally the length of a man's outstretched arms to the tip of the hands, including the longest finger. Although Tolkien devised some hobbit measures, including a 'fathom' (see note for p. 5), he did not include them in *The Lord of the Rings*, and the primary world *fathom* must be meant here.

301 (I: 314): 'Indeed things have changed!'

301 (I: 314). Stair Falls – 'Falls of the Sirannon beside the steps leading up onto the level before the West-door of Moria' (*Index*).

301 (I: 315): 'There are the Walls

301 (I: 315). Walls of Moria – 'The great cliffs above the West-gate of Moria looking on Eregion' (*Index*).

301 (I: 315). And there the Gate stood once upon a time, the Elven Door at the end of the road from Hollin – In the first version of this chapter there were two secret gates on the west side of Moria. In the second version Gandalf says that 'there was the Elven-door at the end of the road from Hollin by which we have come [*struck through:* and the Dwarven-door further south]. We must get across [*struck through:* to the Elven-door] as quickly as we can'. Christopher Tolkien explains:

> The idea that there were two distinct western entrances to Moria had appeared in the original version, where Gandalf said . . . : 'There were two secret gates on the western side, though the chief entrance was on the East'. Gandalf's words in the present passage in FR [*The Fellowship of the Ring*] . . . *the Elven Door* . . . derive from this, although in the context of FR, where there is no 'Dwarven Door', the 'Elven Door' is understood in relation to what Gandalf said subsequently: 'the West-

door was made chiefly for [the Elves'] use in their traffic with the Lords of Moria'. [*The Treason of Isengard*, p. 178]

302 (I: 315): When they came to the northernmost corner

302 (I: 315). creek – In this context, a recess or inlet in a body of water, not a flowing stream.

303 (I: 316): 'Well, here we are at last!'

303 (I: 316). traffic – Here used in the sense 'trade'.

303 (I: 316). Those were happier days, when there was still close friendship at times between folk of different race, even between Dwarves and Elves. – In *The Lord of the Rings* little more is said of this friendship, but Christopher Tolkien notes that in the late work *Concerning Galadriel and Celeborn* it is said that

> Celebrimbor had 'an almost "dwarvish" obsession with crafts'; and he soon became the chief artificer of Eregion, entering into a close relationship with the Dwarves of Khazad-dûm, among whom his greatest friend was Narvi. . . . Both Elves and Dwarves had great profit from this association: so that Eregion became far stronger, and Khazad-dûm far more beautiful, than either would have done alone. [*Unfinished Tales*, pp. 235–6]

303 (I: 316–17): Turning to the others

303 (I: 317). water-skins – Leather containers for carrying water.

304 (I: 317): 'Dwarf-doors were not made to be seen

304 (I: 317). not made to be seen when shut – This was established in *The Hobbit*, where a side door into the halls of Erebor could be revealed only when the setting sun on a particular day shone on the position of the key-hole.

304 (I: 317). their own makers – In editions prior to 2004 this passage read 'their own masters'. The error for 'makers' was made in the first typescript of the chapter and perpetuated in print. See *The Treason of Isengard*, p. 187, n. 6.

304 (I: 318): The Moon now shone

304 (I: 318). The Moon now shone upon the grey face of the rock . . . where the Moon caught them – It is the evening of 13 January. The moon had been full five nights earlier, and could not possibly shine on a westward-facing surface in the evening: it would rise in the east after sunset and set the next day after sunrise. This description also contradicts Gandalf's statement later in the chapter, when the Company halt after several hours' journey in Moria, that 'outside the late Moon is riding westward and the middle-night has passed' (p. 312, I: 326).

In the earliest version of this chapter the departure date from Rivendell and the phases of the moon were different. In the manuscript and typescript of the second version the moon is almost at the full, rather than full during the Company's first night in Hollin; yet, although it still would not have been in the west when the Company reached the Wall of Moria, Tolkien introduced eight references to it. He later emended the typescript, removing six references to the moon, leaving only the two in this paragraph. The first emendation was the change on p. 302, I: 315 from 'The day was drawing to an end, and the moon was already shining on the edge of the sunset' (indicating that a young moon is setting in the west) to 'The day was drawing to an end, and cold stars were glinting in the sky high above the sunset'. In *The Treason of Isengard* Christopher Tolkien lists the six changes and comments on the second version:

> My father had said that six nights before, the first night march of the Company from Hollin . . . , the Moon was 'almost at the full' ('at the full', FR [*The Fellowship of the Ring*]); and on the previous night, when the Wargs attacked again, 'the night was old, and westward the waning moon was setting' (so also in FR). My father had forgotten this, and as he wrote the present version he evidently saw a young moon in the West ('shining on the edge of the sunset'). When he realised that the moon must now be almost into its last quarter and rising late he changed the text . . . ; but surely the reference to the moon shining on the cliff-face should have been removed with all the others? [pp. 179–80]

In editing the text for the edition of 2004 we considered whether this paragraph should be emended, perhaps substituting references to the stars for those to the moon, but felt that this would destroy Tolkien's vision of the scene. Christopher Tolkien agreed and said: 'I *suspect* that my father "saw" the scene at the doors of Moria as moonlit, but the need to get the moon's phase consistent was at odds with this' (private correspondence).

304 (I: 318): At the top

304 (I: 318). an arch of interlacing letters in an Elvish character. Below . . . the outline could be seen of an anvil and a hammer surmounted by a crown and seven stars. Beneath these again were two trees, each bearing crescent moons. More clearly than all else there shone in the middle of the door a single star with many rays. – Tolkien changed the description of the design on the doors in successive texts, and made at least four drawings which mirror these changes; see *Artist and Illustrator*, figs. 150–3. The picture of the Doors of Durin reproduced in *The Lord of the Rings* (p. 304, I: 319) was made by a blockmaker's copyist after Tolkien's final design. The trees were revised, with Tolkien's consent, so that their outer branches curved in front of the pillars rather than behind. Tolkien would have liked the design to 'appear in white line on a black background, since it represents a silver line in the darkness' (letter to Rayner Unwin,

11 April 1953, *Letters*, p. 167), but this was rejected on the grounds that a solid black illustration would be overly noticeable in the middle of the book.

304 (I: 318): 'There are the emblems of Durin!'

304 (I: 318). the emblems of Durin! – The anvil and hammer, and the crown with seven stars. Material added by Tolkien to the entry for 'Star' in the *1966 Index* includes 'Seven stars (above a crown and anvil), emblems of Durin'. The stars are said to have eight rays and to represent the Plough (see note for p. 174).

304 (I: 318): 'And there is the Tree

304 (I: 318). the Tree of the High Elves! – Legolas mentions only one tree, though the design shows the same tree twice, with crescent moons. The *1966 Index* identifies the *Tree of the High Elves* as Galathilion. According to Tolkien's mythology, the moon was fashioned from the last flower of Telperion (see note for p. 158); but long before that, the Vala Yavanna had made for the Elves living in Tirion in Valinor 'a tree like to a lesser image of Telperion, save that it did not give light of its own being; Galathilion [probably "tree of shining silver"] it was named in the Sindarin tongue' (*The Silmarillion*, p. 59). (See also note for p. 971.)

304, 306 (I: 318): 'And the Star of the House of Fëanor'

304 (I: 318). the Star of the House of Fëanor – For *Fëanor*, see notes for pp. 79, 193.

In the *1966 Index* it is said that the *Star of the House of Fëanor* had eight rays and was of silver. This probably represents one of the Silmarils: among 'heraldic' devices that Tolkien drew *c.* 1960 is one showing three Silmarils, each with eight points. In the device he drew for Fëanor (thus the Sindarin form of the name, from Quenya *Fëanáro* 'spirit of fire') flames are the most prominent element, but at the centre is a tiny eight-pointed star (*Pictures by J.R.R. Tolkien*, 2nd edn., no. 47).

304 (I: 318). *ithildin* that mirrors only starlight and moonlight – On p. 317, I: 331 Gandalf says that *ithildin* is (Sindarin) 'starmoon' ('moon-star' would be closer), and that it was made by the Elves from mithril.

306 (I: 318): 'What does the writing say?'

306 (I: 318). What does the writing say? – Frodo cannot decipher it; according to the inscription below the reproduced design of the door, it is in 'the Feänorian [*sic*, for "Fëanorian"] characters according to the mode of Beleriand'. In Appendix F it is said that although the oldest Eldarin letters had been devised by Rúmil, 'the later letters, the Tengwar of Fëanor, were largely a new invention, though they owed something to the letters of Rúmil' and 'in the Third Age had spread over much the same area as that in which the Common Speech was known' (p. 1117, I: 395). David

Doughan and Julian Bradfield explain in 'An Introduction to the Writing Systems of Middle-earth. Part I: The Fëanorian Letters', (*Quettar* Special Publication no. 1 (1987), that

> the writing system originally devised in Valinor by Fëanor to express the High-elven languages, above all the antique form of Quenya, was brought to Middle-earth by the Exiles. There it was adapted and developed into a variety of forms, depending partly on the scriptorial preferences of the users, but more on the peculiarities of the tongues for which it was used. Four such 'modes' are represented in the published works: one 'full' mode (i.e. using *tengwar* to represent vowels), called 'the mode of Beleriand', which itself has three main variants; and two modes using *tehtar* '[diacritic] marks' over consonants (or 'carriers') for vowels, in a manner similar to Arabic or Classical Hebrew, one of which has three significant variants; and the vestigial mode used for 'Arctic' [in *The Father Christmas Letters*]. [p. 2]

306 (I: 318): 'The words are in the elven-tongue

306 (I: 318). the elven-tongue of the West of Middle-earth in the Elder Days – Sindarin.

306 (I: 318). They say only – The Sindarin text (here translated by Gandalf) is given only in the illustration: '*Ennyn Durin Aran Moria; pedo mellon a minno. Im Narvi hain echant: Celebrimbor o Eregion teithant i thiw hin*'.

306 (I: 318). *Durin, Lord of Moria* – Durin III was the ruler of Khazad-dûm when the Doors were made.

It has often been pointed out that *Moria* was hardly what the ruler of Khazad-dûm would have chosen to have inscribed on his doors. In Book II, Chapter 3 Gimli refers to 'Khazad-dûm, the Dwarrowdelf, that is now called the Black Pit, Moria in the Elvish tongue' (p. 283, I: 296), which indicates that it was not always called 'Moria'. Most commentators have taken the view that this name did not come into use until after the appearance of the Balrog in Third Age 1980, and have queried the use of *Moria* on the West-gate as both anachronistic and undiplomatic; compare, in *The Silmarillion*: 'Greatest of all the mansions of the Dwarves was Khazad-dûm, the Dwarrowdelf, Hadhodrond in the Elvish tongue, that was afterwards *in the days of its darkness* called Moria' (p. 91, emphasis ours). But in Appendix F Tolkien says that 'Moria is an Elvish name, and given without love; for the Eldar, though they might at need, in their bitter wars with the Dark Power and his servants, contrive fortresses underground, were not dwellers in such places of choice. They were lovers of the green earth and the lights of heaven; and Moria in their tongue means the Black Chasm' (p. 1137, I: 415). This suggests that the name was given because Khazad-dûm was underground, not because of any particular horror or darkness.

Jeff Stevenson comments in a letter to *Amon Hen* 103 (May 1990) that

> if MORIA was in fact inscribed on the doors when Frodo arrived there, this can only mean either: (1) Celebrimbor foresaw the name; (2) a later craftsman had re-worked the inscription; or (3) the magic lettering had re-arranged itself when the name 'Moria' was first uttered by the Elves. Alternatively HADHODROND was on the Doors all along, but Gandalf read out 'Moria' for this, in the same way that he read out 'Hollin' when EREGION was inscribed. In this scenario, the illustrator of the Red Book derived his calligraphy by translating Gandalf's interpretation back into Elvish, without considering the history of the Doors. [p. 25]

306 (I: 318). Narvi – See note for p. 303.

306 (I: 318): 'Yes,' said Gandalf

306 (I: 318). doorwards – The wardens or keepers of the door.

307 (I: 320): 'I once knew every spell

307 (I: 320). the secret dwarf-tongue that they teach to none – Tolkien explains in Appendix F that Dwarves used the languages of Men in the areas where they dwelt and, for relations with other races, had names in those languages. But in secret they 'used their own strange tongue, changed little by the years, for it had become a tongue of lore rather than a cradle-speech. . . . Few other races have succeeded in learning it. . . . Their own secret and "inner" names, their true names, the Dwarves have never revealed to anyone of alien race. Not even on their tombs do they inscribe them' (pp. 1132–3, III: 410–11). In work on the *Quenta Silmarillion* after the publication of *The Lord of the Rings* he says that

> the father-tongue of the Dwarves Aulë himself devised for them, and their languages have thus no kinship with those of the Quendi [Elves]. The Dwarves do not gladly teach their tongue to those of alien race; and in use they have made it harsh and intricate, so that of those few whom they have received in full friendship fewer still have learned it well. [*The War of the Jewels*, p. 205]

307 (I: 320): ***Annon edhellen, edro hi ammen!***

307 (I: 320). ***Annon edhellen, edro hi ammen! / Fennas nogothrim, lasto beth lammen!*** – Christopher Tolkien translates this command in Sindarin as 'Elvish gate open now for us; doorway of the Dwarf-folk listen to the word (*beth*) of my tongue' (*The Return of the Shadow*, p. 463, n. 14). The words are analyzed by Carl F. Hostetter in 'Settled Spells', *Amon Hen* 122 (July 1993).

308 (I: 321): Picking up his staff

308 (I: 321). ***Mellon!*** – Sindarin 'friend'.

308 (I: 321–2): 'I was wrong after all'

308 (I: 321). too simple for a learned lore-master in these suspicious days – On 17 December 1972 Tolkien wrote to Richard Jeffery: '*pedo mellon.* I do not know why you are not satisfied with G[andalf]'s own interpretation ... *Say "friend"*: i.e. utter the word "friend". Because it makes G[andalf] seem rather dense? But he admits that he was, and explains why – adequately for those who realize what a burden of responsibility, haste, and fear he bore' (*Letters*, p. 424).

308 (I: 322): Out from the water

308 (I: 322). a long sinuous tentacle – Tolkien never explains what this creature is (if it is indeed one creature and not many, as Frodo wonders on the following page). We learn later that the dwarves that accompanied Balin to Moria called it the 'Watcher in the Water'. Its description recalls a cephalopod, like an octopus or squid, but this creature has at least twenty-one tentacles or arms rather than eight or ten.

310 (I: 323–4): 'I cannot say'

310 (I: 323–4). It cannot be less than forty miles from West-door to East-gate in a direct line. – The Company enter Moria in the evening on 13 January and escape on 15 January, probably about midday, having made brief halts as well as two longer halts to sleep. They make better speed through Moria than in their journey from Rivendell to Hollin.

In his unfinished index Tolkien defines *East-gate* as 'the Great Gates of Moria in Dimrill Dale'.

311 (I: 324–5): 'Do not be afraid!'

311 (I: 324). tales in Rivendell – This was the reading in the first printing of the first edition (1954). In the unauthorized resetting of *The Fellowship of the Ring* for its second printing (1954) 'in Rivendell' was mistakenly altered to 'of Rivendell'. The error was corrected in the edition of 2004.

311 (I: 325). He is surer of finding the way home in a blind night than the cats of Queen Berúthiel. – In his letter to W.H. Auden of 7 June 1955 Tolkien wrote: 'I have yet to discover anything about the cats of Queen Berúthiel' (*Letters*, p. 217); and on 10 November 1955 he wrote to Lord Halsbury: 'I do not think that anything is referred to in *The L. of the R.* which does not actually exist in legends written before it was begun, or at least belonging to an earlier period – except only the "cats of Queen Berúthiel"' (*Letters*, p. 228). Christopher Tolkien comments in *Unfinished Tales*, however, that

> even the story of Queen Berúthiel does exist ... if only in a very 'primitive' outline. ... She was the nefarious, solitary, and loveless wife of Tarannon, twelfth King of Gondor (Third Age 830–913) and first of

the 'Ship-kings', who took the crown in the name of Falastur 'Lord of Coasts', and was the first childless king (*The Lord of the Rings*, Appendix A, I, ii and iv). Berúthiel lived in the King's House in Osgiliath, hating the sounds and smells of the sea and the house that Tarannon built below Pelargir 'upon arches whose feet stood deep in the wide waters of Ethir Anduin'; she hated all making, all colours and elaborate adornment, wearing only black and silver and living in bare chambers, and the gardens of the house in Osgiliath were filled with tormented sculptures beneath cypresses and yews. She had nine black cats and one white, her slaves, with whom she conversed, or read their memories, setting them to discover all the dark secrets of Gondor, so that she knew those things 'that men wish most to keep hidden', setting the white cat to spy upon the black, and tormenting them. No man in Gondor dared touch them; all were afraid of them, and cursed when they saw them pass. What follows is almost totally illegible in the unique manuscript, except for the ending, which states that her name was erased from the Book of the Kings ('but the memory of men is not wholly shut in books, and the cats of Queen Berúthiel never passed wholly out of men's speech'), and that King Tarannon had her set on a ship alone with her cats and set adrift in the sea before a north wind. The ship was last seen flying past Umbar under a sickle moon with a cat at the masthead and another as a figure-head on the prow. [pp. 401–2, n. 7]

It was probably before writing this outline that Tolkien told Daphne Castell in an interview ('The Realms of Tolkien', *New Worlds* 50 (November 1966)):

> Berúthiel. I don't really know anything of her. . . . She just popped up, and obviously called for attention, but I don't really know anything certain about her; though oddly enough I have a notion that she was the wife of one of the ship-kings of Pelargir. She loathed the smell of the sea, and fish, and the gulls. Rather like Skadi the giantess who came to the gods in Valhalla, demanding a recompense for the accidental death of her father. She wanted a husband. The gods all lined up behind a curtain, and she selected the pair of feet that appealed to her most. She thought she'd got Baldur, the beautiful god, but it turned out to be Njord the sea-god, and after she'd married him she got absolutely fed up with the sea-side life, and the gulls kept her awake, and finally she went back to live in Jötunheim.
>
> Well, Berúthiel went back to live in the inland city, and went to the bad (or returned to it – she was a black Númenórean in origin, I guess). She was one of these people who loathe cats, but cats will jump on them and follow them about – you know how sometimes they pursue people who hate them? . . . I'm afraid she took to torturing them for amusement, but she kept some and used them – trained them to go on evil errands by night, to spy on her enemies or terrify them. [p. 147]

312 (I: 325–6): The Company behind him

312 (I: 325–6). Yet Frodo began to hear, or to imagine that he heard, something else: like the faint fall of soft bare feet. It was never loud enough, or near enough, for him to feel certain that he heard it, but once it had started it never stopped, while the Company was moving. But it was not an echo, for when they halted it pattered on for a little while by itself, and then grew still. – These are the sounds of Gollum. In the *Hunt for the Ring* papers it is said that, after escaping the Elves of Mirkwood and

> pursued both by Elves and Orcs Gollum crossed the Anduin, probably by swimming, and so eluded the hunt of Sauron; but being still hunted by Elves, and not yet daring to pass near Lórien (only the lure of the Ring itself made him dare to do this afterwards), he hid himself in Moria. That was probably in the autumn of the year; after which all trace of him was lost.
>
> What then happened to Gollum cannot be known for certain. He was peculiarly well fitted to survive in such straits, though at cost of great misery; but he was in great peril of discovery by the servants of Sauron that lurked in Moria*, especially since such bare necessity of food as he must have he could only get by thieving dangerously. No doubt he had intended to use Moria simply as a secret passage westward, his purpose being to find 'Shire' himself as quickly as he could; but he became lost, and it was a very long time before he found his way about. It thus seems probable that he had not long found his way toward the West-gate when the Nine Walkers arrived. He knew nothing, of course, about the action of the doors. To him they would seem huge and immovable; and though they had no lock or bar and opened outwards to a thrust, he did not discover that. In any case he was now far away from any source of food, for the Orcs were mostly in the East-end of Moria, and was become weak and desperate, so that even if he had known all about the doors he still could not have thrust them open. It was thus a piece of singular good fortune for Gollum that the Nine Walkers arrived when they did. (*These were in fact not very numerous, it would seem. But sufficient to keep any intruders out, if no better armed or prepared than Balin's company and not in v. great numbers.) [*Unfinished Tales*, pp. 345, 353 n.11, revised from Marquette 4/2/34]

312 (I: 326): 'I have no memory of this place

312 (I: 326). outside the late Moon is riding westward and the middle-night has passed – It is now very early on 14 January 1419. An early chronology, when the Company entered Moria on 11 December rather than 13 January, indicates that they travelled about fifteen miles to the well-chamber.

314 (I: 328): For eight dark hours

314 (I: 328). will-o'-the-wisp – A phosphorescent light sometimes seen hovering over marshy ground, supposed to be due to the spontaneous combustion of gas from decaying organic matter. In folklore the *Will-o'-the-wisp* (*Jack-a-lantern*, *Ignis fatuus*, etc.) is sometimes thought to be a mischievous sprite.

315 (I: 329): The Company spent the night

315 (I: 329). dolven – Past participle of *delve* 'to dig'.

315–17 (I: 329–30): *The world was young*

315–17 (I: 329–30). *The world was young . . .* – A recording by Tolkien of this poem is included on Disc 1 of *The J.R.R. Tolkien Audio Collection.*

315 (I: 329). *The world was young . . . / No stain yet on the Moon was seen . . . / When Durin woke and walked alone.* – It is told in *The Silmarillion* that the Dwarves were made by the Vala Aulë, impatient for the coming of the Children of Ilúvatar (Elves and Men). 'Since they were to come in the days of the power of Melkor, Aulë made the Dwarves strong to endure. Therefore they are stone-hard, stubborn, fast in friendship and in enmity, and they suffer toil and hunger and hurt of body more hardily than all other speaking peoples; and they live long, far beyond the span of Men, yet not for ever.' Although such creation was beyond Aulë's authority, Ilúvatar had compassion for him, and gave being to the Dwarves, but would not allow them to come before the Firstborn of his design (the Elves). 'Then Aulë took the Seven Fathers of the Dwarves, and laid them to rest in far-sundered places' (p. 44). When at last Durin woke, the Moon had not yet been created.

In Appendix F it is said that the Dwarves 'are a tough, thrawn race for the most part, secretive, laborious, retentive of the memory of injuries (and of benefits), lovers of stone, of gems, of things that take shape under the hands of the craftsman rather than things that live by their own life. But they are not evil by nature, and few ever served the Enemy of free will, whatever the tales of Men may have alleged' (p. 1132, III: 410).

316 (I: 329). *No words were laid on stream or stone* – The streams and other features of the landscape had not yet been named.

316 (I: 329). *He named the nameless hills* – One of Durin's first acts when he woke was to perform the Adam-like function of naming, at least features of the landscape (animals are not mentioned).

316 (I: 329). *He stooped and looked in Mirrormere, / And saw a crown of stars appear, / As gems upon a silver thread, / Above the shadow of his head.* – In Book II, Chapter 6 Frodo, Sam, and Gimli will look in Mirrormere after leaving Moria: 'slowly they saw the forms of the encircling mountains mirrored in a profound blue, and the peaks were like plumes of white flame above them; beyond there was a space of sky. There like jewels sunk in the deep shone glinting stars, though sunlight was in the sky above' (p. 334, I: 348).

316 (I: 330). ***before the fall / Of mighty kings in Nargothrond / And Gondolin, who now beyond / the Western Seas have passed away*** – *Nargothrond* (Sindarin 'Narog-fortress, city in underground caves') was a great underground stronghold of the Elves on the steep western shore of the gorge of the river Narog. The fortress gave its name also to the surrounding territory. It was established by Finrod Felagund. When he was killed after ruling Nargothrond for over 360 years, he was succeeded by his brother Orodreth, who ruled for another thirty years before he in turn was killed and Nargothrond destroyed by the forces of Morgoth and the dragon Glaurung.

Gondolin 'the hidden rock' was a secret realm, surrounded by the Encircling Mountains. Established by the Elf-king Turgon, it was the last of the kingdoms of the Noldor to fall to Morgoth.

Since Finrod, Orodreth, and Turgon were all killed in Beleriand, *beyond the Western Seas have passed away* does not mean a bodily return into the West, but rather the passing of their spirits to the dwellings of Mandos in Aman.

316 (I: 330). ***Durin's Day*** – That is, in the days in which Durin lived. In *The Hobbit* 'Durin's Day' has a different meaning: 'The first day of the dwarves' New Year is . . . the first day of the last moon of Autumn on the threshold of Winter. We still call it Durin's Day when the last moon of Autumn and the sun are in the sky together' (Chapter 3).

316 (I: 330). ***graver*** – Archaic 'engraver'.

316 (I: 330). ***Buckler and corslet*** – A *buckler* is a small round shield. A *corslet* is a piece of armour to cover the trunk of the body.

316 (I: 330). ***No harp is wrung*** – *Wrung*, the past participle of *wring*, is here used poetically to suggest the twisting (plucking) of strings and the ringing tones of the harp.

317 (I: 331): 'For *mithril*'

317 (I: 331). here alone in the world was found Moria-silver – In *The Disaster of the Gladden Fields* it is said that mithril was also found in Númenor, before that land was lost beneath the waves.

317 (I: 331). Durin's Bane – For its identification as a Balrog, see note for p. 330. In *The Treason of Isengard* Christopher Tolkien comments that 'there seems to be some ambiguity' as to whether Gandalf knew what Durin's Bane was:

> He says that the Dwarves fled from Durin's Bane; but when the Balrog appeared, and Gimli cried out 'Durin's Bane!', he muttered: 'A Balrog! Now I understand.' . . . What did Gandalf mean? That he understood now that the being that had entered the Chamber of Mazarbul and striven with him for the mastery through the closed door was a Balrog? Or that he understood at last what it was that had destroyed Durin? Perhaps he meant both; for if he had known what Durin's Bane was, would he not have surmised, with horror, what was on the other side of the door? – 'I have never felt such a challenge', 'I have met my match, and have nearly been destroyed.' [pp. 188–9, n. 16]

318 (I: 332): When he lay down

318 (I: 332). He woke – It is the morning of 15 January 1419.

319 (I: 333): 'It looks like a tomb'

319 (I: 333). On the slab runes were deeply graven – A straightforward transliteration of the runes is:

BALIN
FUNDINUL
UZBADKHAZADDÛMU
BALINSONOVFUNDINLORDOVMORIA

That is, 'Balin Fundinul Uzbad Khazaddûmu, Balin Son of Fundin Lord of Moria' (*ov* = *of* phonetically). The first three lines are in the Dwarf-language Khuzdul, the fourth in the Common Speech (English). Gandalf reads the final line as if two on p. 320, I: 334.

As for the Moria Gate illustration, the inscription on Balin's tomb was re-lettered by a blockmaker's artist after a drawing by Tolkien. Tolkien felt that the new lettering was 'neater and firmer than the original; but I should have preferred a much closer copy. The style of the original has not been caught. The heavy strokes are now far too heavy, and irregularly so. . . . The characteristic thickening at some of the acute angles has been removed, making the letter-forms look much more "ordinary" and modern' (letter to W.N. Beard, 23 September 1953, Tolkien-George Allen & Unwin archive, HarperCollins).

320 (I: 334): 'These are Daeron's Runes

320 (I: 334). Daeron's Runes – In all but the earliest versions of 'The Silmarillion' Daeron (Sindarin ?'shadow') was the minstrel and chief lore-master of King Thingol of Doriath. The Runes or *Cirth* (from KIR- 'to cut, cleave') were devised by the Sindar in Beleriand; a richer and more ordered form, somewhat influenced by the Tengwar of the Noldor, was developed during the First Age and attributed to Daeron. See further, Appendix E, and the 'Appendix on Runes' in *The Treason of Isengard.*

320 (I: 334). Balin son of Fundin / Lord of Moria – In a late essay, published as *Of Dwarves and Men* in *The Peoples of Middle-earth*, Tolkien comments on difficulties presented by this inscription:

> This is effective in its place: giving an idea of the style of the Runes when incised with more care for a solemn purpose, and providing a glimpse of a strange tongue; though all that is really necessary for the tale is the six lines on I.334 [i.e. the final lines of the chapter, from 'These are Daeron's Runes . . .'] (with the translation of the inscription in bigger and bolder lettering). The actual representation of the inscription has however landed in some absurdities.
>
> The use in the inscription of the older and more 'correct' values and shapes of the *Angerthas* [runic alphabet], and not the later 'usage of Erebor' is not absurd (though possibly an unnecessary elaboration); it is in accord with the history of the Runes as sketched in the Appendix E. The older Runes would be used for such a purpose, since they were used in Moria before the flight of the Dwarves, and would appear in other inscriptions of like kind – and Balin was claiming to be the descendant and successor of the former Lord of Moria. The use of the Dwarf-tongue (Khuzdul) is possible in so short an inscription, since this tongue has been sketched in some detail of structure, if with a very small vocabulary. But the names *Balin* and *Fundin* are in such a context absurd. [pp. 299–300]

That is, 'such names as *Balin*, etc. would not have appeared in any contemporary inscription using actual Khuzdul' (p. 301). 'My father's point', Christopher Tolkien explains (p. 322, n. 22), 'was that *Balin* and *Fundin* are actual Old Norse names used as "translations" for the purpose of *The Lord of the Rings*. What he should have done in a visual representation of the tomb-inscription was to use, not of course their "inner" names in Khuzdul, but their *real* "outer" names which in the text of *The Lord of the Rings* are represented by *Balin* and *Fundin*.' The use of English rather than genuine Common Speech in the last line of the inscription is similarly absurd.

On the use of 'Moria' also in this inscription, see again note for p. 306. It was evidently the accepted name for Khazad-dûm in the 'tongue of Men' (Common Speech) by this point in time.

Chapter 5

THE BRIDGE OF KHAZAD-DÛM

For drafts and history of this chapter, see *The Treason of Isengard*, pp. 190–206.

321 (I: 335): The Company of the Ring

321 (I: 335). Balin's visit to the Shire long ago – Presumably the visit described at the end of *The Hobbit*, recorded in *The Tale of Years* as occurring in Third Age 2949 (S.R. 1349).

321 (I: 335): At length they stirred

321 (I: 335). By both the doors they could now see that many bones were lying, and among them were broken swords and axe-heads, and cloven shields and helms. – In *The Hobbit*, Chapter 13, Bilbo and his companions come upon a similar scene in the Lonely Mountain, in the 'great chamber of Thror': 'Tables were rotting there; chairs and benches were lying there overturned, charred and decaying. Skulls and bones were upon the floor among flagons and bowls and broken drinking-horns and dust.' In both that book and *The Lord of the Rings* the protagonists visit a once glorious realm from which the Dwarves have been driven out.

321 (I: 335). Some of the swords were crooked: orc-scimitars – A *scimitar* is a 'short, curved, single-edged sword, used among Orientals, especially Turks and Persians' (*OED*). Tolkien had already associated goblins (orcs) with scimitars in *The Hobbit*, Chapter 17, where 'the bodyguard of Bolg, goblins of huge size' bore 'scimitars of steel'.

321 (I: 335): There were many recesses

321 (I: 335). the leaves cracked – This was the reading in the first printing of the first edition (1954). In the unauthorized resetting of *The Fellowship of the Ring* for its second printing (1954) 'cracked' was mistakenly altered to 'crackled'. The error was corrected in the edition of 2004.

321 (I: 335). He pored over it for some time – In *Artist and Illustrator* Wayne G. Hammond and Christina Scull suggest that here Tolkien may have been thinking 'of the Cottonian *Beowulf* manuscript, which was scorched and made brittle by fire in 1731 and further damaged by attempts at restoration' (p. 163).

321 (I: 335). in runes, both of Moria and of Dale, and here and there in Elvish script – See note for p. 337 concerning 'facsimile' pages.

321 (I: 335): At last Gandalf looked up

321 (I: 335). their coming to Dimrill Dale nigh on thirty years ago – According to *The Tale of Years* Balin went to Moria in Third Age 2989; it is now early in 3019 (S.R. 1419).

321 (I: 335): *'We drove out orcs*

321 (I: 335). *Flói* – The name *Flói* does not appear in either the *Dvergatal* in the *Elder Edda* or in Snorri Sturluson's *Prose Edda.*

321 (I: 335). *twentyfirst hall of North end* – One of the upper halls of the North-end, the latter being 'excavations of Moria north of the older halls and the Great Gate' (*Index*).

322 (I: 336): 'Well, I can read no more

322 (I: 336). Third Deep – The Deeps are numbered according to stages below Gate-level.

322 (I: 336): 'I fear he had ill tidings

322 (I: 336). He seems to have kept the title that he took for less than five years – According to *The Tale of Years* Balin was killed and the dwarf-colony in Moria destroyed in Third Age 2994 (S.R. 1394).

322 (I: 336): 'It is grim reading

322 (I: 336). *Frár and Lóni and Náli* – All of these names appear in the *Dvergatal* in the *Elder Edda.*

323 (I: 337): Gandalf raised his head

323 (I: 337). the Book of Mazarbul – Tolkien spent a great deal of time and effort in producing a series of 'facsimiles' of the three damaged pages of the *Book of Mazarbul* that Gandalf is able to read. These would have helped to 'authenticate' his fiction, and support the pretence he had established in his original foreword to *The Lord of the Rings*, that he had derived his text from ancient records. He made at least four preliminary sketches of the first of the three pages, and at least one sketch of each of the other two, chiefly in coloured pencil. The three finished 'facsimiles' were made before March 1947. They feature genuine tears, losses, burn marks, and 'stab holes' through which the leaves of the book had supposedly once been sewn together.

Tolkien hoped that the pages could be published at the beginning of Book II, Chapter 5 of *The Lord of the Rings*, and was disappointed when for reasons of cost that plan had to be abandoned. They were eventually reproduced in 1976 in the Allen & Unwin *Lord of the Rings 1977 Calendar*, and then in *Pictures by J.R.R. Tolkien* (1979, no. 23; 2nd edn. (1992), no. 24) with notes by Christopher Tolkien and transcriptions of the text, including some words that in the story Gandalf is unable to read. In

Pictures by J.R.R. Tolkien Christopher Tolkien says that the first, runic page is written in 'the late form of the Angerthas, called "the usage of Erebor". This use would be expected in a kind of diary, written, hastily and without attempt at calligraphy or meticulous consistency of spelling, by Dwarves coming from Dale.' He describes the second page, in Elvish script, as 'written in the later or Westron convention, in its northern variety, in the application of the Elvish signs to the Common Western Speech'. And he comments on the third page that 'the runes employed are the same as those on the first of these facsimiles, though the hand is different and the shapes differ in detail. The last line is in the same Elvish alphabet as that used on the second page.' See further, *The Treason of Isengard*, pp. 457–9, 465.

The three finished facsimiles were first published in *The Fellowship of the Ring* in the Croatian edition of 1995, but not in an English language edition until 2004 (by HarperCollins and Houghton Mifflin). The second (preliminary) version of the first page and the final version of the third page were published in *Artist and Illustrator*, figs. 155–6. Another, later, sketch for the first page was published in *The Invented Worlds of J.R.R. Tolkien: Drawings and Original Manuscripts from the Marquette University Collection* (2004).

In *Of Dwarves and Men* Tolkien wrote that in creating the 'Book of Mazarbul' facsimiles

> I followed the general principle followed throughout: the Common Speech was to be represented as English of today, literary or colloquial as the case demanded. Consequently the text was cast into English spelt as at present, but modified as it might be by writers in haste whose familiarity with the written form was imperfect, and who were also (on the first and third pages) transliterating the English into a different alphabet – one which did not for instance employ any letter in more than one distinct value, so that the distribution of English *k*, *c* — *c*, *s* was reduced to *k* — *s*; while the use of the letters for *s* and *z* was variable since English uses *s* frequently as = *z*. In addition, since documents of this kind nearly always show uses of letters or shapes that are peculiar and rarely or never found elsewhere, a few such features are also introduced: as the signs for the English vowel pairs *ea*, *oa*, *ou* (irrespective of their sounds). . . .
>
> But it is of course in fact an erroneous extension of the general linguistic treatment. It is one thing to represent all the dialogue of the story in varying forms of English: this must be supposed to be done by 'translation' – from memory of unrecorded sounds, or from documents lost or not printed, whether this is stated or not, whenever it is done in any narrative dealing with past times or foreign lands. But it is quite another thing to provide *visible* facsimiles or representations of writings or carvings supposed to be of the date of the events in the narrative. [*The Peoples of Middle-earth*, pp. 298–9]

323 (I: 337). You had better keep it, Gimli – The Book of Mazarbul is never mentioned again.

323 (I: 337): Gandalf had hardly spoken

323 (I: 337). *Doom, doom* – Tolkien uses the sound *doom* to emphasize an atmosphere fraught with danger, made greater as the Company realize that they are now in much the same situation as the dwarves of whom they have just been reading in the Book of Mazarbul. Tolkien comments in the manuscript of *Nomenclature* that the

> word *doom*, original sense 'judgement' (formal and legal, or personal), has in English, partly owing to its sound, and largely owing to its special use in *Doomsday*, become a word loaded with senses of death; finality; fate (impending or foretold). . . .
>
> The use in the text as a word . . . associated with *boom* is of course primarily descriptive of sound, but is meant (and by most English readers would be felt) to recall the noun *doom*, with its sense of disaster.

Robert Boenig in 'The Drums of Doom: H.G. Wells' *First Men in the Moon* and *The Lord of the Rings*', *Mythlore* 14, no. 3, whole no. 53 (Spring 1988), suggests that the 'Boom . . . Boom . . . Boom' of the Selenite machinery heard when the travellers arrive on the Moon in Wells' book may have influenced this scene in *The Lord of the Rings*. Bedford and Cavor are also faced underground with a long narrow bridge extending from the edge of a precipice, and at that point turn on their captors and escape.

324 (I: 338): 'There are Orcs, very many of them'

324 (I: 338). Uruks – In Appendix A it is said that the *Uruks* are 'black orcs of great strength' (p. 1053, III: 333) employed by Mordor and Isengard during the War of the Ring. They first appeared out of Mordor *c.* Third Age 2475.

324 (I: 338): Heavy feet were heard

324 (I: 338). A huge arm and shoulder, with a dark skin of greenish scales . . . then a great, flat, toeless foot – This is presumably the cave-troll just mentioned. In Tolkien's illustration *The Trolls* in *The Hobbit* the creatures appear to have a scaly skin. The flat, toeless foot suggests a lumpish, ill-formed appearance.

325 (I: 339): But even as they retreated

325 (I: 339). a huge orc-chieftain, almost man-high. . . . His broad flat face was swart, his eyes were like coals, and his tongue was red – That even a *huge* orc was only *almost man-high* suggests that orcs generally were shorter than Men.

The *flat face* of the orc-chieftain agrees with the description given by Tolkien to Forrest J. Ackerman in June 1958, that Orcs are 'are (or were) squat, broad, flat-nosed, sallow-skinned, with wide mouths and slant eyes' (*Letters*, p. 274); see note for p. 5.

Swart is an archaic or poetic word meaning 'dark, dusky'. A comparison with coal is commonly used to suggest extreme blackness.

325 (I: 339). thrust his spear . . . and it broke. But even as the orc flung down the truncheon – *Truncheon* here is used in the obsolete or archaic sense 'a fragment of a spear or lance; a piece broken off from a spear' (*OED*).

327 (I: 341): 'It is getting hot!'

327 (I: 341). all the orcs ever spawned – *Spawned* here suggests 'to produce or generate . . . in large numbers' (*OED*), not 'to reproduce through eggs' (as for fish etc.). In *The Silmarillion* it is said that 'the Orcs had life and multiplied after the manner of the Children of Ilúvatar' (p. 50).

328 (I: 342): 'You take after Bilbo'

328 (I: 342). There is more about you than meets the eye, as I said of him long ago. – Gandalf does not use these precise words in *The Hobbit*, but in Chapter 6 of that book says: 'What did I tell you? . . . Mr Baggins has more about him than you guess', and in Chapter 16, to Bilbo: 'There is always more about you than anyone expects!'

328 (I: 342): 'There is some new devilry here'

328 (I: 342). Old Moria – 'The earliest mansions and passages of Moria near the Great Gates' (*Index*).

328 (I: 342): They peered out

328 (I: 342). pillars . . . carved like boles of mighty trees whose boughs upheld the roof with a branching tracery of stone – Similarly in *The Silmarillion* it is said that in Thingol's underground stronghold, Menegroth, the work of Elves and Dwarves, 'the pillars . . . were hewn in the likeness of the beeches of Oromë, stock [trunk], bough, and leaf' (p. 93).

329 (I: 343): 'Now for the last race!'

329 (I: 343). If the sun is shining outside, we may still escape. – Orcs do not like the sunlight.

329 (I: 344): It came to the edge of the fire

329 (I: 344). Its streaming mane – Its *mane*, or long hair, streams presumably because it is impelled backwards by the force of his leap. In *The Lay of Leithian* Tolkien refers to 'the Balrog-lords with fiery manes' (*The Lays of Beleriand*, p. 296).

329 (I: 344). a whip of many thongs – That is, with many narrow strips of leather or some other material.

330 (I: 344): 'Ai! ai!' wailed Legolas

330 (I: 344). Balrog – Sindarin 'demon of might'. In *The Silmarillion* the *Balrogs* are Maiar who were attracted to Melkor by his 'splendour in the days of his greatness, and remained in that allegiance down into his darkness', or whom 'he corrupted afterwards to his service with lies and treacherous gifts. Dread among these spirits were the Valaraukar, the scourges of fire that in Middle-earth were called the Balrogs, demons of terror' (p. 31). Balrogs appeared in *The Fall of Gondolin*, in the earliest version of 'The Silmarillion', where they are described as 'demons with whips of flame and claws of steel' (*The Book of Lost Tales, Part Two*, p. 169). In that tale hundreds of Balrogs take part in the assault on Gondolin; and the idea that Balrogs existed in large numbers remained Tolkien's conception at least until the early 1950s, when Morgoth sent forth 'a host of Balrogs' (*Morgoth's Ring*, pp. 75, 79). But Tolkien emended the latter passage to 'sent forth his Balrogs, the last of his servants that remained faithful to him', and wrote in the margin: 'There should not be supposed more than say 3 or at most 7 ever existed' (p. 80).

On 25 April 1954 Tolkien wrote to Naomi Mitchison:

> The *Balrog* is a survivor from the *Silmarillion* and the legends of the First Age. . . . The *Balrogs*, of whom the whips were the chief weapons, were primeval spirits of destroying fire, chief servants of the primeval Dark Power of the First Age. They were supposed to have been all destroyed in the overthrow of *Thangorodrim*, his fortress in the North. But it is here found (there is usually a hang-over especially of evil from one age to another) that one had escaped and taken refuge under the mountains of Hithaeglin [*sic*] (the Misty Mountains). It is observable that only the Elf knows what the thing is – and doubtless Gandalf. [*Letters*, p. 180]

In the first version of this chapter Tolkien described the Balrog as a figure 'no more than man-high yet terror seemed to go before it. They could see the furnace-fire of its yellow eyes from afar; its arms were very long; it had a red [?tongue]. . . . The flames leaped up to greet it and wreathed about it. Its streaming hair seemed to catch fire, and the sword that it held turned to flame.' But against this he wrote: 'Alter description of Balrog. It seemed to be of man's shape, but its form could not be plainly discerned. It *felt* larger than it looked' (*The Treason of Isengard*, pp. 197, 199). The Balrog in *The Lord of the Rings* is certainly a being of fire and darkness; it uses a whip as a weapon, but also has a sword.

In *J.R.R. Tolkien: Author of the Century* Tom Shippey suggests that Tolkien's Balrogs owe something to the Sigelwara land, the 'land of the Sigelware', mentioned in the Old English poem *Exodus* about which Tolkien wrote an article, *Sigelwara Land*, for *Medium Aevum* (December 1932 and June 1934). 'In modern dictionaries and editions', Shippey comments,

> these 'Sigelware' are invariably translated as 'Ethiopians'. Tolkien thought that the name ... should have been written **sigel-hearwa*. Furthermore, he suggested ... that a **sigel-hearwa* was a kind of fire-giant. The first element in the compound meant both 'sun' and 'jewel'; the second was related to Latin *carbo*, 'soot'. When an Anglo-Saxon of the preliterate Dark Age said *sigelhearwa*, before any Englishman had ever heard of Ethiopia or of the Book of Exodus, Tolkien believed that what he meant was 'rather the sons of Múspell [the fire-giant in Norse mythology who will bring on Ragnarök, the great battle between the gods and the powers of Evil] than of Ham [son of Noah], the ancestors of the Silhearwan with red-hot eyes that emitted sparks, with faces black as soot'. [pp. 85–6]

On possible sources for the Balrog, see also Joe Abbott, 'Tolkien's Monsters: Concept and Function in *The Lord of the Rings*: (Part I) The Balrog of Khazad-dûm', *Mythlore* 16, no. 1, whole no. 59 (Autumn 1989).

330 (I: 344): The Balrog reached the bridge

330 (I: 344). the shadow about it reached out like two vast wings – This and the statement two paragraphs later, that 'it drew itself up to a great height, and its wings were spread from wall to wall', have led to much discussion among readers as to whether Balrogs have wings. *Like two vast wings* in the first describes the shadow surrounding the Balrog, and the second still seems applicable to its shadow: as the Balrog increases its height, so its shadow spreads wider. Other evidence cited for wings, such as that the Balrogs 'arose, and they passed with winged speed over Hithlum' (*Morgoth's Ring*, p. 297), can generally be interpreted as figurative.

330 (I: 344): 'You cannot pass'

330 (I: 344). I am a servant of the Secret Fire, wielder of the flame of Anor – At the beginning of the Music of Creation in *The Silmarillion* Ilúvatar says to the Ainur: 'I have kindled you with the Flame Imperishable' (p. 15); and after showing them a vision of the World: 'Let these things Be! And I will send forth into the Void the Flame Imperishable, and it shall be at the heart of the World' (p. 20). At the beginning of the *Valaquenta*, published in *The Silmarillion*, Ilúvatar's creative act is told again, but with *Secret Fire* replacing *Flame Imperishable*.

In writing after the publication of *The Lord of the Rings* Tolkien said that 'the "Flame Imperishable" ... appears to mean the Creative activity of Eru (in some sense distinct from or within Him), by which things could be given a "real" and independent (though derivative and created) existence' (*Morgoth's Ring*, p. 345). It would appear that the Ainur could use this 'Secret Fire' in actions in accord with the design created in the Music. But Melkor 'had gone often alone into the void places seeking the Imperishable Flame; for desire grew hot within him to bring into Being things of his own. . . . Yet he found not the Fire, for it is with Ilúvatar' (*The Silmarillion*, p. 16); and thus it would seem that those who acted against rather than with the Music could not find or use the Secret Fire – but that Melkor and his servants could use a fire of another sort. In the earliest versions of Book II, Chapter 5, Gandalf says: 'I am the master of White Fire [> Flame]. [Neither Red Fire nor Black Shadow can >] The Red Fire cannot come this way' (*The Treason of Isengard*, pp. 198, 203).

In the manuscript of *Nomenclature* Tolkien notes that *Anor* in *flame of Anor* means 'Sun'. Anor is not mentioned in the early versions of this chapter, and it seems strange that Gandalf should lay such emphasis on the Sun whose light was 'derived from the Trees only after they were sullied by Evil' (letter to Milton Waldman, ?late 1951, *Letters*, p. 148, n.) – except that historically the Sun has been seen as an agent of purification, and *c.* 1946–8 Tolkien wrote a new version of his Creation story, in which the Sun existed from the beginning, and was not derived from the Trees. In late writing, after the publication of *The Lord of the Rings*, he returned to this idea and wrote of the beginning of Arda:

> Now the Sun was designed to be the heart of Arda, and the Valar purposed that it should give light to all that Realm, unceasingly and without wearying or diminution, and that from its light the world should receive health and life and growth. Therefore Varda set there the most ardent and beautiful of all those spirits that had entered with her into Eä [the World] . . . and Varda gave to her keeping a portion of the gift of Ilúvatar [light that is holy] so that the Sun should endure and be blessed and give blessing. [*Morgoth's Ring*, p. 380].

330 (I: 344). Udûn – In his unfinished index Tolkien defines *Udûn* as '"dark pit", the dwelling of Morgoth beneath Thangorodrim . . . called the *Underworld of old*' (distinct from *Udûn* a place in Mordor; see note for p. 928). The *1966 Index* adds 'Udûn *hell*'.

330 (I: 345): The Balrog made no answer

330 (I: 345). wizened – Shrivelled, withered.

331 (I: 345): With a terrible cry

331 (I: 345). 'Fly, you fools!' he cried, and was gone. – In *The Hobbit* Gandalf leaves the dwarves and Bilbo to continue their journey without him, and rejoins them only near the end of the book. In his absence, Bilbo develops previously unexpected abilities, and in some ways even steps into Gandalf's place, winning the respect of the dwarves. In *The Lord of the Rings* Tolkien removes Gandalf twice for purposes of the story: near the beginning, so that Frodo and his companions have to make the journey to Rivendell without the Wizard's support, and again in Book II, so that Frodo and Sam travel on their own into Mordor. Tolkien anticipated Gandalf's fall into the abyss already in autumn 1939, in an outline for the

Moria chapters: 'Of course Gandalf must reappear later – probably fall is not so deep as it seemed. Gandalf thrusts Balrog under him . . . and eventually following the subterranean stream in the gulf he found a way out – but he does not turn up until they [the rest of the Company] have had many adventures' (*The Return of the Shadow*, p. 462).

Chapter 6
LOTHLÓRIEN

For drafts and history of this chapter, see *The Treason of Isengard*, pp. 217–44.

333 (I: 347): They rose and looked about them

333 (I: 347). glen – A narrow valley.

333 (I: 347): 'Yonder is the Dimrill Stair'

333 (I: 347). Dimrill Stair – In his unfinished index Tolkien includes: '*Dimrill*: name of a stream and falls flowing down mountain-side from the N[orth] into Mirrormere'; and '*Dimrill Stair*: steep way down beside the Dimrill from the Redhorn Gate'.

333 (I: 347): To the east the outflung arm

333 (I: 347). sward – An expanse of short grass, turf.

333–4 (I: 347–8): The Company now went down the road

333 (I: 348). whin – The common furze or gorse, a spiny yellow-flowered shrub.

334 (I: 348). from the lowlands to the Dwarf-kingdom – This was the reading in the first printing of the first edition (1954). In the unauthorized resetting of *The Fellowship of the Ring* for its second printing (1954) the passage was mistakenly altered to: 'from the lowlands *of* the Dwarf-kingdom' (emphasis ours). The erroneous reading suggests that the kingdom included extensive lands outside the Great Gates of Moria on the eastern side of the Misty Mountains. The phrase was restored to its correct form in the edition of 2004.

334 (I: 348): 'Be swift then!'

334 (I: 348). The Moon is almost spent – It is just about to enter its last quarter, and will not rise until just after midnight.

334 (I: 348): They stooped over the dark water

334 (I: 348). There like jewels sunk in the deep shone glinting stars – In the next paragraph, and previously in the poem he chanted in Moria, Gimli refers to these as 'the Crown of Durin', evidently the seven stars (representing the Plough) noted previously. Tolkien seems to suggest that the stars shining in the deep 'though sunlight was in the sky above' (when stars would not be visible) are a reflection from Durin's time in the distant past.

334 (I: 348): The road now turned south

334 (I: 348). freshet – A rush of fresh water.

335 (I: 349): 'There lie the woods

335 (I: 349). Lothlórien – In one place in his unfinished index Tolkien partially 'translates' *Lothlórien* as 'Lórien of the Blossom', but in another as 'The Dream Flower'. The name combines Sindarin *loth* 'flower' with Quenya *Lórien* '?Dream Land', the name of the dwelling in Valinor of the Vala Irmo, 'the master of visions and dreams', whose gardens 'are the fairest of all places in the world' (*The Silmarillion*, p. 28). Lothlórien is often referred to simply as *Lórien*, or 'the Golden Wood'.

In a note to the late work *Concerning Galadriel and Celeborn*, Christopher Tolkien explains, it is said that

> *Lórinand* was the Nandorin name of this region . . . and contained the Elvish word meaning 'golden light': 'valley of gold'. The Quenya form would be *Lurenandë*, the Sindarin *Glornan* or *Nan Laur*. Both here and elsewhere the meaning of the name is explained by reference to the golden mallorn-trees of Lothlórien; . . . and in another, later, discussion the name *Lórinand* is said to have been itself a transformation, after the introduction of the mallorns, of a yet older name *Lindórinand*, 'Vale of the Land of the Singers'. From many other discussions of the names of Lothlórien, to some extent at variance among themselves, it emerges that all the later names were probably due to Galadriel herself, combining different elements: *laurë* 'gold', *nan(d)* 'valley', *ndor* 'land', *lin-* 'sing'; and in *Laurelindórinan* 'Valley of Singing Gold' . . . deliberately echoing the name of the Golden Tree that grew in Valinor [Laurelin], 'for which, as is plain, Galadriel's longing increased year by year to, at last, an overwhelming regret'. . . .
>
> The further change from *Lórinand* 'Valley of Gold' to *Lórien* 'may well be due to Galadriel herself', for 'the resemblance cannot be accidental. She had endeavoured to make Lórien a refuge and an island of peace and beauty, a memorial of ancient days, but was now filled with regret and misgiving, knowing that the golden dream was hastening to a grey awakening.' [*Unfinished Tales*, pp. 252–3, n. 5]

335 (I: 349). There are no trees like the trees of that land. For in the autumn their leaves fall not, but turn to gold. Not till the spring comes and the new green opens do they fall, and then the boughs are laden with yellow flowers; and the floor of the wood is golden, and golden is the roof, and its pillars are of silver, for the bark of the trees is smooth and grey. – Tolkien illustrated this description by Legolas in his drawing *The Forest of Lothlórien in Spring* (*Artist and Illustrator*, fig. 157).

The name of the trees is not given until later in the chapter: *mallorn*, Sindarin 'golden tree', plural *mellyrn*. In Middle-earth, with one exception, the mallorn grew only in Lothlórien, and came there from Númenor. According to *A Description of Númenor*, written *c.* 1960, in one part of Númenor

> grew the mighty golden tree [Quenya] *malinornë*, reaching after five centuries a height scarce less than it achieved in Eressëa itself. Its bark was silver and smooth, and its boughs somewhat upswept after the manner of the beech; but it never grew save with a single trunk. Its leaves, like those of the beech but greater, were pale green above and beneath were silver, glistering in the sun; in the autumn they did not fall, but turned to pale gold. In the spring it bore golden blossom in clusters like a cherry, which bloomed on during the summer; and as soon as the flowers opened the leaves fell, so that through spring and summer a grove of *malinorni* was carpeted and roofed with gold, but its pillars were of grey silver. Its fruit was a nut with a silver shale; and some were given as a gift by Tar-Aldarion, the sixth King of Númenor, to King Gil-galad of Lindon. They did not take root in that land; but Gil-galad gave some to his kinswoman, Galadriel, and under her power they grew and flourished in the guarded land of Lothlórien beside the River Anduin, until the High Elves at last left Middle-earth; but they did not reach the height or girth of the great groves of Númenor. [*Unfinished Tales*, pp. 167–8]

335 (I: 349): Soon afterwards they came

335 (I: 349). harts-tongue and shrubs of whortle-berry – *Harts-tongue* is a fern with long, narrow fronds said to resemble the tongues of deer.

Whortle-berry is another name for 'bilberry': see note for p. 209. The word is spelt without a hyphen in Book IV, Chapter 7.

336 (I: 350): 'Look, my friends!'

336 (I: 350). Here's a pretty hobbit-skin to wrap an elven-princeling in! – Surely a deliberate echo of the nursery rhyme 'Bye, baby bunting, / daddy's gone a-hunting, / Gone to get a rabbit skin / to wrap the baby bunting in.'

338 (I: 352): It is long since any of my own folk

338 (I: 352). It is long since any of my own folk journeyed hither back to the land whence we wandered in ages long ago – In writing of the Elves after publication of *The Lord of the Rings* Tolkien said that the folk of Thranduil's realm in northern Mirkwood 'had migrated from the south, being the kin and neighbours of the Elves of Lórien; but they had dwelt in Greenwood the Great east of Anduin. In the Second Age their king, Oropher [the father of Thranduil, father of Legolas], had withdrawn northward beyond the Gladden Fields' (appendix to *The History of Galadriel and Celeborn* in *Unfinished Tales*, p. 258).

338–9 (I: 353): 'Here is Nimrodel!'

338 (I: 353). Nimrodel – In his unfinished index Tolkien writes that *Nimrodel* 'lady of the white grotto' is the 'name of an Elven-maid, and of a mountain-stream falling into the Celebrant (Silverlode)'. In late writing he said that the name 'cannot be fully explained from Sindarin, though fitting it in form' (*Unfinished Tales*, p. 257).

338 (I: 353). Silvan Elves – In a late etymological discussion Tolkien comments that the Silvan Elves (Wood-elves)

> were in origin Teleri, and so remoter kin of the Sindar, though even longer separated from them than the Teleri of Valinor. They were descended from those of the Teleri who, on the Great Journey, were daunted by the Misty Mountains and lingered in the Vale of Anduin, and so never reached Beleriand or the Sea . . . but they still remembered that they were in origin Eldar . . . and they welcomed those of the Noldor and especially the Sindar who did not pass over the Sea but migrated eastward [i.e. at the beginning of the Second Age]. . . .
>
> In Lórien, where many of the people were Sindar in origin, or Noldor, survivors from Eregion . . . , Sindarin had become the language of all the people. [appendix to *The History of Galadriel and Celeborn* in *Unfinished Tales*, pp. 256–7]

339 (I: 353): 'Do you hear the voice

339 (I: 353). our woodland tongue – Later in this chapter an elf of Lothlórien speaks to Legolas 'in an elven-tongue. Frodo could understand little of what was said, for the speech that the Silvan folk east of the mountains used among themselves was unlike that of the West. Legolas looked up and answered in the same language' (p. 342, I: 356). In the second edition (1965) Tolkien added a footnote to this passage, directing the reader to Appendix F, where it is said (in a passage also added in the second edition): 'In Lórien at this period Sindarin was spoken, though with an "accent", since most of its folk were of Silvan origin. This "accent" and his own limited acquaintance with Sindarin misled Frodo . . .' (p. 1127, III: 405). In Appendix F it is also noted that Sindarin and Quenya are only two of the Elvish tongues, of which Sindarin was most commonly used in Middle-earth; and from this it follows that other languages were spoken, of which little or nothing is said in *The Lord of the Rings*: the 'Silvan tongues' as they are called elsewhere in Tolkien's writings. In one late linguistic discussion Tolkien states that Sindarin was spoken in the house of Thranduil (and thus by Legolas, son of the Elven-king) 'though not by all his folk', i.e. other Elves of Mirkwood; and in another late work it is said that 'by the end of the Third Age the Silvan tongues [distinct from Sindarin] had probably ceased to be spoken in the two regions that had importance at the time of the War of the Ring: Lórien and the realm of Thranduil in northern Mirkwood' (appendix to *The History of Galadriel and Celeborn* in *Unfinished Tales*, pp. 256, 257).

339–40 (I: 354–5): *An Elven-maid there was of old*

339–40 (I: 354–5). *An Elven-maid there was of old . . .* – A recording by Tolkien of this poem is included on Disc 1 of *The J.R.R. Tolkien Audio Collection.*

340 (I: 354). *yore* – In poetic or literary usage, 'long ago'.

340 (I: 354). *haven grey* – Apart from this poem, there are only a few references to this particular haven in *The Lord of the Rings*: the comment by Legolas later in this chapter that the Elves of Lórien set sail from the Bay of Belfalas; Haldir's statement, also in this chapter, that the haven in the south no longer exists; and the greeting of Legolas to Imrahil of Dol Amroth: 'It is long since the people of Nimrodel left the woodlands of Lórien, and yet still one may see that not all sailed from Amroth's haven west over water' (Book V, Chapter 9, p. 872, III: 148). Tolkien mentions this haven also in his Preface to *The Adventures of Tom Bombadil and Other Verses from The Red Book*: 'In Langstrand and Dol Amroth there were many traditions of the ancient Elvish dwellings, and of the haven at the mouth of the Morthond from which "westward ships" had sailed as far back as the fall of Eregion in the Second Age' (p. 8). On his instructions, Pauline Baynes placed the haven at the mouth of the Morthond on her decorated map with the name *Edhellond* (Sindarin *edhel* 'elf' + *lond* 'land-locked haven'). Christopher Tolkien therefore included it in his revised map of Middle-earth in *Unfinished Tales*. Tolkien mentions the Elvish haven on the Bay of Belfalas in several late writings, but the accounts vary greatly: see *Unfinished Tales*, pp. 246–8.

340 (I: 354). *mountain-lee* – The side of the mountain away from the wind, the sheltered side.

340 (I: 354). *A wind by night in Northern lands / Arose . . . / And drove the ship* – According to a late text by Tolkien 'there came a great night of storm. . . . It came from the Northern Waste, and roared down through Eriador into the lands of Gondor, doing great havoc; the White Mountains were no shield against it' (*Amroth and Nimrodel* in *Unfinished Tales*, p. 242).

340 (I: 354). *Amroth* – In his unfinished index Tolkien says merely that *Amroth* is the 'name of a prince of the Silvan Elves of Lórien in the Elder Days'. In a late etymological work he says that 'the name Amroth is explained as being a nickname derived from his living in a high *talan* or *flet*, the wooden platforms built high up in the trees of Lothlórien in which the Galadhrim dwelt: it meant "upclimber, high climber"' (*Unfinished Tales*, p. 245). Christopher Tolkien comments: 'This explanation supposes that the first element of the name *Amroth* is the same Elvish word as Quenya *amba* "up", found also in Sindarin *amon*, a hill or mountain with steep sides; while the second element is a derivative from the stem *rath-* meaning "climb"' (*Unfinished Tales*, p. 255, n. 16). In other late writing Tolkien says that the name 'cannot be fully explained from Sindarin, though fitting it in form' (*Unfinished Tales*, p. 257).

340 (I: 355). ***As mew upon the wing*** – *Mew* 'a gull'.

341 (I: 355): The voice of Legolas

341 (I: 355). That is but a part – Tolkien tried to fill out the story of Amroth and Nimrodel in writings after the publication of *The Lord of the Rings*, but with significant variations in the accounts told in different texts (see *The History of Galadriel and Celeborn* in *Unfinished Tales*, pp. 233 ff.). In *Concerning Galadriel and Celeborn*, which deals mainly with events in the Second Age up to the defeat of Sauron in 1701, Amroth is the son of Galadriel and Celeborn, and Nimrodel is not mentioned. Soon after Second Age 1701 Galadriel left Lórien, where she had been living, in the care of Amroth and moved to Imladris. Later (but Tolkien does not indicate how much later) Galadriel and Celeborn settled in 'the little-inhabited lands between the mouth of the Gwathló and Ethir Anduin. There they dwelt in Belfalas, at the place that was afterwards called Dol Amroth; there Amroth their son at times visited them. . . . It was not until far on in the Third Age, when Amroth was lost and Lórinand in peril, that Galadriel returned there, in the year 1981' (*Unfinished Tales*, p. 240). In *The Tale of Years* Third Age 1981 is the date that the Dwarves fled from Moria after a Balrog appeared there in 1980.

In a later text Amroth succeeds to the rule of Lothlórien in succession to his father Amdir, who was slain in the Battle of Dagorlad at the end of the Second Age. 'Though Sindarin in descent he lived after the manner of the Silvan Elves and housed in the tall trees of a great green mound, ever after called Cerin Amroth.' He loved a Silvan Elf, Nimrodel, who returned his love but would not wed him because she

> regretted the incoming of the Elves from the West, who (as she said) brought wars and destroyed the peace of old. She would speak only the Silvan tongue even after it had fallen into disuse among the folk of Lórien; and she dwelt alone beside the falls of the river Nimrodel to which she gave her name. But when the terror came out of Moria and the Dwarves were driven out, and in their stead Orcs crept in, she fled distraught alone south into empty lands [in the year 1981]. [*Amroth and Nimrodel* in *Unfinished Tales*, pp. 240–1]

Amroth followed, and found her on the edge of Fangorn; there they plighted their troth and agreed to pass over the Sea into the West together. But they became separated on their way south. When Amroth reached the

Elf-haven he found the few Elves still there about to depart in their only seaworthy ship. They delayed their departure in response to Amroth, who still hoped that Nimrodel might reach the haven, but, as they had already stripped their houses, they lived on the ship:

> then in the autumn there came a great night of storm. . . . The light Elven-ship was torn from its moorings and driven into the wild waters towards the coasts of Umbar. No tidings of it were ever heard in Middle-earth; but the Elven-ships made for this journey did not founder, and doubtless it left the Circles of the World and came at last to Eressëa. . . . The storm fell on the coast just as dawn was peering through the flying clouds; but when Amroth woke the ship was already far from land. Crying aloud in despair *Nimrodel!* he leapt into the sea and swam towards the fading shore. The mariners with their Elvish sight for a long time could see him battling with the waves, until the rising sun gleamed through the clouds and far off lit his bright hair like a spark of gold. No eyes of Elves or Men ever saw him again in Middle-earth. [p. 242].

See further, note for p. 875 on the River Gilrain.

341 (I: 355). Celebrant – See note for p. 274.

341 (I: 355). neither Nimrodel nor Amroth came ever back – This was the reading in the first printing of the first edition (1954). In the unauthorized resetting of *The Fellowship of the Ring* for its second printing (1954) 'came ever back' was mistakenly altered to 'ever came back'. The error was corrected in the edition of 2004.

341 (I: 355): 'It is told that

341 (I: 355). Galadhrim, the Tree-People – In *The Lord of the Rings* as first published *Galadhrim* was spelt *Galadrim*. Here and elsewhere (except for a few missed examples which were emended later) *Galadrim* became *Galadhrim* in the second printing (1967) of the Allen & Unwin second edition. Christopher Tolkien has said of this change:

> *Galadhrim* is the correct spelling of the name of the Elves of Lórien, and similarly *Caras Galadhon*. My father originally altered the voiced form of *th* (as in Modern English *then*) in Elvish names to *d*, since (as he wrote) *dh* is not used in English and looks uncouth. Afterwards he changed his mind on the point, but *Galadrim* and *Caras Galadhon* remained uncorrected until after the appearance of the revised edition of *The Lord of the Rings*. [*Unfinished Tales*, p. 267]

See also Tolkien's note in his letter to Richard Jeffery, 17 December 1972 (*Letters*, p. 426).

341–2 (I: 356): 'I will climb up'

342 (I: 356). *Mellyrn* – See note for p. 335.

342 (I: 356): '*Daro!*' it said

342 (I: 356). *Daro!* – Sindarin 'stop, halt'.

342 (I: 356): There was a sound

342 (I: 356). Frodo could understand little of what was said – See note for p. 339.

342–3 (I: 357): Out of the shadows

342 (I: 357). there had been built a wooden platform, or *flet* as such things were called in those days: the Elves called it a *talan* – *Flet* is an Old English word meaning 'the ground, floor of a house'. Bosworth and Toller's *Anglo-Saxon Dictionary* cites from *Ancient Laws and Institutes of England*, ed. by Benjamin Thorpe (1840): *Ne cume on bedde ac licge on flette* 'let him not come into a bed, but lie on a floor'. See also note for p. 354.

Talan is Sindarin 'floor, ground'.

343 (I: 357): 'Welcome!'

343 (I: 357). Haldir is my name. My brothers, Rúmil and Orophin – In tales of the First Age *Haldir* (Sindarin 'hidden hero') was briefly the name of the son of Orodreth, second ruler of the Noldorin realm of Nargothrond, but in later accounts became the ruler of the Men of Brethil, who was slain in battle against Morgoth.

Rúmil in *The Silmarillion* is the name of a Noldorin sage of Tirion, the first deviser of written characters (p. 347).

343 (I: 357): 'But we have heard rumours

343 (I: 357). for the messengers of Elrond passed by Lórien on their way home up the Dimrill Stair – In Book II, Chapter 3 it is said that messengers 'had climbed the pass at the sources of the Gladden River, and had come down into Wilderland . . . and they had returned home over the high pass that was called the Redhorn Gate' (p. 274, I: 287). The passage in the present chapter dates from the earliest text, long before the introduction of Elladan and Elrohir into *The Lord of the Rings*, and survives as a shadow of a version before the sons of Elrond journeyed 'down the Silverlode into a strange country', i.e. went to Lothlórien as messengers of their father (also p. 274, I: 287).

343 (I: 358): 'The name of Aragorn

343 (I: 358). he has the favour of the Lady – See note for p. 375.

344 (I: 359): Pippin went on talking

344 (I: 359). bird-loft – In editions prior to 2004 this read 'bed-loft'. The term is *bird-loft* in Tolkien's manuscript of this chapter, but became *bed-loft* in the first (amanuensis) typescript, and the error continued in print. See *The Treason of Isengard*, p. 243, n. 47.

344 (I: 359): 'Once I do get to sleep'

344 (I: 359). the sooner I'll drop off – That is, fall asleep, not roll off the *flet* as Pippin fears.

345 (I: 359): '*Yrch!*'

345 (I: 359). *Yrch!* – Plural 'orcs' in the elven-tongue.

346 (I: 360): Day came pale from the East

346 (I: 360). Day came – It is 16 January 1419.

347 (I: 361): He breathed with relief

347 (I: 361). not even my uncle Andy ever did a trick like that – Andwise Roper of Tighfield, eldest brother of Gaffer Gamgee, a rope-maker; see note for p. 611.

347 (I: 361): When at length all the Company

347 (I: 361). the Elves untied the ropes and coiled two of them. Rúmil, who had remained on the other side, drew back the last one – As first published this passage read: 'the Elves untied the ropes and coiled them. Rúmil, who had remained on the other side, picked one up'. It was revised in the second edition (1965).

347 (I: 361): 'Now, friends'

347 (I: 361). Naith of Lórien, or the Gore . . . that lies like a spearhead between the arms of Silverlode and Anduin – *Naith* means 'triangle, gore' (*Index*). Christopher Tolkien notes that 'Old English *gāra* (in modern use meaning a wedge-shaped piece of cloth, but in Old English an angular point of land) was related to *gār* "spear", the connection lying in the shape of the spear-head' (*The Treason of Isengard*, p. 244, n. 49).

347 (I: 361): 'As was agreed

347 (I: 361). down in Egladil, in the Angle between the waters – *Egladil* (Sindarin 'elven-point') is 'the narrow land near [the] junction of Anduin and Celebrant (Silverlode)' (*Index*). It is also called the *Angle*, 'the Southern end of the Naith of Lórien' (*Index*).

347 (I: 362): Gimli drew his axe

347 (I: 362). A plague on Dwarves and their stiff necks – This (and 'a plague on the stiff necks of Elves', p. 347, I: 362) seems to echo 'a plague o' both your houses', in Shakespeare's *Romeo and Juliet*, Act III, Scene 1.

347 (I: 362): 'Now let us cry

347 (I: 362). But the Company shall all fare alike. – Aragorn shows true leadership in diffusing a difficult situation.

349 (I: 363–4): As they spoke thus

349 (I: 363). the thin clear voices of birds high in the sky – This was the reading in the first printing of the first edition (1954). In the unauthorized resetting of *The Fellowship of the Ring* for its second printing (1954) the word 'high' was omitted. The error was corrected in the edition of 2004.

349 (I: 364): As soon as he set foot

349 (I: 364). As soon as he [Frodo] set foot upon the far bank of Silverlode a strange feeling had come upon him, and it deepened as he walked on into the Naith: it seemed to him that he had stepped over a bridge of time into a corner of the Elder Days, and was now walking in a world that was no more. – In his letter to Milton Waldman, ?late 1951, Tolkien wrote of the chapters set in Lothlórien: 'I make the perilous and difficult attempt to catch at close quarters the air of timeless Elvish enchantment' (*Waldman LR*). Wisely he brings the Company into Lothlórien by stages, revealing the Elvish realm gradually to both his characters and his readers, cushioning the sensation that one has passed into a land that is almost another world. In the process, the Company cross three physical barriers: the river Nimrodel, which washes 'the stain of travel and all weariness' from Frodo's limbs; the river Silverlode, the crossing of which seems to Frodo like stepping *over a bridge of time*; and the bridge and gates to Caras Galadhon. On this subject, see further, Marjorie Burns, *Perilous Realms: Celtic and Norse in Tolkien's Middle-earth* (2005), Chapter 3.

349 (I: 364): All that day

349 (I: 364). In the morning – It is 17 January 1419.

350 (I: 364): He removed the bandage

350 (I: 364). the first Dwarf . . . since Durin's Day – Is Haldir referring to the first Durin, one of the Seven Fathers of the Dwarves, or to one of his successors? Since Gimli's chant in Book II, Chapter 4 also refers to 'Durin's Day' (see note for p. 316) and clearly to the first Durin, that may be meant here.

350 (I: 364–5): When his eyes were in turn uncovered

350 (I: 364). Frodo looked up and caught his breath – An analysis of this chapter by a Tolkien discussion group points out that the blindfolding of the Company also serves a literary purpose: 'Cerin Amroth revealed all at once as the reader's eyes are uncovered with Frodo's has much more impact than it would have had had it had been come upon gradually' (*Rómenna Meeting Report*, 12 May 1985, p. 2).

350 (I: 365). the grass was studded with small golden flowers shaped like stars. Among them, nodding on slender stalks, were other flowers, white and palest green: they glimmered as a mist amid the rich hue of the grass. – The flowers are elanor and niphredil: see note for p. 351.

350 (I: 365): 'Behold! You are come to Cerin Amroth'

350 (I: 365). Cerin Amroth . . . the heart of the ancient realm as it was long ago – *Cerin* is Sindarin for 'circular mound or artificial hill'; thus *Cerin Amroth* 'Amroth's Mound' (*Index*).

For *the ancient realm as it was long ago*, see note for p. 341.

On 25 December 1963 Tolkien wrote to Nancy Smith: 'But now (when [*The Lord of the Rings*] is no longer hot, immediate, or so personal) certain features of it, and especially certain places, still move me very powerfully. The heart remains in the description of Cerin Amroth' (*Letters*, p. 221).

351 (I: 365–6): They followed him

351 (I: 366). elanor and niphredil – *Elanor* is the small golden flower shaped like a star described on p. 350. Its name contains the Sindarin elements for 'star' + 'sun'.

Niphredil is the flower described as white and pale green on a slender stalk. Compare Noldorin (later Sindarin) *nifred* 'pallor' and *nifredil* 'snowdrop' in the *Etymologies* (*The Lost Road and Other Writings*, base NIK-W-). In *The Silmarillion* it is said that when Lúthien was born 'the white flowers of *niphredil* came forth to greet her as stars from the earth' (p. 91). Tolkien drew two devices for Lúthien, *c.* 1960 (*Artist and Illustrator*, figs. 194–5): one of these definitely depicts a *niphredil*, the other a flower with petals white on the outside and yellow inside which may be *elanor.*

On 16 November 1969 Tolkien wrote to Amy Ronald, after she had sent him a book on wildflowers of the Cape Peninsula:

> I have not seen anything that immediately recalls *niphredil* or *elanor* . . . but I think that is because those imagined flowers are lit by a light that would not be seen ever in a growing plant and cannot be recaptured by paint. Lit by that light, *niphredil* would be simply a delicate kin of a snowdrop; and *elanor* a pimpernel (perhaps a little enlarged) growing sun-golden flowers and star-silver ones on the same plant, and sometimes the two combined. [*Letters*, p. 402]

352 (I: 366): 'There lies the fastness

352 (I: 366). In the midst upon a stony height stands Dol Guldur – A note by Tolkien to *The Disaster of the Gladden Fields* reads: '*Amon Lanc*, "Naked Hill", was the highest point in the highland at the south-west corner of the Greenwood, and was so called because no trees grew on its summit. In later days it was Dol Guldur, the first stronghold of Sauron after his awakening' (*Unfinished Tales*, p. 280, n. 12).

352 (I: 366–7): At the hill's foot

352 (I: 366). He was wrapped in some fair memory – In *The Tale of Aragorn and Arwen* in Appendix A it is told how, on the evening of Midsummer in Third Age 2980, over thirty-eight years earlier, Aragorn and Arwen plighted their troth on Cerin Amroth.

352 (I: 366). he seemed clad in white, a young lord tall and fair – *The Tale of Aragorn and Arwen* also tells that when Aragorn arrived in Lórien Galadriel 'clothed him in silver and white, with a cloak of elven-grey and a bright gem on his brow. Then more than any king of Men he appeared, and seemed rather like an Elf-lord from the Isles of the West' (p. 1060, III: 341).

352 (I: 366). *Arwen vanimelda, namárië!* – The reading in the first edition was *Arwen vanimalda namárië*, but in the Allen & Unwin second edition (1966) the acute accent was omitted on the last word. This error was corrected in the edition of 2004. Also in the second edition Tolkien changed *vanimalda* to *vanimelda*.

Chapter 7

THE MIRROR OF GALADRIEL

For drafts and history of this chapter, see *The Treason of Isengard*, pp. 245–66.

353 (I: 368): Suddenly they came

353 (I: 368). ***fosse*** – 'A long narrow trench or ditch, especially in fortification' (*Concise OED*).

353 (I: 368): 'Welcome to Caras Galadhon!'

353 (I: 368). Caras Galadhon – *Galadhon*, spelt with an *h*, replaced *Galadon* in the second printing (1967) of the Allen & Unwin second edition: see note for p. 341.

In his unfinished index Tolkien notes *caras* as a 'circular earthwall with dike', and (using the earlier spelling) *Caras Galadon* as 'City of Trees', the 'chief dwelling of the Elves of Lórien'. In late writing Tolkien says that the name '*Caras* seems to be an old word for a moated fortress not found in Sindarin' (*Unfinished Tales*, p. 257).

354 (I: 369): As he climbed slowly

354 (I: 369). On it was built a house so large – In a late etymological discussion by his father, Christopher Tolkien reports in *Unfinished Tales*, it is said

> that the custom of dwelling in trees was not a habit of the Silvan Elves in general, but was developed in Lórien by the nature and situation of the land: a flat land with no good stone, except what might be quarried in the mountains westward and brought with difficulty down the Silverlode. . . . But the dwelling in trees was not universal even in Lórien, and the *telain* [plural of *talan*] or *flets* were in origin either refuges to be used in the event of an attack, or most often (especially those high up in great trees) outlook posts from which the land and its borders could be surveyed by Elvish eyes: for Lórien after the end of the first millennium of the Third Age became a land of uneasy vigilance, and Amroth must have dwelt in growing disquiet ever since Dol Guldur was established in Mirkwood.

'Such an outlook post', Tolkien says,

> used by the wardens of the north marches, was the *flet* in which Frodo spent the night. The abode of Celeborn in Caras Galadhon was also of the same origin: its highest *flet*, which the Fellowship of the Ring did

> not see, was the highest point in the land. Earlier the *flet* of Amroth at the top of the great mound or hill of Cerin Amroth, piled by the labour of many hands, had been the highest, and was primarily designed to watch Dol Guldur across the Anduin. The conversion of these *telain* into permanent dwellings was a later development, and only in Caras Galadhon were such dwellings numerous. But Caras Galadhon was itself a fortress, and only a small part of the Galadhrim dwelt within its walls. [*Unfinished Tales*, pp. 245–6]

354 (I: 369): The chamber was filled with a soft light

354 (I: 369). Very tall they were – In a note associated with *The Disaster of the Gladden Fields* Tolkien indicates that Celeborn, who (according to a late version of his origin) was one of the Teleri, 'was held by them to be tall, as his name indicated ("silver-tall"); but the Teleri were in general somewhat less in build and stature than the Noldor'. Galadriel was 'the tallest of all the women of the Eldar of whom tales tell', and was said to be man-high 'according to the measure of the Dúnedain and the men of old', about six feet four inches (*Unfinished Tales*, p. 286).

354 (I: 369). No sign of age was upon them, unless it were in the depths of their eyes – Tolkien wrote to W.H. Auden on 7 June 1955: 'of Lothlórien no word had reached my mortal ears till I came there' (*Letters*, p. 216). Nor is there evidence that he knew anything of Galadriel (or of Celeborn) until he came to write 'The Mirror of Galadriel', and he went on 'discovering' more about her until the end of his life.

Several commentators, most notably John D. Rateliff in '*She* and Tolkien', *Mythlore* 8, no. 2, whole no. 28 (Summer 1981), have pointed out possible influences on Galadriel by aspects of Ayesha in works by H. Rider Haggard: *She* (1887), *Ayesha: The Return of She* (1905), *She and Allan* (1921), and *Wisdom's Daughter* (1923). Rateliff writes:

> The most obvious parallel is She herself – Ayesha, Wisdom's daughter, She-Who-Must-Be-Obeyed. An exceedingly beautiful woman, so beautiful that all who see her remember the sight ever after, She rules a small, isolated, ancient kingdom, the borders of which no one is allowed to pass. Strangers are admitted only if she has sent word beforehand to admit them, and even then they must make part of the journey blindfolded. Beautiful and terrible, worshipful but fearsome, she is not only wise and beautiful but also immortal. . . . Like She, Galadriel is immortal, wise, queenly, and beautiful beyond belief. There are important differences between Ayesha and Galadriel, but the similarities are striking. [p. 6]

Steve Linley in 'Tolkien and Haggard: Some Thoughts on Galadriel', *Anor* 23 (1991) comments that both Galadriel and Ayesha 'have a powerful gaze, the effect of which on the recipient being the feeling of being laid bare or psychologically "denuded"', and 'both live amidst a culture of preservation; Ayesha, however, preserves only herself, for selfish reasons. . . . She treats all other human beings as a lesser species. . . . Ayesha actively seeks power and world domination', whereas Galadriel rejects the power the Ring would have given her. However, Linley points out that had Galadriel accepted the Ring 'the reader familiar with *She* might recognise that Galadriel would come to resemble Ayesha more closely in respect of her less appealing characteristics' (pp. 12, 13, 14).

In 1966 Tolkien told Henry Resnik: 'I suppose as a boy *She* interested me as much as anything' ('An Interview with Tolkien', *Niekas* 18 (Spring 1967), p. 40).

355 (I: 370): 'Nay, there was no change

355 (I: 370). But I cannot see him from afar, unless he comes within the fences of Lothlórien: a grey mist is about him, and the ways of his feet and of his mind are hidden from me. – It is not clear whether Galadriel means that she can never see Gandalf from afar, or that now she cannot see him. Readers have interpreted it both ways. At the time she speaks, Gandalf is still fighting with the Balrog underground.

356 (I: 371): 'Alas!' said Celeborn

356 (I: 371). had I known that the Dwarves had stirred up this evil in Moria again, I would have forbidden you to pass the northern borders, you and all that went with you – Celeborn presumably is referring to Balin's attempt to resettle Moria. In an unpublished letter to Eileen Elgar, begun 22 September 1963, Tolkien suggests that Celeborn was worried about what might pursue the Company out of Moria and into Lothlórien. Also, as Tolkien wrote of Celeborn in the Second Age, he 'had no liking for Dwarves of any race (as he showed to Gimli in Lothlórien), and had never forgiven them for their part in the destruction of Doriath' (*Unfinished Tales*, p. 235), 'passing over Morgoth's part in this (by angering of Húrin), and Thingol's own faults' (*The War of the Jewels*, p. 353). See also note for p. 255.

356 (I: 371): He would be rash indeed

356 (I: 371). Do not repent of your welcome to the Dwarf. – In the late *Concerning Galadriel and Celeborn*, dealing with events in the Second Age, Tolkien says that 'Galadriel was more far-sighted' than Celeborn in her attitude to Dwarves. She saw the need for a union of all the peoples against the evil surviving from the First Age, even though this had not yet been identified as Sauron:

> She looked upon the Dwarves also with the eye of a commander, seeing in them the finest warriors to pit against the Orcs. Moreover Galadriel was a Noldo, and she had a natural sympathy with their minds and

their passionate love of crafts of hand, a sympathy much greater than that found among many of the Eldar: the Dwarves were 'the Children of Aulë', and Galadriel, like others of the Noldor, had been a pupil of Aulë and Yavanna in Valinor. [*Unfinished Tales*, p. 235]

356 (I: 371): 'Dark is the water

356 (I: 371). the many-pillared halls of Khazad-dûm – In *Concerning Galadriel and Celeborn* it is said that on at least two occasions Galadriel chose to travel through Khazad-dûm rather than over the Misty Mountains.

356–7 (I: 372): 'Your quest is known to us

357 (I: 372). the Lord of the Galadhrim is accounted the wisest of the Elves of Middle-earth, and a giver of gifts beyond the power of kings – Some readers have doubted Galadriel's statement, since she has just shown herself to have better judgement than her husband. Celeborn does, however, later give help and useful advice for the Company's onward journey. When the Company leave they are given gifts by the Lord and Lady of the Galadhrim, but at least two of the gifts seem to come from Galadriel alone: Frodo's phial with the light of Eärendil, and the contents of Sam's box which will help restore the Shire.

It is difficult to assess the relationship and relative positions of the two rulers of Lothlórien: Celeborn greets the Company, speaking first, but Galadriel wears one of the Three Rings and seems to have the greater innate power. The apparent contradiction may arise from the fact that it took Tolkien some time to appreciate fully the characters who had now entered the story, apparently unplanned; indeed, at first it was the Lord of Lothlórien (as 'King Galdaran'), rather than the Lady, who was to show Frodo visions in a mirror (see *The Treason of Isengard*, p. 249).

357 (I: 372). He has dwelt in the West since the days of dawn – This may refer to the time since the creation of the Sun, or metaphorically 'since the beginning'.

357 (I: 372). ere the fall of Nargothrond or Gondolin I passed over the mountains, and together through ages of the world we have fought the long defeat – On this Christopher Tolkien has said:

> There is no part of the history of Middle-earth more full of problems than the story of Galadriel and Celeborn, and it must be admitted that there are severe inconsistencies 'embedded in the traditions'; or, to look at the matter from another point of view, that the role and importance of Galadriel only emerged slowly, and that her story underwent continual refashionings.
>
> Thus, at the outset, it is certain that the earliest conception was that Galadriel went east over the mountains from Beleriand alone, before

> the end of the First Age, and met Celeborn in his own land of Lórien; this is explicitly stated in unpublished writing, and the same idea underlies Galadriel's words to Frodo in *The Fellowship of the Ring* . . . , where she says of Celeborn that 'He has dwelt in the West since the days of dawn, and I have dwelt with him years uncounted; for ere the fall of Nargothrond or Gondolin I passed over the mountains, and together through ages of the world we have fought the long defeat.' In all probability Celeborn was in this conception a Nandorin Elf (that is, one of the Teleri who refused to cross the Misty Mountains on the Great Journey from Cuiviénen).
>
> On the other hand, in Appendix B to *The Lord of the Rings* appears a later version of the story; for it is stated there that at the beginning of the Second Age 'In Lindon south of the Lune dwelt for a time Celeborn, kinsman of Thingol; his wife was Galadriel, greatest of Elven women.' And in the notes to *The Road Goes Ever On* . . . it is said that Galadriel 'passed over the Mountains of Eredluin with her husband Celeborn (one of the Sindar) and went to Eregion'. [*The History of Galadriel and Celeborn* in *Unfinished Tales*, p. 228]

Neither Galadriel nor Celeborn had appeared in any of the earlier 'Silmarillion' writings, but obviously both, and especially Galadriel, subsequent to *The Lord of the Rings* had to be found a place in that work. Galadriel, Tolkien decided, was born in Aman, a Noldo of the highest family, the daughter of Finrod (later Finarfin), third son of Finwë, ruler of the Noldor. One of her brothers was Inglor (later Finrod Felagund), later ruler of Nargothrond. But she also had Vanyar blood through her paternal grandmother, Finwë's second wife, Indis, from whom she also inherited her golden hair; and Telerin blood from her mother, Eärwen, daughter of King Olwë of Alqualondë, the ruler of the Teleri in Aman and brother of King Thingol of Doriath in Beleriand. Galadriel was among the Noldor who participated in Fëanor's revolt against the Valar and went to Middle-earth to recover the Silmarils from Morgoth. According to the *Annals of Aman* the words of Fëanor 'kindled her heart, and she yearned to see the wide untrodden lands and to rule there a realm maybe at her own will' (*Morgoth's Ring*, p. 113). As first written, the *Annals* made no mention as to whether Galadriel played any part in the kin-slaying at Alqualondë when Fëanor seized the ships of the Teleri.

In Middle-earth Galadriel spent much time in Doriath with Thingol and his wife, Melian, who by her power as a Maia protected Doriath against intruders and the power of Morgoth. In an addition to the *Quenta Silmarillion* it is said that Galadriel 'remained long in Doriath and received the love of Melian and there learned great lore and wisdom' (*The War of the Jewels*, p. 178). The guarded realm of Lórien which few were allowed to enter has some similarities with Doriath.

This is the story that Christopher Tolkien used in editing his father's papers for *The Silmarillion*. He accepted Celeborn as a kinsman of Thingol, indicating that Galadriel met him in Doriath. He gives no explanation of why Celeborn and Galadriel remained in Middle-earth at the end of the First Age, other than that they were among the Elves who were unwilling to forsake the lands 'where they had long suffered and had long dwelt' (*The Silmarillion*, p. 254). It would have been impossible for Christopher to introduce other material from his father's later, and often not fully developed, ideas without substantial rewriting. From this material, however, he compiled *The History of Galadriel and Celeborn*, published in *Unfinished Tales* together with a discussion of his father's developing ideas.

Tolkien's 'refashionings' of the story of Galadriel in the years following the publication of *The Lord of the Rings* dealt with several aspects of her life, of which the most significant were the related questions of whether she had participated in the revolt of the Noldor, and why she remained in Middle-earth at the end of the First Age when most of the surviving Noldor returned into the West. *The Lord of the Rings* is ambiguous on the latter question: when she rejects the Ring at the end of this chapter, she says: 'I pass the test. I will diminish, and go into the West, and remain Galadriel' (p. 366, I: 381). This suggests that she believes she has the option to return to the West, and yet her song of farewell to the Fellowship of the Ring ends with the words: 'But if of ships I now should sing, what ship would come to me / What ship would bear me ever back across so wide a Sea?' (p. 366, I: 381). This may be a symbolic question, for she surely knew about the Grey Havens, but it might indicate that there was a prohibition against her return to Valinor.

Christopher Tolkien is inclined to think that a ban on Galadriel's return into the West was not in his father's mind when he wrote Book II, Chapter 8 of *The Lord of the Rings*. He notes that in the later *Concerning Galadriel and Celeborn* it is said that it was for love of Celeborn, 'who would not leave Middle-earth (and probably with some pride of her own, for she had been one of those eager to adventure there)', that Galadriel did not return into the West, and that later in the Second Age 'she deemed it her duty to remain in Middle-earth while Sauron was still unconquered' (*Unfinished Tales*, pp. 234, 240). Yet by 1967 it was Tolkien's view that Galadriel

> was the last survivor of the princes and queens who had led the revolting *Noldor* to exile in Middle-earth. After the overthrow of *Morgoth* at the end of the First Age a ban was set upon her return, and she had replied proudly that she had no wish to do so. She passed over the Mountains of *Eredluin* with her husband *Celeborn* (one of the *Sindar*) and went to *Eregion*. But it was impossible for one of the High-elves to overcome the yearning for the Sea, and the longing to pass over it again to the land of their former bliss. She was now burdened with this desire. In the event, after the fall of *Sauron*, in reward for all that she had done to oppose him, but above all for her rejection of the Ring when it came

> within her power, the ban was lifted, and she returned over the Sea. [*The Road Goes Ever On: A Song Cycle*, p. 60]

Tolkien said much the same in his draft letter to Mr Rang, August 1967:

> The Exiles were allowed to return – save for a few chief actors in the rebellion of whom at the time of the *L.R.* only *Galadriel* remained.... At the time of her lament in Lórien she believed this [the ban] to be perennial, as long as Earth endured. Hence she concludes her lament with a wish or prayer that Frodo may as a special grace be granted a purgatorial (but not penal) sojourn in *Eressëa*, the Solitary Isle in sight of *Aman*, though for her the way is closed.... Her prayer was granted – but also her personal ban was lifted, in reward for her services against Sauron, and above all for her rejection of the temptation to take the Ring when offered to her. So at the end we see her taking ship. [*Letters*, p. 386]

On 25 January 1971 Tolkien wrote to Ruth Austin:

> I think it is true that I owe much of this character [Galadriel] to Christian and Catholic teaching and imagination about Mary, but actually Galadriel was a penitent: in her youth a leader in the rebellion against the Valar (the angelic guardians). At the end of the First Age she proudly refused forgiveness or permission to return. She was pardoned because of her resistance to the final and overwhelming temptation to take the Ring for herself. [*Letters*, p. 407]

This notion of a pardon in the First Age, in addition to one in the Third, is of a piece with the 'distinctively different' story of Galadriel, as it is described by Christopher Tolkien, told by his father in a very late essay:

> Galadriel was the greatest of the Noldor, except Fëanor maybe, though she was wiser than he, and her wisdom increased with the long years ... she was strong of body, mind, and will, and a match for both the loremasters and the athletes of the Eldar in the days of their youth.... She was proud, strong, and selfwilled ... she had dreams of far lands and dominions that might be her own to order as she would without tutelage. Yet deeper still there dwelt in her the noble and generous spirit of the Vanyar, and a reverence for the Valar that she could not forget. From her earliest years she had a marvellous gift of insight into the minds of others, but judged them with mercy and understanding, and she withheld her goodwill from none save only Fëanor. In him she perceived a darkness that she hated and feared, though she did not perceive that the shadow of the same evil had fallen upon the minds of all the Noldor, and upon her own.
>
> So it came to pass that when the light of Valinor failed ... she joined the rebellion against the Valar who commanded them to stay; and once she had set her foot upon that road of exile she would not relent, but

> rejected the last message of the Valar, and came under the Doom of Mandos. Even after the merciless assault upon the Teleri and the rape of their ships, though she fought fiercely against Fëanor in defence of her mother's kin, she did not turn back. Her pride was unwilling to return, a defeated suppliant for pardon; but now she burned with desire to follow Fëanor with her anger to whatever lands he might come, and to thwart him in all ways that she could. Pride still moved her when, at the end of the Elder Days after the final overthrow of Morgoth, she refused the pardon of the Valar for all who had fought against him, and remained in Middle-earth. It was not until two long ages more had passed, when at last all that she had desired in her youth came to her hand, the Ring of Power and the dominion of Middle-earth of which she had dreamed, that her wisdom was full grown and she rejected it, and passing the last test departed from Middle-earth for ever. [*The History of Galadriel and Celeborn* in *Unfinished Tales*, pp. 229–31]

Then at the very end of his life Tolkien changed his mind yet again. On 4 August 1973 he wrote to Lord Halsbury:

> Galadriel was 'unstained': she had committed no evil deeds. She was an enemy of Fëanor. She did not reach Middle-earth with the other Noldor, but independently. Her reasons for desiring to go to Middle-earth were legitimate, and she would have been permitted to depart, but for the misfortune that before she set out the revolt of Fëanor broke out, and she became involved in the desperate measures of Manwë, and the ban on all emigration. [*Letters*, p. 431]

Christopher Tolkien reports that a new account of Galadriel 'set down in the last month of his life' was probably his father's last writing on Middle-earth and Valinor. He summarizes it in *Unfinished Tales*: Galadriel 'did indeed wish to depart from Valinor and go into the wide world of Middle-earth for the exercise of her talents'. Manwë knew of her desire, and 'had not forbidden her; but nor had she been given formal leave to depart'. Galadriel therefore went to stay with her mother's kindred in Alqualondë.

> There she met Celeborn . . . a Telerin prince, the grandson of Olwë of Alqualondë and thus her close kinsman. Together they planned to build a ship and sail in it to Middle-earth; and they were about to seek leave from the Valar for their venture when Melkor fled from Valmar and returning with Ungoliant destroyed the light of the Trees. In Fëanor's revolt that followed . . . Galadriel had no part: indeed she with Celeborn fought heroically in defence of Alqualondë against the assault of the Noldor, and Celeborn's ship was saved from them. Galadriel, despairing now of Valinor and horrified by the violence and cruelty of Fëanor, set sail into the darkness without waiting for Manwë's leave, which would have undoubtedly been withheld in that hour, however legitimate her desire in itself. It was thus that she came under the ban set upon all

> departure, and Valinor was shut against her return. [*Unfinished Tales*, pp. 231–2]

In Middle-earth Galadriel and Celeborn took no part in the war against Morgoth, which they thought hopeless, but advocated trying to build up strength further east, and to this end themselves crossed the Ered Lindon (i.e. Ered Luin). At the end of the First Age, when they received permission to return into the West, they rejected it. Christopher Tolkien comments that this would have meant much revision of 'The Silmarillion', but he thinks that his father intended to atempt it.

In *The Lord of the Rings* almost nothing is said of the actions of Galadriel and Celeborn during the Second and Third Ages, other than 'in Lindon north of the Lune dwelt for a time Celeborn, kinsman of Thingol; his wife was Galadriel' (Appendix B, p. 1082, III: 363). Christopher Tolkien notes that 'the absence of any indication to the contrary in *The Lord of the Rings* had led commentators to the natural assumption that Galadriel and Celeborn passed the latter half of the Second Age and all the Third in Lothlórien; but this was not so' (*Unfinished Tales*, p. 240).

357 (I: 372). the long defeat – This echoes Elrond's comment in Book II, Chapter 2: 'I have seen three ages in the West of the world, and many defeats, and many fruitless victories' (p. 243, I: 256), and reiterates an underlying theme of *The Lord of the Rings*: that no victory is complete, that evil rises again, that even victory brings loss.

357 (I: 372): It was I who first summoned the White Council

357 (I: 372). if my designs had not gone amiss, it would have been governed by Gandalf the Grey – In *Of the Rings of Power and the Third Age* it is said of the White Council that Saruman

> was chosen to be their chief, for he had most studied the devices of Sauron of old. Galadriel indeed had wished that Mithrandir should be head of the Council, and Saruman begrudged them that, for his pride and desire of mastery was grown great; but Mithrandir refused the office, since he would have no ties and no allegiance, save to those who sent him, and he would abide in no place nor be subject to any summons. [*The Silmarillion*, p. 300]

357 (I: 372). Yet hope remains while all the Company is true – In fact, Boromir's temporary yielding to temptation on Amon Hen played a significant part in the success of the quest, as it helped Frodo to make a difficult decision, and to remove himself and the Ring from the vicinity of the band of orcs who carry off Merry and Pippin.

357 (I: 372): And with that word

357 (I: 372). she held them with her eyes, and in silence looked searchingly at each of them in turn – As noted above, in late writing Tolkien said that Galadriel 'had a marvellous gift of insight into the minds of others, but judged them with mercy and understanding' (*The History of Galadriel and Celeborn* in *Unfinished Tales*, p. 230).

357 (I: 372): 'Go now!'

357 (I: 372). we will not speak of your further road for a while – It will be a month before the question of their further road is considered, though it seems a much shorter time to the Company in Lothlórien. No reason is given in *The Lord of the Rings* for their long stay, but entries in some of Tolkien's time-schemes suggest that Celeborn and Galadriel had their reasons. *Scheme* notes: 'Celeborn and Galadriel send out messengers to Elrond; and seek for news of Gandalf. Galadriel orders the eagles to watch.' And an earlier note, in Marquette MSS 4/2/17, says that Celeborn and Galadriel 'keep company while they send messages to Elrond to learn his advice, since G[andalf] has fallen. Also they seek to discover news of G[andalf].'

357 (I: 373): That night the Company

357 (I: 373). the travellers talked of their night before in the tree-tops – Christopher Tolkien has commented that this statement survived from an earlier version of the chapter in which the Company

> met the northbound Elves at Cerin Amroth, and had their blindfolds removed, on the same day as they left Nimrodel . . . the whole journey to Caras Galadon thus took a single day, and so it was indeed 'the night before' that they passed in the tree-tops. In FR [*The Fellowship of the Ring*] the journey was extended, and they passed the first night after Nimrodel in the woods: 'Then they rested and slept without fear upon the ground for their guides would not permit them to unbind their eyes, and they could not climb. In the light of this the passage in FR (pp. [III] 372–3) required revision that it did not receive: the words 'the travellers talked of their night before in the tree-tops' survive from the [earlier] version, as does Aragorn's 'But tonight I shall sleep without fear for the first time since I left Rivendell [Book II, Chapter 7, p. 358, I: 373]'. [*The Treason of Isengard*, p. 258]

359 (I: 374): *Mithrandir, Mithrandir*

359 (I: 374). *Mithrandir . . . O Pilgrim Grey* – *Mithrandir*, Gandalf's name in Sindarin, is derived from *mith* 'grey' + *rhandir* 'wanderer, pilgrim'. It is variously 'translated' as 'Grey Pilgrim' or 'Grey Wanderer'.

359–60 (I: 374–5): *When evening in the Shire*

359–60 (I: 374–5). *When evening in the Shire was grey . . .* – A recording by Tolkien of this poem is included on Disc 1 of *The J.R.R. Tolkien Audio Collection*.

360 (I: 375). *brand* – A piece of burning or smouldering wood; poetically, a torch, perhaps here referring to Gandalf's fiery nature when roused, or that he fired hearts against Sauron.

360 (I: 375): One evening Frodo and Sam

360 (I: 375). One evening – It is the evening of 15 February 1419. (See further, note for p. 1092.)

361 (I: 376): Turning aside, she led them

361 (I: 376). The evening star had risen and was shining with white fire above the western woods. – If by *evening star* Tolkien meant Venus, it would not visibly rise, but become visible as the sun sank in the west, and would set while the night was young. Venus can visibly rise only when it is the morning star. Nonetheless this is what Tolkien wrote, and is probably significant since the light of Eärendil has a particular importance at this point in the chapter.

361 (I: 377): With water from the stream

361 (I: 377). Here is the Mirror of Galadriel – In '*She* and Tolkien', *Mythlore* 8, no. 2, whole no. 28 (Summer 1981), John D. Rateliff further notes that in Rider Haggard's *She*, Chapter 13, 'we are told of "a vessel like a font cut in carved stone . . . full of pure water" (described in *She and Allan* [Chapter 22] as "a marble tripod on which stood a basin half full of water"). Both Galadriel and Ayesha use this "mirror" to show the heroes visions of distant places and use it themselves to see what is happening in the outer world' (p. 7). But there are differences in what the mirror shows. Ayesha says:

> That water is my glass; in it I see what passes if I care to summon up the pictures which is not often. Therein I can show thee what thou wilt of the past, if be anything that has to do with this country and with what I have known, or anything that thou, the gazer hast known. Think of a face if thou wilt, and it shall be reflected from thy mind upon the water. I know not all the secret yet – I can read nothing in the future. [*She*, Chapter 13]

362 (I: 377): 'And you?' she said

362 (I: 377). For this is what your folk would call magic – In his letter to Milton Waldman, ?late 1951, Tolkien said:

> I have not used 'magic' consistently, and indeed the Elven-queen Galadriel is obliged to remonstrate with the Hobbits on their confused use of the word both for the devices and operations of the Enemy, and for those of the Elves. I have not, because there is not a word for the latter (since all human stories have suffered the same confusion). But the Elves are there (in my tales) to demonstrate the difference. Their 'magic'

> is Art, delivered from many of its human limitations: more effortless, more quick, more complete (product, and vision in unflawed correspondence). And its object is Art not Power, sub-creation not domination and tyrannous re-forming of Creation. The 'Elves' are 'immortal', at least as far as this world goes: and hence are concerned rather with the griefs and burdens of deathlessness in time and change, rather than with death. The Enemy in successive forms is always 'naturally' concerned with sheer Domination, and so the Lord of magic and machines. [*Letters*, p. 146]

This was a subject which concerned Tolkien greatly. In a draft letter to Naomi Mitchison, 25 September 1954, he said (in part):

> I do not intend to involve myself in any debate whether 'magic' in any sense is real or really possible in the world. But I suppose that, for the purposes of the tale, some would say that there is a latent distinction such as once was called the distinction between *magia* [enchantment, wizardry] and *goeteia* [cheatery; the distinction seems to be between true magic and conjuring; see note for p. 24]. Galadriel speaks of the 'deceits of the Enemy'. Well enough, but *magia* could be, was, held good (per se), and *goeteia* bad. Neither is, in this tale, good or bad (per se), but only by motive or purpose or use. Both sides use both, but with different motives. The supremely bad motive is (for this tale, since it is specially about it) domination of other 'free wills'. The Enemy's operations are by no means all goetic deceits, but 'magic' that produces real effects in the physical world. But his *magia* he uses to bulldoze both people and things, and his *goeteia* to terrify and subjugate. Their *magia* the Elves and Gandalf use (sparingly): a *magia*, producing real results (like fire in a wet faggot) for specific beneficent purposes. Their goetic effects are entirely *artistic* and not intended to deceive: they never deceive Elves (but they may deceive or bewilder unaware Men) since the difference is to them as clear as the difference to us between fiction, painting, and sculpture, and 'life'. [*Letters*, pp. 199–200]

362 (I: 377): 'Many things I can command

362 (I: 377). it shows things that were, and things that are, and things that yet may be – Further, on the following page, it 'shows many things, and not all have yet come to pass. Some never come to be, unless those that behold the visions turn aside from their path to prevent them. The mirror is dangerous as a guide of deeds'. In *Master of Middle-earth* Paul H. Kocher comments that the Mirror

> mixes up past, present, and future so indistinguishably that the gazer cannot be sure which is which, and in striving to avert a danger he thinks he sees lying ahead he may take the very measures which are necessary to bring it about. All finite knowledge about the future is

cursed by this Oedipean paradox. Necessarily so, because it is incomplete and therefore blind in its information about the means which must precede any given consequence. [p. 43]

362 (I: 377–8): 'There's only stars

362 (I: 377). he thought he saw Frodo with a pale face lying fast asleep under a great dark cliff. Then he seemed to see himself going along a dim passage, and climbing an endless winding star – This is a true vision of the future, of Frodo after he has been stung by Shelob, and of Sam searching for Frodo in the Tower of Cirith Ungol.

362–3 (I: 378): But now Sam noticed

362–3 (I: 378). the Old Mill had vanished, and a large red-brick building was being put up where it had stood. . . . There was a tall red chimney nearby. – This too will come to pass, as will the digging up of Bagshot Row, but Sam will see in person only the aftermath.

363 (I: 378): 'There's some devilry at work

363 (I: 378). the poor old Gaffer – In editions prior to 2004 'Gaffer' was here spelt 'gaffer', and inconsistently capitalized elsewhere in the text. The word has been regularized to the capitalized form when used in 'the Gaffer' and similar phrases, to mean specifically Hamfast Gamgee called by his nickname, and to lower-case 'gaffer' when referring generically to an old male rustic, or to Hamfast by Sam as 'my gaffer' (as one would say 'my father') or by Frodo as 'your gaffer'.

363–4 (I: 378): 'I will look'

363 (I: 378). the figure was clothed not in grey but in white, in a white that shone faintly in the dusk – The shining white clothing suggests that the vision is of Gandalf after his return.

364 (I: 379): Then there was a pause

364 (I: 379). The sea rose and raged in a great storm. Then he saw against the Sun . . . the black outline of a tall ship with torn sails riding up out of the West. – This seems to be a vision of the past, possibly of the ship of Elendil escaping the destruction of Númenor.

364 (I: 379). a wide river flowing through a populous city. Then a white fortress with seven towers – Surely the *populous city* is Osgiliath on the river Anduin before it was conquered by the forces of Sauron, and the *white fortress with seven towers* is a vision of Minas Tirith.

364 (I: 379). then again a ship with black sails, but now it was morning again . . . and a banner bearing the emblem of a white tree – Presumably a vision of the future, when Aragorn arrives at Minas Tirith during the Battle of the Pelennor Fields.

364 (I: 379). into the mist a small ship passed away, twinkling with lights – Undoubtedly a vision of the ship in which Frodo will sail into the West.

364 (I: 379): But suddenly the Mirror

364 (I: 379). In the black abyss there appeared a single Eye that slowly grew, until it filled nearly all the Mirror. . . . The Eye was rimmed with fire, but was itself glazed, yellow as a cat's, watchful and intent, and the black slit of its pupil opened on a pit, a window into nothing. – In 'The Eye of Sauron', *Beyond Bree*, June 1992, Donald O'Brien considers at length the use of the Eye as an image or symbol of Sauron and his power. He points out that one of Sauron's precursors in Tolkien's early mythology was the cat Tevildo, a demonic servant of Melko, whose eyes 'were long and very narrow and slanted, and gleamed both red and green' (*The Book of Lost Tales, Part Two*, p. 16), and when Tinúviel mentions the hound Huan 'the light of his eyes was red' (p. 26). In *The Lay of Leithian* Thû (an early name for Sauron) watches from Tol Sirion 'with sleepless eyes of flame' (*The Lays of Beleriand*, p. 227), and later 'his flaming eyes he on them bent' (p. 230). When Sauron returned to Middle-earth after the downfall of Númenor 'he took up again his great Ring in Barad-dûr, and dwelt there, dark and silent, until he wrought himself a new guise, an image of malice and hatred made visible; and the Eye of Sauron the Terrible few could endure' (*The Silmarillion*, pp. 280–1). O'Brien comments:

> The later Eye of Sauron in the Mirror of Galadriel 'rimmed with fire' echoes the earlier 'eyes of flame' of Tevildo and the 'flaming eyes of Thû'. . . . The Eye of Sauron was not the replacement of the ocular characteristics of Tevildo or Thû, but stands as the culmination of a tradition of sleepless, slanted, flaming eyes with red or yellow colouration where the feline basis of some of the characteristics is explicitly maintained even into *The Lord of the Rings*. . . .
>
> I believe that the Eye of Sauron is the image of the will of Sauron the Maia. It is not only used visually as the emblem of Sauron's authority and arrogance, but also metaphorically as the verbal expression of the sense of the presence or projection of Sauron's will. [pp. 2–4]

365 (I: 380): 'Yes', she said

365 (I: 380). divining his thought – To *divine* is to determine or interpret by supernatural insight.

365 (I: 380). This is Nenya, the Ring of Adamant – Also called the Ring of Water (*Nenya*, from Quenya *nen* 'water' + *-ya* a suffix of association). See also note for p. 1028.

Adamant is the precious stone specific to the ring (see note for p. 234), but the word also means 'stubbornly resolute', not an inapt description of Galadriel's resistance to the Dark Lord.

365 (I: 380): 'He suspects, but he does not know

365 (I: 380). Yet if you succeed, then our power is diminished, and Lothlórien will fade, and the tides of Time will sweep it away. We must depart into the West, or dwindle to a rustic folk of dell and cave, slowly to forget and to be forgotten. – Galadriel has no doubt that if the One Ring is destroyed, the Three will lose their powers. In Book VI, Chapter 5, after the destruction of the Ring, Gandalf says to Aragorn: 'the time comes of the Dominion of Men, and the Elder Kindred shall fade or depart' (p. 971, III: 249).

365–6 (I: 381): And now at last it comes

365–6 (I: 381). In place of the Dark Lord you will set up a Queen. – Tolkien suggested in his draft letter to Eileen Elgar, September 1963, that neither Galadriel nor Elrond, even with the One Ring, would have been powerful enough to confront Sauron outright:

> In the 'Mirror of Galadriel' . . . it appears that Galadriel conceived of herself as capable of wielding the Ring and supplanting the Dark Lord. If so, so also were the other guardians of the Three, especially Elrond. But this is another matter. It was part of the essential deceit of the Ring to fill minds with imaginations of supreme power. But this the Great had well considered and had rejected, as is seen in Elrond's words at the Council. Galadriel's rejection of the temptation was founded upon previous thought and resolve. In any case Elrond or Galadriel would have proceeded in the policy now adopted by Sauron: they would have built up an empire with great and absolutely subservient generals and armies and engines of war, until they could challenge Sauron and destroy him by force. Confrontation of Sauron alone, unaided, self to self was not contemplated. [*Letters*, p. 332]

366 (I: 381): She lifted up her hand

366 (I: 381). She lifted up her hand and from the Ring that she wore there issued a great light that illumined her alone and left all else dark. She stood before Frodo seeming now tall beyond measurement, and beautiful beyond enduring, terrible and worshipful. Then she let her hand fall, and the light faded . . . and lo! she was shrunken: a slender elf-woman, clad in simple white – John D. Rateliff in '*She* and Tolkien', *Mythlore* 8, no. 2, whole no. 28 (Summer 1981), cites the following from H. Rider Haggard's *Ayesha: The Return of She*, Chapter 19, as a possibly unconscious influence on this scene:

> She began slowly to stroke her abundant hair, then her breast and body. Wherever her fingers passed the mystic light was born, until . . . she shimmered from head to foot like the water of the phosphorescent sea, a being glorious yet fearful to behold. Then she waved her hand, and save for the gentle radiance on her brow, became as she had been. [p. 6]

366 (I: 381): They stood for a long while

366 (I: 381). the tides of fate are flowing – An echo, perhaps, of 'There is a tide in the affairs of men, which taken at the flood leads on to fortune' (Shakespeare, *Julius Caesar*, Act IV, Scene 3).

366 (I: 381): 'I would ask one thing

366 (I: 381). why cannot *I* see – As first published these words read 'why cannot I see'. '*I*' was italicized in the HarperCollins resetting of 1994, but reverted to Roman 'I' in the edition of 2002. It was again made italic in the edition of 2004, supported by Tolkien's manuscript of the chapter at Marquette. See also Christopher Tolkien's note in *The Treason of Isengard*, p. 266, n. 34.

366 (I: 381–2): 'You have not tried'

366 (I: 381). Only thrice have you set the Ring upon your finger since you knew what you possessed. – More precisely, Frodo has set it on his finger twice, in the house of Tom Bombadil and under Weathertop. In the third instance, at the *Prancing Pony*, it slipped onto his finger by accident, or on its own accord.

Chapter 8

FAREWELL TO LÓRIEN

For drafts and history of this chapter, see *The Treason of Isengard*, pp. 267–94.

367 (I: 383): That night the Company was again summoned

367 (I: 383). That night – It is still 15 February 1419, but presumably late evening.

367 (I: 383): 'Now is the time'

367 (I: 383). the long home of those that fall in battle – Celeborn is using a grand phrase with an echo of the Norse Valhalla, but not really applicable in Middle-earth. The spirits of Elves who are killed go to Mandos (see note for p. 209), and not even the Valar know where the spirits of slain Men (or Hobbits) go after a time of waiting in the halls of Mandos (see note for p. 193). The Dwarves, who are not Children of Ilúvatar but the creation of Aulë, believe that after death 'Aulë . . . cares for them, and gathers them to Mandos in halls set apart; and that he declared to their Fathers of old that Ilúvatar will hallow them and give them a place among the Children in the End. Their part shall be to serve Aulë and to aid him in remaking Arda after the Last Battle' (*The Silmarillion*, p. 44).

367 (I: 383): 'I see that you do not yet know what to do'

367 (I: 383). Forest River – A river in Mirkwood.

368 (I: 384): 'That is well'

368 (I: 384). Sarn Gebir – In the manuscript for *Nomenclature* (as part of the entry for *Sarn Ford*, see note for p. 172) Tolkien notes that '*Sarn Gebir* "the rapids of the spikes" in the R[iver] Anduin was so named because of upjutting spikes and snags of rocks that made this part of Anduin's course impassable by boats unless they were steered with great skill (or good fortune) into a clear, but narrow and dangerously swift, central channel'. In his unfinished index he writes that *Sarn Gebir* 'stone-spiked' was the 'name of rapids in Anduin, above the Argonath, so called because of the upright stake-like spikes of rock at their beginning'. In *Index* he also notes the derivation of *Sarn Ford*, from Sindarin *sarn* '(small) stone' + *ceber* (plural *cebir*) 'stake'.

368 (I: 384). the great falls of Rauros – '*Rauros* "roaring spray", the great falls of Anduin at south-end of the Emyn Muil' (*Index*).

368 (I: 384). Nen Hithoel – In his unfinished index Tolkien defines *Nen Hithoel* as 'the lake in the midst of the Emyn Muil', and notes that Sindarin *nen* 'water' is 'used both of lakes, pools, and (lesser) rivers'. Sindarin *Hithoel* means 'mist-cool'.

369 (I: 385): In the morning

369 (I: 385). In the morning – It is the morning of 16 February 1419.

369 (I: 385): '*Cram*,' he said

369 (I: 385). *cram* – *Cram* is first mentioned in *The Hobbit*, Chapter 13: 'If you want to know what *cram* is, I can only say that I don't know the recipe; but it is biscuitish, keeps good indefinitely, is supposed to be sustaining, and is certainly not entertaining being in fact very uninteresting except as a chewing exercise. It was made by the Lake-men for long journeys.' In the *Etymologies* Tolkien notes under the base KRAB- 'press' 'N[oldorin, i.e. Sindarin] *cramb, cram* cake of compressed flour or meal (often containing honey and milk) used on long journey' (*The Lost Road and Other Writings*, p. 365). There is also an English dialect word *cram*, however, defined by the *Oxford English Dictionary* as 'a mass of dough or paste used for cramming fowls, etc.: any food used to fatten'. The *OED* also includes the combination *cram-cake* '?fried-cake, pancake', and Joseph Wright in his *English Dialect Dictionary* notes one meaning of the verb *cram* as 'to stuff, to eat to repletion'. Compare *cramsome bread* and *cramsome cake* in Tolkien's poem *Perry-the-Winkle*, published in *The Adventures of Tom Bombadil and Other Verses from the Red Book*.

369 (I: 385): 'So it is,' they answered

369 (I: 385). *lembas* or waybread – In June 1958 Tolkien wrote to Forrest J. Ackerman:

> In the book *lembas* has two functions. It is a 'machine' or device for making credible the long marches with little provision, in a world in which ... 'miles are miles'. But this is relatively unimportant. It also has a much larger significance, of what one might hesitatingly call a 'religious' kind. This becomes later apparent, especially in the chapter 'Mount Doom' [Book VI, Chapter 3, p. 936, III: 213: 'The *lembas* had a virtue without which they would long ago have lain down to die. It did not satisfy desire.... And yet this waybread ... had a potency that increased as travellers relied on it alone and did not mingle it with other foods. It fed the will, and it gave strength to endure, and to master sinew and limb beyond the measure of mortal kind.']. [*Letters*, p. 275]

On 25 October 1958 Tolkien commented to Deborah Webster that a reader 'saw in the waybread (lembas) = viaticum and the reference to it feeding the *will* and being more potent when fasting, a derivation from the Eucharist' (*Letters*, p. 288).

In a work written in the 1950s, *Of Lembas*, Tolkien wrote:

> This food the Eldar alone knew how to make. It was made for the comfort of those who had need to go on a long journey in the wild, or of the hurt whose life was in peril. Only these were permitted to use it. . . . The Eldar say that they first received this food from the Valar in the beginning of their days in the Great Journey. For it was made of a kind of corn which Yavanna brought forth in the fields of Aman, and some she sent to them by the hand of Oromë for their succour upon the long march.
>
> Since it came from Yavanna, the queen, or the highest among the elven-women of any people, great or small, had the keeping and gift of the *lembas*. . . . [*The Peoples of Middle-earth*, pp. 403–4]

Tolkien continues with an account of the growing of the special grain, and says that the Eldar 'gathered its great golden ears, each one, by hand, and set no blade of metal to it', and that 'from the ear to the wafer none were permitted to handle this grain, save those elven-women who were called . . . the maidens of Yavanna; and the art of the making of the *lembas*, which they learned of the Valar, was a secret among them, and so ever has remained' (p. 404).

At the end of the essay Tolkien says that '*Lembas* is the Sindarin name, and comes from the older form *lenn-mbass* "journey-bread". In Quenya it was most often named *coimas* which "life-bread"' (p. 404). In the *1966 Index* the derivation is given as *len-bas* 'way-bread'.

369–70 (I: 386): 'Indeed it is'

369 (I: 386). honey-cakes of the Beornings – In *The Hobbit*, Chapter 7 Bilbo and the dwarves stay with Beorn, who keeps large bees. When the travellers leave, among the supplies Beorn gives them for their journey are 'twice-baked cakes that would keep good a long time, and on a little of which they could march far. The making of these was one of his secrets; but honey was in them . . . and they were good to eat, though they made one thirsty.'

370 (I: 386): 'I do not know what you mean by that'

370 (I: 386). the web is good – *Web* here means 'woven fabric'.

370 (I: 386). They are Elvish robes certainly – The elf seems to deny any 'magic', but events will prove that these cloaks provide a better camouflage than anything in our world: in Book III, Chapter 2, for instance, Éomer and his Riders, even though they are keeping watch ahead and to both sides and it is broad daylight, do not see Aragorn, Legolas, and Gimli in their elven-cloaks sitting beside the trail.

370 (I: 386): After their morning meal

370 (I: 386). though they could not count the days and nights they had passed there – In Tolkien's first time-scheme for the period following the

Company's escape from Moria, they crossed the Silverlode and came to Caras Galadon on 14 December and were to leave with the New Year (according to the Gregorian Calendar). But then he wrote: 'Dec. 15 onwards time at Caras does not count, therefore they leave on morning of Dec. 15' (*The Treason of Isengard*, p. 367). It was in accordance with this chronology that in late 1941 Tolkien wrote the first account of 'The Great River'; there, when Sam sees the New Moon and comments, 'Why, anyone would think we had come straight from Nimrodel without stopping a night or seeing Caras Galadon', Trotter replies: 'Whether we were in the past or the future or in a time that does not pass, I cannot say: but not I think till Silverlode bore us back to Anduin did we return to the stream of time that flows through mortal lands to the Great Sea' (*The Treason of Isengard*, pp. 354–5). A similar theory is put forward by Frodo in Book II, Chapter 9 as published, but is repudiated by both Legolas and Aragorn (see notes for pp. 388–9). When Tolkien moved the departure of the Company from Rivendell to 25 December, they crossed the Silverlode on 14 January and left Lórien on 15 January.

Tolkien also considered other possibilities: time might pass faster in the world outside Lothlórien ('Does time cease at Lórien or go on faster? So that it might be Spring or nearly so [when the Company left]', *The Treason of Isengard*, p. 368), or it might pass in Lórien but very slowly ('They spend what seems many days in Lórien, but it is about the same time and date when they leave. [*Added:* In fact, one day later, time moving at about 20 times slower (20 days = 1)]' (p. 369). It was not until he was writing Book V in the period *c.* September 1946–Autumn 1947 that Tolkien decided, after all, that time *did* pass at the same rate both inside and outside Lothlórien, but that the Company should find it difficult to reckon the passing of time while they are there.

Tolkien now also introduced the Shire Reckoning, and reached the chronology of *The Tale of Years*: the Company cross the Silverlode on 16 January 1419, and leave on 16 February. Marquette MSS 4/2/17, headed 'New Time Table allowing 30 days sojourn in Lothlórien' with an added note 'which seems less long than it is (in traditional way)', includes an entry: 'The Coy. [Company] stays in Lórien for many days. They cannot count the time, for they do not *age* in that time, but outside in fact 30 days goes by.' In *Scheme* a similar note says: 'They cannot count the time, for they themselves do not age or only very slowly. Outside in fact about 30 days passes.'

This was one of the effects of the Elven-ring worn by Galadriel. Bilbo had commented on a similar inability to reckon time in Rivendell, where Elrond also wore an Elven-ring (see note for p. 231).

For further discussion of Tolkien's ideas concerning time in Lothlórien, see especially Verlyn Flieger, *A Question of Time: J.R.R. Tolkien's Road to Faërie* (1997), Chapter 4.

370 (I: 386–7): 'I have returned

370 (I: 386). the Northern Fences – 'The north borders of Lórien, between Nimrodel and Anduin' (*Index*).

370 (I: 387). I am sent now to be your guide again. The Dimrill Dale is full of vapour and clouds of smoke, and the mountains are troubled. There are noises in the deeps of the earth. – In both the draft and the fair copy for this chapter, immediately before the sentence now beginning 'The Dimrill Dale is full of vapour', Tolkien wrote, as words by Haldir: '"There are strange things happening away back there," he said. "We do not know the meaning of them."' These words were struck through, then marked *Stet*; and that direction in turn was struck through, so that the two additional sentences by Haldir were omitted from the text as it developed further and was finally published. Christopher Tolkien comments in *The Treason of Isengard* that 'it is very hard to see why my father removed' the words,

> and why he hesitated back and forth before finally doing so. Apparently as a comment on this, he pencilled a note on the manuscript: 'This won't do – if Lórien is timeless, for then *nothing* will have happened since they entered.' I can only interpret this to mean that within Lórien the Company existed in a different Time – with its mornings and evenings and passing days – while in the world outside Lórien no time passed: they had left that 'external' Time, and would return to it at the same moment as they left it. . . . But it does not seem to me to explain why only Haldir's opening words were removed. His announcement, which was allowed to stand, that the Dimrill Dale was full of smoke and that there were noises in the earth, merely explains what the 'strange things' were which the Elves did not understand; and these 'strange things' had obviously only begun *since* the Company had entered the Golden Wood. [pp. 285–6]

With Tolkien's intentions in regard to this passage unclear, no attempt was made to restore the two sentences to the text for the edition of 2004.

Some at least of the vapours, clouds, and noises of which Haldir speaks were probably caused by Gandalf's battle with the Balrog, under the earth and on mountain-top: 'Those that looked up from afar thought that the mountain was crowned with storm. Thunder they heard, and lightning, they said, smote upon Celebdil, and leaped back into tongues of fire. . . . A great smoke rose about us, vapour and steam. Ice fell like rain. I threw down my enemy, and he fell from the high place and broke the mountain-side where he smote it in his ruin' (Book III, Chapter 5, p. 502, II: 105–6). But this battle lasted only until 25 January, and Haldir seems to suggest that the area is still in turmoil.

371 (I: 387): They had gone some ten miles

371 (I: 387). On the further shores the woodlands still marched on southwards as far as eye could see, but all the banks were bleak and bare. No mallorn lifted its gold-hung boughs beyond the Land of Lórien – In editions prior to 2004 the words 'as far as eye could see' read 'as far as the eye could see'. The text in draft read: 'On the far banks the woodlands still marched southwards as far as they could see, but beyond the Naith or Angle (as the Elves called this green sward) and upon the east side of the Great River all the boughs were bare' (*The Treason of Isengard*, p. 280). In the fair copy this became: 'On the further shores the woodlands still marched on southwards, as far as eye could see; but beyond the Tongue and upon the east side of the River all the boughs were bare. No mallorn-trees grew there' (p. 291, n. 27). On this Christopher Tolkien comments:

> The intended meaning seems clear: on the west bank beyond the confluence of Silverlode and Anduin, and all along the east bank of Anduin, there was still forest, but the trees not being mallorns they were leafless. So Keleborn [i.e. Celeborn] says that as they go down the River they will find that 'the trees will fail', and they will come to a barren country. In the following manuscript which I made (undated, but clearly following on my copy of 'Galadriel' dated 4 August 1942 . . .) the sentence reads 'all the *banks* were bare'. This, I think, must have been a mere error (as also was 'the eye could see' for 'eye could see', retained in FR [*The Fellowship of the Ring*]), since (in relation to 'the woodlands still marched on southwards') it is obviously a less well-chosen and somewhat ambiguous word: 'bare banks' suggests treeless banks, not wooded banks in winter.
>
> Probably in order to correct this, but without consulting the earlier manuscript and so not seeing that it was an error, my father at some stage changed 'further shores' to 'further western shores' on my copy, but this still gave a confused picture. The text in FR . . . removes the reference to the west shores of Anduin altogether, but retains the 'bare banks', which must therefore be interpreted as 'wooded banks in winter'. [*The Treason of Isengard*, pp. 291–2, n. 27]

In considering the text for the edition of 2004 we felt that to restore *boughs* for *banks* would introduce a redundant element, given that *boughs* is already present in the following sentence ('gold-hung boughs'). But 'the eye' was emended to 'eye'.

371 (I: 387): On the bank of the Silverlode

371 (I: 387). hythe – 'Small haven or landing-place on a river. Now obsolete except in historical use, and in place-names as . . . Hythe Bridge at Oxford' (*OED*).

371 (I: 388): They are made of *hithlain*

371 (I: 388). *hithlain* – Sindarin 'mist-thread'.

372 (I: 388): The Company was arranged

372 (I: 388). the Tongue – 'The extreme end of the Naith of Lórien' (*Index*).

372 (I: 388): They turned a sharp bend

372 (I: 388). it was a ship wrought and carved . . . in the likeness of a bird – See note for p. 234.

372–3 (I: 388–9): *I sang of leaves, of leaves of gold*

372 (I: 389). *golden Tree* – Since this is described as growing in Eldamar, the dwelling of the Elves in Aman, it cannot be Laurelin, one of the Two Trees which grew in Valinor. The 'golden Tree' is perhaps symbolic of the life of the Elves in the Blessed Realm, compared with the Winter of their life in mortal lands.

372 (I: 389). *Ever-eve* – 'Evereven, Ever-eve, names for Eldamar' (*Index*).

372 (I: 389). *What ship would bear me ever back across so wide a Sea?* – See note for p. 357.

373 (I: 389): The Swan passed on slowly

373 (I: 389). She seemed . . . present and yet remote, a living vision of that which has already been left far behind by the flowing streams of Time. – On several occasions Tolkien uses imagery of flowing water when discussing time and Lothlórien: on p. 366, I: 381 Galadriel says that 'the tides of fate are flowing'; and on p. 388, I: 404 Frodo suggests that 'it was not . . . until Silverlode bore us back to Anduin that we returned to the time that flows though mortal lands to the Great Sea'.

373 (I: 389–90): 'As you go down the water'

373 (I: 389). the tall island of the Tindrock, that we call Tol Brandir – In *Nomenclature* Tolkien says that *Tindrock* is the

> Common Speech name (not a translation) of *Tol Brandir*, the steep inaccessible island of towering rock at the head of the falls of *Rauros*. Though originally Common Speech, the name was given long before the time of the tale, and contains the old word *tind* 'a spike', which if it had survived would have rhymed with *find*, etc. But it now appears as *tine* 'prong' with loss of *d*. . . .

In the manuscript of *Nomenclature* Tolkien says that '*Tol* means a sheer-sided isle, *Brandir* was of uncertain origin and meaning; prob[ably] a corruption of **baradnir* Grey-elven [Sindarin] for *tower-steep* = "steep tower"'. In his unfinished index he notes for *Tol Brandir* '(*tol* a high steep-sided isle) an isle so steep that none could land on it, in the midst of the outlet of Anduin from Nen Hithoel to the falls of Rauros'.

373 (I: 389). cataracts – A *cataract* is 'a waterfall; properly one of considerable size, and falling headlong over a precipice' (*OED*).

373 (I: 389). the Nindalf, the Wetwang as it is called in your tongue – '*Nindalf*, translated as "Wetwang", a wide fenny and marshy district about the foot of Rauros-falls, and the mouths of the Entwash' (*Index*). In *Nomenclature* Tolkien writes that *Wetwang* is the 'Common Speech translation of *Nindalf* (Grey-elven [Sindarin] *nîn* "wet" + *talf* "flat field"). But it is in archaic form, *wang* being an old word for "field, flat area". (*Wetwang* is an actual place-name in Yorkshire.)' Compare Old English *wæt wang* 'wet meadow'. See further, J.S. Ryan, 'The Origin of the Name Wetwang', *Amon Hen* 63 (August 1983).

373 (I: 389). fen – 'Low land covered wholly or partially with shallow water, or subject to frequent inundation' (*OED*).

373 (I: 389). Entwash – In *Nomenclature* Tolkien comments that *Entwash*, as well as *Entwade* and *Entwood*,

> are 'modernized' names in Rohan language, *Entwæd*, *Entwæsc*, *Entwudu*. The second elements *-wæd* 'ford', *-wæsc* 'flood-water', *-wudu* 'wood' are given modern English forms, because the Rohan forms were recognizably akin to the words in the Common Speech: sc. speakers of the Common Speech, especially in Gondor (where, of course, the names and geography of Rohan were well-known), used these forms, assimilated to their own language.

Index has: 'Entwash (*Onodiōl*) [*onod* "ent" + **iôl*], River running through E[ast] Rohan, from Fangorn to the Nindalf'. In the late work *Cirion and Eorl and the Friendship of Gondor and Rohan* Tolkien gives the Sindarin name as *Onodló* 'Ent' + 'fen'. For *Ent*, see note for p. 442.

373 (I: 390). Emyn Muil – '*Emyn*: pl[ural] of *amon*, hill. *The Emyn Muil* "the drear hills", folded, rocky and (espec[ially] on east-side) barren hill-country about Lake Nen Hithoel above Rauros Falls' (*Index*).

373 (I: 390). Noman-lands – In his unfinished index Tolkien defines these as the 'desolate region N[orth] of the Black Gate (Morannon) of Mordor'. The name undoubtedly derives from *no-man's-land* 'disputed ground between two armies', which Tolkien would have known especially as applied to the area between the friendly and enemy trenches in the First World War. He saw action in the Battle of the Somme in 1916.

373 (I: 390). Cirith Gorgor – In his unfinished index Tolkien describes *Cirith Gorgor* as 'the haunted ravine, the defile between Ephel Dúath and Ered Lithui, entrance to Mordor, behind the Morannon, also called the

Haunted Pass', and notes '*cirith* cleft, ravine, defile' and '*gorgor* terror, haunting fear'.

374 (I: 390): 'Indeed we have heard

374 (I: 390). for the most part old wives' tales, such as we tell our children – An *old wives' tale* is a widely held traditional belief now thought to be unscientific or incorrect.

Aragorn will be surprised to learn, in Book III, Chapter 5, that 'there is truth in the old legends about the dwellers in the deep forests and the giant shepherds of the trees'. 'Are there still Ents in the world?' he asks. 'I thought they were only a memory of ancient days, if indeed they were ever more than a legend of Rohan' (p. 499, II: 102). In Book III, Chapter 8, when three ents are seen and Théoden asks what they are, Gandalf replies: 'Is it so long since you listened to tales by the fireside? There are children in your land who, out of the twisted threads of story, could pick the answer to your question' (p. 549, II: 155). The Elves know better: on the present page Celeborn tells Boromir not to 'despise the lore that has come down from distant years; for oft it may chance that old wives keep in memory word of things that once were needful for the wise to know'. Later, in the Houses of Healing in Minas Tirith, Aragorn will find that it is only a veritable old wife who remembers lore about *athelas* in the king's hands bringing healing.

On many occasions in *The Lord of the Rings* Tolkien shows that the traditional lore of simple people or of children may have as much validity as the learning of loremasters. In *On Fairy-Stories* he comments that one reason why fairy-stories are associated with children is that they were told to them by their nurses, 'who were sometimes in touch with rustic and traditional lore forgotten by their "betters"' (*Tree and Leaf*, p. 34).

374 (I: 390). Of old Fangorn lay upon the borders of our realm – It no longer does so, Gondor having ceded the territory adjoining Fangorn Forest to Eorl and his people in Third Age 2510. In *Cirion and Eorl and the Friendship of Gondor and Rohan* the northern bounds of Rohan are defined as: 'in the West the river Angren [Isen] from its junction with the Adorn and thence northwards to the outer fences of Angrenost [Isengard], and thence westwards and northwards along the eaves of Fangorn Forest to the river Limlight' (*Unfinished Tales*, p. 305). In Appendix A of *The Lord of the Rings* it is said that the kingdom of Gondor, at the summit of its power in the days of King Hyarmendacil I (Third Age 1015–1149), extended northwards 'to the field of Celebrant and the southern eaves of Mirkwood' (p. 1045, III: 325). According to late writing:

> The River Celebrant (Silverlode) was within the borders of the realm of Lórien, and the effective bounds of the kingdom of Gondor in the north (west of Anduin) was the river Limlight. The whole of the grasslands between Silverlode and Limlight, into which the woods of Lórien

formerly extended further south, were known in Lórien as Parth Celebrant (i.e. the field or enclosed grassland, of Silverlode) and regarded as part of its realm, though not inhabited by its Elvish folk beyond the eaves of the woods. In later days Gondor built a bridge over the upper Limlight, and often occupied the narrow land between the lower Limlight and Anduin as part of its eastern defences, since the great loops of the Anduin (where it came down swiftly past Lórien and entered low flat lands before its descent again into the chasm of the Emyn Muil) had many shallows and wide shoals over which a determined and well-equipped enemy could force a crossing by rafts or pontoons, especially in the two westward bends, known as the North and South Undeeps. It was to this land that the name Parth Celebrant was applied in Gondor; hence its use in defining the ancient northern boundary. In the time of the War of the Ring, when all the land north of the White Mountains (save Anórien) as far as the Limlight had become part of the Kingdom of Rohan, the name Parth (Field of) Celebrant was only used of the great battle in which Eorl the Young destroyed the invaders of Gondor. [*The History of Galadriel and Celeborn* in *Unfinished Tales*, p. 260]

374 (I: 390): 'I have myself been

374 (I: 390). Northerland – '*Norland* "(belonging to) the north-lands", in this tale those regions envisaged in the action north of Rohan. The longer form *Northerland* . . . has the same reference' (*Nomenclature*, in entry for *Norbury*).

374 (I: 390): Now Galadriel rose

374 (I: 390). mead – An alcoholic beverage, from fermented honey and water, especially popular in the early Middle Ages.

374 (I: 390): 'Now it is time

374 (I: 390). though night must follow noon, and already our evening draweth nigh – In this and other phrases Galadriel indicates that Lothlórien will not endure much longer. Later she laments that the Company has seen Lórien only in winter; then, speaking metaphorically: 'For our Spring and our Summer are gone by, and they will never be seen on earth again save in memory' (Book II, Chapter 8, p. 375, I: 392). In depicting Lothlórien Tolkien succeeds in balancing a sense of timelessness with a perception that a long history is coming to an end.

374 (I: 390): Then she brought the cup

374 (I: 390). Then she brought the cup to each of the Company – In this Galadriel follows ancient customs as portrayed in *Beowulf*:

> Wealhtheow, Hrothgar's queen, went forth, mindful of court usage; gold-adorned, she greeted the men in hall, and then the noble woman

gave the cup first [to Hrothgar]. . . . He, the victorious king, partook in gladness of the feast and hall-cup.

Then the lady of the Helmings went round every part of the hall, to old and young; proffered the costly goblet. [Clark Hall translation, p. 51]

374–5 (I: 391): 'The blade that is drawn

374 (I: 391). The blade that is drawn from this sheath shall not be stained or broken even in defeat – The idea that power may reside in the sheath of a sword recalls the sheath of King Arthur's sword Excalibur, said by Merlin to be 'worth far more than the sword itself' for it 'will protect its bearer from injury' (Norman J. Lacy, ed., *The New Arthurian Encyclopedia* (1996), p. 148).

375 (I: 391): And Aragorn answered

375 (I: 391). Lady, you know all my desire, and long held in keeping the only treasure that I seek. Yet it is not yours to give me – Aragorn is referring to Arwen, Galadriel's granddaughter, who over the years has lived in Lothlórien as well as Rivendell. Galadriel showed her favour to Aragorn on his previous visit to Lórien and seemed to promote their betrothal (see *The Tale of Aragorn and Arwen* in Appendix A, and note for p. 352), but it is Elrond's right to approve his daughter's marriage.

375 (I: 391): 'Yet maybe this will lighten

375 (I: 391). a great stone of clear green, set in a silver brooch, that was wrought in the likeness of an eagle with outspread wings – The name given to the stone, *Elessar*, is Quenya 'elfstone'. At some time after the publication of *The Lord of the Rings* Tolkien turned his attention to the origin of this brooch and produced a rough four-page manuscript entitled *The Elessar*. He was uncertain whether there had been one or two jewels with that name. He was sure, however, that an Elessar had been made in Gondolin for Idril by an Elven jewel-smith named Enerdhil. 'For it is said that those who looked through this stone saw things that were withered or burned healed again or as they were in the grace of their youth, and that the hands of one who held it brought to all that they touched healing from hurt' (*Unfinished Tales*, p. 249). Idril gave the stone to her son Eärendil, who wore it when he sailed into the West (thus Aragorn's insistence that Bilbo include a green stone in his song of Eärendil at Rivendell).

But Tolkien hesitated whether the Elessar that came to Aragorn was the same jewel, or another made in imitation of the first. 'In ages after there was again an Elessar, and of this two things are said, though which is true only those Wise could say who are now gone' (p. 249). In one story, if the stone was the original Elessar, then it had been brought back to Middle-earth from Aman by Gandalf who gave it to Galadriel and told her: 'This I bring you from Yavanna. Use it as you may, and for a while you shall make the land of your dwelling the fairest place in Middle-earth. But it is not for you to possess. You shall hand it on when the time comes. For before you grow weary, and at last forsake Middle-earth one shall come who is to receive it, and his name shall be that of the stone: Elessar he shall be called' (p. 250). This story agrees with Galadriel's statement that the name *Elessar* had been foretold for Aragorn, but not with her giving the brooch to her daughter Celebrían rather than waiting for the one who was to receive it.

In the second story, the stone that Galadriel gives to Aragorn had been made for her by the Elven-smith Celebrimbor in imitation of the first Elessar:

> he set it within a great brooch of silver in the likeness of an eagle rising upon outspread wings. Wielding the Elessar all things grew fair about Galadriel, until the coming of the Shadow to the Forest. But afterwards when Nenya . . . was sent to her by Celebrimbor, she needed it [the brooch] (as she thought) no more, and she gave it to Celebrían her daughter, and so it came to Arwen and to Aragorn who was called Elessar. [p. 251]

375 (I: 391). This stone I gave to Celebrían my daughter, and she to hers, and now it comes to you – In *Of the Laws and Customs Among the Eldar Pertaining to Marriage and Other Matters Related Thereto*, written after the publication of *The Lord of the Rings*, Tolkien gives an account which seems to contradict the history set out in the previous note:

> Among the Noldor also it was the custom that the bride's mother should give to the bridegroom a jewel upon a chain or collar; and that the bridegroom's father should give a like gift to the bride. These gifts were sometimes given before the feast. (Thus the gift of Galadriel to Aragorn, since she was in place of Arwen's mother, was in part a bridal gift and earnest of the wedding that was later accomplished.) [*Morgoth's Ring*, p. 211]

Celebrían is Sindarin for 'silver queen'.

375 (I: 391). In this hour take the name that was foretold for you, Elessar, the Elfstone of the House of Elendil! – One foretelling is noted above, in the account of the Elessars. But according to a rough note by Tolkien this name was also foreseen by Aragorn's maternal grandmother, Ivorwen: 'and his father gave him the name Aragorn, a name used in the House of the Chieftains. But Ivorwen at his naming stood by, and said "Kingly Valour" (for so that name is interpreted): "that he shall have, but I see on his breast a green stone, and from that his true name shall come and his chief renown: for he shall be a healer and a renewer." Above this passage is written: 'and they did not know what she meant, for there was no green stone to be seen by other eyes', followed by illegible words; and beneath it 'for the green Elfstone was given to him by Galadriel' (*The Peoples of Middle-earth*, p. xii).

The Elessar given by Galadriel to Aragorn originally had no connection with Arwen, who was a late addition in the writing of *The Lord of the Rings*. In the first account of the gift-giving the jewel was given to Gimli, who thanked Galadriel and said: 'Elfstone shall be a name of honour in my [?kin] for ever' (*The Treason of Isengard*, p. 275). But while writing of the Company's time in Lothlórien, Tolkien decided (temporarily) that Trotter's (Strider's) real name should be *Elfstone*; and immediately after recording Gimli's words, Tolkien decided that the jewel should be given to Trotter, to whom Galadriel said:

> 'Elfstone is your name, Eldamir in the language of your fathers of old, and it is a fair name. I will add this gift of my own to match it.' She put a hand to her throat and unclasped from a fine chain a gem that hung before her breast. It was a stone of clear green set in a band of silver. 'All growing things that you look at through this,' she said, 'you will see as they were in their youth and in their spring. It is a gift that blends joy and sorrow; yet many things that now appear loathly shall seem otherwise to you hereafter.' [p. 276]

Christopher Tolkien comments: 'The Elfstone was the Lady's gift to him [Trotter], not to Gimli, and in giving it to him she made a play on his name' (p. 277).

375 (I: 391): Then Aragorn took the stone

375 (I: 391). they had not marked before how tall and kingly he stood – From this point Strider, partly because he is now the undoubted leader of the Company (or part of it), grows steadily into his role as the future king and leader of the armies of the West. Paul H. Kocher devotes a chapter of *Master of Middle-earth* to an analysis of Aragorn's character and importance: he considers Aragorn 'unquestionably the leading man in *The Lord of the Rings*', and criticizes those who ignore him while concentrating their attention on Frodo, or who find Aragorn too good to be true. Kocher admits that 'Aragorn is rather more difficult to know truly than any other important person in the story', and considers that this is so partly because Tolkien himself did not know who Strider (or Trotter the Hobbit) was at first, and does not provide the reader with much information about him until the Council of Elrond, 'and only in retrospect can [we] understand his actions and feeling at Bree'. 'Even at Rivendell,' Kocher says, 'we may well miss the bare hints which are all that Tolkien finds space for about Aragorn's love for Arwen since youth. Yet this, along with his concurrent planning to recover the throne of Gondor, is basic motivation without a knowledge of which Aragorn remains a mystery' (p. 130–1).

375 (I: 391–2): 'For you little gardener

375 (I: 391–2). a little box of plain grey wood, unadorned save for a single silver rune upon the lid. 'Here is set G for Galadriel – In the first text there is a 'single flowering rune' on the lid, reproduced in *The Treason of Isengard*, p. 274. Possibly not by coincidence, the Anglo-Saxon 'G' rune is called *gifu*, Old English 'gift'.

376 (I: 392): 'Hear all ye Elves!'

376 (I: 392). Yet surely, Gimli . . . you desire something I could give? – Why has Galadriel no gift for Gimli? She would surely not leave him out, and could easily had provided another belt or brooch. Has she already read in his mind what he wants? Even in the text noted above, in which he was originally to have received the Elfstone, Galadriel apparently did not have anything prepared. After giving gifts to the others, she asks Gimli 'what gift would a dwarf ask of Elves', and he replies: 'None, Lady. . . . It is enough for me to have seen the Lady of the Galadrim and known her graciousness.' In response she unclasps the brooch she is wearing and gives it to him as 'a sign that goodwill may be remade between dwarves and elves' (*The Treason of Isengard*, p. 275).

376 (I: 392): 'Treasure it, Lady'

376 (I: 392). Treasure it, Lady – Marjorie Burns comments in *Perilous Realms: Celtic and Norse in Tolkien's Middle-earth* that Gimli 'devotes himself to Galadriel in much the way a medieval knight devotes himself to his lady (an image of courtly dedication which in its highest form is transferred to *the* Lady, to Mary, the mother of Christ)' (p. 152).

376 (I: 392). smithies – A *smithy* is a forge, the workshop of a smith.

376 (I: 392–3): Then the Lady unbraided

376 (I: 392). and cut off three golden hairs, and laid them in Gimli's hand – In a late essay by Tolkien it is said of Galadriel that

> even among the Eldar she was accounted beautiful, and her hair was held a marvel unmatched. It was golden like the hair of her father and of her foremother Indis, but richer and more radiant, for its gold was touched by some memory of the starlike silver of her mother; and the Eldar said that the light of the Two Trees, Laurelin and Telperion, had been snared in her tresses. Many thought that this saying first gave to Fëanor the thought of imprisoning and blending the light of the Trees that later took shape in his hands as the Silmarils. For Fëanor beheld the hair of Galadriel with wonder and delight. He begged three times for a tress, but Galadriel would not give him even one hair. These two kinsfolk, the greatest of the Eldar of Valinor, were unfriends for ever. [*The History of Galadriel and Celeborn* in *Unfinished Tales*, pp. 229–30]

376 (I: 393): 'And you, Ring-bearer

376 (I: 393). phial – A vessel for holding liquids, usually a small glass bottle.

377 (I: 393): Even as they gazed

377 (I: 393). the ancient tongue of the Elves beyond the Sea – Quenya.

377–8 (I: 394): *Ai! laurië lantar lassi súrinen*

377–8 (I: 394). *Ai! laurië lantar lassi súrinen . . .* – An English translation follows in the text. *The Road Goes Ever On: A Song Cycle* includes a word by word translation, comments on pronunciation and stress, a rendering in tengwar, and a manuscript Quenya text showing verbal construction and accentuation.

Two recordings by Tolkien of Galadriel's lament ('Namárië'), one sung and one read, are included on Disc 2 of *The J.R.R. Tolkien Audio Collection*.

377 (I: 394). *Yéni ve lintë yuldar avánier* – As first published this phrase read '*yéni ve linte yuldar vánier*'. In the second edition (1965) *vánier* was 'given the more correct (perfect) form *avánier*' (*The Road Goes Ever On: A Song Cycle*, p. 58). In the sixth printing (1966) of the Ballantine Books edition the revised *avánier* was incorrectly changed to the earlier *vánier*, and not corrected until the reset edition of autumn 2001.

378 (I: 394): 'Ah! like gold fall the leaves

378 (I: 394). Ah! like gold fall the leaves – *Laure* was translated 'gold', 'but it was not a metallic word. It was applied to those things which we often call "golden" though they do not much resemble metallic gold. . . . The reference is to autumn as in Middle-earth (called *lasselanta*, "leaf-fall"), when the yellow leaves released by a wind may fall fluttering, gleaming in the sun' (*The Road Goes Ever On: A Song Cycle*, p. 62).

378 (I: 394). long years – The Quenya word translated is *yéni.* In his word by word translation in *The Road Goes Ever On: A Song Cycle* (p. 58) Tolkien gives this as 'years (long Elvish years)'. In Appendix D of *The Lord of the Rings* he explains that 'the Quenya word *yén*, often translated "year", really means 144 of our years' (p. 1107, III: 385).

378 (I: 394). all paths are drowned in shadow – In *The Road Goes Ever On: A Song Cycle* Tolkien says: 'After the destruction of the Two Trees, and the flight from *Valinor* of the revolting *Eldar*, *Varda* lifted up her hands, in obedience to the decree of *Manwë*, and summoned up the dark shadows which engulfed the shores and the mountains and last of all the *fana* (figure) of Varda with her hands turned eastward in rejection, standing white upon *Oiolossë*' (p. 60). See also note for p. 234.

378 (I: 394). Valimar – 'Properly the city of the Valar, near the mound upon which the Two Trees stood, but it is here used (it means dwellings of the Valar) to stand for the land of the Valar as a whole' (*The Road Goes Ever On: A Song Cycle*, p. 62).

378 (I: 394). Maybe thou shalt find Valimar – 'The last lines of the chant express a wish (or hope) that though she [Galadriel] could not go, Frodo might perhaps be allowed to do so. *Na-i* > *nai*, "be it that," expresses rather a wish than a hope, and would be more closely rendered "may it be that" (thou wilt find), than by "maybe"' (*The Road Goes Ever On: A Song Cycle*, p. 60).

Chapter 9

THE GREAT RIVER

For drafts and history of this chapter, see *The Treason of Isengard*, pp. 350–69.

380 (I: 396): Frodo was roused

380 (I: 396). Frodo was roused – It is 17 February 1419.

380 (I: 396): They started again

380 (I: 396). husbanding – Saving, preserving.

380 (I: 396): Nonetheless they saw no sign

380 (I: 396). As the third day of their voyage wore on – The day of 18 February 1419.

380 (I: 396). the Brown Lands – In his unfinished index Tolkien describes the *Brown Lands* as a 'translation' of *Berennyn* (Sindarin *baran* 'brown, yellow-brown') 'a devastated region, east of Anduin, between Lórien and the Emyn Muil'. In Book III, Chapter 4 Treebeard tells Merry and Pippin that the Entwives once had rich gardens there, but towards the end of Second Age, when the Ents went to visit them, they found the area 'a desert; it was all burned and uprooted, for war had passed over it' (p. 476, II: 79).

380 (I: 396): Upon the west to their right

380 (I: 396). meads – A poetic or literary form of *meadow*.

381 (I: 397): 'Yes,' said Aragorn

381 (I: 397). black swans – Tolkien never indicates whether the swans are spies for Sauron, but that they are *black* suggests evil motives (see note for p. 846). In his letter to Milton Waldman in ?late 1951 Tolkien wrote: 'All through the book hints of the watchfulness of spies have multiplied' (*Waldman LR*).

381 (I: 397): 'But we have not journeyed

381 (I: 397). You are looking now south-west across the north plains of the Riddermark – On p. 429, II: 32 and on the general map this is named 'the Wold of Rohan'. In his unfinished index Tolkien describes it as the 'northern part of the Eastemnet'.

381 (I: 397). Limlight – In his unfinished index Tolkien describes the Limlight as: 'river flowing from Fangorn to Anduin and forming the extreme north-bound of *Rohan*. ([The] name is a partial tr[anslation] of E[lvish, i.e.

Sindarin] *Limlint* "swift-light".)' (*Sic*, compare *limliht* below.) In *Nomenclature* Tolkien notes that in *Limlight* the element *light* means 'bright, clear'. The name is also mentioned in the late work *Cirion and Eorl and the Friendship of Gondor and Rohan*, on which Christopher Tolkien comments:

> There are two versions of the text and note at this point, from one of which it seems that the Sindarin name was *Limlich*, adapted to the language of Rohan as *Limliht* ('modernized' as Limlight). In the other (later) version *Limlich* is emended, puzzlingly to *Limliht* in the text, so that this becomes the Sindarin form. Elsewhere (in *The Disaster of the Gladden Fields*, *Unfinished Tales*, p. 281) the Sindarin name of this river is given as *Limlaith*. In view of this uncertainty I have given *Limlight* in the text. Whatever the original Sindarin name may have been, it is at least clear that the Rohan form was an alteration of it and not a translation, and that its meaning was not known. [*Unfinished Tales*, p. 318, n. 46]

381 (I: 397). of old all that lay between Limlight and the White Mountains belonged to the Rohirrim – See note for p. 374.

381 (I: 397–8): In the next day or two

381 (I: 397). In the next day or two – Presumably (given the uncertainty of *or*) the fourth and fifth days of the voyage, 19 and 20 February 1419.

381 (I: 397). gravel-shoals – A *shoal* is a place of shallow water, here with a bottom of gravel.

381 (I: 397). wolds – A *wold* is high, open, uncultivated land.

382 (I: 398): As dusk drew down

382 (I: 398). on the fourth day – On 19 February 1419.

382 (I: 398): That night they camped

382 (I: 398). a small eyot – An *eyot* is a small island, especially in a river.

383 (I: 399–400): In the dead hours

383 (I: 400). dead hours – In the early hours after midnight on 20 February 1419.

383–4 (I: 400): He lay down

384 (I: 400). gunwale – The upper edge on the side of a boat.

384 (I: 400): 'Gollum,' answered Frodo

384 (I: 400). Gollum – *Scheme* gives details of Gollum's movements since Moria:

> January 15: Gollum dogs the Coy. [Company] and climbs up flet. Then escapes and haunts west borders of Lórien.

January 17: For many days Gollum lurks near Lórien, moving slowly towards the southern borders.

January 24: Gollum captured by Uglúk [see note for p. 416], but escapes after revealing that Hobbits of Shire were with Gandalf, and enough is said to make Uglúk certain that Ring was with the company

February 16: Observes departure of Company and follows them.

February 18: Follows Coy. on log.

February 19: Seen by Sam on log.

February 20: Driven off by vigilance from Company's camp.

February 23 [Sarn Gebir]: Unable to follow by water, G[ollum] in terror of Orcs makes his way to Eastern Emyn Muil by east bank.

384 (I: 400): 'Ah!' said Aragorn

384 (I: 400). footpad – A figurative use of the term: historically, a highwayman who robbed on foot rather than on a horse. Tolkien may be playing on the verbs *pad* 'to walk steadily with a soft sound' and *paddle* 'to use one's limbs like paddles in the water'. In *The Hobbit*, Chapter 5, Gollum 'had a little boat. . . . He paddled it with large feet dangling over the side, but never a ripple did he make.'

384 (I: 400): The night passed

384 (I: 400). until the seventh day – The seventh day counting the day of departure. It is now 22 January 1419.

384 (I: 400–1): The weather was still grey

384 (I: 400). the white rind of the new Moon – This is the night of 22/23 February. A new moon is visible in the west just before and after sunset.

384–5 (I: 401): The next day

384 (I: 401). The next day – It is 23 February 1419.

384 (I: 401). chimneys – A *chimney* in this sense is a steep, narrow cleft in a rock face.

385 (I: 401). wind-writhen – *Writhen* 'twisted or contorted' (compare *writhe*).

385 (I: 401): There were many birds

385 (I: 401). descried – Caught sight of.

385 (I: 401): The eighth night of their journey

385 (I: 401). The eighth night of their journey came. – It is the night of 23/24 February 1419.

386 (I: 402): At that moment

386 (I: 402). shingle-banks – *Shingle* is small stones or pebbles worn by water.

387 (I: 403): Legolas laid down

387 (I: 403). Stringing the bow – An archer's bow of the traditional kind is carried with the bowstring loose. When ready for use, the bow is bent, and the bowstring fitted into a notch and drawn tight.

387 (I: 403): '*Elbereth Gilthoniel!*'

387 (I: 403). Soon it appeared as a great winged creature – Although not so identified until later, this is a Ringwraith riding on a winged beast.

388 (I: 404): 'Well, I can remember

388 (I: 404). Anyone would think that time did not count in there! – See note for p. 370.

388 (I: 404–5): Legolas stirred in his boat

388 (I: 405). because they need not count the running years – In editions prior to 2004 these words read: 'because they do not count the running years'. Christopher Tolkien notes in *The Treason of Isengard*: 'The phrase as my father wrote it was "because they *need* not count the running years", but in copying I missed out the word *need*. Looking through my copy, but without consulting his own manuscript, he wrote in *do*' (p. 366, n. 23). Although *do* is authorial, Christopher Tolkien felt that it was so only artificially, because of the transcription error, and that *need* should be restored.

389 (I: 405): When the day came

389 (I: 405). When the day came – It is 24 February 1419.

389 (I: 405): 'I do not see why

389 (I: 405). cockle-boats – A *cockle-boat* is small, shallow boat resembling a cockle shell.

389 (I: 406): 'No!' answered Aragorn

389 (I: 406). Rauros-foot – 'The basin at the foot of the [Rauros] falls' (*Index*).

389 (I: 406). the North Stair and the high seat upon Amon Hen – '*North Stair*, a great stair cut by the Númenóreans up beside the falls of Rauros, from the Nindalf to Emyn Muil' (*Index*).

Amon Hen is Sindarin for 'hill of the eye'; see note for p. 400.

390 (I: 406): 'Boats of the Elves

390 (I: 406). No road was made by the Men of Gondor in this region, for even in their great days their realm did not reach up Anduin beyond the Emyn Muil – This is contradicted by statements given in the note for p. 374. Although some of the evidence cited there is later than the publication of *The Lord of the Rings*, Boromir himself says that the boundaries of Gondor had once reached Fangorn Forest, which is considerably north of the Emyn Muil.

390 (I: 406). portage-way – A path along which boats or cargo can be carried between two bodies of water.

392 (I: 408): Nothing happened that night

392 (I: 408). As soon as it was fully light – It is 25 February 1419.

392 (I: 408): The rain, however

392 (I: 408). thrawn – Twisted, crooked.

392 (I: 409): 'Behold the Argonath'

392 (I: 409). Argonath – In the manuscript of *Nomenclature* Tolkien writes that *Argonath* means 'royal stones', containing 'the element *gon–d* = "stone" in Elvish'.

> Cf. Quenya *ondo* stone as a material, or a large mass of stone or great rock; *Ondonóre* = Sindarin *Gondor* lit[erally] 'land of Stone', referring to the great works and buildings of stone for which the Númenóreans were renowned. In Sindarin the shorter *gon-* was used for smaller objects made of stone, especially carved figures. In Sindarin *-ath* was the sign of collective or group plurals, here used because the *Argonath* were a pair of twin statues. . . . *Ar(a)-* was a prefix expressing royalty: Cf. Quenya and Sindarin *aran* 'king'.

In Appendix A it is said that the Argonath was built during the reign of Rómendacil II (1304–1366).

These gigantic figures recall ancient Egyptian statues such as the two Colossi of Memnon, all that remains of the Mortuary Temple of Amenophis III (1417–1379 BC) on the west bank of the Nile near the Valley of the Kings.

In one of his working manuscripts on distance and time in *The Lord of the Rings*, Tolkien states that from the Tongue of Lórien to the Argonath is '230 miles direct: over 300 by water, takes 10 days' (Marquette MSS 4/2/19).

392–3 (I: 409): As Frodo was borne

392 (I: 409). in each right hand there was an axe – The sword seems to have been the usual Númenórean weapon, but *axe* is a deliberate change from *sword* which appeared in the draft.

392 (I: 409). silent wardens of a long-vanished kingdom – Probably a reference to the Númenórean kingdom when it was ruled jointly by Isildur and Anárion at the end of the Second Age.

393 (I: 409): Then the light of his eyes

393 (I: 409). Would that Gandalf were here! How my heart yearns for Minas Anor and the walls of my own city! But whither now shall I go? – Only rarely does Tolkien let us see into Aragorn's mind. He does so here perhaps to stress the difficult choice that Aragorn is facing.

393 (I: 409–10): The chasm was long

393 (I: 410). suddenly the boats shot through, out into a wide clear light – In *Scheme* it is said for 25 February: 'They [the Company] pass Gate of Argonath and come to Lake Hithoel (1.30 pm)'.

393 (I: 410): The sun, already long fallen

393 (I: 410). a long oval lake . . . fenced by steep grey hills. . . . At the far southern end rose three peaks. – An aerial view by Tolkien, looking north from a point just south of Rauros and showing the falls, the three hills, the lake, and the ravine north of the lake, is reproduced in *Artist and Illustrator*, fig. 159. Two circles mark the position of the Argonath.

393 (I: 410). pent waters – *Pent* 'restricted, closely confined'.

393–4 (I: 410): 'Behold Tol Brandir!'

394 (I: 410). Amon Lhaw – Sindarin 'hill of the ear'.

394 (I: 410): The tenth day

394 (I: 410). The tenth day of their journey was over – It is evening on 25 February 1419. The Company left Lórien on 16 February.

Chapter 10

THE BREAKING OF THE FELLOWSHIP

For drafts and history of this chapter, see *The Treason of Isengard*, pp. 370–7.

395 (I: 411): 'Here we will rest

395 (I: 411). Parth Galen – In his unfinished index Tolkien notes: '*Parth* "sward": *Parth Galen* "green sward", a grassy place on the N[orth] slope of Amon Hen by the shore of Lake Nen Hithoel'; and '*calen* "green" '.

395 (I: 411): The day came like fire

395 (I: 411). The day came – It is 26 February 1419.

396 (I: 412): Frodo sat for a moment

396 (I: 412). plain as a pikestaff – Clear, obvious. An earlier form of the phrase is 'plain as a packstaff' (i.e. 'the staff on which a pedlar carried his pack, which was worn plain and smooth', *Brewer's Dictionary of Phrase and Fable*, 15th edn., p. 57).

396 (I: 412). putting in his spoke – In this colloquial sense, to *put in a spoke* is to offer advice.

398 (I: 415): 'No, I am afraid

398 (I: 415). I am glad to have heard you speak so fully. My mind is clearer now. – Boromir has fallen to the temptation of the Ring, but without his actions Frodo might not have had the strength to come to the right decision.

399 (I: 415–16): 'Miserable trickster!'

399 (I: 416). in the lurch – In a difficult situation, without assistance.

400 (I: 416): He rose and passed his hand over his eyes

400 (I: 416). What have I done? – Boromir regrets his actions immediately. Yet, as Tolkien has shown both at the Council of Elrond and on several occasions during the journey from Rivendell, Boromir cannot understand and does not really agree with the decision taken at the Council. He is a tragic figure with many good qualities, but with weaknesses that lay him open to temptation. The Ring has been able to play on his wish to save his country and on his desire for personal glory.

400 (I: 416): Soon he came out alone

400 (I: 416). the summit of Amon Hen – In reply to a query, Tolkien wrote to 'Benjamin' on 19 June 1959: 'I don't know the height of Amon Hen but I doubt if it was much over 1,000 feet' (Waterfield's Catalogue 157, *Modern Literature*, 1995, item 427).

400 (I: 416). battlement – 'A parapet with openings at regular intervals along the top of the wall, forming part of a fortification' (*Concise OED*).

400 (I: 416): At first he could see little

400 (I: 416). He seemed to be in a world of mist in which there were only shadows: the Ring was upon him. – Similarly, when Sam puts on the Ring in Book IV, Chapter 10, 'his sight was dimmed. . . . All things about him now were not dark but vague' (p. 734, II: 343). According to Gandalf in Book II, Chapter 1, when the Ring is worn the wearer is half in the wraith world. In Book I, Chapter 11, Aragorn says that the Ringwraiths 'do not see the world of light as we do' (p. 189, I: 202). This effect is mentioned only in *The Lord of the Rings*, not in *The Hobbit* when Bilbo wears the Ring.

400 (I: 416). He was sitting in the Seat of Seeing, on Amon Hen, the Hill of the Eye of the Men of Númenor. – Frodo certainly sees, even if only as small and remote visions, much further than would be normal even from the height of Amon Hen. The published text seems to say that the Ring interferes with his sight, but that the power of the Seat of Seeing gradually overcomes this. Christopher Tolkien notes that the present text replaced one in which the power of Amon Hen follows immediately and explicitly on the description of the inhibiting effect of the Ring on sight: 'At first he could see little: he seemed to be in a world of mist in which there were only shadows. The Ring was on him. [Then the virtue (*written above:* power) of Amon Hen worked upon him]' (*The Treason of Isengard*, p. 373, square brackets in original). See further, note for p. 413.

Several readers have compared the seat on Amon Hen with the high seat of Odin from which he could see over the whole earth, and which Tolkien mentions in *On Fairy-Stories*.

400 (I: 416). fume – In this sense, spray from the falls.

400 (I: 416). Ethir Anduin . . . the mighty delta of the River. – '*Ethir* "outflow": *Ethir Anduin*, the Mouths of Anduin, with delta in Bay of Belfalas. Called in Gondor simply the *Ethir*' (*Index*).

400 (I: 416–17): But everywhere he looked

400 (I: 416–17). Under the boughs of Mirkwood there was deadly strife of Elves and Men and fell beasts. The land of the Beornings was aflame . . . smoke rose on the borders of Lórien. – Nowhere in the text is it suggested that the Seat of Seeing shows events other than those occurring at the time. But this is 26 February, and the only entries in *The Tale of Years* concerning attacks on the areas named in the description are on later dates: 11 March 'First assault on Lórien'; 15 March 'Battle under the Trees in Mirkwood; Thranduil repels the forces of Dol Guldur. Second assault on Lórien'; 22 March 'Third assault on Lórien'.

The *land of the Beornings* lies 'on either side of Anduin, between [the] Misty Mts. and Mirkwood, immediately east of Rivendell' (*Index*).

400–1 (I: 417): Horsemen were galloping

401 (I: 417). wains – *Wain* is an archaic word for 'wagon'.

401 (I: 417). reek – Smoke, fumes.

401 (I: 417). Mount Doom was burning . . . wall upon wall, battlement upon battlement, black, immeasurably strong, mountain of iron, gate of steel, tower of adamant, he saw it: Barad-dûr – Tolkien drew a picture of Barad-dûr, or rather of a part of the Dark Tower but one which suggests its great strength and size, with Mount Doom in the background: see *Artist and Illustrator*, fig. 145.

401 (I: 417): He heard himself crying

401 (I: 417). *Never, never! . . . Verily I come, I come to you. . . . Take it off! Take it off! Fool, take it off! Take off the Ring!* – In Book III, Chapter 5, Gandalf confirms that the last voice ('Take it off!') is his. Tom Shippey has commented that

> the third voice is Gandalf's, in a 'high place' somewhere striving against the mental force of 'the Dark Power'. But whose are the other two voices? The first one seems to be 'himself', i.e. Frodo. The second one could be, perhaps, the voice of the Ring: the sentient creature obeying the call of its maker, Sauron, as it has been all along. Or could it be, so to speak, Frodo's subconscious, obeying a kind of death-wish, entirely internal but psychically amplified by the Ring? [*J.R.R. Tolkien: Author of the Century*, p. 138]

403 (I: 419): 'It would indeed be a betrayal

403 (I: 419). and myself – Aragorn must know that if he goes east to Mordor with Frodo rather than south to assist Minas Tirith in the war, his chances of regaining the throne of Gondor will be much diminished. Yet here he renounces that path, along with the hope of fulfilling Elrond's conditions for his marriage to Arwen. Aragorn puts duty, for the greater good, before his own desires.

403 (I: 419): 'Now where's he got to?'

403 (I: 419). a bit of schooling – Training, experience in situations wholly alien to Hobbits.

404 (I: 421): It was no good

404 (I: 421). A sudden panic or madness seemed to have fallen on the Company. – Madness, or fate sending them on their appointed paths? Sam to join Frodo and set out on the journey to Mount Doom; Boromir to his good death; Merry and Pippin to rouse the Ents, and then Merry to help destroy the Witch-king, and Pippin to save Faramir; Aragorn, Legolas, and Gimli to help win the battle at Helm's Deep; and Aragorn to be in the right place to go south to summon the Dead.

THE TWO TOWERS

Volume title – For the conception of separate titles for the three volumes of *The Lord of the Rings* as first published, see our 'Brief History' at the beginning of the present book. Tolkien's first suggestion for a title for the second volume, made in a letter to Rayner Unwin on 8 August 1953, was *The Shadow Lengthens*. Later that month, after further discussion with Unwin, Tolkien suggested a new title, *The Two Towers*, which 'gets as near as possible to finding a title to cover the widely divergent Books 3 and 4; and can be left ambiguous – it might refer to Isengard and Barad-dûr, or to Minas Tirith and B; or Isengard and Cirith Ungol' (letter to Rayner Unwin, 17 August 1953, *Letters*, p. 170). But on 22 January 1954 Tolkien wrote again to Unwin: 'I am not at all happy about the title "the Two Towers". It must if there is any real reference in it to Vol. II refer to *Orthanc* and the *Tower of Cirith Ungol*. But since there is so much made of the basic opposition of the Dark Tower and Minas Tirith, that seems very misleading. There is, of course, actually no real connecting link between Books III and IV, when cut off and presented separately as a volume' (*Letters*, p. 173). Unwin replied on 27 January: 'I should not worry over much about the title of this last book; it sounds pleasant and the reader can exercise his imagination (or perhaps his speculative powers) on deciding which two towers were intended' (Tolkien-George Allen & Unwin archive, HarperCollins).

Tolkien's first rough dust-jacket design for *The Two Towers* shows Barad-dûr (probably) and Minas Tirith with Mount Doom between them; but a second sketch has Minas Morgul and Orthanc, and it was from this that Tolkien developed his final design. There Minas Morgul is clearly identified by a crescent moon above and nine rings below, and Orthanc as it appears elsewhere in Tolkien's art, but with a blood-spattered white hand below. See *Artist and Illustrator*, pp. 180–1 and figs. 178–80.

Synopsis (in three-volume editions) – In the penultimate paragraph (II: 9–10) is a reference to the attack on the Fellowship (at Parth Galen) by 'orc-soldiers, some in the service of the Dark Lord of Mordor, some of the traitor Saruman of Isengard'. But no attack is mentioned in *The Fellowship of the Ring*, and the fact that it was a joint operation by the Orcs is not explicitly stated in the text proper.

BOOK THREE

Chapter 1

THE DEPARTURE OF BOROMIR

For drafts and history of this chapter, see *The Treason of Isengard*, pp. 378–88.

413 (II: 15): Aragorn sped on up the hill

413 (II: 15). Aragorn sped on up the hill. – Until this moment the narrative of *The Lord of the Rings* has had only one thread, with Frodo (after Book I, Chapter 1) at the centre of a tale with a varying number of companions. Although attention has been paid to concurrent events, these are invariably told in retrospect at a specific point in Frodo's story. But at the end of Book II the Nine Walkers are scattered, and those that survive will not all be together again until Book VI, Chapter 4. Until that point, Tolkien deals with events experienced by one or more members of the Company in turn, carrying the story forward in overlapping and related chapters.

Richard C. West, in 'The Interlace Structure of *The Lord of the Rings*', *A Tolkien Compass* (1975), points out that this overlapping or 'interlacing' was a medieval form of storytelling, very different from

> the modern structural technique of 'organic unity' . . . [which] seeks to reduce a chaotic flux of reality to manageable terms by imposing a clear and fairly simple pattern on it. It calls for a progressive and uncluttered narrative line in which there is a single major theme to which a limited number of other themes may be related so long as they are kept subordinate. . . . It is considered preferable to have a limited number of characters and to have no more than one or two dominate the action. . . .
>
> Interlace, by contrast, seeks to mirror the perception of the flux of events in the world around us, where everything is happening at once. Its narrative line is digressive and cluttered, dividing our attention among an indefinite number of events, characters, and themes, any one of which may dominate at any given time. . . . The paths of the character cross, diverge, and recross, and the story passes from one to another and then another but does not follow a single line. Also, the narrator implies there are innumerable events that he has not had time to tell us about. . . .
>
> Yet the apparently casual form of the interlace is deceptive: it actually has a very subtle kind of cohesion. No part of the narrative can be removed without damage to the whole, for within any given section there are echoes of previous parts and anticipations of later ones. [pp. 78–9]

In *J.R.R. Tolkien: Author of the Century* Tom Shippey comments on how Tolkien uses this interlace structure in Books III and IV. The adventures of the separated members of the Fellowship of the Ring 'are never told for long in strict chronological order, and continually "leapfrog" each other'. In the first two chapters of Book III

> we follow Aragorn, Legolas and Gimli from February 26th to February 30th. In chapters 3 and 4 we follow Pippin and Merry from their capture by the Uruk-hai to their meeting with Treebeard; but though these chapters start at (almost) the same time as the first two, the story here goes further, to March 2nd. Chapters 5 through 8 return us to Aragorn and his companions, soon including Gandalf, picking up at March 1st and continuing this time on to March 5th. Chapter 5 includes Gandalf's necessary 'flashback' explaining his return from the dead, which runs from January 15th. The two groups meet eventually at Isengard, when Gandalf, Aragorn, Théoden and the others find . . . Merry and Pippin, but their appearance is a complete surprise to all including the reader – all, that is, apart from Gandalf, who had met Pippin during his brief detour to Treebeard in chapter 7. The hobbits' explanation of how they got there . . . is given in their own narrative, which starts where chapter 4 left off on March 2nd and takes them up to the moment, March 5th. The six members of the Fellowship stay together for two chapters, 10 and 11, but then separate again. The story as far as they are concerned does not resume till the start of *The Return of the King* more than a hundred pages later. [p. 105]

In between comes Book IV, devoted to the journey of Frodo and Sam towards Mordor, not interlaced within itself, and ending at a point in the story over a week later than Book III. Shippey comments: 'As a general rule one may say that none of the five or six major strands of narrative in the central section of *The Lord of the Rings* ever matches neatly with any of the others in chronology: some are always being advanced, some retarded' (p. 106). He points out that the interlacing technique creates 'a profound sense of reality, of that being *the way things are*. There is a pattern in Tolkien's story, but his characters can never see it (naturally, because they are in it)' (p. 107).

413 (II: 15): Aragorn hesitated

413 (II: 15). But the sun seemed darkened, and the world dim and remote . . . and saw nothing save the distant hills – It seems strange that Aragorn, who is of Númenórean blood, should see nothing on Amon Hen, when Frodo saw so much, and when it seems clear that it was the Seat and not the Ring that gaye Frodo his enhanced vision. In a draft of this chapter Trotter sees orcs, and an eagle, and the same figure of an old man in rags that Frodo sees in Galadriel's Mirror. At the end of this text Tolkien wrote:

'The second vision on Amon Hen is inartistic. Let Trotter be stopped by noise of orcs, and let him see nothing' (*The Treason of Isengard*, p. 380).

413 (II: 15). a great bird like an eagle high in the air – Legolas saw an eagle on 23 February, the eighth day of the journey down the Anduin, and will see another as he, Aragorn, and Gimli pursue the captured hobbits. When Gandalf meets them in Fangorn Forest, he tells them that at least the last of the eagles seen by Legolas was Gwaihir the Windlord.

413 (II: 15): Even as he gazed

413 (II: 15). a great horn blew – Boromir blowing his horn to summon help recalls Count Roland in the *c.* mid-eleventh-century *Chanson de Roland* who, when as rearguard he was waylaid by the Paynim, blew his horn to call Charlemagne to return.

413–14 (II: 15–16): A mile, maybe, from Parth Galen

413–14 (II: 15–16). He was sitting with his back to a great tree . . . his horn cloven in two was at his side. – Roland also dies beneath a tree, with a broken horn beside him.

414 (II: 16): Aragorn knelt beside him

414 (II: 16). 'I tried to take the Ring from Frodo,' he said. 'I am sorry. I have paid.' – The manner of Boromir's passing has struck some readers as nearly a Christian death, his final words in effect a confession. He makes 'a good end according to the warrior ethic (fighting in a noble cause), and more importantly, he died in a spiritual "state of grace", having at last fought off the spell of the Ring. His death is in part an atonement for trying to take the Ring from Frodo' (*Rómenna Meeting Report*, 21 July 1985, p. 2). It is also significant that his last thought was for the people of his city.

414 (II: 17): 'First we must tend the fallen'

414 (II: 17). carrion – Dead flesh, food for scavenging birds and animals.

415 (II: 17): 'Then let us lay him in a boat

415 (II: 17). lay him in a boat with his weapons, and the weapons of his vanquished foes – Ship-burial, in which the deceased is sent out to sea in a boat, of its nature leaves no traces but is well attested in literature. In *Beowulf*, for instance, Scyld is laid in a ship with many treasures, weapons, and coats of mail (see note for p. 416), then given to the ocean, as it would bear him. In most accounts, however, a pyre is built on the ship before it is sent out to sea, so that ship and body are consumed, as in the funeral of King Haki described by Snorri Sturluson in the *Ynglinga Saga*.

415 (II: 17–18): There were four goblin-soldiers

415 (II: 18). bows of yew – In medieval England *yew* was considered the best wood for making bows, especially the famous English longbow.

416 (II: 18): 'Neither does he use his right name

416 (II: 18). by some means the traitor Saruman has had news of our journey. . . . Pursuers from Moria may have escaped the vigilance of Lórien – *Scheme* gives a detailed account of events since the Company escaped from Moria:

> January 15: Moria-orcs pursue Co[mpan]y over Silverlode. Driven off by Elves. Messengers leave Moria to *Isengard*, bringing news of events to Saruman, and also mentioning the appearance of Gollum. (Moria is 260 miles direct to Isengard; but orc-runners cover this in less than 4 days.) Messages also go to Barad-dûr, some by evil birds. Barad-dûr is about 680 miles from Moria as crow flies, but rumour reaches Sauron in 3 days and Grishnákh and Orcs of Mordor are despatched.
>
> January 18: Orc-runners reach *Isengard*. Saruman is greatly moved but dare not act independently of Sauron, until he is certain. Sends out scouts under his orc-captain *Uglúk*. Grishnákh sets out from Mordor.
>
> January 22: Saruman's scouts return to Moria, and gather a force of mountain-orcs. They cannot penetrate Lórien, but lurk outside especially watching the river-exit.
>
> January 24: Isengarders capture Gollum, and torment him for news. Gollum . . . escapes after revealing that Hobbits of Shire were with Gandalf, and enough is said to make Uglúk certain that Ring was with the Company. Uglúk sends news to Isengard of Hobbits; but not of the Ring.
>
> January 26: Grishnákh, having crossed Anduin near rapids, comes up west side, and intercepts Uglúk's messengers, and learns their news. (He retreats, makes contact with a Nazgûl near Sarn Gebir and awaits orders.)
>
> January 30: Saruman receiving news decides to act on his own. Sends out strong force to join Uglúk, orders them to bring Hobbits *alive* to Isengard.
>
> February 2: Grishnákh reinforced. Ordered to cooperate with Uglúk (Sauron does not yet suspect Saruman).
>
> February 6: Uglúk scours northern Rohan.
>
> February 10: Uglúk & Grishnákh make contact above Sarn Gebir. Rohirrim drive off Isengarders, who retreat to Emyn Muil, leaving west bank unguarded. Grishnákh watches east bank near Sarn Gebir.
>
> February 22: Grishnákh's scouts get wind of approach of Coy. A Nazgûl is summoned, but Sauron will not yet permit the Nazgûl to cross west of Anduin.

February 23: Orcs are foiled. Legolas shoots down Nazgûl. The Orcs dismayed, but Grishnákh crosses Anduin and daringly pushes down west shore in pursuit. He believes Coy. is making for Minas Tirith.

February 25: Grishnákh and Uglúk meet in western Emyn Muil. They go in search of the Coy.

416 (II: 18): At the water-side Aragorn remained

416 (II: 18). Aragorn remained, watching the bier – In 'Funeral Customs in Tolkien's Fiction', *Mythlore* 19, no. 2, whole no. 72 (Spring 1993), Patricia Reynolds comments: 'We can note Aragorn's watch over Boromir's body: the three words used for the activity of sitting by the body on the night before burial in English are "watch", "wake" and "vigil". Sitting by the dead person's body on the eve of the funeral is a practice found in many cultures. . . . It is Aragorn, the most noble of the company, who undertakes to watch Boromir's body. Indeed, the whole funeral is arranged by Aragorn' (p. 48).

In an early draft at this point in the text, Tolkien drew a hasty sketch (reproduced in *The Treason of Isengard*, p. 383), in which 'are seen the rill that flowed through the greensward there, and the two remaining boats (the third having been taken by Frodo) moored at the water's edge, with Tol Brandir and Amon Lhaw beyond; X marks the battle where Boromir died. At the shore is the boat brought back by Legolas, marking the place where Boromir's body was set aboard it' (Christopher Tolkien, p. 381).

416–17 (II: 19): Now they laid Boromir

416 (II: 19). they laid Boromir in the middle of the boat . . . his helm they set beside him, and across his lap they laid his cloven horn and the hilt and shards of his sword; beneath his feet they put the swords of his enemies – In *Beowulf* Scyld's funeral is described:

> They laid then the beloved chieftain, giver of rings, on the ship's bosom, glorious by the mast. There were brought many treasures, ornaments from far-off lands. Never have I heard that a vessel was more fairly fitted-out with war-weapons and battle-raiment, swords and coats of mail. On his bosom lay a host of treasures, which were to travel far with him into the power of the flood. [Clark Hall translation, p. 21]

416 (II: 19). the hilt and shards of his sword – In editions prior to 2004 the word 'hilt' was here printed as 'hilts'. Other instances of the latter form in *The Lord of the Rings* were emended by Tolkien, and posthumously, beginning with the second printing of *The Two Towers* (1955).

417 (II: 19): Sorrowfully they cast loose

417 (II: 19). the White Tower – 'The chief tower of the citadel of Minas Tirith [also called] Tower of Ecthelion, Tower of Denethor. Sometimes used to stand for M[inas] T[irith] and Gondor as opposed to "the Dark Tower"' (*Index*).

417 (II: 19–20): For a while the three companions

417 (II: 19–20). For a while the three companions – A recording by Tolkien from these words to the end of the poem is included on Disc 2 of *The J.R.R. Tolkien Audio Collection.*

417 (II: 19). ***What news from the West*** – The West Wind is addressed first because Boromir rode into the West when he left Minas Tirith.

417 (II: 19). ***seven streams*** – A reference to Boromir's journey from Minas Tirith to Rivendell. In Book II, Chapter 4 Boromir states specifically that on his way to Rivendell he passed through the Gap of Rohan; and in Book III, Chapter 2 Éomer refers to the horse the Rohirrim lent to Boromir. But the general map of Middle-earth does not show seven streams or rivers he would need to cross. This seems to be a shadow of an earlier idea by Tolkien, never fully expressed. In an early text of Book II, Chapter 4 ('A Journey in the Dark') Boromir suggests that the Company 'take the road to my land that I followed on my way hither; through Rohan and the Country of Seven Streams' (*The Treason of Isengard*, p. 311), and on Tolkien's *First Map* is entered 'The Greyflood (Gwathló) or Seventh River' (p. 305). Christopher Tolkien discusses the matter at length in *The Treason of Isengard*, pp. 310–12, but finds no solution to the puzzle.

417–18 (II: 20): Then Legolas sang

417 (II: 20). ***Beyond the gate the seaward road runs south*** – In Book V, Chapter 1, Pippin sitting by the battlements of Minas Tirith looks down on the road from the gate of the city running south (towards the Sea), then bending out of sight.

418 (II: 20): Then Aragorn sang again

418 (II: 20). ***the Gate of Kings*** – The Argonath.

419 (II: 21): 'Let me think!'

419 (II: 21). may I make the right choice and change the evil fate of this unhappy day – Aragorn does indeed make the right choice. It is notable that he does not even consider going to Minas Tirith as an option. It is an *unhappy day* because of the death of Boromir, but though its events appear *evil*, they culminate in good: Frodo escapes from Boromir towards Mordor with Sam, Merry and Pippin come to the Ents and rouse them to action against Saruman, and Aragorn, Legolas, and Gimli, reunited with Gandalf, are led to Rohan in time to free Théoden, ally of Gondor, from the influence of Wormtongue.

420 (I: 22): 'Well, after them!'

420 (II: 22). they have a long start – According to *Scheme* 'Merry and Pippin captured by Orcs (about noon). . . . Aragorn begins pursuit of Orcs about 4 p.m.'

Chapter 2

THE RIDERS OF ROHAN

For drafts and history of this chapter, see *The Treason of Isengard*, pp. 389–407.

421 (II: 23): Dusk deepened

421 (II: 23). Dusk deepened . . . the waxing moon was riding in the West – It is the evening of 26 February 1419. The moon is only four days past new, and still sets in the west early in the night.

421 (II: 23): There in the still cool hour

421 (II: 23). There in the still cool hour before dawn – It is 27 February 1419.

423 (II: 25): *Gondor! Gondor*

423 (II: 25). *Silver Tree* – The emblem of Gondor, from the White Tree planted by Isildur.

423 (II: 25). *O wingéd crown and throne of gold!* – The *wingéd crown* is the crown of Gondor as described in Book VI, Chapter 5. In draft these words originally ended '*many-footed throne of gold!*' (*The Treason of Isengard*, p. 395); thus Tolkien's design for a dust-jacket for *The Return of the King* (*Artist and Illustrator*, fig. 182) shows the throne with four feet, together with the wingéd crown and white-flowering ('silver') tree.

423 (II: 25): The ridge upon which

423 (II: 25). the East Wall of Rohan – The *East Wall* is the 'name in Rohan of the sheer sides of Emyn Muil on [the] east side of Rohan' (*Index*). In *Cirion and Eorl and the Friendship of Gondor and Rohan* the eastern and southern boundaries of Rohan are described:

> In the east its bounds were the Anduin and the west-cliff of the Emyn Muil down to the marshes of the Mouths of Onodló [Entwash], and beyond that river the stream of the Glanhír [Mering Stream, both meaning 'boundary stream'] that flowed though the wood of Anwar [Firien Wood] to join the Onodló; and in the south its bounds were the Ered Nimrais as far as the end of their northward arm, but all those vales and inlets that opened northwards were to belong to the Éothéod, as well as the land south of the Hithaeglir that lay between the rivers Angren [Isen] and Adorn. [*Unfinished Tales*, pp. 305–6]

For the western and northern boundaries of Rohan, see note for p. 374.

423 (II: 25): 'Many things'

423 (II: 25). They are many leagues away: twelve, I guess – Twelve leagues are the equivalent of 36 miles. *Scheme* notes: 'Aragorn reaches East Wall at sunrise'; 'At 8 a.m. the Isengarders are 36 miles out on plain.'

423 (II: 25–6): They followed their enemies

423 (II: 25). escarpment – 'A long steep slope at the edge of a plateau or separating areas of land at different heights' (*Concise OED*).

423–4 (II: 26): At the bottom they came

424 (II: 26). cresses – 'The common name of various cruciferous plants, having mostly edible leaves of a pungent flavour' (*OED*), here probably watercress (*Nasturtium officinale*).

424 (II: 26): 'Yes,' he said, 'they are quite plain

424 (II: 26). He is smaller than the others. – In editions prior to 2004 this sentence read: 'He is smaller than the other.' Christopher Tolkien remarks in *The Treason of Isengard* that Aragorn 'would not refer to Merry [the other hobbit being sought] in such a remote tone' (p. 404, n. 15). The words are intended to mean that Pippin is smaller than Merry, Frodo, and Sam.

425 (II: 27): As nightshade was closing

425 (II: 27). nightshade – Twilight.

426 (II: 28): He cast himself on the ground

426 (II: 28). Before dawn was in the sky – It is 28 February 1419.

426–7 (II: 29): 'The rumour of the earth

426–7 (II: 29). Faint and far are the feet of our enemies. But loud are the hoofs of the horses. It comes to my mind that I heard them, even as I lay on the ground in sleep. . . . But now they are drawing ever further from us, riding northward. – The orcs are far away, but Aragorn hears the sound of the Rohirrim pass to the west, pursuing the orcs northward.

427 (II: 29): All day the track

427 (II: 29). Eastemnet – In his unfinished index Tolkien describes *Eastemnet* as 'the eastern plains (beyond Entwash) of Rohan'. In *Nomenclature* he instructs that the name should be retained in translation because, although 'it contains *east*, it is not a Common Speech name, but Rohan for "east-plain"', and he glosses *emnet* as 'flat land, plain' (compare Old English *emnet* 'level ground, a plain').

428 (II: 30): As before Legolas was first afoot

428 (II: 30). It is a red dawn. Strange things await us by the eaves of the forest. – It is 29 February 1419. At dawn, far to the north, the Rohirrim attack and destroy the orcs.

428 (II: 30–1): 'They rested here a while'

428 (II: 30). It is thrice twelve hours, I guess, since the Orcs stood where we now stand. – They reach the downs at 11.00 a.m. on 29 February. According to *Scheme* the orcs reached that place at 9.00 p.m. on 27 February.

429 (II: 31): 'Nothing can we see to guide us here'

429 (II: 31). Well, now we must halt again – *Scheme* notes that on 29 February 'Aragorn starts at sunrise. At 11 a.m. reaches Downs (85 miles out). Goes on all rest of day and reaches N[orthern]. end of Downs at nightfall. (110 miles out). Wind turns *east* at night.'

429 (II: 31): 'And ere morning it will be in the East'

429 (II: 31). Rede – An archaic word for 'advice, counsel'.

429 (II: 31–2): The night grew ever colder

429 (II: 32). Together they watched the dawn – It is 30 February 1419.

429 (II: 32): Ahead and eastward

429 (II: 32). Methedras – '*Methedras* "last peak", the southernmost of the ?last major peaks of the Misty Mountains' (*Index*).

430 (II: 32): Following with his keen eyes

430 (II: 32). Aragorn saw a shadow on the distant green. . . . But Legolas . . . saw . . . the small figures of horsemen – *Scheme* notes: 'Riders leave battlefield and start out on long ride to *Edoras* at sunrise (7 a.m.)'; 'At sunrise Aragorn sees cold clear day open. About 9 a.m. the Riders approach. About 10 a.m. *Éomer* and *Aragorn* meet at N[orth] end of Downs.'

430–1 (II: 33): 'I have been among them'

430 (II: 33). I have been among them – In *The Tale of Aragorn and Arwen* it is said that Aragorn 'went [abroad] in many guises, and won renown under many names. He rode in the host of the Rohirrim' (p. 1060, III: 341).

430 (II: 33). the children of Men before the Dark Years – The *Dark Years* are presumably the same as the Black Years (see note for p. 51), though reference to 'the children of Men' seems to suggest a time early in the First Age.

431 (II: 33). It was in forgotten years long ago that Eorl the Young brought them out of the North – In fact, it was only just over 500 years earlier, in Third Age 2510, that Cirion, the Steward of Gondor, appealed to Eorl and his people for help against invaders from the East. Eorl and his men rode from the far North, and in reward for their help were granted the northern lands of Gondor, Calenardhon, which became known as Rohan. See further, note for p. 1053.

Most of the names of the kings of Rohan are Old English words or epithets meaning 'king', 'ruler', 'lord', etc. *Eorl* is Old English 'warrior, nobleman', from which derives Modern English *earl.*

431 (II: 33). kinship with the Bardings of Dale, and with the Beornings – That is, kinship with Men still living in the North, rather than with Men native to the lands of Gondor or of Númenórean descent.

431 (II: 33–4): Their horses were of great stature

431 (II: 33). flaxen-pale – The pale yellow colour of dressed flax.

431 (II: 34). their burnished shirts of mail hung down upon their knees – On 14 October 1958 Tolkien wrote to Rhona Beare: 'The Rohirrim were not "mediaeval", in our sense. The styles of the Bayeux Tapestry (made in England) fit them well enough, if one remembers that the kind of tennis-nets [the] soldiers seem to have on are only a clumsy conventional sign for chain-mail of small rings' (*Letters*, pp. 280–1).

431–2 (II: 34): Without a word or cry

432 (II: 34). a man taller than all the rest – Éomer. In a note associated with the late *Disaster of the Gladden Fields* Tolkien says that

> the Rohirrim were generally shorter [than the Dúnedain], for in their far-off ancestry they had been mingled with men of broader and heavier build. Éomer was said to have been tall, of like height with Aragorn; but he with other descendants of King Thengel were taller than the norm of Rohan, deriving this characteristic (together in some cases with darker hair) from Morwen, Thengel's wife, a lady of Gondor of high Númenórean descent. [*Unfinished Tales*, p. 286]

432 (II: 34). from his helm as a crest a white horsetail flowed – Tom Shippey comments in *The Road to Middle-earth* that 'a horsetail plume is the traditional prerogative of the Huns and the Tartars and the steppe-folk, a most un-English decoration, at least by tradition' (2nd edn., pp. 115–16).

432 (I: 35): 'As for that'

432 (I: 35). Éomer son of Éomund – Many of the names and words of the Rohirrim contain Old English *eoh* 'war-horse, charger'. *Éomer* seems to derive from *eoh* + Old English *mǣre* (or *mēre*) 'grand, excellent, famous' (cf. William Howard Green, The Hobbit *and Other Fiction by J.R.R. Tolkien* (1969)). The name *Eomer* appears twice in the *Anglo-Saxon Chronicles*, most notably in a genealogical list as the grandson of Offa, King of Angeln on the Continent, ancestor of the kings of Mercia; the other Eomer was an assassin sent by Cwichelm, King of the West Saxons, to try to kill King Edwin of Northumbria.

Éomund contains the Old English elements *eoh* + *mund* 'protector'.

432 (II: 35). the Third Marshal of Riddermark – In an appendix to the late work *The Battles of the Fords of Isen* it is said that

> Marshal of the Mark (or Riddermark) was the highest military rank and the title of the King's lieutenants (originally three), commanders of the royal forces of fully equipped and trained Riders. The First Marshal's ward was the capital, Edoras, and the adjacent King's Lands (including Harrowdale). He commanded the Riders of the Muster of Edoras, drawn from this ward, and from some parts of the West-mark and East-mark for which Edoras was the most convenient place of assembly. The Second and Third Marshals were assigned commands according to the needs of the time. In the beginning of the year [Third Age] 3019 the threat from Saruman was most urgent, and the Second Marshal, the King's son Théodred, had command over the West-mark with his base at Helm's Deep; the third Marshal, the King's nephew Éomer, had as his ward the East-mark with his base at his home, Aldburg in the Folde.
>
> In the days of Théoden there was no man appointed to the office of First Marshal. He came to the throne as a young man . . . vigorous and of martial spirit, and a great horseman. If war came, he would himself command the Muster of Edoras; but his kingdom was at peace for many years. . . . In this peace the Riders and other armed men of the garrison of Edoras were governed by an officer of the rank of marshal (in the years 3012–19 this was Elfhelm). When Théoden became, as it seemed, prematurely old, this situation continued, and there was no effective central command. [*Unfinished Tales*, p. 367]

433 (II: 35–6): 'I serve only the Lord of the Mark

433 (II: 35). the Lord of the Mark, Théoden King son of Thengel – Théoden is the King of Rohan who, as Gandalf told the Council in Rivendell, would not listen to his warnings and bade Gandalf take a horse and begone. His name is derived from Old English *þēoden* 'chief of a people, prince, king'. *Thengel* is Old English (*þengel*) for 'prince'.

In a galley proof of *The Two Towers* a reader queried the construction 'Théoden King' (as used by the Men of Rohan and by others effecting the style of their speech) instead of 'King Théoden'. Tolkien replied: 'The difference is deliberate. T.K. [Théoden King] represents "Anglo-Saxon" in which the title follows. K.T. [King Théoden] is Modern E[nglish]' (Marquette Series 3/5/38).

434 (II: 37): 'Halflings!' laughed the Rider

434 (II: 37). But they are only a little people in old songs and children's tales out of the North. – The remote ancestors of the Rohirrim, the Éothéod, knew the area by the Anduin once inhabited by hobbits.

435 (II: 37): 'Peace, Éothain!'

435 (II: 37). Éothain – 'Horse-soldier', from Old English *eoh* 'war-horse, charger' + (modernized) *þeg(e)n* (in a military context) 'soldier'.

435 (II: 37). *éored* – Described in the *1966 Index* as 'a troop of Riders of Rohan'. *Ēored* is Old English 'cavalry, band, troop'. In a note to *Cirion and Eorl and the Friendship of Gondor and Rohan* Tolkien states that 'a "full *éored*" in battle order was reckoned to contain not less than 120 men (including the Captain)'; and Christopher Tolkien comments that 'the *éored* with which Éomer pursued the Orcs . . . had 120 Riders: Legolas counted 105 when they were far away, and Éomer said that fifteen men had been lost in battle with the Orcs' (*Unfinished Tales*, p. 315, n. 36).

435 (II: 37). Entwade – 'A ford and road-crossing over the Entwash' (*Index*). See further, note for p. 373.

435 (II: 37): 'Gandalf!' Éomer exclaimed

435 (II: 37). Greyhame – As first published, this by-name was spelt *Grayhame.* It was emended in the second printing (1967) of the Allen & Unwin edition. It is a 'modernization' of Old English *grǣghama* 'grey-coated'.

435 (II: 38): 'Indeed since his last coming

435 (II: 38). *Mearas* – From Old English *mearh* (plural *mēaras*) 'horse, steed'.

435 (II: 38). Seven nights ago Shadowfax returned – Gandalf told the Council of Elrond that after leaving Weathertop he sent Shadowfax back to his master (on or soon after 4 October). Therefore Shadowfax took nearly five months to return to the south, whereas when he and Gandalf travelled north they took only ten days to reach Weathertop, including a diversion to the Shire.

When Shadowfax answers his summons at the end of Book III, Chapter 5, Gandalf says: 'It is a long way from Rivendell, my friend' (p. 504, II: 108). These words can only be interpreted to mean either that Shadowfax has just arrived from Rivendell, or that Rivendell, where they last met, is far away – but according to Gandalf's account to the Council, Shadowfax never went there. But a little later Gandalf indicates that he has only just summoned Shadowfax – 'I bent my thought upon him, bidding him to make haste; for yesterday he was far away in the south of this land' (p. 505, II: 108) – which at least agrees with what Éomer says, but does nothing to explain why Shadowfax took so long to return home. In *The Treason of*

Isengard Christopher Tolkien suggests that his father contemplated having Gandalf take Shadowfax to Rivendell, and that Shadowfax would stay there until summoned, but the alteration to the text was not carried through and left traces in the published book.

An isolated note, written at about the same time as Book III, Chapter 5, says that 'some account of "Shadowfax" in the house of Elrond must be given and what arrangements were made about him. Or did he just run off after Gandalf got to Rivendell: How did Gandalf summon him?' In another note Shadowfax 'reappears – sent for from Rivendell. Arrives later. It is 500–600 miles from Rivendell and would take Shadowfax 10–14 days' (*The Treason of Isengard*, p. 390; if this were so, Shadowfax would have left Rivendell between 9 and 13 February, when Gandalf's body was lying on the peak of Zirakzigil). In an early text of the present chapter Éomer tells Aragorn that Shadowfax had returned seven days before, to which Aragorn replies: 'But Gandalf left Shadowfax far in the North at Rivendell. Or so I thought' (*The Treason of Isengard*, p. 401). And an outline for Book III, Chapter 6 includes: 'Shadowfax had been reported coming from the West through the Gap [of Rohan] and fleeing away north' (*The Treason of Isengard*, p. 434). Christopher Tolkien comments that this last 'surely suggests that he had come from Rivendell in obedience to a summons from Gandalf mysteriously conveyed to him' (p. 439, n. 2).

436 (II: 38): 'Your news is all of woe!

436 (II: 38). East-borders – 'The eastern frontiers of Gondor' (*Index*).

436 (II: 38). sons of Eorl – The Rohirrim.

436 (II: 39): 'It is ill dealing with such a foe

437 (II: 39). dwimmer-crafty – Derived from obsolete *dweomercræft* 'magic art' (*OED*), itself from Old English *(ge)dwimor, -er* 'illusion, phantom'. Thus Saruman is adept at illusion and deception.

437 (II: 39): 'Come now!'

437 (II: 39). Westemnet – 'The western plains of Rohan' (*Index*).

437 (II: 39–40): 'Indeed in this riding

437 (II: 39). But scouts warned me of the orc-host coming down out of the East Wall four nights ago – *Four nights ago* was 26 February. In editions prior to 2004 scouts warned Éomer 'three nights ago', a vestige of an earlier conception of the chapter. As Christopher Tolkien comments in *The Treason of Isengard*:

> 'The Riders of Rohan' is unusual in that the narrative underwent an important change in structure long after it was to all intents and purposes completed. . . .
>
> In [the second text] Aragorn, Legolas and Gimli took two days and

two nights after their descent from the 'East Wall' to reach the isolated hill at the northern end of the downs where they meet the Riders; in T[wo] T[owers] they took three days and two nights to reach that place, and passed the third night there. In [the second text] they encountered the Riders returning in the morning after the battle at dawn; in TT the meeting was on the following day: the Riders had passed a whole further day and night by the eaves of Fangorn before setting off south again.

> This change in the chronology, with very substantial rewriting and reordering . . . of the existing chapter, was introduced in October 1944. [p. 406; see further, pp. 406–7]

On 16 October 1944 Tolkien wrote to Christopher: 'I have been struggling with the dislocated chronology of the Ring, which has proved most vexatious. . . . I think I have solved it all at last by small map alterations, and by inserting an extra day's Entmoot, and extra days into Trotter's chase and Frodo's journey . . .' (*Letters*, p. 97).

According to *Scheme*:

> February 26: Scouts report descent of Orcs out of E[myn] Muil to Éomer. But Éomer hesitates to disobey king, who has ordered him to go to Eastfold and gather his men for defence of Edoras.
>
> February 27: News reaches *Edoras* that Orcs are crossing Rohan. *Háma* (Éomer's friend) sends message to Eastfold (É[omer]'s home) warning É[omer] of king's displeasure, but counselling him to ride against the Orcs. Éomer decides to disobey king and sets out with his *éored* about midnight 27/28, taking the direct N[orthern] route.

437 (II: 40). Entwood – 'Name in Rohan of Fangorn' (*Index*).

438 (II: 41): 'As ever he has judged'

438 (II: 41). Good and ill have not changed since yesteryear; nor are they one thing among Elves and Dwarves and another among Men. It is a man's part to discern them as much in the Golden Wood as in his own house. – A clear expression of one of the major themes underlying *The Lord of the Rings*: that the pursuit of good ends does not justify using evil means to achieve them. The good cannot use the Ring.

438 (II: 41): 'True indeed'

438 (II: 41). Yet I am not free to do all as I would. It is against our law to let strangers wander at will in our land, until the king shall give them leave – Éomer is faced with the choice of obeying orders or acting as he thinks right.

438 (II: 41): 'I do not think your law

438 (II: 41). I have been in this land before . . . and ridden with the host . . . under other name and in other guise. You I have not seen before

. . . but I have spoken with Éomund your father, and with Théoden son of Thengel. – *The Tale of Years* places this, with many other journeys and errantries, during the period Third Age 2957–80; see also Appendix A. Éomer was born in 2991. Thengel was king during Aragorn's time in Rohan. Théoden succeeded Thengel in 2980.

438–9 (II: 41): Éomer was silent for a moment

438 (II: 41). chafes – Frets, is impatient.

439 (II: 41). You may go; and what is more, I will lend you horses . . . when your quest is achieved, or is proved vain, return with the horses . . . to Meduseld. . . . In this I place myself, and maybe my very life, in the keeping of your good faith. – This is the first of six instances in *The Lord of the Rings* when someone decides that it is right to disobey an order and, in so doing, aids the eventual success of the Free Peoples over Saruman and Sauron.

Meduseld is 'the royal hall of Théoden in Edoras' (*Index*). The name, from Old English *meduseld* 'mead-house, house in which feasting takes place', is mentioned also in *Beowulf* (line 3065).

439 (II: 42): A great dark-grey horse

439 (II: 42). Hasufel – From Old English *hasu* 'grey, ash-coloured' + *fel* 'skin, hide'. In *The Road to Middle-earth* Tom Shippey comments that not many have noted that the Old English names common among the Rohirrim 'are not in the "standard" or "classical" West Saxon dialect of Old English but in what is thought to have been its Mercian parallel: so Saruman, Hasufel, Herugrim for "standard" Searuman, Heasufel, Heorugrim' (2nd edn., p. 112).

439 (II: 42). Gárulf – 'Spear-wolf', from Old English *gār* 'spear, weapon' + *wulf* 'wolf'.

439 (II: 42): A smaller and lighter horse

439 (II: 42). Arod – Old English 'quick, swift, ready'.

440 (II: 43): At last as the afternoon

440 (II: 43). a mound . . . about it were planted fifteen spears – The spears of the fifteen fallen Riders.

442 (II: 45): You have journeyed further

442 (II: 45). the Onodrim, that Men call Ents – In *Nomenclature* Tolkien writes that *Ent* 'is supposed to be a name in the language of the Vale of Anduin, including Rohan, for these creatures. It is actually an Old English word for "giant", which is thus rightly according to the system attributed to Rohan, but the *Ents* of this tale are not in form or character derived from Germanic mythology. . . . The Grey-elven name was *Onodrim*. . . .'

He explains in a letter to Richard Jeffery on 7 September 1955 that 'the "correct" plural of *onod* was *enyd*, or general plural *onodrim*: though *ened* might be a form used in Gondor' (*Letters*, p. 224).

On 27 November 1954 Tolkien wrote to Katharine Farrer concerning *Ents*:

> As usually with me they grew rather out of their name, than the other way about. I always felt that something ought to be done about the peculiar A[nglo] Saxon word *ent* for a 'giant' or mighty person of long ago – to whom all old works were ascribed. If it had a slightly philosophical tone (though in ordinary philology it is 'quite unconnected with any present participle of the verb to be') that also interested me. [*Letters*, p. 208]

Tom Shippey has said that in Old English *ent* was the word used to describe a giant such as Goliath.

> The disapproving use of it by biblical translators and commentators is belied, however, by the irritatingly vague use of it in heroic and elegiac poetry to mean just a vanished race, a race of builders. The Swedish King Ongentheow, in *Beowulf*, wears an 'entish helm,' and the sword with which Beowulf beheads Grendel's mother is the 'former work of ents.' But stone is their most common material. The ents made the dragon's den in *Beowulf*, the ruined walls of *The Wanderer*. Most strikingly, they made the cities mentioned in the first two lines of the Cottonian *Maxims*, that mysterious set of 'gnomic verses' which still presents very evident puzzles to Anglo-Saxon scholars. The lines run:
>
> Cyning sceal rice healdan. Ceastra beoð feorran gesyne, orðanc enta geweorc. . . .
>
> 'King shall guard kingdom. Cities are to be seen from far off, skilful (*orthanc*) work of giants (*enta*). . . .' It will be remembered that in *The Lord of the Rings* the stone tower in the middle of Isengard, where Saruman is besieged by the ents, is called Orthanc. . . .

'One might go further', Shippey says, 'and suggest that the true stimulus for Professor Tolkien was the . . . very vagueness [of *ents*]: they are a race people have heard of, but never seen, gigantic in size . . . but very definitely *gone*' ('Creation from Philology', *J.R.R. Tolkien: Scholar and Story-teller: Essays in Memoriam*, pp. 294–5).

See further, note for p. 464.

442 (II: 45): With that he fell asleep

442 (II: 45). his eyes unclosed, blending living night and deep dream, as is the way with Elves – On 5 November 1956 Tolkien wrote to a Mr Britten that 'it is plainly suggested that Elves do "sleep", but not in our mode, having a different relation to what we call "dreaming". Nothing very definite is said about it (a) because except at a length destructive of narrative it would be difficult to describe a different mode of consciousness, and (b) for reasons that you so rightly observe: something must be left not fully explained, and only suggested' (Tolkien-George Allen & Unwin archive, HarperCollins).

443 (I: 45): The horses were gone

443 (I: 45). pickets – Pointed wooden stakes driven into the ground, used to tether a horse.

443 (I: 46): 'If you wish to know

443 (I: 46). I think it was Saruman – *Scheme* confirms Gimli's suspicion: 'February 30: Saruman appears on battlefield and is seen by Aragorn and companions at night.' An earlier time-scheme, written while Tolkien was working on Chapters 7 and 8 of Book III, includes the entry: 'Aragorn and his companions spend night on the battle-field, and see "old man" (Saruman)' (*The Treason of Isengard*, p. 428). They are a considerable way from Orthanc and the reader might wonder with Gimli in Book III, Chapter 5 (p. 488, II: 91) whether it was really Saruman or only 'an evil phantom' of him, especially as he leaves no traces. But Gandalf later explains that it was Saruman: 'He was so eager to lay his hands on his prey [the hobbits and possibly the Ring] that he could not wait at home, and he came forth to meet and to spy on his messengers. But he came too late for once, and the battle was over and beyond his help before he reached these parts. He did not remain here long' (Book III, Chapter 5, p. 498, II: 101).

Chapter 3

THE URUK-HAI

For drafts and history of this chapter, see *The Treason of Isengard*, pp. 408–10.

444 (II: 47): He woke

444 (II: 47). He woke. . . . Evening was coming – It is late afternoon on 26 February 1419.

444 (II: 47). a great company of Orcs – In the *Quenta Silmarillion*, a prose narrative of the 'Silmarillion' mythology begun in the mid-1930s and abandoned at the end of 1937, Tolkien introduced the idea that Orcs originated in mockery of the Elves, as a 'creation' of Morgoth, made of stone and brought into being by the powers of that mighty Vala. Thus Treebeard's statement in Book III, Chapter 4 of *The Lord of the Rings*, that 'Trolls are only counterfeits, made by the Enemy in the Great Darkness, in mockery of Ents, as Orcs were of Elves' (p. 486, II: 89). In work on 'The Silmarillion' between the completion and the publication of *The Lord of the Rings* Tolkien speculated that Morgoth had captured and enslaved some of the Elves soon after they woke in Middle-earth, and 'of these slaves it is held came the Orkor [Orcs] that were afterward chief foes of the Eldar' (*Morgoth's Ring*, p. 73).

In *The Road to Middle-earth* Tom Shippey comments that 'there can be little doubt that orcs entered Middle-earth originally just because the story [of 'The Silmarillion'] needed a continual supply of enemies over whom one need feel no compunction. . . . But several readers [of *The Lord of the Rings*] had pointed out that if evil could not create, was only good perverted, then presumably the orcs had been by nature good and might in some way be saved' (2nd edn., p. 207). On 25 April 1954 Tolkien wrote to Naomi Mitchison that Orcs

> are nowhere clearly stated to be of any particular origin. But since they are servants of the Dark Power, and later of Sauron, neither of whom could, or would, produce living things, they must be 'corruptions'. They are not based on direct experience of mine; but owe, I suppose, a good deal to the goblin tradition . . . especially as it appears in George MacDonald [*The Princess and the Goblin*], except for the soft feet which I never believed in. [*Letters*, p. 178]

Later that same year, he drafted a letter in reply to queries by Peter Hastings, who had noted Treebeard's statement about the creation of Orcs:

> Free Will is derivative, and is therefore only operative within provided circumstances; but in order that it may exist, it is necessary that the Author should guarantee it, whatever betides: sc. when it is 'against his Will', as we say, at any rate as it appears on a finite view. He does not stop or make 'unreal' sinful acts, and their consequences. So in this myth, it is 'feigned' . . . that He [Ilúvatar] gave special 'sub-creative' powers to certain of His highest created beings [the Ainur]: that is a guarantee that what they devised and made should be given the reality of Creation. Of course within limits, and of course subject to certain commands or prohibitions. But if they 'fell', as the Diabolus Morgoth did, and started making things 'for himself, to be their Lord', these would then 'be', even if Morgoth broke the supreme ban against making other 'rational' creatures like Elves or Men. They would at least 'be' real physical realities in the physical world, however evil they might prove, even 'mocking' the Children of God. They would be Morgoth's greatest Sins, abuses of his highest privilege, and would be creatures begotten of Sin, and naturally bad. (I nearly wrote 'irredeemably bad'; but that would be going too far. Because by accepting or tolerating their making – necessary to their actual existence – even Orcs would become a part of the World, which is God's and ultimately good.) But whether they could have 'souls' or 'spirits' seems a different question; and since in my myth at any rate I do not conceive of the making of souls or spirits, things of an equal order if not an equal power to the Valar, as a possible 'delegation', I have represented at least the Orcs as pre-existing beings on whom the Dark Lord has exerted the fullness of his power in remodelling and corrupting them, and not making them. . . . There might be other 'makings' all the same which were more like puppets filled (only at a distance) with their maker's mind and will, or ant-like operating under direction of a queen-centre. [*Letters*, p. 195]

After *The Lord of the Rings* was published Tolkien returned to work on his larger mythology, and in late writings expressed doubts about significant aspects. The nature and origin of Orcs 'require more thought', he wrote. 'They are not easy to work into the theory and system [of the mythology].' Only Eru, Ilúvatar, 'could make creatures with independent wills, and with reasoning powers. But Orcs seem to have both.' Therefore, could they be '*corruptions* of something pre-existing'? Not of Men: 'Men had not yet appeared when the Orcs already existed. . . . Eru would not sanction the work of Melkor [Morgoth] so as to allow the independence of the Orcs [if Melkor had created them]. (Not unless Orcs were ultimately remediable, or could be amended and "saved"?)' He could not contemplate the 'absolute perversion' by Melkor 'of a whole people, or group of peoples, and *his making that state heritable* [capable of being transmitted from parent to offspring].' Thus Elves are 'very unlikely' as a source for Orcs. 'And are Orcs "immortal", in the Elvish sense?' Is it 'likely or possible that even the least of the Maiar would become Orcs? Yes: both outside Arda and in it . . . Melkor had corrupted many spirits – some great, as Sauron, or less so, as Balrogs.' At length Tolkien concluded – for the moment – that 'Orcs were *beasts* of humanized shape (to mock Men and Elves) deliberately perverted / converted into a more close resemblance to Men. Their "talking" was really reeling off "records" set in them by Melkor. Even their rebellious critical words – he knew about them' (*Morgoth's Ring*, pp. 409–10). But the issue lingered.

When at the end of the 1950s Tolkien considered whether to revise the cosmology of Arda, another solution emerged. If the Sun existed from the beginning of the world, and the waking of Men was no longer tied to the first rising of the Sun long after Orcs first appeared, then Men might have been the stock from which Orcs were bred. Tolkien put forward this theory in a brief essay on Orcs, published in *Morgoth's Ring*, pp. 416–22.

445 (II: 48): He struggled a little

445 (II: 48). One of the Orcs sitting near laughed – Until now in *The Lord of the Rings* the reader has seen Orcs only at a distance, as a collective body of evil; now they are shown to be individuals, if singularly unpleasant ones.

445 (II: 48). the Common Speech, which he made almost as hideous as his own tongue – It is said in Appendix F that Orcs 'quickly developed as many barbarous dialects as there were groups or settlements of their race, so that their Orkish speech was of little use to them in intercourse between different tribes. So it was that . . . Orcs used for communication between breed and breed the Westron tongue' (p. 1131, III: 409).

445 (II: 48): 'If I had my way

445 (II: 48). *Uglúk u bagronk sha pushdug Saruman-glob búbhosh skai* – The penultimate draft of the section 'Orcs and the Black Speech' in Appendix F explained that 'the curse of the Mordor-orc in Chapter 3 of Book Three is in the more debased form used by the soldiers of the Dark Tower, of whom Grishnákh was the captain. *Uglúk to the cesspool, sha! the dungfilth; the great Saruman-fool, skai!*' (*The Peoples of Middle-earth*, p. 83, n. 6). In a later typescript the curse is translated as 'Uglúk to the dung-pit with stinking Saruman-filth – pig-guts gah!' (*The Peoples of Middle-earth*, p. xii; see also Carl F. Hostetter, 'Uglúk to the Dung-pit', *Vinyar Tengwar* 26 (November 1992)). Christopher Tolkien discovered a third version, and notes that 'all three differ significantly (*bagronk*, for example, being rendered both as "cesspool" and as "torture (chamber)"); from which it seems clear that my father was at this time devising interpretations of the words, whatever he may have intended them to mean when he first wrote them' (*The Peoples of Middle-earth*, p. xii).

446 (II: 49): 'Is Saruman the master

446 (II: 49). Lugbúrz – The Black Speech name for Barad-dûr, the Dark Tower.

447 (II: 50): 'Now,' thought Pippin

447 (II: 50). snicked – Made a small cut.

447 (II: 50): The Orcs were getting ready to march

447 (II: 50). getting ready to march – According to *Scheme*, 'after attacking and destroying the Co[mpan]y Orcs hurry towards Isengard. Quarrel bet[ween] Uglúk and Grishnákh (sundown). Grish[nákh] flies north to Sarn Gebir. Ug[lúk] descends into Rohan and begins a wild forced march towards Fangorn with his prey (Merry and Pippin).' In his time-schemes Tolkien took great care that times and clues in the account of the Three Hunters' chase should correspond exactly with events as seen and experienced by Pippin and Merry.

448 (II: 51): 'Only a single horseman

448 (II: 51). Only a single horseman – The scout that told Éomer of the Orcs; see note for p. 437.

448 (II: 52): 'Hullo, Pippin!'

448 (II: 52). bed and breakfast – A night's lodging in a hotel or guest house. Even in such fearful captivity, Merry presents a brave face and makes a joke.

It is still the night of 26/27 February 1419.

450 (II: 53): Neither Pippin nor Merry

450 (II: 53). Neither Pippin nor Merry remembered much of the later part of the journey. – According to *Scheme*: 'February 27: At 8 a.m. the Isengarders are 36 miles out on plain: seen by Legolas. By nightfall Orcs are going faster, are 72 miles on way (47 ahead of Aragorn). They reach S[outh] end of Downs at 9 p.m.'

450 (II: 53): Dimly he became aware

450 (II: 53). He came back to the waking world and found it was morning – It is 28 February 1419.

451 (II: 54): At that moment

451 (II: 54). there was Grishnákh again – According to *Scheme*:

> February 27: Grishnákh reaches Sarn Gebir. Another Nazgûl has arrived with advice. He is to pursue Uglúk. Nazgûl sets his Orcs across the river. G[rishnákh] hastens off N.W. [north-west] to intercept Uglúk.
>
> February 28: Isengarders pass N[orth] end of Downs at 4.30 am.;

rest at a point 5 miles beyond [*sic* in both this and the previous time-scheme, with no time allowed to cover the stated 5 miles before starting again]. At 5 a.m. they go on till 10 a.m. (seen by Riders) and are then 25 miles N. of Downs and turn towards eaves of Fangorn (25 m[iles] further on). Rest till 10.30 a.m. They then see Riders following; also they see Grishnákh and his Orcs coming from River. From 11.25 all Orcs fly together without rest; but *one mile* short of Fangorn they are overtaken.

[*With extra note below*: Forced march of Grishnákh. Flies from Emyn Muil when defeated by Uglúk evening 26 [February]. Reaches Sarn Gebir late on 27. He has more than 100 miles to go to point where he intercepts Uglúk about 30 m[iles] N. of Downs, about 11.20 a.m. on 29th. This he does between midnight 27/8 and 11.20 on 29th, about 35 hours.]

[*In another column, also* February 28:] Riders' scouts descry the Orcs (about 10 a.m.) from afar. Main *éored* crosses Entwash, N. of Downs late in afternoon. They break up in companies surrounding and heading off the Orcs. Éomer overtakes Orcs at sunset and besieges them. (Wormtongue's spies report the disobedience of Éomer, and the King is angered.)]

In an early note Tolkien worked out that

Orcs usual pace is a steady 4 m[iles] p[er] h[our]. They can keep this up for 5 hours but then need one hour rest. They can thus cover at need 4 x 20 = 80 miles per diem, and can do this for 5 days & then need long rest so in 5 days they can cover 400 miles but must then rest. At need for short period they can trot ?from 6 mph for about 50 ?miles. Isengarders could go a little faster and need only ½ hr rests. [Marquette MSS 4/2/19]

451 (II: 54): 'I know,' growled Uglúk

451 (II: 54). Snaga – Black Speech 'slave'.

452 (II: 55): 'You seem to know a lot'

452 (II: 55). slavering – Dribbling saliva.

453 (II: 57): Night came down

453 (II: 57). Night came down – It is the night of 28/29 February 1419.

453 (II: 57). Many Orcs had fallen, but fully two hundred remained – One hundred Northerners had run ahead, leaving eighty Isengarders with Uglúk, and Grishnákh had returned with forty, so about twenty had fallen.

454 (II: 58): 'There's only one thing

454 (II: 58). gimlets – That is, with *gimlet-eyes*, sharp or piercing like a gimlet (auger).

457 (II: 60–1): The answer came

457 (II: 61). sortie – 'An attack by troops coming from a position of defence' (*Concise OED*).

458 (II: 61): The sounds had died away

458 (II: 61). the sky was beginning to grow pale – It is early on 29 February 1419.

458 (II: 62): I shall have to brush

458 (II: 62). I shall have to brush up my toes, if I am to get level with you. – A reference to hairy Hobbit feet, while playing on the phrase *to brush up*, 'to regain a previously learned skill'.

459 (II: 62): He led the way

459 (II: 62). lichen – 'A simple composite plant consisting of a fungus in association with an alga, typically growing on rocks, walls, and trees' (*Concise OED*).

459 (II: 52–3): Merry and Pippin heard

459 (II: 63). the Sun's limb – In this context *limb* means 'the edge of the Sun's disk'.

459 (II: 63): So it was that they did not see

459 (II: 63). Third Marshal of the Mark – As first published these words read 'Third Marshal of Rohan'. They were emended in the second printing (1967) of the Allen & Unwin second edition. Tolkien wrote in one of his check copies of *The Two Towers* that *Third Marshal of the Mark* 'was the correct title. *Rohan* was not the name of the country used by the Rohirrim themselves' (courtesy of Christopher Tolkien).

459–60 (II: 63): Then when they had laid their fallen comrades

459–60 (II: 63). the Riders – According to *Scheme*: 'February 29: Riders attack Orcs at sunrise (about 7 a.m.). It takes about 3 hours to round up fugitives. They spend remainder of day in burning bodies of Orcs and burying their own dead. They rest on battlefield that night.'

Chapter 4

TREEBEARD

For drafts and history of this chapter, see *The Treason of Isengard*, pp. 411–21.

463–4 (II: 67): '*Hrum, Hoom*'

463 (II: 67). *Hrum, Hoom* – According to his friend Nevill Coghill, reported in *Biography* (p. 194), Tolkien 'modelled Treebeard's way of speaking . . . on the booming voice of C.S. Lewis'.

464 (II: 67). root and twig – In the fair copy manuscript of this chapter Treebeard said, instead, 'Crack my timbers', words which Tolkien noted were queried by his friend Charles Williams (*The Treason of Isengard*, p. 419, n. 2).

464 (II: 67): A queer look came

464 (II: 67). Ent – On 7 June 1955 Tolkien wrote to W.H. Auden that he 'did not consciously invent' the Ents.

> The chapter called 'Treebeard', from Treebeard's first remark . . . was written off more or less as it stands, with an effect on my self (except for labour pains) almost like reading some one else's work. And I like Ents now because they do not seem to have anything to do with me. I daresay something had been going on in the 'unconscious' for some time, and that accounts for my feeling throughout, especially when stuck, that I was not inventing but reporting (imperfectly) and had at times to wait till 'what really happened' came through. But looking back analytically I should say that the Ents are composed of philology, literature, and life. They owe their name to the *eald enta geweorc* of Anglo-Saxon, and their connexion with stone [from the Old English poem *The Wanderer*, line 87: 'eald enta geweorc idlu stodon' = 'the old creations of giants (i.e. ancient buildings erected by a former race) stood desolate']. Their part in the story is due, I think, to my bitter disappointment and disgust from schooldays with the shabby use made in Shakespeare of the coming of 'Great Birnam wood to high Dunsinane hill' [in *Macbeth*]: I longed to devise a setting in which the trees might really march to war. And into this has crept a mere piece of experience, the difference of the 'male' and 'female' attitude to wild things, the difference between unpossessive love and gardening. [*Letters*, pp. 211–12 n., 445]

In a letter to Mrs L.M. Cutts, 26 October 1958, Tolkien wrote that the Ents could be seen as 'a "mythological" form taken by my life-long love of trees, with perhaps some remote influence from George MacDonald's *Phantastes* (a work I do not actually much like [in which trees take human form]) . . .' (Sotheby's London, *English Literature, History, Fine Bindings* [etc.], 10 July 2003, lot 474, p. 297).

On 20 September 1963 Tolkien explained in a draft letter to Colonel Worskett:

> There are or were no Ents in the older stories – because the Ents in fact only presented themselves to my sight, without premeditation or any previous conscious knowledge, when I came to Chapter IV of Book Three. . . .
>
> No one knew whence they (Ents) came or first appeared. The High Elves said that the Valar did not mention them in the 'Music'. But some (Galadriel) were [of the] opinion that when Yavanna discovered the mercy of Eru to Aulë on the matter of the Dwarves, she besought Eru (through Manwë) asking him to give life to things made of living things not stone, and that the Ents were either souls sent to inhabit trees, or else that slowly took the likeness of trees owing to their inborn love of trees. . . . The Ents thus had mastery *over* stone. The males were devoted to Oromë, but the Wives to Yavanna. [*Letters*, pp. 334–5]

Tolkien produced a finished text dealing with the origin of the Ents, which Christopher Tolkien included in *The Silmarillion* as part of the chapter 'Of Aulë and Yavanna'.

464 (II: 67). *The* Ent – In an unpublished draft letter of late 1968 Tolkien wrote: '*Eldest* was the courtesy title of Treebeard as the oldest surviving Ent. The Ents claimed to be the oldest "speaking people" after the Elves [illegible] until taught the art of speech by the Elves. . . . They were therefore placed after the Dwarves in the Old List . . . since Dwarves had the power of speech from their awaking' (private collection). In any case, according to the account of their origin given in *The Silmarillion*, the Ents were created in response to the creation of the Dwarves, and like the Dwarves did not wake in Middle-earth until after the Elves.

464 (II: 67). *Fangorn* is my name according to some, *Treebeard* others make it. – *Fangorn* is Sindarin for 'beard-(of)-tree' (see Appendix F), including the element *orn* 'tree'. The *Oxford English Dictionary* defines *Treebeard* as a name for the lichen *Usnea barbata*, and also for *Tillandsia usneoides*, both of which produce long trailing beardlike growths. (Compare, p. 459, II: 62, on the trees of Fangorn Forest: 'Great trailing beards of lichen hung from them, blowing and swaying in the breeze.')

464 (II: 67): 'An *Ent*?' said Merry

464 (II: 67). 'An *Ent*?' said Merry. – A recording by Tolkien from these words to Treebeard's 'you do not seem to fit in anywhere' is included on Disc 2 of *The J.R.R. Tolkien Audio Collection*.

464 (II: 67). the old lists – Treebeard's 'lore of living creatures' recalls the list of fish, animals, and so forth, with suitable epithets for poetry, included in the *Skáldskaparmál* in Snorri Sturluson's *Edda*.

465 (II: 68): 'Hm, but you *are* hasty folk, I see'

465 (II: 68). There are Ents and Ents, you know; or there are Ents and things that look like Ents but ain't – *Ain't* is a dialectal contracted form of 'are not', generally pronounced very like 'ent'.

465 (II: 68). Real names tell you the story of the things they belong to in my language – Tolkien felt much the same about words and names, and what they reveal about those who had spoken the language in which they occurred.

465–6 (II: 68): 'But now'

465 (II: 68). *a-lalla-lalla-rumba-kamanda-lind-or-burúmë* – In Appendix F Tolkien writes that this phrase seems to have been an attempt by the Hobbits (who wrote the Red Book of Westmarch) 'to represent shorter murmurs and calls by the Ents', and 'is the only extant (probably very inaccurate) attempt to represent a fragment of actual Entish'. He also describes the Entish language as 'slow, sonorous, agglomerated, repetitive, indeed long-winded; formed of a multiplicity of vowel-shades and distinctions of tone and quality' (pp. 1130–1, III: 409).

466 (II: 69): 'Hill?' suggested Pippin

466 (II: 69). shelf – In this context, a ledge of rock.

467 (II: 70): 'Hmm, did he now?'

467 (II: 70). Laurelindórenan – See note for p. 335.

467 (II: 70): 'And so is this

467 (II: 70). *Laurelindórenan lindelorendor malinornélion ornemalin . . . Taurelilómëa-tumbalemorna Tumbaletaurëa Lómëanor* – This is Quenya. The second line is translated in Appendix F as 'Forestmanyshadowed-deepvalleyblack Deepvalleyforested Gloomyland', meaning 'more or less: "there is a black shadow in the deep dales of the forest"' (p. 1131, III: 409). On 8 June 1961 Tolkien explained the first line in a letter to Rhona Beare:

> Treebeard was not using Entish sounds on this occasion, but using ancient Elvish words mixed up and run together in Entish fashion. The elements are *laure*, gold, not the metal but the colour, what we should call golden light; *ndor*, *nor*, land, country; *lin*, *lind-*, a musical sound; *malina*, yellow; *orne*, tree; *lor*, dream; *nan*, *nand-*, valley. So that roughly he means: 'The valley where the trees in a golden light sing musically, a land of music and dreams; there are yellow trees there, it is a tree-yellow land.' The same applies to the [second line], where the elements

are *taure*, forest; *tumba*, deep valley; *mor*, darkness; *lóme*, night. [*Letters*, pp. 307–8]

468 (II: 71): 'Aye, aye, something like

468 (II: 71). Great Darkness – The time of Morgoth's domination of Middle-earth.

468 (II: 71–2): 'Some of my kin

468 (II: 71). limb-lithe – *Limb* 'large branch of a tree' + *lithe* 'flexible, pliant'.

468 (II: 72). East End – 'Name of Fangorn Forest in the Elder Days' (*Index*).

469 (II: 72): Treebeard fell silent

469 (II: 72). Treebeard fell silent . . . – A recording by Tolkien from these words to the end of the poem is included on Disc 2 of *The J.R.R. Tolkien Audio Collection.*

469 (II: 72). *In the willow-meads of Tasarinan / . . . Nan-tasarion* – '*Tasarinan* "willow-vale" a region of Beleriand in the Elder Days, also called *Nan-Tasarion*', '(*nan*, *nand-* "vale")' (*Index*). Treebeard gives the Quenya names. The Sindarin name is *Nan-tathren* 'vale of willows' or 'land of willows', named thus on the *Silmarillion* map where the river Narog flows into Sirion.

469 (II: 72). *Ossiriand . . . Seven Rivers of Ossir* – '*Ossiriand*, "land of Seven Rivers", a region of Beleriand under east-sides of Ered-Luin part of which survived the Floods and became Lindon. Also called *Ossir.* Otos [*sic*, for *otso*] (odo-) 7 [seven] *Sîr* river' (*Index*). The seven rivers were the Gelion and its six tributaries flowing down from the Ered Luin.

469 (II: 72). *Neldoreth . . . Taur-na-neldor!* – '*Taur-na-neldor* = Beech-forest. *Taur* "forest"' (*Index*). Another name for Neldoreth; see note for p. 193.

469 (II: 72). *Dorthonion . . . Orod-na-Thôn* – In his unfinished index Tolkien says in separate entries: '*Dorthonion*, land of pines, a highland on north borders of Beleriand' and '*Thôn* "pine-tree"; *Orod-na-Thôn* "the Pine-mountain" a mountain in Dorthonion, north of Beleriand, in the Elder days', '*dor* "land"'.

469 (II: 72). *And now all those lands lie under the wave* – As a result of the tumults of the great battle at the end of the First Age in which Morgoth was overthrown, the north-western regions of Middle-earth, including most of Beleriand, were rent asunder and drowned in the Sea.

469 (II: 72). in Ambaróna, in Tauremorna, in Aldalómë . . . Tauremorna-lómë – In his unfinished index Tolkien notes that *Ambaróna* is the 'ancient name of a region'. It means 'uprising, sunrise, orient', from Quenya *amba* 'up(wards)' + *róna* 'east'. An unpublished gloss of the name in Tolkien's linguistic notes gives 'Eastern (land)' with the annotation 'dawn = *amba-róne*'. Compare note for p. 468 (*East End* = Fangorn Forest).

Also noted in *Index* are '*Tauremorna* "black forest"'; '*Aldalómë* "tree-twilight'; '*Alda* "tree"'; and '*Lómë* High Elven [Quenya] dimness, twilight, night'.

470 (II: 73): 'Hm! Here you are'

470 (II: 73). I have brought you about seventy-thousand ent-strides – In Marquette MSS 4/2/19 Tolkien made various calculations of the length and speed of an ent-stride, adjusting both to what he felt the distance and length of the journey required. His final conclusion was probably that 'an Ent would take nearly nine hours to do 70,000 strides and presumably in that time would go 70,000 yards at least, probably 4 ft a stride'. This meant about 2.2 strides of 4 feet per second, covering a distance of 53.3 miles, at a speed of about 6 miles per hour. (Other calculations note that at 2 strides per second, 70,000 strides would take 9⅔ hours, and 70,000 strides of 3 feet would be about 40 miles.)

In another note, Tolkien writes: 'Ents are (as long as they can drink running water) almost tireless. They can go at *c.* 12 m.p.h. – averaging say 10 hours (even 24) at a stretch. Max[imum] speed of Treebeard was 20 m.p.h. when charging' (Marquette MSS 4/2/19).

470 (II: 73). the Last Mountain – Methedras.

470 (II: 73). Wellinghall – In *Nomenclature* Tolkien writes that 'the intended sense' of *Wellinghall* 'is "hall (under or behind) the outflow of the spring"'.

471 (II: 74): At last he set the bowl

471 (II: 74). I will lie down; that will prevent this drink from rising to my head – Trees 'drink' while upright, through capillary action.

473 (II: 76): 'Saruman is a Wizard'

473 (II: 76). They appeared first after the Great Ships came over the Sea – Whether Treebeard is referring to the return of the Númenóreans to Middle-earth during the Second Age, or to Elendil and his ships after the destruction of Númenor near the end of the Second Age, the Wizards did not appear until many years later, *c.* Third Age 1000 according to *The Tale of Years* (Appendix B).

473 (II: 76). settled down at Angrenost, or Isengard – *Angrenost* is Sindarin 'iron fortress', from *angren* 'iron' (adjective) + *ost* 'fortress'. According to *The Tale of Years* Saruman took up residence there in Third Age 2759.

473 (II: 76–7): 'I think that I now understand

473 (II: 76). He has a mind of metal and wheels; and he does not care for growing things – In *J.R.R. Tolkien: Author of the Century* Tom Shippey discusses this aspect of Saruman: 'What does Saruman stand for? One thing certainly is a kind of mechanical ingenuity, smithcraft developed into engineering skills.' He has caught 'not the dragon-sickness associated with gold' but a 'metal sickness associated with iron', a disease which

> starts as intellectual curiosity, develops as engineering skill, turns into greed and the desire to dominate, corrupts further into a hatred and contempt of the natural world which goes beyond any rational desire to use it. Saruman's orcs start by felling trees for the furnaces, but they end up by felling them for fun as Treebeard complains. The 'applicability' of this is obvious, with Saruman becoming an image of one of the characteristic vices of modernity, skill without purpose, bulldozing for the sake of change. [pp. 170–1]

473–4 (II: 77): Treebeard rumbled for a moment

474 (II: 77). Down on the borders they are felling trees – good trees. Some of the trees they just cut down and leave to rot – Treebeard expresses Tolkien's own feelings about the wanton destruction of trees. On 30 June 1972 Tolkien wrote to the *Daily Telegraph* that 'nothing it [the Forestry Commission] has done that is stupid compares with the destruction, torture and murder of trees perpetrated by private individuals and minor official bodies. The savage sound of the electric saw is never silent wherever trees are still found growing' (*Letters*, p. 420).

474 (II: 77): Treebeard raised himself

474 (II: 77). besom – A broom made of twigs tied round a stick.

474–5 (II: 77–8): After some time the hobbits

474 (II: 77–8). Finglas, Fladrif . . . Leaflock and Skinbark – Treebeard translates these names, but in *Nomenclature* Tolkien adds that '*Leaflock* . . . is supposed to be a Common Speech translation of the Elvish *Finglas*: *fing* "lock of hair" + *las(s)* "leaf"'.

474 (II: 78). Only three remain of the first Ents that walked in the woods before the Darkness – *Before the Darkness* must mean before Morgoth exerted his power over Middle-earth. According to Treebeard, Ents do not die, but they can be destroyed, and can grow 'tree-ish'.

475–6 (II: 78–9): 'It is rather a strange and sad story'

475 (II: 79). Fimbrethil, of Wandlimb the lightfooted – *Wandlimb* is not a translation of *Fimbrethil* (see *Nomenclature*), but rather an epithet. In Appendix F *Fimbrethil* is said to mean 'slender-beech', but in the *1966*

Index Tolkien glosses it as 'slim-birch': compare *Nimbrethil* 'white-birches' in *Index* (probably 1953–4, and see note for p. 233), thus Sindarin *brethil* 'birch'. It may be that when writing Appendix F Tolkien recalled the *Etymologies* (written probably in the mid- to late 1930s), where he relates the stem BERÉTH- to 'beech-tree', 'beech-mast', including Exilic Noldorin (i.e. Sindarin) *brethil* 'beech-tree'.

476 (II: 79). When the Darkness came in the North – Again, the darkness that came from Morgoth. The Ents and Entwives therefore separated millennia before the present moment in the story.

476 (II: 79–80): 'I remember it was long ago

476 (II: 79). the war between Sauron and the Men of the Sea – The War of the Last Alliance; see the following note.

476 (II: 79). And now the Entwives are only a memory for us. . . . We believe we may meet again in a time to come – In a letter to Naomi Mitchison on 25 April 1954, Tolkien wrote:

> I think that in fact the Entwives had disappeared for good, being destroyed with their gardens in the War of the Last Alliance (Second Age 3429–3441) when Sauron pursued a scorched earth policy and burned their land against the advance of the Allies down the Anduin. . . . They survived only in the 'agriculture' transmitted to Men (and Hobbits). Some, of course, may have fled east, or even have become enslaved: tyrants in such tales must have an economic and agricultural background to their soldiers and metal-workers. If any survived so, they would indeed be far estranged from the Ents, and any rapprochement would be difficult – unless experience of industrialized and militarized agriculture had made them a little more anarchic. I hope so. I don't know. [*Letters*, p. 179]

And on ?6 June 1972 he wrote to Father Douglas Carter:

> As for the *Entwives* I do not know. . . . But I think in [Book III, Chapter 4] it is plain that there would be for Ents no re-union in 'history' – but Ents and their wives being rational creatures would find some 'earthly paradise' until the end of this world: beyond which the wisdom neither of Elves nor Ents could see. Though maybe they shared the hope of Aragorn that they were 'not bound for ever to the circles of the world and beyond them is more than memory'. [*Letters*, p. 419]

477 (II: 80–81): There was an Elvish song

477 (II: 80–81). There was an Elvish song . . . – A recording by Tolkien from these words to the end of the poem is included on Disc 2 of *The J.R.R. Tolkien Audio Collection*.

477 (II: 80). garth – An archaic word for 'yard' or 'garden'.

478 (II: 81): They woke to find

478 (II: 81). They woke – It is 30 February 1419.

478 (II: 82): 'Hoo, ho! Good morning

478 (II: 82). Entmoot – A *moot* is 'an assembly held for debate, especially in Anglo-Saxon and medieval times' (*Concise OED*).

478 (II: 82): 'Hoo, eh? Entmoot?'

478 (II: 82). Derndingle – In *Nomenclature* Tolkien states that *Derndingle* is 'said by Treebeard to be what Men called the meeting place of the Ents . . .'; therefore the name is meant to be in the Common Speech. 'But the Common Speech name must be supposed to have been given a long time ago, when in Gondor more was known or remembered about the Ents. *Dingle* is still known, meaning "a deep (tree-shadowed) dell", but *dern* "secret, hidden" is long obsolete. . . .' (Compare *Dernhelm*, note for p. 804.)

482 (II: 85): The hobbits turned back

482 (II: 85). conclave – A private meeting or assembly.

482 (II: 86): 'Hm, hoom, here I am again'

482 (II: 86). Bregalad is his Elvish name – Later Bregalad says that his name is *Quickbeam* in the Common Speech. In *Nomenclature* Tolkien writes that *Quickbeam* 'is a translation of Sindarin *Bregalad* "quick (lively) tree" . . . in the story this is represented as a name given to him because he was (for an Ent) "hasty". . . . *Quickbeam* and *Quicken* are actual English names of the rowan/mountain-ash; also given to the related "Service-tree". . . . The rowan is here evidently intended, since *rowan* is actually used in Quickbeam's song. . . .'

483 (II: 87): 'There were rowan-trees in my home'

483 (II: 87). Then Orcs came with axes . . . – A recording by Tolkien from these words to the end of Bregalad's poem is included on Disc 2 of *The J.R.R. Tolkien Audio Collection*.

483–4 (II: 87): *O Orofarnë*

483 (II: 87). *Orofarnë, Lassemista, Carnimírië* – Quenya names for rowan trees. Tolkien translates them in his letter to Richard Jeffery of 7 September 1955: 'mountain-dwelling, leaf-grey, with adornment of red jewels' (*Letters*, p. 224).

484 (II: 87). *Upon your head how golden-red the crown* – In autumn the rowan bears clusters of bright red berries.

484 (II: 87): The next day they spent

484 (II: 87). The next day – It is 1 March 1419.

484 (II: 87). slow and solemn as a dirge – A *dirge* is a lament for the dead, or more generally a mournful song.

484 (II: 88): The third day broke

484 (II: 88). The third day – It is 2 March 1419.

484 (II: 88–9): Then with a crash

484 (II: 88–9). Then with a crash . . . – A recording by Tolkien from these words to the end of the following poem is included on Disc 2 of *The J.R.R. Tolkien Audio Collection*.

486 (II: 89): Ho, hm, well, we could, you know!

486 (II: 89). Trolls are only counterfeits, made by the Enemy in the Great Darkness, in mockery of Ents – In his draft letter to Peter Hastings, September 1954, Tolkien wrote:

> Treebeard does not say that the Dark Lord 'created' Trolls and Orcs. He says he 'made' them in *counterfeit* of certain creatures pre-existing. There is, to me, a wide gulf between the two statements, so wide that Treebeard's statement could (in my world) have possibly been true. It is *not* true actually of the Orcs – who are fundamentally a race of "rational incarnate" creatures, though horribly corrupted, if no more so than many Men to be met today. Treebeard is a *character* in my story, not me; and though he has a great memory and some earthy wisdom, he is not one of the Wise, and there is quite a lot he does not know or understand. . . . I am not sure about Trolls. I think they are mere 'counterfeits', and hence (though here I am of course only using elements of old barbarous mythmaking that had no "aware" metaphysic) they return to mere stone images when not in the dark. But there are other sorts of Trolls beside these rather ridiculous, if brutal, Stone-trolls [like the Trolls in *The Hobbit*], for which other origins are suggested. [*Letters*, pp. 190–1]

487 (II: 90): Pippin looked back

487 (II: 90). At last they stood upon the summit – The narrative indicates that it was late afternoon when the ents began their march. According to *Scheme*, it was fifty miles from Derndingle to Isengard, and the ents arrived at 10.00 p.m.

487 (II: 90). Nan Curunír – In his unfinished index Tolkien defines *Curunír* as 'one of cunning device', and *Nan Curunír* as 'the glen of Isengard (also called Wizard's Vale)'. Saruman was called *Curunír* by the Eldar: see note for p. 48.

Chapter 5

THE WHITE RIDER

For drafts and history of this chapter, see *The Treason of Isengard*, pp. 425–35.

488 (II: 91): 'My very bones are chilled'

488 (II: 91). Day had come at last. – It is 1 March 1419.

489–90 (II: 92–3): 'Maybe, I could'

489–90 (II: 92–3). I guess that it was hands . . . he was carried to this point – Aragorn's skills as a tracker are now shown to full advantage, when the reader already knows what happened to Merry and Pippin from the previous chapter.

490 (II: 93): 'I do not know how it happened'

490 (II: 93). Did they suppose they had captured the Ring-bearer and his faithful comrade? I think not. Their masters would not dare to give such plain orders to Orcs . . . they would not speak openly to them of the Ring: they are not trusty servants. But I think the orcs had been commanded to capture *hobbits*, alive, at all costs. – Aragorn is only partly right, in deducing why the orcs were content with capturing Merry and Pippin. But the actions of Grishnákh and Uglúk, and the entries on Tolkien's time-schemes, show that the orcs did have some knowledge about the Ring. Indeed, both of them show considerable loyalty to their masters.

491 (II: 94): 'That is just as well'

491 (II: 94). There is something happening inside, or going to happen. Do you not feel the tenseness? – It is the second day of Entmoot.

495 (II: 98): He stepped down

495 (II: 98). none of you have any weapon that could hurt me – In a note almost certainly pre-dating the writing of this chapter, Tolkien wrote that Gandalf 'passed through fire – and became *the* White Wizard. "I forgot much that I knew, and learned again much that I had forgotten." *He has thus acquired something of the awe and terrible power of the Ring-wraiths* – only on the good side. Evil things fly from him if he is revealed – when he shines. But he does not as a rule reveal himself' (*The Treason of Isengard*, p. 422). In an outline for the Moria chapters of autumn 1939 (see note for p. 331) Tolkien seems not to have anticipated that there would be anything supernatural about Gandalf's return, but as the story developed a darker and more serious tone, so Gandalf was given increased power and authority: not just a particularly helpful and concerned wizard, but one of the emissaries of the Valar 'sent to contest the power of Sauron, and to unite all those who had the will to resist him; but they were forbidden to match his power with power, or to seek to dominate Elves or Men by force and fear' (Appendix B, p. 1084, III: 365).

See further, note for p. 502.

495 (II: 98): 'The eagle!' said Legolas

495 (II: 98). four days ago – In editions prior to 2004 these words read 'three days ago'. In *The Treason of Isengard* Christopher Tolkien notes:

> At one point . . . the need for correction escaped my father's notice: Legolas' words that the last time he saw the eagle was 'three days ago, above the Emyn Muil'. . . . This should have been changed to 'four days ago' . . . cf. *The Tale of Years* in LR: 'February 27 Aragorn reaches the west-cliff at sunrise', and (February having 30 days) 'March 1 Aragorn meets Gandalf the White'. [p. 425]

495 (II: 99): 'Yes,' said Gandalf

495 (II: 99). Very nearly it [the Ring] was revealed to the Enemy, but it escaped. I had some part in that: for I sat in a high place, and I strove with the Dark Tower; and the Shadow passed. – See note for p. 401.

496–7 (II: 100): 'What then shall I say'

497 (II: 100). for he that strikes the first blow, if he strikes hard enough, may need to strike no more – A version of the traditional saying *The first blow is half the battle.*

499 (II: 102–3): 'Ah! now you are asking much

499 (II: 102). Treebeard is . . . the oldest of the Ents, the oldest living thing that still walks beneath the Sun upon this Middle-earth. – In *The Lord of the Rings* Tolkien makes apparently contradictory statements concerning the priority of age in Middle-earth of Treebeard and Tom Bombadil. For the latter, see notes for pp. 119, 124, and 131, in which the cumulative evidence suggests that Tom Bombadil may have existed before Arda was fully fashioned, or at least before growing things appeared. To these may be compared Gandalf's statement about Treebeard as 'oldest' in the present paragraph, his remarks to Théoden in Book III, Chapter 8 ('Treebeard is . . . the eldest and chief of the Ents, and when you speak with him you will hear the speech of the oldest of all living things', p. 558, II: 164), and Celeborn's address of Treebeard as 'Eldest' in Book VI, Chapter 6. Tolkien explained the latter as a 'courtesy title' in his draft letter of 1968, quoted in the note for p. 464; otherwise it is worth repeating Christopher Tolkien's comment that his father was given to 'rhetorical superlatives', such as 'the oldest living thing' (compare, as already noted for p. 15, the statement at the end of the Prologue that when Celeborn at last sought the Grey Havens 'with him went the last living memory of the Elder Days in Middle-earth').

The balance of the statements in Tolkien's drafts for the 1968 letter indicate that Treebeard was the oldest surviving Ent, *but* no one knew the origin of Tom Bombadil or could remember a time when he was not in the world; and Bombadil 'was therefore often referred to as the oldest speaker'. In the 1968 letter Tolkien also said: 'No one knew whence they [Ents] came or first appeared'; yet in his text on the Ents and the Eagles included in *The Silmarillion* as part of 'Of Aulë and Yavanna', he suggests that the Ents did not wake until after or at the same time as the Elves – and Treebeard's list of 'living peoples' places Elves first.

499 (II: 102–3). I saw him four days ago . . . and I think he saw me . . . but I did not speak, for I was heavy with thought, and weary after my struggle with the Eye of Mordor – *Four days ago* was 27 February. Gandalf's struggle with the Eye of Mordor had been the previous day, when he fought to influence Frodo on Amon Hen.

501 (II: 105): 'Yet it has a bottom

501 (II: 105). His fire was quenched, but now he was a thing of slime, stronger than a strangling snake. – Gandalf's account recalls shape-changers in myth and legend, such as Proteus of whom it is said in Homer's *Odyssey*: 'He'll make you fight – for he can take the forms / of all the beasts, and water, and blinding fire' (Robert Fitzgerald translation (1990), Book IV, ll. 446–7); and in Vergil's *Georgics*, Book IV: 'But when thou shalt hold him caught and fettered in thine hands, even then the form and visage of manifold wild beasts shall cheat thee; for in a moment he will turn to bristly boar or a black tiger, a scaly serpent and tawny-necked lioness, or will roar shrill in flame and so slip out of fetters, or will melt into thin water and be gone' (J.W. Mackail translation (1934), p. 348).

501–2 (II: 105): 'We fought far under the living earth

501 (II: 105). Ever he clutched at me, and ever I hewed at him, till he fled at last into dark tunnels – Gandalf's fight with the Balrog recalls that of Beowulf with Grendel's mother: 'Then she clutched at him, she seized the warrior with her horrid claws'; he 'seized Grendel's mother by the shoulder . . . bursting as he was with rage, so flung the deadly foe that she fell upon the ground. She quickly yielded him a recompense again with fearful graspings, and clutched at him . . .' (Clark Hall translation, pp. 95, 97).

501 (II: 105). Far, far below . . . the world is gnawed by nameless things. Even Sauron knows them not. They are older than he. – But Sauron is a Maia: nothing should exist in Middle-earth that is *older than he*. The phrase is probably rhetorical.

Todd Jensen has suggested that in writing this passage Tolkien may have been influenced by 'the horrible creatures gnawing away at the roots of Yggdrasil', the World Tree in Norse mythology, 'especially the dragon Nidhog, and his terrible brood' ('Nameless Things', *Beyond Bree*, August 1988, p. 8).

502 (II: 105). the Endless Stair – 'A stairway leading from the lowest delving of the Dwarves, in Moria, to the summit of Celebdil (Zirak-zigil)' (*Index*).

502 (II: 105): 'It was made, and it had not been destroyed'

502 (II: 105). Durin's Tower – 'A tower on the summit of Zirak-zigil (Celebdil)' (*Index*).

502 (II: 105–6): 'There upon Celebdil was a lonely window

502 (II: 105). Thunder they heard, and lightning, they said, smote upon Celebdil, and leaped back broken into tongues of fire. . . . A great smoke rose about us, vapour and steam. Ice fell like rain. I threw down my enemy, and he fell from the high place and broke the mountain-side – Compare the battle of Zeus and Typhoeus in Hesiod's *Theogony*:

> *Zeus raised up his strength*
> *Seizing his arms, lightning, the blazing bolt,*
> *And thunder, leaped down from Olympus, struck,*
> *And burned the dreadful monster's ghastly heads.*
> *He lashed him with a whip and mastered him,*
> *And threw him down, all maimed, and great earth groaned.*
> *A flame leaped from the lightning-blasted lord,*
> *When he was struck, on the jagged mountainside.*
> *Great earth was widely scorched by the awful blast. . . .*
> [Dorothea Wender translation (1973), ll. 54–62]

502 (II: 106): 'Naked I was sent back

502 (II: 106). Naked I was sent back – for a brief time, until my task is done. – On 4 November 1954 Tolkien wrote in a draft letter to Robert Murray:

> I think the way in which Gandalf's return is presented is a defect, and one other critic, as much under the spell as yourself, curiously used the same expression 'cheating'. That is partly due to the ever-present compulsions of narrative technique. He must return at that point, and such explanations of his survival as are explicitly set out must be given there – but the narrative is urgent, and must not be held up for elaborate discussions involving the whole 'mythological' setting. . . .
>
> Gandalf really 'died', and was changed: for that seems to me the only real cheating, to represent anything that can be called 'death' as making

no difference. 'I am G[andalf] the *White*, who has returned from death'. . . . I might say much more, but . . . it would not, I fear, get rid of the fact that the return of G. is as presented in this book a 'defect', and one I was aware of, and probably did not work hard enough to mend. But G. is not, of course, a human being (Man or Hobbit). There are naturally no precise modern terms to say what he was. I w[oul]d venture to say that he was an *incarnate* 'angel' – strictly an ἄγγελος: that is, with the other *Istari*, wizards, 'those who know', an emissary from the Lords of the West, sent to Middle-earth as the great crisis of Sauron loomed on the horizon. By 'incarnate' I mean they were embodied in physical bodies capable of pain, and weariness, and of afflicting the spirit with physical fear, and of being 'killed', though supported by the angelic spirit they might endure long, and only show slowly the wearing of care and labour.

[They were given this form] . . . to limit and hinder their exhibition of 'power' on the physical plane, and so that they should do what they were primarily sent for: train, advise, instruct, arouse the hearts and minds of those threatened by Sauron to a resistance with their own strengths; and not just to do the job for them. They thus appeared as 'old' sage figures. But . . . all the 'angelic' powers concerned with this world were capable of many degrees of error. . . . The 'wizards' were not exempt, indeed being incarnate were more likely to stray, or err. Gandalf alone fully passes the tests, on a moral plane anyway (he makes mistakes of judgement). For in his condition it was for him a *sacrifice* to perish on the Bridge in defence of his companions, less perhaps than for a mortal Man or Hobbit, since he had a far greater inner power than they; but also, more, since it was a humbling and abnegation of himself in conformity to 'the Rules': for all he could know at that moment he was the *only* person who could direct the resistance to Sauron successfully, and all *his* mission was vain. He was handing over to the Authority that ordained the Rules, and giving up personal hope of success.

That I should say is what the Authority wished, as a set-off to Saruman. The 'wizards', as such, had failed; or if you like: the crisis had become too grave and needed an enhancement of power. So Gandalf sacrificed himself, was accepted, and enhanced, and returned. . . . Of course he remained similar in personality and idiosyncrasy, but both his wisdom and power are much greater. When he speaks he commands attention; the old Gandalf could not have dealt so with Théoden, nor with Saruman. He is still under the obligation of concealing his power and of teaching rather than forcing or dominating wills, but where the physical powers of the Enemy are too great for the good will of the opposers to be effective he can act in emergency as an 'angel'. . . . He seldom does so, operating rather through others, but in one or two cases in the War [of the Ring] . . . he does reveal a sudden power: he

> twice rescues Faramir. He alone is left to forbid the entrance of the Lord of the Nazgûl to Minas Tirith, when the City has been overthrown and its Gates destroyed. . . . He was sent by a mere prudent plan of the angelic Valar or governors; but Authority had taken up this plan and enlarged it, at the moment of its failure. 'Naked I was sent back – for a brief time, until my task is done'. Sent back by whom, and whence? Not by the 'gods' whose business is only with this embodied world and its time; for he passed 'out of thought and time'. Naked is alas! unclear. It was meant just literally, 'unclothed like a child' (not discarnate), and so ready to receive the white robes of the highest. Galadriel's power is not divine, and his healing in Lórien is meant to be no more than physical healing and refreshment.
>
> But if it is 'cheating' to treat 'death' as making no difference, embodiment must not be ignored. Gandalf may be enhanced in power (that is, under the forms of this fable, in sanctity), but if still embodied he must still suffer care and anxiety, and the needs of flesh. [*Letters*, pp. 201–3]

Although Tolkien does not specifically say that the 'Authority' who sent Gandalf back was Eru (Ilúvatar, God), it is implicit, for only Eru was above the Valar. Tolkien was also anxious that the return of Gandalf should not be seen as comparable to the Resurrection of Christ. He wrote in his draft letter to Michael Straight, ?end of 1955:

> But the situation became so much the worse by the fall of Saruman, that the 'good' were obliged to greater effort and sacrifice. Thus Gandalf faced and suffered death; and came back or was sent back, as he says, with enhanced power. But though one may be in this reminded of the Gospels, it is not really the same thing at all. The Incarnation of God is an *infinitely* greater thing than anything I would dare to write. [*Letters*, p. 237]

Readers have seen other echoes of the Gospels in the return of Gandalf, and also noted his momentary difficulty in remembering his Middle-earth name when meeting Aragorn, Legolas, and Gimli in Fangorn Forest: 'Gandalf himself doesn't seem too sure at this point who he is, at least until his transfiguration. The entire episode [is comparable] to the Biblical story of Christ on the road to Emmaus, where three of the disciples met the risen Jesus and didn't recognize him until he chose to reveal himself' (*Rómenna Meeting Report*, 22 September 1985, p. 1).

503 (II: 106): 'Thus it was that I came

503 (II: 106). Thence by strange roads I came – *Scheme* gives further details:

January 15: [Gandalf] falls in the abyss with the Balrog.

January 16: Wrestles with the Balrog and pursues it through the deeps for many days.

January 23: Pursues Balrog to pinnacle of *Zirakinbar* [Zirakzigil] and there wrestles with him for three days.

January 26: G[andalf] casts down the Balrog, and falls into a long trance.

February 17: Gwaihir finds Gandalf on Zirakinbar and takes him to Lórien.

February 20: Gandalf leaves Lórien and flies south, borne by Gwaihir.

February 25: Gandalf reaches Fangorn; sends Gwaihir to spy out lands for news.

February 26: On a hill in Fangorn wrestles in thought with the Eye of Mordor, and saves Frodo from yielding.

505 (II: 109): For many hours they rode

505 (II: 109). sedge – A coarse grass growing in wet places.

505 (II: 109): 'I see a great smoke'

505 (II: 109). I see a great smoke – A shadow of an earlier version of the story, before Tolkien altered the chronology of events. As the story now stands, Gandalf, Aragorn, Legolas, and Gimli ride to Edoras on 1 March. Entmoot is still continuing: the smoke has nothing to do with the Ents' pending attack on Isengard. The First Battle of the Fords of Isen had taken place on 25 February, and the Second Battle will not begin until the night of 2 March. But when the present chapter was written, Aragorn and his companions met Gandalf on 30 January, and the smoke that Legolas saw was thus the smoke of the Second Battle of the Fords, which took place on the same day. Christopher Tolkien comments in *The War of the Ring* that 'it seems impossible to avoid the conclusion that the end of the chapter . . . escaped revision when the date of the (Second) Battle of the Fords of Isen was changed' (p. 5).

Chapter 6

THE KING OF THE GOLDEN HALL

For drafts and history of this chapter, see *The Treason of Isengard*, pp. 411–51.

506 (II: 110): They rode on

506 (II: 110). They rode on – According to *Scheme*, Gandalf and company set out for Edoras at about 3.00 p.m. on 1 March 1419. 'They ride for 12 hours, rest four and at sunrise next day see the King's Hall (Mar. 2)'.

506 (II: 110): Hours passed and still they rode

506 (II: 110). The waxing moon sank into the cloudy West – The moon is one night past its first quarter, and will be full on 7/8 March. Tolkien correctly indicates the moon setting some hours before dawn.

506 (II: 110): 'Look!' he cried

506 (II: 110). mountains of the South . . . the stream that issued from the dale – The *mountains of the South* are the White Mountains. The *stream* is the Snowbourn.

506–7 (II: 110–11): Legolas gazed ahead

507 (II: 111). The light of it shines far over the land. – Tom Shippey in *The Road to Middle-earth* (2nd edn., p. 112) points out that this sentence is a translation of *Beowulf*, l. 311: *lixte se léoma ofer landa fela.*

507 (II: 111): 'Look!' said Gandalf

507 (II: 111). Evermind they are called, *simbelmynë* in this land of Men, for they blossom in all the seasons of the year – In *Nomenclature* Tolkien writes that *Evermind* is a 'flower-name, translation of Rohan *simbelmyne*. The element *-mind* has the sense "memory". The name thus resembles "forget-me-not", but a quite different kind of flower is intended: an imagined variety of anemone, growing in turf like *Anemone pulsatilla*, the pasque-flower, but smaller and white like the wood anemone.'

The Rohan name *simbelmynë* is derived from Old English *simbel* 'continual, perpetual, ever, always' + *myne* 'mind'. In *Of Tuor and His Coming to Gondor*, written *c.* 1951–2, on his way through the ravine leading to Gondolin 'Tuor saw beside the way a sward of grass, where like stars bloomed the white flowers *uilos*, the Evermind that knows no season and withers not' (*Unfinished Tales*, p. 48). Christopher Tolkien comments:

> These were the flowers that bloomed abundantly on the burial mounds of the Kings of Rohan below Edoras, and which Gandalf named in the language of Rohan (as translated into Old English) *simbelmynë*. . . . The Elvish name *uilos* is only given in this passage, but the word is found also in *Amon Uilos*, as the Quenya name *Oiolossë* ('Ever-snow-white', the Mountain of Manwë) was rendered into Sindarin. In 'Cirion and Eorl' the flower is given another Elvish name, *alfirin* [growing on Elendil's tomb, and described as white]. [*Unfinished Tales*, p. 55, n. 27]

The name *alfirin* is also given to a different, yellow flower in Legolas's song, on which see note for p. 875.

507 (II: 111): 'Seven mounds upon the left

507 (II: 111). Seven mounds upon the left, and nine upon the right – The burial mounds of the Kings of Rohan from the establishment of the realm in Third Age 2510. The division marks a break in the line of descent: the ninth king having left no surviving son, he was succeeded by his sister's son. Burial mounds have a long history (see note for p. 114), and in later times those of a dynasty might be placed close together. Hilda Roderick Ellis comments in *The Road to Hel: A Study of the Conception of the Dead in Old Norse Literature* (1943) that 'perhaps the most impressive graves found are those of Vendel in Sweden, where a line of chiefs has been buried, for the most part in their ships, in a series of graves which seem to date in unbroken succession from the sixth century to the tenth' (p. 10). Other such groups include the Anglo-Saxon burial mounds at Sutton Hoo in Suffolk and royal graves at Uppsala in Sweden. Tolkien's description of *seven mounds upon the left, and nine upon the right* recalls a plate in William Stukeley's *Stonehenge: A Temple Restor'd to the British Druids* (1740), which shows a view of barrows in a line at right angles to the Avenue at Stonehenge, with inscriptions 'The 7 Kings Barrows' and 'The 6 Old Kings Barrows' (p. 52, tab. XXVII).

508 (II: 112): 'That, I guess

508 (II: 112). the language of the Rohirrim – Tolkien notes in Appendix F that he made the language of the Rohirrim 'to resemble ancient [Old] English'; but 'this linguistic procedure does not imply that the Rohirrim closely resembled the ancient English otherwise, in culture or art, in weapons or modes of warfare, except in a general way due to their circumstances: a simpler and more primitive people living in contact with a higher and more venerable culture, and occupying lands that had once been part of its domain' (p. 1136, III: 414).

Tom Shippey, however, argues that 'with one admitted exception, the Riders of Rohan resemble the Anglo-Saxons down to minute details' (*The Road to Middle-earth*, 2nd edn., p. 106). The 'obvious difference', he says, 'is horses'.

> The Rohirrim called themselves the Éothéod (Old English *eoh* = 'horse' + *þéod* = 'people'); this translates into the Common Speech as 'the Riders'. . . . The Rohirrim are nothing if not cavalry. By contrast the Anglo-Saxons' reluctance to have anything militarily to do with horses is notorious. . . . How then can Anglo-Saxons and Rohirrim ever, culturally, be equated? A part of the answer is that the Rohirrim are not to be equated with the Anglo-Saxons of history, but with those of poetry, or legend. [p. 112]

508 (II: 112): 'It runs thus in the Common Speech

508 (II: 112). It runs thus in the Common Speech . . . – A recording by Tolkien from these words (slightly reordered) to the end of the following poem is included on Disc 2 of *The J.R.R. Tolkien Audio Collection.*

508 (II: 112). *Where now the horse and the rider? . . .* – Christopher Tolkien points out that this is 'an echo of the Old English poem known as *The Wanderer*, line 92: *Hwær cwom mearg? Hwær cwom mago?*' (*The Treason of Isengard*, p. 449, n. 8). It follows an old convention, *ubi sunt?* in which the poet comments on the passing of time. The *Wanderer*-poet asks: 'Where has the horse gone? Where the young warrior? Where is the giver of treasure? What has become of the seats for the feasts? Where are the joys of the hall? . . . How has that time gone, vanished beneath night's cover, just as if it had never been!' (E. Talbot Donaldson translation, *The Norton Anthology of English Literature*, rev. edn. (1968), vol. 1, p. 92).

508 (II: 112). hauberk – Armour, originally for the neck and shoulders, later a long coat of mail.

508 (II: 112). Felaróf – 'Very valiant, very strong' (Old English *fela* 'much, very' + *róf* 'valiant, stout, strong').

508 (II: 112): There sat many men

508 (II: 112). 'Stay, strangers here unknown!' they cried in the tongue of the Riddermark, demanding the names and errand of the strangers. – In an early draft the challenge was actually written in Old English and in full (see *The Treason of Isengard*, p. 442–3, translated by Christopher Tolkien on p. 449, n. 5): 'Stay, strangers unknown! Who are ye, friends or foes, that have come thus strangely clad riding to the gates of this town? None may enter in, neither beggarman nor warrior, if we know not his name. Now ye comers from afar, declare to us in haste: what are ye called? What is your errand to Theoden our lord?' Christopher Tolkien points out that here and in the following speech of the guards 'the passage in *Beowulf* (lines 237–57) in which Beowulf and his companions are accosted by the watchman on the coast of Denmark is very distinctly echoed'. The relevant passages are:

> 'What kind of armed men are ye, clad in coats of mail, who have thus come and brought a towering ship over the water-ways, hither over the

seas? For a long time I have been acting as coast-guard. . . . Never have I seen a mightier noble upon earth, a warrior in armour, than is one of you. . . .

'Now, I must know your origin, ere you go further, as faithless spies, on Danish ground. Now, ye strangers from afar, ye sea-traversers . . . it is best to tell me quickly the cause of your coming.' [Clark Hall translation, pp. 31–2]

On the wider subject of *Beowulf* and Rohan, see Clive Tolley, 'And the Word Was Made Flesh', *Mallorn* 32 (September 1995).

508–9 (II: 112–13): 'It is the will of Théoden King

508 (II: 113). Mundburg – '*Guardian-fortress*, name in Rohan of Minas Tirith' (*1966 Index*).

508 (II: 113). Who are you that come heedless over the plain, thus strangely clad, riding horses like to our own horses? Long have we kept guard here, and we have watched you from afar. Never have we seen other riders so strange, nor any horse more proud – A continuation of the echo of *Beowulf.*

509 (II: 113): A troubled look

509 (II: 113). Wormtongue – A '"modernized" form of the nickname of *Gríma*, the evil counsellor of Rohan = Rohan [Old English] *wyrm-tunge* "snake-tongue"' (*Nomenclature*). Tolkien was undoubtedly familiar with the Icelandic tale of Gunnlaug the Worm-tongue, translated by William Morris and Eiríkr Magnússon (published 1869), but there the name *Worm-tongue* was given to a poet because of his sharp wit.

509–10 (II: 114): The dark gates were swung open

509 (II: 114). they seemed more than mortal men – In the original draft of this chapter these words were followed by a description of the exterior of the hall: 'Before Théoden's hall there was a portico, with pillars made of mighty trees hewn in the upland forests and carved with interlacing figures gilded and painted. The doors also were of wood, carven in the likeness of many beasts and birds with jewelled eyes and golden claws.' Christopher Tolkien comments in *The Treason of Isengard* that 'it is curious that in the "fair copy" manuscript, and thence in the final text, there is no description at all of the exterior of the house, and I think that it may have got lost in the complexities of redrafting and reordering of the material' (pp. 443–4). But in discussions of emendations to make to the edition of 2004 Christopher Tolkien felt that it was only his guess that the passage was lost rather than deliberately omitted, and although a good guess it is a guess nonetheless. The text therefore was left as it was.

Most of the Anglo-Saxon decorative carving that survives is in stone, not wood, but several examples of carved wooden doorways and doors from eleventh- to thirteenth-century stave churches can be seen in Norway, especially in the University Museum of National Antiquities in Oslo. Both Anglo-Saxon and Viking examples use interlacing figures in various styles, and may well have been painted when new.

510 (II: 114): 'I am the Doorward of Théoden'

510 (II: 114). Háma – From Old English *hám* 'home, house, dwelling', an appropriate name for the King's doorward.

510 (II: 114). I must bid you lay aside your weapons – The same request was made by the coast-guard to Beowulf and his men. Beowulf did not object, but left two or three men to guard the weapons while he was in the hall.

511 (II: 115): 'Truly,' said Aragorn

511 (II: 115). woodman's cot – A *cot* in this sense is a small, humble house or cottage. Here Aragorn is admitting the right of even the poorest to be master of his own dwelling, however humble, according to the proverb *An Englishman's house is his castle.*

511 (II: 115): 'Come, come!'

511 (II: 115). goodman Háma – *Goodman* is an archaic term of address denoting respect.

511 (II: 115): Slowly Aragorn unbuckled his belt

511 (II: 115). Telchar first wrought it in the deeps of time. – *Telchar* was the most renowned of the Dwarf-smiths of Nogrod in the First Age.

511 (II: 116): 'The staff in the hand of a wizard

511 (II: 116). The staff in the hand of a wizard may be more than a prop for age. . . . Yet in doubt a man of worth will trust his own wisdom. I believe you are friends and folk worthy of honour, who have no evil purpose. – Háma is right to suspect Gandalf's staff, but he also correctly judges the purposes of the strangers. Háma's words echo those of the coast-guard to Beowulf: 'The bold shield-warrior, who judges well, must know the difference between these two – words and deeds. I understand that this is a company friendly to the lord of the Scyldings' (Clark Hall translation, p. 34).

511–12 (II: 116): The guards now lifted the heavy bars

512 (II: 116). louver in the roof – The *Oxford English Dictionary* gives two possible interpretations: 'A domed turret-like erection on the roof of a hall . . . in a medieval building with lateral openings for the passage of smoke or the admission of light', or 'a hole in the roof for the passage of smoke'.

512 (II: 116). the floor was paved with stones of many hues; branching runes and strange devices intertwined beneath their feet. They saw now that the pillars were richly carved, gleaming dully with gold and half-seen colours. . . . Many woven cloths were hung upon the walls, and over their wide spaces marched figures of ancient legend – No such great hall survives from the Anglo-Saxon period, but literature and archaeology indicate that it once existed. Tolkien seems to have used such fragmentary evidence to imagine the interior of Meduseld. In *Beowulf* Hrothgar's great feast-hall, Heorot, is described as having a *fágne flor* 'coloured, variegated floor' and on special occasions *gold-fág scinon web æfter wágum* 'gold colour shone in the woven wall-hangings'. The more detailed description of the floor of Meduseld recalls Roman mosaic floors, or floors with decorative patterns formed with shaped slabs of variously coloured marble or stone from both Roman and medieval times. There is some evidence for woven or embroidered wall hangings in the Anglo-Saxon period, fragments of gold thread (probably from clothes) have been found in graves, and late ninth-century linen wall-hangings embroidered with scenes from mythological and heroic tradition have been retrieved from a burial in Norway.

512 (II: 116): 'Behold Eorl the Young!'

512 (II: 116). Behold Eorl the Young! . . . Thus he rode out of the North to the Battle of the Field of Celebrant. – In Third Age 2510 Cirion, the Steward of Gondor, threatened by invaders from the East, sought help from the Éothéod, descendants of former allies who dwelt in the North. When Cirion was under attack on the Field of Celebrant, 'out of the North there came help beyond hope, and the horns of the Rohirrim were first heard in Gondor. Eorl the Young came with his riders and swept away the enemy, and pursued the Balchoth to the death over the fields of Calenardhon. Cirion granted to Eorl that land to dwell in, and he swore to Cirion the Oath of Eorl, of friendship at need or at call to the Lords of Gondor' (Appendix A, p. 1053, III: 334). See further, note for p. 1053.

512 (II: 116–17): Now the four companions

512 (II: 116). in the middle of the dais was a great gilded chair – In this context, a *dais* is a raised platform at one end of a hall for a throne.

512 (II: 116). a man so bent with age that he seemed almost a dwarf – Théoden was born in 2948, so is now seventy or seventy-one. In *The Battles of the Fords of Isen* it is said that his health began to fail early in Third Age 3014 when he was sixty-six: 'his malady may thus have been due to natural causes, though the Rohirrim commonly lived till near or beyond their eightieth year. But it may well have been induced or increased by subtle poisons, administered by Gríma' (*Unfinished Tales*, p. 355).

512–13 (II: 117): 'I greet you,' he said

512 (II: 117). Troubles follow you like crows – *Crows* are carrion birds and therefore are seen on battlefields and scenes of slaughter. Wormtongue is suggesting that Gandalf preys on disaster.

513 (II: 117): 'You speak justly, lord'

513 (II: 117). It is not yet five days since the bitter tidings came that Théodred your son was slain upon the West Marches – The name *Théodred* is evidently derived from Old English *þēod* 'people' + *rǣd* 'counsel, advice'. Théodred was killed in the First Battle of the Fords of Isen on 25 February. It is now 2 March; news of his death did not reach Edoras until about noon on 27 February. Théodred and Éomer had been opponents of Gríma. In *The Battles of the Fords of Isen* it is said:

> It was clearly seen in Rohan, when the true accounts of the battles at the Fords were known, that Saruman had given special orders that Théodred should at all costs be slain. At the first battle all his fiercest warriors were engaged in reckless assaults upon Théodred and his guard, disregarding other events of the battle, which might otherwise have resulted in a much more damaging defeat for the Rohirrim. When Théodred was at last slain Saruman's commander (no doubt under orders) seemed satisfied for the time being, and Saruman made the mistake, fatal as it proved, of not immediately throwing in more forces and proceeding at once to a massive invasion of Westfold; though the valour of Grimbold and Elfhelm contributed to his delay. If the invasion of Westfold had begun five days earlier, there can be little doubt that the reinforcements from Edoras would never have come near Helm's Deep, but would have been surrounded and overwhelmed in the open plain; if indeed Edoras had not itself been attacked and captured before the arrival of Gandalf. . . .
>
> [At the Fords of Isen] the river was broad and shallow, passing in two arms about a large eyot. . . . Only here, south of Isengard, was it possible for large forces, especially those heavily armed or mounted, to cross the river. Saruman thus had this advantage: he could send his troops down either side of the Isen and attack the Fords, if they were held against him, from both sides. Any force of his west of Isen could if necessary retreat upon Isengard. On the other hand, Théodred might send men across the Fords, either in sufficient strength to engage Saruman's troops or to defend the western bridgehead; but if they were worsted, they would have no retreat except back over the Fords with the enemy at their heels, and possibly also awaiting them on the eastern bank. South and west along the Isen they had no way home, unless they were provisioned for a long journey into Western Gondor. [*Unfinished Tales*, pp. 355–6]

A detailed account of the Battle follows. Saruman sent forces on both sides of the Isen and captured the eastern end of the Fords while Théodred was manning the eyot. Théodred fell just before reinforcements arrived and scattered the Isengarders. The last words of Théodred were: 'Let me lie here – to keep the Fords till Éomer comes!' (p. 359). Then:

> Erkenbrand of Westfold assumed command of the West-mark when news of the fall of Théodred reached him in the Hornburg on the next day. He sent errand-riders to Edoras to announce this and to bear to Théoden his son's last words, adding his own prayer that Éomer should be sent at once with all help that could be spared. 'Let the defence of Edoras be made here in the West,' he said, 'and not wait till it is itself besieged.' But Gríma used the curtness of this advice to further his policy of delay. It was not until his defeat by Gandalf that any action was taken. The reinforcements with Éomer and the King himself set out in the afternoon of March the 2nd, but that night the Second Battle of the Fords was fought and lost, and the invasion of Rohan begun. [pp. 359–60]

513 (II: 117). *Láthspell* . . . ill-news – For *Láthspell* compare Old English *lāð-spell* 'a painful grievous story', from *lāð* 'causing hate, evil, injury' + *spell* 'story, message'.

513 (II: 117–18): 'That is so'

513 (II: 117–18). carrion-fowl – Birds that feed on dead flesh.

514 (II: 118): 'Then it is true

514 (II: 118). Sorceress of the Golden Wood . . . webs of deceit were ever woven in Dwimordene – It is ironic that Gríma, who is deceitfully pretending to have Théoden's welfare at heart while secretly supporting Saruman, should accuse Galadriel of deceit. Of course, in one sense he is right: Galadriel and her maidens wove the cloaks that help to camouflage the Company of the Ring.

Dwimordene 'Phantom-vale' (*Index*) is the name in Rohan of Lothlórien. According to the *1966 Index Dwimordene* means 'Valley of Illusion'.

514 (II: 118): *In Dwimordene, in Lórien*

514 (II: 118). *In Dwimordene, in Lórien . . .* – A recording by Tolkien of this poem is included on Discs 1 and 2 of *The J.R.R. Tolkien Audio Collection*; on the first disc (track 18) it is mislabelled on the sleeve.

514 (II: 118): 'The wise speak only of what they know

514 (II: 118). Gríma son of Gálmód – *Gríma* is Old English 'mask, visor' or 'spectre'. *Gálmód* is Old English 'light-minded, licentious'. Jim Allan comments that this is 'a good name for a traitor who hides his true face and his secret lust for Éowyn' (*An Introduction to Elvish*, p. 217).

514 (II: 118). a witless worm . . . keep your forked tongue behind your teeth – *Worm* implies that Gríma is low, beneath contempt; but also compare Old English *wyrm* 'serpent', recalling the serpent in Eden who spoke falsely and tempted Eve. *Forked tongue*, the tongue of a snake, connoting 'deceitful', reinforces the thought; hence the nickname *Wormtongue.*

514 (II: 118). I have not passed through fire and death to bandy crooked words with a serving-man – In the first three printings of the first edition (1954–5) *fire and death* read 'fire and flood'. The phrase was emended in the fourth printing (1956). In his draft letter to Robert Murray, 4 November 1954, Tolkien wrote that Gandalf probably 'should rather have said to Wormtongue: "I have not passed through death (*not* 'fire and flood') to bandy crooked words with a serving-man"' (*Letters*, p. 201).

To *bandy* is to argue pointlessly or rudely.

Several readers have commented on similarities between Gríma Wormtongue and Unferth, the counsellor who sat at the king's feet in *Beowulf.* Clive Tolley comments in 'Tolkien and the Unfinished', *Scholarship and Fantasy: Proceedings of The Tolkien Phenomenon, May 1992* (1993):

> One of the most puzzling characters of the Old English *Beowulf* is Unferð, the spokesman of the Danish king Hroðgar. His name means 'Strife', and he seems to have been specially invented by the poet for this purpose, for his main role in the poem is to accuse Beowulf of not being up to the job of dealing with the monster Grendel, on the basis of a bad performance in a previous swimming match. Beowulf rounds on him, defending himself and pointing out that not only has Unferð shown himself no hero, but has even been the slayer of his brothers.
>
> It is never explained why the Danish king kept on such an evil-doer in a position of authority, nor why he was allowed to make such a savage attack on the honoured newcomer. . . .
>
> Tolkien was unable to resist the enticement of such an ambiguous character. The whole scene of the arrival of Aragorn and his companions at the court of Théoden is based on the arrival of the Geats at the Danish court in *Beowulf*, and follows it in detail. It is hence not surprising that Unferð has his counterpart in Edoras, in the shape of Wormtongue. His object of attack is Gandalf, and like Beowulf, Gandalf gives a good deal better than he gets, utterly discrediting Wormtongue. [pp. 154–5]

515 (II: 119): 'Go, Éowyn sister-daughter!'

515 (II: 119). Éowyn sister-daughter – *Éowyn* means 'joy or delight in horses', from Old English *eoh* 'horse' + *wyn* 'delight, pleasure'. Éowyn is the daughter of Théoden's sister Théodwyn and her husband Éomund. Théoden took her into his house with her brother Éomer after the early deaths of their parents.

515 (II: 119): The woman turned

515 (II: 119). girt with silver – With a silver belt.

515 (II: 119). Thus Aragorn for the first time . . . beheld Éowyn . . . and thought her fair, fair and cold – For some time while writing this part of *The Lord of the Rings* Tolkien intended that Aragorn and Éowyn should marry. Only later did he develop the story that Éowyn loved Aragorn, but he did not return her love because he was already betrothed to Arwen.

515–16 (II: 120): 'Dark have been my dreams

516 (II: 120). the high hall which Brego son of Eorl built – The great hall Meduseld, from which they have just come, was built by Brego, the second ruler of the Riddermark, and completed in Third Age 2569. *Brego* is Old English 'ruler, prince, king'.

516 (II: 121): 'Verily,' said Gandalf

516 (II: 121). that way lies our hope, where sits our greatest fear. Doom hangs still on a thread. Yet hope there is still, if we can but stand unconquered for a little while. – These words seem to suggest that Gandalf told Théoden about the Ring and Frodo, yet on p. 521, II: 126 Gandalf says to Théoden that Éomer's actions saved from Saruman 'two members of my Company, sharers of a secret hope, of which even to you, lord, I cannot yet speak openly'. In an early version of the chapter Tolkien wrote:

> [Gandalf's] voice was low and secret, and yet to those beside him keen and clear. Of Sauron he told, and the lady Galadriel, and of Elrond in Rivendell far away, of the Council and the setting forth of the Company of Nine, and all the perils of their road. 'Four only have come thus far,' he said. 'One is lost, Boromir prince of Gondor. Two were captured, but are free. And two have gone upon a dark Quest. Look eastward, Theoden! Into the heart of menace they have gone: two small folk, such as you in Rohan deem but the matter of children's tales. Yet doom hangs upon them. Our hope is with them – hope, if we can but stand meanwhile! [*The Treason of Isengard*, pp. 445–6]

The phrase *doom hangs still on a thread* alludes to the story of Damocles, above whose head at a banquet a sword was suspended by a thread (representing the 'happiness' of the tyrant Dionysius of Syracuse), thus 'the Sword of Damocles' as a reference to impending danger.

516–17 (II: 121): The other too now turned

516 (I: 121). Where now was the Ring-bearer? – Frodo by now has reached the south side of the Dead Marshes and is resting, hidden, by day.

516–17 (II: 121). that he caught a glint of white . . . on the pinnacle of the Tower of Guard. And further still . . . a tiny tongue of flame – If

Legolas could really see some 300 miles to Minas Tirith (as the crow flies) and over 370 to Mount Doom, Elvish sight was certainly far superior to that of humans.

517 (II: 121): Slowly Théoden sat down

517 (II: 121). The young perish and the old linger, withering. – In the First World War the young Tolkien witnessed the death of many of his fellow soldiers. R. Cary Gilson, Chief Master of King Edward's School, Birmingham which Tolkien had attended, and whose son, Robert Q. Gilson, was killed on the first day of the Battle of the Somme, wrote to Tolkien: 'Would to God that we men "past military age" could go and do this business instead of you young fellows. We have had a good innings: there would be little difficulty in "declaring"' (quoted in John Garth, *Tolkien and the Great War* (2003), p. 183). In the Second World War, Tolkien was one of the 'old' worrying about his sons and seeing the bereavements suffered by his Oxford colleagues.

517 (II: 122): *Arise now, arise, Riders of Théoden!*

517 (II: 122). *Arise now . . .* – Tom Shippey has suggested that this 'call to arms' is influenced by Hnæf's call in the Old English *Finnesburg Fragment*: 'Awaken now, my warriors! Grasp your coats of mail, think of deeds of valour, bear yourselves proudly, be resolute!' (translation in J.R.R. Tolkien, *Finn and Hengest: The Fragment and the Episode* (1982), p. 147).

517 (II: 122). Eorlingas – The people of Eorl, the Rohirrim, from *Eorl* + Old English *-ingas* 'people'.

518 (II: 122): *Westu Théoden hál!*

518 (II: 122). *Westu Théoden hál!* – 'May you be healthy, Théoden'. Beowulf greets Hrothgar with the words 'Wæs þu, Hrōðgār, hāl!' (*Beowulf*, l. 407).

518 (II: 123): 'Hope, yes,' said Gandalf

518 (II: 123). the Hold of Dunharrow – 'A fortified refuge in the White Mountains' (*Index*). *Dunharrow* is a

> modernization of 'actual' Rohan *Dūnhærg* 'the heathen fane [temple] on the hillside', so-called because this refuge of the Rohirrim at the head of *Harrowdale* was on the site of a sacred place of the old inhabitants (now the Dead Men). The element *hærg* can be modernized in English because it remains an element in place-names, notably *Harrow* (*on the Hill*). The word has no connexion with the [agricultural] implement *harrow*. . . . [*Nomenclature*]

518 (II: 123): 'Nay, Gandalf!'

518 (II: 123). Nay, Gandalf! . . . You do not know your own skill in healing. It shall not be so. I myself will go to war, to fall in the front of

battle, if it must be. Thus shall I sleep better. – In December 1954 Hugh Brogan wrote to Tolkien, criticizing the archaic narrative style of parts of *The Two Towers*, especially the chapter 'The King of the Golden Hall'. In September 1955 Tolkien drafted a reply in which he commented on

> the pain that I always feel when anyone – in an age when almost all auctorial manhandling of English is permitted (especially if disruptive) in the name of art or 'personal expression' – immediately dismisses out of court deliberate 'archaism'. The proper use of 'tushery' is to apply it to the kind of bogus 'medieval' stuff which attempts (without knowledge) to give a supposed temporal colour with expletives, such as *tush, pish, zounds, marry*, and the like. But a real archaic English is far more *terse* than modern; also many of things said could not be said in our slack and often frivolous idiom. Of course, not being specially well read in modern English, and far more familiar with works in the ancient and 'middle' idioms, my own ear is to some extent affected; so that though I could easily recollect how a modern would put this or that, what comes easiest to mind or pen is not quite that. But take an example from the chapter that you specially singled out. . . . 'Nay, Gandalf!' said the King. 'You do not know your own skill in healing. It shall not be so. I myself will go to war, to fall in the front of the battle, if it must be. Thus shall I sleep better.'
>
> This is a fair sample – moderated or watered archaism. Using only words that still are used or known to the educated, the King would really have said: 'Nay, thou (n')wost not thine own skill in healing. It shall not be so. I myself will go to war, to fall . . .' etc. I know well enough what a modern would say. 'Not at all my dear G. You don't know your own skill as a doctor. Things aren't going to be like that. I shall go to war in person, even if I have to be one of the first casualties' – and then what? Theoden would certainly think, and probably say 'thus shall I sleep better'! But people who think like that just do not talk a modern idiom. You can have 'I shall lie easier in my grave', or 'I should sleep sounder in my grave like that rather than if I stayed at home' – if you like. But there would be an insincerity of thought, a disunion of word and meaning. For a King who spoke in a modern style would not really think in such terms at all, and any reference to sleeping quietly in the grave would be a deliberate archaism of expression on his part (however worded) far more bogus than the actual 'archaic' English that I have used. Like some non-Christian making a reference to some Christian belief which did not in fact move him at all. [*Letters*, pp. 225–6]

519 (II: 123): 'Here, lord, is Herugrim

519 (II: 123). Herugrim – 'Very fierce or cruel, savage', from Old English *heorugrim*.

519 (II: 124): 'If this is bewitchment'

519 (II: 124). leechcraft – Archaic 'art of healing', but here used ironically: Wormtongue's aim was not to heal, but to disable. Physicians once commonly treated patients by 'bleeding' them through the application of leeches.

520 (II: 124): 'Nay, Éomer, you do not fully understand

520 (II: 124). Down, snake! . . . Down on your belly! – An echo of Genesis 2:14: 'And the Lord God said unto the serpent, Because thou hast done this . . . upon thy belly thou shalt go.'

520 (II: 125): 'That word comes too oft and easy

520 (II: 125). To slay it would be just. But it was not always as it now is. – As before with Gollum (in speaking with Frodo), and later with Saruman, Gandalf advocates mercy. Near the end of the story, Frodo will do the same with Saruman and Wormtongue.

521 (II: 126): 'How far back his treachery goes

521 (II: 126). He was not always evil. Once I do not doubt that he was the friend of Rohan – In a note to *The Battles of the Fords of Isen* it is said that after the invasions and other troubles of Third Age 2758–9, both Rohan and Gondor welcomed Saruman's offer 'to take command of Isengard and repair it and reorder it as part of the defences of the West'.

> There can be little doubt that Saruman made his offer in good faith, or at least with good will towards the defence of the West, so long as he himself remained the chief person in that defence, and the head of its council. He was wise, and perceived clearly that Isengard with its position and its great strength, natural and by craft, was of utmost importance. The line of the Isen, between the pincers of Isengard and the Hornburg, was a bulwark against invasion from the East (whether incited and guided by Sauron, or otherwise), either aiming at encircling Gondor or at invading Eriador. But in the end he turned to evil and became an enemy; and yet the Rohirrim, though they had warnings of his growing malice towards them, continued to put their main strength in the west at the Fords, until Saruman in open war showed them that the Fords were small protection without Isengard and still less against it. [*Unfinished Tales*, p. 373]

521 (II: 126): 'I owe much to Éomer'

521 (II: 126). Faithful heart may have froward tongue. – In the edition of 1994 'froward' was mistakenly reset as 'forward'. The correct reading was restored in the edition of 2004. *Froward* means 'contrary, perverse'.

522 (II: 126): 'Say also,' said Gandalf

522 (II: 126). to crooked eyes truth may wear a wry face – *Wry* in this sense means 'distorted, crooked'.

522 (II: 127): Now men came bearing raiment of war

522 (II: 127). Helms too they chose – In further response to Hugh Brogan's criticisms of the present chapter, Tolkien wrote in his draft letter of September 1955 that the text on this page is

> an example of 'archaism' that cannot be defended as 'dramatic', since it is not in dialogue, but the author's description of the arming of the guests – which seemed specially to upset you. But such 'heroic' scenes do not occur in a modern setting to which a modern idiom belongs. Why deliberately ignore, refuse to use the wealth of English which leaves us a choice of styles – without any possibility of unintelligibility.
>
> I can see no more reason for not using the much *terser* and more vivid ancient *style*, than for changing the obsolete weapons, helms, shields, hauberks into modern uniforms.
>
> 'Helms too they chose' is archaic. Some (wrongly) class it as an 'inversion', since normal order is 'They also chose helmets' or 'they chose helmets too'. (Real mod[ern] E[nglish] 'They also picked out some helmets and round shields'.) But this is not normal order, and if mod[ern] E[nglish] has lost the trick of putting a word desired to emphasize (for pictorial, emotional or logical reasons) into prominent first place, without addition of a lot of little 'empty' words (as the Chinese say), so much the worse for it. And so much the better for it the sooner it learns the trick again. And *some* one must begin the teaching, by example. [*Letters*, p. 226]

522 (II: 127). Mountain in the North – Erebor, the Lonely Mountain.

522 (II: 127). the running horse, white upon green, that was the emblem of the House of Eorl – The *Oxford English Dictionary* notes (under *horse*) that the white horse is 'reputed (by later writers) as the ensign of the Saxons when they invaded Britain, and the heraldic ensign of Brunswick, Hanover, and Kent'.

522 (II: 127): The king now rose

522 (II: 127). *Ferthu Théoden hál!* – 'May you go forth, Théoden, in health.'

523–4 (II: 128): Gimli walked with Legolas

524 (II: 128). saddlebow – The arched front part of a saddle.

524 (II: 129): At the gate they found a great host of men

524 (II: 129). Snowmane – 'A meaningful name (of King Théoden's horse [i.e. presumably it has white hair along its neck]), but (like *Shadowfax*) translated into modern English form, for [Old English] *snāw-mana*' (*Nomenclature*).

525 (II: 130): The trumpets sounded

525 (II: 130). the last host of Rohan rode thundering into the West – According to *Scheme*:

> A[ragorn] and Gandalf reach Meduseld about 8.30. They interview King Théoden about 10.30 a.m. (Thunder passes over from East at 11 a.m.)
>
> King Théoden is healed by Gandalf. Pardons Éomer. Host of Rohan is mustered; sets out [at] 2 p.m. Camps in plain, 50 miles W[est] of *Edoras* at night.
>
> Wormtongue flies to Isengard (about 1 p.m.): on an old slow horse. Saruman, informed by spies (birds) of riding of Théoden sends out his whole army about 10.30 that night.
>
> Second Battle of Isen Fords. Erkenbrand of Westfold is defeated & retreats towards *Helm's Deep* (night of 2/3 March), sending remaining *horsemen* away back to Edoras.

Chapter 7

HELM'S DEEP

For drafts and history of this chapter, see *The War of the Ring*, pp. 8–24.

526 (II: 131): The host rode on

526 (II: 131). the fords of the Isen – 'Fords from and to an eyot in Isen over which the road from Edoras to Isengard passed' (*Index*). The Sindarin name of the Fords is said in *Cirion and Eorl and the Friendship of Gondor and Rohan* to be *Athrad Angren*; in *The Rivers and Beacon-hills of Gondor* it is given in the plural, *Ethraid Engrin*.

526 (II: 131): Night closed about them

526 (II: 131). They had ridden for some five hours – It is now about 7.00 p.m. According to *Scheme* the host camped after riding 50 miles, which is indeed less than half of the some 120 miles ('forty leagues and more') between Edoras and the fords of the Isen.

526 (II: 131). bivouac – An open encampment, without tents.

526 (II: 131). At dawn the horns sounded – It is 3 March 1419.

526 (II: 131): There were no clouds

526 (II: 131). another darkness . . . a shadow crept down slowly from the Wizard's Vale – *Scheme* notes: 'Gandalf sees shadow of Huorns over Nan Gurunír [earlier form of Curunír]'.

527 (II: 132): As the second day of their riding

527 (II: 132). Thrihyrne – 'A mountain with three peaks, a northward arm of the White Mts. at the head of the glen of Helm's Deep' (*Index*). The name derives from Old English *þrī* 'three' + *hyrne* 'horn, corner, angle' (*þrī-hyrne* 'three-cornered, triangular').

527 (II: 132): He came, a weary man

527 (II: 132). We were overmastered. The shield-wall was broken. – *Overmastered* 'mastered completely, conquered'.

In notes to his edition of *The Battle of Maldon* (1937) E.V. Gordon describes the *shield-wall* as a battle tactic characteristic of Anglo-Saxon armies, who fought on foot rather than on horseback. It 'was a defensive formation made by ranks of men placed closely one behind another and holding their shields side by side and overlapping so as to present a continuous wall. The front rank of men held their shields before their breasts and the ranks behind held theirs over their heads to protect both those in front and themselves. This formation was probably from common Germanic tradition . . .' (p. 50). The Rohirrim may be unlike the Anglo-Saxons in that they are primarily cavalry, but they also fight on foot and use Anglo-Saxon tactics.

A more detailed account of the events referred to by the 'weary man' is given in *The Battles of the Fords of Isen* (*Unfinished Tales*, pp. 360–4). After the death of Théodred, Erkenbrand occupied himself with the gathering of men in the Westfold, towards the preparation of Helm's Deep against attack. He gave command in the field to Grimbold, who thought that the Fords should be manned: for if Saruman learned that all of the opposing forces were on the east bank, he might send another army down the west bank, cross the Fords, and attack the Rohirrim from the rear. But Elfhelm, who had independent command of the Muster of Edoras, felt that Saruman would send his army down the east side of the river Isen, a slower approach but one which avoided forcing the passage of the Fords, and therefore advised that the Fords be abandoned and men placed on the east side of the river to hold up the enemy's advance.

A compromise was struck: Grimbold's foot-soldiers manned the western end of the Fords, while he and the rest of his men and cavalry remained on the east bank; and Elfhelm withdrew his Riders to a position where he wished the main defence to stand. Grimbold's forces at the Fords were attacked first during the day on 2 March, and by sunset were forced to withdraw to the east bank. But Saruman's forces, whose departure from Isengard Merry describes to Aragorn, Legolas, and Gimli in Book III, Chapter 9, marched south on both sides of the Isen. Around midnight those on the west side swept over the Fords. Grimbold formed a great shield-wall, which held for a while. No help came from Elfhelm, who had been attacked by Saruman's army on the east and forced to retreat. Grimbold then realized that 'though his men might fight on till all were slain, and would if he ordered it, such valour would not help Erkenbrand: any man that could break out and escape southwards would be more useful, though he might seem inglorious' (p. 362). He therefore arranged a successful diversion, and 'so it was that the greater part of Grimbold's men survived' (p. 363), though they were scattered.

527 (II: 132). Erkenbrand of Westfold – The name *Erkenbrand* may be derived from Old English *eorcan* 'precious' (as also in *eorcan-stān* 'precious stone', thus the *Arkenstone* in *The Hobbit*) + Old English *brand* 'fire-brand, torch' or, metaphorically, 'sword'. In developing *The Lord of the Rings* Tolkien briefly considered *Erkenbrand*, rather than *Aragorn*, as a name for Trotter.

Westfold is 'the slopes and fields between Thrihyrne and Edoras' (*Index*); see also note for p. 803.

527 (II: 132). Helm's Deep – *Deep* in this sense means 'cavity': 'a deep gorge in the White Mountains' (*Index*). It was named after the ninth King of the Mark, Helm Hammerhand, who took refuge there in Third Age 2758–9 when Rohan was invaded by the Dunlendings.

Among his working drawings for *The Lord of the Rings*, Tolkien made a sketch-plan of Helm's Deep and an illustration, *Helm's Deep & the Hornburg* (*Artist and Illustrator*, figs. 160–1).

527 (II: 132): Théoden had sat silent

527 (II: 132). Ceorl – The Old English word for a freeman of the lowest class, countryman, husbandman. The *Oxford English Dictionary* comments on *ceorl*: 'In the Old English constitution: A man simply without rank; a member of the third or lowest rank of freemen'; and that after the Norman Conquest the word came to mean 'a tenant in pure villeinage; a serf, a bondsman. (The position to which most of the O.E. ceorlas were reduced.)'

528 (II: 133): 'Ride, Théoden!'

528 (II: 133). Helm's Gate – 'The entrance to Helm's Deep guarded by the Hornburg' (*Index*).

528 (II: 133): He spoke a word to Shadowfax

528 (II: 133). Even as they looked he was gone – According to *Scheme*: 'At sunset Gandalf leaves host and rides on Shadowfax to Isengard. Arrives at nightfall. Stays only 20 minutes to speak to Treebeard & then rides to help of Erkenbrand.' According to *The Battles of the Fords of Isen*:

> [Gandalf] received news of the disaster [the defeat of the Riders at the Fords] only in the late afternoon of March the 3rd. The King was then at a point not far east of the junction of the Road with the branch going to the Hornburg. From there it was about ninety miles in a direct line to Isengard; and Gandalf must have ridden there with the greatest speed that Shadowfax could command. He reached Isengard in the early darkness, and left again in no more than twenty minutes. [*Unfinished Tales*, pp. 363–4]

Both the original general map of Middle-earth and the revised map of 1980 agree with a distance of about ninety miles from near the Deeping-coomb to Isengard. But in Book III, Chapter 8, Gandalf says that from a point near the mouth of the Deeping-coomb to Isengard is about 'fifteen leagues [forty-five miles]' as the crow flies to Isengard, 'five [fifteen miles] from the mouth of Deeping-coomb to the Fords; and ten more [thirty miles] from there to the gates of Isengard' (p. 548, II: 154). These shorter distances appear not only in the published text, but also in calculations made by Tolkien while writing the narrative (with little or no variation). See also note for p. 548.

528 (II: 133): The host turned away

528 (II: 133). on the far side of the Westfold Vale, a great bay in the mountains, lay a green coomb – In editions prior to 2004 this passage read: 'on the far side of the Westfold Vale, lay a green coomb, a great bay in the mountains'. The current, correct reading is clear in the manuscript of this chapter, but somehow became partly inverted in typescript. See *The War of the Ring*, p. 12.

528–9 (II: 133–4): At Helm's Gate

528 (II: 133). the Hornburg – 'A fortress on a rocky eminence at the mouth of Helm's Deep' (*Index*). *Hornburg*, and *Hornrock*, 'are so called because of Helm's great horn, supposed still at times to be heard blowing' (*Nomenclature*).

528 (II: 134). culvert – An underground channel for carrying water.

528 (II: 134). Deeping-stream – 'Stream flowing out of Helm's Deep & over into the Westfold' (*Index*). As first published, the name was spelt 'Deeping Stream'; it was emended in the fifth printing (1977) of the Unwin Books three-volume paperback edition. In *Nomenclature* (under *Deeping-coomb*) Tolkien notes that '*Deeping* is not a verbal ending, but one indicating relationship', thus *Deeping-stream* is the stream associated with the Deep.

529 (II: 134). gore – In this context, a triangular piece of land.

529 (II: 134). Helm's Dike – 'An earth wall defending the upland before Helm's Deep' (*Index*).

529 (II: 134). Deeping-coomb – 'The coomb or deep valley belonging to the *Deep* (*Helm's Deep*) to which it led up' (*Nomenclature*). As first published, the name was spelt 'Deeping Coomb'; it was emended in the fifth printing (1977) of the Unwin Books three-volume paperback edition, in accordance with the reference in *Nomenclature.*

529–30 (II: 135): Aragorn and Legolas went now

529 (II: 135). van – A shortened form of *vanguard*, the foremost unit of an advancing military force.

530 (II: 135): The rumour of war

530 (II: 135). rumour – In this sense, clamour, noise.

530 (II: 135): 'They bring fire'

530 (II: 135). rick, cot, and tree – A *rick* is 'a stack of hay, corn, peas, etc., especially one regularly built and thatched' (*OED*). Saruman's army is setting fire to haystacks, cottages, trees – anything that will burn.

530 (II: 135): 'We need not fly

530 (II: 135). rampart – 'A mound of earth raised for the defence of a place . . . wide enough on the top for the passage of troops' (*OED*).

530–1 (II: 136): 'Maybe, we have a thousand

530 (II: 136). Gamling – In *Nomenclature* Tolkien notes that *Gamling* 'the Old', is

> a name of one of the Rohirrim . . . like one or two other names in Rohan, as *Shadowfax*, *Wormtongue*, etc., it has been slightly anglicized and modernized. It should be *Gameling* (with short *ă*). It would be one of the words and names that hobbits recognized as similar to their own, since it is an English (= Common Speech) name, probably the origin of the surname *Gamlen*, *Gam(b)lin*, etc. Cf. *The Tale of Gamelin*, a medieval poem from which ultimately was derived part of Shakespeare's *As You Like It*. (It is derived from the stem *gamal-* 'old', the normal word in Scandinavian languages, but only found in Old English in verse-language and in Old High German only as an element in personal names.)

531 (II: 136): Quickly Éomer set his men

531 (II: 136). Deeping Wall – 'The wall closing entrance to Helm's Deep' (*Index*).

531 (II: 136–7): The Deeping Wall stood twenty feet high

531 (II: 136). parapet – A low wall to shelter troops.

531 (II: 137): Gimli stood leaning against the breastwork

531 (II: 137). breastwork – Usually a temporary low wall erected for defence; in this context, the 'parapet over which only a tall man could look' as described in the preceding paragraph, a defensive wall on top of the Deeping Wall. Gimli, well short of a tall man, is leaning against the parapet, Legolas is sitting on top of it.

532 (II: 137–8): It was now past midnight

532 (II: 137). It was now past midnight – It is 4 March 1419.

532 (II: 138). sable – The heraldic term for 'black'.

533 (II: 138): Brazen trumpets sounded

533 (II: 138). brazen – Brass.

533 (II: 138). blazoned – Painted in a heraldic manner.

533 (II: 139): Running like fire

533 (II: 139). postern-door – In fortifications, a door usually in the angle or the flank, used for small sorties.

533 (II: 139): 'Gúthwinë!' cried Éomer

533 (II: 139). Gúthwinë – The name of Éomer's sword, from Old English *gūþ* 'war, battle, fight' + *wine* 'friend'.

534 (II: 139): For a moment

534 (II: 139). storm-wrack – The remains of the storm.

534 (II: 139): 'We did not come too soon

534 (II: 139). The doors will not withstand another such battering. – These words were omitted in all editions prior to 2004. In *The War of the Ring* Christopher Tolkien notes that they were present in the final manuscript, but 'were left out of the typescript that followed, but there is nothing in the manuscript to suggest that they should be, and it seems clear that their omission was an error (especially since they give point to Éomer's reply: "Yet we cannot stay here beyond the walls to defend them")' (p. 20).

534 (II: 139): They turned and ran

534 (II: 139). *Baruk Khazâd! Khazâd ai-mênu!* – Tolkien translates this in Appendix F (p. 1132, III: 411) as 'Axes of the Dwarves! The Dwarves are upon you'!' In *The War of the Ring* Christopher Tolkien comments that years later, after the publication of *The Lord of the Rings*, his father began an analysis of the various languages of Middle-earth, but these 'diminished to largely uninterpretable jottings. *Baruk* he here translated as "axes", without further comment; *ai-mênu* is analysed as *aya*, *mēnu*, but the meanings are not clearly legible: most probably *aya* "upon", *mēnu* "acc[usative] pl[ural] you"' (p. 20).

534–5 (II: 140): There may be many

535 (II: 140). Till now I have hewn naught but wood since I left Moria. – Gimli's statement cannot be true if one accepts the words of Legolas at Parth Galen in Book III, Chapter 1: 'We [Legolas and Gimli] have hunted and slain many Orcs in the woods' (p. 414, II: 16). See further, comments by Christopher Tolkien, *The War of the Ring*, pp. 20–1; 24, n. 21. When preparing the text of the 2004 edition, it was decided that Gimli's statement was too famous to be omitted, and that if 'Moria' (referring to events two months earlier at this point in the story) were emended to 'Parth Galen' (events only a week before) it would suggest too great a bloodthirstiness for Gimli's character.

535 (II: 140): The sky now was quickly

535 (II: 140). the sinking moon – The moon is four nights before full, and will set several hours before dawn.

536 (II: 142): 'But these creatures of Isengard

536 (II: 142). quail – In this sense, to lose heart, feel fear or apprehension.

536–7 (II: 142): 'Yet there are many that cry

537 (II: 142). Forgoil – Evidently the only word in the Dunland tongue to appear in Tolkien's published works.

537 (II: 142): 'Devilry of Saruman!'

537 (II: 142). fire of Orthanc – A 'blasting fire' as later described, some form of explosives. Saruman has developed modern weaponry: compare the 'liquid fire' with which he attacks the ents at Isengard, described in Book III, Chapter 9.

539 (II: 145): The Orcs yelled and jeered

539 (II: 145). skulking – Hiding, keeping out of sight.

540 (II: 145): 'Get down or we will shoot you

540 (II: 145). parley – A conference with an enemy, under truce.

542 (II: 147): The hosts of Isengard

542 (II: 147). reeled – Wavered, became unsteady.

Chapter 8

THE ROAD TO ISENGARD

For drafts and history of this chapter, see *The War of the Ring*, pp. 25–46.

543 (II: 148): 'That may be

543 (II: 148). and the stout legs of the Westfold-men marching through the night – In *The Battles of the Fords of Isen*, after recording Gandalf's brief visit to Isengard on 3 March, it is said that

> both on the outward journey, when his direct route would take him close to the Fords, and on his return south to find Erkenbrand, he [Gandalf] must have met Grimbold and Elfhelm. They were convinced that he was acting for the King, not only by his appearance on Shadowfax, but also by his knowledge of the name of the errand-rider, Ceorl, and the message that he brought; and they took as orders the advice that he gave. Grimbold's men he sent southward to join Erkenbrand. . . . [*Unfinished Tales*, p. 364]

544 (II: 149): 'Then if not yours

544 (II: 149). sage – In this sense, a wise man.

544–5 (II: 149–50): The King then chose men

544 (II: 150). There the Lord of the Mark would hold an assembly of all that could bear arms, on the third day after the full moon. – In editions prior to 2005 the assembly was on the *second* day after the full moon. This error, and two others concerning the assembly or muster in relation to the securely established dates of the full moon on the night of 7/8 March and the muster on 10 March, were overlooked as the story developed and the chronology of events shifted. See also notes for pp. 778 and 792, and discussion by Christopher Tolkien in *The War of the Ring*, pp. 321–2.

545 (II: 150): In the midst of the field

545 (II: 150). East Dales – The Eastfold; see note for p. 803.

545 (II: 150). But the men of Dunland were set apart in a mound below the Dike. – This sentence was not present in editions prior to 2004. In *The War of the Ring* Christopher Tolkien notes that in the fair copy of the present chapter

> in the account of the burials after the battle of the Hornburg, there were not only the two mounds raised over the fallen Riders: following the words 'and those of the Westfold upon the other' . . . there stands

in the manuscript 'But the men of Dunland were set apart in a mound below the Dike' (a statement that goes back through the first complete manuscript to the original draft of the passage . . .). This sentence was inadvertently omitted in the following typescript (not made by my father), and the error was never observed. [p. 40]

546 (II: 151): The sun was already drawing near

546 (II: 151). The sun was already drawing near the hills . . . when at last Théoden and Gandalf and their companions rode down from the Dike. – According to *Scheme*, they set out at 3.30 p.m.

547 (II: 152): 'And I would give gold

547 (II: 152). And I would give gold to be excused . . . and double to be let out, if I strayed in! – Some readers have found Legolas's statement puzzling, since in *The Hobbit*, Chapter 8, the king of the Elves of Mirkwood, and presumably his son Legolas, lived in a 'great cave, from which countless smaller ones opened out on every side, [and which] wound far underground and had many passages and wide halls'. Moreover, 'it was lighter and more wholesome than any goblin-dwelling, and neither so deep nor so dangerous'. It is also said, however, that 'the subjects of the king mostly lived and hunted in the open woods, and had houses or huts on the ground and in the branches. . . . The king's cave was his palace, and the strong place of his treasure, and the fortress of his people against their enemies.'

547 (II: 152): 'You have not seen

547 (II: 152). where your King dwells under the hills in Mirkwood, and Dwarves helped in their making long ago – This seems to be the only mention that Dwarves helped to make the Elven-king's halls; but in 'The Silmarillion' it is told how dwarves of the First Age helped to build the two great underground strongholds of the Elves: Menegroth for Thingol, and Nargothrond for Finrod.

547 (II: 152). hovels – Squalid or poorly constructed dwellings.

547 (II: 152). immeasurable halls, filled with an everlasting music of water that tinkles into pools – On 4 February 1971 Tolkien wrote to P. Rorke, S.J., that Gimli's description of the Caverns of Helm's Deep 'was based on the caves in Cheddar Gorge and was written just after I had revisited these in 1940 but was still coloured by my memory of them much earlier before they became so commercialized. I had been there during my honeymoon nearly thirty years before' (*Letters*, p. 407). The Cheddar Caves, in the Cheddar Gorge in Somerset, are famous for their beauty, with groups of fantastic stalactites and stalagmites, and other limestone formations, reflected in pools.

547–8 (II: 152–3): 'And, Legolas, when the torches

547 (II: 153). saffron – Orange-yellow, the colour of the spice *saffron.*

548 (II: 154): 'About fifteen leagues

548 (II: 154). About fifteen leagues, as the crows of Saruman make it . . . five from the mouth of the Deeping-coomb to the Fords; and ten more from there to the gates of Isengard. – Some early drafts and working papers for *The Lord of the Rings* indicate a shorter journey to Isengard, but later texts, time-schemes, and calculations by Tolkien of journeys and distances give (with little or no variation) the distances in the published text. These agree with the 40 leagues or more (over 120 miles) from Edoras to the Fords of Isen, given at the beginning of Book III, Chapter 7, and with details of Théoden's ride: he and those with him were 50 miles from Edoras when they halted on 2 March, and on the following day they were close to the Deeping-coomb (15 miles from the Fords) as the sun began to set, having presumably covered at least another 55 miles. The distance from Edoras to the Fords on both the original general map of Middle-earth and the revised map of 1980 seems to be about 120 miles. On both maps, however, the distance from the mouth of the Deeping-coomb to the Fords is much more than 15 miles, and the distance from the Fords to Isengard is little more than that from the mouth of the Deeping-coomb to the Fords. In *The War of the Ring* Christopher Tolkien comments that the working map on which he based his 1943 map (the basis in turn for the 1954 map) 'is here very difficult to interpret and I have probably not placed Helm's Deep at precisely the point my father intended' (p. 78, n. 2).

548 (II: 154): 'I do not know myself

548 (II: 154). the Glittering Caves of Aglarond – *Glittering Caves* is a 'translation' of *Aglarond.* In the manuscript of *Nomenclature* Tolkien notes '*aglar* "brilliance" + *rond* "vault, high roofed cavern"'.

549 (II: 154): Even as he spoke

549 (II: 154). their legs in their long paces beat quicker than the heron's wings – See note for p. 470.

550 (II: 155): 'Yet also I should be sad'

550 (II: 155). For however the fortune of war shall go, may it not so end that much that was fair and wonderful shall pass for ever out of Middle-earth? – Théoden foresees truly. Tom Shippey comments:

> The whole history of Middle-earth seems to show that good is attained only at vast expense while evil recuperates almost at will. . . . And even if [the crisis at the end of the Third Age] is surmounted, it is made extremely clear that this success too will conform to the general pattern of 'fruitlessness' – or maybe one should say that its fruit will be bitter.

> Destruction of the Ring, says Galadriel, will mean that her ring and Gandalf's and Elrond's will also lose their power, so that Lothlórien 'fades' and the elves 'dwindle'. Along with them will go the ents and the dwarves, indeed the whole imagined world of Middle-earth, to be replaced by modernity and the domination of men; all the characters and their story, one might say, will shrink to poetic 'rigmaroles' and misunderstood snatches in plays and ballads. Beauty especially will be a casualty. [*The Road to Middle-earth*, 2nd edn., pp. 139–40]

550 (II: 157): 'With the help of Shadowfax

550 (II: 157). Some men I sent with Grimbold of Westfold to join Erkenbrand. Some I set to make this burial. They have now followed your marshal, Elfhelm. I sent him with many Riders to Edoras. – As first published this passage read: 'Some of them I sent to join Erkenbrand; some I set to this labour that you see, and they by now have gone back to Edoras. Many others also I sent thither before to guard your house.' It was revised in the second printing (1967) of the Allen & Unwin second edition.

553 (II: 158): At dawn they made ready

553 (II: 158). At dawn – It is 5 March 1419. According to *The Tale of Years* they reach Isengard at noon.

555 (II: 160–1): A strong place and wonderful

555 (II: 161). suffered no rival – *Suffered* in this sense means 'tolerated'.

556 (II: 162): 'Welcome, my lords

556 (II: 162). Saradoc – *Saradoc* as the name of Merry's father in draft replaced *Caradoc*, a Welsh name in accordance with Tolkien's decision that Buckland names should have a vaguely 'Celtic' style. Caradoc of Llancarfan wrote a life of St. Gildas, the first known text (*c.* 1130) to associate King Arthur with Glastonbury, and another Caradoc is the hero of the *Livre de Caradoc*, part of the First Continuation of Chrétien de Troyes' *Perceval* (*c.* 1200).

556 (II: 162). Paladin – The name of Pippin's father accords with Tolkien's decision to give names of Frankish or Gothic origin to some members of older families. *Paladin* is a term used to describe 'any of the twelve peers of Charlemagne's court', and by extension 'a knight renowned for heroism and chivalry' (*Concise OED*).

557 (II: 162): 'And what about

557 (II: 162). you woolly-footed and wool-pated – *Woolly-footed* is obviously descriptive of Hobbits' hairy feet; *wool-pated* accurately describes Merry and Pippin's *pates* 'heads', particularly after ent-draughts have curled their hair in Book III, Chapter 4, but it is also a synonym for *dull-witted*, hence a friendly insult. Compare Butterbur's 'Nob, you woolly-pated ninny' in Book VI, Chapter 7 (p. 990, III: 269).

557 (II: 162). Hammer and tongs – An appropriate exclamation for a Dwarf, whose people are renowned for working in metal, but the phrase exists also in English as an adverb meaning 'enthusiastically'.

557 (II: 163): The Riders laughed

557 (II: 163). Holbytlan – Here Tolkien originally wrote *holbylta(n)*, then changed it to *holbytlan*. In *The War of the Ring* Christopher Tolkien comments that '*Holbytla* "Hole-builder" has the consonants *lt* (*Holbylta*) reversed, as in the closely related Old English *botl*, *boðl* beside *bold* "building"' (p. 44, n. 29). In the *1966 Index Holbytlan* is explained as the Rohan word for 'hole-dwellers'. See also note for p. 1.

558 (II: 163): 'That is not surprising

558 (II: 163). It was Tobold Hornblower of Longbottom in the Southfarthing – In the draft of this chapter Merry continued this history with much detail concerning pipe-weed and smoking, but the passage was removed to the Preface; see notes for pp. 8–9.

Chapter 9

FLOTSAM AND JETSAM

For drafts and history of this chapter, see *The War of the Ring*, pp. 47–60.

560 (II: 165). [chapter title] – *Flotsam and jetsam* now means 'odds and ends' or 'useless or discarded items', but properly 'wreckage and other goods found in the sea'. *Flotsam* denotes floating wreckage, and *jetsam* discarded goods washed ashore.

561 (II: 166): 'And you need not turn up your nose

561 (II: 166). broil – Cook food by placing it on a fire or grill.

561 (II: 166): The three were soon busy

561 (II: 166). unabashed – Without embarrassment.

563 (II: 168): 'The fifth of March

563 (II: 168). I reckon that three very horrible days followed – Merry and Pippin were captured at about noon on 26 February, and escaped just before dawn on 29 February.

564 (II: 169): 'Nothing else'

564 (II: 169). One who cannot cast away a treasure at need is in fetters. – A truism, but particularly pertinent in Tolkien's created world where again and again those who place too great value on their treasures end up losing them. The saying is also related to the idea of 'having one's hands tied', being unable to act freely.

564 (II: 169): 'All this about the Orcs

564 (II: 169). Grishnákh evidently sent some message across the River after the quarrel – See note for p. 451.

564 (II: 169). Saruman . . . is in a cleft stick of his own cutting – He is in a situation of his own making, in which any action he takes will have adverse consequences.

564 (II: 169): 'Five nights ago'

564 (II: 169). Five nights ago – This is 5 March 1419. Aragorn, Legolas, and Gimli saw Saruman on the evening of 30 February.

564–5 (II: 169–70): 'Let me see'

564 (II: 169–70). The next morning we went to Entmoot. . . . It lasted all that day and the next . . . then late in the afternoon in the third day – In October 1944 Tolkien solved a chronological problem in *The Lord of the Rings* by extending Entmoot by one day, but did not immediately notice all of the alterations made necessary as a consequence. It was only in the galley proofs that he added 'and the next' here; but for most of the first edition the text continued to read 'in the afternoon in the *second* day' (italics ours). Finally a reader wrote to Allen & Unwin to point out the discrepancy, and on 30 September 1955 Tolkien wrote to Philip Unwin:

> I am afraid your correspondent is correct, and this detail somehow escaped when I completely overhauled the chronology. On p. 170 line 3 read *third* for *second*. The correct chronology is given in Appendix B, Vol. III, p. 373. The technical reason is that originally the Entmoot broke up (or was said to break up) on the second day; but that was found not to fit events elsewhere. An extra day was inserted on page 88 of Vol. II, and 'second' was overlooked: I think because of the feeling that Entmoot had only lasted 2 full days. [Tolkien-George Allen & Unwin archive, HarperCollins]

The text was corrected at this point to 'third' in the fourth printing (1956), but apparently the type suffered damage and was replaced for the fifth printing (1957), but with the earlier reading 'second'. The correction was made again in the second edition (1965).

565 (II: 170): 'There is a great power in them

565 (II: 170). They still have voices, and can speak with the Ents – that is why they are called Huorns – The first element of *Huorn* could be derived from the base KHUG- 'bark, bay', which appears to be supported by unpublished etymological notes by Tolkien. The second element is unquestionably Sindarin *orn* 'tree'.

566 (II: 171): 'Then all at once

566 (II: 171). battalions – Used here probably in its more general sense 'large bodies of soldiers'.

566 (II: 171): 'I thought of him too'

566 (II: 171). It seems plain now that the Southerner was a spy of Saruman's; but whether he was working with the Black Riders, or for Saruman alone – See note for p. 155.

567 (II: 172): 'They pushed, pulled, tore

567 (II: 172). he has not much grit – Here *grit* is a colloquial word for 'courage, spirit, resolve'.

569–70 (II: 175): 'We were just wondering

570 (II: 175). It was already dark – As first published these words read: 'It was getting dark'. They were revised in the second printing (1967) of the Allen & Unwin second edition.

570 (II: 175): 'There was no need

570 (II: 175). 'Gandalf!' I said at last – Although the reader has known for several chapters of Gandalf's return, Pippin still believed that he had died in Moria.

570 (II: 175). tom-fool – 'A foolish or stupid person; one who behaves foolishly. (More emphatic than *fool*)' (*OED*).

570 (II: 175): 'Treebeard heard his voice

570 (II: 175). Gandalf obviously expected to find Treebeard here; and Treebeard might almost have been loitering about near the gates on purpose – In a note to *The Battles of the Fords of Isen* it is said that 'Gandalf must already have made contact with Treebeard, and knew that the patience of the Ents was at an end; and he had already read the meaning of Legolas' words [pp. 526–7, II: 132]: Isengard was veiled in an impenetrable shadow, the Ents had already surrounded it' (*Unfinished Tales*, p. 366, n. 16).

570 (II: 175). I remembered a queer look he gave us at the time. I can only suppose that he had seen Gandalf or had some news of him – In Book III, Chapter 4, when Merry and Pippin tell Treebeard of Gandalf's fall in Moria, he says: '"Hoo, come now! . . . Hoom, hm, ah well." He paused, looking long at the hobbits. "Hoom, ah, well I do not know what to say. Come now!" (p. 466, II: 69). In Book III, Chapter 5 Gandalf knows that Merry and Pippin are with Treebeard.

570 (II: 175): '"Hoom! Gandalf!"

570 (II: 175). stock and stone – Here *stock* means 'the trunk or woody stem of a living tree'. Compare Treebeard's 'by stock or by stone' in Book VI, Chapter 6. Tom Shippey discusses the significance of this phrase to *The Lord of the Rings* in *The Road to Middle-earth*, Chapter 6.

570 (II: 176): '"Wherever I have been

570 (II: 176). I must ride fast – See note for p. 528.

574 (II: 180): '"We want man-food

574 (II: 180). man-food for twenty-five – Actually there were twenty-six: Gandalf, Aragorn, Legolas, Gimli, Théoden, Éomer, and twenty men of Théoden's household, as described in Book III, Chapter 8. In a letter to *Amon Hen* 123 (September 1993) Denis Collins suggests that the ents miscounted because 'Legolas and Gimli were riding on the same horse and in the distance would have looked like a single rider' (p. 14).

Chapter 10

THE VOICE OF SARUMAN

For drafts and history of this chapter, see *The War of the Ring*, pp. 61–7.

576–7 (II: 181–2): 'And how will you learn that

576 (II: 181–2). Saruman could look like me in your eyes, if it suited his purpose with you. – Another expression of Saruman as 'dwimmer-crafty', a master of illusion.

577 (II: 182): 'The last is most likely

577 (II: 182). Beware of his voice! – In June 1958 Tolkien wrote to Forrest J. Ackerman that 'Saruman's voice was not hypnotic but persuasive. Those who listened to him were not in danger of falling into a trance, but of agreeing with his arguments, while fully awake. It was always open to one to reject, *by free will and reason*, both his voice while speaking and its after-impressions. Saruman corrupted the reasoning powers' (*Letters*, pp. 276–7).

577 (II: 182): On the eastern side

577 (II: 182). embrasures – Openings or recesses around the windows, forming enlargements of the area from inside.

578 (II: 183): The window closed

578 (II: 183). gainsaid – Contradicted, denied.

579 (II: 184): It was Gimli the dwarf

579 (II: 184). The words of this wizard stand on their heads – That is, his words say the opposite of what he really means.

579 (II: 184): 'Peace!' said Saruman

579 (II: 184). suave – Charming, confident, agreeable.

579 (II: 184). embroiled – Involved deeply.

579–80 (II: 185): 'Lord, hear me!'

579 (II: 186). an old liar with honey on his forked tongue – He is speaking sweetly, but lying. Compare Gandalf's words concerning Wormtongue, note for p. 514.

580 (II: 186). forsooth – In truth, truly.

580 (II: 186). Remember Théodred at the Fords, and the grave of Háma in Helms's Deep! – As first published this sentence read only: 'Remember the grave of Háma in Helm's Deep!' It was revised in the second edition (1965), but with 'Ford' instead of 'Fords' (corrected in the second printing (1967) of the Allen & Unwin second edition).

580 (II: 185–6): 'We will have peace'

580 (II: 185). gibbet – 'Originally synonymous with gallows, but in later use signifying an upright post with projecting arm from which the bodies of criminals were hung in chains or irons after execution' (*OED*).

580 (II: 186). I do not need to lick your fingers – An adaptation of the saying *to lick someone's boots*, to be abjectly servile.

581 (II: 186): 'Gibbets and crows!'

581 (II: 186). dotard – A senile old man.

581 (II: 186). brigands – A *brigand* is a bandit, one who lives by pillage and robbery.

581–2 (II: 187): So great was the power

582 (II: 187). elusive discourse – That is, a discussion difficult for the listener to follow.

582 (II: 187): 'Saruman, Saruman!'

582 (II: 187). the king's jester and earned your bread, and your stripes – Gandalf is suggesting that Saruman is fit to be only a jester or fool at the king's court, where he would be given food (*bread*), but also be whipped (received a *stripe* 'stroke from a whip') when he offended.

583 (II: 188): 'Reasons for leaving

583 (II: 188). the Key of Orthanc – According to a note to *The Battles of the Fords of Isen* the 'keys' of Orthanc had been entrusted to Saruman, when he took up residence there, by the then Steward of Gondor; see *Unfinished Tales*, p. 373.

583 (II: 188). your staff – See note for p. 279.

583 (II: 188): Saruman's face grew livid

583 (II: 188). the rods of the Five Wizards – Presumably the staffs of the five Istari. Saruman is implying that Gandalf wishes to have sole power among the Wizards.

583 (II: 188). and have purchased yourself a pair of boots many sizes larger than those you now wear – Saruman is accusing Gandalf of 'being too big for his boots', unduly self-confident, conceited.

583 (II: 188). rag-tag – Disreputable people, riffraff, rabble.

583 (II: 188–9): 'I did not give you leave to go'

583 (II: 188). gnaw the ends of your old plots – As a dog might gnaw a bone with no meat on it.

583–4 (II: 189): He raised his hand

584 (II: 189). The stair cracked and splintered in glittering sparks – The Ents, in contrast, had been able to make only a few scorings and flake-like splinters in the tough fabric of Orthanc.

584 (II: 189): 'Here, my lad, I'll take that!

584 (II: 189). It is not a thing, I guess, that Saruman would have chosen to cast away. – The words 'I guess' were added in the second printing (1967) of the Allen & Unwin second edition, the first of several emendations dealing with the *palantír* and what Gandalf knew about it. Writings by Tolkien on the history and use of the *palantíri*, produced while working on these revisions, are published as *The Palantíri* in *Unfinished Tales.*

584–5 (II: 190): 'Not likely'

585 (II: 190). riding the storm – A metaphorical use of a nautical term, denoting a ship which endures a storm, does not drag its anchor, and sustains no great damage.

585 (II: 190): 'I? Nothing!'

585 (II: 190). Strange are the turns of fortune! Often does hatred hurt itself! – The saying is similar in thought to the proverb *Curses, like chickens come home to roost*, a form of which appears in Chaucer's *Canterbury Tales.*

585 (II: 190). I guess that, even if we had entered in, we could have found few treasures in Orthanc more precious – In the text as first published Gandalf said 'I fancy that', not 'I guess that'. The phrase was revised in the second printing (1967) of the Allen & Unwin second edition.

On 7 June 1955 Tolkien wrote to W.H. Auden: 'I knew nothing of the *Palantíri*, though the moment the Orthanc-stone was cast from the window, I recognized it, and knew the meaning of the "rhyme of lore" that had been running in my mind: *seven stars and seven stones and one white tree.* These rhymes and names will crop up; but they do not always explain themselves' (*Letters*, p. 217).

586 (II: 192): 'No,' said Gandalf

586 (II: 192). weave again such webs as he can – Gandalf uses almost the same words to describe Saruman as Wormtongue used of Galadriel. Imagery of webs, weaving, and spiders are commonly used in an negative sense in *The Lord of the Rings.*

In a draft article written after interviewing Tolkien, Charlotte and Denis Plimmer reported him as saying that when C.S. Lewis said to him 'You can do better than that. Better, Tolkien, please!' he would try to do so. 'I'd sit down and write the section over and over. That happened with the scene I think is the best in the book, the confrontation between Gandalf and his rival wizard, Saruman, in the ravaged city of Isengard.' Having received a copy of the Plimmers' draft, Tolkien wrote to them on 8 February 1967:

> I do not think the Saruman passage 'the best in the book'. It is much better than the first draft, that is all. I mentioned the passage because it is in fact one of the very few places where in the event I found L[ewis]'s detailed criticisms useful and just. I cut out some passages of light-hearted hobbit conversation which he found tiresome, thinking that if he did most other readers (if any) would feel the same. I do not think the event has proved him right. To tell the truth he never really liked hobbits very much, least of all Merry and Pippin. But a great number of readers do, and would like more than they have got. [*Letters*, p. 376]

In fact no 'passages of light-hearted hobbit conversation' appear to have been discarded from the present chapter as published (see *The War of the Ring*, Part I, Chapter 5); but the previous chapter, 'Flotsam and Jetsam', in which Tolkien did delete some 'hobbit' material, as originally conceived continued into 'The Voice of Saruman'.

Chapter 11
THE PALANTÍR

For drafts and history of this chapter, see *The War of the Ring*, pp. 68–81.

588 (II: 193): 'So you heard that?'

588 (II: 193). Be thankful no longer words were aimed at you. He had his eyes on you. – As first published this passage read: 'Be thankful that no longer words were aimed at you. He had never met a hobbit before and did not know what kind of thing to say to you. But he had his eyes on you.' In the Ballantine Books edition (1965) the publisher failed to omit the second sentence as instructed (it was a shadow of an earlier idea, untrue according to the completed story), but correctly altered the third. The full revision was made in the Allen & Unwin second edition (1966).

589 (II: 194): 'Yes, we have won

589 (II: 194). There was some link between Isengard and Mordor, which I have not yet fathomed. – One of Tolkien's aims in the *Palantíri* writings associated with the second edition was to explain why the White Council, Gandalf in particular, had not given much thought to the danger the seeing-stones presented. Tolkien explains that when Minas Ithil was taken by the Ringwraiths in Third Age 2002, it was not known in Gondor whether the Ithil-stone had been destroyed or had fallen into Sauron's hands. For fear of the latter, the last kings of Gondor and the Stewards did not dare to use the other two *palantíri* of Gondor; and among their people the stones were generally forgotten or remembered only in legends or rhymes of lore that few understood.

> It is evident that at the time of the War of the Ring the Council had not long become aware of the doubt concerning the fate of the Ithil-stone, and failed (understandably . . . under the weight of their cares) to appreciate its significance, to consider what might be the result if Sauron became possessed of one of the Stones, and anyone else should then make use of another. It needed the demonstration on Dol Baran of the effects of the Orthanc-stone on Peregrin to reveal suddenly that the 'link' between Isengard and Barad-dûr (seen to exist after it was discovered that forces of Isengard had been joined with others directed by Sauron in the attack on the Fellowship at Parth Galen) was in fact the Orthanc-stone – and one other *palantír*. [*Unfinished Tales*, p. 405]

589 (II: 194): The road passed slowly

589 (II: 194). the moon, now waxing round – This is the night of 5/6 March; the moon will be full on the night of 7/8 March.

589 (II: 194–5): At last they halted

589 (II: 194). Dol Baran – In his unfinished index Tolkien defines *Dol Baran* as 'a hill at the S[outhern] end of the Misty Mountains'. He seems to have hesitated over the etymology of the name: he first wrote, but deleted, 'brown head'. Another, mostly illegible sentence which has been struck through seems to be concerned with the etymology of *Dol*, which is given in a separate entry as 'head, hill' with *Dol Baran* among the citations. Another entry for *baran* 'gold brown' continues: '*not* ?sense *Dol Baran* see *Paran*'; and the entry for the latter has '*Paran* smooth, shaven (often applied to hills ?without trees) cf. *Dol Baran*'.

589 (II: 195). bracken, among which the tight-curled fronds – Strictly, *bracken* is 'a tall fern with coarse lobed fronds (*Pteridium aquilinum*)' (*Concise OED*), but in the North of Britain, and more generally speaking, the word is applied to any large fern.

A *frond* is a leaf-like organ formed by the union of stem and foliage.

589 (II: 195). two hours or so before the middle of the night – The company left Isengard about sunset and stopped at about 10.00 p.m. Calculations of distances in Marquette MSS 4/2/19 indicate that Dol Baran was sixteen miles from the gates of Isengard.

591 (II: 196): 'Well, what else could I say?'

591 (II: 196). wheedling – Using flattering words persuasively.

591 (II: 196–7): At last he could stand it no longer

591 (II: 197). hummock – A protuberance of earth or rock above the level ground; here used figuratively.

592 (II: 197): Quickly now he drew off the cloth

592 (II: 197). a smooth globe of crystal, now dark and dead – In *The Palantíri* it is said that the *palantíri* were 'perfect spheres, appearing when at rest to be made of solid glass or crystal deep black in hue' (*Unfinished Tales*, p. 409).

592 (II: 197): Pippin sat with his knees drawn up

592 (III: 197). Pippin sat with his knees drawn up and the ball between them. – In Tolkien's late account of the *palantíri* it is said (among much else on their nature and operation) that the Stones had permanent poles, so that a user who wished to look to the west, for instance, would place himself on the east side of the Stone; but the minor *palantíri*, including that of Orthanc, also had a fixed orientation, so that a face set to one direction would look only in that direction. 'So it was "by chance" as Men call it (as Gandalf would have said) that Peregrin, fumbling with the Stone, must have set it on the ground more or less "upright", and sitting westward of it have had the fixed east-looking face in the proper position' (*Unfinished Tales*, p. 410).

592 (II: 197–8): 'So this is the thief'

592 (II: 198). haggard – With the appearance of exhaustion, worry.

594 (II: 199): He lifted Pippin gently

594 (II: 199). an itch in your palms – A phrase used figuratively of 'an uneasy or restless desire or hankering after something' (*OED*).

594–5 (II: 200): 'Never yet. Do not then stumble

594–5 (II: 200). But my [Gandalf's] mind was bent on Saruman, and I did not at once guess the nature of the Stone. Then I was weary, and as I lay pondering it, sleep overcame me. Now I know! – As first published this passage read: 'But my mind was bent on Saruman, and I did not guess the nature of the stone until it was too late. Only now have I become sure of it.' It was revised in the second printing (1967) of the Allen & Unwin second edition. Tolkien wrote in a check copy of *The Two Towers*: 'This alteration goes together with the insertion of *guess* on p. II 139, [i.e. 190], the recasting of II. 203, and amendment of III. 132. The changes are made necessary by a more careful consideration of the *palantíri,* and of the inconsistencies of Gandalf's references to them (which some readers have queried)' (courtesy of Christopher Tolkien).

Christopher Tolkien notes and cites 'a curious series of shifts in the precise wording of Gandalf's remarks about his failure to understand immediately the nature of the ball thrown down from Orthanc' in the various texts preceding that published in 1954.

> There is, to be sure, among all these formulations no great difference in the actual meaning, but it was evidently a detail that concerned my father: just how much did Gandalf surmise about the *palantír* before Pippin's experience brought certainty, and how soon?
>
> An element of ambiguity does in fact remain in LR. Already in the first manuscript of 'The Voice of Saruman' Gandalf said: 'I fancy that, if we could have come in, we should have found few treasures in Orthanc more precious than the thing which the fool Wormtongue tossed down to us!' The nature of Wormtongue's missile cannot have been fully apparent to my father himself at that stage: it was in that manuscript, only a few lines above, that he changed, as he wrote, the initial story of the globe's having smashed into fragments on the rock. . . . But even when he had fully established the nature of the *palantír* he retained those words of Gandalf . . . at the moment when it

burst upon the story – *although*, as Gandalf said at Dol Baran, 'I did not at once guess the nature of the Stone'. But then why was he so emphatic, as he stood beneath the tower, that 'we could have found few treasures in Orthanc more precious' – even before Wormtongue's shriek gave reinforcement to his opinion? Perhaps we should suppose simply that this much at least was immediately clear to him, that a great ball of dark crystal in Orthanc was most unlikely to have been nothing but an elegant adornment of Saruman's study. [*The War of the Ring*, p. 75]

595 (II: 200): 'Strange powers have our enemies

595 (II: 200). oft evil will shall evil mar – A saying similar to *Often does hatred hurt itself*. Gandalf immediately comments on the proof of the saying, and notes that Pippin's action has saved him from the mistake of probing the Stone.

595 (II: 201): At that moment a shadow fell

595 (II: 201). vast winged shape . . . went north – According to *Scheme*, 'Nazgûl passes over on way to Isengard about 11 p.m.' and 'reached Orthanc and then returned to Barad-dûr'.

595 (II: 201). The stars fainted – Here *fainted* is used in the sense 'to lose colour or brightness; to fade, die away' (*OED*).

595 (II: 201): 'Nazgûl!' he cried

595 (II: 201). Wait not for the dawn! Let not the swift wait for the slow! Ride! – While writing Book V, Chapter 3 ('The Muster of Rohan') Tolkien noted: 'Gandalf must tell the king as he rides off that he will order the muster at Dunharrow and speed it up'. Christopher Tolkien comments that this 'can only refer to his [Gandalf] leaving Dol Baran on Shadowfax after the Nazgûl passed over; but no such change was in fact introduced in that place' (*The War of the Ring*, p. 320, n. 1). Instead, in the published *Lord of the Rings*, as Théoden arrives at Dunharrow he still expects the Riders to assemble at Edoras on the day he appointed; he finds most of them assembled at Dunharrow instead, and is told that when Gandalf arrived at Edoras he brought word from Théoden to hasten the gathering, and that when a Nazgûl passed over Edoras he further advised that the muster take place at Dunharrow. Thus Gandalf took it upon himself to hasten the gathering of the Rohirrim, as he hastened the relief of Helm's Deep by Erkenbrand.

596 (II: 201): Over the plains Shadowfax was flying

596 (II: 201). Less than an hour had passed, and they had reached the Fords of Isen – A distance of fourteen miles (Marquette MSS 4/2/19). According to Marquette MSS 4/2/17, Gandalf and Pippin left Dol Baran at 11.30 p.m. It is now past midnight on 6 March 1419.

597 (II: 202): Pippin was silent again for a while

597 (II: 202). ***Tall ships and tall kings*** – In the *Akallabêth*, the tale of the downfall of Númenor published in *The Silmarillion*, it is said that when, at the instigation of Sauron, Ar-Pharazôn, the King of Númenor, sailed with a great fleet to conquer Valinor, Elendil prepared ships and

> the Faithful put aboard their wives and their children, and their heirlooms, and great store of goods. Many things there were of beauty and power, such as the Númenóreans had contrived in the days of their wisdom, vessels and jewels, and scrolls of lore written in scarlet and black. And Seven Stones they had, the gift of the Eldar; but in the ship of Isildur was guarded the young tree, the scion of Nimloth the Fair. [p. 276]

When Númenor foundered and sank into the abyss, Elendil's ships were blown east to Middle-earth. 'Nine ships there were: four for Elendil, and for Isildur three, and for Anárion two; and they fled before the black gale. . . . And the deeps rose . . . and waves like unto mountains . . . after many days cast them upon the shores of Middle-earth' (p. 280). According to the *1966 Index* the seven stars that were part of the emblem of Elendil and his house 'originally represented the single stars on the banners of each of seven ships (of 9) that bore a *palantír*'.

597 (II: 203): 'The name meant

597 (II: 203). ***that which looks far away*** – Tolkien glosses Quenya *palantír* in *The Road Goes Ever On: A Song Cycle* as *palan-* ' "afar," more accurately "abroad, far and wide" ' and 'the stem TIR "to look at (towards), watch, watch over" ' (pp. 64–5).

According to *Of the Rings of Power and the Third Age*, the *palantíri*

> had the virtue that those who looked in therein might perceive in them things far off, whether in place or in time. For the most part they revealed only things near to another kindred Stone, for the Stones each called to each; but those who possessed great strength of will and of mind might learn to direct their gaze whither they would. . . .
>
> These stones were gifts of the Eldar to Amandil father of Elendil, for the comfort of the Faithful of Númenor in their dark days, when the Elves might come no longer to that land under the shadow of Sauron. [*The Silmarillion*, p. 292]

597 (II: 203): 'No,' said Gandalf.

597 (II: 203). The Noldor made them. Fëanor himself, maybe – Gandalf's speculation that the *palantíri* were made by Fëanor seems to be confirmed in *The Silmarillion*, where it is said that Fëanor made crystals 'wherein things far away could be seen small but clear, as with the eyes of the eagles of Manwë' (p. 64). This idea entered 'The Silmarillion' in writing between the completion of *The Lord of the Rings* and its publication.

In one of his check copies of *The Two Towers* Tolkien wrote:

> Re-casting of page 203 [from '"No," said Gandalf' to 'Minas Morgul it has become']. This unfortunate page, which is at many points inconsistent with what is elsewhere said concerning Gandalf, the Council, and the general history and situation, was regrettably never revised – and is in some points now nonsensical.
>
> . . . .
>
> I urged that the general re-casting was required for a 'revised edition'. This is devised to be consistent with the general narrative and history, and as clear as the limitations of space allow – I have taken care to limit the new matter so that the page may remain intact and not fall short or run over. [courtesy of Christopher Tolkien]

597 (II: 203). We had not yet given thought to the fate of the *palantíri* of Gondor in its ruinous wars. By Men they were almost forgotten. Even in Gondor they were a secret known only to a few; in Arnor they were remembered only in a rhyme of lore among the Dúnedain. – As first published this passage read: 'It was not known to us that any of the *palantíri* had escaped the ruin of Gondor. Outside the Council it was not even remembered among Elves or Men that such things had ever been, save only in a Rhyme of Lore preserved among Aragorn's folk.' It was revised in the second printing (1967) of the Allen & Unwin second edition.

598 (II: 203): 'To see far off and to converse

598 (II: 203). Dome of Stars at Osgiliath – 'Great domed hall of old in Osgiliath' (*Index*).

598 (II: 203). The three others were far away in the North. In the house of Elrond it is told that they were at Annúminas, and Amon Sûl, and Elendil's Stone was on the Tower Hills that look towards Mithlond in the Gulf of Lune – As first published this passage read: 'The others were far away. Few now know where, for no rhyme says. But in the House of Elrond it is told that they were at Annúminas, and Amon Sûl, and on the Tower Hills [etc.]'. It was revised in the second printing (1967) of the Allen & Unwin second edition.

For *Mithlond* (the Grey Havens), see note for p. 7.

598 (II: 203): 'Each *palantír* replied to each

598 (II: 203). Each *palantír* replied to each, but all those in Gondor were ever open to the view of Osgiliath. – As first published this sentence read: 'Each *palantír* spoke to each, but at Osgiliath they could survey them all together at one time.' It was revised in the second printing (1967) of the Allen & Unwin second edition.

598 (II: 203): 'Who knows where the lost Stones

598 (II: 203). Who knows where the lost Stones of Arnor and Gondor now lie, buried, or drowned deep? – As first published this sentence read: 'Who knows where all those other stones now lie, broken, or buried, or drowned deep?' It was revised in the second printing (1967) of the Allen & Unwin second edition.

598 (II: 203). But one at least Sauron must have obtained – In *The Palantíri* it is said that

> in his talk to Peregrin as they rode on Shadowfax from Dol Baran . . . Gandalf's immediate object was to give the Hobbit some idea of the history of the *palantíri*, so that he might begin to realize the ancientry, dignity, and power of things that he had presumed to meddle with. He was not concerned to exhibit his own processes of discovery and deduction, except in its last point: to explain how Sauron came to have control of them, so that they were perilous for *anyone*, however exalted, to use. But Gandalf's mind was at the same time earnestly busy with the Stones, considering the bearings of the revelation at Dol Baran upon many things that he had observed and pondered: such as the wide knowledge of events far away possessed by Denethor, and his appearance of premature old age, first observable when he was not much above sixty years old, although he belonged to a race and family that still normally had longer lives than other men. Undoubtedly Gandalf's haste to reach Minas Tirith, in addition to the urgency of the time and the imminence of war, was quickened by his sudden fear that Denethor also had made use of a *palantír*, the Anor-stone, and his desire to judge what effect this had had on him: whether in the crucial test of desperate war it would not prove that he (like Saruman) was no longer to be trusted and might surrender to Mordor. [*Unfinished Tales*, pp. 405–6]

598 (II: 203–4): 'Easy it is now to guess

598 (II: 204). the biter bit, the hawk under the eagle's foot, the spider in a steel web – *The biter bit*, i.e. the cheater or deceiver is himself cheated or deceived.

598 (II: 204). the White Tree and the Golden – Telperion the White Tree and Laurelin the Golden Tree, the Two Trees sung into being by the Vala Yavanna which gave light in Valinor until they were destroyed by Morgoth and Ungoliant.

> The one had leaves of dark green that beneath were as shining silver, and from each of his countless flowers a dew of silver light was ever falling, and the earth beneath was dappled with the shadows of his

fluttering leaves. The other bore leaves of a young green like the new-opened beech; their edges were of glittering gold. Flowers swung upon her branches in clusters of yellow flame, formed each to a glowing horn that spilled a golden rain upon the ground; and from the blossom of that tree there came forth warmth and a great light. [*The Silmarillion*, p. 38]

598–9 (II: 204): 'Oh yes, you had'

599 (II: 204). the burned hand teaches best – An analogue to the proverb *A burnt child dreads (or fears) the fire* or *Once burnt, twice shy.*

599 (II: 204): 'The names of all the stars

599 (II: 204). Over-heaven – 'A Common Speech equivalent of Elvish [Quenya] *menel* "firmament", *tar-menel* "high Heaven", suggested by Old Norse *uphiminn*' (*Nomenclature*).

599–600 (II: 205): 'But I cannot tell how

599–600 (II: 205). Or that an heir of Elendil lives and stood beside me. If Wormtongue was not deceived by the armour of Rohan, he would remember Aragorn and the title that he claimed. – These sentences were added in the second edition (1965). On 31 July 1965 Tolkien wrote to his American publisher, Houghton Mifflin, about emendations to *The Two Towers*: 'The second on p. 205 . . . stops a small hole in the narrative: Aragorn was not at Orthanc in the earlier version of the chapter. If recognized, he would certainly have been addressed by Saruman' (Tolkien-George Allen & Unwin archive, HarperCollins).

600 (II: 205–6): 'We shall ride now to daybreak

600 (II: 206). You may see the first glimmer of dawn upon the golden roof of the house of Eorl. And in three days thence you shall see the purple shadow of Mount Mindolluin and the walls of the tower of Denethor white in the morning. – In editions prior to 2005 'three days' here read 'two days', a shadow of an earlier time-scheme which Tolkien revised in order to allow an additional day for events surrounding Aragorn and his companions. Several shadows of this sort in Book V were emended in the 2005 edition. As noted above, Gandalf and Pippin left Dol Baran just before midnight on 5 March. Gandalf now refers to dawn on 6 March when they will arrive at Edoras and see the golden roof of Meduseld. 'Two days thence', as previously printed, thus would be 8 March, but it is clear in Book V, and confirmed by *The Tale of Years*, that in fact Gandalf and Pippin arrive at Minas Tirith on 9 March.

In his unfinished index Tolkien describes *Mindolluin* as '(Towering blue-head) the great Mountain behind M[inas] Tirith'.

BOOK FOUR

Chapter 1

THE TAMING OF SMÉAGOL

For drafts and history of this chapter, see *The War of the Ring*, pp. 85–103.

603 (II: 209): It was the third evening

603 (II: 209). It was the third evening since they had fled from the Company – Frodo and Sam fled from Parth Galen around noon on 26 February; it is now 28 February. *Scheme* has the following entries:

> February 26: F[rodo] & S[am] first night in Emyn Muil. Gollum picks up trail of Frodo and Sam in Emyn Muil and dogs them.
> February 27: 2nd day and night wandering in Emyn Muil, along SE. [south-east] edge. They become aware of Gollum.
> February 28: 3rd day. Here Tale picks them up again. They spend cold night under shelter of a rock.

603 (II: 209): 'What a fix!'

603 (II: 209). where we can't get nohow – *Nohow* 'by no means'. The *Oxford English Dictionary* notes that 'in uneducated speech [*nohow* is] frequently used with another negative' (i.e. *can't*).

604 (II: 210): 'I wonder,' said Frodo

604 (II: 210). All my choices have proved ill. – Compare Aragorn's complaints in Book III, Chapter 1 ('all that I do goes amiss', p. 413, II: 15) and Chapter 2 ('Since we passed through the Argonath my choices have gone amiss', p. 426, II: 28). But as with Aragorn, Frodo's choices eventually will prove to have been good.

604 (II: 210). the hard of Battle Plain – The hard ground of Dagorlad (see note for p. 243).

604 (II: 210): 'Did you see them again

604 (II: 210). early morning – It is 29 February 1419.

604 (II: 210): 'Nor me,' said Sam.

604 (II: 210). did give me a turn – Gave him a sudden fright.

605 (II: 211): 'So do I,' said Frodo

605 (II: 211). the dead flats – The Dead Marshes. *Flat* in this sense means 'a tract of low-lying swamp'.

607 (II: 213): The hurrying darkness

607 (II: 213). high shrill shriek – The sound of a Ringwraith in flight. Tom Shippey suggests that it 'was coming back from a fruitless wait for Grishnákh the orc, dead and burnt that same day, with the smoke from his burning "seen by many watchful eyes"' (*The Road to Middle-earth*, 2nd edn., p. 146).

608 (II: 214): 'Rope!' cried Sam

608 (II: 214). numbskulls! You're nowt but a ninnyhammer – A *numbskull* is 'a dull-witted or stupid person' (*OED*).

Nowt is a Northern English dialect word, 'nothing, nought'.

Ninnyhammer means 'simpleton'.

609 (II: 215): Thunder growled and rumbled

609 (II: 215). spate – A sudden flood.

609 (II: 215): Sam paid it out slowly

609 (II: 215). paid it out slowly, measuring it with his arms . . . ells – To *pay out* in this sense is 'to let out or slacken a rope'; here Sam measures the rope in lengths against his arm. In the draft 'Frodo wound it [?round his] elbows' (*The War of the Ring*, p. 89).

The *ell* is an old measure of length based on the length of the arm or forearm. It varies in different countries: the English ell was 45 inches. In *The War of the Ring* Christopher Tolkien notes that the hobbits' rope was originally 80 hobbit-ells, with a note in the margin '2 feet > 2½ feet'; but eventually Tolkien abandoned the 'hobbit-ell' and used the English ell. 'This was the measure in [*The Two Towers*], where the cliff was about 18 fathoms [108 feet], and the rope about 30 ells [112½ feet]; taking these figures as exact, there would be 4½ feet of rope to spare ("there was still a good bight in Frodo's hands, when Sam came to the bottom")' (p. 99, n. 11).

609 (II: 215–16): With that he stood up

609 (II: 216). Thence it turned, smiting the Vale of Anduin with hail and lightning, and casting its shadow upon Minas Tirith with threat of war. Then, lowering in the mountains, and gathering its great spires, it rolled on slowly over Gondor and the skirts of Rohan, until far away the Riders on the plain saw its black towers moving behind the sun, as they rode into the West. – When this chapter was first written Frodo saw the storm towards evening on 1 February, and the Battle of Helm's Deep took place on the night of 1/2 February. Tolkien wrote in a contemporary time-scheme: 'Night Feb. 1–2 Frodo and Sam meet Gollum. (Storm that reached Helm's Deep about midnight on Feb. 1–2 passed over Emyn Muil earlier in the night.)' The storm thus served as a link between the stories of Frodo and Sam east of Anduin and of the rest of the Company to the west, whom it reaches in Book III, Chapter 7. Later changes and adjustments to the chronology, however, meant that Frodo witnessed the storm on 29 February and the Battle of Helm's Deep took place on the night of 3/4 March. Christopher Tolkien notes that his father altered the description of the storm only after the chapter was in proof, 'giving the great storm a more widely curving path, and suggesting, perhaps, a reinforcement of its power and magnitude as it passed slowly over Ered Nimrais' (*The War of the Ring*, see pp. 100–3).

610 (II: 216): It did not, however, turn out

610 (II: 216). bight – A loop of rope.

610–11 (II: 217): But Sam did not answer

610–11 (II: 217). Noodles! – In this context *noodle* has the obscure meaning 'simpleton'. Compare note for p. 608.

611 (II: 217): Sam did not laugh

611 (II: 217). my grand-dad, and my uncle Andy . . . had a rope-walk over by Tighfield – Sam's grandfather was Hobson Gamgee, known as 'Roper Gamgee'.

A *rope-walk* is a 'technical name for a rope-maker's yard' (*Nomenclature*). *Tighfield* is a village in the Westfarthing. Tolkien writes in *Nomenclature* that the name

> is intended to contain an old word for 'rope' (surviving in some of the senses of modern English *tie* [noun] in which the spelling is assimilated to that of the related verb *tie*). It was the site of a 'rope-walk' or rope-maker's yard. . . .
>
> A 'rope-walk' (known in English since the seventeenth century) is so-called because the ropes were stretched out in long lines over trestles at intervals. . . .
>
> There is, however, another place-name element (peculiar to English) that has the same forms as the 'rope' word, though it is probably not related: in modern place-names *tigh*, *teigh*, *tye*, *tey*. This meant 'an enclosed piece of land'. It does not occur as the first element in a compound.

611 (II: 217). as fast a hitch – A *hitch* is a knot by which a rope is secured (or made *fast*) to some object.

611 (II: 218): 'Yes,' said Frodo

611 (II: 218). he won't be full for some days . . . half a moon – This is the night of 29/30 February. The moon will reach its first quarter early on 30 February, and will be full on the night of 7/8 March.

612 (II: 219): Sam looked and breathed in

612 (II: 219). snakes and adders – There is a popular board game called 'Snakes and Ladders', from which derives a figurative use of the phrase to mean 'a series of unpredictable successes and set-backs' (*OED*).

613 (II: 219): Down the face of the precipice

613 (II: 219). a small black shape was moving with its thin limbs splayed out. Maybe its soft clinging hands and toes were finding crevices and holds . . . but it looked as if it was just creeping down on sticky pads, like some large prowling thing of insect-kind. . . . Now and again it lifted its head slowly, turning it right back on its long skinny neck, and the hobbits caught a glimpse of two small pale gleaming lights, its eyes that blinked at the moon and then were quickly lidded again. – As he climbs down the cliff face Gollum comes fully into view for the first time in *The Lord of the Rings.* All that have been seen previously, in Book II, Chapter 9, are 'pale lamplike eyes', 'a dark shape', 'a long whitish hand' (pp. 383–4, II: 400), and 'paddle-feet, like a swan's almost, only they seemed bigger' (p. 382, II: 399). In the first edition of *The Hobbit* (1937), Chapter 5, Gollum is said to be 'as dark as darkness, except for two big round pale eyes [*added in the edition of 1966:* in his thin face]'; he paddles his boat 'with large feet dangling over the side', which are also described as 'webby'; he looks 'out of his pale lamp-like eyes for blind fish', which he grabs 'with his long fingers'; and it emerges that he has six teeth and is not naked ('he thought of all the things he kept in his own pockets').

In *The Lord of the Rings*, when Gollum pauses during his descent of the cliff in Book IV, Chapter 1, 'his large head on its scrawny neck was lolling from side to side' (p. 614, II: 220); and during the struggle that follows he is said to have 'long legs and arms', 'thin lank hair', and a 'long neck' (p. 614, II: 220–1). Later his sharp yellow teeth and colourless lips are noted, and he is described as 'a tiny figure sprawling on the ground: there perhaps lay the famished skeleton of some child of Men, its ragged garment still clinging to it, its long arms and legs almost bone-white and bone-thin: no flesh worth a peck' (Book IV, Chapter 3, p. 644, II: 253). In Book IV, Chapter 6 his figure is also 'froglike' (p. 685, II: 294), and he is said to have 'bulging eyes' with 'heavy pale lids' and 'sparse locks . . . hanging like rank weed over his bony brows' (p. 688, II: 297; p. 689, II: 298). A clear indication of his size is given in Book IV, Chapter 9: 'now he was face to face with a furious enemy [Sam], little less than his own size' (p. 726, II: 336).

The first translation of *The Hobbit*, into Swedish in 1947, included an illustration of Gollum as a gigantic dark triangular shape with huge eyes and barely distinguishable hands, towering over Bilbo. Tolkien commented in a letter to 'Rosemary' on 18 January 1948 that the Swedish edition had 'some dreadful pictures which make Gollum look simply huge. But he was not much bigger than Bilbo, only thin and very wiry, and he had of course large flabby-sticky hands and feet' (reproduced in *Mallorn* 36 (November 1998), p. 34). Even translations of *The Hobbit* which appeared after the publication of *The Lord of the Rings*, when Gollum was more fully described, often depicted him as much larger than Bilbo, or with monster-like features. In the illustrations to the Japanese translations of *The Hobbit* (1965) and *The Lord of the Rings* (1972) Gollum is more or less the right size but, presumably picking up references to his froglike figure and movements, he is rendered like a frog rather than of Hobbit-kind. Tolkien was not happy with such illustrations, and wrote to Joy Hill at Allen & Unwin on 11 October 1963 that if a prospective illustrator of *The Hobbit* intended to include an illustration of Gollum 'it should be noted that G[ollum] is *not* a monster, but a slimy little creature not larger than Bilbo' (Tolkien-George Allen & Unwin archive, HarperCollins).

In a late unpublished manuscript Tolkien commented that

> Gollum was according to Gandalf one of a riverside hobbit people – and therefore in origin a member of a small variety of the human race, although he had become deformed during his long inhabiting of the dark lake. [He had long hands and his feet] are described as *webby* [in *The Hobbit*], *like a swan's* [in *The Lord of the Rings*], but had prehensile toes. But he was very thin – in The L.R. emaciated . . . he had for his size a *large head* and a *long thin neck*, very large eyes (protuberant), and thin lank hair. . . . He is often said to be dark or black. At his first mention [in *The Hobbit*] he was 'dark as darkness': that of course means no more than that he could not be seen with ordinary eyes in the black cavern – except for his own large luminous eyes; similarly 'the dark shape' at night [*The Lord of the Rings*, Book II, Chapter 9]. But that does not apply to the 'black (crawling) shape' [in Book IV, Chapter 1], where he was in moonlight.
>
> Gollum was never *naked*. He had a pocket in which he kept the Ring. . . . His skin was white, no doubt with a pallor increased by dwelling long in the dark, and later by hunger. He remained a human being, not an animal or a mere bogey, even if deformed in mind and body: an object of disgust, but also of pity – to the deep-sighted, such as Frodo had become. There is no need to wonder how he came by clothes or replaced them: any consideration of the tale will show that he had plenty of opportunities by theft, or charity (as of the Wood-elves), throughout his life. [Tolkien Papers, Bodleian Library, Oxford]

613 (II: 220): 'Ach, sss! Cautious, my precious!

613 (II: 220). We musstn't rissk our neck, musst we, precious? – In this paragraph Gollum clearly uses 'precious' to address himself, and therefore the word is in lower case. See note for p. 11.

613 (II: 220): He was getting lower now

613 (II: 220). Where iss it, where iss it: my Precious, my Precious? . . . Where are they with my Precious? – Here Gollum uses 'Precious' to refer to the Ring, and therefore the word is capitalized.

In this and the previous paragraphs, as commonly elsewhere, in talking to himself Gollum uses *we* and *our* rather than *I* and *my*. On occasions when Frodo's pity and understanding affect him, he will use *I* and refer to himself by his true name, *Sméagol*. As Paul H. Kocher notes:

> Nobody who handles the Ring . . . escapes the greed to possess it. Tolkien indicates this avidity by the device of having each of its wearers describe it as 'precious'. Gollum, of course, does so in almost every sentence he speaks. Significantly, by the word *precious* he means sometimes the Ring, sometimes himself, and sometimes both confusedly. This is Tolkien's brilliant literary method of showing that Gollum often is no longer thinking of the Ring as something separate from himself. He is the Ring, the Ring is Gollum. Apart from it he has no individuality of his own. [*Master of Middle-earth*, p. 65]

614 (II: 221): 'Let go! Gollum'

614 (II: 221). This is Sting. You have seen it before – In *The Hobbit*, Chapter 5, Bilbo was carrying Sting when he met Gollum. Gollum thought that Bilbo might make 'a tasty morsel', but on seeing his sword 'became quite polite'.

614 (II: 221): Gollum collapsed

614 (II: 221). whimpering – In 'Studies in Tolkien's Language II: A Mirror of the Soul: On the Indexical Function of Gollum's Speech' (*Arda 3* (1986, for 1982–3)) Nils-Lennart Johannesson points out that Gollum's manner of speaking is one of his most striking characteristics. 'When he is frightened, he speaks in a higher pitch range, as shown by the use of reporting verbs *squeak*, *squeal*, *wail*, *whimper*, and *whine*. . . . When he is excited, upset, or angry, he hisses. . . .' Not only are there over thirty references in *The Lord of the Rings* to his hissing, but it 'is emphasized by the fact that Tolkien on several occasions uses an eye-catching spelling with double *s*': *yess*, *fissh*, *nassty*, *masster*, *musstn't*, etc. (p. 2). Even apart from such instances Gollum's vocabulary includes an unusual number of words with alveolar fricatives (*s/z* sounds). Much of this was already present in *The Hobbit*, but was developed to greater effect in its sequel.

Johannesson notes the frequent use of some words: '*Nice* is typically used as a symptom of obsequiousness in Gollum's more or less fulsome attempts to ingratiate himself to Frodo . . . ; *good* and *poor* are typically used in expressions of self-praise and self-pity. . . . *Nasty* is Gollum's standard epithet for anything that he openly shows his displeasure with . . .' (p. 12). In regard to Gollum's idiosyncratic use of personal pronouns, despite the fact that his talk is 'almost constantly about himself . . . he normally does not use *I* to refer to himself; instead he uses either *we* or *Sméagol/he*. Similarly, he seldom uses *you* to refer to his interlocutors, but prefers *he* or *they* (or a suitable noun phrase such as *the hobbit(s)* or *Master*)' (p. 15).

615 (II: 221): It seemed to Frodo

615 (II: 221). he heard, quite plainly but far off, voices out of the past – Frodo is recalling his conversation with Gandalf in Bag End over ten months earlier, in Book I, Chapter 2, where the wording is slightly different. In *The War of the Ring* Christopher Tolkien discusses the evolution and relationship of these two passages, the earlier of which was rewritten by Tolkien when he wrote the later chapter. The conversations 'remain different in detail of wording, perhaps not intentionally at all points' (p. 97).

615 (II: 222): 'Very well,' he answered aloud

615 (II: 222). For now that I see him, I do pity him. – Although Frodo does not know it, this is the turning point of his quest, the decision that will eventually ensure its success. In Book VI, Chapter 3 he will remark to Sam: 'Do you remember Gandalf's words: *Even Gollum may have something yet to do*? But for him, Sam, I could not have destroyed the Ring. The Quest would have been in vain, even at the bitter end. So let us forgive him! For the Quest is achieved . . .' (p. 947, III: 225).

616 (II: 222–3): 'Yess. Yess. No!'

616 (II: 222). Leave me alone. . . . You hurt me. O my poor hands. . . . I, we, I don't want to come back. I can't find it. I am tired. I, we can't find it. – In this confused monologue Gollum seems to recall being tortured in Mordor, and apparently being told to go and find the Ring. Under this pressure his Sméagol side comes to the fore, thus he uses mainly *I* rather than *we*.

616 (II: 223): 'The big lights hurt our eyes

616 (II: 223). the White Face – The moon. Compare *Yellow Face*, Gollum's name for the sun, p. 621, II: 298.

618 (II: 225): For a moment it appeared to Sam

618 (II: 225). Yet the two were in some way akin and not alien: they could reach one another's minds. – They are linked because both know the burden of bearing the Ring. Some readers have seen Gollum as Frodo's 'shadow'. In *Splintered Light: Logos and Language in Tolkien's World* (2nd edn., 2003) Verlyn Flieger comments that

> [Frodo's] journey into the dark takes him away from everything he holds dear and separates him even from himself. For if Frodo's external

> journey is eastward into Mordor, his inner journey is into his own darkness, where he must meet and acknowledge his unadmitted self, that Grendel-like prowler in the wilderness of the psyche that Jung calls the Shadow. In Frodo's case, the Shadow is personified in Gollum, who embodies with horrible and pitiable clarity the darkness that the Ring evokes. Gollum . . . is a brilliantly realized character, a double self of 'I' and 'we', of Sméagol and Gollum, of Slinker and Stinker. He is Frodo turned inside out. He is the emblem of Frodo's growing division from himself, a division that we do not see in its entirety until the final moment at the Cracks of Doom.
>
> . . . .
>
> Both have left the light to go into the dark, Frodo reluctantly, Gollum by free choice. Light of any kind is hateful and actually painful to Gollum. He avoids both daylight and moonshine. He is nocturnal, a creature of night and nightmare, an image out of the unconscious forced into the light of day to be confronted and recognized. And Frodo, who at first rejected indignantly the notion that Gollum could be in any way connected with hobbits, comes at last by way of his own journey into darkness to see Gollum clearly, to recognize the Gollum in himself, and to pity the external creature. The two are one another's Self and Other, but it is the mark of Frodo's greater humanity that only he can recognize and acknowledge this. [pp. 151–2]

618 (II: 225). pawing . . . fawning – Having referred to Gollum as appearing like 'a little whining dog' at Frodo's feet, Tolkien continues to stress his dog-like actions: he paws, he fawns (shows slavish devotion). Frodo's response, 'Down! down!' is one usually spoken to a dog, and then Gollum's behaviour is compared to that of 'a whipped cur [a worthless dog, mongrel] whose master has patted it', or 'looking back inquiringly, like a dog inviting them for a walk'.

618 (II: 225): 'We promises, yes I promise!'

618 (II: 225). I will serve the Master of the Precious – Gollum's promise is ambiguous: it is not specific to Frodo, but to whoever holds the Ring.

619 (II: 226): In the deep of night

619 (II: 226). they set off – According to *Scheme*: 'February 29: F[rodo] and S[am] descend from Emyn Muil at dusk. Meet Gollum about 10 p.m. That night they journey SE. [south-east] in Gully with Gollum' and 'February 30: Journey in Gully until daybreak. Sleep all day in Gully and go on at dusk'.

Chapter 2

THE PASSAGE OF THE MARSHES

For drafts and history of this chapter, see *The War of the Ring*, pp. 104–20.

620 (II: 227): Gollum cast up and down

620 (II: 227). cast – Searched.

620 (II: 227): He led the way

620–1 (II: 227–8). [Gollum] chuckled to himself . . . – A recording by Tolkien from these words to the end of Gollum's second poem (*'so juicy-sweet!'*) is included on Disc 2 of *The J.R.R. Tolkien Audio Collection.*

620–1 (II: 227–8): 'Ha! ha! What does we wish?'

620–1 (II: 227–8). He guessed it long ago, Baggins guessed it. – Gollum is referring to one of the riddles he set Bilbo in Chapter 5 of *The Hobbit.* His second verse here is an extension of it. The first three lines are the same in both works, but the fourth and final line of the riddle in *The Hobbit* reads: 'All in mail never clinking'. In *The Annotated Hobbit* Douglas A. Anderson notes a slight analogue to the riddle (and so to this verse) 'in the Old Norse *Saga of King Heidrek the Wise,* in a contest of wisdom between King Heidrek and Gestumblindi, who is the Norse god Odin in disguise' (2nd edn., pp. 125–6). One of the questions asked is: 'What lives without breath?' to which Heidrek correctly answers: 'the fish' (*The Saga of King Heidrek the Wise* (1960), ed. by Christopher Tolkien, p. 80).

621 (II: 228): They stumbled along

621 (II: 228). with the first grey of morning – It is 30 February 1419.

624 (II: 231): 'About the food'

624 (II: 231). it doesn't satisfy the innards proper – *Innards* is a colloquialism for 'internal organs'. Sam means that *lembas* nourishes but does not satisfy the appetite.

624 (II: 232): 'Worms or beetles

624 (II: 232). Worms or beetles or something slimy out of holes – Marjorie Burns comments in *Perilous Realms: Celtic and Norse in Tolkien's Middle-earth* that Gollum's 'inability to tolerate Elven food, his disgust for cooked rabbit and herbs, and his preference instead for things raw, for cold fish, worms, or "something slimy out of holes" . . . accentuate his regression, his devolution back to a primordial world of "black mud", wetness, and a "chewing and slavering" state' (p. 164).

624–5 (II: 232): The next stage of their journey

625 (II: 232). the coming of day – It is 1 March 1419.

625 (II: 232): On either side and in front

625 (II: 232). noisome – Having an extremely unpleasant smell.

626 (II: 233–4): As the day wore on

626 (II: 234). seed-plumes – *Plume* in this context is the appendage by which a seed is carried from a plant by the wind.

626–7 (II: 234): So passed the third day

626 (II: 234). the third day of their journey with Gollum – They had begun to travel with Gollum during the night of 29/30 February; it is now 1 March. This would amount to three days only if Tolkien considered that their first journey began before midnight on 29 February and counted that as a 'day'. Christopher Tolkien notes, however, that his father numbered the journeys made in one of his time-schemes, 'and it may well be that "3" against [this journey through the marshes] explains [the third day of their journey] for it was the third journey, but not the third day' (*The War of the Ring*, p. 119).

626 (II: 234). Before the shadows of evening were long – They continue on through the night of 1/2 March. According to *Scheme*: 'March 1: Reach end of Gully at daybreak. At once begin passage of Dead Marshes by day (misty). Continue the march on through the night. Episode of the Corpse-candles occurs about 8 p.m. A Nazgûl passes over them at midnight.'

627 (II: 234): Presently it grew altogether dark

627 (II: 234). the air itself seemed black and heavy to breathe. When lights appeared Sam rubbed his eyes. . . . He first saw . . . a wisp of pale sheen . . . some like misty flames – In H. Rider Haggard's *She* the protagonists also pass through unpleasant marshes:

> Never did I see a more dreary and depressing scene. Miles on miles of quagmire, varied only by bright green strips of comparatively solid ground, and by deep sullen pools fringed with tall rushes. . . . Undoubtedly, however, the worst feature of the swamp was the awful smell of rotting vegetation that hung about it, which at times was positively overpowering, and the malarious exhalations that accompanied it, which we were of course obliged to breathe.

This marsh is by no means dead: it contains many birds and reptiles, including poisonous snakes, and clouds of mosquitoes. At night one of the heroes sees 'impish marsh-born balls of fire, rolled this way and that' (Chapter 10; compare *will-o'-the wisp*, note for p. 314).

627 (II: 234): Gollum looked up

627 (II: 234). Candles of corpses – The *Oxford English Dictionary* defines *corpse-candle* as 'a lambent flame seen in a churchyard or over a grave, and superstitiously believed to appear as an omen of death, or to indicate the route of a coming funeral'.

627 (II: 235): Hurrying forward again

627 (II: 235). There are dead things, dead faces in the water – Tolkien wrote to Professor L.W. Forster on 31 December 1960 that 'the Dead Marshes and the approaches to the Morannon owe something to Northern France after the Battle of the Somme [in the First World War]' (*Letters*, p. 303). Compare, for instance, the comment from the Somme by Captain Alfred Bundy in his diary for 19 October 1916: 'I have never seen such desolation. Mud thin, deep and black, shell holes full of water, corpses all around in every stage of decomposition, some partially devoid of flesh, some swollen and black' (quoted in Malcolm Brown, *The Imperial War Museum Book of the Somme* (2002), p. 223); and that by Siegfried Sassoon in his *Memoirs of an Infantry Officer*: 'Floating on the surface of the flooded trench was the mask of a human face which had detached itself from the skull.' Another inspiration for the Dead Marshes may have been the account in *De Origine Actibusque Getarum* (*The Origin and Deeds of the Goths*) by the sixth-century writer Jordanes, of how a bridge collapsed while an army was crossing, in an area 'surrounded by quaking bogs' and where 'even today one may hear in that neighborhood the lowing of cattle and may find traces of men' (trans. by Charles C. Mierow (1908), p. 8).

628 (II: 235): 'Yes, yes,' said Gollum

628 (II: 235). a great battle long ago, yes, so they told him when Sméagol was young. . . . Tall Men . . . and terrible Elves – The great Battle of Dagorlad in 3434 at the end of the Second Age. It was nearly 2,500 years later that Gollum heard stories about the battle.

628 (II: 236): At last they came to the end

628 (II: 236). cesspool – 'A well sunk to receive the soil [sewage] from a water-closet, kitchen sink, etc.; properly one which retains the solid matter and allows liquid to escape' (*OED*).

628 (II: 236): It was late in the night

628–9 (II: 236). It was late in the night – But apparently not yet midnight, as *Scheme* places the passing over of the Nazgûl at that time.

629 (II: 237): For a moment the sight

628 (II: 237). scudded – To *scud* is to 'move fast in a straight line because or as if driven by the wind' (*Concise OED*).

629–30 (II: 237): They fell forward

630 (II: 237). the shadow of horror wheeled and returned, passing lower now, right above them. . . . And then it was gone, flying back to Mordor – As first conceived, this Nazgûl was to be on his way to Isengard, thus the mention in the previous paragraph of his speeding westward; but shifts in the chronology of *The Lord of the Rings* made this impossible, and Tolkien emended the text so that the Ringwraith swept back over the marshes and returned to Mordor. His notes indicate that it would take about six or seven hours for a Nazgûl to fly from Barad-dûr to Isengard, 600 miles or more. In *The War of the Ring*, pp. 119–20, Christopher Tolkien discusses his father's various attempts to provide links between Book IV, Chapter 2 and Book III, Chapter 11: he concludes that

> according to the final chronology neither of the unseen Nazgûl that passed over high up at the end of the chapter "The Passage of the Marshes" (at dusk on March 4, and again an hour after midnight) can have been the one that wheeled over Dol Baran on the night of March 5, nor the one that passed over Edoras on the morning of March 6. A rigorous chronology led to this disappointing conclusion. [*The War of the Ring*, p. 120]

631 (II: 238): When day came at last

631 (II: 238). When day came at last – It is 2 March 1419.

631 (II: 328). walls of Mordor – As Frodo and Sam approach from the North they will be looking towards the Morannon at the north-west corner of Mordor between the Ephel Dúath, marking the western border of Mordor, and the Ered Lithui in the north.

631 (II: 238). peats – *Peat* is 'vegetable matter decomposed by water and partially carbonized by chemical change, often forming bogs or 'mosses' of large extent' (*OED*).

631 (II: 238–9): While the grey light lasted

631 (II: 238–9). For two more nights – The nights of 2/3 and 3/4 March.

631 (II: 239): At last, on the fifth morning

631 (II: 239). on the fifth morning since they took the road with Gollum – Their first *morning* with Gollum was 30 February. It is now the morning of 4 March.

631 (II: 239). buttresses – In this sense a *buttress* is a projecting part of a hill or mountain.

631 (II: 239). arid – Dry, parched.

631 (II: 239). Noman-lands – In the first edition this was spelt *Nomen's*

Land. It was changed in the second edition (1965) to agree with the spelling used in Book II, Chapter 8. According to *Scheme*:

> March 2: At dawn F[rodo] S[am] and Gollum reach end of Marshes and hide under a stone. At night begin journey in moors of Nomen's Land.
>
> March 3: Journey in Nomen's Land continues.
>
> March 4: Reach Slagmounds and edge of Desolation of Morannon. Stay in a hole all day.

631 (II: 239). more loathsome far was the country that the crawling day now slowly unveiled – Tolkien said in an interview with Keith Brace that from his time at the front in First World War France 'I remember miles and miles of seething tortured earth, perhaps best described in the chapter about the approaches to Mordor. It was a searing experience' ('In the Footsteps of the Hobbits', *Birmingham Post*, 25 May 1968).

631 (II: 239). leprous – A figurative allusion to the disease *leprosy* which eats away at the human body.

632 (II: 239): For a while they stood there

632 (II: 239). flags of smoke – Long trailing plumes.

632 (II: 239–40): Too weary to go further

632 (II: 239). sump – A depression or pit in which water or other fluids collect.

632 (II: 240): Suddenly Sam woke up

632 (II: 240). A pale light and a green light – From this point, a *green light* in Gollum's eyes is a sign that his evil side is dominant. Compare *The Hobbit*, Chapter 5: 'As suspicion grew in Gollum's mind, the light of his eyes burned with a pale flame.'

632–3 (II: 240): 'Yes, yes, my precious

632–3 (II: 240). to save our Precious – Gollum's use of *our* shows that he still considers the Ring to belong to him.

633 (II: 241): 'No, sweet one. See, my precious

633 (II: 241). Eat fish . . . fresh from the sea – It seems unlikely that Gollum has ever eaten fish fresh from the sea, but has evidently heard about them.

634–5 (II: 242): In the falling dusk

635 (II: 242). the menace passed high overhead, going maybe on some swift errand from Barad-dûr – At one stage in the writing of this chapter, this Nazgûl was on its way to Isengard and would pass over Dol Baran en route; see note for p. 630.

635 (II: 242): About an hour after midnight

635 (II: 242). About an hour after midnight – It is now early on 5 March.

635 (II: 242). the fear fell on them a third time . . . rushing with terrible speed into the West – At one point this was to be the Nazgûl that passed over Edoras later in the day, dispatched after Pippin looked into the *palantír*; see note for p. 630.

According to *Scheme*: 'March 4: Go on again at nightfall. Nazgûl passes over soon after they start. Another goes over them about midnight or 1 hr. after.'

Chapter 3

THE BLACK GATE IS CLOSED

For drafts and history of this chapter, see *The War of the Ring*, pp. 121–30.

636 (II: 244): Before the next day dawned

636 (II: 244). Before the next day dawned – It is 5 March 1419.

636 (II: 244): Upon the west of Mordor

636 (II: 244). Ephel Dúath, the Mountains of Shadow – 'Fence of shadow' (*Index*), from Sindarin *ephel* 'encircling ring or fence' + *dúath* 'dark shadow'.

636 (II: 244). Ered Lithui, grey as ash – *Ered Lithui* 'ashen mountains' is derived from Sindarin *orod* (plural *ered*) 'mountain' + *lith* 'ash' + adjectival suffix *-ui*. In *Nomenclature* (entry for *Ashen Mountains*) Tolkien writes that these are 'mountains of ash-grey hue'.

636 (II: 244). the mournful plains of Lithlad and of Gorgoroth – *Lithlad* is Sindarin for 'plain of ashes' (*Index*), at the feet of the Ered Lithui, from *lith* 'ash' + *lad* 'plain'. Both Lithlad and the barren plateau of Gorgoroth are *mournful* in the sense 'sad, dismal'.

636 (II: 244). the bitter inland sea of Núrnen – *Núrnen* is the water (Sindarin *nen*) of the region *Nurn* (as named on the maps of Middle-earth). In his unfinished index Tolkien glosses the name 'sad-water', and in Book VI, Chapter 2 refers to 'the dark sad waters of Lake Núrnen' (p. 923, III: 201). An old definition of *sad* is 'dark-coloured', in particular referring to an unpleasant colour; but by the waters of Núrnen were the great fields of Mordor worked by slaves, and in that context may be recalled the plight of the Hebrew slaves expressed in Psalm 137: 'By the rivers of Babylon, there we sat down, yea, we wept, when we remembered Zion.' Núrnen is *bitter* perhaps by analogy with *sad*, or in the sense 'unpalatable': into it drain the poisonous waters of Mordor.

636 (II: 244). a deep defile – A gorge.

636 (II: 244). the Teeth of Mordor – The Towers of the Teeth, named in Book VI, Chapter 1 *Narchost* on the west and *Carchost* on the east; see note for p. 900.

636 (II: 244): Across the mouth of the pass

636 (II: 244). Morannon, the black gate – The main northern entrance to Mordor. Its name combines Sindarin *mor-* 'dark, black' + *annon* 'great door or gate'.

637 (II: 245–6): 'No, no, master!'

637 (II: 245). He'll eat us all, if He gets it, eat all the world. – In *Perilous Realms: Celtic and Norse in Tolkien's Middle-earth* Marjorie Burns comments: 'That the sins of this now mostly disembodied but still formidable being can be reduced [in this statement by Gollum] to a display of excessive appetite, to something rather like greed at table, places Sauron, for a moment, in the same category as any mortal who contrives to gain more than his or her fair share' (pp. 163–4). Gollum's plea is a very vivid picture, however, perhaps more so than Faramir's description of Sauron as 'a destroyer who would devour all' (Book IV, Chapter 5, p. 672, II: 280).

639 (II: 247): Frodo did not answer Gollum

639 (II: 247). The hollow in which they had taken refuge was delved in the side of a low hill, at some little height above a long trenchlike valley that lay between it and the outer buttresses of the mountain-wall. In the midst of the valley stood the black foundations of the western watch-tower. By morning-light the roads that converged upon the Gate of Mordor could now be clearly seen, pale and dusty; one winding back northwards; another dwindling eastwards into the mists that clung about the feet of Ered Lithui; and a third that ran towards him. As it bent sharply round the tower, it entered a narrow defile and passed not far below the hollow where he stood. Westward, to his right, it turned – As first published this passage read:

> The hollow in which they had taken refuge was delved in the side of a low hill and lay at some little height above the level of the plain. A long trench-like valley ran between it and the outer buttresses of the mountain-wall. In the morning-light the roads that converged upon the Gate of Mordor could now be clearly seen, pale and dusty; one winding back northwards; another dwindling eastwards into the mists that clung about the feet of Ered Lithui; and another that, bending sharply, ran close under the western watch-tower, and then passed along the valley at the foot of the hillside where the hobbits lay and not many feet below them. Soon it turned . . .

It was revised in the second edition (1965). Tolkien submitted the altered text to Houghton Mifflin on 31 July 1965, explaining that it 'attempts to make my vision of the scene clearer: if I did not (as I do) retain a clear picture of what I was trying to describe, I should not get one from the previous text' (Tolkien-George Allen & Unwin archive, HarperCollins). The Ballantine Books edition introduced (among other faults of text) an error, 'mountains' for 'mountain-wall', which persisted for many years.

639 (II: 247). deep shadows that mantled all the western sides – The shadows *mantled* the sides of the mountains as if covering them with a mantle or cloak.

640 (II: 248): 'Sméagol,' he said

640 (II: 248). May the third time prove the best! – The notion underlying this saying dates to medieval times. In *Sir Gawain and the Green Knight*, l. 1680, is the phrase 'þrid tyme þrowe best', which Tolkien and E.V. Gordon gloss in their edition of the poem 'third time, turn out best', noting that it is 'a proverbial expression . . . the modern equivalent [of which] is "third time pays for all"' (p. 109). Similar words are also said later in *The Lord of the Rings*: 'the third turn may turn the best'; 'third time pays for all'; 'thrice shall pay for all'. In a letter to Jared Lobdell, 31 July 1964, Tolkien commented on the proverb as one 'used when a third try is needed to rectify two poor efforts, or when a third occurrence may surpass the others'; see Lobdell, 'A Medieval Proverb in *The Lord of the Rings*', *American Notes and Queries Supplement 1* (1978).

641 (II: 249): 'On, on, on'

641 (II: 249). the Great Water that is never still – The sea.

641 (II: 249): 'Tales out of the South'

641 (II: 249). tall Men with the shining eyes – Númenórean exiles.

642 (II: 250): 'Not nice hobbit, not sensible'

642 (II: 250). That is the only way big armies can come. – But the Black Gate is not the only way: in Book IV, Chapter 8 a great army comes out of the gate at Minas Morgul.

643 (II: 251): Frodo felt a strange certainty

643 (II: 251). The 'escape' may have been allowed or arranged, and well known in the Dark Tower. – Frodo's judgement is correct; see note for p. 255.

644 (II: 252): Its name was Cirith Ungol

644 (II: 252). Cirith Ungol – Sindarin 'cleft of the spider', from *cirith* 'cleft', 'a narrow passage *cut* through earth or rock (like a railway cutting)' (*Nomenclature*, entry for *The Cleft*) + *ungol* 'spider'.

644–5 (II: 253): Frodo's head was bowed

645 (II: 253). vast stretch of pinion – Wide wings, as seen in flight. Compare the description of the Nazgûl's mount in Book V, Chapter 6: 'it was a winged creature: if bird, then greater than all other birds, and it was naked, and neither quill nor feather did it bear, and its vast pinions were as webs of hide between horned fingers' (p. 840, III: 115).

646 (II: 254): 'Were there any oliphaunts?'

646 (II: 254–5). Were there any oliphaunts? . . . – A recording by Tolkien from this sentence to the end of the following poem is included on Disc 2 of *The J.R.R. Tolkien Audio Collection*.

Oliphaunt is an

> archaic form of *elephant* used as a 'rusticism', on the supposition that rumour of the Southern beast would have reached the Shire long ago in the form of legend. . . . *Oliphant* in English is derived from Old French *olifant*, but the *o* is probably derived from old forms of English or German: Old English *olfend*, Old High German *olbenta* 'camel'. The names of foreign animals, seldom or never seen, are often misapplied in the borrowing language. Old English *olfend*, etc. are probably ultimately related to the classical *elephant* (Latin from Greek). [*Nomenclature*]

646 (II: 254–5): *Grey as a mouse*

646 (II: 254–5). *Grey as a mouse . . .* – Sam's poem is a reduction of a much longer work by Tolkien, *Iumbo, or ye Kinde of ye Oliphaunt*, written probably in the 1920s and published as one of the *Adventures in Unnatural History and Medieval Metres, Being the Freaks of Fisiologus* in the Exeter College, Oxford *Stapeldon Magazine* for June 1927. It was inspired by the medieval bestiary, derived especially from earlier verses by *Physiologus* ('Naturalist'), which describes the characteristics of animals and draws from them Christian morals. In *Iumbo* Tolkien followed the bestiary model but added elements of contemporary culture:

> The Indic oliphaunt's a burly lump,
> A moving mountain, a majestical mammal
> (But those that fancy that he wears a hump
> Confuse him incorrectly with the camel).
> His pendulous ears they flap about like flannel;
> He trails a supple elongated nose
> That twixt his tusks of pearly-white enamel
> Performs the functions of a rubber hose
> Or vacuum cleaner as his needs impose. . . . [p. 125]

646 (II: 254). *Never lie on the ground, / Not even to die.* – According to the medieval bestiary 'the Elephant's nature is that if he tumbles down he cannot get up again. Hence it comes that he leans against a tree when he wants to go to sleep, for he has no joints in his knees' (*The Bestiary: A Book of Beasts*, trans. by T.H. White (1960), p. 26). In truth, the elephant does lie down from time to time, as for sleep.

647 (II: 255): 'That,' said Sam

647 (II: 255). big folk down away in the Sunlands. Swertings – *Sunlands* is a Shire name for Harad. 'It is evidently meant as a popular name, in Common Speech or other languages, current in Gondor and the N.W. [North-west of Middle-earth] for the little known countries of the far South' (*Nomenclature*).

The *Swertings* are the Haradrim, 'said by Sam to be the name in the Shire for the legendary (to hobbits) dark-skinned people of the "Sunlands" (far South). It . . . is evidently a derivative of *swart*, which is still in use (= *swarthy*)' (*Nomenclature*).

647 (II: 255). They put houses and towers on the oliphauntses backs and all – The 'house' or 'tower' was historically sometimes used as a platform for archers, etc.; compare the 'war-tower' seen by Sam (in ruins) on a *mûmak* in Book IV, Chapter 4.

Chapter 4

OF HERBS AND STEWED RABBIT

For drafts and history of this chapter, see *The War of the Ring*, pp. 131–43.

648 (II: 256): The dusk was deep

648 (II: 256). The dusk was deep when at length they set out – It is the evening of 5 March 1419.

648 (II: 256): With hearts strangely lightened

648 (II: 256). until the dawn began to spread – It is now 6 March.

649 (II: 256–7): The growing light revealed

649 (II: 257). ling and broom and cornel – *Ling* is a common heather (see note for p. 209).

Broom is a shrub typically with yellow flowers, thin green stems, and small or few leaves.

Cornel is a variety of dogwood, a shrub with dark red branches and greenish-white flowers.

649 (II: 257). uplands – An area of high or hilly land.

649 (II: 257): The day passed uneasily

649 (II: 257). whiffling – Making a light whistling sound.

649–50 (II: 257–8): The road had been made

649–50 (II: 257–8). The handiwork of Men of old could still be seen in its straight sure flight and level course: now and again it cut its way through hillside slopes, or leaped over a stream upon a wide shapely arch . . . but it did not wind: it held on its own sure course – The 'Men of old' were the Númenórean settlers in Gondor. The description of the road recalls those built by the Romans, the straight courses of which are mirrored in the lines of many roads in England today.

650 (II: 258): So they passed into the northern marches

650 (II: 258). At the first signs of day – It is 7 March.

650 (II: 258). a long cutting, deep and sheer-sided in the middle – The site of Faramir's ambush of the Southrons in the present chapter, and of an attempted ambush of the army of the West in Book V, Chapter 10.

650 (II: 258): Day was opening in the sky

650 (II: 258). resinous trees – Trees such as fir and pine, which exude sticky resin.

650 (II: 258). cedar and cypress – Coniferous trees which grow more commonly in a Mediterranean climate. The *cedar* is tall with typically fragrant wood, the *cypress* an evergreen with small, dark foliage.

J.A. Schulp in 'The Flora of Middle-earth', *Inklings-Jahrbuch für Literatur und Ästhetik* 3 (1985), notes that according to the general map of Middle-earth 'North Ithilien is 600 miles South of the Shire. The Shire being comparable in climate and vegetation with Middle or South England, Tolkien is justified in confronting the readers with an all-Mediterranean vegetation . . . the country west of Dagorlad suddenly changes into a Mediterranean aspect' (p. 131). Schulp suggests that since (at this time) Tolkien had not travelled further south in Europe than Switzerland, he must have 'derived his description of the vegetation from classical authors or other literary sources, not from his own experience. It must be admitted that all the trees and herbs summed up by Tolkien make up the essence of Mediterranean vegetation to us Northerners' (p. 132).

650 (II: 258). everywhere there was a wealth of sweet-smelling herbs and shrubs – Tolkien added this account of the flora of Ithilien, including many culinary herbs, after he wrote in the following pages of Sam cooking rabbits.

650 (II: 258). larches – The *larch* is a coniferous tree with bunches of bright green needles.

650 (II: 258). Ithilien, the garden of Gondor now desolate kept still a dishevelled dryad loveliness – In Greek and Latin mythology a *dryad* is a nymph who inhabits a tree. The meaning here is apparently that though no longer tended (*dishevelled* 'untidy, disordered'), Ithilien is still a land in which nature seems especially alive.

On 30 April 1944, after writing the present chapter, Tolkien wrote to his son Christopher that Ithilien was 'proving a lovely land' (*Letters*, p. 76). It surely seems so to most readers, and comes as a relief to them as well as to Frodo and Sam after the desolation of the Dead Marshes and the landscape before the Morannon.

650 (II: 258): South and west it looked

650 (II: 258). of tamarisk and pungent terebinth, of olive and of bay – The *tamarisk* is an evergreen shrub or small tree, with feathery branches and small leaves.

The *terebinth* is a tree from which turpentine is made.

The *olive* is an evergreen with narrow leaves and white flowers.

The *bay*, or *bay-laurel*, is a tree with deep-green leaves and dark purple berries.

650 (II: 258). junipers and myrtles; and thymes – *Juniper* is an evergreen shrub or tree, sometimes with berry-like cones.

Myrtle also is an evergreen shrub, with glossy foliage and white flowers.

Thyme is a familiar low-growing, aromatic herb.

650 (II: 258). sages of many kinds . . . blue flowers, or red, or pale green; and marjorams and new sprouting parsleys – *Sage*, *marjoram*, and *parsley*, like bay and thyme, are aromatic herbs often used in cooking.

650 (II: 258). The grots and rocky walls were already starred with saxifrages and stonecrops. – *Grot* is a poetic word for *grotto*, here probably meaning natural stony recesses.

Saxifrage is a low-growing plant with small white, yellow, or red flowers, which often roots in clefts of rock.

Stonecrop is a small fleshy-leaved plant typically with star-shaped yellow or white flowers, often found among rocks or on walls.

650 (II: 258). Primeroles and anemones . . . in the filbert-brakes – The name *primerole* is given to early spring flowers, such as the cowslip and the field daisy. In 1975 Christopher Tolkien replied to a suggestion that *primeroles* here should be *primroses*: '*Primerole* is not the same word as *primrose*, but is based on Latin *primula*. It was long current and was e.g. used by Chaucer in the Miller's Tale [in the *Canterbury Tales*]' (courtesy of Christopher Tolkien).

The *anemone* (Greek 'windflower') is known for its flowers in bright colours, including scarlet, pink, shades of blue and purple, and yellow, as well as white.

Filbert-brakes are clumps of hazel trees.

650 (II: 258). asphodel and many lily flowers – *Asphodel* is itself a plant of the lily family, with long slender leaves and flowers, mostly white or pink, on a spike.

650–1 (II: 259): The travellers turned their backs

651 (II: 259). iris-swords – The leaves of the iris are shaped like swords. An old name for the iris was *gladden* (see note for p. 52), probably derived from Latin *gladius* 'sword'.

651 (II: 259). in-falling freshet – Presumably the stream as it falls into the lake.

651 (II: 259): Sam scrambling below the outfall

651 (II: 259). with briar and eglantine and trailing clematis – *Briar* denotes a prickly shrub, such as the wild rose *Rosa rubiginosa* and *eglantine* (sweet-briar, *Rosa eglanteria*).

Clematis is typically a climbing plant with white, pink, or purple flowers.

651–2 (II: 260): Sam had been giving earnest thought

652 (II: 260). Six days or more had passed since he reckoned that they had only a bare supply for three weeks. – That had been on 30 February, the day that Sam and Frodo had slept in the gully. It is now 7 March.

653 (II: 261): While Gollum was away

653 (II: 261). coneys – Rabbits. *Cony* or *coney* was formerly the proper name for this animal, while *rabbit* referred only to its young. The *Oxford English Dictionary* comments that rabbits are not mentioned in England before the Norman period, and there is no word for them in Celtic or Teutonic.

654 (II: 262): 'I don't think so'

654 (II: 262). make a smother – Create dense smoke.

654 (II: 262): Gollum withdrew grumbling

654 (II: 262). taters – A dialectal corruption of *potatoes*; see note for p. 22.

654–5 (II: 263): 'Po – ta – toes'

655 (II: 263). fish and chips – A favourite meal in Britain, deep-fried fish with *chips*, long pieces of deep-fried potato, usually larger than American French fries.

655 (II: 263): 'A present from Sméagol'

655 (II: 263). brace – In this sense, a pair of animals killed in hunting.

656 (II: 264): The two hobbits trussed

656 (II: 264). trussed – Fastened, secured.

656 (II: 265): 'Nay! Not Elves'

656 (II: 265). wondrous – Poetic 'wonderfully'.

657 (II: 265): The tall green man laughed

657 (II: 265). I am Faramir, Captain of Gondor – On 6 May 1944 Tolkien wrote to his son Christopher: 'A new character has come on the scene (I am sure I did not invent him, I did not even want him, though I like him, but there he came walking into the woods of Ithilien): Faramir, the brother of Boromir' (*Letters*, p. 79). The character in fact entered the story in draft as 'Falborn, son of Anborn', and only later received his final name and significance. The second element of *Faramir* is probably the same as that in *Boromir*, Quenya *míre* 'jewel'.

657–8 (II: 266): 'I do not know where he is'

657 (II: 266). gangrel – Vagabond, vagrant.

658 (II: 266): 'Boromir son of the Lord Denethor?'

658 (II: 266). Captain-General – Commander-in-chief.

658 (II: 266–7): 'We must learn more of this'

658 (II: 266). hard handstrokes – Hand-to-hand fighting.

658–9 (II: 267): The hobbits sat down again

659 (II: 267). pale-skinned, dark of hair, with grey eyes . . . Dúnedain of the South – Many of the Men who went to Númenor at the beginning of the Second Age were of the House of Bëor, described in *The Silmarillion* as having 'dark or brown hair' and 'grey eyes' (p. 148).

659 (II: 267): After a while he spoke to them

659 (II: 267). Mablung and Damrod – In *The Silmarillion Mablung* is the name of an 'Elf of Doriath, chief captain of Thingol, friend of Túrin; called "of the Heavy Hand"' (which is the meaning of the name *Mablung*); slain in Menegroth by the Dwarves' (p. 339).

Damrod was for a while the name of one of the sons of Fëanor; it means 'hammerer of copper [later metal]'.

659 (II: 267). forayers – Raiders; men who make a sudden attack or incursion into enemy territory.

659 (II: 267–8): 'Aye, curse the Southrons!'

659 (II: 267). Umbar – 'A natural haven on [the] coast south of Gondor, now occupied by hostile people (whose lords were orig[inally] rebel Númenóreans), and now are pirates' (*Index*).

659 (II: 267–8). they were ever ready to His will – as have so many also in the East – The brief history of Gondor told in Appendix A shows that it was constantly under attack from the East. There it is also said that Umbar

> had been Númenórean land since days of old; but it was a stronghold of the King's Men, who were afterwards called the Black Númenóreans, corrupted by Sauron, and who hated above all the followers of Elendil. After the fall of Sauron [at the end of the Second Age] their race swiftly dwindled or became merged with the Men of Middle-earth, but they inherited without lessening their hatred of Gondor. [pp. 1044–5, III: 325]

659–60 (II: 268): 'But still we will not sit idle

659 (II: 268). the cloven way – The long cutting described earlier in the chapter: 'deep, and sheer-sided in the middle, by which the road clove its way through a stony ridge' (p. 650, II: 258).

661 (II: 269): It was Sam's first view of a battle

661 (II: 269). He wondered what the man's name was and where he came from; and if he was really evil of heart, or what lies or threats had led him on the long march from his home; and if he would not really rather have stayed there in peace – Sam sees the fallen Southron as a human being, and considers the possibility that he may have been an innocent participant in the war. In *The Lord of the Rings* the characters who oppose Sauron or Saruman do so because they know that they are about to be attacked. They fight to defend themselves; most do not like to fight and would rather be at peace. Tolkien makes it clear that Sauron is utterly evil and that it is right to resist him. Nonetheless he allows that some of those who fight for Sauron or Saruman may not do so willingly, or may have been deluded. In a letter to his son Christopher on 25 May 1944 he wrote that in the real world the lines between good and evil are less clearly drawn than in 'romance':

> For 'romance' has grown out of 'allegory', and its wars are still derived from the 'inner war' of allegory in which good is on one side and various modes of badness on the other. In real (exterior) life men are on both sides: which means a motley alliance of orcs, beasts, plain naturally honest men, and angels. But it does make some difference who are your captains and whether they are orc-like per se! And what it is all about (or thought to be). It is even in this world possible to be (more or less) in the wrong or in the right. [*Letters*, p. 82]

Not all of those on the 'right' side in *The Lord of the Rings* are entirely good, nor are they perfect: they exhibit weaknesses in varying degrees. Boromir falls to temptation and Théoden to lethargy, but both redeem themselves, while Saruman and Denethor pursue their chosen paths to the bitter end. After achieving victory, both Théoden and Aragorn pardon men who had fought against them (Dunlendings, Easterlings, Haradrim) and make peace.

661 (II: 269). dinning – Resounding, making a noise.

661 (II: 269): 'Ware! Ware!'

661 (II: 269). Ware! – That is, 'beware'.

661 (II: 269). May the Valar turn him aside! – This is one of the few direct religious references in *The Lord of the Rings*. Damrod calls on the Valar, the Rulers, the Powers, who had participated in the Music which envisioned Arda, and to whose guardianship Eru, the One, the Creator, has entrusted the care of the world. *Valar* (singular *Vala*) means 'those with power', from Quenya *val-* 'power'.

661 (II: 269). Mûmak! – The name (plural *Mûmakil*) by which the 'oliphaunt' is known in Gondor.

Chapter 5

THE WINDOW ON THE WEST

For drafts and history of this chapter, see *The War of the Ring*, pp. 144–70.

664 (II: 272): 'Maybe,' he said

664 (II: 272). when I set out six days ago – On 1 March 1419. It is now 7 March.

665 (II: 273): 'See here, Captain!'

665 (II: 273). 'sauce' – Impudence, impertinence.

665 (II: 273): 'Patience!' said Faramir

665 (II: 273). But I do not slay man or beast needlessly, and not gladly even when it is needed. – Faramir quickly develops into one of the most fully rounded and sympathetic characters in *The Lord of the Rings*: perceptive, merciful, brave, responsible, restrained, aware of his position but neither boastful nor arrogant, choosing to do what he feels to be right even if it may be to his disadvantage. In a draft letter of *c.* 1953 Tolkien wrote:

> I think you misunderstand *Faramir.* He was daunted by his father: not only in the ordinary way of a family with a stern proud father of great force of character, but as a Númenórean before the chief of the one surviving Númenórean state [i.e. Denethor]. He was motherless and sisterless . . . and had a 'bossy' brother. He had been accustomed to giving way and not giving his own opinions air, while retaining a power of command among men, such as a man may obtain who is evidently personally courageous and decisive, but also modest, fair-minded and scrupulously just, and very merciful. [*Letters*, p. 323]

In fact Faramir often expresses Tolkien's own thoughts about the world and life. In his draft letter to Mr Thompson, 14 January 1956, Tolkien wrote: 'As far as any character is "like me" it is Faramir – except that I lack what all my characters possess . . . *Courage*' (*Letters*, p. 232, note).

666 (II: 274): 'Five days ere I set out

666 (II: 274). eleven days ago at about this hour of the day – Boromir's death occurred at about noon on 26 February, but this conversation is taking place in late afternoon. The call of Boromir's horn took time to reach Faramir to the south, if sound it was, and not a supernatural 'echo in the mind'.

666 (II: 274). On the third night after – Presumably the night of 28/29 February.

666 (II: 274): 'An awe fell on me

666 (II: 274). It waded deep – It lay deep in the water as it moved.

667 (II: 275–6): Then turning again to Frodo

667 (II: 276). The shards came severally to shore: one . . . among the reeds . . . northwards below the infalls of the Entwash; the other was found spinning on the flood – According to *Scheme*, the *shards* (broken pieces) were found on 28 and 30 February.

667 (II: 276). murder will out – An old proverb, found in this form in Chaucer's *Canterbury Tales*.

668 (II: 277): 'Now you, Frodo and Samwise

668 (II: 277). affray – Attack, disturbance.

669 (II: 277): There was nothing for Frodo to do

669 (II: 277). foray – Raid.

669 (II: 277): 'I do not blame you'

669 (II: 277). hazard – In this sense (as a verb), guess, venture to say.

669 (II: 277). confederates – Allies, those in league with others.

669 (II: 277). hit near the mark – *Near the mark*, here meaning 'close to the truth', derives from archery, as does Frodo's reply: 'Near, but not in the gold' (i.e. not in the centre or bull's-eye of a target, coloured gold).

669 (II: 277): 'Near,' said Frodo

669 (II: 277). ancient tales teach us also the peril of rash words concerning such things as – heirlooms – A theme which Tolkien explored also in the story of the oath sworn by Fëanor and his seven sons, pledging war and undying hatred against Morgoth who had stolen the Silmarils, and 'to pursue with vengeance and hatred to the ends of the World Vala, Demon, Elf or Man . . . whoso should hold or keep a Silmaril from their possession' (*The Silmarillion*, p. 83). This brought only disaster and death, murder and war among kinfolk until the last two survivors were 'sick and weary with the burden of the dreadful oath' (p. 247).

669–70 (II: 278): 'But, Frodo, I pressed you hard

670 (II: 278). Mardil, the good steward, who ruled in the king's stead when he went away to war. And that was King Eärnur, last of the line of Anárion – From the time of King Minardil (Third Age 1621–34) the Kings of Gondor chose their Stewards from the descendants of Húrin, who had been Minardil's Steward. By 2000 the office became hereditary. In 2050 King Eärnur, accepting a challenge from the Witch-king, rode away to Minas Morgul and was never heard of again. Since his death was uncertain and 'no claimant to the crown could be found who was of pure blood, or whose claim all would allow; and all feared the memory of the Kin-strife [a civil war in Gondor many years before], knowing that if any such dissension arose again, then Gondor would perish', Mardil the Steward, and his descendants, continued to rule. 'Each new Steward indeed took office with the oath "to hold rod and rule in the name of the king, until he shall return". But these soon became words of ritual little heeded, for the Stewards exercised all the power of the kings.' But they 'never sat on the ancient throne, and they wore no crown, and held no sceptre' (Appendix A, pp. 1052–3, III: 332–3), nor did they use the royal banner.

In his draft letter to Mr Rang in August 1967 Tolkien explained that 'the element, or verbal base (N)DIL, "to love, be devoted to" – describing the attitude of one to a person, thing, course or occupation to which one is devoted for its own sake' appeared in many Quenya names 'such as *Mardil* the Good Steward (devoted to the House [Quenya *már*], sc. of the Kings)' (*Letters*, p. 386).

670 (II: 278): 'And this I remember

670 (II: 278). our sires – Ancestors.

670 (II: 278). 'How many hundreds of years need it to make a steward a king, if the king returns not?' he [Boromir] asked. 'Few years maybe, in other places of less royalty,' my father [Denethor] answered. 'In Gondor ten thousand years would not suffice.' – Boromir, as eldest son and heir to the Stewardship, can expect to have the power of a king but wants the title as well. In a letter published in *Mythlore* 6, no. 4, whole no. 22 (Fall 1979), Benjamin Urrutia points out that 'two major events of Gondorian history are inversions, most likely conscious, of milestones in French history. The faithful Stewardship is the exact opposite of the treachery of the Carolingian stewards, who deposed the Merovingians', while the Bourbons 'were overthrown by the Republic, which was taken over by the arrogant upstart, Napoleon, who snatched the crown from the Pope's hands, placing it upon his own head. The mirror image of that deed is the humble action of Aragorn, who by law is entitled to crown himself, but instead requests Mithrandir, the spiritual leader, to do so' (p. 41). In 'Steward and King', *Beyond Bree*, February 1983, Ron Sanborn rejects the suggestion of a connection between the Stewards of Gondor and

> the accession of the Stewarts to the throne of Scotland. The head of the family had been the hereditary high steward of Scotland . . . [but] had not previously ruled, and they succeeded to the kingship legitimately: Walter Stewart, the sixth steward, married Marjorie Bruce, the daughter and eventual heiress of the famous king Robert the Bruce. . . .

> The accession of the Carolingian dynasty in France was somewhat different. The family was founded by Pippin [or Pepin] the Old, steward (*major domus*, 'mayor of the palace') of part of France (Austrasia). His son, grandson, and son-in-law were executed for trying to seize the throne.
>
> Nevertheless, Pippin's other grandson, Pippin the Younger, was subsequently restored to the stewardship. He proceeded to make himself ruler of all France. He and his successor, his son Charles Martel, like the ruling stewards of Gondor, exercised all the royal power but did not take the title *king*. The Gondorian stewards, however, ruled only in the king's absence; the French king [of the Merovingians] was a puppet in the hands of the steward. The stewards deposed and appointed kings at will. . . .
>
> At last, Pippin the Short, son and successor of Charles Martel, usurped the throne for himself, in the third generation. I think that this may have been Tolkien's inspiration for Denethor's remark about 'places of less royalty'. [p. 4]

Denethor's reply to Boromir shows that he was content with the title of Steward if with it came the power of the king, but his later refusal even to consider a claimant of the line of Isildur (Aragorn) reveals that he was not willing to give up the power.

670 (II: 278): 'I doubt it not'

670 (II: 278). the pinch – Critical point, moment of stress.

670 (II: 278): 'But I stray

670 (II: 278). in divers characters – In many different (diverse) writing systems.

670 (II: 278–9): 'Mithrandir, we called him

670 (II: 279). *Tharkûn to the Dwarves, Olórin I was in my youth in the West that is forgotten, in the South Incánus, in the North Gandalf* – In Tolkien's writings on the Istari, *Tharkûn*, obviously a Dwarvish name, is said to mean 'Staff-man', that is, a man with a staff.

Olórin, in contrast,

> is a High-elven name, and must therefore have been given to him in Valinor by the Eldar, or be a 'translation' meant to be significant to them. In either case, what was the significance of the name given or assumed? *Olor* is a word often translated 'dream', but that does not refer to (most) human 'dreams', certainly not the dreams of sleep. To the Eldar it included the vivid contents of their memory, as of their *imagination*: it referred in fact to *clear vision*, in the mind, of things not physically present at the body's situation. But not only to an idea, but to a full clothing of this in particular form and detail. [*The Istari* in *Unfinished Tales*, p. 396]

In *The Silmarillion* it is said that although Olórin 'loved the Elves, he walked among them unseen, or in form as one of them, and they did not know whence came the fair visions or the promptings of wisdom that he put into their hearts. In later days he was the friend of all the Children of Ilúvatar, and took pity on their sorrows; and those who listened to him awoke from despair and put away the imaginations of darkness' (p. 31).

Tolkien hesitated about the name *Incánus* and what Gandalf meant by 'the South'. In a note written before the publication of the second edition of *The Lord of the Rings* Tolkien said that Gandalf may have visited the areas of Harad adjoining Gondor, and that 'the name *Incánus* is apparently "alien", that is neither Westron, nor Elvish (Sindarin or Quenya), nor explicable by the surviving tongues of Northern Men. A note in the Thain's Book says that it is a form adapted to Quenya of a word in the tongue of the Haradrim meaning simply "North-spy" (*Inkā* + *nūs*)' (*The Istari* in *Unfinished Tales*, p. 399). But in another note, written in 1967, Tolkien indicated that 'the South' should mean Gondor at its widest extent, and 'Incánus was . . . a Quenya name, but one devised in Gondor in earlier times while Quenya was still much used by the learned, and was still the language of many historical records' (Christopher Tolkien, *Unfinished Tales*, p. 400). He proposed an etymology from Quenya *in(id)-* 'mind' + *kan-* 'ruler'. Christopher Tolkien comments:

> In this note my father referred to the Latin word *incánus* 'grey-haired' in such a way as to suggest that this was the actual origin of this name of Gandalf's when *The Lord of the Rings* was written, which if true would be very surprising; and at the end of the discussion he remarked that the coincidence in form of the Quenya name and the Latin word must be regarded as an 'accident'. . . . [p. 400]

671 (II: 279–80): 'What in truth this Thing is

671 (II: 280). allured – Attracted or tempted.

671 (II: 280): 'But fear no more!

671 (II: 280). I would not take this thing, if it lay by the highway. Not were Minas Tirith falling in ruin and I alone could save her, so, using the weapon of the Dark Lord for her good and my glory. – In this Faramir shows his character, and contrasts with his brother Boromir and, as shown later, with his father. He believes with Tolkien that the end does not justify the means. Although when he makes this statement he does not know what he is renouncing, he considers himself bound by it.

671–2 (II: 280): 'For myself,' said Faramir

671–2 (II: 280). I would see the White Tree in flower again . . . and the Silver Crown return, and Minas Tirith in peace. Minas Anor again as of old, full of light, high and fair, beautiful as a queen among other

queens: not a mistress of many slaves, nay, not even a kind mistress of willing slaves. War must be, while we defend our lives against a destroyer who would devour all; but I do not love the bright sword for its sharpness, nor the arrow for its swiftness, nor the warrior for his glory. I love only that which they defend: the city of the Men of Númenor – In wishing to 'see the White Tree [to be] in flower again' and 'the Silver Crown return' Faramir desires the restoration of a descendant of Elendil to the throne of Gondor. He accepts war when necessary, but would prefer the blessings of peace within the borders of Gondor to the conquest and rule of other nations. Tolkien expressed similar feelings in a wartime letter to his son Christopher on 9 December 1943: 'I love England (not Great Britain and certainly not the British Commonwealth (grr!)), and if I was of military age, I should, I fancy, be grousing away, in a fighting service, and willing to go on to the bitter end – always hoping that things may turn out better for England than they look like doing' (*Letters*, p. 65).

On 27 July 1955 Tolkien commented in a letter to M. Judson that 'technically he [Faramir] is very much needed as a link between the separated strands of the story' (Robert F. Batchelder, *Catalog 97* (February 1995), item 96). Faramir's conversation, during the walk to Henneth Annûn and the evening there, provides the reader with important background information in preparation for Pippin's arrival in Minas Tirith in Book V.

673 (II: 281): So they passed on

673 (II: 281). ilex and dark box-woods – *Ilex* has various applications in botanical nomenclature, including the common holly.

Boxwood is a small evergreen tree or shrub with dark green, leathery leaves.

674 (II: 282): 'At least by good chance

674 (II: 282). the Window of the Sunset, Henneth Annûn – In his unfinished index Tolkien notes: '*Henneth* (window) in *Henneth Annûn* "Window of Sunset" name of a cave ?and waterfall in Ithilien' and '*Annû(n)* Sunset, West'.

674 (II: 282). land of many fountains – Here *fountain* is meant in the poetic sense 'water issuing from the earth'.

674 (II: 282–3): Even as he spoke the sun sank

674 (II: 282). stooping – With a downward slope.

674–5 (II: 283): The hobbits were taken to a corner

674 (II: 283). trestles – A *trestle* is 'a framework consisting of a horizontal beam supported by two pairs of sloping legs, used in pairs to support a flat surface such as a table top' (*Concise OED*).

675 (II: 283–4): 'Well, no, lord'

675 (II: 284). They have black squirrels there, 'tis said. – This is stated to be so in Mirkwood at the beginning of Chapter 8 of *The Hobbit*.

675 (II: 284): 'Perhaps,' said Faramir

675 (II: 284). the escapes of Mirkwood – *Escapes* in this context refers to creatures that have spread out from Mirkwood into other habitats.

676 (II: 284): Now more torches were being lit

676 (II: 284). broached – Opened.

676 (II: 284). laving – Washing.

676 (II: 284): They were led then to seats

676 (II: 284). pelts – Animal skins with hair or fur.

676 (II: 284–5): 'So we always do'

676 (II: 284–5). we look towards Númenor that was, and beyond that to Elvenhome that is, and to that which is beyond Elvenhome and will ever be – Númenor was once in the West, but was drowned near the end of the Second Age when its king sailed with a great fleet against Aman, the land of the Valar, hoping thereby to gain immortality. Aman lay further west beyond Númenor, and near its eastern shore was Elvenhome where many of the Elves lived. When Númenor was destroyed, Aman was removed from the Circles of the World.

This ceremony of facing West for a moment of silence before eating, called 'the Standing Silence' in Book VI, Chapter 4, is almost the only religious observance described in *The Lord of the Rings*. Tolkien wrote to Rhona Beare on 14 October 1958 that in respect of 'theology' the Númenóreans

> were Hebraic and even more puritan . . . there is practically no overt 'religion', or rather religious acts or places or ceremonies among the 'good' or anti-Sauron peoples. . . .
>
> Almost the only vestige of 'religion' is seen on II pp. 284–5 in the 'Grace before Meat'. This is indeed mainly as it were a commemoration of the Departed, and theology is reduced to 'that which is beyond Elvenhome and ever will be', sc. beyond the mortal lands, beyond the memory of unfallen Bliss, beyond the physical world. [*Letters*, p. 281]

Earlier, in 1955, Tolkien, a devout Catholic, wrote to his American publisher, Houghton Mifflin:

> The only criticism [of *The Lord of the Rings*] that annoyed me was one that it 'contained no religion'. . . . It is a monotheistic world of 'natural theology'. The odd fact that there are no churches, temples, or religious

> rites and ceremonies, is simply part of the historical climate depicted. It will be sufficiently explained if . . . the *Silmarillion* and other legends of the First and Second Ages are published. I am in any case myself a Christian; but the 'Third Age" was not a Christian world. [*Letters*, p. 220]

Tolkien intended that the events related in 'The Silmarillion' and *The Lord of the Rings* should be considered to have taken place in a fictional earlier era of our own world, necessarily pre-Christian. But from his earliest writings Arda (the Earth) is created by the One (Eru, Ilúvatar), with the participation of the Ainur, themselves created by him. Tolkien was unwilling to introduce into this world fictional temples and religious observances even on the part of those who recognized Eru, apart from a few allusions to simple ceremonies of thanksgiving or remembrance. It is Sauron who promotes the building of temples, demands sacrifices, and fosters the worship of Morgoth or himself.

Tolkien was more expansive in explaining and defending this religious background to correspondents who had a particular concern with religion. In September 1954, in his draft letter to Peter Hastings, the manager of a Catholic bookshop in Oxford, he wrote that 'the immediate "authorities" are the Valar (the Powers or Authorities): the "gods'. But they are only created spirits – of high angelic order we should say, with their attendant lesser angels – reverend therefore, but not worshipful'. He explained in a note:

> There are thus no temples or 'churches' or fanes in this 'world' among 'good' peoples. They had little or no 'religion' in the sense of worship. For help they may call on a *Vala* (as *Elbereth*), as a Catholic might on a Saint, though no doubt knowing in theory as well as he that the power of the Vala was limited and derivative. But this is a 'primitive age': and these folk may be said to view the Valar as children view their parents or immediate adult superiors, and though they know they are subjects of the King he does not live in their country nor have there any dwelling. I do not think Hobbits practised any form of worship or prayer (unless through exceptional contact with Elves). The Númenóreans (and others . . . that fought against Morgoth, even if they elected to remain in Middle-earth and did not go to Númenor: such as the Rohirrim) were pure monotheists. But there was no temple in Númenor (until Sauron introduced the cult of Morgoth). The top of the mountain, the Meneltarma or Pillar of Heaven, was dedicated to Eru, the One, and there at any time privately, and at certain times publicly, God was invoked, praised, and adored: in imitation of the Valar and the Mountain of Aman. But Númenor fell and was destroyed and the Mountain engulfed, and there was no substitute. Among the exiles, remnants of the Faithful who had not adopted the false religion nor taken part in the rebellion, religion as divine worship (though perhaps

> not as philosophy and metaphysics) seems to have played a small part; though a glimpse of it is caught in Faramir's remark on 'grace at meat'. . . . [*Letters*, pp. 193–4]

In his draft letter to Robert Murray, 4 November 1954, Tolkien elaborates that the High Elves in Middle-earth who were exiles, the Noldor who had left Aman against the wishes of the Valar, 'had no "religion" (or religious practices, rather) for those had been in the hands of the gods [the Valar], praising and adoring *Eru* "the One", *Ilúvatar* the Father of All on the Mt. of Aman' (*Letters*, p. 204). Concerning the Númenóreans in exile, he says that

> the 'hallow' of God and the Mountain had perished, and there was no real substitute. Also when the 'Kings' came to an end there was no equivalent to a 'priesthood': the two being identical in Númenórean ideas. So while God (Eru) was a datum of good Númenórean philosophy, and a prime fact in their conception of history, He had at the time of the War of the Ring no worship and no hallowed place. And that kind of negative truth was characteristic of the West, and all the area under Númenórean influence: the refusal to worship any 'creature', and above all no 'dark Lord' or satanic demon, Sauron, or any other, was almost as far as they got. They had (I imagine) no petitionary prayers to God; but preserved the vestige of thanksgiving. (Those under special Elvish influence might call on the angelic powers for help in immediate peril or fear of evil enemies.) It later appears that there had been a 'hallow' on Mindolluin, only approachable by the King, where he had anciently offered thanks and praise on behalf of his people; but it had been forgotten. It was re-entered by Aragorn, and there he found a sapling of the White Tree [see end of Book VI, Chapter 5]. . . . It is to be presumed that with the reemergence of the lineal priest kings (of whom Lúthien the Blessed Elf-maiden was a foremother) the worship of God would be renewed, and His Name (or title) be again more often heard. But there would be no *temple* of the True God while Númenórean influence lasted. [*Letters*, pp. 206–7]

677 (II: 286): 'What hope have we?'

677 (II: 286). rekindle – Revive.

677 (II: 286): 'The Men of Númenor

677 (II: 286). the Great Lands – Christopher Tolkien notes that *Great Lands* here is a 'survival of old usage' from 'The Silmarillion' writings and is 'its only occurrence in *The Lord of the Rings*'. A subsequent occurrence in manuscripts of this chapter was emended to *Middle-earth* (p. 679, II: 288), 'suggesting that its appearance in the first passage was an oversight' (*The War of the Ring*, p. 167, n. 16). And yet it contradicts nothing, and is part of the flavour of Faramir's speech.

678 (II: 286): 'It is not said that evil arts

678 (II: 286). brought about its own decay falling by degrees into dotage, and thinking the enemy was asleep, who was only banished – *Dotage* 'feebleness, folly, weakness'. Tolkien may have had in mind the failure in the 1930s of various countries to act against the growing power of Hitler and Nazi Germany until it was too late to avoid war.

678 (II: 286): 'Death was ever present

678 (II: 286). Kings made tombs more splendid than houses of the living – On 14 October 1958 Tolkien wrote to Rhona Beare: 'The Númenóreans of Gondor were proud, peculiar, and archaic, and I think are best pictured in (say) Egyptian terms. In many ways they resembled "Egyptians" – the love of, and power to construct, the gigantic and the massive. And in their great interest in ancestry and in tombs' (*Letters*, p. 281).

678 (II: 286). withered men compounded strong elixirs – The phrase recalls the search by alchemists for the elixir of life, a potion to prolong life indefinitely.

678 (II: 287): 'So it came to pass

678 (II: 287). Cirion the Twelfth Steward – Cirion was Steward of Gondor during Third Age 2489–2567. See note for p. 512, and *Unfinished Tales*, pp. 295–308.

678 (II: 287). Calenardhon – Originally the northern part of the realm of Gondor, it became depopulated, and in Third Age 2510 was granted by Cirion to Eorl and his people as a reward for their help against invaders of Gondor. At the time of the War of the Ring it was known as Rohan, or the Riddermark. Tolkien 'translated' the name as 'green province' (*Index*) and 'the (great) green region' (draft letter to Mr Rang, August 1967, *Letters*, p. 383).

678 (II: 287): 'Of our lore and manners

678 (II: 287). those same Three Houses of Men as were the Númenóreans in their beginning – Men allied with the Elves against Morgoth in the First Age, the Houses of Bëor, Hador, and Haleth.

678 (II: 287). not from Hador the Goldenhaired, the Elf-friend, maybe, yet from such of his people as went not over Sea into the West, refusing the call – In editions prior to 2004 the words 'yet from such of his people' read 'yet from such of his sons and people'. In the draft for this chapter (as emended) they read: 'from those same Three Houses of Men as were the Númenóreans, from Beor and Hador and Haleth, but from such as went not over sea' (*The War of the Ring*, p. 157); and in the following manuscript: 'from those same Three Houses of Men as were the Númenóreans, from Hador the Golden-haired, the Elf-friend maybe, but from such of their sons as went not over the Sea into the West, refusing the call' (p. 157). Tolkien later emended 'such of their sons' in the manuscript to 'such of his people' (p. 168, n. 24). These alterations may have been made to suggest that the Rohirrim were more closely linked with the House of Hador, because most of his people had yellow hair and blue eyes, while those of the other two houses were dark-haired, and to take account of the fact that apparently Hador's only descendants at the end of the First Age were Elros and Elrond, who could not have been ancestors of the Rohirrim.

In *The War of the Ring*, p. 168, n. 24, Christopher Tolkien notes that in a late typescript the insertion of 'not' by his father led to the reading 'not from Hador', but 'it was put in very hurriedly, and it seems to me possible that he read the sentence differently from his original meaning – which was certainly "They may be descended from Hador indeed, *but if so*, then of course from those of Hador's descendants who did not pass over the Sea."' In addition, Tolkien's emendation in the manuscript of 'such of their sons' (referring to all three houses) to 'such of his people' (referring to Hador) was misinterpreted by a typist, who produced 'such of his sons and people'. In this complexity of alterations and misunderstandings, it seemed best to remove in the 2004 edition only the obvious error 'sons and'.

679 (II: 287): 'Yet now, if the Rohirrim

679 (II: 287). though we still hold that a warrior should have more skills than only the craft of weapons and slaying, we esteem a warrior, nonetheless, above men of other crafts – Tolkien commented to his son Christopher on 6 May 1944 that Faramir 'is holding up the "catastrophe" by a lot of stuff about the history of Gondor and Rohan (with some very sound reflections no doubt on martial glory and true glory): but if he goes on much more a lot of him will have to be removed to the appendices' (*Letters*, p. 79).

679 (II: 287). prowess – Valour, bravery.

679 (II: 287). so hardy in toil, so onward in battle – *Hardy* can mean 'bold, courageous, daring', but also 'vigorous, capable of enduring fatigue, hardship'. *Toil* also has various meanings: the sense 'battle, strife' is now obsolete, but the word can also denote 'a spell of severe bodily labour' or 'hard and continuous work and exertion'. Perhaps here *so hardy in toil* means 'so vigorous and tireless when engaged in conflict'.

Onward in battle here means 'always at the front'.

679 (II: 288): 'No indeed, Master Samwise'

679 (II: 288). Edain – Sindarin *adan* 'man', plural *edain* 'Men', derived by the Noldor from *Atan, Atani*, 'the name given to Men in Valinor in the lore that told of their coming' (*The Silmarillion*, p. 143).

> Since in Beleriand for a long time the only Men known to the Noldor and Sindar were those of the Three Houses of the Elf-friends, this name (in the Sindarin form *Adan*, plural *Edain*) became specially associated with them, so that it was seldom applied to other Men who came later to Beleriand, or who were reported to be dwelling beyond the Mountains. But in the speech of Ilúvatar . . . the meaning is 'Men (in general)'. [*The Silmarillion*, p. 318]

679–80 (II: 288): 'The Lady of Lórien!

680 (II: 288). daffadowndilly – A poetic and dialect form of the flower name *daffodil*.

680 (II: 288). di'monds – The spelling reflects the common pronunciation of 'diamonds'.

680 (II: 289): 'Save me!' said Sam

680 (II: 289). *When ever you open your big mouth you put your foot in it* – A variation of *to put one's foot in one's mouth*, 'to get into trouble, to say or do the wrong thing'.

682 (II: 290): Frodo had felt himself trembling

682 (II: 290). dissemble – Conceal his intentions.

682 (II: 291): Faramir smiled

682 (II: 291). pert – 'Forward in speech and behaviour; unbecomingly ready to express an opinion' (*OED*).

682 (II: 291): 'Maybe,' said Faramir

682 (II: 291). Good night! – Tom Shippey compares the meeting of Frodo and Sam with Faramir with that of Aragorn, Legolas, and Gimli with Éomer:

> In both cases an armed company comes upon strangers in a disputed borderland. In both cases the leader of the company is under orders to arrest strangers and take them back, but decides not to obey the order, at the risk of his own life. Both scenes begin with a hostile demonstration, indeed a surrounding, and in both a subordinate member of the weaker party (Gimli, Sam) comes close to losing his temper in support of his own leader. In both scenes, finally, there is an initial sequence which is public, heard by all the Riders or Rangers, and then a second one in which the leader of the group speaks more privately and in more conciliatory fashion. However, the scenes make quite a different impression. [*J.R.R. Tolkien: Author of the Century*, p. 100; see further, pp. 100–2]

Chapter 6

THE FORBIDDEN POOL

For drafts and history of this chapter, see *The War of the Ring*, pp. 171–4.

683 (II: 292): 'Not yet, but night

683 (II: 292). night is drawing to an end, and the full moon is setting – It is early on 8 March 1419. According to the 1942 lunar calendar used by Tolkien, the moon became full soon after midnight.

683 (II: 292): They went first along

683 (II: 292). turret stair – A *turret* is a small tower, usually with a spiral staircase.

683 (II: 292): At last they came out

683 (II: 292). race – In this sense, a narrow channel.

684 (II: 293): Faramir heard and answered

684 (II: 293). Moonset over Gondor – *Scheme* notes: 'See Moon-set about 5 a.m.'

684 (II: 293). white locks – Snow-covered peaks.

684 (II: 293): Faramir turned to the man

684 (II: 293). a kingfisher? Are there black kingfishers in . . . Mirkwood? – The *kingfisher* is a bird with a long sharp beak which dives to catch fish in streams, ponds, etc. Most are brightly coloured. Faramir wonders if black kingfishers exist in Mirkwood along with black squirrels (and, as seen in *The Hobbit*, black bats, butterflies, etc.).

685 (II: 294): 'You know, then, what this thing is?'

685 (II: 294). he has done worse trespass – Here *trespass* means both 'committed an offence' and 'entered a place without permission'.

690 (II: 299): 'Then I will declare my doom'

690 (II: 299). This doom shall stand for a year and a day – '*A year and a day* is the period specified in some legal matters to ensure the completion of a full year' (*Concise OED*). The phrase is used in a more general sense of expressing a period of time at the beginning of Book I, Chapter 2.

691 (II: 301): 'Not wholly, perhaps'

691 (II: 301). canker – A spreading sore or ulcer.

691–2 (II: 301): 'No,' said Faramir

691 (II: 301). break troth – Break a solemn agreement.

692 (II: 301). holden – Beholden, under an obligation.

692 (II: 301): 'Nothing certain,' said Faramir

692 (II: 301). there is some dark terror – Some readers have wondered why Faramir did not at least tell Frodo that *ungol* means 'spider'.

692 (II: 301). blanch – Turn pale with fear.

692 (II: 301–2): 'The Valley of Minas Morgul

692 (II: 301). the banished Enemy dwelt yet far away – In Dol Guldur.

692 (II: 301). it [Minas Ithil] was taken by fell men. . . . It is said that their lords were men of Númenor who had fallen into dark wickedness; to them the Enemy had given rings of power, and he had devoured them. . . . After his going they took Minas Ithil and dwelt there, and they filled it and all the valley about, with decay. . . . Nine lords there were, and after the return of their Master, which they aided and prepared in secret, they grew strong again. Then the Nine Riders issued forth from the gates of horror, and we could not withstand them. – According to *The Tale of Years*, Minas Ithil, which Isildur had built after his escape from Númenor in Second Age 3319, was captured by Sauron in 3429. After the overthrow of Sauron at the end of the Second Age, Minas Ithil was resettled; but in Third Age 1636 'a plague came upon dark winds out of the east. . . . Then the forts on the borders of Mordor were deserted, and Minas Ithil was emptied of its people' (*Of the Rings of Power and the Third Age* in *The Silmarillion*, p. 296). In Third Age 2000 the Nazgûl came out of Mordor, whence they had returned 'to prepare the ways of their Master' (*The Silmarillion*, p. 297), besieged Minas Ithil, and took it in 2002. Both mentions by Faramir of the taking of the city, and to the Nazgûl having *issued forth from the gates of horror*, seem to refer to the occasion in the Third Age.

Chapter 7

JOURNEY TO THE CROSS-ROADS

For drafts and history of this chapter, see *The War of the Ring*, pp. 175–82.

694 (II: 303): When they had finished

694 (II: 303). Imlad Morgul, the Valley of Living Death – In his unfinished index Tolkien writes: '*Imlad Morgul* = Morgul Vale', '*Imlad* narrow valley with steep sides but a flat habitable bottom', and '*Morgul* "necromancy"'.

694 (II: 303). portends – To *portend* is to give warning that something momentous or calamitous is about to occur.

694 (II: 303): The hobbits' packs were brought

694 (II: 303). staves – In this context, the plural of *staff*, in the sense 'a stick used as an aid in walking or climbing'.

694 (II: 303): 'I have no fitting gifts

694 (II: 303). the fair tree *lebethron*, beloved of the woodwrights – The casket in which the crown of Gondor is brought to Aragorn in Book VI, Chapter 5 is made of black *lebethron*.

A *woodwright* is one who works in wood, a carpenter or joiner.

696 (II: 305): Darkness came early

696 (II: 305). the first glimmer of light – It is 9 March 1419.

696 (II: 305): As the third stage

696 (II: 305). great ilexes of huge girth – Besides the common holly, which can grow to sixty-five feet, the term *ilex* also encompasses the holm-oak or evergreen oak (*Quercus ilex*), which can reach ninety feet. Frodo, Sam, and Gollum sleep in a holm-oak the following night.

696 (II: 305). launds – A *laund* is an open space in woods, a glade.

696 (II: 305). celandine – According to the *Oxford English Dictionary*, *celandine* is 'the name of two distinct plants bearing yellow flowers; by old herbalists regarded as species of the same plant, and identified (probably correctly) with the greater and lesser *chelidonia* of ancient writers'. The Lesser Celandine, filewort or figwort (*Ranunculus ficaria*), which flowers in March and grows in shady places, is probably meant here. (The Common or Greater Celandine, *Chelidonium majus*, which can grow up to thirty inches tall, would be out of place in this landscape.)

696 (II: 305). woodland hyacinths – Bluebells (*Hyacinthoides nonscripta*).

696–7 (II: 306): Light was fading fast

696–7 (II: 306). Light was fading fast. . . . A dim valley lay before them . . . – Brian Rosebury has commented on the descriptive power of this paragraph:

> Tolkien describes like a painter: his descriptions appeal to the emotions through the senses, not the other way round. . . . Tolkien evokes the human experience of perceiving a landscape. . . . But the analogy of a painter is imperfect, not merely because sound and silence are heard but because the visual scene is not experienced statically. Frodo arrives at this vantage point, after long journeying . . . and his (and our) perception of the land ahead is suffused with an awareness of the continuing journey. The long valley comes out of the darkness, but Frodo must go into it. And the description is full of verbs suggesting movement, though most refer to static features of the landscape. . . . The paradox of movement in stillness reinforces that of an audible silence: we sense the nervously attentive eyes and ears of the travellers. Already the absence of living creatures, and the heavy stifling atmosphere, have been stressed. . . . The landscape becomes suffused with a tension which will be intensified in the following pages. . . . [*Tolkien: A Cultural Phenomenon*, pp. 84–5]

697 (II: 306). the long valley – The vale of Morgulduin. Faramir had said that it was fifteen leagues to that place from Henneth Annûn; therefore Frodo, Sam, and Gollum have covered about forty-five miles in two days.

697 (II: 306). old towers forlorn and dark – Rosebury comments that this 'inversion' (of noun phrase and adjectives) is for euphony and variation:

> Out of context, it might be dismissed as a Gothic cliché; actually it is an example of one of the work's greatest strengths. . . . The point is that the towers are *literally* forlorn: they belong to Osgiliath, the 'populous city' glimpsed in the Mirror of Galadriel, but long ago abandoned in Gondor's retreat before the expansion of Mordor. Not only do we recall this historical detail when we read the phrase, but the visual scene brings home the distinctive kind of forlornness to which Osgiliath is condemned: it stands in no man's land between two opposed powers, East and West; and the haunted impression it makes under the gathering dark reminds us that it is Mordor, rather than Gondor, the spirit of decay rather than the spirit of growth, that dominates in this disputed territory. . . . Tolkien here restores power to a jaded image by constructing around it a new historical and geographical context, which displays afresh its original aptness: the very simplicity which made it a cliché becomes again its virtue. [*Tolkien: A Cultural Phenomenon*, pp. 85–6]

697 (II: 306): Frodo looked down on the road

697 (II: 306). Morgulduin, the polluted stream that flowed from the Valley of the Wraiths – *Morgulduin*, the river that ran out of Morgul Vale, also called Imlad Morgul, Morgul Valley, the Valley of the Wraiths; see note for p. 694.

697–8 (II: 306–7): Gollum reluctantly agreed to this

697 (II: 306). the crotch of a large holm-oak – *Crotch* in this sense means 'a place in the limbs of a tree where they divide in two'.

698 (II: 307): It must have been a little after midnight

698 (II: 307). a little after midnight – It is early on 10 March.

698 (II: 307): As soon as they were down

698 (II: 307). There seemed to be a great blackness looming slowly out of the East, eating up the faint blurred stars. – According to *The Tale of Years*, 'Darkness begins to flow out of Mordor' on 9 March, presumably late, since in the narrative Frodo notices nothing during that evening. *Scheme* notes that on 9 March Frodo, Sam, and Gollum reach the Osgiliath Road at dusk and sleep in a tree. Then: 'March 10: Darkness begins to flow out of Mordor at night. F. & S. [Frodo and Sam] go on during early hours, and reach Hogback. No dawn. Lie hid till afternoon. Reach *Cross-Roads* at dusk, & see last glimpse of sun.'

698 (II: 307): He quickened his pace

698 (II: 307). hog-back – A long steep hill or ridge.

698 (II: 307). gorse – A shrub with yellow flowers and spine-shaped leaves. (Compare *whin*, note for p. 333.)

698–9 (II: 308): On the further edge

699 (II: 308). covert – In this sense (as a noun), a hiding-place.

700 (II: 309): The afternoon, as Sam supposed

700 (II: 309). dun – Dull greyish-brown.

700 (II: 310): Sam stared at him

700 (II: 310). tea-time – The time of an afternoon or early evening meal with which tea is drunk, traditionally at about four o'clock.

701 (II: 310): 'The Cross-roads, yes'

701 (II: 310). Cross-roads – The point at which the Southward Road from the Morannon through Ithilien to Harad crosses the road running east from Osgiliath to Minas Morgul.

701–2 (II: 311): As furtively as scouts

701 (II: 311). campment – A shortened form of *encampment*, a place where troops camp in tents or other temporary shelter.

702 (II: 311): Standing there for a moment

702 (II: 311). pall – Here used figuratively 'of something that covers or conceals . . . especially something such as a cloud that extends over a thing or region and produces an effect of gloom' (*OED*).

702 (II: 311). unsullied – In this figurative sense, not yet made gloomy or dull.

702 (II: 311). a huge sitting figure. . . . The years had gnawed it. . . . Its head was gone – The description and the ravages of time and hostility on a once imposing figure recall Percy Bysshe Shelley's poem *Ozymandias*, which commemorates a battered statue of an Egyptian pharaoh:

> *Two vast and trunkless legs of stone*
> *Stand in the desert. . . . Near them, on the sand,*
> *Half sunk, shattered visage lies . . .*
>
> . . . .
>
> *Nothing beside remains. Round the decay*
> *Of that colossal wreck, boundless and bare*
> *The lone and level sands stretch far away.*

702 (II: 311): The eyes were hollow

702 (II: 311). carven beard – And yet, the kings of Gondor had Elven blood in their ancestry, and in a note written by Tolkien in December 1972 it is said that 'the Elvish strain in Men [is] . . . observable in the beardlessness of those who were so descended (it was a characteristic of all Elves to be beardless)' (*Unfinished Tales*, p. 247). But this is a late note, and the concept might not have been in Tolkien's mind when he wrote *The Lord of the Rings* (in Book VI, Chapter 9, the Elf Círdan, the Shipwright, is described as having a long beard). The note was evidently prepared to explain how Legolas recognized an Elvish strain in the ancestry of Imrahil of Dol Amroth (Book V, Chapter 9).

702 (II: 311). coronal – A garland or wreath for the head.

Chapter 8

THE STAIRS OF CIRITH UNGOL

For drafts and history of this chapter, see *The War of the Ring*, pp. 183–226.

704 (II: 313): So they came slowly to the white bridge

704 (II: 313). Here the road . . . passed over the stream in the midst of the valley, and went on, winding deviously up towards the city's gate: a black mouth opening in the outer circle of the northward walls. – See Tolkien's sketch-map, captioned 'Minas Morghul and the Cross-roads', in *The War of the Ring*, p. 181, and his 1941 sketch of the city gate shaped like a gaping mouth with teeth and an eye on either side (*Artist and Illustrator*, fig. 170).

704 (II: 313). charnel-smell – An 'odour of rottenness', as of dead bodies.

706 (II: 315): All that host was clad in sable

706 (II: 315). wan walls – *Wan* 'pale'.

708 (II: 317): Frodo raised his head

708 (II: 317). whether Faramir or Aragorn or Elrond or Galadriel or Gandalf or anyone else ever knew about it – It seems odd that Frodo should include Gandalf in this list, when he believes Gandalf to have been killed in Moria.

708 (II: 317): They did not answer

708 (II: 317). they followed him on to the climbing ledge – From this point, as Frodo and Sam begin their ascent towards Cirith Ungol on the evening of 10 March 1419, the chronology of their story is no longer straightforward until Sam comes out of his swoon on 14 March. Internally, this reflects the hobbits' difficulty in counting the passage of time within the darkness both outside and inside the tunnel through the mountains ('One hour, two hours, three hours: how many had they passed in this lightless hole? Hours – days, weeks rather', p. 718, II: 327); but also externally, the timing of events within the period 10–14 March (as it became after revision) became confused as Tolkien made adjustments in the course of writing.

If *The Tale of Years* is taken in conjunction with *Scheme* and with the immediately preceding time-scheme (Marquette MSS 4/2/17, with a difference of one day in dating), a clearer chronology can be expressed:

March 10: Frodo and Sam reach the Cross-roads at dusk and see a last glimpse of the sun. They pass Minas Morgul, and see the host ride out. They begin climbing in the Ephel Dúath.

March 11: Climbing in Ephel Dúath. They rest and sleep in a crevice of rocks. Gollum slips off to see Shelob.

March 12: Gollum returns, and seeing the sleeping Frodo nearly repents, but finally surrenders to evil. In the afternoon he leads Frodo and Sam into Shelob's lair.

March 13: Escape from Shelob's lair in the morning. Frodo is struck down. Sam's agony. Frodo is captured by Orcs in the late afternoon or evening. Sam lies in a swoon outside the Undergate of the Tower.

March 14: Sam lies in a swoon until late morning. Seeking a way in, he comes to the front gate of the Tower in the afternoon or evening. He enters and finds Frodo.

March 15: Frodo and Sam escape early in the day.

See also note for p. 715.

711 (II: 320): In a dark crevice

711 (II: 320). In a dark crevice . . . they sat down. – It is 11 March 1419. Frodo, Sam, and Gollum have probably been walking and climbing for well over twenty-four hours.

712 (II: 321): 'No, they never end as tales'

712 (II: 321). the people in them come, and go when their part's ended – The phrase recalls Jacques' soliloquy in Shakespeare's *As You Like It*, Act II, Scene 7: 'All the world's a stage, / And all the men and women merely players. / They have their exits and their entrances, / And one man in his time plays many parts'.

712 (II: 321): 'And then we can have some rest

712 (II: 321). I wonder if we shall ever be put into songs or tales . . . told by the fireside, or read out of a great big book with red and black letters – Apart from the tale that Frodo and Sam are in literally – *The Lord of the Rings* – they enter a song within the tale sung by a minstrel at the Field of Cormallen (Book VI, Chapter 4), and the abandoned Epilogue to *The Lord of the Rings* opens with Sam and his children sitting by the fireside in Bag End, where (in the first version, though similarly in the second) 'he had been reading aloud (as was usual) from a big Red Book on a stand' (*Sauron Defeated*, p. 114). In Book VI, Chapter 9, Frodo tells Sam that he 'will read things out of the Red Book, and keep alive the memory of the age that is gone, so that people will remember the Great Danger and so love their beloved land all the more. And that will keep you as busy and as happy as anyone can be, as long as your part of the Story goes on' (p. 1029, III: 309).

713 (II: 323): 'Well, I suppose you're right

713 (II: 323). I don't doubt he'd hand *me* over to Orcs as gladly as kiss his hand. – That is, Gollum would have no difficulty in betraying Sam to the Orcs (compare the slang phrase *as easy as kiss your hand*).

714 (II: 323): 'No, but we'd better keep our eyes skinned

714 (II: 323). keep our eyes skinned – Stay watchful, alert.

714 (II: 323). have a wink – Take a nap.

714 (II: 324): 'Hey you!' he said roughly

714 (II: 324). 'Hey you!' he said roughly. 'What are you up to?' – Gollum has engaged in 'some interior debate', Gollum vs. Sméagol, in which Sméagol has nearly won. But Sam sees Gollum's touch of Frodo's knee not as 'almost a caress' but as 'pawing at master'. Suddenly awakened, he speaks out roughly, and the moment is lost. Gollum withdraws, and a green light appears in his eyes, a sign that his evil side is ascendant. In September 1963 Tolkien wrote in his draft letter to Eileen Elgar: 'For me perhaps the most tragic moment in the Tale comes in II 323 ff. when Sam fails to note the complete change in Gollum's tone and aspect.' Gollum's 'repentance is blighted and all Frodo's pity [given to him to this point] is (in a sense) wasted.' But in the context of the story, 'Sam could hardly have acted differently' (*Letters*, p. 330).

715 (II: 324): 'It's tomorrow

715 (II: 324). 'It's tomorrow,' said Gollum, 'or this was tomorrow when hobbits went to sleep. – *The Tale of Years* indicates for 11 March: 'Gollum visits Shelob, but seeing Frodo asleep nearly repents'; and for 12 March: 'Gollum leads Frodo into Shelob's lair'. But both the glossed passage and Tolkien's working time-schemes make it clear that although Gollum left Sam and Frodo sleeping on one day, he did not return until the next. The phrase 'but seeing Frodo asleep nearly repents' is not meant to refer to an event on 11 March, only to an aspect of Gollum's character in opposition to his treachery involving Shelob. Marquette MSS 4/2/17, probably the penultimate synoptic time-scheme, with slightly different dating, has:

> 10 March: F[rodo] & Sam in Ephel Dúath and sleep in rocks (while Gollum visits Shelob).
>
> 11 March: Gollum returns and leads F & S into Shelob's Lair. (It was prob[ably] afternoon or late morning).

And compare *Scheme*, in which the idea of repentance was introduced into the chronology:

> 11 March: Climbing in Ephel Dúath. They [Frodo and Sam] rest and

sleep in a crevice of rocks. (Gollum slips off to see Shelob: nearly repents but finally surrenders to evil.)

12 March: Gollum returns and leads F. and S. into Shelob's Lair (in afternoon).

Chapter 9

SHELOB'S LAIR

For drafts and history of this chapter, see *The War of the Ring*, pp. 183–226.

717 (II: 326): Presently they were under the shadow

717 (II: 326). Torech Ungol, Shelob's Lair – *Torech Ungol* is Sindarin for 'tunnel of the spider', from *torech* 'hole, excavation' + *ungol* 'spider' (*Index*).

Shelob is simply composed of *she* 'female' + dialectal English *lob* 'spider'. Compare Bilbo's taunt to the spiders, 'Lazy Lob', in *The Hobbit*, Chapter 8. The creature's name was originally to be *Ungoliant*, borrowed from 'The Silmarillion'; see following note.

717–18 (II: 326–7): Drawing a deep breath

717 (II: 327). a black vapour wrought of veritable darkness that, as it was breathed, brought blindness not only to the eyes but to the mind – *The Silmarillion* tells of Ungoliant, who 'took shape as a spider of monstrous form, weaving her black webs in a cleft of the mountains. There she sucked up all light that she could find, and spun it forth again in dark nets of strangling gloom, until no light more could come to her abode' (p. 73). With Melkor she attacked the Two Trees of Valinor, draining them of their sap. As she did so, she 'belched forth black vapours', and 'so soon as any [in pursuit] came up with the Cloud of Ungoliant the riders of the Valar were blinded and dismayed' (p. 76).

720 (II: 329): Frodo gazed in wonder

720 (II: 329). *Aiya Eärendil Elenion Ancalima!* – In his draft letter to Mr Rang, August 1967, Tolkien wrote that this phrase in Quenya means 'Hail Eärendil brightest of stars', and that it 'is derived at long remove from *Éala Éarendel engla beorhtast*', a line from the Old English poem *Crist* (*Letters*, p. 385). See also note for p. 194.

720 (II: 329–30): But other potencies there are

720 (II: 329). potencies – In this sense, beings possessed of power.

720 (II: 329). She that walked in darkness had heard the Elves cry that cry far back in the deeps of time – 'She' is Shelob, but the Elves cannot have cried thus until the end of the First Age and the transformation of the mariner Eärendil into a star.

720 (II: 329). a deadly regard – *Regard* in this sense means 'gaze'.

720 (II: 329). two great clusters of many-windowed eyes – In this and other respects Shelob is not like normal spiders, which do not have compound eyes. See further, note for p. 724.

721 (II: 330): Frodo and Sam, horror-stricken

721 (II: 330). baleful – Menacing.

721 (II: 330): 'Galadriel!' he called

721 (II: 330). flickered – In editions prior to 2004 this word was printed 'flicked', an original error overlooked in proof. See *The War of the Ring*, p. 223, n. 30.

721 (II: 330): They wavered

721 (II: 330). One by one they [Shelob's eyes] dimmed, and slowly they drew back. No brightness so deadly had ever afflicted them before. From sun and moon and star they had been safe underground – Whereas Ungoliant in *The Silmarillion* lusted for light and gorged herself on it, Shelob is repelled by it.

722 (II: 331): 'That would not help us now'

722 (II: 331). There were webs of horror in the dark ravines of Beleriand where it was forged. – Frodo's sword Sting was 'made in Gondolin for the Goblin-wars' (*The Hobbit*, Chapter 3). In *The Silmarillion* it is said that Ungoliant, fleeing the Balrogs of Morgoth,

> went down into Beleriand, and dwelt beneath Ered Gorgoroth [east of Gondolin], in that dark valley that was afterwards called Nan Dungortheb, the Valley of Dreadful Death, because of the horror that she bred there. For other foul creatures of spider form had dwelt there since the days of the delving of Angband, and she mated with them, and devoured them; and even after Ungoliant herself departed, and went whither she would into the forgotten south of the world, her offspring abode there and wove their hideous webs. [p. 81]

722 (II: 332): It seemed light in that dark land

722 (II: 332). The great smokes had risen and grown thinner, and the last hours of a sombre day were passing. Yet it seemed to Frodo that he looked upon a morning of sudden hope. – According to *Scheme* it is the morning of 13 March. Tolkien's revisions to the 'Cirith Ungol' sequence (the final chapters of Book IV, and the beginning of Book VI) were complex, involving changes both to the topography of the passage through the mountains (working sketch-plans are reproduced in *The War of the Ring*, Chapter 8, and see also *Artist and Illustrator*, figs. 172–4) and to the chronology of events. Here *the last hours of a sombre day were passing* are a vestige of the earlier chronology, in which Frodo and Sam entered Shelob's lair in the morning and escaped in the afternoon.

723 (II: 332): There agelong she had dwelt

723 (II: 332). an evil thing in spider-form, even such as once of old had lived in the Land of the Elves in the West that is now under the Sea, such as Beren fought in the Mountains of Terror in Doriath. . . . How Shelob came there, flying from ruin, no tale tells. . . . But still she was there, who was there before Sauron, and before the first stone of Barad-dûr; and she served none but herself, drinking the blood of Elves and Men, bloated and grown fat with endless brooding on her feasts, weaving webs of shadow; for all living things were her food, and her vomit darkness. Far and wide her lesser broods, bastards of the miserable mates, her own offspring, that she slew, spread from glen to glen, from the Ephel Dúath to the eastern hills, to Dol Guldur and the fastnesses of Mirkwood. But none could rival her, Shelob the Great, last child of Ungoliant to trouble the unhappy world. – Thus Shelob in *The Lord of the Rings* is related to the giant spiders of Mirkwood in *The Hobbit* and to a creature Tolkien had envisioned long before in 'The Silmarillion'. On 25 April 1954 he wrote to Naomi Mitchison that Shelob is represented as a 'descendant of the giant spiders of the glens of *Nandungorthin*, which come into the legends of the First Age, especially into the chief of them, the tale of Beren and Lúthien. . . . The giant spiders were themselves only the offspring of Ungoliante the primeval devourer of light, that in spider-form assisted the Dark Power, but ultimately quarrelled with him' (*Letters*, p. 180). Of Ungoliant *The Silmarillion* says that 'the Eldar knew not whence she came'; she took 'all things to herself to feed her emptiness', and she 'crept towards the light of the Blessed Realm; for she hungered for light and hated it' (p. 73). Of Beren's terrible southward journey through the Mountains of Terror (Ered Gorgoroth), *The Silmarillion* tells that in 'the wilderness of Dungortheb, where the sorcery of Sauron and the power of Melian came together, . . . horror and madness walked. There spiders of the fell race of Ungoliant abode, spinning their unseen webs in which all living things were snared' (p. 164).

The first stone of Barad-dûr was laid *c.* Second Age 1000.

In drafts for this section of *The Lord of the Rings* Frodo and Sam were menaced by a host of spiders, as Bilbo encountered in *The Hobbit* but more deadly. Eventually Tolkien chose to write of one great spider, at first named *Ungoliant*, finally the *last child of Ungoliant* (i.e. the last descendant, if not literally the offspring of a creature of the distant First Age of the world).

Some readers have supposed that Tolkien had a fear of spiders, which manifested itself in Shelob. 'If that has anything to do with my being stung by a tarantula when a small child,' he wrote to W.H. Auden on 7 June 1955, 'people are welcome to the notion. . . . I can only say that I remember nothing about it, should not know it if I had not been told; and I do not dislike spiders particularly, and have no urge to kill them. I usually rescue those whom I find in the bath!' (*Letters*, p. 217).

724 (II: 333): And as for Sauron

724 (II: 333). unabated – Not lessened.

724 (II: 333). *his cat* he calls her, but she owns him not – That is, she does not acknowledge Sauron's authority.

724–5 (II: 334): Dread was round him

724 (II: 334). a fey mood – *Fey* 'overexcited or elated, as formerly associated with the state of mind of a person about to die' (*Concise OED*).

725 (II: 334): Hardly had Sam hidden the light

725 (II: 334). Most like a spider she was – In a late unpublished work Tolkien noted that Shelob is not described in *The Lord of the Rings*

> in precise spider terms; but she was 'most like a spider'. As such she was enormously magnified; and she had two horns and two great clusters of eyes. But she had the characteristic tight constriction of spiders between the front section (head and thorax) and the rear (belly) – this is called ... her 'neck', because the rear portion is swollen and bloated out of proportion. She was black, except for the underpart of her belly, which was 'pale and luminous' with corruption. [Tolkien Papers, Bodleian Library, Oxford]

Chapter 10

THE CHOICES OF MASTER SAMWISE

For drafts and history of this chapter, see *The War of the Ring*, pp. 183–226.

728 (II: 337): Now the miserable creature

728 (II: 337). Her vast belly . . . with its putrid light – *Putrid* 'rotten, foul, noxious'. It has already been said, in Book IV, Chapter 9, that Shelob's 'pale and luminous belly . . . gave forth a stench' (p. 725, II: 334), while in the next paragraph her hide is 'knobbed and pitted with corruption'.

728–9 (II: 337–8): But Shelob was not as dragons are

729 (II: 337). But Shelob was not as dragons are, no softer spot had she save only her eyes. – Dragons by tradition have a soft spot in their under-parts. In Norse legend Sigurd slew Fafnir by stabbing him from underneath, and Túrin uses the same method to kill Glaurung in *The Silmarillion*. In *The Hobbit* Bilbo notices an unprotected soft spot on Smaug's left breast, and by this knowledge Bard the archer knows where to aim to kill the dragon over Lake-town.

729 (II: 337–8). not though Elf or Dwarf should forge the steel or the hand of Beren or of Túrin wield it – No weapon could pierce her skin, even if wielded by the greatest of heroes. But Sam holds his sword in such a way that Shelob drives it into herself. In his letter to Milton Waldman in ?late 1951 Tolkien referred to Sam's 'supreme plain dogged common-sensible heroism in aid of his master', and said that as he confronts Shelob 'Sam now begins his rise to supremely heroic stature. He fights the Spider, rescues his master's body, assumes the ghastly burden of the Ring, and is preparing to stagger on alone in an attempt to carry out the impossible errand' (*Waldman LR*).

729 (II: 338): No such anguish had Shelob

729 (II: 338). had ever thus endured her – Here *endured* means 'persisted, continued to attack'.

729 (II: 338): Sam had fallen to his knees

729 (II: 338). drabbling – Bespattering.

729 (II: 338): 'Galadriel!' he said faintly

729 (II: 338). ***Gilthoniel A Elbereth!*** – As first published, the reading here and in the verse below was '*O Elbereth*'. These expressions were emended in the second edition (1965). On 14 October 1958 Tolkien wrote to Rhona Beare:

> The use of *O* on II p. 339 [2004 edn., p. 729] is an error. Mine in fact, taken over from p. 338, where *Gilthoniel O Elbereth* is, of course, a quotation of I p. 88 [p. 79], which was a 'translation', English in all but proper names. Sam's invocation is, however, in pure Elvish and should have had *A* as in I p. 250 [p. 238]. Since hobbit-language is represented as English, *O* could be defended as an inaccuracy of his own; but I do not propose to defend it. He was 'inspired' to make this invocation in a language he did not know. . . . Though it is, of course, in the style and metre of the hymn-fragment, I think it is composed or inspired for his particular situation. [*Letters*, p. 278]

729 (II: 338–9): And then his tongue was loosed

729 (II: 338). And then his tongue was loosed and his voice cried in a language which he did not know – The language Sam uses is Sindarin. In Shelob's lair Frodo cried out in Quenya.

729 (II: 339). ***A Elbereth Gilthoniel . . .*** – In his letter to Rhona Beare, 14 October 1958, Tolkien says that the verse

> means, more or less: '*O Elbereth Starkindler* (in the past tense: the title belongs to mythical pre-history and does not refer to a permanent function) *from heaven gazing-afar, to thee I cry now in the shadow of (the fear of) death. O look towards me, Everwhite!*' *Everwhite* is an inadequate translation; as is equally the *snow-white* of I 88. The element *ui* (Primitive Elvish *oio*) means *ever*; both *fan-* and *los(s)* convey *white*, but *fan* connotes the whiteness of clouds (in the sun); *loss* refers to *snow*.
>
> *Amon Uilos*, in High-elven *Oiolosse*, was one of the names of the highest peak of the Mountains of Valinor, upon which Manwe and Varda dwelt. So that an Elf using or hearing the name *Fanuilos*, would not think of (or picture) only a majestic figure robed in white, standing in a high place and gazing eastwards to mortal lands, he would at the same time picture an immense peak, snow-capped, crowned with a piercing or dazzling white cloud. [*Letters*, p. 278]

Prior to the second printing (1967) of the Allen and Unwin second edition the *i* in *palan-díriel* and in *tíro* was marked as long. Tolkien comments in *The Road Goes Ever On: A Song Cycle* (p. 64) that these vowels in fact should be short.

730 (II: 339): As if his indomitable spirit

730 (II: 339). indomitable – Impossible to overcome or subdue.

730 (II: 339). firmament – 'The arch or vault of heaven overhead, in which the clouds and the stars appear; the sky or heavens. In modern use, poetical' (*OED*).

730 (II: 339): Sam was left alone

730 (II: 339). as the evening of the Nameless Land fell – Evidently another vestige of the earlier chronology of this episode, when Frodo and Sam escaped from Shelob's lair in the late afternoon rather than in the morning.
The *Nameless Land* is Mordor.

730 (II: 339): 'Master, dear master!'

730 (II: 339). had stung him in the neck – Real spiders in fact do not have stings, but poison or paralyze their prey with a bite. Again, however, Tolkien does not say that Shelob *is* a spider, only that she is 'in spider-form' and 'most like a spider'.

730 (II: 339–40): Then as quickly as he could

730 (II: 340). chafed – Rubbed to restore warmth or feeling.

730 (II: 340): 'Frodo, Mr. Frodo!'

730 (II: 340). O wake up, Frodo, me dear, me dear. – In his distress, as he attempts to rouse Frodo, Sam forgets to address him formally, omitting 'Mr'. Helen Saunders in a letter to *Amon Hen* 57 (August 1982) points out that

> there is nothing embarrassing in Sam calling Frodo 'M'dear'. I think it highly possible that JRRT was called 'M'dear' during his family holidays in Cornwall. It used to be the recognised form of address, between almost anyone, irrespective of sex. Sometimes varied with 'My lover'. Sam's family was based on an old Cornishman named by JRRT Gaffer Gamgee. Gaffer Gamgee would probably address any member of the Tolkien family as 'M'dear'. [p. 21]

731 (II: 340): Then anger surged over him

731 (II: 340). suddenly he saw that he was in the picture that was revealed to him in the mirror of Galadriel – See note for p. 362.

731 (II: 340). 'He's dead!' he said. . . . And as he said it . . . it seemed to him that the hue of the face grew livid green. – As noted for p. 271, Tolkien commented in a letter to his son Christopher on 7–8 November 1944: 'in the last chapter of The Ring that I have yet written I hope you'll note, when you receive it . . . that Frodo's face goes livid and convinces Sam that he's dead, just when Sam gives up *hope*' (*Letters*, p. 101).

731 (II: 340): When at last the blackness passed

731 (II: 340). When at last the blackness passed – Tolkien intended that Sam should be unconscious of the world for a long time. In an early outline, when the attack on Frodo was to take place much later in the day, he wrote: 'Make Sam *sit* long by Frodo all through night' (*The War of the Ring*, p. 190). In the final chronology Frodo is struck down in the morning, and his unconscious body is found by orcs in the late afternoon or evening.

731 (II: 340): 'What shall I do, what shall I do?'

731 (II: 340). And then he remembered his own voice speaking words that at the time he did not understand himself – On the morning after the hobbits spent the night with Gildor and the Elves, in Book I, Chapter 4.

732 (II: 341): He looked on the bright point

732 (II: 341). He looked on the bright point of the sword. . . . 'What am I to do then?' . . . *see it through.* – Sam contemplates revenge and suicide but, although his grief at Frodo's apparent death is as great, and probably greater, than Denethor's grief for Faramir in Book V, he sees that these would be useless actions. Instead, without hope, he makes the decision to assume Frodo's task. He will soon think that he made the wrong choice, but his reasoning is sound, and his actions will lead to the successful outcome of the Quest. Even if he had realized that Frodo was not dead, there was nowhere safe he could have taken him to wait until the effect of the sting wore off; if he had stayed beside him, both would have been captured and the Ring taken; and without the fight over Frodo's mithril coat which destroyed the garrison of Cirith Ungol, it is unlikely that they would have been able to pass the tower undetected. Sam's choice is perhaps a constructive expression of the Northern spirit of fighting against all odds until the last.

733 (II: 342–3): As the sheer sides of the Cleft

733 (II: 343). He fancied there was a glimmer on the ground – In *The War of the Ring* Christopher Tolkien speculates that this is a shadow of an earlier text in which Sam left the Phial of Galadriel clasped in Frodo's hand, and that its original meaning was that 'there was a faint shining from the Phial' (p. 214).

735 (II: 344): 'Orders, you lubber'

735 (II: 344). lubber – 'A big, clumsy, stupid fellow; especially one who lives in idleness' (*OED*). Gorbag and Shagrat accuse each other of avoiding more active service.

735 (II: 344). Shagrat – Tolkien deliberately invented Orc names with sounds which seem harsh and unpleasant to English ears or have unpleasant associations. *Shag*, for instance, has many meanings including 'rough matted hair' and 'a low rascally fellow', while *rat* can mean 'vermin', 'a despicable person', 'one who deserts a cause', etc.

735 (II: 344): 'Hai! Hola! Here's something!

735 (II: 344). babel of baying voices – A *babel* is a confused noise of voices, derived from the biblical story in Genesis that at a time when all men spoke the same language they attempted to build a tower to reach the heavens, but God responded by confusing their language and scattering them over the earth.

Baying is the sound made by dogs, especially used of hounds in a hunt.

736 (II: 345): There was a wild clamour

736 (II: 345). Ya hoi! Ya harri hoi! Up! Up! – In *The Annotated Hobbit* Douglas A. Anderson compares these words with the song of the goblins in *The Hobbit*, Chapter 6, as they dance around the trees in which Gandalf, Bilbo, and the dwarves have taken refuge: '*Ya hey! Ya-harri-hey! Ya hoy!*':

> It may be that Tolkien intended the phrases to be Common Speech renderings of Orkish curses. In section I of Appendix F ('The Languages and Peoples of the Third Age') of *The Lord of the Rings*, Tolkien wrote of the Orcs: 'It is said that they had no language of their own, but took what they could of other tongues and perverted it to their own liking; yet they made only brutal jargons, scarcely sufficient even to their own needs, unless it were for curses and abuse.' [2nd edn., p. 152]

736 (II: 345): Then a voice shouted

736 (II: 345). Undergate – 'An underground entrance to [the] rear of the Tower of C[irith] U[ngol] reached by a passage from Torech Ungol' (*Index*).

736 (II: 345–6): It no longer seemed very dark

736 (II: 345). His weariness was growing but his will hardened all the more – An obvious echo of the Northern ethic as described in the Old English poem *The Battle of Maldon*: 'Hige sceal þe heardra, heorte þe cenre, / mod sceal þe mare þe ure mægen lytlað', translated by Tolkien in *The Homecoming of Beorhtnoth Beorhthelm's Son* (*Essays and Studies 1953* (1953), p. 3) as 'Will shall be the sterner, heart the bolder, spirit the greater, as our strength lessens'.

736 (II: 346). the swiftest way from the Dead City over the mountains – That is, from Minas Morgul. Considering the difficulty of the stairs, even apart from the need to watch out for Shelob, one would expect the longer route along the road that ran past Minas Morgul and up the cutting by which Sam and Frodo escaped to be quicker; but Orcs had longer legs than the hobbits.

736 (II: 346). In what far-off time the main tunnel and the great round pit had been made, where Shelob had taken up her abode, they did not know – In an earlier version Tolkien wrote:

> Goblins go fast in tunnels, especially those which they have themselves made, and all the many passages in this region of the mountains were their work, even the main tunnel and the great deep pit where Shelob housed. In the Dark Years they had been made, until Shelob came and made her lair there, and to escape her they had bored new passages, too narrow for her growth, that crossed and recrossed the straight way. [*The War of the Ring*, p. 215]

737 (II: 347): 'No, I don't know'

737 (II: 347). Those Nazgûl give me the creeps – To *give someone the creeps* is 'to induce a feeling of revulsion of fear' (*Concise OED*). In early drafts Trotter the hobbit said to Frodo at Bree that the Black Riders 'give me the creeps' (*The Return of the Shadow*, p. 153).

738 (II: 347): 'It's going well, they say'

738 (II: 347). It's going well, they say. . . . – Official news, especially at a time of war, is typically optimistic.

738 (II: 347): 'Yes,' said Gorbag

738 (II: 347). if they get topsides on Him – If they defeat Sauron.

738 (II: 347): 'Bad business'

738 (II: 347). our Silent Watchers were uneasy more than two days ago. . . . But my patrol wasn't ordered out for another day, nor any message sent to Lugbúrz either: owing to the Great Signal going up, and the High Nazgûl going off to the war. . . . And then they couldn't get Lugbúrz to pay attention for a good while – It is now late on 13 March; *more than two days ago* would be 10 or 11 March. Frodo and Sam reached Minas Morgul and began the ascent on 10 March; therefore Gorbag's patrol presumably set out on 11 or 12 March. The latter seems possible, as the orcs had speed and knowledge of the paths. If the former, this passage may be a shadow of an earlier text, when Frodo was captured two rather than three days after passing Minas Morgul.

It is lucky that in the confusion of the beginning of the war action was not taken more quickly, and that Minas Morgul could not get Sauron's attention. Otherwise Frodo and Sam would have been intercepted on the stairs or in the tunnel or as they emerged. The inattention of Sauron and his forces is due partly to the fact that on 6 March Aragorn had looked in the Orthanc-stone and revealed himself to Sauron. *Scheme* states:

March 6: Sauron sees Aragorn & Sword in the Stone, and is disturbed in plans. Decides eventually on immediate War. Draws off forces from North and aims all thrust at Minas Tirith.

March 7: Sauron bids Lord of Nazgûl lead out a great Orc force from Morgul on 10 of March. Sauron prepares a great smoke and darkness.

The *Great Signal* was the red flash described on p. 705, II: 314–15.

738–9 (II: 348): You must have seen him

738 (II: 348). Came *out* of Lugbúrz the first time, years ago, and we had word from High Up to let him pass. – This is further confirmation that Gollum was allowed to leave Mordor, but suggests that he was allowed to believe that he had escaped. *The Tale of Years* says that Gollum was released in 3017.

738 (II: 348). He's been up the Stairs once or twice since then. . . . Early last night we saw him. – It is now probably evening on 13 March. Gollum might have been seen when he visited Shelob on the night of 11/12 March, but *early last night* suggests early on 12/13 March. After leading Frodo and Sam into Shelob's lair on the afternoon of 12 March, Gollum disappeared after only a short distance, and knowing the way, he could have reached the upper exit well before they did. But this too may be a shadow of an earlier conception, when Frodo and Sam traversed the whole of Shelob's lair on the same day, and Gollum's visit to Shelob would have been the previous night.

739 (II: 349): 'You may well put your thinking cap on

739 (II: 349). put your thinking cap on – Think carefully about the problem.

739 (II: 349). since the Great Siege – By *Great Siege* Gorbag is probably referring to the Siege of Barad-dûr in the Second Age, rather than to the Siege of Angband in the First Age. This remark has led some readers to wonder if Gorbag and Shagrat were alive in an earlier age, and thus (extrapolating still further) whether Orcs, like Elves, are to be considered immortal unless killed. Tolkien's later writings, however, indicate that Orcs led comparatively short lives, 'indeed they appear to have been by nature short-lived compared with the span of Men of higher race, such as the Edain' (*Morgoth's Ring*, p. 418).

739–40 (II: 349): 'It's my guess you won't find much

739 (II: 349). the real mischief – Here *mischief* is used in the sense 'harm, evil'.

740 (II: 349). just left him lying: regular Elvish trick – Tom Shippey comments in 'Orcs, Wraiths, Wights: Tolkien's Images of Evil', *Tolkien and His Literary Resonances: Views of Middle-earth*: 'There is no mistaking the disapproval in Gorbag's last three words. Like other characters in *LR* (not all of them on the side of Sauron), "elvish" to him is pejorative. It is clear that he regards abandoning one's comrades as contemptible, and also characteristic of the other side. And yet only a page later it is exactly what characterizes his own side': Shagrat describes how they found 'old Ufthak' still alive, but chose not to interfere with Shelob and her prey. 'Regular orcish trick', Shippey remarks, but notes the implications of the conversation between Gorbag and Shagrat: 'that orcs are moral beings, with an underlying morality much the same as ours. But if that is true, it seems that an underlying morality has no effect at all on actual behaviour. How, then, is an essentially correct theory of good and evil corrupted? If one starts from a sound moral basis, how can things go so disastrously wrong?' He points out the relevance of this question to the twentieth century, 'in which the worst atrocities have often been committed by the most civilized people' (pp. 183–4).

Shippey carefully analyzes other fragments of Orc-conversation in *The Lord of the Rings* and finds that they 'recognize the idea of goodness, appreciate humor, value loyalty, trust, group cohesion, and the ideal of a higher cause than themselves, and condemn failings from these ideals in others. So, if they know what is right, how does it happen that they persist in wrong?' (p. 186). He concludes that Orcish behaviour is also human behaviour, 'and their inability to judge their own actions by their own moral criteria is a problem all too sadly familiar' (p. 189).

740 (II: 350): 'Garn!' said Shagrat

740 (II: 350). Garn! – 'Colloquial (chiefly Cockney [East End of London]) pronunciation of *go on* often used to express disbelief or ridicule of a statement' (*OED*).

740 (II: 350). Nar – Colloquial pronunciation 'ne'er, never'.

742 (II: 352): The great doors slammed to

742 (II: 352). Frodo was alive but taken by the Enemy. – It is late on 13 March 1419. Tolkien wrote to his son Christopher on 29 November 1944: 'I have got the hero into such a fix that not even an author will be able to extricate him without labour and difficulty' (*Letters*, p. 103).

THE RETURN OF THE KING

Synopsis (in three-volume editions) – In the paragraph beginning 'In the parley before the door' (III: 12), in editions prior to 2005, the words 'four surviving *palantíri*' read 'three surviving *palantíri*' (and in some printings the acute accent in *palantíri* was mistakenly omitted). But, as a reader pointed out to Christopher Tolkien in 1987, in fact *four* seeing-stones survived: those held by Sauron, Saruman, and Denethor, and the one kept by the Elves in the Tower on Emyn Beraid. The last named of these is not revealed until Appendix A, and one could argue that it was not known to Gandalf when he spoke with Pippin en route to Minas Tirith in Book III, Chapter 11. But, as Christopher Tolkien has remarked, it 'is incredible that the Stone of Emyn Beraid, guarded by Círdan and the elves of Lindon, should not have been known to Gandalf' (private correspondence).

BOOK FIVE

Chapter 1

MINAS TIRITH

For drafts and history of this chapter, see *The War of the Ring*, pp. 229–35, 255–65, 274–95.

747 (III: 19): Pippin looked out from the shelter

747 (III: 19). Pippin looked out – It is the night of 7/8 March 1419.

747 (III: 19). Sleepily he tried to reckon the times and stages of their journey – In Tolkien's original scheme the Battle of the Pelennor Fields took place on 14 March. But when he came to write the story of Aragorn's journey from Helm's Deep to Minas Tirith, originally to be told wholly in retrospect after the battle, he found that more time was needed for that sequence than he had allowed. He considered that the 'Fellowship could be broken sooner giving 2 days (5) [i.e. presumably 5 days instead of 3] to F[rodo and] S[am] in [the] Emyn Muil and moving [the] Hornburg etc. back 2 days. But this would throw all out of gear in rest [of] story. Best would be to make Pelennor later' (Marquette MSS 4/2/17). The Battle of the Pelennor Fields was thus moved to 15 March, and an extra day was added to Gandalf and Pippin's journey from Dol Baran to Minas Tirith: they still left Dol Baran late on 5 March, but arrived at Minas Tirith early on 9 March instead of 8 March. In Marquette MSS 4/2/17 Tolkien worked out 'Gandalf's ride' with meticulous attention to detail, although concomitantly the speed and endurance of Shadowfax became less remarkable:

> March 5: 11.30 leaves Dolbaran [*sic*].
> March 6: 7.30 sights Edoras having ridden (with brief rest) at 16 mph. 136 miles.
> Rides on to Edoras (139 mi.).
> Stays there during day, resting Shadowfax and ordering things anew.
> Leaves Edoras with 294 miles to go to M[inas] T[irith].

[In the following, the first figure indicates the miles travelled in the period stated, and the second the total miles travelled during the ride:]

Mar. 6	8 p.m. > 10 p.m.	32	32
Mar. 7	midnight > 2 a.m.	32	64
	4 > 6 a.m.	32	96
	(hides)		
	8 > 10 [p.m.]	32	128
Mar. 8	mid[night] > 2 a.m.	32 passes into Anórien	160
	4 > 6 a.m.	32	192

	8 > 10 [p.m.]	32	224
Mar. 9	mid[night] > 2 a.m.	32	256
	4 [>] 6.20 [a.m.]	38	294
	reaches Rammas Echor at 6.20		

> Errand-riders reach DH [Dunharrow] at dark on 9th. When do they pass Gandalf?
>
> Episode of moon must be therefore in early hours of 8 [March] (5 a.m.) and the errand-riders would then be about 176 miles out from Gondor which they should reach [i.e. reach Dunharrow] by dark next day.

Having worked out these details, Tolkien also emended or rewrote his original entries in *Scheme* for 6 and 7 March:

> March 6: Gandalf and Pippin sight Edoras at dawn (139 miles between 11.30 p.m. on 5 March and 7.30 a.m.) Remain at Edoras during day. Proceed at night, and ride [*deleted*: another 60 miles before 11.30 [p.m.] and then rest 199 [*i.e. total miles from Dol Baran*]] > on (with pauses) through night 6/7.
>
> March 7: G[andalf] and Pippin [*deleted*: ride 69 miles and pass into Anórien and lie hid in foothills at 3 a.m. (10 miles over border). Go on again at 4 a.m. until 7 a.m. doing another 50 miles. Gandalf has then still 119 miles to go to reach wall of Rammas Echor. Rides on at 8 p.m. Pippin sees moon rise at 9 p.m. and about 9.20 the errand-riders of Gondor go by to Rohan and the beacons are kindled. G[andalf] now rides faster, and when he rests at 11 p.m. he is only 69 miles from the Pelennor] > 96 miles from Edoras rest and hide. Ride on at night.

From 8 March the account of the ride (and other events) is continued on a new sheet but with the revised chronology *ab initio*:

> March 8: *Pippin* sees moon soon after midnight 7/8, and beacons in Anórien. Errand-riders of Gondor pass, 176 miles from Edoras. Gandalf halts 192 miles from Edoras.
>
> March 9: Gandalf rides through night and reaches *Rammas Echor* about 6.15 a.m.

No hint of this careful division of the journey of Gandalf and Pippin into thirty-two-mile stretches, each taking two hours and with two-hour breaks in between, is suggested in the narrative, which mentions only halts during the day. The only alteration made to the text to indicate an extra day was the addition of the words on p. 748 (III: 20): 'Another day of hiding and a night of journey had fleeted by.'

747 (III: 19): There had been the first ride

747 (III: 19). the great empty house on the hill – Meduseld, empty because most of the inhabitants had withdrawn to safer places.

747 (III: 19). the winged shadow . . . and Gandalf giving orders – According to *Scheme*: 'Second Nazgûl swoops over Edoras in morning and terrifies all men. Gandalf orders the Muster to remove up the Snowbourn valley to Dunharrow.'

747 (III: 19). the third night since he looked in the Stone – Pippin looked in the *palantír* during the evening of 5 March; the three nights are 5/6, 6/7, and 7/8 March.

747 (III: 19): A light kindled in the sky

747 (III: 19). the moon was rising above the eastern shadows, now almost at the full. So the night was not yet old and for hours the dark journey would go on. – Here the narrative fits better with Tolkien's earlier time-scheme, when Pippin saw the moon at 9 p.m. In the revised scheme (not apparent in the text) he does not see the moon until after midnight, when it had become full. Some hours later, Frodo at Henneth Annûn will see this moon setting over Gondor.

747 (III: 19): 'In the realm of Gondor'

747 (III: 19). Anórien – In *Nomenclature* (entry for *Sunlending*) Tolkien writes that *Anórien* was 'the name of the land immediately attached to *Minas Anor* (originally including that city and inhabited country as far as the River *Erui*). It is thus "heraldic" rather than climatic, and related to the heraldic names of Elendil's sons *Anárion* and *Isildur*, being the counterpart of *Ithilien*.'

747 (III: 19): For answer Gandalf cried aloud

747 (III: 19). The beacons of Gondor are alight, calling for aid. – On reading this, almost every English man, woman, and child would immediately think of the beacons lit in 1588 to warn of the approach of the Spanish Armada. Tolkien almost certainly knew Thomas Babington Macaulay's poem *The Armada*, which recounts the event:

Till Belvoir's lordly terraces the sign to Lincoln sent,
And Lincoln sped the message on o'er the wide vale of Trent;
Till Skiddaw saw the fire that burned on Gaunt's embattled pile,
And the red glare on Skiddaw roused the burghers of Carlisle.

Beacons have long been used to signal warnings and to call for aid. In the eighth and ninth centuries, for instance, the news of a Saracen invasion on the Cilician frontier was flashed to Constantinople by eight beacon fires. Even earlier, Homer wrote in the *Iliad*: 'Thus, from some far-away beleaguered island, where all day long the men have fought a desperate battle from their city walls, the smoke goes up to heaven; but no sooner has the sun gone down than the light from the line of beacons blazes up and shoots into the sky to warn the neighbouring islanders and bring them to the rescue in their ships' (trans. by E.V. Rieu (1950), p. 342).

747 (III: 19). Amon Dîn . . . Eilenach; . . . Nardol, Erelas, Min-Rimmon, Calenhad . . . Halifirien – In *The Rivers and Beacon-hills of Gondor* Tolkien says that

> the full beacon system, that was still operating in the War of the Ring, can have been no older than the settlement of the Rohirrim in Calenardhon about 500 years before; for its principal function was to warn the Rohirrim that Gondor was in danger or (more rarely) the reverse. How old the names then used were cannot be said. The beacons were set on hills or on the high ends of ridges running out from the mountains, but some were not very notable objects. [*Vinyar Tengwar* 42 (July 2001), p. 18; partly published in *Unfinished Tales*, p. 315, n. 35]

In the same essay, Tolkien discusses the situation of the beacons and their names. *Amon Dîn* (Sindarin 'silent hill')

> was perhaps the oldest, with the original function of a fortified outpost of Minas Tirith, from which its beacon could be seen, to keep watch over the passage into North Ithilien from Dagorlad and any attempt by enemies to cross the Anduin at or near Cair Andros. Why it was given this name is not recorded. Probably because it was distinctive, a rocky and barren hill standing out and isolated from the heavily wooded hills of the Drúadan Forest (Tawar-in-Drúedain), little visited by men, beasts or birds. [*Unfinished Tales*, p. 319, n. 51]

Eilenach (or *Eilienach*) is 'probably an alien name; not Sindarin, Númenórean, or Common Speech. In true Sindarin *eilen* could only be derived from **elyen*, **alyen*, and would normally be written *eilien*' (*Vinyar Tengwar* 42, p. 19). That hill

> was the highest point of the Drúadan Forest. It could be seen far to the West, and its function in the days of the beacons was to transmit the warning of Amon Dîn; but it was not suitable for a large beacon-fire, there being little space on its sharp summit. Hence the name *Nardol* 'Fire-hilltop' [compare Sindarin *naur* 'fire'] of the next beacon westward; it was on the end of a high ridge, originally part of the Drúadan Forest, but long deprived of trees by masons and quarriers who came up the Stonewain Valley. Nardol was manned by a guard, who also protected the quarries; it was well-stored with fuel and at need a great blaze could be lit, visible on a clear night even as far as the last beacon (Halifirien) some hundred and twenty miles to the westward. The line of beacons from Nardol to Halifirien lay in a shallow curve bending a little southward, so that the three intervening beacons did not cut off the view. [*Unfinished Tales*, p. 319, n. 51; *Vinyar Tengwar* 42, p. 19]
>
> *Erelas* was a small beacon, as also was *Calenhad*. These were not always lit; their lighting as in *The Lord of the Rings* was a signal of great urgency. *Erelas* is Sindarin in style, but has no suitable meaning in that

> language. It was a green hill without trees, so that neither *er-* 'single' nor *las(s)* 'leaf' seem applicable.
>
> *Calenhad* was similar but rather larger and higher. *Calen* was the usual word in Sindarin for 'green' (its older sense was 'bright', Q[uenya] *kalina*). *-had* appears to be for *sad* . . . seen in S[indarin] *sad* 'a limited area naturally or artificially defined, a place, spot', etc. . . . *Calenhad* would thus mean simply 'green space', applied to the turf-covered crown of the hill. But *had* may stand for S[indarin] *-hadh* . . . *-hadh* would then be for *sadh* (in isolated use *sâdh*) 'sward, turf'. . . . [*Vinyar Tengwar* 42, pp. 19–20]

Min-Rimmon (Sindarin *min* 'peak') is a 'peak of the Rimmon (a group of crags)' (*Index*).

In *Nomenclature* Tolkien notes that *Firien* represents 'an old word (Old English *firgen*, pronounced *firien*) for "mountain". Cf. *Halifirien* "holy-mount".' In *The Rivers and Beacon-hills of Gondor* he says more extensively about the name *Halifirien* that it is

> in the language of Rohan. It was a mountain with easy approach to its summit. Down its northern slopes grew the great wood called in Rohan the Firien Wood. This became dense in lower ground, westward along the Mering Stream and northwards out into the moist plain through which the Stream flowed into the Entwash. The great West Road passed through a long ride or clearing through the wood to avoid the wet land beyond its eaves. The name Halifirien (modernized in spelling for *Háligfirgen*) meant Holy Mountain. The older name in Sindarin had been *Fornarthan* 'North Beacon'; the wood had been called *Eryn Fuir* 'North Wood'. The reason for the Rohan name is not now known for certain. [*Vinyar Tengwar* 42, p. 20]

Tolkien goes on in this work to develop the idea that the Rohirrim considered Halifirien holy because, according to their traditions, it was on the summit that Eorl and Cirion had sworn 'perpetual friendship and alliance' between Rohan and Gondor, and looking forth over the land had 'fixed the bounds' of the realm that Cirion granted to Eorl. Tolkien suggests that in the Oath Cirion may have invoked the One (Eru), which would have hallowed the place. He also mentions that it was recorded that on the top was an ancient monument, perhaps a tomb – and at that point the manuscript ceases. Christopher Tolkien suggests that 'these last words may well signify the precise moment at which the tomb of Elendil on Halifirien entered the history' (*Vinyar Tengwar* 42, pp. 20, 22). At this point Tolkien abandoned the essay and marked the part on Halifirien for deletion; its explanation, however, probably accords closely with what Tolkien had in mind while writing *The Lord of the Rings*.

A later and more extensive account of Halifirien was published as part of *Cirion and Eorl and the Friendship of Gondor and Rohan* in *Unfinished Tales*, pp. 300 ff.:

> The Halifirien was the highest of the beacons, and like Eilenach, the next in height, appeared to stand up alone out of a great wood; for behind it there was a deep cleft, the dark Firien-dale, in the long northward spur of the Ered Nimrais. . . . The Beacon-wardens were the only inhabitants of the Wood, save wild beasts; they housed in lodges in the trees near the summit, but they did not stay long, unless held there by foul weather, and they came and went in turns of duty. For the most part they were glad to return home. Not because of the peril of the wild beasts, nor did any evil shadow out of the dark days lie upon the Wood; but beneath the sounds of the winds, the cries of the birds and beasts, or at times the noise of horsemen riding in haste upon the Road, there lay a silence, and a man would find himself speaking to his comrades in a whisper, as if he expected to hear the echo of a great voice that called from far away and long ago. [p. 300]

748 (III: 20): Pippin woke to the sound of voices

748 (III: 20). Another day of hiding and a night of journey – 8 March, and the night of 8/9 March.

748–9 (III: 20–1): 'Yea truly, we know you

748 (III: 20). the Seven Gates – 'The Gates of the [seven] circles of M[inas] T[irith]' (*Index*).

749 (III: 21): 'Because I come seldom

749 (III: 21). the Pelennor – '"Fenced, encircled land", the "townlands" of the City of Minas Tirith, guarded by the wall of the Rammas Echor' (*Index*). Also called the *Fields of Pelennor* and the *Pelennor Fields.*

750 (III: 22): Gandalf passed now into the wide land

750 (III: 22). Rammas Echor – '(*Rammas* "a great wall", *echor* "outer circle") the great wall about the Pelennor, built under Denethor's lordship. Also called *the Rammas*' (*Index*).

750 (III: 22). frowning bank – *Frowning* here suggests 'steep, not easily climbed'.

750 (III: 22). embattled – Fortified, having battlements.

750 (III: 22). Emyn Arnen – The *Emyn Arnen* are 'low hills in Ithilien, on [the] east bank of the Anduin which made a loop about their feet' (*Index*). In *The Rivers and Beacon-hills of Gondor* it is said that

> suggestions of the historians of Gondor that *arn-* is an element in some pre-Númenórean language meaning 'rock' is merely a guess. More probable is the view of the author (unknown) of the fragmentarily preserved *Ondonóre Nómesseron Minaþurie* ('Enquiry into the Place-names of Gondor') . . . that *Arnen* originally was intended to mean

> 'beside the water, sc. Anduin'; but *ar-* in this sense is Quenya not Sindarin. Though since in the full name *Emyn Arnen* the *Emyn* is Sindarin plural of *Amon* 'hill', *Arnen* cannot be a Sindarin adjective, since an adjective of such shape would have a Sindarin plural *ernain* or *ernin*. The name must therefore have meant 'the hills of Arnen'. It is now forgotten, but it can be seen from old records that *Arnen* was the older name of the greater part of the region later called *Ithilien*. [*Vinyar Tengwar* 42 (July 2001), pp. 16–17]

750 (III: 22). Harlond – '"Southhaven", the haven on the Anduin within [the] south walls of the Pelennor' (*Index*).

750 (III: 22). southern fiefs – In *Nomenclature* (entry for *Sunlending*) Tolkien notes that the *southern fiefs*, 'also called the Outlands' are 'the sea-board lands south of *Anórien*'.

750 (III: 22): The townlands were rich

750 (III: 22). wide tilth . . . oast and garner, fold and byre – *Tilth* refers to cultivation of the soil.

An *oast* is 'a kiln for drying hops' (*Concise OED*).

A *garner* is a storehouse for grain.

A *fold* in this sense is an 'enclosure for livestock, especially sheep' (*Concise OED*).

A *byre* is a cowshed.

750 (III: 22). husbandmen – Farmers.

750 (III: 22). Lossarnach – In his unfinished index Tolkien notes '*Lossarnach* "flowery Arnach" (a pre N[úmenórean' name], the region of NW [north-west] Lebennin about the sources of Sirith and Erui'. In *The Rivers and Beacon-hills of Gondor* he rejects the idea that the name was related to *Arnen* in *Emyn Arnen*: '*Arnach* is not Sindarin. . . . [It] was applied to the valleys in the south of the mountains and their foothills between Celos and Erui. There were many rocky outcrops there, but hardly more than in the higher valleys of Gondor generally.' But if *Arnach* is not related to *Arnen*,

> its origin and source are . . . now lost. It was generally called in Gondor *Lossarnach*. *Loss* is Sindarin for 'snow', especially fallen and long-lying snow. For what reason this was prefixed to Arnach is unclear. Its upper valleys were renowned for their flowers, and below them there were great orchards, from which at the time of the War of the Ring much of the fruit needed in Minas Tirith still came. Though no mention of this is found in any chronicles – as is often he case with matters of common knowledge – it seems probable that the reference was in fact to the fruit blossom. Expeditions to Lossarnach to see the flowers and trees were frequently made by the people of Minas Tirith. . . . This use of 'snow'

would be specially likely in Sindarin, in which the words for fallen snow and flower were much alike, though different in origin: *loss* and *loth*, [the latter] meaning 'inflorescence, a head of small flowers'. [*Vinyar Tengwar* 42 (July 2001), pp. 17, 18]

750 (III: 22). Prince Imrahil in his castle of Dol Amroth – In Appendix E it is said that '*Imrahil* is a Númenórean name' (p. 1113, III: 391). Carl F. Hostetter and Patrick Wynne note in 'An Adûnaic Dictionary', *Vinyar Tengwar* 25 (September 1992), that the name contains the element *hil* 'heir, follower', hence *Imrahil* is perhaps intended to mean 'heir of Imrazôr', a Númenórean whose son Galador was the first Lord of Dol Amroth (see *The Peoples of Middle-earth*, p. 221).

In a note to *Cirion and Eorl and the Friendship of Gondor and Rohan* it is said that the title *Prince* held by the Lord of Dol Amroth had been 'given to his ancestors by Elendil, with whom they had kinship. They were a family of the Faithful who had sailed from Númenor before the Downfall and had settled in the land of Belfalas, between the mouths of Ringló and Gilrain, with a stronghold upon the high promontory of Dol Amroth (named after the last King of Lórien)' (*Unfinished Tales*, p. 316, n. 39). See further, notes for pp. 771, 872.

750–1 (III: 22–3): Now after Gandalf had ridden

751 (III: 23). the Guarded City – Minas Tirith, the 'Tower of Guard'.

751 (III: 23). not builded but carven by giants – In the Anglo-Saxon era the remains of buildings from earlier times were often thought to have been built by giants, as in the beginning of the Old English poem *The Ruin*: 'Wondrous is this stone wall, smashed by fate. / The buildings have crumbled, the work of giants [*enta geweorc*] decays' (*Old and Middle English: An Anthology*, ed. by Elaine Treharne (2000), pp. 84–5).

751 (III: 23): Even as Pippin gazed

751 (III: 23). the Tower of Ecthelion – '*The White Tower*, the chief tower of the Citadel of Minas Tirith', also called 'the Tower of Denethor' (*Index*). According to *The Tale of Years* the Tower was originally built by King Calimehtar in Third Age 1900 and rebuilt by the Steward Ecthelion I in 2698.

751 (III: 23). white banners – The banner of the Stewards.

751 (III: 23–4): For the fashion of Minas Tirith

751 (III: 23–4). it was built on seven levels, each delved into a hill, and about each was set a wall, and in each wall was a gate. But the gates were not set in a line – Some readers have suggested that in creating the seven circles of Minas Tirith (once Minas Anor, the Tower of the Sun) Tolkien may have been influenced by the City of the Sun in *Civitas Solis*, written by the philosopher Tommaso Campanella in 1602 and first published in 1613–14. That city also is said to have been built on a high hill and divided into seven rings or circles. Unlike Minas Tirith, however, it has four gates, one at each point of the compass, from which four streets lead up through the circles.

Two drawings of Minas Tirith by Tolkien, made before he introduced its great pier of rock, are reproduced in *Artist and Illustrator*, figs. 167–8. The first, the earliest sketch of the city, is also reproduced in *The War of The Ring*, p. 261. Sketch-plans of the city and its relation to Mount Mindolluin are reproduced in *The War of the Ring*, pp. 280, 290.

752 (III: 24). a vast pier of rock whose huge out-thrust bulk divided in two all the circles of the City save the first – A sketch of the city with this pier is reproduced in *Artist and Illustrator*, fig. 169.

752 (III: 24). partly in the primeval shaping – Partly from the original natural shaping of the hill.

752 (III: 24). bastion – A projecting part of a fortification.

752 (III: 24). the High Court and the Place of the Fountain – The *High Court* is 'the topmost circle of M[inas] T[irith]' and 'the square about the feet of the White Tower in the Citadel of M[inas] T[irith]' (*Index*).

The *Place of the Fountain*, also called the Court of the Fountain, is a part of the High Court 'before the doors of the Tower Hall (under the W[hite] Tower)' (*Index*).

752 (III: 24). tall and shapely, fifty fathoms from its base to the pinnacle, where the banner of the Stewards floated a thousand feet above the plain – As first published this passage read: '. . . tall and shapely it was, one hundred and fifty fathoms from its base to the pinnacle, where the banner of the Stewards floated a thousand feet above the plain'. Thus the Tower was 900 feet tall, leaving only 100 feet for the seven circles of the city. As emended in the second edition (1965), the height of the tower is 300 feet.

752 (III: 24). the Hill of Guard – In *Nomenclature* Tolkien writes that *Hill of Guard* is the 'Common Speech name of *Amon Tirith*, the hill on which *Minas Tirith* was built'.

752 (III: 24–5): At last they came out of Shadow

752 (III: 25). the Citadel – 'The topmost circle of M[inas] Tirith' (*Index*; compare note for *High Court*, above).

752–3 (III: 25): The Guards of the Gate

753 (III: 25). Upon the black surcoats were embroidered in white a tree blossoming like snow beneath a silver crown and many-pointed stars. This was the livery of the heirs of Elendil – A *surcoat* is an outer garment worn by people of rank, often over armour, bearing heraldic arms.

For the white tree and crown, see notes for p. 423.

In regard to *many-pointed stars*, in the *1966 Index* as first published each of the seven stars of Elendil (see note for p. 597) is said to have *six* points. But in the Allen & Unwin de luxe edition of 1969 this was changed to *five* points, possibly because the binding art of that book is an adaptation of Tolkien's dust-jacket design for *The Return of the King* (see 'Preliminaries', above), in which each of the stars has five points.

The colour *black* is frequently met in *The Lord of the Rings* in connection with evil, following traditional symbolism in Western culture: names such as *Mordor* and *Morgul* contain the element 'black'; the Ringwraiths appear first as Black Riders; Saruman's avian spies are black crows; the sails of the Corsairs are black (Book V, Chapter 6); the Nazgûl spread despair with the Black Breath (Book V, Chapter 8). But black is also the ground colour of the livery of the heirs of Elendil. Christian Weichman in 'Black (Not) a Colour in Middle-earth', *Lembas-extra 2002* (2002), explores possible reasons for this departure, one of which is simply that black provides a good contrast to silver (and white). Tolkien was well aware of the strong graphic effect of such a combination: see note for p. 304, concerning the design of the doors of Moria. See also note for p. 847.

Livery in this sense is clothing worn by retainers or servants with which they may be recognized as such.

754 (III: 26): Gandalf halted before a tall door

754 (III: 26). birds-nesting – Hunting for birds' nests in order to take eggs, often for a collection.

754 (III: 26): The door opened

754 (III: 26). the wide vaulting gleamed with dull gold. The floor was of polished stone, white-gleaming, inset with flowing traceries of many colours. – In editions prior to 2004 this passage read: 'the wide vaulting gleamed with dull gold, inset with flowing traceries of many colours'. Christopher Tolkien notes in *The War of the Ring* that the present, longer text appears in the fair copy manuscript and the following typescript of this chapter, but that in the typescript made for the printer the two sentences became compressed. 'Since there is no indication on the second typescript that any change was intended, it seems certain that this was a casual "line-jumping" error, causing the "flowing traceries" to be ascribed to the vaulting' (p. 288).

754 (III: 26). No hangings nor storied webs, nor any things of woven stuff or of wood – For *hangings*, i.e. wall-hangings, see note for p. 512. These and *storied* (i.e. pictorial) *webs* are *woven stuff*, woven cloth.

Here Tolkien is making a deliberate comparison between the interior of the hall at Minas Tirith and that of Meduseld. The former, the throne-room of a great empire, reflects the architecture of Rome in the use of stone and vaulting, and with its columns and aisles incorporates some of the elements of the Roman basilica or court of justice. Meduseld is basically Northern European in style, structure, and decoration, as befits the Anglo-Saxon associations given to the Rohirrim.

754 (III: 26). a silent company of tall images graven in cold stone. – At Rivendell in Book II, Chapter 2, Aragorn had said to Boromir: 'Little do I resemble the figures of Elendil and Isildur as they stand carven in their majesty in the halls of Denethor' (p. 248, I: 261).

755 (III: 27): 'Verily,' said Denethor

755 (III: 27). Vorondil father of Mardil hunted the wild kine of Araw in the far fields of Rhûn – *Vorondil* the Hunter was Steward to King Eärnil during Third Age 1998–2029.

For *Mardil*, see note for p. 670.

In Appendix A it is said that 'the wild white kine that were still to be found near the Sea of Rhûn were said in legend to be descended from the Kine of Araw, the huntsman of the Valar. . . . *Oromë* is the High-elven [Quenya] form of his name' (p. 1039, III: 319). *Kine* is an archaic word meaning 'a collection of cattle'. See also note for p. 279.

755 (III: 27). thirteen days ago – It is 9 March. Boromir fell on 26 February.

755–6 (III: 27): Then Pippin looked

755–6 (III: 27). Pippin drew forth his small sword and laid it at Denethor's feet. – The ceremonies by which Pippin swears loyalty to Denethor and Merry devotes himself to Théoden (Book V, Chapter 2) reveal cultural differences and the characters and feelings of the participants. In *J.R.R. Tolkien: Author of the Century* Tom Shippey comments:

> Merry's action is spontaneous, prompted only by 'love for this old man', and is received in the same spirit. The ceremony, in so far as there is one, consists only of Merry saying 'Receive my service, if you will', and Théoden replying 'Gladly will I take it . . . Rise now, Meriadoc, esquire of Rohan of the household of Meduseld'. There is no doubt about the binding quality of what has happened, but it takes few words. By contrast Pippin's offer has more complex motives: pride, and anger at the 'scorn and suspicion' in Denethor's questioning. His offer is not immediately accepted: Denethor looks at his sword first, the one taken from the Barrow-wight, and seems to be affected by that before he says 'I accept your service' (not quite the same words as Théoden's, for the one uses the colloquial 'take', the other the formal 'accept'). Both parties in the Minas Tirith scene then make a formal statement, naming themselves in full and giving both patronymics and titles: Denethor's is not without an element of threat, a promise to reward 'oath-breaking with vengeance', far removed from Théoden's 'Take your sword and bear it unto

good fortune'. It is probably fair to say that the scene between Merry and Théoden makes much the better impression, kindlier, more casual, and with more concern for the feelings of the junior party. [pp. 98–9]

Sarah Beach in 'Specific Derivation', *Mythlore* 12, no. 4, whole no. 46 (Summer 1986), suggests that Tolkien was influenced by 'two slightly different procedures, different in the quality of the relationship implied between the lord and the warrior giving his sword' (p. 16) which he discusses in *Finn and Hengest*:

> (1) There is a passage in Saxo [Grammaticus] Book II where after the death of Hrólfr Kraki (Rolvo) only Viggo is left alive. Hiartvarus . . . [the slayer of Rolvo] asks Viggo if he is willing to become his man, and when he says yes offers him a drawn sword; but Viggo refuses the blade, and seizes the hilt, saying that was the way Rolvo used to offer the sword to his men . . . 'for formerly those who were about to engage themselves as members of the king's *comitatus* were accustomed to promise service while touching the sword hilt', sc. of the king's sword lying in his lap. . . .
>
> (2) That a sword could be laid on the lap as a mere *present* accompanying a gift of vassalship, or a request to be accepted as a vassal, is shown [in a passage] . . . from the *Annales Fuldenses* (anno 873) . . . : 'The ambassadors of Halbdenus, brother of King Sigifridus, offered to the king (Hludovicus) as a gift a sword which had a golden hilt, earnestly beseeching that the king should deign to have their masters in place of sons, while they would honour him as a father all the days of their life. . . .' [Tolkien, *Finn and Hengest*, pp. 133–4]

Beach comments that 'Pippin's encounter with Denethor follows the first example Tolkien gave in *Finn and Hengest*. Denethor has spoken slightingly of hobbits and Pippin's pride stirs him to offer his sword.' Pippin swears his oath holding the hilt. But when Merry offers his service to Théoden the scene has a completely different tone, as in the second example in *Finn and Hengest*. 'It contains the offer of the sword as part of a gift of vassalship, and the personal relationship between the lord and warrior wherein the lord stands as father to his follower' (pp. 16, 36).

756 (III: 28): 'I see that strange tales

756 (III: 28). you have courteous speech, strange though the sound of it may be to us in the South – In Appendix F it is said that Hobbits 'spoke for the most part a rustic dialect [of the Westron or Common Speech], whereas in Gondor and Rohan a more antique language was used, more formal and more terse'. One point of divergence, which 'proved impossible to represent', was the distinction between 'familiar' and 'deferential' forms in pronouns of the second person (and often of the third). The deferential forms were no longer widely used in the Shire.

> This was one of the things referred to when people of Gondor spoke of the strangeness of Hobbit-speech. Peregrin Took, for instance, in his first few days in Minas Tirith used the familiar for people of all ranks, including the Lord Denethor himself. This may have amused the aged Steward, but it must have astonished his servants. No doubt this free use of the familiar forms helped to spread the popular rumour that Peregrin was a person of very high rank in his own country. [p. 1133, III: 411]

756 (III: 28): 'Here I do swear fealty

756 (III: 28). fealty – 'The obligation of fidelity on the part of a . . . vassal to his lord' (*OED*).

757 (III: 29): Denethor looked indeed

757 (III: 29). What was Gandalf? In what far time and place did he come into the world, and when would he leave it? – Gandalf is a Maia, one of the Ainur, the offspring of Eru's thought, who, in the great Music they made before Eru, created a vision of Arda and then entered the still unshaped world to fashion it according to the vision. The Ainur who chose to enter Arda were bound to stay within it.

757 (III: 29): 'Yea,' he said

757 (III: 29). for though the Stones be lost . . . still the lords of Gondor have keener sight than lesser men – The extract from *The Palantíri* quoted in the note for p. 598 indicates that one reason for Gandalf's concern to reach Minas Tirith quickly was his fear that Denethor, like Saruman, may have made use of a *palantír* and was no longer to be trusted. Tolkien continues:

> Gandalf's dealings with Denethor on arrival in Minas Tirith, and in the following days, and all things that they are reported to have said to one another, must be viewed in the light of this doubt in Gandalf's mind.
>
> Denethor was evidently aware of Gandalf's guesses and suspicions, and at once both angered and sardonically amused by them. Note his words to Gandalf at their meeting in Minas Tirith . . . : 'I know already sufficient of these deeds for my own counsel against the menace of the East', and especially his mocking words that followed: 'Yea; for though the Stones be lost, they say, still the lords of Gondor have keener sight than lesser men, and many messages come to them.' Quite apart from the *palantíri*, Denethor was a man of great mental powers, and a quick reader of thoughts behind faces and words, but he may well also have actually seen in the Anor-stone visions of events in Rohan and Isengard. [*Unfinished Tales*, pp. 406, 412, n. 8]

757 (III: 29–30): Then men came bearing

757 (III: 29). a salver with a silver flagon – Here a *salver* is a tray used for handing refreshments.

A *flagon* is a large vessel for serving drinks.

757 (III: 30): 'Now tell me your tale

757 (III: 30). liege – Vassal, one sworn to service.

758 (III: 30): 'If you understand it

758 (III: 30). to him there is no purpose higher in the world as it now stands than the good of Gondor; and the rule of Gondor . . . is mine – In ?1956 Tolkien wrote in notes on W.H. Auden's review of *The Return of the King* that

> Denethor *was* tainted with mere politics: hence his failure. . . . It had become for him a prime motive to preserve the polity of Gondor, as it was, against another potentate, who had made himself stronger and was to be feared and opposed for that reason rather than because he was ruthless and wicked. Denethor despised lesser men, and one may be sure did not distinguish between orcs and the allies of Mordor. If he had survived as victor, even without the use of the Ring, he would have taken a long stride towards becoming himself a tyrant, and the terms and treatment he accorded to the deluded peoples of east and south would have been cruel and vengeful. He had become a "political" leader: sc. Gondor against the rest. [*Letters*, p. 241]

758 (III: 30–1): 'Unless the king should come again?'

758 (III: 30–1). all worthy things that are in peril as the world now stands, those are my care. . . . I shall not wholly fail of my task, though Gondor should perish, if anything passes through this night that can still grow fair or bear fruit or flower again in days to come. For I also am a steward. – The report of a Tolkien discussion group meeting for 29 June 1986 comments that

> Gandalf's rejoinder . . . carries a great many implications in a few words. He is reminding Denethor that he [Gandalf] is a representative of a higher authority than Denethor is (i.e., the Valar and/or Ilúvatar). He is reproving Denethor: 'You are also answerable to a higher authority.' He is implying that Gondor is part of his own stewardship too, and finally he is pointing out that Gondor is only part of a larger battle. [*Rómenna Meeting Report*, p. 2]

759–60 (III: 32): He fell silent and sighed

759–60 (III: 32). The board is set, and the pieces are moving . . . the Enemy has the move, and he is about to open his full game. And pawns are likely to see as much of it as any – Allusions to the game of chess.

760 (III: 33): 'I am named Beregond

760 (III: 33). Beregond – *Beregond* may mean 'valiant stone', but perhaps should be interpreted as 'valiant [man of] Gondor'.

761 (III: 33): 'Well, yes, to speak in courtesy

761 (III: 33). to speak in courtesy – To be strictly truthful.

761 (III: 33). racked – Caused mental stress.

761 (III: 33–4): Beregond laughed

761 (III: 34). nuncheon, at noon . . . men gather for the daymeal . . . about the hour of sunset – *Nuncheon* is 'a slight refreshment of liquor etc., originally taken in the afternoon; a light refreshment taken between meals; a lunch' (*OED*).

Daymeal is evidently intended to mean 'the main meal of the day'.

761 (III: 34): 'One moment!' said Pippin

761 (III: 34). the apple of the king's eye – *Apple of one's eye* means 'something cherished, regarded highly'.

762 (III: 34): 'I am glad to learn it'

762 (III: 34). strange accents do not mar fair speech – See note for p. 756.

762 (III: 34). butteries – A *buttery* was originally a place for storing liquor, but was early extended to a place where provisions are kept. It is used especially of communities such as colleges.

762 (III: 34): Shadowfax lifted up his head

762 (III: 34). manger – A box or trough in a stable in which food for a horse is be placed. In the next paragraph Beregond uses *manger* figuratively for his and Pippin's meal.

763 (III: 35): 'I do,' said Pippin

763 (III: 35). it will be four years yet before I "come of age" – It is 1419; Pippin was born in 1390, so will not be thirty-three ('of age') until 1423.

763 (III: 35–6): The sun was now climbing

763 (III: 36). standards – A *standard* in this sense is a distinctive banner or flag, signifying a king, noble, or commander.

764 (III: 36): 'That is the road

764 (III: 36). vales of Tumladen – 'A *flat valley with steep sides* [= Sindarin *tumladen*] . . . : a name of a vale in Beleriand [in which Gondolin was built, cf. *The Silmarillion*] transferred to the flatlands at east of Lebennin' (*Index*).

765 (III: 37): 'When?' said Pippin

765 (III: 37). For I saw the beacons two nights ago and the errand riders – In editions prior to 2005 Pippin 'saw the beacons last night'. It is now 9 March; Pippin saw the beacons and the errand riders on the night of the full moon, 7/8 March. In *The War of the Ring* Christopher Tolkien notes that as originally written, 'the beacons were fired on the last night of Gandalf's ride; in the final form it was on the night preceding the last (the journey taking four nights), and so when Pippin woke in the dawn beside the wall of the Pelennor "Another day of hiding and a night of journey had fleeted by"' (p. 264, n. 3).

765 (III: 37): 'But why were the beacons

765 (III: 37). But why were the beacons lit two nights ago? – In editions prior to 2005 the beacons were 'lit last night'. See the preceding note.

765 (III: 37–8): 'It is over-late to send for aid

765 (III: 37). Some say that as he sits alone in his high chamber in the Tower at night, and bends his thought this way and that, he can read somewhat of the future; and that he will at times search even the mind of the Enemy, wrestling with him. – It will later become clear that Denethor uses the *palantír* of Minas Anor to see from afar the designs of Sauron, unaware that he is being deceived.

765 (III: 38): 'But if you would know

765 (III: 38). if you would know what I think set the beacons ablaze, it was the news that came that eve out of Lebennin – In editions prior to 2005 the news 'came yestereve out of Lebennin'. See preceding notes on the firing of the beacons.

765 (III: 38). corsairs of Umbar – A *corsair* in this sense is a pirate, a privateer. In *Nomenclature* Tolkien notes that the Corsairs of Umbar 'are imagined as similar to the Mediterranean corsairs: sea-robbers with fortified bases'.

For *Umbar*, see note for p. 659.

765 (III: 38): 'And yet' – he paused

765 (III: 38). the Inland Sea – Tolkien's unfinished index makes it clear that Beregond is referring to 'the "Sea of Rhûn" far East beyond Mirkwood', though elsewhere Tolkien uses 'Inland Sea' to refer to the Sea of Núrnen.

767 (III: 39–40): 'Will you come with me?'

767 (III: 39). mess – A place where a company or section of an army eat together.

767–8 (III: 40): Though Pippin had regretfully

767 (III: 40). outlands – Here *outlands* cannot bear its specific meaning in Gondor (see note for p. 769, for capitalized *Outlands*), but rather means 'foreign parts'. Compare note for p. 24.

768 (III: 40–1): At length Beregond rose

769 (III: 40). Old Guesthouse in the Rath Celerdain, the Lampwrights' Street – In his unfinished index Tolkien includes '*Old Guesthouse* (Sennas Iaur) in M[inas] T[irith]'; '*Rath* street (in a city)'; and '*calar* a portable lamp; *calardan* a lampwright', plural *Celerdain*. In *Unfinished Tales* Christopher Tolkien notes 'a stem *rath-* meaning "climb" (whence also the noun *rath*, which in the Númenórean Sindarin used in Gondor in the naming of places and persons was applied to all the longer roadways and streets of Minas Tirith, nearly all of which were on an incline' (p. 255, n. 16).

768 (III: 41): People stared much as he passed

768 (III: 41). ***Ernil i Pheriannath*** – Prince of the Halflings. In *The Road Goes Ever On: A Song Cycle* Tolkien comments that in Sindarin

> plurals were mostly made with vowel-changes. . . . But the suffix *-ath* (originally a collective noun-suffix) was used as a group plural, embracing all things of the same name, or those associated in some special arrangement or organization. So . . . *Periannath*, 'the Hobbits (as a race),' as collective pl[ural] of *perian*, 'halfling' (pl. *periain*). . . . In S[indarin] the simple genitive was usually expressed by placing the genitival noun in adjectival position (in S[indarin] *after* the primary noun). So . . . *Ernil i Pheriannath*, 'Prince (of) the Halflings'. . . . [pp. 66–7]

769 (III: 41): 'Which question shall I answer first?'

769 (III: 41). Whitwell – 'A village on the Downs near Tuckborough, home of Peregrin' (*Index*). Tolkien comments in *Nomenclature* (entry for *Whitfurrows*) that *whit-* is 'the usual shortening of *white* in personal . . . and local names'. There are several places in Britain with the name *Whitwell* ('white spring or stream').

769 (III: 42): 'The Captains of the Outlands

769 (III: 42). Outlands – In this context, capitalized, *Outlands* refers to 'the "southern fiefs" . . . the sea-board lands south of *Anórien*' (*Nomenclature*); 'the fiefs of Gondor beyond the Pelennor' (*Index*).

770 (III: 43): 'Forlong has come'

770 (III: 43). Forlong the Fat, the Lord of Lossarnach – In Appendix F it is said that *Forlong* was a name 'of forgotten origin, and descended doubtless from days before the ships of the Númenóreans sailed the Sea' (p. 1129, III: 407).

770 (III: 43): Leading the line

770 (III: 43). shorter and somewhat swarthier than any men that Pippin had yet seen in Gondor – Faramir told Frodo during their conversation at Henneth Annûn in Book IV, Chapter 5 (p. 678, II: 286) that the Stewards had 'recruited the strength of our people from the sturdy folk of the sea-coast, and from the hardy mountaineers of the Ered Nimrais', people not of Númenórean descent.

770 (III: 43): 'Forlong!' men shouted

770 (III: 43). a tithe – One tenth.

770–1 (III: 43–4): And so the companies came

770 (III: 43). And so the companies came – Tolkien wrote on a working synopsis for *The Lord of the Rings*: 'Homeric catalogue. Forlong the Fat. The folk of Lebennin' (*The War of the Ring*, p. 229), thus comparing the arrival of the reinforcements at Minas Tirith to the catalogue of ships in Homer's *Iliad*. Todd Jensen, in 'Elements of the Classical Epic in *The Lord of the Rings*', *Beyond Bree*, March 1990, comments that one of the traditional features of the epic is a catalogue or list of chieftains or officers in an army. Homer includes in Book 2 of the *Iliad*

> a list of each of the Greek leaders before Troy, including a description of each one's kingdom (listing all the towns in it), and how many ships he brought with him. There is also a similar list of Trojan leaders, at the end of the same book. When Vergil wrote the *Aeneid*, and got to the point of the war that Aeneas has to fight to ensure the preservation of the Trojan kingdom that he has founded in Italy, there is a similar catalogue of the leaders in the stories on both sides. Finally, Milton, in Book One of *Paradise Lost*, gives a catalogue of Satan's foremost officers in his army. . . . [Jensen, p. 2]

770 (III: 43). Ringló Vale – The land about the '*Ringló* a river (joint tributary of Morthond in S[outh] Gondor' (*Index*). Its name is derived from Sindarin *ring* 'cold, chill' + *lô* 'fenland'. In *The Rivers and Beacon-hills of Gondor* it is said that 'there is no record of any swamps or marsh in' the course of the Ringló. 'It was a swift (and cold) river, as the element *ring-* implies. It drew its first waters from a high snowfield that fed an icy tarn in the mountains. If this at seasons of snowmelting spread into a shallow lake, it would account for the name, another of the many that refer to a river's source' (*Vinyar Tengwar* 42 (July 2001), p. 13).

770 (III: 43). the uplands of Morthond, the great Blackroot Vale – In *Nomenclature* Tolkien writes that *Blackroot* is the 'Common Speech translation of *Morthond* (name of a river, given because its source was in the dark caverns of the Dead Men)'. In *The Rivers and Beacon-hills of Gondor* he says that the river 'rose in a dark valley in the mountains due south of Edoras, called *Mornan* [*mor-* "dark" + *nan* "valley"], not only because of the shadow of the two high mountains between which it lay, but because through it passed the road from the Gate of the Dead Men, and living men did not go there' (*Vinyar Tengwar* 42 (July 2001), p. 14).

770 (III: 43). Lamedon – Tolkien notes in his unfinished index that *Lamedon* is a 'region close to [the] upper waters of Ciril and Ringló', and that its name is pre-Númenórean.

770 (III: 43). the Green Hills from Pinnath Gelin – Tolkien notes in his unfinished index that *Pinnath Gelin* ('Green Downs') are 'hills behind the Langstrand in the West of S[outh] Gondor . . . (*pinnath* = "group of downs" [?might] properly be *penneth* (*penn* "slope" pl[ural] *pinn*) but is formed from the pl[ural])'. In the *1966 Index* the name is translated 'green ridges'.

771 (III: 43). Imrahil, Prince of Dol Amroth, kinsman of the Lord – In writings on the lineage of the House of Dol Amroth, prepared for the *Lord of the Rings* Appendices but ultimately omitted, Imrahil is shown to be the brother-in-law of Denethor, Steward of Gondor, through Denethor's wife Finduilas. See *The Peoples of Middle-earth*, pp. 220–4.

Chapter 2

THE PASSING OF THE GREY COMPANY

For drafts and history of this chapter, see *The War of the Ring*, pp. 296–311, 397–9, 405–11, 416–17, 419–24, 427–9.

773 (III: 46): Gandalf was gone

773 (III: 46). Gandalf was gone – It is late on 5 March 1419. Aragorn and the others will ride through the night of 5/6 March.

773 (III: 46): 'I cannot say yet'

773 (III: 46). four nights from now – The night of 9/10 March. In Book V, Chapter 3, Théoden arrives at Dunharrow late on 9 March and expects the muster to take place on 10 March.

773 (III: 46): 'Well, for myself'

773 (III: 46). it is dark before me. I must go down also to Minas Tirith, but I do not yet see the road. – Aragorn is still uncertain (*it is dark*, i.e. not clear), but is probably also pondering Galadriel's message in Book III, Chapter 5: 'But dark is the path appointed for thee: / The Dead watch the road that leads to the Sea' (p. 503, II: 106).

773 (III: 46). an hour long prepared – Aragorn was twenty in Third Age 2951 (sixty-eight years before the present point in the story) when Elrond revealed to him his lineage. Aragorn went out into the wild, and spent the intervening years in becoming 'the most hardy of living Men, skilled in their crafts and lore' (Appendix A, p. 1060, III: 341), preparing himself to help lead the opposition to Sauron, and to reveal himself in Gondor as the heir of Elendil.

773 (III: 46): Soon all were ready to depart

773 (III: 46). Soon all were ready to depart – Gandalf and Pippin left at 11.30 p.m. on 5 March (see note for p. 747). It is probably now about midnight, at the beginning of 6 March 1419.

775 (III: 48): 'I bring word to you

775 (III: 48). *the Paths of the Dead* – '([*Raith* >] *Fui 'Ngorthrim*), the road believed to lead under the Dwimorberg from the Dark Door to some end S[outh] of the [White] Mts., but guarded by the Unquiet Dead cursed by Isildur' (*Index*).

775 (III: 48): 'It is a gift that I bring you

775 (III: 48). the Lady of Rivendell – Arwen Undómiel, daughter of Elrond.

775 (III: 48). *Either our hope cometh, or all hope's end.* – This was the reading in all editions and printings until *c.* 1978, when in the standard Allen & Unwin edition '*hope's*' was erroneously changed to '*hopes*', possibly as a result of a repair to a printing plate, and in that form carried over into subsequent editions. The word was returned to its correct form in the edition of 2004. By chance, either form makes sense in context; but the sentence began in rough manuscript (Marquette Series 3/7/38): '*For either our hope cometh soon, or the end of all hope.*' Tolkien then emended the latter part, in the same manuscript, to '*all hope's end*'.

775 (III: 48). *I send thee what I have made for thee.* – The *th-* forms of second person singular pronouns (nominative *thou*, objective *thee*, possessive *thine*, *thy*) largely disappeared in standard English in the eighteenth century, though they are still to be encountered in dialects, in poetry, and in older works that continue to be quoted, such as the King James Bible. Also lost is the distinction Tolkien applies in some of his dialogue between high-born characters, in which *th-* forms are used between intimates – such as in the quoted phrase from Arwen to Aragorn – while *ye*, *you*, *your* are used formally. This developed in imitation of the French distinction between *tu* and *vous*, but in English was not always used consistently. See further, notes for pp. 852, 977.

776 (III: 49–50): Legolas stood before the gate

776 (III: 50). They have no need to ride to war; war already marches on their own lands. – According to *The Tale of Years*, on 15 March 'Thranduil repels the forces of Dol Guldur', and on 17 March 'Battle of Dale. King Brand and King Daín Ironfoot fall. Many Dwarves and Men take refuge in Erebor and are besieged.'

777 (III: 50): For a while the three companions

777 (III: 50). Dunlendings – People of Dunland; see note for p. 3.

777 (III: 50): 'I doubt it not,' said the king.

777 (III: 50). sword-thain – Defined as 'esquire' in the *1966 Index*.

777 (III: 50–1): 'Gladly will I take it'

777 (III: 50–1). Take your sword and bear it to good fortune – For comparison with Pippin's oath of allegiance before Denethor, see note for pp. 755–6.

778 (III: 51): The king with his guard

778 (III: 51). weapontake – Here the word must mean 'muster of armed men'. Compare *wapentake* 'a division of certain English shires'. The *Oxford English Dictionary* notes that in Old Norse the equivalent word meant '(1) a vote of consent expressed by waving or brandishing of weapons; (2) a vote or resolution of a deliberative assembly; (3) in Iceland the breaking up of a session of the Althing when the members resumed their weapons that had been laid aside during the sittings. In English there is no trace of these senses and the development of the actual sense can only be explained conjecturally.'

777 (III: 51): A little apart the Rangers sat

777 (III: 51). Roheryn – 'Horse of the lady', so called because it was a gift to Aragorn from Arwen (*The Silmarillion*, p. 363).

777 (III: 51). a brooch of silver shaped like a rayed star – Presumably the insignia of the Dúnedain or Rangers of Arnor, related to the seven stars of the emblem of Elendil. When Aragorn served in Gondor he was called 'Thorongil . . . , the Eagle of the Star, for he was swift and keen-eyed, and wore a silver star upon his cloak' (Appendix A, p. 1055, III: 335). Compare the 'Star of the Dúnedain' which King Elessar presents to Samwise on the king's visit to the North in S.R. 1436 (*The Tale of Years*).

778 (III: 51): The king mounted his horse

778 (III: 51). Stybba – Compare Old English *stybb* 'stub, stump of a tree'.

778 (III: 52): 'It is now a full hour past noon'

778 (III: 52). Before the night of the third day from now we should come to the Hold. – It is now 6 March. *The Tale of Years* agrees with the narrative that Théoden will reach Dunharrow in the evening of 9 March.

778 (III: 52). The Moon will then be two nights past his full – In editions prior to 2005 the final words in this passage read 'one night past his full'. But the full moon was on 7/8 March, and Théoden arrived at Dunharrow on the evening of 9/10 two nights later. Barbara Strachey notes this problem in *Journeys of Frodo*, and the need for alteration accords with the discrepancies or shadows of earlier chronologies noted by Christopher Tolkien in *The War of the Ring*, p. 322.

779 (III: 52): 'That road I will take

779 (III: 52). in battle we may yet meet again, though all the hosts of Mordor should stand between – Aragorn, already shown to have prophetic wisdom, once again foreshadows events to come, in this case his reunion with Éomer on the Pelennor Fields in Book V, Chapter 6.

780 (III: 53): 'You forget to whom you speak

780 (III: 53). What do you fear that I should say to him? Did I not openly proclaim my title before the doors of Edoras? – As first published this passage read: 'What do you fear that I should say: that I had a rascal of a rebel dwarf here that I would gladly exchange for a serviceable orc?' Tolkien sent revised text to Ballantine Books for the second edition (1965), but in printing the order of the sentences was mistakenly reversed and a word was misspelt, thus: 'Did I not openly proclaim my title before the deson [*sic*] of Edoras? What do you fear that I should say to him?' The same order, but with correct 'doors', continued to appear until the Houghton Mifflin edition of 1987: then the order of the sentences was changed in accordance with Tolkien's wishes, though a new error was introduced ('What *did* you fear'). The emended passage was not completely correct until the HarperCollins edition of 1994.

In his unpublished letter begun 22 September 1963 to Eileen Elgar, who apparently had criticized Aragorn's sharp retort as published in the first edition, Tolkien wrote that Gimli should have known better than to question the action and judgement of the greatest Captain of Men and a superior strategist. Gimli's remark was silly and impertinent; but although Aragorn at this point in the story was under great stress, his original reply was more grim humour than serious rebuke. Nonetheless, Tolkien softened Aragorn's words in the second edition.

780 (III: 53). I am the lawful master of the stone. . . . The strength was enough – barely. – In his draft letter to Eileen Elgar, September 1963, Tolkien wrote that 'in the contest with the Palantír Aragorn was the rightful owner. Also the contest took place at a distance, and in a tale which allows the incarnation of great spirits in a physical and destructible form their power must be far greater when actually physically present' (*Letters*, p. 332). In Tolkien's notes on the *palantíri* written while preparing the second edition it is

> noted with regard to the narrative of *The Lord of the Rings* that over and above any such deputed authority, even hereditary, any 'heir of Elendil' (that is, a recognized descendant occupying a throne or lordship in the Númenórean realms by virtue of this descent) had the *right* to use any of the *palantíri*. Aragorn thus claimed the right to take the Orthanc-stone into his possession, since it was now, for the time being, without owner or warden; and also because he was *de jure* the rightful King of both Gondor and Arnor, and could, if he willed, for just cause withdraw all previous grants to himself. [*Unfinished Tales*, p. 409]

780 (III: 53–4): He drew a deep breath

780 (III: 53). The eyes in Orthanc did not see through the armour of Théoden, but Sauron has not forgotten Isildur – As first published these words read simply: 'But he has not forgotten Isildur'. They were emended in the second edition (1965).

780 (III: 54): 'The hasty stroke goes oft astray'

780 (III: 54). a grave peril I saw coming unlooked-for from the South – It is now 6 March; Beregond (as emended, see notes for p. 765) says that news of the fleet reached Minas Tirith on the evening of 7 March.

781 (III: 54): 'Thus spoke Malbeth the Seer

781 (III: 54). *Stone of Erech* – '*Erech* (pre-N[úmenórean] name) a hill in South Gondor in Morthond Vale. . . . On it was the great black Stone of Isildur' (*Index*). In *1966 Index* Tolkien notes that the latter was 'a tryst-stone (symbol of Isildur's overlordship)'.

Tolkien wrote in his draft letter to Mr Rang, August 1967, of

> two cases where I was *not*, at the time of making use of them, aware of 'borrowing', but where it is probable, but by no means certain, that the names were nonetheless 'echoes'. *Erech*, the place where Isildur set the covenant-stone. This of course fits the style of the predominantly Sindarin nomenclature of Gondor (or it would not have been used), as it would do historically, even if it was, as it is now convenient to suppose, actually a pre-Númenórean name of long-forgotten meaning. Since naturally, as one interested in antiquity and notably the history of languages and 'writing', I knew and had read a good deal about Mesopotamia, I must have known *Erech* the name of that most ancient city. Nonetheless at the time of writing *L.R.* Book V chs. II and IX (originally a continuous narrative, but divided for obvious constructional reasons) and devising a legend to provide for the separation of Aragorn from Gandalf, and his disappearance and unexpected return, I was probably more influenced by the important element ER (in Elvish) = 'one, single, alone'. In any case the fact that *Erech* is a famous name is of *no* importance to *The L.R.* and no connexions in my mind or intention between Mesopotamia and the Númenóreans or their predecessors can be deduced. [*Letters*, p. 384]

782 (III: 55): 'That we shall know

782 (III: 55). the Men of the Mountains – In a note to the late *Battles of the Fords of Isen* it is said that 'the Dunlendings were a remnant of the peoples that had dwelt in the vales of the White Mountains in ages past. The Dead Men of Dunharrow were of their kin' (*Unfinished Tales*, p. 370).

782 (III: 55): 'Then Isildur said to their king

782 (III: 55). this curse I lay upon thee and thy folk: to rest never until your oath is fulfilled – The importance of oaths or promises, and the consequences of their fulfilment or of their breaking, is a recurring theme in Tolkien's fiction, most elaborately and tragically in 'The Silmarillion' with the oath of Fëanor to recover the Silmarils (see note for p. 669). In Book IV, Chapter 1 of *The Lord of the Rings* Gollum makes a qualified and ultimately empty promise to 'serve the Master of the Precious' (p. 618, II: 225), and oaths of service are given variously to Théoden, Denethor, and Aragorn (see especially note for pp. 755–6), or referred to in other respects, notably the pledge by Eorl the Young that the Rohirrim would come to the aid of Gondor at need (see note for p. 431, and Appendix A). Oaths as legal and social contracts were central to medieval society, in particular oaths of fealty to lords and kings; and to break an oath was tantamount to treason (in accepting Pippin's service, Denethor promises, *inter alia*, to 'reward . . . oath-breaking with vengeance', p. 756, III: 28). The case of those who had broken their oath of alliance with Isildur in the fight against Sauron, and found no rest in death for over 3,000 years, is an extreme expression of this idea but emphasizes the point. See further, Alain Renoir, 'The Heroic Oath in *Beowulf*, the *Chanson de Roland*, and the *Nibelungenlied*', in *Studies in Old English Literature in Honor of Arthur G. Brodeur* (1963), and John R. Holmes, 'Oaths and Oath Breaking: Analogues of Old English *Comitatus* in Tolkien's Myth', *Tolkien and the Invention of Myth: A Reader* (2004).

782 (III: 55–6): Legolas and Gimli made no answer

782 (III: 56). stared in amaze – *Amaze* is an older, now poetic equivalent of *amazement*.

As Tolkien first planned and wrote Book V, this paragraph concluded the account dealing with Aragorn and those who went with him, while the rest of the chapter (originally entitled 'Many Roads Lead Eastward') contained what became 'The Muster of Rohan' (Book V, Chapter 3). Tolkien intended that the tale of Aragorn's journey from Helm's Deep to Minas Tirith should be told to Merry and Pippin in retrospect after the Battle of the Pelennor Fields. Some time later, however, he decided to extend the direct narrative to cover the journey through the Paths of the Dead and the summoning of the Dead at the Stone of Erech, and make it a separate chapter, while leaving only the latter part of the journey to be told in retrospect. Thus the story continues to flow unimpeded for a greater length, and Aragorn's arrival during the battle before Minas Tirith still comes as a surprise.

782 (III: 56): And while Théoden went

782 (III: 56). on the next day in the afternoon they came to Edoras – On 7 March 1419. According to *Scheme*, on 6 March they left Helm's Deep at about 4.00 p.m., and camped '20 miles or so on way'. On 7 March: 'Aragorn reaches Edoras during day, and after brief halt rides to Dunharrow which he reaches at nightfall.'

783 (III: 56): And she answered as one

783 (III: 56). Harrowdale – 'Valley at head of Snowbourn, under walls of Dunharrow' (*Index*).

783 (III: 56): 'They may suffer me to pass'

783 (III: 56). adventure it – Take a chance, though success might be doubtful.

783–4 (III: 57): But as Aragorn came

783 (III: 57). the booth where he was to lodge – *Booth* in this sense means 'a temporary shelter, a tent'.

784 (III: 57): 'Because I must'

784 (III: 57). Were I to go where my heart dwells, far in the North I would now be wandering in the fair valley of Rivendell. – Aragorn gently suggests to Éowyn both that he has already given his love to another, and that she must fulfil her duty as he is fulfilling his, regardless of desires.

784 (III: 57): 'Too often have I heard of duty'

784 (III: 57). a shieldmaiden and not a dry-nurse – For *shieldmaiden*, compare *shieldmay*, 'a female warrior, an Amazon' (*OED*), from Old Norse *skjaldmær* 'shieldmaid'.

Dry-nurse is used here in its general sense 'nurse' (Éowyn has been caring for Théoden in his dotage induced by Wormtongue), rather than as a woman who attends to a child but does not suckle it.

785 (III: 58): 'Neither have those others'

785 (III: 58). Neither have those others who go with thee. They go only because they would not be parted from thee – because they love thee. – Éowyn began this conversation with Aragorn using formal *you*, *your* (see note for p. 775), but here pointedly changes to the intimate *thee*, expressing her feelings. When their conversation resumes the next day, she continues to use *thee*, *thou*, but Aragorn consistently addresses her with *you*, *your*, painfully polite.

785 (III: 58): When the light of day was come

785 (III: 58). When the light of day was come – It is 8 March 1419.

785 (III: 59): But Éowyn stood still

785 (III: 59). Dwimorberg, the Haunted Mountain – '*Dwimorberg* (Phantom Mt.) = Haunted Mountain, mountain east of Firienfeld in Dunharrow' (*Index*).

785 (III: 59). Door of the Dead – In Houghton Mifflin printings prior to 1987, and British editions prior to 1994, these words read 'Gate of the

Dead'. Tolkien entered this change in one of his check copies, but it was overlooked for many years.

786 (III: 59): The light was still grey

786 (III: 59). even as they passed between the lines of ancient stones – This is the first mention of the stones in *The Return of the King* as published. But as the chapter was originally written (see note for p. 782), the reader first came to Dunharrow with Théoden and Merry, and heard about Aragorn's visit only in retrospect. A detailed description 'of the Dwimorberg, the Firienfeld, the line of standing stones, the Dimholt, and the great monolith before the Dark Door' as seen by Merry was therefore given in what became Book V, Chapter 3. In *The War of the Ring* Christopher Tolkien notes that

> when afterwards the structure of the narrative was changed my father largely retained this description in the chapter 'The Muster of Rohan' . . . : he treated the coming of the Grey Company to Dunharrow two nights before the arrival of Théoden in a single sentence ('they passed up the valley, and so came to Dunharrow as darkness fell' [p. 782, III: 56], and said almost nothing of the scene. . . . The approach of the Company to the Dark Door next morning is described with a mysterious brevity: the double line of standing stones across the Firienfeld is mentioned cursorily, as if their existence were already known to the reader. . . . [p. 313]

786 (III: 59). Dimholt – In *Nomenclature* Tolkien describes *Dimholt* as '"wood of dark trees at entrance to the Dark Door". The name is given in the form of the language of Rohan . . . *dim* is still current in English (but here used in an older sense "obscure, secret"), and *holt* [Old English "wood"] is in occasional poetic use.'

786 (III: 60): His knees shook

786 (III: 60). he was wroth with himself – Gimli was angry with himself. Since no hobbit takes part in the journey through the Paths of the Dead and South Gondor, the reader experiences it instead through Gimli's eyes.

787 (III: 60–1): Nonetheless he drew near

787 (III: 60–1). the bones of a mighty man. . . . He had fallen near the far wall of the cave – It is the body of Baldor, son of Brego, grandson of Eorl, who in Third Age 2569 dared to tread the Paths of the Dead but never returned. See Book VI, Chapter 3.

787 (III: 61): Aragorn did not touch him

787 (III: 61). Hither shall the flowers of *simbelmynë* come never unto the world's end. . . . Nine mounds and seven there are now – Aragorn is referring to the white flower, Evermind, that grew on the burial mounds of the kings of Rohan. Baldor has been dead for 450 years, during which time all but one of the mounds were raised.

787 (III: 61). the door that he could not unlock. Whither does it lead? Why would he pass? None shall ever know! – Much later Tolkien wrote, in a note to *The Rivers and Beacon-hills of Gondor*:

> The Men of Darkness built temples, some of great size, usually surrounded by dark trees, often in caverns (natural or delved) in secret valleys of mountain-regions; such as the dreadful halls and passages under the Haunted Mountain beyond the Dark Door (Gate of the Dead) in Dunharrow. The special horror of the closed door before which the skeleton of Baldor was found was probably due to he fact that the door was the entrance to an evil temple hall to which Baldor had come, probably without opposition up to that point. But the door was shut in his face, and enemies that had followed him silently came up and broke his legs and left him to die in the darkness, unable to find any way out. [*Vinyar Tengwar* 42 (July 2001), p. 22]

787 (III: 61): 'For that is not my errand!'

787 (III: 61). the Accursed Years – Presumably the same as the Dark Years, during which the Men of the Mountains worshipped Sauron.

788 (III: 61): Suddenly he heard the tinkle

788 (III: 61). So deep and narrow was that chasm that the sky was dark, and in it small stars glinted. Yet as Gimli after learned it was still two hours ere sunset – David Cofield comments in 'Harbinger of Fate: The Eclipse of 3019' in *Beyond Bree*, October 1993, that it was an 'ancient tradition that observers at the bottom of a deep gorge, cavern, well, or chimney are able to see stars in the daylight sky', but recent research has shown 'that the glare of the sun and the atmospheric scattering of its light make it impossible to see any star (except the sun itself) from the earth's surface [in daylight] with the naked eye' (p. 3). In reply, Carl F. Hostetter comments in a letter to *Beyond Bree* for November 1993 that even if the 'chimney effect' is disproved, 'it is clear from Tolkien's own explanation that *he* believed [it] to be an authentic phenomenon, which is really all that matters' (p. 8).

789 (III: 62): Lights went out in house

789 (III: 62). hamlet – A group of houses or a small village.

789 (III: 62). The King of the Dead is come upon us! – Gill Page in 'The Wild Hunt', *Amon Hen* 42 (December 1979), suggests that there are parallels between the Dead Men of Dunharrow and the Wild Hunt, 'one of the most common elements in the folklore of Northern Europe; and especially Britain. The Hunt is led by a great warrior or hero god . . . accompanied by either wild hounds; or warriors similar to himself. . . . The Hunter and his followers are fierce, terrible to look upon or to hear, and dangerous' (p. 7). See also Margaret A. Sinex, '"Oathbreakers, why have ye come?": Tolkien's "Passing of the Grey Company" and the Twelfth-century *Exercitus Mortuorum*', in *Tolkien the Medievalist* (2003).

789 (III: 62): Bells were ringing far below

789 (III: 62). they came at last to the Hill of Erech – In *The War of the Ring* Christopher Tolkien notes that his father gave varying distances for the journey from Dunharrow to Erech, probably because of changing ideas of the former's exact position. He notes that 'the Second Map ([reproduced on] p. 434) gives (probably) 45 miles; and this is also the distance on my father's large-scale map of Rohan, Gondor and Mordor (and on my reproduction of it published in *The Return of the King*)' (p. 308, n. 2). The 'distance from the issue of the Paths of the Dead to the Stone of Erech' was probably 25 miles (p. 422, n. 3).

789 (III: 62–3): Long had the terror

789 (III: 62). For upon the top [of the hill] stood a black stone, round as a globe, the height of a man, though its half was buried in the ground. Unearthly it looked . . . but those who remembered still the lore of Westernesse told that it had been brought out of the ruin of Númenor and there set by Isildur at his landing. – If this passage refers to the height of an ordinary man, the stone was over eleven feet in diameter, with five or six feet above the surface of the hill; if to the height of a Númenórean (see note for p. 242), it was over thirteen feet in diameter. Readers have pointed out that it therefore must have been very heavy, and its transportation by ship problematical; and that it must have been of major significance (nowhere explained by Tolkien) to be loaded with other treasures on one of the ships that waited off the coast of Númenor in anticipation of disaster. One draft manuscript suggests that the Stone was brought from Númenor before its fall.

789 (III: 63): Then Aragorn said: 'The hour

789 (III: 63). Pelargir – '(Garth of the Royal Ships) haven above the delta of Anduin, where N[úmenórean] landings had taken place in [the] Second Age' (*Index*). In the *Akallabêth* it is said that Pelargir was the haven of the Elf-friends, and that the King's Men established havens much further south (*The Silmarillion*, p. 267).

790 (III: 63): But when the dawn came

790 (III: 63). the dawn came – It is 9 March 1419.

790 (III: 63): They passed Tarlang's Neck

790 (III: 63). Tarlang's Neck – In the final *Nomenclature* Tolkien writes only that 'the *Neck* was a long ridge of rock, over which the road climbed, joining the main mass of the range to the branch (containing three peaks) which separated the plain of *Erech* from *Lamedon. Tarlang*, originally the name of this ridge, was later taken as a personal name.' This was preceded in the manuscript, however, by two variant texts of much greater length and complexity (in the end, perhaps, thought irrelevant to the *Nomenclature* as a guide to translators). The first note read:

> *Tarlang's Neck* . . . is an explanation in C[ommon] S[peech] of a name that was no longer certain in meaning at that time. The *Neck* was a ridge (over which the road climbed) joining the main range of mountains to the mountainous spur that separated the plain of Erech from Lamedon. This was [*double erased and illegible*] called in Sindarin *tarch-lang* 'stiff, rough[or tough]-neck', which in its later form *tarlang* was no longer clear in meaning, and *Neck* was usually added in C[ommon] Speech]. *Tarlang* in local legend was the name of a giant of 'long ago' of one of the giants who in 'ancient days' had built the White Mountains as a wall to keep Men out of their land by the Sea. But Tarlang, while carrying a load of rock on his head, tripped and fell, and the other giants used him to finish the wall at that point, leaving his neck lying southward, while his head and the load made up the S[outhern] mts of the ridge, [?called] Tarlangs, that separate the plain of Erech from [?Lamedon].

This was replaced by a new text, the first part of which was retained in the final version:

> The *Neck* was a long ridge of rock, over which the road climbed. joining the main mass of the range to the branch (containing three peaks) which separated the plain of Erech from Lamedan. [*added*: Tarlang originally the name of this ridge was later taken as a personal name]. [*The following bracketed and marked* 'don't copy this':] Actually *Tarlang* was probably the original name of this ridge or neck (it means "stiff neck"), for the road over it was hard and laborious, and was only used by those in great need or haste. But owing to the facts that *lang* 'neck', though frequently used geographically, was also applied to the neck of men and animals, while *Tarlang* was a not uncommon man's name* [*added*: *in origin a nickname "Stiff neck" applied to men of haughty carriage or mood], there grew up a local legend to explain the name. It was said that when 'in ancient days' some giants were building the White Mountains as a wall to keep Men out of their land by the Sea, one of them called Tarlang tripped and fell on his face and as he was carrying a heavy load of rocks on his head he broke his neck and was killed. The other giants used his body to complete the wall at that point, but left his neck lying southward, leading to the three mountains of the spur: *Dol Tarlang* 'Tarlang's Head', *Cûl Veleg* 'Bigload' and *Cûl Bîn* 'Little Load'. The break in his neck was shown by a depression in the ridge, near the junction with Tarlang's Head, over which the road went.

In consequence the *Tarlang* was called *Achad Tarlang* using another word for 'neck' (Q[uenya] *axo*), properly referring only to the bony vertebral part and not including the throat, this was generally called in the vernacular C[ommon] S[peech] *Tarlang's Neck*.

790 (III: 63). Calembel upon Ciril – '*Calembel* ("Greenham") a town by the Fords on the Ciril' (*Index*).

In *The Rivers and Beacon-hills of Gondor* it is said of the derivation of *Ciril* (or *Kiril*): 'Uncertain, but probably from KIR "cut". It rose in Lamedon and flowed westward for some way in a deep rocky channel' (*Vinyar Tengwar* 42 (July 2001), p. 13).

790 (III: 63). the sun went down like blood – In Book IV, Chapter 7 Frodo and Sam see the same sunset as they reach the road from Minas Morgul to Osgiliath: 'a fire-flecked sky' (p. 697, II: 306; described in *Scheme* as 'ominous sunset'); and in Book V, Chapter 1 Pippin sees it from Minas Tirith: 'in the West the dying sun had set all the fume on fire, and now Mindolluin stood black against a burning smoulder flecked with embers' (p. 771, III: 44).

790 (III: 63). the next day there came no dawn – It is 10 March 1419, the Dawnless Day.

Chapter 3

THE MUSTER OF ROHAN

For drafts and history of this chapter, see *The War of the Ring*, pp. 231–67.

791 (III: 64): Now all roads were running together

791 (III: 64). the King of Rohan came down out of the hills – It is the evening of 9 March 1419.

791 (III: 64): All day far below them

791 (III: 64). Snowbourn – In his unfinished index Tolkien notes that the *Snowbourn* is a 'river rising under Starkhorn and flowing out down Harrowdale and so past Edoras to join [the] Entwash in Fenmarch'. In *Nomenclature* he says that the name is a modernized form of 'the actual Rohan (i.e. Old English) *snāw-burna*'. Compare, in Modern English, *bourn* or *bourne* (Scottish *burn*) 'small stream or brook'.

791 (III: 64). Starkhorn – In his unfinished index Tolkien describes the *Starkhorn* as a mountain of the Ered Nimrais at the head of Harrowdale. In *Nomenclature* its name is said to derive from Rohan, meaning 'a horn (peak) "standing up stiff like a spike". . . . To an English reader *stark* has now implications of nakedness and grimness (not originally present, but due to applications to *rigor mortis* in corpses, and to the expression *stark-naked*). . . .'

791–2 (III: 64–5): He was very tired

791 (III: 64). though they had ridden slowly – According to *Scheme* they had ridden 'slowly by hidden path in lower mountains. Doing only about 35 m[iles] p[er] day'.

792 (III: 65): 'This journey is over, maybe'

792 (III: 65). Two nights ago the moon was full – In printings prior to 2005 this read: 'Last night the moon was full'. But this is the evening of 9/10 March and the moon was full on 7/8 March. This is a shadow of an earlier chronology when Théoden arrived on the evening of 8 March. Christopher Tolkien notes the discord in *The War of the Ring*, p. 322.

793 (III: 66): 'At dawn three days ago, lord'

793 (III: 66). three days ago – It is the evening of 9 March. Gandalf reached Edoras at dawn on 6 March.

794 (III: 67): On all the level spaces

794 (III: 67). a great concourse of men – *Concourse* 'a coming together, a gathering'.

794 (III: 67): Merry wondered how many

794 (III: 67). Púkel-men – *Púkel-men* is 'a Rohan name for the effigies of men of a vanished race. It represents Old English *pūcel* (still surviving as *puckle*), one of the forms of the *pūk-* stem (widespread in England, Wales, Ireland, Norway and Iceland) referring to a devil, or to a minor sprite, e.g. Puck, and often applied to ugly misshapen persons' (*Nomenclature*). When Merry sees the Wose, Ghân-buri-Ghân, in Book V, Chapter 5, he thinks that he is like one of the Púkel-men brought to life. Tolkien later wrote that the Púkel-men, or Drúedain, ancestors of the Woses,

> occupied the White Mountains (on both sides) in the First Age. When the occupation of the coastlands by the Númenóreans began in the Second Age they survived in the mountains of the promontory [of Andrast], which was never occupied by the Númenóreans. Another remnant [Ghân-buri-Ghân's people] survived at the eastern end of the range [in Anórien]. At the end of the Third Age the latter, much reduced in numbers, were believed to be the only survivors; hence the other region was called 'the Old Púkel-wilderness' (Drúwaith Iaur). [*The Drúedain* in *Unfinished Tales*, p. 384]

794–5 (III: 67–8): At last the king's company

794 (III: 67). Firienfeld – In *Nomenclature* (entry for *Firien*) Tolkien writes that the name *Firienfeld* denotes 'the flat upland of Dunharrow'. For *firien*, see note for p. 747 (*Halifirien*). The element *-feld* is Old English 'field'.

794 (III: 68). Írensaga – A name of Rohan (i.e. from Old English) which means '"iron-saw" with reference to its serrated ridge, crest' (*Nomenclature*).

794 (III: 68). a double line of unshaped standing stones – For this Tolkien may have been inspired by lines (single or double) of uncarved or roughly shaped standing stones in several places in North-west Europe, notably Carnac in Brittany, the West Kennet Avenue near Avebury in Wiltshire, and at Callanash on the Isle of Lewis in the Hebrides.

795 (III: 68): Such was the dark Dunharrow

795 (III: 68). Such was the dark Dunharrow – The final conception of Dunharrow took a long time to emerge in Tolkien's mind, and as he explored various possibilities he made several drawings. See *The War of the Ring*, with illustrations as frontispiece and on pp. 239, 314, *Sauron Defeated*, pp. 136–7, with illustrations on pp. 140–1, and *Artist and Illustrator*, pp. 171–2 and figs. 165–6. Tolkien's finished drawing of Dunharrow

(*Artist and Illustrator*, fig. 166) bears a remarkable resemblance to a photograph of Mürren, Switzerland seen by the authors.

795 (III: 69): 'I do not know'

795 (III: 69). he rode away yestermorn – It is late on 9 March. Aragorn left early on 8 March.

797 (III: 70): 'No man knows'

797 (III: 70). Baldor, son of Brego – See note for p. 787. *Baldor* is Old English 'prince, ruler', closely related to *bald* (*beald*) 'bold, brave'.

798 (III: 71–2): A tall man entered

798 (III: 72). In his hand he bore a single arrow, black-feathered and barbed with steel, but the point was painted red. – In *A Tale of the House of the Wolfings* by William Morris the Wolfings are summoned to war against the Romans in part by a messenger who carries 'the token of the war-arrow ragged and burnt and bloody' (Chapter 2).

799–800 (III: 73): 'But we will speak no longer

800 (III: 73). a week it may be from tomorrow's morn – *Tomorrow* will be 10 March; the Rohirrim will arrive at Minas Tirith at dawn on 15 March, two days less than Théoden's estimate. With the coming of the Great Darkness Théoden will decide that there is no need for hiding, and he and his forces can ride by the open road.

800 (III: 73): 'A week!' said Hirgon

800 (III: 73). Swarthy Men – The Haradrim (*1966 Index*).

800 (III: 73–4): He was wakened

800 (III: 73). He was wakened – It is 10 March 1419.

803 (III: 76): On down the grey road

803 (III: 76). Underharrow – 'Village on the Snowbourn beneath the cliff of the Hold' (*Index*). See also note for p. 518.

803 (III: 76). Upbourn – 'Village on the Snowbourn a mile below Underharrow' (*Index*). In *Nomenclature* Tolkien writes that '*Up-* is used in English place-names for river-side villages far up the named river (as *Upavon* in Wilts. [Wiltshire]), especially in contrast to larger places near its mouth, as *Upwey* above *Weymouth*. This village was some way up the *Snowbourn* above *Edoras*, but not so far up as *Underharrow*.' The 'proper Rohan form' is *Upburnan*.

803 (III: 76–7). so without horn or harp . . . – A recording by Tolkien from these words to the end of the following poem is included on Disc 2 of *The J.R.R. Tolkien Audio Collection*.

803 (III: 76–7): *From dark Dunharrow in the dim morning*

803 (III: 76). *Mark-wardens* – Kings of the Mark.

803 (III: 77). *Five nights and days* – According to *Scheme*: 'Théoden leaves Dunharrow in morn; reaches Edoras; leaves Edoras after midday.' He will arrive at Minas Tirith at dawn on 15 March.

803 (III: 77). *Folde and Fenmarch and the Firienwood* – In *Nomenclature* Tolkien writes that *Folde* is 'a Rohan name' which also occurs in *Eastfold*.

> This is Old English *folde* (Old Norse *fold*) 'earth, land, country', not connected either with the English verb *fold*, or with (*sheep*)*fold*. . . .
>
> The *Folde* was the centre of the kingdom, in which the royal house and its kin had their dwellings; its boundary eastward was roughly a line S.W. [south-west] from the junction of the Snowbourn and Entwash to the mountains; the *Eastfold* was the land from that line east to the *Fenmark* between Entwash and the mountains; the *Westfold* was the similar land along the mountains as far as the R[iver] Isen. The defensive centre of the *Folde* and *Eastfold* was at *Edoras*; of *Westfold* at *Helm's Deep*.

Fenmarch is also a 'Rohan name: the fenny (marshy) border-land about the *Mering Stream* . . . forming the boundary of *Rohan* and *Anórien*. This should have been called *Fenmark*, but since appears in III 78 [2004 edn., p. 804; Book V, Chapter 3] and on the map to vol. III, I have retained it; the meaning of *-mark*, or the French form (of Germanic origin) *marche* is the same: boundary, border (land)' (*Nomenclature*).

The *Firienwood* is the 'wood about and on the slopes of the *Halifirien*' (*Nomenclature*, entry for *Firien*); see note for p. 747. Tolkien later wrote that *Firien Wood* is a 'modernized spelling' for Old English *firgen-wudu* (*Unfinished Tales*, p. 314, n. 33).

803 (III: 77). *Sunlending* – 'A translation into the language of Rohan of *Anórien* [see note for p. 747]. . . . It only occurs in the verses . . . purporting to translate the minstrelsy of Rohan. . . . It might well be spelt (indeed more accurately) *Sunnlending*', Old English 'sun-land-people' (*Nomenclature*).

803 (III: 77). *foe-beleaguered* – Under siege.

804 (III: 77): 'I received you for your safe-keeping'

804 (III: 77). a hundred leagues and two to Mundburg – Three hundred and six miles. This agrees with the 294 miles of Gandalf's ride from Edoras to the Rammas Echor, plus the 4 leagues (12 miles) from the Rammas to Minas Tirith.

804 (III: 77): Merry bowed and went away

804 (III: 77). tightening their girths – A *girth* is 'a belt or band of leather or cloth, placed round the body of a horse . . . and drawn tight, so as to secure a saddle, pack etc. upon its back' (*OED*).

804 (III: 78): 'Do you not?'

804 (III: 78). Dernhelm – A name derived from obsolete *dern* 'secret, hidden' + *helm* 'helmet'.

804 (III: 78): Thus it came to pass

804 (III: 78). Windfola – Old English 'Wind-foal'.

804 (III: 78): On into the shadow they rode

804 (III: 78). In the willow-thickets where Snowbourn flowed into Entwash, twelve leagues east of Edoras, they camped that night. – This seems to be out of their way: surely the Great West Road, shown prominently on the map of Rohan, Gondor, and Mordor as running direct from Edoras to Minas Tirith, would have been the quickest route. According to *Scheme* they camp '30 miles east on way', compared with 36 miles ('twelve leagues') in the text.

804 (III: 78). And then on again through the Folde – It is 11 March 1419.

804–5 (III: 78): And so King Théoden departed

804 (III: 78). and mile by mile the long road wound away – According to *Scheme*:

> March 11: Théoden rides on and camps 110 miles east.
>
> March 12: Théoden rides on and camps under Minrimmon. Ents destroy orc-host on plains of Rohan and so save Rohirrim from flank-attack or destruction of Edoras behind them.
>
> March 13: Théoden camps beyond Eilenach in Drúadan Forest and interviews Wild Men at night.

Chapter 4

THE SIEGE OF GONDOR

For drafts and history of this chapter, see *The War of the Ring*, pp. 323–42.

806 (III: 79): Pippin was roused by Gandalf

806 (III: 79). Pippin was roused – It is 10 March 1419.

806 (III: 79): Before long he was walking

806 (III: 79). Tower Hall – 'Hall of the White Tower, the great hall of the throne under the White Tower' (*Index*).

806 (III: 79): 'I will, when I learn

806 (III: 79). out-garrison – Those defending a position some distance from the main fortress. Also referred to as 'the out-companies'.

808 (III: 81): It was the sunset-hour

808 (III: 81). the great pall now stretched far into the West – It had already reached Dunharrow by dawn: it was dark when Merry woke on this same day.

809 (III: 82): Reluctantly Pippin climbed

809 (III: 82). five birdlike forms, horrible as carrion fowl yet greater than eagles – As first published, 'five birdlike forms' read 'huge birdlike forms'. The phrase was altered in the second edition (1965).

More detail of the winged steeds of the Nazgûl is given in Book V, Chapter 6 when that ridden by the Witch-king is seen at close quarters: 'it was a winged creature: if bird, then greater than all other birds, and its vast pinions were as webs of hide between horned fingers; and it stank. A creature of an older world maybe it was, whose kind, lingering in forgotten mountains cold beneath the Moon, outstayed their day . . .' (p. 840, III: 115). In a draft letter of 14 October 1958 to Rhona Beare, who had asked if the Witch-king rode a pterodactyl, Tolkien wrote:

> Yes and no. I did not intend the steed of the Witch-king to be what is now called a 'pterodactyl', and often is drawn (with rather less shadowy evidence than lies behind many monsters of the new and fascinating semi-scientific mythology of the 'Prehistoric'). But obviously it is *pterodactylic* and owes much to the new mythology, and its description even provides a sort of way in which it could be a last survivor of older geological eras. [*Letters*, p. 282]

In a draft manuscript of Book V, Chapter 6 the Witch-king rides a beast like a 'huge vulture' (*The War of the Ring*, p. 365).

811 (III: 84): So at length they came

811 (III: 84). brazier – A container for burning coals.

811 (III: 84): When Faramir had taken

811 (III: 84). he sat upon a low chair at his father's left hand. Removed a little upon the other side sat Gandalf in a chair of carven wood – According to formal protocol, Gandalf sits on the more prestigious (right-hand) side of Denethor. Faramir's *low chair* indicates his relationship with his lord and father.

811 (III: 84). ten days before – This is the evening of 10 March. Faramir had set out on 1 March, probably in the morning (*The Tale of Years*).

812 (III: 85): 'I parted with them

812 (III: 85). in the morning two days ago – On 8 March.

812 (III: 85). accursed Tower – Minas Morgul.

812 (III: 85). At swiftest they could not come there before today, and maybe they have not come there yet. – It must now be an hour or more past sunset in Minas Tirith. Frodo was at the Cross-roads at sunset and probably came to Morgul Vale at about this time. Brian Rosebury points out in *Tolkien: A Cultural Phenomenon* that Faramir's news provides Gandalf

> with the information about Frodo's progress necessary to guide his later strategy. His fear that Frodo may have perished or been captured in the valley of Minas Morgul, and Sauron already regained the Ring, is not less moving because we already know that . . . it is both well-founded and ill-founded: Frodo has indeed been captured, but the Ring is in the possession of Sam, still at liberty. [p. 65]

This news also will lead Gandalf and Aragorn to decide to assault the Morannon, rather than Minas Morgul, lest they draw Sauron's attention nearer to Frodo. Gandalf, as the bearer of Narya, would surely have known if Sauron had regained the Ring.

812 (III: 85). It is clear to me that the Enemy has long planned an assault on us, and its hour had already been determined before ever the travellers left my keeping. – Sauron had indeed long been planning an assault, but moved his plans forward after Aragorn looked in the *palantír* on 6 March. See Gandalf's explanation, p. 815, III: 88–9.

812 (III: 85): 'Some twenty-five leagues

812 (III: 85). Cair Andros – 'This name means "Ship of Long-foam"; for the isle was shaped like a great ship, with a high prow pointing north, against which the white foam of Anduin broke on sharp rocks' (Appendix A, p. 1054, III: 335, n. 1).

812 (III: 85): 'Ill?' cried Denethor

812 (III: 85). 'Ill?' cried Denethor, and his eyes flashed suddenly. – Tolkien now skilfully begins to depict the fraught relationship between Faramir and his father, and how Denethor's grief at the death of his favoured son, Boromir, has made him even harder on Faramir, though deep down he loves him too. In early drafts Denethor was less harsh in his dealings with Faramir, and it was Faramir, not Denethor, who urged the defence of Osgiliath and the forts. But Tolkien wrote in a note to himself:

> The early conversation of Faramir and his father and motives must be altered. Denethor must be *harsh.* He must say he did wish Boromir had been at Henneth Annûn – for he *would* have been loyal to his father and brought him the Ring. . . . Faramir grieved but patient. Then Denethor must be all for holding Osgiliath 'like Boromir did', while Faramir (and Gandalf?) are against it, using the arguments previously given to Denethor. At length in submission, but proudly, to please his father and show him that not only Boromir was brave [he] accepts the command at Osgiliath. Men in City do not like it.
>
> This will not only be truer to previous situation, but will explain Denethor's breaking up when Faramir is brought back *dying*, as it seems. [*The War of the Ring*, p. 333]

812 (III: 86): 'My son, your father

812 (III: 86). as was my wont – *Wont* 'custom, habit', here indicating 'as well as ever I could'.

814 (III: 87): 'And where will other men look

814 (III: 87). 'And where will other men look for help, if Gondor falls? . . . If I had this thing now in the deep vaults of this citadel, we should not then shake with dread – Again Denethor thinks only of Gondor, and does not imagine that anything could survive if Gondor falls, in contrast to Gandalf's broader point of view which encompasses 'other men and other lives'. Denethor also believes that he could resist the temptation of the Ring, but we will learn that he has succumbed to temptation by using the *palantír*, and Gandalf implies that Denethor would wish to use the Ring (the first person singular, *if* I *had this thing*, is telling), no less than had Boromir.

815 (III: 88): Gandalf stood for a moment

815 (III: 88). some five days ago now he would discover that we had thrown down Saruman, and had taken the Stone – It is now the evening of 10 March; it was on the evening of 5 March that Pippin looked in the *palantír*. One Nazgûl flew over Isengard soon afterward, and a second the next day.

815 (III: 89): The next day came

815 (III: 89). The next day came – It is 11 March.

816 (III: 89): 'Yet, said Denethor

816 (III: 89). we should not lightly abandon the outer defences, the Rammas made with so great a labour – In his unfinished index Tolkien says that the *Rammas* was built under Denethor's lordship, which would explain his reluctance to abandon it, though it surely enclosed too great an area to be adequately defended.

816 (III: 90): 'Much must be risked in war'

816 (III: 90). Cair Andros is manned – According to *The Tale of Years* an army which issued from the Morannon had taken Cair Andros the previous day and passed into Anórien. According to *Scheme*:

> March 10: Orc-host from Morannon with Easterlings assault Cair Andros after Faramir has gone. They cross into Anórien and march west at great speed.
>
> March 12: Easterlings pass the Pelennor and march west to waylay Rohirrim.
>
> March 13: Orcs and Easterlings from Cair Andros camp near Amon Dín [*sic*] to bar way of Rohirrim.

817 (III: 90): 'Yes, he will come'

817 (III: 90). At best the Red Arrow cannot have reached him more than two days ago – The Red Arrow reached Théoden late on 9 March.

817 (III: 90): It was night again

817 (III: 90). news came . . . saying that a host had issued from Minas Morgul – This is the army that Frodo saw leaving Minas Morgul after sunset on 10 March. It is now late on 11 March.

817 (III: 91): The next day

817 (III: 91). The next day – It is 12 March.

817 (III: 91). Causeway Forts – Two towers guarding the eastern gate in the Rammas Echor, four leagues distant from Minas Tirith, from which a causeway or raised road led over the flats to Osgiliath.

818 (III: 91): The bells of day

818 (III: 91). The bells of day – It is now 13 March 1419.

818 (III: 91): 'They have taken the wall!'

818 (III: 91). blasting breaches – Sauron, like Saruman, uses explosives, which is depicted as if evil sorcery. There is no indication that Gondor, or any other of the 'Free Peoples', has this technology.

819 (III: 92): Pippin trembled

819 (III: 92). if words spoken of old be true, not by the hand of man shall he fall – In Third Age 1975 the Host of the West defeated the Witch-king of Angmar at the Battle of Fornost. Eärnur, son of the King of Gondor, wished to pursue the Witch-king in his flight, but was restrained by Glorfindel who said of their foe: 'Far off yet is his doom, and not by the hand of man will he fall' (Appendix A, p. 1051, III: 332). Here Tolkien introduces the prophecy, to prepare the reader for the dénouement in Book V, Chapter 6.

819 (III: 92). Captain of Despair – The Witch-king, Lord of the Nazgûl.

820 (III: 93): The retreat became a rout

820 (III: 93). rout – In this sense, a disorderly retreat by a defeated army.

820 (III: 94): The Nazgûl screeched

820 (III: 94). taken at unawares in wild career – That is, taken by surprise as they attacked in a disorganized way.

820 (III: 94). smote – Attacked.

821 (III: 94): Last of all he came

821 (III: 94). his kinsman – Faramir is the nephew of Prince Imrahil, son of his sister Finduilas, deceased wife of Denethor.

821 (III: 94). the stricken field – The field of battle.

821 (III: 94): 'Faramir! Faramir!'

821 (III: 94). a deadly dart – An arrow.

821 (III: 94–5): The Prince Imrahil brought

821 (III: 95). saw a pale light that gleamed and flickered – Presumably Denethor is looking in the *palantír* of Minas Tirith. When Pippin looked in the Stone of Orthanc 'all the inside seemed on fire; the ball was spinning, or the lights within were revolving' (Book III, Chapter 11, p. 592, II: 197).

821 (III: 95). And when Denethor descended again . . . the face of the Lord was grey, more deathlike than his son's. – What did he see in the *palantír* to have this effect? Tom Shippey suggests in *J.R.R. Tolkien: Author of the Century* (p. 172) that it may have been the capture of Frodo, since Denethor cannot have seen the fleet coming up the Anduin until 14 or

15 March: Aragorn captures the fleet on this day, 13 March, but it will not begin to move up river until early on the 14th. In any case, Denethor already knows about the fleet – it was the reason he had the beacons lit – though he does not know that it is now under Aragorn's command ('the wind of thy hope cheats thee [Gandalf] and wafts up Anduin a fleet with black sails', Book V, Chapter 7, p. 853, III: 129). Shippey supports his suggestion with Denethor's words to Pippin in Book V, Chapter 4 (pp. 823–4, III: 97): 'The fool's [Gandalf] hope has failed. The enemy has found it, and now his power waxes; he sees our very thoughts, and all we do is ruinous.'

In opposition to this, however, even though Frodo was indeed held by the enemy at the time that Denethor looked in the *palantír*, no news of his capture reached Sauron for some time, there is no clear indication that Denethor used the *palantír* to look upon Cirith Ungol, and he makes no mention of Frodo and the Ring in his final words to Gandalf in Book VI, Chapter 7, only of the forces of the enemy approaching the city. One could argue instead that Denethor assumes that only the power of the Ring could have led so quickly to the imminent downfall of Minas Tirith, described as 'a strong citadel indeed, and not to be taken by a host of enemies, if there were any within that could hold weapons' (Book V, Chapter 1, p. 752, III: 24). In fact the attack is succeeding quickly because of the enemy's technology and the fear inspired by the Nazgûl, so much so that it hardly deserves to be called a 'siege'. Also, Gandalf will later suggest (Book V, Chapter 7, p. 856, III: 132) that when Denethor looked in the *palantír* 'he saw nonetheless only those things which the Power permitted him to see . . . the vision of the great might of Mordor that was shown to him fed the despair of his heart until it overthrew his mind'; and Denethor himself says, just before he destroys himself, 'to this City only the first finger of his hand has yet been stretched. All the East is moving' (Book V, Chapter 7, p. 853, III: 129).

Of course, at this stage the reader new to the book does not know that Denethor has a *palantír*, nor that Aragorn has captured the fleet.

821 (III: 95): So now at last the City was besieged

821 (III: 95). who had admitted Gandalf and Pippin less than five days before – They had arrived just before dawn on 9 March; it is now late on 13 March.

821–2 (III: 95): The Gate was shut

822 (III: 95). when morning or its dim shadow – It is now 14 March.

822 (III: 95): Busy as ants hurrying

822 (III: 95). digging lines of deep trenches . . . and as the trenches were made each was filled with fire . . . and soon yet more companies of the enemy were swiftly setting up, each behind the cover of a trench, great

engines for the casting of missiles – The trenches were presumably to impede any sorties to destroy the siege engines. Later Théoden will learn that those forces of Sauron sent to waylay the Rohirrim 'have cast trenches and stakes across the road. We cannot sweep them away in sudden onset' (Book V, Chapter 5, p. 832, III: 106).

Engines for the casting of missiles are noted in writings as early as the eighth century BC, but not much developed until the time of Philip of Macedon and Alexander, and then further perfected by the Romans. 'The missile engines threw stones from 75 lb. up to 600 lb., heavy darts from six to 12 ft. long, and Greek fire. Archimedes at the siege of Syracuse [*c.* 212 BC] even made some throwing 1,800 lb. The ranges varied, according to the machine and the weight thrown, up to 600 yd. for direct fire and 1,000 yd. for curved fire' (*Encyclopædia Britannica*, 14th edn., vol. 9, p. 525).

822–3 (III: 96): Soon there was great peril of fire

822–3 (III: 96). For the enemy was flinging into the City all the heads of those who had fallen fighting at Osgiliath, or on the Rammas, or in the fields . . . and all were branded with the foul token of the Lidless Eye. – This was evidently a form of psychological warfare. Adrienne Mayor in *Greek Fire, Poison Arrows & Scorpion Bombs: Biological and Chemical Warfare in the Ancient World* (2003) describes the Mongols catapulting bubonic plague-ridden corpses of their own soldiers over the walls of Kaffa, a Genoese fortress on the Black Sea in AD 1346, an early form of biological warfare; but 'terrifying the enemy was the sole object of a catapulting incident in 207 BC, when the Romans hurled the head of the Carthaginian general Hasdrubal into the camp of his brother, Hannibal . . . the act served to demoralize Hannibal, dashing his hopes of getting the reinforcements he needed to conquer Italy' (pp. 119–20).

824 (III: 97): 'I sent my son forth

824 (III: 97). unthanked, unblessed, out into needless peril . . . whatever may now betide in war, my line too is ending. . . . Mean folk shall rule the last remnant of the Kings of Men – Denethor is undoubtedly truly grieved that Faramir seems to be dying, but he grieves not only for his son, but also for the loss of an heir. He does not mention the impending fall of Minas Tirith, only that any survivors will be ruled by 'mean folk', among whom evidently he includes Aragorn, 'last of a ragged house long bereft of lordship and dignity' (Book V, Chapter 7, p. 854, III: 130).

824 (III: 98): Far beyond the battle

824 (III: 98). siege-towers – Comparable structures, made by the Romans (masters of siegecraft) are described in the *Encyclopædia Britannica* as

> movable towers of wood . . . built so high that from their tops the parapet walk of the wall [under attack] could be swept with arrows and stones. . . . The height of the towers was from 70 to 150 ft. They were moved on wheels of solid oak or elm, six to 12 ft. in diameter and three to four feet thick. The ground floor contained one or two rams. The upper floors, of which there might be as many as 15, were furnished with missile engines of a smaller kind. The archers occupied the top floor. There were also placed reservoirs of water to extinguish fire. . . . Drawbridges, either hanging or worked on rollers, were placed at the proper height to give access to the top of the wall. . . . The siege towers had of course to be very solidly built of strong timbers to resist the heavy stones thrown by the engines of the defence. They were protected against fire by screens of osiers [willow], plaited rope or raw hides. [14th edn., vol. 9, p. 525]

825 (III: 98–9): 'Why do the fools fly?'

825 (III: 98–9). before ever a ship sailed hither from the West – Denethor is referring to the earlier years of Númenor, when the men of that country first sailed back to Middle-earth as teachers and friends of men still living there, under threat from Sauron.

825 (III: 99): Now Denethor stood up

825 (III: 99). The house of his spirit crumbles. – As first published this sentence read: 'His house crumbles', and in that form may have referred either to the body of Faramir or to the House of the Stewards. It was altered in the second edition (1965). The new text recalls Tolkien's later work on 'The Silmarillion', in which he discusses the relationship of the *fëa* (spirit) and the *hröa* (bodily form) of an Elf, and uses such words as: 'This destruction of the *hröa*, causing death or the unhousing of the *fëa*' (*Morgoth's Ring*, p. 218)

825 (III: 99): 'I will not say farewell

825 (III: 99). I will not think of dying until he despairs of life. . . . I do not wish to be released – Pippin has matured a great deal in his few days in Minas Tirith. He has a hobbit's tenacity and will not give up hope, but is ready to fight to the last. His sympathy for Denethor helps to soften the reader's attitude towards the Steward, who abandons not only hope but the rule and care of his city (breaking his own oath of service), and in desiring death does not seek it honourably in the defence of Minas Tirith.

826 (III: 99–100): All was silent save for the rumour

826 (III: 99). Fen Hollen – '*Fen* "door". *Fen Hollen* (prop[erly] *chollen*) the "Closed Door" leading to the Street of Tombs in M[inas] T[irith]' (*Index*). Later this is called the 'Steward's Door'.

826 (III: 100): A porter sat in a little house

826 (III: 100). many pillared balusters – The *Oxford English Dictionary* defines a single *baluster* as 'a short pillar or column, or circular section of curving outline (properly double-curved), slender above and swelling below into an elliptical or pear shaped bulge; usually applied to a series called a *balustrade*'; but also notes an archaic use as a collective singular, 'a balustrade or protective railing'.

826 (III: 100). the Silent Street, Rath Dínen – Here Tolkien precedes the Sindarin name with a translation. In his unfinished index he gives '*Rath* street (in a city)' and '*Tîn* silent, quiet, *tínen* silent in *Rath Dínen*'.

826 (III: 100): There Pippin, staring uneasily

826 (III: 100). upon each table a sleeping form – The sleeping forms may be effigies, or the embalmed bodies of former Stewards. It is said in Appendix A that after Aragorn departed his life in Rath Dínen 'long there he lay, an image of the splendour of the Kings of Men in glory undimmed before the breaking of the world' (p. 1063, III: 344).

827 (III: 101): 'Well, you must choose

827 (III: 101). you must choose between orders and the life of Faramir . . . as for orders, I think you have a madman to deal with – This is perhaps Tolkien's clearest expression of the view that obedience to orders should not be absolute, that in some circumstances it is right to disobey and yet fulfil a greater duty.

827 (III: 101): He ran on, down

827 (III: 101). the Second Gate – 'Gate from [the] Outer Circle of M[inas] T[irith] to the next stone circle' (*Index*).

828 (III: 101–2): Ever since the middle night

828 (III: 101). Yet their Captain cared not greatly what they did or how many might be slain – W.A. Senior in 'Loss Eternal in J.R.R. Tolkien's Middle-earth', *J.R.R. Tolkien and His Literary Resonances: Views of Middle-earth* (2000), compares this with the acceptance by General Haig and the British Command of appalling losses during the Battle of the Somme in 1916. When he was informed that estimated casualties on the first day of the battle were 40,000 (killed, wounded, and missing; later revised to 58,000 including 19,240 killed), Haig is said to have remarked: 'This cannot be considered severe in view of the numbers engaged and the length of the front attacked' (quoted in Malcolm Brown, *The Imperial War Museum Book of the Somme*, p. 119). Though wave after wave of Allied troops were killed as they climbed out of the trenches to attack the German line, there was no change in tactics in the following months.

828 (III: 102): The drums rolled louder

828 (III: 102). a huge ram, great as a forest-tree a hundred feet in length, swinging on mighty chains . . . its hideous head, forged of black steel, was shaped in the likeness of a ravening wolf – A battering-ram, 'an ancient military engine employed for battering down walls, consisting of a beam of wood, with a mass of iron at one end, sometimes in the form of a ram's head' (*OED*). The head shaped like a wolf is appropriate to Sauron, called in *The Silmarillion* 'lord of werewolves' (p. 156).

828 (III: 102). Grond they named it, in memory of the Hammer of the Underworld of old. – *Grond* was the name of the mace used by Morgoth in his battle with Fingolfin, King of the Noldor, in the First Age.

829 (III: 102): Thrice he cried

829 (III: 102). Thrice he cried. Thrice the great ram boomed. And suddenly upon the last stroke the Gate of Gondor broke. – It is only just over twenty-four hours after the arrival of Sauron's forces at the walls of Minas Tirith that the main gate is destroyed. Sauron relies on force of arms and technology, but also on sorcery, on 'spells of ruin' laid on the ram, and words of power and terror spoken by the Lord of the Nazgûl. In June 1958 Tolkien wrote to Forrest J. Ackerman that the Nazgûl had 'no great physical power against the fearless; but what they have, and the fear they inspire, is enormously increased by *darkness*. The Witch-king, their leader, is more powerful in all ways than the others; but he must not yet [in Book I] be raised to the stature of Vol. III. There, put in command by Sauron, he is given an added demonic force' (*Letters*, p. 272).

829 (III: 103): The Black Rider flung back his hood

829 (III: 103). he had a kingly crown; and yet upon no head visible was it set. the red fires shone between it and the mantled shoulders vast and dark. – The Witch-king is a wraith, his body no longer visible, but his clothing can be seen, here as during the attack on Weathertop in Book I, Chapter 11. When Bilbo, Frodo, and Sam have worn the One Ring, even their clothes have vanished; but the Nazgûl no longer wear the Nine Rings, which are held by Sauron (see note for p. 250), and thus can pass unseen only if unclad. (See further, *Unfinished Tales*, p. 338.)

829 (III: 103): Gandalf did not move

829 (III: 103). a cock crowed – Douglas A. Anderson in *The Annotated Hobbit* (2nd edn., p. 150) compares this scene with the end of a battle against werewolves in S.R. Crockett's *The Black Douglas*:

> The howling stopped and there fell a silence. Lord James would have spoken.
>
> 'Hush!' said Malise, yet more solemnly.

And far off, like an echo from another world, thin and sweet and silver clear, a cock crew.

The blue leaping flame of the wild-fire abruptly ceased. The dawn arose red and broad in the east. The piles of dead beasts shone out black on the grey plain of the forest glade, and on the topmost bough of a pine tree a thrush began to sing.

829 (III: 103). Recking nothing – Paying no heed.

829 (III: 103): And as if in answer

829 (III: 103). Great horns of the North, wildly blowing. Rohan had come at last. – Tolkien wrote to Nancy Smith in a letter begun on 25 December 1963: 'But now (when the work is no longer hot, immediate or so personal) certain features of it, and especially certain places, still move me very powerfully. . . . I am most stirred by the sound of the horns of the Rohirrim at cockcrow' (J.R.R. Tolkien Papers, Marquette University Libraries; published, unidentified, in *Letters*, p. 221, with 'horses' for 'horns').

In *The Road to Middle-earth* Tom Shippey comments that

> challenging horns echo through Northern stories, from the trumpets of Hygelac, Beowulf's uncle, coming to rescue his dispirited compatriots from death by torture, to the war-horns of the 'Forest Cantons' . . . lowing to each other across the field of Marignano, as the Swiss pikemen rallied in the night for a second suicidal assault on overwhelming numbers of French cavalry and cannon' [2nd edn., pp. 194–5].

The arrival of Hygelac as translated by Clark Hall is described thus:

> Then with a mighty army he [Ongentheow, King of the Swedes] encompassed those whom the sword had not despatched, faint from their wounds, and through the livelong night he often threatened the wretched band with misery – said he would destroy them by morn with edge of sword – hang some on gallows-trees as sport for birds. Once more came help to the sad-hearted ones with early dawn, when they became aware of Hygelac's horn, his trumpet blast, – when the hero came bearing down on their track with a picked body of his troops. [*Beowulf and the Finnesburg Fragment*, pp. 164–5]

Chapter 5

THE RIDE OF THE ROHIRRIM

For drafts and history of this chapter, see *The War of the Ring*, pp. 343–58.

830 (III: 104): It was dark

830 (III: 104). It was dark – It is not long before dawn on 14 March 1419.

830 (III: 104): He could not see them

830 (III: 104). Drúadan Forest – In editions prior to 2004 the name 'Drúadan' was printed, here and in other instances, variously with and without the acute accent, but the accented form predominated, in one instance 'Druadan' was emended to 'Drúadan' in the second edition (1965), and the accented form appears also in *Unfinished Tales*. All instances of the name were regularized to 'Drúadan' for the latest text.

In his unfinished index Tolkien defines *D[rúadan] Forest* as 'the woods between Eilenach and Dîn', and *Druadan* [*sic*] as 'firth or enclosure of the *Drúad* (*drû* wild, untamed) . . . a woodwose'. In *Unfinished Tales* Christopher Tolkien gives the Sindarin name of the forest as *Tawar-in-Drúedain* (p. 319, n. 51).

830 (III: 104): Tired as he was

830 (III: 104). He had ridden now for four days on end – Presumably Tolkien is counting four calendar days from the riders' departure from Dunharrow or Edoras on 10 March to the present date, 14 March.

831 (III: 105): 'Nay, nay,' said Elfhelm

831 (III: 105). the Woses, the Wild Men of the Woods – In *Nomenclature* Tolkien says that *Woses*

> represents (modernized) the Rohan word for 'wild men of the woods'. It is not a purely invented word. The supposed genuine Rohan word was *wāsa*, pl[ural] *wāsan*, which if it had survived into modern English would be *woses*. It would have been better to call the 'wild men' *woodwoses*, for that actually occurs in Old English *wudewāsa* glossing '*faunus, satyrus*, savage men, evil creatures'. (This word survived into the Tudor period as *woodoses* (often corrupted to *woodhouses*), and survives in heraldry, since a *woodhouse* = 'a wild hairy man clad in leaves', common as a supporter to arms.) The *wāsa* element meant originally a forlorn or abandoned person. . . . The origin of this idea was no doubt the actual existence of wild folk, remnants of former peoples driven out by invaders, or outlaws, living a debased and savage life in forests and mountains.

Christopher Tolkien notes that 'the actual word employed by the Rohirrim (of which "wose" is a translation, according to the method employed throughout) is once mentioned: *róg*, plural *rógin*' (*Unfinished Tales*, p. 387, n. 14). The term *wodwos* is met in *Sir Gawain and the Green Knight*, translated by Tolkien in 1975 (p. 43) as 'wood-trolls'. See further, Tom Shippey, 'A Wose by Any Other Name . . .', *Amon Hen* 45 (July 1980).

831 (III: 105). they use poisoned arrows – As have some peoples in our history, such as those natives of South America with arrows tipped with *curare*, an extract of *Strychnos toxifera*.

831 (III: 105). they are woodcrafty beyond compare – Compare many so-called 'primitive' peoples in our history, who by living close to nature have greater tracking and hunting skills than are possessed by more 'civilized' cultures. Tolkien remarked in his lecture *On Fairy-Stories* that he had enjoyed tales of (North) American Indians as a child: 'there were bows and arrows . . . and strange languages, and glimpses of an archaic mode of life, and above all, forests in such stories' (*Tree and Leaf*, pp. 39–40).

831–2 (III: 105–6): Presently he came

831 (III: 105–6). a strange squat shape of a man, gnarled as an old stone, and the hairs of his scanty beard straggled on his lumpy chin like dry moss. He was short-legged and fat-armed, thick and stumpy, and clad only with grass about his waist. – After writing *The Lord of the Rings* Tolkien introduced the Drúedain into the stories of the First Age (see especially *Unfinished Tales*, pp. 380–7). He described the First Age ancestors of Ghân-buri-Ghân thus:

> To the eyes of Elves and other Men [than those of the Folk of Haleth] they were unlovely in looks: they were stumpy (some four foot high) but very broad, with heavy buttocks and short thick legs; their wide faces had deep-set eyes with heavy brows, and flat noses, and they grew no hair beneath their eyebrows, except in a few men (who were proud of the distinction) a small tail of black hair in the midst of the chin. Their features were usually impassive, the most mobile being their wide mouths; and the movement of their wary eyes could not be observed save from close at hand, for they were so black that the pupils could not be distinguished, but in anger they glowed red. Their voices were deep and guttural, but their laughter was a surprise: it was rich and rolling, and set all who heard it, Elves or Men, laughing too for its pure merriment untainted by scorn or malice. In peace they often laughed at work or play when other Men might sing. But they could be relentless enemies, and when once aroused their red wrath was slow to cool, though it showed no sign save the light in their eyes; for they fought in silence and did not exult in victory, not even over Orcs, the only creatures for whom their hatred was implacable.

> The Eldar called them Drúedain, admitting them to the rank of Atani [Men who were friends of the Elves], for they were much loved while they lasted. Alas! they were not long-lived, and were ever few in number, and their losses were heavy in their feud with the Orcs, who returned their hatred and delighted to capture them and torture them. When the victories of Morgoth destroyed all the realms and strongholds of Elves and Men in Beleriand, it is said that they had dwindled to a few families. . . .
>
> They had a marvellous skill as trackers of all living creatures . . . for the Drúedain used their scent, like hounds, save that they were also keen-eyed. They boasted that they could smell an Orc to windward further away than other Men could see them, and they could follow its scent for weeks except through running water. Their knowledge of all growing things was almost equal to that of the Elves (though untaught by them); and it is said that if they removed to a new country they knew within a short time all things that grew there, great or minute, and gave names to those that were new to them, discerning those that were poisonous, or useful as food. [*The Drúedain* in *Unfinished Tales*, pp. 377–8]

In an isolated note it is said that most of the Drúedain 'remained in the White Mountains, in spite of their persecution by later-arrived Men, who had relapsed into the service of the Dark' (*Unfinished Tales*, p. 383).

832 (III: 106). suddenly he remembered the Púkel-men of Dunharrow. Here was one of those old images brought to life, or maybe a creature descended in true line through endless years from the models used by the forgotten craftsmen long ago. – In Beleriand during the First Age the Drúedain 'showed great talent for carving in wood or stone . . . they delighted in carving figures of men and beasts, whether toys and ornaments or large images, to which the most skilled among them could give vivid semblance of life. . . . They made also images of themselves and placed them at the entrances to tracks or at turnings of woodland paths. These they called "watch-stones"' (*Unfinished Tales*, p. 379).

832 (III: 106): There was a silence

832 (III: 106). guttural – Producing sounds in the throat.

832 (III: 106): 'No, father of Horse-men'

832 (III: 106). *gorgûn* – Orcs. *Gorgûn* is the only word of the language of the Woses given in *The Lord of the Rings*.

832 (III: 106). Stone-houses – 'Drú[edain] name = Gondor, also Stone-City' (*Index*).

832 (III: 106): 'Bring news,' said the Wild Man

832 (III: 106). Stone-city is shut. Fire burns there outside; now inside too. – This seems to occur near dawn on 14 March. The previous chapter suggests that there were no fires inside the city until daylight.

832 (III: 106): The old man's flat face

832 (III: 106). I count many things. . . . You have a score of scores counted ten times and five. – Ghân-buri-Ghân seems able to count both accurately and in quantities that many would find difficult. A *score of scores counted ten times and five* is 20 x 20 x (10 + 5) = 6,000, the 'six thousand spears to Sunlending' recorded in the poem in Book V, Chapter 3.

832 (III: 106–7): 'Let Ghân-buri-Ghân finish!'

832 (III: 106–7). They went through Drúadan to Rimmon with great wains. They go no longer, the Road is forgotten. . . . Over hill and behind hill it lies still under grass and tree, there behind Rimmon and down to Dîn, and back at the end to Horse-men's road. – In *The Lord of the Rings* the beacon nearest Minas Tirith is Amon Dîn, and then moving west, Eilenach (near which the Rohirrim are encamped in Drúadan Forest), Nardol, Erelas, and Min-Rimmon. In *The War of the Ring* Christopher Tolkien notes that originally the order of the first three beacons from Minas Tirith was Amon Dîn, Min Rimmon, and Eilenach. In an early draft the Rohirrim are bivouacked in the forest of Taur-rimmon, out of which rises the hill of Min Rimmon, and Ghân-buri-Ghân says that the men of Gondor 'went to Eilenach with great wains. . . . Long road runs still under trees and grass behind Rimmon down to Dîn' (p. 351). In the first complete text

> the Rohirrim are still camped in 'Taur-rimmon Forest' from which rises Min Rimmon beacon. Ghân-buri-Ghân tells of the wains that went to Eilenach passing 'through Rimmon', where he clearly means 'the forest of Rimmon'; and he speaks as in the draft of the lost road that lies 'there behind Rimmon and down to Dîn'. Changes made to the manuscript in these passages produced the text of RK [*The Return of the King*] . . . but this development is rather puzzling. The host [of Rohan] now lies in the Druadan Forest out of which rises Eilenach beacon; and Ghân-buri-Ghân now says that the wains went 'through Druadan to Rimmon'; but his words about the old road remain unchanged from the draft, 'there behind Rimmon and down to Dîn'. If we suppose that after the order of the beacons had been changed the ancient wain-road went all the way to Min Rimmon (and the change of 'They went through Rimmon to Eilenach' to 'They went through Druadan to Rimmon' was not casually made: my father wrote *Rimmon* twice and twice crossed it out before finally settling on this name), it nonetheless seems strange that Ghân-buri-Ghân, in the Druadan Forest, should say 'there behind Rim-

> mon', since Min Rimmon was now the third beacon, not the sixth, and some seventy-five miles to the west of Eilenach. [pp. 351–2]

It is possible, given Tolkien's deliberation over *Rimmon*, that he did indeed intend to extend the road considerably further west, in which case 'there behind Rimmon' should probably be 'there behind Eilenach'. But it is more likely that both instances of *Rimmon* are in error. On the large-scale map of Rohan, Gondor, and Mordor the road through the Valley seems to reach only as far as Nardol; and it may be significant that in his late *Rivers and Beacon-hills of Gondor* Tolkien says that Nardol 'was on the end of a high ridge, originally part of the Drúadan Forest, but long deprived of trees by masons and quarriers who came up the Stonewain Valley. Nardol was manned by a guard who also protected the quarries' (*Unfinished Tales*, p. 319, n. 51). If the latter was the case, then the text of *The Lord of the Rings* should probably read 'through Drúadan to Nardol . . . there behind Eilenach'. But since Tolkien's intent is not clear, it seemed best to leave the text unaltered in the revised edition of 2004.

833 (III: 107): 'Dead men are not friends

833 (III: 107). leave Wild Men alone in the woods and do not hunt them like beasts any more – In a late scrap of writing Tolkien says that

> in Rohan the identity of the statues of Dunharrow called 'Púkel-men' with the 'Wild Men' of the Drúadan Forest was not recognized, neither was their 'humanity': hence the reference by Ghân-buri-Ghân to persecution of the 'Wild Men' by the Rohirrim in the past. . . . Since Ghân-buri-Ghân was attempting to use the Common Speech he called his people 'Wild Men' (not without irony); but this was not of course their own name for themselves. [*Unfinished Tales*, p. 384]

833 (III: 107): 'Wild Men go quick on feet'

833 (III: 107). Stonewain Valley – 'The Common Speech name of the long narrow defile along which the wains (sleds or drays) passed to and fro from the stone-quarries' (*Nomenclature*). In his unfinished index Tolkien says that the name is a 'translation of *Imrath Gondraith*', and notes *Imrath* as 'a long narrow valley with road or water course running ?lengthwise'.

835 (III: 109): 'Then since we must look for fell deeds

835–8 (III: 109–13). Then since we must look for fell deeds . . . – A recording by Tolkien from these words to the end of the chapter is included on Disc 2 of *The J.R.R. Tolkien Audio Collection*.

835 (III: 109). fell deeds – Here Tolkien uses *fell* in yet another sense, 'fierce, ruthless'.

835 (III: 109): To this the king assented

835 (III: 109). Grey Wood – 'The wood near the junction of Stonewain Valley and the main West R[oa]d' (*Index*). Prior to the edition of 2004, this instance of the name read 'grey wood', but the reference is surely to that area elsewhere called the (capitalized) 'Grey Wood'.

835 (III: 109–10): 'This, lord: they were errand-riders

835 (III: 110). they found the enemy already on the out-wall, or assailing it, when they returned – and that would be two nights ago – It is now the evening of 14 March; the errand-riders presumably left Edoras at about mid-day on 10 March, having ridden there with Théoden from Dunharrow. If they were approaching Gondor late on 12 March, they would have found the road held by Easterlings, who according to *Scheme* on 12 March 'pass the Pelennor and march west to waylay Rohirrim'.

836 (III: 110): It was night

836 (III: 110). the host of Rohan was moving silently – It is probably now the early hours of 15 March.

836 (III: 110): 'Do you remember

836 (III: 110). Wídfara – Old English 'far-traveller', from *wīd* 'wide' + *fara* 'farer, traveller'.

836 (III: 110): 'Now is the hour come

836 (III: 110). Oaths ye have taken: now fulfil them all, to lord and land and league of friendship! – The Riders owe allegiance to Théoden as their king, and he by the Oath of Eorl is bound by alliance with Gondor. In the message carried by the errand-riders Denethor asked Théoden 'to remember old friendship and oaths long spoken' (Book V, Chapter 3, p. 799, III: 72).

837 (III: 111): It was no more than a league

837 (III: 111). the north gate in the Rammas – 'The gate by which the "north-way" [*North-way* in the text] from the Gate of M[inas] T[irith] reached the West Road' (*Index*).

837–8 (III: 112): But at that same moment

837–8 (III: 112). a flash, as if lightning had sprung from the earth . . . a great *boom* – The flash of light is mentioned in the previous chapter (p. 829, III: 102). The *boom* must be the sound of the Gate collapsing.

838 (III: 112): At that sound the bent shape

838 (III: 112). Guthláf – Old English 'battle-leaving', i.e. 'survivor', from *gūþ* 'war, battle, fight' + *lāf* 'leaving'. Despite his name, Guthláf will not survive the coming battle.

838 (III: 112–13): Suddenly the king cried

838 (III: 113). as Oromë the Great in the battle of the Valar when the world was young – Oromë was one of the Valar, a great hunter. His name means 'horn-blowing' or 'sound of horns'. The battle was perhaps the one that took place soon after the awakening of the Elves, when the Valar attacked the strongholds of Morgoth in Middle-earth and brought him to Valinor as a prisoner.

Chapter 6

THE BATTLE OF THE PELENNOR FIELDS

For drafts and history of this chapter, see *The War of the Ring*, pp. 365–73.

839 (III: 114): But it was no orc-chieftain

839 (III: 114). the darkness was breaking too soon – It is dawn on 15 March 1419. The wind from the south is blowing away the darkness that flowed out of Mordor, and speeding the Haradrim ships captured by Aragorn up the Anduin. Some readers have speculated that this is due to the unseen intervention of Manwë, chief of the Valar, whose province is the winds and breezes and regions of the air; see also notes for pp. 868, 920, 949.

839 (III: 114): Théoden King of the Mark

839 (III: 114). black serpent upon scarlet – The serpent is a traditional emblem of evil, a sense emphasized by the colour *black*.

839 (III: 114): Then Théoden was aware

839 (III: 114). long spears and bitter – That is, the spears are long and *bitter* 'sharp, keen, cutting'.

839 (III: 114). shivered – Broken, shattered.

840 (III: 115): The great shadow descended

840 (III: 115). its vast pinions were as webs of hide between horned fingers – *Pinions* here must indicate the entire wings of the creature, apparently similar to those of a bat in which 'the hand is formed into a wing with a membrane of skin extending between the hand bones to the forearm, side of body and hind leg' (W.H. Burt and R.P. Grosseneheider, *A Field Guide to the Mammals* (1952), p. 14).

840 (III: 115). A creature of an older world maybe it was – See note for p. 809.

840 (III: 115). nursed it with fell meats – This recalls Morgoth in the First Age who, knowing that it was decreed that the hound Huan could be killed only by the mightiest wolf ever to live, chose a young whelp 'and fed him with his own hand upon living flesh, and put his power upon him. Swiftly the wolf grew, until he could creep into no den, but lay huge and hungry before the feet of Morgoth. There the fire and anguish of hell entered into him, and he became filled with a devouring spirit, tormented, terrible, and strong. Carcharoth, the Red Maw . . .' (*The Silmarillion*, p. 180).

840 (III: 115): Upon it sat a shape

840 (III: 115). mace – A heavy club with a spiked metal head.

840 (III: 115): But Théoden was not utterly forsaken

840 (III: 115). Merry crawled on all fours – Théoden's charge has been described in heroic language by the narrator, viewing the entire battlefield, but we see the encounter between Éowyn and the Witch-king through Merry's eyes. Merry's horror at the scene contrasts with Éowyn's bravery and strength of mind.

841 (III: 116): 'Begone, foul dwimmerlaik

841 (III: 116). dwimmerlaik – In the *1966 Index* Tolkien says that *dwimmerlaik* in the language of Rohan means 'work of necromancy, spectre'. It is derived from Middle English *dweomer*, Old English *(ge)dwimor, -er* 'illusion, phantom' + Middle English *-layk, -laik* 'play'. Compare obsolete *demerlayk* (or *dweomerlak*, etc.) 'magic, practice of occult art' (*OED*), and see also *The War of the Ring*, p. 372, n. 2. The *OED* notes also under *-laik* that 'occasionally the suffix representing Old English *-lāc* was in northern or north Midland texts written *-laik*, so that it became coincident in form with the Scandinavian suffix [Old Norse *-leikr*], e.g. in *dwimerlaik*'.

841 (III: 116): 'Hinder me? Thou fool

841 (III: 116). No living man may hinder me – The prophecy by Glorfindel (see note for p. 819) recalls one of those made to Macbeth in Shakespeare's play (Act IV, Scene 1), that 'none of woman born' shall harm him. In both cases the wording is deceptive. Macbeth is killed by Macduff, who was 'from his mother's womb / Untimely ripped' (Act V, Scene 8), while the Lord of the Nazgûl will be destroyed by Éowyn, who is of humankind but not male, and by Merry who is male but, strictly speaking, a Hobbit and not a Man. In draft texts it was foretold first that the Witch-king would be overthrown 'by one young and gallant' (i.e. not by Gandalf), then that he would be slain not by 'men of war or wisdom' but 'by one who has slain no living thing' (*The War of the Ring*, pp. 326, 334–5). The latter, at least, would be unlikely on a busy field of battle, and a less satisfying dénouement than that Tolkien finally devised.

Readers have debated, inevitably to no firm conclusion, whether Éowyn or Merry killed the Witch-king. Some have held that Merry plays the greater part, because of the remark that 'no other blade, not though mightier hands had wielded it, would have dealt that foe a wound so bitter, cleaving the undead flesh, breaking the spell that knit his unseen sinews to his will' (Book V, Chapter 6, p. 844, III: 120). Writing in *Beyond Bree* for October 1990, Nancy Martsch says that she took this passage to mean 'that Merry was able to hamstring the Witch-king and Éowyn was able to finish him off with a thrust to the throat. Perhaps an enchanted blade could do greater damage' (p. 6). Later, in *Beyond Bree* for February 1992, in light of draft texts for *The Lord of the Rings*, she concludes that the larger question of credit for the Witch-king's death is best summed up in Gandalf's words in the fair copy manuscript: 'Not by the hand of man was the Lord of the Nazgûl doomed to fall, and in that doom placed his trust. But he was felled by a woman and with the aid of a halfling' (*The War of the Ring*, p. 390).

841 (III: 116): The winged creature screamed

841 (III: 116). she whom he had called Dernhelm. But the helm of her secrecy had fallen from her, and her bright hair, released from its bonds – *Dernhelm* means literally 'helm of secrecy', that with which Éowyn concealed her hair and identity.

842 (III: 117): Still she did not blench

842 (III: 117). blench – Flinch, shrink, give way.

842 (III: 117): 'Éowyn! Éowyn!' cried Merry

842 (III: 117). and was never heard again in that age of this world – Surely Tolkien is being merely rhetorical, and not suggesting that the Lord of the Nazgûl would return in a later age. Ten days later, the Ring that had extended the Witch-king's life will lose all power when the One is destroyed.

842 (III: 117): And there stood Meriadoc

842 (III: 117). he looked on the face of the king, fallen in the midst of his glory. For Snowmane in his agony had rolled away from him again; yet he was the bane of his master. – In *The Road to Middle-earth* Tom Shippey suggests that 'on a larger scale the Battle of the Pelennor Fields closely follows the account, in Jordanes' *Gothic History*, of the Battle of the Catalaunian Plains, in which also the civilisation of the West was preserved from the "Easterlings", and in which the Gothic king Theodorid was trampled by his own victorious cavalry with much the same mixture of grief and glory as Tolkien's Théoden' (2nd edn., p. 14).

843 (III: 118): New forces of the enemy

843 (III: 118). footmen – Foot soldiers, infantry.

843–4 (III: 119): But Éomer said to them

843 (III: 119). *meet was his ending* – That is, he died in a way that was worthy, fitting.

844 (III: 119): And still Meriadoc the hobbit

844 (III: 119). there lay his weapon, but the blade was smoking like a dry branch that has been thrust in a fire; and as he watched it writhed and withered and was consumed. – Compare Aragorn's statement in Book I, Chapter 12, of Frodo's sword: 'all blades perish that pierce that dreadful King' (p. 198, I: 210). See further, note for p. 198.

844 (III: 119–20): So passed the sword

844 (III: 119–20). But glad would he have been to know its fate who wrought it slowly long ago in the North-kingdom when the Dúnedain were young, and chief among their foes was the dread realm of Angmar and its sorcerer king. No other blade, not though mightier hands had wielded it, would have dealt that foe a wound so bitter, cleaving the undead flesh, breaking the spell that knit his unseen sinews to his will. – On 18 April and 6 May 1963 Tolkien wrote to Anneke C. Kloos-Adriaansen and P. Kloos that the incidents of the Witch-king's knife in Book I, Chapter 12, and of Merry's sword in the present chapter

> were intended to be integrated with the entire mytho-historical background, events in an agelong war. Frodo received his wound from the Witchking under Weathertop, the bulwark of the ancient fortified line made by the Numenoreans against his kingdom; Meriadoc's dagger was taken from the gravemounds of the same people. It was made by smiths who knew all about Sauron and his servants, and made in prophetic vision or hope of ending just as it did. [spellings *sic*; courtesy of Christopher Tolkien]

845 (III: 120): Men now raised the king

845 (III: 120). Snowmane's Howe – A *howe* is an artificial mound, a barrow or burial mound.

845 (III: 120): Now slowly and sadly

845 (III: 120). A great rain came out of the Sea, and it seemed that all things wept for Théoden and Éowyn, quenching the fires in the City with grey tears. – In *The War of the Ring* Christopher Tolkien describes this passage as 'recalling the grief for Baldr', one of the Norse gods (p. 369). According to Norse legend, when Baldr was killed Hel agreed to release him 'if all things in the world, alive and dead, weep for him', and 'all did this, the people and animals and the earth and the stones and trees and every metal, just as you will have seen that these things weep when they come out of frost and into heat' (Snorri Sturluson, *Edda*, trans. by Anthony Faulkes (1995), pp. 50–1).

845 (III: 121): Then the prince seeing her beauty

845 (III: 121). leeches – Healers, physicians; see note for p. 519.

845 (III: 121). the bright-burnished vambrace – Highly polished armour for the forearm.

845 (III: 121). a little mist was laid on it – This is one of several similarities to *King Lear* which Michael D.C. Drout ('Tolkien's Prose Style and its Literary and Rhetorical Effects', *Tolkien Studies* 1 (2004)) finds in this part of *The Lord of the Rings*. In Act V, Scene 3 of Shakespeare's play, Lear, hoping that Cordelia is not dead, says: 'Lend me a looking glass / If that her breath will mist or stain the stone, / Why, then she lives.'

845–6 (III: 121): And now the fighting

846 (III: 121). Húrin the Tall – The same name was earlier borne by one of the great heroes of the First Age: see note for pp. 270–1.

846 (III: 121): Not too soon came their aid

846 (III: 121). But wherever the *mûmakil* came there the horses would not go, but blenched and swerved away – In *Greek Fire, Poison Arrows & Scorpion Bombs* Adrienne Mayor comments that in the Hellenistic era

> elephants were carefully trained from birth [for use in war] by the traditional suppliers in India and they were very effective, especially against men and horses who had never set eyes on such creatures before. Elephants . . . were fitted with coats of armor and iron tusk covers, and carried crenellated 'castles' with archers on top. An elephant could charge at fifteen miles per hour (but at that momentum, it had difficulty coming to a halt). The stampeding animals could plow through tight phalanxes of men, crushing them or causing them to scatter to avoid being trampled.
>
> The Romans were first introduced to war elephants when Pyrrhus of Epirus invaded Italy in 280 BC with Indian war elephants. The 'bulk and uncommon appearance' of Pyrrhus's twenty pachyderms, each one carrying a tower with one or two men with bows and javelins, undid the Romans, and their terrified cavalry horses refused to face the beasts. In the panic, many Roman soldiers were impaled by the elephants' tusks and crushed under their feet. [pp. 194–5]

846 (III: 121). Gothmog the lieutenant of Morgul – Christopher Tolkien notes that 'the name *Gothmog* is one of the original names of the tradition, going back to *The Book of Lost Tales*; Lord of Balrogs, slayer of Fëanor and Fingon', himself slain in the assault on Gondolin (*The War of the Ring*, p. 372, n. 9). Readers' suggestions that the later Gothmog was a Nazgûl or a Black Númenórean are no more than speculation, in the absence of further details by Tolkien.

It is not clear if *lieutenant* here means the second-in-command of Minas Morgul or, more likely, second-in-command to the Witch-king, who is sometimes called the *Morgul-lord*.

846 (III: 121). Variags of Khand – According to *Index Khand* is a land south-east of Mordor 'inhabited by Variags'. The *Oxford English Dictionary* notes that 'in the old Russian chronicle of Nestor' *Variags* is used of the people usually named *Varangians*, 'the Scandinavian rovers who in the 9th and 10th centuries overran parts of Russia and reached Constantinople', a group of whom formed the Varangian Guard of the Byzantine Emperor.

846 (III: 122): For Anduin, from the bend

846 (III: 122). dromunds – A *dromund* (or *dromon*) was

> a large vessel of the Mediterranean which operated between the 9th and 15th centuries. Byzantine in origin, the name was at first used to denote a royal ship, but came into general use as describing any very large ship propelled by many oars and with a single mast and a large square sail. They were used principally for trade or as transports in war. Most of the Christian armies used in the Crusades were transported in dromons, which also carried the horses of the cavalry. [*The Oxford Companion to Ships and the Sea*, ed. by Peter Kemp (1988), p. 272]

846 (III: 122). ships of great draught – Ships which displace a great depth of water.

846 (III: 122). bellying in the breeze – Filled by the wind.

847 (III: 122): Stern now was Éomer's mood

847 (III: 122). to make a great shield-wall at the last, and stand, and fight there on foot till all fell – Another example of the Northern ethic; see note for p. 736.

847 (III: 122–3): These staves he spoke

847 (III: 122). staves – Verses.

847 (III: 123): And then wonder took him

847 (III: 123). a great standard broke – As established in Book V, Chapter 2, Aragorn's standard is made of black cloth, like the livery of the heirs of Elendil in Minas Tirith (see note for p. 753): thus a sign of hope to the people of Gondor is the same colour as the black sails they had seen as a sign of evil.

The ships of the Corsairs recall at least two ancient legends in which black sails convey bad news. In Greek mythology, when Theseus is taken as tribute to Crete, he tells his father, Aegeus, King of Athens, that if he succeeds in destroying the Minotaur he will change the black sails on his ships to white when he returns home. But he forgets to do so, and when Aegeus sees the black sails he thinks that the ship is bringing news of his son's death, and throws himself into the sea in despair. In another story, Tristan, after parting from his beloved Isolde who is also his uncle's wife, in an effort to forget her marries Iseult of the White Hands. Later, when he is desperately ill he sends a message to Isolde, who has great healing powers, and asks that if she agrees to come the ship carrying her should have a white sail, but if she refuses a black one. The ship is seen in the distance with a white sail, but Iseult, who has secretly overheard Tristan's request, tells him the sail is black and he dies of despair. In *The Lord of the Rings* Denethor is similarly driven to despair and suicide when he believes that the ships he has seen in the *palantír* will arrive filled with enemies.

In this regard Christian Weichman, 'Black (Not) a Colour in Middle-earth', *Lembas-extra 2002*, points also to Tolkien's unfinished story *Tal-Elmar*, in particular to its final part written in January 1955, as he was completing *The Return of the King* for publication. In 1968 Tolkien wrote on the paper in which the manuscript of *Tal-Elmar* is wrapped:

> Beginning of a tale that sees the Númenóreans from the point of view of the Wild Men. It was begun without much consideration of geography (or the situation as envisaged in *The Lord of the Rings*). But either it must remain as a separate tale only vaguely linked with the developed *Lord of the Rings* history, or – and I think so – it must recount the coming of the Númenóreans (Elf-friends) *before the Downfall.* [*The Peoples of Middle-earth*, p. 422]

Tal-Elmar is a youth of the Wild Men, but has inherited the fair skin of his grandmother who had been captured in battle. One day he sees four ships, three with white sails and one with black. His father tells him of the High Men of the Sea, dangerous enemies who worship Death and slay men cruelly in honour of the Dark, and that sometimes they trade, but often carry away on ships with black sails men, women, and children who are never seen again. If what the father says is true, black is here again used by those who commit evil deeds, and almost certainly these are the ships of Númenóreans of the King's party, probably under the influence of Sauron.

Tal-Elmar, sent to find out more, discovers where the three ships with white sails have landed. He approaches the men and is taken before their leader. He looks like them, and they recognize him as kin. They want to take him with them, but he is afraid and asks:

> 'What would you do to me? Would you lure me to the black-winged boat and give me to the Dark?'
>
> 'You or your kin at least belong already to the Dark,' they answered. 'But why do you speak so of the black sails? The black sails are to us a sign of honour, for they are the fair night before the coming of the Enemy, and upon the black are set the silver stars of Elbereth. The black sails of our captain have passed further up the water.'
>
> Still Tal-Elmar was afraid because he was not yet able to imagine black as anything but the symbol of the night of fear. [*The Peoples of Middle-earth*, pp. 436–7]

847–8 (III: 123): Thus came Aragorn

848 (III: 123). tides of fate – *Brewer's Dictionary of Phrase and Fable* comments that *tide* is often 'used figuratively of a tendency, a current or flow of events or the like, as in a tide of feeling, and in Shakespeare's "There is a tide in the affairs of men, / Which taken at the flood, leads on to fortune; / Omitted, all the voyage of their life / Is bound in shallows and in miseries' (*Julius Caesar*, Act IV, Scene 3).

848 (III: 123): East rode the knights

848 (III: 123). dour-handed – *Dour* 'bold, stern, fierce'.

848 (III: 123). a great valour of the folk – Here, presumably, *valour* means 'strength, brave fighting force'.

848 (III: 123). upon his brow was the Star of Elendil – The *Elendilmir* or Star of Elendil was 'of diamond and represented the Star of Eärendil' (*1966 Index*). It entered the text only in proof; previously the reading here was: 'about his helm there was a kingly crown'. In writings by Tolkien after the publication of *The Lord of the Rings* it is said that the original Elendilmir had belonged to Silmarien, daughter and eldest child daughter of Tar-Elendil, the fourth King of Númenor. This white star of Elvish crystal upon a fillet of mithril passed to her descendants, the Lords of Andunië, coming at last to Elendil, and 'had been taken by him as the token of royalty in the North Kingdom' (*The Disaster of the Gladden Fields* in *Unfinished Tales*, p. 277).

Some years later than Silmarien, Aldarion, who would become the sixth king of Númenor, brought back from Middle-earth a diamond for his future wife, Erendis, and she had it 'set as a star in a silver fillet; and at her asking he bound it on her forehead'. 'Thus came, it is said, the manner of the Kings and Queens afterwards to wear as a star a white jewel upon the brow, and they had no crown' (*Aldarion and Erendis* in *Unfinished Tales*, pp. 184 and 215, n. 18). Christopher Tolkien comments that 'this tradition cannot be unconnected with that of the Elendilmir, a star-like gem borne on the brow as a token of royalty in Arnor; but the original Elendilmir itself, since it belonged to Silmarien, was in existence in Númenor . . . before Aldarion brought Erendis' jewel from Middle-earth, and they cannot be the same' (p. 284, n. 32).

The Elendilmir that came from Silmarien passed to Isildur and was lost with him in the river by the Gladden Fields. Elven-smiths in Imladris made a new jewel for Isildur's son Valandil which was borne by the kings and chieftains of Arnor. But though it was of great beauty, 'it had not the ancientry nor potency of the one that had been lost when Isildur fled into the dark and came back no more' (*Unfinished Tales*, p. 277). This is the Elendilmir that Aragorn wears on the Pelennor Fields, and will wear at his coronation.

It is also said in *The Disaster of the Gladden Fields* that when Aragorn later visited Orthanc, among other stolen treasures he found in a steel closet 'a small case of gold, attached to a fine chain; it was empty, and bore no letter or token, but beyond all doubt it had once borne the Ring about Isildur's neck. Next to it lay a treasure without price, long mourned as lost for ever': the Elendilmir of Silmarien. 'Elessar took it up with reverence' and wore it on high days when he was in the North Kingdom. 'Otherwise, when in kingly raiment he bore the Elendilmir which had descended to him' (p. 277).

848 (III: 124): Hard fighting and long labour

848 (III: 124). the Southrons were bold men and grim, and fierce in despair; and the Easterlings were strong and war-hardened – Tolkien allows men who fought for Sauron the same ethos as those fighting on the side of Gondor. This accords with feelings he expressed about Germans during the Second World War:

> I cannot understand the line taken by the BBC [British Broadcasting Corporation] (and papers, and so, I suppose, emanating from M[inistry] O[f] I[nformation]) that the German troops are a motley collection of sutlers and broken men, while yet recording the bitterest defence against the finest and the best equipped armies . . . that have ever taken the field. . . . But it is distressing to see the press grovelling in the gutter as low as Goebbels in his prime, shrieking that any German commander who holds out in a desperate situation (when, too, the military needs of his side clearly benefit) is a drunkard, and a besotted fanatic. [letter to Christopher Tolkien, 23–5 September 1944, *Letters*, p. 93]

848 (III: 124). asked no quarter – Did not ask for clemency or mercy in return for surrender; fought to the death.

848 (III: 124). so in this place and that, by burned homestead or barn, upon hillock or mound, under wall or on field, still they gathered and rallied and fought – Tolkien began Book V of *The Lord of the Rings* in earnest at the earliest in August 1946, but the Second World War, and especially the pushing back of German troops in Europe after D-Day, would have been fresh in his mind.

848 (III: 124): Then the Sun went down at last

848 (III: 124). And in that hour the great battle of the field of Gondor was over – Two historical sieges have been suggested as possible influences on Tolkien's account of the siege of Minas Tirith. The first is that of Constantinople, the capital of the Byzantine or Eastern Roman Empire which had survived for a thousand years after the Western Empire disintegrated, overrun by various invaders. After periods of great power and glory, by 1453 the Byzantine Empire had lost most of its territories and was facing the growing power of invaders from the east, the Ottoman Turks. Tolkien himself recognized the parallels between this and the once great Númenórean realms in exile. He wrote to Milton Waldman in ?late 1951: 'But in the north Arnor dwindles . . . and finally vanishes. In the south Gondor rises to a peak of power, almost reflecting Númenor, and then fades slowly to decayed Middle Age, a kind of proud, venerable, but increasingly impotent Byzantium. The watch on Mordor is relaxed. The pressure of the Easterlings and Southrons increases' (*Letters*, p. 157); and, describing Book V, 'we come to the half-ruinous Byzantine City of Minas Tirith' (*Waldman LR*).

Constantinople had a commanding position on the Bosporus, the narrow waterway connecting the Black Sea and the Mediterranean, not dissimilar to the position of Minas Tirith on the Anduin. The walls and defences of Constantinople were perhaps the strongest ever built and withstood many assaults:

> Any attacking army had first to negotiate a deep ditch some sixty feet across, which could be flooded to a depth of about thirty feet in an emergency. Beyond this was a low crenellated breastwork with a terrace behind it about thirty feet wide; then the outer wall, seven feet thick and nearly thirty feet high, with ninety-six towers at regular intervals along it. Within this wall came another broad terrace, and then the principal element of the defence, the great inner wall, about sixteen feet thick at the base and rising to a height of forty feet above the city. It too had ninety-six towers, alternating in position with those of the outer wall. [John Julius Norwich, *Byzantium: The Decline and Fall* (1996), p. 423]

The Ottoman army of probably 100,000 men arrived before Constantinople at the beginning of April 1453. In addition to greatly superior numbers, it had far greater cannon power, including one weapon said to have been able to hurl 'a ball weighing some 1,340 pounds . . . through the air for well over a mile before burying itself six feet deep in the ground' (p. 419). Against this Constantinople had fewer than 7,000 men to defend fourteen miles of walls; nonetheless the city did not fall until 29 May.

In July 1683 a Turkish army of 150,000, led by the grand vizier Kara (Black) Mustafa began to lay siege to Vienna, the capital of the Habsburg empire. In the area before the moat and walls of the city the Ottoman Turks dug a network of tunnels and deep trenches, not to be filled with fire, but used to approach selected points of attack with explosives, and with linking trenches providing protection for guns and soldiers. At the end of August 1683 John III Sobieski of Poland, and contingents from some German states (including Saxony, Franconia, and Bavaria), assembled to take part in the relief of Vienna, joining with Charles of Lorraine who was in command of the imperial cavalry. On 12 September this combined army of about 80,000 attacked the Turks. They advanced slowly during the morning, and in late afternoon, as the attack continued elsewhere on the field, Sobieski led a cavalry charge. The Turks had neglected to fortify their positions; they were defeated and put to flight. The successful charge of the Polish hussaria caught the general imagination so strongly that some accounts omit the fact that it was the culmination of a day's fighting, that other armies were involved, and that though John Sobieski was recognized as supreme commander, the leaders of the other contingents were involved with the planning and decisions.

849–50 (III: 124): Aragorn and Éomer and Imrahil

849 (III: 124). nor Grimbold to Grimslade – Tolkien says in his unfinished index that *Grimslade* was the home of Grimbold of Westfold. In *Nomenclature* (entry for *Great Smials*) he explains that '*Grimslade* . . . contains *Grim* (evidently the name of an ancestor [of Grimbold]) + *slade* (Old English *slæd* . . .) widely used in English place-names, and still in use, mostly with the sense "forest glade, dell" (especially one on the slope up a hillside).'

849 (III: 124–5). No few had fallen . . . – A recording by Tolkien from these words to the end of the following poem is included on Disc 2 of *The J.R.R. Tolkien Audio Collection.*

849 (III: 124–5): *We heard of the horns*

849 (III: 124). ***There Théoden fell, Thengling mighty*** – *Thengling* 'son of Thengel'. See note for p. 433.

849 (III: 125). ***Harding and Guthláf, / Dúnhere and Déorwine, doughty Grimbold, / Herefara and Herubrand, Horn and Fastred*** – Again Tolkien derives names of the Rohirrim from Old English:

Harding 'hard one', from *heard* 'hard'.

Dúnhere 'hill-warrior', in effect, from *dūn* 'hill' + *here* 'army, host'.

Déorwine 'brave-friend', presumably, from *dēor* 'brave, bold (as a wild beast)' + *wine* 'friend'.

Herefara 'host-traveller', from *here* 'army, host', used in personal names with the meaning 'warrior' + *fara* 'farer, traveller'.

Herubrand 'sword-brand', literally, from *heoru* 'sword' + *brand* 'fire-brand, torch', but *brand* was also metaphorically 'sword'; compare *Erkenbrand*, note for p. 527.

Fastred 'firm-counsel', from *fæst* 'firm, solid' + *rǣd* 'counsel, advice'

849 (III: 124). Mounds of Mundburg – 'The funeral mounds of those slain in Battle of Pelennor' (*Index*). Because written by a maker (poet) of Rohan it refers to *Mundburg*, not 'Minas Tirith'; see note for p. 508.

849 (III: 124). the South-kingdom – Gondor, as opposed to Arnor. The song was made 'long afterwards' when even the Rohirrim would have become accustomed to the idea of the two kingdoms.

849 (III: 124). Stoningland – This name 'represents Rohan *Stāning-(land)*, a translation of Gondor . . . this has been "modernized" (sc. accommodated to the forms of English)' (*Nomenclature*).

Chapter 7

THE PYRE OF DENETHOR

For drafts and history of this chapter, see *The War of the Ring*, pp. 374–82.

851–2 (III: 128): Even as Gandalf and Pippin

852 (III: 128). Slay me this renegade – A *renegade* is 'one who deserts a party, person, or principle, in favour of another; a turn-coat' (*OED*).

The order of Denethor's words (rather than 'Slay this renegade for me') is another example of archaism used by Tolkien for dramatic effect; see note for p. 518.

852 (III: 129): 'What is this, my lord?'

852 (III: 129). Hallows – 'A Common Speech translation . . . of the Gondor name (not given) for the Sacred Places of the tombs' (*Nomenclature*).

852 (III: 129): 'Since when has the Lord of Gondor

852 (III: 129). answerable to thee – Compare also p. 853, III: 129 ('Didst thou think that the eyes of the White Tower were blind? Nay, I have seen more than thou knowest, Grey Fool. For thy hope is but ignorance.'), etc., in which Denethor addresses Gandalf with *thee, thou, thy*. In an isolated note related to work on Appendix F Tolkien wrote:

> Where *thou, thee, thy* appears it is used mainly to mark a use of the familiar form where that was not usual. For instance its use by Denethor in his last madness to Gandalf, and by the Messenger of Sauron [Book V, Chapter 10], was in both cases intended to be contemptuous. But elsewhere it is occasionally used to indicate a deliberate change to a form of affection or endearment. [*The Peoples of Middle-earth*, p. 68]

(See note for p. 775.) Christopher Tolkien notes that 'in Denethor's speeches to Gandalf there are some occurrences of "you" that were not corrected' (*The Peoples of Middle-earth*, p. 68); see further, final note for p. 853.

853 (III: 129): 'Authority is not given

853 (III: 129). Authority is not given to you, Steward of Gondor – As first published this passage read: 'Authority is not given to you, nor to any other lord'. It was revised in the second edition (1965). The change was made possibly because it was realized that in *The Tale of Aragorn and Arwen* Aragorn, as a descendant of the kings of Númenor, did choose the hour of his death, though he did not slay himself, but fell asleep.

853 (III: 129). only the heathen kings, under the domination of the Dark Power, did thus, slaying themselves in pride and despair, murdering their kin to ease their own death – Alexei Kondratiev has pointed out that

> Tolkien's view of suicide as presented in this chapter is different from that of the source cultures he was drawing from (Anglo-Saxon, for instance), in which suicide was an honorable way out for a man who, like Denethor, had lost everything he most cared for. While the trappings of Middle-earth come from pagan cultures, Christian elements enter in when you come to ethical structures. Gandalf, certainly the voice of the author here (among other things) tells Denethor that 'authority is not given to you to order the hour of your death'. [*Rómenna Meeting Report*, 26 October 1986, p. 1]

Suicide is regarded as a sin by many Christians, notably by Roman Catholics like Tolkien. During this same discussion it was also observed that 'Denethor's sin, in Christian terms, is despair, the denial of hope, and that if he wanted to die, what he should have done was gone out on the battlefield to fight to the death' (p. 1).

In *The Road to Middle-earth* Tom Shippey comments that

> 'heathen' of course is a word used normally only by Christians and so out of place in Middle-earth. In Appendix (c) to his British Academy lecture [*Beowulf: The Monsters and the Critics*] Tolkien had remarked on the one place where the *Beowulf*-poet used this word of men, thinking it a mistake or an interpolation. By the 1950s he may have changed his mind, accepting stronger Christian and anti-heroic elements in *Beowulf*, *Maldon* and his own fiction. [2nd edn., p. 316, n. 14]

If asked about the word *heathen* in *The Lord of the Rings*, Tolkien might have replied that he was only 'translating', and had used the most suitable word available. What he meant by *heathen* was someone who did not recognize Eru, and especially anyone who worshipped Morgoth or Sauron: see notes for pp. 267 and 676.

Examples in our history of leaders slaying themselves in defeat rather than face capture and ignominy include Hannibal, Brutus, and Cleopatra, and contemporary with Tolkien, leaders of Nazi Germany who murdered their own children before committing suicide as the Russian army closed on Berlin. Archaeology meanwhile has revealed many instances of burials of important persons which also contain the bodies of those deliberately killed to accompany the primary occupant, e.g. the Royal Tombs of Ur (*c.* 2750 BC). It is generally thought that those so slain were servants and concubines who (it was believed) would continue to serve their master in the afterlife.

853 (III: 129). throes – Intense struggle, agony of mind. Denethor hesitates before rejecting the last chance offered him by Gandalf.

853 (III: 129): Then suddenly Denethor laughed

853 (III: 129). and lo! he had between his hands a *palantír* – In Tolkien's writings on the *palantíri* it is said that the last kings of Gondor, and then the Stewards, realized that the Ithil-stone had probably fallen into Sauron's hands when Minas Ithil was captured in Third Age 2002. But

> the Stone would be of little use to him for the damage of Gondor, unless it made contact with another Stone that was in accord with it. It was for this reason, it may be supposed, that the Anor-stone, about which all the records of the Stewards are silent until the War of the Ring, was kept a closely-guarded secret, accessible only to the Ruling Stewards and never by them used (it seems) until Denethor II. [*Palantíri*: *Unfinished Tales*, p. 403]

853 (III: 129): 'Pride and despair!'

853 (III: 129). I have seen more than thou knowest. . . . For a little space you may triumph on the field, for a day. But against the Power that now arises there is no victory. To this City only the first finger of his hand has yet been stretched. All the East is moving. And even now the wind of thy hope cheats thee and wafts up Anduin a fleet with black sails. – Denethor must have looked in the *palantír* again since 13 August. It is now 15 August, and it was not until after midnight, early on 15 August, that the wind began to blow and the black fleet was able to make sail. In draft texts Denethor knew that Aragorn was leading the fleet and would seek to displace him as ruler of Gondor, but Tolkien rejected this idea (see further, note for p. 855). The fact that Denethor does not taunt Gandalf with Sauron having captured the Ring seems to confirm that his earlier statement to this effect was only a surmise (see note for p. 821). It is clearly the sight of the vast forces of Sauron, which Gondor cannot hope to overcome, which has led him to despair.

853 (III: 129–30): 'Hope on then!'

853 (III: 129). Do I not know that this halfling was commanded by thee to keep silence? That he was brought hither to be a spy within my very chamber? – Prior to the edition of 2004 these sentences read: 'Do I not know that you commanded this halfling here to keep silence? That you brought him hither to be a spy within my very chamber?' In *The War of the Ring* Christopher Tolkien comments:

> When writing a very rapid draft my father would move from 'thou' to 'you' in the same speech, but his intention from the first was certainly that in this scene Denethor should 'thou' Gandalf, while Gandalf should use 'you'. In one passage confusion between 'thou' and 'you' remains in [*The Return of the King*]. . . . In the fair copy manuscript my father wrote: 'Do I not know that you commanded this halfling here to

keep silence?'; subsequently he changed 'you commanded' to 'thou commandedst', but presumably because he disliked this form he changed the sentence to 'Do I not know that this halfling was commanded by thee . . .' At the same time he added the sentence 'That you brought him hither to be a spy within my very chamber?' changing it immediately and for the same reason to 'That he was brought hither . . .' For some reason the 'you' constructions reappeared in the first typescript and so remained. [p. 382, n. 4]

853–4 (III: 130): 'But I say to thee, Gandalf

854 (III: 130). I will not step down to be the dotard chamberlain of an upstart. – That is, 'I will not yield rule to be the weak (or senile) attendant (steward, subordinate) of one who has newly risen to importance'.

854 (III: 130). Even were his claim proved to me, still he comes but of the line of Isildur. I will not bow to such a one, last of a ragged house long bereft of lordship and dignity. – Denethor pays lip-service to being a Steward, as when he told Boromir that in Gondor no length of time would suffice to make a steward a king; but when the possibility of not wielding royal power arises, he refuses to accept a subordinate position.

854 (III: 130): 'I would have things

854 (III: 130). longfathers – Forefathers, ancestors.

854 (III: 131): 'Come hither!' he cried

854 (III: 131). recreant – Cowardly, faint-hearted, but also 'false, unfaithful to duty'.

854–5 (III: 131): 'So passes Denethor

855 (III: 131). You have been caught in a net of warring duties that you did not weave. But think, you servants of the Lord, blind in your obedience, that but for the treason of Beregond Faramir, Captain of the White Tower, would now also be burned. – That is, it is not the servants' fault that they were faced with opposing duties of obeying the orders of Denethor to whom they had sworn service, and of saving Faramir. But Gandalf's next words, that the servants were 'blind in your obedience', imply that he thinks that they made the wrong choice. In a draft manuscript of this chapter Gandalf argued more expansively that the servants owed obedience to Denethor only, 'and he who says: "my master is not in his mind, and knows not what he bids; I will not do it", is in peril, unless he has knowledge and wisdom. But to Berithil [later Beregond] of the guard such discernment was a duty, whereas also he owed allegiance first to his captain, Faramir, to succour him while he lived' (*The War of the Ring*, p. 379).

855–6 (III: 132): But even as Gandalf

855 (III: 132). a great cry went up – The cry that marked the passing of the Witch-king in Book V, Chapter 6. Thus Tolkien synchronizes Gandalf's arrival at the Houses of Healing with events on the battlefield. In the previous chapter little time seemed to elapse between the charge of the Rohirrim at dawn, the unhorsing of Théoden, and the defeat of the Witch-king, while during the same period Gandalf rode through six circles of the city, made his way to the House of Stewards, rescued Faramir, argued with Denethor, and carried Faramir to the Houses of Healing.

856 (III: 132): 'Though the Stewards deemed

856 (III: 132). long ago I guessed that here in the White Tower, one at least of the Seven Seeing Stones was preserved – As first published this passage read: 'long have I known that here in the White Tower, as at Orthanc, one of the Seven Stones was preserved'. It was revised in the second printing (1967) of the Allen & Unwin edition.

856 (III: 132). In the days of his wisdom Denethor would not presume to use it – Prior to the edition of 1994 'would not presume' read 'did not presume'. In Tolkien's writings on the *palantíri* while preparing the second edition it is said that 'Gandalf should have been reported as saying that he did not *think* that Denethor had presumed to use [the Anor-stone], until his wisdom failed. He could not state it as a known fact, for when and why Denethor had dared to use the Stone was and remains a matter of conjecture' (*Unfinished Tales*, p. 406). On this Christopher Tolkien comments: 'My father's emendation (arising from the present discussion) of "Denethor did not presume to use it" to "Denethor would not presume to use it" was (apparently by mere oversight) not incorporated in the revised edition' (*Unfinished Tales*, p. 413, n. 11).

The Palantíri also includes a lengthy discussion of Denethor and how at least one of his motives for consulting the Anor-stone soon after he succeeded his father as Steward was jealousy of 'Thorongil', the captain who had achieved such fame (i.e. Aragorn in other guise) that Denethor's own position was weakened, and hostility to Gandalf, whom Denethor also saw as a 'usurper' of knowledge and information. Denethor had, in any case, inherited authority to use the Stone if he wished. Among much else, it is said that

> Denethor remained steadfast in his rejection of Sauron, but was made to believe [through Sauron's mental deceits] that his [Sauron's] victory was inevitable, and so fell into despair. . . . Denethor was a man of great strength of will, and maintained the integrity of his personality until the final blow of the (apparently) mortal wound of his only surviving son. He was proud, but this was by no means merely personal: he loved Gondor and its people, and deemed himself appointed by destiny to

lead them in this desperate time. And in the second place the Anor-stone was his *by right*, and nothing but expediency was against his use of it in his grave anxieties. [p. 408]

857 (III: 133): 'Now I must go down

857 (III: 133). I have seen a sight upon the field that is very grievous to my heart – The *sight* is the death of Théoden.

Chapter 8

THE HOUSES OF HEALING

For drafts and history of this chapter, see *The War of the Ring*, pp. 384–96.

858 (III: 134): Already men were labouring

858 (III: 134). litters – A *litter* is a 'framework supporting a bed or couch for the transport of the sick and wounded' (*OED*).

859 (III: 135): 'Don't!' said Pippin

859 (III: 135). *perian* – See note for p. 768.

859–60 (III: 135–6): It was not long before Gandalf

859 (III: 135–6). He has well repaid my trust; for if Elrond had not yielded to me, neither of you would have set out; and then far more grievous would the evils of this day have been. – Prior to the galley proof of *The Return of the King* this passage read: 'Greater was the wisdom of Elrond than mine; for if I had had my way, neither you, Pippin, nor he would have set out; and then far more grievous would the evils of this day have been.' In *The War of the Ring* Christopher Tolkien notes that this statement

> is decidedly strange: for the form of the Choosing of the Company in *The Fellowship of the Ring* . . . in which it was through Gandalf's advocacy *against* Elrond that Merry and Pippin were included, had been reached long before in the second version of 'The Ring Goes South' [Book II, Chapter 3]. . . . Earlier than this, it is true, Gandalf had also been opposed to their inclusion ("Elrond's decision is wise", he had said [*The Treason of Isengard*, p. 115]), but only here, and again in [an early text of] 'The Last Debate' [Book V, Chapter 9], is there any suggestion that it was Elrond who advocated their inclusion in opposition to Gandalf. [p. 387]

860 (III: 136): So at last Faramir

860 (III: 136). Save old age only. For that they had found no cure; and indeed the span of their lives had now waned to little more than that of other men, and those among them who passed the tale of five score years with vigour were grown few, save in some houses of purer blood. – In Appendix A it is said that the Númenóreans had originally been granted a life-span 'thrice that of lesser Men' (p. 1035, III: 315). This span is also mentioned in *The Line of Elros*, written some years after the publication of *The Lord of the Rings*. Christopher Tolkien comments, however, that in his father's latest writing 'to the Númenórean people as a whole is ascribed a life-span some five times the length of that of other Men' (*Unfinished Tales*, p. 224, n. 1).

860 (III: 136). Still at whiles – At times.

860 (III: 136): Then an old wife

860 (III: 136). Ioreth – On 28 August 1967 Tolkien wrote in his letter to Mr Joukes that *Ioreth* (in draft spelt *Yoreth*) 'was invented just to fit the character of the old nurse in the hospital, and its Elvish meaning is "old woman". . . . Quenya *yāra* – old, Sindarin *iaur* in composition *ior-*; *eth* is a feminine ending' (reproduced in René van Rossenberg, *Hobbits in Holland*, p. 68).

860 (III: 136). as there were once upon a time, they say – To the people of Minas Tirith the kings are at best a distant memory, the stuff of story. The last king rode to Minas Morgul in Third Age 2050 and never returned; it is now 3019.

860 (III: 136). *The hands of the king are the hands of a healer.* – In his article 'The Hands of a King', *Beyond Bree*, September 1986, David Cofield writes:

> During the Middle ages the monarchs of France and England were believed to possess the divine power to heal scrofula, a term then applied to various skin diseases and infections. Indeed, another name for scrofula was 'King's Evil'. The power to heal scrofula was believed to descend on the rulers at their coronations when they were anointed with holy oil. French monarchs claimed this ability from the time of Clovis in AD 481 through Louis XVI, who was beheaded in 1793. In England, the practice evidently began with King Edward the Confessor before the Norman Conquest and lasted until the death of Queen Anne in 1714. [p. 2]

Cofield argues that Tolkien gave 'Aragorn, the Heir of Elendil, a similar but greater ability as part of his royal inheritance' (p. 2). Healing involved the sovereign touching the sores and ulcers. The practice is mentioned in Shakespeare's *Macbeth*, Act IV, Scene 3:

> A most miraculous work in this good king,
> Which often since my here-remain in England
> I have seen him do. How he solicits heaven
> Himself best knows; but strangely-visited people,
> All swol'n and ulcerous, pitiful to the eye,
> The mere despair of surgery, he cures,
> Hanging a golden stamp about their necks,
> Put on with holy prayers; and 'tis spoken,
> To the succeeding royalty he leaves
> The healing benediction.

862 (III: 138): And Gandalf answered

862 (III: 138). his house is in ashes – The burial place of his House is literally in ashes. But the phrase also recalls 'ashes to ashes', an expression of finality, as used in the Christian burial service.

863 (III: 139): 'Strider! How splendid!

863 (III: 139). I guessed it was you in the black ships. – It is not explained why Pippin should think so; in fact these words are a shadow of Tolkien's abandoned idea that Denethor had known from the *palantír* that Aragorn was in command of the black fleet (see note for p. 853). In drafts of Book V, Chapter 7 Pippin learned of this from Denethor, and in draft for the present chapter conveyed the news to Berithil (= Beregond), later remarking to Aragorn when he appeared at the Houses of Healing that 'Denethor was right after all' (*The War of the Ring*, p. 390).

863 (III: 139): And Aragorn hearing him

863 (III: 139). in the high tongue of old I am *Elessar*, the Elfstone, and *Envinyatar*, the Renewer – *Envinyatar*, the Quenya word for *Renewer*, was added in the second printing (1967) of the Allen & Unwin second edition. It is an appropriate name for one who will restore the kingship to both Gondor and Arnor.

863 (III: 139). the high tongue – Quenya.

863 (III: 139). Telcontar – Presumably from Quenya *telko* 'leg'.

863 (III: 139). the heirs of my body – A legal phrase, meaning 'heirs who are direct descendants'.

864 (III: 140): 'I drew it forth'

864 (III: 140). staunched the wound – *Staunched* (or *stanched*) 'stopped the flow of blood'.

864 (III: 140–1): 'Weariness, grief for his father's mood

864 (III: 140). staunch will – Strong, resolute.

864 (III: 141): Thereupon the herb-master

864 (III: 141). for *kingsfoil* as the rustics name it . . . or *athelas* in the noble tongue, or to those who know somewhat of the Valinorean – In *Nomenclature* Tolkien notes of *kingsfoil*: 'translate: *-foil* (from Old French *foil*) = "leaf", as in *cinquefoil*, etc. Only the *-leaf* of *asëa* was valued.'

The *Valinorean* language is Quenya. In the following paragraph Aragorn gives the corresponding name of the plant in Quenya, *asëa aranion* 'leaf of kings'.

Rustics are country folk.

864 (III: 141). no virtue that we know of, save perhaps to sweeten a fouled air, or to drive away some passing heaviness – The herb-master quotes 'virtues' of the plant in the manner of medieval herbals, compendia which describe the physical attributes and purported uses of plants (or of animals, minerals, etc.) according to the wisdom of the ancients, supplemented by more recent authorities. At this moment in the history of Gondor knowledge of the special virtue of *athelas* has been lost, for it depends upon a king, and there has been no king in Gondor for nearly a thousand years.

865 (III: 141): 'Your pardon lord!'

865 (III: 141). doggrel – Misspelt 'doggerel' in some printings, the more common spelling, but *doggrel* here is original and intended. 'An epithet applied to comic or burlesque verse, usually of irregular rhythm; or to mean, trivial, undignified verse' (*OED*).

865 (III: 141). infusion of the herb – An *infusion* is a drink or extract made by soaking leaves, as for tea.

865 (III: 141): 'Then in the name of the king

865 (III: 141). less lore and more wisdom – Gandalf is making a distinction between knowledge without understanding, and wisdom as defined in the *Oxford English Dictionary*: 'capacity of judging rightly in matters relating to life and conduct; soundness of judgement in the choice of means and ends; sometimes, less strictly, sound sense, especially in practical affairs'.

865 (III: 141): Now Aragorn knelt beside Faramir

865 (III: 141). and walked afar in some dark vale, calling for one that was lost – This seems to echo, perhaps deliberately, Psalm 23:4, 'though I walk through the valley of the shadow of death'.

865 (III: 141–2): But Aragorn smiled

865 (III: 141). breathed on them – An analysis of this chapter by a Tolkien discussion group comments: 'We felt it significant that Aragorn *breathes* on the *athelas* leaves before infusing them. Symbolically he is imparting his life-force, his *mana*, to the victims of the Black Breath, countering the evil Breath with his own' (*Rómenna Meeting Report*, 26 October 1986, p. 3).

865 (III: 142). the fragrance that came to each was like a memory of dewy mornings of unshadowed sun in some land of which the fair world in spring is itself but a fleeting memory – In *J.R.R. Tolkien* Katharyn W. Crabbe points out that it is significant that the three individuals tended by Aragorn

> wake to impressions of those things that are most important to them. For Faramir, the image of 'some land of which the fair world of Spring

is but a fleeting memory' is appropriate because it evokes the pervasive myth of the golden age, to which he has always felt allegiance, though to his father's sorrow. For Éowyn, the image of unbreathed air and high stars is appropriate because it represents the purity for which she had pined during the long years she has felt her life and that of her race being defiled by the works of Wormtongue. Placed next to the elevated images associated with Éowyn, those associated with Merry strike the reader as distinguished by their domesticity. The evocation of orchards, heather, and bees is an evocation of the rural paradise that is the Shire.

What this tailoring of sense impressions to the greatest joys of the three wounded warriors suggests is that *athelas* heals by helping people to be more fully themselves. [rev. and expanded edn., pp. 95–6]

865–6 (III: 142): 'Well now! Who would have believed it?'

866 (III: 142). Imloth Melui – In his unfinished index Tolkien notes: '*Imloth* flowery vale in *Imloth Melui* (lovely) . . . [*illegible*] vale in Lossarnach'. In *The Rivers and Beacon-hills of Gondor* the name is glossed 'sweet flower-valley' (*Vinyar Tengwar* 42 (July 2001), p. 18).

867 (III: 143): 'Think you that Wormtongue

867 (III: 143). the bitter watches of the night – Those times (*watches*) when Éowyn was wakeful, when she did not or could not sleep for *bitter* feelings of misery or grief.

867 (III: 143). the walls of her bower closing in about her, a hutch to trammel some wild thing in – A *bower* is a lady's private rooms, here compared with a *hutch*, a box or cage for a small domesticated animal such as a rabbit.

Trammel is 'to restrain, fetter, confine'. Éowyn felt herself a prisoner with no freedom of movement.

868 (III: 144): Then, whether Aragorn

868 (III: 144). it seemed to those who stood by that a keen wind blew through the window, and it bore no scent, but was an air wholly fresh and clean and young, as if it had not before been breathed by any living thing and came new-made from snowy mountains high beneath a dome of stars, or from shores of silver far away washed by seas of foam. – If, as some readers familiar with *The Silmarillion* have thought and as Tolkien sometimes seems to hint, the peoples arrayed against the evil of Sauron are watched over by powers that occasionally and in small ways intervene, the wind that at this moment blows into the Houses of Healing again suggests the agency of Manwë (see note for p. 839). 'Snowy mountains high beneath a dome of stars' recalls Manwë's home on Taniquetil (see note for p. 79), and 'shores of silver far away' brings to mind the shining beaches of Eldamar in the Uttermost West.

868 (III: 144): 'Awake, Éowyn, Lady of Rohan!'

868 (III: 144). he took her right hand in his and felt it warm with life returning – The words 'and felt it warm with life returning' were added in the second edition (1965).

868 (III: 144): 'That is grievous'

868 (III: 144). the House of Eorl was sunk in honour less than any shepherd's cot – Here *House of Eorl*, with capitalized *House*, must mean 'descendants of Eorl', i.e. the honour of Éowyn's family was at its ebb while Théoden was under the influence of Wormtongue. But the comparison to a shepherd's cottage seems more suited to lower-case *house* 'dwelling': that is, Éowyn says that there was at that time more honour in even the humblest cottage than in Théoden's house, Meduseld, the Golden Hall. In the *1966 Index*, entry for *Eorl*, Tolkien indicates that here he meant *House* in both senses.

869 (III: 146): 'Master Meriadoc,' said Aragorn

869 (III: 146). it is called *westmansweed* by the vulgar, and *galenas* by the noble – *Westmansweed* is 'a Common Speech rendering of "herb of Men of the West" (sc. of *Westernesse, Númenor*)' (*Nomenclature*).

Here *vulgar* means the language used by the common people, the vernacular, native speech as opposed to a different language used only by some of the population (such as Latin in various circles in Europe in the Middle Ages, or French among the ruling class in England after the Norman Conquest).

Galenas is the Sindarin equivalent of *pipe-weed.*

871 (III: 147): At the doors of the Houses

871 (III: 147). men came and prayed that he would heal their kinsmen or their friends. . . . And Aragorn arose and went out, and he sent for the sons of Elrond, and together they laboured far into the night. – In a draft letter to Naomi Mitchison, September 1954, Tolkien wrote following a discussion of magic that

> a difference in the use of 'magic' in this story [*The Lord of the Rings*] is that it is not to be come by by 'lore' or spells; but is in an inherent power not possessed or attainable by Men as such. Aragorn's 'healing' might be regarded as 'magical', or at least a blend of magic with pharmacy and 'hypnotic' processes. But it is (in theory) reported by hobbits who have very little notions of philosophy and science; while A[ragorn] is not a pure 'Man', but at long remove one of the 'children of Lúthien'. [*Letters*, p. 200]

That is, Aragorn has the power to heal not because he is king *per se*, but because the kings are descended from Lúthien. Ioreth's words, '*The hands of the king are the hands of the healer.* And so the rightful king could ever be known' (Book V, Chapter 8, p. 860, III: 136), suggest that in those descended from Lúthien through Elros, the first King of Númenor, the power, or the full power, of healing was given to the king, and not to others of the same blood. But Elrond and his sons all have power in this regard: Aragorn calls on the sons to help him at Minas Tirith, but also says that 'Elrond is the eldest of all our race, and has the greater power' (Book V, Chapter 8, p. 863, III: 139). Only Elrond was able to detect and remove from Frodo the fragment of the Morgul-knife and to heal him after he was stabbed under Weathertop – in what manner, Tolkien does not say.

Aragorn's power of healing seems to have several elements. He has a general knowledge and skill for dealing with more ordinary situations: he knows that the wound Sam received in Moria was not poisoned, and he binds his and Frodo's injuries; and he is able to judge both that Faramir's wound is healing and that Éowyn's arm has been dealt with correctly. The 'pharmacy' referred to by Tolkien in his letter presumably means Aragorn's use of *athelas*, while '"hypnotic" processes' must refer to his calling the three patients back to life as if he himself 'was removed from them, and walked afar in some dark vale, calling for one that was lost' (Book V, Chapter 8, p. 865, III: 141). This last ability is perhaps his strongest: in the cases of Faramir and Merry it is clear that Aragorn considers the worst over even before he applies *athelas*, and Éowyn begins to breathe more deeply when he calls her.

Chapter 9

THE LAST DEBATE

For drafts and history of this chapter, see *The War of the Ring*, pp. 397–429.

872 (III: 148): The morning came

872 (III: 148). The morning came – It is 16 March 1419.

872 (III: 148): 'They need more gardens'

872 (III: 148). people of the Wood – The Elves of Mirkwood, Greenwood the Great.

872 (III: 148): At length they came to the Prince Imrahil

872 (III: 148). Legolas . . . saw that here was one who had elven-blood in his veins. . . . It is long since the people of Nimrodel left the woodlands of Lórien, and yet still one may see that not all sailed from Amroth's haven west – In a note written in December 1972 or later, discussing the Elvish strain in Men as being observable in the beardlessness (a characteristic of Elves) of those who were so descended, Tolkien said:

> As Legolas's mention of Nimrodel shows, there was an ancient Elvish port near Dol Amroth, and a small settlement of Silvan Elves there from Lórien. The legend of the prince's line was that one of their earliest fathers had wedded an Elf-maiden: in some versions it was indeed (evidently improbably) said to have been Nimrodel herself. In other tales, and more probably, it was one of Nimrodel's companions who was lost in the upper mountain glens. [*Unfinished Tales*, p. 248]

Elsewhere he wrote that 'Galador, first Lord of Dol Amroth (*c.* Third Age 2004–2129) . . . was the son of Imrazôr the Númenórean, who dwelt in Belfalas, and the Elven-lady Mithrellas', one of the companions of Nimrodel, lost on the journey to the haven. 'But when she had borne him a son, Galador, and a daughter, Gilmith, she slipped away by night and he saw her no more. But although Mithrellas was of the lesser Silvan race (and not of the High Elves or the Grey) it was ever held that the house and kin of the Lords of Dol Amroth was noble by blood as they were fair in face and mind' (p. 248). The disappearance of a fairy or selkie bride after bearing a child or children to a mortal is a common theme in folk- and fairy-lore.

874 (III: 150): 'And by the love of him also'

874 (III: 150). It was at early morn of the day ere you came there . . . that we left Dunharrow – The Grey Company left Dunharrow early on 8 March. Merry arrived there on the evening of 9 March.

874 (III: 150): He fell silent

874 (III: 150). I will tell you enough – On 24 June 1957 Tolkien wrote to Caroline Everett about difficulties in writing *The Return of the King*:

> The last volume was naturally the most difficult, since by that time I had accumulated a large number of narrative debts, and set some awkward problems of presentation in drawing together the separated threads. But the problem was not so much 'what happened?', about which I was only occasionally in doubt . . . as how to order the account of it. The solution is imperfect. Inevitably.
>
> Obviously the chief problem of this sort, is how to bring up Aragorn unexpectedly to the raising of the Siege, and yet inform readers of what he had been up to. Told in full in its proper place (Vol. III [Book V], ch. 2), though it would have been better for the episode, it would have destroyed Chapter 6. Told in full, or indeed in part, in retrospect it would be out of date and hold up the action (as it does in Chapter 9).
>
> The solution, imperfect, was to cut down the whole episode (which in full would belong rather to a *Saga of Aragorn Arathorn's Son* than to my story) and tell the ending of it briefly during the inevitable pause after the Battle of the Pelennor. [*Letters*, p. 258]

Tolkien's first attempt at telling the story in retrospect (called by Christopher Tolkien for convenience in *The War of the Ring*, and here as well, 'The Tale of Gimli and Legolas') was fuller than the published text, and no doubt he abandoned some of the material for the reasons given in his letter to Caroline Everett.

874–5 (III: 150–1): Swiftly then he told

874 (III: 150). ninety leagues and three from Erech to Pelargir . . . four days and nights and on into the fifth – 'Ninety leagues and three' is 279 miles. The Company left Erech on the morning of 9 March and reached Pelargir on 13 March. In 'The Tale of Gimli and Legolas' Gimli reckons that it is 'some 60 leagues as birds fly from Erech, over Tarlang's Neck into Lamedon, and so, crossing Kiril [later Ciril] and Ringlo [later Ringló], to Linhir beside the waters of Gilrain, where there are fords that lead into Lebennin. And from Linhir it is a hundred miles . . . to Pelargir on Anduin' (*The War of the Ring*, pp. 411–12) – that is, 280 miles, which differs by only one mile from the distance given in *The Return of the King*.

875 (III: 151): 'One day of light we rode

875 (III: 151). One day of light we rode – This was 9 March, the last day before the Great Darkness. The day has already been described at the end of Book V, Chapter 2: 'They passed Tarlang's Neck and came into Lamedon . . . until they came to Calembel upon Ciril, and the sun went down like blood behind Pinnath Gelin away in the West behind them. The township and the fords of Ciril they found deserted. . . . But the next day there came no dawn . . .' (p. 790, III: 63). *The Tale of Years* agrees with this account: 'Aragorn sets out from Erech and comes to Calembel'. *Scheme* has: 'March 9: Aragorn leaves Erech at 8 a.m. and crosses Tarlang's Neck into Lamedon reaching Calembel on Ciril.' The large-scale map of Rohan, Gondor, and Mordor places Calembel a short distance east of the Ciril (*Kiril*), though the text indicates that it was on the river.

875 (III: 151). then came the day without dawn, and still we rode on, and Ciril and Ringló we crossed – This was 10 March. Both *The Tale of Years* and *Scheme* mention only the crossing of the Ringló on that date. Here Legolas seems to suggest that the Company crossed both rivers on 10 March.

For *Ringló*, see note for p. 770 on the Ringló Vale.

875 (III: 151). on the third day we came to Linhir above the mouth of Gilrain. And there the men of Lamedon contested the fords – The 'third day' was 11 March. For this *The Tale of Years* has 'Aragorn reaches Linhir and crosses into Lebennin', and *Scheme* has 'Aragorn reaches Linhir on Gilrain and forces crossing into Lebennin.' In 'The Tale of Gimli and Legolas', omitting slight differences of timing between draft and final accounts, Gimli says

> Thus we came at nightfall . . . to Linhir. There the men of Lamedon had been contesting the passage of Gilrain with a great strength of the Haradrim, and of their allies the Shipmen of Umbar, who had sailed up Gilrain-mouth and far up the waters of Anduin with a host of ships and were now ravaging Lebennin and the coast of Belfalas. But defenders and invaders alike fled at our approach. And thus we crossed into Lebennin unopposed, and there we rested. . . . [*The War of the Ring*, p. 412]

Linhir is defined in Tolkien's unfinished index as 'a haven with ferry-bridge over Gilrain near its mouth, prop[erly] a river name = fair stream, name of the joint course of Gilrain and Ringló [i.e. Serni] bet[ween] their junction and the sea'.

Gilrain is a 'river of Gondor, joining Serni and fl[owing] to [the] Sea beyond the Ethir' (*Index*). Tolkien discusses the name in *The Rivers and Beacon-hills of Gondor*:

> This resembles the name of Aragorn's mother, *Gilraen*; but unless it is misspelt must have had a different meaning. . . . The element *gil-* in both is no doubt S[indarin] *gil* 'spark, twinkle of light, star', often used of the stars of heaven in place of the older and more elevated *el-*, *elen-* stem. . . . The element *raen* was the Sindarin form of Q[uenya] *raina* 'netted, enlaced'. . . .
>
> In *Gilrain* the element *-rain* though similar was distinct in origin.

Probably it was derived from base RAN 'wander, stray, go on uncertain course', the equivalent of Q[uenya] *ranya*. . . . This would not seem suitable to any of the rivers of Gondor; but the names of rivers may often apply only to part of their course, to their source, or to their lower reaches, or to other features that struck explorers who named them. In this case, however, the fragments of the legend of Amroth and Nimrodel offer an explanation. The Gilrain came swiftly down from the mountains as did the other rivers of that region; but as it reached the end of the outlier of Ered Nimrais that separated it from the Celos it ran into a wide shallow depression. In this it wandered for a while, and formed a small mere at the southern end before it cut through a ridge and went on swiftly again to join the Serni. When Nimrodel fled from Lórien it is said that seeking for the sea she became lost in the White Mountains, until at last (by what road or pass is not told) she came to a river that reminded her of her own stream in Lórien. Her heart was lightened, and she sat by a mere, seeing the stars reflected in its dim waters, and listening to the waterfalls by which the river went again on its journey down to the sea. There she fell into a deep sleep of weariness, and so long she slept that she did not come down into Belfalas until Amroth's ship had been blown out to sea, and he was lost trying to swim back to Belfalas. This legend was well known in the Dor-en-Ernil (the Land of the Prince), and no doubt the name [*Gilrain*] was given in memory of it, or rendered in Elvish form from an older name of the same meaning. [*Vinyar Tengwar* 42 (July 2001), pp. 11–12, and *Unfinished Tales*, pp. 242–3]

875 (III: 151). Angbor – Sindarin 'iron-fist'.

875 (III: 151): 'Thus we crossed over Gilrain

875 (III: 151). But soon Aragorn arose – It was still dark, early on 12 March. On that date Faramir retreated from Osgiliath to the Causeway Forts.

875 (III: 151): Legolas paused and sighed

875 (III: 151). ***from Celos to Erui*** – *Celos* is one of the rivers of Lebennin, a tributary of the Sirith. Tolkien wrote in *The Rivers and Beacon-hills of Gondor*: 'The name must be derived from the root *kelu-* "flow out swiftly", formed with an ending *-sse*, *-ssa*, seen in Quenya *kelussë* "freshet, water falling out swiftly from a rocky spring"' (*Unfinished Tales*, p. 426). On the original *Unfinished Tales* map the branching of the River Sirith and its tributary, the Celos, were marked in reverse order; this was corrected in 2004. The name is spelt *Kelos* on the large-scale map made for *The Return of the King*.

Erui is the first river of Lebennin, and the first tributary of the Anduin south of Minas Tirith. Tolkien wrote of the Erui in *The Rivers and Beacon-hills of Gondor*:

Though this was the first of the Rivers of Gondor it cannot be used for 'first'. In Eldarin *er* was not used in counting in series: it meant 'one, single, alone'. *Erui* is not the usual Sindarin for 'single, alone': that was *ereb* . . . but it has the very common adjectival ending *-ui* of Sindarin. The name must have been given because of the Rivers of Gondor it was the shortest and swiftest and was the only one without a tributary. [*Vinyar Tengwar* 42 (July 2001), p. 10]

875 (III: 151). *the golden bells are shaken of mallos and alfirin* – Tolkien says nothing more of these flowers. In *Cirion and Eorl and the Friendship of Gondor and Rohan* he uses *alfirin* as another name of the white flower *simbelmynë*; but Christopher Tolkien comments (*Unfinished Tales*, p. 316, n. 38) that this is apparently a different flower to that in Legolas's song.

875 (III: 151): 'Green are those fields

875 (III: 151). we hunted our foes through a day and a night – From early on 12 March and through the night of 12/13 March, reaching Pelargir the next day. According to *The Tale of Years*, on 12 March 'Aragorn drives the enemy towards Pelargir', and on 13 March 'Aragorn reaches Pelargir and captures the fleet'. According to *Scheme*, on 13 March Aragorn 'reaches Pelargir and destroys enemy. Captures large part of the fleet, and prepares to embark. Musters men of Lamedon & Lebennin and sends those marching north that he does not put on board.'

876 (III: 152): 'To every ship they came

876 (III: 152). save the slaves chained to the oars – Large ships propelled primarily by oars, such as those of the Barbary pirates in the Mediterranean, were often manned by slaves or prisoners or convicted criminals, secured to rowing benches by a fetter round the ankle.

876 (III: 152): 'Strange indeed,' said Legolas

876 (III: 152). I . . . thought how great and terrible a Lord he might have become . . . had he taken the Ring to himself – In his draft letter to Eileen Elgar, September 1963, Tolkien wrote that no mortal, not even Aragorn, could have withheld the Ring from Sauron 'in his actual presence' (*Letters*, p. 332).

877 (III: 153): 'That night we rested

877 (III: 153). That night we rested – The night of 13/14 March.

877 (III: 153): 'And that is near the end

877 (III: 158). in the morning the fleet set forth – On 14 March.

877 (III: 158). yet it was but the morn of the day ere yesterday, the sixth since we rode from Dunharrow – This is being told on 16 March. The Company left Dunharrow on 8 March, and Pelargir on 14 March.

877 (III: 153): 'But at midnight

877 (III: 153). Long ere day – Very early on 15 March.

877 (III: 153). we came in the third hour of the morning . . . and we unfurled the great standard in battle – There is some confusion in the various accounts about the timing of the sighting of the fleet and its reaching the Harlond. Gimli's account is deliberately brief, and 'we unfurled' could refer to raising the standard on sighting Minas Tirith or to carrying it into battle after arrival. The hours in Minas Tirith, at least, were marked from the rising of the sun. On p. 757, III: 30 Pippin reckons that 'it cannot be more than nine o'clock', and soon after, on p. 758, III: 30, Denethor orders the Captains to wait on him 'as soon as may be after the third hour has rung'. On p. 846, III: 122 it is mid-morning, probably about 9.00 a.m., when the fleet is first sighted, still some leagues away. It is not clear how long it then was before the ships reached the Harlond. *Scheme* has: 'March 14: In morning Aragorn sets sail in black fleet up Anduin, but as wind is still east makes at first slow progress mainly by rowing. By midnight fleet is about 60 miles above Pelargir' (i.e. still 66 miles from Minas Tirith). And 'March 15: SW [south wind] springs up in early hours and fleet hoists sail and begins to go at speed. They come into sight of haven at Harlond about noon.' 'Noon' here may mean the time the troops disembarked, but even so that seems rather late in relation to what is said in Book V, Chapter 6. In an early outline Tolkien said that watchers on the walls of Minas Tirith could see down the Anduin for ten miles, and that at 'about 9 a.m. they [the black ships] can be seen by watchers from Minas Tirith who are dismayed. As soon as Aragorn catches sight of the city and of the enemy, he hoists his standard' (*The War of the Ring*, p. 399). Although this outline differs in several other respects from the published text, here it seems to agree. At any rate, one should not expect people taking part in a desperate battle to keep careful account of time.

878 (III: 154): 'And I for the folk

878 (III: 154). the Great Wood – Mirkwood, Greenwood the Great.

878 (III: 154): When Imrahil parted

878 (III: 154). there they took counsel together – Evidently only Aragorn, Gandalf, Éomer, Imrahil, Elladan, and Elrohir are present.

878–9 (III: 155): 'Concerning this thing

878–9 (III: 155). Concerning this thing, my lords, you now all know enough for the understanding of our plight – Aragorn and the sons of Elrond presumably have been given Faramir's news of Frodo, and Imrahil and Éomer told the whole story.

879 (III: 155): 'Other evils there are

879 (III: 155). Other evils there are that may come, for Sauron is himself but a servant or emissary. Yet it is not our part to master all the tides of the world, but to do what is in us for the succour of those wherein we are set, uprooting the evil in the fields that we know, so that those who live after may have clean earth to till. What weather they shall have is not ours to rule. – This is a passage much quoted in Tolkien criticism. Gandalf did not think a final victory to be possible; while the history of Arda in Tolkien's mythology shows that any triumph over evil, however long-lived, is only temporary. At the Council in Rivendell Elrond said he had 'seen three ages in the West of the world, and many defeats, and many fruitless victories' (Book II, Chapter 2, p. 243, I: 257). Morgoth was defeated, but Sauron took his place. Even after Sauron's defeat in *The Lord of the Rings*, when Tolkien looked forward into the Fourth Age he found 'secret societies practising dark cults, and "orc-cults" among adolescents' (letter to Fr. Douglas Carter, ?6 June 1972, *Letters*, p. 419). But nothing is achieved by giving way to despair and inaction. Through hope, action, and resistance, something may be saved. Gandalf tells Denethor: 'I shall not wholly fail of my task, though Gondor should perish, if anything passes through this night that can still grow fair or bear fruit and flower again in days to come' (Book V, Chapter 1, p. 758, III: 30–1). In *The Silmarillion*, as Elves and Men were slaughtered by the armies of Morgoth in the Nirnaeth Arnoediad (Battle of Unnumbered Tears) and Turgon feared that Gondolin would soon fall, Huor foresaw the birth of Eärendil: 'Yet if it stands but a little while, then out of your house shall come the hope of Elves and Men . . . from you and from me a new star shall arise' (p. 194). On 15 December 1956 Tolkien wrote to Amy Ronald: 'Actually I am a Christian, and indeed a Roman Catholic, so that I do not expect "history" to be anything but a "long defeat" – though it contains (and in legend may contain more clearly and movingly) some samples or glimpses of final victory' (*Letters*, p. 255).

For *Sauron is himself but a servant or emissary*, see note for p. 15.

879 (III: 155): 'I did so ere I rode

879 (III: 155). I deemed . . . that the Stone had come to me for just such a purpose. – Although both Gandalf and Aragorn believe that some higher power is influencing events against Sauron, they also know that this does not eliminate their responsibility to act. 'God helps them that help themselves.'

879 (III: 155). it was then ten days since the Ringbearer went east from Rauros – Aragorn looked in the Orthanc-stone on 6 March. Frodo left the Company on 26 February.

880 (III: 156): 'As Aragorn has begun

880 (III: 156). We must push Sauron to his last throw. – An analogy to the last throw of dice in a game of chance, to a final gamble while the odds seem to be in Sauron's favour. Compare note for p. 882.

880–1 (III: 157): 'As for me,' said Imrahil

880 (III: 157). liege-lord – A ruler, entitled to allegiance and service.

881 (III: 157). an army still unfought upon our northern flank – The army camped on the road to prevent the arrival of the Rohirrim, which the Riders avoided with the assistance of Ghân-buri-Ghân.

881 (III: 157): 'All are weary

881 (III: 157). very many have wounds light or grievous . . . I cannot hope to lead even two thousands, and yet leave as many for the defence of the City. – Of the 6,000 who rode to Minas Tirith, at least 2,000 were killed or are not fit for further immediate service.

881–2 (III: 158): This then was the end

882 (III: 158). some three thousand under the command of Elfhelm – As first published this passage read only: 'some three thousand'. The words 'under the command of Elfhelm' were added in the second edition (1965).

882 (III: 158): 'Surely,' he cried

882 (III: 158). a bow of string and green willow – Useless as a weapon.

882 (III: 158): 'Neither shall we'

882 (III: 158). the last move in a great jeopardy – Another analogy to a game. *Jeopardy* here is 'a position in a game, undertaking etc. in which the chances of winning and losing hang in the balance; an even chance; an undecided state of affairs' (*OED*).

Chapter 10

THE BLACK GATE OPENS

For drafts and history of this chapter, see *The War of the Ring*, pp. 430–2.

883 (III: 159): Two days later

883 (III: 159). Two days later – It is 18 March 1419.

883 (III: 159). they had broken and fled – According to *Scheme*: 'March 17: Rohirrim destroy the Easterlings on the North Road.'

883 (III: 159): At last the trumpets rang

883 (III: 159). they wheeled – To *wheel* 'of a rank or body of troops: to turn, with a movement like that of the spokes of a wheel, about a pivot, so as to change front' (*OED*).

884 (III: 160): Ere noon the army

884 (III: 160). Ere noon the army came to Osgiliath. – It was twelve miles to the Causeway Forts in the Pelennor, which were probably close to Osgiliath, as there 'the wall overlooked the long flats to the river' (Book V, Chapter 1, p. 750, III: 22).

884 (III: 160): The vanguard passed on

884 (III: 160). Old Gondor – Osgiliath (*Index*).

884 (III: 160). Five miles beyond Osgiliath they halted – The main host did not join the vanguard until the next day. It may have taken some time for all the men to cross the river.

884 (III: 160): Now in their debate

884 (III: 160). Now in their debate – Presumably on 16 March; a subject not mentioned in the previous chapter.

884–5 (III: 160–1): But against this Gandalf

885 (III: 161). So the next day – It is 19 March.

885 (III: 161): It was dark and lifeless

885 (III: 161). they broke the evil bridge and set red flames in the noisome fields – 'From mead to mead the bridge sprang. Figures stood at its head, carven with cunning in forms human and bestial, but all corrupt and loathsome' (Book IV, Chapter 8, p. 704, II: 313). For the *noisome fields* see note for p. 253.

885 (III: 161): The day after

885 (III: 161). The day after – It is 20 March.

885 (III: 161). it was some hundred miles by that way from the Cross-roads to the Morannon – They are close to the Morannon by the end of 24 March, but do not use the road for the last part of the journey so that they can approach the Morannon from the north-west.

885 (III: 161). ghylls and crags – A *ghyll* (*gill*) is 'a deep cleft or ravine, usually wooded and forming the course of a stream' (*OED*).

A *crag* is 'a steep or precipitous rugged rock' (*OED*).

885 (III: 161–2): Nonetheless, though they marched

885 (III: 161). It was near the end of the second day of their march from the Cross-roads – Near the end of 21 March.

885 (III: 161). attempted to take their leading companies in ambush – This is clearly on 21 March, and unusually here *Scheme* does not agree with the published text, stating instead that the host halted twenty miles north of the Cross-roads on 20 March, forty-five miles north on 21 March, and sixty-five miles north on 22 March after defeating and scattering an ambush above Henneth Annûn. For 23 March, however, both *Scheme* and *The Tale of Years* note that the host passed on that date out of Ithilien.

886 (III: 162): But the victory did little

886 (III: 162). feint – A pretended attack, to deceive the enemy.

886 (III: 162): So time and the hopeless journey

886 (III: 162). So time and the hopeless journey wore away – Paul H. Kocher comments: 'Much has been written, and justly, about the self-sacrificial courage of Frodo and Sam in the last stages of their journey through Mordor. But few or none have remarked on the equal if less solitary unselfish daring displayed by the mere seven thousand men whom Aragorn and his peers lead up to the Black Gate to challenge the ten times ten thousands inside' (*Master of Middle-earth*, p. 157).

The leaders know the faint hope behind this desperate march, that somehow Frodo and Sam will be able to destroy the Ring before the army of the West is annihilated, or at the least, that the destruction of the army will distract Sauron long enough for the quest to be achieved, even if many do not live to see it. The men they lead know nothing of that slender hope, but follow on trust what must seem a hopeless undertaking.

886 (III: 162). Upon the fourth day from the Cross-roads and the sixth from Minas Tirith – On 23 March.

886 (III: 162). unmanned – 'Deprived of courage; made weak or timid' (*OED*).

887 (III: 163): They advanced now slowly

887 (III: 163). at nightfall of the fifth day of the march from Morgul Vale – At nightfall on 24 March.

887 (III: 163). the waxing moon was four nights old – The moon had been new on 21 March; it is four nights old on the night of 24/25 March.

887 (III: 163): It grew cold

887 (III: 163). As morning came the wind began to stir again, but now it came from the North, and soon it freshened to a rising breeze. – This wind plays a notable part in the events of the day. In Book VI, Chapter 4 the eagles come 'from the northern mountains, speeding on a gathering wind' (p. 948, III: 226); the same wind takes the shadow of Sauron and blows it away (p. 949, III: 227); and it is the 'cold blast rising to a gale, which drove back the darkness and the ruin of the clouds' witnessed by Sam (p. 951, III: 229); while in Book VI, Chapter 5 it is the 'wind that had sprung up in the night . . . blowing now keenly from the North' witnessed by Faramir and Éowyn on the walls of Minas Tirith (p. 961, III: 239).

887 (III: 163): The two vast iron doors

887 (III: 163). The two vast iron doors of the Black Gate under its frowning arch were fast closed. – As first published this sentence read: 'The three vast doors of the Black Gate under their frowning arches were fast closed.' It was revised in the second printing (1967) of the Allen & Unwin second edition, to accord with the description of a single gate in Book IV, Chapter 3.

888 (III: 164): There was a long silence

888 (III: 164). the door of the Black Gate – Prior to the Houghton Mifflin edition of 1987 and the HarperCollins edition of 1994, these words read 'the middle door of the Black Gate'.

888 (III: 164). braying of horns – They are making a loud, harsh, unpleasant sound.

888 (III: 164): At its head there rode

888 (III: 164). yet this was no Ringwraith but a living man. The Lieutenant of the Tower of Barad-dûr he was, and his name is remembered in no tale; for he himself had forgotten it, and he said: 'I am the Mouth of Sauron.' – Paul H. Kocher comments that the Mouth of Sauron 'is firmly material. But he hideously resembles' the Ringwraiths

> in the extent to which he has become absorbed into his master's aims and methods. . . . He ends by being transformed into a replica of his

> teacher. 'Mouth of Sauron' he calls himself, a man without any name of his own, 'for he himself had forgotten it.' Considering the high value placed in Tolkien's Middle-earth upon real names as indices of identity – Treebeard and the whole race of dwarves refuse to reveal their names to anybody, and virtually nobody will even pronounce Sauron's aloud in the Black Speech – such namelessness is the acme of total surrender. [*Master of Middle-earth*, p. 67]

It has been pointed out that Aragorn said that Sauron 'does not use his right name, nor permit it to be spelt or spoken' (Book III, Chapter 1, p. 416, II: 18), but presumably that means, without his special approval.

888 (III: 164). it is told that he was a renegade who came of the race of those that are named the Black Númenóreans; for they established their dwellings in Middle-earth during the years of Sauron's domination, and they worshipped him, being enamoured of evil knowledge. And he entered the service of the Dark Tower when it first rose again – In *The War of the Ring* Christopher Tolkien notes his father's various rejected ideas for the background of the Mouth of Sauron. In the draft manuscript it is said

> '. . . that he was a living man, who being captured as a youth became a servant of the Dark Tower, and because of his cunning grew high in the Lord's favour. . . .' In the fair copy this was repeated, but was changed subsequently to: 'But it is said that he was a renegade, son of a house of wise and noble men in Gondor, who becoming enamoured of evil knowledge entered the service of the Dark Tower, and because of his cunning [and the fertile cruelty of his mind] [and servility] he grew ever higher in the Lord's favour . . .' (these phrases being thus bracketed in the original). [*The War of the Ring*, p. 431]

In Appendix A it is said that in the Second Age the area around Umbar was Númenórean land, 'but it was a stronghold of the King's Men, who were afterwards called the Black Númenóreans, corrupted by Sauron, and who hated above all the followers of Elendil. After the fall of Sauron their race swiftly dwindled or became merged with the Men of Middle-earth, but they inherited without lessening their hatred of Gondor' (pp. 1044–5, III: 325, n. 1).

According to *The Tale of Years*, Sauron began to rebuild Barad-dûr in Third Age 2951.

888 (III: 165): 'Is there anyone in this rout

888 (III: 165). rout – In this sense, 'disorderly, tumultuous, or disreputable crowd of persons' (*OED*).

888 (III: 165). Not thou at least – The use of the familiar *thou* is meant to be insulting. See note for p. 852.

889 (III: 165): Aragorn said naught

889 (III: 165). I am a herald and ambassador, and may not be assailed! – *Herald* here has a similar meaning to ambassador, but refers especially to someone who carries messages between states or opposing sides in time of war, and who by custom may not be attacked or harmed while carrying out his duties.

889 (III: 165): The Messenger put these aside

889 (III: 165). the short sword that Sam had carried – As first published these words read 'a short sword such as Sam had carried'. They were revised in the second printing (1967) of the Allen & Unwin second edition.

890 (III: 166): No one answered him

890 (III: 166). the Great Tower – Barad-dûr.

890 (III: 166): 'These are the terms

890 (III: 166). These are the terms – Tom Shippey sees similarities in the terms offered by the Mouth of Sauron to those imposed on defeated France in the Second World War. He suggests that the demanded cession of the lands east of Anduin (Ithilien) is similar to the return of the disputed territory of Alsace-Lorraine to German sovereignty; while the area west of Anduin, tributary to Mordor, disarmed, nominally governing its own affairs but under the eye of Sauron's lieutenant at Isengard, 'is in effect . . . a demilitarized zone, with what one can only call Vichy status, which will pay war-reparations' (*J.R.R. Tolkien: Author of the Century*, p. 166). Vichy was the seat of Marshal Pétain's government from 1940 to 1944, which operated with limited independence but took part in collecting the money, raw materials, and foodstuffs exacted by the occupying Germans.

890 (III: 166): But Gandalf said

890 (III: 166). This is much to demand for the delivery of one servant. . . . Where is this prisoner? – Gandalf has surely noticed that the Mouth speaks of only one 'imp', and although the tokens come from both Frodo and Sam, only one of each item is present, suggesting that only one of the hobbits has been captured. In an early synopsis looking forward to this scene, Tolkien described Gandalf's rejection of the terms and wrote: 'Gandalf explains that Frodo is probably *not* captive – for at any rate Sauron has not got the Ring. Otherwise he would not seek to parley' (*The War of the Ring*, p. 230). Gandalf surely knew enough of Sauron's ways to think that, even if Sauron had regained the Ring and was playing a cruel game with them before striking, he would surely have mentioned the Ring itself, to increase the anguish of his foes and reduce them to utter despair. And as the bearer of the Elven-ring Narya Gandalf again would have been aware that Sauron was still not in possession of the One.

This is a case where even the first-time reader knows more than Gandalf: that although Frodo has been captured, Sam is still free and may attempt a rescue.

891 (III: 167): Then the Messenger of Mordor

891 (III: 167). the muzzle – 'The projecting part of the head of an animal which includes the nose and the mouth' (*OED*).

891 (III: 167): Drums rolled and fires leaped up

891 (III: 167). The great doors of the Black Gate – As first published these words read: 'All the doors of the Morannon'. They were revised in the second printing (1967) of the Allen & Unwin second edition (compare notes for pp. 887, 888).

892 (III: 168–9): Then even as he thought

892 (III: 168). knotted hands – 'Characterized by knobs, protuberances, excrescences or concretions; gnarled, as a trunk or branch; having swollen joints' (*OED*).

892 (III: 169): Then Pippin stabbed upwards

892 (III: 169). written blade – Engraved or inscribed with writing.

893 (III: 169): 'So it ends as I guessed

893 (III: 169). The Eagles are coming! . . . That came in his [Bilbo's] tale – In *The Hobbit*, Chapter 17, during the Battle of Five Armies Bilbo, who is watching miserably as the Goblins seem to be winning, looks around:

> He gave a great cry: he had seen a sight that made his heart leap, dark shapes small yet majestic against the distant glow.
>
> 'The Eagles! The Eagles!' he shouted. 'The Eagles are coming!'
>
> Bilbo's eyes were seldom wrong. The eagles were coming down the wind, line after line, in such a host as must have gathered from all the eyries of the North.

The Eagles help to turn the tide of battle.

BOOK SIX

Chapter 1

THE TOWER OF CIRITH UNGOL

For drafts and history of this chapter, see *Sauron Defeated*, pp. 18–30.

897 (III: 173): Sam roused himself

897 (III: 173). Sam roused himself – It is 14 March 1419. Frodo was captured in the late afternoon or evening of 13 March; Sam followed the orcs and listened to their conversation at the under-gate late on the 13th.

897 (III: 173–4): 'I wonder if they think of us at all'

897 (III: 173–4). I wonder if they think of us – As Book VI begins, Tolkien carefully ensures that his readers know the present date and time, and how the situation described in this chapter relates to events in the West.

898 (III: 174): There he halted and sat down

898 (III: 174). he drew out the Ring and put it on again – A reader pointed out to Christopher Tolkien that Sam put on the Ring at the end of Book IV, and now 'put it on again', but there is no intervening reference to him taking it off. Christopher agreed that 'this does seem to be a most remarkable case of the author nodding' (courtesy of Christopher Tolkien).

899 (III: 175): Hard and cruel

899 (III: 175). Morgai – '"Black Fence", an inner ridge much lower than [the] Ephel Dúath and separated from it by a deep trough (shallower at either end): the inner ring of the fences of Mordor' (*Index*).

899–900 (III: 176): In that dreadful light

899 (III: 176). Its eastern face stood up in three great tiers from a shelf in the mountain-wall far below – In a draft manuscript of this chapter Cirith Ungol rose in four tiers, as shown in an accompanying drawing (*Artist and Illustrator*, fig. 174). Later this was changed to three tiers, which projected 40, 30, and 20 yards from the cliff, with their heights 100, 75, and 50 feet.

900 (III: 176): As he gazed at it

900 (III: 176). Narchost and Carchost, the Towers of the Teeth – '*Carchost* "fang fort" eastern of 2 *Towers of the Teeth*'; '*Narchost* bitter-biting fort ("narch") the western of the 2 Towers of the Teeth' (*Index*).

901 (III: 177): In that hour of trial

901 (III: 177). In that hour of trial it was the love of his master that helped most to hold him firm; but also deep down in him lived still

unconquered his plain hobbit-sense – Sam has come to play an increasingly important role. From late in Book V, when Frodo falls unconscious and is captured, until the end of the quest at the Crack of Doom, the reader sees the story mainly from Sam's point of view rather than Frodo's. And Sam now becomes, as Tolkien wrote to Milton Waldman, the 'chief hero' (see note for p. 1024), unlikely though that seemed earlier in the book; and yet he retains his rustic outlook. In his draft letter to Eileen Elgar, September 1963, Tolkien noted that Sam 'did not think of himself as heroic or even brave, or in any way admirable – except in his service and loyalty to his master. That had an ingredient (probably inevitable) of pride and possessiveness: it is difficult to exclude it from the devotion of those who perform such service' (*Letters*, p. 329).

902 (III: 178): They were like great figures

902 (III: 178). Each had three jointed bodies and three heads facing outward, and inward, and across the gateway. The heads had vulture-faces – Bird-headed gods were depicted in ancient Egypt, three-dimensional or in profile in low relief or painted, but always as individual figures. Some columns had a head on each face as part of the 'capital'. Hybrid figures also occur in the art of Mesopotamia and the Near East. At Sargon's palace, built *c.* 700 BC at Khorsabad in northern Iraq, winged human-headed bulls were carved in high relief at the entrance to the citadel, to represent protecting genii; they face outwards, while other winged human figures were carved on the walls of the gateway. Griffin-headed human figures representing genii or demons appear in other Assyrian reliefs.

A diagrammatic sketch by Tolkien of the Two Watchers is reproduced in *The Treason of Isengard*, p. 348.

905 (III: 181): All at once, when he felt

905 (III: 181). There the stair was covered by a small domed chamber in the midst of the roof, with low doors facing east and west. – In *Sauron Defeated* Christopher Tolkien notes that his father added the sentence 'Both were open.' following 'east and west' in the fair copy manuscript of this chapter, but that the words were omitted in the second manuscript, 'perhaps inadvertently' (p. 26). The words were not added to the 2004 edition, absent adequate proof of Tolkien's intent.

905 (III: 181–2): 'You won't go again, you say?'

905 (III: 182). I'll squeeze your eyes out, like I did to Radbug just now – Presumably the cause of the 'dreadful choking shriek' Sam has just heard (pp. 903–4, III: 180).

On 18 February 1956, in response to corrections suggested by a reader, Tolkien wrote to Rayner Unwin:

> As for [the reader's] pedantry about *like / as* [as in 'like I did to Radbug'], you may inform him, if you think there is any need to do so, that he is in my opinion being very silly. First of all, his . . . examples are taken from 'reported speech'. Since this use of *like* has been current in English for many centuries, especially in the freer and more conversational styles, I see no reason why dramatic propriety should be sacrificed to [the reader's] prejudices. In any case, two of the speakers (Sam and an Orc!) are nowhere represented as using 'correct' English. However the notion that *like* is either 'vulgar' or incorrect as a conjunction has no foundation either in the observed usage of so-called 'good writers'; nor in the history of English syntax. No doubt, like other pedantic 'rules' of correctness, it was invented by those ignorant of both. [Tolkien-George Allen & Unwin archive, HarperCollins]

905 (III: 182): 'Then you must go

905 (III: 182). he [Gorbag] knifed me, the dung – Possibly by coincidence, one meaning of Old English *gor* is 'dung'.

905 (III: 182). the Black Pits – 'Dungeons of torment under Barad-dûr' (*Index*).

906 (III: 182): 'Well, you put his back up

906 (III: 182). put his back up – Annoyed, offended him.

906 (III: 182). *tarks* – In Appendix F (as directed by the footnote, added in the Allen & Unwin second edition, 1966) it is said that 'in this jargon *tark*, "man of Gondor", was a debased form of *tarkil*, a Quenya word used in Westron for one of Númenórean descent' (p. 1139, III: 409). In *The Treason of Isengard*, p. 8, Christopher Tolkien comments that at one point his father gave the true name of Trotter as *Tarkil*. 'The Name *Tarkil* appears in the *Etymologies* in V.364 [*The Lost Road and Other Writings*, p. 364] . . . (stem KHIL "follow"): **tāra-khil*, in which the second element evidently bears the sense "mortal man" (*Hildi* "the Followers", an Elvish name for Men . . .).'

907–8 (III: 184): Softly Sam began to climb

907 (III: 184). the guttering torch – The verb *gutter* is usually used of a candle, to mean 'melting rapidly', the wax flowing down the sides, until the flame goes out. The latest *Concise Oxford English Dictionary* adds the definition '(of a flame) flicker and burn unsteadily'.

908 (III: 184–5): His voice sounded thin

908 (III: 185). And then suddenly new strength rose in him, and his voice rang out – This episode, in which Frodo reveals his location by responding to Sam's song, was surely inspired by the legend of King Richard I of England, taken prisoner while returning from the Crusades, and his loyal minstrel Blondel de Nesle. According to one version, Blondel went from castle to castle, searching for the king who was held in an unknown location, and singing one of Richard's favourite songs. When he came to where Richard was imprisoned, the king joined in, revealing his presence. (See Tolkien's letter of 7 June 1965 to the composer Donald Swann, in the Marion E. Wade Center, Wheaton College, Wheaton, Illinois, in which he refers to 'Richard Coeur de Lion and the minstrel', apparently in connection with Sam's song *In Western Lands.*)

Tolkien used the same motif in *The Silmarillion*, where the Noldo Fingon sings to discover where Morgoth has imprisoned his cousin Maedhros: 'suddenly above him, far and faint his song was taken up, and a voice answering called to him. Maedhros it was that sang amid his torment' (p. 110). Later in the same work, Lúthien sings to discover if Beren is held prisoner in Sauron's Tol-in-Gaurhoth (Isle of Werewolves): 'In that hour Lúthien came, and standing on the bridge that led to Sauron's isle she sang a song that no walls of stone could hinder. Beren heard. . . . And in answer he sang a song of challenge' (p. 174). A similar episode was also to feature in the (abandoned) sequel to *Farmer Giles of Ham*, with the pig boy Suet imitating the sounds of farm animals to discover where the giant Caurus held Giles' son George captive.

909 (III: 186): 'You lie quiet

909 (III: 186). keep your trap shut – Snaga is not referring to the trap-door by which he has just entered but using a slang phrase meaning 'Quiet, keep your mouth shut'.

911–12 (III: 188): 'No, no!' cried Frodo

912 (III: 188). bemused – Stupefied, bewildered.

913 (III: 189): He opened the bundle

913 (III: 189). stabbing-sword – A short sword used for close fighting; compare the *gladius*, one of the primary weapons of the Roman soldier along with the spear or javelin.

913–4 (III: 190): 'Save me, but so I had!'

914 (III: 190). I don't know when drop or morsel last passed my lips – The last time it is mentioned that Frodo and Sam ate or drank was Book IV, Chapter 8, when they 'took what they expected to be their last meal before they went down into the Nameless Land' (p. 711, II: 320), some time on 11 March. Presumably Sam must have sipped some water since then, as it is now early on 15 March.

914 (III: 190): 'No, they eat and drink

914 (III: 190). The Shadow that bred them [orcs] can only mock, it cannot make: not real new things of its own. I don't think it gave life

to the orcs, it only ruined them and twisted them – See note for p. 444. In a letter to W.H. Auden on 12 May 1965 Tolkien wrote:

> With regard to *The Lord of the Rings*, I cannot claim to be a sufficient theologian to say whether my notion of orcs is heretical or not. I don't feel under any obligation to make my story fit with formalized Christian theology, though I actually intended it to be consonant with Christian thought and belief, which is asserted somewhere, Book Five [i.e. VI], page 190, where Frodo asserts that orcs are not evil in origin. We believe that, I suppose, of all human kinds and sorts and breeds, though some appear, both as individuals and groups to be, by us at any rate, unredeemable. [*Letters*, p. 355]

Chapter 2

THE LAND OF SHADOW

For drafts and history of this chapter, see *Sauron Defeated*, pp. 31–6.

916 (III: 193): The eastern faces

916 (III: 193). hue and cry – 'An early system for apprehending suspected criminals. Neighbours were bound to join in a hue and cry and to pursue a suspect to the bounds of the manor' (*Brewer's Dictionary of Phrase and Fable*).

916 (III: 193): The eastern faces of the Ephel Dúath

916 (III: 193). flying bridge – A bridge without any intermediate supports.

917 (III: 194): 'Orc-mail doesn't keep

917 (III: 194). jerkin – A close-fitting jacket or short coat.

917 (III: 194): Day was coming again

917 (III: 194). Day was coming – It is dawn on 15 March 1419. *Scheme* and *The Tale of Years* agree that Sam entered the Tower and found Frodo on 14 March, but that they did not escape from the Tower until 15 March.

917 (III: 195): Sam scrambled to his feet

917 (III: 195). It's a long time . . . since I had a proper sleep – It is not long after dawn on 15 March, and excluding the hours he was unconscious at the under-gate during the night of 13/14 March, Sam had last slept the night of 11/12 March and probably well into 12 March, before entering Shelob's lair.

919 (III: 196): As Frodo and Sam stood

919 (III: 196). a cry of woe and dismay – Presumably this is one of the surviving Nazgûl bringing news of the destruction of the Witch-king.

919 (III: 196): 'Well no, not much, Sam'

919 (III: 196). a great wheel of fire – This image, which recurs as Frodo nears the end of his quest, is known also in Classical and Christian mythology as a symbol of hellish torture. Perhaps its best-known expression is in the Greek myth of Ixion, who for his attempted seduction of Hera was bound everlastingly to a fiery wheel.

920 (III: 197): Sharing a wafer

920 (III: 197). the narrows of Isenmouthe, the iron jaws of Carach Angren. – In *Nomenclature* Tolkien writes that *Isenmouthe* is intended to represent a 'translation' into the Common Speech of Sindarin *Carach Angren*, but 'made at so early a date that at the period of the tale' it 'had become archaic in form' and its original meaning was obscured. '*Isen* is an old variant form in English of *iron* . . . ; *mouthe* is a derivative of *mouth*, representing Old English *mūtha* (from *mūth* "mouth") "an opening", especially used of the mouths of rivers, but also applied to other openings (not parts of a body). . . . The *Isenmouthe* was so called because of the great fence of pointed iron posts that closed the gap leading into *Udûn*, like teeth in jaws. . . .' In his unfinished index Tolkien describes the Isenmouthe as a 'rampart and dike guarding [the] entr[ance] to Udûn', and notes '*carach* "jaws, rows of teeth"'.

921 (III: 198): The river-bed was now

921 (III: 198). Marges – Poetic 'margins'.

922 (III: 199): 'Now you go to sleep first

922 (III: 199). I reckon this day is nearly over. – *Scheme* has 'sleep under brambles' at the end of the entry for 15 March.

922 (III: 199): Frodo sighed and was asleep

922 (III: 199). Sam saw a white star twinkle for a while. The beauty of it smote his heart . . . and hope returned to him. For like a shaft . . . the thought pierced him that in the end the Shadow was only a small and passing thing: there was light and high beauty for ever beyond its reach. – A frequently quoted passage which stresses the importance of hope and suggests that there are limits to what Evil can achieve. When Eärendil first sailed the sky as a star at the end of the First Age, the people of Middle-earth 'took it for a sign, and called it Gil-Estel, the Star of High Hope' (*The Silmarillion*, p. 250).

922 (III: 199–200): They woke together

922 (III: 199). They woke – It is 16 March 1419.

922 (III: 200). screes – A *scree* is 'a mass of small loose stones that form or cover a slope on a mountain' (*Concise OED*).

923 (III: 200): Still far away

923 (III: 200). forty miles at least – But Frodo and Sam will take a much longer route. In *Sauron Defeated* Christopher Tolkien notes that this was a late change from shorter distances, and comments: 'On the large-scale map of Rohan, Gondor and Mordor the distance is somewhat under 60 miles, as Mount Doom was first placed; but when it was moved further to the west it became about 43 miles (under 40 in my redrawing of the map published in *The Return of the King*), with which the text of RK agrees' (pp. 34–5).

923 (III: 200). Ashen Mountains – The Ered Lithui; see note for p. 636.

923 (III: 200). the Eye turned inward, pondering tidings of doubt and danger; a bright sword, and a stern and kingly face – According to *Scheme*, on the previous day, 15 March, 'news of escape of prisoners [*sic*] of Tower reaches Baraddûr almost at same time as news of their capture', but evidently Sauron was more concerned with other matters. It is ten days since Aragorn revealed himself in the *palantír*, but since then Sauron has seen his army defeated on the Pelennor Fields and the Witch-king annihilated, and, according to Gandalf, probably thinks that Aragorn is now the wielder of the Ring.

923 (III: 200): Frodo and Sam gazed out

923 (III: 200). As far as their eyes could reach . . . there were camps, some of tents, some ordered like small towns. . . . Barely a mile out into the plain it clustered . . . with straight dreary streets of huts and long low drab buildings. – The description recalls some of the extensive army camps to which Tolkien was posted during the First World War, in particular those situated in Staffordshire on Cannock Chase.

925 (III: 202): 'Not much use are you

925 (III: 202). snotty noses – Literally, stuffed with mucus and therefore unable to follow a scent, but *snotty* is also slang for 'dirty, paltry, contemptible'.

925 (III: 202): 'All right, all right!'

925 (III: 202). gobbler with the flapping hands – Gollum. A *gobbler* swallows hurriedly and in a noisy fashion. In *The Hobbit*, Chapter 5 it is said that when Gollum 'said *gollum* he made a horrible swallowing noise in his throat. That is how he got his name.'

925 (III: 203): 'Who to?

925 (III: 203). Not to your precious Shagrat. He won't be captain any more. – Both *The Tale of Years* and *Scheme* state that on 17 March Shagrat brings Frodo's cloak, mail-shirt, and (Sam's) sword to Barad-dûr. *Scheme* adds that he is slain by Sauron.

925–6 (III: 203): The other halted

925 (III: 203). peaching sneakthief – *Peaching* 'to give incriminating evidence, to inform against'.

Sneakthief is here probably intended to have its slang meaning of 'informer, telltale'.

925 (III: 203). Shriekers – The Two Watchers of Minas Morgul.

926–7 (III: 204): It was difficult

926 (III: 204). It was difficult and dangerous moving in the night – Frodo and Sam travel during the night of 16/17 March and rest during the day on 17 March.

927 (III: 204): 'No, not any clear notion

927 (III: 204). I only remember vaguely – Frodo reckons that he and Sam have covered about twelve of the twenty leagues from the bridge below the Tower to the Isenmouthe, from which point they would be about sixty miles from Orodruin. Therefore they still have some eighty-four miles to cover, which Frodo thinks will take about a week, about twelve miles a day. In *Sauron Defeated* Christopher Tolkien comments that the distance from the Morgai bridge below Cirith Ungol to the Isenmouthe was less in early texts, but 'on the large-scale map it becomes 56 miles or just under 19 leagues, agreeing with the twenty leagues of [*The Return of the King*]'. He also notes that

> Frodo's [original] estimation of the distance from the Isenmouthe to Mount Doom as about fifty miles likewise remained through all the texts until replaced at the very end by sixty. This distance is roughly 50 miles on the Second Map, about 80 on the Third Map, and 62 on the large-scale map as Mount Doom was first placed; when it was moved further west the distance from the Isenmouthe became 50 miles. The change of 50 to 60 at the end of the textual history of RK is thus strangely the reverse of the development of the map. [p. 35]

927 (III: 205): It was not yet quite dark

927 (III: 205). At the first hint of grey light – It is 18 March. Frodo and Sam have travelled through the night of 17/18 March.

927–8 (III: 205): Slowly the light grew

928 (III: 205). the deep dale of Udûn – '*Udûn* . . . name of the defile bet[ween] [the] arms of [Ephel] Dúath and [Ered] Lithui' (*Index*). This has the same name, but is not the same place, as that mentioned by Gandalf when confronting the Balrog: see note for p. 330.

928 (III: 205). there now their Lord was gathering in haste great forces to meet the onslaught of the Captains of the West – In a Tolkien discussion group report published in *Beyond Bree* for May 1982, pp. 5–6, the point is made that 'Frodo and Sam approached the Isenmouthe on the same day that the Captains of the West left Minas Tirith'.

> How, then, did the Dark Lord know to rush all his troops to the north – before the enemy had indicated their direction of attack? Perhaps the Black Gate was the only practical passage for a large army into Mordor. . . . Did the Dark Lord consider the natural defenses of the

Nameless Pass so great that he did not even leave a guard there? Or was it because the only successful invasion of Mordor had been through the Black Gate – and both Sauron and Aragorn knew their history? Even so, it smacks of foreknowledge: perhaps the Dark Lord used the *palantír*.

928 (III: 205): A few miles north

928 (III: 205). Durthang – 'Dark press or oppression' (*Index*).

929–30 (III: 207): Mordor-dark had returned

929 (III: 207). when the hobbits set out again – It is the evening of 18 March.

930 (III: 207): After doing some twelve miles

930 (III: 207). twelve miles – Of the twenty miles estimated to the Isenmouthe. In *Sauron Defeated* Christopher Tolkien notes that as late as the printer's typescript the length of the road to the Isenmouthe was about ten miles, the hobbits had been on it only for about an hour when they halted, and they were soon overtaken with about six miles yet to go.

> On the typescript my father emended 'ten miles' to 'twenty miles', and 'an hour' to 'three hours', but the final reading of [*The Return of the King*] was 'after doing some twelve miles, they halted.' On the large-scale map [of Rohan, Gondor, and Mordor] the track of Frodo and Sam up the valley below the Morgai is marked, and the point where their track joined the road from Durthang is 20 miles from the Isenmouthe; the change in the text was thus very probably made to accommodate it to the map. The change whereby the hobbits had gone for three hours or twelve miles along the road before being overtaken clearly followed the increased distance to the Isenmouthe, in order to reduce the time that Frodo and Sam had to submit to the punishing pace set by the orcs before they escaped. [pp. 35–6]

930 (III: 208): They did not have to wait long

930 (III: 203). to hide their feet – Sam did not bring any footwear to Frodo in Cirith Ungol, so presumably both are barefoot as usual for hobbits, and their hairy feet are likely to betray the fact that they are not Orcs.

931 (III: 208): It was hard enough for poor Sam

931 (III: 208). he bent all his will to draw his breath and to make his legs keep going – Sam's effort recalls that of the typical foot soldier – of any army. As an officer in France during the First World War, Tolkien was not expected to carry his kit during lengthy marches, but still had to cover the distance.

931 (III: 208–9): 'There now!' he laughed

931 (III: 208). Where there's whip there's a will – A play on the proverb *Where there's a will there's a way.*

931 (III: 209). Don't you know we're at war? – An echo of the Second World War catch-phrase *Don't you know there's a war on?*

932 (III: 209): With a last despairing effort

932 (III: 209). Then he pitched down into a shallow pit – It is now early, before dawn, on 18 March. *The Tale of Years* says that Frodo and Sam are captured on 18 March and escape on 19 March. During their time with the orcs they cover about eight miles. This incident and the forced march of Frodo and Sam echoes that of Merry and Pippin in Book III, but the former are not prisoners, only mistaken for orcs. Like Merry and Pippin, they manage to escape, and in both cases apparent disaster turns out for the good: Merry and Pippin are brought to Fangorn, which leads to the destruction of Isengard; and it is only being mistaken for orcs and the greater speed of the forced march that enable Frodo and Sam to pass a dangerous point and so reach Mount Doom in time to destroy the Ring before the armies of the West are annihilated.

Chapter 3

MOUNT DOOM

For drafts and history of this chapter, see *Sauron Defeated*, pp. 37–43.

933 (III: 210): In the morning

933 (III: 210). In the morning – It is 19 March 1419.

933–4 (III: 210–11): Sam tried to guess

933 (III: 210). It looks every step of fifty miles – That is, from the opening of the Isenmouthe. Frodo had reckoned that it might be sixty miles from the point where the spur towards Isenmouthe jutted out of the Ephel Dúath.

934 (III: 211): 'So that was the job

934 (III: 211). Rosie Cotton – This is the first mention of Rose Cotton, and the first hint of Sam's feelings for her. Nor did she appear in any extant drafts until this chapter.

According to *Nomenclature* the name *Cotton*

> is a place-name in origin (as are many modern surnames): from *cot* 'a cottage or humble dwelling' + *-ton*, the usual English element in place-names, a shortening of *town* (Old English *tūn* 'village'). . . .
>
> It is a common English surname, and has of course in origin no connexion with *cotton* the textile material; though it is naturally associated with it at the present day. Hobbits are represented as using tobacco, and this is made more or less credible by the suggestion that the plant was brought over the Sea by the Men of Westernesse . . . ; but it is not intended that 'cotton' should be supposed to be known or used at that time.

In Appendix F Tolkien attempts an 'internal' or Westron etymology for the name: 'Cotton . . . represents *Hlothran*, a fairly common village-name in the Shire, derived from *hloth*, 'a two-roomed dwelling or hole', and *ran(u)* a small group of such dwellings on a hill-side. As a surname it may be an alteration of *hlothram(a)* 'cottager'. *Hlothram*, which I have rendered Cotman, was the name of Farmer Cotton's grandfather' (p. 1138, III: 416). See also note for p. 22, on *Gamgee*, and further, J.S. Ryan, 'Wherefore the Surname Cotton?' *Amon Hen* 72 (March 1985).

934 (III: 211). her brothers – Rose has four brothers; see note for p. 939.

934 (III: 211). Marigold – Sam's younger sister, who will marry the eldest of the Cotton brothers. Like Rose and many other female hobbits, she has a flower-name. Tolkien used *Marigold* 'because it is suitable as a name in English, and because, containing *gold* and referring to a golden flower, it suggests that there was a "Fallohide" strain . . . in Sam's family – which, increased by the favour of Galadriel, became notable in his children: especially *Elanor*, but also *Goldilocks* (a name sometimes given to flowers of buttercup-kind), who married the heir of Peregrin Took' (*Nomenclature*).

934 (III: 211): But even as hope died

934 (III: 211). But even as hope died . . . or seemed to die, it was turned to new strength. . . . the will hardened in him – Another reference to the Northern spirit (see note for p. 736), combined with the Christian virtue, hope.

934 (III: 211): With a new sense of responsibility

934 (III: 211). The whole surface . . . was pocked with great holes, as if while it was still a waste of soft mud, it had been smitten with a shower of bolts and slingstones. – In a letter to *The Listener* Graham Tayar, who like Tolkien had attended King Edward's School, Birmingham, wrote that Tolkien 'once told me that the physical setting [of Mordor] derived directly from the trenches of World War One, the wasteland of shell-cratered battlefields where he had fought in 1916', rather than from the industrial Birmingham of Tolkien's youth as Humphrey Carpenter had suggested ('Tolkien's Mordor', 14 July 1977).

A *bolt* in this sense is an arrow.

A *slingstone* is a stone cast by a slingshot or by some engine of war working on a similar principle.

935 (III: 212): He was taking

935 (III: 212). for the Captains of the West had passed the Cross-roads and set flames in the deadly fields of Imlad Morgul – The narrative, *The Tale of Years*, and *Scheme* all agree that the fields were burnt on 19 March.

935–6 (III: 212–13): There came at last a dreadful nightfall

935 (III: 212). Then came at last a dreadful nightfall; and even as the Captains of the West drew near to the end of the living lands. . . . Four days had passed since they had escaped from the orcs – This is the night of 22 March. *The Tale of Years* and *Scheme* note that on 23 March the Host of the West will leave Ithilien. In *The Tale of Years* there is no intervening entry between that for 19 March, recording Sam and Frodo's escape and that they 'begin their journey along the road to Barad-dûr', and for 22 March: 'The dreadful nightfall. Frodo and Samwise leave the road and turn south to Mount Doom.' In *Sauron Defeated*, p. 43, Christopher Tolkien notes that in the margins of the first complete manuscript his father wrote, against nightfall of the day Frodo and Sam escaped, '18 ends' (19 March in the published text), and against the words 'There came at last a dreadful evening' he wrote 'end of 22'. Christopher comments that the latter is the same date as in *The Return of the King*, 'and thus there follows in the original text "Five days had passed since they escaped the orcs" (i.e. March 18–22), where RK has "Four" [19–22 March].'

936 (III: 213): 'Water, water!'

936 (III: 213). cisterns – Water storage tanks.

936–7 (III: 213–14): The hateful night passed

936 (III: 213–14). such daylight as followed – It is 23 March.

936 (III: 214): A wild light came

936 (III: 214). I am almost in its power now. I could not give it up – Tolkien prepares us for Frodo's failure at the Crack of Doom. In a draft letter to Miss J. Burn on 26 July 1956 he wrote: 'If you re-read all the passages dealing with Frodo and the Ring, I think you will see that not only was it *quite impossible* for him to surrender the Ring, in act or will, especially at its point of maximum power, but that this failure was adumbrated from far back' (*Letters*, p. 251).

938–9 (III: 216): At their last halt he sank down

939 (III: 216). Jolly Cotton and Tom and Nibs – These are nicknames: Jolly's real name is *Wilcome*, Tom is *Tolman*, and Nibs is *Carl*. Here Sam omits the third Cotton son, Nick (actually *Bowman*).

939 (III: 216): He could not sleep

939 (III: 216). he held a debate with himself – Sam's debate provides an interesting contrast with that of Sméagol/Gollum, between despair and hope, or between surrender and stubborn devotion to duty.

939 (III: 217): The last stage of their journey

939 (III: 217). The last stage of their journey to Orodruin came – It is 24 March.

939 (III: 217). it was a torment greater than Sam had ever thought he could bear. . . . And yet their wills did not yield, and they struggled on. – In '*The Lord of the Rings* as Romance', *J.R.R. Tolkien, Scholar and Storyteller: Essays in Memoriam* (1979), Derek S. Brewer comments that

> in the last stages of the journey to the Crack of Doom Tolkien succeeds in creating the sense of physical difficulty and cost that romance sometimes fails to achieve. He realises most vividly the appalling landscape, the aching struggle towards the repellent yet desired objective, barely relieved by the blessed brief oblivion of exhausted sleep. This is a hopelessness which is not despair; an assertion of the will which denies the self. No doubt Tolkien's war-experience contributed to the imagery. . . . [p. 257]

In a letter to Forrest J. Ackerman, probably between 11 April and 5 May 1958, objecting to a proposed film treatment, Tolkien wrote that 'the most important part of the whole work, the journey through Mordor and the martyrdom of Frodo, has been cut in preference for battles; though it is the chief point of *The Lord of the Rings* that the battles were of subordinate significance' (Marquette Series 7/17/03).

940 (III: 217): 'I didn't ought to have

940 (III: 217). the last day of their quest – It is 25 March.

941 (III: 218): As Frodo clung upon his back

941 (III: 218). pig-a-back – A ride on someone's back and shoulders, also called *piggyback*.

941 (III: 218–19): He looked back

941 (III: 218–19). The confused and tumbled shoulders of its great base rose for maybe three thousand feet above the plain, and above them was reared half as high again its tall central cone. . . . As he looked up . . . he saw plainly a path or road. It climbed like a rising girdle from the west and wound snakelike about the Mountain, until before it went round out of view it reached the foot of the cone upon its eastern side. – In *Sauron Defeated*, p. 40, Christopher Tolkien comments that his father's drawing of Mount Doom reproduced in *Pictures by J.R.R. Tolkien* (2nd edn., no. 30) and *Sauron Defeated* (p. 42) 'seems to show the final conception, with the cone "half as high again" in relation to the "base"; but in this drawing the door of the Sammath Naur is at the foot of the cone, whereas in all versions of the text the climbing road came "high in the upper cone, but still far from the reeking summit, to a dark entrance" [Book VI, Chapter 3, p. 942, III: 219].'

942 (III: 219): The path was not

942 (III: 219). Sammath Naur, the Chambers of Fire – The Sindarin name is followed by its meaning in the Common Speech. Curiously, *Index* describes the Sammath Naur as 'the cave at [the] base of the cone of Orodruin'; compare note for p. 941.

942 (III: 219). Window of the Eye – 'In the topmost tower of Barad-dûr' (*Index*).

942 (III: 219): Sam drew a deep breath

942 (III: 219). Suddenly a sense of urgency which he did not understand came to Sam. It was almost as if he had been called. . . . Frodo also seemed to have felt the call. – At this moment the Host of the West is facing the might of Sauron at the Morannon.

943 (III: 220): Again he lifted Frodo

943–5 (III: 220–2). There at the bend it was cut deep . . . – A recording by Tolkien from these words to 'all other powers were here subdued' (in the paragraph beginning 'At first he could see nothing') is included on Disc 2 of *The J.R.R. Tolkien Audio Collection*.

943 (III: 220–1): With a violent heave

943 (III: 221). griping – Grasping, clutching.

944 (III: 221): 'Begone, and trouble me

944 (III: 221). Begone, and trouble me no more! If you touch me ever again, you shall be cast yourself into the Fire of Doom. – Some readers have argued that this is the Ring itself speaking, rather than Frodo, because the 'commanding voice' emanates from the 'wheel of fire' seen by Sam. To say so, however, is to argue for a sentience within the Ring beyond its ability, established early in the story, to 'look after itself' with the aim of eventual return to Sauron. A simpler interpretation, borne out within two pages, is that the voice is Frodo's, and that he is on the brink of claiming the Ring for himself.

944 (III: 221): 'Don't kill us'

944 (III: 221). when Precious goes we'll die, yes, die into the dust – See note for p. 974.

944 (III: 221–2): Sam's hand wavered

944 (III: 222). there was something that restrained him . . . now dimly he guessed the agony of Gollum's shrivelled mind and body – At the last, Sam expresses pity for Gollum, as Bilbo and Frodo had done before, thus ensuring the success of the quest.

945 (III: 223): 'I have come,' he said

945 (III: 223). I do not choose now to do what I came to do. I will not do this deed. The Ring is mine! – In a draft of this chapter Frodo says, instead: 'I have come. But I cannot do what I have come to do. I will not do it. The Ring is mine.' Christopher Tolkien comments: 'I do not think that the difference [between the two texts] is very significant, since it was already a central element in the outlines that Frodo would *choose* to keep the Ring himself; the change in his words does no more than emphasize that he fully willed his act' (*Sauron Defeated*, p. 38).

In his letter to Milton Waldman, ?late 1951, Tolkien comments: 'We reach the brink of the Fire, *and the whole plan fails*. The Ring conquers. Frodo cannot bear to destroy it. He renounces the Quest, and claims the Ring and puts it on his finger' (*Waldman LR*). Later, in his draft letter to Eileen Elgar, September 1963, he wrote:

> From the point of view of the storyteller the events on Mt Doom proceed simply from the logic of the tale up to that time. They were not deliberately worked up to nor foreseen until they occurred. (Actually, since the events at the Cracks of Doom would obviously be vital to the Tale, I made several sketches or trial versions at various stages in the narrative – but none of them were used, and none of them much resembled what is actually reported in the finished story.) But, for one thing, it became at last quite clear that Frodo after all that had happened would be incapable of voluntarily destroying the Ring. Reflecting on the solution after it was arrived at (as a mere event) I feel that it is central to the whole 'theory' of true nobility and heroism that is presented. [*Letters*, pp. 325–6]

Indeed, from very early in the writing of *The Lord of the Rings* Tolkien knew that Frodo would not be able to destroy the Ring, but was uncertain exactly how nonetheless the Ring would go into the fire. Probably as early as August 1939, when the story had not got beyond Rivendell, he wrote:

> When Bingo [*written above:* Frodo] at last reaches Crack and Fiery Mountain *he cannot make himself throw the Ring away.* ? He hears Necromancer's voice offering him great reward – to share power with him, if he will keep it.
>
> At that moment Gollum – who had seemed to reform and had guided them by secret ways through Mordor – comes up and treacherously tries to take Ring. They wrestle and Gollum *takes Ring* and falls into the Crack. [*The Return of the Shadow*, p. 380]

In undated notes and synopses, *c.* late 1940–1, he tried out other ideas:

> [Frodo] comes to a flat place on the mountain-side where the fissure is full of fire. . . . The Vultures [i.e. Nazgûl] are coming. He *cannot* throw Ring in. . . . All goes dark in his eyes and he falls to his knees. At that moment Gollum comes up and wrestles with him, and takes Ring. Frodo falls flat.
>
> Here perhaps Sam comes up, beats off a vulture and hurls himself and Gollum into the gulf? . . .
>
> It is *Sam* that wrestles with Gollum and [?throws] him finally in the Gulf. [*The Treason of Isengard*, p. 209]

In response to questions from correspondents Tolkien wrote several lengthy accounts explaining Frodo's failure and why nonetheless he was still deserving of honour. In his draft letter to Michael Straight, ?end of 1955, he comments that Frodo was placed in an untenable position, in which the good of the world depended on his behaviour in circumstances which demanded a strength which he did not possess. Frodo was, therefore, 'doomed to fall to temptation or be broken by pressure against his "will": that is against any choice he could make or would make unfettered, not under the duress'.

> Frodo was in such a position: an apparently complete trap: a person of greater native power could probably never have resisted the Ring's lure to power so long; a person of less power could not hope to resist it in the final decision. (Already Frodo had been unwilling to harm the Ring before he set out, and was incapable of surrendering it to Sam.)
>
> The Quest therefore was bound to fail as a piece of world-plan, and also was bound to end in disaster as the story of humble Frodo's development to the 'noble', his sanctification. Fail it would and did as far as Frodo considered alone was concerned. He apostatized – and I have had one savage letter, crying out that he shd. have been executed as a traitor, not honoured. Believe me, it was not until I read this that I had myself any idea how 'topical' such a situation might appear. . . . I did not foresee that before the tale was published we should enter a dark age in which the technique of torture and disruption of personality would rival that of Mordor and the Ring and present us with the practical problem of honest men of good will broken down into apostates and traitors. [*Letters*, pp. 233–4]

On 26 July 1956 Tolkien wrote similarly in his draft letter to Miss J. Burn:

> I think . . . of the mysterious last petitions of the Lord's Prayer: Lead us not into temptation, but deliver us from evil. A petition against something that cannot happen is unmeaning. There exists the possibility of being placed in positions beyond one's power. In which case (as I believe) salvation from ruin will depend on something apparently unconnected: the general sanctity (and humility and mercy) of the sacrificial person. I did not 'arrange' the deliverance in this case: it again follows the logic of the story. (Gollum had had his chance of repentance, and of returning generosity with love; and had fallen off the knife-edge.) In the case of those who now issue from prison 'brainwashed', broken, or insane, praising their torturers, no such immediate deliverance is as a rule to be seen. But we can at least judge them by the will and intentions with which they entered the *Sammath Naur*; and not demand impossible feats of will, which could only happen in stories unconcerned with real moral and mental probability. [*Letters*, p. 252]

In his draft letter to Eileen Elgar, September 1963, Tolkien argues at length that Frodo's failure was not *moral*, given that the power of the Ring had become impossible for anyone to resist, especially 'after long possession, months of increasing torment, and when starved and exhausted'. Moreover, 'Frodo had done what he could and spent himself completely (as an instrument of Providence) and had produced a situation in which the object of his quest could be achieved. His humility (with which he began) and his sufferings were justly rewarded by the highest honour; and his exercise of patience and mercy towards Gollum gained him Mercy: his failure was redressed.' A *moral* failure, Tolkien said, 'can only be asserted

. . . when a man's effort or endurance falls *short* of his limits, and the blame decreases as that limit is approached'. Frodo's quest was undertaken out of love, and his pledge no more than 'to do what he could, to try to find a way, and to go as far on the road as his strength of mind and body allowed. He did that. I do not myself see that the breaking of his mind and will under demonic pressure after torment was any more a *moral* failure than the breaking of his body would have been – say, by being strangled by Gollum, or crushed by a falling rock' (*Letters*, pp. 326–7).

In his draft letter to Michael Straight, ?end of 1955, Tolkien comments that both the world and Frodo himself were saved by the pity and forgiveness he had shown to Gollum.

> To 'pity' him [Gollum], to forbear to kill him, was a piece of folly, or a mystical belief in the ultimate value-in-itself of pity and generosity even if disastrous in the world of time. He did rob him and injure him in the end – but by a 'grace', that last betrayal was at a precise juncture when the final evil deed was the most beneficial thing any one c[oul]d have done for Frodo! [*Letters*, p. 234]

Katharyn W. Crabbe points out that

> the insidiousness of evil makes Tolkien's version of the sacrificing hero even more poignant and moving than its archetype. Frodo's danger is not simply a danger to his physical life, with the assurance of a reward in another world; he risks his spiritual life as well, for the very proximity to the Ring that will allow him to save the world threatens to make of him the source of its destruction. That is, on the edges of the cracks of doom the Ring succeeds in making of Frodo a hobbit Sauron. He claims the Ring, and it is taken from him as it was taken from Sauron at the end of the Second Age, by the severing of his finger.
>
> This pairing of Frodo with Sauron not only suggests the dual nature of man, it also suggests just how close Frodo has come to becoming the enemy he has offered his life to defeat. The ultimate defeat, then, in *The Lord of the Rings* is not simply to lose the battle with evil, but to become incorporated into it. [*J.R.R. Tolkien*, rev. edn., p. 87]

946 (III: 223–4): Sam got up

946 (III: 223). Gollum on the edge of the abyss was fighting like a mad thing with an unseen foe. – It is not explained how Gollum was able to find his foe while Frodo was invisible. Readers have suggested, among other solutions, that he did so by means of a keen sense of hearing or smell, or by sensing the presence of the Ring, having become attuned to it through long years of possession; or that Frodo cast a shadow, as Bilbo did while wearing the Ring in *The Hobbit*, Chapter 5; or that Gollum found Frodo by sheer chance. Chance, however, would seem to be ruled out by Tolkien's comment to Amy Ronald on 27 July 1956, that at the point when

Frodo's will failed and he claimed the Ring, 'the Other Power then took over: the Writer of the Story (by which I do not mean myself)', i.e. God (*Letters*, p. 253).

946 (III: 224): 'Precious, precious, precious!'

946 (III: 224). he stepped too far, toppled, wavered for a moment on the brink, and then with a shriek he fell – Thus does Frodo's prediction earlier in the chapter come true ('If you touch me ever again, you shall be cast yourself into the Fire of Doom', p. 944, III: 221).

946 (III: 224). *Precious* – As first published, Gollum's wail was spelt '*precious*'. It was revised to capitalized '*Precious*', thus indicating the Ring rather than Gollum himself (see note for p. 11), in the second printing (1967) of the Allen & Unwin second edition.

947 (III: 224): 'Well, this is the end

947 (III: 224). this is the end – According to *Scheme*: 'About noon (or after?) Ring destroyed and Barad-dûr crumbles in ruin. Nazgûl flying back in last effort are caught in eruption and burned. End of the reign of Sauron; and nothing is left of his power.'

947 (III: 224). in his eyes there was peace now – Tolkien wrote in his draft letter to Eileen Elgar, September 1963, that Frodo 'appears at first to have had no sense of guilt (III 224–5); he was restored to *sanity* and peace. But then he thought that he had given his life in sacrifice: he expected to die very soon. But he did not, and one can observe the disquiet growing in him' (*Letters*, p. 327).

Chapter 4

THE FIELD OF CORMALLEN

For drafts and history of this chapter, see *Sauron Defeated*, pp. 44–53.

948 (III: 226): There came Gwaihir the Windlord

948 (III: 226). Gwaihir the Windlord, and Landroval his brother, greatest of all the Eagles of the North, mightiest of the descendants of old Thorondor, who built his eyries in the inaccessible peaks of the Encircling Mountains when Middle-earth was young – In Tolkien's *Quenta Silmarillion* text written in 1937 Gwaewar and Lhandroval ('wide-wing'), led by Thorondor ('king of eagles', from Sindarin *thoron* 'eagle' + *-dor* 'lord'), rescue Beren and Lúthien after they escape from Angband with a Silmaril. *Gwaewar* was later revised to *Gwaihir*, as also occurred with the Gwaihir of *The Lord of the Rings*. In *Sauron Defeated* Christopher Tolkien comments that he suppressed the names *Gwaihir* and *Landroval*

> in the published *Silmarillion* (p. 182) on account of the present passage in [*The Return of the King*], but this was certainly mistaken: it is clear that my father deliberately repeated the names. As in so many other cases in *The Lord of the Rings*, he took the name *Gwaewar* for the great eagle, friend of Gandalf, from *The Silmarillion*, and when *Gwaihir* replaced *Gwaewar* in *The Lord of the Rings*, he made the same change to the eagle's name in *The Silmarillion*. Now he took also *Lhandroval* [thus in the draft for Book VI, Chapter 4] to be the name of Gwaihir's brother; and added a new name *Meneldor*. . . . [p. 45]

In *The Silmarillion* Thorondor is described as 'mightiest of all birds that have ever been, whose outstretched wings spanned thirty fathoms' (p. 110).

The *Encircling Mountains* are the Eryd Echor, the mountains 'about Gondolin in the lost land of B[eleriand]' (*Index*).

948 (III: 226). vassals – Here, in a more general sense, followers, subjects.

948 (III: 226–7): Then all the Captains of the West

948 (III: 226). close-serried – Close together, shoulder to shoulder.

949 (III: 227): 'The realm of Sauron

949 (III: 227). a huge shape of shadow. . . . Enormous it reared above the world, and stretched out towards them a vast threatening hand – In a design for a dust-jacket for *The Return of the King* Tolkien drew in the background, behind the throne of Gondor and a stylized White Tree, the Shadow of Mordor given gigantic form as a long arm reaching out across red and black mountains, at its end a clawed hand. See *Artist and Illustrator*, fig. 182.

Hugh Brogan, in 'Tolkien's Great War', *Children and Their Books: A Celebration of the Work of Iona and Peter Opie* (1989), compares Tolkien's description of the shadow of Sauron with that of a First World War shell-burst as written by Siegfried Sassoon in *Memoirs of a Fox-hunting Man*: 'Against the clear morning sky a cloud of dark smoke expands and drifts away. Slowly its dingy wrestling vapours take the form of a hooded giant with clumsy expostulating arms. Then, with a gradual gesture of acquiescence, it lolls sideways, falling over into the attitude of a swimmer on his side. And so it dissolves into nothingness.' Brogan comments: 'The similarities between these passages cannot be coincidental. . . . It is possible that Tolkien used Sassoon's description as a model, but it is surely much likelier that he, as well as Sassoon, could remember what a shell-burst looked like, and exploit it for literary purposes' (pp. 353–4).

949 (III: 227). a great wind took it, and it was all blown away – In 1987 a Tolkien discussion group observed 'that Sauron's "shadow" is dissipated by wind, . . . the province of Manwë', with whom also are associated the Great Eagles (*Rómenna Meeting Report*, 29 March 1987, p. 5; see also notes for p. 261, above, and p. 1020).

949 (III: 227): The Captains bowed their heads

949 (III: 227). As when death smites the swollen brooding thing that inhabits their crawling hill and holds them all in sway, ants will wander witless and purposeless – The 'swollen brooding thing' in this context is the queen ant. Some readers have compared this passage to the elaborate similes often found in Homer. In his letter to Milton Waldman, ?late 1951, Tolkien used a comparable phrase, 'like termites with a dead queen' (*Waldman LR*).

949 (III: 227–8): 'Twice you have borne me

949 (III: 227). Twice you have borne me – Gandalf names one of these occasions, when he flew from Zirakzigil to Lothlórien; the other must be when Gwaihir rescued Gandalf from Orthanc. This would appear to preclude Gwaihir being the Lord of the Eagles (later King of All Birds) who rescues Gandalf in Chapter 6 of *The Hobbit* and later took part in the Battle of Five Armies, but some have argued that Gandalf may have been miscounting. Anders Stenström (Beregond) has discussed the question at length in 'Is Gwaihir to Be Identified with the Lord of the Eagles and the King of All Birds?', *Beyond Bree*, April and May 1987; both he and Douglas A. Anderson in *The Annotated Hobbit* (2nd edn.) reject the identification.

Many readers have asked why the Council of Elrond did not simply give the Ring to Gwaihir to drop into the crater of Orodruin. Apart from the fact that there would then be no story, Tolkien wrote to Forrest J.

Ackerman in June 1958: 'The Eagles are a dangerous "machine". I have used them sparingly, and that is the absolute limit of their credibility or usefulness' (*Letters*, p. 271).

950 (III: 228): 'The North Wind blows

950 (III: 228). Meneldor – A Sindarin name, presumably 'lord of the sky', from *menel* 'firmament, heavens' + *-dor* 'lord'.

951 (III: 229): When Sam awoke

951 (III: 229). When Sam awoke – It is 8 April 1419.

951 (III: 229): He remembered that smell

951 (III: 229). third finger – The third finger from the thumb, also called the ring finger.

952 (III: 230): 'The fourteenth of the New Year

952 (III: 230). The fourteenth of the New Year . . . or . . . the eighth day of April in the Shire-reckoning . . . in Gondor the New Year will always now begin upon the twenty-fifth of March when Sauron fell – Frodo and Sam have slept for fourteen days. Since in the Shire Reckoning March has thirty days, it is now 8 April.

In *The Road to Middle-earth* Tom Shippey comments that 'in Anglo-Saxon belief, and in European popular tradition both before and after that, 25 March is the date of the Crucifixion; also of the Annunciation (nine months before Christmas); also of the last day of Creation' (p. 181), all asserted in *Byrhtferth's Manual*, written by Byrhtferth, a monk of Ramsey, *c*. 970–*c* 1020. From the latter part of the twelfth century the feast of the Annunciation, 'Lady Day', 25 March, was the beginning of the year for most purposes in England. It remained so, for legal and official purposes, until the reform of the calendar in 1751.

952 (III: 230): 'The clothes that you wore

952 (III: 230). 'The clothes that you wore on your way to Mordor,' said Gandalf. 'Even the orc-rags that you bore in the black land, Frodo, shall be preserved. No silks and linens, nor any armour or heraldry could be more honourable. But later I will find some other clothes, perhaps.' – As first published this passage read: '"The clothes that you journeyed in," said Gandalf. "No silks and linens, nor any armour or heraldry could be more honourable. But later we shall see."' It was revised in the second edition (1965), though Ballantine Books at first misprinted 'silks or linens' for 'silks and linens'.

952 (III: 230–1): Then he held out his hands

952 (III: 230–1). Then he held out his hands to them, and they saw that one shone with light. 'What have you got there?' Frodo cried. 'Can it

be—?' [*paragraph:*] **'Yes, I have brought your two treasures. They were found on Sam when you were rescued, the Lady Galadriel's gifts: your glass, Frodo, and your box, Sam. You will be glad to have these safe again.'** – These two paragraphs were added in the second edition (1965). Ballantine Books misprinted 'Light' for 'light' and 'Galadnil's' for 'Galadriel's', and erroneously divided the sentence 'They were found . . .' into two. The first two errors were corrected in the Allen & Unwin second edition (1966); the third was not completely corrected until the edition of 2004, having been variously punctuated in the interim.

953 (III: 231): As they came to the opening

953 (III: 231). a long wooded isle – Cair Andros.

953 (III: 231): *'Long live the Halflings!*

953 (III: 231). *Long live the Halflings! Praise them with great praise! / Cuio i Pheriain anann! Aglar'ni Pheriannath!* . . . – Tolkien wrote to Rhona Beare on 8 June 1961 in regard to these phrases:

> The second, fourth and sixth lines are Sindarin or Grey Elvish. The seventh and ninth are High Elvish. Line 2 [*Cuio i Pheriain anann! Aglar'ni Pheriannath!*] means 'May the Halflings live long, glory to the Halflings.' The fourth line [*Daur a Berhael, Conin en Annûn! Eglerio!*] means 'Frodo and Sam, princes of the west, glorify (them)', the sixth [*Eglerio!*], 'glorify (them)'. The seventh line [*A laita te, laita te! Andave laituvalmet!*] means 'Bless them, bless them, long will we praise them.' The ninth line [*Cormacolindor, a laita tárienna!*] means 'The Ring bearers, bless (or praise) them to the height.' [*Letters*, p. 308]

In his letter to Milton Waldman, ?late 1951, he wrote:

> In the scene where all the hosts of the West unite to do honour and praise to the two humble Hobbits, Frodo and Sam, we reach the 'eucatastrophe' of the whole romance: that is the sudden joyous 'turn' and fulfilment of hope, the opposite of tragedy, that should be the hallmark of a 'fairy-story' of higher or lower tone, the resolution and justification of all that has gone before. It brought tears to my eyes to write it, and still moves me, and I cannot help believing that it is a supreme moment of its kind. [*Waldman LR*]

Christopher Tolkien notes that earlier forms of the praise differed considerably from that published, and included Old English as well as Sindarin and Quenya. The final form was typed onto the galley proof, replacing: '*Long live the Halflings! Praise them with great praise! Cuio i Pheriannath anann! Aglar anann! Praise them with great praise! Wilcuman, wilcuman, Fróda and Samwís! Praise them! Uton herian holbytlan! A laita te, laita te! Andave laituvalmet! Praise them! The Ringbearers, praise them with great praise!*' (*Sauron Defeated*, p. 47).

954 (III: 232–3): Frodo and Sam were led apart

954 (III: 233). the soils and hurts that it had suffered; and then he laid before them two swords. . . . And when they were arrayed they went to the great feast; and they sat at the King's table with Gandalf – As first published this passage read: 'the soils and hurts that it had suffered; and when the hobbits were made ready, and circlets of silver were set upon their heads, they went to the King's feast, and they sat at his table with Gandalf'. It was revised in the second edition (1965), introducing several lines of dialogue in which Frodo agrees to wear a sword though he does not wish to do so.

Nancy Martsch suggests in 'Frodo's Failure', *Beyond Bree*, June 1997, that Frodo may not have wanted to wear a sword because he felt that he had failed: 'The sword was a badge of honour among Men, the emblem of a successful warrior. Frodo probably felt that he did not merit such an honour' (p. 4). But Frodo had said, not long after escaping from Cirith Ungol: 'I do not think it will be my part to strike any blow again' (Book VI, Chapter 2, p. 926, III: 204). Nor does he, even in the battle with the ruffians in Book VI, Chapter 8.

955 (III: 233): But when, after the Standing Silence

955 (III: 233). after the Standing Silence – These words were added in the second edition (1965). Compare, in Book IV, Chapter 5: 'Before they ate, Faramir and all his men turned and faced west in a moment of silence' (p. 676, II: 284).

955 (III: 233): At last the glad day ended

955 (III: 233). the round Moon rose slowly – It is the night of 8/9 April. The moon had been full the previous night.

956 (III: 234): 'And not only Sam and Frodo

956 (III: 234). I made sure you were dead – That is, he was convinced that Pippin was dead.

956 (III: 234–5): *To the Sea, to the Sea!*

956 (III: 235). *the Last Shore* – 'The Shores of Elvenhome, beyond the G[rea]t Sea' (*Index*).

956 (III: 235). *in the Lost Isle calling, in Eressëa* – The *Lost Isle* is another name for Eressëa; see note for p. 244.

957 (III: 235): Then the others also departed

957 (III: 235). Field of Cormallen – In his unfinished index Tolkien defines *Cormallen* ('golden circle', from Sindarin *cor* 'ring' + *mallen* 'golden') as 'a region in Ithilien (originally called after the laburnum that grew there)', and *Field of Cormallen* as 'a mead in C[ormallen] in Ithilien not far from east b[ank] of Anduin, opposite Cair Andros, where the rejoicings at the Victory were held S.R. 1419'. *Index* also includes an entry for a word which does not appear in *The Lord of the Rings* but is evidently meant as a source of the name *Cormallen*: '*culumalda*: a tree with hanging yellow blossoms (prob[ably] a laburnum) growing in Ithilien espec[ially] at *Cormallen*'.

957 (III: 235): But at last when the month of May

957 (III: 235). they sailed from Cair Andros – According to *Scheme*:

April 27: Captains set sail from Cair Andros.
April 28: Victorious host reaches Osgiliath.
April 30: Host camps in the Pelennor.

Chapter 5

THE STEWARD AND THE KING

For drafts and history of this chapter, see *Sauron Defeated*, pp. 54–60.

958 (III: 236): When the Captains

958 (III: 236). When the Captains were but two days gone – It is 20 March 1419.

958 (III: 236): 'Lady,' he answered

958 (III: 236). You should not have risen from your bed for seven days yet – On 15 March Aragorn told the Warden that Éowyn should not be permitted from rising 'until at least ten days be passed' (Book V, Chapter 8, p. 870, III: 147). Five days have passed since then, leaving five more under Aragorn's prescription, not *seven* as the Warden says here. Perhaps he is taking Aragorn's 'at least' to heart and adding two days.

958 (III: 236): 'There are no tidings'

958 (III: 236). rents – In this context, wounds made by *rending* with blades.

959 (III: 237): The Warden looked at her

959 (III: 237). her right hand clenched – As originally written and set in type, these words read: 'her left hand clenched'. Tolkien recorded an emendation, 'left hand' changed to 'right hand' (because Éowyn's left arm, her shield arm, had been broken in the battle), on the galley proof of *The Return of the King* (Marquette Series 3/9/29), but evidently in attempting to make the change the typesetters deleted 'left' without inserting 'right'. 'Her hand' was corrected to 'her right hand' in the edition of 2005.

959 (III: 237): 'I do not rightly know'

959 (III: 237). There is a marshal over the Riders of Rohan – As first published, the word 'marshal' here read 'captain'. It was altered in the second edition (1965).

961 (III: 239): 'Alas, not me, lord!'

961 (III: 239). she did him a courtesy – Expressed respect through an action or gesture.

961 (III: 239): But in the morning

961 (III: 239). But in the morning – It is 21 March.

961 (III: 239): And so the fifth day

961 (III: 239). the fifth day came since the lady Éowyn went first to Faramir – It is now 25 March.

961 (III: 239–40): They were clad in warm raiment

961 (III: 239–40). his mother, Finduilas of Amroth, who died untimely – Finduilas was born in Third Age 2950 and died in 2988; Boromir had been born in 2978, and Faramir only in 2983. In Appendix A it is said that Denethor

> married late (2976), taking to wife Finduilas, daughter of Adrahil of Dol Amroth. She was a lady of great beauty and gentle heart, but before twelve years had passed she died. Denethor loved her, in his fashion, more dearly than any other. . . . But it seemed to men that she withered in the guarded city, as a flower of the seaward vales set upon a barren rock. The shadow in the east filled her with horror, and she turned her eyes ever south to the sea that she missed. [p. 1056, III: 336]

A *Finduilas* also figures in Tolkien's tales of the First Age, the daughter of Orodreth, loved by Gwindor. She was captured in the sack of Nargothrond and killed by Orcs at the Crossings of Teiglin. In drafts of *The Lord of the Rings* the name was first given to Elrond's daughter (later *Arwen*).

962 (III: 240): And as they stood so

962 (III: 240). it seemed to them that above the ridges of the distant mountains another vast mountain of darkness rose, towering like a wave that should engulf the world, and about it lightnings flickered; and then a tremor ran through the earth, and they felt the walls of the City quiver – The description here, and that of the scene witnessed by Frodo and Sam from Mount Doom in Book VI, Chapter 3 (p. 947, III: 224: 'Towers fell and mountains slid; walls crumbled and melted, crashing down; vast spires of smoke and spouting steams went billowing up, up, until they toppled like an overwhelming wave, and its wild crest curled and came foaming down upon the land . . . the earth shook, the plain heaved and cracked. . . . The skies burst into thunder seared with lightning'), recall the destruction of Númenor as described in the *Akallabêth*: 'Then suddenly fire burst from the Meneltarma, and there came a mighty wind and a tumult of the earth, and the sky reeled, and the hills slid, and Númenor went down into the sea. . . . And last of all the mounting wave, green and cold and plumed with foam, climbing over the land . . .' (*The Silmarillion*, p. 279). Since Númenor was destroyed in response to its king's attempted invasion of Aman, at the instigation of Sauron, it is only fitting that more than an Age later Sauron's own realm should be destroyed in a similar manner.

962 (III: 240): 'Yes,' said Faramir

962 (III: 240). the great dark wave climbing over the green lands and above the hills, and coming on, darkness unescapable. I often dream of it. – In his draft letter to Mr Thompson, 14 January 1956, Tolkien says that 'when Faramir speaks of his private vision of the Great Wave, he speaks for me. That vision and dream has been ever with me' (*Letters*, p. 232). On 7 June 1955 he wrote to W.H. Auden:

> I have what some might call an Atlantis complex. Possibly inherited, though my parents died too young for me to know such things about them, and too young to transfer such things by words. Inherited from me (I suppose) by one only of my children [Michael], though I did not know that about my son until recently, and he did not know it about me. I mean the terrible recurrent dream (beginning with memory) of the Great Wave, towering up, and coming in ineluctably over the trees and green fields. (I bequeathed it to Faramir.) I don't think I have had it since I wrote the 'Downfall of Númenor' as the last of the legends of the First and Second Age. [*Letters*, p. 213]

963 (III: 241): And so they stood on the walls

963 (III: 241). And the Shadow departed, and the Sun was unveiled, and light leaped forth; and the waters of Anduin shone like silver, and in all the houses of the City men sang for the joy that welled up in their hearts from what source they could not tell. – In *On Fairy-Stories* Tolkien writes of *eucatastrophe*, 'the Consolation of the Happy Ending' or 'the sudden joyous "turn"' provided in many fairy-stories that is 'a sudden and miraculous grace . . . it denies . . . universal final defeat and in so far is *evangelium*, giving a fleeting glimpse of Joy, Joy beyond the Walls of the World, poignant as grief' (*Tree and Leaf*, p. 62). In *The Lord of the Rings* the 'turn' is spread over two chapters, concentrating in Book VI, Chapter 4 on Frodo and Sam ('all my wishes have come true', p. 954, III: 232), and now in the present chapter with a wider focus.

In 'Goldberry and Galadriel: The Quality of Joy', *Mythlore* 16, no. 2, whole no. 60 (Winter 1989), L. Eugene Startzman notes that in the passages immediately preceding the Eagle's song

> the language describing the threat and the change is biblical and apocalyptic: earthquake and lightning accompany the "vast mountain of darkness"; the use of the coordinate conjunction *and* to join together a series of primarily independent clauses suggests the narrative style of the King James translation. The effect is to celebrate and further ground that joy which we experience in the turn of the story in the very structure of the universe. That is, Sun and Stars are always there behind the Darkness; they are permanent, and have their ultimate origin in the Flame Imperishable of Ilúvatar. . . .

> [The language of *The Return of the King*] conveys the real nature of the joy experienced in the Ringbearer's victory. The Sun, for example, doesn't just emerge from behind the clouds: it is 'unveiled,' and the style suggests that the departure of the Shadow is not necessarily the cause. The coordinate conjunctions separate and emphasize each action: 'And the Shadow departed, and the Sun was unveiled, and light leaped forth; . . .' The semicolon after *forth* allows a brief pause between the vigorous action of the light and its immediate consequences, thus giving final emphasis to the meaning of the light: 'and the waters of Anduin shone like silver, and in all the houses of the City men sang for the joy that welled up in their hearts from what source they could not tell.' The effect on the water is connected to the effect on the people because the joy 'welled up' as if from some underground, hidden source, which is exactly what joy (and the Sun in the third volume) has been throughout the story – hidden because of the menace of darkness and despair. . . . [pp. 11–12]

963 (III: 241): And before the Sun had fallen

963 (III: 241). And before the Sun had fallen . . . – A recording by Tolkien from these words to the sentence following the poem ('And the people sang in all the ways of the City') is included on Disc 2 of *The J.R.R. Tolkien Audio Collection.*

963 (III: 241). he bore tidings beyond hope from the Lords of the West – Thus the Eagle seems to have been sent by the Valar, the Authorities or Powers in Aman, whose title *Lords of the West* is established in the *Akallabêth.*

963 (III: 241). ***Sing now, ye people of the Tower of Anor . . .*** – Tom Shippey comments in *The Road to Middle-earth* concerning the Eagle's message:

> There is no doubt here about Tolkien's stylistic model, which is the Bible and particularly the Psalms. The use of 'ye' and 'hath' is enough to indicate that to most English readers, familiar with those words only from the Authorised Version. But 'Sing and rejoice' echoes Psalm 33, 'Rejoice in the Lord', while the whole of the poem is strongly reminiscent of Psalm 24, 'Lift up your heads, O ye gates, and be ye lift up, ye everlasting doors for the King of glory shall come in.' 'Who is the King of glory?' asks the Psalm, and one traditional answer is Christ, crucified but not yet ascended, come to the city of Hell to rescue from it those especially virtuous pre-Christians. . . . Of course the eagle's song is *not about that.* When it says 'the Black Gate is broken' it means the Morannon . . . and when it says 'your King shall come again', it means Aragorn. Yet the first statement could very *easily* apply to Death and Hell (Matthew xvi, 18 'and the gates of hell shall not prevail'), the second to Christ and the Second Coming. [2nd edn., pp. 180–1]

963–4 (III: 241–2): The days that followed were golden

963 (III: 241). and Spring and Summer joined and made revel together – Tolkien wrote to Forrest J. Ackerman in May–June 1958: '*Seasons* are carefully regarded in [*The Lord of the Rings*]. . . . The main action begins in autumn and passes through winter to a brilliant spring: this is basic to the purport and tone of the tale' (*Letters*, pp. 271–2)

964 (III: 242): 'Then if you will have it so

964 (III: 242). you do not go, because only your brother called for you. . . . Or because I do not go . . . . And maybe for both these reasons, and you yourself cannot choose between them. Éowyn, do you not love me, or will you not? – In his meetings with Frodo and Sam in Book IV Faramir is shown to be a shrewd judge of character and of circumstances. Here he makes a fairly accurate assessment of Éowyn's feelings, which to her are still confused. He forces the issue with the question: do you really feel nothing for me, or do you refuse to acknowledge what you feel?

964 (III: 242): 'That I know,' he said

964 (III: 242). puissant – Having great power, authority.

964 (III: 243): Then the heart of Éowyn changed

964 (III: 243). Then the heart of Éowyn changed, or else at last she understood it. – Tolkien drafted a reply *c.* 1963 to an unnamed correspondent concerning Faramir and Éowyn:

> It is possible to love more than one person (of the other sex) at the same time, but in a different mode and intensity. I do not think that Eowyn's feelings for Aragorn really changed much; and when he was revealed as so lofty a figure, in descent and office, she was able to go on *loving* and admiring him. He was *old*, and that is not only a physical quality: when not accompanied by any physical decay age can be alarming or awe-inspiring. Also she was *not* herself ambitious in the true political sense. Though not a 'dry nurse' in temper, she was also not really a soldier or 'amazon', but like many brave women was capable of great military gallantry at a crisis. . . .
>
> [Regarding] criticism of the speed of the relationship or 'love' of Faramir and Eowyn. In my experience feelings and decisions ripen very quickly (as measured by mere 'clock-time', which is actually not justly applicable) in periods of great stress, and especially under the expectation of imminent death. And I do *not* think that persons of high estate and breeding need all the petty fencing and approaches in matters of 'love'. This tale does not deal with a period of 'Courtly Love' and its pretences; but with a culture more primitive (sc. less corrupt) and nobler. [*Letters*, pp. 323–4]

Some critics have objected to Éowyn's acceptance of a 'domestic' role as Faramir's wife; but her role would have been no different had she married Aragorn, as she had earlier hoped. Her change of heart most especially reflects Tolkien's belief that conflict and battle should not be exalted, but embraced only at need. Éowyn turns from the more martial ethos of the Rohirrim to the higher ideals described by Faramir (p. 679, II: 287), in which craft and skill are more valued than prowess at war.

965–6 (III: 243–4): At last an evening came

965 (III: 243). an evening came – The evening of 30 April.

965 (III: 244). the sun rose in the clear morning – The morning of 1 May.

966 (III: 244). argent – Silvery white.

966 (III: 244): So now there was a wide space

966 (III: 244). but his head was bare save for a star upon his forehead bound by a slender fillet of silver – As first published this passage read: 'but his head was bare'. It was extended in the second edition (1965). See note for p. 848.

A *fillet* is a narrow band worn around the head as an ornament.

966 (III: 244): 'Nay, cousin!

966 (III: 244). Those are *Periain* – As first published this phrase read: 'They are Periannath'. It was revised in the second printing (1967) of the Allen & Unwin second edition.

966 (III: 244). the Black Country – 'Common Speech translation of *Mordor*' (*Nomenclature*).

967 (III: 245): Faramir met Aragorn

967 (III: 245). Faramir met Aragorn in the midst of those there assembled . . . – The ceremony includes elements of an English coronation: the presentation of the monarch to those assembled for their recognition, acceptance and acclamation, and an oath taken by the monarch to uphold Law and Justice.

967 (III: 245): Then Faramir stood up

967 (III: 245). chieftain of the Dúnedain of Arnor, Captain of the Host of the West, bearer of the Star of the North, wielder of the Sword Reforged – As first published this passage read: 'chieftain of the Dúnedain of the North, Captain of the Host of the West, wielder of the Sword Reforged'.

967 (III: 245): Then the Guards stepped forward

967 (III: 245). held up an ancient crown – It is said in Appendix A that

> the crown of Gondor was derived from the form of a Númenórean war-helm. In the beginning it was indeed a plain helm; and it is said to have been the one that Isildur wore in the Battle of Dagorlad (for the helm of Anárion was crushed by the stone-cast from Barad-dûr that slew him). But in the days of Atanatar Alcarin this was replaced by the jewelled helm used in the crowning of Aragorn. [p.1043, III: 323]

Tolkien wrote on 14 October 1958 to Rhona Beare: 'I think the crown of Gondor (the S[outh] Kingdom) was very tall, like that of Egypt, but with wings attached, not set straight back but at an angle. The N[orth] Kingdom had only a *diadem* (III 323). Cf. the difference between the N[orth] and S[outh] kingdoms of Egypt' (*Letters*, p. 281). Here he illustrates the crown of Gondor, clearly based on the White Crown of Upper or Southern Egypt.

967 (III: 245). emblem of kings who came over the Sea – See note for p. 597.

967 (III: 245): Then Aragorn took the crown

967 (III: 245). *Et Eärello Endorenna utúlien. Sinome maruvan ar Hildinyar tenn' Ambar-metta!* – Tolkien translates this Quenya passage in the following paragraph: 'Out of the Great Sea. . . .'

968 (III: 246): 'Now come the days of the King

968 (III: 246). and may they be blessed while the thrones of the Valar endure! – As first published this passage read only: 'and may they be blessed!' It was extended in the second edition (1965). This is a rare reference to the Valar in *The Lord of the Rings*, appropriately made by their envoy, Gandalf (see note for p. 48). In *The Silmarillion* it is said that when Yavanna sang the Two Trees into being, the Valar 'sat silent upon their thrones of council in the Máhanaxar, the Ring of Doom near to the golden gates of Valmar' (p. 38).

968 (III: 246): But when Aragorn arose

968 (III: 246). ancient of days he seemed and yet in the flower of manhood – That is, in manner Aragorn displayed a maturity of long years, but in appearance was young and vigorous. He was born on 1 March 2931; at this point in the story it is 1 May 3019, so Aragorn has not long passed his 88th birthday, and he will not lay down his life until the age of 210.

According to *The Tale of Years* Elrond and Arwen set out from Rivendell on 1 May, the day that Aragorn fulfils the condition set by Elrond ('Arwen Undómiel . . . shall not be the bride of any Man less than the King of both Gondor and Arnor', p. 1016, III: 342). How they knew when to set out is not explained. They will reach Lothlórien on 20 May. The escort of Arwen will leave Lórien on 27 May, and on 14 June will be met by the sons of Elrond and reach Edoras.

968 (III: 246–7): In the days that followed

968 (III: 246). the Hall of Kings – The hall in which Denethor received Gandalf and Pippin.

968 (III: 247). And the King pardoned the Easterlings that had given themselves up, and sent them away free, and he made peace with the peoples of Harad; and the slaves of Mordor he released and gave them all the lands about Lake Núrnen to be their own. – Aragorn deals mercifully and justly with those who surrender and are willing to make peace. It is a telling contrast with the terms demanded by the Mouth of Sauron: cessation of land, tribute, disarmament, and under the eye of an alien governor.

Tolkien commented to Charlotte and Denis Plimmer that *The Lord of the Rings* 'ends in what is far more like the re-establishment of an effective Holy Roman Empire with its seat in Rome than anything that would be devised by a "Nordic"' (8 February 1967, *Letters*, p. 376).

969 (III: 247): 'So it must be

969 (III: 247). Prince of Ithilien – In Appendix A Faramir is called 'Lord of Emyn Arnen' (p. 1039, III: 319). The first Steward, Húrin, was of that land.

969 (III: 247): And then Beregond

969 (III: 247). Aragorn gave to Faramir Ithilien to be his princedom – In a draft letter of *c.* 1963, in reply to criticism of his treatment of Faramir, Tolkien wrote that

> to be Prince of Ithilien, the greatest noble after Dol Amroth in the revived Númenórean state of Gondor, soon to be of imperial power and prestige, was not a 'market-garden job' as you term it. Until much had been done by the restored King, the P[rince] of Ithilien would be the resident march-warden of Gondor, in its main eastward outpost – and also would have many duties in rehabilitating the lost territory, and clearing it of outlaws and orc-remnants, not to speak of the dreadful vale of Minas Ithil (Morgul). I did not, naturally, go into details about the way in which Aragorn, as King of Gondor, would govern the realm. But it was made clear that there was much fighting, and in the earlier years of A[ragorn]'s reign expeditions against enemies in the East. The chief commanders, under the King, would be Faramir and Imrahil; and one of these would normally remain a military commander at home in the King's absence. A Númenórean King was *monarch*, with the power of unquestioned decision in debate; but he governed the realm with the frame of ancient law, of which he was administrator (and interpreter)

but not the maker. In all debatable matters of importance domestic, or external, however, even Denethor had a Council, and at least listened to what the Lords of the Fiefs and the Captains of the Forces had to say. Aragorn re-established the Great Council of Gondor, and in that Faramir, who remained by inheritance the *Steward* (or representative) of the King during his absence abroad, or sickness, or between his death and the accession of his heir) would [be] the chief counsellor. [*Letters*, pp. 323–4]

969–70 (III: 248): So the glad days passed

969 (III: 248). the North-way – 'The Road from the Gate to the Rammas to join the West Road' (*Index*).

969–70 (III: 248). with them went the sons of Elrond – Evidently to meet their father and sister at Edoras, as revealed in *The Tale of Years*.

970 (III: 248): In those days the Companions

970 (III: 248). In those days the Companions of the Ring dwelt together in a fair house with Gandalf, and they went to and fro as they wished. – In *Sauron Defeated* Christopher Tolkien notes that the reading in the draft manuscript at this point is 'the Companions of the Ring lived with Gandalf in a house in the Citadel, and went to and fro as they wished; but Legolas sat most[ly] on the walls and looked south towards the sea', but 'that the house was in the Citadel is not repeated in [the fair copy], which retained however the words concerning Legolas; these were lost, possibly unintentionally in [the following manuscript]' (p. 57).

970–1 (III: 248–9): There came a day

970 (III: 248). There came a day – 25 June, according to *The Tale of Years*, but see note for p. 972.

970 (III: 249). it led up on to the mountain to a high hallow where only the kings had been wont to go. – See note for p. 676.

971 (III: 249): And Gandalf said

971 (III: 249). For though much has been saved, much must now pass away; and the power of the Three Rings also is ended. – This is the first mention of how the destruction of the One Ring has affected the Three. As the bearer of one of the Three, Gandalf knows that, as Elrond believed, with the passing of the One the Three have failed. This is also one of many references in the final chapters of the book to loss even in victory, contrary to the views of critics who have claimed that all ends 'happily'.

971 (III: 249). the time comes of the Dominion of Men, and the Elder Kindred shall fade or depart – Tolkien wrote to Milton Waldman in ?late 1951 that Men are 'Followers', after the Elves, the 'First-born'. 'The doom of the Elves is to be immortal, to love the beauty of the world, to bring it to full flower with their gifts of delicacy and perfection, to last while it lasts, never leaving it even when "slain", but returning – and yet, when the Followers come, to teach them, and make way for them, to "fade" as the Followers grow and absorb the life from which both proceed' (*Letters*, p. 147).

In *Nomenclature* Tolkien notes of *Elder Kindred* that 'in English the older [more archaic] form *elder* implies both seniority and kinship'.

971 (III: 249): 'But I shall die'

971 (III: 249). though being what I am and of the race of the West unmingled – Rhona Beare evidently queried this statement, presumably pointing out that Arvedui, the last king of Arnor, had married Fíriel, daughter of King Ondoher of Gondor, among whose ancestors was Vidumavi, the non-Númenórean wife of King Valacar. Tolkien replied on 8 June 1961:

> With regard to Aragorn's boast, I think he was reckoning his ancestry through the paternal line for this purpose; but in any case I imagine that Númenóreans, before their knowledge dwindled, knew more about heredity than other people. To this of course they refer by the common symbol of blood. They recognized the fact that in spite of intermarriages, some characteristics would appear in pure form in later generations. Aragorn's own longevity was a case in point. Gandalf I think refers to the curious fact that even in the much less well preserved house of the stewards Denethor had come out as almost purely Númenórean. [*Letters*, p. 307]

971 (III: 249). I shall have life far longer than other men, yet that is but a little while; and when those who are now in the wombs of women are born and have grown old, I too shall grow old – On the page proofs of *The Return of the King* Tolkien changed 'I have still twice the span of other men' to the reading of the first edition: 'I may have life far longer than other men' (*Sauron Defeated*, p. 57). *The Tale of Years* in the first edition gives Aragorn's death date as Shire Reckoning 1521; in the second edition (Ballantine Books, 1965) Tolkien changed this to Shire Reckoning *1541*, with a footnote that the year is equivalent to Fourth Age 120. Thus Aragorn now was said to live to be 210, exactly three times the biblical 'three-score years and ten'. In the Allen & Unwin second edition (1966) Tolkien made a further change to Aragorn's words to Gandalf, from 'I may' to 'I shall' (possibly omitted in error in the Ballantine edition). Since on p. 860 (III: 136) it is said that few in Gondor now 'passed the tale of five score years with vigour', the lengthening of Aragorn's life makes the rest of his statement less apt than it was in the first edition.

971 (III: 250): Then Aragorn cried

971 (III: 250). *Yé! utúvienyes!* – This Quenya phrase is immediately rendered in English: 'I have found it!'

971–2 (III: 250): And Gandalf coming looked at it

971 (III: 250). this is a sapling of the line of Nimloth the fair; and that was a seedling of Galathilion, and that a fruit of Telperion of many names, Eldest of Trees – *Telperion* (Quenya ?'silver-white') was the first of the Two Trees which came into being at the song of Yavanna and gave light to Valinor. In *The Silmarillion* it is described as having 'leaves of dark green that beneath were as shining silver' and flowers from which fell 'a dew of silver light'; and in addition to *Telperion* it was called 'Silpion, and Ninquelótë, and many other names' (p. 38). *Nimloth* was the White Tree of Númenor, which grew in the king's courts, of which a fruit was stolen by Isildur before Sauron prevailed on the king to destroy the tree. *Nimloth* ('white blossom' or 'white flower') is the Sindarin form of *Ninquelótë.*

Galathilion is a more complex problem. In 'Silmarillion' writings prior to *The Lord of the Rings* there is no mention of any sapling, fruit, memorial, or image of Telperion. In an early text of the *Akallabêth* as emended, it is said the Eldar 'brought to Númenor many gifts. . . . And a seedling they brought of the White Tree Galathilion that grew in the midst of Eressëa, and was in his turn a seedling of the Eldest Tree, Telperion of many names, the light of Valinor. And the tree grew and blossomed in the courts of the King. . . . Nimloth the fair it was named . . .' (*The Peoples of Middle-earth*, p. 147). This seems to be the history of the sapling discovered by Aragorn in the hallow, but Tolkien later emended the *Akallabêth* so that the Elves brought to Númenor a seedling 'of the White Tree that grew in the midst of Eressëa, and was in its turn a seedling of the Tree of Túna, Galathilion, that Yavanna gave to the Eldar in the Land of the Gods to be a memorial of Telperion. . . . Nimloth the Fair it was named' (p. 148). The Tree of Túna (Tirion), described as either an image or memorial of Telperion and given the name *Galathilion* previously given to the Tree of Eressëa, also appears in the *Annals of Aman* and additions to the *Quenta Silmarillion* which can be dated to 1951. This is the lineage which appears in the *Quenta Silmarillion* and the *Akallabêth*, as published in *The Silmarillion*: Telperion (Valinor) > Galathilion (Tirion/Túna) > Celeborn (Eressëa) > Nimloth (Númenor).

Christopher Tolkien discusses the various texts in *The Peoples of Middle-earth* (pp. 147–9) and concludes that the account in *The Lord of the Rings* 'agrees with the emended form of the passage in the first phase . . . of the *Akallabêth*: for Galathilion (as the parent of Nimloth) is here the Tree of Eressëa, there is no mention of the Tree of Túna, and Galathilion is a 'fruit' of Telperion (not an "image", or a "memorial"). The conclusion must be that this passage was not revised when the Tree of Túna entered the history' (pp. 148–9).

972 (III: 250): Then Aragorn laid his hand

972 (III: 250). and when the month of June entered in it was laden with blossom. [*paragraph:*] 'The sign has been given . . . and the day is not far off.' – Here the narrative cannot be reconciled with *The Tale of Years*. By itself, the former makes perfect sense: Aragorn finds the Tree in May, at some time after 8 May when the Riders of Rohan left Minas Tirith, and before 'the month of June entered in'; the Tree flowers around the beginning of June, evidently the 'sign' Aragorn refers to; and Arwen enters the City on 'the day before Midsummer' (this page). In that sequence the gap of time between the 'sign' and Arwen's arrival is four weeks, arguably 'not far off' to Aragorn, who has waited to marry Arwen for nearly forty years. But according to *The Tale of Years*, Aragorn did not find the Tree until 25 June, only six days before Arwen's arrival. If that date is correct, then 'when the month of June entered in' must be an error, the Tree blossoms in an impossibly short period of time, and Arwen appears at Minas Tirith almost before Aragorn sets his watchers on the walls.

972 (III: 250): It was the day before Midsummer

972 (III: 250). the day before Midsummer – It is 1 Lithe 1419. In the Shire Calendar there were three days between June and July: 1 Lithe, Mid-year's Day (Midsummer), and 2 Lithe.

972 (III: 250–1): Upon the very Eve

972 (III: 251). bearing the sceptre of Annúminas – These words were added only in page proof. In Appendix A (p. 1043, III: 323) it is said that

> the sceptre was the chief mark of royalty in Númenor . . . and that was also so in Arnor, whose kings wore no crown, but bore a single white gem, the Elendilmir, Star of Elendil, bound on their brows with a silver fillet. . . . In speaking of a crown . . . Bilbo [in the Red Book] no doubt referred to Gondor; he seems to have become well acquainted with matters concerning Aragorn's line. The sceptre of Númenor is said to have perished with Ar-Pharazôn. That of Annúminas was the silver rod of the Lords of Andúnië. . . . It was already more than five thousand years old when Elrond surrendered it to Aragorn. . . .

Elrond had withheld the sceptre when Aragorn on reaching manhood received other heirlooms of his house. 'The Sceptre of Annúminas I withhold,' Elrond said, 'for you have yet to earn it' (Appendix A, p. 1057, III: 338).

972 (III: 251). palfrey – 'A saddle-horse for ordinary riding as distinguished from a war-horse; especially a small saddle-horse for ladies' (*OED*).

972–3 (III: 251): Then the King welcomed

972 (III: 251). High City – 'The Citadel or 7th Circle of M[inas] T[irith]' (*Index*).

Chapter 6

MANY PARTINGS

For drafts and history of this chapter, see *Sauron Defeated*, pp. 61–74.

974 (III: 252). [chapter title] – The title 'Many Partings' is an intentional contrast to the title of the first chapter of Book II, 'Many Meetings'.

974 (III: 252): When the days of rejoicing

974 (III: 252). When the days of rejoicing were over – It is 15 July 1419.

974 (III: 252): 'Do you wonder at that

974 (III: 252). For you know the power of that thing which is now destroyed; and all that was done by that power is now passing away. But your kinsman possessed this thing longer than you. He is ancient in years now, according to his kind; and he awaits you, for he will not again make any long journey save one. – Among many other things, the power of the Ring gave Bilbo long life, and evidently continued to sustain him until the Ring was destroyed. Gollum, too, was sustained, for hundreds of years since the Ring came to him, and for nearly seventy years after losing it to Bilbo; and it seems clear from his words to Sam on Mount Doom ('when Precious goes we'll die, yes, die into the dust', p. 944, III: 221) that he is aware that his life depends upon the Ring surviving – he is far more 'ancient in years' than Bilbo – apart from his emotional ties to his 'Precious'.

Having given up the Ring, Bilbo had clearly aged by the time Frodo spoke with him at Rivendell before the Council of Elrond; and now his true physical age has caught up with him. The 'long journey' he will make is that which Frodo will share, into the West, as Arwen is about to offer; but the words also refer metaphorically to Bilbo's inevitable death.

974 (III: 252): 'In seven days we will go'

974 (III: 252). In three days now Éomer will return hither – In *Scheme* the following additional information is given, omitted from *The Tale of Years* possibly for reasons of space:

> Mid-year's Day: Aragorn and Arwen wed. That day and the [six > seven >] 14 following are made days of festival.
>
> July [6 > 14 >] 12: End of the festival [in fact, 2 Lithe plus 1–12 July = only 13 days].
>
> July [7 >] 15: Frodo begs leave of the King to depart.
>
> July [10 >] 18: Éomer returns from Rohan with picked body of Riders.

974–5 (III: 252–3): But the Queen Arwen said

974 (III: 252). A gift I will give you. For I am the daughter of Elrond. I shall not go with him now when he departs to the Havens; for mine is the choice of Lúthien. . . . But in my stead you shall go, Ring-bearer, when the time comes, and if you then desire it. If your hurts grieve you still and the memory of your burden is heavy, then you may pass into the West, until all your wounds and weariness are healed. – To this point in the narrative there has been no suggestion that Frodo could not be fully healed. In his draft letter to Eileen Elgar, September 1963, Tolkien wrote that Frodo

> appears at first to have had no sense of guilt . . . ; he was restored to *sanity* and peace. But . . . one can observe the disquiet growing in him. Arwen was the first to observe the signs, and gave him her jewel for comfort, and thought of a way of healing him. . . .
>
> It is not made explicit how she could arrange this. She could not of course just transfer her ticket on the boat like that! For any except those of Elvish race 'sailing west' was not permitted, and any exception required 'authority', and she was not in direct communication with the Valar, especially not since her choice to become 'mortal'. What is meant is that it was Arwen who first thought of sending Frodo into the West, and put in a plea for him to Gandalf (direct or through Galadriel, or both), and she used her own renunciation of the right to go West as an argument. Her renunciation and suffering were related to and enmeshed with Frodo's: both were parts of a plan for the regeneration of the state of Men. Her prayer might therefore be specially effective, and her plan have a certain equity of exchange. No doubt it was Gandalf who was the authority that accepted her plea. The Appendices show clearly that he was an emissary of the Valar, and virtually their plenipotentiary in accomplishing the plan against Sauron. He was also in special accord with Círdan the Ship-master, who had surrendered to him his ring and so placed himself under Gandalf's command. Since Gandalf himself went on the Ship there would be so to speak no trouble either at embarking or at the landing. [*Letters*, p. 327]

Tolkien comments later in the draft: 'It is clear, of course, that the plan had actually been made and concerted (by Arwen, Gandalf and others) before Arwen spoke. But Frodo did not immediately take it in; the implications would slowly be understood on reflection' (p. 328). See further, note for p. 1029.

975 (III: 253): In three days, as the King had said

975 (III: 253). In three days – On 18 July.

975 (III: 253). Merethrond, the Great Hall of Feasts – In *Sauron Defeated* Christopher Tolkien notes that on a page of rough drafting for this passage my father dashed off a little plan of the Citadel. This is shown as a circle with seven small circles (towers) at equal distances within the circumference, one of these standing beside the entrance. Beyond the Court of the Fountain is marked, at the centre, the White Tower and Hall of Kings, and beyond that again, on the west side of the Citadel, the King's House. To the right (north) of the White Tower is the Hall of Feasts. The outlines of other buildings are roughed in between the towers. [p. 67]

975 (III: 253): At last the day of departure came

975 (III: 253). the day of departure – 22 July. *Scheme* includes for this date: 'The cortège of Théoden leaves Minas Tirith with all the chieftains, and the four hobbits. They proceed slowly and take 15 days [to reach Edoras].'

976 (III: 254): Without haste and at peace

976 (III: 254). the Grey Wood – Described in Book V, Chapter 5 as 'wide grey thickets' (p. 834, III: 108). Tolkien defines *Grey Wood* in his unfinished index as 'the wood near the junction of Stonewain Valley and the main West Rd.'

976 (III: 254): At length after fifteen days

976 (III: 254). after fifteen days of journey – They arrive at Edoras on 7 August.

976 (III: 254). there was held the highest feast that it had known – This is probably looking ahead to the feast after the funeral, rather than to a separate feast held on the travellers' arrival at Edoras.

976 (III: 254). after three days – On 10 August.

976 (III: 254). now there were eight mounds on the east side of the Barrowfield. – See note for p. 507. When Éomer dies a third line will begin, since he is Théoden's sister-son, not his son.

Index defines the *Barrowfield* (written 'Barrow-field') as 'the field before Edoras beside Snowbourn where the Kings' mounds stood'.

976 (III: 254): Then the Riders of the King's House

976 (III: 254). Gléowine – Old English 'lover of music, lover of minstrelsy', from *glēo* 'music, song' + *wine* 'friend'.

977 (III: 255): When the burial was over

977 (III: 255). the burial – Apart from the absence of a religious ceremony, Théoden's funeral includes elements recorded as having been part of the burial of famous leaders in the early medieval period in Europe: burial with arms and other possessions; the raising of a mound over the grave;

followers riding around the barrow; the singing of a song recording the deeds of the deceased; and expressions of grief.

In his *De Origine Actibusque Getarum* Jordanes describes the funeral of Attila, the leader of the Huns, in AD 453:

> His body was placed in the midst of a plain and lay in state in a silken tent as a sight for men's admiration. The best horsemen of the entire tribe of the Huns rode around in circles, after the manner of circus games, in the place to which he had been brought and told of his deeds in a funeral dirge. . . . When they had mourned him with such lamentations, a *strava*, as they call it, was celebrated over his tomb with great revelling. They gave way in turn to the extremes of feeling and displayed funereal grief alternating with joy. Then in the secrecy of night they buried his body in the earth. They bound his coffins, the first with gold, the second with silver and the third with the strength of iron. . . . They also added the arms of foemen won in the fight, trappings of rare worth, sparkling with various gems, and ornaments of all sorts whereby princely state is maintained. And that so great riches might be kept from human curiosity, they slew those appointed to the work. . . . [*The Origin and Deeds of the Goths*, trans. by Charles C. Mierow, pp. 80–1]

In *Beowulf* the hero's body was burned on a funeral pyre 'hung round with helmets, battle-shields, bright corslets' and 'the roaring flame mingled with the noise of weeping. . . . Depressed in soul, they [the warriors] uttered forth their misery, and mourned their lord's death. Moreover, the aged woman with hair bound up, sang in memory of Beowulf a doleful dirge. . . .' Over Beowulf's ashes, and the treasure taken from the dragon's hoard, his people build a mound upon a cliff; 'then the warriors brave in battle, sons of nobles, twelve in all, rode round the barrow; they would lament their loss, mourn for their king, utter a dirge, and speak about their hero. They reverenced his manliness, extolled highly his deeds of valour . . .' (Clark Hall translation, pp. 174–5).

977 (III: 255). then folk gathered to the Golden Hall for the great feast. . . . And when the time came that in the custom of the Mark they should drink to the memory of the kings, Éowyn Lady of Rohan came forth . . . and she bore a filled cup to Éomer. [*paragraph:*] . . . And when Théoden was named Éomer drained the cup. – Hilda Roderick Ellis writes in *The Road to Hel: A Study of the Conception of the Dead in Old Norse Literature* p. 59, that

> throughout the sagas it is made clear that an important way of paying honour to the dead was to hold a funeral feast in his memory; and this was important for the living as well as for the dead, since it was at the feast that the son took over the inheritance of his father. Snorri [*Ynglinga Saga*] describes the proceedings at such a feast:

> It was the custom at that time when a funeral feast should be made in honour of king or jarl that he who held it and who was to succeed to the inheritance should sit on the step before the high-seat up to the time when the cup was borne in which was called Bragi's cup. Then he should stand up with the cup of Bragi and make a vow, and drink off the cup afterwards; then he should proceed to the high-seat which his father had had, and then he succeeded to all the inheritance after him. [p. 59]

After giving other examples Ellis continues: 'What then was the original motive behind this custom? Was there some idea of well-being for the dead dependent on the holding of a feast for them? We know that poems in honour of the dead man were recited, for in the famous scene in *Egil's Saga* Egil's daughter proposes that her father shall make a poem to be recited at his son's funeral feast' (p. 60). The *Icelandic-English Dictionary* by Cleasby, Vigfusson, and Craigie notes for *bragr* 'best, foremost', and for *bragar-full* or *braga-full*:

> *a toasting cup*, to be drunk esp[ecially] at funeral feasts; it seems properly to mean *the king's toast* (cp. Bragi = *princeps*), i.e. the toast in the memory of the deceased king or earl, which was to be drunk first; the heir to the throne rose to drink this toast, and while doing so put his feet on the footstool of his seat and made a solemn vow; he then for the first time took his father's seat, and the other guests in their turn made similar vows.

977 (III: 255): Then a minstrel and loremaster stood up

977 (III: 255). Aldor brother of Baldor the hapless; and Fréa, and Fréawine, and Goldwine, and Déor, and Gram. . . . Fréaláf . . . and Léofa, and Walda, and Folca, and Folcwine, and Fengel – *Aldor* is Old English 'chief, prince' and 'elder, parent'.

Baldor, who failed to pass the Paths of the Dead (see note for p. 787), is unlucky (*hapless*).

Fréa is Old English (*frēa*) 'lord, master'.

Fréawine 'dear or beloved lord' is derived from Old English *frēa* + *wine* 'friend', in the sense 'one who can help or protect'.

Goldwine 'liberal and kindly prince' is derived from Old English *gold* 'gold' + *wine* 'friend' (as above).

Déor is Old English (*dēor*) 'brave, bold'.

Gram is Old English 'furious, fierce'.

Fréaláf means 'surviving lord', from Old English *frēa* 'lord, master' + *lāf* 'leaving'. In editions through 2004 the name is given here erroneously without the second accent. The second accent was overlooked also for the 2005 hardback edition, but was added in the 2005 paperback. Fréaláf became king after the death of his mother's brother, Helm, and of Helm's two sons.

As first published, the passage 'Léofa, and Walda, and Folca, and Folcwine, and Fengel' read: 'Léof, and Walda, and Folca, and Fengel'. It was revised in the second edition (1965) to be consistent with the list of Kings of the Mark in Appendix A; see note for pp. 1068–9.

In Appendix A it is said that Léofa was born *Brytta* (Old English 'bestower, distributor, prince, lord'), but was called *Léofa* because he was loved by all of his people (from Old English *lēof* 'loved, beloved, dear'; on III: 255 in the first edition his name is given as *Léof*).

Walda is derived from Old English *wealda* 'ruler'.

Folca is derived from Old English *folc* 'folk, people'.

Folcwine 'friend of the people' is derived from Old English *folc* + *wine*. His name was added to the present list in the second edition (1965), having been omitted in error in the first edition.

Fengel is Old English 'prince', related to *feng* 'booty' (in Appendix A Fengel is said to have been 'greedy of food and of gold', p. 1069, III: 350).

977 (III: 255): At the last when the feast

977 (III: 255). trothplighted – Betrothed.

977 (III: 255): 'No niggard are you

977 (III: 255). niggard – A mean, stingy, or miserly person.

977 (III: 256): And he answered

977 (III: 256). I have wished thee joy ever since first I saw thee. It heals my heart to see thee now in bliss. – Paul H. Kocher concludes a sensitive survey of the difficult relationship between Aragorn and Éowyn by noting: 'It is symptomatic of his ease that he now dares to use to her the familiar *thee* with which she addressed him in her wooing but which he avoided in addressing her' (*Master of Middle-earth*, p. 156).

978 (III: 256): When the feast was over

978 (III: 256). When the feast was over – On 14 August.

978 (III: 256): At the last before the guests set out

978 (III: 256). Holdwine of the Mark – This additional name for Merry, derived from Old English *hold* 'faithful, loyal' + *wine* 'friend', was added only in page proof.

978 (III: 256): Then Éowyn gave to Merry

978 (III: 256). came from the hoard of Scatha the Worm – These words were added in galley proof. According to Appendix A, pp. 1064–5, III: 346, Fram, a chieftain of the ancestors of the Rohirrim living in the North, 'slew Scatha, the great dragon of Ered Mithrin, and the land had peace from the long-worms afterwards. Thus Fram won great wealth, but was at feud with the Dwarves, who claimed the hoard of Scatha.' In *Nomenclature* Tolkien comments that *Scatha* is 'Old English ("injurer, enemy, robber") and so is from the language of Rohan'.

978 (III: 256): Now the guests were ready

978 (III: 256). stirrup-cup – 'A cup of wine or other drink handed to a man when already on horseback setting out for a journey; a parting glass' (*OED*).

978 (III: 256). came at length to Helm's Deep – According to *The Tale of Years* they arrive on 18 August. *Scheme* adds 'at eve'.

978 (III: 256). Legolas repaid his promise to Gimli and went with him to the Glittering Caves – According to *Scheme* they visit the caves on 19 August.

978–9 (III: 257): From Deeping-coomb

978 (III: 257). they rode to Isengard – According to *Scheme* they leave Helm's Deep on 21 August, and according to both *Scheme* and *The Tale of Years* they reach Isengard on 22 August.

979 (III: 257): '*Hoom*, well, that is fair enough'

979 (III: 257). *morimaite-sincahonda* – Quenya 'blackhanded-flint-hearted'.

979 (III: 257). all round the wood of Laurelindórenan, which they could not get into – According to *The Tale of Years* three attacks were made on Lothlórien on 11, 15, and 22 March 'from Dol Guldur, but besides the valour of the elven people of that land, the power that dwelt there was too great for any to overcome, unless Sauron had come there himself. Though grievous harm was done to the fair woods on the borders, the assaults were driven back' (p. 1104, III: 375).

979 (III: 257): 'And these same foul creatures

979 (III: 257). these same foul creatures were more than surprised to meet us on the wold – *The Tale of Years* indicates: for 11 March, Eastern Rohan is invaded from the north; and for 12 March, the Ents defeat the invaders of Rohan.

980 (III: 258): 'No, not dead, so far as I know'

980 (III: 258). Yes, he is gone seven days. – As first published this sentence read only: 'Yes, he is gone.' The words 'seven days' were added in the second edition (1965). Treebeard released Saruman on 15 August, a date added to *The Tale of Years* in the edition of 2004 in accordance with a note by Tolkien in one of his check copies of *The Lord of the Rings*.

980 (III: 258): 'That will be seen later'

980 (III: 258). I will give to Ents all this valley – Aragorn grants the valley to the Ents, requiring only a light service in return, such as was required of the Hobbits when granted the land that became the Shire: see note for p. 4. In both cases there is no suggestion that military service was required in return for land; and this, together with the fact that Denethor could not demand a certain number of soldiers from Rohan or the southern fiefs, nor that they should be led by the man of highest rank, shows that Gondor and Arnor were not feudal states.

981 (III: 259): 'Here then at last

981 (III: 259). the Fellowship of the Ring – Only now, very late in *The Lord of the Rings*, is this phrase used, other than in the title of the first volume or part. Heretofore there have been only references to a 'fellowship', fewer than those to the 'Company' (of the Ring).

981 (III: 259): 'We will come

981 (III: 259). We will come, if our own lords allow it – In the first version of the abandoned Epilogue to *The Lord of the Rings* (see note for p. 1031) Sam tells his children:

> Legolas, he came with his people and they live in the land across the River, Ithilien . . . and they've made it very lovely, according to Mr. Pippin. . . .
>
> Gimli, he came down to work for the King in the City, and he and his folk worked so long they got used to it and proud of their work, and in the end they settled up in the mountains up away west behind the City, and there they are still. And Gimli goes once every year to see the Glittering Caves. [*Sauron Defeated*, p. 116].

A slightly different account is given in Appendix A, which shows Tolkien's later thoughts:

> After the fall of Sauron, Gimli brought south a part of the Dwarf-folk of Erebor, and he became Lord of the Glittering Caves. He and his people did great works in Gondor and Rohan. For Minas Tirith they forged gates of *mithril* and steel to replace those broken by the Witch-king. Legolas his friend also brought south Elves out of Greenwood, and they dwelt in Ithilien, and it became once again the fairest country in all the westlands. [p. 1080, III: 360, 362]

981 (III: 259): Then Treebeard said farewell

981 (III: 259). *A vanimar, vanimálion nostari!* – On 8 June 1961 Tolkien wrote to Rhona Beare that 'Treebeard's greeting to Celeborn and Galadriel meant "O beautiful ones, parents of beautiful children"' (*Letters*, p. 308). In *The Lord of the Rings* only one child of Galadriel and Celeborn is recorded. Christopher Tolkien comments in *Unfinished Tales*, p. 234, that he thinks it unlikely that his father had any thought, while writing *The Lord of the Rings*, of Amroth being their son, or the fact surely would have been mentioned. Treebeard probably is referring more generally to their descendants.

981 (III: 259): And Celeborn said

981 (III: 259). Eldest – See note for p. 409.

981 (III: 259). nor until the lands that lie under the wave are lifted up again – Galadriel is referring to Beleriand and other lands drowned at the end of the First Age as a result of the cataclysmic strife that overthrew Morgoth. More generally she is referring to the hope also expressed at the end of the *Quenta Silmarillion*: 'If ["The Silmarillion"] has passed from the high and the beautiful to darkness and ruin, that was of old the fate of Arda Marred; and if any change shall come and the Marring be amended, Manwë and Varda may know; but they have not revealed it, and it is not declared in the dooms of Mandos' (*The Silmarillion*, p. 255).

982 (III: 260): But Celeborn said

982 (III: 260). Kinsman, farewell! May your doom be other than mine, and your treasure remain with you to the end! – Celeborn is his kinsman, because Aragorn is now married to his granddaughter. He is expressing the hope that Arwen will never leave Aragorn, as he knows that Galadriel will soon be leaving him, to return to Valinor across the Sea. In the first version of the abandoned Epilogue, some seventeen years later in Shire Reckoning 1436, Sam tells his daughter Elanor that there are still Elves living in Lórien, including Celeborn. She asks if Celeborn is sad that Galadriel has gone. Sam tells her that, though Celeborn may be sad, 'he lives in his own land as he always has done. Lórien is his land and he loves trees . . . he is happy in his Elvish way, I don't doubt. They can afford to wait, Elves can. His time is not come yet. The Lady came to his land, and now she is gone; and he has the land still. When he tires of it he can leave it' (*Sauron Defeated*, pp. 115–16). This was presumably Tolkien's idea of the earlier history of Celeborn and Galadriel when he finished *The Lord of the Rings*, but he later changed his mind: see note for p. 357.

In Appendix B it is said that 'after the passing of Galadriel in a few years Celeborn grew weary of his realm and went to Imladris to dwell with the sons of Elrond' (p. 1094, III: 375), his grandsons. In the second edition (1965) Tolkien added a similar statement at the end of the Prologue: 'It is said that Celeborn went to dwell there [Rivendell] after the departure of Galadriel; but there is no record of the day when at last he sought the Grey Havens . . .' (p. 15, I: 25).

These comments imply that Celeborn could have left Middle-earth with Galadriel if he had wished, and Tolkien's replies to queries from readers seem to confirm this. In his unpublished letter to Eileen Elgar, begun 22 September 1963, he comments that Celeborn and Galadriel were of different kin: Celeborn was of that branch of the Elves that, in the First Age, was so in love with Middle-earth that they had refused the call of the Valar to go to Valinor; he had never seen the Blessed Realm. Now he remained until he had seen the coming of the Dominion of Men. But to an immortal Elf, for whom time was not as it is to mortals, the period in which he was parted from Galadriel would seem brief.

It is Arwen, rather than Aragorn, who in some part shares Celeborn's fate. She stays with Aragorn until he lays down his life; left alone, she does not then try to alter her choice. See further, note for p. 1063.

982 (III: 260): With that they parted

982 (III: 260). With that they parted – Whereas the entry in *The Tale of Years* for 22 August says only: 'They come to Isengard; they take leave of the King of the West at sunset', *Scheme* has a longer entry and more information about 22 August:

> They visit Treebeard; and learn of the release of Saruman and Wormtongue. Legolas and Gimli say farewell and go N[orth] through Fangorn. The rest of the Company proceed to Dolbaran [*sic*].
>
> At sunset Aragorn says farewell on the west-margin of Gondor. Rest of company go on over the Isen. They then ride northward passing through eastern edge of Dunland.

982 (III: 260–1): Soon the dwindling company

982 (III: 260–1). Soon the dwindling company, following the Isen, turned west and rode through the Gap into the waste lands beyond, and then they turned northwards, and passed over the borders of Dunland. The Dunlendings fled . . . to their country; but the travellers . . . when they would. – As first published this passage read: 'Soon the dwindling company came to the Isen, and crossed over it, and came into the waste lands beyond, and then they turned northwards, and passed by the borders of Dunland. And the Dunlendings fled . . . to their country. But the travellers . . . when they would; and as they went the summer wore away.' It was revised in the second edition (1965). The comma between 'company' and 'following', omitted in the Ballantine Books edition, was added in the second printing (1967) of the Allen & Unwin second edition.

982–3 (III: 261): On the sixth day

982 (III: 261). On the sixth day since their parting from the King they journeyed . . . into the open country at sundown they overtook an old man – As first published this passage read: 'After they had passed by Dunland and were come to places where few folk dwelt, and even birds and beasts were seldom to be seen, they journeyed . . . into open country they overtook an old man'. It was revised in the second edition (1965).

According to *The Tale of Years*, the 'sixth day since their parting' is 28 August.

983 (III: 261): 'To me?' said Saruman

983 (III: 261). she always hated me, and schemed for your part – See note for p. 357.

983 (III: 261–2): For a moment his eyes kindled

983 (III: 261). you have doomed yourselves – With the destruction of the One Ring, the three Elven-rings have also lost their powers.

983 (III: 262). what ship will bear you ever back across so wide a sea? – Saruman mocks a sentiment expressed by Galadriel in her song before the parting feast in Lothlórien (Book II, Chapter 8); how he knows of these words, or that Galadriel intends to sail into the West, Tolkien does not say.

984–5 (III: 263): Next day they went on into northern Dunland

984–5 (III: 263). Next day they went on into northern Dunland, where no men now dwelt, though it was a green and pleasant country. September came in with golden days and silver nights, and they rode at ease until they reached the Swanfleet river, and found the old ford, east of the falls where it went down suddenly into the lowlands. Far to the west in a haze lay the meres and eyots through which it wound its way to the Greyflood: there countless swans housed in a land of reeds. [*paragraph:*] So they passed into Eregion, and at last a fair morning dawned – As first published this passage read only: 'September came in with golden days and silver nights. At last a fair morning dawned'. It was revised in the second edition (1965). In *Sauron Defeated* Christopher Tolkien notes that 'by this change the company was still in Dunland when they came upon Saruman', and the added text in the second edition concerning the following day led to 'northern Dunland, rather than the country north of Dunland, now becoming the uninhabited region' (p. 69).

The travellers reach northern Dunland on 29 August.

On 30 June 1969 Tolkien wrote to Paul Bibire, in response to a query as to whether the River Glanduin was the same as the Swanfleet:

> The Glanduin is the same river as the Swanfleet, but the names are not related. I find on the map with corrections that are to be made for the new edition to appear at the end of this year [the India paper edition, Allen & Unwin, 1969] that this river is marked by me as both Glanduin and various compounds with *alph* 'swan'. The name *Glanduin* was meant to be 'border-river', a name given as far back as the Second Age when it was the southern border of Eregion, beyond which were the unfriendly people of Dunland. In the earlier centuries of the Two King-

> doms *Enedwaith* (Middle-folk) was a region between the realm of Gondor and the slowly receding realm of Arnor (it originally included Minhiriath (Mesopotamia)). Both kingdoms shared an interest in the region, but were mainly concerned with the upkeep of the great road that was their main way of communication except by sea, and the bridge at Tharbad. People of Númenórean origin did not live there, except at Tharbad, where a large garrison of soldiers and river-wardens was once maintained. In those days there were drainage works, and the banks of the Hoarwell and Greyflood were strengthened. But in the days of *The Lord of the Rings* the region had long become ruinous and lapsed into its primitive state: a slow wide river running through a network of swamps, pools and eyots: the haunt of hosts of swans and other water-birds.
>
> If the name Glanduin was still remembered it would apply only to the upper course where the river ran down swiftly, but was soon lost in the plains and disappeared into the fens. I think I may keep Glanduin on the map for the upper part, and mark the lower part as fenlands with the name *Nîn-in-Eilph* (water-lands of the Swans), which will adequately explain Swanfleet river, III.263. [*Vinyar Tengwar* 42, pp. 6–7]

The names *Swanfleet* and *Glanduin* (misspelt *Glandin*) were added to the general map as revised for the edition of 1969, but in the wrong location; see the essay on maps, above. *Nîn-in-Eilph* first appeared on Christopher Tolkien's new map of 1980.

In his long essay *The Rivers and Beacon-hills of Gondor*, inspired by Bibire's questions, Tolkien repeated much of this information, and continued: 'If the river had any name it was in the language of the Dunlendings. In *The Return of the King* VI 6 it is called the Swanfleet river (not River), simply as being the river that went down into Nîn-in-Eilph, "the Water-lands of the Swans"' (*Unfinished Tales*, pp. 264–5).

September came in with *silver nights* presumably because there was a full moon on 1 September.

985 (III: 263): So they passed into Eregion

985 (III: 263). at last a fair morning dawned – *The Tale of Years* indicates that on 6 September the company halted in sight of the Mountains of Moria.

985 (III: 263): Here now for seven days

985 (III: 263). for seven days they tarried – Until 13 September.

985 (III: 263). little would he have seen or heard. . . . For they did not move or speak with mouth, looking from mind to mind; and only their shining eyes stirred and kindled as their thoughts went to and fro. – A rare reference in Tolkien's works to extrasensory communication among the Elves. See further, his essay *Ósanwe-kenta* ('Enquiry into the Communication of Thought'), *Vinyar Tengwar* 39 (July 1998).

985 (III: 264): At last one evening

985 (III: 264). At last one evening – It is the evening of 21 September.

986 (III: 264): When nearly a fortnight had passed

986 (III: 264). When nearly a fortnight had passed – It is 4 October.

986–7 (III: 265): In the evening they went

987 (III: 265). three books of lore that he had made at various times . . . *Translations from the Elvish, by B.B.* – As first published 'three books' read 'some books'. This was revised in the second edition (1965). In the 'Note on the Shire Records' added to the Prologue in the second edition it is said that 'these three volumes were found to be a work of great skill and learning in which, between 1403 and 1418, he [Bilbo] had used all the sources available to him in Rivendell, both living and written . . . almost entirely concerned with the Elder Days' (p. 15, I: 24).

987 (III: 265): To Sam he gave a little bag of gold

987 (III: 265). Almost the last drop of the Smaug vintage – That is, the end of the treasure that Bilbo had brought back from Smaug's hoard (see note for p. 24). *Drop* and *vintage* here together make a wine metaphor, the latter word commonly used of the year in which a wine is produced.

987 (III: 265): 'I have nothing much to give

987 (III: 265). Don't let your heads get too big for your hats! – A variation on *to be too big for one's boots*, 'to be unduly self-confident, to be above oneself, conceited, cocksure' (*Brewer's Dictionary of Phrase and Fable*).

987 (III: 266): *The Road Goes Ever On and On*

987 (III: 266). *But I at last with weary feet / Will turn toward the lighted inn, / My evening-rest and sleep to meet.* – This is literally true, in that Bilbo no longer wishes to travel; it contrasts with the 'eager feet' with which he left Bag End after his birthday party in Book I, Chapter 1. But the new words may also be seen as a metaphor for death.

988 (III: 266): At that Bilbo opened an eye

988 (III: 266). Collect all my notes and papers, and my diary too, and take them with you – As first published this passage read: 'Collect all my notes and papers and take them with you'. It was revised in the second edition (1965).

988 (III: 267): The next day Gandalf

988 (III: 267). The next day – It is 5 October.

988 (III: 267): 'I think, Frodo, that maybe

988 (III: 267). about this time of the year, when the leaves are gold before they fall, look for Bilbo in the woods of the Shire – This is all that Elrond says, with no indication as to which year, or exactly where in the woods; but two years later, Frodo will seem to know exactly when and where to meet Elrond and Bilbo.

Chapter 7

HOMEWARD BOUND

For drafts and history of this chapter, see *Sauron Defeated*, pp. 75–8.

989 (III: 268): At last the hobbits

989 (III: 268). At last the hobbits had their faces turned to home – It is 5 October 1419 as Gandalf and the hobbits leave Rivendell.

989 (III: 268): By the end of the next day

989 (III: 268). By the end of the next day – It is now 7 October.

989 (III: 268). At length they came to Weathertop – According to *Scheme*, from the Ford the hobbits and Gandalf 'ride at leisure, having good weather as far as Weathertop and often linger on way in autumn woods. (It is 285 miles *by road* from Rivendell to Weathertop.) They pass Weathertop on Oct[ober] 23. The weather then changes and they ride more quickly.'

989 (III: 268–9): So it was that near the end

989 (III: 268). near the end of a wild and wet evening in the last days of October – According to *The Tale of Years* it is 28 October. *Scheme* notes that the distance from Weathertop to Bree is ninety-five miles.

989 (III: 268). Bree-hill – Here, as first published, 'Bree-hill' was printed 'Bree Hill', though all other instances of the name in *The Lord of the Rings* have the hyphenated form. It was emended to 'Bree-hill' in the edition of 2004. Both forms are found variously in Tolkien's manuscripts.

990 (III: 269): 'Come in!' he said

990 (III: 269). a ruffianly evening – In this context (referring to the weather), windy, blustery.

991 (III: 270): When he came back

991 (III: 270). Southlinch – 'Hill fields on the S[outh] side of Bree Hill' (*Index*).

992 (III: 271): But he did say much

992 (III: 271). Outside – 'Outside Bree' (*Index*). See also notes for pp. 22 and 154.

992 (III: 271): 'Three and two'

992 (III: 271). up-away – This probably refers to hobbits living higher on Bree-hill, as described on p. 149, I: 161: 'They lived mostly in Staddle though there were some in Bree itself, especially on the higher slopes of the hill, above the houses of the Men.'

992 (III: 271). Pickthorn – Another example of the botanical surnames common in Bree. See notes for pp. 148 and 155.

994 (III: 273): 'I hope so, I'm sure'

994 (III: 273). a month of Mondays – A play on the saying *a month of Sundays*, i.e. a long time.

994–5 (III: 274): The travellers stayed in Bree

994 (III: 274). The travellers stayed in Bree all the next day – On 29 October.

995 (III: 274): No trouble by day

995 (III: 274). The next morning they got up early – The morning of 30 October.

996 (III: 275): 'Deep in, but not at the bottom'

996 (III: 275). He [Saruman] began to take an interest in the Shire before Mordor did. – See note for p. 75.

996 (III: 275): 'But if you would know

996 (III: 275). He [Bombadil] is a moss-gatherer, and I have been a stone doomed to rolling. – A play on the proverb *A rolling stone gathers no moss*, i.e. 'someone who is always on the move and does not settle down will never become prosperous or wealthy' (*Brewer's Dictionary of Phrase and Fable*).

996 (III: 275): 'As well as ever

996 (III: 275). I should press on now for home, or you will not come to the Brandywine Bridge before the gates are locked – Gandalf is either deducing that there are now gates at the Bridge, in light of the disturbing news that he and the hobbits have heard about the Shire, or he has knowledge not indicated in the text.

996 (III: 276): 'But there aren't any gates'

996 (III: 276). Buckland Gate – See note for p. 107.

Chapter 8

THE SCOURING OF THE SHIRE

For drafts and history of this chapter, see *Sauron Defeated*, pp. 79–107.

998 (III: 277): It was after nightfall

998 (III: 277). It was after nightfall – On 30 October 1419.

998 (III: 277). two-storeyed with narrow straight-sided windows, bare and dimly lit, all very gloomy and un-Shirelike – In the Prologue it is said that when hobbits built houses, rather than excavating holes, they 'were usually long, low and comfortable . . . [with] a preference for round windows' (p. 7, I: 16).

998 (III: 277): 'Come along!'

998 (III: 277). Hob Hayward – In *Nomenclature* Tolkien explains that a *hayward* is 'a local official with the duty of inspecting fences and keeping cattle from straying. . . .' The word is 'now obsolescent, and surviving chiefly in the very common surname *Hayward*; but *Hob* . . . was supposed actually to be a hayward'. 'The word is derived from *hay* "fence" (*not* "grass") + *ward* "guard".' (See also note for p. 107.)

998 (III: 277). Hay Gate – See note for p. 107.

999 (III: 278): 'So much for your Big Man'

999 (III: 278). Bridge Inn – 'Inn by the Brandywine Bridge' (*Index*).

1000 (III: 279): 'All right, all right!'

1000 (III: 279). no smoke – No smoking allowed (*smoke* = 'tobacco').

1000 (III: 279): 'The new 'Chief'

1000 (III: 279). It was a good forty miles from the Bridge to Bag End – David Cofield points out in 'The Size of the Shire: A Problem in Cartography', *Beyond Bree*, July 1994, p. 4, that this statement does not agree with others made by Tolkien, including, in the first edition, 'Fifty leagues it [the Shire] stretched from the Westmarch under the Tower Hills to the Brandywine Bridge', and the emended text in the second edition, 'Forty leagues [120 miles] it stretched from the Far Downs to the Brandywine Bridge'.

> Here at the end of the book is a major problem. . . . It is stated specifically that it was a 'good 40 miles' from the Brandywine Bridge to Bag End. . . . This means that more than two-thirds of the Shire lay west of the Hobbiton-Bywater region, which was known as 'the comfortable

> heart of the Shire' [Book I, Chapter 2, p. 44, I: 53]. It also means that the Eastfarthing must be squeezed into less than a third of the whole country and the Westfarthing must be swollen enormously. . . . Finally it makes nonsense of the claim of the Three-Farthing Stone (which was south and east of Bag End) to be 'as near the centre of the Shire as no matter' [Book VI, Chapter 9, p. 1023, III: 303].

(See note for p. 1023.) Cofield suggests that Tolkien did not deal with this problem probably 'due to the haste with which the 1965 revisions had to be made', or 'he may have been concerned that lengthening the Bridge to Bag End distance could have made it impossible for Frodo, Sam, Merry, and Pippin to traverse it in two days, especially with an escort of Shirriffs on foot'. He also thinks, 'although it is hard to be certain since mileage is rarely given', that 'Tolkien envisaged a greater distance between Bag End and the Brandywine when writing the first chapters of his book than he did when near the end' (p. 4).

At any rate, there is an inconsistency. Unfortunately there is no scale on the map *A Part of the Shire*, but if one extrapolates from Frodo's estimate, made just below Woodhall, that 'they had about eighteen miles to go in a straight line' to the Bucklebury Ferry (Book I, Chapter 4, p. 88, I: 98), then the distance from Hobbiton to the Ferry, even as the crow flies, is about 69 miles, and the hobbits took a less direct and longer route; and the (cross-country) distance from the Bridge to Bag End is about 62 miles. In the present chapter it is said that, travelling by the Road, Frogmorton is 'about twenty-two miles from the Bridge' and Bywater a further 18 miles from Frogmorton; again extrapolating from the 18 miles between Woody End and the Ferry, these distances (in a straight line, not allowing for the curves in the road) would be about 30 miles and 27 miles respectively. The distance between the Bridge and the Three-Farthing Stone (4 miles short of Bywater) is about 51 miles, which is closer to the middle of a Shire 120 miles from east to west than the 36 miles suggested by the narrative in this chapter. On the other hand, the distance from Hobbiton to the Ferry appears on the general map of Middle-earth to be closer to 50 miles.

1000 (III: 279–80): They had not made any definite plans

1000 (III: 280). the fag-end of autumn – A *fag-end* is 'the last part or remnant of anything after the best has been used; the extreme end, e.g. of a portion of space or time' (*OED*).

1001 (III: 280): As evening fell

1001 (III: 280). Frogmorton – In *Nomenclature* Tolkien states that *Frogmorton* 'is not an actual English place-name, but has the same element as in *Frogmore* (Bucks [Buckinghamshire]): *frog + moor + town*. . . . N.B. *moor/mor* has the meaning "marshy land", as usually in place-names of southern and midland England.' In his notes for the Dutch translator Tolkien says that '*Frogmorton* represents an older *froggan-mere-tun* "village by the frog-mere". It possibly does not actually occur in mod[ern] England, but familiar names of a similar pattern do (e.g. *Throckmorton, Throgmorton*).'

1001 (III: 280). *The Floating Log* – A name probably chosen to suit the wetlands around Frogmorton.

1001 (III: 280). Shirriffs . . . feathers in their caps – See notes for p. 10.

1001 (III: 280): 'There now, Mister

1001 (III: 280). Lockholes – 'Old storage tunnels in M[ichel] Delving, used as prisons by the Ruffians' (*Index*). In *Nomenclature* they are described as 'the hobbit version of "lock-up (house)": a place of detention'.

1001 (III: 280–1): Sam had been looking

1001 (III: 281). Smallburrow – Another Hobbit surname derived from the custom of living in holes.

1001 (III: 281): 'Look here, Cock-robin!'

1001 (III: 281). Cock-robin – 'A familiar or pet name for a male robin, also slang for 'a soft, easy fellow' (*OED*).

1002 (III: 281): 'Can't say as I'd be sorry

1002 (III: 281). old Flourdumpling – The origin of Will Whitfoot's nick-name was given in Book I, Chapter 9, where Pippin gives 'an account of the collapse of the roof of the Town Hole in Michel Delving: Will Whitfoot, the Mayor, and the fattest hobbit in the Westfarthing, had been buried in chalk, and came out like a floured dumpling' (p. 156, I: 168).

1002 (III: 282): 'That's right

1002 (III: 282). One came in from Whitfurrows last night . . . and another took it on from here. And a message came back this afternoon – As first published the place-name in the first of these sentences read 'Bamfurlong', not referring to Maggot's farm but to a place on the Road about half way between the Bridge and Frogmorton. It was altered to 'Whitfurrows' in the second edition (1965), but an entry for *Bamfurlong* at this point in the text appeared nonetheless in the index of the Ballantine Books edition. *Bamfurlong* first appeared as the name of Maggot's farm in the second printing (1967) of the Allen & Unwin second edition; see note for p. 91.

Whitfurrows is derived from *whit-* 'white' (see note for p. 769) + *furrows* 'grooves in the soil made by a plough'. The earth in Whitfurrows is presumably chalky. See also *Nomenclature.*

Obviously one of the hobbits at the Brandywine Bridge was a spy for the 'Chief'. It was after nightfall the previous day when the travellers reached the Bridge, but already some time 'last night' a message had travelled twenty-two miles to Frogmorton. By the next afternoon it had travelled eighteen more miles to Bywater, and an order had travelled eighteen miles back – fifty-eight miles in about twenty hours (ignoring the calculations in the note for p. 1000, since Tolkien was considering the distances as he conceived them at this time).

1003 (III: 282): The Shirriff-house at Frogmorton

1003 (III: 282). they set off at ten o'clock in the morning – On 2 November.

1003 (III: 282): At the Three-Farthing Stone

1003 (III: 282). Three-Farthing Stone – This was 'on the East Road at junction of lands of W[est], S[outh], E[ast] Farthings' (*Index*). In Book VI, Chapter 9 it is said that the *Three-Farthing Stone* 'is as near the centre of the Shire as no matter' (p. 1023, III: 303). The problem of its location only forty miles from the Brandywine Bridge, while the Shire is said to be 120 miles from East to West, is discussed in the note to p. 1000. Barbara Strachey also notes this in her *Journeys of Frodo*, map 50: 'this being so, the Stone can only have been central in a north-south direction, unless the Hobbits' "no matter" was unusually elastic'. Tolkien may have been thinking mainly of the Stone being at the meeting point of three of the four Farthings, with the fourth not too far distant.

1004 (III: 284): 'Garn, what did I say?'

1004 (III: 284). Sharkey – In *Nomenclature* Tolkien writes that *Sharkey* 'is supposed to be a nickname modified to fit Common Speech (in the English text anglicized), based on Orkish *sharkû* "old man"'. He describes the ending *-ey* as 'diminutive and quasi-affectionate'. In *The Road to Middle-earth* Tom Shippey suggests that 'to a medievalist the name [*Sharkey*] might well suggest the "Old Man of the Mountains" or leader of the Assassins as described in *Mandeville's Travels*. "Old Man" is simply Arabic *shaikh*' (2nd edn., p. 154).

1005 (III: 284): The man stared at him

1005 (III: 284). cock-a-whoop – The more usual term is *cock-a-hoop*, one who is 'in a state of elation; crowing with exultation. . . . Elated, exultant, boastfully and loudly triumphant' (*OED*).

1005 (III: 285): 'I am a messenger of the King'

1005 (III: 285). this troll's bane – The sword from the barrow with which Pippin killed the troll before the Morannon in Book V, Chapter 10.

1005–6 (III: 285): The sword glinted

1005 (III: 285). but Frodo did not move – In *Sauron Defeated* Christopher Tolkien notes that in the original draft of this chapter 'Frodo is portrayed

... at every stage as an energetic and commanding intelligence, warlike and resolute in action; and the final text of the chapter had been largely achieved when the changed conception of Frodo's part in the Scouring of the Shire entered' (pp. 93–4). Many of his words and actions were then transferred to Merry.

1006 (III: 285): 'Fight?' said Frodo

1006 (III: 285). But remember: there is to be no slaying of hobbits, not even if they have gone over to the other side. Really gone over, I mean; not just obeying ruffians' orders because they are frightened. – Early readers of *The Lord of the Rings* no doubt were reminded in this passage of the problem of collaborators in German-occupied countries in the Second World War.

1006 (III: 285). And nobody is to be killed at all, if it can be helped. Keep your tempers and hold your hands to the last possible moment! – Tolkien is not advocating pacifism, but that violence should be only a last resort. He personally fought in the First World War, and supported the fight against the Axis in 1939–45. He accepted that fighting is sometimes necessary in a just cause, and especially in defence when attacked, but he objected to excessive force, the pursuit of revenge, or national aggrandizement. In wishing to spare even the ruffians, Frodo is following Aragorn's example of mercy towards the former allies of Sauron.

1006 (III: 286): 'I've an idea'

1006 (III: 286). old Tom Cotton's – Tom Cotton is the father of Rose Cotton and four sons (see note for p. 939), and second cousin to Sam's father. In Tolkien's unfinished index *Cotton's (farm)* is said to be 'on s[outh] side of Bywater reached by South Lane', and *South Lane* 'in Bywater leading to Cotton's farm'.

1006 (III: 286): 'No!' said Merry

1006 (III: 286). It's no good getting under cover – In the story in draft, the hobbits do go to Cotton's farm, but Tolkien could not work out a satisfactory plan of action from that point and abandoned the idea.

1007 (III: 286): 'Raise the Shire!'

1007 (III: 286). Raise the Shire! – *Raise* is used here in the sense 'rouse people for the purpose of common action'.

1007 (III: 287): 'It's Sam, Sam Gamgee

1007 (III: 287). It's Sam, Sam Gamgee. – In his draft letter to Eileen Elgar, September 1963, Tolkien wrote that

> Sam is meant to be lovable and laughable. Some readers he irritates and even infuriates. I can well understand it. All hobbits at times affect

> me in the same way, though I remain very fond of them. But Sam can be very 'trying'. He is a more representative hobbit than any of the others that we have to see much of; and he has consequently a stronger ingredient of that quality which even some hobbits found at times hard to bear: a vulgarity – by which I do not mean a mere 'down-to-earthiness' – a mental myopia which is proud of itself, a smugness (in varying degrees) and cocksureness, and a readiness to measure and sum up all things from a limited experience, largely enshrined in sententious traditional 'wisdom'. We only meet exceptional hobbits in close companionship – those who had a grace or gift: a vision of beauty, and a reverence for things nobler than themselves, at war with their rustic self-satisfaction. Imagine Sam without his education by Bilbo and his fascination with things Elvish! Not difficult. The Cotton family and the Gaffer, when the 'Travellers' return are a sufficient glimpse. [*Letters*, p. 329]

Later in this chapter, on Sam's arrival, Farmer Cotton remarks (with evident disapproval) on his 'queer' dress and that he had 'been in foreign parts, seemingly'. And when the Gaffer reappears a few pages later, he too complains that Frodo and his friends have been 'trapessing in foreign parts' while the ruffians have 'dug up Bagshot Row and ruined my taters!' (p. 1014, III: 293).

1009 (III: 288): 'No, more's the pity'

1009 (III: 288). Waymeet – In *Sauron Defeated* Christopher Tolkien comments: 'My original large-scale map of the Shire made in 1943 has *Waymoot*, as also that published in *The Fellowship of the Ring*; but the second manuscript of 'The Scouring of the Shire' [and published text] has *Waymeet*. Presumably my father changed his mind about the form but neglected the map' (p. 106, n. 24). Tolkien, however, rationalized in *Nomenclature* that *Waymeet* is 'modernized' in the text as the name of 'a village at the *meeting* of three *ways*' (emphasis ours). In Tolkien's unfinished index *Waymeet* is defined as a 'vill[age] at [the] junctions of [the] East Road branching N[orth and] S[outh] of the White Downs'.

1009–10 (III: 289): 'Not exactly,' said Cotton

1009 (III: 289). they got no change out of him – A colloquialism for 'they received no satisfaction'.

1013 (III: 292): 'The biggest ruffian

1013 (III: 292). it was about last harvest, end o' September maybe, that we first heard of him – *Scheme*, after noting the meeting with Saruman on 28 August on the way north, continues: 'Saruman changes his course, and when they are gone strikes NW [north-west] towards the Shire.' Both *Scheme* and *The Tale of Years* indicate Saruman's arrival in the Shire on 22 September. It is now 2 November.

1013 (III: 292). what he says is mostly: hack, burn, and ruin. . . . They cut down trees and let 'em lie – In 1968 Tolkien reminisced about his childhood: 'There was a willow hanging over the mill-pool, and I learned to climb it. . . . One day they cut it down. They didn't do anything with it; the log just lay there. I never forgot that' (interview with Keith Brace, 'In the Footsteps of the Hobbits', *Birmingham Post Midland Magazine*, 25 May 1968).

1013 (III: 293): '"Sharkey," says they

1013 (III: 293). old hagling – A *hag* is an ugly old woman. The diminutive suffix *-ling* brings the word down to Hobbit size.

1014 (III: 294): 'It takes a lot o' believing

1014 (III: 294). I don't hold with wearing ironmongery, whether it wears well or no – By *ironmongery* the Gaffer means Sam's mail shirt; the word generally refers to goods made of iron.

In this sentence Tolkien is playing with *wear*, first in the sense of what one does with clothing, and then in the sense of withstanding continued use.

1014 (III: 294): Farmer Cotton's household

1014 (III: 294). early the next morning – It is 3 November.

1014 (III: 294): After breakfast a messenger

1014 (III: 294). the big gang down that way – Those described earlier in this chapter as 'down south in Longbottom and by Sarn Ford' (p. 1009, III: 288).

1014 (III: 294): The next news was less good

1014 (III: 294). about ten o' clock . . . a big band about four miles away . . . coming along the road from Waymeet – Messengers had been sent to Waymeet by the ruffians from Bag End before they came to Bywater. It was about fifteen miles from Waymeet to Bywater; the ruffians now approaching at 'about ten o'clock' evidently waited for daybreak before setting out.

1015 (III: 294–5): The ruffians came tramping along

1015 (III: 294–5). the Bywater Road, which ran for some way sloping up between high banks with low hedges on top. Round a bend . . . they met a stout barrier. . . . At the same moment they became aware that the hedges on both sides . . . were all lined with hobbits. Behind them other hobbits now pushed out some more waggons . . . and so blocked the way back. – Merry's plan is similar to Faramir's ambush of the Haradrim, and to the attempt to ambush the army of the West on its way to the Morannon.

1016 (III: 295): At last all was over

1016 (III: 295). The fallen hobbits were laid together in a grave on the hill-side, where later a great stone was set up with a garden about it. – Patricia Reynolds observes in 'Funeral Customs in Tolkien's Fiction', *Mythlore* 19, no 2, whole no. 72 (Spring 1993), that 'the setting of memorial stones . . . is a widespread tradition, however the planting of the garden recalls the tradition of the war-memorial with its garden of remembrance, a feature common to many English villages after the First World War' (p. 50).

1016 (III: 295). the names of all those who took part were made into a Roll – A *roll* in this context is an official register of names to honour or commemorate those who took part in a noble cause.

1016 (III: 295–6): Frodo had been in the battle

1016 (III: 295). Frodo had been in the battle, but he had not drawn sword – Tolkien wrote to Amy Ronald on 15 December 1956: 'Frodo's attitude to weapons was personal. He was not in modern terms a "pacifist". Of course, he was mainly horrified at the prospect of civil war among Hobbits; but he had (I suppose) also reached the conclusion that physical fighting is actually less ultimately effective than most (good) men think it!' (*Letters*, p. 255).

1016 (III: 296): It was one of the saddest hours

1016 (III: 296). rows of new mean houses . . . the new mill in all its frowning and dirty ugliness . . . every tree had been felled – The hobbits' feelings of sadness reflect those often felt by Tolkien himself: see note for p. xxv, concerning Sarehole.

1016–17 (III: 296): As they crossed the bridge

1016 (III: 296). The Old Grange on the west side – The Old Grange has not been previously mentioned, but appears in Tolkien's drawing *The Hill: Hobbiton across the Water* in the first printing of *The Hobbit* (1937), and in the watercolour that replaced it in the second Allen & Unwin printing (1937), reproduced in *Artist and Illustrator* as figs. 97–8. The *Oxford English Dictionary* defines *grange* as 'a repository for grain; a granary, barn (*archaic*)'; and 'an establishment where farming is carried on. . . . Now applied to: a country house with farm buildings attached, usually the residence of a gentleman-farmer.'

1016 (III: 296). All the chestnuts were gone – The chestnut trees, with pink flowers, are readily identifiable as such in the watercolour version of *The Hill* (*Artist and Illustrator*, fig. 98).

1016 (III: 296). tarred sheds – Wooden sheds painted with tar as protection against wind and water.

1017 (III: 296): A laugh put an end

1017 (III: 296). prattle – 'Foolish or inconsequential talk' (*Concise OED*).

1017 (III: 296–7): Ted Sandyman spat over the wall

1017 (III: 297). any more of your mouth – *Mouth* in this context means 'spoken impudence'.

1018 (III: 297): Merry looked round in dismay

1018 (III: 297). If I had known all the mischief he had caused, I should have stuffed my pouch down Saruman's throat. – Although both Merry and Frodo realize that Saruman is behind what has happened in the Shire, neither has thought that Saruman might actually be present until he emerges. Nor, for that matter, did Tolkien until he had written most of the first text of the present chapter. In *Sauron Defeated* Christopher Tolkien comments on how striking it is 'that here, virtually at the end of *The Lord of the Rings* and in an element in the whole that my father had long meditated, the story when he first wrote it down should have been so different from its final form (or that he so signally failed to see "what really happened"!) . . . He did not perceive that it was Saruman who was the real 'Boss', Sharkey, at Bag End' (p. 93).

The earliest indication in the writing of *The Lord of the Rings* that the hobbits would find that all was not well when they returned to the Shire is in a note written probably in 1939 (see note for p. xxiv). Most of the hints to the hobbits (and the reader) in the published text, such as Elrond wishing to send Merry and Pippin back to deal with trouble in the Shire, Sam's vision in the Mirror of Galadriel, and the discovery of Shire-produced pipe-weed at Isengard, were included as the work was written.

Despite Tolkien's protestations in his Foreword to the second edition that 'The Scouring of the Shire' does not reflect the situation in England after the Second World War, many readers nonetheless have found it applicable to their own experience in those years. Tom Shippey has commented that most British readers in the 1950s would find points of similarity to Britain in the years following the end of the war in 1945, including 'the curious "socialism" of Sharkey and his men' supposedly gathering 'for fair distribution' but not sharing much; 'the disillusionment of returning from victory to poor food, ration-books, endemic shortages, and a rash of "prefabs" and jerry-built "council houses"' (*J.R.R. Tolkien: Author of the Century*, pp. 167–8).

1018 (III: 297): Saruman laughed again

1018 (III: 297). I will get ahead of them and teach them a lesson – See notes for p. 1013 on Saruman turning towards the Shire, and Farmer Cotton's comments. In *Sauron Defeated* Christopher Tolkien records an interesting note written by his father beside this episode in a copy of the first edition (when those riding north had already left Dunland when they met Saruman; see notes for pp. 984, 1013):

> Saruman turned back into Dunland on Aug. 28. He then made for the old South Road and went north over the Greyflood at Tharbad, and thence NW. [north-west] to Sarn Ford, and so into the Shire and to Hobbiton on Sept. 22: a journey of about 460 [miles] in 25 days. He thus averaged about 18 miles a day – evidently hastening as well as he could. He had thus only 38 days in which to work his mischief in the Shire; but much of it had already been done by the ruffians according to his orders – already planned and issued before the sack of Isengard. [p. 103]

1020 (III: 300): To the dismay of those

1020 (III: 300). To the dismay of those . . . and turned away. – These two paragraphs were added to the chapter in page proof. In *Tolkien: A Cultural Phenomenon* Brian Rosebury rewrites the first of these in 'a more commonplace syntactical mode', in which 'subject and main verb initiate each sentence' and each sentence contains no more than a single conjunction, in order to show how much less effective the stylistically modern version is than Tolkien's with its 'more idiosyncratic phrase-order'. Tolkien abandons modern inhibitions of style 'while avoiding archaism' and 'achieves greater clarity and fluency as well as an appropriately grave tone' (p. 73).

1020 (III: 300). For a moment it wavered, looking to the West; but out of the West came a cold wind – Some readers have inferred that the spirit of Saruman the Maia here seeks to return to Valinor, but is rejected by the Valar.

1020 (III: 300). it shrank, and the shrivelled face became rags of skin upon a hideous skull. – Readers, including John D. Rateliff and Jared Lobdell, have noted a similarity between Tolkien's description of the death of Saruman and the sudden ageing and death of Ayesha in H. Rider Haggard's *She*:

> Smaller she grew and smaller yet, till she was no larger than a monkey. Now the skin had puckered into a million wrinkles, and on the shapeless face was the stamp of unutterable age . . . nobody ever saw anything like the frightful age that was graven on that fearful countenance, no bigger now than that of a two-months' child, though the skull remained the same size, or nearly so. . . . I took up Ayesha's kirtle and the gauzy scarf . . . and, averting my head so that I might not look upon it, covered up that dreadful relic. . . . [*She*, Chapter XXVI]

Chapter 9

THE GREY HAVENS

For drafts and history of this chapter, see *Sauron Defeated*, pp. 108–13.

1021 (III: 301): The clearing up certainly needed

1021 (III: 301). The day after the battle – It is 4 November 1419.

1021 (III: 301). the Brockenbores by the hills of Scary – *Brockenbores* is given thus in the text, but as *Brockenborings* on the map *A Part of the Shire*. The name suggests 'holes made by the brock', i.e. the badger (from Old English *brocc*); compare *Brockhouse* (note for p. 28). In Tolkien's unfinished index *Brockenbores* is defined as 'holes in the quarried hills of Scary'. In *Nomenclature* Tolkien writes of *Scary*: 'a meaningless name in the Shire; but since it was in a region of caves and rock-holes . . . and of a stone-quarry . . . it may be supposed to contain English dialectal *scar* "rocky cliff"'.

1021 (III: 301): Then there was Lobelia

1021 (III: 301). Hardbottle – In his unfinished index Tolkien says that *Hardbottle* is a village in the Southfarthing; but in *Nomenclature* he explains that it is the 'home of the Bracegirdles (in North Farthing, not on the map). *-bottle* is an English place-name element, Old English *botl*, variant of *bold* (from which modern English *build* is derived), meaning "(large) dwelling"; it is not connected with *bottle* "glass container".' *Hardbottle* means '"hard dwelling"; "hard" because excavated in or built of stone (in the rocky Northfarthing).'

1022 (III: 302): Meanwhile the labour

1022 (III: 302). gammers – *Gammer* is a rustic word for 'old woman'; compare *gaffer* for a man (see note for p. 22).

1022 (III: 302). Yule – In the Shire Calendar there were two Yule days between 30 December and 1 January: 1 Yule, the last day of the old year, and 2 Yule, the beginning of the new year.

1022 (III: 302): It's an ill wind as blows

1022 (III: 302). All's well as ends Better – A play on the proverb *All's well that ends well.*

1022 (III: 302): There was some discussion

1022 (III: 302). Sharkey's End – In one sense, the place where Sharkey met his end; but *end* is also a familiar element in English street- or place-names, meaning the 'the end of an estate, district, village etc.' (compare *Bag End*, note for p. 21).

1022 (III: 302): Inside it was filled

1022 (III: 302). like a small nut with a silver shale – See note for p. 335.

1023 (III: 303): So Sam planted saplings

1023 (III: 303). the Three-Farthing Stone, which is as near the centre of the Shire as no matter – See note for p. 1003.

1023 (III: 303): Spring surpassed his wildest hopes

1023 (III: 303). Spring surpassed his wildest hopes – The spring of 1420.

1023 (III: 303). and burst into golden flowers in April – On 6 April, according to *The Tale of Years*.

1023 (III: 303). people would come long journeys to see it: the only *mallorn* west of the Mountains and east of the Sea – Presumably this excluded Men, after Aragorn in 1427 forbade them to enter the Shire.

1023 (III: 303): Altogether 1420 in the Shire

1023 (III: 303). Altogether 1420 in the Shire was a marvellous year . . . an air of richness and growth, and a gleam of beauty beyond that of mortal summers. . . . All the children born or begotten in that year . . . were fair to see . . . and most of them had rich golden hair – The splendour of 1420 is greater than can be explained merely by the passing of the Shadow. Tolkien seems to imply that at least some of it may be due to Galadriel's elven-dust, every grain of which (Frodo believes) has a value. He hints at this also in *Nomenclature* (entry for *Marigold*), where it is said that 'there was a "Fallohide" strain . . . in Sam's family – which, *increased by the favour of Galadriel*, became notable in his children', several of whom had golden hair (emphasis ours).

1024 (III: 304): Sam stayed at first

1024 (III: 304). on the thirteenth of that month [March] – The first anniversary of Shelob's attack.

1024 (III: 304): 'It is gone for ever'

1024 (III: 304). It is gone for ever . . . and now all is dark and empty. – Frodo is not healed, and at times regrets the destruction of the Ring. See further, note for p. 1025.

1024 (III: 304): 'There is no need to come yet

1024 (III: 304). Widow Rumble – *Rumble* is the 'name of an old hobbit-woman. It had no meaning (at that time) in the Shire' (*Nomenclature*).

1024 (III: 304): 'It's Rosie, Rose Cotton'

1024 (III: 304). But as I hadn't spoken, she couldn't say so. And I didn't speak . . . . But now I have spoken – Sam uses *speak, spoke* in the sense 'to propose marriage, to make one's intentions known'.

1024–5 (III: 304–5): So it was settled

1024 (III: 304). Sam Gamgee married Rose Cotton – According to *The Tale of Years* Sam and Rose were married on 1 May 1420. Tolkien wrote to Milton Waldman in ?late 1951: 'I think the simple "rustic" love of Sam and his Rosie (nowhere elaborated) is *absolutely essential* to the study of his (the chief hero's) character, and to the theme of the relation of ordinary life (breathing, eating, working, begetting) and quests, sacrifice, causes, and the "longing for Elves", and sheer beauty' (*Letters*, p. 161).

1025 (III: 305): Merry and Pippin lived together

1025 (III: 305). cut a great dash – To *cut a dash* is to 'be stylish or impressive in one's dress or behaviour' (*Concise OED*).

1025 (III: 305): All things now went well

1025 (III: 305). Frodo dropped quietly out of all the doings of the Shire, and Sam was pained to notice how little honour he had in his own country. – In his draft letter to Eileen Elgar, September 1963, Tolkien wrote:

> Slowly [Frodo] fades 'out of the picture', saying and doing less and less. I think it is clear on reflection to an attentive reader that when his dark times came upon him and he was conscious of being 'wounded by knife, sting, and tooth, and a long burden' (III 268) it was not only nightmare memories of past horrors that afflicted him, but also unreasoning self-reproach: he saw himself and all that he had done as a broken failure. 'Though I may come to the Shire, it will not seem the same, for I shall not be the same.' That was actually a temptation out of the Dark, a last flicker of pride: desire to have returned as a 'hero', not content with being a mere instrument of good. And it was mixed with another temptation, blacker and yet (in a sense) more merited, for however that may be explained, he had not in fact cast away the Ring by a voluntary act: he was tempted to regret its destruction, and still to desire it. 'It is gone for ever, and now all is dark and empty', he said as he wakened from his sickness in 1420. [*Letters*, pp. 327–8]

'How little honour [Frodo] had in his own country' echoes the proverb *A prophet is not without honour save in his own country.* Tolkien's changed conception of the part that Frodo played in the Shire and how it affected his subsequent reputation is shown by comparing the published text with the first draft:

> Even Sam could find no fault with Frodo's fame and honour in his own country. The Tooks were too secure in their traditional position – and after all their folkland was the only one that had never given in to the ruffians – and also too generous to be really jealous; yet it was plain that the name of Baggins would become the most famous in Hobbit-history. [*Sauron Defeated*, p. 108]

In *Tolkien and the Land of Heroes* Anne C. Petty comments that Frodo's return to the Shire

> takes the form of the hero who sadly can't fit back into the society he left behind. He has sacrificed all, and not even Elrond can heal the damage done. If you want to look at him in terms of war imagery, mirroring Tolkien's experience at the front, Frodo comes back to the Shire shell-shocked . . . like many veterans of combat [he] suffers from post-traumatic stress syndrome that causes him to become more withdrawn and troubled as the days go by. He has saved the world, yet the magnitude of what he accomplished can never be appreciated or even comprehended by his old community. [p. 282]

See also John Garth, 'Frodo and the Great War', in the proceedings of the October 2004 Marquette University Tolkien conference, forthcoming.

1025–6 (III: 305–6): Time went on

1025 (III: 305). Frodo was ill again in March – On 13 March 1421, according to *The Tale of Years*.

1026 (III: 306). The first of Sam and Rosie's children was born on the twenty-fifth of March, a date that Sam noted. – It was the second anniversary of the destruction of the Ring. According to *The Tale of Years* it was also the 'day on which the Fourth Age began in the reckoning of Gondor'. In Appendix D (p. 1120, III: 390) it is said that 'the Fourth Age was held to have begun with the departure of Master Elrond, which took place in September 3021 [S.R. 1421]; but for purposes of record in the Kingdom Fourth Age 1 was the year that began according to the New Reckoning in March 25, 3021, old style.'

1026 (III: 306): 'It will be Bilbo's birthday

1026 (III: 306). It will be Bilbo's birthday on Thursday – On Thursday it will be 22 September.

1026 (III: 306): 'Of course not

1026 (III: 306). You can see me on my way . . . you won't be away very long, not more than a fortnight – In fact he will be away for fifteen nights: Frodo and Sam will leave on 21 September, and Sam will return home on 6 October. Tolkien does not say how Frodo knows exactly when and where to meet Elrond, Bilbo, and the others. Sam's response shows that he thinks that Frodo is going to Rivendell; Frodo delays revealing the truth.

1026–7 (III: 306–7): In the next day or two

1027 (III: 307). It was divided into chapters but Chapter 80 was unfinished, and after that there were some blank leaves. . . . Together with extracts from Books of Lore translated by Bilbo in Rivendell. . . . 'I have quite finished. . . . The last pages are for you.' – Kristin Thompson asserts in '*The Hobbit* as a Part of *The Red Book of Westmarch*', *Mythlore* 15, no. 2, whole no. 56 (Winter 1988), that the volume Frodo gave Sam 'was meant to include only Bilbo's and Frodo's memoirs, not Bilbo's *Translations from the Elvish*. Taken together, *The Hobbit* and *The Lord of the Rings* contain 81 chapters' (p. 13). This total is the sum of the nineteen chapters of *The Hobbit* and the sixty-two of *The Lord of the Rings*. (The Prologue to the latter is presumably intended to be Tolkien's own work as 'editor'.) The sticking point is the statement in the present text, 'Chapter 80 was unfinished': for it seems logical to infer that Frodo has completed his portion of the account up to the time that he gives the volume to Sam, who in turn will write the rest of the final chapter. By the same token, it does not seem logical to suppose that Frodo wrote only part of the eightieth chapter ('The Scouring of the Shire'), which recounts events in which he took part.

In *Sauron Defeated* (pp. 109; 112, n. 2) Christopher Tolkien notes that in successive versions of the text his father changed the number of chapters from '77?' to '72' to '80'. It is not clear what Tolkien had in mind, or if he miscounted, a possibility made more likely by the fact that in draft form some chapters were conjoined, and only later separated; or it may be that '80' is meant to refer to the original Red Book but not to the work Tolkien 'edited' or 'translated'. In fact Tolkien's 'source' for *The Hobbit* and *The Lord of the Rings* is said in the Prologue ('Note on the Shire Records') to be later copies and extracts, not the actual Red Book begun by Bilbo and Frodo and completed by Sam.

The abandoned Epilogue seems to confirm the view that only a little of the manuscript was left for Sam to write. In his letter to Milton Waldman, ?late 1951, Tolkien said that in the Epilogue Sam is 'struggling to finish off the Red Book, begun by Bilbo and nearly completed by Frodo, in which all the events (told in The Hobbit and The Lord [of the Rings]) are recorded' (*Waldman LR*; also quoted in *Sauron Defeated*, p. 132). In the second version of the Epilogue Sam tells Elanor that Frodo 'left the last pages of the Book to me, but I have never yet durst to put hand to them. I am still making notes, as old Mr Bilbo would have said' (*Sauron Defeated*, p. 122). He also makes it clear that he has been collecting questions which need answering, such as whether Gimli and Legolas went back to Gondor, but he does not know how to write them as part of the story. He discusses some of these questions with his daughter Elanor, who says near the end:

'I know what your chapter should be. Write down our talk together' (p. 127).

In the present chapter Frodo is said to give Sam only 'a big book with plain red leather covers' (p. 1026, III: 307). But he must have given him the three volumes of Bilbo's *Translations from the Elvish* as well, since they were afterwards preserved by Elanor and her descendants. The phrase on Frodo's title-page, 'Together with extracts from Books of Lore translated by Bilbo in Rivendell', may indicate that the page applies to the four volumes together, or only that Frodo incorporated parts of Bilbo's work in his own narrative. In the Prologue it is said that Bilbo's translations were 'little used by Frodo, being almost entirely concerned with the Elder Days' (p. 15, I: 24).

1027 (III: 307): On September the twenty-first

1027 (III: 307). On September the twenty-first – It is 21 September. Three years earlier, the hobbits had set out two days later, on 23 September 1418.

1028 (III: 308): It was evening

1028 (III: 308). It was evening – On 22 September.

1028 (III: 308): *Still round the corner*

1028 (III: 308). *And though I oft have passed them by, / A day will come at last when I / Shall take the hidden paths that run / qWest of the Moon, East of the Sun.* – These lines are an adaptation of part of the hobbits' walking-song in Book I, Chapter 3: '*And though we pass them by today / Tomorrow we may come this way / And take the hidden paths that run / Towards the Moon or to the Sun*' (p. 77, I: 87). Frodo implies that the day *will* come, and that he knows it is near. Seven days later he will set sail from the Grey Havens on the Straight Road into the True West.

Tolkien perhaps first met the phrase 'West of the Moon, East of the Sun' as *East o' the Sun & West o' the Moon*, the title of a Norwegian folk tale included in *Popular Tales from the Norse* (1859), translated by George Webbe Dasent, which Tolkien mentions several times in *On Fairy-Stories*. One of the earliest poems of Tolkien's mythology, *The Shores of Faery*, written in 1915 (published in *The Book of Lost Tales, Book Two*, pp. 271–2), begins 'East of the Moon, West of the Sun' (altered from 'West of the Moon, East of the Sun'), referring to Aman.

1028 (III: 308): There was Gildor

1028 (III: 308). upon his finger was a ring of gold with a great blue stone, Vilya, mightiest of the Three – Vilya, one of the three Elven-rings, also called the Ring of Air and the Ring of Sapphire, was given by Celebrimbor to Gil-galad, and by Gil-galad to Elrond at the end of the Second Age. Here it is first revealed that Elrond wore one of the Rings. The words 'Vilya, mightiest of the Three' were added only in proof. *Vilya* is Quenya, from *vilwa* 'lower air, sky'. In *Of the Rings of Power and the Third Age* it is said, concerning the three Elven-rings: 'Narya, Nenya, and Vilya, they were named, the Rings of Fire, and of Water, and of Air, set with ruby and adamant and sapphire' (*The Silmarillion*, p. 288). In an early text of Book I, Chapter 2 of *The Lord of the Rings*, while his ideas concerning the Rings were still developing, Tolkien named them '*Kemen*, *Ëar*, and *Menel*, the Rings of Earth, Sea and Heaven' (Marquette Series 3/1/12).

1028 (III: 308). Galadriel was . . . robed all in glimmering white – Here 'robed' was correct in the first Allen & Unwin printing in 1955, but by the fourth printing (1958) it was inexplicably changed to 'roped'. This error survived in the standard three-volume hardcover edition until at least the seventh printing (1973) of the Allen & Unwin second edition, but was corrected by the ninth printing (1978).

1028 (III: 308). On her finger was Nenya, the ring wrought of *mithril*, that bore a single white stone flickering like a frosty star. – That Galadriel bore one of the Elven-rings was revealed at the end of Book II, Chapter 7, where it is called the Ring of Adamant. The present reading was added in proof; previously the text was: 'On her finger was a great ring bearing a single white stone that flickered like a frosty star' (Marquette Series 3/8/44).

1029 (III: 309): 'No, Sam

1029 (III: 309). Not yet anyway. . . . Your time may come. – According to *The Tale of Years*, after the death of Rose 'on 22 September [1482] Master Samwise rides out from Bag End. He comes to the Tower Hills, and is last seen by Elanor, to whom he gives the Red Book afterwards kept by the Fairbairns. Among them the tradition is handed down from Elanor that Samwise passed the Towers, and went to the Grey Havens, and passed over Sea, last of the Ring-bearers' (p. 1097, III: 378).

1029 (III: 309): 'So I thought too, once

1029 (III: 309). But I have been too deeply hurt – Tolkien explained in his draft letter to Eileen Elgar, September 1963:

> 'Alas! there are some wounds that cannot be wholly cured', said Gandalf [Book VI, Chapter 7, p. 989, III: 268] – not in Middle-earth. Frodo was sent or allowed to pass over Sea to heal him – if that could be done, *before he died*. He would have eventually to 'pass away': no mortal could, or can, abide for ever on earth, or within Time. So he went both to a purgatory and to a reward, for a while: a period of reflection and peace and a gaining of a truer understanding of his position in littleness and in greatness, spent still in Time amid the natural beauty of 'Arda Unmarred', the Earth unspoiled by Evil.
>
> Bilbo went too. No doubt as a completion of the plan due to Gandalf himself. Gandalf had a very great affection for Bilbo, from the hobbit's

> childhood onwards. His companionship was really necessary for Frodo's sake – it is difficult to imagine a hobbit, even one who had been through Frodo's experiences, being really happy even in an earthly paradise without a companion of his own kind, and Bilbo was the person Frodo most loved. . . . But he also needed and deserved the favour on his own account. He bore still the mark of the Ring that needed to be finally erased: a trace of pride and personal possessiveness. . . . As for reward for his part, it is difficult to feel that his life would be complete without an experience of 'pure Elvishness', and the opportunity of hearing the legends and histories in full the fragments of which had so delighted him. . . .
>
> Such a journey would at first seem [to Frodo] something not necessarily to be feared, even as something to look forward to – so long as undated and postponable. His real desire was hobbitlike (and humanlike) just 'to be himself' again and get back to the old familiar life that had been interrupted. Already on his journey back from Rivendell he suddenly saw that was not for him possible. Hence his cry 'Where shall I find rest?' . . . From the onset of the first sickness (Oct. 5, 3019) Frodo must have been thinking about 'sailing', though still resisting a final decision – to go with Bilbo, or to go at all. It was no doubt after his grievous illness in March 3020 that his mind was made up. [*Letters*, pp. 328–9]

In a letter to Roger Lancelyn Green on 17 July 1971 Tolkien was more explicit about Frodo's ultimate fate. Mortals, he said, 'could only dwell in *Aman* for a limited time – whether brief or long. The *Valar* had neither the power nor the right to confer "immortality" upon them. Their sojourn was a "purgatory", but one of peace and healing, and they would eventually pass away (*die* at their own desire and of free will) to destinations of which the Elves knew nothing' (*Letters*, p. 411).

1029 (III: 309). and Frodo-lad will come, and Rosie-lass, and Merry, and Goldilocks, and Pippin; and perhaps more that I cannot see – Sam had told Frodo that if his first child had been a boy he and Rose wanted to call him Frodo, so the mention of 'Frodo-lad' needed no foresight; the following four children will be named as Frodo says here, except that Pippin will precede Goldilocks. 'The Longfather-Tree of Master Samwise' in Appendix C seems to indicate that *Merry* and *Pippin* were the actual names given to those sons, rather than *Meriadoc* and *Peregrin*. Another seven children will follow (one of them named Bilbo); in draft Tolkien originally wrote that there would be eight more, but Lily, the youngest, was removed in the first proof (see further, note for p. 1105).

1029 (III: 309). You will be the Mayor, of course, as long as you want to be – According to *The Tale of Years* Sam will be elected Mayor seven times, serving from 1427 to 1476.

1029 (III: 309): Then Elrond and Galadriel rode on

1029 (III: 309). for the Third Age was over, and the Days of the Rings were passed, and an end was come of the story and song of those times – Sauron has been destroyed and the Free Peoples saved from his domination, and the Shire has been restored, but this 'happy ending' has not been achieved without loss, and *The Lord of the Rings* ends in a minor key as most of the Elves leave Middle-earth and the Age of Man begins, in which other evils will come. Tolkien wrote to Milton Waldman in ?late 1951 to explain why the narrative continues so long after the fall of Sauron:

> But it ['The Field of Cormallen', Chapter 4] is not the end of the 'Sixth Book', or of *The Lord of the Rings* as a whole. For various reasons. The chief artistic one that the music cannot be cut off short at its peak. Also the history is left in the air, unfinished. Also I like tying up loose ends, and hate them in other people's books; I like to wind up the clues, as do not only children, but most folk of hearty appetite. Again, the story began in the simple Shire of the Hobbits, and it must end there, back to common life and earth (the ultimate foundation) again. Finally and cogently, it is the function of the longish *coda* to show the *cost* of victory (as always), and to show that no victory, even on a world-shaking scale, is final. The war will go on, taking other modes. [courtesy of Christopher Tolkien]

Tom Shippey comments in *The Road to Middle-earth* that wise men and women in *The Lord of the Rings* 'accept defeat as a long-term prospect'.

> Thus Galadriel says of her life, 'Through ages of the world we have fought the long defeat'. Elrond agrees, 'I have seen three ages in the West of the world, and many defeats and many fruitless victories'. Later he queries his own adjective 'fruitless', but still repeats that the victory long ago in which Sauron was overthrown but not destroyed 'did not achieve its end'. The whole history of Middle-earth seems to show that good is attained only at vast expense while evil recuperates almost at will.

And even if the crisis at the end of the Third Age leads to the defeat of Sauron, Tolkien makes it clear that this will bear only bitter fruit: the Elven-rings lose their power, Lothlórien 'fades', the Elves, Ents, and Dwarves retreat before the Dominion of Men;

> all the characters and their story, one might say, will shrink to poetic 'rigmaroles' and misunderstood snatches in plays and ballads. Beauty especially will be a casualty. 'However the fortunes of war shall go . . .', asks Théoden, 'may it not so end that much that was fair and wonderful shall pass for ever out of Middle-earth?' 'The evil of Sauron cannot be wholly cured', replies Gandalf, 'nor made as if it had not been.' Fangorn agrees when he says of his own dying species, 'songs like trees bear fruit

only in their own time and their own way, and sometimes they are withered untimely'. [2nd edn., pp. 139–40]

1029 (III: 309). High Kindred – The High Elves, Noldor; see note for p. 79.

1029–30 (III: 310): Though they rode through the midst

1030 (III: 310). so they rode down at last to Mithlond, to the Grey Havens – They arrive at the Grey Havens on 29 September.

1030 (III: 310). firth of Lune – A *firth* is a narrow inlet of the sea.

1030 (III: 310): As they came to the gates

1030 (III: 310). Círdan the Shipwright. . . . Very tall he was, and his beard was long, and he was grey and old – Readers have remarked that not only did Círdan appear old, he also had a long beard despite the fact that Elves, as immortals, did not usually show physical signs of aging, and beardlessness is supposed to be a sign of Elvish blood (see note for p. 872). Iwan Morus, in 'The Ageing of the Elves', *Anor* 1 [?January 1983], comments that

> Círdan would appear to be the oldest elf living in Middle-earth at the time of the War of the Ring. He is first mentioned in the early pages of the [*Silmarillion*] as leader of those Telerin elves of the Falas who listened to the pleas of Ossë and remained, rather than departing to the West. He had therefore dwelt in Middle-earth throughout all three Ages, and for unknown thousands of years before the rising of the Sun and Moon. It may possibly be surmised that a sojourn of this length in the mortal lands is sufficient time for even an Elda of noble race to lose some of his youthful vigour. [p. 4]

In a note in papers associated with *The Shibboleth of Fëanor*, written *c.* 1968, Tolkien says that 'Elves did not have beards until they entered the third cycle of life. Nerdanel's father was exceptional, being only early in his second' (*Vinyar Tengwar* 41 (July 2000), p. 9).

Tolkien wrote a brief manuscript in late 1972 or early 1973 in which it is said that *Círdan*

> is the Sindarin for 'Shipwright', and describes his later functions in the history of the First Three Ages; but his 'proper' name, sc. his original name among the Teleri [one of the kindreds of the Elves], to whom he belonged, is never used. He is said . . . to have seen further and deeper into the future than anyone else in Middle-earth [Appendix B, p. 1085, III: 366]. This does not include the Istari (who came from Valinor), but must include even Elrond, Galadriel, and Celeborn. [*The Peoples of Middle-earth*, p. 385]

He wished to follow his kin into the West, and built a ship in which to sail, but as he stood on the shore he received in his heart a message, which he knew to come from the Valar, telling him to stay in Middle-earth, for the time would come when his work there would be of 'utmost worth' (p. 386) – in particular, concerning the construction of the ship with which Eärendil reached Valinor (see note for p. 194).

1030 (III: 310): Then Círdan led them

1030 (III: 310). upon the quay beside a great grey horse stood a figure robed all in white awaiting them. As he turned and came towards them Frodo saw that Gandalf now wore openly on his hand the Third Ring, Narya the Great – As first published the first part of this passage read: 'upon the quay stood a figure robed all in white awaiting them. As he turned and came towards them Frodo saw that it was Gandalf'. It was revised in the Allen & Unwin second edition (1966). In one of his check copies of *The Return of the King* Tolkien noted that this was done 'to satisfy queries what became of Shadowfax, also to remove the suggestion of the text that Frodo would not have immediately recognized Gandalf with or without a horse'. On 19 January 1965 he wrote to Miss A.P. Northey:

> I think Shadowfax certainly went with Gandalf [across the Sea], though this is not stated [in the first edition]. I feel it is better not to state everything (and indeed it is more realistic, since in chronicles and accounts of 'real' history, many facts that some enquirer would like to know are omitted, and the truth has to be discovered or guessed from such evidence as there is). I should argue so: Shadowfax came of a special race . . . being as it were an Elvish equivalent of ordinary horses: his 'blood' came from 'West over Sea'. It would not be unfitting for him to 'go West'. Gandalf was not 'dying', or going by a special grace to the Western Land, before passing on 'beyond the circles of the world': he was going home, being plainly one of the 'immortals', an angelic emissary of the angelic governors (Valar) of the Earth. He would take or could take what he loved. Gandalf was last seen riding Shadowfax. . . . He must have ridden to the Havens, and it is inconceivable that he would [have] ridden any beast but Shadowfax; so Shadowfax must have been there. A chronicler winding up a long tale, and for the moment moved principally by the sorrow of those left behind (himself among them!) might omit mention of the horse; but had the horse also shared in the grief of sundering, he could hardly have been forgotten. [*Letters*, p. 354]

Indeed, in the fair copy of the first version of the Epilogue it is said (by Sam) that 'Shadowfax went in the White Ship with Gandalf: of course Gandalf couldn't a' left him behind' (*Sauron Defeated*, p. 120).

Until the Houghton Mifflin edition of 1987, and then the HarperCollins edition of 1994, 'on his hand' was misprinted 'upon his hand'.

Grey is often used to mean 'white' when describing the colour of a horse.

Tolkien commented in his letter to Michael Straight, ?end of 1955, that Gandalf was not the 'original holder of the Ring – but it was surrendered to him by Círdan, to assist him in his task. Gandalf was returning, his labour and errand finished, to his home, the land of the Valar' (*Letters*, pp. 236–7). In *The Tale of Years* it is said that when Gandalf arrived in Middle-earth Círdan welcomed him, 'knowing whence he came and whither he would return'.

> 'Take this ring, Master,' he said, 'for your labours will be heavy, but it will support you in the weariness that you have taken upon yourself. For this is the Ring of Fire, and with it you may rekindle hearts in a world that grows chill. But as for me, my heart is with the Sea, and I will dwell by the grey shores until the last ship sails. I will await you.' [p. 1083, III: 366]

The name *Narya the Great* was added only when this chapter was in proof.

1030 (III: 310): But Sam was now sorrowful

1030 (III: 310). up rode Merry and Pippin – It is curious that Frodo did not contrive to say farewell to these other close friends and relations, but their last-minute arrival contributes more drama to the close of the tale than if all four hobbits had joined the Elves in the Shire.

1030 (III: 310): Then Frodo kissed Merry and Pippin

1030 (III: 310). And the ship went out into the High Sea – On 17 July 1971 Tolkien wrote to Roger Lancelyn Green:

> The 'immortals' who were permitted to leave Middle-earth and seek *Aman* . . . set sail in ships specially made and hallowed for this voyage, and steered due West. . . . They only set out after sundown; but if any keen-eyed observer from that shore had watched one of these ships he might have seen that it never became hull-down but dwindled only by distance until it vanished in the twilight: it followed the straight road to the true West and not the bent road of the earth's surface. As it vanished it left the physical world. There was no return. The Elves who took this road and those few 'mortals' who by special grace went with them, had abandoned the 'History of the world' and could play no further part in it.
>
> The angelic immortals (incarnate only at their own will), the *Valar* or regents under God and others of the same order but less power and majesty (such as Olórin = Gandalf) needed no transport, unless they for a time remained incarnate, and they could, if allowed or commanded, return. [*Letters*, p. 410–11]

1030 (III: 310). as in his dream in the house of Bombadil – This phrase was added only in proof. See note for p. 135.

1030 (III: 310). he beheld white shores and beyond them a far green country under a swift sunrise – Frodo's departure echoes that of King Arthur to Avalon to be healed of his wounds, but with no suggestion of return. Tolkien wrote to Milton Waldman, ?late 1951: 'To Bilbo and Frodo the special grace is granted to go with the Elves they loved – an Arthurian ending, in which it is, of course, not made explicit whether this is an "allegory" of death, or a mode of healing and restoration leading to a return. . . . It is hinted that they come to Eressëa' (quoted in *Sauron Defeated*, p. 132). The resonance is made greater by the fact in other writings by Tolkien that the name of the Elves' haven and city on Tol Eressëa is *Avallónë*.

1031 (III: 311): At last the three companions

1031 (III: 311). until they came back to the Shire – At this time the Shire extended only as far west as the Far Downs.

1031 (III: 311): At last they rode over the downs

1031 (III: 311). At last they rode over the downs and took the East Road – Presumably *downs* here means the White Downs. On the general map of Middle-earth the Road extends only that far to the west.

1031 (III: 311). as day was ending once more – It is evening on 6 October.

1031 (III: 311): He drew a deep breath

1031 (III: 311). 'Well, I'm back' – Christopher Tolkien comments in *Sauron Defeated*, p. 114:

> The words that end *The Lord of the Rings*, '"Well, I'm back," he said', were not intended to do so when my father wrote them in the long [first] draft manuscript [of the later chapters of Book VI]. It is obvious from the manuscript that the text continued on without break; and there is in fact no indication that my father thought of what he was writing as markedly separate from what preceded.

The Epilogue takes place nearly fifteen years later, in March 1436. In its first version, written probably in late summer or early autumn 1948, Sam is reading to his children from the Red Book and answering their questions. He tells them that the King is coming north, that they are all to meet him at the Brandywine Bridge and travel with him to his house by Lake Evendim, and he reads them the King's letter to this effect. In the second version of the Epilogue, which must date from after 1951, Sam is alone with Elanor, all the younger children being in bed. Both versions serve to tie up loose ends and to provide information about events subsequent to Frodo's departure.

But the Epilogue was 'universally condemned', as Tolkien wrote to Naomi Mitchison (25 April 1954, *Letters*, p. 179), possibly because it was anti-climactic, and Tolkien abandoned it, though he felt the picture to be 'incomplete without something on Samwise and Elanor' (letter to Katharine Farrer, *Letters*, p. 227). See further, *Sauron Defeated*, pp. 114–35; and *Vinyar Tengwar* 29 and 31 (May and September 1993).

*

In the 1950s Tolkien began a story set in Middle-earth, which he called *The New Shadow*. It is set in the days of Eldarion, son of King Elessar, long after the fall of Sauron, when the tale of that time was little heeded 'by most of the people of Gondor, though a few were still living who could remember the War of the Ring as a shadow upon their early childhood'. Now, as it seems, Evil is rising again. But Tolkien felt that the story was not worth continuing after only a few pages (though he twice revised them). On 13 May 1964 he wrote to Colin Bailey that *The New Shadow*

> proved both sinister and depressing. Since we are dealing with *Men* it is inevitable that we should be concerned with the most regrettable feature of their nature: their quick satiety with good. So that the people of Gondor in times of peace, justice and prosperity, would become discontented and restless – while the dynasts descended from Aragorn would become just kings and governors – like Denethor or worse. I found that even so early there was an outcrop of revolutionary plots, about a centre of secret Satanistic religion; while Gondorian boys were playing at being Orcs and going round doing damage. I could have written a 'thriller' about the plot and its discovery and overthrow – but it would be just that. Not worth doing. [*Letters*, p. 344]

See further, *The Peoples of Middle-earth*, pp. 409–21.

APPENDIX A

ANNALS OF THE KINGS AND RULERS

For drafts and history of Appendix A, see *The Peoples of Middle-earth*, pp. 188–24, 253–89.

Space permits us to annotate the Appendices only very selectively; but the Appendices themselves are intended to be a work of reference for readers of *The Lord of the Rings*, and should be used as such. Many of the names given in the Appendices, if not (like *Thingol* and *Tuor* on p. 1034, III: 314) directly and adequately explained within the text, are glossed by Christopher Tolkien in the indexes to *The Silmarillion* and *Unfinished Tales*.

In his original Foreword to *The Lord of the Rings* Tolkien called the attention of the reader to supplementary material then projected to appear at the end of the final volume, including

> some abridged family-trees, which show how the Hobbits mentioned were related to one another, and what their ages were at the time when the story opens. There is an index of names and strange words with some explanations. And for those who like such lore in an appendix some brief account is given of the languages, alphabets, and calendars that were used in the West-lands in the Third Age of Middle-earth. [1954 edn., I: 8]

Such 'lore' had accumulated as the story was written, and was further developed by Tolkien after he brought the main text to completion in draft in 1948. An appendix or appendices, indeed, were long contemplated as an essential adjunct to the tale proper. Tolkien handed over some of the ancillary material to Allen & Unwin in 1954, but was still working on the Appendices in March 1955 while his readers, having had *The Fellowship of the Ring* and *The Two Towers* already months earlier, were clamouring for *The Return of the King*. On 2 March 1955 Rayner Unwin pleaded with Tolkien to deliver the remainder of the Appendices, or Allen & Unwin would have to 'yield to the intense pressure that is accumulating and publish [*The Return of the King*] without all the additional material' (quoted in *Letters*, p. 209). Tolkien replied that he would have to 'make do with what material' he could produce in a short time.

> I now wish that no appendices had been promised! For I think their appearance in truncated and compressed form will satisfy nobody: certainly not me; clearly from the (appalling mass of) letters I receive not those people who like that kind of thing – astonishingly many. . . .

> It is, I suppose, a tribute to the curious effect that story has, when based on very elaborate and detailed workings of geography, chronology, and language, that so many should clamour for sheer 'information', or 'lore'. But the demands such people make would again require a book, at least the size of Vol. I.
>
> In any case the 'background' matter is very intricate, useless unless exact, and compression within the limits available leaves it unsatisfactory. [*Letters*, p. 210]

In April 1956, in his draft letter to H. Cotton Minchin, Tolkien wrote of plans for a 'specialist volume' to include much additional material concerning Middle-earth, especially about the Elvish tongues (*Letters*, pp. 247–8). Similarly he mentioned an 'accessory volume' in his original Foreword to *The Lord of the Rings*. This separate book never materialized, but some of the abundant material it might have contained, in draft if not finished form, or which was prepared for the Appendices but omitted due to insufficient space, has appeared in posthumous volumes such as *Unfinished Tales* and *The Peoples of Middle-earth*.

In the event, the Appendices occupied more than one hundred pages in the first edition. In the second edition (1965) they were extensively revised, but in such a way as to occupy the same amount of space when published in hardcover.

On 27 May 1958 Tolkien wrote to Rayner Unwin concerning the index to *The Lord of the Rings* that Nancy Smith had prepared (see our 'Brief History', above): 'All [readers of the book] miss an index (with indications of the meaning of names in other tongues).' But there was some doubt whether the inclusion of an index would require the omission of an equivalent amount of the Appendices; and in that respect Tolkien felt that

> some of what exists could be dropped without any damage at all. . . . I should say (1) most of Appendix D [The Calendars] (other than p. III 384 [the Shire Calendar table]; probably most of App. E II [Writing], and most of F II [On Translation], for a start: possibly some 15 pages. If the *Silmarillion* could be finished A I (i) [on the Númenórean kings] and probably (v) [the *Tale of Aragorn and Arwen*] would also be unnecessary. [Tolkien-George Allen & Unwin archive, HarperCollins]

On 24 January 1961, however, Tolkien wrote to Alina Dadlez at Allen & Unwin concerning a Swedish edition of *The Lord of the Rings* which the publisher, Gebers, had proposed to issue without the Appendices so as to reduce costs:

> I have no objection . . . to the omission of C [Hobbit family trees], D (except for the Shire Calendar, iii 384), E ii and Fii. Omission of the remainder would be, in different degrees, damaging to the book as a whole. In the case of Het Spectrum [the Dutch translation of *The Lord*

> *of the Rings*, *In de ban van de ring*, 1956–7], A and B and the Shire Calendar were retained, and that is the arrangement that I favour. I feel strongly that the absolute minimum is the retention of A (v) 'Of Aragorn and Arwen', and the Shire Calendar: two items essential to the understanding of the main text in many places. If Messrs. Gebers will include these in vol. iii, they may do as they wish with the remainder. . . .
>
> I do not believe that they [the Appendices] give the work a 'scholarly' . . . look, and they play a major part in producing the total effect: as Messrs. Gebers' translator has himself pointed out (selecting the detail and the *documentation* as two chief ingredients in producing the compelling sense of historical reality). In any case, purchasers of vol. iii will presumably be already involved: vol. iii is not a separate book to be purchased solely on its own merits. Actually, an analysis of many hundreds of letters shows that the Appendices have played a very large part in readers' pleasure, in turning library readers into purchasers (since the Appendices are needed for reference), and in creating a demand for another book [*The Silmarillion*]. A sharp distinction must be drawn between the tastes of reviewers ('donnish folly' and all that) and of readers! I think I understand the tastes of simple-minded folk (like myself) pretty well. But I do appreciate the question of costs and retail prices. There is a price beyond which simple-minded folk cannot go, even if they would like to. [Tolkien-George Allen & Unwin archive, HarperCollins; partly printed in *Letters*, p. 304]

The first Swedish edition (*Sagan om ringen*, 1959–61) ultimately omitted the Appendices except for *A Part of the Tale of Aragorn and Arwen* and Appendix D, much as Tolkien insisted (now emphasizing the importance of the *Tale*); and when an opportunity arose to add an index to the second English and American editions of *The Lord of the Rings*, this was done with no loss to the Appendices (indeed, for the sake of obtaining a new copyright, it was in the author's and publishers' interests to add as much new material to the book as feasible). When, in 1968, the first one-volume edition was published, limited in its page count by practicalities of binding a thick volume in paperback, the Appendices were omitted except for *The Tale of Aragorn and Arwen*.

THE NÚMENÓREAN KINGS

1033 (III: 313): Concerning the sources

1033 (III: 313). Concerning the sources for most of the matter. . . . – As first published, the introduction to Appendix A (I: 313) read thus:

> Until the War of the Ring the people of the Shire had little knowledge of the history of the Westlands beyond the traditions of their own wanderings; but afterwards all that concerned the King Elessar became

of deep interest to them; while in the Buckland the tales of Rohan were no less esteemed. Thus the Red Book contained many annals, genealogies, and traditions of the realms of the South and the North, derived through Bilbo from the books of lore in Rivendell; or through Frodo and Peregrin from the King himself, and from the records of Gondor that he opened to them: such as *The Book of the Kings*, *The Book of the Stewards*, and the *Akallabêth* (that is, *The Downfall of Númenor*). From Gimli no doubt is derived the information concerning the Dwarves of Moria, for he remained much attached to both Peregrin and Meriadoc. But through Meriadoc alone, it seems, were derived the tales of the House of Eorl; for he went back to Rohan many times, and learned the language of the Mark, it is said. For this matter the authority of Holdwine is often cited, but that appears to have been the name which Meriadoc himself was given in Rohan. Some of the notes and tales, however, were plainly added by other hands at later dates, after the passing of King Elessar.

Much of this lore appears as notes to the main narrative, in which case it has usually been included in it; but the additional material is very extensive, even though it is often set out in brief and annalistic form. Only a selection from it is here presented, again greatly reduced, but with the same object as the original compilers appear to have had: to illustrate the story of the War of the Ring and its origins and fill up some of the gaps in the main account.

Actual extracts from the longer annals and tales that are found in the Red Book are placed within quotation marks. These can often be seen to be copies of matter not composed in the Shire. Notes made at later times are printed as notes or placed in square brackets.

The dates given are those of the Third Age, according to the reckoning of Gondor, unless they are marked S.A. (Second Age) or F.A. (Fourth Age). The Second Age was held to have ended with the year 3441; but although a new era and calendar was begun in Gondor from the day of the final overthrow of Sauron, March 25, 3019, the Third Age was held to have ended with the year 3021 in which the Three Rings passed away [i.e. were taken by their bearers over sea into the West]. On the equation of this reckoning with Shire Reckoning see I, 14.

In lists the dates set after the names of kings and rulers are the dates of their deaths, where only one date is given. The sign † indicates a death in battle or other violent manner, though an annal of the event has not always been included. A few references are given to *The Lord of the Rings* by volume and page, and to *The Hobbit* by page (add 5 after p. 96 for the second edition).

In the second edition of *The Lord of the Rings* (1965) some of this material was moved and adapted to the Prologue, in the 'Note on the Shire Records'.

1033–4 (III: 313–14): Fëanor was the greatest

1033–4 (III: 313–14). Fëanor was the greatest of the Eldar . . . allies of the Eldar against the Enemy. – This paragraph was added in the second edition (1965), providing in a short space essential background concerning Fëanor, the Silmarils, and the struggle of the Eldar and the Edain against Morgoth which lay behind the paragraphs with which Appendix A.I.i originally began.

1034 (III: 314): There were three unions

1034 (III: 314). There were three unions of the Eldar and the Edain – As first published this passage read: 'There were only three unions of the High Elves and Men'. It was revised in the second edition (1965). As noted earlier (see note for p. 79), Tolkien in his letter to Naomi Mitchison of 14 April 1954 distinguished between the *High Elves* who had dwelt in Aman before returning to Middle-earth, and the *Eldar* who accepted the invitation of the Valar to pass from Middle-earth into the West but did not necessarily reach it; and it may be that it occurred to him when revising the text that although Lúthien's mother was a Maia and her father an Elf who had been to Aman, she herself had not actually lived there, nor indeed had Arwen. *Edain* likewise is more specific than *Men*, generally used to mean those of the Three Houses who allied with the Elves in the First Age, from whom Aragorn was descended.

Other unions between Elf and Man are noted or implied in Tolkien's writings, but it is debatable whether they are strictly 'of the Eldar and the Edain'. Mithrellas, a Silvan Elf, married a Lord of Dol Amroth (see note for p. 872); she had not lived in Aman, so was not a High Elf, but could be considered one of the Eldar if that term is taken to mean those Elves that began the journey West, including the Silvan folk; but in Appendix F Tolkien distinguishes *Eldar* 'the West-elves', i.e. of Beleriand, from 'the East-elves', i.e. 'most of the Elven-folk of Mirkwood and Lórien' (p. 1126, III: 405; see also *The Lost Road and Other Writings*, pp. 182–3). A stronger argument could be made for Dior (see note for p. 194), the son of Beren and Lúthien: born after his mother had become mortal, he would seem to be fully mortal himself, but in late writings by Tolkien he seems to be considered Half-elven. In *The Problem of Ros* he says of himself 'I am the first of the *Peredil* (Half-elven)', and in a late plot synopsis for the *Narn i Chîn Húrin* he is called 'Dior Halfelven' (*The Peoples of Middle-earth*, p. 369 and *The War of the Jewels*, p. 257). Although Dior's two sons and his daughter Elwing appeared early in 'Silmarillion' writings, their mother is not identified, or even mentioned until after the publication of *The Lord of the Rings*. In the late plot synopsis Dior is said to have married the Elf Lindis of Ossiriand; in late writings she is variously named Lindis, Elulin, and (as in *The Silmarillion*) Nimloth, and said to be from Ossiriand, or from Doriath and kin to Thingol and Celeborn (*The War of the Jewels*, pp. 349–50) – in any case, one of the Eldar.

1034 (III: 314): Lúthien Tinúviel was the daughter

1034 (III: 314). the First House of the Edain – One of the three houses of the Elf-friends; see note for p. 130.

1034 (III: 314): Idril Celebrindal was the daughter

1034 (III: 314). Idril Celebrindal – The story of Tuor and Idril, and of their escape with Eärendil from Morgoth's destruction of Gondolin, was the first tale of 'The Silmarillion' that Tolkien wrote, *The Fall of Gondolin*. A partial list of names appended to the tale notes that *Idril* means 'beloved', 'but often do Elves say *Idhril* which more rightly compares with *Irildë* and that meaneth "mortal maiden", and perchance signifies her wedding with Tuor son of Men' (*The Book of Lost Tales, Part Two*, p. 343).

Celebrindal 'silverfoot' is derived from Sindarin *celebrin* 'like silver, in hue or worth' + *tal* 'foot').

1034 (III: 314): Eärendil wedded Elwing

1034 (III: 314). the First Age. Of these things the full tale, and much else concerning Elves and Men, is told in *The Silmarillion*. – As first published this passage read more briefly: 'the First Age, as is told in the Silmarillion'. It was extended in the second edition (1965).

1034 (III: 314): The sons of Eärendil

1034 (III: 314). Elros – See notes for pp. 15 and 194.

1034–5 (III: 314–15): At the end of the First Age

1035 (III: 315). But to the children of Elrond a choice also was appointed: to pass with him from the circles of the world; or if they remained to become mortal and die in Middle-earth. – Since it is said at the end of the Prologue (p. 15, I: 25) that 'though Elrond had departed, his sons long remained' in Rivendell, some readers have assumed that Elladan and Elrohir, like their sister Arwen, chose to be of mortal kind. But in his draft letter to Peter Hastings in September 1954 Tolkien said that the end of Elladan and Elrohir 'is not told: they delay their choice, and remain for a while' (*Letters*, p. 193).

1035 (III: 315): Elros chose to be of Man-kind

1035 (III: 315). a great life-span was granted to him many times – As first published this passage read: 'a great life-span was granted to him (and to his descendants), many times'. It was revised in the second edition (1965).

1035 (III: 315): As a reward for their sufferings

1035 (III: 315). guided by the Star of Eärendil came to the great Isle of Elenna – *Elenna* is Quenya 'starwards', 'from the guidance of the Edain by Eärendil on their voyage to Númenor at the beginning of the Second Age' (*The Silmarillion*, p. 327).

1035 (III: 315): There was a tall mountain

1035 (III: 315). Meneltarma – Quenya 'pillar of heaven'; see note for p. 676.

1035 (III: 315). Undying Lands – Aman and Eressëa, the lands of the immortals (the Ainur and the Elves) beyond the Western Seas.

1035 (III: 315). though a long span of life had been granted to them, in the beginning thrice that of lesser Men – See notes for pp. 860 and 1062.

1035 (III: 315): Elros was the first King

1035 (III: 315). Tar-Minyatur – The prefix *Tar-* of the first nineteen rulers of Númenor is Quenya 'king, queen', from a root meaning 'high, noble'. *Minyatur* is Quenya for 'first ruler' (*minya* 'first' + *tur* 'power, mastery').

1035 (III: 315). *Akallabêth* – The account of the downfall of Númenor, published in *The Silmarillion*. *Akallabêth* is Adûnaic (Númenórean) for 'the Downfallen'.

1035 (III: 315): *These are the names*

1035 (III: 315). Elros Tar-Minyatur . . . – The Kings and Queens of Númenor are discussed in detail in *The Line of Elros*, written after (and not always in agreement with) *The Lord of the Rings* and published in *Unfinished Tales*.

1035 (III: 315). Tar-Calmacil, Tar-Ardamin – The name 'Tar-Ardamin' was added in the edition of 2004. In *Unfinished Tales* Christopher Tolkien comments that as the list of rulers was originally published, Tar-Calmacil was followed by Ar-Adûnakhôr, and that the latter is described later in Appendix A (p. 1036, III: 316) as 'the twentieth king' though he is nineteenth in the list.

> In 1964 my father replied to a correspondent who had enquired about this: 'As the genealogy stands he should be called the sixteenth king and nineteenth ruler. Nineteen should possibly be read for twenty; but it is also possible that a name has been left out.' . . .
>
> When editing the *Akallabêth* [for *The Silmarillion*, since corrected] . . . I had not observed that in 'The Line of Elros' [published in *Unfinished Tales*] the ruler following Tar-Calmacil was not Ar-Adûnakhôr but Tar-Ardamin; but it now seems perfectly clear, from the fact alone that Tar-Ardamin's death date is here given as 2899, that he

was omitted in error from the list in *The Lord of the Rings*. [*Unfinished Tales*, pp. 226–7, n. 11]

1035 (III: 315–16): After Ardamin the Kings

1035 (III: 315). After Ardamin – As first published these words read: 'After Calmacil'. They were emended in the edition of 2004; see previous note.

1035 (III: 315). Ar-Adûnakhôr – The Adûnaic prefix *Ar-* 'king, *queen' is the equivalent of Quenya *Tar-*. The Adûnaic names of the rulers of Númenor are glossed in 'An Adûnaic Dictionary' by Carl F. Hostetter and Patrick Wynne, *Vinyar Tengwar* 25 (September 1992).

1035–6 (III: 316): In the days of Tar-Elendil

1035 (III: 316). the Lords of Andúnië . . . renowned for their friendship with the Eldar – *Andúnië* was a great haven on the west coast of Númenor; its name is derived from Quenya *andúnë* 'sunset, west'. In the *Akallabêth* it is said that the *Lords of Andúnië* were

> highest in honour after the house of the kings . . . for they were of the line of Elros, being descended from Silmarien, daughter of Tar-Elendil the fourth king of Númenor. And these lords were loyal to the kings, and revered them; and the Lord of Andúnië was ever among the chief councillors of the Sceptre. Yet also from the beginning they bore especial love to the Eldar and reverence for the Valar; and as the Shadow grew they aided the Faithful as they could. [*The Silmarillion*, p. 268]

1036 (III: 316): The realm of Númenor

1036 (III: 316). The realm of Númenor endured to the end of the Second Age . . . – In ?late 1951 Tolkien wrote to Milton Waldman:

> *The Downfall* [of Númenor] is partly the result of an inner weakness in Men – consequent, if you will, upon the first Fall (unrecorded in these tales), repented but not finally healed. . . . The Fall [of Númenor] is achieved by the cunning of Sauron in exploiting this weakness. Its central theme is (inevitably, I think, in a story of Men) a Ban, or Prohibition.
>
> The Númenóreans dwell within far sight of the easternmost 'immortal' land, Eressëa; and as the only men to speak an Elvish tongue (learned in the days of their Alliance) they are in constant communication with their ancient friends and allies [the Eldar], either in the bliss of Eressëa, or in the kingdom of Gilgalad on the shores of Middle-earth. They became thus in appearance, and even in powers of mind, hardly distinguishable from the Elves – but they remained mortal, even though rewarded by a triple, or more than a triple, span of years. Their reward is their undoing – or the means of their temptation. Their long life aids

> their achievements in art and wisdom, but breeds a possessive attitude to these things, and desire awakes for more *time* for their enjoyment. Foreseeing this in part, the gods laid a Ban on the Númenóreans from the beginning: they must never sail to Eressëa, nor westward out of sight of their own land. . . . They must not set foot on 'immortal' lands, and so become enamoured of an immortality (within the world), which was against their law, the special doom or gift of Ilúvatar (God), and which their nature could not in fact endure. [*Letters*, pp. 154–5]

1036–7 (III: 317): He resolved to challenge Sauron

1036–7 (III: 317). So great was the might and splendour of the Númenóreans that Sauron's own servants deserted him; and Sauron humbled himself, doing homage, and craving pardon. . . . – On 14 October 1958 Tolkien wrote to Rhona Beare, who had asked how Ar-Pharazôn could defeat Sauron when Sauron had the One Ring:

> You cannot press the One Ring too hard, for it is of course a mythical feature, even though the world of the tales is conceived in more or less historical terms. The Ring of Sauron is only one of the various mythical treatments of the placing of one's life, or power, in some external object, which is thus exposed to capture or destruction with disastrous results to oneself. If I were to 'philosophize' this myth, or at least the Ring of Sauron, I should say it was a mythical way of representing the truth that *potency* (or rather *potentiality*) if it is to be exercised, and produce results, has to be externalized and so as it were passes, to a greater or lesser degree, out of one's direct control. A man who wishes to exert 'power' must have subjects, who are not himself. But he then depends on them.
>
> Ar-Pharazôn, as is told in the 'Downfall' or *Akallabêth*, conquered or terrified Sauron's *subjects*, not Sauron. Sauron's personal 'surrender' was voluntary and cunning: he got free transport to Númenor! He naturally had the One Ring, and so very soon dominated the minds and wills of most of the Númenóreans. (I do not think Ar-Pharazôn knew anything about the One Ring. The Elves kept the matter of the Rings very secret, as long as they could. In any case Ar-Pharazôn was not in communication with them. . . .)
>
> Sauron was first defeated by a 'miracle': a direct action of God the Creator, changing the fashion of the world, when appealed to by Manwë. . . . Though reduced to 'a spirit of hatred borne on a dark wind', I do not think one need boggle at this spirit carrying off the One Ring, upon which his power of dominating minds now largely depended. That Sauron was not himself destroyed in the anger of the One is not my fault: the problem of evil, and its apparent toleration, is a permanent one for all who concern themselves with our world. The indestructibility of *spirits* with free wills, even by the Creator of them,

> is also an inevitable feature, if one either believes in their existence, or feigns it in a story. [*Letters*, pp. 279–80]

1037 (III: 317): And Sauron lied to the King

1037 (III: 317). And Sauron lied to the King, declaring that everlasting life would be his who possessed the Undying Lands – In his draft letter to Robert Murray, 4 November 1954, Tolkien observes that this

> was a delusion of course, a Satanic lie. For as emissaries from the Valar clearly inform him [Ar-Pharazôn], the Blessed Realm does not confer immortality. The land is blessed because the Blessed dwell there, not vice versa, and the Valar are immortal by right and nature, while Men are mortal by right and nature. But cozened by Sauron he dismisses all this as a diplomatic argument to ward off the power of the King of Kings. It might or might not be 'heretical', if these myths were regarded as statements about the actual nature of Man in the real world: I do not know. But the view of the myth is that Death – the mere shortness of human life-span – is not a punishment for the Fall, but a biologically (and therefore also spiritually, since body and spirit are integrated) inherent part of Man's nature. The attempt to escape is wicked because 'unnatural', and silly because Death in that sense is the Gift of God (envied by the Elves), release from the weariness of Time. [*Letters*, p. 205]

1037 (III: 317): At length Ar-Pharazôn

1037 (III: 317). Aman the Blessed – The Undying Lands, the Blessed Realm, where immortals dwell; see note for p. 1035. *Aman* is Quenya for 'blessed, free from evil'.

1037 (III: 317). called upon the One – *The One* is Eru (Quenya 'he that is alone'), i.e. God.

1037 (III: 317): But it was not so

1037 (III: 317). [Sauron] was unable ever again to assume a form that seemed fair to men – On 25 June 1957 Tolkien wrote to Major R. Bowen that Sauron

> was always de-bodied when vanquished. The theory, if one can dignify the modes of the story with such a term, is that he was a spirit, a minor one but still an 'angelic' spirit. According to the mythology of these things that means that, though of course a creature, he belonged to the race of intelligent beings that were made before the physical world, and were permitted to assist in their measure in the making of it. Those who became most involved in this work of Art . . . desired to enter into it. . . .

> They were self-incarnated, if they wished; but their incarnate forms were more analogous to our clothes than to our bodies, except that they were more than are clothes the expression of their desires, moods, wills and functions. . . .

Because of the pre-occupation of the Spirits with the Children of God – Elves and Men – they

> often took the form and likeness of the Children. . . . It was thus that Sauron appeared in this shape. It is mythologically supposed that when this shape was 'real', that is a physical actuality in the physical world and not a vision transferred from mind to mind, it took some time to build up. It was then destructible like other physical organisms. But that of course did not destroy the spirit, nor dismiss it from the world to which it was bound until the end. After the battle with Gilgalad and Elendil, Sauron took a long while to re-build, longer than he had done after the Downfall of Númenor (I suppose because each building-up used up some of the inherent energy of the spirit, which might be called the 'will' or the effective link between the indestructible mind and being and the realization of its imagination). The impossibility of re-building after the destruction of the Ring, is sufficiently clear 'mythologically' in the present book. [*Letters*, pp. 259–60]

1038 (III: 318–19): THE REALMS IN EXILE

1038 (III: 318–19). *The Northern Line . . . The Southern Line* – The division of the Númenórean realms in exile into two kingdoms bears some similarity to the Western and Eastern subdivision of the late Roman Empire. One empire, Byzantium, long outlasted the other and had periods of great glory, as did Gondor in Middle-earth; and just as Arnor split into smaller kingdoms (see note for p. 1039), the Western Empire soon disintegrated, and whole provinces were lost to invaders such as Gaul to the Franks and Spain to the Visigoths. In both Byzantium and the Western Empire, however, not one but a succession of different families ruled; and whereas the Kin-strife in Gondor was an isolated episode, in both the Eastern and Western Empires internecine fighting among members of the ruling families was frequent, and murder of rivals a common occurrence. Byzantium eventually fell, but a kind of successor to the Western Empire was established by Charlemagne, and as the Holy Roman Empire survived until 1806 under a succession of dynasties ruling different parts of Western and Central Europe. (Cf. note for p. 848.)

1038 (III: 318): *Arnor*

1038 (III: 318). Eärendur – In his draft letter to Mr Rang, August 1967, Tolkien glosses *Eärendur* as '(professional) mariner', with the Quenya suffix *-n(dur)* 'to serve (a legitimate master)' (*Letters*, p. 386).

1038 (III: 318): *Chieftains*

1038 (III: 318). Aragorn II F.A. 120. – As first published this reference was to 'F.A. 100'. It was revised in the second edition (1965).

1038–9 (III: 318–19): *Kings of Gondor*

1038 (III: 318). Valacar 1432 – The date '1432' was added (from *The Tale of Years*) in the edition of 2004.

1039 (III: 319): *Ruling Stewards*

1039 (III: 319). Ecthelion – The name of two Stewards, *Ecthelion* was also the name in the First Age of an Elf-lord of Gondolin, who slew, and was slain by, Gothmog, Lord of Balrogs.

1039 (III: 319–20): 'At its greatest Arnor

1039 (III: 319). Glanduin – See note for pp. 984–5.

1039 (III: 320). Lindon – 'A name of Ossiriand in the First Age. . . . After the tumults at the end of the First Age the name Lindon was retained for the lands west of the Blue Mountains that still remained above the Sea' (*The Silmarillion*, p. 338). See also notes for pp. 243 and 469.

1039–40 (III: 320): After Elendil and Isildur

1039 (III: 320). After Eärendur, owing to dissensions among his sons their realm was divided into three: Arthedain, Rhudaur, and Cardolan. – This seems to be the one exception in Tolkien's writings to the general rule of the eldest son (in Númenor, the eldest child) of a ruler inheriting the entire kingdom. Here the division seems to have been the result of rivalry among the sons, and there appear to have been no further subdivisions. Similar divisions occurred in medieval Europe, such as William I leaving his original inheritance, Normandy, to his eldest son Robert, and his conquered realm, England, to his second son William; but the closest analogues to the subdivision of a single realm were among the Merovingian and Carolingian rulers of the Franks, according to the Frankish custom of inheritance by which all sons had the right to share their father's property, even if that meant dividing a kingdom. Among the most notable examples are Clovis (AD 465–511), who established his rule over territory which included modern France and parts of western Germany and subdivided it among his four sons, and Louis the Pious (778–840), the son of Charlemagne, who produced various schemes during his lifetime for the division of his empire, with the result that his sons not only fought each other but also attacked their father, each vying to secure a larger share of patrimony.

The names *Arthedain*, *Rhudaur*, and *Cardolan* are Sindarin. They mean, probably: *Arthedain* 'realm of the Edain' (*arth* 'region, realm' + *Edain*); *Rhudaur* 'east forest' (*rhû* (*rhu-*) 'east' + *taur* 'forest'); *Cardolan* 'red hill country' (*carn* 'red' + *dol* 'hill, mount' + *an(n)* 'land'). See note for p. 185.

1039, n. 1 (III: 319, n. 1): See p. 755 [See III, 27]

1039, n. 1 (III: 319, n. 1). the Sea of Rhûn – See note for p. 765. On the general map of Middle-earth a wooded island is marked within the boundaries of the Sea of Rhûn: at so small a scale, its trees appear only as dots.

1041 (III: 321): In the days of Argeleb II

1041 (III: 321). Minhiriath – 'Between the rivers' (*Unfinished Tales*, p. 261), from Sindarin *min-* 'between' + *siriath* 'rivers', i.e. the land between the rivers Baranduin and Gwathló.

1041 (III: 321): 'It is said that the mounds

1041 (III: 321). Tyrn Gorthad – 'Haunted downs', from Sindarin *tyrn* 'downs' + *gorth* 'dread' + *sad* (*-had*) 'place'.

1041 (III: 321–2): 'For a while Arvedui

1041 (III: 321). Lossoth, the Snowmen of Forochel – *Lossoth* 'snowmen' is derived from Sindarin *loss* 'snow' + *-hoth* 'men, people'. The Lossoth seem to have been roughly equivalent to the Lapps or the Inuit: they 'house in the snow, and it is said that they can run on the ice with bones on their feet [snowshoes], and have carts without wheels [sleighs]' (p. 1041, III: 321, n. 1).

Forochel 'northern ice' contains the Sindarin element *for(od)* 'north, northern'. For *-chel*, compare the stem KHEL- 'freeze' in *The Etymologies* (in *The Lost Road and Other Writings*).

1041, n. 1 (III: 321, n. 1): These are a strange, unfriendly people

1041, n. 1 (III: 321, n. 1). Forodwaith – 'North land', from Sindarin *forod* 'north' + *gwaith* (*-waith*) 'folk, land'.

1041, n. 1 (III: 321, n. 1). the great Cape of Forochel – In *Unfinished Tales* Christopher Tolkien comments that the body of water marked on his 1954 map of Middle-earth (see essay on Maps, above) as 'The Icebay of Forochel' 'was in fact only a small part of the Bay (referred to in [the present note] as "immense") which extended much further to the north-east: its northern and western shores being formed by the great Cape of Forochel, of which the tip, unnamed, appears on my original map' (p. 13, n.).

1042, n. 1 (III: 322, n. 2): These were the Stones

1042, n. 1 (III: 322, n. 2). Emyn Beraid – The Tower Hills; see note for p. 7.

1043 (III: 323–4): 'When the kingdom ended

1043 (III: 323). the Watchful Peace – The period from Third Age 2063 to 2460, 'during which Sauron withdrew before the power of the White

Council and the Ringwraiths remained hidden in Morgul Vale' (Appendix A, p. 1053, III: 333).

1043–4 (III: 324): There were fifteen Chieftains

1043 (III: 324). There were fifteen Chieftains, before the sixteenth and last was born. – As first published this sentence read: 'There were fourteen Chieftains, before the fifteenth and last was born'. It was revised *c.* 1978, no later than the ninth printing of the second Allen & Unwin edition, according to a correction indicated by Tolkien but not accomplished earlier.

1043, n. 1 (III: 323, n. 1): The sceptre was the chief mark

1043, n. 1 (III: 323, n. 1). the Elendilmir, Star of Elendil – See note for p. 848.

1044 (III: 324): It was the pride and wonder

1044 (III: 324). Aragorn indeed lived to be two hundred and ten years old – As first published this passage read: 'Aragorn indeed lived to be one hundred and ninety years old'. It was revised in the fourth or fifth printing (1966) of the Ballantine Books edition, but not altered in a primary edition until the HarperCollins resetting of 1994.

1045 (III: 325): The might of Hyarmendacil

1045 (III: 325). north to the field of Celebrant – As first published these words read: 'north to Celebrant'. In *Unfinished Tales*, p. 260, Christopher Tolkien comments that his father 'stated several times' that 'to Celebrant' was an error for 'to the field of Celebrant', but no correction was made until the edition of 2004. On the *field of Celebrant* (Parth Celebrant), see note for p. 374.

1045 (III: 325): So ended the line

1045 (III: 325). Nonetheless it was not until the days of Valacar . . . – As first published this sentence was broken off as a separate paragraph, with 'Rómendacil II' rather than 'Valacar'. It was revised in the second edition (1965).

1045 (III: 325–6): Minalcar, son of Calmacil

1045 (III: 325–6). Minalcar, son of Calmacil . . . with the Northmen. – This paragraph was added in the second edition (1965). At that time also, the beginning of the following paragraph (p. 1045, III: 326) was slightly revised, and the opening quotation marks with which that and the next three paragraphs had begun were omitted (thus indicating that they are *not* 'actual extracts from longer annals and tales', p. 1033, III: 313).

1046 (III: 326): In the days of Narmacil I

1046 (III: 326). In the days of Narmacil I their attacks began again . . . but it was learned by the regent – As first published this passage read: 'In the days of Rómendacil II their attacks began again . . . but it was learned by the King'. It was revised in the second edition (1965).

1046 (III: 326). Minalcar therefore in 1248 led out a great force, and between Rhovanion and the Inland Sea he defeated a large army of the Easterlings and destroyed all their camps and settlements east of the Sea. He then took the name of Rómendacil. – These sentences were added in the second edition (1965).

For *Rhovanion*, see note for p. 3 (Wilderland).

Rómendacil is Quenya for 'east-victor', from *rómen* 'east' + *-dacil* 'victor'.

1046 (III: 326): On his return Rómendacil

1046 (III: 326). On his return Rómendacil fortified – As first published these words read: 'Rómendacil therefore fortified'. They were revised in the second edition (1965).

1046 (III: 326): Rómendacil showed especial favour

1046 (III: 326). Rómendacil showed especial favour to Vidugavia. . . . He called himself King of Rhovanion . . . though his own realm lay between Greenwood and the River Celduin. In 1250 Rómendacil sent his son Valacar as an ambassador to dwell for a while with Vidugavia . . . he married Vidumavi, daughter of Vidugavia. . . . From this marriage came later the war of the Kin-strife. – In the second edition (1965) this paragraph replaced the following: 'In return he sent his son Valacar to dwell for a while with Vidugavia, who called himself the King of Rhovanion, and was indeed the most powerful of their princes, though his own realm lay between Greenwood and the River Running. There Valacar was wedded to Vidugavia's daughter, and so caused later the evil war of the Kin-strife.'

Regarding *Vidugavia*, in *Unfinished Tales* Christopher Tolkien notes

> that the names of the early kings and princes of the Northmen and the Éothéod are Gothic in form, not Old English. . . . *Vidugavia* is Latinized in spelling, representing Gothic *Widugauja* ('wood-dweller'), a recorded Gothic name, and similarly *Vidumavi* Gothic *Widumawi* ('wood-maiden'). . . . Since, as is explained in Appendix F (II) the language of Rohan was 'made to resemble ancient English', the names of the ancestors of the Rohirrim are cast into the forms of the earliest recorded Germanic language. [p. 311, n. 6]

1046 (III: 326): 'For the high men of Gondor

1046 (III: 326). looked askance at the Northmen – Regarded them with disapproval, as a 'lesser and alien race'.

1046 (III: 326–7): 'Therefore when Eldacar

1046 (III: 327). the Tower of the Dome of Osgiliath – As first published this phrase read: 'the Tower of the Stone of Osgiliath', referring to 'the *palantír* [that] was lost in the waters' as the sentence still concludes. This was the reading until at least the seventh printing (1973) of the second Allen & Unwin edition, after which it was emended to 'the Tower of the Dome of Osgiliath', according to a correction submitted to the publisher by Christopher Tolkien. Later it was truncated to 'the Dome of Osgiliath', then restored to 'the Tower of the Dome of Osgiliath'. Both of these later readings, one would surmise, reflect the statement in Book III, Chapter 11: 'The chief and master of these [the *palantíri*] was under the Dome of Stars at Osgiliath before its ruin' (p. 598, II: 203); and thus some have thought 'Dome of Osgiliath' likely to be correct in Appendix A.

Another consideration has been the curiousness of the phrase 'Tower of the Dome', as domes (as a matter of engineering) cannot have towers. Presumably the words are meant to indicate that the tower in question contained a dome or a domed chamber. Or possibly the tower was attached to a larger building containing the dome; but that is not the most obvious interpretation of the phrase. Neither of these suggestions fits well with Tolkien's description in his unfinished index of the Dome of Stars as 'the great domed hall of old in Osgiliath', which sounds more substantial than a chamber in a tower.

Nonetheless, 'Tower of the Dome of Osgiliath' must be considered the intended reading. Christopher Tolkien informs us that his father twice and apparently at different times, in check copies of *The Lord of the Rings*, crossed out 'Stone' in the original reading and wrote 'Dome' in the margin. Neither he nor we can explain why this was done, when the reading 'Tower of the Stone' was of long standing (and before that, in manuscript, 'Tower of the palantír'), but the later reading is clear and authorial.

1048 (III: 328): The second and greatest evil

1048 (III: 328). a deadly plague came with dark winds out of the East – In Third Age 1636. The plague reached the Shire the following year (Shire Reckoning 37), as noted on p. 5. More details of the plague are given in *Cirion and Eorl and the Friendship of Gondor and Rohan*, in *Unfinished Tales*, pp. 288–9.

1048 (III: 328). Angamaitë and Sangahyando – In his letter to Richard Jeffery, 17 December 1972, Tolkien wrote that these names mean, in Quenya, 'iron-handed' and 'throng-cleaver' (*throng* 'a closely formed body of enemy soldiers'). 'They were, however, possibly "aggressive" in being personal warrior names (or nicknames), whereas the other (few) warlike Q[uenya] names [in *The Lord of the Rings*], like *Rómendacil*, were "political": assumed by a king in celebration of victories against a public enemy' (*Letters*, p. 425).

1048–9 (III: 329): The third evil was the invasion

1048 (III: 329). King Narmacil II was slain. . . . The people of eastern and southern Rhovanion were enslaved – In *Cirion and Eorl and the Friendship of Gondor and Rohan* it is said (among much else) that 'King Narmacil II took a great army north into the plains south of Mirkwood, and gathered all that he could of the scattered remnants of the Northmen; but he was defeated, and himself fell in battle. The remnant of his army retreated over the Dagorlad into Ithilen, and Gondor abandoned all lands east of the Anduin save Ithilien' (*Unfinished Tales*, p. 289). Further:

> The escape of the army of Gondor from total destruction was in part due to the courage and loyalty of the horsemen of the Northmen under Marhari (a descendant of Vidugavia 'King of Rhovanion') who acted as rearguard. But the forces of Gondor had inflicted such losses on the Wainriders that they had not strength enough to press their invasion, until reinforced from the East, and were content for the time to complete their conquest of Rhovanion. [p. 311, n. 5]

1049 (III: 329): Calimehtar, son of Narmacil II

1049 (III: 329). Calimehtar, son of Narmacil II, helped by a revolt in Rhovanion, avenged his father – In *Cirion and Eorl and the Friendship of Gondor and Rohan* it is told how messengers came to Calimehtar from Marhwini, leader of the Northmen, with news of an impending invasion by the Wainriders, and that a revolt of enslaved Northmen was being prepared. Calimehtar led an army out of Ithilien and lured the Wainriders onto the Dagorlad, where horsemen of Calimehtar joined with an *éored* led by Marhwini achieved an overwhelming victory, 'though not in the event decisive'. Great loss was inflicted on the enemy, but in the revolt of the Northmen most perished in the attempt, and 'in the end Marhwini was obliged to retire again to his land beside the Anduin', while 'Calimehtar withdrew to Gondor' (*Unfinished Tales*, p. 290).

1049 (III: 329): Many of the Wainriders

1049 (III: 329). in this great assault from north and south, Gondor came near to destruction – The story of this invasion is told at length in *Cirion and Eorl and the Friendship of Gondor and Rohan*, in *Unfinished Tales*.

1050 (III: 330): 'He sent messages to Arvedui

1050 (III: 330). the royalty of Arnor – In some editions these words were incorrectly printed 'the loyalty of Arnor'.

1051 (III: 331): 'But the Host of the West

1051 (III: 331). Nenuial – Lake Evendim; see note for p. 244.

1052 (III: 332–3): So it was that no claimant

1052 (III: 333). the crown of Elendil – The crown is so called, though Elendil never wore it. Earlier in Appendix A (p. 1043, III: 323, n. 1) it is said that the later crown of Gondor was made during the reign of Atanatar Alcarin, replacing Isildur's war-helm which had served as a crown from the time of Meneldil, son of Anárion. Nothing is said about any insignia of royalty worn or carried by Isildur and Anárion as rulers of Gondor. The rulers of Arnor, and probably Elendil as High-king, wore the Elendilmir and carried the sceptre of Annúminas.

1053 (III: 334): 'Foreseeing the storm, Cirion sent north for aid

1053 (III: 334). Cirion sent north for aid. . . . Then out of the North there came help beyond hope. . . . Eorl the Young came with his riders and swept away the enemy, and pursued the Balchoth to the death over the fields of Calenardhon. Cirion granted to Eorl that land to dwell in, and he swore to Cirion the Oath of Eorl, of friendship at need or at call to the Lords of Gondor. – In *Cirion and Eorl and the Friendship of Gondor and Rohan* it is said that only one of six riders sent by Cirion reach Eorl at last after a journey of fifteen days. Upon hearing his message, Eorl said: 'I will come. If the Mundburg falls, whither shall we flee from the Darkness?' (*Unfinished Tales*, p. 297). The description of the ride of the Éothéod recalls that of the Rohirrim in the War of the Ring:

> At last the whole host was assembled; and only a few hundreds were left behind to support the men unfitted for such desperate venture by youth or age . . . in silence the great *éohere* set out, leaving fear behind, and taking with them small hope; for they knew not what lay before them, either on the road or at its end. It is said that Eorl led forth some seven thousand fully-armed riders and some hundreds of horsed archers. [p. 298]

When they passed Dol Guldur a gleaming mist came out of Lothlórien, driving back the darkness that came from the tower glooms of Dol Guldur'. The riders meanwhile under the canopy of the mist 'were lit with a clear and shadowless light, while to left and right they were guarded as it were by white walls of secrecy' (p. 298).

Tolkien never wrote an account of the Battle of the Field of Celebrant, which he intended should follow that of the journey of the Éothéod, and only took up the story with an account of the history of the hill called Halifirien (see note for p. 747), the gift of Cirion, and the oaths sworn by Cirion and Eorl. At the bottom of the stair leading to the top of the hill Cirion said:

> I will now declare what I have resolved, with the authority of the Stewards of the Kings, to offer to Eorl son of Léod, Lord of the Éothéod, in recognition of the valour of his people and of the help beyond hope

> that he brought to Gondor in time of dire need. To Eorl I will give in free gift all the great land of Calenardhon from Anduin to Isen. There, if he will, he shall be king, and his heirs after him, and his people shall dwell in freedom while the authority of the Stewards endures, until the Great King returns. No bond shall be laid upon them other than their own laws and will, save this only: they shall live in perpetual friendship with Gondor and its enemies shall be their enemies while both realms endure. But the same bond shall be laid also on the people of Gondor. [*Unfinished Tales*, p. 303]

Then Eorl vowed:

> in my own name and on behalf of the Éothéod of the North that between us and the Great People of the West there shall be friendship for ever: their enemies shall be our enemies, their need shall be our need, and whatsoever evil, or threat, or assault may come upon them we will aid them to the utmost end of our strength. This vow shall descend to my heirs, all such as may come after me in our new land, and let them keep it in faith unbroken, lest the Shadow fall upon them and they become accursed. [pp. 304–5]

'Such an oath', it is said, 'had not been heard in Middle-earth since Elendil himself had sworn alliance with Gil-galad King of the Eldar' (p. 305).

The granting of Calenardhon to the Rohirrim for very special service bears some resemblance to the grant by the Roman Empire of land to tribes such as the Ostrogoths in return for protecting the Empire against the more barbaric invaders, though the Rohirrim were given far greater autonomy and proved more loyal than any of the peoples taken into the imperial sphere.

1055 (III: 335): 'Ecthelion II, son of Turgon

1055 (III: 335). Thorongil . . . the Eagle of the Star – *Thorongil* derives from Sindarin *thoron* 'eagle' + *gil* 'star'; see also note for p. 171.

1057 (III: 337): 'Arador was the grandfather of the King

1057 (III: 337). Gilraen – In *The Rivers and Beacon-hills of Gondor* Tolkien comments that

> the element *gil-* in both [*Gilraen* and the name of the river Gilrain] is no doubt S[indarin] *gil* 'spark, twinkle of light, star', often used of the stars of heaven in place of the older and more elevated *el-*, *elen-* stem. . . . The meaning of *Gilraen* as a woman's name is not in doubt. It meant 'one adorned with a tressure set with gems in its network', such as the tressure of Arwen described in L.R. I 239 [see note for p. 227]. It may have been a second name given to her after she had come to womanhood, which as often happened in legends had replaced her true name, no longer recorded. More likely, it was her true name, since it had

become a name given to women of her people, the remnants of the Númenóreans of the North Kingdom of unmingled blood. The women of the Eldar were accustomed to wear such tressures; but among other peoples they were used only by women of high rank among the 'Rangers', descendants of Elros, as they claimed. Names such as *Gilraen*, and others of similar meaning, would thus be likely to become first names given to maid-children of the kindred of the 'Lords of the Dúnedain'. The element *raen* was the Sindarin form of Q[uenya] *raina* 'netted, enlaced'. [*Vinyar Tengwar* 42 (July 2001), p. 11]

1057 (III: 338): 'Then Aragorn, being now the Heir of Isildur

1057 (III: 338). Then Aragorn, being now the Heir of Isildur, was taken with his mother to dwell in the house of Elrond; and Elrond took the place of his father and came to love him as a son of his own. But . . . his true name and lineage were kept secret. . . . – Aragorn's upbringing recalls in some respects that of King Arthur as related by Sir Thomas Malory in the medieval *Morte Darthur*, where it is said that Arthur, son of King Uther Pendragon, was raised as the son of Sir Ector, his true identity long concealed on the advice of Merlin.

1058 (III: 338): 'For Aragorn had been singing

1058 (III: 338). the Lay of Lúthien – Some readers have suggested that this should read 'the Lay of Leithian', according to the title given in *The Lays of Beleriand*. But Christopher Tolkien has said, in private correspondence, that the published reading is correct, and that his father often referred to the poem as 'Lúthien'.

1060 (III: 340–1): 'Then Aragorn took leave

1060 (III: 340). he became a friend of Gandalf the Wise, from whom he gained much wisdom – Readers have frequently compared Gandalf to Merlin in some of the Arthurian legends, as mentor of the young king; but the differences are far greater than the similarities. Gandalf had nothing to do with Aragorn's conception or his fostering at Rivendell, and little to do with his basic education and training, or with his eventual acceptance as King of Gondor. Although Gandalf visited Rivendell during the time the young Aragorn was growing up, according to *The Tale of Years* it was only in Third Age 2956, when Aragorn was 25, that he met Gandalf and their friendship began. Undoubtedly Aragorn benefited greatly from their association, but despite Gandalf's status as a Maia and an envoy of the Valar, they appear more as colleagues in the fight against Sauron, rather than tutor and pupil.

1060 (III: 341). He rode in the host of the Rohirrim, and fought for the Lord of Gondor by land and by sea – See note for p. 438, and comments in 'The Stewards' (pp. 1055–6, III: 335–6).

1060 (III: 341): 'He did not know it

1060 (III: 341). Then more than any king of Men he appeared – This is the reading of the first edition, and correct. In many editions, beginning with the second (1965), 'king of Men' was misprinted 'kind of Men'.

1061 (III: 342): "'My son, years come

1061 (III: 342). Therefore, though I love you, I say to you: Arwen Undómiel shall not diminish her life's grace for less cause. She shall not be the bride of any Man less than the King of both Gondor and Arnor. – While this echoes the demand of Thingol, that Beren recover a Silmaril in return for the hand of Lúthien (see note for p. 193), the circumstances are very different. There was no prior relationship between Thingol and Beren; Thingol was seeking Beren's death while keeping a promise not to harm him; and the task Beren was set was not one that he had any personal obligation to fulfil. Elrond, in contrast, is Aragorn's foster-father; he is not seeking Aragorn's death; and though he sets Aragorn a hard task, it is one which Aragorn is bound by duty of lineage to attempt, even without the hand of Arwen as a reward. In these circumstances both Arwen and Aragorn respect Elrond's conditions. Some readers, looking at the situation from a modern perspective, have felt that Elrond was unduly harsh, and have wondered why Arwen and Aragorn accepted his conditions. But in *Master of Middle-earth* Paul H. Kocher comments perceptively that

> Tolkien has so drawn the characters of the lovers as to make their obedience entirely in character, without detracting from the ardor of their love. Arwen is deeply devoted to her father and her kin. . . . Marrying Aragorn will mean that she must surrender her immortality as an elf and become a mortal being whose soul at death will be separated from the souls of her people while time endures, and perhaps eternally. She will do it, but she owes it to her father to fulfil his conditions before taking the hardly imaginable parting step.
>
> On his side Aragorn has many reasons for respecting Elrond's wishes. He has been saved since infancy and trained by Elrond, incurring a heavy debt of gratitude and at the same time feeling for him something of the affection due to a father. Moreover, Aragorn is a man who, as later developments will show, has a strong sense of the importance of authority, propriety, law. It is by these principles that he governs when he himself becomes king in the end. He knows that if he expects his subjects to obey him freely out of respect for these principles he must first learn to obey them himself. It is unthinkable that he would urge Arwen to run off with him into the woods without her father's consent, or perhaps even with it.

Aragorn realizes that to ask Arwen to marry him is to ask her eventually to accept her own death, 'an intolerable gift for any sensitive man to bestow on the woman he loves' (and something utterly foreign, perhaps even fearsome, to an immortal; see note for p. 1062). The one thing Aragorn 'cannot do in that position is to press his suit hard upon her. Hence his apparent inactivity in wooing, and also the deep inner convulsions of his mind, the outward grimness, as he confronts the complex ironies of his lot' (p. 138).

1061 (III: 342): 'But she answered only with this *linnod*

1061 (III: 342). she answered only with this *linnod*: *Ónen i-Estel Edain, ú-chebin estel anim* – In 'Three Elvish Verse Modes', in *Tolkien's* Legendarium*: Essays on* The History of Middle-earth (2000), Patrick Wynne and Carl F. Hostetter comment: 'We might suppose from this single pithy line of verse, laden with grim irony, that the *linnod* was a mode traditionally used for aphorisms or similar brief utterances of grave import. This aphoristic quality also suggests that the *linnod* typically consisted of one line only, as in our sole example.' They suggest that *linnod*, apparently derived from Sindarin *linn* *'song, chant' and *od* *'seven', means 'seven-chant' or 'chant of seven', a fitting description of Gilraen's single line which divides into 'two identical halves, each with seven syllables' (pp. 131–2).

'*Ónen*' is the reading in both the first edition and the Ballantine Books second edition, but became '*Onen*' in the first printing of the Allen & Unwin second edition (1966). The accent was restored in the edition of 2004. There seems to be no documentation to show whether the accent was omitted at Tolkien's direction, or the omission occurred by accident in resetting, but the latter seems most likely. Arden R. Smith informs us that the vowel is marked as long in two manuscript instances of the linnod.

1062 (III: 343): 'As Queen of Elves and Men

1062 (III: 343). As Queen of Elves and Men she dwelt with Aragorn for six-score years – As first published, 'six-score years' read 'five-score years'. The phrase was revised in the second edition (1965).

Tolkien does not state over which elves Arwen was considered queen, at a time when most of her people were taking ship into the West. She and her brothers (as long as they remained) were, however, the sole descendants in Middle-earth of Finwë, ruler of the Noldor, and of Elwë (Thingol), ruler of the Sindar.

1062 (III: 343): "'Not before my time"

1062 (III: 343). I must soon go perforce. – *Perforce* 'necessarily'.

1062 (III: 343). Eldarion our son is a man full-ripe for kingship. – In the *Akallabêth* it is said 'the Lords of Númenor had been wont to wed late in their long lives and to depart and leave the mastery to their sons when these were come to full stature of body and mind' (*The Silmarillion*, p. 266).

1062 (III: 343): 'Then going to the House of the Kings

1062 (III: 343). She was not yet weary of her days – In his unpublished letter to Eileen Elgar, begun 22 September 1963, Tolkien suggests that Arwen could have surrendered her life at the same time as Aragorn, but she was not yet prepared to do so. Although she had become mortal, by nature she was still Elvish, with the long view of life held by that immortal race, to whom 'the gift of the One to Men . . . is bitter to receive' (p. 1063, III: 344).

1062 (III: 343): "'Lady Undómiel," said Aragorn

1062 (III: 343). I am the last of the Númenóreans . . . and to me has been given not only a span of years thrice that of Men of Middle-earth, but also the grace to go at my will, and give back the gift. Now, therefore, I will sleep. – Some readers have considered Aragorn's willingness that his life should end as he felt the weariness of age upon him to be akin to suicide. Rather, his decision conforms to the view in Tolkien's mythology that Death is not to be feared, and that 'a good Númenórean died of free will when he felt it to be time to do so' (draft letter to Robert Murray, 4 November 1954, *Letters*, p. 205). Tolkien also wrote that it was 'the Elvish (and uncorrupted Númenórean) view that a "good" Man would or should *die* voluntarily by surrender with trust *before being compelled* (as did Aragorn). This may have been the nature of *unfallen* Man; though *compulsion* would not threaten him: he would desire and ask to be allowed to "go on" to a higher state' (note added later to a draft letter to Rhona Beare written in October 1958, *Letters*, p. 286 n.). In a summary of his father's later writings on the extended life-span of the Númenóreans, Christopher Tolkien writes that

> they grew at much the same rate as other Men, but when they had achieved 'full-growth' they then aged, or 'wore out', very much more slowly. The first approach of 'world-weariness' was indeed for them a sign that their period of vigour was nearing its end. When it came to an end, if they persisted in living, then decay would proceed, as growth had done, no more slowly than among other Men. Thus a Númenórean would pass quickly, in ten years maybe, from health and vigour of mind to decrepitude and senility. In the earlier generations they did not 'cling to life', but resigned it voluntarily. 'Clinging to life', and so in the end dying perforce and involuntarily, was one of the changes brought about by the Shadow and the rebellion of the Númenóreans. [*Unfinished Tales*, p. 225, n. 1]

1062–3 (III: 343): "'I speak no comfort to you

1062 (III: 343). the circles of the world – Arda, the Earth, after Númenor was destroyed and the world was 'made round', that is, there was no longer a road to the Blessed Realm except for the Eldar. In the *Akallabêth* it is said that mariners 'that sailed far came only to . . . new lands, and found them like to the old lands, and subject to death. And those that sailed furthest set but a girdle about the Earth and returned weary at last to the place of their beginning; and they said: "All roads are now bent"' (*The Silmarillion*, p. 281).

1063 (III: 343–4): "'Nay, dear lord," she said

1063 (III: 344). There is now no ship that would bear me hence, and I must indeed abide the Doom of Men, whether I will or I nill – It is not clear whether Arwen means that she would not be granted a place on a ship, or that the Havens are deserted and even Círdan has left Middle-earth (see p. 1039, III: 319–20: 'At the Grey Havens dwelt Círdan the Shipwright, and some say he dwells there still, until the Last Ship sets sail into the West'). The latter may be implied by Aragorn's statement that Rivendell is now deserted, and later in the tale Lothlórien is said to be silent.

Whether I will or I nill, i.e. 'willingly or unwillingly', 'whether I wish it or not'.

1063 (III: 344): "'So it seems," he said

1063 (III: 344). In sorrow we must go, but not in despair. Behold! we are not bound for ever to the circles of the world, and beyond them is more than memory. – Tolkien wrote to Michael Straight, probably at the end of 1955, that in *The Lord of the Rings* his concern with Death was only 'as part of the nature, physical and spiritual, of Man, and with Hope without guarantees' (*Letters*, p. 237). In his unpublished letter to Eileen Elgar, begun 22 September 1963, he says that although no one knew the purposes of the One in regard to Men beyond the end of the world, or beyond their death, Aragorn trusted that they were good, and that if he and Arwen bound themselves in obedience to that trust they would be reunited.

1063 (III: 344): "'Estel, Estel!'"

1063 (III: 344). an image of the splendour of the Kings of Men in glory undimmed before the breaking of the world – That is, an image of the Kings of Númenor at the height of their glory, before the Downfall and the reshaping of the world.

1063 (III: 344): 'But Arwen went forth

1063 (III: 344). dwelt there alone under the fading trees until winter came. Galadriel had passed away and Celeborn also was gone, and the land was silent. [*paragraph:*] 'There at last when the mallorn-leaves were falling, but spring had not yet come, she laid herself to rest upon Cerin Amroth; and there is her green grave, until the world is changed – As first published this passage read: 'dwelt there alone under the fading trees; for Galadriel also was gone, and the elven-leaves were withering. [*paragraph:*] 'There at last she laid herself to rest.' It was revised in the second edition (1965). The new passage seems to suggest that it was less than a year after Aragorn's death, rather than an unspecified time, when Arwen at last surrendered her life. Tolkien's description of her grave may be intended to stress her destiny as a mortal, whose physical body would not be restored to life, and whose spirit faced an unknown fate beyond the halls of Mandos (compare the fate of Elves, notes for pp. 193, 209).

On *The Tale of Aragorn and Arwen*, see further, Helen Armstrong, 'There Are Two People in This Marriage', *Mallorn* 36 (November 1998). On the romance of Aragorn and Arwen in general, see Richard C. West, '"Her Choice Was Made and Her Doom Appointed": Tragedy and Divine Comedy in the Tale of Aragorn and Arwen', forthcoming in the proceedings of the October 2004 Marquette University Tolkien conference.

THE HOUSE OF EORL

1063–4 (III: 344–5): 'Eorl the Young

1063 (III: 344). That land lay near the sources of Anduin, between the furthest ranges of the Misty Mountains and the northernmost parts of Mirkwood. – In *Cirion and Eorl and the Friendship of Gondor and Rohan* it is said that the 'new land of the Éothéod' into which the Northmen moved in Second Age 1977

> lay north of Mirkwood, between the Misty Mountains westward and the Forest River eastward. Southward it extended to the confluence of the two short rivers that they named Greylin and Langwell. Greylin flowed down from the Ered Mithrin, the Grey Mountains, but Langwell came from the Misty Mountains, and this name it bore because it was the source of Anduin, which from its junction with Greylin they called Langflood. [*Unfinished Tales*, p. 295]

1064–5 (III: 345–6): 'Many lords and warriors

1064 (III: 345). Frumgar – From Old English *frumgār* 'chieftain, leader, prince, patriarch', literally 'first spear'.

1064 (III: 346). Fram – Old English 'valiant, stout, firm'.

1065 (III: 346): 'Léod was the name

1065 (III: 346). Léod – Old English (poetic) 'prince'.

1065 (III: 346): 'Of the Kings of the Mark

1065 (III: 346). Freca – Old English 'bold man, warrior, hero'.

1065 (III: 346). Adorn – A tributary of the Isen, together forming the western boundary of Rohan. In *The Rivers and Beacon-hills of Gondor* it is said that *Adorn*, 'as would be expected in any name in the region not of Rohanese origin, [is] of a form suitable to Sindarin; but it is not interpretable in Sindarin. It must be supposed to be of pre-Númenórean origin adapted to Sindarin' (*Vinyar Tengwar* 42 (July 2001), p. 8).

1066 (III: 347): Four years later

1066 (III: 347). Lefnui – In *The Rivers and Beacon-hills of Gondor* Tolkien writes that the river *Lefnui*, or Levnui, is 'the longest and widest of the Five [Rivers of Gondor]. This was held to be the boundary of Gondor in this direction [to the west]; for beyond it lay the promontory of Angast and the wilderness of "Old Púkel-land" (Drúwaith Iaur) which the Númenóreans had never attempted to occupy with permanent settlements, though they maintained a Coast-guard force and beacons at the end of Cape Angast [marked 'Andrast' on maps]' (*Vinyar Tengwar* 42 (July 2001), p. 14). The name is said to mean 'fifth', because the Lefnui comes after the Erui, Sirith, Serni, and Morthond, counted by their mouths from east to west. (The region of Gondor known as Lebennin, 'five rivers', does not encompass the Morthond and Lefnui, but took its name from the Erui, Sirith, Serni, Gilrain, and Celos; see note for p. 296.)

1066 (III: 347): The Rohirrim were defeated

1066 (III: 347). Haleth – Old English (*hæleþ*) 'man, warrior, hero'. Haleth, Helm's son is not to be confused with Haleth, the woman in the First Age who led the Haladin, the Second House of the Edain (also called the House of Haleth).

1068–9 (III: 349–50): [*Second Line*]

1068 (III: 349). 2726–2798 10. *Fréaláf Hildeson* – Fréaláf (see note for p. 977) was the son of Hild, Helm's sister.

1068–9 (III: 349–50). 2752–2842 11. *Brytta* . . . the tusk-wounds that it gave him. – In the first edition Brytta, Walda, and Folca are only listed, with their dates. The present notes were added in the second edition (1965) in concert with changes to Book VI, Chapter 6; see note for p. 977.

1069 (III: 350). 2804–64 13. *Folca* . . . the great boar of Everholt – *Everholt* is derived from Old English *eofor* 'wild boar' + *holt* 'wood'.

1069 (III: 350). 2905–80 16. *Thengel* . . . Morwen of Lossarnach – In a note associated with the late *Disaster of the Gladden Fields* Tolkien wrote that Thengel's wife

> was known as Morwen of Lossarnach, for she dwelt there; but she did not belong to the people of that land. Her father had removed thither, for love of its flowering vales, from Belfalas; he was a descendant of a former Prince of that fief, and thus a kinsman of Prince Imrahil. His

> kinship with Éomer of Rohan, though distant, was recognized by Imrahil, and great friendship grew between them. Éomer wedded Imrahil's daughter [Lothíriel], and their son, Elfwine the Fair, had a striking likeness to his mother's father. [*Unfinished Tales*, p. 286]

In the First Age *Morwen* was the name of a daughter of Baragund (nephew of Barahir, the father of Beren) who became the wife of Húrin and the mother of Túrin and Nienor.

1069 (III: 350). 2948–3019 17. *Théoden* . . . Ednew – The epithet *Ednew* is derived from Old English *ednēowe* 'renewed'.

1070 (III: 351): Not long after Théodwyn took sick

1070 (III: 351). Elfhild – In a draft text the queen is called 'Elfhild of Eastfold'; see *The Peoples of Middle-earth*, p. 274, n. 4.

1071 (III: 352): In Éomer's day

1071 (III: 352). He [Elessar] renewed to Éomer the gift of Cirion, and Éomer took again the Oath of Eorl – In a note to *Cirion and Eorl and the Friendship of Gondor and Rohan* in *Unfinished Tales* (p. 317, n. 44) it is said that the Oath was renewed at the summit of Halifirien, where long before Eorl had taken his Oath beside the tomb of Elendil (see note for p. 747).

DURIN'S FOLK

1071 (III: 352): Concerning the beginning of the Dwarves

1071 (III: 352). the Seven Fathers of their race, and the ancestor of all the kings of the Longbeards – See note for p. 315. In his late essay *Of Dwarves and Men* Tolkien names the descendants of the Seven Fathers (or Seven Ancestors) as the Blacklocks, Broadbeams, Firebeards, Ironfists, Longbeards, Stiffbeards, and Stonefoots (*The Peoples of Middle-earth*, p. 301). In *The Hobbit* until Tolkien's revisions of 1966 Durin's line represented one of only two races of Dwarves.

In *The Annotated Hobbit* Douglas A. Anderson suggests that in using the name *Longbeards* 'Tolkien is probably recalling the Lombards ("Longbeards," Old English *Longbeardan*), a Germanic people renowned for their ferocity' (2nd edn., p. 98).

1071 (III: 352). Kheled-zâram – See note for p. 273. As first published, here and on p. 1074, III: 355 ('a wood of great trees that then still grew not far from Kheled-zâram'), this name was spelt *Kheledzâram*. A hyphen was added, to be consistent with the spelling elsewhere in the text, probably with the ninth printing (1978) of the Allen & Unwin second edition.

1072 (III: 353): Most of those that escaped

1072 (III: 353). the great jewel, the Arkenstone, Heart of the Mountain – *Arkenstone* is derived from Old English *eorcnanstān* 'precious stone'. The Arkenstone features in *The Hobbit* as the chief object of Thorin Oakenshield's desire for his ancestral treasure in Erebor: 'It was like a globe with a thousand facets; it shone like silver in the firelight, like water in the sun, like snow under the stars, like rain upon the Moon!' (Chapter 12). See further, note by Douglas A Anderson in *The Annotated Hobbit*, 2nd edn., pp. 293–4.

1072 (III: 353). a great cold-drake – *Drake* in this context is an obsolete word for 'dragon' (compare Latin *draco*). A *cold-drake* is evidently to be distinguished from a *fire-drake*. In Tolkien's tale of *Turambar and the Foalókë* it is said that 'the least mighty' of the dragons of Melko (later Melkor, Morgoth) 'are cold as is the nature of snakes and serpents . . . ; but the mightier are hot and very heavy and slow-going, and some belch flame, and fire flickereth beneath their scales' (*The Book of Lost Tales, Part Two*, pp. 96–7).

1073 (III: 354): Then Nár turned the head

1073 (III: 354). Then Nár turned the head and saw branded on the brow in Dwarf-runes so that he could read it the name azog. That name was branded in his heart and in the hearts of all the Dwarves afterwards. – In *The Hobbit*, Chapter 1, as first published it was said only that Thrór was killed 'in the mines of Moria by a goblin'. In the third edition (1966), published after *The Lord of the Rings*, Thrór's killer was named specifically 'Azog the Goblin'.

1073, n. 1 (III: 354, n. 2): Azog was the father of Bolg

1073, n. 1 (III: 354, n. 2). Azog was the father of Bolg – In *The Hobbit*, Chapter 17, Bolg is the leader of the goblins in the Battle of Five Armies, and is killed by Beorn.

1074 (III: 355): Thráin at once sent messengers

1074 (III: 355). When all was ready they assailed and sacked one by one all the strongholds of the Orcs that they could find from Gundabad to the Gladden. – This is the reading of the first edition, and correct. In the Allen & Unwin second edition (1966) 'they could find from' was mistakenly reset as 'they could from'. The error was corrected in the edition of 2004. See *The Peoples of Middle-earth*, p. 323, n. 25.

In his late essay *Of Dwarves and Men* Tolkien wrote that *Gundabad* was 'in origin a Khuzdul [Dwarvish] name', and that the mountain had been the place at which 'the ancestor of the Longbeards' (Durin) awoke. Mount Gundabad 'was therefore revered by the Dwarves, and its occupation in the Third Age by the Orks [*sic*] was one of the chief reasons for their great hatred of the Orks' (*The Peoples of Middle-earth*, p. 301).

1074 (III: 355): At first fortune

1074 (III: 355). mattocks – *Mattock* is generally used for 'an agricultural tool similar to a pickaxe, but with one arm of the head curved like an adze and the other like a chisel edge' (*Concise OED*).

1075 (III: 356): Then Thráin turned to Dáin

1075 (III: 356). The world must change and some other power than ours must come before Durin's Folk walk again in Moria. – Balin tried unsuccessfully to return to Moria 190 years later. In the second version of the abandoned Epilogue to *The Lord of the Rings*, set several years after the destruction of the Rings, in response to a question about whether the Dwarves have returned to Moria Sam writes: 'I have heard no news. Maybe the foretelling about Durin is not for our time. Dark places still need a lot of cleaning up. I guess it will take a lot of trouble and daring deeds yet to root out the evil creatures from the halls of Moria. For there are certainly plenty of Orcs left in such places. It is not likely that we shall ever get quite rid of them' (*Sauron Defeated*, p. 122).

1077–8, 1080 (III: 358–60): But at last there came

1077–8, 1080 (III: 358–60). But at last there came about. . . . A chance-meeting, as we say in Middle-earth. – These paragraphs are an abridgement of a much longer account that Tolkien once intended to include here. On 27 September 1963 he wrote to Colonel Worskett:

> There are, of course, quite a lot of links between *The Hobbit* and The L.R. that are not clearly set out. They were mostly written or sketched out, but cut out to lighten the boat: such as Gandalf's exploratory journeys, his relations with Aragorn and Gondor; all the movements of Gollum, until he took refuge in Moria, and so on. I actually wrote in full an account of what really happened before Gandalf's visit to Bilbo and the subsequent 'Unexpected Party', as seen by Gandalf himself. It was to have come in during a looking-back conversation in Minas Tirith; but it had to go, and is only represented in brief in App. A pp. 358 to 360, though the difficulties Gandalf had with Thorin are omitted. [*Letters*, p. 334]

The idea of saying more about events immediately preceding *The Hobbit* seems to have come to Tolkien while drafting a new version of 'Durin's Folk' for Appendix A. He wrote four versions of the account, probably between summer vacation 1954 and spring 1955: each presents information learned by Frodo, his fellow hobbits, and Gimli from Gandalf in Minas Tirith in the days following the coronation of King Elessar, and said to have been added to the Red Book by Frodo but 'which because of its length was not included in the tale of the war' (*The Peoples of Middle-earth*, p. 282). Tolkien's initial manuscript was followed by a fair copy and then by a typescript, each incorporating emendations, the latter with the added title *The Quest of Erebor*. A fourth, manuscript version 'tells the story in a more economical and tightly-constructed form, omitting a good deal . . . and introducing some new elements' (*Unfinished Tales*, p. 327), possibly an (insufficient) attempt to reduce the account for Appendix A. The final abridgement, incorporated within 'Durin's Folk', appears to date between 6 March 1955, when (with parts of the Appendices already in proof) Tolkien informed his publisher, Rayner Unwin, that he was still trying to compress material to fit the available space, and 12 April when Allen & Unwin sent the printer copy for the remainder of the Appendices.

In the third, typescript version of *The Quest of Erebor* Gandalf is asked whether, when he planned the dwarves' quest to the Lonely Mountain and Bilbo's inclusion in the company, he saw beyond the destruction of Smaug to the fall of Sauron. He explains that his most immediate thought was to protect Rivendell and Lothlórien from attack by Sauron, by preventing the use of Smaug by the Dark Lord and by persuading the White Council to drive Sauron from Dol Guldur. Gandalf is said to have met Thorin by chance in Bree and, hearing of his desire for vengeance on Smaug, accepted an invitation to visit him in the Ered Luin. It was only when he heard more of Thorin's history that Gandalf realized that the dying dwarf he had found in the pits of Dol Guldur was Thorin's father, Thráin. He remembered the map and key that Thráin had given him, and suggested to Thorin that rather than wage open war he should deal with the dragon by stealth, with the help of a hobbit, whose smell would be unknown to Smaug. The dwarves however did not have a high opinion of Hobbits; and when Gandalf pointed out that Bilbo had courage and professional stealth (meaning the usual hobbit ability to disappear quietly and quickly), the dwarves leapt to the conclusion that Bilbo was a professional thief. Gandalf said that he would put the thief's mark on Bilbo's door, and with sudden foresight told Thorin that if he wanted to succeed he must persuade the hobbit to accompany them. In this Gandalf was relying on his memory of Bilbo as a child; upon seeing Bilbo as an adult, his confidence was shaken. After the bad impression Bilbo made on the dwarves, Gandalf had great difficulty in persuading Thorin to add Bilbo to his company. (This version is published in full, with an introductory note by Douglas A. Anderson, in *The Annotated Hobbit*, 2nd edn., pp. 367–77; and in part in *Unfinished Tales*, pp. 328–36.)

In the fourth version, when Gandalf hears Thorin's story, he promises to help him if he can, but has no immediate plan. Then he visits the Shire and hears news of Bilbo: 'He was already growing a bit queer, they said, and went off for days by himself. He could be seen talking to strangers, even Dwarves.' Thus the plan for the quest of Erebor came suddenly into Gandalf's mind. He tried unsuccessfully to see Bilbo, who was away from home; and relying on what he had heard, Gandalf persuaded Thorin to accept the plan. Gandalf admits that this was a mistake: 'For Bilbo had changed.... He was altogether bewildered, and made a complete fool of himself... he did not realize at all how fatuous the Dwarves thought him, nor how angry they were with me' (*Unfinished Tales*, p. 323). Gandalf explains that it was only by producing the map and key at the right moment, and arguing with Thorin far into the night, that he persuaded him to accept the plan. The account of why the dwarves thought Bilbo was a professional burglar is omitted. (This version is published in full in *Unfinished Tales*, pp. 321–6.)

When Christopher Tolkien edited *The Quest of Erebor* for *Unfinished Tales* he was unaware of the earliest version. Later, in *The Peoples of Middle-earth*, he explained its relationship to Tolkien's work on Appendix A and to the later texts. Some brief extracts from the first manuscript are included in *The Peoples of Middle-earth*, pp. 280–4, 287–9; some very brief extracts from the second version are published in *Unfinished Tales* (pp. 329, 330). In addition, two brief extracts which might be from either of the first two versions are published and discussed in *The War of the Ring*, pp. 357–8.

1077 (III: 358–9): But at last there came about

1077 (III: 359). He [Gandalf] was on his way to the Shire, which he had not visited for some twenty years – In *The Hobbit*, Chapter 1, it is said that when Gandalf visited Bilbo before the 'unexpected party' (in Third Age 2941) 'he had not been down that way under The Hill for ages and ages, not since his friend the Old Took died', i.e. not since 2920.

1079 (III: 361): The Line of the Dwarves of Erebor

1079 (III: 361). Dwalin 2772–3112 – Tom Delaney observes in a letter to *Beyond Bree*, July 1986, p. 9, that Dwalin 'lived to be 340, a full 78 years longer than every other known dwarf'. In *The Peoples of Middle-earth* Christopher Tolkien quotes from his father's 'Notes on Chronology of Durin's Line', made while he was evolving the Dwarf family tree:

> Dwarves of different 'breeds' vary in their longevity. Durin's race were originally long-lived (especially those named Durin), but like most other peoples they had become less so during the Third Age. Their average age (unless they met a violent death) was about 250 years, which they seldom fell far short of, but could occasionally far exceed (up to 300). [*Christopher Tolkien comments:* It will be found in the genealogical table that the life-span of all the 'kings of Durin's folk' from Thráin I to Náin II varied only between 247 and 256 years, and no Dwarf in the table exceeded that, save Borin (261) and Dwalin, who lived to the vast age of 340 (the date of his death appears in all the later texts of the table, although the first to give dates seems – it is hard to make out the

figures – to make him 251 years old at his death.] A dwarf of 300 was about as rare and aged as a Man of 100.

Dwarves remained young – e.g. regarded as too tender for really hard work or for fighting – until they were 30 or nearly that (Dáin II was very young in 2799 (32) and his slaying of Azog was a great feat). After that they hardened and took on the appearance of age (by human standards) very quickly. By forty all Dwarves looked much alike in age, until they reached what they regarded as old age, about 240. They then began to age and wrinkle and go white quickly (baldness being unknown among them), unless they were going to be long-lived, in which case the process was delayed. Almost the only physical order they suffered from (they were singularly immune from diseases such as affected Men, and Halflings) was corpulence. If in prosperous circumstances, many grew very fat at or before 200, and could not do much (save eat) afterwards. Otherwise 'old age' lasted not much more than ten years, and from say 40 or a little before to near 240 (two hundred years) the capacity for toil (and for fighting) of most Dwarves was equally great. [pp. 284–5; p. 288, n. 17]

1079 (III: 361). Gimli Elf-friend 2879–3141 (F.A. 120). – As first published, through early printings of the second edition, these dates read: '2879–3121' and 'F.A. [Fourth Age] 100'. The latter date is not the year of Gimli's death, but that in which he sailed from Middle-earth with Legolas after the passing of King Elessar. In the second edition (1965) the date of the King's death was altered from Fourth Age 100 to Fourth Age 120, but not all of the emendations consequent upon this change were noticed and made at the same time. An incomplete change to '2879–3141 (F.A. 100)' appeared in the fourth or fifth printing (1966) of the Ballantine Books edition. The complete emendation, with 'F.A. 120', first appeared probably in the ninth printing (1978) of the Allen & Unwin second edition.

1080 (III: 360): Dís was the daughter of Thráin II

1080 (III: 360). there are few dwarf-women . . . other peoples cannot tell them apart – In *The Peoples of Middle-earth* Christopher Tolkien comments that what is said about dwarf-women in his father's 'Notes on Chronology of Durin's Line' is similar to that published in Appendix A 'except for the statements that they are never forced to wed against their will (which "would of course be impossible"), and that they have beards' (p. 285). Tolkien expanded on the importance of beards to dwarves in a revision to the *Quenta Silmarillion* in 1951:

> The Naugrim [Dwarves] were ever, as they still remain, short and squat in stature; they were deep-breasted, strong in the arm, and stout in the leg, and their beards were long. Indeed this strangeness they have that no Man nor Elf has ever seen a beardless Dwarf – unless he were shaven

in mockery, and would then be more like to die of shame than of many other hurts that to us would be more deadly. For the Naugrim have beards from the beginning of their lives, male and female alike; nor indeed can their womenkind be discerned by those of other race, be it in feature or in gait or in voice, nor in any wise save this: that they go not to war, and seldom save at direst need issue from their deep bowers and halls. [*The War of the Jewels*, p. 205]

APPENDIX B

THE TALE OF YEARS

(CHRONOLOGY OF THE WESTLANDS)

For drafts and history of Appendix B, see *The Peoples of Middle-earth*, pp. 140, 166–87, 225–52.

1082 (III: 363). [section title] – The word *Tale* in *The Tale of Years* means 'counting or reckoning' (*Nomenclature*).

1082 (III: 363): In the beginning of this age

1082 (III: 363). . . . still remained. Most of these dwelt in Lindon west of the Ered Luin; but before the building of the Barad-dûr many of the Sindar passed eastward, and some established realms in the forests far away, where their people were mostly Silvan Elves. Thranduil, king in the north of Greenwood the Great, was one of these. In Lindon north of the Lune dwelt Gil-galad, last heir of the kings of the Noldor in exile. He was acknowledged as High King of the Elves of the West. In Lindon south of the Lune dwelt for a time Celeborn, kinsman of Thingol; his wife was Galadriel, greatest of Elven women. She was sister of Finrod Felagund, Friend-of-Men, once king of Nargothrond, who gave his life to save Beren son of Barahir. – As first published this paragraph, following its first sentence, read only: 'The exiled Noldor dwelt in Lindon, but many of the Sindar passed eastward and established realms in the forests far away. The chief of these were Thranduil in the north of Greenwood the Great, and Celeborn in the south of the forest. But the wife of Celeborn was Noldorin: Galadriel, sister of Felagund of the House of Finrod.' The present text was introduced in the second edition (1965). (On changes to names in the lineage of Galadriel, see note for p. 80.)

For *Lindon*, see note for p. 469.

The name *Sindar* (Quenya 'grey ones', i.e. Grey-elves) was applied by the Noldor, returning to Middle-earth from Aman, to the elves they met in Beleriand. In *The Silmarillion* Christopher Tolkien notes that

> the Noldor may have devised this name because the first Elves of this origin whom they met with were in the north, under the grey skies and mists about Lake Mithrim [the great lake in the east of Hithlum] . . . ; or perhaps because the Grey-elves were not of the Light (of Valinor) nor yet of the Dark (Avari ['The Unwilling, the Refusers', those Elves who refused to join the westward march from Cuiviénen], but were *Elves of the Twilight*. [p. 348]

In late philological writing by Tolkien Thranduil's realm is said to have

> extended into the woods surrounding the Lonely Mountain and growing along the west shores of the Long Lake, before the coming of the Dwarves exiled from Moria and the invasion of the Dragon. The Elvish folk of this realm had migrated from the south, being the kin and neighbours of the Elves of Lórien; but they had dwelt in Greenwood the Great east of Anduin. In the Second Age their king, Oropher [the father of Thranduil, father of Legolas], had withdrawn northward beyond the Gladden Fields. This he did to be free from the power and encroachments of the Dwarves of Moria, which had grown to be the greatest of the mansions of the Dwarves recorded in history; and also he resented the intrusions of Celeborn and Galadriel into Lórien. But as yet there was little to fear between the Greenwood and the Mountains and there was constant intercourse between his people and their kin across the River, until the War of the Last Alliance. [*Unfinished Tales*, p. 258]

When, in the Third Age, the Shadow fell upon Greenwood the Great, the Silvan Elves under Thranduil

> retreated before it as it spread ever northward, until at last Thranduil established his realm in the north-east of the forest and delved there a fortress and great halls underground. Oropher was of Sindarin origin, and no doubt Thranduil his son was following the example of King Thingol long before, in Doriath; though his halls were not to be compared with Menegroth. He had not the arts nor the wealth nor the aid of the Dwarves; and compared with the Elves of Doriath his Silvan folk were rude and rustic. [*Unfinished Tales*, p. 259]

The name *Felagund* is that by which Finrod was known after the establishment of Nargothrond; it was Dwarvish in origin, from *felak-gundu* 'cave-hewer', translated in *The Silmarillion* as 'Lord of Caves'.

1084 (III: 365): When maybe a thousand years

1084 (III: 365). *Istari* – See note for p. 502.

1082–3 (III: 363): Later some of the Noldor

1083 (III: 363). Celebrimbor was lord of Eregion and the greatest of their craftsmen; he was descended from Fëanor. – This sentence was added in the second edition (1965).

1083–4 (III: 363–4): [*The Second Age*]

1083 (III: 364): 521 Birth in Númenor of Silmariën. – As first published this date was given as '548'. It was emended in the edition of 2004. In *The Line of Elros: Kings of Númenor* it is said that the eldest child of Tar-Elendil 'was a daughter, Silmarien, born in the year 521' (*Unfinished Tales*, p. 219); and in an accompanying note Christopher Tolkien expresses the opinion that the date '548' in *The Tale of Years*, which survived from the first drafts of that text, 'should have been revised but escaped notice' (p. 225, n. 4).

1083 (III: 364). 2251 Death of Tar-Atanamir. Tar-Ancalimon takes the sceptre. – As first published this passage read: 'Tar-Atanamir takes the sceptre.' It was revised in the edition of 2004. In *Unfinished Tales* Christopher Tolkien comments that the original reading 'is altogether discrepant with the present text [*The Line of Elros*], according to which Tar-Atanamir died in 2221. This date 2221 is, however, itself an emendation from 2251; and his death is given elsewhere as 2251. Thus the same year appears in different texts as both the date of his accession and the date of his death; and the whole structure of the chronology shows clearly that the former must be wrong' (p. 226, n. 10).

1084 (III: 364). 3175 Repentance of Tar-Palantir. – In *The Line of Elros* the death date of Ar-Gimilzôr was originally given as 3175, but later emended to 3177, in contradiction to *The Tale of Years*. Christopher Tolkien thinks it 'almost certain' that 3175 was the year of the succession of Tar-Palantir (*Unfinished Tales*, p. 227, n. 15).

1085 (III: 366): Throughout the Third Age

1085 (III: 366). Gil-galad before he died gave his ring to Elrond; Círdan later surrendered his to Mithrandir. – As first published this passage read: 'The ring of Gil-galad was given by him to Elrond; but Círdan surrendered his to Mithrandir.' It was revised in the Allen & Unwin second edition (1966).

1085–90 (III: 366–71): [*The Third Age*]

1085 (III: 366). 109 Elrond weds Celebrían, daughter of Celeborn. – As first published this read: '100 Elrond weds Celebrían of Lórien.' In the second edition (1965) it was emended to: '100 Elrond weds daughter of Celeborn.' In the Allen & Unwin second edition (1966) Tolkien further emended the date '100' to '109'. The present reading entered only in the eighth (1974) or ninth (1978) printing of the Allen & Unwin second edition.

1085 (III: 366). 130 Birth of Elladan and Elrohir, sons of Elrond. – As first published this passage read: '139 Birth of Elladan and Elrohir, sons of Elrond.' In the Allen & Unwin second edition (1966) Tolkien emended the date '139' to '130'.

1085 (III: 366). 1149 Reign of Atanatar Alcarin begins. – As first published, 'Atanatar' read 'Atanamir'. The name was corrected in the Allen & Unwin second edition (1966).

1087 (III: 368). 1981 Náin I slain. The Dwarves flee from Moria. Many of the Silvan Elves of Lórien flee south. Amroth and Nimrodel are lost. – This is the correct reading, as published in the first edition (1955) and the Ballantine Books second edition (1965). As first printed in the Allen & Unwin second edition (1966), however, a section was omitted, producing the erroneous reading: 'Náin I slain. The Dwarves of Lórien flee south.' This was corrected in the eighth (1974) or ninth (1978) printing of that edition.

1088 (III: 369). 2683 Isengrim II becomes tenth Thain – The apparent contradiction of Isengrim (Took) II as tenth Thain with Isumbras I as 'thirteenth Thain, and first of the Took line' (entry for 2340) is explained by an early version of *The Tale of Years* which includes the entry: '2620 Isengrim II, tenth Thain *of the Took-line*, born in the Shire' (*The Peoples of Middle-earth*, p. 236, emphasis ours).

1088 (III: 369). 2758 . . . The Long Winter follows. Great suffering and loss of life in Eriador and Rohan. Gandalf comes to the aid of the Shire-folk. – In the third version of *The Quest of Erebor* Gandalf says:

> And then there was the Shire-folk. I began to have a warm place in my heart for them in the Long Winter. . . . They were very hard put to it then: one of the worst pinches they have been in, dying of cold, and starving in the dreadful dearth that followed. But that was the time to see their courage, and their pity for one another. It was by their pity as much as by their tough uncomplaining courage that they survived. [*The Annotated Hobbit*, 2nd edn., p. 370]

1088 (III: 369). 2799 . . . They settle in the South of Ered Luin beyond the Shire (2802). – This sentence was added in the second edition (1965), but with 'shire' for 'Shire'. The latter was corrected in the Allen & Unwin second edition (1966).

1088 (III: 369). 2851 The White Council meets. Gandalf urges an attack on Dol Guldur. Saruman overrules him. – In papers published as part of *The Hunt for the Ring* it is said that this meeting was held at Rivendell. A passage is quoted giving details of the debate and of a confrontation between Gandalf and Saruman; see *Unfinished Tales*, pp. 350–2.

1088 (III: 369). 2872 Belecthor II of Gondor dies. The White Tree dies, and no seedling can be found. The Dead Tree is left standing. – In editions prior to 2005 this was entered for the year 2852, though correctly dated 2872 in the list of Stewards. Christopher Tolkien notes in *The Peoples of Middle-earth*: 'The date of the death of the Steward Belecthor II in all three texts of *The Heirs of Elendil* [precursors of Appendix A.I.ii–iv] is 2872. The date 2852 in the later typescripts of the Tale of Years and in Appendix B is evidently a casual error' (p. 250, n. 38).

1089 (III: 370). 2951 . . . Sauron sends three of the Nazgûl to reoccupy Dol Guldur. – One text of *The Hunt for the Ring* states that in June 3018 'the second to the Chief [of the Ringwraiths], Khamûl the Shadow of the East, abode in Dol Guldur as Sauron's lieutenant, with one other [Nazgûl] as his messenger' (*Unfinished Tales*, p. 338). Christopher Tolkien comments:

> According to the entry in the Tale of Years for 2951 Sauron sent three, not two, of the Nazgûl to reoccupy Dol Guldur. The two statements can be reconciled on the assumption that one of the Ringwraiths of Dol Guldur returned afterwards to Minas Morgul, but I think it more likely that the formulation of the present text [of *The Hunt for the Ring*] was superseded when the Tale of the Years was compiled; and it may be noted that in a rejected version of the present passage there was only one Nazgûl in Dol Guldur (not named as Khamûl, but referred to as "the Second Chief (the Black Easterling)"), while one remained with Sauron as his chief messenger. [p. 352, n. 1]

1089 (III: 371). 2956 Aragorn meets Gandalf and their friendship begins. – Gandalf visited Rivendell at least twice during Aragorn's fostering there, in 2941 and 2942 while on his way to and from Erebor. There is no indication that he encountered Aragorn at Rivendell; at any rate, the present entry marks the beginning of their close relationship.

1090 (III: 371). 2957–80 . . . As Thorongil he serves in disguise both Thengel of Rohan and Ecthelion of Gondor. – The words 'As Thorongil' were added in the Allen & Unwin second edition (1966).

1090 (III: 371). 2968 Birth of Frodo. – This entry was added in the second edition (1965).

1090 (III: 371). 2980 . . . Birth of Samwise. – This reading was introduced in the edition of 2004, replacing the entry for Sam under 2983. 'Birth of Samwise' was added to *The Tale of Years* for Third Age 2983 in the second edition (1965), after the mention of the birth of Faramir; but the date of Sam's birth in 'The Longfather Tree of Master Samwise' (Appendix C) has been given, since the first edition, as Shire Reckoning 1380 (= Third Age 2980), and this is supported by the entry near the end of *The Tale of Years* for Shire Reckoning 1469, which states that Sam was 'in 1476 [= Third Age 3076], at the end of his office, ninety-six years old'.

1090 (III: 371). 3009 . . . Elrond sends for Arwen, and she returns to Imladris; the Mountains and all lands eastward are becoming dangerous. – Prior to the second edition (1965) this passage was printed as a separate entry for the year 3016.

1090 (III: 371) 3009 Gandalf and Aragorn renew their hunt for Gollum at intervals during the next eight years. . . . At some time during these years Gollum himself ventured into Mordor, and was captured by

Sauron. . . . [*paragraph:*] **3017 Gollum is released from Mordor. He is taken by Aragorn in the Dead Marshes, and brought to Thranduil in Mirkwood.** – The uncertain date for the capture of Gollum by Sauron, and the entry in *The Tale of Years* for 3017, do not agree with dates given in *The Hunt for the Ring*. There it is said in one text that 'Gollum was captured in Mordor in the year 3017' (*Unfinished Tales*, p. 337), and in another that Aragorn captured Gollum 'at nightfall on February 1st' (3018) and took fifty days for a journey 'not much short of nine hundred miles' to bring him to Thranduil 'on the twenty-first of March' (p. 343), and that 'Gandalf arrived two days later, and left on the 29th March early in the morning. After the Carrock he had a horse, but he had the High Pass over the Mountains to cross. He got a fresh horse at Rivendell, and making the greatest speed he could he reached Hobbiton late on the 12th April, after a journey of nearly eight hundred miles' (p. 353, n. 6).

Appendix B was one of the last parts of *The Lord of the Rings* to be completed. Tolkien did not send it to Allen & Unwin until early April 1955, and in compiling it abandoned some of the ideas he had tried out in *The Hunt for the Ring*. He may have decided to be less definite about the date of Gollum's capture by Sauron, since the only (unreliable) source for this date would be Gollum himself. Tolkien apparently also came to think that more time was needed between Aragorn's capture of Gollum and Gandalf's arrival in Hobbiton. On the carbon copy of the latest typescript of Appendix B (Marquette Series 3/9/7, dating from March or the beginning of April 1955) he calculated the minimum time between Gollum's capture and 12 April, at the same time emending his calculation for some of the distances involved:

Gandalf would go as soon as possible to Frodo after questioning Gollum. Ar[agorn] took Gollum in Dead Marshes and then took him to Thranduil – over ?700 or poss[ibly] 800 miles say 44 days.
Gandalf arrived later say 10 days.
Gandalf questions Gollum say 5.
Gandalf then went to Shire also 700 miles = 40 days. [Although presumably, as stated in *The Hunt for the Ring* but with a different chronology, he had a horse for part of the time, whereas Aragorn's journey was entirely on foot, he had to cross the Misty Mountains, and he would have needed to discuss the situation with Elrond.]
Total 99
Yule 1
Jan 30
Feb 30
March 30
April 12 Gandalf comes to Frodo
Total 103
Gollum must therefore have been captured at beginning of 3018
say about Jan 1–3

Tolkien may have removed this history to 3017 in order to begin the section 'The Great Years' with an event related in the direct narrative of *The Lord of the Rings*: Gandalf's arrival at Hobbiton on 12 April 3018.

1091–94 (III: 372–5): [THE GREAT YEARS]

1091 (III: 372). *Mid-year's Day* Gandalf meets Radagast. – As first published *The Tale of Years* included an entry for 29 June: 'Gandalf meets Radagast.' This was omitted beginning with the Allen & Unwin second edition (1966); the present entry was added in the edition of 2004. The original entry was removed presumably because it did not agree with the narrative: Gandalf says at the Council of Elrond (Book II, Chapter 2) that at the end of June he met Radagast 'not far from Bree'. 'I could not follow him then and there. I had ridden very far already that day, and I was as weary as my horse. . . . I stayed the night in Bree. . . . I wrote a message to Frodo. . . . I rode away at dawn' (pp. 256, 257–8, I: 269, 271). During his conversation with Gandalf, Radagast says that 'Midsummer . . . is now here' (Book II, Chapter 2, p. 257, I: 279), and Gandalf dates his letter to Frodo 'Midyear's Day' (*sic*, Book I, Chapter 10, p. 169, I: 182). Butterbur's report of his own conversation with Gandalf (Book I, Chapter 10, p. 167, I: 179) makes it clear that the letter was written and given to him the day that Gandalf arrived. In the Shire Calendar *Mid-year's day* is the middle of the three days between June and July. The entry for this day in 3018 may have been overlooked in resetting the Appendices for the Allen & Unwin edition of 1966, or it may have been omitted at the direction of the author but not replaced with a revised entry at this place for typographical reasons, because the centred month subheadings do not readily permit an entry that falls *between* months.

1092 (III: 373). [*February*] 15 The Mirror of Galadriel. – In editions prior to 2005 *The Tale of Years* dated this episode (Book II, Chapter 7) to 14 February, and the farewell to Lothlórien to 16 February, yet the narrative indicates that the day of the Company's departure was the day *immediately following* Frodo and Sam looking into the Mirror. After they have done so, Galadriel says: 'In the morning you must depart' (p. 366, I: 381); and the next chapter begins (p. 367, I: 383): 'That night the Company was again summoned', thus the same night; and then on p. 368 (III: 384) Celeborn says: 'All shall be prepared for you and await you at the haven before noon tomorrow', and there is a reference to the Company's 'last night in Lothlórien'. There is no evidence of an extra day intervening. Therefore it seems clear that if the Mirror of Galadriel occurs on 14 February, the farewell must be on 15 February; but all subsequent dating depends upon a departure on 16 February.

1094 (III: 375): In the North also

1094 (III: 375). But after the passing of Galadriel in a few years Celeborn

grew weary of his realm and went to Imladris to dwell with the sons of Elrond. In the Greenwood the Silvan Elves remained untroubled, but in Lórien there lingered sadly only a few of its former people, and there was no longer light or song in Caras Galadhon. – This passage was added in the second edition (1965), but ending 'Caras' Galadon', with an extraneous apostrophe. This became 'Caras Galadon' in the Allen & Unwin second edition (1966), but 'Caras Galadhon' in the edition of 1994; cf. note for p. 341.

1095 (III: 376): When news came of the great victories

1095 (III: 376). When news came of the great victories. . . . They sent ambassadors to the crowning of King Elessar – News of the fall of Sauron travelled swiftly to Erebor and Dale: according to *The Tale of Years*, only two days passed between the downfall of Barad-dûr and the expulsion of the enemy from Dale. It is not said how word was conveyed to the Dwarves and Men in the North (by Eagles?), nor how they learned that there was to be a coronation.

1095–6 (III: 376–7): [THE CHIEF DAYS FROM THE FALL OF BARAD-DÛR TO THE END OF THE THIRD AGE]

1095 (III: 376). [*May*] 8. Éomer and Éowyn depart from Rohan with the sons of Elrond. – The words 'with the sons of Elrond' were added in the second edition (1965).

1095 (III: 376). *June* 14. The sons of Elrond meet the escort and bring Arwen to Edoras. – This entry was added in the second edition (1965)

1095 (III: 376). [*July*] 22. The funeral escort of King Théoden set out. – As first published this entry was dated '*July* 19'. It was corrected in the edition of 2004. Christopher Tolkien notes in *Sauron Defeated* that

> in [the fair copy of 'Many Partings', Book VI, Chapter 6] Aragorn tells Frodo they will leave in seven days, and that 'in three days now Éomer will return hither to bear Théoden back to rest in the Mark', as he duly did; and all this is retained in *The Lord of the Rings*, together with the fifteen days of the journey to Rohan. . . . It is a curious fact that the chronology of 'The Chief Days from the Fall of Barad-dûr to the End of the Third Age' in Appendix B . . . does not agree with the text of 'Many Partings' in respect either of Éomer's return in relation to the setting out for Edoras or of the time taken on that journey. In the chronology of 'The Chief Days' Éomer returned to Minas Tirith on July 18, and the riding from the City with King Théoden's wain took place on the following day, July 19, not four days later as in 'Many Partings'; while the arrival at Edoras is dated August 7, eighteen days later, not fifteen, as in the text. [pp. 73–4]

The change of departure date of the funeral escort from 19 to 22 July brings 'The Chief Days' into accord with the narrative.

1095 (III: 376). [*August*] 15. Treebeard releases Saruman. – This entry was added in the edition of 2004. In *Sauron Defeated* Christopher Tolkien notes: 'On a copy of a First Edition that my father used to make alterations for incorporation in the Second Edition he added . . . the entry "*August 15* Treebeard releases Saruman", but this was not for some reason included in the Second Edition' (p. 72, n. 13). This date agrees with Treebeard's statement made on 22 August that Saruman 'is gone seven days' (Book VI, Chapter 6, p. 980, III: 258).

1096–8 (III: 377–8): [LATER EVENTS CONCERNING THE MEMBERS OF THE FELLOWSHIP OF THE RING]

1097 (III: 378). 1436 King Elessar rides north, and dwells for a while by Lake Evendim. . . . He gives the Star of the Dúnedain to Master Samwise – This is the first mention in the published text of Aragorn visiting Arnor, nearly seventeen years after his coronation. No doubt there was a great deal for him to do in the South, but the North was also important. In the second version of the abandoned Epilogue, however, Sam refers to an earlier visit, remarking that the King had not been north since Elanor was 'a mite' (*Sauron Defeated*, p. 126). Christopher Tolkien comments: 'I do not know of any other reference to this northern journey of Aragorn in the early years of his reign' (p. 135, n. 17).

Aragorn's dwelling *by Lake Evendim* was presumably on the site of Elendil's former capital, Annúminas, rather than Fornost, the chief city of the later kings of Arnor.

In *Unfinished Tales* (pp. 284–5, n. 33) Christopher Tolkien rejects the identification of *the Star of the Dúnedain* with the Elendilmir by both Robert Foster (in *The Complete Guide to Middle-earth*) and J.E.A. Tyler (in *The Tolkien Companion*, 1976), but is uncertain of the distinction given to Samwise. In *The War of the Ring* he reports that subsequent to the publication of *Unfinished Tales* two readers 'independently suggested to me that the Star of the Dúnedain was very probably the same as the silver brooch shaped like a rayed star that was worn by the Rangers' who joined Aragorn in Rohan. One of the readers also drew attention to the star on the cloak worn by Aragorn when he served in Gondor and received the name *Thorongil*. Christopher comments: 'These suggestions are clearly correct' (p. 309, n. 8).

1097 (III: 378). 1451 Elanor the Fair marries Fastred of Greenholm on the Far Downs. – The words 'on the Far Downs' were added in the second edition (1965).

1097 (III: 378). 1452 The Westmarch, from the Far Downs to the Tower Hills (*Emyn Beraid*), is added to the Shire by the gift of the King. Many

hobbits remove to it. – This entry, and a footnote with relevant page references, were added in the second edition (1965).

1097 (III: 378). 1455 Master Samwise becomes Mayor for the fifth time. [*paragraph:*] 1462 Master Samwise becomes Mayor for the sixth time. At his request the Thain makes Fastred Warden of Westmarch. Fastred and Elanor make their dwelling at Undertowers on the Tower Hills, where their descendants, the Fairbairns of the Towers, dwelt for many generations. – As first published the latter part of the entry for 1462 read: 'At his request the Thain makes Fastred and Elanor Wardens of the Westmarch (a region newly inhabited); they take up their dwelling on the slopes of the Tower Hills, where their descendants, the Fairbairns of Westmarch, dwell for many generations.' This was revised in the second edition (1965).

In parallel with his addition of the entry for 1452 concerning the addition of the Westmarch to the Shire, Tolkien proposed that the entry for 1462 should be changed to its present reading. The change was incorrectly made, however, in the second edition (Ballantine Books, 1965), and the entries for 1455 and 1462 were replaced with a single entry: '1455 Master Samwise becomes Mayor for the fifth time. At his request . . . for many generations.' Thus no mention appeared of Sam's sixth term of office, and Fastred became Warden in 1455 rather than 1462. This error was continued in the Allen & Unwin second edition (1966). An attempted correction in the fourth or fifth printing (1966) of the Ballantine Books edition led to a partial duplication:

> 1455 Master Samwise becomes Mayor for the fifth time. At his request the Thain makes Fastred Warden of Westmarch. Fastred and Elanor make their dwelling at Undertowers on the Tower Hills, where their descendants, the Fairbairns of the Towers, dwelt for many generations.
>
> 1462 Master Samwise becomes Mayor for the sixth time. At his request the Thain makes Fastred and Elanor Wardens of the Westmarch (a region newly inhabited); they take up their dwelling on the slopes of the Tower Hills, where their descendants, the Fairbairns of Westmarch, dwell for many generations.

An attempt to correct the reading in the 1987 Houghton Mifflin edition added the entry: '1462 Master Samwise becomes Mayor for the sixth time'.

The dates for Sam's fifth and sixth terms as Mayor clearly began in 1455 and 1462. It is also clear that the revised wording of the 1965 edition concerning the request to the Thain which omits the superfluous 'a region newly inhabited' is correct, but it is not immediately clear whether Tolkien intended to move the creation of Fastred as Warden back to 1455, or whether this was merely a typesetting error, though from the way the entries have been joined the latter seems most likely. Evidence for 1462 is provided by the note in the Prologue concerning the Fairbairns of

Westmarch (p. 14, I: 23) which directs the reader to the entries for 1451, 1462, and 1482: this was added in the second edition (1965) together with the section 'Note on the Shire Records'. Unless the creation of Fastred as Warden is placed in 1462, there is no mention of Westmarch, Elanor, or Fastred in that entry. The present reading was introduced in the edition of 2004.

1098 (III: 378). 1541 In this year on March 1st came at last the Passing of King Elessar. – As first published this passage read: '1521 In this year came at last the Passing of King Elessar.' It was revised in the second edition (1965). The accompanying footnote 'Fourth Age (Gondor) 120' was added at that time.

APPENDIX C

FAMILY TREES

For drafts and history of Appendix C, see *The Peoples of Middle-earth*, pp. 85–118.

In his draft letter to A.C. Nunn, probably late 1958–early 1959, Tolkien wrote:

> As far as I know Hobbits were universally monogamous (indeed they very seldom married a second time, even if wife or husband died very young); and I should say that their family arrangements were 'patrilinear' rather than patriarchal. That is, their family names descended in the male-line (and women were adopted into their husband's name); also the titular head of the family was usually the eldest male. In the case of large powerful families (such as the Tooks), still cohesive even when they had become very numerous, and more what we might call clans, the head was properly the eldest male of what was considered the most direct line of descent. But the government of a 'family', as of the real unit: the 'household', was not a monarchy (except by accident). It was a 'dyarchy', in which master and mistress had equal status, if different functions. Either was held to be the proper representative of the other in case of absence (including death). There were no 'dowagers'. If the master died first, his place was taken by his wife, and this included (if he had held that position) the titular headship of a large family or clan. This title did not descend to the son, or other heir, while she lived, unless she voluntarily resigned. . . .
>
> Customs differed in cases where the 'head' died leaving no son. In the Took-family, since the headship was also connected with the title and (originally military) office of Thain, descent was strictly through the male line. (This title and office descended immediately, and was not held by a widow. . . .) In other great families the headship might pass through a *daughter of the deceased* to his *eldest* grandson (irrespective of the daughter's age). This latter custom was usual in families of more recent origin, without ancient records or ancestral mansions. In such cases the heir (if he accepted the courtesy title) took the name of his mother's family – though he often also retained that of his father's family also (placed second). [*Letters*, pp. 293–4, 295]

1101–2. [Bolger and Boffin family trees] – These were prepared by Tolkien for the first edition, but omitted for lack of space. They were first published in *The Peoples of Middle-earth*, and added to *The Lord of the Rings* with the edition of 2004.

1103 (III: 381). [Took family tree] – Those who held the office of Thain are marked with an asterisk (*).

In his draft letter to A.C. Nunn, probably late 1958–early 1959, Tolkien comments that Fortinbras II, son of Isumbras IV, married Lalia the Great ('or less courteously the Fat'), *née* Clayhanger, 'in 1314, when he was 36 and she was 31. He died in [S.R.] 1380 at the age of 102, but she long outlived him, coming to an unfortunate end in 1402 at the age of 119.' She was prevented from attending Bilbo's 'long-expected party' 'rather by her great size and immobility than by her age. Her son, *Ferumbras* [Ferumbras III, noted in the family tree as "unmarried"], had no wife, being unable (it was alleged) to find anyone willing to occupy apartments in the Great Smials, under the rule of Lalia' (*Letters*, pp. 294–5). Lalia is said to have died when her attendant (rumoured to be Pippin's sister Pearl) let her wheeled chair slip down a flight of steps.

As first published the Took genealogy states that Adelard Took had '3 daughters' (in addition to sons Reginard and Everard). In a list of errors in the Ballantine Books edition Tolkien emended '3 daughters' to '2 daughters': this was corrected at last in the edition of 2004.

1104 (III: 382). [Brandybuck family tree] – Estella Bolger was added to the Brandybuck family tree as the wife of Meriadoc, and to the Took family tree as the sister of Fredegar (children of Odovacar Bolger, who married Rosamunda Took), in the third printing (1966) of the Ballantine Books edition. But she appears in the family trees only in some subsequent editions, beginning with the Houghton Mifflin edition of 1987. In all cases her name should be underlined to indicate that she was present at Bilbo's birthday party, a late revision entered by Tolkien in one of his personal copies of *The Lord of the Rings*.

1105 (III: 383). [Longfather-tree of Master Samwise] – In the version of this genealogy sent to the printer in 1955 Samwise and Rose had fourteen children, including Lily, the youngest, born in 1444. But Tolkien removed Lily from the family tree in proof, feeling that the number of Sam's children (now thirteen) should surpass that of the Old Took (twelve) by one only.

APPENDIX D

THE CALENDARS

For drafts and history of Appendix D, see *The Peoples of Middle-earth*, pp. 119–39.

1106 (III: 384). [Shire Calendar] – The names of the months in the Shire Calendar are adaptations, or modernizations, of names in Old English:

Afteryule from *æfter Gēola* 'after Winter Solstice'.

Solmath from *Solmōnað*, apparently 'mud-month' (from *sol* 'mud'; the Venerable Bede thought that *Solmōnað* was named after cakes offered to the Gods).

Rethe from *Hrēðmōnað* 'glory-month'. (Tolkien considered the name *Luyde* for the third month, derived from Old English *Hlȳda*, probably related to Modern English *loud* after roaring March winds; see *The Peoples of Middle-earth*, p. 137, n. 3)

Astron from *Ēastermōnað* 'Easter-month', in turn derived from *Eostre*, the name of a goddess whose festival was celebrated at the vernal equinox (compare Germanic **austrōn-* cognate with words for 'dawn' in Sanskrit etc.).

Thrimidge from *Þri-milce* 'three milk-givings'.

Forelithe from *ǣrra Līða* 'before Līða'. *Līða* 'gentle, mild' suits the summer months.

Afterlithe from *æfter Līða* 'after Līða'.

Wedmath from *Wēodmōnað* 'weed-month'.

Halimath from *Hāligmōnað* 'holy-month'. The Venerable Bede refers to it as the 'Month of Offerings', i.e. a harvest month (see *The Peoples of Middle-earth*, p. 122).

Winterfilth from *Winterfylleð* 'winter fullness', compare 'the filling or completion of the year before Winter', p. 1110, n. 1 (III: 388, n. 1). In *The Peoples of Middle-earth* Christopher Tolkien notes that Bede 'explained the name by reference to the ancient English division of the year into two parts of six months each, Summer and Winter: *Winterfylleth* was so called because it was the first month of Winter, but *fylleth*, Bede supposed, referred to the full moon of October, marking the beginning of that period of the year' (p. 137, n. 4).

Blotmath from *Blōtmōnað* 'sacrifice-month', so called because at this season the Saxons offered in sacrifice many of the animals they killed in setting aside provisions for winter.

Foreyule from *ǣrra Gēola* 'before Winter Solstice'.

See also Jim Allan, 'The Giving of Names' in *An Introduction to Elvish*, pp. 227–8; and Adrian Knighton, letter to the editor, *Amon Hen* 36 (December 1978), pp. 15–16.

1106 (III: 384): Every year began on the first day of the week

1106 (III: 384). The Lithe before Mid-year's Day was called 1 Lithe, and the one after was called 2 Lithe. The Yule at the end of the year was 1 Yule, and that at the beginning was 2 Yule. – In *Nomenclature* Tolkien writes about *Lithe* and *Yule*:

> The former and later *Lithe* (Old English *līða*) were the old names for June and July respectively. All the month-names in the Shire-Calendar are (worn-down) forms of the Old English names. In the Hobbit Calendar *(the) Lithe* was the middle-day (or 183rd day) of the year. Since all the Hobbit month-names are supposed *not* to be Common Speech, but conservative survivals from their former language before migration, it would be best to keep *Lithe* unaltered [in translations of *The Lord of the Rings*]. . . . (The word was peculiar to English and no related calendar word is found elsewhere.) . . .
>
> *Yule*, the midwinter counterpart, only occurs in Appendix D, but in translating this, it should like *Lithe* be treated as an alien word not generally current in Common Speech. . . . *Yule* is found in modern English (mostly as a literary archaism), but this is an accident, and cannot be taken to imply that a similar or related word was also found in the Common Speech at that time: the hobbit calendar differed throughout from the official Common Speech calendars. It may, however, be supposed that a form of the same word had been used by the Northmen who came to form a large part of the population of Gondor . . . and was later in use in Rohan, so that some word like *Yule* was well-known in Gondor as a 'northern name' for the midwinter festival.

(In the course of writing *Nomenclature* Tolkien changed his mind in regard to *Yule*. In an earlier, deleted entry he wrote: 'Since it [*Yule*] does occur in modern English, though not in common use, it must be assumed to represent a Common Speech word of similar status at that time. It should therefore be translated in the language used in translation, if possible by a related word, of some similar kind – so long as this has no recognizable Christian reference.')

1107 (III: 385): The Calendar in the Shire

1107 (III: 385). The year no doubt was of the same length – The footnote accompanying this phrase ('365 days, 5 hours, 48 minutes, 46 seconds') was added in the second edition (1965).

1107 (III: 385): It seems clear that the Eldar

1107 (III: 385). the Eldar in Middle-earth, who had, as Samwise

remarked, more time at their disposal – The reference is probably to Sam's remark in Book II, Chapter 9 in regard to Lothlórien: 'Anyone would think that time did not count in there', to which Legolas replies that the Elves 'do not count the running years, not for themselves. The passing seasons are but ripples ever repeated in the long long stream' (p. 388, I: 404–5).

1107 (III: 385). contained 52,596 days – In the first edition a footnote was included at this point: 'The *ré* contained *aurë* day(light) and *lómë* (night); in Sindarin the terms were *aur* containing *calan* and *fuin*.' It was deleted in the second edition (1965).

1108 (III: 386): *Lairë* and *hrívë*

1108 (III: 386). doubling the *enderi* (adding 3 days) in every twelfth year – This is the equivalent of adding *one* day every fourth year in the Gregorian Calendar.

1108 (III: 386): How any resulting inaccuracy

1108 (III: 386). If the year was then of the same length as now, the *yén* would have been more than a day too long. – In the 144 years of the *yén*, a total of 36 days would have been added at the rate of 3 days every twelfth year. But 36 days (864 hours) more than compensates for the deficit, about 837 hours over 144 years (5 hours 48 minutes 46 seconds per year). Thus the surplus in one total *yén* was nearly 27 hours, 'more than a day too long'.

1108 (III: 386): The Númenórean system

1108 (III: 386). The Númenórean system – Tolkien wrote to Naomi Mitchison on 8 December 1955: 'I am sorry about my childish amusement with arithmetic; but there it is: the Númenórean calendar was just a bit better than the Gregorian: the latter being on average 26 sec[ond]s fast p.a. [per annum], and the N[úmenórean] 17.2 secs slow' (*Letters*, p. 229). The Gregorian Calendar adjusts for an extra 5 hours 48 minutes 46 seconds each year beyond 365 days, by adding in February one extra day every fourth (leap) year, defined as years the number of which is divisible by four, excepting the last years of each century unless the number is divisible by 400. This provides 97 leap years in 400 years, but leaves a surplus of 26 seconds per year, or 1 day in 3,323 years.

1108 (III: 386). In every fourth year, except the last of a century (*haranyë*), two *enderi* or 'middle-days' were substituted for the *loëndë* [or middle-day]. – This is similar to the Gregorian system, adding (though in midsummer, not February) one day every fourth year, except at the end of a century.

1108 (III: 386–7): In Númenor calculation started

1108–9 (III: 386–7). In Númenor calculation started with S.A. 1. . . . between the ninth and tenth (September, October). – As first published these paragraphs read:

> This system was originally reckoned from Year 1 of the Second Age, not from 32, the date of the foundation of Númenor. Millennial adjustments were made by adding 2 days to S.A. 1000, 2000 and 3000. A new numeration, however, was begun with Third Age 1. No addition was made until T.A. 1000 (repeated in 2000). Also S.A. 3440 had been an *atendëa* ('double-middle' or leap-year), but the first *atendëa* of the Third Age was in T.A. 4 (that is, in 3445). It was probably to correct this and other inaccuracies accruing since S.A. 3000 that Mardil the Steward added 2 days to T.A. 2060. Hador added another in 2360. These alterations seem to have become recognized eventually throughout the westlands; but there were no further corrections during the Third Age.
>
> Mardil also in the same year, 2060, introduced a revised system which was called Stewards' Reckoning and was adopted eventually by most of the users of the Westron language, except the Hobbits. The months were all of 30 days, and 2 days outside the months were introduced between the third and fourth months (March, April) and 1 between the ninth and tenth (September, October). These 5 days outside the months, *yestarë, tuilérë, loëndë, yáviérë,* and *mettarë*, were holidays.

The text was revised in the second edition (1965).

1108 (III: 386). The *Deficit* caused by deducting 1 day from the last year of a century was not adjusted until the last year of a millennium, leaving a *millennial deficit* of 4 hours, 46 minutes, 40 seconds. This addition was made in Númenor in S.A. 1000, 2000, 3000. – The wording here is curious, since in the previous paragraph there is no mention of *deducting* a day from the last year of a century, only of not *adding* one. The deficit arose because the Númenórean calendar did not add an extra day at the end of 400 years as in the Gregorian system, but made an adjustment at the end of a millennium, by which time more that two days would have accumulated. In the first edition it is quite clear that in S.A. 1000, etc. 2 days were added (equivalent to the extra days in 400, 800, etc. in the Gregorian Calendar), but this feature was omitted, perhaps inadvertently, in the second edition. By S.A. 1000 another part of a day would have accumulated. As Åke Jönsson (Bertenstam) comments in 'The King's Reckoning: Did Tolkien Reckon Correct?' *Beyond Bree* (November 1985): 'The phrase "This addition" may mislead us into believing that Tolkien states that the millennial deficit of the King's Reckoning is 4 hours etc., but it isn't so. What Tolkien says is that the error *remaining* after an unspecified addition is 4 hours etc. This addition must be 2 days' (p. 5).

Indeed, the addition of 2 extra days in S.A. 1000 would still leave 4 hours 46 minutes 40 seconds not accounted for.

1108 (III: 386). To reduce the errors so caused, and the accumulation of the millennial deficit, Mardil the Steward issued a revised calendar to take effect in T.A. 2060, after a special addition of 2 days to 2059 (S.A. 5500), which concluded 5½ millennia since the beginning of the Númenórean system. But this still left about 8 hours deficit. – The deficit of 5½ millennia after adding 2 days three times in the Second Age and twice in the Third Age would be 50 hours 16 minutes 40 seconds. The addition of two days to T.A. 2059 would reduce this to 2 hours 16 minutes 40 seconds. Tolkien presumably reached '8 hours deficit' by adding 5 hours 48 minutes 46 seconds for the late leap year in T.A. 4, or taking into account that with no extra day in 2060 it would be 5 years before the next leap year, T.A. 2064. Åke Jönsson, 'The King's Reckoning: Did Tolkien Reckon Correct?' agrees that the deficit was 8 hours 5 minutes 26 seconds.

1108 (III: 386–7). Hador to 2360 added 1 day though this deficiency had not quite reached that amount. – Adding the deficit surviving from Mardil's revision to the deficiency accumulated in 300 years gives a total of 23 hours 55 minutes 26 seconds.

1108 (III: 387). After that no more adjustments were made. By the end of the Third Age, after 660 more years, the Deficit had not yet amounted to 1 day. – Åke Jönsson in 'The King's Reckoning: Did Tolkien Reckon Correct?' seems to be correct when he says that with no further adjustments in the 660 years following 2360, the deficit must have amounted to more than 1 day. In a millennium it reached 2 days 4 hours 46 minutes 40 seconds. And since the 660-year period 2360–3020 included seven centennial years, in which an extra day was not added, the deficit was proportionately more, over 44 hours.

1108–9 (III: 387): The Revised Calendar

1109 (III: 387). These 5 days outside the months – That is, the three days outside the months since the beginning (*yestarë, loëndë, mettarë*), plus the two new days added by Mardil: *tuilérë* between the third and fourth months, and *yáviérë* between the ninth and the tenth.

1109 (III: 387–8): In the above notes

1109 (III: 387–8). It appears, however, that Mid-year's Day was intended to correspond as nearly as possible to the summer solstice. In that case the Shire dates were actually in advance of ours by some ten days, and our New Year's Day corresponded more or less to the Shire January 9. – As first published this passage read: 'It appears, however, that Mid-year's Day and Year's End were originally intended to correspond as nearly as possible to the summer and winter solstices, and still did so. In that case the Shire dates were actually in advance of ours by some nine days, and our New Year's Day corresponded more or less to the Shire January 8.' In both the Ballantine Books second edition (1965) and the Allen & Unwin second edition (1966) 'summer solstice' was incorrectly printed 'summer solstices'. This was corrected in the eighth (1974) or ninth (1978) printing of the Allen & Unwin edition.

The statements quoted here, from both the first and second editions, have puzzled and perplexed readers trying to correlate the Shire Reckoning (S.R.) and the Gregorian Calendar (G.C). It is not clear that Shire dates can be ten (or nine) days in advance of Gregorian dates *and* that our New Year's Day (January 1) could 'correspond more or less to the Shire January 9' (or 8). S.R. January 9 is only *eight* days, not *ten*, in advance of our January 1. And if one were to assume that Tolkien meant that S.R. January 9 was the *tenth* day of the Shire Year (which began with 2 Yule), that would still make the Shire Calendar only nine days in advance of the Gregorian.

If, however, one ignores this problem and constructs parallel calendars with G.C. January 1 = S.R January 9, then Mid-year's Day in the Shire Reckoning corresponds with June 23 and 1 Yule (Year's End) with December 22, close to the solstices. These vary slightly: the summer solstice is usually on June 21 but can fall on June 22, the winter solstice falls on December 21 or 22. This agrees reasonably well with Tolkien's other statement in regard to both solstices in the first edition, and with the summer solstice in the second edition. Mid-year's Day is in fact less close to a solstice than Year's End, but another factor may be significant: in much of Europe June 24, the Feast of the Nativity of St John the Baptist, is known and sometimes celebrated with traditional ceremonies as Midsummer's Day. (See also note for p. 10.)

See further, Nancy Martsch, 'Calendar Concordance', *Beyond Bree* (March 1993), with charts for the year in three columns: in the first, the Gregorian Calendar beginning with January 1; in the second, the Shire Calendar starting with 2 Yule; and in the third, the Shire Calendar starting with January 9 (= January 1 in the Gregorian Calendar).

1109, n. 2 (III: 387, n. 2): It will be noted if one glances

1109 (III: 387). Friday the first of Summerfilth – Just as there is no 'Friday the first' in any month in Shire Reckoning, so there is no month called *Summerfilth*. The name is obviously intended to echo *Winterfilth*.

1110 (III: 388): The Shire names are set out

1110 (III: 388). In Bree the names [of the months] differed, being *Frery, Solmath, Rethe, Chithing, Thrimidge, Lithe, The Summerdays, Mede, Wedmath, Harvestmath, Wintring, Blooting,* and *Yulemath.* – Like the month-names in the Shire, the variant Bree names are also derived from Old English:

Frery, the Bree equivalent of the Shire's Afteryule, evidently from *frēorig* 'freezing, frigid'.

Chithing (for Astron) from *cīþing* 'growing thing' (*cīþ* 'young shoot, sprout').

Mede (for Afterlithe) from *mǣd* 'mead, meadow'.

Harvestmath (for Halimath) from *Hærfestmōnað*, literally 'harvest-month' (i.e. September).

Wintring (for Winterfilth) from *wintrig* 'wintry, winter'.

Blooting (for Blotmath) from *blōt* 'sacrifice'.

Yulemath (for Foreyule) from *Gēolmōnað* 'Yule-month'.

1110 (III: 388): In this nomenclature

1110 (III: 388). In this nomenclature the Hobbits, however, both of the Shire and of Bree, diverged from the Westron usage, and adhered to old-fashioned local names of their own, which they seem to have picked up in antiquity from the Men of the vales of Anduin; at any rate similar names were found in Dale and Rohan (cf. the notes on the languages, pp. 1130, 1135–6 [pp. 414–15]). – As first published, the note at the end of this passage referred the reader to p. 408 of volume III, Appendix F, 'Of Hobbits', which includes a reference to the Mannish language of the upper Anduin (p. 1130 in the edition of 2004). In early printings of the Ballantine Books second edition (1965) the note incorrectly referred to a page in Appendix A, but by the seventh printing (1966) it directed the reader to 'Of Hobbits'. The Allen & Unwin second edition (1966) and later printings, however, directed the reader to pp. 414–15, part of 'On Translation' in Appendix F, which also discusses Mannish languages. When queried, Christopher Tolkien could find no evidence that his father made this deliberate change, but thought that he must have done so. The current citation therefore safely refers to both locations.

1111 (III: 389): Not many ancient documents

1111 (III: 389). Yellowskin, or the Yearbook of Tuckborough – Lester Simons comments in 'Writing and Allied Technologies in Middle-earth', *Proceedings of the J.R.R. Tolkien Centenary Conference 1992* (1995), that 'the earliest Shire records would seem to be inscribed on vellum . . . which in European history has been used for the most formal and permanent documents; the so-called "Yellowskin" document of the Thain's library may indeed be vellum, if the name is any guide to the material' (p. 340).

1111 (III: 389). In these the weekday names appear in archaic forms, of which the following are the oldest: (1) *Sterrendei*, (2) *Sunnendei*, (3) *Monendei*, (4) *Trewesdei*, (5) *Hevenesdei*, (6) *Meresdei*, (7) *Hihdei*. – These are derived from Old English words, each with the final element *dæg* 'day': *Sterrendei* from *steorra* 'star'; *Sunnendei* from *sunne* 'the sun'; *Monendei* from *mōna* 'the moon'; *Trewesdei* from *trēow* 'tree'; *Hevensdei* from *heofon*, *heofen* 'heaven'; *Meresdei* from *mere* 'sea'; and *Hihdei* from *hēah* 'high, tall, lofty, sublime'.

In editions prior to 2005 *Hihdei* was incorrectly printed *Highdei*. The form *Hihdei* appears in the initial draft of Appendix D; see *The Peoples of Middle-earth*, p. 137, n. 6.

1111 (III: 389): I have translated these names

1111 (III: 398). I have translated these names – In the narrative Tolkien uses familiar names for months and days, not those given in Appendix D. In *The Peoples of Middle-earth* Christopher Tolkien comments:

> In writing of the names of the months and days of the week my father used the word 'translation'. He was referring, of course, to the substitution of e.g. *Thursday* for *Mersday* or *March* for *Rethe*. But it is to be remembered that *Mersday*, *Rethe*, etc. were themselves feigned to be 'translations' of the true Hobbit names . . . the theory is that my father devised a translation of the Hobbit name, which he knew, in archaic English form, *Meresdei* later *Mersday*, and then substituted *Thursday* in the narrative. The rhyming of 'Trewsday, Hensday, Mersday, Hiday' [in a draft of Appendix D] with our 'Tuesday, Wednesday (Wensday), Thursday, Friday' he naturally called an accidental likeness; but it was an astonishing coincidence! I am much inclined to think that the Hobbit calendar was the original conception, and that the names of the days were in fact devised precisely in order to provide this 'accidental likeness'. If this is so, then of course the earlier history of the names of the week (going back to the six-day week of the Eldar) was a further evolution in this extraordinarily ingenious and attractive conception. It is notable, I think, that the Elvish names do not appear until [the second version of Appendix D]. . . . [p. 125]

1111 (III: 389): A few other names

1111 (III: 389). *quellë* (or *lasselanta*) – The alternative '(or *lasselanta*)' was added in the second edition (1965).

1111 (III: 389–90): The Shire Reckoning and dates

1111 (III: 389). All the days, months, and dates – As first published this phrase read: 'All the days and dates'. It was revised in the second edition (1965).

1111 (III: 390). March 25, the date of the downfall of the Barad-dûr, would correspond to our March 27, if our years began at the same seasonal point. – In each calendar this is the eighty-sixth day of the year, but since, as already noted, the years do not begin at the same seasonal point, this is a theoretical correspondence governed by *if*. It has nothing to do with the actual correspondence discussed elsewhere. (N.B. the chart in 'Chronologies, Calendars, and Moons' earlier in the present volume is concerned only with Tolkien's method of adjusting the lunar calendar for 1941–2 to his changing ideas within the narrative. It has no relation to the correspondences discussed in Appendix D.)

1112, n. 2 (III: 390, n. 2): Anniversary of its first blowing

1112, n. 2 (III: 390, n. 2). Anniversary of its first blowing in the Shire in 3019. – This note was added in the second edition (1965).

APPENDIX E

WRITING AND SPELLING

For drafts and history of Appendix E, see *The Peoples of Middle-earth*, pp. 22–3, 28.

PRONUNCIATION OF WORDS AND NAMES

1113–14 (III: 391–2): [CONSONANTS]

1114 (III: 392). PH . . . *alph* 'swan' . . . and (*d*) in Adûnaic and Westron – On 30 June 1969 Tolkien wrote to Paul Bibire that *alph* 'could not be Quenya, as *ph* is not used in my transcription of Quenya, and Quenya does not tolerate final consonants other than the dentals, *t*, *n*, *l*, *r* after a vowel. Quenya for "swan" was *alqua* (*alkwā*)' (quoted in *The Rivers and Beacon-hills of Gondor*, *Vinyar Tengwar* 42 (July 2001), p. 7). *Alph* is Sindarin (*alf*).

The words 'and Westron' were added in the Allen & Unwin second edition (1966).

1114 (III: 392). S . . . SH, occurring in Westron, Dwarvish and Orkish – 'Westron' was added in the Allen & Unwin second edition (1966).

1114 (III: 392). TH . . . This had become *s* in spoken Quenya – As first published these words read: 'This became in Quenya of the Third Age *s*'.

1114–15 (III: 392–3). Y . . . represents a sound like that often heard – The word 'often' was added in the Allen & Unwin second edition (1966).

1115 (III: 393): In Sindarin the combinations

1115 (III: 393). *ng* remained unchanged except initially and finally – The words 'initially and' were added in the Allen & Unwin second edition (1966).

1115 (III: 393). *Endóre* – On 7 September 1955 Tolkien wrote to Richard Jeffery that *en*, *ened* = middle, centre as in *Endor*, *Endóre* Middle-earth (S[indarin] *ennorath*)' (*Letters*, p. 224).

WRITING

1117 (III: 395): The alphabets were of two main

1117 (III: 395). *Cirth*, translated as 'runes' – On 25 June 1963 Tolkien wrote to Rhona Beare:

> The 'cirth' or runes in the 'L.R.' were invented for that story and, within it, have no supposed historical connexion with the Germanic Runic alphabet, to which the English gave its most elaborate development. There is thus nothing to be surprised at if similar signs have different values. The similarity of shapes is inevitable in alphabets devised primarily for cut[ting] or scratching on wood and so made of lines directly or diagonally cut across the grain. [*Letters*, pp. 324–5]

The signs used in the *Cirth* are nearly all extracted from a basic pattern, given in the letter quoted above and reproduced in *Letters*.

In *The Hobbit* Tolkien used genuine Anglo-Saxon runes for the Dwarvish lettering. On runes in *The Lord of the Rings*, see further, *The Treason of Isengard*, pp. 452–65.

1117 (III: 395): The *Tengwar* were the more ancient

1117 (III: 395). Rúmil – The Noldorin Elf of Tirion in the First Age (see note for p. 343), to whom is attributed the *Ainulindalë*.

1120 (III: 398): Within these general applications

1120 (III: 398). *th, f, sh, ch* – As first published this read: '*th, f, sh, kh*'. It was revised (i.e. *kh* > *ch*) in the second edition (1965).

1120, n. 1 (III: 398, n. 1): The representation of the sounds

1120, n. 1 (III: 398, n. 1). The representation of the sounds here is the same as that employed in transcription and described above, except that here *ch* represents the *ch* in English *church*; *j* represents the sound of English *j*, and *zh* the sound heard in *azure* and *occasion*. – As first published this footnote read: 'The representation of the sounds is not strictly phonetic, but is the same as that employed in transcription and described on pp. 391–5, except that here *ch* represents the *ch* in English *church*, and to distinguish it the back 'spirant' *ch* is represented by *kh*; *j* represents the sound of English *j*, and *zh* the sound heard in *azure* and *occasion*; *ŋ* is used for *ng* in *sing*.' It was replaced in the second edition (Ballantine Books, 1965) with: 'The representation of the sounds here is the same as that employed in transcription and described on pp. 487–9, except that here *ch* represents the *ch* in English *church*; *j* represents the sound of English *j*, and *zh* the sound heard in *azure* and *occasion*, *n* [*error, for ŋ*] is used for *ng* in *sing*.' The portion of text following *occasion* was deleted, and the page reference made more general, in the Allen & Unwin second edition (1966).

1121 (III: 399): The standard spelling of Quenya

1121 (III: 399). The standard spelling of Quenya . . . Quenya letter-names pp. 1122–3 [400, 401]. – This paragraph was added in the Ballantine Books second edition (1965), though with errors of transcription (corrected in the Allen & Unwin second edition, 1966).

1121 (III: 399–400): *The vowels* were in many modes

1121 (III: 399). The three dots, most usual in formal writing – In the Ballantine Books and Allen & Unwin second editions (1965, 1966) 'formal' was erroneously set as 'forming'. The correct reading, as in the first edition, was restored in the HarperCollins edition of 2002.

1122–3 (III: 400–1): *The names of the letters*

1123 (III: 401). *noldo* (older *ngoldo*) . . . *nwalme* (older *ngwalme*) . . . *úre* heat – As first published, '*ngoldo*' read '*ŋoldo*', and '*úre*' read '*úr*'. The first was altered, and the words '(older *ngwalme*)' added, in the second edition (1965). The word *ngwalme* was misprinted *ywalme* in the Ballantine Books printings, but corrected in the Allen & Unwin second edition (1966). Also in the latter, the word *úr* was changed to *úre*.

1123 (III: 401). the spirant *ch* . . . distinct signs for *chw* – As first published this passage read: 'the spirant *kh* . . . distinct sounds for *khw*'. The sounds *kh* and *khw* were altered to *ch* and *chw* in the second edition (1965).

APPENDIX F

For drafts and history of Appendix F, see *The Peoples of Middle-earth*, pp. 19–84.

THE LANGUAGES AND PEOPLES OF THE THIRD AGE

1127 (III: 405): Of the *Eldarin* tongues

1127 (III: 405). Of the *Eldarin* tongues two are found in this book – On 25 April 1954 Tolkien wrote to Naomi Mitchison:

> Two of the Elvish tongues appear in this book. They have some sort of existence, since I have composed them in some sort of completeness, as well as their history and account of their relationship. They are intended (a) to be definitely of a European kind in style and structure (not in detail); and (b) to be specially pleasant. The former is not difficult to achieve; but the latter is more difficult, since individuals' personal predilections, especially in the phonetic structure of languages, varies widely, even when modified by the imposed languages (including their so-called 'native' tongue).
>
> I have therefore pleased myself. The archaic language of lore is meant to be a kind of 'Elven-latin', and by transcribing it into a spelling closely resembling that of Latin (except that *y* is only used as a consonant, as *y* in E[nglish] *Yes*) the similarity to Latin had been increased ocularly. Actually it might be said to be composed on a Latin basis with two other (main) ingredients that happened to give me 'phonaesthetic' pleasure: Finnish and Greek. It is however less consonantal than any of the three. This language is High-elven or in its own terms *Quenya* (Elvish).
>
> The living language of the Western Elves (*Sindarin* or Grey-elven) is the one usually met, especially in names. This is derived from an origin common to it and *Quenya*; but the changes have been deliberately devised to give it a linguistic character very like (though not identical with) British-Welsh: because that character is one that I find, in some linguistic moods, very attractive; and because it seems to fit the rather 'Celtic' type of legends and stories told of its speakers. [*Letters*, pp. 175–6]

1127, n. 1 (III: 405, n. 1): In Lórien at this period

1127, n. 1 (III: 405, n. 1). In Lórien at this period . . . adapted to Sindarin. – This footnote was added in the second edition (1965).

1128 (III: 406): The Exiles, dwelling

1128 (III: 406). the Lady Galadriel of the royal house of Finarfin and sister of Finrod Felagund, King of Nargothrond – As first published this passage read: 'the Lady Galadriel of the royal house of Finrod, father of Felagund, lord of Nargothrond'. In the second edition (1965) it was altered to: 'the Lady Galadriel of the royal house of Finarphir and sister of Finrod Felagund, King of Nargothrond'. By the ninth printing (1978) of the Allen & Unwin second edition 'Finarphir' was changed by Christopher Tolkien to 'Finarfin', as in *The Silmarillion*. See also note for p. 1137.

1128–9 (III: 406): The *Dúnedain* alone of all races

1128 (III: 406). The *Dúnedain* alone of all races of Men knew and spoke an Elvish tongue – On 17 December 1972 Tolkien wrote to Richard Jeffery:

> At the time of the L.R. . . . Quenya had been a 'dead' [language] (sc. not one inherited in childhood, but learnt) for many centuries (act[ually] about 6,000 years). The 'High-Elves' or exiled Noldor had, for reasons that the legend of their rebellion and exile from Valinor explains, at once adopted Sindarin, and even translated their Q[uenya] names into S[indarin] or adapted them. . . . It may be noted that at the end of the Third Age there were prob[ably] more people (Men) that knew Q[uenya], or spoke S[indarin], than there were Elves that did either! Though dwindling, the population of Minas Tirith and its fiefs must have been much greater than that of *Lindon*, *Rivendell*, and *Lórien*. (The Silvan Elves of Thranduil's realm did not speak S[indarin] but a related language or dialect.) In Gondor the generally used language was 'Westron', a lang[uage] about as mixed as mod[ern] English, but basically derived from the native lang[uage] of the Númenóreans; but Sindarin was an acquired polite language and used by those of more pure N[úmenórean] descent, esp[ecially] in *Minas Tirith*, if they wished to be polite (as in the cry *Ernil i Pheriannath* . . . and Master *Perian* . . .). [*Letters*, p. 425]

1128, n. 1 (III: 406, n. 1): Quenya, for example

1128, n. 1 (III: 406, n. 1). Most of the names of the other men and women. . . . Some few are of mixed forms, as *Boromir*. – As first published these sentences read: 'The names of other lords of the Dúnedain, such as *Aragorn*, *Denethor*, *Faramir*, are of Sindarin form, being often the names of Elves or Men remembered in the songs and histories of the First Age.' They were revised in the second edition (1965).

1131 (III: 409): So it was that in the Third Age

1131 (III: 409). less unlovely than Orkish. In this jargon *tark*, 'man of Gondor', was a debased form of *tarkil*, a Quenya word used in Westron

for one of Númenórean descent; see p. 906 [see III, 182]. – The sentence following 'Orkish' was added in the Allen & Unwin second edition (1966).

1131–2 (III: 409–10): It is said that the Black Speech

1131 (III: 409). the Black Speech – Tolkien commented to Naomi Mitchison on 25 April 1954: 'The Black Speech was used only in Mordor. . . . It was never used willingly by any other people, and consequently even the names of places in Mordor are in English (for the C.S. [Common Speech]) or Elvish' (*Letters*, p. 178).

1132 (III: 410). *Sharkû* in that tongue means *old man*. – This sentence was added in the second edition (1965), originally with the name spelt 'Sharkū'. Tolkien later emended the macron to a circumflex in a check copy of *The Return of the King*. (Cf. Appendix E, p. 1116, III: 393–4: 'In Sindarin long vowels in stressed monosyllables are marked with the circumflex, since they tended in such cases to be specially prolonged'.)

ON TRANSLATION

1133 (III: 411): The Common Speech

1133 (III: 411). The Common Speech . . . has inevitably been turned into modern English. – On 25 April 1954 Tolkien wrote to Naomi Mitchison that the issue of translation had given him much thought.

> It seems seldom regarded by other creators of imaginary worlds, however gifted as narrators (such as [E.R.] Eddison [author of *The Worm Ouroboros*, etc.]). But then I am a philologist, and much though I should like to be precise on other cultural aspects and features, that is not within my competence. Anyway 'language' is the most important, for the story has to be told, and the dialogue conducted in a language; but English cannot have been the language of any people at that time. What I have, in fact done, is to equate the Westron or wide-spread Common Speech of the Third Age with English; and translate everything, including names such as *The Shire*, that was in the Westron into English terms, with some differentiation of style to represent dialectal differences. Languages quite alien to the C.S. [Common Speech] have been left alone. Except for a few scraps in the Black Speech of Mordor, and a few names and a battle-cry in Dwarvish, these are almost entirely Elvish (*Eldarin*).
>
> Languages, however, that were related to the Westron presented a special problem. I turned them into forms of speech related to English. Since the *Rohirrim* are represented as recent comers out of the North, and users of an archaic Mannish language relatively untouched by the influence of *Eldarin*, I have turned their names into forms like (but not identical with) Old English. The language of Dale and the Long Lake

> would, if it appeared, be represented as more or less Scandinavian in character; but it is only represented by a few names, especially those of the Dwarves that came from that region. These are all Old Norse Dwarf-names. [*Letters*, pp. 174–5]

In *The Peoples of Middle-earth* Christopher Tolkien comments that, as it seems from the available evidence, the idea of 'translation' in *The Lord of the Rings* 'evolved gradually, as the history, linguistic and other, was consolidated and became increasingly coherent' (p. 70). See further, *The Peoples of Middle-earth*, Chapter 2.

1134 (III: 412–13): The name of the Shire

1134 (III: 412). The name of the Shire (*Sûza*) – In *Nomenclature* Tolkien comments, in regard to *Shire* and words in other languages with the meaning 'district', that 'the Old Norse and modern Icelandic *sýsla* (Swedish *syssla*, Danish *syssel*, now obsolete in sense *amt*, but occurring in place-names) was in mind when I said that the real untranslated name of the Shire was *Súza*. . . .'

1136–7 (III: 415): The still more northerly language

1137 (III: 415). Naugrim – The Sindarin name ('the stunted people') for the Dwarves.

1137 (III: 415–16): *Elves* has been used

1137 (III: 416). They were tall, fair of skin and grey-eyed, though their locks were dark, save in the golden house of Finarfin – As first published, 'Finarfin' read 'Finrod'. In the Allen & Unwin three-volume paperback edition (1974) 'Finrod' was changed to 'Finarphir' (first and second printings), then to 'Finarphin' (third printing, 1975), and finally 'Finarfin' (fourth printing, 1976), as Christopher Tolkien determined the name to be used in *The Silmarillion* (1977).

In context, these words seem to apply to the Eldar as a whole. In *The Book of Lost Tales, Part One*, pp. 43–4 (compare *The Peoples of Middle-earth*, pp. 76–7), however, Christopher Tolkien quotes a draft for the final paragraph of Appendix F in which it is said that 'the Noldor belonged to a race high and beautiful, the elder Children of the world, who now are gone. Tall they were, fair-skinned and grey-eyed, and their locks were dark, save in the golden house of Finrod.' Christopher explains:

> Thus these words describing characters of face and hair were actually written of the Noldor only, and *not* of all the Eldar: indeed the Vanyar had golden hair, and it was from Finarfin's Vanyarin mother Indis that he, and Finrod Felagund and Galadriel his children, had their golden hair that marked them out among the princes of the Noldor. But I am unable to determine how this extraordinary perversion of meaning arose. [p. 44]

In the edition of 2004 a footnote by the present authors was added to p. 1137 ('These words describing characters of face and hair in fact applied only to the Noldor: see *The Book of Lost Tales, Part One*, p. 44') to explain the distinction, in preference to rewriting Tolkien's words, within a finely cadenced paragraph.

EXTRACTS FROM A LETTER BY J.R.R. TOLKIEN TO MILTON WALDMAN, ?LATE 1951, ON THE LORD OF THE RINGS

As mentioned already in our 'Brief History', when Tolkien had completed *The Lord of the Rings* in 1949 (excepting final revisions and the Appendices) he greatly desired to see it published in conjunction with 'The Silmarillion', though only parts of the latter yet existed in fair copy. Because George Allen & Unwin had earlier rejected 'The Silmarillion' as a successor to *The Hobbit*, Tolkien now felt that he should change his publisher; and around this time Milton Waldman, an editor with the London firm Collins, expressed an interest in publishing both 'The Silmarillion' and *The Lord of the Rings*, which Allen & Unwin judged impractical due to their combined length, given costs and the continued rationing of paper after the Second World War.

Probably in late 1951 Tolkien wrote a long letter to Milton Waldman to demonstrate the relationship of the two works, which Tolkien considered interdependent, 'one long Saga of the Jewels and the Rings' (as he wrote to Waldman in earlier correspondence, *Letters*, p. 139). Most of this text was published in *Letters of J.R.R. Tolkien*, pp. 143–61, but parts were omitted, in particular a summary of *The Lord of the Rings*, a work already well known to the intended audience of the collection. (A short extract later appeared in *Sauron Defeated*, pp. 129, 132.) It seems appropriate, however, to include that omitted text in the present book as further documentation of the history of *The Lord of the Rings*, together with related preceding and following paragraphs. The making and nature of the One Ring belong to the Second Age, and are described in *Letters* pp. 152–4. At the time of this letter Tolkien still intended to include an Epilogue at the end of Book VI.

For the present text we have followed a copy kindly supplied to us by Christopher Tolkien of that part of the typescript made by order of Milton Waldman from Tolkien's original manuscript letter (apparently not extant). Except for a few silent corrections of minor typographical errors, we have retained capitalization, punctuation, etc. as found. Other portions of the letter are given as published in *Letters*. (An independent edition of the portion omitted from *Letters* was published, together with the complete letter to Waldman translated into French and with notes by Michaël Devaux, in *Tolkien: Les racines du légendaire, La Feuille de la Compagnie Cahier d'études tolkieniennes* 2 (Genève: Ad Solem), autumne 2003, pp. 19–81. Devaux earlier published the complete letter in French, with commentary, as 'Lettre à Milton Waldman: L'horizon de la Terre du Milieu' in *Conférence* 12 (Printemps 2001), pp. 707–56.)

*

The sequel [to *The Hobbit*], *The Lord of the Rings*, much the largest, and I hope also in proportion the best, of the entire cycle [including also 'The Silmarillion'], concludes the whole business – an attempt is made to include in it, and wind up, all the elements and motives of what has preceded: elves, dwarves, the Kings of Men, heroic 'Homeric' horsemen, orcs and demons, the terrors of the Ring-servants and Necromancy, and the vast horror of the Dark Throne, even in style it is to include the colloquialism and vulgarity of Hobbits, poetry and the highest style of prose. We are to see the overthrow of the last incarnation of Evil, the unmaking of the Ring, the final departure of the Elves, and the return in majesty of the true King, to take over the Dominion of Men, inheriting all that can be transmitted of Elfdom in his high marriage with Arwen daughter of Elrond, as well as the lineal royalty of Númenor. But as the earliest Tales are seen through Elvish eyes, as it were, this last great Tale, coming down from myth and legend to the earth, is seen mainly through the eyes of Hobbits: it thus becomes in fact anthropocentric. But through Hobbits, not Men so-called, because the last Tale is to exemplify most clearly a recurrent theme: the place in 'world politics' of the unforeseen and unforeseeable acts of will, and deeds of virtue of the apparently small, ungreat, forgotten in the places of the Wise and Great (good as well as evil). A moral of the whole (after the primary symbolism of the Ring, as the will to mere power, seeking to make itself objective by physical force and mechanism, and so also inevitably by lies) is the obvious one that without the high and noble the simple and vulgar is utterly mean; and without the simple and ordinary the noble and heroic is meaningless.

It is not possible even at great length to 'pot' *The Lord of the Rings* in a paragraph or two. . . . It was begun in 1936 [*sic*, for 1937], and every part has been written many times. Hardly a word in its 600,000 or more has been unconsidered. And the placing, size, style, and contribution to the whole of all the features, incidents, and chapters has been laboriously pondered. I do not say this in recommendation. It is, I feel, only too likely that I am deluded, lost in a web of vain imaginings of not much value to others – in spite of the fact that a few readers have found it good, on the whole.* [* But as each has disliked this or that, I should (if I took all the criticisms together and obeyed them) find little left, and am forced to the conclusion that so great a work (in size) cannot be perfect, nor even if perfect, be liked entirely by any *one* reader.] What I intend to say is this: I cannot substantially alter the thing. I have finished it, it is 'off my mind': the labour has been colossal; and it must stand or fall, practically as it is.

The Lord of the Rings opens on the same scene as *The Hobbit*: some sixty years later. It begins with a chapter, somewhat similar in style, that in title (*A Long-expected Party*) and content is a deliberate parallel to the first chapter of the earlier book. *Bilbo* is now 111 years old – old age for a hobbit.* [* The normal span of hobbits is represented as being roughly in the proportion of 100 to our 80.] He has adopted as his heir his favourite kinsman of a younger generation, *Frodo*. He is generally envied for his wealth and apparently unaging health; but conversation between Bilbo and Gandalf reveals that all is not well with the old hobbit: he is finding life 'thin' and wearisome. Gandalf shows a certain anxious curiosity about his ring.

The introduction ends with the sudden disappearance in the midst of his own birthday-party of the Hobbit, Bilbo, never to be seen in the Shire again. It is his last use of the ring. Gandalf induces him to leave it behind with his heir, Frodo. All his other trophies of the old adventure he takes with him, and departs – to an 'unknown destination' (but of course to the House of Elrond and peaceful memory of the past).

Some seventeen years elapse. Frodo is now of the age that Bilbo was when he went on his Quest. He also preserves his youth, but is afflicted with restlessness. Rumours of troubles in the great world outside reach the Hobbits, especially of the rise again of the Enemy or Dark Lord. Gandalf, after long absences on perilous journeys of search, returns and reveals that Bilbo's ring is The Ring, the One; and that the Enemy is aware of its existence, and probably through the treachery of Gollum knows where it is. Something of the history of the Ring is sketched (mainly how it came into the 'accidental' keeping of Gollum).

Frodo makes plans to fly in secret – to the House of Elrond. A tryst is made for the autumn, but Gandalf fails to keep it*, and *Frodo* and his hobbit-servant *Sam* and two younger kinsmen go off alone into the wild – in the nick of time, just as the Black Riders of Mordor (the Nine Ring-slaves in disguise) reach the Shire. [* It is later revealed that this is owing to the treason of *Saruman*, chief wizard, who attempts to imprison Gandalf and force him to join the Enemy party.] Over all the 400 miles to Elrond they are pursued by the terror, and are brought through only by the help of a strange man met in an inn, known to some as Strider. His stature and power are only slowly manifested. Frodo receives a desperate wound from the Captain of the Black Riders, and is at Death's door, when at last the fugitives escape and come to Elrond. The First Book ends with the destruction of the Black Riders (in that form) and the reception of the Ring-bearer by Elrond.

The Second Book – which must, as explained before, begin with a pause, before a complete change of direction, after healing and refreshment and the gaining of wisdom – begins with the healing of *Frodo*, the meeting of Frodo and Bilbo again, the council of the Wise, and the making of the plan for the Final Quest: the unmaking of the Ring. At the end of the year in the mid-winter (the most unlooked-for time) the Company of the Ring sets out, in the most unlooked-for direction: towards the land of the Enemy.

The Company of Nine, as counterpart to the Nine Riders, and as representing all the chief elements of resistance to the Dark Power, contains Gandalf, the four Hobbits, Boromir, a lord of Gondor; Strider, now revealed as Aragorn, heir of Isildur, and hidden claimant to the Ancient Crown; an Elf; and a Dwarf. Their adventures start on a plane and in a style resembling that of *The Hobbit* but rise steadily to a higher level. All the characters are slowly revealed in their nature and in their change [*sic*, apparently a typist's error, omitting a word or words].

There is a sense throughout of a hidden watch on their movements, a constant hostility even of beasts and inanimate things. The Company is driven to attempt the passage of the ominous Mines of Moria, and there Gandalf falls into an abyss in the act of saving them from a trap. Aragorn leads them on through Lórien, a guarded Elvish land – at which point I make the perilous and difficult attempt to catch at close quarters the air of timeless Elvish enchantment; and they proceed down the Great River, until they pass the water-gate into the old realm of Gondor. At last halting at the vast Falls of Rauros they are almost in sight of the Black Land east, and of the last City of Gondor westward. Decision what to do, long put off, must now be faced, for with the loss of Gandalf much of his plans and purpose remain unknown even to Aragorn.

The Second Book ends in disaster, and the breaking up of the Company (owing to the secret working of the Ring, that excites the lust of Boromir of Gondor). Frodo and Sam go off east alone on their desperate mission to bring the Ring to the Enemy's own country, and cast it in the Fire. Aragorn is placed in a dilemma. He may go after Frodo with small hope of finding him, or even so of helping him, and abandon the two hobbits that have been captured by Orcs, the enemies' soldiers. Or he may rescue the Hobbits, and leave Frodo and Sam to their hopeless errand. All through the book hints of the watchfulness of spies have multiplied. Also it becomes at last clear that Gollum himself has picked up their trail and is dogging the footsteps of the Ringbearer. At the last the Black Riders reappear in still more terrible form, winged riders in the air. The book ends with the death of Boromir fighting the Orcs in an effort to redeem himself for his fall – he had tried to take the Ring from Frodo by force.

The Third Book deals with the fate and adventures of all the Companions save Frodo and Sam, who have passed beyond knowledge and aid. It treats of the adventures of the two young hobbits captured by Orcs, and their rise to heroism; and of the desperate effort of Aragorn and the Elf and Dwarf to overtake them and rescue them. But it also introduces one to the greater politics of the defence of the West, and to the preparations for the last war and battle with Sauron. It is crossed by the lesser war with Saruman chief of the Wise who has turned himself to evil, and seeks for domination, playing into the hands (more or less wittingly) of the Dark Lord. We meet the noble Riders of Rohan, the Rohirrim, and their King in his Golden Hall; and the book ends with the destruction of Saruman's stronghold in Isengard and the reunion of all the Companions (save Frodo and Sam).

Gandalf reappears – changed and more evidently superhuman after his combat in the abyss. The book ends with the appearance of a great Nazgûl (Black Rider of the Air), a signal that the major and final war is about to open. A great darkness spreads from Mordor over all the lands. Gandalf with one hobbit rides like the wind to Gondor.

The Fourth Book deals with the perils and labours of Frodo and Sam. Gollum reappears, and is 'tamed' by Frodo: that is by the power of the Ring he is cowed to a Caliban-like servitude at first, but slowly Frodo awakes his long-buried better self: he begins to love Frodo as a good and kind master. This regeneration is constantly hindered by the suspicion and dislike of the faithful Sam. It is finally frustrated by an impatient and impulsive rebuke of Sam's at a critical moment, when Gollum was poised on the brink of repentance. Gollum relapses into hatred and treachery. But he is essential: only by his guidance could the hobbits even approach the Black Land. They pass the Dead Marshes. They come to the desolation before the Black Gates of Mordor. They are impassable. Gollum leads them away southward to a secret pass in the western walls of the land. They meet and are aided by Faramir, Boromir's brother, of Gondor, who is conducting perilous forays upon the Forces of Sauron. They pass at last into the Mountains of Shadow, and here are delivered into a trap by the treachery of Gollum. The Book ends in apparent disaster. Frodo stricken down by the monstrous Spider – guardian of the pass, lies as dead. Sam now begins his rise to supremely heroic stature. He fights the Spider, rescues his master's body, assumes the ghastly burden of the Ring, and is preparing to stagger on alone in an attempt to carry out the impossible errand. But at the last moment, Orcs come, carry off his beloved Master's body, and his primary loyalty to [his] master triumphs. He pursues them, learns that Frodo is only poison-drugged, and flings himself senseless and in despair against the brazen door of the Orcs, as it closes. So the book ends.

The Fifth Book returns to the precise point at which Book Three ended. Gandalf on his great horse (with the Hobbit Peregrin Took) passing along the great 'north-road', South to Gondor. Now we come to the half-ruinous Byzantine City of Minas Tirith, and meet its grim lord, the old proud wizard-like Steward, Denethor. He prepares for war and hopeless siege. The last levies from the remaining fiefs march in. The great darkness comes. The Nazgûl ride the air, cowing all hearts. Slowly the assault begins and mounts in fire and terror. Denethor commits suicide. The Sorcerer-King, Captain of the Black Riders, overthrows the 'unbreakable' gates of the City. Gandalf alone is left to face him.

The siege is raised at the last moment by the coming at last of the Riders of Rohan, led by their ancient king Théoden. The charge of their horsemen saves the field. Then the great battle of the Pelennor Fields is joined. Théoden falls. Victory turns towards the Enemy, but Aragorn appears in the Great River with a fleet, coming as the Númenóreans of old as it were up out of the Sea, and he raises for the first time in many ages the Banner of the King. After the victory (and destruction of the Captain of the Black Riders) the Book ends in the last desperate deed of the West. To draw off the eyes of the Enemy, in case Frodo is indeed come to his land, and also because sitting still in a fortress would end at last only in ruin, all that can be mustered of the Men of Rohan and Gondor march away openly to assault the very gates of Mordor. In the last pages of this Book we see the hopeless defeat of the forlorn hope. The hobbit among them (Peregrin) falls under the weight of the slain, and as consciousness fails and he passes into forgetfulness, he seems to hear the cry of 'The Eagles'. But he remembers that was the turning point of Bilbo's story, which he knew well, and laughing at his fancy his spirit flies away, and he remembers no more.

The Sixth and Last Book begins where the Fourth left off. We now have the *αριστεία* [prowess] of Sam, his supreme plain dogged common-sensible heroism in aid of his master. I cannot 'pot' these chapters in which I have told (and, I think, even made credible in their mode) how he rescued his master, how he guided and aided him through the horrors and deadly perils of Mordor, until at the very edge of death (by hunger, thirst and fear and the growing burden of the Ring), they reach the Mountain of Doom and the high chamber of the Fire – dogged still by the relentless Gollum, over whom the Ring that he no longer possesses has a power that nothing but death could heal.

We reach the brink of the First, *and the whole plan fails*. The Ring conquers. Frodo cannot bear to destroy it. He renounces the Quest, and claims the Ring and puts it on his finger. The Dark Lord is suddenly aware of him and all the plot. His whole appalling will is withdrawn from the battle at the Gates and concentrated on the Mountain (within sight of his throne). Gollum comes up, and wrestles on the brink for mastery with Frodo. He bits off finger and Ring, and screams with exultation, but falls in his mad capering into the abyss, and so ends. And so the Ring is after all unmade – and even the treachery of Gollum has served its end (as Gandalf foretold).

The Hobbits are nearly overwhelmed in the resulting cataclysm. From afar they glimpse through the clouds the catastrophic downfall of the Dark Tower, and the disintegration of Sauron. The Mountain erupts. At last they lie choked in fume and flame on a last rock-isle in a sea of molten lava.

The scene shifts back to the exact moment at which Book Five ended. We see and hear now from afar the same shattering ruin. The forces of Sauron, bereft (like termites with a dead queen) of all direction and will, fly and disintegrate. The vast figure of Sauron rears up, 'terrible but impotent', as it passes away on the wind, a shadow that shall never again take substance. The cry of 'the Eagles' really is heard. They come down the wind from the North, and directed by Gandalf, bear up the bodies of Frodo and Sam and bring them out of the ruin of Mordor.

The story reaches its end (as a tale of Hobbits!) in the celebration of victory in which all the Nine Companions are reunited. In the scene where all the hosts of the West unite to do honour and praise to the two humble Hobbits, Frodo and Sam, we reach the 'eucatastrophe' of the whole romance: that is the sudden joyous 'turn' and fulfilment of hope, the opposite of tragedy, that should be the hallmark of a 'fairy-story' of higher or lower tone, the resolution and justification of all that has gone before. It brought tears to my eyes to write it, and still moves me, and I cannot help believing that it is a supreme moment of its kind.

But it is not the end of the 'Sixth Book', or of *The Lord of the Rings* as a whole. For various reasons. The chief artistic one that the music cannot be cut off short at its peak. Also the history is left in the air, unfinished. Also I like tying up loose ends, and hate them in other people's books; I like to wind up the clues, as do not only children, but most folk of hearty appetite. Again, the story began in the simple Shire of the Hobbits, and it must end there, back to common life and earth (the ultimate foundation) again. Finally and cogently, it is the function of the longish *coda* to show the *cost* of victory (as always), and to show that no victory, even on a world-shaking scale, is final. The war will go on, taking other modes.

We pass thus to wind up the affairs of Gondor, and witness the Crowning of the King, and his marriage with the lady high and fair, daughter of Elrond, destined queen of the throne restored. And the Companions depart, dropping off one by one in a series of farewells as we go back north to Elrond's House, and then west again to the Shire. Saruman the Great is passed on the road, a whining malicious beggar. In Rivendell farewell is said to the old Hobbit Bilbo, now dozing to his end, as the power of the destroyed Ring fades and he is released from unnatural prolongation. The Hobbits, still hobbits in idiom and stature, but clad now in the arms and garb of the high chivalry of the South, fearless and ennobled, approach the Shire and Gandalf says farewell. They go on to discover that the tentacles of the evil of that time have reached even to their beloved land in their absence. Greed and ambition has touched even the Hobbits, and one of Frodo's kin has tried to corner all the wealth and the power of the community. He had long been in secret communication with Saruman, only to be outwitted: for evil Men, servants of Saruman, have really usurped him, ruling all by pillage and force. Barracks disfigure the villages, trees are felled far and wide, rivers fouled, and mills turned to machines. The 'scouring of the Shire' ending in the last battle ever fought there occupies a chapter. It is followed by a second spring, a marvellous restoration and enhancement of bounty, chiefly wrought by Sam (with the help of gifts given him in Lórien). But Frodo cannot be healed. For the preservation of the Shire he has sacrificed himself, even in health and has no heart to enjoy it. Sam has to choose between love of master and of wife. In the end he goes with Frodo on a last journey. At night in the woods, where Sam first met Elves on the outward journey, they meet the twilit cavalcade from Rivendell. The Elves and the Three Rings, and Gandalf (Guardian of the Third Age) are going to the Grey Havens, to set sail for the West, never to return. Bilbo is with them. To Bilbo and Frodo the special grace is granted to go with the Elves they loved – an Arthurian ending, in which it is, of course, not made explicit whether this is an 'allegory' of death, or a mode of healing and restoration leading to a return. They ride to the Grey Havens, and take Ship: Gandalf with the Red Ring, Elrond (with the Blue) and the greater part of his household, and Galadriel of Lórien with the White Ring, and with them depart Bilbo and Frodo. It is hinted that they come to Eressëa. But Sam standing stricken on the stone quay sees only the white ship slip down the grey estuary and fade into the darkling West. He stays long unmoving listening to the sound of the Sea on the shores of the world.

Then he rides home; his wife welcomes him to the firelight and his first child, and he says simply 'Well, I've come back'. There is a brief epilogue in which we see Sam among his children, a glance at his love for Elanor (the Elvish name of a flower in Lórien) his eldest, who by a strange gift has the looks and beauty of an elven-maid: in her all his love and longing for Elves is resolved and satisfied. He is busy, contented, many times mayor of the Shire, and struggling to finish off the Red Book, begun by Bilbo and nearly completed by Frodo, in which all the events (told in The Hobbit and The Lord) are recorded. The whole ends with Sam and his wife standing outside Bag-end, as the children are asleep, looking at the stars in the cool spring-sky. Sam tells his wife of his bliss and content, and goes in, but as he closes the door he hears the sighing of the Sea on the Shores of the world.

That is a long and yet bald résumé. Many characters important to the tale are not even mentioned. Even some whole inventions like the remarkable *Ents*, oldest of living rational creatures, *Shepherds of the Trees*, are omitted. Since we now try to deal with 'ordinary life', springing up ever unquenched under the trample of world policies and events, there are love-stories touched in, or love in different modes, wholly absent from *The Hobbit*. But the highest love-story, that of Aragorn and Arwen Elrond's daughter is only alluded to as a known thing. It is told elsewhere in a short tale, *Of Aragorn and Arwen Undómiel*. I think the simple 'rustic' love of Sam and his Rosie (nowhere elaborated) is *absolutely essential* to the study of his (the chief hero's) character, and to the theme of the relation of ordinary life (breathing, eating, working, begetting) and quests, sacrifice, causes, and the 'longing for Elves', and sheer beauty. But I will say no more, nor defend the theme of mistaken love seen in Éowyn and her first love for Aragorn. I do not feel much can now be done to heal the faults of this large and much-embracing tale – or to make it 'publishable', if it is not so now. . . .

NOMENCLATURE OF THE LORD OF THE RINGS

The first translations of *The Lord of the Rings* were those in Dutch (*In de ban van de ring*) and Swedish (*Sagan om ringen*), published in 1956–7 and 1959–61 respectively. In each instance Tolkien objected strongly to the work while in progress, especially in regard to the alteration of names as he had written them. On 3 July 1956 he wrote to Rayner Unwin concerning the version in Dutch:

> *In principle* I object as strongly as is possible to the 'translation' of the *nomenclature* at all (even by a competent person). I wonder why a translator should think himself called on or entitled to do any such thing. That this is an 'imaginary' world does not give him any right to remodel it according to his fancy, even if he could in a few months create a new coherent structure which it took me years to work out.

The correct way to translate *The Lord of the Rings*, he felt, 'is to leave the maps and nomenclature alone as far as possible, but to substitute for some of the least-wanted Appendices a glossary of names (with meanings but no ref[erence]s.). I could supply one for translation. May I say at once that I will *not* tolerate any similar tinkering with the *personal nomenclature.* Nor with the name/word *Hobbit*' (*Letters*, pp. 249–51). But he was only partly successful in turning the Dutch translator to his point of view, despite lengthy correspondence. Later he had a similar experience with the Swedish *The Lord of the Rings*, all the more distressing because the translator of the first Swedish *Hobbit* (*Hompen*, 1947) had also taken liberties with the text. On 7 December 1957 Tolkien wrote to Rayner Unwin: 'I do hope that it can be arranged, if and when any further translations are negotiated [after the Dutch and Swedish], *that I should be consulted at an early stage*. . . . After all, I charge nothing, and can save a translator a good deal of time and puzzling; and if *consulted* at an early stage my remarks will appear far less in the light of peevish criticisms' (*Letters*, p. 263).

At length Tolkien himself took the initiative. He continued to prefer that *The Lord of the Rings* in translation preserve the essential *Englishness* of many of its personal and place-names; but he came to accept that other translators were likely to take a line similar to those of the Dutch and Swedish editions, who had sometimes misunderstood their source, and instead of insisting on *no* translation of nomenclature, he attempted to influence the translator through an explanatory document. On 2 January 1967 he wrote to Otto B. Lindhardt, of the Danish publisher Gyldendals Bibliotek, who were planning to publish *The Lord of the Rings* in Danish, that 'experience in attempting to help translators or in reading their versions has made me realize that the nomenclature of persons and places offers particular difficulty', but is important 'since it was constructed with considerable care, to fit with the supposed history of the period described. I have therefore recently been engaged in making, and have nearly completed, a commentary on the names in this story, with explanations and suggestions for the use of a translator, having especially in mind Danish and German' (Tolkien-George Allen & Unwin archive, HarperCollins).

Tolkien's 'commentary' for many years was photocopied by Allen & Unwin and sent to translators of *The Lord of the Rings* as an aid to their work. After Tolkien's death it was edited by his son Christopher and published in *A Tolkien Compass* (1975) as *Guide to the Names in The Lord of the Rings*. For the present book it has been newly transcribed from the professional typescript as corrected by Tolkien, with reference also to an earlier version in manuscript and typescript. For the sake of a more general audience, we have slightly edited the work for clarity and consistency of form, most often by the addition or emendation of articles, conjunctions, and marks of punctuation (thus also by Christopher Tolkien for *A Tolkien Compass*); but to convey the flavour of the original, we have retained (for the most part, but have regularized) Tolkien's abbreviations of language names, etc., and have restored the original title of the work. Citations by Tolkien to the Prologue in the first edition of *The Lord of the Rings* (1954) have been silently emended to the pagination of the Allen & Unwin second edition (1966). Significant insertions by the editors are indicated by [square brackets].

Notes removed by Tolkien from the final *Nomenclature* are quoted earlier in this book, in annotations for pp. 5 (on *Angmar*), 296 (on *Barad-dûr*), 330 (on *Anor*), 392 (on *Argonath*), and 548 (on *Aglarond*). Other notes from the same source are cited or quoted below.

*

All names not in the following list should be left *entirely* unchanged in any language used in translation (LT), except that inflexional *s, es* should be rendered according to the grammar of the LT.

It is desirable that the translator should read Appendix F, and follow the theory there set out. In the original text English represents the Common Speech (CS) of the supposed period. Names that are given in modern English therefore represent names in the CS, often but not always being translations of older names in other languages, especially Sindarin (Grey-elven, G.). The LT now replaces English as the equivalent of the CS; the names in English form should therefore be translated into the LT *according to their meaning* (as closely as possible).

Most of the names of this type should offer no difficulty to a translator, especially not to one using a LT of Germanic origin, related to English: Dutch, German, and the Scandinavian languages; e.g. Black Country, Battle Plain, Dead Marshes, Snowmane, etc. Some names, however, may prove less easy. In a few cases the author, acting as translator of Elvish names already devised and used in this book or elsewhere, has taken pains to produce a CS name that is both a translation and also (to English ears) a euphonious name of familiar English style, even if it does not actually occur in England. *Rivendell* is a successful example, as a translation of G. *Imladris* 'Glen of the Cleft'. It is desirable to translate such names into the LT, since to leave them unchanged would disturb the carefully devised scheme of nomenclature and introduce an unexplained element without a place in the feigned linguistic history of the period. But of course the translator is free to devise a name in the LT that is suitable in sense and/or topography: not all the CS names are precise translations of those in other languages.

A further difficulty arises in some cases. Names (of places and persons) occur, especially in the Shire, which are not 'meaningless', but are English in form (sc. in theory the author's translation of CS names), and contain elements that are in the current language obsolete or dialectal, or are worn-down and obscured in form. (See Appendix F.) From the author's point of view it is desirable that translators should have some knowledge of the nomenclature of persons and places in the LT, and of words that occur in them that are obsolete in the current LT, or only preserved locally. The notes I offer are intended to assist a translator in distinguishing 'inventions', made of elements current in modern English, such as *Rivendell*, *Snow-mane*, from actual names in use in England, independently of this story, and therefore elements in the modern English language that it is desirable to match by equivalents in the LT, with regard to their original meaning, and also where feasible with regard to their archaic or altered form. I have sometimes referred to old, obsolescent, or dialectal words in the Scandinavian and German languages which might possibly be used as the equivalents of similar elements in the English names found in the text. I hope that these references may be sometimes found helpful, without suggesting that I claim any competence in these modern languages beyond an interest in their early history.

Abbreviations

CS = *Common Speech*, in original text represented by English.

LT = the language used in translation, which must now replace English as representing CS.

E. = English.

G. or **S.** = *Grey-elven* or *Sindarin*, the Elvish language to which most of the names (outside the Shire) belong.

Q. = *Quenya*, the archaic Elvish language in which 'Galadriel's Lament' (I 394) [pp. 377–8 in the 2004 edn., in Book II, Chapter 8].

R. = *Rohan*: the language used in Rohan, related to that used by Hobbits before their migration.

[Also: **cf.** = Latin *confer* 'compare'; **Dan.** = Danish; **e.g.** = *exempli gratia* 'for example'; **Fr.** = French; **Ger.** = German; **Icel.** = Icelandic; **ME** = Middle English; **MHG** = Middle High German; **mod.** = modern; **N.B.** = *nota bene* 'take notice'; **Norw.** = Norwegian; **OE** = Old English; **OHG** = Old High German; **ON** = Old Norse; **O.Swed.** = Old Swedish; **pl.** = plural; **q.v.** = *quod vide* 'which see'; **sb.** = substantive (noun); **sc.** = *scilicet* 'that is'; **Scand.** = Scandinavian; **Swed.** = Swedish; ***The H.*** = *The Hobbit*; ***The L.R.*** = *The Lord of the Rings*]

Persons, Peoples, Creatures

Appledore. Old word for 'apple-tree' (survives in E. place-names). Should be translated by the equivalent in the LT of *apple-tree* (i.e. by a dialectal or archaic word of same meaning). In Germanic languages this may be a word of the same origin: e.g. Ger. (MHG) *aphalter*; Icel. *apuldur*; Norw., O.Swed. *apald.*

Baggins. Intended to recall *bag* – cf. Bilbo's conversation with Smaug in *The H.* [Chapter 12] – and meant to be associated (by hobbits) with *Bag End* (sc. the end of a 'bag' or 'pudding bag' = cul-de-sac), the local name for Bilbo's house. (It was the local name for my aunt's farm in Worcestershire, which was at the end of a lane leading to it and no further.) Cf. also *Sackville-Baggins.* The LT should contain an element meaning 'sack, bag'.

Banks. Clearly a topographical name containing *bank* in the sense 'steep slope or hill-side'. It should be represented by something similar.

Barrow-wights. Creatures dwelling in a *barrow* 'grave-mound'. (See *Barrow* under Places.) It is an invented name: an equivalent should be invented. The Dutch [edition] has *grafghest* 'grave-ghast'; Swed. *Kummelgast* 'gravemound-ghost'.

Beechbone. This is meant to be significant (being a translation into CS of some Entish or Elvish equivalent). It should be translated similarly (e.g. as *Buchbein* or probably better *Büchenbein*?).

Big Folk, Big People. Translate.

Black Captain. Translate.

Black One. Translate.

Black Riders. Translate.

Bolger. See *Budgeford* [under Places].

Bounders. Evidently intended to mean 'persons watching the bounds (sc. boundaries)'. This word exists in E. and is not marked as obsolete in dictionaries, though I have seldom heard it used. Probably because the late nineteenth-century slang *bounder* – 'an offensively pushing and ill-bred man' – was for a time in very general use and soon became a term of contempt equivalent to 'cad'. It is a long time since I heard it, and I think it is now forgotten by younger people. [Max] Schuchart [the Dutch translator] used *Poenen* 'cads', probably because a well-known dictionary only gives *patser* 'bounder, cad' as the meaning of *bounder* (labelled as slang). In the text the latter sense is meant to be recalled by English readers, but the primary functional sense to be clearly understood. (This slender jest is not, of course, worth imitating, even if possible.)

Bracegirdle. A genuine English surname. Used in the text, of course, with reference to the hobbit tendency to be fat and so to strain their belts. A desirable translation would recognize this by some equivalent meaning: *Tight-belt*, or *Belt-tightener/strainer/stretcher.* (The name is a genuine English one; a compound of the Romance type with verbal element first, as *Drinkwater* = *Boileau*; but it is not necessary that the representation should be a known surname in the language of translation.) Would not *Gürtelspanner* do?

Brandybuck. A rare E. name which I have come across. Its origin in E. is not concerned. In *The L.R.* it is obviously meant to contain elements of the *Brandywine River* (q.v.) and the family name *Oldbuck* (q.v.). The latter contains the word *buck* (animal); either OE *bucc* 'male deer' (fallow or roe), or *bucca* 'he-goat'.

N.B. *Buckland* (see Places) is also meant to contain the same animal name (Ger. *Bock*), though *Buckland*, an English place-name, is frequently in fact derived from 'book-land', land originally held by a written charter.

Brockhouse. *Brock* is an old word (in OE) for the badger (*Dachs*) still widely current in country-speech up to the end of the nineteenth century and appearing in literature, and hence in good dictionaries, including bilinguals. So there is not much excuse for the Dutch and Swedish translators' having misrendered it.* It occurs in numerous place-names, from which surnames are derived, such as *Brockbanks*. *Brockhouse* is of course feigned to be a hobbit-name, because the 'brock' builds complicated and well-ordered underground dwellings or 'setts'. The Ger. rendering should be *Dachsbau*, I think. In Danish use *Grævling*.

*Dutch *Broekhuis* (not a misprint since repeated in the four places where this name occurs) seems absurd: what is a 'breech-house'? Swed. *Galthus* 'wild-boar house' is not much better, since swine do not burrow! The translator evidently did not know or look up *brock*, since he uses *Grävlingar* for the name *Burrows* (Swed. *gräflingar*, *gräfsvin* 'badgers').

Butterbur. So far as I know, not found as a name in England. Though *Butter* is so used, as well as combinations (in origin place-names) such as *Butterfield*. These have in the tale been modified, to fit the generally botanical names of Bree, to the plant-name *butterbur* (*Petasites vulgaris*).

If the popular name for this contains an equivalent of 'butter', so much the better. Otherwise use another plant-name containing 'butter' (as Ger. *Butterblume*, *Butterbaum*, Dutch *boterbloeme*) or referring to a fat thick plant. (The butterbur is a fleshy plant with heavy flower-head on thick stalk, and very large leaves.)

Butterbur's first name *Barliman* is simply an altered spelling of *barley* and *man* (suitable to an innkeeper and ale-brewer), and should be translated.

Captains of the West. Translate.

Chief, The. Translate.

Chubb. A genuine English surname. Chosen because its immediate association in E. is with the adjective *chubby* 'round and fat in bodily shape' (said to be derived from the *chub*, a name of a river-fish).

Corsairs. Translate. They are imagined as similar to the Mediterranean corsairs: sea-robbers with fortified bases.

Cotton. This is a place-name in origin (as are many modern surnames): from *cot* 'a cottage or humble dwelling' + *-ton*, the usual E. element in place-names, a shortening of *town* (OE *tūn* 'village'). It should be translated in these terms.

It is a common E. surname, and has of course in origin no connexion with *cotton* the textile material; though it is naturally associated with it at the present day. Hobbits are represented as using tobacco, and this is made more or less credible by the suggestion that the plant was brought over the Sea by the Men of Westernesse (Prologue, I 19 [2004 edn., p. 8]); but it is not intended that 'cotton' should be supposed to be known or used at that time. Since it is highly improbable that in any other language a normal and frequent village-name should in any way resemble the equivalent of *cotton* (the material), this resemblance in the original text may be passed over. It has no importance for the narrative. See *Gamgee*.

Cotman occurs as a first name in the genealogies, an old word meaning 'cottager, cot-dweller', to be found in larger dictionaries, also a well-known E. surname.

Dark Lord, Dark Power. Translate.

Dead, The. Translate.

Dunlendings. Leave unchanged except in the plural ending. It represents Rohan *dun(n)lending*, an inhabitant of *Dun(n)land*.

Easterlings. Translate, as 'Easterners, men from the East' (in the story men from the little known regions beyond the Sea of Rhûn).

Elder Kindred, Elder Race, Elder People. Translate. In a LT which possesses two forms of the comparative of *old*, use the more archaic form. (In E. the older form *elder* implies both seniority and kinship.)

The similarity between *Elda-r* plural, the western Elves, and *Elder* is accidental. (The name *Elda* 'Elf' had been devised long before *The L.R.* was written.) There is no need to seek to imitate it; it is not useful or significant. Cf. *Elder Days*, which again implies a more ancient epoch in the history of people of *the same kin*, sc. in the days of their far-off ancestors.

Elf-friend. Translate. (It was suggested by *Ælfwine*, the English form of an old Germanic name (represented for instance in the Lombardic *Alboin*), though its analysable meaning was probably not recognized or thought significant by the many recorded bearers of the name *Ælfwine* in OE.)

Elven-smiths. Translate. N.B. The archaic adjectival or composition form *elven* used in *The L.R.* should on no account be equated with the debased E. word *elfin*, which has entirely wrong associations. Use either the LT [word] for *elf*, or a first element in a compound, or divide into *Elvish* (+ *smiths*, etc.), using an equivalent in the LT for the correct adjective *Elvish*.

With regard to German: I would suggest with diffidence that *Elf*, *elfen*, are perhaps to be avoided as equivalents of *Elf*, *elven*. *Elf* is, I believe, borrowed from English, and may retain some of the associations of a kind that I should particularly desire not to be present (if possible): e.g. those of Drayton or of *A Midsummer Night's Dream* (in the translation of which, I believe, *Elf* was first used in German). That is, the pretty fanciful reduction of *elf* to a butterfly-like creature inhabiting flowers.

I wonder whether the word *Alp* (or better still the form *Alb*, still given in modern dictionaries as a variant, which is historically the more normal form) could not be used. It is the true cognate of English *elf*; and if it has senses nearer to English *oaf*, referring to puckish and malicious sprites, or to idiots regarded as 'changelings', that is true also of English *elf*. I find these debased rustic associations less damaging than the 'pretty' literary fancies. The Elves of the 'mythology' of *The L.R.* are not actually equatable with the folklore traditions about 'fairies', and as I have said (Appendix F, *The L.R.* III 415 [2004 edn., p. 1137]) I should prefer the oldest available form of the name to be used, and leave it to acquire its own associations for readers of my tale. In Scandinavian languages *alf* is available.

Enemy, The. Translate.

Ent. Retain this, alone or in compounds, such as *Entwives*. It is supposed to be a name in the languages of the Vale of Anduin, including R., for these creatures. It is actually an OE word for 'giant', which is thus rightly according to the system attributed to Rohan, but the *Ents* of this tale are not in form or character derived from Germanic mythology. *Entings* 'descendants [children] of Ents' (II 78 [2004 edn., p. 475; Book III, Chapter

4]) should also be unchanged (except in the plural ending). The Grey-elven name was *Onodrim* (II 45 [2004 edn., p. 442; Book III, Chapter 2]).

Evenstar. As the title of *Arwen Undómiel.* When used in the text this translation of *Undómiel* (a Q. name) should be translated.

Fair Folk. The beautiful people. (Based on Welsh *Tylwyth teg* 'the Beautiful Kindred' = Fairies.) Title of the Elves. Translate.

Fairbairns. Translate. It is an English surname, a northern variant of the name *Fairchild.* It is used by me to suggest that the Elvish beauty of Elanor, daughter of Sam, was long inherited by her descendants. Elanor was also remarkable for her golden hair: and in modern English *fair,* when used of complexion or hair, means primarily blond, but though this association was meant to be present in the minds of English readers, it need not be represented.

Fallohide. This has given difficulty. It should if possible be translated, since it is meant to represent a name with a meaning in CS, though one devised in the past and so containing archaic elements. It is made of E. *fallow* + *hide* (cognates of Ger. *falb* and *Haut*) and means 'paleskin'. It is archaic since *fallow* 'pale, yellowish' is not now in use, except in *fallow deer*; and *hide* is no longer applied to human skin (except as a transference back from its modern use of animal hides, used for leather). But this element of archaism need not be imitated. See *Marcho and Blanco.* See also note on relation of special Hobbit words to the language of Rohan [in Appendix F, p. 1136, III: 414].

Fang. A dog's name in Book I, Chapter 4. Translate. Meant of course to be the English *fang* 'canine or prominent tooth' (OE *fengtōþ*, Ger. *Fangzahn*); but since it is associated with *Grip*, the sense of the now lost verb *fang*, I should think that Ger. *Fang* would be a good version.

Fatty Lumpkin. Translate. The *kin* is of course a diminutive suffix.

Fell Riders. Translate.

Fellowship of the Ring. Translate in the text. Also if possible in the title.

Ferny. A name in Bree. Translate. *Fern* and *Ferny, Fernie* are E. surnames, but whatever their origin the name is here used to fit the predominantly botanical names current in Bree.

Firefoot. Translate.

Firstborn, The. Title of the Elves. Translate. ('Firstborn' since the Elves appeared in the world before all other 'speaking peoples', not only Men, but also Dwarves, of independent origin. Hobbits are of course meant to be a special variety of the human race.)

Flourdumpling. Translate.

Free Folk, Free Lords of the Free, Free Peoples. Translate.

Gamgee. A surname found in England though uncommon. I do not know its origin; it does not appear to be English. It is also a word for 'cotton-wool' (now obsolescent but known to me in childhood), derived from the name of *S. Gamgee*, died 1886, a distinguished surgeon, who invented 'Gamgee tissue'. In a translation it would be best to treat this name as 'meaningless' and retain it with any spelling changes that may seem necessary to fit it to the style of the LT. [See also note for p. 22, containing a long further comment on *Gamgee* from the manuscript of *Nomenclature.*]

Gamling (the Old). A name of one of the Rohirrim, and best left unchanged, though like one or two other names in Rohan, as *Shadowfax*, *Wormtongue*, etc., it has been slightly anglicized and modernized. It should be *Gameling* (with short *ă*). It would be one of the words and names that hobbits recognized as similar to their own, since it is an English (= CS) name, probably the origin of the surnames *Gamlen*, *Gam(b)lin*, etc. Cf. *The Tale of Gamelin*, a medieval poem from which ultimately was derived part of Shakespeare's *As You Like It.* (It is derived from the stem *gamal-* 'old', the normal word in Scandinavian languages, but only found in OE in verse-language and in OHG only as an element in personal names.)

Goatleaf. A Bree-name of botanical type, an old name of honeysuckle/woodbine. Cf. Fr. *chèvrefeuille* (medieval Latin *caprifolium*, probably from the vernaculars). Presents no difficulty in Ger., as LT since *Geiszblad* [i.e. *Geissblatt*] seems one of the names in use.

Goldberry. Translate by sense.

Great Enemy. Translate.

Grey Company. Translate.

Grey Host. Translate.

Grey Pilgrim. Another by-name of Gandalf, translation of *Mithrandir*, should be translated by sense into the LT.

Greyhame. [Spelt *Grayhame* in typescript, as in the first edition of *The Lord of the Rings*, altered to *Greyhame* in the second edition.] Modernized 'Rohanese'. Rohan grēg-hama 'greycoat'. By-name in Rohan of Gandalf. Since both *Grēghama* and *Greyhame* would probably be unintelligible in a LT, whereas at least the *Grey-* is meant to be intelligible to readers, it would be right, I think, to translate this epithet: sc. to represent *Éomer* (*The L.R.* II 37 [2004 edn., p. 435; Book III, Chapter 2]) as translating its sense into CS. So Dutch correctly *Grijsmantel*; but Swed. wrongly *gråhamn* 'grey phantom'. Ger. might be *Graumantel*?

Grip. Dog-name. Translate. See *Fang.*

Grubb. Hobbit-name. (*Grubbs,* I 36 [2004 edn., p. 28; Book I, Chapter 1], is plural.) Translate in the LT, if possible in some way more or less suitable to sound and sense. The name is meant to recall the E. verb *grub* 'dig, root in the ground'.

Guardians. Translate.

Halfling. CS name for *Hobbit.* It is not actually an E. word, but might be (i.e. it is suitably formed with an appropriate suffix). The sense is 'a half-sized man/person'. Translate with similar invention containing the LT word for 'half'. The Dutch translation used *Halfling* (presumably an intelligible derivative of *half,* though not in use in Dutch any more than in E.).

Harfoots. (Plural.) Meant to be intelligible (in its context) and recognized as an altered form of an old name = 'hairfoot': sc. 'one with hairy feet'. (Technically supposed to represent archaic *hǣr-fōt* > *hērfot* > *hĕrfoot* with the usual change of *er* > *ar* in English. Mod. E. *hair,* though related, is not a direct descendant of OE *hǣr/hēr* = Ger. *Haar.*) Ger. *Harfuss* would adequately represent form, meaning, and slight change of spelling in an old proper name. See *Fallohide.*

Harry < Herry < Henry. Any popular man's name of similar sort will do.

Hayward. Translate. A local official with the duty of inspecting fences and keeping cattle from straying. Cf. *The L.R.* I (Prologue) p. 19 [2004 edn., p. 10]. (Now obsolescent, and surviving chiefly in the very common surname *Hayward;* but *Hob* (*The L.R.* III, p. 277, 279 [2004 edn., pp. 998, 1000; Book VI, Chapter 8]) was supposed actually to be a hayward.) The word is derived from *hay* 'fence' (*not* 'grass') + *ward* 'guard'. Cf. *High Hay, Hay Gate, Haysend,* place-names in *Buckland.* If the LT possesses an old compound of similar sense, so much the better. The Dutch translation used *Schutmeester* (which is very close: 'keeper of a pound or fenced-enclosure'). Swed. *stängselvakt* 'hedge-watch' is, I think, made for the purpose.

Healer, the Healers. Translate.

Heathertoes. Bree-name. No parallel in English, though *Heather-* appears in some surnames. Translate. [In German it might be translated as] ?*Heidezehn.* The Dutch translation has *Heideteen.* (Presumably a joke of the Big Folk, meaning that the Little Folk, wandering unshod, collected heather, twigs, and leaves between their toes.)

Hobbit. Do not translate, since the name is supposed no longer to have had a recognized meaning in the Shire, and is supposed not to have been derived from CS (= English or the LT).

Holman. An English surname; but here supposed to = 'hole-man' (pronounced the same). Translate by this sense.

Hornblower. *Hornblow, -er,* are E. surnames, in the Shire evidently occupational surnames. Translate by sense.

Isengrim. See *The L.R.* III 413 [2004 edn., p. 1135; Appendix F], 'In some old families. . . .' It is an old Germanic name, perhaps best known now as that adopted for the Wolf as a character in the romance of *Reynard the Fox.* It is best left untranslated since it is not supposed to be made of CS elements (see the place-name *Isengard*).

Leaflock. Translate by sense, since this is supposed to be a CS translation of the Elvish *Finglas*: *fing* 'lock of hair' + *las(s)* 'leaf'. Similarly the Ent-name *Fladrif,* translated as *Skinbark.*

Maggot. Intended to be a 'meaningless' name, hobbit-like in sound. (Actually it is an accident that *maggot* is an E. word = 'grub, larva'. The Dutch translation has *Van der Made* (*made* = Ger. *Made,* OE *maðe* 'maggot'), but the name is probably best left alone, as in the Swed. translation, though some assimilation to the style of the LT would be in place.

Marigold. Translate this flower-name (see *The L.R.* III 413 [2004 edn., p. 1135; Appendix F]). The name is used because it is suitable as a name in E., and because, containing *gold* and referring to a golden flower, it suggests that there was a 'Fallohide' strain (see *The L.R.* I 12 [2004 edn., p. 3; Prologue]) in Sam's family – which, increased by the favour of Galadriel, became notable in his children: especially *Elanor,* but also *Goldilocks* (a name sometimes given to flowers of buttercup-kind), who married the heir of Peregrin Took. Unfortunately the name of the flower in the LT may be unsuitable as a name in form or meaning (e.g. French *souci*). In such a case it would be better to substitute the name of some other yellow flower. The Swed. translator solved the difficulty by translating the name as *Majagull* and adding *Ringblom* (Swed. *ringblomma* 'marigold'; cf. Ger. *Ringelblume*). The Dutch translator was content with *Meizoentje* 'daisy': which is good enough. He did not include the genealogies in his translation, and ignored the fact that Daisy was the name of a much older sister of Sam and not a playmate of Rosie Cotton.

Mugwort. Bree name. A plant-name (*Artemisia,* Fr. *armoise,* akin to Wormwood, Fr. *armoise amère*). Translate by LT name of plant, e.g. Ger. *Beifusz* [*Beifuss*] if suitable; or by some other herb-name of more or less similar shape. There is no special reason for the choice of *Mugwort,* except its hobbit-like sound.

Necromancer. Translate.

Neekerbreekers. Invented insect-name. Represent by some LT invention of similar sound (supposed to be like that of a cricket).

Noakes. Adapt to LT or substitute some suitable name in LT of similar style. (*Noake(s)*, *Noke(s)* is an E. surname, derived probably from the not uncommon minor place-name *No(a)ke*, from early E. *atten oke* 'at the oak'; but since this is no longer recognized, this need not be considered. The name is in the tale unimportant.)

Oldbuck. See *Brandywine* [in Places], *Brandybuck*. The *-buck* is derived from a personal name *Buck*, in archaic form *Bucca* (Appendix B, III 368 [2004 edn., p. 1087], year 1979). The first name *Gorhendad* (*The L.R.* I 108 [2004 edn., p. 98; Book I, Chapter 5]) should be left unchanged. It is a Welsh word meaning 'great-grandfather'; but the reason for giving the folk of Buckland Welsh names or ones of similar style is given in Appendix F (*The L.R.* III 413 [2004 edn., p. 1135]).

Oliphaunt. Retain this. It is an archaic form of *elephant* used as a 'rusticism', on the supposition that rumour of the Southern beast would have reached the Shire long ago in the form of legend. This detail might be retained simply by substituting *O* for the initial *E* of the ordinary name of the elephant in the LT: the meaning would remain sufficiently obvious, even if the LT had no similar archaic form. In Dutch *olifant* remains the current form, and so is used by the translator, but with loss of the archaic colouring. *Oliphant* in E. is derived from Old Fr. *olifant*, but the *o* is probably derived from old forms of E. or Ger.: OE *olfend*, OHG *olbenta* 'camel'. The names of foreign animals, seldom or never seen, are often misapplied in the borrowing language. OE *olfend*, etc. are probably ultimately related to the classical *elephant* (Latin from Greek).

Orald. *Forn* and *Orald* as names of Bombadil are meant to be names in foreign tongues (not CS) and should according to the system be left unchanged. *Forn* is actually the Scand. word for '(belonging to) ancient (days)'. All the dwarf-names in this tale are Norse, as representing a northern language of Men, different from but closely related to that of the Rohirrim who came from the other side of Mirkwood (see *The L.R.* III, p. 410, 415 [2004 edn., pp. 1132, 1136–7; Appendix F]). *Orald* is an OE word for 'very ancient', evidently meant to represent the language of the Rohirrim and their kin. It may be left unchanged. But since it is the exact counterpart in form and sense of Ger. *uralt*, this might well be used in a Ger. translation.

Orc. This is supposed to be the CS name of these creatures at that time. It should therefore according to the system be translated into E. or the LT. It was translated 'goblin' in *The H.*, except in one place; but this word, and other words of similar sense in other European languages (as far as I know), are not really suitable. The *orc* in *The L.R.* and *The Silmarillion*, though of course partly made out of traditional features, is not really comparable in supposed origin, functions, and relation to the Elves. In any case *orc* seemed to me, and seems, in sound a good name for these creatures. It should be retained.

It should be spelt *ork* (so the Dutch translation) in a Germanic LT, but I had used the spelling *orc* in so many places that I have hesitated to change it in the E. text, though the adjective is necessarily spelt *orkish*. (The Grey-elven form is *orch*, pl. *yrch*.

(I originally took the word from OE *orc* (*Beowulf* 112, *orc-neas* and the gloss *orc* = *þyrs* 'ogre', *heldeofol* 'hell-devil'). This is supposed not to be connected with mod. E. *orc*, *ork*, a name applied to various sea-beasts of the dolphin-order.)

Pickthorn. Bree name. Meant to be 'meaningful'. Translate.

Pimple. Opprobrious nickname. Translate.

Proudfoot. Hobbit surname. Translate. (It is an English surname.)

Puddifoot. Surname in the muddy Marish. Meant to suggest *puddle* + *foot*. Translate.

Quickbeam. (Ent.) This is a translation of S. *Bregalad* 'quick (lively) tree'. Since in the story this is represented as a name given to him because he was (for an Ent) 'hasty', it would be best to translate the name in the LT by a compound (made for the purpose) having this sense (e.g. Ger. *Quickbaum*?). It is unlikely that the LT would possess an actual tree-name having or appearing to have this sense. *Quickbeam* and *Quicken* are actual E. names of the rowan/mountain-ash; also given to the related 'Service-tree'. (According to dictionaries, Ger. *Vogenbeere*, *-beerbaum* and *Eberesche*.) The rowan is here evidently intended, since *rowan* is actually used in Quickbeam's song (II 87 [2004 edn., p. 483; Book III, Chapter 4]).

Ring-wraiths. This is a translation of the Black Speech *Nazgûl*, from *nazg* 'ring' and *gûl*, any one of the major invisible servants of Sauron dominated entirely by his will. A compound must be made of suitable elements in the LT that has the sense of *ring-wraith* as nearly as possible.

Rumble. Name of an old hobbit-woman. It had no meaning (at that time) in the Shire. A form of similar pattern to suit the LT will suffice.

Sackville-Baggins. *Sackville* is an E. name (of more aristocratic association than *Baggins*). It is of course joined in the story with *Baggins* because of the similar meaning in E. (= CS) *sack* and *bag*, and because of the slightly comic effect of this conjunction. Any compound in the LT containing elements meaning (more or less) equivalent to *sack/bag* will do.

Scatha. This is OE ('injurer, enemy, robber') and so is from the language of Rohan and should be left unchanged.

Shadowfax. This is an anglicized form of Rohan (= OE) *Sceadu-fæx* 'having shadow-grey mane (and coat)'. (It does not actually occur in OE.)

Since it is not CS it may be retained, though better so in a simplified form of the Rohan name: *Scadufax*. But since in the text this name has been assimilated to modern E. (= CS), it would be satisfactory to do the same in a Germanic LT, using related elements. *Fax* 'hair' is now obsolete in E., except in the name *Fairfax* (no longer understood). It was used in OHG (*faks*) and MHG (*vahs*, *vachs*, etc.), but is, I believe, also now obsolete; but it could be revived in this name, as it is in the E. text: e.g. *Schattenvachs*? *Fax* (*faks*) is still in use in Iceland and Norway for 'mane'; but *shadow* has no exact equivalents in Scandinavian languages. The Dutch version has *Schaduwschicht* ('shadow-flash'), Swed. *Skuggfaxe*.

Sharkey. This is supposed to be a nickname modified to fit CS (in the E. text anglicized), based on Orkish *sharkû* 'old man'. The word should therefore be kept with modification of spelling to fit LT; alteration of the diminutive and quasi-affectionate ending *-ey* to fit the LT would also be in place.

Shelob. Though it sounds (I think) a suitable name for the Spider, in some foreign (Orkish) tongue, it is actually composed of *She* and *lob* (a dialectal E. word for 'spider'). (Cf. *The Hobbit*, Chapter 8.) The Dutch version retains *Shelob*, but the Swed. has the rather feeble *Honmonstret*.

Shirriff(s). Actually a now obsolete form of E. *sheriff* 'shire-officer', used by me to make the connexion with *Shire* plainer. In the story it and *Shire* are supposed to be special hobbit-words, not generally current in the CS of the time, and so derived from their former language related to that of the *Rohirrim*. Since the word is thus not supposed to be CS, but a local word, it is not necessary to translate it, or do more than accommodate its spelling to the style of the LT. It should, however, resemble in its first part whatever word is used to represent *Shire* (q.v.).

Skinbark. E. (= CS) translation of *Fladrif*. The name should therefore be suitably translated by sense into the LT.

Smallburrow. A meaningful hobbit-name. Translate by sense.

Snowmane. A meaningful name (of King Théoden's horse), but (like *Shadowfax*) translated into modern E. form, for *snāw-mana*. It should therefore be represented by its proper Rohan form *Snawmana*, or translated (especially in a Germanic LT), as e.g. Ger. *Schneemähne*.

Stoors. Name of a third kind of hobbit, of heavier build. This is early E. *stor*, *stoor* 'large, strong', now obsolete. Since it is thus supposed to be a special hobbit-word not current in CS, it need not be translated, and may be represented by a more or less 'phonetic' spelling according to the LT use of letters. But an archaic or dialectal word of this sense in the LT would also be acceptable.

Swertings. Said by Sam to be the name in the Shire for the legendary (to hobbits) dark-skinned people of the 'Sunlands' (far South). It may be left unchanged as a special local word (not in CS); but since it is evidently a derivative of *swart*, which is still in use (= *swarthy*), it could be represented by some similar derivative of the word for 'black/dark' in the LT. Cf. *Swarthy Men*, the CS equivalent, III, 73 [2004 edn., p. 800; Book V, Chapter 3].

Thistlewool. Translate by sense.

Took. Hobbit-name of unknown origin representing actual Hobbit *Tūk* (see Appendix F, III 413 [2004 edn., p. 1135]). It should thus be kept and spelt phonetically according to the LT.

The Took personal names should be kept in form and spelling of text as *Peregrin*, *Paladin*, *Adelard*, *Bandobras*, etc. Note that *Bandobras*' nickname 'Bullroarer' is in CS and should be translated by sense (if possible alliterating on B). This nickname also appeared in *Bullroarer Took* in *The Hobbit*, new edn. p. 17 [Chapter 1]. I believed when I wrote it that *bullroarer* was a word used by anthropologists, etc. for instrument(s) used by uncivilized peoples that made a roaring sound; but I cannot find it in any dictionaries (not even in O.E.D. Suppl. [i.e. the *Oxford English Dictionary* Supplement; but see note for *The Lord of the Rings* p. 2]).

Treebeard. Translation of *Fangorn*. Translate by sense.

Twofoot. Translate by sense.

Underhill. Translate by sense.

Wandlimb. = *Fimbrethil*, of which it is *not* a translation. Translate by sense. An Entwife's name.

Whitfoot. Translate by 'white' and 'foot'.

Windfola. = 'Wind-foal', but leave unaltered since it is in the alien (not CS) language of Rohan.

Wingfoot. Nickname. Translate by sense 'winged-foot'.

Wizard. See Index in 2nd edition [i.e. *1966 Index*; the pertinent elements are retained in the new index of 2005].

Wormtongue. 'Modernized' form of the nickname of *Gríma*, the evil counsellor of Rohan = Rohan *wyrm-tunge* 'snake-tongue'. Translate by sense.

Woses. Represents (modernized) the Rohan word for 'wild men of the woods'. It is not a purely invented word. The supposed genuine Rohan word was *wāsa*, pl. *wāsan*, which if it had survived into modern E. would be *woses*. It would have been better to call the 'wild men' *woodwoses*, for that actually occurs in OE *wudewāsa*, glossing '*faunus*, *satyrus*, savage men, evil creatures'. (This word survived into the Tudor period as *woodoses* (often corrupted to *woodhouses*), and survives in heraldry, since a *woodhouse* = 'a wild hairy man clad in leaves', common as a supporter to arms.) The *wāsa* element meant originally a forlorn or abandoned person and now (e.g. in Ger. *Waise* and Dutch *wees*) means 'orphan'. The origin of this idea was no doubt the actual existence of wild folk, remnants of former peoples driven out by invaders, or outlaws, living a debased and savage life in forests and mountains.

Places

Archet. Actually an English place-name of Celtic origin. Used in the nomenclature of Bree to represent a stratum of names older than those in CS or the Hobbit language. So also *Bree*, an English place-name from a Celtic word for 'hill'. Therefore retain *Archet* and *Bree* unaltered, since these names no longer have a recognized meaning in English. *Chetwood* is a compound of Celtic and E., both elements = 'wood'. Cf. *Brill* (Oxon [i.e. in Oxfordshire]) derived from *bree* + *hill*. Therefore in *Chetwood* retain *Chet* and translate *wood*. [In the manuscript of *Nomenclature* Tolkien writes further that *Archet* descended 'from British **ar(e)cait-* > Old English *ar-cæt* (Welsh *argoed* [obsolete 'trees, edge of forest'])'.]

Ashen Mountains. CS translation of *Ered Lithui* (S. *orod*, pl. *eryd/ered* 'mountain', *lith* 'ash' + adjectival *ui*). Translate in LT by sense: mountains of ash-grey hue.

Bag End. A popular term for 'pudding-bag', a house or place at end of a cul-de-sac. Translate by sense. See *Baggins*. N.B. The same element in the LT should appear in *Baggins* and *Bag End*.

Bagshot Row. Row of small 'holes' in the lane below Bag End. (Said to have been so named because the earth removed in excavating 'Bag End' was shot over the edge of the sudden fall in the hillside on the ground which later became the gardens and earthwalls of the humbler dwelling.) Translate by approximate sense, including the same LT element = 'bag'.

Bamfurlong. An English place-name, probably from *bean* 'bean' + *furlong* (in sense: 'a division of a common field'), the name being given to a strip of land usually reserved for beans. The name is now, and so is supposed to have been at that time in the Shire, without clear meaning. It is the name of Farmer Maggot's farm. Translate as seems suitable in the LT, but some compound containing the LT [word] for 'bean' + 'field/cultivated ground' would seem desirable.

Baránduin. Meaning 'the long gold-brown river'. Leave untranslated: *Brandywine* is represented as a corruption of S. *Baranduin* with the accent on the middle syllable *ánd*. (S. *baran* 'brown yellow-brown' + *duin*: see *Anduin* [an entry ultimately omitted from *Nomenclature*: '*and* "long" +

duin "large river": in CS *the Great River*'.]) The common Elvish was *duinē*: stem *dui-* 'flow (in volume)'. The Q. form would have been *luine* (Q. initial *d* > *l*), but the word was not used. Retain when so spelt. Usually by hobbits altered to *Brandywine* (q.v.).

Barrow-downs. Translate by sense: low treeless hills on which there are many 'barrows', sc. tumuli and other prehistoric grave-mounds. This *barrow* is not related to modern *barrow* 'an implement with a wheel'; it is a recent adoption by archaeologists of dialectal *barrow* (< *berrow*, < OE *beorg*, *berg* 'hill, mound').

Barrowfield. See preceding. Translate by sense: 'a field containing a grave-mound'.

Battle Gardens, Battle Pit. Translate by sense.

Better Smials. See *Smials*.

Black Country, Black Land. CS translation of *Mordor*. Translate in LT.

Black Stone. Translate by sense.

Blackroot Vale. Translate by sense. [*Blackroot* is the] CS translation of *Morthond* (name of a river, given because its source was in the dark caverns of the Dead Men).

Blessed Realm. Translate by sense. CS name for the Far Western Land in which the Valar (guardian powers) and the High Elves dwelt, called in Q. *Aman*, the region where the Valar dwelt being *Valimar*, *Valinor*; that of the Elves *Eldamar*. The Blessed Realm was at this time no longer part of the physical world, and could not, except in rare cases, be reached by mortals.

Bonfire Glade. Translate by sense.

Brandy Hall. Should be translated, but contain the same element as that used in the river-name [*Brandywine*]. In this case the whole LT word, e.g. *Branntwein* or *Brendevin*, could be used, since the Hall was on the east bank of the river. In the personal name *Brandybuck* it could be reduced to the first element, e.g. *Brendebuk*?

Brandywine. This is represented as a hobbit alteration (cf. I 13 [2004 edn., p. 4; Prologue]) of the Elvish (S.) *Baránduin* (stressed on the middle syllable). Since this is meant to have been intelligible at that time it should be translated by sense; but a difficulty arises, since the translation should if possible also be a possible corruption of *Baranduin*. Dutch *Brandewijn* was used; the Swed. translation missed the point, using *Vinfluden*, though *Brännavin* would have served. Danish *Brendevin* or Ger. *Branntwein* would also do. See *Brandybuck* [in Persons].

Bree. Retain, since it was an old name, of obsolete meaning in an older language. See *Archet*. For *Bree-hill*, *Bree-land* retain the first element, and translate the *hill*, and *land*.

Brockenbores. Not (I think) a genuine E. place-name; but intended to have the recognized sense: 'badgers' borings/tunnellings'. Translate in this sense. See note to the personal name *Brockhouse*.

Buck Hill, Buckland. The element *buck* should be translated. See note under the personal names *Brandybuck*, *Oldbuck*.

Bucklebury. Name of the chief village in the *Buckland*. Translate with a name containing the *buck* element (as above) + some equivalent of E. *-bury* (= OE *burg* 'a place occupying a defensive position, walled or enclosed, a town'; cf. *Norbury*). The *le* in *Buckle-* is either an alteration of *Buckenbury*, with old genitive pl. *en(a)*, or a reduction of *Buckland*.

Budgeford. *Budge-* was an obscured element, having at the time no clear meaning. Since it [Budgeford] was the main residence of the *Bolger* family (a hobbit-name *not* to be translated) it [*budge-*] may be regarded as a corruption of the element *bolge*, *bulge*. Both *Bolger* and *Bulger* occur as surnames in England. Whatever their real origin, they are used in the story to suggest that they were in origin nicknames referring to fatness, tubbiness.

Bywater. Village name: as being beside the wide pool occurring in the course of the Water, the main river of the Shire, a tributary of the Brandywine. Translate by sense.

Chetwood. See note on *Archet*.

Cleft, The. (sc. 'of the Spider') = *Cirith Ungol*. The [second edition] Index is deficient. Read II 332, 342, 343, III 174, 175 [2004 edn., pp. 723, 733, 734, 898, 899; Book IV, Chapters 9, 10, and Book VI, Chapter 1]. *Cirith* = a 'cleft', a narrow passage *cut* through earth or rock (like a railway cutting). Translate by sense.

Cloudyhead. (Translation of Dwarvish *Bundu-shathûr*.) Translate by sense.

Coomb. A deep (but usually not very large) valley. [The word is] very frequent as an element in place-names spelt *-comb*, *-cumb*, *-combe*, etc. In this story it is used in the name *Deeping Coomb*, or with reference to it. See *Deeping* [*Coomb*].

Crack of Doom. In modern use derived from *Macbeth* IV, i, 117, in which *the cracke of Doome* means 'the announcement of the Last Day', by a crack/peal of thunder: so commonly supposed, but it may mean 'the sound of the last trump', since *crack* could be applied to the sudden sound of horns or trumpets (so *Sir Gawain* [*and the Green Knight*, lines] 116, 1166). In this story *crack* is here used in the sense 'fissure', and refers to the volcanic fissure in the crater of *Orodruin* in *Mordor*. (I think that this use is ultimately derived from Algernon Blackwood, who as my memory seems to recall used it in this way in one of his books read very many years ago.) See further [in Places] under *Doom* [with] *Mount Doom*.

Crickhollow. Place-name in Buckland. It is meant to be taken as composed of an obsolete element + the known word *hollow*. The *-hollow* 'a small depression in the ground' can be translated by sense, the *crick* retained (in LT spelling).

Deadman's Dike. So [the second edition] index, [should be] correct[ed] to *Deadmen's* as in the text. [The correction was made in the new index of 2005.]

Deeping Coomb. This should have been spelt *Deeping-coomb*, since *Deeping* is not a verbal ending, but one indicating relationship: the coomb or deep valley belonging to the *Deep* (*Helm's Deep*) to which it led up. So also *Deeping Stream*. [Both names were emended in 1977.]

Derndingle. Said by Treebeard to be what Men called the meeting place of the Ents (II 82 [2004 edn., p. 478; Book III, Chapter 4]); therefore meant to be in CS. But the CS name must be supposed to have been given a long time ago, when in Gondor more was known or remembered about the Ents. *Dingle* is still known, meaning 'a deep (tree-shadowed) dell', but *dern* 'secret, hidden' is long obsolete, as are the related words in other Germanic languages – except *Tarn-* in Ger. *Tarnkappe* (from MHG). Translate by sense, preferably by obsolete, poetic, or dialectal elements.

Dimholt. Wood of dark trees at the entrance to the Dark Door. The name is given in the form of the language of Rohan and so should be retained unchanged, though *dim* is still current in E. (but here used in an older sense 'obscure, secret'), and *holt* is in occasional poetic use.

Dimrill Dale. CS name of Dwarvish *Azanulbizar*, Grey-elven *Nan Duhirion*. The CS form is an accurate translation: the valley of the dim (overshadowed) rills that ran down the mountain-side. Translate by sense. Similarly *Dimrill Gate/Stair*. [See also note for p. 283, quoting a related comment from the manuscript of *Nomenclature*.]

Doom, Mount Doom. This word *doom*, original sense 'judgement' (formal and legal, or personal), has in E., partly owing to its sound, and largely owing to its special use in *Doomsday*,* become a word loaded with senses of death; finality; fate (impending or foretold). (*Now outside E. only preserved in Scandinavian languages: Icel. *dómsdagur*, Swed. *domedag*, Dan. *dómmedag*, Finnish *tumoipäivä*.)

The use in the text as a word descriptive of sound (e.g. especially in Book II, Chapter 5) associated with *boom* is of course primarily descriptive of sound, but is meant (and would by most E. readers be felt) to recall the noun *doom*, with its sense of disaster. This is probably not possible to represent in a LT. The Dutch version represents *doom/boom* phonetically by *doem/boem*, which is sufficient, and at any rate has the support of the verb *doemen* which especially in the past participle *gedoemd* has the same sense as E. *doomed* (to death or an evil fate). The Swed. version usually has *dom/bom*, but occasionally has *dum/bom*. This seems (as far as I can judge) unsatisfactory, since the associations of *dum* are quite out of place, and *dumbom* is a word for a 'blockhead' (Ger. *Dummkopf*).

Mount Doom was (in Gondor) the CS name of the volcano *Orodruin* ('mountain of red flame'), but was [also] a translation of its other name *Amon Amarth* 'hill of doom', given to Sauron's forge-mountain because it was linked in little-understood prophecies with the 'doom' that it was foretold would befall when Isildur's Bane came to light again: cf. verses in I 259 [2004 edn., p. 246; Book II, Chapter 2].

Dunharrow. A modernization of 'actual' Rohan *Dūnhærg* 'the heathen fane on the hillside', so-called because this refuge of the Rohirrim at the head of *Harrowdale* was on the site of a sacred place of the old inhabitants (now the Dead Men). The element *hærg* can be modernized in E. because it remains an element in place-names, notably *Harrow* (*on the Hill*). The word has no connexion with the [agricultural] implement *harrow*, it is the OE equivalent of ON *hörg-r* (modern Icel. *hörgur*), OHG *harug*. In the LT it is best represented by an approximation to the genuine Rohan form. The Dutch version *Dunharg* is satisfactory. The Swed. *Dunharva* may be suspected to have taken *harrow* as the implement (*harf*).

Dunland. Contains the E. adjective *dun* 'dark, dusky, dull-hued'. See Appendix F, III 408 [2004 edn., p. 1130].

Dwarrowdelf. See Appendix F, III 415 [2004 edn., p. 1137]. Said to be a translation of the actual CS name of Moria: *Phurunargian*, given an archaic E. form, since *Phurunargian* was already itself archaic in form. The 'archaism' is not of much importance; the name should be translated by the same element as that used to translate *Dwarf* (or a variety of that) + a word meaning 'mine, digging, excavation', e.g. Ger. *Zwergengrube*?

Eastemnet. Rohan; retain (though it contains *east*, it is not a CS name, but R. for 'east-plain'). Similarly *Eastfold*.

Eastfarthing. See *The Farthings*.

Elvenhome; Elven Door, Elven river. See note to *Elven-smiths* in the section: Persons.

Entwade, Entwash, Entwood. These are 'modernized' names in Rohan language, *Entwæd*, *Entwæsc*, *Entwudu*. The second elements *wæd* 'ford', *wæsc* 'flood-water', *wudu* 'wood' are given modern E. forms, because the R. forms were recognizably akin to the words in the CS: sc. speakers of the CS, especially in Gondor (where, of course, the names and geography of Rohan were well-known), used these forms, assimilated to their own language. The *-wade, -wash, -wood* may, therefore, be translated by sense in the LT, especially if the LT contains related elements, as Swed. *vad* 'ford'. On *Ent* see *Ent* in section: Persons.

Ettendales. Meant to be a CS (not Elvish) name, though it contains an obsolete element *eten* 'troll, ogre'. This should be retained, except in a LT which preserves a form of the same word, as Dan. *jætte*, Swed. *jätte*, Icel. *jötunn* = OE *eoten*, ME *eten*, E. dialect *eten*, *yeten*.

Similarly *Ettenmoors*; *moor* here has the northern sense of 'high barren land'.

Farthings, The. See I 19 [2004 edn., p. 9; Prologue]. This [the name *Farthing*, and the second element in *Eastfarthing, Northfarthing, Southfarthing, Westfarthing*] is the same word as E. *farthing* (OE *feorðing*, ME *ferthing*), quarter of a penny; but used in its original sense, 'a fourth part, a quarter'. This is modelled on *thriding* 'third part', still used of the divisions of Yorkshire, with loss of *th* after the *th*, *t* in *Northriding, Eastriding, Westriding*. The application to divisions of other measures than money has long been obsolete in E., and *farthing* has been used since early ME for a negligible amount, so that to E. ears the application to the divisions of the Shire (an area of about 18,000 square miles) is comical. This tone can hardly be reproduced. But related words in a LT could perhaps be used: as Dan. *fjerding*, Swed. *fjärding*; or Ger. *Viertal* (which is applied to 'regions, districts'). [See also note for p. 9, quoting a further comment on *farthing* from the manuscript of *Nomenclature.*]

Fenmarch. Rohan name: the fenny (marshy) border-land about the *Mering Stream* ([large-scale] map) forming the boundary of *Rohan* and *Anórien*. This should have been called *Fenmark*, but since it appears in III 78 [2004 edn., p. 804; Book V, Chapter 3] and on the map to vol. III, I have retained it; the meaning of *-mark*, or the French form (of Germanic origin) *marche* is the same: 'boundary, border (land)'. As a Rohan name use in translation *Fenmark*.

Firien. Rohan: representing an old word (OE *firgen*, pronounced *firien*) for 'mountain'. Cf. *Halifirien* 'holy-mount'. As belonging to the language of Rohan, *firien* should be retained. Inconsistently *Firienfeld*, the flat upland of Dunbarrow, has been left unmodernized (the *Firienfield* of the [second edition] Index is in error), but *Firienholt* has been altered to *Firienwood*, the wood about and on the slopes of the *Halifirien*. In a translation it would be best to leave both unaltered, *Firienfeld, Firienholt*, as being alien (not CS) names.

Folde. A Rohan name, to remain unaltered. The same word occurs in *Eastfold*, which should also remain unchanged (cf. *Eastemnet*). This is OE *folde* (ON *fold*) 'earth, land, country', not connected either with the E. verb *fold*, or with *(sheep)fold*. Cf. *Vestfold* and *Østfold* in Norway.

(The *Folde* was the centre of the kingdom, in which the royal house and its kin had their dwellings; its boundary eastward was roughly a line S.W. [south-west] from the junction of the Snowbourn and Entwash to the mountains; the *Eastfold* was the land from that line east to the *Fenmark* between Entwash and the mountains; the *Westfold* was the similar land along the mountains as far as the R. Isen. The defensive centre of the *Folde* and *Eastfold* was at *Edoras*; of *Westfold* at *Helm's Deep*.)

Frogmorton. This is not an actual E. place-name, but has the same element as in *Frogmore* (Bucks [Buckinghamshire]): *frog* + *moor* + *town*. Since this is an intelligible name, it may be translated. N.B. *moor/mor* has the meaning 'marshy land', as usually in place-names of southern and midland England.

Gladden Fields. *Gladden* is here the name for the 'flag' or iris (OE *glædene*), now usually spelt *gladdon*, and has no connexion with E. *glad*; *gladden*, verb. Translate by sense, but avoid if possible the 'learned' name *iris*. Similarly in *Gladden River* which flowed into the *Gladden Fields*.

Golden Perch. An inn name; probably one favoured by anglers. In any case *Perch* is the fish-name (and not a land-measure or bird-perch).

Great Smials. For *Smials*, see *smials* under Things. From here to the end of G in the Index translate by sense: all the names are in modern E. (= CS). But note: *Grimslade*, mentioned III 124 [2004 edn., p. 849; Book V, Chapter 6] as the home of *Grimbold*, killed in battle, contains *Grim* (evidently the name of an ancestor) + *slade* (OE *slæd*, Norw. dialect *slad*) widely used in E. place-names, and still in use, mostly with the sense 'forest glade, dell (especially one on a slope up a hillside)'.

Halifirien. Rohan [name]. Retain unaltered: see *Firien*.

Hallows, The. A CS translation (III 247, 253 [2004 edn., pp. 969, 975; Book VI, Chapters 5, 6]) of the Gondor name (not given) for the Sacred Places of the tombs (cf. III 24 [2004 edn., p. 752; Book V, Chapter 1]). Translate into the LT (if possible with a word of archaic or poetic tone).

Hardbottle. [A place in the] Shire; home of the Bracegirdles (in the North Farthing, not on the map). *-bottle* is an E. place-name element, OE *botl*, variant of *bold* (from which modern E. *build* is derived), meaning '(large) dwelling'; it is not connected with *bottle* 'glass container'. Cf. *ottle* on the small Shire-map, which is an actual place-name in England (Northumberland). Translate by suitable elements in the LT: meaning 'hard dwelling'; 'hard' because excavated in or built of stone (in the rocky Northfarthing). The equivalent and related elements in Ger. place-names is *-büttel*; in Scandinavian *-bol* (especially in Norway).

Harrowdale. See *Dunharrow.*

Haysend. Sc. the end of the *hay* or boundary hedge (not *hay* 'dried grass'). Translate as 'hedge's end'. Cf. *High Hay.*

Helm's Deep, Helm's Dike, Helm's Gate. *Helm* is the name of a man and should be retained.

Hill of Guard. Translate, since this is CS name of *Amon Tirith*, the hill on which *Minas Tirith* was built.

Hoarwell. CS translation of *Mith-eithel* 'pale grey' + 'spring, source'; *well*, as usually in place-names, has this sense (not that of a deep water-pit). Translate.

Hobbiton. See *Hobbit* under Persons. The village name should be translated by *hobbit* + an element = 'village'.

Hold. In the *Hold of Dunharrow* it has the sense 'stronghold, defended refuge'.

Hollin. The CS name (short for *Hollin-land*) of the country called in Elvish *Eregion* 'holly-region'. *Hollin* is an old form, still used locally, of *holly*; the region abounded in holly-trees. Translate.

Hornburg, Hornrock. So called because of Helm's great horn, supposed still at times to be heard blowing. Translate.

Írensaga. [A name of] Rohan. It means 'iron-saw' with reference to its serrated ridge, crest; but it may be left unchanged as an alien name or translated as in the next.

Isengard, Isenmouthe. These names were intended to represent translations into the CS of the (Elvish) names *Angrenost* and *Carach Angren*, but ones made at so early a date that at the period of the tale they had become archaic in form and their original meanings were obscured. They can therefore be left unchanged, though translation (of one or both elements in either name) would be suitable, and I think desirable when the LT is a Germanic language, possessing related elements.

Isen is an old variant form in E. of *iron*; *gard* a Germanic word meaning 'an enclosure', especially one round a dwelling or group of buildings; *mouthe* is a derivative of *mouth*, representing OE *mūtha* (from *mūth* 'mouth') 'an opening', especially used of the mouths of rivers, but also applied to other openings (not parts of a body). *Isengard* 'the iron-court' was so called because of the great hardness of the stone in that place and especially in the central tower. The *Isenmouthe* was so called because of the great fence of pointed iron posts that closed the gap leading into *Udûn*, like teeth in jaws (cf. III 197, 209 [2004 edn., pp. 920, 931; Book VI, Chapter 2]).

In the Dutch and Swed. version *Isengard* is left unchanged. For *Isen-*

mouthe the Dutch uses *Isenmonde*, translating or assimilating to Dutch only the second element. (A more complete translation to *Ijzermonde* would seem to me better.) The Swed. renders it *Isensgap*, which is incorrect, since *Isen* is not a proper name but adjectival.

The *gard* element appears in ON *garðr* whence current or dialectal Swed. *gård*, Dan. *gaard*, and E. *garth* (beside genuine E. *yard*); this though usually of more lowly associations (as E. *farmyard*) appears e.g. in ON *Ás-garðr*, now widely known as *Asgard* in mythology. The word was early lost in German, except in OHG *mittin-* or *mittil-gart* (the inhabited lands of Men) = ON *miðgarðr*, and OE *middan-geard*: see *Middle-earth* below. Would not this old element in German form *-gart* be suitable for a translation or assimilation to German such as *Eisengart*?

Of *-mouthe* the German equivalent appears to be *mündung* (? or in place-names: *-münde*); in Scandinavian, Dan. *munding*, Swed. *mynning*.

N.B. Whatever form is used in *Isengard* must be also used in the name of the *River Isen*, since the river-name was derived from *Isengard* in which it had its source.

Lake Evendim. CS version of *Nen Uial* 'water of twilight'. Translate by sense: 'evening – dust/twilight/gloaming'.

Langstrand. (Translation of *Anfalas*.) This is a CS name, so translate by sense 'long strand'. The shortening of *long* > *lang*, very frequent in E. place-names, can be disregarded.

Limlight (river). The spelling *-light* indicates that this is a CS name; but leave the obscured element *lim-* unchanged, and translate *-light*: the adjective *light* = 'bright, clear'.

Lockholes. The hobbit version of 'lock-up (house)': a place of detention. Translate by sense.

Longbottom. The second element retains its original sense (as locally and frequently in place-names and derived surnames such as *Ramsbottom*) of 'valley' (especially the head or inner end of a valley); related words are Swed. *botten*, Dan. *bund*, Ger. *Boden*, but the last does not agree closely in sense. Translate by sense.

Lune. An Anglicized, that is a Hobbit-version of the Elvish *Lhûn* (so on the [general] map). It is thus an alien name, and should be retained in the LT, assimilated if required to its spelling of such a sound as *lūn*.

Marish. An old form of E. *marsh*. Translate (using if possible a word or form that is understood but local or out of date).

Mathomhouse. See *Mathom* under Things.

Mering Stream. On the final [large-scale] map: 'boundary stream'. Retain *Mering* as a Rohan word not in CS. (OE *mǣre*, *mēre* 'boundary'.)

Middle-earth. Not a special land, or world, or 'planet' as too often supposed, though it is made plain in the Prologue (I 11 etc. [2004 edn., pp. 2 etc.]), text, and Appendices that the story takes place on this earth and under skies in general the same as now visible. The sense is 'the inhabited lands of (Elves and) Men', envisaged as lying between the Western Sea and that of the Far East (only known in the West by rumour). *Middle-earth* (see dictionaries) is a modern alteration of medieval *middel-erde* from OE *middan-geard* (see *Isengard*). The Dutch and Swed. versions correctly use the old 'mythological' name, assimilated to the modern LT: Dutch *Midden-aarde*, Swed. *Midgård.*

Midgewater Marshes. Translate by sense. (The name was suggested by *Mývatn* in Iceland of the same meaning.)

Mirkwood. A name borrowed from ancient Germanic geography and legend, chiefly preserved in ON *myrkviðr*, though the oldest recorded form is Old Ger. *mirkiwidu.* Not preserved in E., though *Mirkwood* is now used to represent ON *myrkviðr.* Primitive form *mirkwi-widu.* Translate by sense, if possible using elements of poetic or antique tone. The Dutch version has *Demsterwold*, the Swed. *Mörkmården*, the last part of which I do not understand, since the only *mård* known to me is the name of the fur-animal 'marten' (Dan. *maar*). (The translators of Norse mythology into Ger. or Scand. languages must have desired something better?)

Mirrormere. CS translation of Dwarvish *Kheledzâram* ('glass-lake'). Translate by sense.

Mount Doom. See *Doom.* [In the typescript *Nomenclature* Tolkien included a separate entry for *Mount Doom*, but had dealt with the name already under *Doom*, and in much the same words.]

Norbury. CS translation of *Forn-ost.* The form that OE *north-burg* would take in mod. E. place-names, meaning 'north-(fortified) town'. Translate by sense, and by related elements in the LT when available. Similarly *Norland* '(belonging to) the north-lands', in this tale those regions envisaged in the action north of Rohan. The longer form *Northerland* (I 390 [2004 edn., p. 374; Book II, Chapter 8]) has the same reference.

Northfarthing. See *The Farthings.*

Over-heaven. (*-heavens* in [the second edition] index is an error.) Translate by sense. This is a CS equivalent of Elvish *menel* 'firmament', *tar-menel* 'high heaven' (I 247 [2004 edn., p. 235; Book II, Chapter 1]), suggested by ON *upphiminn*, and correctly translated *Upphimlen* in the Swed. version. The Dutch has *Boven-hemel.*

Rivendell. 'Cloven-dell': CS translation of *Imlad-ris(t)* 'deep dale of the cleft'. Translate by sense, or retain as seems best. The Dutch version retains the name as *Rivendel.* (The Swed. version has *Vattnadal*, which is incorrect and suggests that the translator thought *Riven-* was related to *river.*)

Rushey. 'Rush-isle' (sc. in origin a 'hard' among the fens of the Marish). The element *-ey, y* in the sense 'small island' = Swed. *ö*, Dan. *ø*, ON *ey* is very frequent in E. place-names. (The Ger. equivalent is *Aue* 'riverside land, water-meadow', which would not be unsuitable in this case.)

Sarn Ford. Retain *Sarn*. The name is a half-translation (of *Sarn-thrad* 'stony-ford'), a process frequent in place-names. The Elvish *Sarn* is also seen in *Sarn Gebir.* [See also notes for p. 172 and 368, quoting further notes on *Sarn Ford* and *Sarn Gebir* respectively, from the manuscript of *Nomenclature.*]

Scary. A meaningless name in the Shire; but since it was in a region of caves and rock-holes (III 301 [2004 edn., p. 1021; Book VI, Chapter 9]), and of a stone-quarry ([marked on the Shire] map) it may be supposed to contain E. dialectal *scar* 'rocky cliff'. Leave unchanged except as required by the LT spelling.

Shire. An organized region with a 'county-town' (cf. I 14 [2004 edn., p. 5; Prologue]). (In the case of the hobbits' Shire this was *Michel Delving.*) Since this word is current in mod. E. and therefore is in the tale CS, translate by sense.

Shire, OE *scīr*, seems very early to have replaced the ancient Germanic word for a 'district', found in its oldest form in Gothic *gawi*, surviving now in Dutch *gouw*, Ger. *Gau.* (In E., owing to its reduction to *gē*, it survived only in a few old place-names, the best known of which is *Surrey* (from *Suðer-ge*) 'southern district'.) This word would seem the nearest equivalent in antiquity and general sense to the Shire of the story. The Dutch version uses *Gouw*; *Gau* seems to me suitable in Ger., unless its recent use in regional reorganization under Hitler has spoilt this very old word. In Scand. languages (in which a related word does not exist) some other (preferably old) word for a 'district, province, etc.' should be used. The Swed. version uses *Fylki* (apparently borrowing the ON, especially Norw. *fylki* 'district, province'). Actually the ON and mod. Icelandic *sýsla* (Swed. *syssla*, Dan. *syssel*, now obsolete in sense *amt*, but occurring in place-names) was in mind when I said that the real untranslated name of the Shire was *Súza* (III 412 [2004 edn., p. 1134; Appendix F]); hence it was also said (I 14 [2004 edn., p. 5; Prologue]) that it was so named as a 'district of well-ordered *business*'.

Silverlode. (Translation of Elvish *Celeb-rant.*) Translate by sense: *silver* + *lode* 'course, water-channel'.

Silvertine. (Translation of *Celeb-dil.*) Translate by sense: *silver* + *tine* 'spike, sharp horn'.

Smials. See *Smial* under *Things.*

Snowbourn. Modernized [form of] the actual Rohan (i.e. OE) *snāw-burna.* Either use *Snawburna,* or in a LT possessing related elements modernize the name to suit it: e.g. *Schneebrunnen, Snebrønd, Snöbrunn.*

Staddle. Village-name in Bree. *Staddle* is now dialectal, but occurs in place-names = 'foundation', of buildings, sheds, ricks, etc.: from OE *stathol.* Use a related equivalent in the LT (if any) as Ger. *Stadel,* or assimilate to LT spelling.

Starkhorn. Mountain-name in Rohan. This may be retained, as a name not in CS; it meant a horn (peak) 'standing up stiff like a spike'. The occurrence of *stark* in Ger. (and Swed.) should make it sufficiently intelligible. The Dutch version has *Sterkhorn,* Swed. *Starkhorn.* (To an E. reader *stark* now has implications of nakedness and grimness (not originally present, but due to applications to *rigor mortis* in corpses, and to the expression *stark-naked*), which would perhaps (?) be better represented in Ger. by *starr.*)

Stonewain Valley. Translate by sense. The CS name of the long narrow defile along which the wains (sleds or drays) passed to and fro from the stone-quarries.

Stoningland. Represents Rohan *Stāning-(land),* a translation of *Gondor.* Since this has been 'modernized' (sc. accommodated to the forms of E.) use the etymological equivalent of 'stone' in the LT, as *sten, stein,* for the first element.

Sunlands. Translate by sense. It is evidently meant as a popular name, in CS or other languages, current in Gondor and the N.W. [North-west] for the little known countries of the far South.

Sunlending. This, however, is a translation into the language of Rohan of *Anórien,* the name of the land immediately attached to *Minas Anor* (originally including that city and inhabited country as far as the River *Erui*). It is thus 'heraldic' rather than climatic, and related to the heraldic names of Elendil's sons *Anárion* and *Isildur,* being the counterpart of *Ithilien.* It only occurs in the verses (III 77 [2004 edn., p. 803; Book V, Chapter 3]) purporting to translate the minstrelsy of Rohan, and should be *retained.* It might well be spelt (indeed more accurately) *Sunnlending,* as in the Swed. version. But the translation in Dutch, *Zuiderleen* 'southern-fief', is erroneous, since the 'southern fiefs', also called the Outlands, referred to the sea-board lands south of *Anórien.*

Tarlang's Neck. Translate *Neck* (as representing CS) and retain *Tarlang.* The Swed. version has *Tarlangs hals;* the Dutch *Engte van Tarlang.*

The *Neck* was a long ridge of rock, over which the road climbed, joining the main mass of the range to the branch (containing three peaks) which separated the plan of *Erech* from *Lamedon*. *Tarlang*, originally the name of this ridge, was later taken as a personal name. [See also note for p. 790, quoting two lengthy variant explanations of the name *Tarlang's Neck* from the manuscript of *Nomenclature*.]

Teeth of Mordor. Translate *Teeth of* in the LT.

Three-farthing Stone. See *The Farthings*. Translate, using whatever word is adopted to represent *farthing*.

Tighfield. This is intended to contain an old word for 'rope' (surviving in some of the senses of mod. E. *tie* sb., in which the spelling is assimilated to that of the related verb *tie*). It was the site of a 'rope-walk' or rope-maker's yard. It would be best translated by some other word for 'rope' than that used in *rope-walk*. (Related are Icel. *taug*, and also the word with various forms *toug*, *tov*, *tog*, in Dan. and Norw.; also nautical Ger. (from Low Ger.) *tou*.)

N.B. The E. *rope-walk* seems to have been misunderstood by other translators; certainly the Swed. which has (II 249) *en repbro över älven borta vid Slättäng*. There is no mention of a river in my text (II 217 [2004 edn., p. 611; Book IV, Chapter 1]). Nor is it easy to see why having a 'rope-bridge' over a river would beget an inherited knowledge in the family about the nature of ropes, and their making. The Dutch has *touwbrug* which I suspect is also due to misunderstanding. I do not know the technical equivalent of *rope-walk* in other languages: dictionaries give Ger. *Seilerbahn*, and Dan. *reberbane*, but these also are possibly mistaken? A *rope-walk* (known in E. since the seventeenth century) is so-called because the ropes were stretched out in long lines over trestles at intervals.

(The Swed. *Slättäng* and Dutch *Weideveld* do not, of course, translate *Tighfield* as above defined, and are probably mere contextual guesses. There is, however, another place-name element (peculiar to E.) that has the same forms as the 'rope' word, though it is probably not related: in mod. place-names *tigh*, *teigh*, *tye*, *tey*. This meant 'an enclosed piece of land'. It does not occur as the first element in a compound.)

Tindrock. CS name (not a translation) of *Tol Brandir*, the steep inaccessible island of towering rock at the head of the falls of *Rauros*. Though originally CS, the name was given long before the time of the tale, and contains the old word *tind* 'a spike', which if it had survived would have rhymed with *find*, etc. But it now appears as *tine* 'prong' with loss of *d*. The ON equivalent was *tind-r*, OHG *zint*. It might be possible to use the latter as an archaic form; but the current (probably related) Ger. *Zinne* has precisely the right sense. Of this *Zinne* the Swed. equivalent is *Tinne*, Dan. *Tind*(e) – which also seem suitable. *Tol Brandir* should be retained as an Elvish name. [A further note on the name, from the manuscript of *Nomenclature*, is quoted in our annotation for p. 373, 'the tall island of the Tindrock'.]

Tower. All the place-names under *Tower(s)* are contemporary CS translations, or author's translations of the Grey-elven names, and should be translated, in those parts that are E.

Treegarth (of Orthanc). On *garth* see *Isengard.* Translate by sense: a *garth* is an enclosed space or garden, usually round a central building (here *Orthanc*).

Udûn. Retain.

Umbar. Retain.

Underharrow. See *Dunharrow, Harrowdale.* A hamlet in the valley below the *Dunharrow.* Use the same word as that used for *harrow* ('fane') in *Dunharrow.*

Upbourn. *Up-* is used in E. place-names for river-side villages far up the named river (as *Upavon* in Wilts. [Wiltshire]), especially in contrast to larger places near its mouth, as *Upwey* above *Weymouth.* This village was some way up the *Snowbourn* above *Edoras,* but not so far up as *Underharrow.* Since the name is given in modernized E. form, it may be translated if that presents no difficulty, or retained in its proper Rohan form *Upburnan.*

Watchwood. Translate.

Waymeet. In the map [printed as] *Waymoot,* in the text modernized as *Way-meet,* a village at the meeting of three ways. Translate by sense, as convenient.

Weathertop. Translate. It is the CS name of the hill called in Grey-elven *Amon Sûl* 'hill of the wind'.

Wellinghall. Treebeard's translation into CS of ('part of') the name of his dwelling. Translate. The intended sense is 'hall (under or behind) the outflow of the spring'.

West Marches (in Rohan). This is given in the CS form and may be translated into the LT for 'the West(ern) Borderlands': in Rohan the land bordering the *Isen.*

Westemnet. Rohan: *emnet* 'flat land, plain', equivalent of Dan. *slette,* and of Ger. *Ebene* (to which it is related). Retain as a non-CS name, but *West-* may be spelt (e.g. with *V*) in a language that does not use *W,* since the word for *West* was the same or similar in CS and the language of Rohan.

Westernesse. The CS name of *Númenor* (which means 'West-land'). It is meant to be *western* + *ess,* an ending used in partly francized names of 'romantic' lands, as *Lyonesse,* or *Logres* (England in Arthurian Romance). The name actually occurs in the early romance *King Horn,* of some kingdom reached by ship. Translate by some similar invention containing *West-* or its equivalent in the LT. The Swed. [translation] has *Västerness*, the Dutch *Westernisse*.

Westfarthing. See *The Farthings*.

Westfold. See *Folde*.

Westmarch. (in the Shire). Translate: *march* = 'borderland'.

Wetwang. CS translation of *Nindalf* (Grey-elven *nîn* 'wet' + *talf* 'flat field'). But it is in archaic form, *wang* being an old word for 'field, flat area'. (*Wetwang* is an actual place-name in Yorkshire.) *Wet-* should be translated in the LT, and *wang* by sense. But in Scand. languages this should not be difficult since the equivalent of both E. *wet* and *wang* are found in them: Icel. *votur* and *vangur*; Swed. *våt, vång*; Dan. *vaad, vang*. The Dutch version retains *Wetwang*, though *Natwang* would have been better; the Swed. has *Våta vägen*, which is not the meaning, and is quite unsuitable: the *Wetwang* was a pathless fen. *Wang* did not survive in Dutch, or in German (except in place-names or dialect). Ger. *Wange*, Dutch *Wang* 'cheek', is a different (but related) word.

Whitfurrows (in the Shire). Translate by sense, *whit-* being the usual shortening of *white* in personal (*Whitlock*) and local names (*Whitley*). Similarly *Whitwell* in the Shire (an actual E. place-name). The reference in E. place-names is usually to the colour of the soil.

Wilderland. An invention (not actually found in E.), based on *wilderness* (originally meaning 'country of wild creatures, not inhabited by Men'), but with a side-reference to the verb *wilder* 'wander astray', and *bewilder*. Supposed to be the CS name of *Rhovanion* (in the map, not in the text), the lands east of the Misty Mountains (including Mirkwood) as far as the River Running. The Dutch version has *Wilderland*: Dutch has *wildernis*, but not Ger. or Scand. languages (Ger. *Wildnis*, Dan. *Vildnis*).

Withywindle. River-name in the Old Forest, intended to be in the language of the Shire. It was a winding river bordered by willows (withies). *Withy-* is not uncommon in E. place-names, but *-windle* does not actually occur (*withywindle* was modelled on *withywind*, a name of the convolvulus or bindweed). An invention of suitable elements in the LT would be desirable. Very good in the Dutch version *Wilgewinde* (with *wilg* = E. willow). I do not understand the Swed. version *Vittespring*. Words related to *withy* are found in the Scand. languages; related also is Ger. *Weide*.

Things

Few of these entries require comment, since they are either in alien (especially Elvish) languages, or simply in modern E. (= CS) and require normal translation.

Elder Days. This is naturally taken by E. readers to mean 'older' (sc. former) but with an archaic flavour, since this original form of the comparative is now only applied to persons, or used as a noun in *Elders* (seniors). In inventing the expression I intended this, as well as association with the poetic word *eld* 'old age, antiquity'. I have since (recently) come across the expression in early E.: *be eldern dawes* 'in the days of our forefathers, long ago'. This, meaning 'days of the seniors', might help in devising a translation that is not just the LT equivalent of 'the older days'. The Swed. version has simply *i Aldre tiden*; the Dutch *de Oude Tid* (less correctly, since this would naturally also apply to the other ages before the Third).

(The similarity to *Eldar*, pl. of *Elda* 'Elf', is accidental and unintentional. *Elda* is the Q. form of the Grey-elven word *edhel*.) [Compare *Elder Kindred* under Persons.]

Elven. With regard to this old adjectival form, see note upon it under Persons [i.e. under *Elven-smiths*].

Evermind. Flower-name, translation of Rohan *simbelmyne*. The element *-mind* has the sense 'memory'. The name thus resembles 'forget-me-not', but a quite different kind of flower is intended: an imagined variety of anemone, growing in turf like *Anemone pulsatilla*, the pasque-flower, but smaller and white like the wood anemone. Translate by sense. The Swed. and Dutch versions both omit the element *-mind*, and so produce names equivalent to 'everlasting flower', which is not the point. Though the plant bloomed at all seasons its flowers were not 'immortelles'. (Swed. *evighets-blommor*, Dutch *Immerdaar.*)

Ithilstone. [Spelt *Ithil-stone* in the text.] Translate the second element *-stone.*

Kingsfoil. Translate: *-foil* (from Old French *foil*) = 'leaf', as in *cinquefoil*, etc. Only the *-leaf* of *asëa* was valued.

Lithe. The former and later *Lithe* (OE *līða*) were the old names for June and July respectively. All the month-names in the Shire Calendar are (worn-down) forms of the OE names. In the Hobbit Calendar *(the) Lithe* was the middle-day (or 183rd day) of the year. Since all the Hobbit month-names are supposed *not* to be CS, but conservative survivals from their former language before migration, it would be best to keep *Lithe* unaltered – as would be necessary with the other calendar names in any translation of the Appendices. The Dutch version keeps *Lithe.* (The word was peculiar to E. and no related calendar word is found elsewhere.) The Swed. version rewrites the passage I 20 (new edition I 19) [2004 edn., p. 10; Prologue] 'who was elected . . . at Midsummer': *Han valdes vart sjunde år vid midsommarvakan uppe pä Kritklipporna i sommarsolståndets natt.* This, besides omitting *the Free Fair* and misrendering *the White Downs* (a name) as 'the chalk cliffs' (!), misrepresents the passage and the customs plainly alluded to. It was not a night festival or 'wake', but a day-celebration marked by a 'Free Fair' (Dutch version *Vrije Markt*), so-called because anyone who wished could set up a booth without charge. The [Swedish] translator has assimilated the passage to the Scandinavian summer-solstice festival, christianized in name by association with St. John the Baptist's day (June 24), which occurred at more or less the right date (Icel. *Jónsvaka, Jónsmessa,* Dan. *Sankthansnat, Skaersommernat*; etc.) But the affair was not a Midsummer Night's Dream!

Yule, the midwinter counterpart, only occurs in Appendix D*, but in translating this, it should like *Lithe* be treated as an alien word not generally current in CS. It should therefore be retained, though with a spelling suitable to the LT: so e.g. in Dan. or Ger. spelt *Jule,* to match *Lithe. Yule* is found in modern E. (mostly as a literary archaism), but this is an accident, and cannot be taken to imply that a similar or related word was also found in the CS at that time: the hobbit calendar differed throughout from the official CS calendars. It may, however, be supposed that a form of the same word had been used by the Northmen who came to form a large part of the population of Gondor (III 328 [2004 edn., p. 1047; Appendix A]), and was later in use in Rohan, so that some word like *Yule* was well-known in Gondor as a 'northern name' for the midwinter festival. Somewhat like the appearance in modern Ger. of *Jul* (? as a loan from the North), in such words as *Julblock* 'Yule-log' and *Julklapp* (as in Swed. and similarly in Dan.). In Scandinavia, of course, *Jule* would be well understood.

*Midwinter only occurs once during the main narrative. The midwinter festival was not an Elvish custom, and so would not have been celebrated in Rivendell. The Fellowship, however, left on Dec. 25, which [date] had then no significance, since the Yule, or its equivalent, was then the last day of the year and the first of the next year. Though Dec. 25 (setting out) and March 25 (accomplishment of quest) were intentionally chosen by me.

[See also note for p. 1106, quoting part of a deleted entry for *Yule* in the manuscript of *Nomenclature.*]

Longbottom Leaf. See *Longbottom* under Places.

Old Toby. Variety of tobacco, named after *Tobold* (*Hornblower*). Use whatever equivalent of 'Toby' is used for the personal name on the same page.

Old Winyards. A wine – but, of course, in fact a place-name, meaning 'the Old Vineyards'. *Winyard* is actually preserved as a place-name in England, descending from OE before the assimilation to French and Latin *vin-*. This cannot, I think, be imitated, and one must remain content with the LT word for 'vineyard', as *weingarten*, *vingaard*, etc. (Dutch *Oude Wijngaarden.*) The Swed. version for no obvious reason (unless failure to recognize *winyards* as a relative of *vingård*) simply omits the name.

Púkel-men. A Rohan name for the effigies of men of a vanished race. It represents OE *pūcel* (still surviving as *puckle*), one of the forms of the *pūk-* stem (widespread in England, Wales, Ireland, Norway and Iceland) referring to a devil, or to a minor sprite, e.g. Puck, and often applied to ugly misshapen persons. The *púkel-men* are adequately described, and the element *púkel* may be retained – or replaced by some words of similar (possibly related) form and sense in the LT. (Dutch version *de Púkel-mensen*, Swed. *Pukel-männen.*)

Rope-walk. Not in the index: occurs II 217 [2004 edn., p. 611; Book IV, Chapter 1] as the technical name for a rope-maker's yard. See *Tighfield* [under Places].

Springle-ring. An invention. Render by a similar one suitable to the LT, implying a vigorous ring-dance in which dancers often leaped up.

Tale. in *Tale of Years* means 'counting' or 'reckoning'.

Westmansweed. Translate, as a CS rendering of 'herb of Men of the West' (sc. of *Westernesse*, *Númenor*).

Yule. See *Lithe.*

CHANGES TO THE EDITIONS OF 2004–5

As generally described in the Preface and 'Brief History' earlier in this volume, numerous emendations were made to *The Lord of the Rings* for the 2004 (fiftieth anniversary one-volume) edition, using the 2002 revised typesetting by HarperCollins as the copy-text. Many of these were corrections to errors introduced at various points, most frequently the 'second printing' of *The Fellowship of the Ring* (1954) and the resetting of 1994. Further errors, old and new (introduced in the 2004 setting), having been discovered in the course of writing this book, additional emendations were made in the reprint edition of 2005, which also includes a new, expanded index by the present authors. Excepting only a few corrections of spacing, indentation, and misaligned marks of punctuation, all of the emendations of the 2002 copy-text in 2004, and of the 2004 edition in 2005, are documented below in two parts, with page citations to the new edition as published by HarperCollins, London, and the Houghton Mifflin Company, Boston, Massachusetts. Emendations marked with an asterisk (*) are explained in notes in the present book.

2004 EDITION

THE FELLOWSHIP OF THE RING

FOREWORD

xxiii 1 forced myself to tackle > I forced myself to tackle [*numeral 1 > capital I*]

PROLOGUE

2 Bandobras Took (Bullroarer), son of Isengrim the Second, > Bandobras Took (Bullroarer), son of Isumbras the Third, [*'Isengrim the Second' > 'Isumbras the Third'*] *

3 The Stoors were broader, heavier in build; their feet and hands were larger, and they preferred > The Stoors were broader, heavier in build; their feet and hands were larger; and they preferred [*comma after 'larger' > semi-colon*]

They moved westward early, and roamed over Eriador as far as Weathertop while the others were still in the Wilderland. > They moved westward early, and roamed over Eriador as far as

Weathertop while the others were still in Wilderland. [*'in the Wilderland' > 'in Wilderland'*]

9 The Thain was the master of the Shire-moot, and captain of the Shire-muster and the Hobbitry-in-arms, but > The Thain was the master of the Shire-moot, and captain of the Shire-muster and the Hobbitry-in-arms; but [*comma after 'arms' > semi-colon*]

11 It was the one thing he loved, his 'precious', > It was the one thing he loved, his 'Precious', [*'precious' > 'Precious'*] *

12 He was hungry now, and angry, and once his 'precious' was with him > He was hungry now, and angry, and once his 'Precious' was with him [*'precious' > 'Precious'*]

The light in his eyes was like a green flame as he sped back to murder the hobbit and recover his 'precious'. > The light in his eyes was like a green flame as he sped back to murder the hobbit and recover his 'Precious'. [*'precious' > 'Precious'*]

For just as he ran > For as he ran [*'just as' > 'as'*]

Warily Bilbo followed him, as he went along, cursing, and talking to himself about his 'precious'; > Warily Bilbo followed him, as went along, cursing, and talking to himself about his 'Precious'; [*'precious' > 'Precious'*]

13 It was suggested to Bilbo . . . for Gollum did, in fact, call the ring his 'birthday present', > It was suggested to Bilbo . . . for Gollum did, in fact, call the ring his 'birthday-present', [*'birthday present' > 'birthday-present'*] *

BOOK I

23 But I reckon it was a nasty shock > But I reckon it was a nasty knock [*'shock' > 'knock'*] *

24 Crazy about stories of the old days he is, > Crazy about stories of the old days, he is, [*added comma after 'days'*]

At the end of the second week in September a cart came in through Bywater from the direction of the Brandywine Bridge > At the end of the second week in September a cart came in through Bywater from the direction of Brandywine Bridge [*deleted 'the' before 'Brandywine Bridge'*]

25 [*bold black dot following the elf-rune > full stop of a more appropriate size*]

They knew him by sight . . . they now belonged to the legendary past. > They knew him by sight . . . they now belonged to a legendary past. [*'the legendary past'* > *'a legendary past'*]

27 Actually in Hobbiton and Bywater every day in the year it was somebody's birthday, > Actually in Hobbiton and Bywater every day in the year was somebody's birthday, [*'it was'* > *'was'*]

28 Some of these were only very distantly connected with Bilbo, and some of them had hardly ever been in Hobbiton before, > Some of these were only very distantly connected with Bilbo, and some had hardly ever been in Hobbiton before, [*'some of them'* > *'some'*]

The purchase of provisions . . . but as Bilbo's catering had depleted the stocks of most stores, cellars and warehouses for miles around, > but as Bilbo's catering had depleted the stocks of most of the stores, cellars and warehouses for miles around, [*'most stores'* > *'most of the stores'*]

29 Seizing a horn from a youngster near by, > Seizing a horn from a youngster nearby, [*'near by'* > *'nearby'*] *

30 Many of his guests, and especially the Sackville-Bagginses, > Many of the guests, and especially the Sackville-Bagginses, [*'his guests'* > *'the guests'*]

31 He walked briskly back to his hole, and stood for a moment listening with a smile to the din in the pavilion and > He walked briskly back to his hole, and stood for a moment listening with a smile to the din in the pavilion, and [*added comma after 'pavilion'*]

33 'It is mine, I tell you. My own. My precious. Yes, my precious.' > 'It is mine, I tell you. My own. My Precious. Yes, my Precious.' [*'precious'* > *'Precious', twice*]

34 I won't give my precious away, I tell you.' > I won't give my Precious away, I tell you.' [*'precious'* > *'Precious'*]

After all that's what this party business was all about, really: to give away lots of birthday presents, > After all that's what this party business was all about, really: to give away lots of birthday-presents, [*'birthday presents'* > *'birthday-presents'*]

36 Then without another word he turned away from the lights and voices in the fields and tents, > Then without another word he turned away from the lights and voices in the field and tents, [*'fields'* > *'field'*] *

39 A little later Frodo came out of the study to see how things were going on and found her still about the place, investigating nooks and corners and tapping the floors. > A little later Frodo came out of the study to see how things were going on, and found her still about the place, investigating nooks and corners, and tapping the floors. [*added commas after 'going on' and 'corners'*]

The legend of Bilbo's gold . . . as every one knows, any one's for the finding > The legend of Bilbo's gold . . . as everyone knows, anyone's for the finding [*'every one' > 'everyone', 'any one's' > 'anyone's'*] *

42 Frodo went tramping all over the Shire > Frodo went tramping over the Shire [*deleted 'all'*]

45 But I warrant you haven't seen them doing it; nor any one else in the Shire.' > But I warrant you haven't seen them doing it; nor anyone else in the Shire.' [*'any one' > 'anyone'*]

46 'Ah well eh?' said Gandalf. > 'All well eh?' said Gandalf. [*'Ah' > 'All'*]

Everything looked fresh, the new green of Spring > Everything looked fresh, the new green of spring [*'Spring' > 'spring'*] *

47 And if he often uses the Ring . . . walks in the twilight under the eye of the dark power that rules the Rings. > And if he often uses the Ring . . . walks in the twilight under the eye of the Dark Power that rules the Rings. [*'dark power' > 'Dark Power'*] *

Yes, sooner or later . . . the dark power will devour him.' > Yes, sooner or later . . . the Dark Power will devour him.' [*'dark power' > 'Dark Power'*]

'Let me see – it was in the year that the White Council drove the dark power from Mirkwood, > 'Let me see – it was in the year that the White Council drove the Dark Power from Mirkwood, [*'dark power' > 'Dark Power'*]

48 Much like Gollum with his "birthday present". > Much like Gollum with his "birthday-present". [*'birthday present' > 'birthday-present'*]

54 But as he lowered his eyes, he saw far above the tops of the Misty Mountains, > But as he lowered his eyes, he saw far ahead the tops of the Misty Mountains, [*'above' > 'ahead'*]

55 'Surely the Ring was his precious > 'Surely the Ring was his Precious [*'precious' > 'Precious'*]

56 For instance, he called the Ring his "birthday present", > For instance, he called the Ring his "birthday-present", [*'birthday present' > 'birthday-present'*]

The murder of Déagol haunted Gollum, and he had made up a defence, repeating it to his "precious" > The murder of Déagol haunted Gollum, and he had made up a defence, repeating it to his "Precious" [*'precious' > 'Precious'*]

57 It *was* his birthday present, > It *was* his birthday-present, [*'birthday present'* > *'birthday-present'*]

But from hints dropped among the snarls I even gathered > But from hints dropped among the snarls I gathered [*'even gathered'* > *'gathered'*]

58 But at last, when I had given up the chase and turned to other parts, > But at last, when I had given up the chase and turned to other paths, [*'parts'* > *'paths'*] *

65 To tell the truth, he was very reluctant to start, now that it had come to the point. Bag End > To tell the truth, he was very reluctant to start, now that it had come to the point: Bag End [*full stop after 'point'* > *colon*]

70 'No, you don't, Sam!' > 'No you don't, Sam!' [*deleted comma after 'No'*]

71 It climbed away . . . towards Woody-End, > It climbed away . . . towards Woody End, [*'Woody-End'* > *'Woody End'*] *

79 They don't live in the Shire, but they wander into it in Spring and Autumn, > They don't live in the Shire, but they wander into it in spring and autumn, [*'Spring'* > *'spring'*, *'Autumn'* > *'autumn'*]

81 '*Elen síla lúmenn' omentielvo*, a star shines on the hour of our meeting,' he added in the high-elven speech. > '*Elen síla lúmenn' omentielvo*, a star shines on the hour of our meeting,' he added in the High-elven speech. [*'high-elven'* > *'High-elven'*]

87 *I am going with him, if he climbs to the Moon, and* > *I am going with him, if he climbs to the Moon; and* [*comma after 'Moon'* > *semi-colon*]

88 'I will go along with you, Mr. Frodo,' said Sam (in spite of private misgiving > 'I will go along with you, Mr. Frodo,' said Sam (in spite of private misgivings [*'misgiving'* > *'misgivings'*]

93 'Well, if that isn't queerer than ever?' > 'Well, if that isn't queerer than ever!' [*question mark after 'ever'* > *exclamation mark*]

96 'It's going to be thick,' said Maggot; 'but I'll not light my lantern > 'It's going to be thick,' said Maggot; 'but I'll not light my lanterns [*'lantern'* > *'lanterns'*]

99 They can go twenty miles north to Brandywine Bridge > They can go ten miles north to Brandywine Bridge [*'twenty'* > *'ten'*] *

104 To tell you the truth, I had been watching > To tell you the truth, I have been watching [*'had been watching'* > *'have been watching'*]

105 I kept my knowledge to myself, till this Spring > I kept my knowledge to myself, till this spring [*'Spring' > 'spring'*]

107 There are six ponies > There are five ponies [*'six ponies' > 'five ponies'*] *

109 In their shed they found the ponies; sturdy little beasts > In their shed they found the ponies: sturdy little beasts [*semi-colon after 'ponies' > colon*]

124 But I see you are an elf-friend; > But I see that you are an Elf-friend; [*added 'that' after 'see', 'elf-friend' > 'Elf-friend'*]

128 There was a fold or channel where the mist was broken into many plumes and billows; the valley of the Withywindle. > There was a fold or channel where the mist was broken into many plumes and billows: the valley of the Withywindle. [*semi-colon after 'billows' > colon*]

I wakened Goldberry singing under window; but nought > I wakened Goldberry singing under window; but naught [*'nought' > 'naught'*] *

133 'I am no weather-master,' he said; > 'I am no weather-master,' said he; [*'he said' > 'said he'*]

136 Their way wound . . . over the shoulder of further hills, > Their way wound . . . over the shoulders of further hills, [*'shoulder' > 'shoulders'*]

137 Then their hearts rose, for > Then their hearts rose; for [*comma after 'rose' > semi-colon*]

However, that may be: > However that may be: [*deleted comma after 'However'*]

138 When they reached the bottom it was so cold > When they reached the bottom it was so chill [*'cold' > 'chill'*] *

145 Most of these he made into a pile that glistened > Most of these he made into a pile that glistered [*'glistened' > 'glistered'*] *

149 There were also many families of hobbits in the Bree-land and *they* > There were also many families of hobbits in the Bree-land; and *they* [*added semi-colon after 'Bree-land'*]

151 They came to the West-gate and found it shut, but > They came to the West-gate and found it shut; but [*comma after 'shut' > semi-colon*]

He wondered why the man was so suspicious, and whether any one > He wondered why the man was so suspicious, and whether anyone [*'any one' > 'anyone'*]

153 Might I ask your names, sir?' > Might I ask your names, sirs?' [*'sir' > 'sirs'*]

It never rains but it pours, we say in Bree. > It never rains but it pours, we say in Bree.' [*added quotation mark after full stop*]

Well find him! > Well, find him! [*added comma after 'Well'*]

'Well, now, what was I going to say?' > 'Well now, what was I going to say?' [*deleted comma after 'Well'*]

156 The hobbits did not pay much attention to all this, and it did not at the moment > The hobbits did not pay much attention to all this, as it did not at the moment [*'and it did not' > 'as it did not'*]

160 Presently he slipped out of the door, followed by the squint-eyed southerner: the two had been whispering together a good deal during the evening. Harry the gatekeeper also went out just behind them. > Presently he slipped out of the door, followed by the squint-eyed southerner: the two had been whispering together a good deal during the evening. [*deleted 'Harry the gatekeeper also went out just behind them.'*] *

163 'I am called Strider,' he answered: 'and > 'I am called Strider,' he answered; 'and [*colon after 'answered' > semi-colon*]

163–4 I need not repeat all that they said to old Bombadil or to one another, but > I need not repeat all that they said to old Bombadil or to one another; but [*comma after 'another' > semi-colon*]

164 'I don't see what interest my name has for any one in Bree,' > 'I don't see what interest my name has for anyone in Bree,' [*'any one' > 'anyone'*]

165 Frodo made no answer, his mind > Frodo made no answer; his mind [*comma after 'answer' > semi-colon*]

168–9 You can let Mr. Underhill stay here tonight, as Mr. Underhill, and > You can let Mr. Underhill stay here tonight, as Mr. Underhill; and [*comma after 'Underhill' > semi-colon*]

172 Strider shall be your guide. We shall have a rough road tomorrow. > Strider shall be your guide. And now I think it is time you went to bed and took what rest you can. We shall have a rough road tomorrow. [*added sentence 'And now . . . you can.'*] *

177 Far-away answering horns > Far away answering horns [*'Far-away' > 'Far away'*] *

180 Strider had changed his mind, and he decided to leave > Strider had changed his mind, and had decided to leave [*'he decided' > 'had decided'*]

187 Frodo saw some scratches: 'There seems to be a stroke > [*restored missing graphic of scratches*]

191 'Tell us of Gil-galad,' said Merry suddenly, when he paused at the end of a story of the Elf-Kingdoms. > 'Tell us of Gil-galad,' said Merry suddenly, when he paused at the end of a story of the Elf-kingdoms. [*'Elf-Kingdoms' > 'Elf-kingdoms'*]

192 *He called her by her elvish name; > He called her by her Elvish name;* [*'elvish' > 'Elvish'*] *

201 He recalled Bilbo's account of his journey . . . near the Troll's wood > He recalled Bilbo's account of his journey . . . near the Trolls' wood [*'Troll's wood' > 'Trolls' wood'*]

213 Two rode towards Frodo: two galloped > Two rode towards Frodo; two galloped [*colon after 'Frodo' > semi-colon*]

214 White flames seemed to Frodo to flicker on their crests and he > White flames seemed to Frodo to flicker on their crests, and he [*added comma after 'crests'*]

BOOK II

219 In the House of Elrond, > In the house of Elrond, [*'House' > 'house'*] *

221 But then we don't know much about Men in the Shire, except perhaps the Breelanders. > But then we don't know much about Men in the Shire, except perhaps the Bree-landers. [*'Breelanders' > 'Bree-landers'*] *

223 Gandalf moved his chair to the bedside, and > Gandalf moved his chair to the bedside and [*deleted comma after 'bedside'*]

226 The Lord of the Ring is not Frodo, but the master of the Dark Tower of Mordor, whose power is again stretching out over the world! > The Lord of the Ring is not Frodo, but the master of the Dark Tower of Mordor, whose power is again stretching out over the world. [*exclamation mark after 'world' > full stop*]

Though at the moment I feel more like eating and drinking! > Though at the moment I feel more like eating and drinking. [*exclamation mark after 'drinking' > full stop*]

Frodo looked at them in wonder, for > Frodo looked at them in wonder; for [*comma after 'wonder' > semi-colon*]

227 But her brothers, Elladan and Elrohir, were out upon errantry: for > But her brothers, Elladan and Elrohir, were out upon errantry; for [*colon after 'errantry' > semi-colon*]

230 As Elrond entered and went towards the seat prepared for him, elvish minstrels > As Elrond entered and went towards the seat prepared for him, Elvish minstrels [*'elvish' > 'Elvish'*]

232 I am sorry: sorry you have come in for this burden: sorry about everything. > I am sorry: sorry you have come in for this burden; sorry about everything. [*colon after 'burden' > semi-colon*]

233 Man of the West, Númenorean. > Man of the West, Númenórean. [*'Númenorean' > 'Númenórean'; instances of* Númenorean(s) *were emended to* Númenórean(s) *also on pp. 244, 678, 679, 888, 1033, 1035, 1036, 1037, 1043, 1044, 1048, 1052, 1061, 1062, 1063, 1083, 1084, 1108, 1110, 1113, 1114, 1117, 1128, 1129, and 1131*] *

234 *her prow was fashioned > her prow he fashioned* [*'was fashioned' > 'he fashioned'*] *

from west to east and errandless, > from west to east, and errandless, [*added comma after 'east'*]

and crowned him with the living light > and crowned him with the living light, [*added comma after 'light'*]

237 Not that hobbits would ever acquire quite the elvish appetite > Not that hobbits would ever acquire quite the Elvish appetite [*'elvish' > 'Elvish'*]

238 He stood still enchanted, while the sweet syllables of the elvish song > He stood still enchanted, while the sweet syllables of the Elvish song [*'elvish' > 'Elvish'*]

I am getting very old, and I began to wonder if I should ever live to see > I am getting very old, and I began to wonder if I should live to see [*'should ever live' > 'should live'*]

243 Small wonder it is > Small wonder is it [*'it is' > 'is it'*]

245 For few, I deem, know of our deeds, and therefore guess little of their peril, > For few, I deem, know of our deeds, and therefore guess little at their peril, [*'of their peril' > 'at their peril'*]

249 'But not yet, I beg, Master!' said Bilbo. > 'But not yet, I beg, Master!' cried Bilbo. [*'said' > 'cried'*] *

Galdor of the Havens, who sat near by, > Galdor of the Havens, who sat nearby, [*'near by' > 'nearby'*]

252 And yet there lie in his hoards many records that few now can read, even of the lore-masters, for their scripts > And yet there lie in his hoards many records that few even of the lore-masters now can read, for their scripts [*'few now can read, even of the lore-masters' > 'few even of the lore-masters now can read'*] *

255 'Alas! alas!' cried Legolas, and in his fair elvish face > 'Alas! alas!' cried Legolas, and in his fair Elvish face [*'elvish' > 'Elvish'*]

Pray do not interrupt, > Pray, do not interrupt, [*added comma after 'Pray'*]

260 Wolves and orcs were housed in Isengard, for Saruman was mustering a great force on his own account, in rivalry of Sauron and not in his service yet. > Wolves and orcs were housed in Isengard, for Saruman was mustering a great force on his own account, in rivalry of Sauron and not in his service, yet. [*added comma after 'service'*]

263 How it happened I could not then guess, > How it had happened I could not then guess, [*'How it happened' > 'How it had happened'*]

It's the best news I have had since midsummer: it's worth > It's the best news I have had since Midsummer; it's worth [*'midsummer:' > 'Midsummer;'*] *

264 It took me nearly fourteen days from Weathertop, > It took me nearly fifteen days from Weathertop, [*'fourteen' > 'fifteen'*] *

But so it was that I came to Rivendell only three days before the Ring, > But so it was that I came to Rivendell only two days before the Ring, [*'three days' > 'two days'*] *

266 The Nine have been unhorsed indeed but > The Nine have been unhorsed indeed, but [*added comma after 'indeed'*]

270 Can't you think of some names > Can't we think of some names [*'Can't you' > 'Can't we'*] *

But if you take it freely, I will say that your choice is right; and though all the mighty elf-friends > But if you take it freely, I will say that your choice is right; and though all the mighty Elf-friends [*'elf-friends' > 'Elf-friends'*]

271 [*restored paragraph missing at the end of Book II, Chapter 2:*] Sam sat down, blushing and muttering. 'A nice pickle we have landed ourselves in, Mr. Frodo!' he said, shaking his head.

274 The hobbits had been nearly two months in the House of Elrond, > The hobbits had been nearly two months in the house of Elrond, [*'House' > 'house'*]

Many had gone east and south . . . while others had climbed the pass at the source of the Gladden River, > Many had gone east and south . . . while others had climbed the pass at the sources of the Gladden River, [*'source' > 'sources'*] *

Radagast was not there; and they had returned over the high pass that was called the Dimrill Stair. > Radagast was not there; and they had returned over the high pass that was called the Redhorn Gate. [*'Dimrill Stair' > 'Redhorn Gate'*] *

276 Even if you chose for us an elf-lord, > Even if you chose for us an Elf-lord, [*'elf-lord' > 'Elf-lord'*]

297 'I will *not* go,' said Boromir; 'not unless the vote of the whole company > 'I will *not* go,' said Boromir; 'not unless the vote of the whole Company [*'company' > 'Company'*]

298 There was a hideous yell, and the leaping shape thudded to the ground; the elvish arrow > There was a hideous yell, and the leaping shape thudded to the ground; the Elvish arrow [*'elvish' > 'Elvish'*]

304 'They are invisible, and their own masters > 'They are invisible, and their own makers [*'masters' > 'makers'*] *

311 I have been with him . . . ; and there are tales of Rivendell of greater deeds > I have been with him . . . ; and there are tales in Rivendell of greater deeds [*'of Rivendell' > 'in Rivendell'*] *

312 There was no sound but the sound of their own feet; the dull stump > There was no sound but the sound of their own feet: the dull stump [*semi-colon after 'feet' > colon*]

'Steady! Steady!' cried Gandalf as > 'Steady! Steady!' cried Gandalf, as [*added comma after 'Gandalf'*]

315 He raised his staff, and for a brief instant there was blaze > He raised his staff, and for a brief instant there was a blaze [*'was blaze' > 'was a blaze'*]

321 Gandalf lifted it carefully, but the leaves crackled > Gandalf lifted it carefully, but the leaves cracked [*'crackled' > 'cracked'*] *

330 The Balrog fell back and > The Balrog fell back, and [*added comma after 'back'*]

331 They stumbled wildly up the great stairs beyond the door. Aragorn leading, Boromir at the rear. > They stumbled wildly up the great stairs beyond the door, Aragorn leading, Boromir at the rear. [*full stop after 'door' > comma*]

333–4 But still it could be seen that once long ago a great paved highway had wound upwards from the lowlands of the Dwarf-kingdom. > But still it could be seen that once long ago a great paved highway had wound upwards from the lowlands to the Dwarf-kingdom. [*'lowlands of the Dwarf-kingdom' > 'lowlands to the Dwarf-kingdom'*] *

341 But neither Nimrodel nor Amroth ever came back. > But neither Nimrodel nor Amroth came ever back. [*'ever came back' > 'came ever back'*] *

343–4 We have been keeping watch on the rivers, ever since we saw a great troop of Orcs going north toward Moria, > We have been keeping watch on the rivers, ever since we saw a great troop of Orcs going north towards Moria, [*'toward' > 'towards'*]

344 I hope, if I do go to sleep in this bed-loft, > I hope, if I do go to sleep in this bird-loft, [*'bed-loft' > 'bird-loft'*] *

Late in the night he awoke. > Late in the night he woke. [*'awoke' > 'woke'*]

349 He could hear many different notes in the rustle of the leaves overhead, the river murmuring away on his right, and the thin clear voices of birds in the sky. > He could hear many different notes in the rustle of the leaves overhead, the river murmuring away on his right, and the thin clear voices of birds high in the sky. [*'birds in the sky' > 'birds high in the sky'*] *

A marching host of Elves had come up silently: they were hastening toward the northern borders > A marching host of Elves had come up silently: they were hastening towards the northern borders [*'toward' > 'towards'*]

351 'I thought that Elves were all for moon and stars: but this is more elvish > 'I thought that Elves were all for moon and stars: but this is more Elvish [*'elvish' > 'Elvish'*]

As he stepped out at last upon the lofty platform, Haldir took his hand and turned him toward the South. > As he stepped out at last upon the lofty platform, Haldir took his hand and turned him towards the South. [*'toward' > 'towards'*]

352 *Arwen vanimelda, namarië!* > *Arwen vanimelda, namárië!* [*'namarië' > 'namárië'*]

355 'Why has nothing of this been told to me before?' he asked in the Elven-tongue. > 'Why has nothing of this been told to me before?' he asked in the elven-tongue. [*'Elven-tongue' > 'elven-tongue'*]

357 The Elves spread for them a pavilion among the trees near the fountain, and in it they laid soft couches; then speaking words of peace with fair elvish voices > The Elves spread for them a pavilion among the trees near the fountain, and in it they laid soft couches; then speaking words of peace with fair Elvish voices [*'elvish' > 'Elvish'*]

360 They're all elvish enough, > They're all Elvish enough, [*'elvish' > 'Elvish'*]

361 Turning aside, she led them toward the southern slopes > Turning aside, she led them towards the southern slopes [*'toward'* > *'towards'*]

363 They've dug up Bagshot Row, and there's the poor old gaffer > They've dug up Bagshot Row, and there's the poor old Gaffer [*'gaffer'* > *'Gaffer'*] *

366 I am permitted to wear the One Ring: why cannot I see > I am permitted to wear the One Ring: why cannot *I* see [*roman 'I'* > *italic 'I'*] *

You'd stop them digging up the gaffer > You'd stop them digging up the Gaffer [*'gaffer'* > *'Gaffer'*]

370 They are elvish robes > They are Elvish robes [*'elvish'* > *'Elvish'*]

371 On the further shores the woodlands still marched on southwards as far as the eye could see, > On the further shores the woodlands still marched on southwards as far as eye could see, [*'the eye'* > *'eye'*] *

372 They turned a sharp bend in the river, and there, sailing proudly down the stream toward them, > They turned a sharp bend in the river, and there, sailing proudly down the stream towards them, [*'toward'* > *'towards'*]

375 In this hour take the name that was foretold for you, Elessar, the Elfstone of the house of Elendil!' > In this hour take the name that was foretold for you, Elessar, the Elfstone of the House of Elendil!' [*'house'* > *'House'*]

For our spring and our summer are gone by, > For our Spring and our Summer are gone by, [*'spring'* > *'Spring'*, *'summer'* > *'Summer'*]

380 Nonetheless they saw no sign of an enemy that day, > Nonetheless they saw no sign of any enemy that day, [*'an'* > *'any'*]

On the eastern bank to their left they saw long formless slopes stretching up and away toward the sky; > On the eastern bank to their left they saw long formless slopes stretching up and away towards the sky; [*'toward'* > *'towards'*]

388 Slow, because they do not count > Slow, because they need not count [*'do not count'* > *'need not count'*] *

391 Of what tree growing in the elvish country > Of what tree growing in the Elvish country [*'elvish'* > *'Elvish'*]

393 Under their shadow Elessar, the Elfstone son of Arathorn of the House of Valandil Isildur's son, heir of Elendil, has nought to dread!' > Under their shadow Elessar, the Elfstone son of Arathorn of the House of Valandil Isildur's son, heir of Elendil, has naught to dread!' [*'nought'* > *'naught'*]

398 And I have seen it only for an instant in the House of Elrond. > And I have seen it only for an instant in the house of Elrond. [*'House'* > *'house'*]

401 Suddenly he was aware of himself again. Frodo, > Suddenly he was aware of himself again, Frodo, [*full stop after 'again' > comma*]

THE TWO TOWERS

BOOK III

416 'Sauron does not use the Elf-runes.' > 'Sauron does not use the elf-runes.' [*'Elf-runes'* > *'elf-runes'*]

His helm they set beside him, and across his lap they laid the cloven horn and the hilts > His helm they set beside him, and across his lap they laid the cloven horn and the hilt [*'hilts'* > *'hilt'*] *

424 He is smaller than the other. > He is smaller than the others. [*'other'* > *'others'*] *

427 Over the wide solitude they passed . . . ; even in the cool sunlight of mid-day few but elvish eyes > Over the wide solitude they passed . . . ; even in the cool sunlight of mid-day few but Elvish eyes [*'elvish'* > *'Elvish'*]

429 Only Legolas still stepped as lightly as ever . . . resting his mind in the strange paths of elvish dreams, > Only Legolas still stepped as lightly as ever . . . resting his mind in the strange paths of Elvish dreams, [*'elvish'* > *'Elvish'*]

432 Are you elvish folk?' > Are you Elvish folk?' [*'elvish'* > *'Elvish'*]

437 But scouts warned me of the orc-host coming down out of the East Wall three nights ago, > But scouts warned me of the orc-host coming down out of the East Wall four nights ago, [*'three nights'* > *'four nights'*] *

438 'We reached the forest-eaves before them, and if after that any living thing broke through our ring, then it was no Orc and had some elvish power.' > 'We reached the forest-eaves before them, and if after that any living thing broke through our ring, then it was no Orc and had some Elvish power.' [*'elvish'* > *'Elvish'*]

439 'I need them not,' he said . . . such was the elvish way > 'I need them not,' he said . . . such was the Elvish way [*'elvish'* > *'Elvish'*]

445–6 I heard that one of them has got something, something that's wanted for the War, some elvish plot > I heard that one of them has got something, something that's wanted for the War, some Elvish plot [*'elvish'* > *'Elvish'*]

465 That does not sound elvish to me. > That does not sound Elvish to me. [*'elvish'* > *'Elvish'*]

467 But it is a queer place, and not for just any one > But it is a queer place, and not for just anyone [*'any one'* > *'anyone'*]

493 An Elf, a Man, and a Dwarf, all clad in elvish fashion. > An Elf, a Man, and a Dwarf, all clad in Elvish fashion. [*'elvish'* > *'Elvish'*]

495 'I have seen an eagle high and far off: the last time was three days ago, > 'I have seen an eagle high and far off: the last time was four days ago, [*'three days'* > *'four days'*] *

499 I thought Fangorn was dangerous. > I thought Fangorn was dangerous.' [*added closing quotation mark*]

503 'Yes, if she had nought else > 'Yes, if she had naught else [*'nought'* > *'naught'*]

511 In this elvish sheath > In this Elvish sheath [*'elvish'* > *'Elvish'*]

521 'Faithful heart may have forward tongue.' > 'Faithful heart may have froward tongue.' [*'forward'* > *'froward'*] *

528 Still some miles away, on the far side of the Westfold Vale, lay a green coomb, a great bay in the mountains, out of which a gorge opened in the hills. > Still some miles away, on the far side of the Westfold Vale, a great bay in the mountains, lay a green coomb, out of which a gorge opened in the hills. [*reversed order of 'lay a green coomb' and 'a great bay in the mountains'*] *

534 Their great hinges and iron bars were wrenched and bent; many of their timbers were cracked. [*paragraph:*] 'Yet we cannot stay here > Their great hinges and iron bars were wrenched and bent; many of their timbers were cracked. 'The doors will not withstand another such battering.' [*paragraph:*] 'Yet we cannot stay here [*added sentence 'The doors will not withstand . . .' after 'cracked'*] *

545 In the midst of the field before the Hornburg two mounds were raised, and beneath them were laid all the Riders of the Mark who fell in the defence, those of the East Dales upon one side, and those of Westfold upon the other. In a grave alone > In the midst of the field before the Hornburg two mounds were raised, and beneath them were laid all the Riders of the Mark who fell in the defence, those of the East Dales upon one side, and those of

Westfold upon the other. But the men of Dunland were set apart in a mound below the Dike. In a grave alone [*added sentence 'But the men of Dunland . . .' after 'other'*] *

556 Meriadoc, son of Saradoc is my name; and my companion . . . is Peregrin, son of Paladin, of the house of Took. > Meriadoc, son of Saradoc is my name; and my companion . . . is Peregrin, son of Paladin, of the House of Took. [*'house' > 'House'*]

590 'You had the luck, Merry,' said Pippin softly, after a long pause. > 'You had the luck, Merry,' said Pippin softly, after a pause. [*'a long pause' > 'a pause'*]

That – glass ball, now. > That—glass ball, now. [*en dash > em dash, to better indicate pause*]

596 The horror of the stone > The horror of the Stone [*'stone' > 'Stone'*]

BOOK IV

609 Maybe you remember them putting the ropes in the boats, as we started off: in the elvish country > Maybe you remember them putting the ropes in the boats, as we started off: in the Elvish country [*'elvish' > 'Elvish'*]

611 And I put as fast a hitch over the stump as any one > And I put as fast a hitch over the stump as anyone [*'any one' > 'anyone'*]

622 Leaves out of the elf-country, > Leaves out of the Elf-country, [*'elf-country' > 'Elf-country'*]

648 By his reckoning it was nearly thirty leagues from the Morannon to the cross-roads > By his reckoning it was nearly thirty leagues from the Morannon to the Cross-roads [*'cross-roads' > 'Cross-roads'*]

655 But there's nought > But there's naught [*'nought' > 'naught'*]

659 To his amazement, as he listened Frodo became aware that it was the Elven-tongue > To his amazement, as he listened Frodo became aware that it was the elven-tongue [*'Elven-tongue' > 'elven-tongue'*]

668 Though,' and now he smiled, 'there is something strange about you, Frodo, an elvish air, > Though,' and now he smiled, 'there is something strange about you, Frodo, an Elvish air, [*'elvish' > 'Elvish'*]

678 Indeed it is said by our lore-masters . . . not from Hador the Goldenhaired, the Elf-friend, maybe, yet from such of his sons and people > Indeed it is said by our lore-masters . . . not from Hador the Goldenhaired, the Elf-friend, maybe, yet from such of his people [*'such of his sons and people' > 'such of his people'*] *

682 'Ah well, sir,' said Sam, 'you said my master had an elvish air; > 'Ah well, sir,' said Sam, 'you said my master had an Elvish air; [*'elvish'* > *'Elvish'*]

721 Sting flashed out, and the sharp elven-blade sparkled in the silver light, but at its edges a blue fire flicked. > Sting flashed out, and the sharp elven-blade sparkled in the silver light, but at its edges a blue fire flickered. [*'flicked'* > *'flickered'*] *

723 Run, run, and we'll be through – through before any one can stop us! > Run, run, and we'll be through – through before anyone can stop us! [*'any one'* > *'anyone'*]

733 And for a moment he lifted up the Phial . . . and in that light Frodo's face was fair of hue again, pale but beautiful with an elvish beauty, > And for a moment he lifted up the Phial . . . and in that light Frodo's face was fair of hue again, pale but beautiful with an Elvish beauty, [*'elvish'* > *'Elvish'*]

739–40 The big fellow with the sharp sword . . . just left him lying: regular elvish trick.' > The big fellow with the sharp sword . . . just left him lying: regular Elvish trick.' [*'elvish'* > *'Elvish'*]

742 'You're forgetting the great big elvish warrior > 'You're forgetting the great big Elvish warrior [*'elvish'* > *'Elvish'*]

THE RETURN OF THE KING

BOOK V

754 Monoliths of black marble, they rose to great capitals carved in many strange figures of beasts and leaves; and far above in shadow the wide vaulting gleamed with dull gold, inset with flowing traceries of many colours. > Monoliths of black marble, they rose to great capitals carved in many strange figures of beasts and leaves; and far above in shadow the wide vaulting gleamed with dull gold. The floor was of polished stone, white-gleaming, inset with flowing traceries. [*inserted 'The floor was of polished stone, white-gleaming,' after new full stop following 'gold'*] *

771 We might have journeyed to Lossarnach; . . . it is good to be there in Spring, > We might have journeyed to Lossarnach; . . . it is good to be there in spring, [*'Spring'* > *'spring'*]

775 *Either our hope cometh, or all hopes end.* > *Either our hope cometh, or all hope's end.* [*'hopes'* > *'hope's'*] *

786 The company halted, > The Company halted, [*'company'* > *'Company'*]

786–7 He could see nothing but the dim flame of the torches; but if the company halted > He could see nothing but the dim flame of the torches; but if the Company halted, [*'company'* > *'Company'*]

787 Nothing assailed the company > Nothing assailed the Company [*'company'* > *'Company'*]

The road was wide, as far as he could judge, but now the company > The road was wide, as far as he could judge, but now the Company [*'company'* > *'Company'*]

788 Light grew, and lo! the company > Light grew, and lo! the Company [*'company'* > *'Company'*]

830 The host was bivouacked in the pine-woods that clustered about Eilenach Beacon, a tall hill standing up from the long ridges of the Druadan Forest > The host was bivouacked in the pine-woods that clustered about Eilenach Beacon, a tall hill standing up from the long ridges of the Drúadan Forest [*'Druadan'* > *'Drúadan'*] *

831 They still haunt Druadan Forest, > They still haunt Druadan Forest, [*'Druadan'* > *'Drúadan'*]

835 The scouts have found naught to report beyond the grey wood, > The scouts have found naught to report beyond the Grey Wood, [*'grey wood'* > *'Grey Wood'*] *

853 Do I not know that you commanded this halfling here to keep silence? That you brought him hither to be a spy within my very chamber? > Do I not know that this halfling was commanded by thee to keep silence? That he was brought hither to be a spy within my very chamber? [*sentences changed to second form*] *

858 'This is a tunnel leading to a tomb; there we shall stay forever.' > 'This is a tunnel leading to a tomb; there we shall stay for ever.' [*'forever'* > *'for ever'*]

865 For the fragrance that came to each was like a memory of dewy mornings of unshadowed sun in some land of which the fair world in Spring > For the fragrance that came to each was like a memory of dewy mornings of unshadowed sun in some land of which the fair world in spring [*'Spring'* > *'spring'*]

870 Was there ever any one > Was there ever anyone [*'any one'* > *'anyone'*]

874 'For all those who come to know him come to love him after his own fashion, even the cold maiden of the Rohirrim. > 'For all those who come to know him come to love him after their own fashion, even the cold maiden of the Rohirrim. [*'his' > 'their'*]

883 Peregrin shall go and represent the Shirefolk; > Peregrin shall go and represent the Shire-folk; [*'Shirefolk' > 'Shire-folk'*]

888–9 It needs more to make a king than a piece of elvish glass, > It needs more to make a king than a piece of Elvish glass, [*'elvish' > 'Elvish'*]

BOOK VI

899 He listened; and as he did a gleam of hope > He listened; and as he did so a gleam of hope [*'he did' > 'he did so'*]

901 Well, all I can say is: things look as hopeless as a frost in spring. > Well, all I can say is: things look as hopeless as a frost in Spring. [*'spring' > 'Spring'*]

903 It was dimly lit with torches flaring in brackets on the walls but > It was dimly lit with torches flaring in brackets on the walls, but [*added comma after 'walls'*]

917 'Wake up, Samı' > 'Wake up, Sam!' [*numeral 1 after 'Sam' > exclamation mark*]

952 They were found on Sam when you were rescued; the Lady Galadriel's gifts: your glass, Frodo; and > They were found on Sam when you were rescued, the Lady Galadriel's gifts: your glass, Frodo, and [*semi-colons after 'rescued' and 'Frodo' > commas*] *

954 And he sang to them, now in the Elven-tongue, > And he sang to them, now in the elven-tongue, [*'Elven-tongue' > 'elven-tongue'*]

960 She did not answer, but . . . something in her softened, as though a bitter frost were yielding at the first presage of Spring. > She did not answer, but . . . something in her softened, as though a bitter frost were yielding at the first presage of spring. [*'Spring' > 'spring'*]

964 For you are a lady high and valiant and have yourself won renown that shall not be forgotten; and you are a lady beautiful, I deem, beyond even the words of the Elven-tongue > For you are a lady high and valiant and have yourself won renown that shall not be forgotten; and you are a lady beautiful, I deem, beyond even the words of the elven-tongue [*'Elven-tongue' > 'elven-tongue'*]

976 The Forest of Drúadan he gives to Ghân-buri-ghân > The Forest of Drúadan he gives to Ghân-buri-Ghân [*'Ghân-buri-ghân' > 'Ghân-buri-Ghân'*]

989 When they came to the Chetwood already the boughs were almost bare, and a great curtain of rain veiled Bree Hill > When they came to the Chetwood already the boughs were almost bare, and a great curtain of rain veiled Bree-hill [*'Bree Hill'* > *'Bree-hill'*] *

993 'There is room enough for realms between Isen and Greyflood, or along the shore-lands south of the Brandywine, without any one > 'There is room enough for realms between Isen and Greyflood, or along the shore-lands south of the Brandywine, without anyone [*'any one'* > *'anyone'*]

1000 The wind had dropped . . . but it was after all the first of November and the fag-end of Autumn. > The wind had dropped . . . but it was after all the first of November and the fag-end of autumn. [*'Autumn'* > *'autumn'*]

1005 Scaring Breeland peasants, > Scaring Bree-land peasants, [*'Breeland'* > *'Bree-land'*]

1008 I've been expecting you since the Spring. > I've been expecting you since the spring. [*'Spring'* > *'spring'*]

1014 'Well, you can't say fairer than that,' said the gaffer. > 'Well, you can't say fairer than that,' said the Gaffer. [*'gaffer'* > *'Gaffer'*]

'It takes a lot o' believing,' said the gaffer, > 'It takes a lot o' believing,' said the Gaffer, [*'gaffer'* > *'Gaffer'*]

1021 When the poor creature died next Spring > When the poor creature died next spring [*'Spring'* > *'spring'*]

1024 Sam Gamgee married Rose Cotton in the Spring > Sam Gamgee married Rose Cotton in the spring [*'Spring'* > *'spring'*]

1025 He resigned the office of Deputy Mayor at the Free Fair that mid-summer, > He resigned the office of Deputy Mayor at the Free Fair that Midsummer, [*'midsummer'* > *'Midsummer'*]

1026 Though as pretty a maidchild as any one > Though as pretty a maidchild as anyone [*'any one'* > *'anyone'*]

APPENDICES

1033 The Third Age was held to have ended . . . but for the purposes of records in Gondor F.A. I > The Third Age was held to have ended . . . but for the purposes of records in Gondor F.A. 1 [*capital 'I'* > *numeral '1'*]

1035 These are the names of the Kings and Queens of Númenor: . . . Tar-Calmacil. [*paragraph:*] After Calmacil the Kings took the sceptre in names of the Númenorean > These are the names of the Kings and Queens of Númenor: . . . Tar-Calmacil, Tar-Ardamin. [*paragraph:*] After Ardamin the Kings took the sceptre in names of the Númenórean [*'Tar-Calmacil.'* > *'Tar-Calmacil, Tar-Ardamin.'*, *'After Calmacil'* > *'After Ardamin'*, *'Númenorean'* > *'Númenórean'*] *

1038 *Kings of Gondor.* Elendil (Isildur and) > *Kings of Gondor.* Elendil, (Isildur and) [*added comma after 'Elendil'*]

Atanatar II . . . Calmacil 1304, Minalcar (regent 1240–1304), crowned as Rómendacil II 1304, died 1366, Valacar. > Calmacil 1304, Minalcar (regent 1240–1304), crowned as Rómendacil II 1304, died 1366, Valacar 1432. [*added '1432' after 'Valacar'*] *

1040 The Tower of Amon Sûl was burned and razed; but the *palantír* was saved and carried back in retreat to Fornost, Rhudaur was occupied > The Tower of Amon Sûl was burned and razed; but the *palantír* was saved and carried back in retreat to Fornost. Rhudaur was occupied [*comma after 'Fornost'* > *full stop*]

1041 It is said that the mounds of Tyrn Gorthad, as the Barrowdowns > It is said that the mounds of Tyrn Gorthad, as the Barrow-downs [*'Barrowdowns'* > *'Barrow-downs'*]

1043 It was at this time that a large band came so far west as to enter the Shire, and were driven off by Bandobras Took. > It was at this time that a large band came so far west as to enter the Shire, and were driven off by Bandobras Took.' [*added closing quotation mark*]

1045 The realm then extended north to Celebrant > The realm then extended north to the field of Celebrant [*'to Celebrant'* > *'to the field of Celebrant'*] *

1054 Long it stood, *Haudh in Gwanur,* > Long it stood, *Haudh in Gwanûr,* [*'Gwanur'* > *'Gwanûr'*]

1056–7 It did not seem possible to Faramir that any one in Gondor > It did not seem possible to Faramir that anyone in Gondor [*'any one'* > *'anyone'*]

1059 "'That will indeed be your fate," said Gilraen; but though she had in a measure the foresight of her people, she said no more to him of her foreboding, nor did she speak to any one > "'That will indeed be your fate," said Gilraen; but though she had in a measure the foresight of her people, she said no more to him of her foreboding, nor did she speak to anyone [*'any one'* > *'anyone'*]

1060 Then more than any kind of Men he appeared > Then more than any king of Men he appeared [*'kind'* > *'king'*] *

1061 But neither, lady, is the Twilight for me; for I a mortal, > But neither, lady, is the Twilight for me; for I am mortal, [*'I a mortal'* > *'I am mortal'*]

Onen i-Estel > *Ónen i-Estel* [*'Onen'* > *'Ónen'*] *

1064 A great host of wild men from the North-east swept over Rhovanion and coming down out of the Brown-lands > A great host of wild men from the North-east swept over Rhovanion and coming down out of the Brown Lands [*'Brown-lands'* > *'Brown Lands'*]

1065 It was upon Felaróf that Eorl rode to the Field of Celebrant; for that horse proved as long lived as Men, > It was upon Felaróf that Eorl rode to the Field of Celebrant; for that horse proved as long-lived as Men, [*'long lived'* > *'long-lived'*]

1066 The were in great force > They were in great force [*'The were'* > *'They were'*]

1072 It was not long before all that realm was destroyed, and the town of Dale near by > It was not long before all that realm was destroyed, and the town of Dale nearby [*'near by'* > *'nearby'*]

1073 Nár stayed near by > Nár stayed nearby [*'near by'* > *'nearby'*]

Then Nár turned the head and saw branded on the brow in Dwarf-runes > Then Nár turned the head and saw branded on the brow in dwarf-runes [*'Dwarf-runes'* > *'dwarf-runes'*]

1074 When all was ready they assailed and sacked one by one all the strongholds of the Orcs that they could from Gundabad > When all was ready they assailed and sacked one by one all the strongholds of the Orcs that they could find from Gundabad [*'they could from'* > *'they could find from'*]

1083 548 Birth in Númenor of Silmariën. > 521 Birth in Númenor of Silmariën. [*'548'* > *'521'*] *

2251 Tar-Atanamir takes the sceptre. > 2251 Death of Tar-Atanamir. Tar-Ancalimon takes the sceptre. * [*'Tar-Atanamir'* > *'Death of Tar-Atanamir. Tar-Ancalimon'*]

1085 Mithrandir was closest in friendship with the Eldar, and wandered mostly in the West and never > Mithrandir was closest in friendship with the Eldar, and wandered mostly in the West, and never [*added comma after 'West'*]

1090 2980 Aragorn enters Lórien . . . King of Rohan. [*paragraph:*] 2983 Faramir son of Denethor born. Birth of Samwise > 2980 Aragorn enters Lórien . . . King of Rohan. Birth of Samwise. [*paragraph:*]

2983 Faramir son of Denethor born [*'Birth of Samwise' moved to end of entry for 2980*] *

c. 3000 . . . Saruman dares to use the *palantír* of Orthanc, but becomes ensnared by Sauron, who has the Ithil Stone > *c.* 3000 . . . Saruman dares to use the *palantír* of Orthanc, but becomes ensnared by Sauron, who has the Ithil-stone [*'Ithil Stone' > 'Ithil-stone'*]

1091 *Mid-year's Day* Gandalf meets Radagast. [*entry added*] *

1093 10 [March] . . . Frodo passes the Cross Roads, > 10 . . . Frodo passes the Cross-roads, [*'Cross Roads' > 'Cross-roads'*]

12 [March] . . . Théoden camps under Minrimmon. > 12 . . . Théoden camps under Min-rimmon. [*'Minrimmon' > 'Min-rimmon' (in error; see below for 2005)*]

1094 19 [March] The Host comes to Morgul-vale. > 19 The Host comes to Morgul Vale. [*'Morgul-vale' > 'Morgul Vale'*]

1095 [July] 19. The funeral escort of King Théoden sets out. > 22. The funeral escort of King Théoden sets out. [*'19' > '22'*] *

[August] 14. The guests take leave of King Éomer. [*paragraph:*] 18. They come to Helm's Deep. > 14. The guests take leave of King Éomer. [*paragraph:*] 15. Treebeard releases Saruman. [*paragraph:*] 18. They come to Helm's Deep. [*added entry for 15 August*] *

1097 1455 Master Samwise becomes Mayor for the fifth time. At his request the Thain makes Fastred Warden of Westmarch. Fastred and Elanor make their dwelling at Undertowers on the Tower Hills, where their descendants, the Fairbairns of the Towers, dwelt for many generations. [*paragraph:*] 1462 Master Samwise becomes Mayor for the sixth time. > 1455 Master Samwise becomes Mayor for the fifth time. [*paragraph:*] 1462 Master Samwise becomes Mayor for the sixth time. At his request the Thain makes Fastred Warden of Westmarch. Fastred and Elanor make their dwelling at Undertowers on the Tower Hills, where their descendants, the Fairbairns of the Towers, dwelt for many generations. [*moved 'At his request . . . for many generations.' from 1455 to 1462*] *

1101–2 [*added Bolger and Boffin family trees, including Estella Bolger as sister to Fredegar*] *

1103 [*in Took family tree, '3 daughters' of Adelard > '2 daughters', line of descent drawn to them between 'Reginard' and 'Everard', Estella Bolger added as child of Rosamunda Took and Odovacar Bolger*]

1104 [*in Brandybuck family tree, Estella Bolger added as wife of Meriadoc Brandybuck*] *

1110 They were: *Narvinyë, Nénimë, . . . Cermië, Urimë,* > They were: *Narvinyë, Nénimë, . . . Cermië, Urimë,* [*'Urimë' > 'Úrimë'*]

1115 [*in sentence beginning 'In Sindarin long* e*', restored superscript '2' after 'correctly'*]

For this sound *y* has been used (as in ancient English): as in *lyg* > For this sound *y* has been used (as in ancient English): as in *lŷg* [*'lyg' > 'lŷg'*]

[*note 2:*] Those therefore who pronounce *yéni ûnótime* > Those therefore who pronounce *yéni únótime* [*'ûnótime' > 'únótime'*]

1116 [*note 2:*] But *iu* in Quenya was in the Third Age usually pronounced as a rising dipthong > But *iu* in Quenya was in the Third Age usually pronounced as a rising diphthong [*'dipthong' > 'diphthong'*]

1118 This script was not in origin an 'alphabet', that is, > This script was not in origin an 'alphabet': that is, [*comma after "'alphabet'" > colon*]

1120 They were not needed in the languages of the Third Age . . . distinguished from Grade l) > They were not needed in the languages of the Third Age . . . distinguished from Grade 1) [*'Grade l', i.e. with lower case el > 'Grade 1', i.e. with numeral one*]

[*note 1:*] The representation of the sounds . . . heard in *azure* and *occasion.* > The representation of the sounds . . . heard in *azure* and *occasion*; *ŋ* is used for *ng* in *sing.* [*'occasion.' > 'occasion; ŋ is used for ng in sing.'*)

1123 [*added section number '(ii)' before subheading 'THE CIRTH'*]

1126 The consequent use of 12 for *r*, . . . and the consequent use of 36 as *η* > The consequent use of 12 for *r*, . . . and the consequent use of 36 as *ŋ* [*Greek character eta > International Phonetic Alphabet character eng (ŋ)]*

1127 Of the latter kind were most of the elven-folk > Of the latter kind were most of the Elven-folk [*'elven-folk' > 'Elven-folk'*]

1129 They used therefore the Common Speech in their dealing with other folk and in the government of their wide realms; they enlarged the language and enriched it with many words drawn from Elven-tongues. > They used therefore the Common Speech in their dealing with other folk and in the government of their wide realms; they enlarged the language and enriched it with many words drawn from elven-tongues. [*'Elven-tongues' > 'elven-tongues'*]

In the days of the Númenorean kings this ennobled Westron speech spread far and wide, even among their enemies; and it became used more and more by the Dúnedain themselves, so that at the time of The War of the Ring the Elven-tongue > In the days of the Númenórean kings this ennobled Westron speech spread far and wide, even among their enemies; and it became used more and more by the Dúnedain themselves, so that at the time of The War of the Ring the elven-tongue [*'Elven-tongue' > 'elven-tongue'*]

1133 Their own secret and 'inner' names, their true names, the Dwarves have never revealed to any one > Their own secret and 'inner' names, their true names, the Dwarves have never revealed to anyone [*'any one' > 'anyone'*]

1134 Some differed in meaning: as Mount Doom for *Orodruin* 'burning mountain', or Mirkwood for *Taur e-Ndaedelos* 'forest of great fear'. > Some differed in meaning: as Mount Doom for *Orodruin* 'burning mountain', or Mirkwood for *Taur e-Ndaedelos* 'forest of the great fear'. [*'of great fear' > 'of the great fear'*]

1137 They were tall, fair of skin and grey-eyed, though their locks were dark, save in the golden house of Finarfin; > They were tall, fair of skin and grey-eyed, though their locks were dark, save in the golden house of Finarfin[1]; [*added superscript reference number after 'Finarfin'; added editors' footnote on this page:*]

[1] [These words describing characters of face and hair in fact applied only to the Noldor: see *The Book of Lost Tales, Part One*, p. 44.] *

2005 EDITION

THE FELLOWSHIP OF THE RING

PROLOGUE

9 Outside the Farthings were the East and West Marches: the Buckland (p. 97); and the Westmarch added to the Shire in S.R. 1462. > Outside the Farthings were the East and West Marches: the Buckland (p. 98); and the Westmarch added to the Shire in S.R. 1452. [*'(p. 97)' > '(p. 98)', '1462' > '1452'*] *

BOOK I

45 'Well I don't know,' said Sam thoughtfully. > 'Well, I don't know,' said Sam thoughtfully. [*restored comma after 'Well'*]

50 [*restored the drawing of the Ring inscription that Tolkien approved*] *

212 The hobbits ran down the slope, Glorfindel and Strider followed as rear-guard. > The hobbits ran down the slope, Glorfindel and Strider followed as rearguard. [*'rear-guard' > 'rearguard'*]

BOOK II

243 I was at the Battle of Dagorlad before the Black Gate of Mordor, where we had the mastery: for the Spear of Gil-galad and the Sword of Elendil, Aiglos and Narsil, > I was at the Battle of Dagorlad before the Black Gate of Mordor, where we had the mastery: for the Spear of Gil-galad and the Sword of Elendil, Aeglos and Narsil, [*'Aiglos'* > *'Aeglos'*] *

334 He bowed, and turned away, and hastened back up the green-sward > He bowed, and turned away, and hastened back up the greensward [*'green-sward'* > *'greensward'*]

361 No fireworks like poor Gandalf > No fireworks like poor old Gandalf [*'poor Gandalf'* > *'poor old Gandalf'*]

388 'I think – No, I will not say', > 'I think–No, I will not say', [*en dash > em dash, to better indicate pause*]

THE TWO TOWERS

BOOK III

544 There the Lord of the Mark would hold an assembly of all that could bear arms, on the second day after the full moon. > There the Lord of the Mark would hold an assembly of all that could bear arms, on the third day after the full moon. [*'second day'* > *'third day'*] *

600 And in two days thence > And in three days thence [*'two days'* > *'three days'*] *

BOOK IV

608 Never mind your Gaffer! > Never mind your gaffer! [*'Gaffer'* > *'gaffer'*]

611 'If you can think of any way we could have both used the rope and yet brought it down with us, then you can pass on to me ninny-hammer, or any other name your Gaffer gave you,' > 'If you can think of any way we could have both used the rope and yet brought it down with us, then you can pass on to me ninnyhammer, or any other name your gaffer gave you,' [*'Gaffer'* > *'gaffer'*]

624 'Don't think of any of your Gaffer's hard names,' > 'Don't think of any of your gaffer's hard names,' [*'Gaffer'* > *'gaffer'*]

700 'Maybe,' said Sam; 'but *where there's life there's hope*, as my Gaffer used to say; > 'Maybe,' said Sam; 'but *where there's life there's hope*, as my gaffer used to say; [*'Gaffer'* > *'gaffer'*]

THE RETURN OF THE KING

BOOK V

765 For I saw the beacons last night and the errand-riders; > For I saw the beacons two nights ago and the errand-riders; [*'last night'* > *'two nights ago'*] *

But why were the beacons lit last night? > But why were the beacons lit two nights ago? [*'last night'* > *'two nights ago'*] *

But if you would know what I think set the beacons ablaze, it was the news that came yestereve out of Lebennin. > But if you would know what I think set the beacons ablaze, it was the news that came that eve out of Lebennin. [*'yestereve'* > *'that eve'*] *

778 The Moon will then be one night past his full, > The Moon will then be two nights past his full [*'one night'* > *'two nights'*] *

792 Last night the moon was full, > Two nights ago the moon was full, [*'Last night'* > *'Two nights ago'*] *

BOOK VI

952 'The fourteenth of the New Year,' said Gandalf; 'or if you like, the eighth day of April in the Shire reckoning. > 'The fourteenth of the New Year,' said Gandalf; 'or if you like, the eighth day of April in the Shire-reckoning. [*'Shire reckoning'* > *'Shire-reckoning'*]

959 Tall she stood there, her eyes bright in her white face, her hand clenched > Tall she stood there, her eyes bright in her white face, her right hand clenched [*'her hand'* > *'her right hand'*] *

APPENDICES

1035 These are the names of the Kings and Queens of Númenor: > *These are the names of the Kings and Queens of Númenor:* [*italicized introductory phrase*]

1039 The wild kine > The wild white kine [*'kine'* > *'white kine'*]

1040 A remnant of the faithful . . . also held out in Tyrn Gorthas (the Barrowdowns) > A remnant of the faithful . . . also held out in Tyrn Gorthas (the Barrow-downs) [*'Barrowdowns'* > *'Barrow-downs'*]

1068 2594–2680 5. *Frëawine* > 2594–2680 5. *Fréawine* [*'Frëawine'* > *'Fréawine'*]

1072 At last Dáin I . . . was slain at the door of his hall > At last Dáin I . . . was slain at the doors of his hall [*'door'* > *'doors'*]

1088 [*date entry:*] 2852 > 2872 *

1091 Gandalf meets Radagast > Gandalf meets Radagast. [*added full stop after 'Radagast'*]

1092 [*entry for 14 February:*] 14 > 15 *

1093 Théoden camps under Min-rimmon. > Théoden camps under Min-Rimmon. [*'Min-rimmon'* > *'Min-Rimmon'*]

1095 Éomer and Éowyn depart from Rohan > Éomer and Éowyn depart for Rohan [*'from Rohan'* > *'for Rohan'*]

1101 [*Bolger family tree:*] Aldadrida > Adaldrida

Poppy Chubb Baggins > Poppy Chubb-Baggins [*'Chubb Baggins'* > *'Chubb-Baggins'*]

1102 [*Boffin family tree:*] Otto S-Baggins > Otho S-Baggins [*'Otto'* > *'Otho'*]

1107 In the west-lands of Eriador, . . . they adopted the King's reckoning > In the west-lands of Eriador, . . . they adopted the Kings' Reckoning [*'King's reckoning'* > *'Kings' Reckoning'*]

1108 The Númenórean system . . . was called King's Reckoning. > The Númenórean system . . . was called Kings' Reckoning. [*'King's Reckoning'* > *'Kings' Reckoning'*]

1109 The months were all of 30 days . . . 1 between the third and four months > The months were all of 30 days . . . 1 between the third and fourth months [*'four months'* > *'fourth months'*]

1111 In these the weekday names appear . . . (7) *Highdei.* > In these the weekday names appear . . . (7) *Hihdei.* [*'Highdei'* > *'Hihdei'*] *

1113 It is usually related to *d*, as in S. *galadh* 'tree' compared with Q. *alda*; but is sometimes derived from *n r*, > It is usually related to *d*, as in S. *galadh* 'tree' compared with Q. *alda*; but is sometimes derived from *n+r*, [*'n r'* > *'n+r'*]

1114 It was derived mainly from *c* or *t y*. > It was derived mainly from *c* or *t+y*. [*'t y'* > *'t+y'*]

1115 [*note 1:*] *Remmirath* (p. 81) contains *rem* 'mesh', Q. *rembe*, *mîr* 'jewel'. > *Remmirath* (p. 81) contains *rem* 'mesh', Q. *rembe*, + *mîr* 'jewel'. [*'rembe, mîr'* > *'rembe, + mîr'*]

[*Note 2:*] Frodo said to have shown > Frodo is said to have shown [*'Frodo said' > 'Frodo is said'*]

1116 In the following examples the stressed vowel is marked by a capital letter: *isIldur, Orome, erEssëa, fanor, ancAlima, elentri,* > In the following examples the stressed vowel is marked by a capital letter: *isIldur, Orome, erEssëa, fËanor, ancAlima, elenÁtri,* [*'fanor' > 'fËanor', 'elentri' > 'elentÁri'*]

Words of the type *elentri* . . . they are commoner with the vowels *í, ú,* as *andne* > Words of the type *elentÁri* . . . they are commoner with the vowels *í, ú,* as *andÚne* [*'elentri' > 'elentÁri', 'andne' > 'andÚne'*]

1120 These usually represented aspirated consonants (e.g. *th, ph, kh*), > These usually represented aspirated consonants (e.g. *t+h, p+h, k+h*), [*'th, ph, kh' > 't+h, p+h, k+h'*]

1121 (For *lv*, not for *lw*, many speakers, especially Elves, used *lb*: this was written with 276, since *lmb* could not occur.) > (For *lv*, not for *lw*, many speakers, especially Elves, used *lb*: this was written with 27+6, since *lmb* could not occur.) [*'276' > '27+6'*]

1122 The sign for following *w* . . . was in this mode the *u*-curl or a modification of it . > The sign for following *w* . . . was in this mode the *u*-curl or a modification of it ~. [*restored missing tilde*]

1122–3 The names of the letters in the table were . . . *silme* light, > The names of the letters in the table were . . . *silme* starlight, [*'light' > 'starlight'*]

1123 The names of the letters most widely known and used were 17 *n*, 33 *hy*, 25 *r*, 9 *f*: > The names of the letters most widely known and used were 17 *n*, 33 *hy*, 25 *r*, 10 *f*: [*'9 f' > '10 f'*]

1131 Orc is the form of the name > *Orc* is the form of the name [*italicized 'Orc'*]

1134 But some were derived, as already noted, from old hobbit-words no longer in use, and these have been represent by similar English things, > But some were derived, as already noted, from old hobbit-words no longer in use, and these have been represented by similar English things, [*'represent' > 'represented'*]

Minor corrections were made also to the synopses preceding *The Two Towers* and *The Return of the King*.

ADDENDA

A few additional textual errors came to our attention too late for correction in the 2005 hardback edition, but have been noted by the publisher for the 2005 paperback and future printings: p. 977, l. 19, for 'Fréalaf' read 'Fréaláf'; p. 1136, l. 7, for '*hámfœst*' (with an oe digraph) read '*hámfæst*' (with an ae digraph); and p. 1137, l. 29, for 'butterflies to the falcon' read 'butterflies to the swift falcon'.

WORKS CONSULTED

WORKS BY J.R.R. TOLKIEN

(In general, the citation is to the first edition of the work)

Adventures in Unnatural History and Medieval Metres, being the Freaks of Fisiologus: (i) Fastitocalon, (ii) Iumbo, or ye Kinde of ye Oliphaunt. Stapledon Magazine 7, no. 40 (June 1927), pp. 123–7.

The Adventures of Tom Bombadil. Oxford Magazine, 15 February 1934, pp. 464–5.

The Adventures of Tom Bombadil and Other Verses from the Red Book. London: George Allen & Unwin, 1962.

The Annotated Hobbit. Annotated by Douglas A. Anderson. Rev. and expanded edn. Boston: Houghton Mifflin, 2002.

The Book of Lost Tales, Part One. Ed. by Christopher Tolkien. London: George Allen & Unwin, 1983. Vol. I of *The History of Middle-earth.*

The Book of Lost Tales, Part Two. Ed. by Christopher Tolkien. London: George Allen & Unwin, 1984. Vol. II of *The History of Middle-earth.*

Farmer Giles of Ham. Ed. by Christina Scull and Wayne G. Hammond. London: HarperCollins, 1999.

Finn and Hengest: The Fragment and the Episode. Ed. by Alan Bliss. London: George Allen & Unwin, 1982.

'From *The Shibboleth of Fëanor*'. *Vinyar Tengwar* 41 (July 2000), pp. 7–10.

The Homecoming of Beorhtnoth Beorhthelm's Son. Essays and Studies 1953. Ed. by Geoffrey Bullough. London: John Murray, 1953. Pp. 1–18.

Iumonna Gold Galdre Bewunden. Oxford Magazine, 4 March 1937, p. 473. An earlier version was published in *The Gryphon*, January 1923. The poem was revised as *The Hoard* in *The Adventures of Tom Bombadil and Other Verses from the Red Book* (1962).

The J.R.R. Tolkien Audio Collection. New York: Caedmon, 2001. 4 compact discs. Tolkien's recordings of extracts from *The Lord of the Rings* were previously released (1975) on LP and cassette tape as *J.R.R. Tolkien Reads and Sings His The Hobbit and The Fellowship of the Ring* and *J.R.R. Tolkien Reads and Sings His Lord of the Rings: The Two Towers/The Return of the King*, augmented in the compact disc issue.

J.R.R. Tolkien's Letters to Rhona Beare. St. Louis, Mo.: New England Tolkien Society, 1985.

The Lays of Beleriand. Ed. by Christopher Tolkien. London: George Allen & Unwin, 1985. Vol. III of *The History of Middle-earth.*

The Letters of J.R.R. Tolkien. Sel. and ed. by Humphrey Carpenter, with the assistance of Christopher Tolkien. London: George Allen & Unwin, 1981.

'Lettre à Milton Waldman: L'horizon de la Terre du Milieu'. *Conférence* 12 (Printemps 2001), pp. 707–56. The complete letter to Waldman, ?late 1951, translated with commentary by Michaël Devaux. Also published in *Tolkien: Les racines du légendaire* (*La Feuille de la Compagnie Cahier d'études tolkieniennes* 2), Genève: Ad Solem, autumne 2003, pp. 19–81, again with notes by Devaux, and, in English, the previously unpublished portion concerning *The Lord of the Rings*.

The Lord of the Rings. Various editions consulted, including: London: George Allen & Unwin, 1954–5; 2nd edn., New York: Ballantine Books, 1965; 2nd Allen & Unwin edition, 1966 and 1967 printings; Boston: Houghton Mifflin, 1987; London: HarperCollins, 1994 (dated '1991'); London: HarperCollins, 2002 (illustrated by Alan Lee); London: HarperCollins, 2004 (also Boston: Houghton Mifflin, 2004).

The Lost Road and Other Writings: Language and Legend before The Lord of the Rings. Ed. by Christopher Tolkien. London: Unwin Hyman, 1987. Vol. V of *The History of Middle-earth*.

The Monsters and the Critics and Other Essays. Ed. by Christopher Tolkien. London: George Allen & Unwin, 1983.

Morgoth's Ring: The Later Silmarillion, Part One. Ed. by Christopher Tolkien. London: HarperCollins, 1993. Vol. X of *The History of Middle-earth*.

Ósanwe-kenta ('Enquiry into the Communication of Thought'). Ed. with introduction, glossary, and additional notes by Carl F. Hostetter. *Vinyar Tengwar* 39 (July 1998), pp. 21–34.

The Peoples of Middle-earth. Ed. by Christopher Tolkien. London: HarperCollins, 1996. Vol. XII of *The History of Middle-earth*.

Pictures by J.R.R. Tolkien. Foreword and notes by Christopher Tolkien. London: George Allen & Unwin, 1979.

Qenyaqetsa: The Qenya Phonology and Lexicon, together with the Poetic and Mythologic Words of Eldarissa. Ed. by Christopher Gilson, Carl F. Hostetter, Patrick Wynne, and Arden R. Smith. Published as *Parma Eldalamberon* 12 (1998).

The Return of the Shadow: The History of The Lord of the Rings, Part One. Ed. by Christopher Tolkien. London: Unwin Hyman, 1988. Vol. VI of *The History of Middle-earth*.

The Rivers and Beacon-hills of Gondor. Excerpts from this work appeared in *Unfinished Tales* (see below). The remainder of the text was published in *Vinyar Tengwar* 42 (July 2001), pp. 5–34, ed. by Carl F. Hostetter with his notes on philological matters, and with additional commentary by Christopher Tolkien.

The Road Goes Ever On: A Song Cycle. Poems by J.R.R. Tolkien, music by Donald Swann. Boston: Houghton Mifflin, 1967.

Roverandom. Ed. by Christina Scull and Wayne G. Hammond. London: HarperCollins, 1998.

Sauron Defeated: The End of the Third Age (The History of The Lord of the Rings, Part Four), The Notion Club Papers, and The Drowning of Anadûnê. Ed. by Christopher Tolkien. London: HarperCollins, 1992. Vol. IX of *The History of Middle-earth*.

The Shaping of Middle-earth: The Quenta, the Ambarkanta, and the Annals. Ed. by Christopher Tolkien. London: George Allen & Unwin, 1986. Vol. IV of *The History of Middle-earth*.

The Silmarillion. Ed. by Christopher Tolkien. London: George Allen & Unwin, 1977.

Sir Gawain and the Green Knight. Ed. by J.R.R. Tolkien and E.V. Gordon. Oxford: Clarendon Press, 1925.

Sir Gawain and the Green Knight, Pearl, and Sir Orfeo. Trans. by J.R.R. Tolkien. London: George Allen & Unwin, 1975.

Tolkien and Basil Bunting. London: BBC Cassettes, 1980. Includes 1964 interview of Tolkien by Denys Gueroult. Additional audio material is held in the National Sound Archive, British Library.

The Treason of Isengard: The History of The Lord of the Rings, Part Two. Ed. by Christopher Tolkien. London: Unwin Hyman, 1989. Vol. VII of *The History of Middle-earth*.

Tree and Leaf. London: Unwin Hyman, 1988. Includes the lecture *On Fairy-Stories*.

'[Two] Letters by J.R.R. Tolkien'. *Mallorn* 36 (November 1998), pp. 31–4.

Unfinished Tales of Númenor and Middle-earth. Ed. by Christopher Tolkien. London: George Allen & Unwin, 1980.

The War of the Jewels: The Later Silmarillion, Part Two: The Legends of Beleriand. Ed. by Christopher Tolkien. London: HarperCollins, 1994. Vol. XI of *The History of Middle-earth*.

The War of the Ring: The History of The Lord of the Rings, Part Three. London: Unwin Hyman, 1990. Vol. VIII of *The History of Middle-earth*.

WORKS BY OTHER AUTHORS

Abbott, Joe. 'Tolkien's Monsters: Concept and Function in *The Lord of the Rings*: (Part I) The Balrog of Khazad-dûm'. *Mythlore* 16, no. 1, whole no. 59 (Autumn 1989), pp. 19–26, 33.

Allan, Jim, ed. *An Introduction to Elvish*. Hayes, Middlesex: Bran's Head Books, 1978.

The Anglo-Saxon Chronicles. Trans. and ed. by Michael Swanton. London: Phoenix Press, 2000.

Armstrong, Helen. Letter to the Editor. *Amon Hen* 111 (August 1991), p. 17.

—— 'There Are Two People in This Marriage'. *Mallorn* 36 (November 1998), pp. 5–12.

Auden, W.H. 'At the End of the Quest, Victory' (review of *The Return of the King*). *New York Times Book Review*, 22 January 1956, p. 5.

Barnfield, Marie. 'The Roots of Rivendell'. *Þe Lyfe ant þe Auncestrye* 3 (Spring 1996), pp. 4–18.

Bartlett, Robert. *England under the Norman and Angevin Kings, 1075–1225*. Oxford: Clarendon Press, 2000.

The Battle of Maldon. Ed. by E.V. Gordon. London: Methuen, 1937.

Baynes, Pauline. *A Map of Middle-earth*. London: George Allen & Unwin, 1970.

Beach, Sarah. 'Specific Derivation'. *Mythlore* 12, no. 4, whole no. 46 (Summer 1986), pp. 16, 36.

Beare, Rhona. 'Tolkien's Calendar & Ithildin'. *Mythlore* 9, no. 4, whole no. 34 (Winter 1982), pp. 23–4.

Beowulf and the Finnesburg Fragment. Trans. by John R. Clark Hall. Prefatory remarks by J.R.R. Tolkien. London: George Allen & Unwin, 1940.

Beowulf with the Finnesburg Fragment. Ed. by C.L. Wrenn. New edn., rev. by W.F. Bolton. London: Harrap, 1973.

The Bestiary: A Book of Beasts. Trans. by T.H. White. New York: Capricorn Books, 1960.

Blackburn, Bonnie, and Leofranc Holford-Strevens. *The Oxford Companion to the Year*. Oxford: Oxford University Press, 1999.

Blackwelder, Richard E. 'Reflections on Literary Criticism and Middle-earth'. Unpublished paper, presented at the Marquette University Tolkien Conference, 1983.

Boenig, Robert. 'The Drums of Doom: H.G. Wells' *First Men in the Moon* and *The Lord of the Rings*'. *Mythlore* 14, no. 3, whole no. 52 (Spring 1988), pp. 57–8.

Bosworth, Joseph. *An Anglo-Saxon Dictionary Based on the Manuscript Collections of the Late Joseph Bosworth*. Ed. and enlarged by T. Northcote Toller. Oxford: Clarendon Press, 1898.

Brace, Keith. 'In the Footsteps of the Hobbits'. *Birmingham Post Midland Magazine*, 25 May 1968.

Bradfield, J.C. *A Dictionary of Quenya*. 2nd edn. Cambridge: J.C. Bradfield, 1983.

Bratman, David. 'A Corrigenda to *The Lord of the Rings*'. *Tolkien Collector* 6, March 1994, pp. 17–25.

Brewer, Derek S. '*The Lord of the Rings* as Romance'. *J.R.R. Tolkien, Scholar and Storyteller*. Ed. by Mary Salu and Robert T. Farrell. Ithaca, N.Y.: Cornell University Press, 1979. Pp. 249–64.

Brewer's Dictionary of Phrase and Fable. 15th edn. Rev. by Adrian Room. London: HarperCollins, 1995.

Briggs, Katharine. *An Encyclopedia of Fairies: Hobgoblins, Brownies, Bogies, and Other Supernatural Creatures*. New York: Pantheon Books, 1976. First published as *A Dictionary of Fairies*.

—— *The Folklore of the Cotswolds*. Totowa, N.J.: Rowman and Littlefield, 1974.

Brogan, Hugh. 'Tolkien's Great War'. *Children and Their Books: A Celebration of the Work of Iona and Peter Opie*. Ed. by Gillian Avery and Julia Briggs. Oxford: Clarendon Press, 1989. Pp. 351–67.

Brown, Malcolm. *The Imperial War Museum Book of the Somme*. London: Pan Books, 2002.

Burns, Marjorie. 'Gandalf and Odin'. *Tolkien's* Legendarium*: Essays on* The History of Middle-earth. Ed. by Verlyn Flieger and Carl F. Hostetter. Westport, Conn.: Greenwood, 2000. Pp. 219–31.

—— *Perilous Realms: Celtic and Norse in Tolkien's Middle-earth*. Toronto: University of Toronto Press, 2005.

Burt, William Henry. *A Field Guide to the Mammals*. Boston: Houghton Mifflin, 1952.

Caldecott, Stratford. *Secret Fire: The Spiritual Vision of J.R.R. Tolkien*. London: Darton, Longman & Todd, 2003.

Campanella, Tommaso. *The City of the Sun*. Uncredited translation of *Civitas Solis* at http://www.gutenberg.org/dirs/etext01/tcots10.txt.

Carpenter, Humphrey. *J.R.R. Tolkien: A Biography*. London: George Allen & Unwin, 1977.

Castell, Daphne. 'The Realms of Tolkien'. *New Worlds* 50 (November 1966), pp. 143–54.

Chaij, Kenneth. *Sindarin Lexicon*. Ed. by Richard Crawshaw. Telford: Tolkien Society, 2001.

Churchill, Winston S. *The Gathering Storm*. Boston: Houghton Mifflin, 1948.

Clark, Stuart, and Rosie Clark. 'Oxonmoot '74 Report'. *Amon Hen* 13 (October 1974), pp. 6–13.

Cleasby, Richard. *An Icelandic-English Dictionary*. Rev., enlarged, and completed by Gudbrand Vigfusson. 2nd edn., with a supplement by Sir William A. Craigie. Oxford: Clarendon Press, 1957.

Cofield, David. 'The Hands of a King'. *Beyond Bree*, September 1986, pp. 2–3.

—— 'Harbinger of Fate: The Eclipse of 3019'. *Beyond Bree*, October 1993, pp. 3–4.

—— 'The Size of the Shire: A Problem in Cartography'. *Beyond Bree*, July 1994, pp. 4–5.

Collingwood, R.G., and J.N.L. Myres. *Roman Britain and the English Settlements*. 2nd edn. Oxford: Clarendon Press, 1937 (1968 printing).

Collins, Denis. Letter to the Editor. *Amon Hen* 123 (September 1993), p. 14.

The Concise Oxford English Dictionary. 10th edn., rev. Ed. by Judy Pearsall. Oxford: Oxford University Press, 2002.

Crabbe, Katharyn W. *J.R.R. Tolkien*. Rev. and expanded edn. New York: Continuum, 1988.

Cremona, David. Letter to the Editor. *Beyond Bree*, June 1991, p. 10.

Davidson, Hilda Ellis. 'Archaeology and *Beowulf*'. *Beowulf and Its Analogues*. Trans. by G.N. Garmonsway and Jacqueline Simpson. London: J.M. Dent & Sons, 1980.

—— (as Hilda Roderick Ellis). *The Road to Hel: A Study of the Conception of the Dead in Old Norse Literature*. Cambridge: Cambridge University Press, 1943.

—— *The Sword in Anglo-Saxon England: Its Archaeology and Literature*. Woodbridge, Suffolk: Boydell Press, 1962 (corrected 1994 printing).

Dickerson, Matthew T. *Following Gandalf: Epic Battles and Moral Victories in* The Lord of the Rings. Grand Rapids, Mich.: Brazos Press, 2003.

Donaldson, E. Talbot. 'The Middle Ages'. *The Norton Anthology of English Literature*, vol. I. Rev. edn. New York: W.W. Norton, 1968.

Doughan, David, and Julian Bradfield. *An Introduction to the Writing Systems of Middle-earth*. *Quettar* Special Publication no. 1. London: Tolkien Society, 1987.

Drout, Michael D.C. 'Tolkien's Prose Style and Its Literary and Rhetorical Effects'. *Tolkien Studies* 1. Morgantown: West Virginia University Press, 2004. Pp. 137–62.

Ead, James. Letter to the Editor. *Mallorn* 3 (1971), p. 23.

Ekwall, Eilert. *The Concise Oxford Dictionary of English Place-names*. 4th edn. Oxford: Clarendon Press, 1960.

—— *English River-names*. Oxford: Clarendon Press, 1928.

The Elder Edda: A Selection. Trans. by Paul B. Taylor and W.H. Auden. London: Faber and Faber, 1973. First published 1969.

Elliott, Ralph W.V. *Runes: An Introduction*. Manchester: Manchester University Press, 1959.

Emery, Walter B. *Archaic Egypt*. Harmondsworth, Middlesex: Penguin Books, 1961.

Encyclopædia Britannica. 14th edn. New York: Encyclopædia Britannica, 1938.

'The Epic of Westernesse' (review of *The Two Towers*). *Times Literary Supplement*, 17 December 1954, p. 817.

Evans, H. Meurig, and Thomas, W.O. *Y Geiriadur Mawr: The Complete Welsh–English English–Welsh Dictionary*. Llandysul: Gwasg Gomer, 1995.

Ezard, John. 'The Hobbit Man'. *Oxford Mail*, 3 August 1966, p. 4.

Falconer, Joan O. Letter to the Editor. *Mythprint* 8, no. 3 (September 1973), p. 3.

Fettes, Christopher. Letter to the Editor. *Amon Hen* 173 (January 2002), pp. 31–2.

Field Guide to the Trees and Shrubs of Britain. London: Reader's Digest, 1981.

Flieger, Verlyn. 'In the Footsteps of Ælfwine'. *Tolkien's* Legendarium*: Essays on* The History of Middle-earth. Ed. by Verlyn Flieger and Carl F. Hostetter. Westport, Conn.: Greenwood, 2000. Pp. 183–98.

—— *A Question of Time: J.R.R. Tolkien's Road to Faërie*. Kent, Ohio: Kent State University Press, 1997.

—— *Splintered Light: Logos and Language in Tolkien's World*. Rev. edn. Kent, Ohio: Kent State University Press, 2002.

—— 'Taking the Part of Trees: Eco-Conflict in Middle-earth'. *J.R.R. Tolkien and His Literary Resonances: Views of Middle-earth*. Ed. by George Clark and Daniel Timmons. Westport, Conn.: Greenwood Press, 2000. Pp. 147–58.

Flood, Robert H. 'Hobbit Hoax?' *Books on Trial*, February 1955, pp. 169–70.

Fonstad, Karen Wynn. *The Atlas of Middle-earth*. Rev. edn. Boston: Houghton Mifflin, 1991.

Foster, Robert. *The Complete Guide to Middle-earth: From* The Hobbit *to* The Silmarillion. London: HarperCollins, 2003.

—— Letter to the Editor. *Tolkien Journal* 3, no. 2 (1967), pp. 19–20.

Frazer, James George. *The Golden Bough: A Study in Magic and Religion*. Abridged edn. New York: Collier Books, 1985.

Frisby, Steven M. 'Identifying First Edition Printings of the Houghton Mifflin *Lord of the Rings*'. *Tolkien Collector* 20 (July 1999), 21 (September 1999), 22 (January 2000), pp. 25–34, 20–7, 22–30 respectively.

Fuller, Edmund. 'The Lord of the Hobbits: J.R.R. Tolkien'. Originally published in *Books with Men behind Them* (1962), reprinted in *Tolkien and the Critics: Essays on J.R.R. Tolkien's The Lord of the Rings*. Ed. by Neil D. Isaacs and Rose A. Zimbardo. Notre Dame, Indiana: University of Notre Dame Press, 1968. Pp. 17–39.

Fussell, Paul. *The Great War and Modern Memory*. New York: Oxford University Press, 1977. First published 1975.

Garth, John. 'Frodo and the Great War'. Forthcoming in the proceedings of the October 2004 Marquette University Tolkien conference.

—— *Tolkien and the Great War: The Threshold of Middle-earth*. London: HarperCollins, 2003.

Gay, David Elton. 'J.R.R. Tolkien and the *Kalevala*: Some Thoughts on the Finnish Origins of Tom Bombadil and Treebeard'. *Tolkien and the Invention of Myth: A Reader*. Ed. by Jane Chance. Lexington: University Press of Kentucky, 2004. Pp. 295–304.

Gelling, Margaret. *The Place-names of Oxfordshire*. Based on material collected by Doris Mary Stenton. Cambridge: Cambridge University Press, 1953–4.

Getty, Naomi. 'Stargazing in Middle-earth: Stars and Constellations in the Work of Tolkien'. *Beyond Bree*, April 1984, pp. 1–3.

Gould, Chester Nathan. 'Dwarf-names: A Study in Old Icelandic Religion'. *PMLA* 44, no. 4 (December 1929), pp. 939–67.

Grahame, Kenneth. *The Wind in the Willows*. London: Methuen, 1959. First published 1908.

Graves, Robert. *The Greek Myths*. Rev. edn. Harmondsworth, Middlesex: Penguin Books, 1960. 2 vols.

Green, Peter. 'Outward Bound by Air to an Inappropriate Ending' (review of *The Fellowship of the Ring*). *Daily Telegraph* (London), 27 August 1954, p. 8.

Green, William Howard. The Hobbit *and Other Fiction by J.R.R. Tolkien: Their Roots in Medieval Heroic Literature and Language*. Ph.D. thesis, Louisiana State University and Agricultural and Mechanical College, 1969.

Greene, Deirdre. 'Higher Argument: Tolkien and the Tradition of Vision, Epic and Prophecy'. *Proceedings of the J.R.R. Tolkien Centenary Conference 1992*. Ed. by Patricia Reynolds and Glen H. GoodKnight. Milton Keynes: Tolkien Society; Altadena, Calif.: Mythopoeic Press, 1995. Pp. 45–52.

Gregory of Tours. *The History of the Franks*. Trans. by Lewis Thorpe. Harmondsworth, Middlesex: Penguin Books, 1974.

Grimm, Jacob. *Teutonic Mythology*. Trans. by James Steven Stallybrass. New York: Dover, 2004. 4 vols. First published in English 1883–8.

Haggard, H. Rider. *The Annotated* She. Introduction and notes by Norman Etherington. Bloomington: Indiana University Press, 1991.

—— *She and Allan*. New York: Ballantine Books, 1978. First published 1921.

Haigh, Walter E. *A New Glossary of the Dialect of the Huddersfield District*. London: Oxford University Press, 1928.

Hammond, Wayne G. 'All the Comforts: The Image of Home in *The Hobbit* and *The Lord of the Rings*'. *Mythlore* 14, no. 1, whole no. 51 (Autumn 1987), pp. 29–33.

—— 'The Critical Response to Tolkien's Fiction'. *Proceedings of the J.R.R. Tolkien Centenary Conference 1992*. Ed. by Patricia Reynolds and Glen H. GoodKnight. Milton Keynes: Tolkien Society; Altadena, Calif.: Mythopoeic Press, 1995. Pp. 226–32.

—— and Christina Scull. *J.R.R. Tolkien: Artist and Illustrator*. London: HarperCollins, 1995.

—— with the assistance of Douglas A. Anderson. *J.R.R. Tolkien: A Descriptive Bibliography*. Winchester: St Paul's Bibliographies; New Castle, Del.: Oak Knoll Books, 1993. Supplemented in issues of the *Tolkien Collector*, an occasional publication ed. by Christina Scull.

Hanks, Patrick, and Flavia Hodges. *A Dictionary of First Names*. Oxford: Oxford University Press, 1990 (1995 corrected printing).

Hargrove, Gene. 'Who is Tom Bombadil'. *Mythlore* 13, no. 1, whole no. 47 (Autumn 1986), pp. 20–4.

Harvey, Paul, ed. *The Oxford Companion to English Literature*. 4th edn. Rev. by Dorothy Eagle. Oxford: Oxford University Press, 1967.

'Heroic Endeavour' (review of *The Fellowship of the Ring*). *Times Literary Supplement*, 27 August 1954, p. 541.

Hesiod. *Theogony [and] Works and Days; [and] Elegies [of] Theogonis.* Trans. and with introductions by Dorothea Wender. Harmondsworth, Middlesex: Penguin, 1973.

Hollister, C. Warren. *The Making of England 55 B.C.–1399.* 2nd edn. Lexington, Mass.: D.C. Heath, 1971.

Holmes, John R. 'Oaths and Oath Breaking: Analogues of Old English *Comitatus* in Tolkien's Myth'. *Tolkien and the Invention of Myth: A Reader.* Ed. by Jane Chance. Lexington: University Press of Kentucky, 2004. Pp. 249–61.

Homer. *The Iliad.* Trans. by E.V. Rieu. Harmondsworth: Penguin, 1950 (1960 printing).

—— *The Odyssey.* Trans. by Robert Fitzgerald. New York: Vintage, 1990.

Honey, Derek S. *An Encyclopaedia of Oxford Pubs, Inns and Taverns.* Usk, Mon.: Oakwood Press, 1998.

Honegger, Thomas. 'The Man in the Moon: Structural Depth in Tolkien'. *Root and Branch: Approaches towards Understanding Tolkien.* Ed. by Thomas Honegger. Zurich: Walking Tree Publishers, 1999. Pp. 9–76.

Hooker, Mark T. 'In a Hole in the Ground There Lived a . . .' *Beyond Bree,* November 2002, pp. 3–5.

Hoskins, W.G. *English Landscapes.* London: British Broadcasting Corporation, 1973.

Hostetter, Carl F. 'The "King's Letter": An Historical and Comparative Analysis', *Vinyar Tengwar* 31 (September 1993), pp. 12–34.

—— Letter to the Editor. *Beyond Bree,* November 1993, p. 8.

—— '*Sauron Defeated*: A Linguistic Review'. *Vinyar Tengwar* 24 (July 1992), pp. 4–13.

—— 'Settled Spells'. *Amon Hen* 122 (July 1993), p. 11.

—— 'Uglúk to the Dung-pit'. *Vinyar Tengwar* 26 (November 1992), p. 16.

—— and Patrick Wynne. 'An Adûnaic Dictionary'. *Vinyar Tengwar* 25 (September 1992), pp. 8–26.

—— and Patrick Wynne. 'Stone Towers'. *Mythlore* 19, no. 4, whole no. 74 (Autumn 1993), pp. 47–55, 65.

Hyde, Ron. 'A Revised Map of the Shire'. *Beyond Bree,* May 1994, pp. 2–3.

The Invented Worlds of J.R.R. Tolkien: Drawings and Original Manuscripts from the Marquette University Collection. Milwaukee: Patrick and Beatrice Haggerty Museum of Art, Marquette University, 2004.

Jensen, Todd. 'The Animals of Middle-earth: Part 1, Mammals'. *Beyond Bree,* May 1995, pp. 1–5.

—— 'Elements of the Classical Epic in *The Lord of the Rings*'. *Beyond Bree,* March 1990, pp. 1–3.

—— 'Frodo's Delay'. *Beyond Bree,* May 1991, p. 7. Reply (letter) by David Cremona, *Beyond Bree,* June 1991, p. 10.

—— 'Hobbits and the Little People'. *Beyond Bree,* August 1994, p. 3.

—— 'Nameless Things'. *Beyond Bree,* August 1988, p. 8.

Johannesson, Nils-Lennart. 'Studies in Tolkien's Language II: A Mirror of the Soul: On the Indexical Function of Gollum's Speech'. *Arda* 3 (1986, for 1982–3), pp. 1–31.

—— 'Studies in Tolkien's Language III: Sure as Shiretalk: On Linguistic Variation in Hobbit Speech'. *Arda* 5 (1988, for 1985), pp. 38–55; *Arda* 7 (1992, for 1987), pp. 92–126. A revision, 'The Speech of the Individual and of the Community in *The Lord of the Rings*', was published in *News from the Shire and Beyond: Studies on Tolkien*, ed. by Peter Buchs and Thomas Honegger (Zurich: Walking Tree Publishers, 1997), pp. 11–47.

Johnson, Judith A. *J.R.R. Tolkien: Six Decades of Criticism*. Westport, Conn.: Greenwood Press, 1986.

Johnston, George Burke. 'The Poetry of J.R.R. Tolkien'. *The Tolkien Papers*. Mankato Studies in English, no. 2. Mankato, Minn.: Mankato State University, 1967. Pp. 63–75.

Jones, Chris. Letter to the Editor. *Tolkien Journal* 3, no. 4, whole no. 10 (November 1969), pp. 21–2.

Jones, Gwyn. *A History of the Vikings*. Rev. edn. Oxford: Oxford University Press, 1984.

Jönsson, Åke (*now* Åke Bertenstam). 'The King's Reckoning: Did Tolkien Reckon Correct?' *Beyond Bree*, November 1985, pp. 5–6.

Jordanes. *The Origin and Deeds of the Goths*. Trans. by Charles C. Mierow. Princeton, N.J.: Princeton University, 1908.

Kemp, Peter, ed. *The Oxford Companion to Ships and the Sea*. Oxford: Oxford University Press, 1976 (1988 printing, with corrections).

Kipling, Rudyard. *Puck of Pook's Hill*. London: Piccolo, 1975. First published 1906.

Knighton, Adrian. Letter to the Editor, *Amon Hen* 36 (December 1978), pp. 15–16.

Kocher, Paul H. *Master of Middle-earth: The Fiction of J.R.R. Tolkien*. Boston: Houghton Mifflin, 1972.

Lacy, Norris J., ed. *The New Arthurian Encyclopedia*. New York: Garland, 1996.

Lang, Andrew, ed. *The Red Fairy Book*. London: Longmans, Green, 1895. First published 1890.

Lewis, C.S. 'The Dethronement of Power' (review of *The Two Towers* and *The Return of the King*). *Time and Tide*, 22 October 1955, pp. 1373–4.

—— 'The Gods Return to Earth' (review of *The Fellowship of the Ring*). *Time and Tide*, 14 August 1954, pp. 1082–3.

Linley, Steve. 'Tolkien and Haggard: Some Thoughts on Galadriel'. *Anor* 23 (1991), pp. 11–16.

Lion Heart Autographs. *Catalogue No. 12*. New York, April 1985.

Lobdell, Jared. 'A Medieval Proverb in *The Lord of the Rings*'. *American Notes and Queries Supplement* 1 (1978): 330–1.

Martsch, Nancy. 'Calendar Concordance'. *Beyond Bree*, March 1993, pp. 4–6.

—— 'Éowyn and the Witch-king'. *Beyond Bree*, February 1992, pp. 2–3.

—— 'Éowyn, Merry, and the Witch-king'. *Beyond Bree*, October 1990, p. 6.

—— 'Frodo's Failure'. *Beyond Bree*, June 1997, pp. 1–4.

—— 'Hobbit Nomenclature'. *Beyond Bree*, March 1984, pp. 5–6.

—— 'The "Squint-eyed Southerner"'. *Beyond Bree*, May 1990, p. 9.

—— 'The Two Towers and the Nazgûl's Mount'. *Beyond Bree*, June 1993, p. 2.

—— 'What You Always Wanted to Know about Middle-earth but Were Too Embarrassed to Ask: Being the Report of a Discussion by the Hobbiton (Los Angeles) Fellowship and Suggestions by Readers of "Beyond Bree"'. *Beyond Bree*, May 1982, pp. 5–6.

Mayor, Adrienne. *Greek Fire, Poison Arrows, and Scorpion Bombs: Biological and Chemical Warfare in the Ancient World*. Woodstock, N.Y.: Overlook Duckworth, 2003.

Mitchison, Naomi. 'One Ring to Bind Them' (review of *The Fellowship of the Ring*). *New Statesman and Nation*, 18 September 1954, p. 331.

Morford, Mark P.O., and Robert J. Lenardon. *Classical Mythology*. 3rd edn. New York: Longman, 1985.

Morris, William. *A Tale of the House of the Wolfings and All the Kindreds of the Mark*. Pocket edn. London: Longmans, Green, 1913. First published 1888.

Morus, Iwan. 'The Ageing of the Elves'. *Anor* 1 [?January 1983], pp. 3–4.

Muir, Richard. *The English Village*. London: Thames and Hudson, 1980.

Murray, Robert. 'Sermon at Thanksgiving Service, Keble College Chapel, 23rd August 1992'. *Proceedings of the J.R.R. Tolkien Centenary Conference 1992*. Ed. by Patricia Reynolds and Glen H. GoodKnight. Milton Keynes: Tolkien Society; Altadena, Calif.: Mythopoeic Press, 1995. Pp. 17–20.

Noad, Charles E. 'The Natures of Tom Bombadil: A Summary'. *Leaves from the Tree: J.R.R. Tolkien's Shorter Fiction*. London: Tolkien Society, 1991. Pp. 79–83.

Norwich, John Julius. *Byzantium: The Decline and Fall*. New York: Alfred A. Knopf, 1996.

O'Brien, Donald. 'The Eye of Sauron'. *Beyond Bree*, June 1992, pp. 1–5.

—— 'On the Origin of the Name "Hobbit"'. *Mythlore* 16, no. 2, whole no. 60 (Winter 1989), pp. 32–8.

Opie, Iona and Peter, eds. *The Oxford Dictionary of Nursery Rhymes*. New edn. Oxford: Oxford University Press, 1997.

Oxford Dictionary of Quotations. 2nd edn. Oxford: Oxford University Press, 1955.

Oxford English Dictionary. Compact edn. Oxford: Oxford University Press, 1971 (1987 issue with supplement, in 3 vols.).

Page, Gill. 'The Wild Hunt'. *Amon Hen* 42 (December 1979), pp. 7–8.

Partridge, Eric. *A Dictionary of Slang and Unconventional English*. 5th edn. New York: Macmillan, 1961.

Petty, Anne C. *Tolkien in the Land of Heroes: Discovering the Human Spirit*. Cold Spring Harbor, N.Y.: Cold Spring Press, 2003.

Phillips, Roger. *Wild Flowers of Britain*. Assisted by Sheila Grant. New York: Quick Fox, 1977.

Plotz, Dick. Letter to the Editor. *Mythprint* 10, no. 1 (July 1974), p. 3.

The Poetic Edda. Trans. by Carolyne Larrington. Oxford: Oxford University Press, 1996.

Polunin, Oleg. *A Concise Guide to the Flowers of Britain and Europe*. Assisted by Robin S. Wright. Oxford: Oxford University Press, 1972.

Pool, Daniel. *What Jane Austen Ate and Charles Dickens Knew*. New York: Simon & Schuster, 1993.

Previté-Orton, C.W. *The Shorter Cambridge Medieval History*. Cambridge: At the University Press, 1953. 2 vols.

Pulsiano, Phillip, *et al.*, eds. *Medieval Scandinavia: An Encyclopedia*. New York: Garland, 1993.

Pyles, Thomas. *The Origins and Development of the English Language*. 2nd edn. New York: Harcourt Brace Jovanovich, 1971.

Quiñonez, Jorge, and Ned Raggett. 'Nólë i Meneldilo: Lore of the Astronomer'. *Vinyar Tengwar* 12 (July 1990), pp. 5–9, 11–15.

Ransome, Arthur. *Signalling from Mars: The Letters of Arthur Ransome*. Ed. by Hugh Brogan. London: Jonathan Cape, 1997.

Rateliff, John D. '*She* and Tolkien'. *Mythlore* 8, no. 2, whole no. 28 (Summer 1981), pp. 6–8.

Reaney, P.H. *A Dictionary of English Surnames*. Rev. 3rd edn., with corrections and additions by R.M. Wilson. Oxford: Oxford University Press, 1997.

Reeves, Compton. *Pleasures and Pastimes in Medieval England*. New York: Oxford University Press, 1995.

Renoir, Alain. 'The Heroic Oath in *Beowulf*, the *Chanson de Roland*, and the *Nibelungenlied*'. *Studies in Old English Literature in Honor of Arthur G. Brodeur*. Ed. by Stanley B. Greenfield. Eugene: University of Oregon Books, 1963. Pp. 237–66.

Resnik, Henry. 'An Interview with Tolkien'. *Niekas* 18 (Late Spring 1967), pp. 37–43.

Reynolds, Patricia. 'Funeral Customs in Tolkien's Fiction'. *Mythlore* 19, no. 2, whole no. 72 (Spring 1993), pp. 45–53.

—— Letter to the Editor. *Amon Hen* 121 (May 1993), p. 25.

—— 'The Real Tom Bombadil'. *Leaves from the Tree: J.R.R. Tolkien's Shorter Fiction*. London: Tolkien Society, 1991. Pp. 85–8.

Richardson, Maurice. 'New Novels' (review of *The Two Towers*). *New Statesman and Nation*, 18 December 1954, pp. 835–6.

Robert F. Batchelder. *Catalog 97*. Ambler, Pa., February 1995.

Rockow, Karen. *Funeral Customs in Tolkien's Trilogy*. Baltimore: T-K Graphics, 1973.

Roessler, Bernie. 'More on Technology and the Middle Ages'. *Beyond Bree*, July 1996, p. 8.

Rojkin, Rony. 'The Istari'. *Beyond Bree*, April 1999, p. 8.

Rómenna Meeting Report. 12 May 1985; 21 July 1985; 24 August 1985; 22 September 1985; 29 June 1986; 26 October 1986; 29 March 1987.

Rosebury, Brian. *Tolkien: A Cultural Phenomenon.* Basingstoke, Hampshire: Palgrave Macmillan, 2003.

Rossenberg, René van. *Hobbits in Holland: Leven en Werk van J.R.R. Tolkien (1892–1973).* Den Haag: Koninklijke Bibliotheek, 1992.

Ryan, J.S. 'The Origin of the Name Wetwang'. *Amon Hen* 63 (August 1983), pp. 10–13.

—— 'Wherefore the Surname Cotton?' *Amon Hen* 72 (March 1985), pp. 12–13.

The Saga of King Heidrek the Wise. Trans. with introduction, notes, and appendices by Christopher Tolkien. Edinburgh: Thomas Nelson and Sons, 1960.

'The Saga of Middle Earth' (review of *The Return of the King*). *Times Literary Supplement*, 25 November 1955, p. 704.

Sanborn, Ron. 'Steward and King'. *Beyond Bree*, February 1983, p. 4.

Sanders, Helen. Letter to the Editor. *Amon Hen* 57 (August 1982), p. 21.

Schulp, J.A. 'The Flora of Middle-earth'. *Inklings-Jahrbuch für Literatur und Ästhetik* 3 (1985), pp. 129–39.

Scull, Christina. '*The Hobbit* and Tolkien's Other Pre-War Writings'. *Mallorn* 30 (September 1993), pp. 14–20.

—— 'The Influence of Archaeology & History on Tolkien's World'. *Scholarship & Fantasy: Proceedings of The Tolkien Phenomenon, May 1992.* Ed. by K.J. Battarbee. Turku: University of Turku, 1993. Pp. 33–51.

—— 'Open Minds, Closed Minds in *The Lord of the Rings*'. *Proceedings of the J.R.R. Tolkien Centenary Conference 1992.* Ed. by Patricia Reynolds and Glen H. GoodKnight. Milton Keynes: Tolkien Society; Altadena, Calif.: Mythopoeic Press, 1995. Pp. 151–6.

—— 'Tom Bombadil and *The Lord of the Rings*'. *Leaves from the Tree: J.R.R. Tolkien's Shorter Fiction.* London: Tolkien Society, 1991. Pp. 73–7.

—— 'What Did He Know and When Did He Know It?: Planning, Inspiration, and *The Lord of the Rings*'. Forthcoming in the proceedings of the October 2004 Marquette University Tolkien conference.

—— and Wayne G. Hammond. *The J.R.R. Tolkien Companion and Guide.* London: HarperCollins, forthcoming.

Selections from the Marquette J.R.R. Tolkien Collection. Milwaukee: Marquette University Library, 1987.

Senior, W.A. 'Loss Eternal in J.R.R. Tolkien's Middle-earth'. *J.R.R. Tolkien and His Literary Resonances: Views of Middle-earth.* Ed. by George Clark and Daniel Timmons. Westport, Conn.: Greenwood Press, 2000. Pp. 173–82.

Shakespeare, William. *The Complete Works of Shakespeare.* Ed. by Irving Ribner and George Lyman Kittredge. Waltham, Mass.: Ginn, 1971.

Shelley, Percy Bysshe. *The Complete Poetical Works of Percy Bysshe Shelley.* Ed. by Thomas Hutchinson. London: Oxford University Press, 1905 (reset 1934).

Shippey, T.A. 'Creation from Philology'. *J.R.R. Tolkien: Scholar and Storyteller: Essays in Memoriam*. Ed. by Mary Salu and Robert T. Farrell. Ithaca, N.Y.: Cornell University Press, 1979. Pp. 286–316.

—— *J.R.R. Tolkien: Author of the Century*. London: HarperCollins, 2000.

—— 'Orcs, Wraiths, Wights: Tolkien's Images of Evil'. *J.R.R. Tolkien and His Literary Resonances: Views of Middle-earth*. Ed. by George Clark and Daniel Timmons. Westport, Conn.: Greenwood Press, 2000. Pp. 183–98.

—— *The Road to Middle-earth*. 2nd edn. London: Grafton, 1992. We have found this the most convenient edition to cite, but our references may be found also in earlier and later editions. Except for a new final chapter, the text of the 1992 edn. is identical to that of the 1st edn. (1982), but with different pagination. A further 'revised and expanded edition', reset, was published by Houghton Mifflin, Boston, in 2003.

—— 'A Wose by Any Other Name . . .' *Amon Hen* 45 (July 1980), pp. 8–9.

Simek, Rudolf. *Dictionary of Northern Mythology*. Trans. by Angela Hall. Woodbridge, Suffolk: D.S. Brewer, 1993.

Simons, Lester. 'Writing and Allied Technologies in Middle-earth'. *Proceedings of the J.R.R. Tolkien Centenary Conference 1992* (1995). Ed. by Patricia Reynolds and Glen H. GoodKnight. Milton Keynes: Tolkien Society; Altadena, Calif.: Mythopoeic Press, 1995. Pp. 340–3.

Sinex, Margaret A. '"Oathbreakers, why have ye come?": Tolkien's "Passing of the Grey Company" and the Twelfth-century *Exercitus Mortuorum*'. *Tolkien the Medievalist*. Ed. by Jane Chance. London: Routledge, 2003. Pp. 155–68.

Smith, A.H. *English Place-Name Elements*. Cambridge: Cambridge University Press, 1970. 2 vols.

Smith, Arden R. 'Possible Sources of Tolkien's Bullroarer'. *Mythprint* 37, no. 12, whole no. 225 (December 2000), pp. 3–4.

—— 'The Tengwar Versions of the King's Letter'. *Vinyar Tengwar* 29 (May 1993), pp. 7–20.

The Song of Roland. Trans. by Dorothy L. Sayers. Harmondsworth: Penguin, 1963. First published 1957.

Sotheby's. *English Literature and History, Private Press and Illustrated Books, Related Drawings and Animation Art* [auction catalogue]. London, 21–2 July 1992.

—— *English Literature, History, Fine Bindings, Private Press Books, Children's Books, Illustrated Books and Drawings* [auction catalogue]. London, 10 July 2003.

Speake, Jennifer, ed. *The Oxford Dictionary of Proverbs*. 4th edn. Oxford: Oxford University Press, 2003.

Spence, Lewis. *The Fairy Tradition in Britain*. London: Rider, 1948.

Startzman, L. Eugene. 'Goldberry and Galadriel: The Quality of Joy'. *Mythlore* 16, no. 2, whole no. 60 (Winter 1989), pp. 5–13.

Stenström, Anders (Beregond). 'Is Gwaihir to Be Identified with the Lord

of the Eagles and the King of All Birds?' *Beyond Bree*, April 1987, pp. 1–4; and May 1987, pp. 3–5.
—— 'Något om pipor, blad och rökning' ('Some Notes on Pipes, Leaf, and Smoking'). *Arda* 4 (1988, for 1984), pp. 32–93. In Swedish, with a summary in English.
—— 'Striking Matches: An Exegesis of H [*The Hobbit*] V: 4'. *Arda* 5 (1988, for 1985), pp. 56–69.
Stenton, F.M. *Anglo-Saxon England*. 2nd edn. Oxford: Clarendon Press, 1947.
Stephens, Meic, ed. *The Oxford Companion to the Literature of Wales*. Oxford: Oxford University Press, 1986 (1990 corrected printing).
Stevenson, Jeff. Letter to the Editor. *Amon Hen* 103 (May 1990), p. 25.
Stoye, John. *The Siege of Vienna*. New York: Holt, Rinehart and Winston, 1964.
Strachey, Barbara. *Journeys of Frodo: An Atlas of J.R.R. Tolkien's The Lord of the Rings*. London: George Allen & Unwin, 1981.
Stratyner, Leslie. 'Ðe Us Ðas Beagas Geaf (He Who Gave Us These Rings): Sauron and the Perversion of Anglo-Saxon Ethos'. *Mythlore* 16, no. 1, whole no. 59 (Autumn 1989), pp. 5–8.
Ström, Fredrik. 'Letters to *VT*'. *Vinyar Tengwar* 42 (July 2001), pp. 3–4.
Stukeley, William. *Stonehenge: A Temple Restor'd to the British Druids*. London: Printed for W. Innys and R. Manby, 1740.
Sturluson, Snorri. *Edda*. Trans. and ed. by Anthony Faulknes. London: J.M. Dent, 1995. The *Prose* or *Younger Edda*.
—— *Heimskringla: The Norse King Sagas*. London: J.M. Dent, 1930.
Tacitus on Britain and Germany. Trans. by H. Mattingly. Harmondsworth, Middlesex: Penguin Books, 1948.
Talbot, Norman. 'Where Do Elves Go To? Tolkien and a Fantasy Tradition'. *Proceedings of the J.R.R. Tolkien Centenary Conference 1992*. Ed. by Patricia Reynolds and Glen H. GoodKnight. Milton Keynes: Tolkien Society; Altadena, Calif.: Mythopoeic Press, 1995. Pp. 94–106.
Tayar, Graham. 'Tolkien's Mordor'. *The Listener*, 14 July 1977.
Thompson, Eric J. Letter to the Editor. *Amon Hen* 121 (May 1993), p. 25.
Thompson, Kristin. '*The Hobbit* as Part of *The Red Book of Westmarch*'. *Mythlore* 15, no. 2, whole no. 56 (Winter 1988), pp. 11–16.
Timmons, Daniel. *Mirror on Middle-earth: J.R.R. Tolkien and the Critical Perspectives*. Ph.D. thesis, University of Toronto, 1998.
Tinkler, John. 'Old English in Rohan'. *Tolkien and the Critics: Essays on J.R.R. Tolkien's* The Lord of the Rings. Ed. by Neil D. Isaacs and Rose A. Zimbardo. Notre Dame, Ind.: University of Notre Dame Press, 1968. Pp. 164–9.
Tolkien, John, and Priscilla Tolkien. *The Tolkien Family Album*. London: HarperCollins, 1992.
Tolley, Clive. 'And the Word Was Made Flesh'. *Mallorn* 32 (September 1995), pp. 5–14.

—— 'Tolkien and the Unfinished'. *Scholarship and Fantasy: Proceedings of The Tolkien Phenomenon, May 1992*. Ed. by K.J. Battarbee. Turku: University of Turku, 1993. Pp. 151–64.

Toynbee, Philip. 'Dissension among the Judges'. *The Observer*, 6 August 1961.

Treharne, Elaine, ed. *Old and Middle English: An Anthology*. Oxford: Blackwell, 2000.

Unwin, Rayner. *George Allen & Unwin: A Remembrancer*. Ludlow: Privately printed for the author by Merlin Unwin Books, 1999.

Urrutia, Benjamin. Letter to the Editor. *Mythlore* 6, no. 4, whole no. 22 (Fall 1979), p. 41.

Vergil. *Vergil's Works: The Aeneid, Eclogues, Georgics*. Trans. by J.W. Mackail. New York: Modern Library, 1934.

Vickery, Roy. *A Dictionary of Plant Lore*. Oxford: Oxford University Press, 1995.

Volsunga Saga: The Story of the Volsungs and Niblungs. Trans. by William Morris. London: Walter Scott, [1888].

Waterfield's (bookseller). Catalogue 157, *Modern Literature*. Oxford, 1995.

Watts, Victor, ed. *The Cambridge Dictionary of English Place-names*. Cambridge: Cambridge University Press, 2004.

Webster, Leslie, and Janet Backhouse, eds. *The Making of England: Anglo-Saxon Art and Culture, AD 600–900*. London: British Museum Press, 1991.

Webster's Geographical Dictionary. Springfield, Mass.: G. & C. Merriam, 1957.

Weichman, Christian. 'Black (Not) a Colour in Middle-earth'. *Lembas-extra 2002*. Leiden: Tolkien Genootschap Unquendor, 2002. Pp. 7–13.

Welden, Bill. 'Negation in Quenya'. *Vinyar Tengwar* 42 (July 2001), pp. 32–4.

West, Richard C. '"Her Choice Was Made and Her Doom Appointed": Tragedy and Divine Comedy in the Tale of Aragorn and Arwen'. Forthcoming in the proceedings of the October 2004 Marquette University Tolkien conference.

—— 'The Interlace Structure of *The Lord of the Rings*'. *A Tolkien Compass*. Ed. by Jared Lobdell. La Salle, Ill.: Open Court, 1975. Pp. 77–94.

—— *Tolkien Criticism: An Annotated Checklist*. Rev. edn. Kent, Ohio: Kent State University Press, 1981.

Whitaker's Almanack. London: J. Whitaker; issues for 1941, 1942, 1944.

Whitelock, Dorothy. *The Beginnings of English Society*. Harmondsworth, Middlesex: Penguin Books, 1952; reprinted with revisions, 1965.

—— ed. *English Historical Documents, c. 500–1042*. New York: Oxford University Press, 1955.

Wilson, Edmund. 'Oo, Those Awful Orcs!' (review of *The Lord of the Rings*). *The Nation*, 14 April 1956, pp. 312–13.

Wolfe, Gene. 'The Tolkien Toll-free Fifties Freeway to Mordor & Points beyond Hurray!' *Vector* (British Science Fiction Association) 67/68 (Spring 1974), pp. 7–11.

Wood, Steve. 'Tolkien & the O.E.D.' *Amon Hen* 28 (August 1977), p. 10.

Worthington, Margaret. 'Offa's Dyke'. *The Blackwell Encyclopaedia of Anglo-Saxon England.* Ed. by Michael Lapidge, John Blair, Simon Keynes, and Donald Scragg. Oxford: Blackwell, 1999. P. 341.

Wright, Joseph, ed. *The English Dialect Dictionary.* London: Henry Frowde, 1898–1905. 6 vols.

Wyke-Smith, E.A. *The Marvellous Land of Snergs.* London: Ernest Benn, 1927.

Wynne, Patrick, and Carl F. Hostetter. 'Three Elvish Verse Modes: *Ann-thennath, Minlamad thent/estent,* and *Linnod*'. *Tolkien's* Legendarium*: Essays on* The History of Middle-earth. Ed. by Verlyn Flieger and Carl F. Hostetter. Westport, Conn.: Greenwood, 2000. Pp. 114–39.

Zimmermann, Manfred. 'Miscellaneous Remarks: On Gimli and on Rhythmic Prose'. *Mythlore* 11, no. 3, whole no. 41 (Winter–Spring 1985), p. 32.

—— 'The Origin of Gandalf and Josef Madlener'. *Mythlore* 9, no. 4, whole no. 34 (Winter 1983), pp. 22, 24.

LIBRARY AND ARCHIVAL SOURCES

BBC Written Archives Centre, Caversham Park, Reading.

Department of Western Manuscripts, Bodleian Library, University of Oxford.

Department of Manuscripts, British Library, London.

HarperCollinsPublishers, London.

Special Collections and University Archives, Marquette University Libraries, Milwaukee, Wisconsin.

Department of Archives and Manuscripts, Reading University Library.

Marion E. Wade Center, Wheaton College, Wheaton, Illinois.

Private collections.

INDEX

The following is concerned with the *Reader's Companion* beginning with our 'Brief History' and ending with our notes for the Appendices to *The Lord of the Rings*. We have not indexed the self-contained extract from Tolkien's letter to Milton Waldman or the separate *Nomenclature* (both of which are covered, however, as quoted in the text proper), or the rest of the back matter to this book.

In compiling this index it seemed to us that the merely mechanical accounting of every name or significant word or phrase in the *Reader's Companion* would tend to help the reader less than a selective index in which elements are included only when they carry a sufficient weight of meaning. Whether or not an element carries such 'weight' is, of course, a matter of subjective judgement, and such judgement may vary in the course of indexing a lengthy book; but we hope that we have been reasonably consistent in this respect. The entries include names of persons, places, and things, excepting the recipients of Tolkien's letters; invented languages and writing systems, when mentioned substantively; Tolkien's own writings and works of art; publishers concerned with *The Lord of the Rings*; authors and subjects considered as influences or analogues, or which otherwise figure in the history of the work; cited authors and reference sources; and glossed words and selected phrases.

Primary entry elements have been chosen usually according to predominance in *The Lord of the Rings*, but sometimes based on familiarity or ease of reference: thus (for instance) predominant *Nazgûl* rather than *Ringwraiths* or even less frequent *Black Riders*, and predominant and familiar *Treebeard* rather than *Fangorn*, with cross-references from (as they seem to us) the most important alternate terms. Names of bays, bridges, fords, gates, towers, vales, etc. including 'Bay', 'Bridge', etc. are entered usually under the principal element, e.g. *Belfalas, Bay of* rather than *Bay of Belfalas*. Names of battles and mountains are entered directly, e.g. *Battle of Bywater, Mount Doom*. With one exception (Rose Cotton), married female hobbits are indexed under the husband's surname. The abbreviation *LR* for *The Lord of the Rings* has been used freely.